Jules Verne's Early Novels 1864-70

Cover Photograph: Saturn h

ISBN: 978-1-78139-248-5

© 2012 Benediction Classics, Oxford.

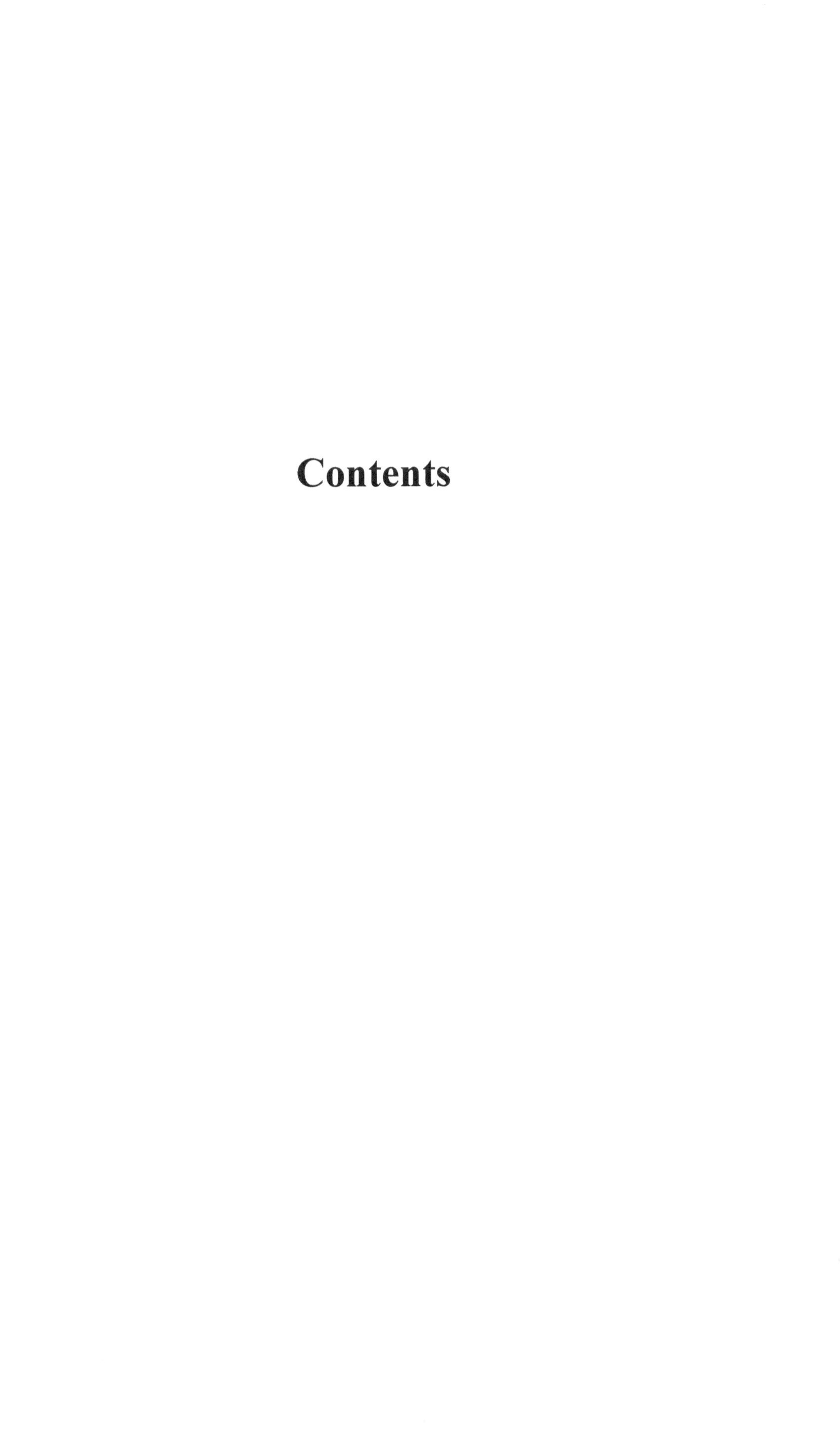

Contents

A JOURNEY INTO THE INTERIOR OF THE EARTH

FROM THE EARTH TO THE MOON

ROUND THE MOON

THE ENGLISH AT THE NORTH POLE

THE FIELD OF ICE

IN SEARCH OF THE CASTAWAYS

SOUTH AMERICA

AUSTRALIA

NEW ZEALAND

TWENTY THOUSAND LEAGUES UNDER THE SEA

PART ONE

PART TWO

A JOURNEY INTO THE INTERIOR OF THE EARTH

PREFACE

THE "Voyages Extraordinaires" of M. Jules Verne deserve to be made widely known in English-speaking countries by means of carefully prepared translations. Witty and ingenious adaptations of the researches and discoveries of modern science to the popular taste, which demands that these should be presented to ordinary readers in the lighter form of cleverly mingled truth and fiction, these books will assuredly be read with profit and delight, especially by English youth. Certainly no writer before M. Jules Verne has been so happy in weaving together in judicious combination severe scientific truth with a charming exercise of playful imagination.

Iceland, the starting point of the marvellous underground journey imagined in this volume, is invested at the present time with a painful interest in consequence of the disastrous eruptions last Easter Day, which covered with lava and ashes the poor and scanty vegetation upon which four thousand persons were partly dependent for the means of subsistence. For a long time to come the natives of that interesting island, who cleave to their desert home with all that *amor patriae* which is so much more easily understood than explained, will look, and look not in vain, for the help of those on whom fall the smiles of a kindlier sun in regions not torn by earthquakes nor blasted and ravaged by volcanic fires. Will the readers of this little book, who, are gifted with the means of indulging in the luxury of extended beneficence, remember the distress of their brethren in the far north, whom distance has not barred from the claim of being counted our "neighbours"? And whatever their humane feelings may prompt them to bestow will be gladly added to the Mansion-House Iceland Relief Fund.

In his desire to ascertain how far the picture of Iceland, drawn in the work of Jules Verne is a correct one, the translator hopes in the course of a mail or two to receive a communication from a leading man of science in the island, which may furnish matter for additional information in a future edition.

The scientific portion of the French original is not without a few errors, which the translator, with the kind assistance of Mr. Cameron of H. M. Geological Survey, has ventured to point out and correct. It is scarcely to be expected in a work in which the element of amusement is intended to enter more largely than that of scientific instruction, that any great degree of accuracy should be arrived at. Yet the translator hopes that what trifling deviations from the text or corrections in foot notes he is responsible for, will have done a little towards the increased usefulness of the work.

F. A. M.

The Vicarage,
Broughton-in-Furness

CHAPTER I. THE PROFESSOR AND HIS FAMILY

On the 24th of May, 1863, my uncle, Professor Liedenbrock, rushed into his little house, No. 19 Königstrasse, one of the oldest streets in the oldest portion of the city of Hamburg.

Martha must have concluded that she was very much behindhand, for the dinner had only just been put into the oven.

"Well, now," said I to myself, "if that most impatient of men is hungry, what a disturbance he will make!"

"M. Liedenbrock so soon!" cried poor Martha in great alarm, half opening the dining-room door.

"Yes, Martha; but very likely the dinner is not half cooked, for it is not two yet. Saint Michael's clock has only just struck half-past one."

"Then why has the master come home so soon?"

"Perhaps he will tell us that himself."

"Here he is, Monsieur Axel; I will run and hide myself while you argue with him."

And Martha retreated in safety into her own dominions.

I was left alone. But how was it possible for a man of my undecided turn of mind to argue successfully with so irascible a person as the Professor? With this persuasion I was hurrying away to my own little retreat upstairs, when the street door creaked upon its hinges; heavy feet made the whole flight of stairs to shake; and the master of the house, passing rapidly through the dining-room, threw himself in haste into his own sanctum.

But on his rapid way he had found time to fling his hazel stick into a corner, his rough broadbrim upon the table, and these few emphatic words at his nephew:

"Axel, follow me!"

I had scarcely had time to move when the Professor was again shouting after me:

"What! not come yet?"

And I rushed into my redoubtable master's study.

Otto Liedenbrock had no mischief in him, I willingly allow that; but unless he very considerably changes as he grows older, at the end he will be a most original character.

He was professor at the Johannæum, and was delivering a series of lectures on mineralogy, in the course of every one of which he broke into a passion once or twice at least. Not at all that he was over-anxious about the improvement of his class, or about the degree of attention with which they listened to him, or the success which might eventually crown his labours. Such little matters of detail never troubled him much. His teaching was as the German philosophy calls it, 'subjective'; it was to benefit himself, not others. He was a learned egotist. He was a well of science, and the pulleys worked uneasily when you wanted to draw anything out of it. In a word, he was a learned miser.

Germany has not a few professors of this sort.

To his misfortune, my uncle was not gifted with a sufficiently rapid utterance; not, to be sure, when he was talking at home, but certainly in his public delivery; this is a want much to be deplored in a speaker. The fact is, that during the course of his lectures at the Johannæum, the Professor often came to a complete standstill; he fought with wilful words that refused to pass his struggling lips, such words as resist and distend the cheeks, and at last break out into the unasked-for shape of a round and most unscientific oath: then his fury would gradually abate.

Now in mineralogy there are many half-Greek and half-Latin terms, very hard to articulate, and which would be most trying to a poet's measures. I don't wish to say a word against so respectable a science, far be that from me. True, in the august presence of rhombohedral crystals, retinasphaltic resins, gehlenites, Fassaites, molybdenites, tungstates of manganese, and titanite of zirconium, why, the most facile of tongues may make a slip now and then.

It therefore happened that this venial fault of my uncle's came to be pretty well understood in time, and an unfair advantage was taken of it; the students laid wait for him in dangerous places, and when he began to stumble, loud was the laughter, which is not in good taste, not even in Germans. And if there was always a full audience to honour the Liedenbrock courses, I should be sorry to conjecture how many came to make merry at my uncle's expense.

Nevertheless my good uncle was a man of deep learning—a fact I am most anxious to assert and reassert. Sometimes he might irretrievably injure a specimen by his too great ardour in handling it; but still he united the genius of a true geologist with the keen eye of the mineralogist. Armed with his hammer, his steel pointer, his magnetic needles, his blowpipe, and his bottle of nitric acid, he was a powerful man of science. He would refer any mineral to its proper place among the six hundred[1] elementary substances now enumerated, by its fracture, its appearance, its hardness, its fusibility, its sonorousness, its smell, and its taste.

The name of Liedenbrock was honourably mentioned in colleges and learned societies. Humphry Davy[2], Humboldt, Captain Sir John Franklin, General Sabine, never failed to call upon him on their way through Hamburg. Becquerel, Ebelman, Brewster, Dumas, Milne-Edwards, Saint-Claire-Deville frequently consulted him upon the most difficult problems in chemistry, a science which was indebted to him for considerable discoveries, for in 1853 there had appeared at Leipzig an imposing folio by Otto Liedenbrock, entitled, "A Treatise upon Transcendental Chemistry," with plates; a work, however, which failed to cover its expenses.

To all these titles to honour let me add that my uncle was the curator of the museum of mineralogy formed by M. Struve, the Russian ambassador; a most valuable collection, the fame of which is European.

Such was the gentleman who addressed me in that impetuous manner. Fancy a tall, spare man, of an iron constitution, and with a fair complexion which took off a good ten years from the fifty he must own to. His restless eyes were in incessant motion behind his full-sized spectacles. His long, thin nose was like a knife blade. Boys have been heard to

---

[1] Sixty-three. (Tr.)

[2] As Sir Humphry Davy died in 1829, the translator must be pardoned for pointing out here an anachronism, unless we are to assume that the learned Professor's celebrity dawned in his earliest years. (Tr.)

remark that that organ was magnetised and attracted iron filings. But this was merely a mischievous report; it had no attraction except for snuff, which it seemed to draw to itself in great quantities.

When I have added, to complete my portrait, that my uncle walked by mathematical strides of a yard and a half, and that in walking he kept his fists firmly closed, a sure sign of an irritable temperament, I think I shall have said enough to disenchant any one who should by mistake have coveted much of his company.

He lived in his own little house in Königstrasse, a structure half brick and half wood, with a gable cut into steps; it looked upon one of those winding canals which intersect each other in the middle of the ancient quarter of Hamburg, and which the great fire of 1842 had fortunately spared.

It is true that the old house stood slightly off the perpendicular, and bulged out a little towards the street; its roof sloped a little to one side, like the cap over the left ear of a Tugendbund student; its lines wanted accuracy; but after all, it stood firm, thanks to an old elm which buttressed it in front, and which often in spring sent its young sprays through the window panes.

My uncle was tolerably well off for a German professor. The house was his own, and everything in it. The living contents were his god-daughter Gräuben, a young Virlandaise of seventeen, Martha, and myself. As his nephew and an orphan, I became his laboratory assistant.

I freely confess that I was exceedingly fond of geology and all its kindred sciences; the blood of a mineralogist was in my veins, and in the midst of my specimens I was always happy.

In a word, a man might live happily enough in the little old house in the Königstrasse, in spite of the restless impatience of its master, for although he was a little too excitable— he was very fond of me. But the man had no notion how to wait; nature herself was too slow for him. In April, after he had planted in the terra-cotta pots outside his window seedling plants of mignonette and convolvulus, he would go and give them a little pull by their leaves to make them grow faster. In dealing with such a strange individual there was nothing for it but prompt obedience. I therefore rushed after him.

CHAPTER II. A MYSTERY TO BE SOLVED AT ANY PRICE

That study of his was a museum, and nothing else. Specimens of everything known in mineralogy lay there in their places in perfect order, and correctly named, divided into inflammable, metallic, and lithoid minerals.

How well I knew all these bits of science! Many a time, instead of enjoying the company of lads of my own age, I had preferred dusting these graphites, anthracites, coals, lignites, and peats! And there were bitumens, resins, organic salts, to be protected from the least grain of dust; and metals, from iron to gold, metals whose current value altogether disappeared in the presence of the republican equality of scientific specimens; and stones too, enough to rebuild entirely the house in Königstrasse, even with a handsome additional room, which would have suited me admirably.

But on entering this study now I thought of none of all these wonders; my uncle alone filled my thoughts. He had thrown himself into a velvet easy-chair, and was grasping between his hands a book over which he bent, pondering with intense admiration.

"Here's a remarkable book! What a wonderful book!" he was exclaiming.

These ejaculations brought to my mind the fact that my uncle was liable to occasional fits of bibliomania; but no old book had any value in his eyes unless it had the virtue of being nowhere else to be found, or, at any rate, of being illegible.

"Well, now; don't you see it yet? Why I have got a priceless treasure, that I found his morning, in rummaging in old Hevelius's shop, the Jew."

"Magnificent!" I replied, with a good imitation of enthusiasm.

What was the good of all this fuss about an old quarto, bound in rough calf, a yellow, faded volume, with a ragged seal depending from it?

CHAPTER II. A MYSTERY TO BE SOLVED AT ANY PRICE

But for all that there was no lull yet in the admiring exclamations of the Professor.

"See," he went on, both asking the questions and supplying the answers. "Isn't it a beauty? Yes; splendid! Did you ever see such a binding? Doesn't the book open easily? Yes; it stops open anywhere. But does it shut equally well? Yes; for the binding and the leaves are flush, all in a straight line, and no gaps or openings anywhere. And look at its back, after seven hundred years. Why, Bozerian, Closs, or Purgold might have been proud of such a binding!"

While rapidly making these comments my uncle kept opening and shutting the old tome. I really could do no less than ask a question about its contents, although I did not feel the slightest interest.

"And what is the title of this marvellous work?" I asked with an affected eagerness which he must have been very blind not to see through.

"This work," replied my uncle, firing up with renewed enthusiasm,
"this work is the Heims Kringla of Snorre Turlleson, the most famous
Icelandic author of the twelfth century! It is the chronicle of the
Norwegian princes who ruled in Iceland."

"Indeed;" I cried, keeping up wonderfully, "of course it is a German translation?"

"What!" sharply replied the Professor, "a translation! What should I do with a translation? This *is* the Icelandic original, in the magnificent idiomatic vernacular, which is both rich and simple, and admits of an infinite variety of grammatical combinations and verbal modifications."

"Like German." I happily ventured.

"Yes," replied my uncle, shrugging his shoulders; "but, in addition to all this, the Icelandic has three numbers like the Greek, and irregular declensions of nouns proper like the Latin."

"Ah!" said I, a little moved out of my indifference; "and is the type good?"

"Type! What do you mean by talking of type, wretched Axel? Type! Do you take it for a printed book, you ignorant fool? It is a manuscript, a Runic manuscript."

"Runic?"

"Yes. Do you want me to explain what that is?"

"Of course not," I replied in the tone of an injured man. But my uncle persevered, and told me, against my will, of many things I cared nothing about.

"Runic characters were in use in Iceland in former ages. They were invented, it is said, by Odin himself. Look there, and wonder, impious young man, and admire these letters, the invention of the Scandinavian god!"

Well, well! not knowing what to say, I was going to prostrate myself before this wonderful book, a way of answering equally pleasing to gods and kings, and which has the advantage of never giving them any embarrassment, when a little incident happened to divert conversation into another channel.

This was the appearance of a dirty slip of parchment, which slipped out of the volume and fell upon the floor.

My uncle pounced upon this shred with incredible avidity. An old document, enclosed an immemorial time within the folds of this old book, had for him an immeasurable value.

"What's this?" he cried.

And he laid out upon the table a piece of parchment, five inches by three, and along which were traced certain mysterious characters.

Here is the exact facsimile. I think it important to let these strange signs be publicly known, for they were the means of drawing on Professor Liedenbrock and his nephew to undertake the most wonderful expedition of the nineteenth century.

The Professor mused a few moments over this series of characters; then raising his spectacles he pronounced:

"These are Runic letters; they are exactly like those of the manuscript of Snorre Turlleson. But, what on earth is their meaning?"

Runic letters appearing to my mind to be an invention of the learned to mystify this poor world, I was not sorry to see my uncle suffering the pangs of mystification. At least, so it seemed to me, judging from his fingers, which were beginning to work with terrible energy.

"It is certainly old Icelandic," he muttered between his teeth.

And Professor Liedenbrock must have known, for he was acknowledged to be quite a polyglot. Not that he could speak fluently in the two thousand languages and twelve thousand dialects which are spoken on the earth, but he knew at least his share of them.

So he was going, in the presence of this difficulty, to give way to all the impetuosity of his character, and I was preparing for a violent outbreak, when two o'clock struck by the little timepiece over the fireplace.

At that moment our good housekeeper Martha opened the study door, saying:

"Dinner is ready!"

I am afraid he sent that soup to where it would boil away to nothing, and Martha took to her heels for safety. I followed her, and hardly knowing how I got there I found myself seated in my usual place.

I waited a few minutes. No Professor came. Never within my remembrance had he missed the important ceremonial of dinner. And yet what a good dinner it was! There was parsley soup, an omelette of ham garnished with spiced sorrel, a fillet of veal with compote of prunes; for dessert, crystallised fruit; the whole washed down with sweet Moselle.

All this my uncle was going to sacrifice to a bit of old parchment. As an affectionate and attentive nephew I considered it my duty to eat for him as well as for myself, which I did conscientiously.

"I have never known such a thing," said Martha. "M. Liedenbrock is not at table!"

"Who could have believed it?" I said, with my mouth full.

"Something serious is going to happen," said the servant, shaking her head.

My opinion was, that nothing more serious would happen than an awful scene when my uncle should have discovered that his dinner was devoured. I had come to the last of the fruit when a very loud voice tore me away from the pleasures of my dessert. With one spring I bounded out of the dining-room into the study.

CHAPTER III. THE RUNIC WRITING EXERCISES THE PROFESSOR

"Undoubtedly it is Runic," said the Professor, bending his brows; "but there is a secret in it, and I mean to discover the key."

A violent gesture finished the sentence.

"Sit there," he added, holding out his fist towards the table. "Sit there, and write."

I was seated in a trice.

"Now I will dictate to you every letter of our alphabet which corresponds with each of these Icelandic characters. We will see what that will give us. But, by St. Michael, if you should dare to deceive me—"

The dictation commenced. I did my best. Every letter was given me one after the other, with the following remarkable result:

mm rnlls esrevel seecIde sgtssmf vnteief niedrke kt,samn atrateS saodrrn emtnaeI nvaect rrilSa Atsaar .nvcrc ieaabs ccrmi eevtVl frAntv dt,iac oseibo KediiI

When this work was ended my uncle tore the paper from me and examined it attentively for a long time.

"What does it all mean?" he kept repeating mechanically.

Upon my honour I could not have enlightened him. Besides he did not ask me, and he went on talking to himself.

"This is what is called a cryptogram, or cipher," he said, "in which letters are purposely thrown in confusion, which if properly arranged would reveal their sense. Only think that under this jargon there may lie concealed the clue to some great discovery!"

As for me, I was of opinion that there was nothing at all, in it; though, of course, I took care not to say so.

Then the Professor took the book and the parchment, and diligently compared them together.

"These two writings are not by the same hand," he said; "the cipher is of later date than the book, an undoubted proof of which I see in a moment. The first letter is a double m, a letter which is not to be found in Turlleson's book, and which was only added to the alphabet in the fourteenth century. Therefore there are two hundred years between the manuscript and the document."

I admitted that this was a strictly logical conclusion.

"I am therefore led to imagine," continued my uncle, "that some possessor of this book wrote these mysterious letters. But who was that possessor? Is his name nowhere to be found in the manuscript?"

My uncle raised his spectacles, took up a strong lens, and carefully examined the blank pages of the book. On the front of the second, the title-page, he noticed a sort of stain which looked like an ink blot. But in looking at it very closely he thought he could distinguish some half-effaced letters. My uncle at once fastened upon this as the centre of interest, and he laboured at that blot, until by the help of his microscope he ended by making out the following Runic characters which he read without difficulty.

"Arne Saknussemm!" he cried in triumph. "Why that is the name of another Icelander, a savant of the sixteenth century, a celebrated alchemist!"

I gazed at my uncle with satisfactory admiration.

"Those alchemists," he resumed, "Avicenna, Bacon, Lully, Paracelsus, were the real and only savants of their time. They made discoveries at which we are astonished. Has not this Saknussemm concealed under his cryptogram some surprising invention? It is so; it must be so!"

The Professor's imagination took fire at this hypothesis.

"No doubt," I ventured to reply, "but what interest would he have in thus hiding so marvellous a discovery?"

"Why? Why? How can I tell? Did not Galileo do the same by Saturn? We shall see. I will get at the secret of this document, and I will neither sleep nor eat until I have found it out."

My comment on this was a half-suppressed "Oh!"

"Nor you either, Axel," he added.

"The deuce!" said I to myself; "then it is lucky I have eaten two dinners to-day!"

"First of all we must find out the key to this cipher; that cannot be difficult."

At these words I quickly raised my head; but my uncle went on soliloquising.

"There's nothing easier. In this document there are a hundred and thirty-two letters, viz., seventy-seven consonants and fifty-five vowels. This is the proportion found in southern languages, whilst northern tongues are much richer in consonants; therefore this is in a southern language."

These were very fair conclusions, I thought.

"But what language is it?"

Here I looked for a display of learning, but I met instead with profound analysis.

"This Saknussemm," he went on, "was a very well-informed man; now since he was not writing in his own mother tongue, he would naturally select that which was currently adopted by the choice spirits of the sixteenth century; I mean Latin. If I am mistaken, I can but try Spanish, French, Italian, Greek, or Hebrew. But the savants of the sixteenth century generally wrote in Latin. I am therefore entitled to pronounce this, à priori, to be Latin. It is Latin."

I jumped up in my chair. My Latin memories rose in revolt against the notion that these barbarous words could belong to the sweet language of Virgil.

"Yes, it is Latin," my uncle went on; "but it is Latin confused and in disorder; "*pertubata seu inordinata,*" as Euclid has it."

"Very well," thought I, "if you can bring order out of that confusion, my dear uncle, you are a clever man."

"Let us examine carefully," said he again, taking up the leaf upon which I had written. "Here is a series of one hundred and thirty-two letters in apparent disorder. There are words consisting of consonants only, as *nrrlls;* others, on the other hand, in which vowels predominate, as for instance the fifth, *uneeief,* or the last but one, *oseibo*. Now this arrangement has evidently not been premeditated; it has arisen mathematically in obedience to the unknown law which has ruled in the succession of these letters. It appears to me a certainty that the original sentence was written in a proper manner, and afterwards distorted by a law which we have yet to discover. Whoever possesses the key of this cipher will read it with fluency. What is that key? Axel, have you got it?"

I answered not a word, and for a very good reason. My eyes had fallen upon a charming picture, suspended against the wall, the portrait of Gräuben. My uncle's ward was at that time at Altona, staying with a relation, and in her absence I was very downhearted; for I may confess it to you now, the pretty Virlandaise and the professor's nephew loved each other with a patience and a calmness entirely German. We had become engaged unknown to my uncle, who was too much taken up with geology to be able to enter into such feelings as ours. Gräuben was a lovely blue-eyed blonde, rather given to gravity and seriousness; but that did not prevent her from loving me very sincerely. As for me, I adored her, if there is such a word in the German language. Thus it happened that the picture of my pretty Virlandaise threw me in a moment out of the world of realities into that of memory and fancy.

There looked down upon me the faithful companion of my labours and my recreations. Every day she helped me to arrange my uncle's precious specimens; she and I labelled them together. Mademoiselle Gräuben was an accomplished mineralogist; she could have taught a few things to a savant. She was fond of investigating abstruse scientific questions. What pleasant hours we have spent in study; and how often I envied the very stones which she handled with her charming fingers.

Then, when our leisure hours came, we used to go out together and turn into the shady avenues by the Alster, and went happily side by side up to the old windmill, which forms such an improvement to the landscape at the head of the lake. On the road we chatted hand in hand; I told her amusing tales at which she laughed heartily. Then we reached the banks of the Elbe, and after having bid good-bye to the swan, sailing gracefully amidst the white water lilies, we returned to the quay by the steamer.

That is just where I was in my dream, when my uncle with a vehement thump on the table dragged me back to the realities of life.

"Come," said he, "the very first idea which would come into any one's head to confuse the letters of a sentence would be to write the words vertically instead of horizontally."

"Indeed!" said I.

"Now we must see what would be the effect of that, Axel; put down upon this paper any sentence you like, only instead of arranging the letters in the usual way, one after the other, place them in succession in vertical columns, so as to group them together in five or six vertical lines."

I caught his meaning, and immediately produced the following literary wonder:

I y l o a u l o l w r b o u , n G e v w m d r n e e y e a !

"Good," said the professor, without reading them, "now set down those words in a horizontal line."

I obeyed, and with this result:

Iyloau lolwrb ou,nGe vwmdrn eeyea!

"Excellent!" said my uncle, taking the paper hastily out of my hands. "This begins to look just like an ancient document: the vowels and the consonants are grouped together in equal disorder; there are even capitals in the middle of words, and commas too, just as in Saknussemm's parchment."

I considered these remarks very clever.

"Now," said my uncle, looking straight at me, "to read the sentence which you have just written, and with which I am wholly unacquainted, I shall only have to take the first letter of each word, then the second, the third, and so forth."

And my uncle, to his great astonishment, and my much greater, read:

"I love you well, my own dear Gräuben!"

"Hallo!" cried the Professor.

Yes, indeed, without knowing what I was about, like an awkward and unlucky lover, I had compromised myself by writing this unfortunate sentence.

"Aha! you are in love with Gräuben?" he said, with the right look for a guardian.

"Yes; no!" I stammered.

"You love Gräuben," he went on once or twice dreamily. "Well, let us apply the process I have suggested to the document in question."

My uncle, falling back into his absorbing contemplations, had already forgotten my imprudent words. I merely say imprudent, for the great mind of so learned a man of course had no place for love affairs, and happily the grand business of the document gained me the victory.

Just as the moment of the supreme experiment arrived the Professor's eyes flashed right through his spectacles. There was a quivering in his fingers as he grasped the old parchment. He was deeply moved. At last he gave a preliminary cough, and with profound gravity, naming in succession the first, then the second letter of each word, he dictated me the following:

mmessvnkaSenrA.icefdoK.segnittamvrtn ecertserrette,rotaisadva,ednecsedsadne lacart-niiilvIsiratracSarbmvtabiledmek meretarcsilvcoIsleffenSnI.

I confess I felt considerably excited in coming to the end; these letters named, one at a time, had carried no sense to my mind; I therefore waited for the Professor with great pomp to unfold the magnificent but hidden Latin of this mysterious phrase.

But who could have foretold the result? A violent thump made the furniture rattle, and spilt some ink, and my pen dropped from between my fingers.

"That's not it," cried my uncle, "there's no sense in it."

Then darting out like a shot, bowling down stairs like an avalanche, he rushed into the Königstrasse and fled.

CHAPTER IV. THE ENEMY TO BE STARVED INTO SUBMISSION

"He is gone!" cried Martha, running out of her kitchen at the noise of the violent slamming of doors.

"Yes," I replied, "completely gone."

"Well; and how about his dinner?" said the old servant.

"He won't have any."

"And his supper?"

"He won't have any."

"What?" cried Martha, with clasped hands.

"No, my dear Martha, he will eat no more. No one in the house is to eat anything at all. Uncle Liedenbrock is going to make us all fast until he has succeeded in deciphering an undecipherable scrawl."

"Oh, my dear! must we then all die of hunger?"

I hardly dared to confess that, with so absolute a ruler as my uncle, this fate was inevitable.

The old servant, visibly moved, returned to the kitchen, moaning piteously.

When I was alone, I thought I would go and tell Gräuben all about it. But how should I be able to escape from the house? The Professor might return at any moment. And suppose he called me? And suppose he tackled me again with this logomachy, which might vainly have been set before ancient Oedipus. And if I did not obey his call, who could answer for what might happen?

The wisest course was to remain where I was. A mineralogist at Besançon had just sent us a collection of siliceous nodules, which I had to classify: so I set to work; I sorted, labelled, and arranged in their own glass case all these hollow specimens, in the cavity of each of which was a nest of little crystals.

But this work did not succeed in absorbing all my attention. That old document kept working in my brain. My head throbbed with excitement, and I felt an undefined uneasiness. I was possessed with a presentiment of coming evil.

In an hour my nodules were all arranged upon successive shelves. Then I dropped down into the old velvet armchair, my head thrown back and my hands joined over it. I lighted my long crooked pipe, with a painting on it of an idle-looking naiad; then I amused myself watching the process of the conversion of the tobacco into carbon, which was by slow degrees making my naiad into a negress. Now and then I listened to hear whether a well-known step was on the stairs. No. Where could my uncle be at that moment? I fancied him running under the noble trees which line the road to Altona, gesticulating, making shots with his cane, thrashing the long grass, cutting the heads off the thistles, and disturbing the contemplative storks in their peaceful solitude.

Would he return in triumph or in discouragement? Which would get the upper hand, he or the secret? I was thus asking myself questions, and mechanically taking between my fingers the sheet of paper mysteriously disfigured with the incomprehensible succession of letters I had written down; and I repeated to myself "What does it all mean?"

I sought to group the letters so as to form words. Quite impossible! When I put them together by twos, threes, fives or sixes, nothing came of it but nonsense. To be sure the fourteenth, fifteenth and sixteenth letters made the English word 'ice'; the eighty-third and two following made 'sir'; and in the midst of the document, in the second and third lines, I observed the words, "rots," "mutabile," "ira," "net," "atra."

"Come now," I thought, "these words seem to justify my uncle's view about the language of the document. In the fourth line appeared the word "luco", which means a sacred wood. It is true that in the third line was the word "tabiled", which looked like Hebrew, and in the last the purely French words "mer", "arc", "mere.""

All this was enough to drive a poor fellow crazy. Four different languages in this ridiculous sentence! What connection could there possibly be between such words as ice, sir, anger, cruel, sacred wood, changeable, mother, bow, and sea? The first and the last might have something to do with each other; it was not at all surprising that in a document written in Iceland there should be mention of a sea of ice; but it was quite another thing to get to the end of this cryptogram with so small a clue. So I was struggling with an insurmountable difficulty; my brain got heated, my eyes watered over that sheet of paper; its hundred and thirty-two letters seemed to flutter and fly around me like those motes of mingled light and darkness which float in the air around the head when the blood is rushing upwards with undue violence. I was a prey to a kind of hallucination; I was stifling; I wanted air. Unconsciously I fanned myself with the bit of paper, the back and front of which successively came before my eyes. What was my surprise when, in one of those rapid revolutions, at the moment when the back was turned to me I thought I caught sight of the Latin words "craterem," "terrestre," and others.

A sudden light burst in upon me; these hints alone gave me the first glimpse of the truth; I had discovered the key to the cipher. To read the document, it would not even be necessary to read it through the paper. Such as it was, just such as it had been dictated to me, so it might be spelt out with ease. All those ingenious professorial combinations were coming right. He was right as to the arrangement of the letters; he was right as to the language. He had been within a hair's breadth of reading this Latin document from end to end; but that hair's breadth, chance had given it to me!

You may be sure I felt stirred up. My eyes were dim, I could scarcely see. I had laid the paper upon the table. At a glance I could tell the whole secret.

At last I became more calm. I made a wise resolve to walk twice round the room quietly and settle my nerves, and then I returned into the deep gulf of the huge armchair.

"Now I'll read it," I cried, after having well distended my lungs with air.

I leaned over the table; I laid my finger successively upon every letter; and without a pause, without one moment's hesitation, I read off the whole sentence aloud.

Stupefaction! terror! I sat overwhelmed as if with a sudden deadly blow. What! that which I read had actually, really been done! A mortal man had had the audacity to penetrate! . . .

"Ah!" I cried, springing up. "But no! no! My uncle shall never know it. He would insist upon doing it too. He would want to know all about it. Ropes could not hold him, such a determined geologist as he is! He would start, he would, in spite of everything and everybody, and he would take me with him, and we should never get back. No, never! never!"

My over-excitement was beyond all description.

"No! no! it shall not be," I declared energetically; "and as it is in my power to prevent the knowledge of it coming into the mind of my tyrant, I will do it. By dint of turning this document round and round, he too might discover the key. I will destroy it."

There was a little fire left on the hearth. I seized not only the paper but Saknussemm's parchment; with a feverish hand I was about to fling it all upon the coals and utterly destroy and abolish this dangerous secret, when the study door opened, and my uncle appeared.

CHAPTER V. FAMINE, THEN VICTORY, FOLLOWED BY DISMAY

I had only just time to replace the unfortunate document upon the table.

Professor Liedenbrock seemed to be greatly abstracted.

The ruling thought gave him no rest. Evidently he had gone deeply into the matter, analytically and with profound scrutiny. He had brought all the resources of his mind to bear upon it during his walk, and he had come back to apply some new combination.

He sat in his armchair, and pen in hand he began what looked very much like algebraic formula: I followed with my eyes his trembling hands, I took count of every movement. Might not some unhoped-for result come of it? I trembled, too, very unnecessarily, since the true key was in my hands, and no other would open the secret.

For three long hours my uncle worked on without a word, without lifting his head; rubbing out, beginning again, then rubbing out again, and so on a hundred times.

I knew very well that if he succeeded in setting down these letters in every possible relative position, the sentence would come out. But I knew also that twenty letters alone could form two quintillions, four hundred and thirty-two quadrillions, nine hundred and two trillions, eight billions, a hundred and seventy-six millions, six hundred and forty thousand combinations. Now, here were a hundred and thirty-two letters in this sentence, and these hundred and thirty-two letters would give a number of different sentences, each made up of at least a hundred and thirty-three figures, a number which passed far beyond all calculation or conception.

So I felt reassured as far as regarded this heroic method of solving the difficulty.

But time was passing away; night came on; the street noises ceased; my uncle, bending over his task, noticed nothing, not even Martha half opening the door; he heard not a sound, not even that excellent woman saying:

"Will not monsieur take any supper to-night?"

And poor Martha had to go away unanswered. As for me, after long resistance, I was overcome by sleep, and fell off at the end of the sofa, while uncle Liedenbrock went on calculating and rubbing out his calculations.

When I awoke next morning that indefatigable worker was still at his post. His red eyes, his pale complexion, his hair tangled between his feverish fingers, the red spots on his cheeks, revealed his desperate struggle with impossibilities, and the weariness of spirit, the mental wrestlings he must have undergone all through that unhappy night.

To tell the plain truth, I pitied him. In spite of the reproaches which I considered I had a right to lay upon him, a certain feeling of compassion was beginning to gain upon me. The poor man was so entirely taken up with his one idea that he had even forgotten how to get angry. All the strength of his feelings was concentrated upon one point alone; and as their usual vent was closed, it was to be feared lest extreme tension should give rise to an explosion sooner or later.

I might with a word have loosened the screw of the steel vice that was crushing his brain; but that word I would not speak.

Yet I was not an ill-natured fellow. Why was I dumb at such a crisis?

Why so insensible to my uncle's interests?

"No, no," I repeated, "I shall not speak. He would insist upon going; nothing on earth could stop him. His imagination is a volcano, and to do that which other geologists have never done he would risk his life. I will preserve silence. I will keep the secret which mere chance has revealed to me. To discover it, would be to kill Professor Liedenbrock! Let him find it out himself if he can. I will never have it laid to my door that I led him to his destruction."

Having formed this resolution, I folded my arms and waited. But I had not reckoned upon one little incident which turned up a few hours after.

When our good Martha wanted to go to Market, she found the door locked. The big key was gone. Who could have taken it out? Assuredly, it was my uncle, when he returned the night before from his hurried walk.

Was this done on purpose? Or was it a mistake? Did he want to reduce us by famine? This seemed like going rather too far! What! should Martha and I be victims of a position of things in which we had not the smallest interest? It was a fact that a few years before this, whilst my uncle was working at his great classification of minerals, he was forty-eight hours without eating, and all his household were obliged to share in this scientific fast. As for me, what I remember is, that I got severe cramps in my stomach, which hardly suited the constitution of a hungry, growing lad.

Now it appeared to me as if breakfast was going to be wanting, just as supper had been the night before. Yet I resolved to be a hero, and not to be conquered by the pangs of hunger. Martha took it very seriously, and, poor woman, was very much distressed. As for me, the impossibility of leaving the house distressed me a good deal more, and for a very good reason. A caged lover's feelings may easily be imagined.

My uncle went on working, his imagination went off rambling into the ideal world of combinations; he was far away from earth, and really far away from earthly wants.

About noon hunger began to stimulate me severely. Martha had, without thinking any harm, cleared out the larder the night before, so that now there was nothing left in the house. Still I held out; I made it a point of honour.

Two o'clock struck. This was becoming ridiculous; worse than that, unbearable. I began to say to myself that I was exaggerating the importance of the document; that my uncle would surely not believe in it, that he would set it down as a mere puzzle; that if it came to the worst, we should lay violent hands on him and keep him at home if he thought on venturing on the expedition; that, after all, he might himself discover the key of the cipher, and that then I should be clear at the mere expense of my involuntary abstinence.

These reasons seemed excellent to me, though on the night before I should have rejected them with indignation; I even went so far as to condemn myself for my absurdity in having waited so long, and I finally resolved to let it all out.

I was therefore meditating a proper introduction to the matter, so as not to seem too abrupt, when the Professor jumped up, clapped on his hat, and prepared to go out.

Surely he was not going out, to shut us in again! no, never!

"Uncle!" I cried.

He seemed not to hear me.

"Uncle Liedenbrock!" I cried, lifting up my voice.

"Ay," he answered like a man suddenly waking.

"Uncle, that key!"

"What key? The door key?"

"No, no!" I cried. "The key of the document."

The Professor stared at me over his spectacles; no doubt he saw something unusual in the expression of my countenance; for he laid hold of my arm, and speechlessly questioned me with his eyes. Yes, never was a question more forcibly put.

I nodded my head up and down.

He shook his pityingly, as if he was dealing with a lunatic. I gave a more affirmative gesture.

His eyes glistened and sparkled with live fire, his hand was shaken threateningly.

This mute conversation at such a momentous crisis would have riveted the attention of the most indifferent. And the fact really was that I dared not speak now, so intense was the excitement for fear lest my uncle should smother me in his first joyful embraces. But he became so urgent that I was at last compelled to answer.

"Yes, that key, chance—"

"What is that you are saying?" he shouted with indescribable emotion.

"There, read that!" I said, presenting a sheet of paper on which I had written.

"But there is nothing in this," he answered, crumpling up the paper.

"No, nothing until you proceed to read from the end to the beginning."

I had not finished my sentence when the Professor broke out into a cry, nay, a roar. A new revelation burst in upon him. He was transformed!

"Aha, clever Saknussemm!" he cried. "You had first written out your sentence the wrong way."

And darting upon the paper, with eyes bedimmed, and voice choked with emotion, he read the whole document from the last letter to the first.

It was conceived in the following terms:

In Sneffels Joculis craterem quem delibat
Umbra Scartaris Julii intra calendas descende,
Audax viator, et terrestre centrum attinges.
Quod feci, Arne Saknussemm[1].

Which bad Latin may be translated thus:

"Descend, bold traveller, into the crater of the jokul of Sneffels, which the shadow of Scartaris touches before the kalends of July, and you will attain the centre of the earth; which I have done, Arne Saknussemm."

In reading this, my uncle gave a spring as if he had touched a Leyden jar. His audacity, his joy, and his convictions were magnificent to behold. He came and he went; he seized his head between both his hands; he pushed the chairs out of their places, he piled up his books; incredible as it may seem, he rattled his precious nodules of flints together; he sent a kick here, a thump there. At last his nerves calmed down, and like a man exhausted by too lavish an expenditure of vital power, he sank back exhausted into his armchair.

"What o'clock is it?" he asked after a few moments of silence.

"Three o'clock," I replied.

"Is it really? The dinner-hour is past, and I did not know it. I am half dead with hunger. Come on, and after dinner—"

"Well?"

---

[1] In the cipher, *audax* is written *avdas,* and *quod* and *quem, hod* and *ken.* (Tr.)

CHAPTER V. FAMINE, THEN VICTORY, FOLLOWED BY DISMAY

"After dinner, pack up my trunk."
"What?" I cried.
"And yours!" replied the indefatigable Professor, entering the dining-room.

CHAPTER VI. EXCITING DISCUSSIONS ABOUT AN UNPARALLELED ENTERPRISE

At these words a cold shiver ran through me. Yet I controlled myself; I even resolved to put a good face upon it. Scientific arguments alone could have any weight with Professor Liedenbrock. Now there were good ones against the practicability of such a journey. Penetrate to the centre of the earth! What nonsense! But I kept my dialectic battery in reserve for a suitable opportunity, and I interested myself in the prospect of my dinner, which was not yet forthcoming.

It is no use to tell of the rage and imprecations of my uncle before the empty table. Explanations were given, Martha was set at liberty, ran off to the market, and did her part so well that in an hour afterwards my hunger was appeased, and I was able to return to the contemplation of the gravity of the situation.

During all dinner time my uncle was almost merry; he indulged in some of those learned jokes which never do anybody any harm. Dessert over, he beckoned me into his study.

I obeyed; he sat at one end of his table, I at the other.

"Axel," said he very mildly; "you are a very ingenious young man, you have done me a splendid service, at a moment when, wearied out with the struggle, I was going to abandon the contest. Where should I have lost myself? None can tell. Never, my lad, shall I forget it; and you shall have your share in the glory to which your discovery will lead."

"Oh, come!" thought I, "he is in a good way. Now is the time for discussing that same glory."

"Before all things," my uncle resumed, "I enjoin you to preserve the most inviolable secrecy: you understand? There are not a few in the scientific world who envy my success, and many would be ready to undertake this enterprise, to whom our return should be the first news of it."

"Do you really think there are many people bold enough?" said I.

"Certainly; who would hesitate to acquire such renown? If that document were divulged, a whole army of geologists would be ready to rush into the footsteps of Arne Saknussemm."

"I don't feel so very sure of that, uncle," I replied; "for we have no proof of the authenticity of this document."

"What! not of the book, inside which we have discovered it?"

"Granted. I admit that Saknussemm may have written these lines. But does it follow that he has really accomplished such a journey? And may it not be that this old parchment is intended to mislead?"

CHAPTER VI. EXCITING DISCUSSIONS ABOUT AN UNPARALLELED ENTERPRISE

I almost regretted having uttered this last word, which dropped from me in an unguarded moment. The Professor bent his shaggy brows, and I feared I had seriously compromised my own safety. Happily no great harm came of it. A smile flitted across the lip of my severe companion, and he answered:

"That is what we shall see."

"Ah!" said I, rather put out. "But do let me exhaust all the possible objections against this document."

"Speak, my boy, don't be afraid. You are quite at liberty to express your opinions. You are no longer my nephew only, but my colleague. Pray go on."

"Well, in the first place, I wish to ask what are this Jokul, this
Sneffels, and this Scartaris, names which I have never heard before?"

"Nothing easier. I received not long ago a map from my friend, Augustus Petermann, at Liepzig. Nothing could be more apropos. Take down the third atlas in the second shelf in the large bookcase, series Z, plate 4."

I rose, and with the help of such precise instructions could not fail to find the required atlas. My uncle opened it and said:

"Here is one of the best maps of Iceland, that of Handersen, and I believe this will solve the worst of our difficulties."

I bent over the map.

"You see this volcanic island," said the Professor; "observe that all the volcanoes are called jokuls, a word which means glacier in Icelandic, and under the high latitude of Iceland nearly all the active volcanoes discharge through beds of ice. Hence this term of jokul is applied to all the eruptive mountains in Iceland."

"Very good," said I; "but what of Sneffels?"

I was hoping that this question would be unanswerable; but I was mistaken. My uncle replied:

"Follow my finger along the west coast of Iceland. Do you see Rejkiavik, the capital? You do. Well; ascend the innumerable fiords that indent those sea-beaten shores, and stop at the sixty-fifth degree of latitude. What do you see there?"

"I see a peninsula looking like a thigh bone with the knee bone at the end of it."

"A very fair comparison, my lad. Now do you see anything upon that knee bone?"

"Yes; a mountain rising out of the sea."

"Right. That is Snæfell."

"That Snæfell?"

"It is. It is a mountain five thousand feet high, one of the most remarkable in the world, if its crater leads down to the centre of the earth."

"But that is impossible," I said shrugging my shoulders, and disgusted at such a ridiculous supposition.

"Impossible?" said the Professor severely; "and why, pray?"

"Because this crater is evidently filled with lava and burning rocks, and therefore—"

"But suppose it is an extinct volcano?"

"Extinct?"

"Yes; the number of active volcanoes on the surface of the globe is at the present time only about three hundred. But there is a very much larger number of extinct ones. Now, Snæfell is one of these. Since historic times there has been but one eruption of this mountain, that of 1219; from that time it has quieted down more and more, and now it is no longer reckoned among active volcanoes."

To such positive statements I could make no reply. I therefore took refuge in other dark passages of the document.

"What is the meaning of this word Scartaris, and what have the kalends of July to do with it?"

My uncle took a few minutes to consider. For one short moment I felt a ray of hope, speedily to be extinguished. For he soon answered thus:

"What is darkness to you is light to me. This proves the ingenious care with which Saknussemm guarded and defined his discovery. Sneffels, or Snæfell, has several craters. It was therefore necessary to point out which of these leads to the centre of the globe. What did the Icelandic sage do? He observed that at the approach of the kalends of July, that is to say in the last days of June, one of the peaks, called Scartaris, flung its shadow down the mouth of that particular crater, and he committed that fact to his document. Could there possibly have been a more exact guide? As soon as we have arrived at the summit of Snæfell we shall have no hesitation as to the proper road to take."

Decidedly, my uncle had answered every one of my objections. I saw that his position on the old parchment was impregnable. I therefore ceased to press him upon that part of the subject, and as above all things he must be convinced, I passed on to scientific objections, which in my opinion were far more serious.

"Well, then," I said, "I am forced to admit that Saknussemm's sentence is clear, and leaves no room for doubt. I will even allow that the document bears every mark and evidence of authenticity. That learned philosopher did get to the bottom of Sneffels, he has seen the shadow of Scartaris touch the edge of the crater before the kalends of July; he may even have heard the legendary stories told in his day about that crater reaching to the centre of the world; but as for reaching it himself, as for performing the journey, and returning, if he ever went, I say no—he never, never did that."

"Now for your reason?" said my uncle ironically.

"All the theories of science demonstrate such a feat to be impracticable."

"The theories say that, do they?" replied the Professor in the tone of a meek disciple. "Oh! unpleasant theories! How the theories will hinder us, won't they?"

I saw that he was only laughing at me; but I went on all the same.

"Yes; it is perfectly well known that the internal temperature rises one degree for every 70 feet in depth; now, admitting this proportion to be constant, and the radius of the earth being fifteen hundred leagues, there must be a temperature of 360,032 degrees at the centre of the earth. Therefore, all the substances that compose the body of this earth must exist there in a state of incandescent gas; for the metals that most resist the action of heat, gold, and platinum, and the hardest rocks, can never be either solid or liquid under such a temperature. I have therefore good reason for asking if it is possible to penetrate through such a medium."

"So, Axel, it is the heat that troubles you?"

"Of course it is. Were we to reach a depth of thirty miles we should have arrived at the limit of the terrestrial crust, for there the temperature will be more than 2372 degrees."

"Are you afraid of being put into a state of fusion?"

"I will leave you to decide that question," I answered rather sullenly. "This is my decision," replied Professor Liedenbrock, putting on one of his grandest airs. "Neither you nor anybody else knows with any certainty what is going on in the interior of this globe, since not the twelve thousandth part of its radius is known; science is eminently perfectible; and every new theory is soon routed by a newer. Was it not always believed until Fourier that the temperature of the interplanetary spaces decreased perpetually? and is it not known at the present time that the greatest cold of the ethereal regions is never lower than 40 degrees below zero Fahr.? Why should it not be the same with the internal heat? Why should it not, at a certain depth, attain an impassable limit, instead of rising to such a point as to fuse the most infusible metals?"

As my uncle was now taking his stand upon hypotheses, of course, there was nothing to be said.

"Well, I will tell you that true savants, amongst them Poisson, have demonstrated that if a heat of 360,000 degrees[1] existed in the interior of the globe, the fiery gases arising from the fused matter would acquire an elastic force which the crust of the earth would be unable to resist, and that it would explode like the plates of a bursting boiler."

"That is Poisson's opinion, my uncle, nothing more."

"Granted. But it is likewise the creed adopted by other distinguished geologists, that the interior of the globe is neither gas nor water, nor any of the heaviest minerals known, for in none of these cases would the earth weigh what it does."

"Oh, with figures you may prove anything!"

"But is it the same with facts! Is it not known that the number of volcanoes has diminished since the first days of creation? and if there is central heat may we not thence conclude that it is in process of diminution?"

"My good uncle, if you will enter into the legion of speculation, I can discuss the matter no longer."

"But I have to tell you that the highest names have come to the support of my views. Do you remember a visit paid to me by the celebrated chemist, Humphry Davy, in 1825?"

"Not at all, for I was not born until nineteen years afterwards."

"Well, Humphry Davy did call upon me on his way through Hamburg. We were long engaged in discussing, amongst other problems, the hypothesis of the liquid structure of the terrestrial nucleus. We were agreed that it could not be in a liquid state, for a reason which science has never been able to confute."

"What is that reason?" I said, rather astonished.

"Because this liquid mass would be subject, like the ocean, to the lunar attraction, and therefore twice every day there would be internal tides, which, upheaving the terrestrial crust, would cause periodical earthquakes!"

"Yet it is evident that the surface of the globe has been subject to the action of fire," I replied, "and it is quite reasonable to suppose that the external crust cooled down first, whilst the heat took refuge down to the centre."

"Quite a mistake," my uncle answered. "The earth has been heated by combustion on its surface, that is all. Its surface was composed of a great number of metals, such as potassium and sodium, which have the peculiar property of igniting at the mere contact with air and water; these metals kindled when the atmospheric vapours fell in rain upon the soil; and by and by, when the waters penetrated into the fissures of the crust of the earth, they broke out into fresh combustion with explosions and eruptions. Such was the cause of the numerous volcanoes at the origin of the earth."

"Upon my word, this is a very clever hypothesis," I exclaimed, in spite rather of myself.

"And which Humphry Davy demonstrated to me by a simple experiment. He formed a small ball of the metals which I have named, and which was a very fair representation of

---

[1] The degrees of temperature are given by Jules Verne according to the centigrade system, for which we will in each case substitute the Fahrenheit measurement. (Tr.)

our globe; whenever he caused a fine dew of rain to fall upon its surface, it heaved up into little monticules, it became oxydized and formed miniature mountains; a crater broke open at one of its summits; the eruption took place, and communicated to the whole of the ball such a heat that it could not be held in the hand."

In truth, I was beginning to be shaken by the Professor's arguments, besides which he gave additional weight to them by his usual ardour and fervent enthusiasm.

"You see, Axel," he added, "the condition of the terrestrial nucleus has given rise to various hypotheses among geologists; there is no proof at all for this internal heat; my opinion is that there is no such thing, it cannot be; besides we shall see for ourselves, and, like Arne Saknussemm, we shall know exactly what to hold as truth concerning this grand question."

"Very well, we shall see," I replied, feeling myself carried off by his contagious enthusiasm. "Yes, we shall see; that is, if it is possible to see anything there."

"And why not? May we not depend upon electric phenomena to give us light? May we not even expect light from the atmosphere, the pressure of which may render it luminous as we approach the centre?"

"Yes, yes," said I; "that is possible, too."

"It is certain," exclaimed my uncle in a tone of triumph. "But silence, do you hear me? silence upon the whole subject; and let no one get before us in this design of discovering the centre of the earth."

CHAPTER VII. A WOMAN'S COURAGE

Thus ended this memorable seance. That conversation threw me into a fever. I came out of my uncle's study as if I had been stunned, and as if there was not air enough in all the streets of Hamburg to put me right again. I therefore made for the banks of the Elbe, where the steamer lands her passengers, which forms the communication between the city and the Hamburg railway.

Was I convinced of the truth of what I had heard? Had I not bent under the iron rule of the Professor Liedenbrock? Was I to believe him in earnest in his intention to penetrate to the centre of this massive globe? Had I been listening to the mad speculations of a lunatic, or to the scientific conclusions of a lofty genius? Where did truth stop? Where did error begin?

I was all adrift amongst a thousand contradictory hypotheses, but I could not lay hold of one.

Yet I remembered that I had been convinced, although now my enthusiasm was beginning to cool down; but I felt a desire to start at once, and not to lose time and courage by calm reflection. I had at that moment quite courage enough to strap my knapsack to my shoulders and start.

But I must confess that in another hour this unnatural excitement abated, my nerves became unstrung, and from the depths of the abysses of this earth I ascended to its surface again.

"It is quite absurd!" I cried, "there is no sense about it. No sensible young man should for a moment entertain such a proposal. The whole thing is non-existent. I have had a bad night, I have been dreaming of horrors."

But I had followed the banks of the Elbe and passed the town. After passing the port too, I had reached the Altona road. I was led by a presentiment, soon to be realised; for shortly I espied my little Gräuben bravely returning with her light step to Hamburg.

"Gräuben!" I cried from afar off.

The young girl stopped, rather frightened perhaps to hear her name called after her on the high road. Ten yards more, and I had joined her.

"Axel!" she cried surprised. "What! have you come to meet me? Is this why you are here, sir?"

But when she had looked upon me, Gräuben could not fail to see the uneasiness and distress of my mind.

"What is the matter?" she said, holding out her hand.

"What is the matter, Gräuben?" I cried.

In a couple of minutes my pretty Virlandaise was fully informed of the position of affairs. For a time she was silent. Did her heart palpitate as mine did? I don't know about that, but I know that her hand did not tremble in mine. We went on a hundred yards without speaking.

At last she said, "Axel!"

"My dear Gräuben."

"That will be a splendid journey!"

I gave a bound at these words.

"Yes, Axel, a journey worthy of the nephew of a savant; it is a good thing for a man to be distinguished by some great enterprise."

"What, Gräuben, won't you dissuade me from such an undertaking?"

"No, my dear Axel, and I would willingly go with you, but that a poor girl would only be in your way."

"Is that quite true?"

"It is true."

Ah! women and young girls, how incomprehensible are your feminine hearts! When you are not the timidest, you are the bravest of creatures. Reason has nothing to do with your actions. What! did this child encourage me in such an expedition! Would she not be afraid to join it herself? And she was driving me to it, one whom she loved!

I was disconcerted, and, if I must tell the whole truth, I was ashamed.

"Gräuben, we will see whether you will say the same thing to-morrow."

"To-morrow, dear Axel, I will say what I say to-day."

Gräuben and I, hand in hand, but in silence, pursued our way. The emotions of that day were breaking my heart.

After all, I thought, the kalends of July are a long way off, and between this and then many things may take place which will cure my uncle of his desire to travel underground.

It was night when we arrived at the house in Königstrasse. I expected to find all quiet there, my uncle in bed as was his custom, and Martha giving her last touches with the feather brush.

But I had not taken into account the Professor's impatience. I found him shouting—and working himself up amidst a crowd of porters and messengers who were all depositing various loads in the passage. Our old servant was at her wits' end.

"Come, Axel, come, you miserable wretch," my uncle cried from as far off as he could see me. "Your boxes are not packed, and my papers are not arranged; where's the key of my carpet bag? and what have you done with my gaiters?"

I stood thunderstruck. My voice failed. Scarcely could my lips utter the words:

"Are we really going?"

"Of course, you unhappy boy! Could I have dreamed that you would have gone out for a walk instead of hurrying your preparations forward?"

"Are we to go?" I asked again, with sinking hopes.

"Yes; the day after to-morrow, early."

I could hear no more. I fled for refuge into my own little room.

All hope was now at an end. My uncle had been all the morning making purchases of a part of the tools and apparatus required for this desperate undertaking. The passage was encumbered with rope ladders, knotted cords, torches, flasks, grappling irons, alpenstocks, pickaxes, iron shod sticks, enough to load ten men.

I spent an awful night. Next morning I was called early. I had quite decided I would not open the door. But how was I to resist the sweet voice which was always music to my ears, saying, "My dear Axel?"

I came out of my room. I thought my pale countenance and my red and sleepless eyes would work upon Gräuben's sympathies and change her mind.

"Ah! my dear Axel," she said. "I see you are better. A night's rest has done you good."

"Done me good!" I exclaimed.

I rushed to the glass. Well, in fact I did look better than I had expected. I could hardly believe my own eyes.

"Axel," she said, "I have had a long talk with my guardian. He is a bold philosopher, a man of immense courage, and you must remember that his blood flows in your veins. He has confided to me his plans, his hopes, and why and how he hopes to attain his object. He will no doubt succeed. My dear Axel, it is a grand thing to devote yourself to science! What honour will fall upon Herr Liedenbrock, and so be reflected upon his companion! When you return, Axel, you will be a man, his equal, free to speak and to act independently, and free to —"

The dear girl only finished this sentence by blushing. Her words revived me. Yet I refused to believe we should start. I drew Gräuben into the Professor's study.

"Uncle, is it true that we are to go?"

"Why do you doubt?"

"Well, I don't doubt," I said, not to vex him; "but, I ask, what need is there to hurry?"

"Time, time, flying with irreparable rapidity."

"But it is only the 16th May, and until the end of June—"

"What, you monument of ignorance! do you think you can get to Iceland in a couple of days? If you had not deserted me like a fool I should have taken you to the Copenhagen office, to Liffender & Co., and you would have learned then that there is only one trip every month from Copenhagen to Rejkiavik, on the 22nd."

"Well?"

"Well, if we waited for the 22nd June we should be too late to see the shadow of Scartaris touch the crater of Sneffels. Therefore we must get to Copenhagen as fast as we can to secure our passage. Go and pack up."

There was no reply to this. I went up to my room. Gräuben followed me. She undertook to pack up all things necessary for my voyage. She was no more moved than if I had been starting for a little trip to Lübeck or Heligoland. Her little hands moved without haste. She talked quietly. She supplied me with sensible reasons for our expedition. She delighted me, and yet I was angry with her. Now and then I felt I ought to break out into a passion, but she took no noticc and went on her way as methodically as ever.

Finally the last strap was buckled; I came downstairs. All that day the philosophical instrument makers and the electricians kept coming and going. Martha was distracted.

"Is master mad?" she asked.

I nodded my head.

"And is he going to take you with him?"

I nodded again.

"Where to?"

I pointed with my finger downward.

"Down into the cellar?" cried the old servant.

"No," I said. "Lower down than that."

Night came. But I knew nothing about the lapse of time.

"To-morrow morning at six precisely," my uncle decreed "we start."

At ten o'clock I fell upon my bed, a dead lump of inert matter. All through the night terror had hold of me. I spent it dreaming of abysses. I was a prey to delirium. I felt myself grasped by the Professor's sinewy hand, dragged along, hurled down, shattered into little bits. I dropped down unfathomable precipices with the accelerating velocity of bodies falling through space. My life had become an endless fall. I awoke at five with shattered nerves, trembling and weary. I came downstairs. My uncle was at table, devouring his breakfast. I stared at him with horror and disgust. But dear Gräuben was there; so I said nothing, and could eat nothing.

At half-past five there was a rattle of wheels outside. A large carriage was there to take us to the Altona railway station. It was soon piled up with my uncle's multifarious preparations.

"Where's your box?" he cried.

"It is ready," I replied, with faltering voice.

"Then make haste down, or we shall lose the train."

It was now manifestly impossible to maintain the struggle against destiny. I went up again to my room, and rolling my portmanteaus downstairs I darted after him.

At that moment my uncle was solemnly investing Gräuben with the reins of government. My pretty Virlandaise was as calm and collected as was her wont. She kissed her guardian; but could not restrain a tear in touching my cheek with her gentle lips.

"Gräuben!" I murmured.

"Go, my dear Axel, go! I am now your betrothed; and when you come back I will be your wife."

I pressed her in my arms and took my place in the carriage. Martha and the young girl, standing at the door, waved their last farewell. Then the horses, roused by the driver's whistling, darted off at a gallop on the road to Altona.

CHAPTER VIII. SERIOUS PREPARATIONS FOR VERTICAL DESCENT

Altona, which is but a suburb of Hamburg, is the terminus of the Kiel railway, which was to carry us to the Belts. In twenty minutes we were in Holstein.

At half-past six the carriage stopped at the station; my uncle's numerous packages, his voluminous *impedimenta,* were unloaded, removed, labelled, weighed, put into the luggage vans, and at seven we were seated face to face in our compartment. The whistle sounded, the engine started, we were off.

Was I resigned? No, not yet. Yet the cool morning air and the scenes on the road, rapidly changed by the swiftness of the train, drew me away somewhat from my sad reflections.

As for the Professor's reflections, they went far in advance of the swiftest express. We were alone in the carriage, but we sat in silence. My uncle examined all his pockets and his travelling bag with the minutest care. I saw that he had not forgotten the smallest matter of detail.

Amongst other documents, a sheet of paper, carefully folded, bore the heading of the Danish consulate with the signature of W. Christiensen, consul at Hamburg and the Professor's friend. With this we possessed the proper introductions to the Governor of Iceland.

I also observed the famous document most carefully laid up in a secret pocket in his portfolio. I bestowed a malediction upon it, and then proceeded to examine the country.

It was a very long succession of uninteresting loamy and fertile flats, a very easy country for the construction of railways, and propitious for the laying-down of these direct level lines so dear to railway companies.

I had no time to get tired of the monotony; for in three hours we stopped at Kiel, close to the sea.

The luggage being labelled for Copenhagen, we had no occasion to look after it. Yet the Professor watched every article with jealous vigilance, until all were safe on board. There they disappeared in the hold.

My uncle, notwithstanding his hurry, had so well calculated the relations between the train and the steamer that we had a whole day to spare. The steamer *Ellenora,* did not start until night. Thence sprang a feverish state of excitement in which the impatient irascible traveller devoted to perdition the railway directors and the steamboat companies and the governments which allowed such intolerable slowness. I was obliged to act chorus to him when he attacked the captain of the *Ellenora* upon this subject. The captain disposed of us summarily.

At Kiel, as elsewhere, we must do something to while away the time. What with walking on the verdant shores of the bay within which nestles the little town, exploring the thick woods which make it look like a nest embowered amongst thick foliage, admiring the villas, each provided with a little bathing house, and moving about and grumbling, at last ten o'clock came.

The heavy coils of smoke from the *Ellenora's* funnel unrolled in the sky, the bridge shook with the quivering of the struggling steam; we were on board, and owners for the time of two berths, one over the other, in the only saloon cabin on board.

At a quarter past the moorings were loosed and the throbbing steamer pursued her way over the dark waters of the Great Belt.

The night was dark; there was a sharp breeze and a rough sea, a few lights appeared on shore through the thick darkness; later on, I cannot tell when, a dazzling light from some lighthouse threw a bright stream of fire along the waves; and this is all I can remember of this first portion of our sail.

At seven in the morning we landed at Korsor, a small town on the west coast of Zealand. There we were transferred from the boat to another line of railway, which took us by just as flat a country as the plain of Holstein.

Three hours' travelling brought us to the capital of Denmark. My uncle had not shut his eyes all night. In his impatience I believe he was trying to accelerate the train with his feet.

At last he discerned a stretch of sea.

"The Sound!" he cried.

At our left was a huge building that looked like a hospital.

"That's a lunatic asylum," said one of or travelling companions.

Very good! thought I, just the place we want to end our days in; and great as it is, that asylum is not big enough to contain all Professor Liedenbrock's madness!

At ten in the morning, at last, we set our feet in Copenhagen; the luggage was put upon a carriage and taken with ourselves to the Phoenix Hotel in Breda Gate. This took half an hour, for the station is out of the town. Then my uncle, after a hasty toilet, dragged me after him. The porter at the hotel could speak German and English; but the Professor, as a polyglot, questioned him in good Danish, and it was in the same language that that personage directed him to the Museum of Northern Antiquities.

The curator of this curious establishment, in which wonders are gathered together out of which the ancient history of the country might be reconstructed by means of its stone weapons, its cups and its jewels, was a learned savant, the friend of the Danish consul at Hamburg, Professor Thomsen.

My uncle had a cordial letter of introduction to him. As a general rule one savant greets another with coolness. But here the case was different. M. Thomsen, like a good friend, gave the Professor Liedenbrock a cordial greeting, and he even vouchsafed the same kindness to his nephew. It is hardly necessary to say the secret was sacredly kept from the excellent curator; we were simply disinterested travellers visiting Iceland out of harmless curiosity.

M. Thomsen placed his services at our disposal, and we visited the quays with the object of finding out the next vessel to sail.

I was yet in hopes that there would be no means of getting to Iceland. But there was no such luck. A small Danish schooner, the *Valkyria*, was to set sail for Rejkiavik on the 2nd of June. The captain, M. Bjarne, was on board. His intending passenger was so joyful that he almost squeezed his hands till they ached. That good man was rather surprised at his energy. To him it seemed a very simple thing to go to Iceland, as that was his business;

but to my uncle it was sublime. The worthy captain took advantage of his enthusiasm to charge double fares; but we did not trouble ourselves about mere trifles. .

"You must be on board on Tuesday, at seven in the morning," said

Captain Bjarne, after having pocketed more dollars than were his due.

Then we thanked M. Thomsen for his kindness, "and we returned to the

Phoenix Hotel.

"It's all right, it's all right," my uncle repeated. "How fortunate we are to have found this boat ready for sailing. Now let us have some breakfast and go about the town."

We went first to Kongens-nye-Torw, an irregular square in which are two innocent-looking guns, which need not alarm any one. Close by, at No. 5, there was a French "restaurant," kept by a cook of the name of Vincent, where we had an ample breakfast for four marks each (2s. 4d.).

Then I took a childish pleasure in exploring the city; my uncle let me take him with me, but he took notice of nothing, neither the insignificant king's palace, nor the pretty seventeenth century bridge, which spans the canal before the museum, nor that immense cenotaph of Thorwaldsen's, adorned with horrible mural painting, and containing within it a collection of the sculptor's works, nor in a fine park the toylike chateau of Rosenberg, nor the beautiful renaissance edifice of the Exchange, nor its spire composed of the twisted tails of four bronze dragons, nor the great windmill on the ramparts, whose huge arms dilated in the sea breeze like the sails of a ship.

What delicious walks we should have had together, my pretty Virlandaise and I, along the harbour where the two-deckers and the frigate slept peaceably by the red roofing of the warehouse, by the green banks of the strait, through the deep shades of the trees amongst which the fort is half concealed, where the guns are thrusting out their black throats between branches of alder and willow.

But, alas! Gräuben was far away; and I never hoped to see her again.

But if my uncle felt no attraction towards these romantic scenes he was very much struck with the aspect of a certain church spire situated in the island of Amak, which forms the south-west quarter of Copenhagen.

I was ordered to direct my feet that way; I embarked on a small steamer which plies on the canals, and in a few minutes she touched the quay of the dockyard.

After crossing a few narrow streets where some convicts, in trousers half yellow and half grey, were at work under the orders of the gangers, we arrived at the Vor Frelsers Kirk. There was nothing remarkable about the church; but there was a reason why its tall spire had attracted the Professor's attention. Starting from the top of the tower, an external staircase wound around the spire, the spirals circling up into the sky.

"Let us get to the top," said my uncle.

"I shall be dizzy," I said.

"The more reason why we should go up; we must get used to it."

"But—"

"Come, I tell you; don't waste our time."

I had to obey. A keeper who lived at the other end of the street handed us the key, and the ascent began.

My uncle went ahead with a light step. I followed him not without alarm, for my head was very apt to feel dizzy; I possessed neither the equilibrium of an eagle nor his fearless nature.

As long as we were protected on the inside of the winding staircase up the tower, all was well enough; but after toiling up a hundred and fifty steps the fresh air came to salute my face, and we were on the leads of the tower. There the aerial staircase began its gyrations, only guarded by a thin iron rail, and the narrowing steps seemed to ascend into infinite space!

"Never shall I be able to do it," I said.

"Don't be a coward; come up, sir"; said my uncle with the coldest cruelty.

I had to follow, clutching at every step. The keen air made me giddy; I felt the spire rocking with every gust of wind; my knees began to fail; soon I was crawling on my knees, then creeping on my stomach; I closed my eyes; I seemed to be lost in space.

At last I reached the apex, with the assistance of my uncle dragging me up by the collar.

"Look down!" he cried. "Look down well! You must take a lesson in abysses."

I opened my eyes. I saw houses squashed flat as if they had all fallen down from the skies; a smoke fog seemed to drown them. Over my head ragged clouds were drifting past, and by an optical inversion they seemed stationary, while the steeple, the ball and I were all spinning along with fantastic speed. Far away on one side was the green country, on the other the sea sparkled, bathed in sunlight. The Sound stretched away to Elsinore, dotted with a few white sails, like sea-gulls' wings; and in the misty east and away to the north-east lay outstretched the faintly-shadowed shores of Sweden. All this immensity of space whirled and wavered, fluctuating beneath my eyes.

But I was compelled to rise, to stand up, to look. My first lesson in dizziness lasted an hour. When I got permission to come down and feel the solid street pavements I was afflicted with severe lumbago.

"To-morrow we will do it again," said the Professor.

And it was so; for five days in succession, I was obliged to undergo this anti-vertiginous exercise; and whether I would or not, I made some improvement in the art of "lofty contemplations."

CHAPTER IX. ICELAND! BUT WHAT NEXT?

The day for our departure arrived. The day before it our kind friend M. Thomsen brought us letters of introduction to Count Trampe, the Governor of Iceland, M. Picturssen, the bishop's suffragan, and M. Finsen, mayor of Rejkiavik. My uncle expressed his gratitude by tremendous compressions of both his hands.

On the 2nd, at six in the evening, all our precious baggage being safely on board the *Valkyria,* the captain took us into a very narrow cabin.

"Is the wind favourable?" my uncle asked.

"Excellent," replied Captain Bjarne; "a sou'-easter. We shall pass down the Sound full speed, with all sails set."

In a few minutes the schooner, under her mizen, brigantine, topsail, and topgallant sail, loosed from her moorings and made full sail through the straits. In an hour the capital of Denmark seemed to sink below the distant waves, and the *Valkyria* was skirting the coast by Elsinore. In my nervous frame of mind I expected to see the ghost of Hamlet wandering on the legendary castle terrace.

"Sublime madman!" I said, "no doubt you would approve of our expedition. Perhaps you would keep us company to the centre of the globe, to find the solution of your eternal doubts."

But there was no ghostly shape upon the ancient walls. Indeed, the castle is much younger than the heroic prince of Denmark. It now answers the purpose of a sumptuous lodge for the doorkeeper of the straits of the Sound, before which every year there pass fifteen thousand ships of all nations.

The castle of Kronsberg soon disappeared in the mist, as well as the tower of Helsingborg, built on the Swedish coast, and the schooner passed lightly on her way urged by the breezes of the Cattegat.

The *Valkyria* was a splendid sailer, but on a sailing vessel you can place no dependence. She was taking to Rejkiavik coal, household goods, earthenware, woollen clothing, and a cargo of wheat. The crew consisted of five men, all Danes.

"How long will the passage take?" my uncle asked.

"Ten days," the captain replied, "if we don't meet a nor'-wester in passing the Faroes."

"But are you not subject to considerable delays?"

"No, M. Liedenbrock, don't be uneasy, we shall get there in very good time."

At evening the schooner doubled the Skaw at the northern point of Denmark, in the night passed the Skager Rack, skirted Norway by Cape Lindness, and entered the North Sea.

In two days more we sighted the coast of Scotland near Peterhead, and the *Valkyria* turned her lead towards the Faroe Islands, passing between the Orkneys and Shetlands.

Soon the schooner encountered the great Atlantic swell; she had to tack against the north wind, and reached the Faroes only with some difficulty. On the 8th the captain made out Myganness, the southernmost of these islands, and from that moment took a straight course for Cape Portland, the most southerly point of Iceland.

The passage was marked by nothing unusual. I bore the troubles of the sea pretty well; my uncle, to his own intense disgust, and his greater shame, was ill all through the voyage.

He therefore was unable to converse with the captain about Snæfell, the way to get to it, the facilities for transport, he was obliged to put off these inquiries until his arrival, and spent all his time at full length in his cabin, of which the timbers creaked and shook with every pitch she took. It must be confessed he was not undeserving of his punishment.

On the 11th we reached Cape Portland. The clear open weather gave us a good view of Myrdals jokul, which overhangs it. The cape is merely a low hill with steep sides, standing lonely by the beach.

The *Valkyria* kept at some distance from the coast, taking a westerly course amidst great shoals of whales and sharks. Soon we came in sight of an enormous perforated rock, through which the sea dashed furiously. The Westman islets seemed to rise out of the ocean like a group of rocks in a liquid plain. From that time the schooner took a wide berth and swept at a great distance round Cape Rejkianess, which forms the western point of Iceland.

The rough sea prevented my uncle from coming on deck to admire these shattered and surf-beaten coasts.

Forty-eight hours after, coming out of a storm which forced the schooner to scud under bare poles, we sighted east of us the beacon on Cape Skagen, where dangerous rocks extend far away seaward. An Icelandic pilot came on board, and in three hours the *Valkyria* dropped her anchor before Rejkiavik, in Faxa Bay.

The Professor at last emerged from his cabin, rather pale and wretched-looking, but still full of enthusiasm, and with ardent satisfaction shining in his eyes.

The population of the town, wonderfully interested in the arrival of a vessel from which every one expected something, formed in groups upon the quay.

My uncle left in haste his floating prison, or rather hospital. But before quitting the deck of the schooner he dragged me forward, and pointing with outstretched finger north of the bay at a distant mountain terminating in a double peak, a pair of cones covered with perpetual snow, he cried:

"Snæfell! Snæfell!"

Then recommending me, by an impressive gesture, to keep silence, he went into the boat which awaited him. I followed, and presently we were treading the soil of Iceland.

The first man we saw was a good-looking fellow enough, in a general's uniform. Yet he was not a general but a magistrate, the Governor of the island, M. le Baron Trampe himself. The Professor was soon aware of the presence he was in. He delivered him his letters from Copenhagen, and then followed a short conversation in the Danish language, the purport of which I was quite ignorant of, and for a very good reason. But the result of this first conversation was, that Baron Trampe placed himself entirely at the service of Professor Liedenbrock.

My uncle was just as courteously received by the mayor, M. Finsen, whose appearance was as military, and disposition and office as pacific, as the Governor's.

CHAPTER IX. ICELAND! BUT WHAT NEXT?

As for the bishop's suffragan, M. Picturssen, he was at that moment engaged on an episcopal visitation in the north. For the time we must be resigned to wait for the honour of being presented to him. But M. Fridrikssen, professor of natural sciences at the school of Rejkiavik, was a delightful man, and his friendship became very precious to me. This modest philosopher spoke only Danish and Latin. He came to proffer me his good offices in the language of Horace, and I felt that we were made to understand each other. In fact he was the only person in Iceland with whom I could converse at all.

This good-natured gentleman made over to us two of the three rooms which his house contained, and we were soon installed in it with all our luggage, the abundance of which rather astonished the good people of Rejkiavik.

"Well, Axel," said my uncle, "we are getting on, and now the worst is over."

"The worst!" I said, astonished.

"To be sure, now we have nothing to do but go down."

"Oh, if that is all, you are quite right; but after all, when we have gone down, we shall have to get up again, I suppose?"

"Oh I don't trouble myself about that. Come, there's no time to lose;
I am going to the library. Perhaps there is some manuscript of
Saknussemm's there, and I should be glad to consult it."

"Well, while you are there I will go into the town. Won't you?"

"Oh, that is very uninteresting to me. It is not what is upon this island, but what is underneath, that interests me."

I went out, and wandered wherever chance took me.

It would not be easy to lose your way in Rejkiavik. I was therefore under no necessity to inquire the road, which exposes one to mistakes when the only medium of intercourse is gesture.

The town extends along a low and marshy level, between two hills. An immense bed of lava bounds it on one side, and falls gently towards the sea. On the other extends the vast bay of Faxa, shut in at the north by the enormous glacier of the Snæfell, and of which the *Valkyria* was for the time the only occupant. Usually the English and French conservators of fisheries moor in this bay, but just then they were cruising about the western coasts of the island.

The longest of the only two streets that Rejkiavik possesses was parallel with the beach. Here live the merchants and traders, in wooden cabins made of red planks set horizontally; the other street, running west, ends at the little lake between the house of the bishop and other non-commercial people.

I had soon explored these melancholy ways; here and there I got a glimpse of faded turf, looking like a worn-out bit of carpet, or some appearance of a kitchen garden, the sparse vegetables of which (potatoes, cabbages, and lettuces), would have figured appropriately upon a Lilliputian table. A few sickly wallflowers were trying to enjoy the air and sunshine.

About the middle of the tin-commercial street I found the public cemetery, inclosed with a mud wall, and where there seemed plenty of room.

Then a few steps brought me to the Governor's house, a but compared with the town hall of Hamburg, a palace in comparison with the cabins of the Icelandic population.

Between the little lake and the town the church is built in the Protestant style, of calcined stones extracted out of the volcanoes by their own labour and at their own expense; in high westerly winds it was manifest that the red tiles of the roof would be scattered in the air, to the great danger of the faithful worshippers.

On a neighbouring hill I perceived the national school, where, as I was informed later by our host, were taught Hebrew, English, French, and Danish, four languages of which, with shame I confess it, I don't know a single word; after an examination I should have had to stand last of the forty scholars educated at this little college, and I should have been held unworthy to sleep along with them in one of those little double closets, where more delicate youths would have died of suffocation the very first night.

In three hours I had seen not only the town but its environs. The general aspect was wonderfully dull. No trees, and scarcely any vegetation. Everywhere bare rocks, signs of volcanic action. The Icelandic huts are made of earth and turf, and the walls slope inward; they rather resemble roofs placed on the ground. But then these roofs are meadows of comparative fertility. Thanks to the internal heat, the grass grows on them to some degree of perfection. It is carefully mown in the hay season; if it were not, the horses would come to pasture on these green abodes.

In my excursion I met but few people. On returning to the main street I found the greater part of the population busied in drying, salting, and putting on board codfish, their chief export. The men looked like robust but heavy, blond Germans with pensive eyes, conscious of being far removed from their fellow creatures, poor exiles relegated to this land of ice, poor creatures who should have been Esquimaux, since nature had condemned them to live only just outside the arctic circle! In vain did I try to detect a smile upon their lips; sometimes by a spasmodic and involuntary contraction of the muscles they seemed to laugh, but they never smiled.

Their costume consisted of a coarse jacket of black woollen cloth called in Scandinavian lands a 'vadmel,' a hat with a very broad brim, trousers with a narrow edge of red, and a bit of leather rolled round the foot for shoes.

The women looked as sad and as resigned as the men; their faces were agreeable but expressionless, and they wore gowns and petticoats of dark 'vadmel'; as maidens, they wore over their braided hair a little knitted brown cap; when married, they put around their heads a coloured handkerchief, crowned with a peak of white linen.

After a good walk I returned to M. Fridrikssen's house, where I found my uncle already in his host's company.

CHAPTER X. INTERESTING CONVERSATIONS WITH ICELANDIC SAVANTS

Dinner was ready. Professor Liedenbrock devoured his portion voraciously, for his compulsory fast on board had converted his stomach into a vast unfathomable gulf. There was nothing remarkable in the meal itself; but the hospitality of our host, more Danish than Icelandic, reminded me of the heroes of old. It was evident that we were more at home than he was himself.

The conversation was carried on in the vernacular tongue, which my uncle mixed with German and M. Fridrikssen with Latin for my benefit. It turned upon scientific questions as befits philosophers; but Professor Liedenbrock was excessively reserved, and at every sentence spoke to me with his eyes, enjoining the most absolute silence upon our plans.

In the first place M. Fridrikssen wanted to know what success my uncle had had at the library.

"Your library! why there is nothing but a few tattered books upon almost deserted shelves."

"Indeed!" replied M. Fridrikssen, "why we possess eight thousand volumes, many of them valuable and scarce, works in the old Scandinavian language, and we have all the novelties that Copenhagen sends us every year."

"Where do you keep your eight thousand volumes? For my part—"

"Oh, M. Liedenbrock, they are all over the country. In this icy region we are fond of study. There is not a farmer nor a fisherman that cannot read and does not read. Our principle is, that books, instead of growing mouldy behind an iron grating, should be worn out under the eyes of many readers. Therefore, these volumes are passed from one to another, read over and over, referred to again and again; and it often happens that they find their way back to their shelves only after an absence of a year or two."

"And in the meantime," said my uncle rather spitefully, "strangers—"

"Well, what would you have? Foreigners have their libraries at home, and the first essential for labouring people is that they should be educated. I repeat to you the love of reading runs in Icelandic blood. In 1816 we founded a prosperous literary society; learned strangers think themselves honoured in becoming members of it. It publishes books which educate our fellow-countrymen, and do the country great service. If you will consent to be a corresponding member, Herr Liedenbrock, you will be giving us great pleasure."

My uncle, who had already joined about a hundred learned societies, accepted with a grace which evidently touched M. Fridrikssen.

"Now," said he, "will you be kind enough to tell me what books you hoped to find in our library and I may perhaps enable you to consult them?"

My uncle's eyes and mine met. He hesitated. This direct question went to the root of the matter. But after a moment's reflection he decided on speaking.

"Monsieur Fridrikssen, I wished to know if amongst your ancient books you possessed any of the works of Arne Saknussemm?"

"Arne Saknussemm!" replied the Rejkiavik professor. "You mean that learned sixteenth century savant, a naturalist, a chemist, and a traveller?"

"Just so!"

"One of the glories of Icelandic literature and science?"

"That's the man."

"An illustrious man anywhere!"

"Quite so."

"And whose courage was equal to his genius!"

"I see that you know him well."

My uncle was bathed in delight at hearing his hero thus described. He feasted his eyes upon M. Fridrikssen's face.

"Well," he cried, "where are his works?"

"His works, we have them not."

"What—not in Iceland?"

"They are neither in Iceland nor anywhere else."

"Why is that?"

"Because Arne Saknussemm was persecuted for heresy, and in 1573 his books were burned by the hands of the common hangman."

"Very good! Excellent!" cried my uncle, to the great scandal of the professor of natural history.

"What!" he cried.

"Yes, yes; now it is all clear, now it is all unravelled; and I see why Saknussemm, put into the Index Expurgatorius, and compelled to hide the discoveries made by his genius, was obliged to bury in an incomprehensible cryptogram the secret—"

"What secret?" asked M. Fridrikssen, starting.

"Oh, just a secret which—" my uncle stammered.

"Have you some private document in your possession?" asked our host.

"No; I was only supposing a case."

"Oh, very well," answered M. Fridrikssen, who was kind enough not to pursue the subject when he had noticed the embarrassment of his friend. "I hope you will not leave our island until you have seen some of its mineralogical wealth."

"Certainly," replied my uncle; "but I am rather late; or have not others been here before me?"

"Yes, Herr Liedenbrock; the labours of MM. Olafsen and Povelsen, pursued by order of the king, the researches of Troïl the scientific mission of MM. Gaimard and Robert on the French corvette *La Recherche*[1], and lately the observations of scientific men who came in the *Reine Hortense,* have added materially to our knowledge of Iceland. But I assure you there is plenty left."

"Do you think so?" said my uncle, pretending to look very modest, and trying to hide the curiosity was flashing out of his eyes.

---

[1] *Recherche* was sent out in 1835 by Admiral Duperré to learn the fate of the lost expedition of M. de Blosseville in the *Lilloise* which has never been heard of.

CHAPTER X. INTERESTING CONVERSATIONS WITH ICELANDIC SAVANTS

"Oh, yes; how many mountains, glaciers, and volcanoes there are to study, which are as yet but imperfectly known! Then, without going any further, that mountain in the horizon. That is Snæfell."

"Ah!" said my uncle, as coolly as he was able, "is that Snæfell?"

"Yes; one of the most curious volcanoes, and the crater of which has scarcely ever been visited."

"Is it extinct?"

"Oh, yes; more than five hundred years."

"Well," replied my uncle, who was frantically locking his legs together to keep himself from jumping up in the air, "that is where I mean to begin my geological studies, there on that Seffel—Fessel—what do you call it?"

"Snæfell," replied the excellent M. Fridrikssen.

This part of the conversation was in Latin; I had understood every word of it, and I could hardly conceal my amusement at seeing my uncle trying to keep down the excitement and satisfaction which were brimming over in every limb and every feature. He tried hard to put on an innocent little expression of simplicity; but it looked like a diabolical grin.

"Yes," said he, "your words decide me. We will try to scale that

Snæfell; perhaps even we may pursue our studies in its crater!"

"I am very sorry," said M. Fridrikssen, "that my engagements will not allow me to absent myself, or I would have accompanied you myself with both pleasure and profit."

"Oh, no, no!" replied my uncle with great animation, "we would not disturb any one for the world, M. Fridrikssen. Still, I thank you with all my heart: the company of such a talented man would have been very serviceable, but the duties of your profession—"

I am glad to think that our host, in the innocence of his Icelandic soul, was blind to the transparent artifices of my uncle.

"I very much approve of your beginning with that volcano, M.

Liedenbrock. You will gather a harvest of interesting observations.

But, tell me, how do you expect to get to the peninsula of Snæfell?"

"By sea, crossing the bay. That's the most direct way."

"No doubt; but it is impossible."

"Why?"

"Because we don't possess a single boat at Rejkiavik."

"You don't mean to say so?"

"You will have to go by land, following the shore. It will be longer, but more interesting."

"Very well, then; and now I shall have to see about a guide."

"I have one to offer you."

"A safe, intelligent man."

"Yes; an inhabitant of that peninsula. He is an eider-down hunter, and very clever. He speaks Danish perfectly."

"When can I see him?"

"To-morrow, if you like."

"Why not to-day?"

"Because he won't be here till to-morrow."

"To-morrow, then," added my uncle with a sigh.

This momentous conversation ended in a few minutes with warm acknowledgments paid by the German to the Icelandic Professor. At this dinner my uncle had just elicited important facts, amongst others, the history of Saknussemm, the reason of the mysterious document, that his host would not accompany him in his expedition, and that the very next day a guide would be waiting upon him.

CHAPTER XI. A GUIDE FOUND TO THE CENTRE OF THE EARTH

In the evening I took a short walk on the beach and returned at night to my plank-bed, where I slept soundly all night.

When I awoke I heard my uncle talking at a great rate in the next room. I immediately dressed and joined him.

He was conversing in the Danish language with a tall man, of robust build. This fine fellow must have been possessed of great strength. His eyes, set in a large and ingenuous face, seemed to me very intelligent; they were of a dreamy sea-blue. Long hair, which would have been called red even in England, fell in long meshes upon his broad shoulders. The movements of this native were lithe and supple; but he made little use of his arms in speaking, like a man who knew nothing or cared nothing about the language of gestures. His whole appearance bespoke perfect calmness and self-possession, not indolence but tranquillity. It was felt at once that he would be beholden to nobody, that he worked for his own convenience, and that nothing in this world could astonish or disturb his philosophic calmness.

I caught the shades of this Icelander's character by the way in which he listened to the impassioned flow of words which fell from the Professor. He stood with arms crossed, perfectly unmoved by my uncle's incessant gesticulations. A negative was expressed by a slow movement of the head from left to right, an affirmative by a slight bend, so slight that his long hair scarcely moved. He carried economy of motion even to parsimony.

Certainly I should never have dreamt in looking at this man that he was a hunter; he did not look likely to frighten his game, nor did he seem as if he would even get near it. But the mystery was explained when M. Fridrikssen informed me that this tranquil personage was only a hunter of the eider duck, whose under plumage constitutes the chief wealth of the island. This is the celebrated eider down, and it requires no great rapidity of movement to get it.

Early in summer the female, a very pretty bird, goes to build her nest among the rocks of the fiords with which the coast is fringed. After building the nest she feathers it with down plucked from her own breast. Immediately the hunter, or rather the trader, comes and robs the nest, and the female recommences her work. This goes on as long as she has any down left. When she has stripped herself bare the male takes his turn to pluck himself. But as the coarse and hard plumage of the male has no commercial value, the hunter does not take the trouble to rob the nest of this; the female therefore lays her eggs in the spoils of her mate, the young are hatched, and next year the harvest begins again.

Now, as the eider duck does not select steep cliffs for her nest, but rather the smooth terraced rocks which slope to the sea, the Icelandic hunter might exercise his calling without any inconvenient exertion. He was a farmer who was not obliged either to sow or reap his harvest, but merely to gather it in.

This grave, phlegmatic, and silent individual was called Hans Bjelke; and he came recommended by M. Fridrikssen. He was our future guide. His manners were a singular contrast with my uncle's.

Nevertheless, they soon came to understand each other. Neither looked at the amount of the payment: the one was ready to accept whatever was offered; the other was ready to give whatever was demanded. Never was bargain more readily concluded.

The result of the treaty was, that Hans engaged on his part to conduct us to the village of Stapi, on the south shore of the Snæfell peninsula, at the very foot of the volcano. By land this would be about twenty-two miles, to be done, said my uncle, in two days.

But when he learnt that the Danish mile was 24,000 feet long, he was obliged to modify his calculations and allow seven or eight days for the march.

Four horses were to be placed at our disposal—two to carry him and me, two for the baggage. Hams, as was his custom, would go on foot. He knew all that part of the coast perfectly, and promised to take us the shortest way.

His engagement was not to terminate with our arrival at Stapi; he was to continue in my uncle's service for the whole period of his scientific researches, for the remuneration of three rixdales a week (about twelve shillings), but it was an express article of the covenant that his wages should be counted out to him every Saturday at six o'clock in the evening, which, according to him, was one indispensable part of the engagement.

The start was fixed for the 16th of June. My uncle wanted to pay the hunter a portion in advance, but he refused with one word:

"*Efter,*" said he.

"After," said the Professor for my edification.

The treaty concluded, Hans silently withdrew.

"A famous fellow," cried my uncle; "but he little thinks of the marvellous part he has to play in the future."

"So he is to go with us as far as—"

"As far as the centre of the earth, Axel."

Forty-eight hours were left before our departure; to my great regret I had to employ them in preparations; for all our ingenuity was required to pack every article to the best advantage; instruments here, arms there, tools in this package, provisions in that: four sets of packages in all.

The instruments were:

1. An Eigel's centigrade thermometer, graduated up to 150 degrees (302 degrees Fahr.), which seemed to me too much or too little. Too much if the internal heat was to rise so high, for in this case we should be baked, not enough to measure the temperature of springs or any matter in a state of fusion.

2. An aneroid barometer, to indicate extreme pressures of the atmosphere. An ordinary barometer would not have answered the purpose, as the pressure would increase during our descent to a point which the mercurial barometer[1] would not register.

---

[1] In M. Verne's book a 'manometer' is the instrument used, of which very little is known. In a complete list of philosophical instruments the translator cannot find the name. As he is assured by a first-rate instrument maker, Chadburn, of Liverpool, that an aneroid can be constructed to measure any depth, he has thought it best to furnish the adventurous profes-

3. A chronometer, made by Boissonnas, jun., of Geneva, accurately set to the meridian of Hamburg.

4. Two compasses, viz., a common compass and a dipping needle.

5. A night glass.

6. Two of Ruhmkorff's apparatus, which, by means of an electric current, supplied a safe and handy portable light[1]

The arms consisted of two of Purdy's rifles and two brace of pistols. But what did we want arms for? We had neither savages nor wild beasts to fear, I supposed. But my uncle seemed to believe in his arsenal as in his instruments, and more especially in a considerable quantity of gun cotton, which is unaffected by moisture, and the explosive force of which exceeds that of gunpowder.

The tools comprised two pickaxes, two spades, a silk ropeladder, three iron-tipped sticks, a hatchet, a hammer, a dozen wedges and iron spikes, and a long knotted rope. Now this was a large load, for the ladder was 300 feet long.

And there were provisions too: this was not a large parcel, but it was comforting to know that of essence of beef and biscuits there were six months' consumption. Spirits were the only liquid, and of water we took none; but we had flasks, and my uncle depended on springs from which to fill them. Whatever objections I hazarded as to their quality, temperature, and even absence, remained ineffectual.

To complete the exact inventory of all our travelling accompaniments, I must not forget a pocket medicine chest, containing blunt scissors, splints for broken limbs, a piece of tape of unbleached linen, bandages and compresses, lint, a lancet for bleeding, all dreadful articles to take with one. Then there was a row of phials containing dextrine, alcoholic ether, liquid acetate of lead, vinegar, and ammonia drugs which afforded me no comfort. Finally, all the articles needful to supply Ruhmkorff's apparatus.

My uncle did not forget a supply of tobacco, coarse grained powder, and amadou, nor a leathern belt in which he carried a sufficient quantity of gold, silver, and paper money. Six pairs of boots and shoes, made waterproof with a composition of indiarubber and naphtha, were packed amongst the tools.

"Clothed, shod, and equipped like this," said my uncle, "there is no telling how far we may go."

---

sor with this more familiar instrument. The 'manometer' is generally known as a pressure gauge.—TRANS.

[1] Ruhmkorff's apparatus consists of a Bunsen pile worked with bichromate of potash, which makes no smell; an induction coil carries the electricity generated by the pile into communication with a lantern of peculiar construction; in this lantern there is a spiral glass tube from which the air has been excluded, and in which remains only a residuum of carbonic acid gas or of nitrogen. When the apparatus is put in action this gas becomes luminous, producing a white steady light. The pile and coil are placed in a leathern bag which the traveller carries over his shoulders; the lantern outside of the bag throws sufficient light into deep darkness; it enables one to venture without fear of explosions into the midst of the most inflammable gases, and is not extinguished even in the deepest waters. M. Ruhmkorff is a learned and most ingenious man of science; his great discovery is his induction coil, which produces a powerful stream of electricity. He obtained in 1864 the quinquennial prize of 50,000 franc reserved by the French government for the most ingenious application of electricity.

The 14th was wholly spent in arranging all our different articles. In the evening we dined with Baron Tramps; the mayor of Rejkiavik, and Dr. Hyaltalin, the first medical man of the place, being of the party. M. Fridrikssen was not there. I learned afterwards that he and the Governor disagreed upon some question of administration, and did not speak to each other. I therefore knew not a single word of all that was said at this semi-official dinner; but I could not help noticing that my uncle talked the whole time.

On the 15th our preparations were all made. Our host gave the Professor very great pleasure by presenting him with a map of Iceland far more complete than that of Hendersen. It was the map of M. Olaf Nikolas Olsen, in the proportion of 1 to 480,000 of the actual size of the island, and published by the Icelandic Literary Society. It was a precious document for a mineralogist.

Our last evening was spent in intimate conversation with M. Fridrikssen, with whom I felt the liveliest sympathy; then, after the talk, succeeded, for me, at any rate, a disturbed and restless night.

At five in the morning I was awoke by the neighing and pawing of four horses under my window. I dressed hastily and came down into the street. Hans was finishing our packing, almost as it were without moving a limb; and yet he did his work cleverly. My uncle made more noise than execution, and the guide seemed to pay very little attention to his energetic directions.

At six o'clock our preparations were over. M. Fridrikssen shook hands with us. My uncle thanked him heartily for his extreme kindness. I constructed a few fine Latin sentences to express my cordial farewell. Then we bestrode our steeds and with his last adieu M. Fridrikssen treated me to a line of Virgil eminently applicable to such uncertain wanderers as we were likely to be:

"Et quacumque viam dedent fortuna sequamur."

"Therever fortune clears a way,
Thither our ready footsteps stray."

CHAPTER XII. A BARREN LAND

We had started under a sky overcast but calm. There was no fear of heat, none of disastrous rain. It was just the weather for tourists.

The pleasure of riding on horseback over an unknown country made me easy to be pleased at our first start. I threw myself wholly into the pleasure of the trip, and enjoyed the feeling of freedom and satisfied desire. I was beginning to take a real share in the enterprise.

"Besides," I said to myself, "where's the risk? Here we are travelling all through a most interesting country! We are about to climb a very remarkable mountain; at the worst we are going to scramble down an extinct crater. It is evident that Saknussemm did nothing more than this. As for a passage leading to the centre of the globe, it is mere rubbish! perfectly impossible! Very well, then; let us get all the good we can out of this expedition, and don't let us haggle about the chances."

This reasoning having settled my mind, we got out of Rejkiavik.

Hans moved steadily on, keeping ahead of us at an even, smooth, and rapid pace. The baggage horses followed him without giving any trouble. Then came my uncle and myself, looking not so very ill-mounted on our small but hardy animals.

Iceland is one of the largest islands in Europe. Its surface is 14,000 square miles, and it contains but 16,000 inhabitants. Geographers have divided it into four quarters, and we were crossing diagonally the south-west quarter, called the 'Sudvester Fjordungr.'

On leaving Rejkiavik Hans took us by the seashore. We passed lean pastures which were trying very hard, but in vain, to look green; yellow came out best. The rugged peaks of the trachyte rocks presented faint outlines on the eastern horizon; at times a few patches of snow, concentrating the vague light, glittered upon the slopes of the distant mountains; certain peaks, boldly uprising, passed through the grey clouds, and reappeared above the moving mists, like breakers emerging in the heavens.

Often these chains of barren rocks made a dip towards the sea, and encroached upon the scanty pasturage: but there was always enough room to pass. Besides, our horses instinctively chose the easiest places without ever slackening their pace. My uncle was refused even the satisfaction of stirring up his beast with whip or voice. He had no excuse for being impatient. I could not help smiling to see so tall a man on so small a pony, and as his long legs nearly touched the ground he looked like a six-legged centaur.

"Good horse! good horse!" he kept saying. "You will see, Axel, that there is no more sagacious animal than the Icelandic horse. He is stopped by neither snow, nor storm, nor impassable roads, nor rocks, glaciers, or anything. He is courageous, sober, and surefooted. He never makes a false step, never shies. If there is a river or fiord to cross (and we shall meet with many) you will see him plunge in at once, just as if he were amphibious, and gain the opposite bank. But we must not hurry him; we must let him have his way, and we shall get on at the rate of thirty miles a day."

"We may; but how about our guide?"

"Oh, never mind him. People like him get over the ground without a thought. There is so little action in this man that he will never get tired; and besides, if he wants it, he shall have my horse. I shall get cramped if I don't have a little action. The arms are all right, but the legs want exercise."

We were advancing at a rapid pace. The country was already almost a desert. Here and there was a lonely farm, called a boër built either of wood, or of sods, or of pieces of lava, looking like a poor beggar by the wayside. These ruinous huts seemed to solicit charity from passers-by; and on very small provocation we should have given alms for the relief of the poor inmates. In this country there were no roads and paths, and the poor vegetation, however slow, would soon efface the rare travellers' footsteps.

Yet this part of the province, at a very small distance from the capital, is reckoned among the inhabited and cultivated portions of Iceland. What, then, must other tracts be, more desert than this desert? In the first half mile we had not seen one farmer standing before his cabin door, nor one shepherd tending a flock less wild than himself, nothing but a few cows and sheep left to themselves. What then would be those convulsed regions upon which we were advancing, regions subject to the dire phenomena of eruptions, the offspring of volcanic explosions and subterranean convulsions?

We were to know them before long, but on consulting Olsen's map, I saw that they would be avoided by winding along the seashore. In fact, the great plutonic action is confined to the central portion of the island; there, rocks of the trappean and volcanic class, including trachyte, basalt, and tuffs and agglomerates associated with streams of lava, have made this a land of supernatural horrors. I had no idea of the spectacle which was awaiting us in the peninsula of Snæfell, where these ruins of a fiery nature have formed a frightful chaos.

In two hours from Rejkiavik we arrived at the burgh of Gufunes, called Aolkirkja, or principal church. There was nothing remarkable here but a few houses, scarcely enough for a German hamlet.

Hans stopped here half an hour. He shared with us our frugal breakfast; answering my uncle's questions about the road and our resting place that night with merely yes or no, except when he said "Gardär."

I consulted the map to see where Gardär was. I saw there was a small town of that name on the banks of the Hvalfiord, four miles from Rejkiavik. I showed it to my uncle.

"Four miles only!" he exclaimed; "four miles out of twenty-eight.

What a nice little walk!"

He was about to make an observation to the guide, who without answering resumed his place at the head, and went on his way.

Three hours later, still treading on the colourless grass of the pasture land, we had to work round the Kolla fiord, a longer way but an easier one than across that inlet. We soon entered into a 'pingstaoer' or parish called Ejulberg, from whose steeple twelve o'clock would have struck, if Icelandic churches were rich enough to possess clocks. But they are like the parishioners who have no watches and do without.

There our horses were baited; then taking the narrow path to left between a chain of hills and the sea, they carried us to our next stage, the aolkirkja of Brantär and one mile farther on, to Saurboër 'Annexia,' a chapel of ease built on the south shore of the Hvalfiord.

CHAPTER XII. A BARREN LAND

It was now four o'clock, and we had gone four Icelandic miles, or twenty-four English miles.

In that place the fiord was at least three English miles wide; the waves rolled with a rushing din upon the sharp-pointed rocks; this inlet was confined between walls of rock, precipices crowned by sharp peaks 2,000 feet high, and remarkable for the brown strata which separated the beds of reddish tuff. However much I might respect the intelligence of our quadrupeds, I hardly cared to put it to the test by trusting myself to it on horseback across an arm of the sea.

If they are as intelligent as they are said to be, I thought, they won't try it. In any case, I will tax my intelligence to direct theirs.

But my uncle would not wait. He spurred on to the edge. His steed lowered his head to examine the nearest waves and stopped. My uncle, who had an instinct of his own, too, applied pressure, and was again refused by the animal significantly shaking his head. Then followed strong language, and the whip; but the brute answered these arguments with kicks and endeavours to throw his rider. At last the clever little pony, with a bend of his knees, started from under the Professor's legs, and left him standing upon two boulders on the shore just like the colossus of Rhodes.

"Confounded brute!" cried the unhorsed horseman, suddenly degraded into a pedestrian, just as ashamed as a cavalry officer degraded to a foot soldier.

"*Färja,*" said the guide, touching his shoulder.

"What! a boat?"

"*Der,*" replied Hans, pointing to one.

"Yes," I cried; "there is a boat."

"Why did not you say so then? Well, let us go on."

"*Tidvatten,*" said the guide.

"What is he saying?"

"He says tide," said my uncle, translating the Danish word.

"No doubt we must wait for the tide."

"*Förbida,*" said my uncle.

"*Ja,*" replied Hans.

My uncle stamped with his foot, while the horses went on to the boat.

I perfectly understood the necessity of abiding a particular moment of the tide to undertake the crossing of the fiord, when, the sea having reached its greatest height, it should be slack water. Then the ebb and flow have no sensible effect, and the boat does not risk being carried either to the bottom or out to sea.

That favourable moment arrived only with six o'clock; when my uncle, myself, the guide, two other passengers and the four horses, trusted ourselves to a somewhat fragile raft. Accustomed as I was to the swift and sure steamers on the Elbe, I found the oars of the rowers rather a slow means of propulsion. It took us more than an hour to cross the fiord; but the passage was effected without any mishap.

In another half hour we had reached the aolkirkja of Gardär

CHAPTER XIII. HOSPITALITY UNDER THE ARCTIC CIRCLE

It ought to have been night-time, but under the 65th parallel there was nothing surprising in the nocturnal polar light. In Iceland during the months of June and July the sun does not set.

But the temperature was much lower. I was cold and more hungry than cold. Welcome was the sight of the boër which was hospitably opened to receive us.

It was a peasant's house, but in point of hospitality it was equal to a king's. On our arrival the master came with outstretched hands, and without more ceremony he beckoned us to follow him.

To accompany him down the long, narrow, dark passage, would have been impossible. Therefore, we followed, as he bid us. The building was constructed of roughly squared timbers, with rooms on both sides, four in number, all opening out into the one passage: these were the kitchen, the weaving shop, the badstofa, or family sleeping-room, and the visitors' room, which was the best of all. My uncle, whose height had not been thought of in building the house, of course hit his head several times against the beams that projected from the ceilings.

We were introduced into our apartment, a large room with a floor of earth stamped hard down, and lighted by a window, the panes of which were formed of sheep's bladder, not admitting too much light. The sleeping accommodation consisted of dry litter, thrown into two wooden frames painted red, and ornamented with Icelandic sentences. I was hardly expecting so much comfort; the only discomfort proceeded from the strong odour of dried fish, hung meat, and sour milk, of which my nose made bitter complaints.

When we had laid aside our travelling wraps the voice of the host was heard inviting us to the kitchen, the only room where a fire was lighted even in the severest cold.

My uncle lost no time in obeying the friendly call, nor was I slack in following.

The kitchen chimney was constructed on the ancient pattern; in the middle of the room was a stone for a hearth, over it in the roof a hole to let the smoke escape. The kitchen was also a dining-room.

At our entrance the host, as if he had never seen us, greeted us with the word "*Sællvertu,*" which means "be happy," and came and kissed us on the cheek.

After him his wife pronounced the same words, accompanied with the same ceremonial; then the two placing their hands upon their hearts, inclined profoundly before us.

I hasten to inform the reader that this Icelandic lady was the mother of nineteen children, all, big and little, swarming in the midst of the dense wreaths of smoke with which the fire on the hearth filled the chamber. Every moment I noticed a fair-haired and rather melancholy face peeping out of the rolling volumes of smoke—they were a perfect cluster of unwashed angels.

My uncle and I treated this little tribe with kindness; and in a very short time we each had three or four of these brats on our shoulders, as many on our laps, and the rest between our knees. Those who could speak kept repeating "*Sœllvertu,*" in every conceivable tone; those that could not speak made up for that want by shrill cries.

This concert was brought to a close by the announcement of dinner. At that moment our hunter returned, who had been seeing his horses provided for; that is to say, he had economically let them loose in the fields, where the poor beasts had to content themselves with the scanty moss they could pull off the rocks and a few meagre sea weeds, and the next day they would not fail to come of themselves and resume the labours of the previous day.

"*Sœllvertu,*" said Hans.

Then calmly, automatically, and dispassionately he kissed the host, the hostess, and their nineteen children.

This ceremony over, we sat at table, twenty-four in number, and therefore one upon another. The luckiest had only two urchins upon their knees.

But silence reigned in all this little world at the arrival of the soup, and the national taciturnity resumed its empire even over the children. The host served out to us a soup made of lichen and by no means unpleasant, then an immense piece of dried fish floating in butter rancid with twenty years' keeping, and, therefore, according to Icelandic gastronomy, much preferable to fresh butter. Along with this, we had 'skye,' a sort of clotted milk, with biscuits, and a liquid prepared from juniper berries; for beverage we had a thin milk mixed with water, called in this country 'blanda.' It is not for me to decide whether this diet is wholesome or not; all I can say is, that I was desperately hungry, and that at dessert I swallowed to the very last gulp of a thick broth made from buckwheat.

As soon as the meal was over the children disappeared, and their elders gathered round the peat fire, which also burnt such miscellaneous fuel as briars, cow-dung, and fishbones. After this little pinch of warmth the different groups retired to their respective rooms. Our hostess hospitably offered us her assistance in undressing, according to Icelandic usage; but on our gracefully declining, she insisted no longer, and I was able at last to curl myself up in my mossy bed.

At five next morning we bade our host farewell, my uncle with difficulty persuading him to accept a proper remuneration; and Hans signalled the start.

At a hundred yards from Gardär the soil began to change its aspect; it became boggy and less favourable to progress. On our right the chain of mountains was indefinitely prolonged like an immense system of natural fortifications, of which we were following the counter-scarp or lesser steep; often we were met by streams, which we had to ford with great care, not to wet our packages.

The desert became wider and more hideous; yet from time to time we seemed to descry a human figure that fled at our approach, sometimes a sharp turn would bring us suddenly within a short distance of one of these spectres, and I was filled with loathing at the sight of a huge deformed head, the skin shining and hairless, and repulsive sores visible through the gaps in the poor creature's wretched rags.

The unhappy being forbore to approach us and offer his misshapen hand. He fled away, but not before Hans had saluted him with the customary "*Sœllvertu.*"

"*Spetelsk,*" said he.

"A leper!" my uncle repeated.

This word produced a repulsive effect. The horrible disease of leprosy is too common in Iceland; it is not contagious, but hereditary, and lepers are forbidden to marry.

These apparitions were not cheerful, and did not throw any charm over the less and less attractive landscapes. The last tufts of grass had disappeared from beneath our feet. Not a tree was to be seen, unless we except a few dwarf birches as low as brushwood. Not an animal but a few wandering ponies that their owners would not feed. Sometimes we could see a hawk balancing himself on his wings under the grey cloud, and then darting away south with rapid flight. I felt melancholy under this savage aspect of nature, and my thoughts went away to the cheerful scenes I had left in the far south.

We had to cross a few narrow fiords, and at last quite a wide gulf; the tide, then high, allowed us to pass over without delay, and to reach the hamlet of Alftanes, one mile beyond.

That evening, after having forded two rivers full of trout and pike, called Alfa and Heta, we were obliged to spend the night in a deserted building worthy to be haunted by all the elfins of Scandinavia. The ice king certainly held court here, and gave us all night long samples of what he could do.

No particular event marked the next day. Bogs, dead levels, melancholy desert tracks, wherever we travelled. By nightfall we had accomplished half our journey, and we lay at Krösolbt.

On the 19th of June, for about a mile, that is an Icelandic mile, we walked upon hardened lava; this ground is called in the country 'hraun'; the writhen surface presented the appearance of distorted, twisted cables, sometimes stretched in length, sometimes contorted together; an immense torrent, once liquid, now solid, ran from the nearest mountains, now extinct volcanoes, but the ruins around revealed the violence of the past eruptions. Yet here and there were a few jets of steam from hot springs.

We had no time to watch these phenomena; we had to proceed on our way. Soon at the foot of the mountains the boggy land reappeared, intersected by little lakes. Our route now lay westward; we had turned the great bay of Faxa, and the twin peaks of Snæfell rose white into the cloudy sky at the distance of at least five miles.

The horses did their duty well, no difficulties stopped them in their steady career. I was getting tired; but my uncle was as firm and straight as he was at our first start. I could not help admiring his persistency, as well as the hunter's, who treated our expedition like a mere promenade.

June 20. At six p.m. we reached Büdir, a village on the sea shore; and the guide there claiming his due, my uncle settled with him. It was Hans' own family, that is, his uncles and cousins, who gave us hospitality; we were kindly received, and without taxing too much the goodness of these folks, I would willingly have tarried here to recruit after my fatigues. But my uncle, who wanted no recruiting, would not hear of it, and the next morning we had to bestride our beasts again.

The soil told of the neighbourhood of the mountain, whose granite foundations rose from the earth like the knotted roots of some huge oak. We were rounding the immense base of the volcano. The Professor hardly took his eyes off it. He tossed up his arms and seemed to defy it, and to declare, "There stands the giant that I shall conquer." After about four hours' walking the horses stopped of their own accord at the door of the priest's house at Stapi.

CHAPTER XIV. BUT ARCTICS CAN BE INHOSPITABLE, TOO

Stapi is a village consisting of about thirty huts, built of lava, at the south side of the base of the volcano. It extends along the inner edge of a small fiord, inclosed between basaltic walls of the strangest construction.

Basalt is a brownish rock of igneous origin. It assumes regular forms, the arrangement of which is often very surprising. Here nature had done her work geometrically, with square and compass and plummet. Everywhere else her art consists alone in throwing down huge masses together in disorder. You see cones imperfectly formed, irregular pyramids, with a fantastic disarrangement of lines; but here, as if to exhibit an example of regularity, though in advance of the very earliest architects, she has created a severely simple order of architecture, never surpassed either by the splendours of Babylon or the wonders of Greece.

I had heard of the Giant's Causeway in Ireland, and Fingal's Cave in Staffa, one of the Hebrides; but I had never yet seen a basaltic formation.

At Stapi I beheld this phenomenon in all its beauty.

The wall that confined the fiord, like all the coast of the peninsula, was composed of a series of vertical columns thirty feet high. These straight shafts, of fair proportions, supported an architrave of horizontal slabs, the overhanging portion of which formed a semi-arch over the sea. At intervals, under this natural shelter, there spread out vaulted entrances in beautiful curves, into which the waves came dashing with foam and spray. A few shafts of basalt, torn from their hold by the fury of tempests, lay along the soil like remains of an ancient temple, in ruins for ever fresh, and over which centuries passed without leaving a trace of age upon them.

This was our last stage upon the earth. Hans had exhibited great intelligence, and it gave me some little comfort to think then that he was not going to leave us.

On arriving at the door of the rector's house, which was not different from the others, I saw a man shoeing a horse, hammer in hand, and with a leathern apron on.

"*Sællvertu,*" said the hunter.

"*God dag,*" said the blacksmith in good Danish.

"*Kyrkoherde,*" said Hans, turning round to my uncle.

"The rector," repeated the Professor. "It seems, Axel, that this good man is the rector."

Our guide in the meanwhile was making the 'kyrkoherde' aware of the position of things; when the latter, suspending his labours for a moment, uttered a sound no doubt understood between horses and farriers, and immediately a tall and ugly hag appeared from the hut. She must have been six feet at the least. I was in great alarm lest she should treat me to the Icelandic kiss; but there was no occasion to fear, nor did she do the honours at all too gracefully.

The visitors' room seemed to me the worst in the whole cabin. It was close, dirty, and evil smelling. But we had to be content. The rector did not to go in for antique hospitality. Very far from it. Before the day was over I saw that we had to do with a blacksmith, a fisherman, a hunter, a joiner, but not at all with a minister of the Gospel. To be sure, it was a week-day; perhaps on a Sunday he made amends.

I don't mean to say anything against these poor priests, who after all are very wretched. They receive from the Danish Government a ridiculously small pittance, and they get from the parish the fourth part of the tithe, which does not come to sixty marks a year (about £4). Hence the necessity to work for their livelihood; but after fishing, hunting, and shoeing horses for any length of time, one soon gets into the ways and manners of fishermen, hunters, and farriers, and other rather rude and uncultivated people; and that evening I found out that temperance was not among the virtues that distinguished my host.

My uncle soon discovered what sort of a man he had to do with; instead of a good and learned man he found a rude and coarse peasant. He therefore resolved to commence the grand expedition at once, and to leave this inhospitable parsonage. He cared nothing about fatigue, and resolved to spend some days upon the mountain.

The preparations for our departure were therefore made the very day after our arrival at Stapi. Hans hired the services of three Icelanders to do the duty of the horses in the transport of the burdens; but as soon as we had arrived at the crater these natives were to turn back and leave us to our own devices. This was to be clearly understood.

My uncle now took the opportunity to explain to Hans that it was his intention to explore the interior of the volcano to its farthest limits.

Hans merely nodded. There or elsewhere, down in the bowels of the earth, or anywhere on the surface, all was alike to him. For my own part the incidents of the journey had hitherto kept me amused, and made me forgetful of coming evils; but now my fears again were beginning to get the better of me. But what could I do? The place to resist the Professor would have been Hamburg, not the foot of Snæfell.

One thought, above all others, harassed and alarmed me; it was one calculated to shake firmer nerves than mine.

Now, thought I, here we are, about to climb Snæfell. Very good. We will explore the crater. Very good, too, others have done as much without dying for it. But that is not all. If there is a way to penetrate into the very bowels of the island, if that ill-advised Saknussemm has told a true tale, we shall lose our way amidst the deep subterranean passages of this volcano. Now, there is no proof that Snæfell is extinct. Who can assure us that an eruption is not brewing at this very moment? Does it follow that because the monster has slept since 1229 he must therefore never awake again? And if he wakes up presently, where shall we be?

It was worth while debating this question, and I did debate it. I could not sleep for dreaming about eruptions. Now, the part of ejected scoriae and ashes seemed to my mind a very rough one to act.

So, at last, when I could hold out no longer, I resolved to lay the case before my uncle, as prudently and as cautiously as possible, just under the form of an almost impossible hypothesis.

I went to him. I communicated my fears to him, and drew back a step to give him room for the explosion which I knew must follow. But I was mistaken.

"I was thinking of that," he replied with great simplicity.

CHAPTER XIV. BUT ARCTICS CAN BE INHOSPITABLE, TOO

What could those words mean?—Was he actually going to listen to reason? Was he contemplating the abandonment of his plans? This was too good to be true.

After a few moments' silence, during which I dared not question him, he resumed:

"I was thinking of that. Ever since we arrived at Stapi I have been occupied with the important question you have just opened, for we must not be guilty of imprudence."

"No, indeed!" I replied with forcible emphasis.

"For six hundred years Snæfell has been dumb; but he may speak again. Now, eruptions are always preceded by certain well-known phenomena. I have therefore examined the natives, I have studied external appearances, and I can assure you, Axel, that there will be no eruption."

At this positive affirmation I stood amazed and speechless.

"You don't doubt my word?" said my uncle. "Well, follow me."

I obeyed like an automaton. Coming out from the priest's house, the Professor took a straight road, which, through an opening in the basaltic wall, led away from the sea. We were soon in the open country, if one may give that name to a vast extent of mounds of volcanic products. This tract seemed crushed under a rain of enormous ejected rocks of trap, basalt, granite, and all kinds of igneous rocks.

Here and there I could see puffs and jets of steam curling up into the air, called in Icelandic 'reykir,' issuing from thermal springs, and indicating by their motion the volcanic energy underneath. This seemed to justify my fears: But I fell from the height of my newborn hopes when my uncle said:

"You see all these volumes of steam, Axel; well, they demonstrate that we have nothing to fear from the fury of a volcanic eruption."

"Am I to believe that?" I cried.

"Understand this clearly," added the Professor. "At the approach of an eruption these jets would redouble their activity, but disappear altogether during the period of the eruption. For the elastic fluids, being no longer under pressure, go off by way of the crater instead of escaping by their usual passages through the fissures in the soil. Therefore, if these vapours remain in their usual condition, if they display no augmentation of force, and if you add to this the observation that the wind and rain are not ceasing and being replaced by a still and heavy atmosphere, then you may affirm that no eruption is preparing."

"But—"

'No more; that is sufficient. When science has uttered her voice, let babblers hold their peace.'

I returned to the parsonage, very crestfallen. My uncle had beaten me with the weapons of science. Still I had one hope left, and this was, that when we had reached the bottom of the crater it would be impossible, for want of a passage, to go deeper, in spite of all the Saknussemm's in Iceland.

I spent that whole night in one constant nightmare; in the heart of a volcano, and from the deepest depths of the earth I saw myself tossed up amongst the interplanetary spaces under the form of an eruptive rock.

The next day, June 23, Hans was awaiting us with his companions carrying provisions, tools, and instruments; two iron pointed sticks, two rifles, and two shot belts were for my uncle and myself. Hans, as a cautious man, had added to our luggage a leathern bottle full of water, which, with that in our flasks, would ensure us a supply of water for eight days.

It was nine in the morning. The priest and his tall Megæra were awaiting us at the door. We supposed they were standing there to bid us a kind farewell. But the farewell was put in the unexpected form of a heavy bill, in which everything was charged, even to the very air we breathed in the pastoral house, infected as it was. This worthy couple were fleecing us just as a Swiss innkeeper might have done, and estimated their imperfect hospitality at the highest price.

My uncle paid without a remark: a man who is starting for the centre of the earth need not be particular about a few rix dollars.

This point being settled, Hans gave the signal, and we soon left
Stapi behind us.

CHAPTER XV. SNÆFELL AT LAST

Snæfell is 5,000 feet high. Its double cone forms the limit of a trachytic belt which stands out distinctly in the mountain system of the island. From our starting point we could see the two peaks boldly projected against the dark grey sky; I could see an enormous cap of snow coming low down upon the giant's brow.

We walked in single file, headed by the hunter, who ascended by narrow tracks, where two could not have gone abreast. There was therefore no room for conversation.

After we had passed the basaltic wall of the fiord of Stapi we passed over a vegetable fibrous peat bog, left from the ancient vegetation of this peninsula. The vast quantity of this unworked fuel would be sufficient to warm the whole population of Iceland for a century; this vast turbary measured in certain ravines had in many places a depth of seventy feet, and presented layers of carbonized remains of vegetation alternating with thinner layers of tufaceous pumice.

As a true nephew of the Professor Liedenbrock, and in spite of my dismal prospects, I could not help observing with interest the mineralogical curiosities which lay about me as in a vast museum, and I constructed for myself a complete geological account of Iceland.

This most curious island has evidently been projected from the bottom of the sea at a comparatively recent date. Possibly, it may still be subject to gradual elevation. If this is the case, its origin may well be attributed to subterranean fires. Therefore, in this case, the theory of Sir Humphry Davy, Saknussemm's document, and my uncle's theories would all go off in smoke. This hypothesis led me to examine with more attention the appearance of the surface, and I soon arrived at a conclusion as to the nature of the forces which presided at its birth.

Iceland, which is entirely devoid of alluvial soil, is wholly composed of volcanic tufa, that is to say, an agglomeration of porous rocks and stones. Before the volcanoes broke out it consisted of trap rocks slowly upraised to the level of the sea by the action of central forces. The internal fires had not yet forced their way through.

But at a later period a wide chasm formed diagonally from south-west to north-east, through which was gradually forced out the trachyte which was to form a mountain chain. No violence accompanied this change; the matter thrown out was in vast quantities, and the liquid material oozing out from the abysses of the earth slowly spread in extensive plains or in hillocky masses. To this period belong the felspar, syenites, and porphyries.

But with the help of this outflow the thickness of the crust of the island increased materially, and therefore also its powers of resistance. It may easily be conceived what vast quantities of elastic gases, what masses of molten matter accumulated beneath its solid surface whilst no exit was practicable after the cooling of the trachytic crust. Therefore a time would come when the elastic and explosive forces of the imprisoned gases would upheave this ponderous cover and drive out for themselves openings through tall chimneys. Hence then the volcano would distend and lift up the crust, and then burst through a crater suddenly formed at the summit or thinnest part of the volcano.

To the eruption succeeded other volcanic phenomena. Through the outlets now made first escaped the ejected basalt of which the plain we had just left presented such marvellous specimens. We were moving over grey rocks of dense and massive formation, which in cooling had formed into hexagonal prisms. Everywhere around us we saw truncated cones, formerly so many fiery mouths.

After the exhaustion of the basalt, the volcano, the power of which grew by the extinction of the lesser craters, supplied an egress to lava, ashes, and scoriae, of which I could see lengthened screes streaming down the sides of the mountain like flowing hair.

Such was the succession of phenomena which produced Iceland, all arising from the action of internal fire; and to suppose that the mass within did not still exist in a state of liquid incandescence was absurd; and nothing could surpass the absurdity of fancying that it was possible to reach the earth's centre.

So I felt a little comforted as we advanced to the assault of Snæfell.

The way was growing more and more arduous, the ascent steeper and steeper; the loose fragments of rock trembled beneath us, and the utmost care was needed to avoid dangerous falls.

Hans went on as quietly as if he were on level ground; sometimes he disappeared altogether behind the huge blocks, then a shrill whistle would direct us on our way to him. Sometimes he would halt, pick up a few bits of stone, build them up into a recognisable form, and thus made landmarks to guide us in our way back. A very wise precaution in itself, but, as things turned out, quite useless.

Three hours' fatiguing march had only brought us to the base of the mountain. There Hans bid us come to a halt, and a hasty breakfast was served out. My uncle swallowed two mouthfuls at a time to get on faster. But, whether he liked it or not, this was a rest as well as a breakfast hour and he had to wait till it pleased our guide to move on, which came to pass in an hour. The three Icelanders, just as taciturn as their comrade the hunter, never spoke, and ate their breakfasts in silence.

We were now beginning to scale the steep sides of Snæfell. Its snowy summit, by an optical illusion not unfrequent in mountains, seemed close to us, and yet how many weary hours it took to reach it! The stones, adhering by no soil or fibrous roots of vegetation, rolled away from under our feet, and rushed down the precipice below with the swiftness of an avalanche.

At some places the flanks of the mountain formed an angle with the horizon of at least 36 degrees; it was impossible to climb them, and these stony cliffs had to be tacked round, not without great difficulty. Then we helped each other with our sticks.

I must admit that my uncle kept as close to me as he could; he never lost sight of me, and in many straits his arm furnished me with a powerful support. He himself seemed to possess an instinct for equilibrium, for he never stumbled. The Icelanders, though burdened with our loads, climbed with the agility of mountaineers.

To judge by the distant appearance of the summit of Snæfell, it would have seemed too steep to ascend on our side. Fortunately, after an hour of fatigue and athletic exercises, in the midst of the vast surface of snow presented by the hollow between the two peaks, a kind of staircase appeared unexpectedly which greatly facilitated our ascent. It was formed by one of those torrents of stones flung up by the eruptions, called 'sting' by the Icelanders. If this torrent had not been arrested in its fall by the formation of the sides of the mountain, it would have gone on to the sea and formed more islands.

Such as it was, it did us good service. The steepness increased, but these stone steps allowed us to rise with facility, and even with such rapidity that, having rested for a moment while my companions continued their ascent, I perceived them already reduced by distance to microscopic dimensions.

At seven we had ascended the two thousand steps of this grand staircase, and we had attained a bulge in the mountain, a kind of bed on which rested the cone proper of the crater.

Three thousand two hundred feet below us stretched the sea. We had passed the limit of perpetual snow, which, on account of the moisture of the climate, is at a greater elevation in Iceland than the high latitude would give reason to suppose. The cold was excessively keen. The wind was blowing violently. I was exhausted. The Professor saw that my limbs were refusing to perform their office, and in spite of his impatience he decided on stopping. He therefore spoke to the hunter, who shook his head, saying:

"*Ofvanför.*"

"It seems we must go higher," said my uncle.

Then he asked Hans for his reason.

"*Mistour,*" replied the guide.

"*Ja Mistour,*" said one of the Icelanders in a tone of alarm.

"What does that word mean?" I asked uneasily.

"Look!" said my uncle.

I looked down upon the plain. An immense column of pulverized pumice, sand and dust was rising with a whirling circular motion like a waterspout; the wind was lashing it on to that side of Snæfell where we were holding on; this dense veil, hung across the sun, threw a deep shadow over the mountain. If that huge revolving pillar sloped down, it would involve us in its whirling eddies. This phenomenon, which is not unfrequent when the wind blows from the glaciers, is called in Icelandic 'mistour.'

"*Hastigt! hastigt!*" cried our guide.

Without knowing Danish I understood at once that we must follow Hans at the top of our speed. He began to circle round the cone of the crater, but in a diagonal direction so as to facilitate our progress. Presently the dust storm fell upon the mountain, which quivered under the shock; the loose stones, caught with the irresistible blasts of wind, flew about in a perfect hail as in an eruption. Happily we were on the opposite side, and sheltered from all harm. But for the precaution of our guide, our mangled bodies, torn and pounded into fragments, would have been carried afar like the ruins hurled along by some unknown meteor.

Yet Hans did not think it prudent to spend the night upon the sides of the cone. We continued our zigzag climb. The fifteen hundred remaining feet took us five hours to clear; the circuitous route, the diagonal and the counter marches, must have measured at least three leagues. I could stand it no longer. I was yielding to the effects of hunger and cold. The rarefied air scarcely gave play to the action of my lungs.

At last, at eleven in the sunlight night, the summit of Snæfell was reached, and before going in for shelter into the crater I had time to observe the midnight sun, at his lowest point, gilding with his pale rays the island that slept at my feet.

CHAPTER XVI. BOLDLY DOWN THE CRATER

Supper was rapidly devoured, and the little company housed themselves as best they could. The bed was hard, the shelter not very substantial, and our position an anxious one, at five thousand feet above the sea level. Yet I slept particularly well; it was one of the best nights I had ever had, and I did not even dream.

Next morning we awoke half frozen by the sharp keen air, but with the light of a splendid sun. I rose from my granite bed and went out to enjoy the magnificent spectacle that lay unrolled before me.

I stood on the very summit of the southernmost of Snæfell's peaks. The range of the eye extended over the whole island. By an optical law which obtains at all great heights, the shores seemed raised and the centre depressed. It seemed as if one of Helbesmer's raised maps lay at my feet. I could see deep valleys intersecting each other in every direction, precipices like low walls, lakes reduced to ponds, rivers abbreviated into streams. On my right were numberless glaciers and innumerable peaks, some plumed with feathery clouds of smoke. The undulating surface of these endless mountains, crested with sheets of snow, reminded one of a stormy sea. If I looked westward, there the ocean lay spread out in all its magnificence, like a mere continuation of those flock-like summits. The eye could hardly tell where the snowy ridges ended and the foaming waves began.

I was thus steeped in the marvellous ecstasy which all high summits develop in the mind; and now without giddiness, for I was beginning to be accustomed to these sublime aspects of nature. My dazzled eyes were bathed in the bright flood of the solar rays. I was forgetting where and who I was, to live the life of elves and sylphs, the fanciful creation of Scandinavian superstitions. I felt intoxicated with the sublime pleasure of lofty elevations without thinking of the profound abysses into which I was shortly to be plunged. But I was brought back to the realities of things by the arrival of Hans and the Professor, who joined me on the summit.

My uncle pointed out to me in the far west a light steam or mist, a semblance of land, which bounded the distant horizon of waters.

"Greenland!" said he.

"Greenland?" I cried.

"Yes; we are only thirty-five leagues from it; and during thaws the white bears, borne by the ice fields from the north, are carried even into Iceland. But never mind that. Here we are at the top of Snæfell and here are two peaks, one north and one south. Hans will tell us the name of that on which we are now standing."

The question being put, Hans replied:

"Scartaris."

My uncle shot a triumphant glance at me.

CHAPTER XVI. BOLDLY DOWN THE CRATER

"Now for the crater!" he cried.

The crater of Snæfell resembled an inverted cone, the opening of which might be half a league in diameter. Its depth appeared to be about two thousand feet. Imagine the aspect of such a reservoir, brim full and running over with liquid fire amid the rolling thunder. The bottom of the funnel was about 250 feet in circuit, so that the gentle slope allowed its lower brim to be reached without much difficulty. Involuntarily I compared the whole crater to an enormous erected mortar, and the comparison put me in a terrible fright.

"What madness," I thought, "to go down into a mortar, perhaps a loaded mortar, to be shot up into the air at a moment's notice!"

But I did not try to back out of it. Hans with perfect coolness resumed the lead, and I followed him without a word.

In order to facilitate the descent, Hans wound his way down the cone by a spiral path. Our route lay amidst eruptive rocks, some of which, shaken out of their loosened beds, rushed bounding down the abyss, and in their fall awoke echoes remarkable for their loud and well-defined sharpness.

In certain parts of the cone there were glaciers. Here Hans advanced only with extreme precaution, sounding his way with his iron-pointed pole, to discover any crevasses in it. At particularly dubious passages we were obliged to connect ourselves with each other by a long cord, in order that any man who missed his footing might be held up by his companions. This solid formation was prudent, but did not remove all danger.

Yet, notwithstanding the difficulties of the descent, down steeps unknown to the guide, the journey was accomplished without accidents, except the loss of a coil of rope, which escaped from the hands of an Icelander, and took the shortest way to the bottom of the abyss.

At mid-day we arrived. I raised my head and saw straight above me the upper aperture of the cone, framing a bit of sky of very small circumference, but almost perfectly round. Just upon the edge appeared the snowy peak of Saris, standing out sharp and clear against endless space.

At the bottom of the crater were three chimneys, through which, in its eruptions, Snæfell had driven forth fire and lava from its central furnace. Each of these chimneys was a hundred feet in diameter. They gaped before us right in our path. I had not the courage to look down either of them. But Professor Liedenbrock had hastily surveyed all three; he was panting, running from one to the other, gesticulating, and uttering incoherent expressions. Hans and his comrades, seated upon loose lava rocks, looked at him with as much wonder as they knew how to express, and perhaps taking him for an escaped lunatic.

Suddenly my uncle uttered a cry. I thought his foot must have slipped and that he had fallen down one of the holes. But, no; I saw him, with arms outstretched and legs straddling wide apart, erect before a granite rock that stood in the centre of the crater, just like a pedestal made ready to receive a statue of Pluto. He stood like a man stupefied, but the stupefaction soon gave way to delirious rapture.

"Axel, Axel," he cried. "Come, come!"

I ran. Hans and the Icelanders never stirred.

"Look!" cried the Professor.

And, sharing his astonishment, but I think not his joy, I read on the western face of the block, in Runic characters, half mouldered away with lapse of ages, this thrice-accursed name:

"Arne Saknussemm!" replied my uncle. "Do you yet doubt?"

I made no answer; and I returned in silence to my lava seat in a state of utter speechless consternation. Here was crushing evidence.

How long I remained plunged in agonizing reflections I cannot tell; all that I know is, that on raising my head again, I saw only my uncle and Hans at the bottom of the crater. The Icelanders had been dismissed, and they were now descending the outer slopes of Snæfell to return to Stapi.

Hans slept peaceably at the foot of a rock, in a lava bed, where he had found a suitable couch for himself; but my uncle was pacing around the bottom of the crater like a wild beast in a cage. I had neither the wish nor the strength to rise, and following the guide's example I went off into an unhappy slumber, fancying I could hear ominous noises or feel tremblings within the recesses of the mountain.

Thus the first night in the crater passed away.

The next morning, a grey, heavy, cloudy sky seemed to droop over the summit of the cone. I did not know this first from the appearances of nature, but I found it out by my uncle's impetuous wrath.

I soon found out the cause, and hope dawned again in my heart. For this reason.

Of the three ways open before us, one had been taken by Saknussemm. The indications of the learned Icelander hinted at in the cryptogram, pointed to this fact that the shadow of Scartaris came to touch that particular way during the latter days of the month of June.

That sharp peak might hence be considered as the gnomon of a vast sun dial, the shadow projected from which on a certain day would point out the road to the centre of the earth.

Now, no sun no shadow, and therefore no guide. Here was June 25. If the sun was clouded for six days we must postpone our visit till next year.

My limited powers of description would fail, were I to attempt a picture of the Professor's angry impatience. The day wore on, and no shadow came to lay itself along the bottom of the crater. Hans did not move from the spot he had selected; yet he must be asking himself what were we waiting for, if he asked himself anything at all. My uncle spoke not a word to me. His gaze, ever directed upwards, was lost in the grey and misty space beyond.

On the 26th nothing yet. Rain mingled with snow was falling all day long. Hans built a hut of pieces of lava. I felt a malicious pleasure in watching the thousand rills and cascades that came tumbling down the sides of the cone, and the deafening continuous din awaked by every stone against which they bounded.

My uncle's rage knew no bounds. It was enough to irritate a meeker man than he; for it was foundering almost within the port.

But Heaven never sends unmixed grief, and for Professor Liedenbrock there was a satisfaction in store proportioned to his desperate anxieties.

The next day the sky was again overcast; but on the 29th of June, the last day but one of the month, with the change of the moon came a change of weather. The sun poured a flood of light down the crater. Every hillock, every rock and stone, every projecting surface, had its share of the beaming torrent, and threw its shadow on the ground. Amongst them all, Scartaris laid down his sharp-pointed angular shadow which began to move slowly in the opposite direction to that of the radiant orb.

My uncle turned too, and followed it.

At noon, being at its least extent, it came and softly fell upon the edge of the middle chimney.

"There it is! there it is!" shouted the Professor.

"Now for the centre of the globe!" he added in Danish.

I looked at Hans, to hear what he would say.

"*Forüt!*" was his tranquil answer.

"Forward!" replied my uncle.

It was thirteen minutes past one.

CHAPTER XVII. VERTICAL DESCENT

Now began our real journey. Hitherto our toil had overcome all difficulties, now difficulties would spring up at every step.

I had not yet ventured to look down the bottomless pit into which I was about to take a plunge. The supreme hour had come. I might now either share in the enterprise or refuse to move forward. But I was ashamed to recoil in the presence of the hunter. Hans accepted the enterprise with such calmness, such indifference, such perfect disregard of any possible danger that I blushed at the idea of being less brave than he. If I had been alone I might have once more tried the effect of argument; but in the presence of the guide I held my peace; my heart flew back to my sweet Virlandaise, and I approached the central chimney.

I have already mentioned that it was a hundred feet in diameter, and three hundred feet round. I bent over a projecting rock and gazed down. My hair stood on end with terror. The bewildering feeling of vacuity laid hold upon me. I felt my centre of gravity shifting its place, and giddiness mounting into my brain like drunkenness. There is nothing more treacherous than this attraction down deep abysses. I was just about to drop down, when a hand laid hold of me. It was that of Hans. I suppose I had not taken as many lessons on gulf exploration as I ought to have done in the Frelsers Kirk at Copenhagen.

But, however short was my examination of this well, I had taken some account of its conformation. Its almost perpendicular walls were bristling with innumerable projections which would facilitate the descent. But if there was no want of steps, still there was no rail. A rope fastened to the edge of the aperture might have helped us down. But how were we to unfasten it, when arrived at the other end?

My uncle employed a very simple expedient to obviate this difficulty. He uncoiled a cord of the thickness of a finger, and four hundred feet long; first he dropped half of it down, then he passed it round a lava block that projected conveniently, and threw the other half down the chimney. Each of us could then descend by holding with the hand both halves of the rope, which would not be able to unroll itself from its hold; when two hundred feet down, it would be easy to get possession of the whole of the rope by letting one end go and pulling down by the other. Then the exercise would go on again *ad infinitum.*

"Now," said my uncle, after having completed these preparations, "now let us look to our loads. I will divide them into three lots; each of us will strap one upon his back. I mean only fragile articles."

Of course, we were not included under that head.

"Hans," said he, "will take charge of the tools and a portion of the provisions; you, Axel, will take another third of the provisions, and the arms; and I will take the rest of the provisions and the delicate instruments."

CHAPTER XVII. VERTICAL DESCENT

"But," said I, "the clothes, and that mass of ladders and ropes, what is to become of them?"

"They will go down by themselves."

"How so?" I asked.

"You will see presently."

My uncle was always willing to employ magnificent resources. Obeying orders, Hans tied all the non-fragile articles in one bundle, corded them firmly, and sent them bodily down the gulf before us.

I listened to the dull thuds of the descending bale. My uncle, leaning over the abyss, followed the descent of the luggage with a satisfied nod, and only rose erect when he had quite lost sight of it.

"Very well, now it is our turn."

Now I ask any sensible man if it was possible to hear those words without a shudder.

The Professor fastened his package of instruments upon his shoulders; Hans took the tools; I took the arms: and the descent commenced in the following order; Hans, my uncle, and myself. It was effected in profound silence, broken only by the descent of loosened stones down the dark gulf.

I dropped as it were, frantically clutching the double cord with one hand and buttressing myself from the wall with the other by means of my stick. One idea overpowered me almost, fear lest the rock should give way from which I was hanging. This cord seemed a fragile thing for three persons to be suspended from. I made as little use of it as possible, performing wonderful feats of equilibrium upon the lava projections which my foot seemed to catch hold of like a hand.

When one of these slippery steps shook under the heavier form of

Hans, he said in his tranquil voice:

"*Gif akt!*"

"Attention!" repeated my uncle.

In half an hour we were standing upon the surface of a rock jammed in across the chimney from one side to the other.

Hans pulled the rope by one of its ends, the other rose in the air; after passing the higher rock it came down again, bringing with it a rather dangerous shower of bits of stone and lava.

Leaning over the edge of our narrow standing ground, I observed that the bottom of the hole was still invisible.

The same manoeuvre was repeated with the cord, and half an hour after we had descended another two hundred feet.

I don't suppose the maddest geologist under such circumstances would have studied the nature of the rocks that we were passing. I am sure I did trouble my head about them. Pliocene, miocene, eocene, cretaceous, jurassic, triassic, permian, carboniferous, devonian, silurian, or primitive was all one to me. But the Professor, no doubt, was pursuing his observations or taking notes, for in one of our halts he said to me:

"The farther I go the more confidence I feel. The order of these volcanic formations affords the strongest confirmation to the theories of Davy. We are now among the primitive rocks, upon which the chemical operations took place which are produced by the contact of elementary bases of metals with water. I repudiate the notion of central heat altogether. We shall see further proof of that very soon."

No variation, always the same conclusion. Of course, I was not inclined to argue. My silence was taken for consent and the descent went on.

Another three hours, and I saw no bottom to the chimney yet. When I lifted my head I perceived the gradual contraction of its aperture. Its walls, by a gentle incline, were drawing closer to each other, and it was beginning to grow darker.

Still we kept descending. It seemed to me that the falling stones were meeting with an earlier resistance, and that the concussion gave a more abrupt and deadened sound.

As I had taken care to keep an exact account of our manoeuvres with the rope, which I knew that we had repeated fourteen times, each descent occupying half an hour, the conclusion was easy that we had been seven hours, plus fourteen quarters of rest, making ten hours and a half. We had started at one, it must therefore now be eleven o'clock; and the depth to which we had descended was fourteen times 200 feet, or 2,800 feet.

At this moment I heard the voice of Hans.

"Halt!" he cried.

I stopped short just as I was going to place my feet upon my uncle's head.

"We are there," he cried.

"Where?" said I, stepping near to him.

"At the bottom of the perpendicular chimney," he answered.

"Is there no way farther?"

"Yes; there is a sort of passage which inclines to the right. We will see about that tomorrow. Let us have our supper, and go to sleep."

The darkness was not yet complete. The provision case was opened; we refreshed ourselves, and went to sleep as well as we could upon a bed of stones and lava fragments.

When lying on my back, I opened my eyes and saw a bright sparkling point of light at the extremity of the gigantic tube 3,000 feet long, now a vast telescope.

It was a star which, seen from this depth, had lost all scintillation, and which by my computation should be 46; *Ursa minor.* Then I fell fast asleep.

CHAPTER XVIII. THE WONDERS OF TERRESTRIAL DEPTHS

At eight in the morning a ray of daylight came to wake us up. The thousand shining surfaces of lava on the walls received it on its passage, and scattered it like a shower of sparks.

There was light enough to distinguish surrounding objects.

"Well, Axel, what do you say to it?" cried my uncle, rubbing his hands. "Did you ever spend a quieter night in our little house at Königsberg? No noise of cart wheels, no cries of basket women, no boatmen shouting!"

"No doubt it is very quiet at the bottom of this well, but there is something alarming in the quietness itself."

"Now come!" my uncle cried; "if you are frightened already, what will you be by and by? We have not gone a single inch yet into the bowels of the earth."

"What do you mean?"

"I mean that we have only reached the level of the island, long vertical tube, which terminates at the mouth of the crater, has its lower end only at the level of the sea."

"Are you sure of that?"

"Quite sure. Consult the barometer."

In fact, the mercury, which had risen in the instrument as fast as we descended, had stopped at twenty-nine inches.

"You see," said the Professor, "we have now only the pressure of our atmosphere, and I shall be glad when the aneroid takes the place of the barometer."

And in truth this instrument would become useless as soon as the weight of the atmosphere should exceed the pressure ascertained at the level of the sea.

"But," I said, "is there not reason to fear that this ever-increasing pressure will become at last very painful to bear?"

"No; we shall descend at a slow rate, and our lungs will become inured to a denser atmosphere. Aeronauts find the want of air as they rise to high elevations, but we shall perhaps have too much: of the two, this is what I should prefer. Don't let us lose a moment. Where is the bundle we sent down before us?"

I then remembered that we had searched for it in vain the evening before. My uncle questioned Hans, who, after having examined attentively with the eye of a huntsman, replied:

"*Der huppe!*"

"Up there."

And so it was. The bundle had been caught by a projection a hundred feet above us. Immediately the Icelander climbed up like a cat, and in a few minutes the package was in our possession.

"Now," said my uncle, "let us breakfast; but we must lay in a good stock, for we don't know how long we may have to go on."

The biscuit and extract of meat were washed down with a draught of water mingled with a little gin.

Breakfast over, my uncle drew from his pocket a small notebook, intended for scientific observations. He consulted his instruments, and recorded:

"Monday, July 1.

"Chronometer, 8.17 a.m.; barometer, 297 in.; thermometer, 6° (43°
F.). Direction, E.S.E."

This last observation applied to the dark gallery, and was indicated by the compass.

"Now, Axel," cried the Professor with enthusiasm, "now we are really going into the interior of the earth. At this precise moment the journey commences."

So saying, my uncle took in one hand Ruhmkorff's apparatus, which was hanging from his neck; and with the other he formed an electric communication with the coil in the lantern, and a sufficiently bright light dispersed the darkness of the passage.

Hans carried the other apparatus, which was also put into action. This ingenious application of electricity would enable us to go on for a long time by creating an artificial light even in the midst of the most inflammable gases.

"Now, march!" cried my uncle.

Each shouldered his package. Hans drove before him the load of cords and clothes; and, myself walking last, we entered the gallery.

At the moment of becoming engulfed in this dark gallery, I raised my head, and saw for the last time through the length of that vast tube the sky of Iceland, which I was never to behold again.

The lava, in the last eruption of 1229, had forced a passage through this tunnel. It still lined the walls with a thick and glistening coat. The electric light was here intensified a hundredfold by reflection.

The only difficulty in proceeding lay in not sliding too fast down an incline of about forty-five degrees; happily certain asperities and a few blisterings here and there formed steps, and we descended, letting our baggage slip before us from the end of a long rope.

But that which formed steps under our feet became stalactites overhead. The lava, which was porous in many places, had formed a surface covered with small rounded blisters; crystals of opaque quartz, set with limpid tears of glass, and hanging like clustered chandeliers from the vaulted roof, seemed as it were to kindle and form a sudden illumination as we passed on our way. It seemed as if the genii of the depths were lighting up their palace to receive their terrestrial guests.

"It is magnificent!" I cried spontaneously. "My uncle, what a sight! Don't you admire those blending hues of lava, passing from reddish brown to bright yellow by imperceptible shades? And these crystals are just like globes of light."

"Ali, you think so, do you, Axel, my boy? Well, you will see greater splendours than these, I hope. Now let us march: march!"

He had better have said slide, for we did nothing but drop down the steep inclines. It was the facifs *descensus Averni* of Virgil. The compass, which I consulted frequently, gave our direction as south-east with inflexible steadiness. This lava stream deviated neither to the right nor to the left.

CHAPTER XVIII. THE WONDERS OF TERRESTRIAL DEPTHS

Yet there was no sensible increase of temperature. This justified Davy's theory, and more than once I consulted the thermometer with surprise. Two hours after our departure it only marked 10° (50° Fahr.), an increase of only 4°. This gave reason for believing that our descent was more horizontal than vertical. As for the exact depth reached, it was very easy to ascertain that; the Professor measured accurately the angles of deviation and inclination on the road, but he kept the results to himself.

About eight in the evening he signalled to stop. Hans sat down at once. The lamps were hung upon a projection in the lava; we were in a sort of cavern where there was plenty of air. Certain puffs of air reached us. What atmospheric disturbance was the cause of them? I could not answer that question at the moment. Hunger and fatigue made me incapable of reasoning. A descent of seven hours consecutively is not made without considerable expenditure of strength. I was exhausted. The order to 'halt' therefore gave me pleasure. Hans laid our provisions upon a block of lava, and we ate with a good appetite. But one thing troubled me, our supply of water was half consumed. My uncle reckoned upon a fresh supply from subterranean sources, but hitherto we had met with none. I could not help drawing his attention to this circumstance.

"Are you surprised at this want of springs?" he said.

"More than that, I am anxious about it; we have only water enough for five days."

"Don't be uneasy, Axel, we shall find more than we want."

"When?"

"When we have left this bed of lava behind us. How could springs break through such walls as these?"

"But perhaps this passage runs to a very great depth. It seems to me that we have made no great progress vertically."

"Why do you suppose that?"

"Because if we had gone deep into the crust of earth, we should have encountered greater heat."

"According to your system," said my uncle. "But what does the thermometer say?"

"Hardly fifteen degrees (59° Fahr), nine degrees only since our departure."

"Well, what is your conclusion?"

"This is my conclusion. According to exact observations, the increase of temperature in the interior of the globe advances at the rate of one degree (1 4/5° Fahr.) for every hundred feet. But certain local conditions may modify this rate. Thus at Yakoutsk in Siberia the increase of a degree is ascertained to be reached every 36 feet. This difference depends upon the heat-conducting power of the rocks. Moreover, in the neighbourhood of an extinct volcano, through gneiss, it has been observed that the increase of a degree is only attained at every 125 feet. Let us therefore assume this last hypothesis as the most suitable to our situation, and calculate."

"Well, do calculate, my boy."

"Nothing is easier," said I, putting down figures in my note book. "Nine times a hundred and twenty-five feet gives a depth of eleven hundred and twenty-five feet."

"Very accurate indeed."

"Well?"

"By my observation we are at 10,000 feet below the level of the sea."

"Is that possible?"

"Yes, or figures are of no use."

The Professor's calculations were quite correct. We had already attained a depth of six thousand feet beyond that hitherto reached by the foot of man, such as the mines of Kitz Bahl in Tyrol, and those of Wuttembourg in Bohemia.

The temperature, which ought to have been 81° (178° Fahr.) was scarcely 15° (59° Fahr.). Here was cause for reflection.

CHAPTER XIX. GEOLOGICAL STUDIES IN SITU

Next day, Tuesday, June 30, at 6 a.m., the descent began again.

We were still following the gallery of lava, a real natural staircase, and as gently sloping as those inclined planes which in some old houses are still found instead of flights of steps. And so we went on until 12.17, the, precise moment when we overtook Hans, who had stopped.

"Ah! here we are," exclaimed my uncle, "at the very end of the chimney."

I looked around me. We were standing at the intersection of two roads, both dark and narrow. Which were we to take? This was a difficulty.

Still my uncle refused to admit an appearance of hesitation, either before me or the guide; he pointed out the Eastern tunnel, and we were soon all three in it.

Besides there would have been interminable hesitation before this choice of roads; for since there was no indication whatever to guide our choice, we were obliged to trust to chance.

The slope of this gallery was scarcely perceptible, and its sections very unequal. Sometimes we passed a series of arches succeeding each other like the majestic arcades of a gothic cathedral. Here the architects of the middle ages might have found studies for every form of the sacred art which sprang from the development of the pointed arch. A mile farther we had to bow our heads under corniced elliptic arches in the romanesque style; and massive pillars standing out from the wall bent under the spring of the vault that rested heavily upon them. In other places this magnificence gave way to narrow channels between low structures which looked like beaver's huts, and we had to creep along through extremely narrow passages.

The heat was perfectly bearable. Involuntarily I began to think of its heat when the lava thrown out by Snæfell was boiling and working through this now silent road. I imagined the torrents of fire hurled back at every angle in the gallery, and the accumulation of intensely heated vapours in the midst of this confined channel.

I only hope, thought I, that this so-called extinct volcano won't take a fancy in his old age to begin his sports again!

I abstained from communicating these fears to Professor Liedenbrock. He would never have understood them at all. He had but one idea—forward! He walked, he slid, he scrambled, he tumbled, with a persistency which one could not but admire.

By six in the evening, after a not very fatiguing walk, we had gone two leagues south, but scarcely a quarter of a mile down.

My uncle said it was time to go to sleep. We ate without talking, and went to sleep without reflection.

Our arrangements for the night were very simple; a railway rug each, into which we rolled ourselves, was our sole covering. We had neither cold nor intrusive visits to fear. Travellers who penetrate into the wilds of central Africa, and into the pathless forests of the New World, are obliged to watch over each other by night. But we enjoyed absolute safety and utter seclusion; no savages or wild beasts infested these silent depths.

Next morning, we awoke fresh and in good spirits. The road was resumed. As the day before, we followed the path of the lava. It was impossible to tell what rocks we were passing: the tunnel, instead of tending lower, approached more and more nearly to a horizontal direction, I even fancied a slight rise. But about ten this upward tendency became so evident, and therefore so fatiguing, that I was obliged to slacken my pace.

"Well, Axel?" demanded the Professor impatiently.

"Well, I cannot stand it any longer," I replied.

"What! after three hours' walk over such easy ground."

"It may be easy, but it is tiring all the same."

"What, when we have nothing to do but keep going down!"

"Going up, if you please."

"Going up!" said my uncle, with a shrug.

"No doubt, for the last half-hour the inclines have gone the other way, and at this rate we shall soon arrive upon the level soil of Iceland."

The Professor nodded slowly and uneasily like a man that declines to be convinced. I tried to resume the conversation. He answered not a word, and gave the signal for a start. I saw that his silence was nothing but ill-humour.

Still I had courageously shouldered my burden again, and was rapidly following Hans, whom my uncle preceded. I was anxious not to be left behind. My greatest care was not to lose sight of my companions. I shuddered at the thought of being lost in the mazes of this vast subterranean labyrinth.

Besides, if the ascending road did become steeper, I was comforted with the thought that it was bringing us nearer to the surface. There was hope in this. Every step confirmed me in it, and I was rejoicing at the thought of meeting my little Gräuben again.

By mid-day there was a change in the appearance of this wall of the gallery. I noticed it by a diminution of the amount of light reflected from the sides; solid rock was appearing in the place of the lava coating. The mass was composed of inclined and sometimes vertical strata. We were passing through rocks of the transition or silurian[1] system.

"It is evident," I cried, "the marine deposits formed in the second period, these shales, limestones, and sandstones. We are turning away from the primary granite. We are just as if we were people of Hamburg going to Lübeck by way of Hanover!"

I had better have kept my observations to myself. But my geological instinct was stronger than my prudence, and uncle Liedenbrock heard my exclamation.

"What's that you are saying?" he asked.

"See," I said, pointing to the varied series of sandstones and limestones, and the first indication of slate.

"Well?"

"We are at the period when the first plants and animals appeared."

---

[1] The name given by Sir Roderick Murchison to a vast series of fossiliferous strata, which lies between the non-fossiliferous slaty schists below and the old red sandstone above. The system is well developed in the region of Shropshire, etc., once inhabited by the Silures under Caractacus, or Caradoc. (Tr.)

"Do you think so?"

"Look close, and examine."

I obliged the Professor to move his lamp over the walls of the gallery. I expected some signs of astonishment; but he spoke not a word, and went on.

Had he understood me or not? Did he refuse to admit, out of self-love as an uncle and a philosopher, that he had mistaken his way when he chose the eastern tunnel? or was he determined to examine this passage to its farthest extremity? It was evident that we had left the lava path, and that this road could not possibly lead to the extinct furnace of Snæfell.

Yet I asked myself if I was not depending too much on this change in the rock. Might I not myself be mistaken? Were we really crossing the layers of rock which overlie the granite foundation?

If I am right, I thought, I must soon find some fossil remains of primitive life; and then we must yield to evidence. I will look.

I had not gone a hundred paces before incontestable proofs presented themselves. It could not be otherwise, for in the Silurian age the seas contained at least fifteen hundred vegetable and animal species. My feet, which had become accustomed to the indurated lava floor, suddenly rested upon a dust composed of the *debris* of plants and shells. In the walls were distinct impressions of fucoids and lycopodites.

Professor Liedenbrock could not be mistaken, I thought, and yet he pushed on, with, I suppose, his eyes resolutely shut.

This was only invincible obstinacy. I could hold out no longer. I picked up a perfectly formed shell, which had belonged to an animal not unlike the woodlouse: then, joining my uncle, I said:

"Look at this!"

"Very well," said he quietly, "it is the shell of a crustacean, of an extinct species called a trilobite. Nothing more."

"But don't you conclude—?"

"Just what you conclude yourself. Yes; I do, perfectly. We have left the granite and the lava. It is possible that I may be mistaken. But I cannot be sure of that until I have reached the very end of this gallery."

"You are right in doing this, my uncle, and I should quite approve of your determination, if there were not a danger threatening us nearer and nearer."

"What danger?"

"The want of water."

"Well, Axel, we will put ourselves upon rations."

CHAPTER XX. THE FIRST SIGNS OF DISTRESS

In fact, we had to ration ourselves. Our provision of water could not last more than three days. I found that out for certain when supper-time came. And, to our sorrow, we had little reason to expect to find a spring in these transition beds.

The whole of the next day the gallery opened before us its endless arcades. We moved on almost without a word. Hans' silence seemed to be infecting us.

The road was now not ascending, at least not perceptibly. Sometimes, even, it seemed to have a slight fall. But this tendency, which was very trifling, could not do anything to reassure the Professor; for there was no change in the beds, and the transitional characteristics became more and more decided.

The electric light was reflected in sparkling splendour from the schist, limestone, and old red sandstone of the walls. It might have been thought that we were passing through a section of Wales, of which an ancient people gave its name to this system. Specimens of magnificent marbles clothed the walls, some of a greyish agate fantastically veined with white, others of rich crimson or yellow dashed with splotches of red; then came dark cherry-coloured marbles relieved by the lighter tints of limestone.

The greater part of these bore impressions of primitive organisms. Creation had evidently advanced since the day before. Instead of rudimentary trilobites, I noticed remains of a more perfect order of beings, amongst others ganoid fishes and some of those sauroids in which palaeontologists have discovered the earliest reptile forms. The Devonian seas were peopled by animals of these species, and deposited them by thousands in the rocks of the newer formation.

It was evident that we were ascending that scale of animal life in which man fills the highest place. But Professor Liedenbrock seemed not to notice it.

He was awaiting one of two events, either the appearance of a vertical well opening before his feet, down which our descent might be resumed, or that of some obstacle which should effectually turn us back on our own footsteps. But evening came and neither wish was gratified.

On Friday, after a night during which I felt pangs of thirst, our little troop again plunged into the winding passages of the gallery.

After ten hours' walking I observed a singular deadening of the reflection of our lamps from the side walls. The marble, the schist, the limestone, and the sandstone were giving way to a dark and lustreless lining. At one moment, the tunnel becoming very narrow, I leaned against the wall.

When I removed my hand it was black. I looked nearer, and found we were in a coal formation.

"A coal mine!" I cried.

"A mine without miners," my uncle replied.

"Who knows?" I asked.

"I know," the Professor pronounced decidedly, "I am certain that this gallery driven through beds of coal was never pierced by the hand of man. But whether it be the hand of nature or not does not matter. Supper time is come; let us sup."

Hans prepared some food. I scarcely ate, and I swallowed down the few drops of water rationed out to me. One flask half full was all we had left to slake the thirst of three men.

After their meal my two companions laid themselves down upon their rugs, and found in sleep a solace for their fatigue. But I could not sleep, and I counted every hour until morning.

On Saturday, at six, we started afresh. In twenty minutes we reached a vast open space; I then knew that the hand of man had not hollowed out this mine; the vaults would have been shored up, and, as it was, they seemed to be held up by a miracle of equilibrium.

This cavern was about a hundred feet wide and a hundred and fifty in height. A large mass had been rent asunder by a subterranean disturbance. Yielding to some vast power from below it had broken asunder, leaving this great hollow into which human beings were now penetrating for the first time.

The whole history of the carboniferous period was written upon these gloomy walls, and a geologist might with ease trace all its diverse phases. The beds of coal were separated by strata of sandstone or compact clays, and appeared crushed under the weight of overlying strata.

At the age of the world which preceded the secondary period, the earth was clothed with immense vegetable forms, the product of the double influence of tropical heat and constant moisture; a vapoury atmosphere surrounded the earth, still veiling the direct rays of the sun.

Thence arises the conclusion that the high temperature then existing was due to some other source than the heat of the sun. Perhaps even the orb of day may not have been ready yet to play the splendid part he now acts. There were no 'climates' as yet, and a torrid heat, equal from pole to equator, was spread over the whole surface of the globe. Whence this heat? Was it from the interior of the earth?

Notwithstanding the theories of Professor Liedenbrock, a violent heat did at that time brood within the body of the spheroid. Its action was felt to the very last coats of the terrestrial crust; the plants, unacquainted with the beneficent influences of the sun, yielded neither flowers nor scent. But their roots drew vigorous life from the burning soil of the early days of this planet.

There were but few trees. Herbaceous plants alone existed. There were tall grasses, ferns, lycopods, besides sigillaria, asterophyllites, now scarce plants, but then the species might be counted by thousands.

The coal measures owe their origin to this period of profuse vegetation. The yet elastic and yielding crust of the earth obeyed the fluid forces beneath. Thence innumerable fissures and depressions. The plants, sunk underneath the waters, formed by degrees into vast accumulated masses.

Then came the chemical action of nature; in the depths of the seas the vegetable accumulations first became peat; then, acted upon by generated gases and the heat of fermentation, they underwent a process of complete mineralization.

Thus were formed those immense coalfields, which nevertheless, are not inexhaustible, and which three centuries at the present accelerated rate of consumption will exhaust unless the industrial world will devise a remedy.

These reflections came into my mind whilst I was contemplating the mineral wealth stored up in this portion of the globe. These no doubt, I thought, will never be discovered; the working of such deep mines would involve too large an outlay, and where would be the use as long as coal is yet spread far and wide near the surface? Such as my eyes behold these virgin stores, such they will be when this world comes to an end.

But still we marched on, and I alone was forgetting the length of the way by losing myself in the midst of geological contemplations. The temperature remained what it had been during our passage through the lava and schists. Only my sense of smell was forcibly affected by an odour of protocarburet of hydrogen. I immediately recognised in this gallery the presence of a considerable quantity of the dangerous gas called by miners firedamp, the explosion of which has often occasioned such dreadful catastrophes.

Happily, our light was from Ruhmkorff's ingenious apparatus. If unfortunately we had explored this gallery with torches, a terrible explosion would have put an end to travelling and travellers at one stroke.

This excursion through the coal mine lasted till night. My uncle scarcely could restrain his impatience at the horizontal road. The darkness, always deep twenty yards before us, prevented us from estimating the length of the gallery; and I was beginning to think it must be endless, when suddenly at six o'clock a wall very unexpectedly stood before us. Right or left, top or bottom, there was no road farther; we were at the end of a blind alley. "Very well, it's all right!" cried my uncle, "now, at any rate, we shall know what we are about. We are not in Saknussemm's road, and all we have to do is to go back. Let us take a night's rest, and in three days we shall get to the fork in the road." "Yes," said I, "if we have any strength left." "Why not?" "Because to-morrow we shall have no water." "Nor courage either?" asked my uncle severely. I dared make no answer.

CHAPTER XXI. COMPASSION FUSES THE PROFESSOR'S HEART

Next day we started early. We had to hasten forward. It was a three days' march to the cross roads.

I will not speak of the sufferings we endured in our return. My uncle bore them with the angry impatience of a man obliged to own his weakness; Hans with the resignation of his passive nature; I, I confess, with complaints and expressions of despair. I had no spirit to oppose this ill fortune.

As I had foretold, the water failed entirely by the end of the first day's retrograde march. Our fluid aliment was now nothing but gin; but this infernal fluid burned my throat, and I could not even endure the sight of it. I found the temperature and the air stifling. Fatigue paralysed my limbs. More than once I dropped down motionless. Then there was a halt; and my uncle and the Icelander did their best to restore me. But I saw that the former was struggling painfully against excessive fatigue and the tortures of thirst.

At last, on Tuesday, July 8, we arrived on our hands and knees, and half dead, at the junction of the two roads. There I dropped like a lifeless lump, extended on the lava soil. It was ten in the morning.

Hans and my uncle, clinging to the wall, tried to nibble a few bits of biscuit. Long moans escaped from my swollen lips.

After some time my uncle approached me and raised me in his arms.

"Poor boy!" said he, in genuine tones of compassion.

I was touched with these words, not being accustomed to see the excitable Professor in a softened mood. I grasped his trembling hands in mine. He let me hold them and looked at me. His eyes were moistened.

Then I saw him take the flask that was hanging at his side. To my amazement he placed it on my lips.

"Drink!" said he.

Had I heard him? Was my uncle beside himself? I stared at, him stupidly, and felt as if I could not understand him.

"Drink!" he said again.

And raising his flask he emptied it every drop between my lips.

Oh! infinite pleasure! a slender sip of water came to moisten my burning mouth. It was but one sip but it was enough to recall my ebbing life.

I thanked my uncle with clasped hands.

"Yes," he said, "a draught of water; but it is the very last—you hear!—the last. I had kept it as a precious treasure at the bottom of my flask. Twenty times, nay, a hundred times, have I fought against a frightful impulse to drink it off. But no, Axel, I kept it for you."

"My dear uncle," I said, whilst hot tears trickled down my face.

"Yes, my poor boy, I knew that as soon as you arrived at these cross roads you would drop half dead, and I kept my last drop of water to reanimate you."

"Thank you, thank you," I said. Although my thirst was only partially quenched, yet some strength had returned. The muscles of my throat, until then contracted, now relaxed again; and the inflammation of my lips abated somewhat; and I was now able to speak. .

"Let us see," I said, "we have now but one thing to do. We have no water; we must go back."

While I spoke my uncle avoided looking at me; he hung his head down; his eyes avoided mine.

"We must return," I exclaimed vehemently; "we must go back on our way to Snæfell. May God give us strength to climb up the crater again!"

"Return!" said my uncle, as if he was rather answering himself than me.

"Yes, return, without the loss of a minute."

A long silence followed.

"So then, Axel," replied the Professor ironically, "you have found no courage or energy in these few drops of water?"

"Courage?"

"I see you just as feeble-minded as you were before, and still expressing only despair!"

What sort of a man was this I had to do with, and what schemes was he now revolving in his fearless mind?

"What! you won't go back?"

"Should I renounce this expedition just when we have the fairest chance of success! Never!"

"Then must we resign ourselves to destruction?"

"No, Axel, no; go back. Hans will go with you. Leave me to myself!"

"Leave you here!"

"Leave me, I tell you. I have undertaken this expedition. I will carry it out to the end, and I will not return. Go, Axel, go!"

My uncle was in high state of excitement. His voice, which had for a moment been tender and gentle, had now become hard and threatening. He was struggling with gloomy resolutions against impossibilities. I would not leave him in this bottomless abyss, and on the other hand the instinct of self-preservation prompted me to fly.

The guide watched this scene with his usual phlegmatic unconcern. Yet he understood perfectly well what was going on between his two companions. The gestures themselves were sufficient to show that we were each bent on taking a different road; but Hans seemed to take no part in a question upon which depended his life. He was ready to start at a given signal, or to stay, if his master so willed it.

How I wished at this moment I could have made him understand me. My words, my complaints, my sorrow would have had some influence over that frigid nature. Those dangers which our guide could not understand I could have demonstrated and proved to him. Together we might have over-ruled the obstinate Professor; if it were needed, we might perhaps have compelled him to regain the heights of Snæfell.

I drew near to Hans. I placed my hand upon his. He made no movement. My parted lips sufficiently revealed my sufferings. The Icelander slowly moved his head, and calmly pointing to my uncle said:

"Master."

"Master!" I shouted; "you madman! no, he is not the master of our life; we must fly, we must drag him. Do you hear me? Do you understand?"

I had seized Hans by the arm. I wished to oblige him to rise. I strove with him. My uncle interposed.

"Be calm, Axel! you will get nothing from that immovable servant.

Therefore, listen to my proposal."

I crossed my arms, and confronted my uncle boldly.

"The want of water," he said, "is the only obstacle in our way. In this eastern gallery made up of lavas, schists, and coal, we have not met with a single particle of moisture. Perhaps we shall be more fortunate if we follow the western tunnel."

I shook my head incredulously.

"Hear me to the end," the Professor went on with a firm voice. "Whilst you were lying there motionless, I went to examine the conformation of that gallery. It penetrates directly downward, and in a few hours it will bring us to the granite rocks. There we must meet with abundant springs. The nature of the rock assures me of this, and instinct agrees with logic to support my conviction. Now, this is my proposal. When Columbus asked of his ships' crews for three days more to discover a new world, those crews, disheartened and sick as they were, recognised the justice of the claim, and he discovered America. I am the Columbus of this nether world, and I only ask for one more day. If in a single day I have not met with the water that we want, I swear to you we will return to the surface of the earth."

In spite of my irritation I was moved with these words, as well as with the violence my uncle was doing to his own wishes in making so hazardous a proposal.

"Well," I said, "do as you will, and God reward your superhuman energy. You have now but a few hours to tempt fortune. Let us start!"

CHAPTER XXII. TOTAL FAILURE OF WATER

This time the descent commenced by the new gallery. Hans walked first as was his custom.

We had not gone a hundred yards when the Professor, moving his lantern along the walls, cried:

"Here are primitive rocks. Now we are in the right way. Forward!"

When in its early stages the earth was slowly cooling, its contraction gave rise in its crust to disruptions, distortions, fissures, and chasms. The passage through which we were moving was such a fissure, through which at one time granite poured out in a molten state. Its thousands of windings formed an inextricable labyrinth through the primeval mass.

As fast as we descended, the succession of beds forming the primitive foundation came out with increasing distinctness. Geologists consider this primitive matter to be the base of the mineral crust of the earth, and have ascertained it to be composed of three different formations, schist, gneiss, and mica schist, resting upon that unchangeable foundation, the granite.

Never had mineralogists found themselves in so marvellous a situation to study nature in situ. What the boring machine, an insensible, inert instrument, was unable to bring to the surface of the inner structure of the globe, we were able to peruse with our own eyes and handle with our own hands.

Through the beds of schist, coloured with delicate shades of green, ran in winding course threads of copper and manganese, with traces of platinum and gold. I thought, what riches are here buried at an unapproachable depth in the earth, hidden for ever from the covetous eyes of the human race! These treasures have been buried at such a profound depth by the convulsions of primeval times that they run no chance of ever being molested by the pickaxe or the spade.

To the schists succeeded gneiss, partially stratified, remarkable for the parallelism and regularity of its lamina, then mica schists, laid in large plates or flakes, revealing their lamellated structure by the sparkle of the white shining mica.

The light from our apparatus, reflected from the small facets of quartz, shot sparkling rays at every angle, and I seemed to be moving through a diamond, within which the quickly darting rays broke across each other in a thousand flashing coruscations.

About six o'clock this brilliant fete of illuminations underwent a sensible abatement of splendour, then almost ceased. The walls assumed a crystallised though sombre appearance; mica was more closely mingled with the feldspar and quartz to form the proper rocky foundations of the earth, which bears without distortion or crushing the weight of the four terrestrial systems. We were immured within prison walls of granite.

CHAPTER XXII. TOTAL FAILURE OF WATER

It was eight in the evening. No signs of water had yet appeared. I was suffering horribly. My uncle strode on. He refused to stop. He was listening anxiously for the murmur of distant springs. But, no, there was dead silence.

And now my limbs were failing beneath me. I resisted pain and torture, that I might not stop my uncle, which would have driven him to despair, for the day was drawing near to its end, and it was his last.

At last I failed utterly; I uttered a cry and fell.

"Come to me, I am dying."

My uncle retraced his steps. He gazed upon me with his arms crossed; then these muttered words passed his lips:

"It's all over!"

The last thing I saw was a fearful gesture of rage, and my eyes closed.

When I reopened them I saw my two companions motionless and rolled up in their coverings. Were they asleep? As for me, I could not get one moment's sleep. I was suffering too keenly, and what embittered my thoughts was that there was no remedy. My uncle's last words echoed painfully in my ears: "it's all over!" For in such a fearful state of debility it was madness to think of ever reaching the upper world again.

We had above us a league and a half of terrestrial crust. The weight of it seemed to be crushing down upon my shoulders. I felt weighed down, and I exhausted myself with imaginary violent exertions to turn round upon my granite couch.

A few hours passed away. A deep silence reigned around us, the silence of the grave. No sound could reach us through walls, the thinnest of which were five miles thick.

Yet in the midst of my stupefaction I seemed to be aware of a noise. It was dark down the tunnel, but I seemed to see the Icelander vanishing from our sight with the lamp in his hand.

Why was he leaving us? Was Hans going to forsake us? My uncle was fast asleep. I wanted to shout, but my voice died upon my parched and swollen lips. The darkness became deeper, and the last sound died away in the far distance.

"Hans has abandoned us," I cried. "Hans! Hans!"

But these words were only spoken within me. They went no farther. Yet after the first moment of terror I felt ashamed of suspecting a man of such extraordinary faithfulness. Instead of ascending he was descending the gallery. An evil design would have taken him up not down. This reflection restored me to calmness, and I turned to other thoughts. None but some weighty motive could have induced so quiet a man to forfeit his sleep. Was he on a journey of discovery? Had he during the silence of the night caught a sound, a murmuring of something in the distance, which had failed to affect my hearing?

CHAPTER XXIII. WATER DISCOVERED

For a whole hour I was trying to work out in my delirious brain the reasons which might have influenced this seemingly tranquil huntsman. The absurdest notions ran in utter confusion through my mind. I thought madness was coming on!

But at last a noise of footsteps was heard in the dark abyss. Hans was approaching. A flickering light was beginning to glimmer on the wall of our darksome prison; then it came out full at the mouth of the gallery. Hans appeared.

He drew close to my uncle, laid his hand upon his shoulder, and gently woke him. My uncle rose up.

"What is the matter?" he asked.

"*Watten!*" replied the huntsman.

No doubt under the inspiration of intense pain everybody becomes endowed with the gift of divers tongues. I did not know a word of Danish, yet instinctively I understood the word he had uttered.

"Water! water!" I cried, clapping my hands and gesticulating like a madman.

"Water!" repeated my uncle. "Hvar?" he asked, in Icelandic.

"*Nedat,*" replied Hans.

"Where? Down below!" I understood it all. I seized the hunter's hands, and pressed them while he looked on me without moving a muscle of his countenance.

The preparations for our departure were not long in making, and we were soon on our way down a passage inclining two feet in seven. In an hour we had gone a mile and a quarter, and descended two thousand feet.

Then I began to hear distinctly quite a new sound of something running within the thickness of the granite wall, a kind of dull, dead rumbling, like distant thunder. During the first part of our walk, not meeting with the promised spring, I felt my agony returning; but then my uncle acquainted me with the cause of the strange noise.

"Hans was not mistaken," he said. "What you hear is the rushing of a torrent."

"A torrent?" I exclaimed.

"There can be no doubt; a subterranean river is flowing around us."

We hurried forward in the greatest excitement. I was no longer sensible of my fatigue. This murmuring of waters close at hand was already refreshing me. It was audibly increasing. The torrent, after having for some time flowed over our heads, was now running within the left wall, roaring and rushing. Frequently I touched the wall, hoping to feel some indications of moisture: But there was no hope here.

Yet another half hour, another half league was passed.

CHAPTER XXIII. WATER DISCOVERED

Then it became clear that the hunter had gone no farther. Guided by an instinct peculiar to mountaineers he had as it were felt this torrent through the rock; but he had certainly seen none of the precious liquid; he had drunk nothing himself.

Soon it became evident that if we continued our walk we should widen the distance between ourselves and the stream, the noise of which was becoming fainter.

We returned. Hans stopped where the torrent seemed closest. I sat near the wall, while the waters were flowing past me at a distance of two feet with extreme violence. But there was a thick granite wall between us and the object of our desires.

Without reflection, without asking if there were any means of procuring the water, I gave way to a movement of despair.

Hans glanced at me with, I thought, a smile of compassion.

He rose and took the lamp. I followed him. He moved towards the wall. I looked on. He applied his ear against the dry stone, and moved it slowly to and fro, listening intently. I perceived at once that he was examining to find the exact place where the torrent could be heard the loudest. He met with that point on the left side of the tunnel, at three feet from the ground.

I was stirred up with excitement. I hardly dared guess what the hunter was about to do. But I could not but understand, and applaud and cheer him on, when I saw him lay hold of the pickaxe to make an attack upon the rock.

"We are saved!" I cried.

"Yes," cried my uncle, almost frantic with excitement. "Hans is right. Capital fellow! Who but he would have thought of it?"

Yes; who but he? Such an expedient, however simple, would never have entered into our minds. True, it seemed most hazardous to strike a blow of the hammer in this part of the earth's structure. Suppose some displacement should occur and crush us all! Suppose the torrent, bursting through, should drown us in a sudden flood! There was nothing vain in these fancies. But still no fears of falling rocks or rushing floods could stay us now; and our thirst was so intense that, to satisfy it, we would have dared the waves of the north Atlantic.

Hans set about the task which my uncle and I together could not have accomplished. If our impatience had armed our hands with power, we should have shattered the rock into a thousand fragments. Not so Hans. Full of self possession, he calmly wore his way through the rock with a steady succession of light and skilful strokes, working through an aperture six inches wide at the outside. I could hear a louder noise of flowing waters, and I fancied I could feel the delicious fluid refreshing my parched lips.

The pick had soon penetrated two feet into the granite partition, and our man had worked for above an hour. I was in an agony of impatience. My uncle wanted to employ stronger measures, and I had some difficulty in dissuading him; still he had just taken a pickaxe in his hand, when a sudden hissing was heard, and a jet of water spurted out with violence against the opposite wall.

Hans, almost thrown off his feet by the violence of the shock, uttered a cry of grief and disappointment, of which I soon under-. stood the cause, when plunging my hands into the spouting torrent, I withdrew them in haste, for the water was scalding hot.

"The water is at the boiling point," I cried.

"Well, never mind, let it cool," my uncle replied.

The tunnel was filling with steam, whilst a stream was forming, which by degrees wandered away into subterranean windings, and soon we had the satisfaction of swallowing our first draught.

Could anything be more delicious than the sensation that our burning intolerable thirst was passing away, and leaving us to enjoy comfort and pleasure? But where was this water from? No matter. It was water; and though still warm, it brought life back to the dying. I kept drinking without stopping, and almost without tasting.

At last after a most delightful time of reviving energy, I cried,

"Why, this is a chalybeate spring!"

"Nothing could be better for the digestion," said my uncle. "It is highly impregnated with iron. It will be as good for us as going to the Spa, or to Töplitz."

"Well, it is delicious!"

"Of course it is, water should be, found six miles underground. It has an inky flavour, which is not at all unpleasant. What a capital source of strength Hans has found for us here. We will call it after his name."

"Agreed," I cried.

And Hansbach it was from that moment.

Hans was none the prouder. After a moderate draught, he went quietly into a corner to rest.

"Now," I said, "we must not lose this water."

"What is the use of troubling ourselves?" my uncle, replied. "I fancy it will never fail."

"Never mind, we cannot be sure; let us fill the water bottle and our flasks, and then stop up the opening."

My advice was followed so far as getting in a supply; but the stopping up of the hole was not so easy to accomplish. It was in vain that we took up fragments of granite, and stuffed them in with tow, we only scalded our hands without succeeding. The pressure was too great, and our efforts were fruitless.

"It is quite plain," said I, "that the higher body of this water is at a considerable elevation. The force of the jet shows that."

"No doubt," answered my uncle. "If this column of water is 32,000 feet high—that is, from the surface of the earth, it is equal to the weight of a thousand atmospheres. But I have got an idea."

"Well?"

"Why should we trouble ourselves to stop the stream from coming out at all?"

"Because—" Well, I could not assign a reason.

"When our flasks are empty, where shall we fill them again? Can we tell that?"

No; there was no certainty.

"Well, let us allow the water to run on. It will flow down, and will both guide and refresh us."

"That is well planned," I cried. "With this stream for our guide, there is no reason why we should not succeed in our undertaking."

"Ah, my boy! you agree with me now," cried the Professor, laughing.

"I agree with you most heartily."

"Well, let us rest awhile; and then we will start again."

I was forgetting that it was night. The chronometer soon informed me of that fact; and in a very short time, refreshed and thankful, we all three fell into a sound sleep.

CHAPTER XXIV. WELL SAID, OLD MOLE! CANST THOU WORK I' THE GROUND SO FAST?

By the next day we had forgotten all our sufferings. At first, I was wondering that I was no longer thirsty, and I was for asking for the reason. The answer came in the murmuring of the stream at my feet.

We breakfasted, and drank of this excellent chalybeate water. I felt wonderfully stronger, and quite decided upon pushing on. Why should not so firmly convinced a man as my uncle, furnished with so industrious a guide as Hans, and accompanied by so determined a nephew as myself, go on to final success? Such were the magnificent plans which struggled for mastery within me. If it had been proposed to me to return to the summit of Snæfell, I should have indignantly declined.

Most fortunately, all we had to do was to descend.

"Let us start!" I cried, awakening by my shouts the echoes of the vaulted hollows of the earth.

On Thursday, at 8 a.m., we started afresh. The granite tunnel winding from side to side, earned us past unexpected turns, and seemed almost to form a labyrinth; but, on the whole, its direction seemed to be south-easterly. My uncle never ceased to consult his compass, to keep account of the ground gone over.

The gallery dipped down a very little way from the horizontal, scarcely more than two inches in a fathom, and the stream ran gently murmuring at our feet. I compared it to a friendly genius guiding us underground, and caressed with my hand the soft naiad, whose comforting voice accompanied our steps. With my reviving spirits these mythological notions seemed to come unbidden.

As for my uncle, he was beginning to storm against the horizontal road. He loved nothing better than a vertical path; but this way seemed indefinitely prolonged, and instead of sliding along the hypothenuse as we were now doing, he would willingly have dropped down the terrestrial radius. But there was no help for it, and as long as we were approaching the centre at all we felt that we must not complain.

From time to time, a steeper path appeared; our naiad then began to tumble before us with a hoarser murmur, and we went down with her to a greater depth.

On the whole, that day and the next we made considerable way horizontally, very little vertically.

On Friday evening, the 10th of July, according to our calculations, we were thirty leagues south-east of Rejkiavik, and at a depth of two leagues and a half.

At our feet there now opened a frightful abyss. My uncle, however, was not to be daunted, and he clapped his hands at the steepness of the descent.

"This will take us a long way," he cried, "and without much difficulty; for the projections in the rock form quite a staircase."

The ropes were so fastened by Hans as to guard against accident, and the descent commenced. I can hardly call it perilous, for I was beginning to be familiar with this kind of exercise.

This well, or abyss, was a narrow cleft in the mass of the granite, called by geologists a 'fault,' and caused by the unequal cooling of the globe of the earth. If it had at one time been a passage for eruptive matter thrown out by Snæfell, I still could not understand why no trace was left of its passage. We kept going down a kind of winding staircase, which seemed almost to have been made by the hand of man.

Every quarter of an hour we were obliged to halt, to take a little necessary repose and restore the action of our limbs. We then sat down upon a fragment of rock, and we talked as we ate and drank from the stream.

Of course, down this fault the Hansbach fell in a cascade, and lost some of its volume; but there was enough and to spare to slake our thirst. Besides, when the incline became more gentle, it would of course resume its peaceable course. At this moment it reminded me of my worthy uncle, in his frequent fits of impatience and anger, while below it ran with the calmness of the Icelandic hunter.

On the 6th and 7th of July we kept following the spiral curves of this singular well, penetrating in actual distance no more than two leagues; but being carried to a depth of five leagues below the level of the sea. But on the 8th, about noon, the fault took, towards the south-east, a much gentler slope, one of about forty-five degrees.

Then the road became monotonously easy. It could not be otherwise, for there was no landscape to vary the stages of our journey.

On Wednesday, the 15th, we were seven leagues underground, and had travelled fifty leagues away from Snæfell. Although we were tired, our health was perfect, and the medicine chest had not yet had occasion to be opened.

My uncle noted every hour the indications of the compass, the chronometer, the aneroid, and the thermometer the very same which he has published in his scientific report of our journey. It was therefore not difficult to know exactly our whereabouts. When he told me that we had gone fifty leagues horizontally, I could not repress an exclamation of astonishment, at the thought that we had now long left Iceland behind us.

"What is the matter?" he cried.

"I was reflecting that if your calculations are correct we are no longer under Iceland."

"Do you think so?"

"I am not mistaken," I said, and examining the map, I added, "We have passed Cape Portland, and those fifty leagues bring us under the wide expanse of ocean."

"Under the sea," my uncle repeated, rubbing his hands with delight.

"Can it be?" I said. "Is the ocean spread above our heads?"

"Of course, Axel. What can be more natural? At Newcastle are there not coal mines extending far under the sea?"

It was all very well for the Professor to call this so simple, but I could not feel quite easy at the thought that the boundless ocean was rolling over my head. And yet it really mattered very little whether it was the plains and mountains that covered our heads, or the Atlantic waves, as long as we were arched over by solid granite. And, besides, I was getting used to this idea; for the tunnel, now running straight, now winding as capriciously in its inclines as in its turnings, but constantly preserving its south-easterly direction, and always running deeper, was gradually carrying us to very great depths indeed.

CHAPTER XXIV. WELL SAID, OLD MOLE! CANST THOU WORK I' THE GROUND SO FAST?

Four days later, Saturday, the 18th of July, in the evening, we arrived at a kind of vast grotto; and here my uncle paid Hans his weekly wages, and it was settled that the next day, Sunday, should be a day of rest.

CHAPTER XXV. DE PROFUNDIS

I therefore awoke next day relieved from the preoccupation of an immediate start. Although we were in the very deepest of known depths, there was something not unpleasant about it. And, besides, we were beginning to get accustomed to this troglodyte[1] life. I no longer thought of sun, moon, and stars, trees, houses, and towns, nor of any of those terrestrial superfluities which are necessaries of men who live upon the earth's surface. Being fossils, we looked upon all those things as mere jokes.

The grotto was an immense apartment. Along its granite floor ran our faithful stream. At this distance from its spring the water was scarcely tepid, and we drank of it with pleasure.

After breakfast the Professor gave a few hours to the arrangement of his daily notes.

"First," said he, "I will make a calculation to ascertain our exact position. I hope, after our return, to draw a map of our journey, which will be in reality a vertical section of the globe, containing the track of our expedition."

"That will be curious, uncle; but are your observations sufficiently accurate to enable you to do this correctly?"

"Yes; I have everywhere observed the angles and the inclines. I am sure there is no error. Let us see where we are now. Take your compass, and note the direction."

I looked, and replied carefully:

"South-east by east."

"Well," answered the Professor, after a rapid calculation, "I infer that we have gone eighty-five leagues since we started."

"Therefore we are under mid-Atlantic?"

"To be sure we are."

"And perhaps at this very moment there is a storm above, and ships over our heads are being rudely tossed by the tempest."

"Quite probable."

"And whales are lashing the roof of our prison with their tails?"

"It may be, Axel, but they won't shake us here. But let us go back to our calculation. Here we are eighty-five leagues south-east of Snæfell, and I reckon that we are at a depth of sixteen leagues."

"Sixteen leagues?" I cried.

"No doubt."

---

[1] tpwgln, a hole; dnw, to creep into. The name of an Ethiopian tribe who lived in caves and holes.

"Why, this is the very limit assigned by science to the thickness of the crust of the earth."

"I don't deny it."

"And here, according to the law of increasing temperature, there ought to be a heat of 2,732° Fahr.!"

"So there should, my lad."

"And all this solid granite ought to be running in fusion."

"You see that it is not so, and that, as so often happens, facts come to overthrow theories."

"I am obliged to agree; but, after all, it is surprising."

"What does the thermometer say?"

"Twenty-seven, six tenths (82° Fahr.)."

"Therefore the savants are wrong by 2,705°, and the proportional increase is a mistake. Therefore Humphry Davy was right, and I am not wrong in following him. What do you say now?"

"Nothing."

In truth, I had a good deal to say. I gave way in no respect to Davy's theory. I still held to the central heat, although I did not feel its effects. I preferred to admit in truth, that this chimney of an extinct volcano, lined with lavas, which are non-conductors of heat, did not suffer the heat to pass through its walls.

But without stopping to look up new arguments I simply took up our situation such as it was.

"Well, admitting all your calculations to be quite correct, you must allow me to draw one rigid result therefrom."

"What is it. Speak freely."

"At the latitude of Iceland, where we now are, the radius of the earth, the distance from the centre to the surface is about 1,583 leagues; let us say in round numbers 1,600 leagues, or 4,800 miles. Out of 1,600 leagues we have gone twelve!"

"So you say."

"And these twelve at a cost of 85 leagues diagonally?"

"Exactly so."

"In twenty days?"

"Yes."

"Now, sixteen leagues are the hundredth part of the earth's radius. At this rate we shall be two thousand days, or nearly five years and a half, in getting to the centre."

No answer was vouchsafed to this rational conclusion. "Without reckoning, too, that if a vertical depth of sixteen leagues can be attained only by a diagonal descent of eighty-four, it follows that we must go eight thousand miles in a south-easterly direction; so that we shall emerge from some point in the earth's circumference instead of getting to the centre!"

"Confusion to all your figures, and all your hypotheses besides," shouted my uncle in a sudden rage. "What is the basis of them all? How do you know that this passage does not run straight to our destination? Besides, there is a precedent. What one man has done, another may do."

"I hope so; but, still, I may be permitted—"

"You shall have my leave to hold your tongue, Axel, but not to talk in that irrational way."

I could see the awful Professor bursting through my uncle's skin, and

I took timely warning.

"Now look at your aneroid. What does that say?"

"It says we are under considerable pressure."

"Very good; so you see that by going gradually down, and getting accustomed to the density of the atmosphere, we don't suffer at all."

"Nothing, except a little pain in the ears."

"That's nothing, and you may get rid of even that by quick breathing whenever you feel the pain."

"Exactly so," I said, determined not to say a word that might cross my uncle's prejudices. "There is even positive pleasure in living in this dense atmosphere. Have you observed how intense sound is down here?"

"No doubt it is. A deaf man would soon learn to hear perfectly."

"But won't this density augment?"

"Yes; according to a rather obscure law. It is well known that the weight of bodies diminishes as fast as we descend. You know that it is at the surface of the globe that weight is most sensibly felt, and that at the centre there is no weight at all."

"I am aware of that; but, tell me, will not air at last acquire the density of water?"

"Of course, under a pressure of seven hundred and ten atmospheres."

"And how, lower down still?"

"Lower down the density will still increase."

"But how shall we go down then."

"Why, we must fill our pockets with stones."

"Well, indeed, my worthy uncle, you are never at a loss for an answer."

I dared venture no farther into the region of probabilities, for I might presently have stumbled upon an impossibility, which would have brought the Professor on the scene when he was not wanted.

Still, it was evident that the air, under a pressure which might reach that of thousands of atmospheres, would at last reach the solid state, and then, even if our bodies could resist the strain, we should be stopped, and no reasonings would be able to get us on any farther.

But I did not advance this argument. My uncle would have met it with his inevitable Saknussemm, a precedent which possessed no weight with me; for even if the journey of the learned Icelander were really attested, there was one very simple answer, that in the sixteenth century there was neither barometer or aneroid and therefore Saknussemm could not tell how far he had gone.

But I kept this objection to myself, and waited the course of events.

The rest of the day was passed in calculations and in conversations. I remained a steadfast adherent of the opinions of Professor Liedenbrock, and I envied the stolid indifference of Hans, who, without going into causes and effects, went on with his eyes shut wherever his destiny guided him.

CHAPTER XXVI. THE WORST PERIL OF ALL

It must be confessed that hitherto things had not gone on so badly, and that I had small reason to complain. If our difficulties became no worse, we might hope to reach our end. And to what a height of scientific glory we should then attain! I had become quite a Liedenbrock in my reasonings; seriously I had. But would this state of things last in the strange place we had come to? Perhaps it might.

For several days steeper inclines, some even frightfully near to the perpendicular, brought us deeper and deeper into the mass of the interior of the earth. Some days we advanced nearer to the centre by a league and a half, or nearly two leagues. These were perilous descents, in which the skill and marvellous coolness of Hans were invaluable to us. That unimpassioned Icelander devoted himself with incomprehensible deliberation; and, thanks to him, we crossed many a dangerous spot which we should never have cleared alone.

But his habit of silence gained upon him day by day, and was infecting us. External objects produce decided effects upon the brain. A man shut up between four walls soon loses the power to associate words and ideas together. How many prisoners in solitary confinement become idiots, if not mad, for want of exercise for the thinking faculty!

During the fortnight following our last conversation, no incident occurred worthy of being recorded. But I have good reason for remembering one very serious event which took place at this time, and of which I could scarcely now forget the smallest details.

By the 7th of August our successive descents had brought us to a depth of thirty leagues; that is, that for a space of thirty leagues there were over our heads solid beds of rock, ocean, continents, and towns. We must have been two hundred leagues from Iceland.

On that day the tunnel went down a gentle slope. I was ahead of the others. My uncle was carrying one of Ruhmkorff's lamps and I the other. I was examining the beds of granite.

Suddenly turning round I observed that I was alone.

Well, well, I thought; I have been going too fast, or Hans and my uncle have stopped on the way. Come, this won't do; I must join them. Fortunately there is not much of an ascent.

I retraced my steps. I walked for a quarter of an hour. I gazed into the darkness. I shouted. No reply: my voice was lost in the midst of the cavernous echoes which alone replied to my call.

I began to feel uneasy. A shudder ran through me.

"Calmly!" I said aloud to myself, "I am sure to find my companions again. There are not two roads. I was too far ahead. I will return!"

For half an hour I climbed up. I listened for a call, and in that dense atmosphere a voice could reach very far. But there was a dreary silence in all that long gallery. I stopped. I could not believe that I was lost. I was only bewildered for a time, not lost. I was sure I should find my way again.

"Come," I repeated, "since there is but one road, and they are on it, I must find them again. I have but to ascend still. Unless, indeed, missing me, and supposing me to be behind, they too should have gone back. But even in this case I have only to make the greater haste. I shall find them, I am sure."

I repeated these words in the fainter tones of a half-convinced man. Besides, to associate even such simple ideas with words, and reason with them, was a work of time.

A doubt then seized upon me. Was I indeed in advance when we became separated? Yes, to be sure I was. Hans was after me, preceding my uncle. He had even stopped for a while to strap his baggage better over his shoulders. I could remember this little incident. It was at that very moment that I must have gone on.

Besides, I thought, have not I a guarantee that I shall not lose my way, a clue in the labyrinth, that cannot be broken, my faithful stream? I have but to trace it back, and I must come upon them.

This conclusion revived my spirits, and I resolved to resume my march without loss of time.

How I then blessed my uncle's foresight in preventing the hunter from stopping up the hole in the granite. This beneficent spring, after having satisfied our thirst on the road, would now be my guide among the windings of the terrestrial crust.

Before starting afresh I thought a wash would do me good. I stooped to bathe my face in the Hansbach.

To my stupefaction and utter dismay my feet trod only—the rough dry granite. The stream was no longer at my feet.

CHAPTER XXVII. LOST IN THE BOWELS OF THE EARTH

To describe my despair would be impossible. No words could tell it. I was buried alive, with the prospect before me of dying of hunger and thirst.

Mechanically I swept the ground with my hands. How dry and hard the rock seemed to me!

But how had I left the course of the stream? For it was a terrible fact that it no longer ran at my side. Then I understood the reason of that fearful, silence, when for the last time I listened to hear if any sound from my companions could reach my ears. At the moment when I left the right road I had not noticed the absence of the stream. It is evident that at that moment a deviation had presented itself before me, whilst the Hansbach, following the caprice of another incline, had gone with my companions away into unknown depths.

How was I to return? There was not a trace of their footsteps or of my own, for the foot left no mark upon the granite floor. I racked my brain for a solution of this impracticable problem. One word described my position. Lost!

Lost at an immeasurable depth! Thirty leagues of rock seemed to weigh upon my shoulders with a dreadful pressure. I felt crushed.

I tried to carry back my ideas to things on the surface of the earth. I could scarcely succeed. Hamburg, the house in the Kŏnigstrasse, my poor Gräuben, all that busy world underneath which I was wandering about, was passing in rapid confusion before my terrified memory. I could revive with vivid reality all the incidents of our voyage, Iceland, M. Fridrikssen, Snæfell. I said to myself that if, in such a position as I was now in, I was fool enough to cling to one glimpse of hope, it would be madness, and that the best thing I could do was to despair.

What human power could restore me to the light of the sun by rending asunder the huge arches of rock which united over my head, buttressing each other with impregnable strength? Who could place my feet on the right path, and bring me back to my company?

"Oh, my uncle!" burst from my lips in the tone of despair.

It was my only word of reproach, for I knew how much he must be suffering in seeking me, wherever he might be.

When I saw myself thus far removed from all earthly help I had recourse to heavenly succour. The remembrance of my childhood, the recollection of my mother, whom I had only known in my tender early years, came back to me, and I knelt in prayer imploring for the Divine help of which I was so little worthy.

This return of trust in God's providence allayed the turbulence of my fears, and I was enabled to concentrate upon my situation all the force of my intelligence.

I had three days' provisions with me and my flask was full. But I could not remain alone for long. Should I go up or down?

Up, of course; up continually.

I must thus arrive at the point where I had left the stream, that fatal turn in the road. With the stream at my feet, I might hope to regain the summit of Snæfell.

Why had I not thought of that sooner? Here was evidently a chance of safety. The most pressing duty was to find out again the course of the Hansbach. I rose, and leaning upon my iron-pointed stick I ascended the gallery. The slope was rather steep. I walked on without hope but without indecision, like a man who has made up his mind.

For half an hour I met with no obstacle. I tried to recognise my way by the form of the tunnel, by the projections of certain rocks, by the disposition of the fractures. But no particular sign appeared, and I soon saw that this gallery could not bring me back to the turning point. It came to an abrupt end. I struck against an impenetrable wall, and fell down upon the rock.

Unspeakable despair then seized upon me. I lay overwhelmed, aghast!

My last hope was shattered against this granite wall.

Lost in this labyrinth, whose windings crossed each other in all directions, it was no use to think of flight any longer. Here I must die the most dreadful of deaths. And, strange to say, the thought came across me that when some day my petrified remains should be found thirty leagues below the surface in the bowels of the earth, the discovery might lead to grave scientific discussions.

I tried to speak aloud, but hoarse sounds alone passed my dry lips. I panted for breath.

In the midst of my agony a new terror laid hold of me. In falling my lamp had got wrong. I could not set it right, and its light was paling and would soon disappear altogether.

I gazed painfully upon the luminous current growing weaker and weaker in the wire coil. A dim procession of moving shadows seemed slowly unfolding down the darkening walls. I scarcely dared to shut my eyes for one moment, for fear of losing the least glimmer of this precious light. Every instant it seemed about to vanish and the dense blackness to come rolling in palpably upon me.

One last trembling glimmer shot feebly up. I watched it in trembling and anxiety; I drank it in as if I could preserve it, concentrating upon it the full power of my eyes, as upon the very last sensation of light which they were ever to experience, and the next moment I lay in the heavy gloom of deep, thick, unfathomable darkness.

A terrible cry of anguish burst from me. Upon earth, in the midst of the darkest night, light never abdicates its functions altogether. It is still subtle and diffusive, but whatever little there may be, the eye still catches that little. Here there was not an atom; the total darkness made me totally blind.

Then I began to lose my head. I arose with my arms stretched out before me, attempting painfully to feel my way. I began to run wildly, hurrying through the inextricable maze, still descending, still running through the substance of the earth's thick crust, a struggling denizen of geological 'faults,' crying, shouting, yelling, soon bruised by contact with the jagged rock, falling and rising again bleeding, trying to drink the blood which covered my face, and even waiting for some rock to shatter my skull against.

I shall never know whither my mad career took me. After the lapse of some hours, no doubt exhausted, I fell like a lifeless lump at the foot of the wall, and lost all consciousness.

CHAPTER XXVIII. THE RESCUE IN THE WHISPERING GALLERY

When I returned to partial life my face was wet with tears. How long that state of insensibility had lasted I cannot say. I had no means now of taking account of time. Never was solitude equal to this, never had any living being been so utterly forsaken.

After my fall I had lost a good deal of blood. I felt it flowing over me. Ah! how happy I should have been could I have died, and if death were not yet to be gone through. I would think no longer. I drove away every idea, and, conquered by my grief, I rolled myself to the foot of the opposite wall.

Already I was feeling the approach of another faint, and was hoping for complete annihilation, when a loud noise reached me. It was like the distant rumble of continuous thunder, and I could hear its sounding undulations rolling far away into the remote recesses of the abyss.

Whence could this noise proceed? It must be from some phenomenon proceeding in the great depths amidst which I lay helpless. Was it an explosion of gas? Was it the fall of some mighty pillar of the globe?

I listened still. I wanted to know if the noise would be repeated. A quarter of an hour passed away. Silence reigned in this gallery. I could not hear even the beating of my heart.

Suddenly my ear, resting by chance against the wall, caught, or seemed to catch, certain vague, indescribable, distant, articulate sounds, as of words.

"This is a delusion," I thought.

But it was not. Listening more attentively, I heard in reality a murmuring of voices. But my weakness prevented me from understanding what the voices said. Yet it was language, I was sure of it.

For a moment I feared the words might be my own, brought back by the echo. Perhaps I had been crying out unknown to myself. I closed my lips firmly, and laid my ear against the wall again.

"Yes, truly, some one is speaking; those are words!"

Even a few feet from the wall I could hear distinctly. I succeeded in catching uncertain, strange, undistinguishable words. They came as if pronounced in low murmured whispers. The word '*forlorad*' was several times repeated in a tone of sympathy and sorrow.

"Help!" I cried with all my might. "Help!"

I listened, I watched in the darkness for an answer, a cry, a mere breath of sound, but nothing came. Some minutes passed. A whole world of ideas had opened in my mind. I thought that my weakened voice could never penetrate to my companions.

"It is they," I repeated. "What other men can be thirty leagues under ground?"

I again began to listen. Passing my ear over the wall from one place to another, I found the point where the voices seemed to be best heard. The word *'forlorad'* again returned; then the rolling of thunder which had roused me from my lethargy.

"No," I said, "no; it is not through such a mass that a voice can be heard. I am surrounded by granite walls, and the loudest explosion could never be heard here! This noise comes along the gallery. There must be here some remarkable exercise of acoustic laws!"

I listened again, and this time, yes this time, I did distinctly hear my name pronounced across the wide interval.

It was my uncle's own voice! He was talking to the guide. And *'forlorad'* is a Danish word.

Then I understood it all. To make myself heard, I must speak along this wall, which would conduct the sound of my voice just as wire conducts electricity.

But there was no time to lose. If my companions moved but a few steps away, the acoustic phenomenon would cease. I therefore approached the wall, and pronounced these words as clearly as possible:

"Uncle Liedenbrock!"

I waited with the deepest anxiety. Sound does not travel with great velocity. Even increased density air has no effect upon its rate of travelling; it merely augments its intensity. Seconds, which seemed ages, passed away, and at last these words reached me:

"Axel! Axel! is it you?"

. . . .

"Yes, yes," I replied.

. . . .

"My boy, where are you?"

. . . .

"Lost, in the deepest darkness."

. . . .

"Where is your lamp?"

. . . .

"It is out."

. . . .

"And the stream?"

. . . .

"Disappeared."

. . . .

"Axel, Axel, take courage!"

. . . .

"Wait! I am exhausted! I can't answer. Speak to me!"

. . . .

"Courage," resumed my uncle. "Don't speak. Listen to me. We have looked for you up the gallery and down the gallery. Could not find you. I wept for you, my poor boy. At last, supposing you were still on the Hansbach, we fired our guns. Our voices are audible to each other, but our hands cannot touch. But don't despair, Axel! It is a great thing that we can hear each other."

. . . .

During this time I had been reflecting. A vague hope was returning to my heart. There was one thing I must know to begin with. I placed my lips close to the wall, saying:

"My uncle!"

. . . .

"My boy!" came to me after a few seconds.

. . . .

"We must know how far we are apart."

. . . .

"That is easy."

. . . .

"You have your chronometer?"

. . .

"Yes."

. . . .

"Well, take it. Pronounce my name, noting exactly the second when you speak. I will repeat it as soon as it shall come to me, and you will observe the exact moment when you get my answer."

"Yes; and half the time between my call and your answer will exactly indicate that which my voice will take in coming to you."

. . . .

"Just so, my uncle."

. . . .

"Are you ready?"

. . . .

"Yes."

. . . . . .

"Now, attention. I am going to call your name."

. . . .

I put my ear to the wall, and as soon as the name 'Axel' came I immediately replied "Axel," then waited.

. . . .

"Forty seconds," said my uncle. "Forty seconds between the two words; so the sound takes twenty seconds in coming. Now, at the rate of 1,120 feet in a second, this is 22,400 feet, or four miles and a quarter, nearly."

. . . .

"Four miles and a quarter!" I murmured.

. . . .

"It will soon be over, Axel."

. . . .

"Must I go up or down?"

. . . .

"Down—for this reason: We are in a vast chamber, with endless galleries. Yours must lead into it, for it seems as if all the clefts and fractures of the globe radiated round this vast cavern. So get up, and begin walking. Walk on, drag yourself along, if necessary slide down the steep places, and at the end you will find us ready to receive you. Now begin moving."

. . . .

These words cheered me up.

"Good bye, uncle." I cried. "I am going. There will be no more voices heard when once I have started. So good bye!"

. . . .

"Good bye, Axel, *au revoir!*"

. . . .

These were the last words I heard.

This wonderful underground conversation, carried on with a distance of four miles and a quarter between us, concluded with these words of hope. I thanked God from my heart, for it was He who had conducted me through those vast solitudes to the point where, alone of all others perhaps, the voices of my companions could have reached me.

This acoustic effect is easily explained on scientific grounds. It arose from the concave form of the gallery and the conducting power of the rock. There are many examples of this propagation of sounds which remain unheard in the intermediate space. I remember that a similar phenomenon has been observed in many places; amongst others on the internal surface of the gallery of the dome of St. Paul's in London, and especially in the midst of the curious caverns among the quarries near Syracuse, the most wonderful of which is called Dionysius' Ear.

These remembrances came into my mind, and I clearly saw that since my uncle's voice really reached me, there could be no obstacle between us. Following the direction by which the sound came, of course I should arrive in his presence, if my strength did not fail me.

I therefore rose; I rather dragged myself than walked. The slope was rapid, and I slid down.

Soon the swiftness of the descent increased horribly, and threatened to become a fall. I no longer had the strength to stop myself.

Suddenly there was no ground under me. I felt myself revolving in air, striking and rebounding against the craggy projections of a vertical gallery, quite a well; my head struck against a sharp corner of the rock, and I became unconscious.

CHAPTER XXIX. THALATTA! THALATTA!

When I came to myself, I was stretched in half darkness, covered with thick coats and blankets. My uncle was watching over me, to discover the least sign of life. At my first sigh he took my hand; when I opened my eyes he uttered a cry of joy.

"He lives! he lives!" he cried.

"Yes, I am still alive," I answered feebly.

"My dear nephew," said my uncle, pressing me to his breast, "you are saved."

I was deeply touched with the tenderness of his manner as he uttered these words, and still more with the care with which he watched over me. But such trials were wanted to bring out the Professor's tenderer qualities.

At this moment Hans came, he saw my hand in my uncle's, and I may safely say that there was joy in his countenance.

"*God dag,*" said he.

"How do you do, Hans? How are you? And now, uncle, tell me where we are at the present moment?"

"To-morrow, Axel, to-morrow. Now you are too faint and weak. I have bandaged your head with compresses which must not be disturbed. Sleep now, and to-morrow I will tell you all."

"But do tell me what time it is, and what day."

"It is Sunday, the 8th of August, and it is ten at night. You must ask me no more questions until the 10th."

In truth I was very weak, and my eyes involuntarily closed. I wanted a good night's rest; and I therefore went off to sleep, with the knowledge that I had been four long days alone in the heart of the earth.

Next morning, on awakening, I looked round me. My couch, made up of all our travelling gear, was in a charming grotto, adorned with splendid stalactites, and the soil of which was a fine sand. It was half light. There was no torch, no lamp, yet certain mysterious glimpses of light came from without through a narrow opening in the grotto. I heard too a vague and indistinct noise, something like the murmuring of waves breaking upon a shingly shore, and at times I seemed to hear the whistling of wind.

I wondered whether I was awake, whether I was dreaming, whether my brain, crazed by my fall, was not affected by imaginary noises. Yet neither eyes, nor ears could be so utterly deceived.

It is a ray of daylight, I thought, sliding in through this cleft in the rock! That is indeed the murmuring of waves! That is the rustling noise of wind. Am I quite mistaken, or have we returned to the surface of the earth? Has my uncle given up the expedition, or is it happily terminated?

I was asking myself these unanswerable questions when the Professor entered.

"Good morning, Axel," he cried cheerily. "I feel sure you are better."

"Yes, I am indeed," said I, sitting up on my couch.

"You can hardly fail to be better, for you have slept quietly. Hans and I watched you by turns, and we have noticed you were evidently recovering."

"Indeed, I do feel a great deal better, and I will give you a proof of that presently if you will let me have my breakfast."

"You shall eat, lad. The fever has left you. Hans rubbed your wounds with some ointment or other of which the Icelanders keep the secret, and they have healed marvellously. Our hunter is a splendid fellow!"

Whilst he went on talking, my uncle prepared a few provisions, which I devoured eagerly, notwithstanding his advice to the contrary. All the while I was overwhelming him with questions which he answered readily.

I then learnt that my providential fall had brought me exactly to the extremity of an almost perpendicular shaft; and as I had landed in the midst of an accompanying torrent of stones, the least of which would have been enough to crush me, the conclusion was that a loose portion of the rock had come down with me. This frightful conveyance had thus carried me into the arms of my uncle, where I fell bruised, bleeding, and insensible.

"Truly it is wonderful that you have not been killed a hundred times over. But, for the love of God, don't let us ever separate again, or we many never see each other more."

"Not separate! Is the journey not over, then?" I opened a pair of astonished eyes, which immediately called for the question:

"What is the matter, Axel?"

"I have a question to ask you. You say that I am safe and sound?"

"No doubt you are."

"And all my limbs unbroken?"

"Certainly."

"And my head?"

"Your head, except for a few bruises, is all right; and it is on your shoulders, where it ought to be."

"Well, I am afraid my brain is affected."

"Your mind affected!"

"Yes, I fear so. Are we again on the surface of the globe?"

"No, certainly not."

"Then I must be mad; for don't I see the light of day, and don't I hear the wind blowing, and the sea breaking on the shore?"

"Ah! is that all?"

"Do tell me all about it."

"I can't explain the inexplicable, but you will soon see and understand that geology has not yet learnt all it has to learn."

"Then let us go," I answered quickly.

"No, Axel; the open air might be bad for you."

"Open air?"

"Yes; the wind is rather strong. You must not expose yourself."

"But I assure you I am perfectly well."

"A little patience, my nephew. A relapse might get us into trouble, and we have no time to lose, for the voyage may be a long one."

"The voyage!"

"Yes, rest to-day, and to-morrow we will set sail."

CHAPTER XXIX. THALATTA! THALATTA!

"Set sail!"—and I almost leaped up.

What did it all mean? Had we a river, a lake, a sea to depend upon?

Was there a ship at our disposal in some underground harbour?

My curiosity was highly excited, my uncle vainly tried to restrain me. When he saw that my impatience was doing me harm, he yielded.

I dressed in haste. For greater safety I wrapped myself in a blanket, and came out of the grotto.

CHAPTER XXX. A NEW MARE INTERNUM

At first I could hardly see anything. My eyes, unaccustomed to the light, quickly closed. When I was able to reopen them, I stood more stupefied even than surprised.

"The sea!" I cried.

"Yes," my uncle replied, "the Liedenbrock Sea; and I don't suppose any other discoverer will ever dispute my claim to name it after myself as its first discoverer."

A vast sheet of water, the commencement of a lake or an ocean, spread far away beyond the range of the eye, reminding me forcibly of that open sea which drew from Xenophon's ten thousand Greeks, after their long retreat, the simultaneous cry, "Thalatta! thalatta!" the sea! the sea! The deeply indented shore was lined with a breadth of fine shining sand, softly lapped by the waves, and strewn with the small shells which had been inhabited by the first of created beings. The waves broke on this shore with the hollow echoing murmur peculiar to vast inclosed spaces. A light foam flew over the waves before the breath of a moderate breeze, and some of the spray fell upon my face. On this slightly inclining shore, about a hundred fathoms from the limit of the waves, came down the foot of a huge wall of vast cliffs, which rose majestically to an enormous height. Some of these, dividing the beach with their sharp spurs, formed capes and promontories, worn away by the ceaseless action of the surf. Farther on the eye discerned their massive outline sharply defined against the hazy distant horizon.

It was quite an ocean, with the irregular shores of earth, but desert and frightfully wild in appearance.

If my eyes were able to range afar over this great sea, it was because a peculiar light brought to view every detail of it. It was not the light of the sun, with his dazzling shafts of brightness and the splendour of his rays; nor was it the pale and uncertain shimmer of the moonbeams, the dim reflection of a nobler body of light. No; the illuminating power of this light, its trembling diffusiveness, its bright, clear whiteness, and its low temperature, showed that it must be of electric origin. It was like an aurora borealis, a continuous cosmical phenomenon, filling a cavern of sufficient extent to contain an ocean.

The vault that spanned the space above, the sky, if it could be called so, seemed composed of vast plains of cloud, shifting and variable vapours, which by their condensation must at certain times fall in torrents of rain. I should have thought that under so powerful a pressure of the atmosphere there could be no evaporation; and yet, under a law unknown to me, there were broad tracts of vapour suspended in the air. But then 'the weather was fine.' The play of the electric light produced singular effects upon the upper strata of cloud. Deep shadows reposed upon their lower wreaths; and often, between two separated fields of cloud, there glided down a ray of unspeakable lustre. But it was not solar light, and there was no heat. The general effect was sad, supremely melancholy. Instead of the shining firmament, spangled with its innumerable stars, shining singly or in clusters, I felt that all these subdued and shaded lights were ribbed in by vast walls of granite, which seemed to overpower me with their weight, and that all this space, great as it was, would not be enough for the march of the humblest of satellites.

Then I remembered the theory of an English captain, who likened the earth to a vast hollow sphere, in the interior of which the air became luminous because of the vast pressure that weighed upon it; while two stars, Pluto and Proserpine, rolled within upon the circuit of their mysterious orbits.

We were in reality shut up inside an immeasurable excavation. Its width could not be estimated, since the shore ran widening as far as eye could reach, nor could its length, for the dim horizon bounded the new. As for its height, it must have been several leagues. Where this vault rested upon its granite base no eye could tell; but there was a cloud hanging far above, the height of which we estimated at 12,000 feet, a greater height than that of any terrestrial vapour, and no doubt due to the great density of the air.

The word cavern does not convey any idea of this immense space; words of human tongue are inadequate to describe the discoveries of him who ventures into the deep abysses of earth.

Besides I could not tell upon what geological theory to account for the existence of such an excavation. Had the cooling of the globe produced it? I knew of celebrated caverns from the descriptions of travellers, but had never heard of any of such dimensions as this.

If the grotto of Guachara, in Colombia, visited by Humboldt, had not given up the whole of the secret of its depth to the philosopher, who investigated it to the depth of 2,500 feet, it probably did not extend much farther. The immense mammoth cave in Kentucky is of gigantic proportions, since its vaulted roof rises five hundred feet[1] above the level of an unfathomable lake and travellers have explored its ramifications to the extent of forty miles. But what were these cavities compared to that in which I stood with wonder and admiration, with its sky of luminous vapours, its bursts of electric light, and a vast sea filling its bed? My imagination fell powerless before such immensity.

I gazed upon these wonders in silence. Words failed me to express my feelings. I felt as if I was in some distant planet Uranus or Neptune—and in the presence of phenomena of which my terrestrial experience gave me no cognisance. For such novel sensations, new words were wanted; and my imagination failed to supply them. I gazed, I thought, I admired, with a stupefaction mingled with a certain amount of fear.

The unforeseen nature of this spectacle brought back the colour to my cheeks. I was under a new course of treatment with the aid of astonishment, and my convalescence was promoted by this novel system of therapeutics; besides, the dense and breezy air invigorated me, supplying more oxygen to my lungs.

It will be easily conceived that after an imprisonment of forty seven days in a narrow gallery it was the height of physical enjoyment to breathe a moist air impregnated with saline particles.

I was delighted to leave my dark grotto. My uncle, already familiar with these wonders, had ceased to feel surprise.

"You feel strong enough to walk a little way now?" he asked.

"Yes, certainly; and nothing could be more delightful."

"Well, take my arm, Axel, and let us follow the windings of the shore."

---

[1] One hundred and twenty. (Trans.)

I eagerly accepted, and we began to coast along this new sea. On the left huge pyramids of rock, piled one upon another, produced a prodigious titanic effect. Down their sides flowed numberless waterfalls, which went on their way in brawling but pellucid streams. A few light vapours, leaping from rock to rock, denoted the place of hot springs; and streams flowed softly down to the common basin, gliding down the gentle slopes with a softer murmur.

Amongst these streams I recognised our faithful travelling companion, the Hansbach, coming to lose its little volume quietly in the mighty sea, just as if it had done nothing else since the beginning of the world.

"We shall see it no more," I said, with a sigh.

"What matters," replied the philosopher, "whether this or another serves to guide us?"

I thought him rather ungrateful.

But at that moment my attention was drawn to an unexpected sight. At a distance of five hundred paces, at the turn of a high promontory, appeared a high, tufted, dense forest. It was composed of trees of moderate height, formed like umbrellas, with exact geometrical outlines. The currents of wind seemed to have had no effect upon their shape, and in the midst of the windy blasts they stood unmoved and firm, just like a clump of petrified cedars.

I hastened forward. I could not give any name to these singular creations. Were they some of the two hundred thousand species of vegetables known hitherto, and did they claim a place of their own in the lacustrine flora? No; when we arrived under their shade my surprise turned into admiration. There stood before me productions of earth, but of gigantic stature, which my uncle immediately named.

"It is only a forest of mushrooms," said he.

And he was right. Imagine the large development attained by these plants, which prefer a warm, moist climate. I knew that the *Lycopodon giganteum* attains, according to Bulliard, a circumference of eight or nine feet; but here were pale mushrooms, thirty to forty feet high, and crowned with a cap of equal diameter. There they stood in thousands. No light could penetrate between their huge cones, and complete darkness reigned beneath those giants; they formed settlements of domes placed in close array like the round, thatched roofs of a central African city.

Yet I wanted to penetrate farther underneath, though a chill fell upon me as soon as I came under those cellular vaults. For half an hour we wandered from side to side in the damp shades, and it was a comfortable and pleasant change to arrive once more upon the sea shore.

But the subterranean vegetation was not confined to these fungi. Farther on rose groups of tall trees of colourless foliage and easy to recognise. They were lowly shrubs of earth, here attaining gigantic size; lycopodiums, a hundred feet high; the huge sigillaria, found in our coal mines; tree ferns, as tall as our fir-trees in northern latitudes; lepidodendra, with cylindrical forked stems, terminated by long leaves, and bristling with rough hairs like those of the cactus.

"Wonderful, magnificent, splendid!" cried my uncle. "Here is the entire flora of the second period of the world—the transition period. These, humble garden plants with us, were tall trees in the early ages. Look, Axel, and admire it all. Never had botanist such a feast as this!"

"You are right, my uncle. Providence seems to have preserved in this immense conservatory the antediluvian plants which the wisdom of philosophers has so sagaciously put together again."

"It is a conservatory, Axel; but is it not also a menagerie?"

"Surely not a menagerie!"

"Yes; no doubt of it. Look at that dust under your feet; see the bones scattered on the ground."

"So there are!" I cried; "bones of extinct animals."

I had rushed upon these remains, formed of indestructible phosphates of lime, and without hesitation I named these monstrous bones, which lay scattered about like decayed trunks of trees.

"Here is the lower jaw of a mastodon[1]," I said. "These are the molar teeth of the deinotherium; this femur must have belonged to the greatest of those beasts, the megatherium. It certainly is a menagerie, for these remains were not brought here by a deluge. The animals to which they belonged roamed on the shores of this subterranean sea, under the shade of those arborescent trees. Here are entire skeletons. And yet I cannot understand the appearance of these quadrupeds in a granite cavern."

"Why?"

"Because animal life existed upon the earth only in the secondary period, when a sediment of soil had been deposited by the rivers, and taken the place of the incandescent rocks of the primitive period."

"Well, Axel, there is a very simple answer to your objection that this soil is alluvial."

"What! at such a depth below the surface of the earth?"

"No doubt; and there is a geological explanation of the fact. At a certain period the earth consisted only of an elastic crust or bark, alternately acted on by forces from above or below, according to the laws of attraction and gravitation. Probably there were subsidences of the outer crust, when a portion of the sedimentary deposits was carried down sudden openings."

"That may be," I replied; "but if there have been creatures now extinct in these underground regions, why may not some of those monsters be now roaming through these gloomy forests, or hidden behind the steep crags?"

And as this unpleasant notion got hold of me, I surveyed with anxious scrutiny the open spaces before me; but no living creature appeared upon the barren strand.

I felt rather tired, and went to sit down at the end of a promontory, at the foot of which the waves came and beat themselves into spray. Thence my eye could sweep every part of the bay; within its extremity a little harbour was formed between the pyramidal cliffs, where the still waters slept untouched by the boisterous winds. A brig and two or three schooners might have moored within it in safety. I almost fancied I should presently see some ship issue from it, full sail, and take to the open sea under the southern breeze.

But this illusion lasted a very short time. We were the only living creatures in this subterranean world. When the wind lulled, a deeper silence than that of the deserts fell upon the arid, naked rocks, and weighed upon the surface of the ocean. I then desired to pierce the distant haze, and to rend asunder the mysterious curtain that hung across the horizon. Anxious queries arose to my lips. Where did that sea terminate? Where did it lead to? Should we ever know anything about its opposite shores?

My uncle made no doubt about it at all; I both desired and feared.

After spending an hour in the contemplation of this marvellous spectacle, we returned to the shore to regain the grotto, and I fell asleep in the midst of the strangest thoughts.

---

[1] These animals belonged to a late geological period, the Pliocene, just before the glacial epoch, and therefore could have no connection with the carboniferous vegetation. (Trans.)

CHAPTER XXXI. PREPARATIONS FOR A VOYAGE OF DISCOVERY

The next morning I awoke feeling perfectly well. I thought a bathe would do me good, and I went to plunge for a few minutes into the waters of this mediterranean sea, for assuredly it better deserved this name than any other sea.

I came back to breakfast with a good appetite. Hans was a good caterer for our little household; he had water and fire at his disposal, so that he was able to vary our bill of fare now and then. For dessert he gave us a few cups of coffee, and never was coffee so delicious.

"Now," said my uncle, "now is the time for high tide, and we must not lose the opportunity to study this phenomenon."

"What! the tide!" I cried. "Can the influence of the sun and moon be felt down here?"

"Why not? Are not all bodies subject throughout their mass to the power of universal attraction? This mass of water cannot escape the general law. And in spite of the heavy atmospheric pressure on the surface, you will see it rise like the Atlantic itself."

At the same moment we reached the sand on the shore, and the waves were by slow degrees encroaching on the shore.

"Here is the tide rising," I cried.

"Yes, Axel; and judging by these ridges of foam, you may observe that the sea will rise about twelve feet."

"This is wonderful," I said.

"No; it is quite natural."

"You may say so, uncle; but to me it is most extraordinary, and I can hardly believe my eyes. Who would ever have imagined, under this terrestrial crust, an ocean with ebbing and flowing tides, with winds and storms?"

"Well," replied my uncle, "is there any scientific reason against it?"

"No; I see none, as soon as the theory of central heat is given up." "So then, thus far," he answered, "the theory of Sir Humphry Davy is confirmed."

"Evidently it is; and now there is no reason why there should not be seas and continents in the interior of the earth."

"No doubt," said my uncle; "and inhabited too."

"To be sure," said I; "and why should not these waters yield to us fishes of unknown species?"

"At any rate," he replied, "we have not seen any yet."

"Well, let us make some lines, and see if the bait will draw here as it does in sublunary regions."

"We will try, Axel, for we must penetrate all secrets of these newly discovered regions."

"But where are we, uncle? for I have not yet asked you that question, and your instruments must be able to furnish the answer."

"Horizontally, three hundred and fifty leagues from Iceland."

"So much as that?"

"I am sure of not being a mile out of my reckoning."

"And does the compass still show south-east?"

"Yes; with a westerly deviation of nineteen degrees forty-five minutes, just as above ground. As for its dip, a curious fact is coming to light, which I have observed carefully: that the needle, instead of dipping towards the pole as in the northern hemisphere, on the contrary, rises from it."

"Would you then conclude," I said, "that the magnetic pole is somewhere between the surface of the globe and the point where we are?"

"Exactly so; and it is likely enough that if we were to reach the spot beneath the polar regions, about that seventy-first degree where Sir James Ross has discovered the magnetic pole to be situated, we should see the needle point straight up. Therefore that mysterious centre of attraction is at no great depth."

I remarked: "It is so; and here is a fact which science has scarcely suspected."

"Science, my lad, has been built upon many errors; but they are errors which it was good to fall into, for they led to the truth."

"What depth have we now reached?"

"We are thirty-five leagues below the surface."

"So," I said, examining the map, "the Highlands of Scotland are over our heads, and the Grampians are raising their rugged summits above us."

"Yes," answered the Professor laughing. "It is rather a heavy weight to bear, but a solid arch spans over our heads. The great Architect has built it of the best materials; and never could man have given it so wide a stretch. What are the finest arches of bridges and the arcades of cathedrals, compared with this far reaching vault, with a radius of three leagues, beneath which a wide and tempest-tossed ocean may flow at its ease?"

"Oh, I am not afraid that it will fall down upon my head. But now what are your plans? Are you not thinking of returning to the surface now?"

"Return! no, indeed! We will continue our journey, everything having gone on well so far."

"But how are we to get down below this liquid surface?"

"Oh, I am not going to dive head foremost. But if all oceans are properly speaking but lakes, since they are encompassed by land, of course this internal sea will be surrounded by a coast of granite, and on the opposite shores we shall find fresh passages opening."

"How long do you suppose this sea to be?"

"Thirty or forty leagues; so that we have no time to lose, and we shall set sail tomorrow."

I looked about for a ship.

"Set sail, shall we? But I should like to see my boat first."

"It will not be a boat at all, but a good, well-made raft."

"Why," I said, "a raft would be just as hard to make as a boat, and I don't see—"

"I know you don't see; but you might hear if you would listen. Don't you hear the hammer at work? Hans is already busy at it."

"What, has he already felled the trees?"

"Oh, the trees were already down. Come, and you will see for yourself."

After half an hour's walking, on the other side of the promontory which formed the little natural harbour, I perceived Hans at work. In a few more steps I was at his side. To my great surprise a half-finished raft was already lying on the sand, made of a peculiar kind of wood, and a great number of planks, straight and bent, and of frames, were covering the ground, enough almost for a little fleet.

"Uncle, what wood is this?" I cried.

"It is fir, pine, or birch, and other northern coniferae, mineralised by the action of the sea. It is called surturbrand, a variety of brown coal or lignite, found chiefly in Iceland."

"But surely, then, like other fossil wood, it must be as hard as stone, and cannot float?"

"Sometimes that may happen; some of these woods become true anthracites; but others, such as this, have only gone through the first stage of fossil transformation. Just look," added my uncle, throwing into the sea one of those precious waifs.

The bit of wood, after disappearing, returned to the surface and oscillated to and fro with the waves.

"Are you convinced?" said my uncle.

"I am quite convinced, although it is incredible!"

By next evening, thanks to the industry and skill of our guide, the raft was made. It was ten feet by five; the planks of surturbrand, braced strongly together with cords, presented an even surface, and when launched this improvised vessel floated easily upon the waves of the Liedenbrock Sea.

CHAPTER XXXII. WONDERS OF THE DEEP

On the 13th of August we awoke early. We were now to begin to adopt a mode of travelling both more expeditious and less fatiguing than hitherto.

A mast was made of two poles spliced together, a yard was made of a third, a blanket borrowed from our coverings made a tolerable sail. There was no want of cordage for the rigging, and everything was well and firmly made.

The provisions, the baggage, the instruments, the guns, and a good quantity of fresh water from the rocks around, all found their proper places on board; and at six the Professor gave the signal to embark. Hans had fitted up a rudder to steer his vessel. He took the tiller, and unmoored; the sail was set, and we were soon afloat. At the moment of leaving the harbour, my uncle, who was tenaciously fond of naming his new discoveries, wanted to give it a name, and proposed mine amongst others.

"But I have a better to propose," I said: "Grauben. Let it be called

Port Gräuben; it will look very well upon the map."

"Port Gräuben let it be then."

And so the cherished remembrance of my Virlandaise became associated with our adventurous expedition.

The wind was from the north-west. We went with it at a high rate of speed. The dense atmosphere acted with great force and impelled us swiftly on.

In an hour my uncle had been able to estimate our progress. At this rate, he said, we shall make thirty leagues in twenty-four hours, and we shall soon come in sight of the opposite shore.

I made no answer, but went and sat forward. The northern shore was already beginning to dip under the horizon. The eastern and western strands spread wide as if to bid us farewell. Before our eyes lay far and wide a vast sea; shadows of great clouds swept heavily over its silver-grey surface; the glistening bluish rays of electric light, here and there reflected by the dancing drops of spray, shot out little sheaves of light from the track we left in our rear. Soon we entirely lost sight of land; no object was left for the eye to judge by, and but for the frothy track of the raft, I might have thought we were standing still.

About twelve, immense shoals of seaweeds came in sight. I was aware of the great powers of vegetation that characterise these plants, which grow at a depth of twelve thousand feet, reproduce themselves under a pressure of four hundred atmospheres, and sometimes form barriers strong enough to impede the course of a ship. But never, I think, were such seaweeds as those which we saw floating in immense waving lines upon the sea of Liedenbrock.

Our raft skirted the whole length of the fuci, three or four thousand feet long, undulating like vast serpents beyond the reach of sight; I found some amusement in tracing these endless waves, always thinking I should come to the end of them, and for hours my patience was vying with my surprise.

What natural force could have produced such plants, and what must have been the appearance of the earth in the first ages of its formation, when, under the action of heat and moisture, the vegetable kingdom alone was developing on its surface?

Evening came, and, as on the previous day, I perceived no change in the luminous condition of the air. It was a constant condition, the permanency of which might be relied upon.

After supper I laid myself down at the foot of the mast, and fell asleep in the midst of fantastic reveries.

Hans, keeping fast by the helm, let the raft run on, which, after all, needed no steering, the wind blowing directly aft.

Since our departure from Port Gräuben, Professor Liedenbrock had entrusted the log to my care; I was to register every observation, make entries of interesting phenomena, the direction of the wind, the rate of sailing, the way we made—in a word, every particular of our singular voyage.

I shall therefore reproduce here these daily notes, written, so to speak, as the course of events directed, in order to furnish an exact narrative of our passage.

Friday, August 14.—Wind steady, N.W. The raft makes rapid way in a direct line. Coast thirty leagues to leeward. Nothing in sight before us. Intensity of light the same. Weather fine; that is to say, that the clouds are flying high, are light, and bathed in a white atmosphere resembling silver in a state of fusion. Therm. 89° Fahr.

At noon Hans prepared a hook at the end of a line. He baited it with a small piece of meat and flung it into the sea. For two hours nothing was caught. Are these waters, then, bare of inhabitants? No, there's a pull at the line. Hans draws it in and brings out a struggling fish.

"A sturgeon," I cried; "a small sturgeon."

The Professor eyes the creature attentively, and his opinion differs from mine.

The head of this fish was flat, but rounded in front, and the anterior part of its body was plated with bony, angular scales; it had no teeth, its pectoral fins were large, and of tail there was none. The animal belonged to the same order as the sturgeon, but differed from that fish in many essential particulars. After a short examination my uncle pronounced his opinion.

"This fish belongs to an extinct family, of which only fossil traces are found in the devonian formations."

"What!" I cried. "Have we taken alive an inhabitant of the seas of primitive ages?"

"Yes; and you will observe that these fossil fishes have no identity with any living species. To have in one's possession a living specimen is a happy event for a naturalist."

"But to what family does it belong?"

"It is of the order of ganoids, of the family of the cephalaspidae; and a species of pterichthys. But this one displays a peculiarity confined to all fishes that inhabit subterranean waters. It is blind, and not only blind, but actually has no eyes at all."

I looked: nothing could be more certain. But supposing it might be a solitary case, we baited afresh, and threw out our line. Surely this ocean is well peopled with fish, for in another couple of hours we took a large quantity of pterichthydes, as well as of others belonging to the extinct family of the dipterides, but of which my uncle could not tell the species; none had organs of sight. This unhoped-for catch recruited our stock of provisions.

Thus it is evident that this sea contains none but species known to us in their fossil state, in which fishes as well as reptiles are the less perfectly and completely organised the farther back their date of creation.

Perhaps we may yet meet with some of those saurians which science has reconstructed out of a bit of bone or cartilage. I took up the telescope and scanned the whole horizon, and found it everywhere a desert sea. We are far away removed from the shores.

I gaze upward in the air. Why should not some of the strange birds restored by the immortal Cuvier again flap their 'sail-broad vans' in this dense and heavy atmosphere? There are sufficient fish for their support. I survey the whole space that stretches overhead; it is as desert as the shore was.

Still my imagination carried me away amongst the wonderful speculations of palæontology. Though awake I fell into a dream. I thought I could see floating on the surface of the waters enormous chelonia, pre-adamite tortoises, resembling floating islands. Over the dimly lighted strand there trod the huge mammals of the first ages of the world, the leptotherium (slender beast), found in the caverns of Brazil; the merycotherium (ruminating beast), found in the 'drift' of iceclad Siberia. Farther on, the pachydermatous lophiodon (crested toothed), a gigantic tapir, hides behind the rocks to dispute its prey with the anoplotherium (unarmed beast), a strange creature, which seemed a compound of horse, rhinoceros, camel, and hippopotamus. The colossal mastodon (nipple-toothed) twists and untwists his trunk, and brays and pounds with his huge tusks the fragments of rock that cover the shore; whilst the megatherium (huge beast), buttressed upon his enormous hinder paws, grubs in the soil, awaking the sonorous echoes of the granite rocks with his tremendous roarings. Higher up, the protopitheca—the first monkey that appeared on the globe—is climbing up the steep ascents. Higher yet, the pterodactyle (wing-fingered) darts in irregular zigzags to and fro in the heavy air. In the uppermost regions of the air immense birds, more powerful than the cassowary, and larger than the ostrich, spread their vast breadth of wings and strike with their heads the granite vault that bounds the sky.

All this fossil world rises to life again in my vivid imagination. I return to the scriptural periods or ages of the world, conventionally called 'days,' long before the appearance of man, when the unfinished world was as yet unfitted for his support. Then my dream backed even farther still into the ages before the creation of living beings. The mammals disappear, then the birds vanish, then the reptiles of the secondary period, and finally the fish, the crustaceans, molluscs, and articulated beings. Then the zoophytes of the transition period also return to nothing. I am the only living thing in the world: all life is concentrated in my beating heart alone. There are no more seasons; climates are no more; the heat of the globe continually increases and neutralises that of the sun. Vegetation becomes accelerated. I glide like a shade amongst arborescent ferns, treading with unsteady feet the coloured marls and the particoloured clays; I lean for support against the trunks of immense conifers; I lie in the shade of sphenophylla (wedge-leaved), asterophylla (star-leaved), and lycopods, a hundred feet high.

Ages seem no more than days! I am passed, against my will, in retrograde order, through the long series of terrestrial changes. Plants disappear; granite rocks soften; intense heat converts solid bodies into thick fluids; the waters again cover the face of the earth; they boil, they rise in whirling eddies of steam; white and ghastly mists wrap round the shifting forms of the earth, which by imperceptible degrees dissolves into a gaseous mass, glowing fiery red and white, as large and as shining as the sun.

And I myself am floating with wild caprice in the midst of this nebulous mass of fourteen hundred thousand times the volume of the earth into which it will one day be condensed, and carried forward amongst the planetary bodies. My body is no longer firm and terrestrial; it is resolved into its constituent atoms, subtilised, volatilised. Sublimed into imponderable vapour, I mingle and am lost in the endless foods of those vast globular volumes of vaporous mists, which roll upon their flaming orbits through infinite space.

But is it not a dream? Whither is it carrying me? My feverish hand has vainly attempted to describe upon paper its strange and wonderful details. I have forgotten everything that surrounds me. The Professor, the guide, the raft—are all gone out of my ken. An illusion has laid hold upon me.

"What is the matter?" my uncle breaks in.

My staring eyes are fixed vacantly upon him.

"Take care, Axel, or you will fall overboard."

At that moment I felt the sinewy hand of Hans seizing me vigorously. But for him, carried away by my dream, I should have thrown myself into the sea.

"Is he mad?" cried the Professor.

"What is it all about?" at last I cried, returning to myself.

"Do you feel ill?" my uncle asked.

"No; but I have had a strange hallucination; it is over now. Is all going on right?"

"Yes, it is a fair wind and a fine sea; we are sailing rapidly along, and if I am not out in my reckoning, we shall soon land."

At these words I rose and gazed round upon the horizon, still everywhere bounded by clouds alone.

CHAPTER XXXIII. A BATTLE OF MONSTERS

Saturday, August 15.—The sea unbroken all round. No land in sight. The horizon seems extremely distant.

My head is still stupefied with the vivid reality of my dream.

My uncle has had no dreams, but he is out of temper. He examines the horizon all round with his glass, and folds his arms with the air of an injured man.

I remark that Professor Liedenbrock has a tendency to relapse into an impatient mood, and I make a note of it in my log. All my danger and sufferings were needed to strike a spark of human feeling out of him; but now that I am well his nature has resumed its sway. And yet, what cause was there for anger? Is not the voyage prospering as favourably as possible under the circumstances? Is not the raft spinning along with marvellous speed?

"-You seem anxious, my uncle," I said, seeing him continually with his glass to his eye.

"Anxious! No, not at all."

"Impatient, then?"

"One might be, with less reason than now."

"Yet we are going very fast."

"What does that signify? I am not complaining that the rate is slow, but that the sea is so wide."

I then remembered that the Professor, before starting, had estimated the length of this underground sea at thirty leagues. Now we had made three times the distance, yet still the southern coast was not in sight.

"We are not descending as we ought to be," the Professor declares. "We are losing time, and the fact is, I have not come all this way to take a little sail upon a pond on a raft."

He called this sea a pond, and our long voyage, taking a little sail!

"But," I remarked, "since we have followed the road that Saknussemm has shown us—"

"That is just the question. Have we followed that road? Did Saknussemm meet this sheet of water? Did he cross it? Has not the stream that we followed led us altogether astray?"

"At any rate we cannot feel sorry to have come so far. This prospect is magnificent, and—"

"But I don't care for prospects. I came with an object, and I mean to attain it. Therefore don't talk to me about views and prospects."

I take this as my answer, and I leave the Professor to bite his lips with impatience. At six in the evening Hans asks for his wages, and his three rix dollars are counted out to him.

Sunday, August 16. —Nothing new. Weather unchanged. The wind freshens. On awaking, my first thought was to observe the intensity of the light. I was possessed with an apprehension lest the electric light should grow dim, or fail altogether. But there seemed no reason to fear. The shadow of the raft was clearly outlined upon the surface of the waves.

Truly this sea is of infinite width. It must be as wide as the

Mediterranean or the Atlantic—and why not?

My uncle took soundings several times. He tied the heaviest of our pickaxes to a long rope which he let down two hundred fathoms. No bottom yet; and we had some difficulty in hauling up our plummet.

But when the pick was shipped again, Hans pointed out on its surface deep prints as if it had been violently compressed between two hard bodies.

I looked at the hunter.

"*Tänder,*" said he.

I could not understand him, and turned to my uncle who was entirely absorbed in his calculations. I had rather not disturb him while he is quiet. I return to the Icelander. He by a snapping motion of his jaws conveys his ideas to me.

"Teeth!" I cried, considering the iron bar with more attention.

Yes, indeed, those are the marks of teeth imprinted upon the metal! The jaws which they arm must be possessed of amazing strength. Is there some monster beneath us belonging to the extinct races, more voracious than the shark, more fearful in vastness than the whale? I could not take my eyes off this indented iron bar. Surely will my last night's dream be realised?

These thoughts agitated me all day, and my imagination scarcely calmed down after several hours' sleep.

Monday, August 17.— I am trying to recall the peculiar instincts of the monsters of the pre-adamite world, who, coming next in succession after the molluscs, the crustaceans and le fishes, preceded the animals of mammalian race upon the earth. The world then belonged to reptiles. Those monsters held the mastery in the seas of the secondary period. They possessed a perfect organisation, gigantic proportions, prodigious strength. The saurians of our day, the alligators and the crocodiles, are but feeble reproductions of their forefathers of primitive ages.

I shudder as I recall these monsters to my remembrance. No human eye has ever beheld them living. They burdened this earth a thousand ages before man appeared, but their fossil remains, found in the argillaceous limestone called by the English the lias, have enabled their colossal structure to be perfectly built up again and anatomically ascertained.

I saw at the Hamburg museum the skeleton of one of these creatures thirty feet in length. Am I then fated—I, a denizen of earth—to be placed face to face with these representatives of long extinct families? No; surely it cannot be! Yet the deep marks of conical teeth upon the iron pick are certainly those of the crocodile.

My eyes are fearfully bent upon the sea. I dread to see one of these monsters darting forth from its submarine caverns. I suppose Professor Liedenbrock was of my opinion too, and even shared my fears, for after having examined the pick, his eyes traversed the ocean from side to side. What a very bad notion that was of his, I thought to myself, to take soundings just here! He has disturbed some monstrous beast in its remote den, and if we are not attacked on our voyage—

I look at our guns and see that they are all right. My uncle notices it, and looks on approvingly.

Already widely disturbed regions on the surface of the water indicate some commotion below. The danger is approaching. We must be on the look out.

Tuesday, August 18. —Evening came, or rather the time came when sleep weighs down the weary eyelids, for there is no night here, and the ceaseless light wearies the eyes with its persistency just as if we were sailing under an arctic sun. Hans was at the helm. During his watch I slept.

Two hours afterwards a terrible shock awoke me. The raft was heaved up on a watery mountain and pitched down again, at a distance of twenty fathoms.

"What is the matter?" shouted my uncle. "Have we struck land?"

Hans pointed with his finger at a dark mass six hundred yards away, rising and falling alternately with heavy plunges. I looked and cried:

"It is an enormous porpoise."

"Yes," replied my uncle, "and there is a sea lizard of vast size."

"And farther on a monstrous crocodile. Look at its vast jaws and its rows of teeth! It is diving down!"

"There's a whale, a whale!" cried the Professor. "I can see its great fins. See how he is throwing out air and water through his blowers."

And in fact two liquid columns were rising to a considerable height above the sea. We stood amazed, thunderstruck, at the presence of such a herd of marine monsters. They were of supernatural dimensions; the smallest of them would have crunched our raft, crew and all, at one snap of its huge jaws.

Hans wants to tack to get away from this dangerous neighbourhood; but he sees on the other hand enemies not less terrible; a tortoise forty feet long, and a serpent of thirty, lifting its fearful head and gleaming eyes above the flood.

Flight was out of the question now. The reptiles rose; they wheeled around our little raft with a rapidity greater than that of express trains. They described around us gradually narrowing circles. I took up my rifle. But what could a ball do against the scaly armour with which these enormous beasts were clad?

We stood dumb with fear. They approach us close: on one side the crocodile, on the other the serpent. The remainder of the sea monsters have disappeared. I prepare to fire. Hans stops me by a gesture. The two monsters pass within a hundred and fifty yards of the raft, and hurl themselves the one upon the other, with a fury which prevents them from seeing us.

At three hundred yards from us the battle was fought. We could distinctly observe the two monsters engaged in deadly conflict. But it now seems to me as if the other animals were taking part in the fray—the porpoise, the whale, the lizard, the tortoise. Every moment I seem to see one or other of them. I point them to the Icelander. He shakes his head negatively.

"*Tva,*" says he.

"What two? Does he mean that there are only two animals?"

"He is right," said my uncle, whose glass has never left his eye.

"Surely you must be mistaken," I cried.

"No: the first of those monsters has a porpoise's snout, a lizard's head, a crocodile's teeth; and hence our mistake. It is the ichthyosaurus (the fish lizard), the most terrible of the ancient monsters of the deep."

"And the other?"

"The other is a plesiosaurus (almost lizard), a serpent, armoured with the carapace and the paddles of a turtle; he is the dreadful enemy of the other."

Hans had spoken truly. Two monsters only were creating all this commotion; and before my eyes are two reptiles of the primitive world. I can distinguish the eye of the ichthyosaurus glowing like a red-hot coal, and as large as a man's head. Nature has endowed it with an optical apparatus of extreme power, and capable of resisting the pressure of the great volume of water in the depths it inhabits. It has been appropriately called the saurian whale, for it has both the swiftness and the rapid movements of this monster of our own day. This one is not less than a hundred feet long, and I can judge of its size when it sweeps over the waters the vertical coils of its tail. Its jaw is enormous, and according to naturalists it is armed with no less than one hundred and eighty-two teeth.

The plesiosaurus, a serpent with a cylindrical body and a short tail, has four flappers or paddles to act like oars. Its body is entirely covered with a thick armour of scales, and its neck, as flexible as a swan's, rises thirty feet above the waves.

Those huge creatures attacked each other with the greatest animosity. They heaved around them liquid mountains, which rolled even to our raft and rocked it perilously. Twenty times we were near capsizing. Hissings of prodigious force are heard. The two beasts are fast locked together; I cannot distinguish the one from the other. The probable rage of the conqueror inspires us with intense fear.

One hour, two hours, pass away. The struggle continues with unabated ferocity. The combatants alternately approach and recede from our raft. We remain motionless, ready to fire. Suddenly the ichthyosaurus and the plesiosaurus disappear below, leaving a whirlpool eddying in the water. Several minutes pass by while the fight goes on under water.

All at once an enormous head is darted up, the head of the plesiosaurus. The monster is wounded to death. I no longer see his scaly armour. Only his long neck shoots up, drops again, coils and uncoils, droops, lashes the waters like a gigantic whip, and writhes like a worm that you tread on. The water is splashed for a long way around. The spray almost blinds us. But soon the reptile's agony draws to an end; its movements become fainter, its contortions cease to be so violent, and the long serpentine form lies a lifeless log on the labouring deep.

As for the ichthyosaurus—has he returned to his submarine cavern? or will he reappear on the surface of the sea?

CHAPTER XXXIV. THE GREAT GEYSER

Wednesday, August 19.—Fortunately the wind blows violently, and has enabled us to flee from the scene of the late terrible struggle. Hans keeps at his post at the helm. My uncle, whom the absorbing incidents of the combat had drawn away from his contemplations, began again to look impatiently around him.

The voyage resumes its uniform tenor, which I don't care to break with a repetition of such events as yesterday's.

Thursday, Aug. 20.—Wind N.N.E., unsteady and fitful. Temperature high. Rate three and a half leagues an hour.

About noon a distant noise is heard. I note the fact without being able to explain it. It is a continuous roar.

"In the distance," says the Professor, "there is a rock or islet, against which the sea is breaking."

Hans climbs up the mast, but sees no breakers. The ocean' is smooth and unbroken to its farthest limit.

Three hours pass away. The roarings seem to proceed from a very distant waterfall.

I remark upon this to my uncle, who replies doubtfully: "Yes, I am convinced that I am right." Are we, then, speeding forward to some cataract which will cast us down an abyss? This method of getting on may please the Professor, because it is vertical; but for my part I prefer the more ordinary modes of horizontal progression.

At any rate, some leagues to the windward there must be some noisy phenomenon, for now the roarings are heard with increasing loudness. Do they proceed from the sky or the ocean?

I look up to the atmospheric vapours, and try to fathom their depths. The sky is calm and motionless. The clouds have reached the utmost limit of the lofty vault, and there lie still bathed in the bright glare of the electric light. It is not there that we must seek for the cause of this phenomenon. Then I examine the horizon, which is unbroken and clear of all mist. There is no change in its aspect. But if this noise arises from a fall, a cataract, if all this ocean flows away headlong into a lower basin yet, if that deafening roar is produced by a mass of falling water, the current must needs accelerate, and its increasing speed will give me the measure of the peril that threatens us. I consult the current: there is none. I throw an empty bottle into the sea: it lies still.

About four Hans rises, lays hold of the mast, climbs to its top. Thence his eye sweeps a large area of sea, and it is fixed upon a point. His countenance exhibits no surprise, but his eye is immovably steady.

"He sees something," says my uncle.

"I believe he does."

Hans comes down, then stretches his arm to the south, saying:

"*Dere nere!*"

"Down there?" repeated my uncle.

Then, seizing his glass, he gazes attentively for a minute, which seems to me an age.

"Yes, yes!" he cried. "I see a vast inverted cone rising from the surface."

"Is it another sea beast?"

"Perhaps it is."

"Then let us steer farther westward, for we know something of the danger of coming across monsters of that sort."

"Let us go straight on," replied my uncle.

I appealed to Hans. He maintained his course inflexibly.

Yet, if at our present distance from the animal, a distance of twelve leagues at the least, the column of water driven through its blowers may be distinctly seen, it must needs be of vast size. The commonest prudence would counsel immediate flight; but we did not come so far to be prudent.

Imprudently, therefore, we pursue our way. The nearer we approach, the higher mounts the jet of water. What monster can possibly fill itself with such a quantity of water, and spurt it up so continuously?

At eight in the evening we are not two leagues distant from it. Its body—dusky, enormous, hillocky—lies spread upon the sea like an islet. Is it illusion or fear? Its length seems to me a couple of thousand yards. What can be this cetacean, which neither Cuvier nor Blumenbach knew anything about? It lies motionless, as if asleep; the sea seems unable to move it in the least; it is the waves that undulate upon its sides. The column of water thrown up to a height of five hundred feet falls in rain with a deafening uproar. And here are we scudding like lunatics before the wind, to get near to a monster that a hundred whales a day would not satisfy!

Terror seizes upon me. I refuse to go further. I will cut the halliards if necessary! I am in open mutiny against the Professor, who vouchsafes no answer.

Suddenly Hans rises, and pointing with his finger at the menacing object, he says:

"*Holm.*"

"An island!" cries my uncle.

"That's not an island!" I cried sceptically.

"It's nothing else," shouted the Professor, with a loud laugh.

"But that column of water?"

"*Geyser,*" said Hans.

"No doubt it is a geyser, like those in Iceland."

At first I protest against being so widely mistaken as to have taken an island for a marine monster. But the evidence is against me, and I have to confess my error. It is nothing worse than a natural phenomenon.

As we approach nearer the dimensions of the liquid column become magnificent. The islet resembles, with a most deceiving likeness, an enormous cetacean, whose head dominates the waves at a height of twenty yards. The geyser, a word meaning 'fury,' rises majestically from its extremity. Deep and heavy explosions are heard from time to time, when the enormous jet, possessed with more furious violence, shakes its plumy crest, and springs with a bound till it reaches the lowest stratum of the clouds. It stands alone. No steam vents, no hot springs surround it, and all the volcanic power of the region is concentrated here. Sparks of electric fire mingle with the dazzling sheaf of lighted fluid, every drop of which refracts the prismatic colours.

"Let us land," said the Professor.

"But we must carefully avoid this waterspout, which would sink our raft in a moment."

Hans, steering with his usual skill, brought us to the other extremity of the islet.

I leaped up on the rock; my uncle lightly followed, while our hunter remained at his post, like a man too wise ever to be astonished.

We walked upon granite mingled with siliceous tufa. The soil shivers and shakes under our feet, like the sides of an overheated boiler filled with steam struggling to get loose. We come in sight of a small central basin, out of which the geyser springs. I plunge a register thermometer into the boiling water. It marks an intense heat of 325°, which is far above the boiling point; therefore this water issues from an ardent furnace, which is not at all in harmony with Professor Liedenbrock's theories. I cannot help making the remark.

"Well," he replied, "how does that make against my doctrine?"

"Oh, nothing at all," I said, seeing that I was going in opposition to immovable obstinacy.

Still I am constrained to confess that hitherto we have been wonderfully favoured, and that for some reason unknown to myself we have accomplished our journey under singularly favourable conditions of temperature. But it seems manifest to me that some day we shall reach a region where the central heat attains its highest limits, and goes beyond a point that can be registered by our thermometers.

"That is what we shall see." So says the Professor, who, having named this volcanic islet after his nephew, gives the signal to embark again.

For some minutes I am still contemplating the geyser. I notice that it throws up its column of water with variable force: sometimes sending it to a great height, then again to a lower, which I attribute to the variable pressure of the steam accumulated in its reservoir.

At last we leave the island, rounding away past the low rocks on its southern shore. Hans has taken advantage of the halt to refit his rudder.

But before going any farther I make a few observations, to calculate the distance we have gone over, and note them in my journal. We have crossed two hundred and seventy leagues of sea since leaving Port Gräuben; and we are six hundred and twenty leagues from Iceland, under England[1].

---

[1] This distance carries the travellers as far as under the Pyrenees if the league measures three miles. (Trans.)

CHAPTER XXXV. AN ELECTRIC STORM

Friday, August 21.—On the morrow the magnificent geyser has disappeared. The wind has risen, and has rapidly carried us away from Axel Island. The roarings become lost in the distance.

The weather—if we may use that term—will change before long. The atmosphere is charged with vapours, pervaded with the electricity generated by the evaporation of saline waters. The clouds are sinking lower, and assume an olive hue. The electric light can scarcely penetrate through the dense curtain which has dropped over the theatre on which the battle of the elements is about to be waged.

I feel peculiar sensations, like many creatures on earth at the approach of violent atmospheric changes. The heavily voluted cumulus clouds lower gloomily and threateningly; they wear that implacable look which I have sometimes noticed at the outbreak of a great storm. The air is heavy; the sea is calm.

In the distance the clouds resemble great bales of cotton, piled up in picturesque disorder. By degrees they dilate, and gain in huge size what they lose in number. Such is their ponderous weight that they cannot rise from the horizon; but, obeying an impulse from higher currents, their dense consistency slowly yields. The gloom upon them deepens; and they soon present to our view a ponderous mass of almost level surface. From time to time a fleecy tuft of mist, with yet some gleaming light left upon it, drops down upon the dense floor of grey, and loses itself in the opaque and impenetrable mass.

The atmosphere is evidently charged and surcharged with electricity. My whole body is saturated; my hair bristles just as when you stand upon an insulated stool under the action of an electrical machine. It seems to me as if my companions, the moment they touched me, would receive a severe shock like that from an electric eel.

At ten in the morning the symptoms of storm become aggravated. The wind never lulls but to acquire increased strength; the vast bank of heavy clouds is a huge reservoir of fearful windy gusts and rushing storms.

I am loth to believe these atmospheric menaces, and yet I cannot help muttering:

"Here's some very bad weather coming on."

The Professor made no answer. His temper is awful, to judge from the working of his features, as he sees this vast length of ocean unrolling before him to an indefinite extent. He can only spare time to shrug his shoulders viciously.

"There's a heavy storm coming on," I cried, pointing towards the horizon. "Those clouds seem as if they were going to crush the sea."

A deep silence falls on all around. The lately roaring winds are hushed into a dead calm; nature seems to breathe no more, and to be sinking into the stillness of death. On the mast already I see the light play of a lambent St. Elmo's fire; the outstretched sail catches not a breath of wind, and hangs like a sheet of lead. The rudder stands motionless in a sluggish, waveless sea. But if we have now ceased to advance why do we yet leave that sail loose, which at the first shock of the tempest may capsize us in a moment?

"Let us reef the sail and cut the mast down!" I cried. "That will be safest."

"No, no! Never!" shouted my impetuous uncle. "Never! Let the wind catch us if it will! What I want is to get the least glimpse of rock or shore, even if our raft should be smashed into shivers!"

The words were hardly out of his mouth when a sudden change took place in the southern sky. The piled-up vapours condense into water; and the air, put into violent action to supply the vacuum left by the condensation of the mists, rouses itself into a whirlwind. It rushes on from the farthest recesses of the vast cavern. The darkness deepens; scarcely can I jot down a few hurried notes. The helm makes a bound. My uncle falls full length; I creep close to him. He has laid a firm hold upon a rope, and appears to watch with grim satisfaction this awful display of elemental strife.

Hans stirs not. His long hair blown by the pelting storm, and laid flat across his immovable countenance, makes him a strange figure; for the end of each lock of loose flowing hair is tipped with little luminous radiations. This frightful mask of electric sparks suggests to me, even in this dizzy excitement, a comparison with pre-adamite man, the contemporary of the ichthyosaurus and the megatherium[1].

The mast yet holds firm. The sail stretches tight like a bubble ready to burst. The raft flies at a rate that I cannot reckon, but not so fast as the foaming clouds of spray which it dashes from side to side in its headlong speed.

"The sail! the sail!" I cry, motioning to lower it.

"No!" replies my uncle.

"*Nej!*" repeats Hans, leisurely shaking his head.

But now the rain forms a rushing cataract in front of that horizon toward which we are running with such maddening speed. But before it has reached us the rain cloud parts asunder, the sea boils, and the electric fires are brought into violent action by a mighty chemical power that descends from the higher regions. The most vivid flashes of lightning are mingled with the violent crash of continuous thunder. Ceaseless fiery arrows dart in and out amongst the flying thunder-clouds; the vaporous mass soon glows with incandescent heat; hailstones rattle fiercely down, and as they dash upon our iron tools they too emit gleams and flashes of lurid light. The heaving waves resemble fiery volcanic hills, each belching forth its own interior flames, and every crest is plumed with dancing fire. My eyes fail under the dazzling light, my ears are stunned with the incessant crash of thunder. I must be bound to the mast, which bows like a reed before the mighty strength of the storm.

(Here my notes become vague and indistinct. I have only been able to find a few which I seem to have jotted down almost unconsciously. But their very brevity and their obscurity reveal the intensity of the excitement which dominated me, and describe the actual position even better than my memory could do.)

Sunday, 23.—Where are we? Driven forward with a swiftness that cannot be measured.

The night was fearful; no abatement of the storm. The din and uproar are incessant; our ears are bleeding; to exchange a word is impossible.

---

[1] Rather of the mammoth and the mastodon. (Trans.)

The lightning flashes with intense brilliancy, and never seems to cease for a moment. Zigzag streams of bluish white fire dash down upon the sea and rebound, and then take an upward flight till they strike the granite vault that overarches our heads. Suppose that solid roof should crumble down upon our heads! Other flashes with incessant play cross their vivid fires, while others again roll themselves into balls of living fire which explode like bombshells, but the music of which scarcely-adds to the din of the battle strife that almost deprives us of our senses of hearing and sight; the limit of intense loudness has been passed within which the human ear can distinguish one sound from another. If all the powder magazines in the world were to explode at once, we should hear no more than we do now.

From the under surface of the clouds there are continual emissions of lurid light; electric matter is in continual evolution from their component molecules; the gaseous elements of the air need to be slaked with moisture; for innumerable columns of water rush upwards into the air and fall back again in white foam.

Whither are we flying? My uncle lies full length across the raft.

The heat increases. I refer to the thermometer; it indicates . . . (the figure is obliterated).

Monday, August 24.—Will there be an end to it? Is the atmospheric condition, having once reached this density, to become final?

We are prostrated and worn out with fatigue. But Hans is as usual. The raft bears on still to the south-east. We have made two hundred leagues since we left Axel Island.

At noon the violence of the storm redoubles. We are obliged to secure as fast as possible every article that belongs to our cargo. Each of us is lashed to some part of the raft. The waves rise above our heads.

For three days we have never been able to make each other hear a word. Our mouths open, our lips move, but not a word can be heard. We cannot even make ourselves heard by approaching our mouth close to the ear.

My uncle has drawn nearer to me. He has uttered a few words. They seem to be 'We are lost'; but I am not sure.

At last I write down the words: "Let us lower the sail."

He nods his consent.

Scarcely has he lifted his head again before a ball of fire has bounded over the waves and lighted on board our raft. Mast and sail flew up in an instant together, and I saw them carried up to prodigious height, resembling in appearance a pterodactyle, one of those strong birds of the infant world.

We lay there, our blood running cold with unspeakable terror. The fireball, half of it white, half azure blue, and the size of a ten-inch shell, moved slowly about the raft, but revolving on its own axis with astonishing velocity, as if whipped round by the force of the whirlwind. Here it comes, there it glides, now it is up the ragged stump of the mast, thence it lightly leaps on the provision bag, descends with a light bound, and just skims the powder magazine. Horrible! we shall be blown up; but no, the dazzling disk of mysterious light nimbly leaps aside; it approaches Hans, who fixes his blue eye upon it steadily; it threatens the head of my uncle, who falls upon his knees with his head down to avoid it. And now my turn comes; pale and trembling under the blinding splendour and the melting heat, it drops at my feet, spinning silently round upon the deck; I try to move my foot away, but cannot.

A suffocating smell of nitrogen fills the air, it enters the throat, it fills the lungs. We suffer stifling pains.

CHAPTER XXXV. AN ELECTRIC STORM

Why am I unable to move my foot? Is it riveted to the planks? Alas! the fall upon our fated raft of this electric globe has magnetised every iron article on board. The instruments, the tools, our guns, are clashing and clanking violently in their collisions with each other; the nails of my boots cling tenaciously to a plate of iron let into the timbers, and I cannot draw my foot away from the spot. At last by a violent effort I release myself at the instant when the ball in its gyrations was about to seize upon it, and carry me off my feet ....

Ah! what a flood of intense and dazzling light! the globe has burst, and we are deluged with tongues of fire!

Then all the light disappears. I could just see my uncle at full length on the raft, and Hans still at his helm and spitting fire under the action of the electricity which has saturated him.

But where are we going to? Where?

* * * *

Tuesday, August 25.—I recover from a long swoon. The storm continues to roar and rage; the lightnings dash hither and thither, like broods of fiery serpents filling all the air. Are we still under the sea? Yes, we are borne at incalculable speed. We have been carried under England, under the channel, under France, perhaps under the whole of Europe.

* * * *

A fresh noise is heard! Surely it is the sea breaking upon the rocks!

But then . . . .

CHAPTER XXXVI. CALM PHILOSOPHIC DISCUSSIONS

Here I end what I may call my log, happily saved from the wreck, and
I resume my narrative as before.

What happened when the raft was dashed upon the rocks is more than I can tell. I felt myself hurled into the waves; and if I escaped from death, and if my body was not torn over the sharp edges of the rocks, it was because the powerful arm of Hans came to my rescue.

The brave Icelander carried me out of the reach of the waves, over a burning sand where I found myself by the side of my uncle.

Then he returned to the rocks, against which the furious waves were beating, to save what he could. I was unable to speak. I was shattered with fatigue and excitement; I wanted a whole hour to recover even a little.

But a deluge of rain was still falling, though with that violence which generally denotes the near cessation of a storm. A few overhanging rocks afforded us some shelter from the storm. Hans prepared some food, which I could not touch; and each of us, exhausted with three sleepless nights, fell into a broken and painful sleep.

The next day the weather was splendid. The sky and the sea had sunk into sudden repose. Every trace of the awful storm had disappeared. The exhilarating voice of the Professor fell upon my ears as I awoke; he was ominously cheerful.

"Well, my boy," he cried, "have you slept well?"

Would not any one have thought that we were still in our cheerful little house on the Königstrasse and that I was only just coming down to breakfast, and that I was to be married to Gräuben that day?

Alas! if the tempest had but sent the raft a little more east, we should have passed under Germany, under my beloved town of Hamburg, under the very street where dwelt all that I loved most in the world. Then only forty leagues would have separated us! But they were forty leagues perpendicular of solid granite wall, and in reality we were a thousand leagues asunder!

All these painful reflections rapidly crossed my mind before I could answer my uncle's question.

"Well, now," he repeated, "won't you tell me how you have slept?"

"Oh, very well," I said. "I am only a little knocked up, but I shall soon be better."

"Oh," says my uncle, "that's nothing to signify. You are only a little bit tired."

"But you, uncle, you seem in very good spirits this morning."

"Delighted, my boy, delighted. We have got there."

"To our journey's end?"

"No; but we have got to the end of that endless sea. Now we shall go by land, and really begin to go down! down! down!"

"But, my dear uncle, do let me ask you one question."

"Of course, Axel."

"How about returning?"

"Returning? Why, you are talking about the return before the arrival."

"No, I only want to know how that is to be managed."

"In the simplest way possible. When we have reached the centre of the globe, either we shall find some new way to get back, or we shall come back like decent folks the way we came. I feel pleased at the thought that it is sure not to be shut against us."

"But then we shall have to refit the raft."

"Of course."

"Then, as to provisions, have we enough to last?"

"Yes; to be sure we have. Hans is a clever fellow, and I am sure he must have saved a large part of our cargo. But still let us go and make sure."

We left this grotto which lay open to every wind. At the same time I cherished a trembling hope which was a fear as well. It seemed to me impossible that the terrible wreck of the raft should not have destroyed everything on board. On my arrival on the shore I found Hans surrounded by an assemblage of articles all arranged in good order. My uncle shook hands with him with a lively gratitude. This man, with almost superhuman devotion, had been at work all the while that we were asleep, and had saved the most precious of the articles at the risk of his life.

Not that we had suffered no losses. For instance, our firearms; but we might do without them. Our stock of powder had remained uninjured after having risked blowing up during the storm.

"Well," cried the Professor, "as we have no guns we cannot hunt, that's all."

"Yes, but how about the instruments?"

"Here is the aneroid, the most useful of all, and for which I would have given all the others. By means of it I can calculate the depth and know when we have reached the centre; without it we might very likely go beyond, and come out at the antipodes!"

Such high spirits as these were rather too strong.

"But where is the compass? I asked.

"Here it is, upon this rock, in perfect condition, as well as the thermometers and the chronometer. The hunter is a splendid fellow."

There was no denying it. We had all our instruments. As for tools and appliances, there they all lay on the ground—ladders, ropes, picks, spades, etc.

Still there was the question of provisions to be settled, and I asked—"How are we off for provisions?"

The boxes containing these were in a line upon the shore, in a perfect state of preservation; for the most part the sea had spared them, and what with biscuits, salt meat, spirits, and salt fish, we might reckon on four months' supply.

"Four months!" cried the Professor. "We have time to go and to return; and with what is left I will give a grand dinner to my friends at the Johannæum."

I ought by this time to have been quite accustomed to my uncle's ways; yet there was always something fresh about him to astonish me.

"Now," said he, "we will replenish our supply of water with the rain which the storm has left in all these granite basins; therefore we shall have no reason to fear anything from thirst. As for the raft, I will recommend Hans to do his best to repair it, although I don't expect it will be of any further use to us."

"How so?" I cried.

"An idea of my own, my lad. I don't think we shall come out by the way that we went in."

I stared at the Professor with a good deal of mistrust. I asked, was he not touched in the brain? And yet there was method in his madness.

"And now let us go to breakfast," said he.

I followed him to a headland, after he had given his instructions to the hunter. There preserved meat, biscuit, and tea made us an excellent meal, one of the best I ever remember. Hunger, the fresh air, the calm quiet weather, after the commotions we had gone through, all contributed to give me a good appetite.

Whilst breakfasting I took the opportunity to put to my uncle the question where we were now.

"That seems to me," I said, "rather difficult to make out."

"Yes, it is difficult," he said, "to calculate exactly; perhaps even impossible, since during these three stormy days I have been unable to keep any account of the rate or direction of the raft; but still we may get an approximation."

"The last observation," I remarked, "was made on the island, when the geyser was—"

"You mean Axel Island. Don't decline the honour of having given your name to the first island ever discovered in the central parts of the globe."

"Well," said I, "let it be Axel Island. Then we had cleared two hundred and seventy leagues of sea, and we were six hundred leagues from Iceland."

"Very well," answered my uncle; "let us start from that point and count four days' storm, during which our rate cannot have been less than eighty leagues in the twenty-four hours."

"That is right; and this would make three hundred leagues more."

"Yes, and the Liedenbrock sea would be six hundred leagues from shore to shore. Surely, Axel, it may vie in size with the Mediterranean itself."

"Especially," I replied, "if it happens that we have only crossed it in its narrowest part. And it is a curious circumstance," I added, "that if my computations are right, and we are nine hundred leagues from Rejkiavik, we have now the Mediterranean above our head."

"That is a good long way, my friend. But whether we are under Turkey or the Atlantic depends very much upon the question in what direction we have been moving. Perhaps we have deviated."

"No, I think not. Our course has been the same all along, and I believe this shore is south-east of Port Gräuben."

"Well," replied my uncle, "we may easily ascertain this by consulting the compass. Let us go and see what it says."

The Professor moved towards the rock upon which Hans had laid down the instruments. He was gay and full of spirits; he rubbed his hands, he studied his attitudes. I followed him, curious to know if I was right in my estimate. As soon as we had arrived at the rock my uncle took the compass, laid it horizontally, and questioned the needle, which, after a few oscillations, presently assumed a fixed position. My uncle looked, and looked, and looked again. He rubbed his eyes, and then turned to me thunderstruck with some unexpected discovery.

"What is the matter?" I asked.

He motioned to me to look. An exclamation of astonishment burst from me. The north pole of the needle was turned to what we supposed to be the south. It pointed to the shore instead of to the open sea! I shook the box, examined it again, it was in perfect condition. In whatever position I placed the box the needle pertinaciously returned to this unexpected quarter. Therefore there seemed no reason to doubt that during the storm there had been a sudden change of wind unperceived by us, which had brought our raft back to the shore which we thought we had left so long a distance behind us.

CHAPTER XXXVII. THE LIEDENBROCK MUSEUM OF GEOLOGY

How shall I describe the strange series of passions which in succession shook the breast of Professor Liedenbrock? First stupefaction, then incredulity, lastly a downright burst of rage. Never had I seen the man so put out of countenance and so disturbed. The fatigues of our passage across, the dangers met, had all to be begun over again. We had gone backwards instead of forwards!

But my uncle rapidly recovered himself.

"Aha! will fate play tricks upon me? Will the elements lay plots against me? Shall fire, air, and water make a combined attack against me? Well, they shall know what a determined man can do. I will not yield. I will not stir a single foot backwards, and it will be seen whether man or nature is to have the upper hand!"

Erect upon the rock, angry and threatening, Otto Liedenbrock was a rather grotesque fierce parody upon the fierce Achilles defying the lightning. But I thought it my duty to interpose and attempt to lay some restraint upon this unmeasured fanaticism.

"Just listen to me," I said firmly. "Ambition must have a limit somewhere; we cannot perform impossibilities; we are not at all fit for another sea voyage; who would dream of undertaking a voyage of five hundred leagues upon a heap of rotten planks, with a blanket in rags for a sail, a stick for a mast, and fierce winds in our teeth? We cannot steer; we shall be buffeted by the tempests, and we should be fools and madmen to attempt to cross a second time."

I was able to develop this series of unanswerable reasons for ten minutes without interruption; not that the Professor was paying any respectful attention to his nephew's arguments, but because he was deaf to all my eloquence.

"To the raft!" he shouted.

Such was his only reply. It was no use for me to entreat, supplicate, get angry, or do anything else in the way of opposition; it would only have been opposing a will harder than the granite rock.

Hans was finishing the repairs of the raft. One would have thought that this strange being was guessing at my uncle's intentions. With a few more pieces of surturbrand he had refitted our vessel. A sail already hung from the new mast, and the wind was playing in its waving folds.

The Professor said a few words to the guide, and immediately he put everything on board and arranged every necessary for our departure. The air was clear—and the northwest wind blew steadily.

What could I do? Could I stand against the two? It was impossible? If Hans had but taken my side! But no, it was not to be. The Icelander seemed to have renounced all will of his own and made a vow to forget and deny himself. I could get nothing out of a servant so feudalised, as it were, to his master. My only course was to proceed.

I was therefore going with as much resignation as I could find to resume my accustomed place on the raft, when my uncle laid his hand upon my shoulder.

"We shall not sail until to-morrow," he said.

I made a movement intended to express resignation.

"I must neglect nothing," he said; "and since my fate has driven me on this part of the coast, I will not leave it until I have examined it."

To understand what followed, it must be borne in mind that, through circumstances hereafter to be explained, we were not really where the Professor supposed we were. In fact we were not upon the north shore of the sea.

"Now let us start upon fresh discoveries," I said.

And leaving Hans to his work we started off together. The space between the water and the foot of the cliffs was considerable. It took half an hour to bring us to the wall of rock. We trampled under our feet numberless shells of all the forms and sizes which existed in the earliest ages of the world. I also saw immense carapaces more than fifteen feet in diameter. They had been the coverings of those gigantic glyptodons or armadilloes of the pleiocene period, of which the modern tortoise is but a miniature representative[1]. The soil was besides this scattered with stony fragments, boulders rounded by water action, and ridged up in successive lines. I was therefore led to the conclusion that at one time the sea must have covered the ground on which we were treading. On the loose and scattered rocks, now out of the reach of the highest tides, the waves had left manifest traces of their power to wear their way in the hardest stone.

This might up to a certain point explain the existence of an ocean forty leagues beneath the surface of the globe. But in my opinion this liquid mass would be lost by degrees farther and farther within the interior of the earth, and it certainly had its origin in the waters of the ocean overhead, which had made their way hither through some fissure. Yet it must be believed that that fissure is now closed, and that all this cavern or immense reservoir was filled in a very short time. Perhaps even this water, subjected to the fierce action of central heat, had partly been resolved into vapour. This would explain the existence of those clouds suspended over our heads and the development of that electricity which raised such tempests within the bowels of the earth.

This theory of the phenomena we had witnessed seemed satisfactory to me; for however great and stupendous the phenomena of nature, fixed physical laws will or may always explain them.

We were therefore walking upon sedimentary soil, the deposits of the waters of former ages. The Professor was carefully examining every little fissure in the rocks. Wherever he saw a hole he always wanted to know the depth of it. To him this was important.

We had traversed the shores of the Liedenbrock sea for a mile when we observed a sudden change in the appearance of the soil. It seemed upset, contorted, and convulsed by a violent upheaval of the lower strata. In many places depressions or elevations gave witness to some tremendous power effecting the dislocation of strata.

We moved with difficulty across these granite fissures and chasms mingled with silex, crystals of quartz, and alluvial deposits, when a field, nay, more than a field, a vast plain,

[1] The glyptodon and armadillo are mammalian; the tortoise is a chelonian, a reptile, distinct classes of the animal kingdom; therefore the latter cannot be a representative of the former. (Trans.)

of bleached bones lay spread before us. It seemed like an immense cemetery, where the remains of twenty ages mingled their dust together. Huge mounds of bony fragments rose stage after stage in the distance. They undulated away to the limits of the horizon, and melted in the distance in a faint haze. There within three square miles were accumulated the materials for a complete history of the animal life of ages, a history scarcely outlined in the too recent strata of the inhabited world.

But an impatient curiosity impelled our steps; crackling and rattling, our feet were trampling on the remains of prehistoric animals and interesting fossils, the possession of which is a matter of rivalry and contention between the museums of great cities. A thousand Cuviers could never have reconstructed the organic remains deposited in this magnificent and unparalleled collection.

I stood amazed. My uncle had uplifted his long arms to the vault which was our sky; his mouth gaping wide, his eyes flashing behind his shining spectacles, his head balancing with an up-and-down motion, his whole attitude denoted unlimited astonishment. Here he stood facing an immense collection of scattered leptotheria, mericotheria, lophiodia, anoplotheria, megatheria, mastodons, protopithecæ, pterodactyles, and all sorts of extinct monsters here assembled together for his special satisfaction. Fancy an enthusiastic bibliomaniac suddenly brought into the midst of the famous Alexandrian library burnt by Omar and restored by a miracle from its ashes! just such a crazed enthusiast was my uncle, Professor Liedenbrock.

But more was to come, when, with a rush through clouds of bone dust, he laid his hand upon a bare skull, and cried with a voice trembling with excitement:

"Axel! Axel! a human head!"

"A human skull?" I cried, no less astonished.

"Yes, nephew. Aha! M. Milne-Edwards! Ah! M. de Quatrefages, how I wish you were standing here at the side of Otto Liedenbrock!"

CHAPTER XXXVIII. THE PROFESSOR IN HIS CHAIR AGAIN

To understand this apostrophe of my uncle's, made to absent French savants, it will be necessary to allude to an event of high importance in a palæontological point of view, which had occurred a little while before our departure.

On the 28th of March, 1863, some excavators working under the direction of M. Boucher de Perthes, in the stone quarries of Moulin Quignon, near Abbeville, in the department of Somme, found a human jawbone fourteen feet beneath the surface. It was the first fossil of this nature that had ever been brought to light. Not far distant were found stone hatchets and flint arrow-heads stained and encased by lapse of time with a uniform coat of rust.

The noise of this discovery was very great, not in France alone, but in England and in Germany. Several savants of the French Institute, and amongst them MM. Milne-Edwards and de Quatrefages, saw at once the importance of this discovery, proved to demonstration the genuineness of the bone in question, and became the most ardent defendants in what the English called this 'trial of a jawbone.' To the geologists of the United Kingdom, who believed in the certainty of the fact—Messrs. Falconer, Busk, Carpenter, and others—scientific Germans were soon joined, and amongst them the forwardest, the most fiery, and the most enthusiastic, was my uncle Liedenbrock.

Therefore the genuineness of a fossil human relic of the quaternary period seemed to be incontestably proved and admitted.

It is true that this theory met with a most obstinate opponent in M. Elie de Beaumont. This high authority maintained that the soil of Moulin Quignon was not diluvial at all, but was of much more recent formation; and, agreeing in that with Cuvier, he refused to admit that the human species could be contemporary with the animals of the quaternary period. My uncle Liedenbrock, along with the great body of the geologists, had maintained his ground, disputed, and argued, until M. Elie de Beaumont stood almost alone in his opinion.

We knew all these details, but we were not aware that since our departure the question had advanced to farther stages. Other similar maxillaries, though belonging to individuals of various types and different nations, were found in the loose grey soil of certain grottoes in France, Switzerland, and Belgium, as well as weapons, tools, earthen utensils, bones of children and adults. The existence therefore of man in the quaternary period seemed to become daily more certain.

Nor was this all. Fresh discoveries of remains in the pleiocene formation had emboldened other geologists to refer back the human species to a higher antiquity still. It is true that these remains were not human bones, but objects bearing the traces of his handiwork, such as fossil leg-bones of animals, sculptured and carved evidently by the hand of man.

Thus, at one bound, the record of the existence of man receded far back into the history of the ages past; he was a predecessor of the mastodon; he was a contemporary of the southern elephant; he lived a hundred thousand years ago, when, according to geologists, the pleiocene formation was in progress.

Such then was the state of palæontological science, and what we knew of it was sufficient to explain our behaviour in the presence of this stupendous Golgotha. Any one may now understand the frenzied excitement of my uncle, when, twenty yards farther on, he found himself face to face with a primitive man!

It was a perfectly recognisable human body. Had some particular soil, like that of the cemetery St. Michel, at Bordeaux, preserved it thus for so many ages? It might be so. But this dried corpse, with its parchment-like skin drawn tightly over the bony frame, the limbs still preserving their shape, sound teeth, abundant hair, and finger and toe nails of frightful length, this desiccated mummy startled us by appearing just as it had lived countless ages ago. I stood mute before this apparition of remote antiquity. My uncle, usually so garrulous, was struck dumb likewise. We raised the body. We stood it up against a rock. It seemed to stare at us out of its empty orbits. We sounded with our knuckles his hollow frame.

After some moments' silence the Professor was himself again. Otto Liedenbrock, yielding to his nature, forgot all the circumstances of our eventful journey, forgot where we were standing, forgot the vaulted cavern which contained us. No doubt he was in mind back again in his Johannæum, holding forth to his pupils, for he assumed his learned air; and addressing himself to an imaginary audience, he proceeded thus:

"Gentlemen, I have the honour to introduce to you a man of the quaternary or post-tertiary system. Eminent geologists have denied his existence, others no less eminent have affirmed it. The St. Thomases of palæontology, if they were here, might now touch him with their fingers, and would be obliged to acknowledge their error. I am quite aware that science has to be on its guard with discoveries of this kind. I know what capital enterprising individuals like Barnum have made out of fossil men. I have heard the tale of the kneepan of Ajax, the pretended body of Orestes claimed to have been found by the Spartans, and of the body of Asterius, ten cubits long, of which Pausanias speaks. I have read the reports of the skeleton of Trapani, found in the fourteenth century, and which was at the time identified as that of Polyphemus; and the history of the giant unearthed in the sixteenth century near Palermo. You know as well as I do, gentlemen, the analysis made at Lucerne in 1577 of those huge bones which the celebrated Dr. Felix Plater affirmed to be those of a giant nineteen feet high. I have gone through the treatises of Cassanion, and all those memoirs, pamphlets, answers, and rejoinders published respecting the skeleton of Teutobochus, the invader of Gaul, dug out of a sandpit in the Dauphiné, in 1613. In the eighteenth century I would have stood up for Scheuchzer's pre-adamite man against Peter Campet. I have perused a writing, entitled Gigan—"

Here my uncle's unfortunate infirmity met him—that of being unable in public to pronounce hard words.

"The pamphlet entitled Gigan—"

He could get no further.

"Giganteo—"

It was not to be done. The unlucky word would not come out. At the Johannæum there would have been a laugh.

CHAPTER XXXVIII. THE PROFESSOR IN HIS CHAIR AGAIN

"Gigantosteologie," at last the Professor burst out, between two words which I shall not record here.

Then rushing on with renewed vigour, and with great animation:

"Yes, gentlemen, I know all these things, and more. I know that Cuvier and Blumenbach have recognised in these bones nothing more remarkable than the bones of the mammoth and other mammals of the post-tertiary period. But in the presence of this specimen to doubt would be to insult science. There stands the body! You may see it, touch it. It is not a mere skeleton; it is an entire body, preserved for a purely anthropological end and purpose."

I was good enough not to contradict this startling assertion.

"If I could only wash it in a solution of sulphuric acid," pursued my uncle, "I should be able to clear it from all the earthy particles and the shells which are incrusted about it. But I do not possess that valuable solvent. Yet, such as it is, the body shall tell us its own wonderful story."

Here the Professor laid hold of the fossil skeleton, and handled it with the skill of a dexterous showman.

"You see," he said, "that it is not six feet long, and that we are still separated by a long interval from the pretended race of giants. As for the family to which it belongs, it is evidently Caucasian. It is the white race, our own. The skull of this fossil is a regular oval, or rather ovoid. It exhibits no prominent cheekbones, no projecting jaws. It presents no appearance of that prognathism which diminishes the facial angle[1]. Measure that angle. It is nearly ninety degrees. But I will go further in my deductions, and I will affirm that this specimen of the human family is of the Japhetic race, which has since spread from the Indies to the Atlantic. Don't smile, gentlemen."

Nobody was smiling; but the learned Professor was frequently disturbed by the broad smiles provoked by his learned eccentricities.

"Yes," he pursued with animation, "this is a fossil man, the contemporary of the mastodons whose remains fill this amphitheatre. But if you ask me how he came there, how those strata on which he lay slipped down into this enormous hollow in the globe, I confess I cannot answer that question. No doubt in the post-tertiary period considerable commotions were still disturbing the crust of the earth. The long-continued cooling of the globe produced chasms, fissures, clefts, and faults, into which, very probably, portions of the upper earth may have fallen. I make no rash assertions; but there is the man surrounded by his own works, by hatchets, by flint arrow-heads, which are the characteristics of the stone age. And unless he came here, like myself, as a tourist on a visit and as a pioneer of science, I can entertain no doubt of the authenticity of his remote origin."

The Professor ceased to speak, and the audience broke out into loud and unanimous applause. For of course my uncle was right, and wiser men than his nephew would have had some trouble to refute his statements.

Another remarkable thing. This fossil body was not the only one in this immense catacomb. We came upon other bodies at every step amongst this mortal dust, and my uncle might select the most curious of these specimens to demolish the incredulity of sceptics.

---

[1] The facial angle is formed by two lines, one touching the brow and the front teeth, the other from the orifice of the ear to the lower line of the nostrils. The greater this angle, the higher intelligence denoted by the formation of the skull. Prognathism is that projection of the jaw-bones which sharpens or lessons this angle, and which is illustrated in the negro countenance and in the lowest savages.

In fact it was a wonderful spectacle, that of these generations of men and animals commingled in a common cemetery. Then one very serious question arose presently which we scarcely dared to suggest. Had all those creatures slided through a great fissure in the crust of the earth, down to the shores of the Liedenbrock sea, when they were dead and turning to dust, or had they lived and grown and died here in this subterranean world under a false sky, just like inhabitants of the upper earth? Until the present time we had seen alive only marine monsters and fishes. Might not some living man, some native of the abyss, be yet a wanderer below on this desert strand?

CHAPTER XXXIX. FOREST SCENERY ILLUMINATED BY ELECTRICITY

For another half hour we trod upon a pavement of bones. We pushed on, impelled by our burning curiosity. What other marvels did this cavern contain? What new treasures lay here for science to unfold? I was prepared for any surprise, my imagination was ready for any astonishment however astounding.

We had long lost sight of the sea shore behind the hills of bones. The rash Professor, careless of losing his way, hurried me forward. We advanced in silence, bathed in luminous electric fluid. By some phenomenon which I am unable to explain, it lighted up all sides of every object equally. Such was its diffusiveness, there being no central point from which the light emanated, that shadows no longer existed. You might have thought yourself under the rays of a vertical sun in a tropical region at noonday and the height of summer. No vapour was visible. The rocks, the distant mountains, a few isolated clumps of forest trees in the distance, presented a weird and wonderful aspect under these totally new conditions of a universal diffusion of light. We were like Hoffmann's shadowless man.

After walking a mile we reached the outskirts of a vast forest, but not one of those forests of fungi which bordered Port Gräuben.

Here was the vegetation of the tertiary period in its fullest blaze of magnificence. Tall palms, belonging to species no longer living, splendid palmacites, firs, yews, cypress trees, thujas, representatives of the conifers, were linked together by a tangled network of long climbing plants. A soft carpet of moss and hepaticas luxuriously clothed the soil. A few sparkling streams ran almost in silence under what would have been the shade of the trees, but that there was no shadow. On their banks grew tree-ferns similar to those we grow in hothouses. But a remarkable feature was the total absence of colour in all those trees, shrubs, and plants, growing without the life-giving heat and light of the sun. Everything seemed mixed-up and confounded in one uniform silver grey or light brown tint like that of fading and faded leaves. Not a green leaf anywhere, and the flowers—which were abundant enough in the tertiary period, which first gave birth to flowers—looked like brown-paper flowers, without colour or scent.

My uncle Liedenbrock ventured to penetrate under this colossal grove. I followed him, not without fear. Since nature had here provided vegetable nourishment, why should not the terrible mammals be there too? I perceived in the broad clearings left by fallen trees, decayed with age, leguminose plants, acerineæ, rubiceæ and many other eatable shrubs, dear to ruminant animals at every period. Then I observed, mingled together in confusion, trees of countries far apart on the surface of the globe. The oak and the palm were growing side by side, the Australian eucalyptus leaned against the Norwegian pine, the birch-tree of the north mingled its foliage with New Zealand kauris. It was enough to distract the most ingenious classifier of terrestrial botany.

Suddenly I halted. I drew back my uncle.

The diffused light revealed the smallest object in the dense and distant thickets. I had thought I saw—no! I did see, with my own eyes, vast colossal forms moving amongst the trees. They were gigantic animals; it was a herd of mastodons—not fossil remains, but living and resembling those the bones of which were found in the marshes of Ohio in 1801. I saw those huge elephants whose long, flexible trunks were grouting and turning up the soil under the trees like a legion of serpents. I could hear the crashing noise of their long ivory tusks boring into the old decaying trunks. The boughs cracked, and the leaves torn away by cartloads went down the cavernous throats of the vast brutes.

So, then, the dream in which I had had a vision of the prehistoric world, of the tertiary and post-tertiary periods, was now realised. And there we were alone, in the bowels of the earth, at the mercy of its wild inhabitants!

My uncle was gazing with intense and eager interest.

"Come on!" said he, seizing my arm. "Forward! forward!"

"No, I will not!" I cried. "We have no firearms. What could we do in the midst of a herd of these four-footed giants? Come away, uncle—come! No human being may with safety dare the anger of these monstrous beasts."

"No human creature?" replied my uncle in a lower voice. "You are wrong, Axel. Look, look down there! I fancy I see a living creature similar to ourselves: it is a man!"

I looked, shaking my head incredulously. But though at first I was unbelieving I had to yield to the evidence of my senses.

In fact, at a distance of a quarter of a mile, leaning against the trunk of a gigantic kauri, stood a human being, the Proteus of those subterranean regions, a new son of Neptune, watching this countless herd of mastodons.

Immanis pecoris custos, immanior ipse[1].

Yes, truly, huger still himself. It was no longer a fossil being like him whose dried remains we had easily lifted up in the field of bones; it was a giant, able to control those monsters. In stature he was at least twelve feet high. His head, huge and unshapely as a buffalo's, was half hidden in the thick and tangled growth of his unkempt hair. It most resembled the mane of the primitive elephant. In his hand he wielded with ease an enormous bough, a staff worthy of this shepherd of the geologic period.

We stood petrified and speechless with amazement. But he might see us! We must fly!

"Come, do come!" I said to my uncle, who for once allowed himself to be persuaded.

In another quarter of an hour our nimble heels had carried us beyond the reach of this horrible monster.

And yet, now that I can reflect quietly, now that my spirit has grown calm again, now that months have slipped by since this strange and supernatural meeting, what am I to think? what am I to believe? I must conclude that it was impossible that our senses had been deceived, that our eyes did not see what we supposed they saw. No human being lives in this subterranean world; no generation of men dwells in those inferior caverns of the globe, unknown to and unconnected with the inhabitants of its surface. It is absurd to believe it!

I had rather admit that it may have been some animal whose structure resembled the human, some ape or baboon of the early geological ages, some protopitheca, or some

---

[1] "The shepherd of gigantic herds, and huger still himself."

mesopitheca, some early or middle ape like that discovered by Mr. Lartet in the bone cave of Sansau. But this creature surpassed in stature all the measurements known in modern palæontology. But that a man, a living man, and therefore whole generations doubtless besides, should be buried there in the bowels of the earth, is impossible.

However, we had left behind us the luminous forest, dumb with astonishment, overwhelmed and struck down with a terror which amounted to stupefaction. We kept running on for fear the horrible monster might be on our track. It was a flight, a fall, like that fearful pulling and dragging which is peculiar to nightmare. Instinctively we got back to the Liedenbrock sea, and I cannot say into what vagaries my mind would not have carried me but for a circumstance which brought me back to practical matters.

Although I was certain that we were now treading upon a soil not hitherto touched by our feet, I often perceived groups of rocks which reminded me of those about Port Gräuben. Besides, this seemed to confirm the indications of the needle, and to show that we had against our will returned to the north of the Liedenbrock sea. Occasionally we felt quite convinced. Brooks and waterfalls were tumbling everywhere from the projections in the rocks. I thought I recognised the bed of surturbrand, our faithful Hansbach, and the grotto in which I had recovered life and consciousness. Then a few paces farther on, the arrangement of the cliffs, the appearance of an unrecognised stream, or the strange outline of a rock, came to throw me again into doubt.

I communicated my doubts to my uncle. Like myself, he hesitated; he could recognise nothing again amidst this monotonous scene.

"Evidently," said I, "we have not landed again at our original starting point, but the storm has carried us a little higher, and if we follow the shore we shall find Port Gräuben."

"If that is the case it will be useless to continue our exploration, and we had better return to our raft. But, Axel, are you not mistaken?"

"It is difficult to speak decidedly, uncle, for all these rocks are so very much alike. Yet I think I recognise the promontory at the foot of which Hans constructed our launch. We must be very near the little port, if indeed this is not it," I added, examining a creek which I thought I recognised.

"No, Axel, we should at least find our own traces and I see nothing—"

"But I do see," I cried, darting upon an object lying on the sand.

And I showed my uncle a rusty dagger which I had just picked up.

"Come," said he, "had you this weapon with you?"

"I! No, certainly! But you, perhaps—"

"Not that I am aware," said the Professor. "I have never had this object in my possession."

"Well, this is strange!"

"No, Axel, it is very simple. The Icelanders often wear arms of this kind. This must have belonged to Hans, and he has lost it."

I shook my head. Hans had never had an object like this in his possession.

"Did it not belong to some pre-adamite warrior?" I cried, "to some living man, contemporary with the huge cattle-driver? But no. This is not a relic of the stone age. It is not even of the iron age. This blade is steel—"

My uncle stopped me abruptly on my way to a dissertation which would have taken me a long way, and said coolly:

"Be calm, Axel, and reasonable. This dagger belongs to the sixteenth century; it is a poniard, such as gentlemen carried in their belts to give the coup *de grace.* Its origin is Spanish. It was never either yours, or mine, or the hunter's, nor did it belong to any of those human beings who may or may not inhabit this inner world. See, it was never jagged like this by cutting men's throats; its blade is coated with a rust neither a day, nor a year, nor a hundred years old."

The Professor was getting excited according to his wont, and was allowing his imagination to run away with him.

"Axel, we are on the way towards the grand discovery. This blade has been left on the strand for from one to three hundred years, and has blunted its edge upon the rocks that fringe this subterranean sea!"

"But it has not come alone. It has not twisted itself out of shape; some one has been here before us!

"Yes—a man has."

"And who was that man?"

"A man who has engraved his name somewhere with that dagger. That man wanted once more to mark the way to the centre of the earth. Let us look about: look about!"

And, wonderfully interested, we peered all along the high wall, peeping into every fissure which might open out into a gallery.

And so we arrived at a place where the shore was much narrowed. Here the sea came to lap the foot of the steep cliff, leaving a passage no wider than a couple of yards. Between two boldly projecting rocks appeared the mouth of a dark tunnel.

There, upon a granite slab, appeared two mysterious graven letters, half eaten away by time. They were the initials of the bold and daring traveller:

"A. S.," shouted my uncle. "Arne Saknussemm! Arne Saknussemm everywhere!"

CHAPTER XL. PREPARATIONS FOR BLASTING A PASSAGE TO THE CENTRE OF THE EARTH

Since the start upon this marvellous pilgrimage I had been through so many astonishments that I might well be excused for thinking myself well hardened against any further surprise. Yet at the sight of these two letters, engraved on this spot three hundred years ago, I stood aghast in dumb amazement. Not only were the initials of the learned alchemist visible upon the living rock, but there lay the iron point with which the letters had been engraved. I could no longer doubt of the existence of that wonderful traveller and of the fact of his unparalleled journey, without the most glaring incredulity.

Whilst these reflections were occupying me, Professor Liedenbrock had launched into a somewhat rhapsodical eulogium, of which Arne Saknussemm was, of course, the hero.

"Thou marvellous genius!" he cried, "thou hast not forgotten one indication which might serve to lay open to mortals the road through the terrestrial crust; and thy fellow-creatures may even now, after the lapse of three centuries, again trace thy footsteps through these deep and darksome ways. You reserved the contemplation of these wonders for other eyes besides your own. Your name, graven from stage to stage, leads the bold follower of your footsteps to the very centre of our planet's core, and there again we shall find your own name written with your own hand. I too will inscribe my name upon this dark granite page. But for ever henceforth let this cape that advances into the sea discovered by yourself be known by your own illustrious name—Cape Saknussemm."

Such were the glowing words of panegyric which fell upon my attentive ear, and I could not resist the sentiment of enthusiasm with which I too was infected. The fire of zeal kindled afresh in me. I forgot everything. I dismissed from my mind the past perils of the journey, the future danger of our return. That which another had done I supposed we might also do, and nothing that was not superhuman appeared impossible to me.

"Forward! forward!" I cried.

I was already darting down the gloomy tunnel when the Professor stopped me; he, the man of impulse, counselled patience and coolness.

"Let us first return to Hans," he said, "and bring the raft to this spot."

I obeyed, not without dissatisfaction, and passed out rapidly among the rocks on the shore.

I said: "Uncle, do you know it seems to me that circumstances have wonderfully befriended us hitherto?"

"You think so, Axel?"

"No doubt; even the tempest has put us on the right way. Blessings on that storm! It has brought us back to this coast from which fine weather would have carried us far away. Suppose we had touched with our prow (the prow of a rudder!) the southern shore of the

Liedenbrock sea, what would have become of us? We should never have seen the name of Saknussemm, and we should at this moment be imprisoned on a rockbound, impassable coast."

"Yes, Axel, it is providential that whilst supposing we were steering south we should have just got back north at Cape Saknussemm. I must say that this is astonishing, and that I feel I have no way to explain it."

"What does that signify, uncle? Our business is not to explain facts, but to use them!"

"Certainly; but—"

"Well, uncle, we are going to resume the northern route, and to pass under the north countries of Europe—under Sweden, Russia, Siberia: who knows where?—instead of burrowing under the deserts of Africa, or perhaps the waves of the Atlantic; and that is all I want to know."

"Yes, Axel, you are right. It is all for the best, since we have left that weary, horizontal sea, which led us nowhere. Now we shall go down, down, down! Do you know that it is now only 1,500 leagues to the centre of the globe?"

"Is that all?" I cried. "Why, that's nothing. Let us start: march!"

All this crazy talk was going on still when we met the hunter.

Everything was made ready for our instant departure. Every bit of
cordage was put on board. We took our places, and with our sail set,
Hans steered us along the coast to Cape Saknussemm.

The wind was unfavourable to a species of launch not calculated for shallow water. In many places we were obliged to push ourselves along with iron-pointed sticks. Often the sunken rocks just beneath the surface obliged us to deviate from our straight course. At last, after three hours' sailing, about six in the evening we reached a place suitable for our landing. I jumped ashore, followed by my uncle and the Icelander. This short passage had not served to cool my ardour. On the contrary, I even proposed to burn 'our ship,' to prevent the possibility of return; but my uncle would not consent to that. I thought him singularly lukewarm.

"At least," I said, "don't let us lose a minute."

"Yes, yes, lad," he replied; "but first let us examine this new gallery, to see if we shall require our ladders."

My uncle put his Ruhmkorff's apparatus in action; the raft moored to the shore was left alone; the mouth of the tunnel was not twenty yards from us; and our party, with myself at the head, made for it without a moment's delay.

The aperture, which was almost round, was about five feet in diameter; the dark passage was cut out in the live rock and lined with a coat of the eruptive matter which formerly issued from it; the interior was level with the ground outside, so that we were able to enter without difficulty. We were following a horizontal plane, when, only six paces in, our progress was interrupted by an enormous block just across our way.

"Accursed rock!" I cried in a passion, finding myself suddenly confronted by an impassable obstacle.

Right and left we searched in vain for a way, up and down, side to side; there was no getting any farther. I felt fearfully disappointed, and I would not admit that the obstacle was final. I stopped, I looked underneath the block: no opening. Above: granite still. Hans passed his lamp over every portion of the barrier in vain. We must give up all hope of passing it.

I sat down in despair. My uncle strode from side to side in the narrow passage.

"But how was it with Saknussemm?" I cried.

"Yes," said my uncle, "was he stopped by this stone barrier?"

CHAPTER XL. PREPARATIONS FOR BLASTING A PASSAGE TO THE CENTRE OF THE EARTH

"No, no," I replied with animation. "This fragment of rock has been shaken down by some shock or convulsion, or by one of those magnetic storms which agitate these regions, and has blocked up the passage which lay open to him. Many years have elapsed since the return of Saknussemm to the surface and the fall of this huge fragment. Is it not evident that this gallery was once the way open to the course of the lava, and that at that time there must have been a free passage? See here are recent fissures grooving and channelling the granite roof. This roof itself is formed of fragments of rock carried down, of enormous stones, as if by some giant's hand; but at one time the expulsive force was greater than usual, and this block, like the falling keystone of a ruined arch, has slipped down to the ground and blocked up the way. It is only an accidental obstruction, not met by Saknussemm, and if we don't destroy it we shall be unworthy to reach the centre of the earth."

Such was my sentence! The soul of the Professor had passed into me. The genius of discovery possessed me wholly. I forgot the past, I scorned the future. I gave not a thought to the things of the surface of this globe into which I had dived; its cities and its sunny plains, Hamburg and the Königstrasse, even poor Gräuben, who must have given us up for lost, all were for the time dismissed from the pages of my memory.

"Well," cried my uncle, "let us make a way with our pickaxes."

"Too hard for the pickaxe."

"Well, then, the spade."

"That would take us too long."

"What, then?"

"Why gunpowder, to be sure! Let us mine the obstacle and blow it up."

"Oh, yes, it is only a bit of rock to blast!"

"Hans, to work!" cried my uncle.

The Icelander returned to the raft and soon came back with an iron bar which he made use of to bore a hole for the charge. This was no easy work. A hole was to be made large enough to hold fifty pounds of guncotton, whose expansive force is four times that of gunpowder.

I was terribly excited. Whilst Hans was at work I was actively helping my uncle to prepare a slow match of wetted powder encased in linen.

"This will do it," I said.

"It will," replied my uncle.

By midnight our mining preparations were over; the charge was rammed into the hole, and the slow match uncoiled along the gallery showed its end outside the opening.

A spark would now develop the whole of our preparations into activity.

"To-morrow," said the Professor.

I had to be resigned and to wait six long hours.

CHAPTER XLI. THE GREAT EXPLOSION AND THE RUSH DOWN BELOW

The next day, Thursday, August 27, is a well-remembered date in our subterranean journey. It never returns to my memory without sending through me a shudder of horror and a palpitation of the heart. From that hour we had no further occasion for the exercise of reason, or judgment, or skill, or contrivance. We were henceforth to be hurled along, the playthings of the fierce elements of the deep.

At six we were afoot. The moment drew near to clear a way by blasting through the opposing mass of granite.

I begged for the honour of lighting the fuse. This duty done, I was to join my companions on the raft, which had not yet been unloaded; we should then push off as far as we could and avoid the dangers arising from the explosion, the effects of which were not likely to be confined to the rock itself.

The fuse was calculated to burn ten minutes before setting fire to the mine. I therefore had sufficient time to get away to the raft.

I prepared to fulfil my task with some anxiety.

After a hasty meal, my uncle and the hunter embarked whilst I remained on shore. I was supplied with a lighted lantern to set fire to the fuse. "Now go," said my uncle, "and return immediately to us." "Don't be uneasy," I replied. "I will not play by the way." I immediately proceeded to the mouth of the tunnel. I opened my lantern. I laid hold of the end of the match. The Professor stood, chronometer in hand. "Ready?" he cried.

"Ay."

"Fire!"

I instantly plunged the end of the fuse into the lantern. It spluttered and flamed, and I ran at the top of my speed to the raft.

"Come on board quickly, and let us push off."

Hans, with a vigorous thrust, sent us from the shore. The raft shot twenty fathoms out to sea.

It was a moment of intense excitement. The Professor was watching the hand of the chronometer.

"Five minutes more!" he said. "Four! Three!"

My pulse beat half-seconds.

"Two! One! Down, granite rocks; down with you."

What took place at that moment? I believe I did not hear the dull roar of the explosion. But the rocks suddenly assumed a new arrangement: they rent asunder like a curtain. I saw a bottomless pit open on the shore. The sea, lashed into sudden fury, rose up in an enormous billow, on the ridge of which the unhappy raft was uplifted bodily in the air with all its crew and cargo.

We all three fell down flat. In less than a second we were in deep, unfathomable darkness. Then I felt as if not only myself but the raft also had no support beneath. I thought it was sinking; but it was not so. I wanted to speak to my uncle, but the roaring of the waves prevented him from hearing even the sound of my voice.

In spite of darkness, noise, astonishment, and terror, I then understood what had taken place.

On the other side of the blown-up rock was an abyss. The explosion had caused a kind of earthquake in this fissured and abysmal region; a great gulf had opened; and the sea, now changed into a torrent, was hurrying us along into it.

I gave myself up for lost.

An hour passed away—two hours, perhaps—I cannot tell. We clutched each other fast, to save ourselves from being thrown off the raft. We felt violent shocks whenever we were borne heavily against the craggy projections. Yet these shocks were not very frequent, from which I concluded that the gully was widening. It was no doubt the same road that Saknussemm had taken; but instead of walking peaceably down it, as he had done, we were carrying a whole sea along with us.

These ideas, it will be understood, presented themselves to my mind in a vague and undetermined form. I had difficulty in associating any ideas together during this headlong race, which seemed like a vertical descent. To judge by the air which was whistling past me and made a whizzing in my ears, we were moving faster than the fastest express trains. To light a torch under these' conditions would have been impossible; and our last electric apparatus had been shattered by the force of the explosion.

I was therefore much surprised to see a clear light shining near me. It lighted up the calm and unmoved countenance of Hans. The skilful huntsman had succeeded in lighting the lantern; and although it flickered so much as to threaten to go out, it threw a fitful light across the awful darkness.

I was right in my supposition. It was a wide gallery. The dim light could not show us both its walls at once. The fall of the waters which were carrying us away exceeded that of the swiftest rapids in American rivers. Its surface seemed composed of a sheaf of arrows hurled with inconceivable force; I cannot convey my impressions by a better comparison. The raft, occasionally seized by an eddy, spun round as it still flew along. When it approached the walls of the gallery I threw on them the light of the lantern, and I could judge somewhat of the velocity of our speed by noticing how the jagged projections of the rocks spun into endless ribbons and bands, so that we seemed confined within a network of shifting lines. I supposed we were running at the rate of thirty leagues an hour.

My uncle and I gazed on each other with haggard eyes, clinging to the stump of the mast, which had snapped asunder at the first shock of our great catastrophe. We kept our backs to the wind, not to be stifled by the rapidity of a movement which no human power could check.

Hours passed away. No change in our situation; but a discovery came to complicate matters and make them worse.

In seeking to put our cargo into somewhat better order, I found that the greater part of the articles embarked had disappeared at the moment of the explosion, when the sea broke in upon us with such violence. I wanted to know exactly what we had saved, and with the lantern in my hand I began my examination. Of our instruments none were saved but the compass and the chronometer; our stock of ropes and ladders was reduced to the bit of cord rolled round the stump of the mast! Not a spade, not a pickaxe, not a hammer was left us; and, irreparable disaster! we had only one day's provisions left.

I searched every nook and corner, every crack and cranny in the raft. There was nothing. Our provisions were reduced to one bit of salt meat and a few biscuits.

I stared at our failing supplies stupidly. I refused to take in the gravity of our loss. And yet what was the use of troubling myself. If we had had provisions enough for months, how could we get out of the abyss into which we were being hurled by an irresistible torrent? Why should we fear the horrors of famine, when death was swooping down upon us in a multitude of other forms? Would there be time left to die of starvation?

Yet by an inexplicable play of the imagination I forgot my present dangers, to contemplate the threatening future. Was there any chance of escaping from the fury of this impetuous torrent, and of returning to the surface of the globe? I could not form the slightest conjecture how or when. But one chance in a thousand, or ten thousand, is still a chance; whilst death from starvation would leave us not the smallest hope in the world.

The thought came into my mind to declare the whole truth to my uncle, to show him the dreadful straits to which we were reduced, and to calculate how long we might yet expect to live. But I had the courage to preserve silence. I wished to leave him cool and self-possessed.

At that moment the light from our lantern began to sink by little and little, and then went out entirely. The wick had burnt itself out. Black night reigned again; and there was no hope left of being able to dissipate the palpable darkness. We had yet a torch left, but we could not have kept it alight. Then, like a child, I closed my eyes firmly, not to see the darkness.

After a considerable lapse of time our speed redoubled. I could perceive it by the sharpness of the currents that blew past my face. The descent became steeper. I believe we were no longer sliding, but falling down. I had an impression that we were dropping vertically. My uncle's hand, and the vigorous arm of Hans, held me fast.

Suddenly, after a space of time that I could not measure, I felt a shock. The raft had not struck against any hard resistance, but had suddenly been checked in its fall. A waterspout, an immense liquid column, was beating upon the surface of the waters. I was suffocating! I was drowning!

But this sudden flood was not of long duration. In a few seconds I found myself in the air again, which I inhaled with all the force of my lungs. My uncle and Hans were still holding me fast by the arms; and the raft was still carrying us.

CHAPTER XLII. HEADLONG SPEED UPWARD THROUGH THE HORRORS OF DARKNESS

It might have been, as I guessed, about ten at night. The first of my senses which came into play after this last bout was that of hearing. All at once I could hear; and it was a real exercise of the sense of hearing. I could hear the silence in the gallery after the din which for hours had stunned me. At last these words of my uncle's came to me like a vague murmuring:

"We are going up."

"What do you mean?" I cried.

"Yes, we are going up—up!"

I stretched out my arm. I touched the wall, and drew back my hand bleeding. We were ascending with extreme rapidity.

"The torch! The torch!" cried the Professor.

Not without difficulty Hans succeeded in lighting the torch; and the flame, preserving its upward tendency, threw enough light to show us what kind of a place we were in.

"Just as I thought," said the Professor "We are in a tunnel not four-and-twenty feet in diameter. The water had reached the bottom of the gulf. It is now rising to its level, and carrying us with it."

"Where to?"

"I cannot tell; but we must be ready for anything. We are mounting at a speed which seems to me of fourteen feet in a second, or ten miles an hour. At this rate we shall get on."

"Yes, if nothing stops us; if this well has an aperture. But suppose it to be stopped. If the air is condensed by the pressure of this column of water we shall be crushed."

"Axel," replied the Professor with perfect coolness, "our situation is almost desperate; but there are some chances of deliverance, and it is these that I am considering. If at every instant we may perish, so at every instant we may be saved. Let us then be prepared to seize upon the smallest advantage."

"But what shall we do now?"

"Recruit our strength by eating."

At these words I fixed a haggard eye upon my uncle. That which I had been so unwilling to confess at last had to be told.

"Eat, did you say?"

"Yes, at once."

The Professor added a few words in Danish, but Hans shook his head mournfully.

"What!" cried my uncle. "Have we lost our provisions?"

"Yes; here is all we have left; one bit of salt meat for the three."

My uncle stared at me as if he could not understand.

"Well," said I, "do you think we have any chance of being saved?"

My question was unanswered.

An hour passed away. I began to feel the pangs of a violent hunger. My companions were suffering too, and not one of us dared touch this wretched remnant of our goodly store.

But now we were mounting up with excessive speed. Sometimes the air would cut our breath short, as is experienced by aeronauts ascending too rapidly. But whilst they suffer from cold in proportion to their rise, we were beginning to feel a contrary effect. The heat was increasing in a manner to cause us the most fearful anxiety, and certainly the temperature was at this moment at the height of 100° Fahr.

What could be the meaning of such a change? Up to this time facts had supported the theories of Davy and of Liedenbrock; until now particular conditions of non-conducting rocks, electricity and magnetism, had tempered the laws of nature, giving us only a moderately warm climate, for the theory of a central fire remained in my estimation the only one that was true and explicable. Were we then turning back to where the phenomena of central heat ruled in all their rigour and would reduce the most refractory rocks to the state of a molten liquid? I feared this, and said to the Professor:

"If we are neither drowned, nor shattered to pieces, nor starved to death, there is still the chance that we may be burned alive and reduced to ashes."

At this he shrugged his shoulders and returned to his thoughts.

Another hour passed, and, except some slight increase in the temperature, nothing new had happened.

"Come," said he, "we must determine upon something."

"Determine on what?" said I.

"Yes, we must recruit our strength by carefully rationing ourselves, and so prolong our existence by a few hours. But we shall be reduced to very great weakness at last."

"And our last hour is not far off."

"Well, if there is a chance of safety, if a moment for active exertion presents itself, where should we find the required strength if we allowed ourselves to be enfeebled by hunger?"

"Well, uncle, when this bit of meat has been devoured what shall we have left?"

"Nothing, Axel, nothing at all. But will it do you any more good to devour it with your eyes than with your teeth? Your reasoning has in it neither sense nor energy."

"Then don't you despair?" I cried irritably.

"No, certainly not," was the Professor's firm reply.

"What! do you think there is any chance of safety left?"

"Yes, I do; as long as the heart beats, as long as body and soul keep together, I cannot admit that any creature endowed with a will has need to despair of life."

Resolute words these! The man who could speak so, under such circumstances, was of no ordinary type.

"Finally, what do you mean to do?" I asked.

"Eat what is left to the last crumb, and recruit our fading strength. This meal will be our last, perhaps: so let it be! But at any rate we shall once more be men, and not exhausted, empty bags."

"Well, let us consume it then," I cried.

My uncle took the piece of meat and the few biscuits which had escaped from the general destruction. He divided them into three equal portions and gave one to each. This made about a pound of nourishment for each. The Professor ate his greedily, with a kind of feverish rage. I ate without pleasure, almost with disgust; Hans quietly, moderately, masticating his small mouthfuls without any noise, and relishing them with the calmness of a man above all anxiety about the future. By diligent search he had found a flask of Hollands; he offered it to us each in turn, and this generous beverage cheered us up slightly.

"*Forträfflig,*" said Hans, drinking in his turn.

"Excellent," replied my uncle.

A glimpse of hope had returned, although without cause. But our last meal was over, and it was now five in the morning.

Man is so constituted that health is a purely negative state. Hunger once satisfied, it is difficult for a man to imagine the horrors of starvation; they cannot be understood without being felt.

Therefore it was that after our long fast these few mouthfuls of meat and biscuit made us triumph over our past agonies.

But as soon as the meal was done, we each of us fell deep into thought. What was Hans thinking of—that man of the far West, but who seemed ruled by the fatalist doctrines of the East?

As for me, my thoughts were made up of remembrances, and they carried me up to the surface of the globe of which I ought never to have taken leave. The house in the Königstrasse, my poor dear Gräuben, that kind soul Martha, flitted like visions before my eyes, and in the dismal moanings which from time to time reached my ears I thought I could distinguish the roar of the traffic of the great cities upon earth.

My uncle still had his eye upon his work. Torch in hand, he tried to gather some idea of our situation from the observation of the strata. This calculation could, at best, be but a vague approximation; but a learned man is always a philosopher when he succeeds in remaining cool, and assuredly Professor Liedenbrock possessed this quality to a surprising degree.

I could hear him murmuring geological terms. I could understand them, and in spite of myself I felt interested in this last geological study.

"Eruptive granite," he was saying. "We are still in the primitive period. But we are going up, up, higher still. Who can tell?"

Ah! who can tell? With his hand he was examining the perpendicular wall, and in a few more minutes he continued:

"This is gneiss! here is mica schist! Ah! presently we shall come to the transition period, and then—"

What did the Professor mean? Could he be trying to measure the thickness of the crust of the earth that lay between us and the world above? Had he any means of making this calculation? No, he had not the aneroid, and no guessing could supply its place.

Still the temperature kept rising, and I felt myself steeped in a broiling atmosphere. I could only compare it to the heat of a furnace at the moment when the molten metal is running into the mould. Gradually we had been obliged to throw aside our coats and waistcoats, the lightest covering became uncomfortable and even painful.

"Are we rising into a fiery furnace?" I cried at one moment when the heat was redoubling.

"No," replied my uncle, "that is impossible—quite impossible!"

"Yet," I answered, feeling the wall, "this well is burning hot."

At the same moment, touching the water, I had to withdraw my hand in haste.

"The water is scalding," I cried.

This time the Professor's only answer was an angry gesture.

Then an unconquerable terror seized upon me, from which I could no longer get free. I felt that a catastrophe was approaching before which the boldest spirit must quail. A dim, vague notion laid hold of my mind, but which was fast hardening into certainty. I tried to repel it, but it would return. I dared not express it in plain terms. Yet a few involuntary observations confirmed me in my view. By the flickering light of the torch I could distinguish contortions in the granite beds; a phenomenon was unfolding in which electricity would play the principal part; then this unbearable heat, this boiling water! I consulted the compass.

The compass had lost its properties! it had ceased to act properly!

CHAPTER XLIII. SHOT OUT OF A VOLCANO AT LAST!

Yes: our compass was no longer a guide; the needle flew from pole to pole with a kind of frenzied impulse; it ran round the dial, and spun hither and thither as if it were giddy or intoxicated.

I knew quite well that according to the best received theories the mineral covering of the globe is never at absolute rest; the changes brought about by the chemical decomposition of its component parts, the agitation caused by great liquid torrents, and the magnetic currents, are continually tending to disturb it—even when living beings upon its surface may fancy that all is quiet below. A phenomenon of this kind would not have greatly alarmed me, or at any rate it would not have given rise to dreadful apprehensions.

But other facts, other circumstances, of a peculiar nature, came to reveal to me by degrees the true state of the case. There came incessant and continuous explosions. I could only compare them to the loud rattle of a long train of chariots driven at full speed over the stones, or a roar of unintermitting thunder.

Then the disordered compass, thrown out of gear by the electric currents, confirmed me in a growing conviction. The mineral crust of the globe threatened to burst up, the granite foundations to come together with a crash, the fissure through which we were helplessly driven would be filled up, the void would be full of crushed fragments of rock, and we poor wretched mortals were to be buried and annihilated in this dreadful consummation.

"My uncle," I cried, "we are lost now, utterly lost!"

"What are you in a fright about now?" was the calm rejoinder. "What is the matter with you?"

"The matter? Look at those quaking walls! look at those shivering rocks. Don't you feel the burning heat? Don't you see how the water boils and bubbles? Are you blind to the dense vapours and steam growing thicker and denser every minute? See this agitated compass needle. It is an earthquake that is threatening us."

My undaunted uncle calmly shook his head.

"Do you think," said he, "an earthquake is coming?"

"I do."

"Well, I think you are mistaken."

"What! don't you recognise the symptoms?"

"Of an earthquake? no! I am looking out for something better."

"What can you mean? Explain?"

"It is an eruption, Axel."

"An eruption! Do you mean to affirm that we are running up the shaft of a volcano?"

"I believe we are," said the indomitable Professor with an air of perfect self-possession; "and it is the best thing that could possibly happen to us under our circumstances."

The best thing! Was my uncle stark mad? What did the man mean? and what was the use of saying facetious things at a time like this?

"What!" I shouted. "Are we being taken up in an eruption? Our fate has flung us here among burning lavas, molten rocks, boiling waters, and all kinds of volcanic matter; we are going to be pitched out, expelled, tossed up, vomited, spit out high into the air, along with fragments of rock, showers of ashes and scoria, in the midst of a towering rush of smoke and flames; and it is the best thing that could happen to us!"

"Yes," replied the Professor, eyeing me over his spectacles, "I don't see any other way of reaching the surface of the earth."

I pass rapidly over the thousand ideas which passed through my mind. My uncle was right, undoubtedly right; and never had he seemed to me more daring and more confirmed in his notions than at this moment when he was calmly contemplating the chances of being shot out of a volcano!

In the meantime up we went; the night passed away in continual ascent; the din and uproar around us became more and more intensified; I was stifled and stunned; I thought my last hour was approaching; and yet imagination is such a strong thing that even in this supreme hour I was occupied with strange and almost childish speculations. But I was the victim, not the master, of my own thoughts.

It was very evident that we were being hurried upward upon the crest of a wave of eruption; beneath our raft were boiling waters, and under these the more sluggish lava was working its way up in a heated mass, together with shoals of fragments of rock which, when they arrived at the crater, would be dispersed in all directions high and low. We were imprisoned in the shaft or chimney of some volcano. There was no room to doubt of that.

But this time, instead of Snæfell, an extinct volcano, we were inside one in full activity. I wondered, therefore, where could this mountain be, and in what part of the world we were to be shot out.

I made no doubt but that it would be in some northern region. Before its disorders set in, the needle had never deviated from that direction. From Cape Saknussemm we had been carried due north for hundreds of leagues. Were we under Iceland again? Were we destined to be thrown up out of Hecla, or by which of the seven other fiery craters in that island? Within a radius of five hundred leagues to the west I remembered under this parallel of latitude only the imperfectly known volcanoes of the north-east coast of America. To the east there was only one in the 80th degree of north latitude, the Esk in Jan Mayen Island, not far from Spitzbergen! Certainly there was no lack of craters, and there were some capacious enough to throw out a whole army! But I wanted to know which of them was to serve us for an exit from the inner world.

Towards morning the ascending movement became accelerated. If the heat increased, instead of diminishing, as we approached nearer to the surface of the globe, this effect was due to local causes alone, and those volcanic. The manner of our locomotion left no doubt in my mind. An enormous force, a force of hundreds of atmospheres, generated by the extreme pressure of confined vapours, was driving us irresistibly forward. But to what numberless dangers it exposed us!

Soon lurid lights began to penetrate the vertical gallery which widened as we went up. Right and left I could see deep channels, like huge tunnels, out of which escaped dense volumes of smoke; tongues of fire lapped the walls, which crackled and sputtered under the intense heat.

"See, see, my uncle!" I cried.

"Well, those are only sulphureous flames and vapours, which one must expect to see in an eruption. They are quite natural."

"But suppose they should wrap us round."

"But they won't wrap us round."

"But we shall be stifled."

"We shall not be stifled at all. The gallery is widening, and if it becomes necessary, we shall abandon the raft, and creep into a crevice."

"But the water—the rising water?"

"There is no more water, Axel; only a lava paste, which is bearing us up on its surface to the top of the crater."

The liquid column had indeed disappeared, to give place to dense and still boiling eruptive matter of all kinds. The temperature was becoming unbearable. A thermometer exposed to this atmosphere would have marked 150°. The perspiration streamed from my body. But for the rapidity of our ascent we should have been suffocated.

But the Professor gave up his idea of abandoning the raft, and it was well he did. However roughly joined together, those planks afforded us a firmer support than we could have found anywhere else.

About eight in the morning a new incident occurred. The upward movement ceased. The raft lay motionless.

"What is this?" I asked, shaken by this sudden stoppage as if by a shock.

"It is a halt," replied my uncle.

"Is the eruption checked?" I asked.

"I hope not."

I rose, and tried to look around me. Perhaps the raft itself, stopped in its course by a projection, was staying the volcanic torrent. If this were the case we should have to release it as soon as possible.

But it was not so. The blast of ashes, scorix, and rubbish had ceased to rise.

"Has the eruption stopped?" I cried.

"Ah!" said my uncle between his clenched teeth, "you are afraid. But don't alarm yourself—this lull cannot last long. It has lasted now five minutes, and in a short time we shall resume our journey to the mouth of the crater."

As he spoke, the Professor continued to consult his chronometer, and he was again right in his prognostications. The raft was soon hurried and driven forward with a rapid but irregular movement, which lasted about ten minutes, and then stopped again.

"Very good," said my uncle; "in ten minutes more we shall be off again, for our present business lies with an intermittent volcano. It gives us time now and then to take breath."

This was perfectly true. When the ten minutes were over we started off again with renewed and increased speed. We were obliged to lay fast hold of the planks of the raft, not to be thrown off. Then again the paroxysm was over.

I have since reflected upon this singular phenomenon without being able to explain it. At any rate it was clear that we were not in the main shaft of the volcano, but in a lateral gallery where there were felt recurrent tunes of reaction.

How often this operation was repeated I cannot say. All I know is, that at each fresh impulse we were hurled forward with a greatly increased force, and we seemed as if we were mere projectiles. During the short halts we were stifled with the heat; whilst we were being projected forward the hot air almost stopped my breath. I thought for a moment how delightful it would be to find myself carried suddenly into the arctic regions, with a cold 30° below the freezing point. My overheated brain conjured up visions of white plains of cool snow, where I might roll and allay my feverish heat. Little by little my brain, weakened by so many constantly repeated shocks, seemed to be giving way altogether. But for the strong arm of Hans I should more than once have had my head broken against the granite roof of our burning dungeon.

I have therefore no exact recollection of what took place during the following hours. I have a confused impression left of continuous explosions, loud detonations, a general shaking of the rocks all around us, and of a spinning movement with which our raft was once whirled helplessly round. It rocked upon the lava torrent, amidst a dense fall of ashes. Snorting flames darted their fiery tongues at us. There were wild, fierce puffs of stormy wind from below, resembling the blasts of vast iron furnaces blowing all at one time; and I caught a glimpse of the figure of Hans lighted up by the fire; and all the feeling I had left was just what I imagine must be the feeling of an unhappy criminal doomed to be blown away alive from the mouth of a cannon, just before the trigger is pulled, and the flying limbs and rags of flesh and skin fill the quivering air and spatter the blood-stained ground.

CHAPTER XLIV. SUNNY LANDS IN THE BLUE MEDITERRANEAN

When I opened my eyes again I felt myself grasped by the belt with the strong hand of our guide. With the other arm he supported my uncle. I was not seriously hurt, but I was shaken and bruised and battered all over. I found myself lying on the sloping side of a mountain only two yards from a gaping gulf, which would have swallowed me up had I leaned at all that way. Hans had saved me from death whilst I lay rolling on the edge of the crater.

"Where are we?" asked my uncle irascibly, as if he felt much injured by being landed upon the earth again.

The hunter shook his head in token of complete ignorance.

"Is it Iceland?" I asked.

"*Nej,*" replied Hans.

"What! Not Iceland?" cried the Professor.

"Hans must be mistaken," I said, raising myself up.

This was our final surprise after all the astonishing events of our wonderful journey. I expected to see a white cone covered with the eternal snow of ages rising from the midst of the barren deserts of the icy north, faintly lighted with the pale rays of the arctic sun, far away in the highest latitudes known; but contrary to all our expectations, my uncle, the Icelander, and myself were sitting half-way down a mountain baked under the burning rays of a southern sun, which was blistering us with the heat, and blinding us with the fierce light of his nearly vertical rays.

I could not believe my own eyes; but the heated air and the sensation of burning left me no room for doubt. We had come out of the crater half naked, and the radiant orb to which we had been strangers for two months was lavishing upon us out of his blazing splendours more of his light and heat than we were able to receive with comfort.

When my eyes had become accustomed to the bright light to which they had been so long strangers, I began to use them to set my imagination right. At least I would have it to be Spitzbergen, and I was in no humour to give up this notion.

The Professor was the first to speak, and said:

"Well, this is not much like Iceland."

"But is it Jan Mayen?" I asked.

"Nor that either," he answered. "This is no northern mountain; here are no granite peaks capped with snow. Look, Axel, look!"

Above our heads, at a height of five hundred feet or more, we saw the crater of a volcano, through which, at intervals of fifteen minutes or so, there issued with loud explosions lofty columns of fire, mingled with pumice stones, ashes, and flowing lava. I could feel the heaving of the mountain, which seemed to breathe like a huge whale, and puff out fire and wind from its vast blowholes. Beneath, down a pretty steep declivity, ran streams of lava for eight or nine hundred feet, giving the mountain a height of about 1,300 or 1,400 feet. But the base of the mountain was hidden in a perfect bower of rich verdure, amongst which I was able to distinguish the olive, the fig, and vines, covered with their luscious purple bunches.

I was forced to confess that there was nothing arctic here.

When the eye passed beyond these green surroundings it rested on a wide, blue expanse of sea or lake, which appeared to enclose this enchanting island, within a compass of only a few leagues. Eastward lay a pretty little white seaport town or village, with a few houses scattered around it, and in the harbour of which a few vessels of peculiar rig were gently swayed by the softly swelling waves. Beyond it, groups of islets rose from the smooth, blue waters, but in such numbers that they seemed to dot the sea like a shoal. To the west distant coasts lined the dim horizon, on some rose blue mountains of smooth, undulating forms; on a more distant coast arose a prodigious cone crowned on its summit with a snowy plume of white cloud. To the northward lay spread a vast sheet of water, sparkling and dancing under the hot, bright rays, the uniformity broken here and there by the topmast of a gallant ship appearing above the horizon, or a swelling sail moving slowly before the wind.

This unforeseen spectacle was most charming to eyes long used to underground darkness.

"Where are we? Where are we?" I asked faintly.

Hans closed his eyes with lazy indifference. What did it matter to him? My uncle looked round with dumb surprise.

"Well, whatever mountain this may be," he said at last, "it is very hot here. The explosions are going on still, and I don't think it would look well to have come out by an eruption, and then to get our heads broken by bits of falling rock. Let us get down. Then we shall know better what we are about. Besides, I am starving, and parching with thirst."

Decidedly the Professor was not given to contemplation. For my part, I could for another hour or two have forgotten my hunger and my fatigue to enjoy the lovely scene before me; but I had to follow my companions.

The slope of the volcano was in many places of great steepness. We slid down screes of ashes, carefully avoiding the lava streams which glided sluggishly by us like fiery serpents. As we went I chattered and asked all sorts of questions as to our whereabouts, for I was too much excited not to talk a great deal.

"We are in Asia," I cried, "on the coasts of India, in the Malay Islands, or in Oceania. We have passed through half the globe, and come out nearly at the antipodes."

"But the compass?" said my uncle.

"Ay, the compass!" I said, greatly puzzled. "According to the compass we have gone northward."

"Has it lied?"

"Surely not. Could it lie?"

"Unless, indeed, this is the North Pole!"

"Oh, no, it is not the Pole; but—"

Well, here was something that baffled us completely. I could not tell what to say.

But now we were coming into that delightful greenery, and I was suffering greatly from hunger and thirst. Happily, after two hours' walking, a charming country lay open before us, covered with olive trees, pomegranate trees, and delicious vines, all of which seemed to belong to anybody who pleased to claim them. Besides, in our state of destitution and famine we were not likely to be particular. Oh, the inexpressible pleasure of pressing those cool, sweet fruits to our lips, and eating grapes by mouthfuls off the rich, full bunches! Not far off, in the grass, under the delicious shade of the trees, I discovered a spring of fresh, cool water, in which we luxuriously bathed our faces, hands, and feet.

Whilst we were thus enjoying the sweets of repose a child appeared out of a grove of olive trees.

"Ah!" I cried, "here is an inhabitant of this happy land!"

It was but a poor boy, miserably ill-clad, a sufferer from poverty, and our aspect seemed to alarm him a great deal; in fact, only half clothed, with ragged hair and beards, we were a suspicious-looking party; and if the people of the country knew anything about thieves, we were very likely to frighten them.

Just as the poor little wretch was going to take to his heels, Hans caught hold of him, and brought him to us, kicking and struggling.

My uncle began to encourage him as well as he could, and said to him in good German:

"*Was heiszt diesen Berg, mein Knablein? Sage mir geschwind!*"

("What is this mountain called, my little friend?")

The child made no answer.

"Very well," said my uncle. "I infer that we are not in Germany."

He put the same question in English.

We got no forwarder. I was a good deal puzzled.

"Is the child dumb?" cried the Professor, who, proud of his knowledge of many languages, now tried French: "*Comment appellet-on cette montagne, mon enfant?*"

Silence still.

"Now let us try Italian," said my uncle; and he said:

"*Dove noi siamo?*"

"Yes, where are we?" I impatiently repeated.

But there was no answer still.

"Will you speak when you are told?" exclaimed my uncle, shaking the urchin by the ears. "*Come si noma questa isola?*"

"STROMBOLI," replied the little herdboy, slipping out of Hans' hands, and scudding into the plain across the olive trees.

We were hardly thinking of that. Stromboli! What an effect this unexpected name produced upon my mind! We were in the midst of the Mediterranean Sea, on an island of the Æolian archipelago, in the ancient Strongyle, where Æolus kept the winds and the storms chained up, to be let loose at his will. And those distant blue mountains in the east were the mountains of Calabria. And that threatening volcano far away in the south was the fierce Etna.

"Stromboli, Stromboli!" I repeated.

My uncle kept time to my exclamations with hands and feet, as well as with words. We seemed to be chanting in chorus!

What a journey we had accomplished! How marvellous! Having entered by one volcano, we had issued out of another more than two thousand miles from Snæfell and from that barren, far-away Iceland! The strange chances of our expedition had carried us into the heart of the fairest region in the world. We had exchanged the bleak regions of perpetual snow and of impenetrable barriers of ice for those of brightness and 'the rich hues of all glorious things.' We had left over our heads the murky sky and cold fogs of the frigid zone to revel under the azure sky of Italy!

After our delicious repast of fruits and cold, clear water we set off again to reach the port of Stromboli. It would not have been wise to tell how we came there. The superstitious Italians would have set us down for fire-devils vomited out of hell; so we presented ourselves in the humble guise of shipwrecked mariners. It was not so glorious, but it was safer.

On my way I could hear my uncle murmuring: "But the compass! that compass! It pointed due north. How are we to explain that fact?"

"My opinion is," I replied disdainfully, "that it is best not to explain it. That is the easiest way to shelve the difficulty."

"Indeed, sir! The occupant of a professorial chair at the Johannæum unable to explain the reason of a cosmical phenomenon! Why, it would be simply disgraceful!"

And as he spoke, my uncle, half undressed, in rags, a perfect scarecrow, with his leathern belt around him, settling his spectacles upon his nose and looking learned and imposing, was himself again, the terrible German professor of mineralogy.

One hour after we had left the grove of olives, we arrived at the little port of San Vicenzo, where Hans claimed his thirteen week's wages, which was counted out to him with a hearty shaking of hands all round.

At that moment, if he did not share our natural emotion, at least his countenance expanded in a manner very unusual with him, and while with the ends of his fingers he lightly pressed our hands, I believe he smiled.

CHAPTER XLV. ALL'S WELL THAT ENDS WELL

Such is the conclusion of a history which I cannot expect everybody to believe, for some people will believe nothing against the testimony of their own experience. However, I am indifferent to their incredulity, and they may believe as much or as little as they please.

The Stromboliotes received us kindly as shipwrecked mariners. They gave us food and clothing. After waiting forty-eight hours, on the 31st of August, a small craft took us to Messina, where a few days' rest completely removed the effect of our fatigues.

On Friday, September the 4th, we embarked on the steamer Volturno, employed by the French Messageries Imperiales, and in three days more we were at Marseilles, having no care on our minds except that abominable deceitful compass, which we had mislaid somewhere and could not now examine; but its inexplicable behaviour exercised my mind fearfully. On the 9th of September, in the evening, we arrived at Hamburg.

I cannot describe to you the astonishment of Martha or the joy of

Gräuben.

"Now you are a hero, Axel," said to me my blushing *fiancée,* my betrothed, "you will not leave me again!"

I looked tenderly upon her, and she smiled through her tears.

How can I describe the extraordinary sensation produced by the return of Professor Liedenbrock? Thanks to Martha's ineradicable tattling, the news that the Professor had gone to discover a way to the centre of the earth had spread over the whole civilised world. People refused to believe it, and when they saw him they would not believe him any the more. Still, the appearance of Hans, and sundry pieces of intelligence derived from Iceland, tended to shake the confidence of the unbelievers.

Then my uncle became a great man, and I was now the nephew of a great man—which is not a privilege to be despised.

Hamburg gave a grand fete in our honour. A public audience was given to the Professor at the Johannæum, at which he told all about our expedition, with only one omission, the unexplained and inexplicable behaviour of our compass. On the same day, with much state, he deposited in the archives of the city the now famous document of Saknussemm, and expressed his regret that circumstances over which he had no control had prevented him from following to the very centre of the earth the track of the learned Icelander. He was modest notwithstanding his glory, and he was all the more famous for his humility.

So much honour could not but excite envy. There were those who envied him his fame; and as his theories, resting upon known facts, were in opposition to the systems of science upon the question of the central fire, he sustained with his pen and by his voice remarkable discussions with the learned of every country.

For my part I cannot agree with his theory of gradual cooling: in spite of what I have seen and felt, I believe, and always shall believe, in the central heat. But I admit that certain circumstances not yet sufficiently understood may tend to modify in places the action of natural phenomena.

While these questions were being debated with great animation, my uncle met with a real sorrow. Our faithful Hans, in spite of our entreaties, had left Hamburg; the man to whom we owed all our success and our lives too would not suffer us to reward him as we could have wished. He was seized with the mal de pays, a complaint for which we have not even a name in English.

"*Farval,*" said he one day; and with that simple word he left us and sailed for Rejkiavik, which he reached in safety.

We were strongly attached to our brave eider-down hunter; though far away in the remotest north, he will never be forgotten by those whose lives he protected, and certainly I shall not fail to endeavour to see him once more before I die.

To conclude, I have to add that this 'Journey into the Interior of the Earth' created a wonderful sensation in the world. It was translated into all civilised languages. The leading newspapers extracted the most interesting passages, which were commented upon, picked to pieces, discussed, attacked, and defended with equal enthusiasm and determination, both by believers and sceptics. Rare privilege! my uncle enjoyed during his lifetime the glory he had deservedly won; and he may even boast the distinguished honour of an offer from Mr. Barnum, to exhibit him on most advantageous terms in all the principal cities in the United States!

But there was one 'dead fly' amidst all this glory and honour; one fact, one incident, of the journey remained a mystery. Now to a man eminent for his learning, an unexplained phenomenon is an unbearable hardship. Well! it was yet reserved for my uncle to be completely happy.

One day, while arranging a collection of minerals in his cabinet, I noticed in a corner this unhappy compass, which we had long lost sight of; I opened it, and began to watch it.

It had been in that corner for six months, little mindful of the trouble it was giving.

Suddenly, to my intense astonishment, I noticed a strange fact, and I uttered a cry of surprise.

"What is the matter?" my uncle asked.

"That compass!"

"Well?"

"See, its poles are reversed!"

"Reversed?"

"Yes, they point the wrong way."

My uncle looked, he compared, and the house shook with his triumphant leap of exultation.

A light broke in upon his spirit and mine.

"See there," he cried, as soon as he was able to speak. "After our arrival at Cape Saknussemm the north pole of the needle of this confounded compass began to point south instead of north."

"Evidently!"

"Here, then, is the explanation of our mistake. But what phenomenon could have caused this reversal of the poles?"

"The reason is evident, uncle."

"Tell me, then, Axel."

"During the electric storm on the Liedenbrock sea, that ball of fire, which magnetised all the iron on board, reversed the poles of our magnet!"

"Aha! aha!" shouted the Professor with a loud laugh. "So it was just an electric joke!"

From that day forth the Professor was the most glorious of savants, and I was the happiest of men; for my pretty Virlandaise, resigning her place as ward, took her position in the old house on the Königstrasse in the double capacity of niece to my uncle and wife to a certain happy youth. What is the need of adding that the illustrious Otto Liedenbrock, corresponding member of all the scientific, geographical, and mineralogical societies of all the civilised world, was now her uncle and mine?

FROM THE EARTH TO THE MOON

CHAPTER I THE GUN CLUB

During the War of the Rebellion, a new and influential club was established in the city of Baltimore in the State of Maryland. It is well known with what energy the taste for military matters became developed among that nation of ship-owners, shopkeepers, and mechanics. Simple tradesmen jumped their counters to become extemporized captains, colonels, and generals, without having ever passed the School of Instruction at West Point; nevertheless; they quickly rivaled their compeers of the old continent, and, like them, carried off victories by dint of lavish expenditure in ammunition, money, and men.

But the point in which the Americans singularly distanced the Europeans was in the science of gunnery. Not, indeed, that their weapons retained a higher degree of perfection than theirs, but that they exhibited unheard-of dimensions, and consequently attained hitherto unheard-of ranges. In point of grazing, plunging, oblique, or enfilading, or point-blank firing, the English, French, and Prussians have nothing to learn; but their cannon, howitzers, and mortars are mere pocket-pistols compared with the formidable engines of the American artillery.

This fact need surprise no one. The Yankees, the first mechanicians in the world, are engineers— just as the Italians are musicians and the Germans metaphysicians— by right of birth. Nothing is more natural, therefore, than to perceive them applying their audacious ingenuity to the science of gunnery. Witness the marvels of Parrott, Dahlgren, and Rodman. The Armstrong, Palliser, and Beaulieu guns were compelled to bow before their transatlantic rivals.

Now when an American has an idea, he directly seeks a second American to share it. If there be three, they elect a president and two secretaries. Given four, they name a keeper of records, and the office is ready for work; five, they convene a general meeting, and the club is fully constituted. So things were managed in Baltimore. The inventor of a new cannon associated himself with the caster and the borer. Thus was formed the nucleus of the "Gun Club." In a single month after its formation it numbered 1,833 effective members and 30,565 corresponding members.

One condition was imposed as a *sine qua non* upon every candidate for admission into the association, and that was the condition of having designed, or (more or less) perfected a cannon; or, in default of a cannon, at least a firearm of some description. It may, however, be mentioned that mere inventors of revolvers, fire-shooting carbines, and similar small arms, met with little consideration. Artillerists always commanded the chief place of favor.

The estimation in which these gentlemen were held, according to one of the most scientific exponents of the Gun Club, was "proportional to the masses of their guns, and in the direct ratio of the square of the distances attained by their projectiles."

The Gun Club once founded, it is easy to conceive the result of the inventive genius of the Americans. Their military weapons attained colossal proportions, and their projectiles, exceeding the prescribed limits, unfortunately occasionally cut in two some unoffending pedestrians. These inventions, in fact, left far in the rear the timid instruments of European artillery.

It is but fair to add that these Yankees, brave as they have ever proved themselves to be, did not confine themselves to theories and formulae, but that they paid heavily, *in propria persona*, for their inventions. Among them were to be counted officers of all ranks, from lieutenants to generals; military men of every age, from those who were just making their *debut* in the profession of arms up to those who had grown old in the gun-carriage. Many had found their rest on the field of battle whose names figured in the "Book of Honor" of the Gun Club; and of those who made good their return the greater proportion bore the marks of their indisputable valor. Crutches, wooden legs, artificial arms, steel hooks, caoutchouc jaws, silver craniums, platinum noses, were all to be found in the collection; and it was calculated by the great statistician Pitcairn that throughout the Gun Club there was not quite one arm between four persons and two legs between six.

Nevertheless, these valiant artillerists took no particular account of these little facts, and felt justly proud when the despatches of a battle returned the number of victims at tenfold the quantity of projectiles expended.

One day, however— sad and melancholy day!— peace was signed between the survivors of the war; the thunder of the guns gradually ceased, the mortars were silent, the howitzers were muzzled for an indefinite period, the cannon, with muzzles depressed, were returned into the arsenal, the shot were repiled, all bloody reminiscences were effaced; the cotton-plants grew luxuriantly in the well-manured fields, all mourning garments were laid aside, together with grief; and the Gun Club was relegated to profound inactivity.

Some few of the more advanced and inveterate theorists set themselves again to work upon calculations regarding the laws of projectiles. They reverted invariably to gigantic shells and howitzers of unparalleled caliber. Still in default of practical experience what was the value of mere theories? Consequently, the clubrooms became deserted, the servants dozed in the antechambers, the newspapers grew mouldy on the tables, sounds of snoring came from dark corners, and the members of the Gun Club, erstwhile so noisy in their seances, were reduced to silence by this disastrous peace and gave themselves up wholly to dreams of a Platonic kind of artillery.

"This is horrible!" said Tom Hunter one evening, while rapidly carbonizing his wooden legs in the fireplace of the smoking-room; "nothing to do! nothing to look forward to! what a loathsome existence! When again shall the guns arouse us in the morning with their delightful reports?"

"Those days are gone by," said jolly Bilsby, trying to extend his missing arms. "It was delightful once upon a time! One invented a gun, and hardly was it cast, when one hastened to try it in the face of the enemy! Then one returned to camp with a word of encouragement from Sherman or a friendly shake of the hand from McClellan. But now the generals are gone back to their counters; and in place of projectiles, they despatch bales of cotton. By Jove, the future of gunnery in America is lost!"

"Ay! and no war in prospect!" continued the famous James T. Maston, scratching with his steel hook his gutta-percha cranium. "Not a cloud on the horizon! and that too at such a critical period in the progress of the science of artillery! Yes, gentlemen! I who address you have myself this very morning perfected a model (plan, section, elevation, etc.) of a mortar destined to change all the conditions of warfare!"

"No! is it possible?" replied Tom Hunter, his thoughts reverting involuntarily to a former invention of the Hon. J. T. Maston, by which, at its first trial, he had succeeded in killing three hundred and thirty-seven people.

"Fact!" replied he. "Still, what is the use of so many studies worked out, so many difficulties vanquished? It's mere waste of time! The New World seems to have made up its mind to live in peace; and our bellicose *Tribune* predicts some approaching catastrophes arising out of this scandalous increase of population."

"Nevertheless," replied Colonel Blomsberry, "they are always struggling in Europe to maintain the principle of nationalities."

"Well?"

"Well, there might be some field for enterprise down there; and if they would accept our services——"

"What are you dreaming of?" screamed Bilsby; "work at gunnery for the benefit of foreigners?"

"That would be better than doing nothing here," returned the colonel.

"Quite so," said J. T. Matson; "but still we need not dream of that expedient."

"And why not?" demanded the colonel.

"Because their ideas of progress in the Old World are contrary to our American habits of thought. Those fellows believe that one can't become a general without having served first as an ensign; which is as much as to say that one can't point a gun without having first cast it oneself!"

"Ridiculous!" replied Tom Hunter, whittling with his bowie-knife the arms of his easy chair; "but if that be the case there, all that is left for us is to plant tobacco and distill whale-oil."

"What!" roared J. T. Maston, "shall we not employ these remaining years of our life in perfecting firearms? Shall there never be a fresh opportunity of trying the ranges of projectiles? Shall the air never again be lighted with the glare of our guns? No international difficulty ever arise to enable us to declare war against some transatlantic power? Shall not the French sink one of our steamers, or the English, in defiance of the rights of nations, hang a few of our countrymen?"

"No such luck," replied Colonel Blomsberry; "nothing of the kind is likely to happen; and even if it did, wc should not profit by it. American susceptibility is fast declining, and we are all going to the dogs."

"It is too true," replied J. T. Maston, with fresh violence; "there are a thousand grounds for fighting, and yet we don't fight. We save up our arms and legs for the benefit of nations who don't know what to do with them! But stop— without going out of one's way to find a cause for war— did not North America once belong to the English?"

"Undoubtedly," replied Tom Hunter, stamping his crutch with fury.

"Well, then," replied J. T. Maston, "why should not England in her turn belong to the Americans?"

"It would be but just and fair," returned Colonel Blomsberry.

"Go and propose it to the President of the United States," cried
J. T. Maston, "and see how he will receive you."

"Bah!" growled Bilsby between the four teeth which the war had left him; "that will never do!"

"By Jove!" cried J. T. Maston, "he mustn't count on my vote at the next election!"

"Nor on ours," replied unanimously all the bellicose invalids.

"Meanwhile," replied J. T. Maston, "allow me to say that, if I cannot get an opportunity to try my new mortars on a real field of battle, I shall say good-by to the members of the Gun Club, and go and bury myself in the prairies of Arkansas!"

"In that case we will accompany you," cried the others.

Matters were in this unfortunate condition, and the club was threatened with approaching dissolution, when an unexpected circumstance occurred to prevent so deplorable a catastrophe.

On the morrow after this conversation every member of the association received a sealed circular couched in the following terms:

BALTIMORE, October 3. The president of the Gun Club has the honor to inform his colleagues that, at the meeting of the 5th instant, he will bring before them a communication of an extremely interesting nature. He requests, therefore, that they will make it convenient to attend in accordance with the present invitation. Very cordially, IMPEY BARBICANE, P.G.C.

CHAPTER II PRESIDENT BARBICANE'S COMMUNICATION

On the 5th of October, at eight p.m., a dense crowd pressed toward the saloons of the Gun Club at No. 21 Union Square. All the members of the association resident in Baltimore attended the invitation of their president. As regards the corresponding members, notices were delivered by hundreds throughout the streets of the city, and, large as was the great hall, it was quite inadequate to accommodate the crowd of *savants*. They overflowed into the adjoining rooms, down the narrow passages, into the outer courtyards. There they ran against the vulgar herd who pressed up to the doors, each struggling to reach the front ranks, all eager to learn the nature of the important communication of President Barbicane; all pushing, squeezing, crushing with that perfect freedom of action which is so peculiar to the masses when educated in ideas of "self-government."

On that evening a stranger who might have chanced to be in Baltimore could not have gained admission for love or money into the great hall. That was reserved exclusively for resident or corresponding members; no one else could possibly have obtained a place; and the city magnates, municipal councilors, and "select men" were compelled to mingle with the mere townspeople in order to catch stray bits of news from the interior.

Nevertheless the vast hall presented a curious spectacle. Its immense area was singularly adapted to the purpose. Lofty pillars formed of cannon, superposed upon huge mortars as a base, supported the fine ironwork of the arches, a perfect piece of cast-iron lacework. Trophies of blunderbuses, matchlocks, arquebuses, carbines, all kinds of firearms, ancient and modern, were picturesquely interlaced against the walls. The gas lit up in full glare myriads of revolvers grouped in the form of lustres, while groups of pistols, and candelabra formed of muskets bound together, completed this magnificent display of brilliance. Models of cannon, bronze castings, sights covered with dents, plates battered by the shots of the Gun Club, assortments of rammers and sponges, chaplets of shells, wreaths of projectiles, garlands of howitzers— in short, all the apparatus of the artillerist, enchanted the eye by this wonderful arrangement and induced a kind of belief that their real purpose was ornamental rather than deadly.

At the further end of the saloon the president, assisted by four secretaries, occupied a large platform. His chair, supported by a carved gun-carriage, was modeled upon the ponderous proportions of a 32-inch mortar. It was pointed at an angle of ninety degrees, and suspended upon truncheons, so that the president could balance himself upon it as upon a rocking-chair, a very agreeable fact in the very hot weather. Upon the table (a huge iron plate supported upon six carronades) stood an inkstand of exquisite elegance, made of a beautifully chased Spanish piece, and a sonnette, which, when required, could give forth a report equal to that of a revolver. During violent debates this novel kind of bell scarcely sufficed to drown the clamor of these excitable artillerists.

In front of the table benches arranged in zigzag form, like the circumvallations of a retrenchment, formed a succession of bastions and curtains set apart for the use of the members of the club; and on this especial evening one might say, "All the world was on the ramparts." The president was sufficiently well known, however, for all to be assured that he would not put his colleagues to discomfort without some very strong motive.

Impey Barbicane was a man of forty years of age, calm, cold, austere; of a singularly serious and self-contained demeanor, punctual as a chronometer, of imperturbable temper and immovable character; by no means chivalrous, yet adventurous withal, and always bringing practical ideas to bear upon the very rashest enterprises; an essentially New Englander, a Northern colonist, a descendant of the old anti-Stuart Roundheads, and the implacable enemy of the gentlemen of the South, those ancient cavaliers of the mother country. In a word, he was a Yankee to the backbone.

Barbicane had made a large fortune as a timber merchant. Being nominated director of artillery during the war, he proved himself fertile in invention. Bold in his conceptions, he contributed powerfully to the progress of that arm and gave an immense impetus to experimental researches.

He was personage of the middle height, having, by a rare exception in the Gun Club, all his limbs complete. His strongly marked features seemed drawn by square and rule; and if it be true that, in order to judge a man's character one must look at his profile, Barbicane, so examined, exhibited the most certain indications of energy, audacity, and *sang-froid.*

At this moment he was sitting in his armchair, silent, absorbed, lost in reflection, sheltered under his high-crowned hat— a kind of black cylinder which always seems firmly screwed upon the head of an American.

Just when the deep-toned clock in the great hall struck eight, Barbicane, as if he had been set in motion by a spring, raised himself up. A profound silence ensued, and the speaker, in a somewhat emphatic tone of voice, commenced as follows:

"My brave, colleagues, too long already a paralyzing peace has plunged the members of the Gun Club in deplorable inactivity. After a period of years full of incidents we have been compelled to abandon our labors, and to stop short on the road of progress. I do not hesitate to state, baldly, that any war which would recall us to arms would be welcome!" (Tremendous applause!) "But war, gentlemen, is impossible under existing circumstances; and, however we may desire it, many years may elapse before our cannon shall again thunder in the field of battle. We must make up our minds, then, to seek in another train of ideas some field for the activity which we all pine for."

The meeting felt that the president was now approaching the critical point, and redoubled their attention accordingly.

"For some months past, my brave colleagues," continued Barbicane, "I have been asking myself whether, while confining ourselves to our own particular objects, we could not enter upon some grand experiment worthy of the nineteenth century; and whether the progress of artillery science would not enable us to carry it out to a successful issue. I have been considering, working, calculating; and the result of my studies is the conviction that we are safe to succeed in an enterprise which to any other country would appear wholly impracticable. This project, the result of long elaboration, is the object of my present communication. It is worthy of yourselves, worthy of the antecedents of the Gun Club; and it cannot fail to make some noise in the world."

A thrill of excitement ran through the meeting.

CHAPTER II PRESIDENT BARBICANE'S COMMUNICATION

Barbicane, having by a rapid movement firmly fixed his hat upon his head, calmly continued his harangue:

"There is no one among you, my brave colleagues, who has not seen the Moon, or, at least, heard speak of it. Don't be surprised if I am about to discourse to you regarding the Queen of the Night. It is perhaps reserved for us to become the Columbuses of this unknown world. Only enter into my plans, and second me with all your power, and I will lead you to its conquest, and its name shall be added to those of the thirty-six states which compose this Great Union."

"Three cheers for the Moon!" roared the Gun Club, with one voice.

"The moon, gentlemen, has been carefully studied," continued Barbicane; "her mass, density, and weight; her constitution, motions, distance, as well as her place in the solar system, have all been exactly determined. Selenographic charts have been constructed with a perfection which equals, if it does not even surpass, that of our terrestrial maps. Photography has given us proofs of the incomparable beauty of our satellite; all is known regarding the moon which mathematical science, astronomy, geology, and optics can learn about her. But up to the present moment no direct communication has been established with her."

A violent movement of interest and surprise here greeted this remark of the speaker.

"Permit me," he continued, "to recount to you briefly how certain ardent spirits, starting on imaginary journeys, have penetrated the secrets of our satellite. In the seventeenth century a certain David Fabricius boasted of having seen with his own eyes the inhabitants of the moon. In 1649 a Frenchman, one Jean Baudoin, published a `Journey performed from the Earth to the Moon by Domingo Gonzalez,' a Spanish adventurer. At the same period Cyrano de Bergerac published that celebrated `Journeys in the Moon' which met with such success in France. Somewhat later another Frenchman, named Fontenelle, wrote `The Plurality of Worlds,' a *chef-d'oeuvre* of its time. About 1835 a small treatise, translated from the New York *American*, related how Sir John Herschel, having been despatched to the Cape of Good Hope for the purpose of making there some astronomical calculations, had, by means of a telescope brought to perfection by means of internal lighting, reduced the apparent distance of the moon to eighty yards! He then distinctly perceived caverns frequented by hippopotami, green mountains bordered by golden lacework, sheep with horns of ivory, a white species of deer and inhabitants with membranous wings, like bats. This *brochure*, the work of an American named Locke, had a great sale. But, to bring this rapid sketch to a close, I will only add that a certain Hans Pfaal, of Rotterdam, launching himself in a balloon filled with a gas extracted from nitrogen, thirty-seven times lighter than hydrogen, reached the moon after a passage of nineteen hours. This journey, like all previous ones, was purely imaginary; still, it was the work of a popular American author— I mean Edgar Poe!"

"Cheers for Edgar Poe!" roared the assemblage, electrified by their president's words.

"I have now enumerated," said Barbicane, "the experiments which I call purely paper ones, and wholly insufficient to establish serious relations with the Queen of the Night. Nevertheless, I am bound to add that some practical geniuses have attempted to establish actual communication with her. Thus, a few days ago, a German geometrician proposed to send a scientific expedition to the steppes of Siberia. There, on those vast plains, they were to describe enormous geometric figures, drawn in characters of reflecting luminosity, among which was the proposition regarding the `square of the hypothenuse,' commonly called the `Ass's Bridge' by the French. `Every intelligent being,' said the geometrician, `must understand the scientific meaning of that figure. The Selenites, do they exist, will respond by a similar figure; and, a communication being thus once established, it will be easy to form an alphabet which shall enable us to converse with the inhabitants of the moon.' So spoke the German geometrician; but his project was never put into practice, and up to the present day there is no bond in existence between the Earth and her satellite. It is reserved for the practical genius of Americans to establish a communication with the sidereal world. The means of arriving thither are simple, easy, certain, infallible— and that is the purpose of my present proposal."

A storm of acclamations greeted these words. There was not a single person in the whole audience who was not overcome, carried away, lifted out of himself by the speaker's words!

Long-continued applause resounded from all sides.

As soon as the excitement had partially subsided, Barbicane resumed his speech in a somewhat graver voice.

"You know," said he, "what progress artillery science has made during the last few years, and what a degree of perfection firearms of every kind have reached. Moreover, you are well aware that, in general terms, the resisting power of cannon and the expansive force of gunpowder are practically unlimited. Well! starting from this principle, I ask myself whether, supposing sufficient apparatus could be obtained constructed upon the conditions of ascertained resistance, it might not be possible to project a shot up to the moon?"

At these words a murmur of amazement escaped from a thousand panting chests; then succeeded a moment of perfect silence, resembling that profound stillness which precedes the bursting of a thunderstorm. In point of fact, a thunderstorm did peal forth, but it was the thunder of applause, or cries, and of uproar which made the very hall tremble. The president attempted to speak, but could not. It was fully ten minutes before he could make himself heard.

"Suffer me to finish," he calmly continued. "I have looked at the question in all its bearings, I have resolutely attacked it, and by incontrovertible calculations I find that a projectile endowed with an initial velocity of 12,000 yards per second, and aimed at the moon, must necessarily reach it. I have the honor, my brave colleagues, to propose a trial of this little experiment."

CHAPTER III EFFECT OF THE PRESIDENT'S COMMUNICATION

It is impossible to describe the effect produced by the last words of the honorable president— the cries, the shouts, the succession of roars, hurrahs, and all the varied vociferations which the American language is capable of supplying. It was a scene of indescribable confusion and uproar. They shouted, they clapped, they stamped on the floor of the hall. All the weapons in the museum discharged at once could not have more violently set in motion the waves of sound. One need not be surprised at this. There are some cannoneers nearly as noisy as their own guns.

Barbicane remained calm in the midst of this enthusiastic clamor; perhaps he was desirous of addressing a few more words to his colleagues, for by his gestures he demanded silence, and his powerful alarum was worn out by its violent reports. No attention, however, was paid to his request. He was presently torn from his seat and passed from the hands of his faithful colleagues into the arms of a no less excited crowd.

Nothing can astound an American. It has often been asserted that the word "impossible" in not a French one. People have evidently been deceived by the dictionary. In America, all is easy, all is simple; and as for mechanical difficulties, they are overcome before they arise. Between Barbicane's proposition and its realization no true Yankee would have allowed even the semblance of a difficulty to be possible. A thing with them is no sooner said than done.

The triumphal progress of the president continued throughout the evening. It was a regular torchlight procession. Irish, Germans, French, Scotch, all the heterogeneous units which make up the population of Maryland shouted in their respective vernaculars; and the "vivas," "hurrahs," and "bravos" were intermingled in inexpressible enthusiasm.

Just at this crisis, as though she comprehended all this agitation regarding herself, the moon shone forth with serene splendor, eclipsing by her intense illumination all the surrounding lights. The Yankees all turned their gaze toward her resplendent orb, kissed their hands, called her by all kinds of endearing names. Between eight o'clock and midnight one optician in Jones'-Fall Street made his fortune by the sale of opera-glasses.

Midnight arrived, and the enthusiasm showed no signs of diminution. It spread equally among all classes of citizens— men of science, shopkeepers, merchants, porters, chairmen, as well as "greenhorns," were stirred in their innermost fibres. A national enterprise was at stake. The whole city, high and low, the quays bordering the Patapsco, the ships lying in the basins, disgorged a crowd drunk with joy, gin, and whisky. Every one chattered, argued, discussed, disputed, applauded, from the gentleman lounging upon the barroom settee with his tumbler of sherry-cobbler before him down to the waterman who got drunk upon his "knock-me-down" in the dingy taverns of Fell Point.

About two A.M., however, the excitement began to subside. President Barbicane reached his house, bruised, crushed, and squeezed almost to a mummy. Hercules could not have resisted a similar outbreak of enthusiasm. The crowd gradually deserted the squares and streets. The four railways from Philadelphia and Washington, Harrisburg and Wheeling, which converge at Baltimore, whirled away the heterogeneous population to the four corners of the United States, and the city subsided into comparative tranquility.

On the following day, thanks to the telegraphic wires, five hundred newspapers and journals, daily, weekly, monthly, or bi-monthly, all took up the question. They examined it under all its different aspects, physical, meteorological, economical, or moral, up to its bearings on politics or civilization. They debated whether the moon was a finished world, or whether it was destined to undergo any further transformation. Did it resemble the earth at the period when the latter was destitute as yet of an atmosphere? What kind of spectacle would its hidden hemisphere present to our terrestrial spheroid? Granting that the question at present was simply that of sending a projectile up to the moon, every one must see that that involved the commencement of a series of experiments. All must hope that some day America would penetrate the deepest secrets of that mysterious orb; and some even seemed to fear lest its conquest should not sensibly derange the equilibrium of Europe.

The project once under discussion, not a single paragraph suggested a doubt of its realization. All the papers, pamphlets, reports— all the journals published by the scientific, literary, and religious societies enlarged upon its advantages; and the Society of Natural History of Boston, the Society of Science and Art of Albany, the Geographical and Statistical Society of New York, the Philosophical Society of Philadelphia, and the Smithsonian of Washington sent innumerable letters of congratulation to the Gun Club, together with offers of immediate assistance and money.

From that day forward Impey Barbicane became one of the greatest citizens of the United States, a kind of Washington of science. A single trait of feeling, taken from many others, will serve to show the point which this homage of a whole people to a single individual attained.

Some few days after this memorable meeting of the Gun Club, the manager of an English company announced, at the Baltimore theatre, the production of "Much ado about Nothing." But the populace, seeing in that title an allusion damaging to Barbicane's project, broke into the auditorium, smashed the benches, and compelled the unlucky director to alter his playbill. Being a sensible man, he bowed to the public will and replaced the offending comedy by "As you like it"; and for many weeks he realized fabulous profits.

CHAPTER IV REPLY FROM THE OBSERVATORY OF CAMBRIDGE

Barbicane, however, lost not one moment amid all the enthusiasm of which he had become the object. His first care was to reassemble his colleagues in the board-room of the Gun Club. There, after some discussion, it was agreed to consult the astronomers regarding the astronomical part of the enterprise. Their reply once ascertained, they could then discuss the mechanical means, and nothing should be wanting to ensure the success of this great experiment.

A note couched in precise terms, containing special interrogatories, was then drawn up and addressed to the Observatory of Cambridge in Massachusetts. This city, where the first university of the United States was founded, is justly celebrated for its astronomical staff. There are to be found assembled all the most eminent men of science. Here is to be seen at work that powerful telescope which enabled Bond to resolve the nebula of Andromeda, and Clarke to discover the satellite of Sirius. This celebrated institution fully justified on all points the confidence reposed in it by the Gun Club. So, after two days, the reply so impatiently awaited was placed in the hands of President Barbicane.

It was couched in the following terms:

The Director of the Cambridge Observatory to the President of the Gun Club at Baltimore.

CAMBRIDGE, October 7. On the receipt of your favor of the 6th instant, addressed to the Observatory of Cambridge in the name of the members of the Baltimore Gun Club, our staff was immediately called together, and it was judged expedient to reply as follows:

The questions which have been proposed to it are these—

"1. Is it possible to transmit a projectile up to the moon?

"2. What is the exact distance which separates the earth from its satellite?

"3. What will be the period of transit of the projectile when endowed with sufficient initial velocity? and, consequently, at what moment ought it to be discharged in order that it may touch the moon at a particular point?

"4. At what precise moment will the moon present herself in the most favorable position to be reached by the projectile?

"5. What point in the heavens ought the cannon to be aimed at which is intended to discharge the projectile?

"6. What place will the moon occupy in the heavens at the moment of the projectile's departure?"

Regarding the *first* question, "Is it possible to transmit a projectile up to the moon?"

Answer.— Yes; provided it possess an initial velocity of 1,200 yards per second; calculations prove that to be sufficient. In proportion as we recede from the earth the action of gravitation diminishes in the inverse ratio of the square of the distance; that is to say, *at three times a given distance the action is nine times less.* Consequently, the weight of a shot will decrease, and will become reduced to *zero* at the instant that the attraction of the moon exactly counterpoises that of the earth; that is to say at 47/52 of its passage. At that instant the projectile will have no weight whatever; and, if it passes that point, it will fall into the moon by the sole effect of the lunar attraction. The *theoretical possibility* of the experiment is therefore absolutely demonstrated; its *success* must depend upon the power of the engine employed.

As to the *second* question, "What is the exact distance which separates the earth from its satellite?"

Answer.— The moon does not describe a *circle* round the earth, but rather an *ellipse*, of which our earth occupies one of the *foci*; the consequence, therefore, is, that at certain times it approaches nearer to, and at others it recedes farther from, the earth; in astronomical language, it is at one time in *apogee*, at another in *perigee.* Now the difference between its greatest and its least distance is too considerable to be left out of consideration. In point of fact, in its apogee the moon is 247,552 miles, and in its perigee, 218,657 miles only distant; a fact which makes a difference of 28,895 miles, or more than one-ninth of the entire distance. The perigee distance, therefore, is that which ought to serve as the basis of all calculations.

To the *third* question.

Answer.— If the shot should preserve continuously its initial velocity of 12,000 yards per second, it would require little more than nine hours to reach its destination; but, inasmuch as that initial velocity will be continually decreasing, it will occupy 300,000 seconds, that is 83hrs. 20m. in reaching the point where the attraction of the earth and moon will be *in equilibrio.* From this point it will fall into the moon in 50,000 seconds, or 13hrs. 53m. 20sec. It will be desirable, therefore, to discharge it 97hrs. 13m. 20sec. before the arrival of the moon at the point aimed at.

Regarding question *four*, "At what precise moment will the moon present herself in the most favorable position, etc.?"

Answer.— After what has been said above, it will be necessary, first of all, to choose the period when the moon will be in perigee, and *also* the moment when she will be crossing the zenith, which latter event will further diminish the entire distance by a length equal to the radius of the earth, *i.e.* 3,919 miles; the result of which will be that the final passage remaining to be accomplished will be 214,976 miles. But although the moon passes her perigee every month, she does not reach the zenith always *at exactly the same moment.* She does not appear under these two conditions simultaneously, except at long intervals of time. It will be necessary, therefore, to wait for the moment when her passage in perigee shall coincide with that in the zenith. Now, by a fortunate circumstance, on the 4th of December in the ensuing year the moon *will* present these two conditions. At midnight she will be in perigee, that is, at her shortest distance from the earth, and at the same moment she will be crossing the zenith.

On the *fifth* question, "At what point in the heavens ought the cannon to be aimed?"

Answer.— The preceding remarks being admitted, the cannon ought to be pointed to the zenith of the place. Its fire, therefore, will be perpendicular to the plane of the horizon; and the projectile will soonest pass beyond the range of the terrestrial attraction. But, in order that the moon should reach the zenith of a given place, it is necessary that the place should not exceed in latitude the declination of the luminary; in other words, it must be comprised within the degrees 0 ° and 28 ° of lat. N. or S. In every other spot the fire must necessarily be oblique, which would seriously militate against the success of the experiment.

As to the *sixth* question, "What place will the moon occupy in the heavens at the moment of the projectile's departure?"

Answer.— At the moment when the projectile shall be discharged into space, the moon, which travels daily forward 13 ° 10' 35", will be distant from the zenith point by four times that quantity, *i.e.* by 52 ° 41' 20", a space which corresponds to the path which she will describe during the entire journey of the projectile. But, inasmuch as it is equally necessary to take into account the deviation which the rotary motion of the earth will impart to the shot, and as the shot cannot reach the moon until after a deviation equal to 16 radii of the earth, which, calculated upon the moon's orbit, are equal to about eleven degrees, it becomes necessary to add these eleven degrees to those which express the retardation of the moon just mentioned: that is to say, in round numbers, about sixty-four degrees. Consequently, at the moment of firing the visual radius applied to the moon will describe, with the vertical line of the place, an angle of sixty-four degrees.

These are our answers to the questions proposed to the

Observatory of Cambridge by the members of the Gun Club:

To sum up—

1st. The cannon ought to be planted in a country situated between 0 ° and 28 ° of N. or S. lat.

2nd. It ought to be pointed directly toward the zenith of the place.

3rd. The projectile ought to be propelled with an initial velocity of 12,000 yards per second.

4th. It ought to be discharged at 10hrs. 46m. 40sec. of the 1st of December of the ensuing year.

5th. It will meet the moon four days after its discharge, precisely at midnight on the 4th of December, at the moment of its transit across the zenith.

The members of the Gun Club ought, therefore, without delay, to commence the works necessary for such an experiment, and to be prepared to set to work at the moment determined upon; for, if they should suffer this 4th of December to go by, they will not find the moon again under the same conditions of perigee and of zenith until eighteen years and eleven days afterward.

The staff of the Cambridge Observatory place themselves entirely at their disposal in respect of all questions of theoretical astronomy; and herewith add their congratulations to those of all the rest of America.

For the Astronomical Staff,

J. M. BELFAST, *Director of the Observatory of Cambridge.*

CHAPTER V THE ROMANCE OF THE MOON

An observer endued with an infinite range of vision, and placed in that unknown center around which the entire world revolves, might have beheld myriads of atoms filling all space during the chaotic epoch of the universe. Little by little, as ages went on, a change took place; a general law of attraction manifested itself, to which the hitherto errant atoms became obedient: these atoms combined together chemically according to their affinities, formed themselves into molecules, and composed those nebulous masses with which the depths of the heavens are strewed. These masses became immediately endued with a rotary motion around their own central point. This center, formed of indefinite molecules, began to revolve around its own axis during its gradual condensation; then, following the immutable laws of mechanics, in proportion as its bulk diminished by condensation, its rotary motion became accelerated, and these two effects continuing, the result was the formation of one principal star, the center of the nebulous mass.

By attentively watching, the observer would then have perceived the other molecules of the mass, following the example of this central star, become likewise condensed by gradually accelerated rotation, and gravitating round it in the shape of innumerable stars. Thus was formed the *Nebulae*, of which astronomers have reckoned up nearly 5,000.

Among these 5,000 nebulae there is one which has received the name of the Milky Way, and which contains eighteen millions of stars, each of which has become the center of a solar world.

If the observer had then specially directed his attention to one of the more humble and less brilliant of these stellar bodies, a star of the fourth class, that which is arrogantly called the Sun, all the phenomena to which the formation of the Universe is to be ascribed would have been successively fulfilled before his eyes. In fact, he would have perceived this sun, as yet in the gaseous state, and composed of moving molecules, revolving round its axis in order to accomplish its work of concentration. This motion, faithful to the laws of mechanics, would have been accelerated with the diminution of its volume; and a moment would have arrived when the centrifugal force would have overpowered the centripetal, which causes the molecules all to tend toward the center.

Another phenomenon would now have passed before the observer's eye, and the molecules situated on the plane of the equator, escaping like a stone from a sling of which the cord had suddenly snapped, would have formed around the sun sundry concentric rings resembling that of Saturn. In their turn, again, these rings of cosmical matter, excited by a rotary motion about the central mass, would have been broken up and decomposed into secondary nebulosities, that is to say, into planets. Similarly he would have observed these planets throw off one or more rings each, which became the origin of the secondary bodies which we call satellites.

Thus, then, advancing from atom to molecule, from molecule to nebulous mass, from that to principal star, from star to sun, from sun to planet, and hence to satellite, we have the whole series of transformations undergone by the heavenly bodies during the first days of the world.

Now, of those attendant bodies which the sun maintains in their elliptical orbits by the great law of gravitation, some few in turn possess satellites. Uranus has eight, Saturn eight, Jupiter four, Neptune possibly three, and the Earth one. This last, one of the least important of the entire solar system, we call the Moon; and it is she whom the daring genius of the Americans professed their intention of conquering.

The moon, by her comparative proximity, and the constantly varying appearances produced by her several phases, has always occupied a considerable share of the attention of the inhabitants of the earth.

From the time of Thales of Miletus, in the fifth century B.C., down to that of Copernicus in the fifteenth and Tycho Brahe in the sixteenth century A.D., observations have been from time to time carried on with more or less correctness, until in the present day the altitudes of the lunar mountains have been determined with exactitude. Galileo explained the phenomena of the lunar light produced during certain of her phases by the existence of mountains, to which he assigned a mean altitude of 27,000 feet. After him Hevelius, an astronomer of Dantzic, reduced the highest elevations to 15,000 feet; but the calculations of Riccioli brought them up again to 21,000 feet.

At the close of the eighteenth century Herschel, armed with a powerful telescope, considerably reduced the preceding measurements. He assigned a height of 11,400 feet to the maximum elevations, and reduced the mean of the different altitudes to little more than 2,400 feet. But Herschel's calculations were in their turn corrected by the observations of Halley, Nasmyth, Bianchini, Gruithuysen, and others; but it was reserved for the labors of Boeer and Maedler finally to solve the question. They succeeded in measuring 1,905 different elevations, of which six exceed 15,000 feet, and twenty-two exceed 14,400 feet. The highest summit of all towers to a height of 22,606 feet above the surface of the lunar disc. At the same period the examination of the moon was completed. She appeared completely riddled with craters, and her essentially volcanic character was apparent at each observation. By the absence of refraction in the rays of the planets occulted by her we conclude that she is absolutely devoid of an atmosphere. The absence of air entails the absence of water. It became, therefore, manifest that the Selenites, to support life under such conditions, must possess a special organization of their own, must differ remarkably from the inhabitants of the earth.

At length, thanks to modern art, instruments of still higher perfection searched the moon without intermission, not leaving a single point of her surface unexplored; and notwithstanding that her diameter measures 2,150 miles, her surface equals the one-fifteenth part of that of our globe, and her bulk the one-forty-ninth part of that of the terrestrial spheroid— not one of her secrets was able to escape the eyes of the astronomers; and these skillful men of science carried to an even greater degree their prodigious observations.

Thus they remarked that, during full moon, the disc appeared scored in certain parts with white lines; and, during the phases, with black. On prosecuting the study of these with still greater precision, they succeeded in obtaining an exact account of the nature of these lines. They were long and narrow furrows sunk between parallel ridges, bordering generally upon the edges of the craters. Their length varied between ten and 100 miles, and their width was about 1,600 yards. Astronomers called them chasms, but they could not get any further. Whether these chasms were the dried-up beds of ancient rivers or not they were unable thoroughly to ascertain.

The Americans, among others, hoped one day or other to determine this geological question. They also undertook to examine the true nature of that system of parallel ramparts discovered on the moon's surface by Gruithuysen, a learned professor of Munich, who considered them to be "a system of fortifications thrown up by the Selenitic engineers." These two points, yet obscure, as well as others, no doubt, could not be definitely settled except by direct communication with the moon.

Regarding the degree of intensity of its light, there was nothing more to learn on this point. It was known that it is 300,000 times weaker than that of the sun, and that its heat has no appreciable effect upon the thermometer. As to the phenomenon known as the "ashy light," it is explained naturally by the effect of the transmission of the solar rays from the earth to the moon, which give the appearance of completeness to the lunar disc, while it presents itself under the crescent form during its first and last phases.

Such was the state of knowledge acquired regarding the earth's satellite, which the Gun Club undertook to perfect in all its aspects, cosmographic, geological, political, and moral.

CHAPTER VI PERMISSIVE LIMITS OF IGNORANCE AND BELIEF IN THE UNITED STATES

The immediate result of Barbicane's proposition was to place upon the orders of the day all the astronomical facts relative to the Queen of the Night. Everybody set to work to study assiduously. One would have thought that the moon had just appeared for the first time, and that no one had ever before caught a glimpse of her in the heavens. The papers revived all the old anecdotes in which the "sun of the wolves" played a part; they recalled the influences which the ignorance of past ages ascribed to her; in short, all America was seized with selenomania, or had become moon-mad.

The scientific journals, for their part, dealt more especially with the questions which touched upon the enterprise of the Gun Club. The letter of the Observatory of Cambridge was published by them, and commented upon with unreserved approval.

Until that time most people had been ignorant of the mode in which the distance which separates the moon from the earth is calculated. They took advantage of this fact to explain to them that this distance was obtained by measuring the parallax of the moon. The term parallax proving "caviare to the general," they further explained that it meant the angle formed by the inclination of two straight lines drawn from either extremity of the earth's radius to the moon. On doubts being expressed as to the correctness of this method, they immediately proved that not only was the mean distance 234,347 miles, but that astronomers could not possibly be in error in their estimate by more than seventy miles either way.

To those who were not familiar with the motions of the moon, they demonstrated that she possesses two distinct motions, the first being that of rotation upon her axis, the second being that of revolution round the earth, accomplishing both together in an equal period of time, that is to say, in twenty-seven and one-third days.

The motion of rotation is that which produces day and night on the surface of the moon; save that there is only one day and one night in the lunar month, each lasting three hundred and fifty-four and one-third hours. But, happily for her, the face turned toward the terrestrial globe is illuminated by it with an intensity equal to that of fourteen moons. As to the other face, always invisible to us, it has of necessity three hundred and fifty-four hours of absolute night, tempered only by that "pale glimmer which falls upon it from the stars."

Some well-intentioned, but rather obstinate persons, could not at first comprehend how, if the moon displays invariably the same face to the earth during her revolution, she can describe one turn round herself. To such they answered, "Go into your dining-room, and walk round the table in such a way as to always keep your face turned toward the center; by the time you will have achieved one complete round you will have completed one turn around yourself, since your eye will have traversed successively every point of the room. Well, then, the room is the heavens, the table is the earth, and the moon is yourself." And they would go away delighted.

So, then the moon displays invariably the same face to the earth; nevertheless, to be quite exact, it is necessary to add that, in consequence of certain fluctuations of north and south, and of west and east, termed her libration, she permits rather more than half, that is to say, five-sevenths, to be seen.

As soon as the ignoramuses came to understand as much as the director of the observatory himself knew, they began to worry themselves regarding her revolution round the earth, whereupon twenty scientific reviews immediately came to the rescue. They pointed out to them that the firmament, with its infinitude of stars, may be considered as one vast dial-plate, upon which the moon travels, indicating the true time to all the inhabitants of the earth; that it is during this movement that the Queen of Night exhibits her different phases; that the moon is *full* when she is in *opposition* with the sun, that is when the three bodies are on the same straight line, the earth occupying the center; that she is *new* when she is in *conjunction* with the sun, that is, when she is between it and the earth; and, lastly that she is in her *first* or *last* quarter, when she makes with the sun and the earth an angle of which she herself occupies the apex.

Regarding the altitude which the moon attains above the horizon, the letter of the Cambridge Observatory had said all that was to be said in this respect. Every one knew that this altitude varies according to the latitude of the observer. But the only zones of the globe in which the moon passes the zenith, that is, the point directly over the head of the spectator, are of necessity comprised between the twenty-eighth parallels and the equator. Hence the importance of the advice to try the experiment upon some point of that part of the globe, in order that the projectile might be discharged perpendicularly, and so the soonest escape the action of gravitation. This was an essential condition to the success of the enterprise, and continued actively to engage the public attention.

Regarding the path described by the moon in her revolution round the earth, the Cambridge Observatory had demonstrated that this path is a re-entering curve, not a perfect circle, but an ellipse, of which the earth occupies one of the *foci*. It was also well understood that it is farthest removed from the earth during its *apogee*, and approaches most nearly to it at its *perigee*.

Such was then the extent of knowledge possessed by every American on the subject, and of which no one could decently profess ignorance. Still, while these principles were being rapidly disseminated many errors and illusory fears proved less easy to eradicate.

For instance, some worthy persons maintained that the moon was an ancient comet which, in describing its elongated orbit round the sun, happened to pass near the earth, and became confined within her circle of attraction. These drawing-room astronomers professed to explain the charred aspect of the moon— a disaster which they attributed to the intensity of the solar heat; only, on being reminded that comets have an atmosphere, and that the moon has little or none, they were fairly at a loss for a reply.

Others again, belonging to the doubting class, expressed certain fears as to the position of the moon. They had heard it said that, according to observations made in the time of the Caliphs, her revolution had become accelerated in a certain degree. Hence they concluded, logically enough, that an acceleration of motion ought to be accompanied by a corresponding diminution in the distance separating the two bodies; and that, supposing the double effect to be continued to infinity, the moon would end by one day falling into the earth. However, they became reassured as to the fate of future generations on being apprised that, according to the calculations of Laplace, this acceleration of motion is confined within very restricted limits, and that a proportional diminution of speed will be certain to succeed it. So, then, the stability of the solar system would not be deranged in ages to come.

There remains but the third class, the superstitious. These worthies were not content merely to rest in ignorance; they must know all about things which had no existence whatever, and as to the moon, they had long known all about her. One set regarded her disc as a polished mirror, by means of which people could see each other from different points of the earth and interchange their thoughts. Another set pretended that out of one thousand new moons that had been observed, nine hundred and fifty had been attended with remarkable disturbances, such as cataclysms, revolutions, earthquakes, the deluge, etc. Then they believed in some mysterious influence exercised by her over human destinies— that every Selenite was attached to some inhabitant of the earth by a tie of sympathy; they maintained that the entire vital system is subject to her control, etc. But in time the majority renounced these vulgar errors, and espoused the true side of the question. As for the Yankees, they had no other ambition than to take possession of this new continent of the sky, and to plant upon the summit of its highest elevation the star- spangled banner of the United States of America.

CHAPTER VII THE HYMN OF THE CANNON-BALL

The Observatory of Cambridge in its memorable letter had treated the question from a purely astronomical point of view. The mechanical part still remained.

President Barbicane had, without loss of time, nominated a working committee of the Gun Club. The duty of this committee was to resolve the three grand questions of the cannon, the projectile, and the powder. It was composed of four members of great technical knowledge, Barbicane (with a casting vote in case of equality), General Morgan, Major Elphinstone, and J. T. Maston, to whom were confided the functions of secretary. On the 8th of October the committee met at the house of President Barbicane, 3 Republican Street. The meeting was opened by the president himself.

"Gentlemen," said he, "we have to resolve one of the most important problems in the whole of the noble science of gunnery. It might appear, perhaps, the most logical course to devote our first meeting to the discussion of the engine to be employed. Nevertheless, after mature consideration, it has appeared to me that the question of the projectile must take precedence of that of the cannon, and that the dimensions of the latter must necessarily depend on those of the former."

"Suffer me to say a word," here broke in J. T. Maston. Permission having been granted, "Gentlemen," said he with an inspired accent, "our president is right in placing the question of the projectile above all others. The ball we are about to discharge at the moon is our ambassador to her, and I wish to consider it from a moral point of view. The cannon-ball, gentlemen, to my mind, is the most magnificent manifestation of human power. If Providence has created the stars and the planets, man has called the cannon-ball into existence. Let Providence claim the swiftness of electricity and of light, of the stars, the comets, and the planets, of wind and sound— we claim to have invented the swiftness of the cannon-ball, a hundred times superior to that of the swiftest horses or railway train. How glorious will be the moment when, infinitely exceeding all hitherto attained velocities, we shall launch our new projectile with the rapidity of seven miles a second! Shall it not, gentlemen— shall it not be received up there with the honors due to a terrestrial ambassador?"

Overcome with emotion the orator sat down and applied himself to a huge plate of sandwiches before him.

"And now," said Barbicane, "let us quit the domain of poetry and come direct to the question."

"By all means," replied the members, each with his mouth full of sandwich.

"The problem before us," continued the president, "is how to

communicate to a projectile a velocity of 12,000 yards per second.

Let us at present examine the velocities hitherto attained.

General Morgan will be able to enlighten us on this point."

"And the more easily," replied the general, "that during the war I was a member of the committee of experiments. I may say, then, that the 100-pounder Dahlgrens, which carried a distance of 5,000 yards, impressed upon their projectile an initial velocity of 500 yards a second. The Rodman Columbiad threw a shot weighing half a ton a distance of six miles, with a velocity of 800 yards per second— a result which Armstrong and Palisser have never obtained in England."

"This," replied Barbicane, "is, I believe, the maximum velocity ever attained?"

"It is so," replied the general.

"Ah!" groaned J. T. Maston, "if my mortar had not burst——"

"Yes," quietly replied Barbicane, "but it did burst. We must take, then, for our starting point, this velocity of 800 yards. We must increase it twenty-fold. Now, reserving for another discussion the means of producing this velocity, I will call your attention to the dimensions which it will be proper to assign to the shot. You understand that we have nothing to do here with projectiles weighing at most but half a ton."

"Why not?" demanded the major.

"Because the shot," quickly replied J. T. Maston, "must be big enough to attract the attention of the inhabitants of the moon, if there are any?"

"Yes," replied Barbicane, "and for another reason more important still."

"What mean you?" asked the major.

"I mean that it is not enough to discharge a projectile, and then take no further notice of it; we must follow it throughout its course, up to the moment when it shall reach its goal."

"What?" shouted the general and the major in great surprise.

"Undoubtedly," replied Barbicane composedly, "or our experiment would produce no result."

"But then," replied the major, "you will have to give this projectile enormous dimensions."

"No! Be so good as to listen. You know that optical instruments have acquired great perfection; with certain instruments we have succeeded in obtaining enlargements of 6,000 times and reducing the moon to within forty miles' distance. Now, at this distance, any objects sixty feet square would be perfectly visible.

"If, then, the penetrative power of telescopes has not been further increased, it is because that power detracts from their light; and the moon, which is but a reflecting mirror, does not give back sufficient light to enable us to perceive objects of lesser magnitude."

"Well, then, what do you propose to do?" asked the general.

"Would you give your projectile a diameter of sixty feet?"

"Not so."

"Do you intend, then, to increase the luminous power of the moon?"

"Exactly so. If I can succeed in diminishing the density of the atmosphere through which the moon's light has to travel I shall have rendered her light more intense. To effect that object it will be enough to establish a telescope on some elevated mountain. That is what we will do."

"I give it up," answered the major. "You have such a way of simplifying things. And what enlargement do you expect to obtain in this way?"

"One of 48,000 times, which should bring the moon within an apparent distance of five miles; and, in order to be visible, objects need not have a diameter of more than nine feet."

"So, then," cried J. T. Maston, "our projectile need not be more than nine feet in diameter."

"Let me observe, however," interrupted Major Elphinstone, "this will involve a weight such as——"

"My dear major," replied Barbicane, "before discussing its weight permit me to enumerate some of the marvels which our ancestors have achieved in this respect. I don't mean to pretend that the science of gunnery has not advanced, but it is as well to bear in mind that during the middle ages they obtained results more surprising, I will venture to say, than ours. For instance, during the siege of Constantinople by Mahomet II., in 1453, stone shot of 1,900 pounds weight were employed. At Malta, in the time of the knights, there was a gun of the fortress of St. Elmo which threw a projectile weighing 2,500 pounds. And, now, what is the extent of what we have seen ourselves? Armstrong guns discharging shot of 500 pounds, and the Rodman guns projectiles of half a ton! It seems, then, that if projectiles have gained in range, they have lost far more in weight. Now, if we turn our efforts in that direction, we ought to arrive, with the progress on science, at ten times the weight of the shot of Mahomet II. and the Knights of Malta."

"Clearly," replied the major; "but what metal do you calculate upon employing?"

"Simply cast iron," said General Morgan.

"But," interrupted the major, "since the weight of a shot is proportionate to its volume, an iron ball of nine feet in diameter would be of tremendous weight."

"Yes, if it were solid, not if it were hollow."

"Hollow? then it would be a shell?"

"Yes, a shell," replied Barbicane; "decidely it must be. A solid shot of 108 inches would weigh more than 200,000 pounds, a weight evidently far too great. Still, as we must reserve a certain stability for our projectile, I propose to give it a weight of 20,000 pounds."

"What, then, will be the thickness of the sides?" asked the major.

"If we follow the usual proportion," replied Morgan, "a diameter of 108 inches would require sides of two feet thickness, or less."

"That would be too much," replied Barbicane; "for you will observe that the question is not that of a shot intended to pierce an iron plate; it will suffice to give it sides strong enough to resist the pressure of the gas. The problem, therefore, is this— What thickness ought a cast-iron shell to have in order not to weight more than 20,000 pounds? Our clever secretary will soon enlighten us upon this point."

"Nothing easier." replied the worthy secretary of the committee; and, rapidly tracing a few algebraical formulae upon paper, among which n^2 and x^2 frequently appeared, he presently said:

"The sides will require a thickness of less than two inches."

"Will that be enough?" asked the major doubtfully.

"Clearly not!" replied the president.

"What is to be done, then?" said Elphinstone, with a puzzled air.

"Employ another metal instead of iron."

"Copper?" said Morgan.

"No! that would be too heavy. I have better than that to offer."

"What then?" asked the major.

"Aluminum!" replied Barbicane.

"Aluminum?" cried his three colleagues in chorus.

"Unquestionably, my friends. This valuable metal possesses the whiteness of silver, the indestructibility of gold, the tenacity of iron, the fusibility of copper, the lightness of glass. It is easily wrought, is very widely distributed, forming the base of most of the rocks, is three times lighter than iron, and seems to have been created for the express purpose of furnishing us with the material for our projectile."

"But, my dear president," said the major, "is not the cost price of aluminum extremely high?"

"It was so at its first discovery, but it has fallen now to nine dollars a pound."

"But still, nine dollars a pound!" replied the major, who was not willing readily to give in; "even that is an enormous price."

"Undoubtedly, my dear major; but not beyond our reach."

"What will the projectile weigh then?" asked Morgan.

"Here is the result of my calculations," replied Barbicane. "A shot of 108 inches in diameter, and twelve inches in thickness, would weigh, in cast-iron, 67,440 pounds; cast in aluminum, its weight will be reduced to 19,250 pounds."

"Capital!" cried the major; "but do you know that, at nine dollars a pound, this projectile will cost——"

"One hundred and seventy-three thousand and fifty dollars ($173,050). I know it quite well. But fear not, my friends; the money will not be wanting for our enterprise. I will answer for it. Now what say you to aluminum, gentlemen?"

"Adopted!" replied the three members of the committee. So ended the first meeting. The question of the projectile was definitely settled.

CHAPTER VII HISTORY OF THE CANNON

The resolutions passed at the last meeting produced a great effect out of doors. Timid people took fright at the idea of a shot weighing 20,000 pounds being launched into space; they asked what cannon could ever transmit a sufficient velocity to such a mighty mass. The minutes of the second meeting were destined triumphantly to answer such questions. The following evening the discussion was renewed.

"My dear colleagues," said Barbicane, without further preamble, "the subject now before us is the construction of the engine, its length, its composition, and its weight. It is probable that we shall end by giving it gigantic dimensions; but however great may be the difficulties in the way, our mechanical genius will readily surmount them. Be good enough, then, to give me your attention, and do not hesitate to make objections at the close. I have no fear of them. The problem before us is how to communicate an initial force of 12,000 yards per second to a shell of 108 inches in diameter, weighing 20,000 pounds. Now when a projectile is launched into space, what happens to it? It is acted upon by three independent forces: the resistance of the air, the attraction of the earth, and the force of impulsion with which it is endowed. Let us examine these three forces. The resistance of the air is of little importance. The atmosphere of the earth does not exceed forty miles. Now, with the given rapidity, the projectile will have traversed this in five seconds, and the period is too brief for the resistance of the medium to be regarded otherwise than as insignificant. Proceeding, then, to the attraction of the earth, that is, the weight of the shell, we know that this weight will diminish in the inverse ratio of the square of the distance. When a body left to itself falls to the surface of the earth, it falls five feet in the first second; and if the same body were removed 257,542 miles further off, in other words, to the distance of the moon, its fall would be reduced to about half a line in the first second. That is almost equivalent to a state of perfect rest. Our business, then, is to overcome progressively this action of gravitation. The mode of accomplishing that is by the force of impulsion."

"There's the difficulty," broke in the major.

"True," replied the president; "but we will overcome that, for the force of impulsion will depend on the length of the engine and the powder employed, the latter being limited only by the resisting power of the former. Our business, then, to-day is with the dimensions of the cannon."

"Now, up to the present time," said Barbicane, "our longest guns have not exceeded twenty-five feet in length. We shall therefore astonish the world by the dimensions we shall be obliged to adopt. It must evidently be, then, a gun of great range, since the length of the piece will increase the detention of the gas accumulated behind the projectile; but there is no advantage in passing certain limits."

"Quite so," said the major. "What is the rule in such a case?"

"Ordinarily the length of a gun is twenty to twenty-five times the diameter of the shot, and its weight two hundred and thirty-five to two hundred and forty times that of the shot."

"That is not enough," cried J. T. Maston impetuously.

"I agree with you, my good friend; and, in fact, following this proportion for a projectile nine feet in diameter, weighing 30,000 pounds, the gun would only have a length of two hundred and twenty- five feet, and a weight of 7,200,000 pounds."

"Ridiculous!" rejoined Maston. "As well take a pistol."

"I think so too," replied Barbicane; "that is why I propose to quadruple that length, and to construct a gun of nine hundred feet."

The general and the major offered some objections; nevertheless, the proposition, actively supported by the secretary, was definitely adopted.

"But," said Elphinstone, "what thickness must we give it?"

"A thickness of six feet," replied Barbicane.

"You surely don't think of mounting a mass like that upon a carriage?" asked the major.

"It would be a superb idea, though," said Maston.

"But impracticable," replied Barbicane. "No, I think of sinking this engine in the earth alone, binding it with hoops of wrought iron, and finally surrounding it with a thick mass of masonry of stone and cement. The piece once cast, it must be bored with great precision, so as to preclude any possible windage. So there will be no loss whatever of gas, and all the expansive force of the powder will be employed in the propulsion."

"One simple question," said Elphinstone: "is our gun to be rifled?"

"No, certainly not," replied Barbicane; "we require an enormous initial velocity; and you are well aware that a shot quits a rifled gun less rapidly than it does a smooth-bore."

"True," rejoined the major.

The committee here adjourned for a few minutes to tea and sandwiches.

On the discussion being renewed, "Gentlemen," said Barbicane, "we must now take into consideration the metal to be employed. Our cannon must be possessed of great tenacity, great hardness, be infusible by heat, indissoluble, and inoxidable by the corrosive action of acids."

"There is no doubt about that," replied the major; "and as we shall have to employ an immense quantity of metal, we shall not be at a loss for choice."

"Well, then," said Morgan, "I propose the best alloy hitherto known, which consists of one hundred parts of copper, twelve of tin, and six of brass."

"I admit," replied the president, "that this composition has yielded excellent results, but in the present case it would be too expensive, and very difficult to work. I think, then, that we ought to adopt a material excellent in its way and of low price, such as cast iron. What is your advice, major?"

"I quite agree with you," replied Elphinstone.

"In fact," continued Barbicane, "cast iron costs ten times less than bronze; it is easy to cast, it runs readily from the moulds of sand, it is easy of manipulation, it is at once economical of money and of time. In addition, it is excellent as a material, and I well remember that during the war, at the siege of Atlanta, some iron guns fired one thousand rounds at intervals of twenty minutes without injury."

"Cast iron is very brittle, though," replied Morgan.

"Yes, but it possesses great resistance. I will now ask our worthy secretary to calculate the weight of a cast-iron gun with a bore of nine feet and a thickness of six feet of metal."

"In a moment," replied Maston. Then, dashing off some algebraical formulae with marvelous facility, in a minute or two he declared the following result:

"The cannon will weigh 68,040 tons. And, at two cents a pound, it will cost——"

"Two million five hundred and ten thousand seven hundred and one dollars."

Maston, the major, and the general regarded Barbicane with uneasy looks.

"Well, gentlemen," replied the president, "I repeat what I said yesterday. Make yourselves easy; the millions will not be wanting."

With this assurance of their president the committee separated, after having fixed their third meeting for the following evening.

CHAPTER IX THE QUESTION OF THE POWDERS

There remained for consideration merely the question of powders. The public awaited with interest its final decision. The size of the projectile, the length of the cannon being settled, what would be the quantity of powder necessary to produce impulsion?

It is generally asserted that gunpowder was invented in the fourteenth century by the monk Schwartz, who paid for his grand discovery with his life. It is, however, pretty well proved that this story ought to be ranked among the legends of the middle ages. Gunpowder was not invented by any one; it was the lineal successor of the Greek fire, which, like itself, was composed of sulfur and saltpeter. Few persons are acquainted with the mechanical power of gunpowder. Now this is precisely what is necessary to be understood in order to comprehend the importance of the question submitted to the committee.

A litre of gunpowder weighs about two pounds; during combustion it produces 400 litres of gas. This gas, on being liberated and acted upon by temperature raised to 2,400 degrees, occupies a space of 4,000 litres: consequently the volume of powder is to the volume of gas produced by its combustion as 1 to 4,000. One may judge, therefore, of the tremendous pressure on this gas when compressed within a space 4,000 times too confined. All this was, of course, well known to the members of the committee when they met on the following evening.

The first speaker on this occasion was Major Elphinstone, who had been the director of the gunpowder factories during the war.

"Gentlemen," said this distinguished chemist, "I begin with some figures which will serve as the basis of our calculation. The old 24-pounder shot required for its discharge sixteen pounds of powder."

"You are certain of this amount?" broke in Barbicane.

"Quite certain," replied the major. "The Armstrong cannon employs only seventy-five pounds of powder for a projectile of eight hundred pounds, and the Rodman Columbiad uses only one hundred and sixty pounds of powder to send its half ton shot a distance of six miles. These facts cannot be called in question, for I myself raised the point during the depositions taken before the committee of artillery."

"Quite true," said the general.

"Well," replied the major, "these figures go to prove that the quantity of powder is not increased with the weight of the shot; that is to say, if a 24-pounder shot requires sixteen pounds of powder;— in other words, if in ordinary guns we employ a quantity of powder equal to two-thirds of the weight of the projectile, this proportion is not constant. Calculate, and you will see that in place of three hundred and thirty-three pounds of powder, the quantity is reduced to no more than one hundred and sixty pounds."

"What are you aiming at?" asked the president.

"If you push your theory to extremes, my dear major," said J. T. Maston, "you will get to this, that as soon as your shot becomes sufficiently heavy you will not require any powder at all."

"Our friend Maston is always at his jokes, even in serious matters," cried the major; "but let him make his mind easy, I am going presently to propose gunpowder enough to satisfy his artillerist's propensities. I only keep to statistical facts when I say that, during the war, and for the very largest guns, the weight of the powder was reduced, as the result of experience, to a tenth part of the weight of the shot."

"Perfectly correct," said Morgan; "but before deciding the quantity of powder necessary to give the impulse, I think it would be as well——"

"We shall have to employ a large-grained powder," continued the major; "its combustion is more rapid than that of the small."

"No doubt about that," replied Morgan; "but it is very destructive, and ends by enlarging the bore of the pieces."

"Granted; but that which is injurious to a gun destined to perform long service is not so to our Columbiad. We shall run no danger of an explosion; and it is necessary that our powder should take fire instantaneously in order that its mechanical effect may be complete."

"We must have," said Maston, "several touch-holes, so as to fire it at different points at the same time."

"Certainly," replied Elphinstone; "but that will render the working of the piece more difficult. I return then to my large-grained powder, which removes those difficulties. In his Columbiad charges Rodman employed a powder as large as chestnuts, made of willow charcoal, simply dried in cast- iron pans. This powder was hard and glittering, left no trace upon the hand, contained hydrogen and oxygen in large proportion, took fire instantaneously, and, though very destructive, did not sensibly injure the mouth-piece."

Up to this point Barbicane had kept aloof from the discussion; he left the others to speak while he himself listened; he had evidently got an idea. He now simply said, "Well, my friends, what quantity of powder do you propose?"

The three members looked at one another.

"Two hundred thousand pounds." at last said Morgan.

"Five hundred thousand," added the major.

"Eight hundred thousand," screamed Maston.

A moment of silence followed this triple proposal; it was at last broken by the president.

"Gentlemen," he quietly said, "I start from this principle, that the resistance of a gun, constructed under the given conditions, is unlimited. I shall surprise our friend Maston, then, by stigmatizing his calculations as timid; and I propose to double his 800,000 pounds of powder."

"Sixteen hundred thousand pounds?" shouted Maston, leaping from his seat.

"Just so."

"We shall have to come then to my ideal of a cannon half a mile long; for you see 1,600,000 pounds will occupy a space of about 20,000 cubic feet; and since the contents of your cannon do not exceed 54,000 cubic feet, it would be half full; and the bore will not be more than long enough for the gas to communicate to the projectile sufficient impulse."

"Nevertheless," said the president, "I hold to that quantity of powder. Now, 1,600,000 pounds of powder will create 6,000,000,000 litres of gas. Six thousand millions! You quite understand?"

"What is to be done then?" said the general.

"The thing is very simple; we must reduce this enormous quantity of powder, while preserving to it its mechanical power."

"Good; but by what means?"

"I am going to tell you," replied Barbicane quietly.

"Nothing is more easy than to reduce this mass to one quarter of its bulk. You know that curious cellular matter which constitutes the elementary tissues of vegetable? This substance is found quite pure in many bodies, especially in cotton, which is nothing more than the down of the seeds of the cotton plant. Now cotton, combined with cold nitric acid, become transformed into a substance eminently insoluble, combustible, and explosive. It was first discovered in 1832, by Braconnot, a French chemist, who called it xyloidine. In 1838 another Frenchman, Pelouze, investigated its different properties, and finally, in 1846, Schonbein, professor of chemistry at Bale, proposed its employment for purposes of war. This powder, now called pyroxyle, or fulminating cotton, is prepared with great facility by simply plunging cotton for fifteen minutes in nitric acid, then washing it in water, then drying it, and it is ready for use."

"Nothing could be more simple," said Morgan.

"Moreover, pyroxyle is unaltered by moisture— a valuable property to us, inasmuch as it would take several days to charge the cannon. It ignites at 170 degrees in place of 240, and its combustion is so rapid that one may set light to it on the top of the ordinary powder, without the latter having time to ignite."

"Perfect!" exclaimed the major.

"Only it is more expensive."

"What matter?" cried J. T. Maston.

"Finally, it imparts to projectiles a velocity four times superior to that of gunpowder. I will even add, that if we mix it with one-eighth of its own weight of nitrate of potassium, its expansive force is again considerably augmented."

"Will that be necessary?" asked the major.

"I think not," replied Barbicane. "So, then, in place of 1,600,000 pounds of powder, we shall have but 400,000 pounds of fulminating cotton; and since we can, without danger, compress 500 pounds of cotton into twenty-seven cubic feet, the whole quantity will not occupy a height of more than 180 feet within the bore of the Columbiad. In this way the shot will have more than 700 feet of bore to traverse under a force of 6,000,000,000 litres of gas before taking its flight toward the moon."

At this juncture J. T. Maston could not repress his emotion; he flung himself into the arms of his friend with the violence of a projectile, and Barbicane would have been stove in if he had not been boom-proof.

This incident terminated the third meeting of the committee.

Barbicane and his bold colleagues, to whom nothing seemed impossible, had succeeding in solving the complex problems of projectile, cannon, and powder. Their plan was drawn up, and it only remained to put it into execution.

"A mere matter of detail, a bagatelle," said J. T. Maston.

CHAPTER X

ONE ENEMY *v.* TWENTY-FIVE MILLIONS OF FRIENDS

The American public took a lively interest in the smallest details of the enterprise of the Gun Club. It followed day by day the discussion of the committee. The most simple preparations for the great experiment, the questions of figures which it involved, the mechanical difficulties to be resolved— in one word, the entire plan of work— roused the popular excitement to the highest pitch.

The purely scientific attraction was suddenly intensified by the following incident:

We have seen what legions of admirers and friends Barbicane's project had rallied round its author. There was, however, one single individual alone in all the States of the Union who protested against the attempt of the Gun Club. He attacked it furiously on every opportunity, and human nature is such that Barbicane felt more keenly the opposition of that one man than he did the applause of all the others. He was well aware of the motive of this antipathy, the origin of this solitary enmity, the cause of its personality and old standing, and in what rivalry of self-love it had its rise.

This persevering enemy the president of the Gun Club had never seen. Fortunate that it was so, for a meeting between the two men would certainly have been attended with serious consequences. This rival was a man of science, like Barbicane himself, of a fiery, daring, and violent disposition; a pure Yankee. His name was Captain Nicholl; he lived at Philadelphia.

Most people are aware of the curious struggle which arose during the Federal war between the guns and armor of iron-plated ships. The result was the entire reconstruction of the navy of both the continents; as the one grew heavier, the other became thicker in proportion. The Merrimac, the Monitor, the Tennessee, the Weehawken discharged enormous projectiles themselves, after having been armor-clad against the projectiles of others. In fact they did to others that which they would not they should do to them— that grand principle of immortality upon which rests the whole art of war.

Now if Barbicane was a great founder of shot, Nicholl was a great forger of plates; the one cast night and day at Baltimore, the other forged day and night at Philadelphia. As soon as ever Barbicane invented a new shot, Nicholl invented a new plate; each followed a current of ideas essentially opposed to the other. Happily for these citizens, so useful to their country, a distance of from fifty to sixty miles separated them from one another, and they had never yet met. Which of these two inventors had the advantage over the other it was difficult to decide from the results obtained. By last accounts, however, it would seem that the armor-plate would in the end have to give way to the shot; nevertheless, there were competent judges who had their doubts on the point.

CHAPTER X

At the last experiment the cylindro-conical projectiles of Barbicane stuck like so many pins in the Nicholl plates. On that day the Philadelphia iron-forger then believed himself victorious, and could not evince contempt enough for his rival; but when the other afterward substituted for conical shot simple 600-pound shells, at very moderate velocity, the captain was obliged to give in. In fact, these projectiles knocked his best metal plate to shivers.

Matters were at this stage, and victory seemed to rest with the shot, when the war came to an end on the very day when Nicholl had completed a new armor-plate of wrought steel. It was a masterpiece of its kind, and bid defiance to all the projectiles of the world. The captain had it conveyed to the Polygon at Washington, challenging the president of the Gun Club to break it. Barbicane, peace having been declared, declined to try the experiment.

Nicholl, now furious, offered to expose his plate to the shock of any shot, solid, hollow, round, or conical. Refused by the president, who did not choose to compromise his last success.

Nicholl, disgusted by this obstinacy, tried to tempt Barbicane by offering him every chance. He proposed to fix the plate within two hundred yards of the gun. Barbicane still obstinate in refusal. A hundred yards? Not even seventy-five!

"At fifty then!" roared the captain through the newspapers.

"At twenty-five yards! and I'll stand behind!"

Barbicane returned for answer that, even if Captain Nicholl would be so good as to stand in front, he would not fire any more.

Nicholl could not contain himself at this reply; threw out hints of cowardice; that a man who refused to fire a cannon-shot was pretty near being afraid of it; that artillerists who fight at six miles distance are substituting mathematical formulae for individual courage.

To these insinuations Barbicane returned no answer; perhaps he never heard of them, so absorbed was he in the calculations for his great enterprise.

When his famous communication was made to the Gun Club, the captain's wrath passed all bounds; with his intense jealousy was mingled a feeling of absolute impotence. How was he to invent anything to beat this 900-feet Columbiad? What armor-plate could ever resist a projectilc of 30,000 pounds weight? Overwhelmed at first under this violent shock, he by and by recovered himself, and resolved to crush the proposal by weight of his arguments.

He then violently attacked the labors of the Gun Club, published a number of letters in the newspapers, endeavored to prove Barbicane ignorant of the first principles of gunnery. He maintained that it was absolutely impossible to impress upon any body whatever a velocity of 12,000 yards per second; that even with such a velocity a projectile of such a weight could not transcend the limits of the earth's atmosphere. Further still, even regarding the velocity to be acquired, and granting it to be sufficient, the shell could not resist the pressure of the gas developed by the ignition of 1,600,000 pounds of powder; and supposing it to resist that pressure, it would be less able to support that temperature; it would melt on quitting the Columbiad, and fall back in a red-hot shower upon the heads of the imprudent spectators.

Barbicane continued his work without regarding these attacks.

Nicholl then took up the question in its other aspects. Without touching upon its uselessness in all points of view, he regarded the experiment as fraught with extreme danger, both to the citizens, who might sanction by their presence so reprehensible a spectacle, and also to the towns in the neighborhood of this deplorable cannon. He also observed that if the projectile did not succeed in reaching its destination (a result absolutely impossible), it must inevitably fall back upon the earth, and that the shock of such a mass, multiplied by the square of its velocity, would seriously endanger every point of the globe. Under the circumstances, therefore, and without interfering with the rights of free citizens, it was a case for the intervention of Government, which ought not to endanger the safety of all for the pleasure of one individual.

In spite of all his arguments, however, Captain Nicholl remained alone in his opinion. Nobody listened to him, and he did not succeed in alienating a single admirer from the president of the Gun Club. The latter did not even take the pains to refute the arguments of his rival.

Nicholl, driven into his last entrenchments, and not able to fight personally in the cause, resolved to fight with money. He published, therefore, in the Richmond *Inquirer* a series of wagers, conceived in these terms, and on an increasing scale:

No. 1 ($1,000).— That the necessary funds for the experiment of the Gun Club will not be forthcoming.

No. 2 ($2,000).— That the operation of casting a cannon of 900 feet is impracticable, and cannot possibly succeed.

No. 3 ($3,000).— That is it impossible to load the Columbiad, and that the pyroxyle will take fire spontaneously under the pressure of the projectile.

No. 4 ($4,000).— That the Columbiad will burst at the first fire.

No. 5 ($5,000).— That the shot will not travel farther than six miles, and that it will fall back again a few seconds after its discharge.

It was an important sum, therefore, which the captain risked in his invincible obstinacy. He had no less than $15,000 at stake.

Notwithstanding the importance of the challenge, on the 19th of
May he received a sealed packet containing the following
superbly laconic reply:

"BALTIMORE, October 19.

"Done.

"BARBICANE."

CHAPTER XI FLORIDA AND TEXAS

One question remained yet to be decided; it was necessary to choose a favorable spot for the experiment. According to the advice of the Observatory of Cambridge, the gun must be fired perpendicularly to the plane of the horizon, that is to say, toward the zenith. Now the moon does not traverse the zenith, except in places situated between 0 ° and 28 ° of latitude. It became, then, necessary to determine exactly that spot on the globe where the immense Columbiad should be cast.

On the 20th of October, at a general meeting of the Gun Club, Barbicane produced a magnificent map of the United States. "Gentlemen," said he, in opening the discussion, "I presume that we are all agreed that this experiment cannot and ought not to be tried anywhere but within the limits of the soil of the Union. Now, by good fortune, certain frontiers of the United States extend downward as far as the 28th parallel of the north latitude. If you will cast your eye over this map, you will see that we have at our disposal the whole of the southern portion of Texas and Florida."

It was finally agreed, then, that the Columbiad must be cast on the soil of either Texas or Florida. The result, however, of this decision was to create a rivalry entirely without precedent between the different towns of these two States.

The 28th parallel, on reaching the American coast, traverses the peninsula of Florida, dividing it into two nearly equal portions. Then, plunging into the Gulf of Mexico, it subtends the arc formed by the coast of Alabama, Mississippi, and Louisiana; then skirting Texas, off which it cuts an angle, it continues its course over Mexico, crosses the Sonora, Old California, and loses itself in the Pacific Ocean. It was, therefore, only those portions of Texas and Florida which were situated below this parallel which came within the prescribed conditions of latitude.

Florida, in its southern part, reckons no cities of importance; it is simply studded with forts raised against the roving Indians. One solitary town, Tampa Town, was able to put in a claim in favor of its situation.

In Texas, on the contrary, the towns are much more numerous and important. Corpus Christi, in the county of Nueces, and all the cities situated on the Rio Bravo, Laredo, Comalites, San Ignacio on the Web, Rio Grande City on the Starr, Edinburgh in the Hidalgo, Santa Rita, Elpanda, Brownsville in the Cameron, formed an imposing league against the pretensions of Florida. So, scarcely was the decision known, when the Texan and Floridan deputies arrived at Baltimore in an incredibly short space of time. From that very moment President Barbicane and the influential members of the Gun Club were besieged day and night by formidable claims. If seven cities of Greece contended for the honor of having given birth to a Homer, here were two entire States threatening to come to blows about the question of a cannon.

The rival parties promenaded the streets with arms in their hands; and at every occasion of their meeting a collision was to be apprehended which might have been attended with disastrous results. Happily the prudence and address of President Barbicane averted the danger. These personal demonstrations found a division in the newspapers of the different States. The New York *Herald* and the *Tribune* supported Texas, while the *Times* and the *American Review* espoused the cause of the Floridan deputies. The members of the Gun Club could not decide to which to give the preference.

Texas produced its array of twenty-six counties; Florida replied that twelve counties were better than twenty-six in a country only one-sixth part of the size.

Texas plumed itself upon its 330,000 natives; Florida, with a far smaller territory, boasted of being much more densely populated with 56,000.

The Texans, through the columns of the *Herald* claimed that some regard should be had to a State which grew the best cotton in all America, produced the best green oak for the service of the navy, and contained the finest oil, besides iron mines, in which the yield was fifty per cent. of pure metal.

To this the *American Review* replied that the soil of Florida, although not equally rich, afforded the best conditions for the moulding and casting of the Columbiad, consisting as it did of sand and argillaceous earth.

"That may be all very well," replied the Texans; "but you must first get to this country. Now the communications with Florida are difficult, while the coast of Texas offers the bay of Galveston, which possesses a circumference of fourteen leagues, and is capable of containing the navies of the entire world!"

"A pretty notion truly," replied the papers in the interest of Florida, "that of Galveston bay *below the 29th parallel!* Have we not got the bay of Espiritu Santo, opening precisely upon *the 28th degree*, and by which ships can reach Tampa Town by direct route?"

"A fine bay; half choked with sand!"

"Choked yourselves!" returned the others.

Thus the war went on for several days, when Florida endeavored to draw her adversary away on to fresh ground; and one morning the *Times* hinted that, the enterprise being essentially American, it ought not to be attempted upon other than purely American territory.

To these words Texas retorted, "American! are we not as much so as you? Were not Texas and Florida both incorporated into the Union in 1845?"

"Undoubtedly," replied the *Times*; "but we have belonged to the Americans ever since 1820."

"Yes!" returned the *Tribune*; "after having been Spaniards or English for two hundred years, you were sold to the United States for five million dollars!"

"Well! and why need we blush for that? Was not Louisiana bought from Napoleon in 1803 at the price of sixteen million dollars?"

"Scandalous!" roared the Texas deputies. "A wretched little strip of country like Florida to dare to compare itself to Texas, who, in place of selling herself, asserted her own independence, drove out the Mexicans in March 2, 1846, and declared herself a federal republic after the victory gained by Samuel Houston, on the banks of the San Jacinto, over the troops of Santa Anna!— a country, in fine, which voluntarily annexed itself to the United States of America!"

"Yes; because it was afraid of the Mexicans!" replied Florida.

"Afraid!" From this moment the state of things became intolerable. A sanguinary encounter seemed daily imminent between the two parties in the streets of Baltimore. It became necessary to keep an eye upon the deputies.

President Barbicane knew not which way to look. Notes, documents, letters full of menaces showered down upon his house. Which side ought he to take? As regarded the appropriation of the soil, the facility of communication, the rapidity of transport, the claims of both States were evenly balanced. As for political prepossessions, they had nothing to do with the question.

This dead block had existed for some little time, when Barbicane resolved to get rid of it all at once. He called a meeting of his colleagues, and laid before them a proposition which, it will be seen, was profoundly sagacious.

"On carefully considering," he said, "what is going on now between Florida and Texas, it is clear that the same difficulties will recur with all the towns of the favored State. The rivalry will descend from State to city, and so on downward. Now Texas possesses eleven towns within the prescribed conditions, which will further dispute the honor and create us new enemies, while Florida has only one. I go in, therefore, for Florida and Tampa Town."

This decision, on being made known, utterly crushed the Texan deputies. Seized with an indescribable fury, they addressed threatening letters to the different members of the Gun Club by name. The magistrates had but one course to take, and they took it. They chartered a special train, forced the Texans into it whether they would or no; and they quitted the city with a speed of thirty miles an hour.

Quickly, however, as they were despatched, they found time to hurl one last and bitter sarcasm at their adversaries.

Alluding to the extent of Florida, a mere peninsula confined between two seas, they pretended that it could never sustain the shock of the discharge, and that it would "bust up" at the very first shot.

"Very well, let it bust up!" replied the Floridans, with a brevity of the days of ancient Sparta.

CHAPTER XII URBI ET ORBI

The astronomical, mechanical, and topographical difficulties resolved, finally came the question of finance. The sum required was far too great for any individual, or even any single State, to provide the requisite millions.

President Barbicane undertook, despite of the matter being a purely American affair, to render it one of universal interest, and to request the financial co-operation of all peoples. It was, he maintained, the right and duty of the whole earth to interfere in the affairs of its satellite. The subscription opened at Baltimore extended properly to the whole world— *Urbi et orbi.*

This subscription was successful beyond all expectation; notwithstanding that it was a question not of lending but of giving the money. It was a purely disinterested operation in the strictest sense of the term, and offered not the slightest chance of profit.

The effect, however, of Barbicane's communication was not confined to the frontiers of the United States; it crossed the Atlantic and Pacific, invading simultaneously Asia and Europe, Africa and Oceanica. The observatories of the Union placed themselves in immediate communication with those of foreign countries. Some, such as those of Paris, Petersburg, Berlin, Stockholm, Hamburg, Malta, Lisbon, Benares, Madras, and others, transmitted their good wishes; the rest maintained a prudent silence, quietly awaiting the result. As for the observatory at Greenwich, seconded as it was by the twenty- two astronomical establishments of Great Britain, it spoke plainly enough. It boldly denied the possibility of success, and pronounced in favor of the theories of Captain Nicholl. But this was nothing more than mere English jealousy.

On the 8th of October President Barbicane published a manifesto full of enthusiasm, in which he made an appeal to "all persons of good will upon the face of the earth." This document, translated into all languages, met with immense success.

Subscription lists were opened in all the principal cities of the Union, with a central office at the Baltimore Bank, 9 Baltimore Street.

In addition, subscriptions were received at the following banks in the different states of the two continents:

At Vienna, with S. M. de Rothschild.
At Petersburg, Stieglitz and Co.
At Paris, The Credit Mobilier.
At Stockholm, Tottie and Arfuredson.
At London, N. M. Rothschild and Son.
At Turin, Ardouin and Co.
At Berlin, Mendelssohn.
At Geneva, Lombard, Odier and Co.

At Constantinople, The Ottoman Bank.
At Brussels, J. Lambert.
At Madrid, Daniel Weisweller.
At Amsterdam, Netherlands Credit Co.
At Rome, Torlonia and Co.
At Lisbon, Lecesne.
At Copenhagen, Private Bank.
At Rio de Janeiro, Private Bank.
At Montevideo, Private Bank.
At Valparaiso and Lima, Thomas la Chambre and Co.
At Mexico, Martin Daran and Co.

Three days after the manifesto of President Barbicane $4,000,000 were paid into the different towns of the Union. With such a balance the Gun Club might begin operations at once. But some days later advices were received to the effect that foreign subscriptions were being eagerly taken up. Certain countries distinguished themselves by their liberality; others untied their purse-strings with less facility—a matter of temperament. Figures are, however, more eloquent than words, and here is the official statement of the sums which were paid in to the credit of the Gun Club at the close of the subscription.

Russia paid in as her contingent the enormous sum of 368,733 roubles. No one need be surprised at this, who bears in mind the scientific taste of the Russians, and the impetus which they have given to astronomical studies—thanks to their numerous observatories.

France began by deriding the pretensions of the Americans. The moon served as a pretext for a thousand stale puns and a score of ballads, in which bad taste contested the palm with ignorance. But as formerly the French paid before singing, so now they paid after having had their laugh, and they subscribed for a sum of 1,253,930 francs. At that price they had a right to enjoy themselves a little.

Austria showed herself generous in the midst of her financial crisis. Her public contributions amounted to the sum of 216,000 florins— a perfect godsend.

Fifty-two thousand rix-dollars were the remittance of Sweden and Norway; the amount is large for the country, but it would undoubtedly have been considerably increased had the subscription been opened in Christiana simultaneously with that at Stockholm. For some reason or other the Norwegians do not like to send their money to Sweden.

Prussia, by a remittance of 250,000 thalers, testified her high approval of the enterprise.

Turkey behaved generously; but she had a personal interest in the matter. The moon, in fact, regulates the cycle of her years and her fast of Ramadan. She could not do less than give 1,372,640 piastres; and she gave them with an eagerness which denoted, however, some pressure on the part of the government.

Belgium distinguished herself among the second-rate states by a grant of 513,000 francs— about two centimes per head of her population.

Holland and her colonies interested themselves to the extent of 110,000 florins, only demanding an allowance of five per cent. discount for paying ready money.

Denmark, a little contracted in territory, gave nevertheless 9,000 ducats, proving her love for scientific experiments.

The Germanic Confederation pledged itself to 34,285 florins. It was impossible to ask for more; besides, they would not have given it.

Though very much crippled, Italy found 200,000 lire in the pockets of her people. If she had had Venetia she would have done better; but she had not.

The States of the Church thought that they could not send less than 7,040 Roman crowns; and Portugal carried her devotion to science as far as 30,000 cruzados. It was the widow's mite— eighty-six piastres; but self-constituted empires are always rather short of money.

Two hundred and fifty-seven francs, this was the modest contribution of Switzerland to the American work. One must freely admit that she did not see the practical side of the matter. It did not seem to her that the mere despatch of a shot to the moon could possibly establish any relation of affairs with her; and it did not seem prudent to her to embark her capital in so hazardous an enterprise. After all, perhaps she was right.

As to Spain, she could not scrape together more than 110 reals. She gave as an excuse that she had her railways to finish. The truth is, that science is not favorably regarded in that country, it is still in a backward state; and moreover, certain Spaniards, not by any means the least educated, did not form a correct estimate of the bulk of the projectile compared with that of the moon. They feared that it would disturb the established order of things. In that case it were better to keep aloof; which they did to the tune of some reals.

There remained but England; and we know the contemptuous antipathy with which she received Barbicane's proposition. The English have but one soul for the whole twenty-six millions of inhabitants which Great Britain contains. They hinted that the enterprise of the Gun Club was contrary to the "principle of non-intervention." And they did not subscribe a single farthing.

At this intimation the Gun Club merely shrugged its shoulders and returned to its great work. When South America, that is to say, Peru, Chili, Brazil, the provinces of La Plata and Columbia, had poured forth their quota into their hands, the sum of $300,000, it found itself in possession of a considerable capital, of which the following is a statement:

United States subscriptions, . . $4,000,000
Foreign subscriptions . . . $1,446,675

Total, ... $5,446,675

Such was the sum which the public poured into the treasury of the Gun Club.

Let no one be surprised at the vastness of the amount. The work of casting, boring, masonry, the transport of workmen, their establishment in an almost uninhabited country, the construction of furnaces and workshops, the plant, the powder, the projectile, and incipient expenses, would, according to the estimates, absorb nearly the whole. Certain cannon-shots in the Federal war cost one thousand dollars apiece. This one of President Barbicane, unique in the annals of gunnery, might well cost five thousand times more.

On the 20th of October a contract was entered into with the manufactory at Coldspring, near New York, which during the war had furnished the largest Parrott, cast-iron guns. It was stipulated between the contracting parties that the manufactory of Coldspring should engage to transport to Tampa Town, in southern Florida, the necessary materials for casting the Columbiad. The work was bound to be completed at latest by the 15th of October following, and the cannon delivered in good condition under penalty of a forfeit of one hundred dollars a day to the moment when the moon should again present herself under the same conditions— that is to say, in eighteen years and eleven days.

The engagement of the workmen, their pay, and all the necessary details of the work, devolved upon the Coldspring Company.

This contract, executed in duplicate, was signed by Barbicane, president of the Gun Club, of the one part, and T. Murchison director of the Coldspring manufactory, of the other, who thus executed the deed on behalf of their respective principals.

CHAPTER XIII STONES HILL

When the decision was arrived at by the Gun Club, to the disparagement of Texas, every one in America, where reading is a universal acquirement, set to work to study the geography of Florida. Never before had there been such a sale for works like "Bertram's Travels in Florida," "Roman's Natural History of East and West Florida," "William's Territory of Florida," and "Cleland on the Cultivation of the Sugar-Cane in Florida." It became necessary to issue fresh editions of these works.

Barbicane had something better to do than to read. He desired to see things with his own eyes, and to mark the exact position of the proposed gun. So, without a moment's loss of time, he placed at the disposal of the Cambridge Observatory the funds necessary for the construction of a telescope, and entered into negotiations with the house of Breadwill and Co., of Albany, for the construction of an aluminum projectile of the required size. He then quitted Baltimore, accompanied by J. T. Maston, Major Elphinstone, and the manager of the Coldspring factory.

On the following day, the four fellow-travelers arrived at New Orleans. There they immediately embarked on board the *Tampico*, a despatch-boat belonging to the Federal navy, which the government had placed at their disposal; and, getting up steam, the banks of Louisiana speedily disappeared from sight.

The passage was not long. Two days after starting, the *Tampico*, having made four hundred and eighty miles, came in sight of the coast of Florida. On a nearer approach Barbicane found himself in view of a low, flat country of somewhat barren aspect. After coasting along a series of creeks abounding in lobsters and oysters, the *Tampico* entered the bay of Espiritu Santo, where she finally anchored in a small natural harbor, formed by the *embouchure* of the River Hillisborough, at seven P.M., on the 22d of October.

Our four passengers disembarked at once. "Gentlemen," said Barbicane, "we have no time to lose; tomorrow we must obtain horses, and proceed to reconnoiter the country."

Barbicane had scarcely set his foot on shore when three thousand of the inhabitants of Tampa Town came forth to meet him, an honor due to the president who had signalized their country by his choice.

Declining, however, every kind of ovation, Barbicane ensconced himself in a room of the Franklin Hotel.

On the morrow some of the small horses of the Spanish breed, full of vigor and of fire, stood snorting under his windows; but instead of four steeds, here were fifty, together with their riders. Barbicane descended with his three fellow- travelers; and much astonished were they all to find themselves in the midst of such a cavalcade. He remarked that every horseman carried a carbine slung across his shoulders and pistols in his holsters.

On expressing his surprise at these preparations, he was speedily enlightened by a young Floridan, who quietly said:

"Sir, there are Seminoles there."

"What do you mean by Seminoles?"

"Savages who scour the prairies. We thought it best, therefore, to escort you on your road."

"Pooh!" cried J. T. Maston, mounting his steed.

"All right," said the Floridan; "but it is true enough, nevertheless."

"Gentlemen," answered Barbicane, "I thank you for your kind attention; but it is time to be off."

It was five A.M. when Barbicane and his party, quitting Tampa Town, made their way along the coast in the direction of Alifia Creek. This little river falls into Hillisborough Bay twelve miles above Tampa Town. Barbicane and his escort coasted along its right bank to the eastward. Soon the waves of the bay disappeared behind a bend of rising ground, and the Floridan "champagne" alone offered itself to view.

Florida, discovered on Palm Sunday, in 1512, by Juan Ponce de Leon, was originally named *Pascha Florida*. It little deserved that designation, with its dry and parched coasts. But after some few miles of tract the nature of the soil gradually changes and the country shows itself worthy of the name. Cultivated plains soon appear, where are united all the productions of the northern and tropical floras, terminating in prairies abounding with pineapples and yams, tobacco, rice, cotton-plants, and sugar-canes, which extend beyond reach of sight, flinging their riches broadcast with careless prodigality.

Barbicane appeared highly pleased on observing the progressive elevation of the land; and in answer to a question of J. T. Maston, replied:

"My worthy friend, we cannot do better than sink our Columbiad in these high grounds."

"To get nearer the moon, perhaps?" said the secretary of the Gun Club.

"Not exactly," replied Barbicane, smiling; "do you not see that among these elevated plateaus we shall have a much easier work of it? No struggles with the water-springs, which will save us long expensive tubings; and we shall be working in daylight instead of down a deep and narrow well. Our business, then, is to open our trenches upon ground some hundreds of yards above the level of the sea."

"You are right, sir," struck in Murchison, the engineer; "and, if I mistake not, we shall ere long find a suitable spot for our purpose."

"I wish we were at the first stroke of the pickaxe," said the president.

"And I wish we were at the *last*," cried J. T. Maston.

About ten A.M. the little band had crossed a dozen miles. To fertile plains succeeded a region of forests. There perfumes of the most varied kinds mingled together in tropical profusion. These almost impenetrable forests were composed of pomegranates, orange-trees, citrons, figs, olives, apricots, bananas, huge vines, whose blossoms and fruits rivaled each other in color and perfume. Beneath the odorous shade of these magnificent trees fluttered and warbled a little world of brilliantly plumaged birds.

J. T. Maston and the major could not repress their admiration on finding themselves in the presence of the glorious beauties of this wealth of nature. President Barbicane, however, less sensitive to these wonders, was in haste to press forward; the very luxuriance of the country was displeasing to him. They hastened onward, therefore, and were compelled to ford several rivers, not without danger, for they were infested with huge alligators from fifteen to eighteen feet long. Maston courageously menaced them with his steel hook, but he only succeeded in frightening some pelicans and teal, while tall flamingos stared stupidly at the party.

At length these denizens of the swamps disappeared in their turn; smaller trees became thinly scattered among less dense thickets— a few isolated groups detached in the midst of endless plains over which ranged herds of startled deer.

"At last," cried Barbicane, rising in his stirrups, "here we are at the region of pines!"

"Yes! and of savages too," replied the major.

In fact, some Seminoles had just came in sight upon the horizon; they rode violently backward and forward on their fleet horses, brandishing their spears or discharging their guns with a dull report. These hostile demonstrations, however, had no effect upon Barbicane and his companions.

They were then occupying the center of a rocky plain, which the sun scorched with its parching rays. This was formed by a considerable elevation of the soil, which seemed to offer to the members of the Gun Club all the conditions requisite for the construction of their Columbiad.

"Halt!" said Barbicane, reining up. "Has this place any local appellation?"

"It is called Stones Hill," replied one of the Floridans.

Barbicane, without saying a word, dismounted, seized his instruments, and began to note his position with extreme exactness. The little band, drawn up in the rear, watched his proceedings in profound silence.

At this moment the sun passed the meridian. Barbicane, after a few moments, rapidly wrote down the result of his observations, and said:

"This spot is situated eighteen hundred feet above the level of the sea, in 27 ° 7' N. lat. and 5 ° 7' W. long. of the meridian of Washington. It appears to me by its rocky and barren character to offer all the conditions requisite for our experiment. On that plain will be raised our magazines, workshops, furnaces, and workmen's huts; and here, from this very spot," said he, stamping his foot on the summit of Stones Hill, "hence shall our projectile take its flight into the regions of the Solar World."

CHAPTER XIV PICKAXE AND TROWEL

The same evening Barbicane and his companions returned to Tampa Town; and Murchison, the engineer, re-embarked on board the Tampico for New Orleans. His object was to enlist an army of workmen, and to collect together the greater part of the materials. The members of the Gun Club remained at Tampa Town, for the purpose of setting on foot the preliminary works by the aid of the people of the country.

Eight days after its departure, the Tampico returned into the bay of Espiritu Santo, with a whole flotilla of steamboats. Murchison had succeeded in assembling together fifteen hundred artisans. Attracted by the high pay and considerable bounties offered by the Gun Club, he had enlisted a choice legion of stokers, iron-founders, lime-burners, miners, brickmakers, and artisans of every trade, without distinction of color. As many of these people brought their families with them, their departure resembled a perfect emigration.

On the 31st of October, at ten o'clock in the morning, the troop disembarked on the quays of Tampa Town; and one may imagine the activity which pervaded that little town, whose population was thus doubled in a single day.

During the first few days they were busy discharging the cargo brought by the flotilla, the machines, and the rations, as well as a large number of huts constructed of iron plates, separately pieced and numbered. At the same period Barbicane laid the first sleepers of a railway fifteen miles in length, intended to unite Stones Hill with Tampa Town. On the first of November Barbicane quitted Tampa Town with a detachment of workmen; and on the following day the whole town of huts was erected round Stones Hill. This they enclosed with palisades; and in respect of energy and activity, it might have been mistaken for one of the great cities of the Union. Everything was placed under a complete system of discipline, and the works were commenced in most perfect order.

The nature of the soil having been carefully examined, by means of repeated borings, the work of excavation was fixed for the 4th of November.

On that day Barbicane called together his foremen and addressed them as follows: "You are well aware, my friends, of the object with which I have assembled you together in this wild part of Florida. Our business is to construct a cannon measuring nine feet in its interior diameter, six feet thick, and with a stone revetment of nineteen and a half feet in thickness. We have, therefore, a well of sixty feet in diameter to dig down to a depth of nine hundred feet. This great work must be completed within eight months, so that you have 2,543,400 cubic feet of earth to excavate in 255 days; that is to say, in round numbers, 2,000 cubic feet per day. That which would present no difficulty to a thousand navvies working in open country will be of course more troublesome in a comparatively confined space. However, the thing must be done, and I reckon for its accomplishment upon your courage as much as upon your skill."

At eight o'clock the next morning the first stroke of the pickaxe was struck upon the soil of Florida; and from that moment that prince of tools was never inactive for one moment in the hands of the excavators. The gangs relieved each other every three hours.

On the 4th of November fifty workmen commenced digging, in the very center of the enclosed space on the summit of Stones Hill, a circular hole sixty feet in diameter. The pickaxe first struck upon a kind of black earth, six inches in thickness, which was speedily disposed of. To this earth succeeded two feet of fine sand, which was carefully laid aside as being valuable for serving the casting of the inner mould. After the sand appeared some compact white clay, resembling the chalk of Great Britain, which extended down to a depth of four feet. Then the iron of the picks struck upon the hard bed of the soil; a kind of rock formed of petrified shells, very dry, very solid, and which the picks could with difficulty penetrate. At this point the excavation exhibited a depth of six and a half feet and the work of the masonry was begun.

At the bottom of the excavation they constructed a wheel of oak, a kind of circle strongly bolted together, and of immense strength. The center of this wooden disc was hollowed out to a diameter equal to the exterior diameter of the Columbiad. Upon this wheel rested the first layers of the masonry, the stones of which were bound together by hydraulic cement, with irresistible tenacity. The workmen, after laying the stones from the circumference to the center, were thus enclosed within a kind of well twenty-one feet in diameter. When this work was accomplished, the miners resumed their picks and cut away the rock from underneath the wheel itself, taking care to support it as they advanced upon blocks of great thickness. At every two feet which the hole gained in depth they successively withdrew the blocks. The wheel then sank little by little, and with it the massive ring of masonry, on the upper bed of which the masons labored incessantly, always reserving some vent holes to permit the escape of gas during the operation of the casting.

This kind of work required on the part of the workmen extreme nicety and minute attention. More than one, in digging underneath the wheel, was dangerously injured by the splinters of stone. But their ardor never relaxed, night or day. By day they worked under the rays of the scorching sun; by night, under the gleam of the electric light. The sounds of the picks against the rock, the bursting of mines, the grinding of the machines, the wreaths of smoke scattered through the air, traced around Stones Hill a circle of terror which thc hcrds of buffaloes and the war parties of the Seminoles never ventured to pass. Nevertheless, the works advanced regularly, as the steam-cranes actively removed the rubbish. Of unexpected obstacles there was little account; and with regard to foreseen difficulties, they were speedily disposed of.

At the expiration of the first month the well had attained the depth assigned for that lapse of time, namely, 112 feet. This depth was doubled in December, and trebled in January.

During the month of February the workmen had to contend with a sheet of water which made its way right across the outer soil. It became necessary to employ very powerful pumps and compressed-air engines to drain it off, so as to close up the orifice from whence it issued; just as one stops a leak on board ship. They at last succeeded in getting the upper hand of these untoward streams; only, in consequence of the loosening of the soil, the wheel partly gave way, and a slight partial settlement ensued. This accident cost the life of several workmen.

No fresh occurrence thenceforward arrested the progress of the operation; and on the tenth of June, twenty days before the expiration of the period fixed by Barbicane, the well, lined throughout with its facing of stone, had attained the depth of 900 feet. At the bottom the masonry rested upon a massive block measuring thirty feet in thickness, while on the upper portion it was level with the surrounding soil.

President Barbicane and the members of the Gun Club warmly congratulated their engineer Murchison; the cyclopean work had been accomplished with extraordinary rapidity.

During these eight months Barbicane never quitted Stones Hill for a single instant. Keeping ever close by the work of excavation, he busied himself incessantly with the welfare and health of his workpeople, and was singularly fortunate in warding off the epidemics common to large communities of men, and so disastrous in those regions of the globe which are exposed to the influences of tropical climates.

Many workmen, it is true, paid with their lives for the rashness inherent in these dangerous labors; but these mishaps are impossible to be avoided, and they are classed among the details with which the Americans trouble themselves but little. They have in fact more regard for human nature in general than for the individual in particular.

Nevertheless, Barbicane professed opposite principles to these, and put them in force at every opportunity. So, thanks to his care, his intelligence, his useful intervention in all difficulties, his prodigious and humane sagacity, the average of accidents did not exceed that of transatlantic countries, noted for their excessive precautions— France, for instance, among others, where they reckon about one accident for every two hundred thousand francs of work.

CHAPTER XV THE FETE OF THE CASTING

During the eight months which were employed in the work of excavation the preparatory works of the casting had been carried on simultaneously with extreme rapidity. A stranger arriving at Stones Hill would have been surprised at the spectacle offered to his view.

At 600 yards from the well, and circularly arranged around it as a central point, rose 1,200 reverberating ovens, each six feet in diameter, and separated from each other by an interval of three feet. The circumference occupied by these 1,200 ovens presented a length of two miles. Being all constructed on the same plan, each with its high quadrangular chimney, they produced a most singular effect.

It will be remembered that on their third meeting the committee had decided to use cast iron for the Columbiad, and in particular the white description. This metal, in fact, is the most tenacious, the most ductile, and the most malleable, and consequently suitable for all moulding operations; and when smelted with pit coal, is of superior quality for all engineering works requiring great resisting power, such as cannon, steam boilers, hydraulic presses, and the like.

Cast iron, however, if subjected to only one single fusion, is rarely sufficiently homogeneous; and it requires a second fusion completely to refine it by dispossessing it of its last earthly deposits. So long before being forwarded to Tampa Town, the iron ore, molten in the great furnaces of Coldspring, and brought into contact with coal and silicium heated to a high temperature, was carburized and transformed into cast iron. After this first operation, the metal was sent on to Stones Hill. They had, however, to deal with 136,000,000 pounds of iron, a quantity far too costly to send by railway. The cost of transport would have been double that of material. It appeared preferable to freight vessels at New York, and to load them with the iron in bars. This, however, required not less than sixty- eight vessels of 1,000 tons, a veritable fleet, which, quitting New York on the 3rd of May, on the 10th of the same month ascended the Bay of Espiritu Santo, and discharged their cargoes, without dues, in the port at Tampa Town. Thence the iron was transported by rail to Stones Hill, and about the middle of January this enormous mass of metal was delivered at its destination.

It will easily be understood that 1,200 furnaces were not too many to melt simultaneously these 60,000 tons of iron. Each of these furnaces contained nearly 140,000 pounds weight of metal. They were all built after the model of those which served for the casting of the Rodman gun; they were trapezoidal in shape, with a high elliptical arch. These furnaces, constructed of fireproof brick, were especially adapted for burning pit coal, with a flat bottom upon which the iron bars were laid. This bottom, inclined at an angle of 25 degrees, allowed the metal to flow into the receiving troughs; and the 1,200 converging trenches carried the molten metal down to the central well.

The day following that on which the works of the masonry and boring had been completed, Barbicane set to work upon the central mould. His object now was to raise within the center of the well, and with a coincident axis, a cylinder 900 feet high, and nine feet in diameter, which should exactly fill up the space reserved for the bore of the Columbiad. This cylinder was composed of a mixture of clay and sand, with the addition of a little hay and straw. The space left between the mould and the masonry was intended to be filled up by the molten metal, which would thus form the walls six feet in thickness. This cylinder, in order to maintain its equilibrium, had to be bound by iron bands, and firmly fixed at certain intervals by cross-clamps fastened into the stone lining; after the castings these would be buried in the block of metal, leaving no external projection.

This operation was completed on the 8th of July, and the run of the metal was fixed for the following day.

"This *fete* of the casting will be a grand ceremony," said J.

T. Maston to his friend Barbicane.

"Undoubtedly," said Barbicane; "but it will not be a public *fete*"

"What! will you not open the gates of the enclosure to all comers?"

"I must be very careful, Maston. The casting of the Columbiad is an extremely delicate, not to say a dangerous operation, and I should prefer its being done privately. At the discharge of the projectile, a *fete* if you like— till then, no!"

The president was right. The operation involved unforeseen dangers, which a great influx of spectators would have hindered him from averting. It was necessary to preserve complete freedom of movement. No one was admitted within the enclosure except a delegation of members of the Gun Club, who had made the voyage to Tampa Town. Among these was the brisk Bilsby, Tom Hunter, Colonel Blomsberry, Major Elphinstone, General Morgan, and the rest of the lot to whom the casting of the Columbiad was a matter of personal interest. J. T. Maston became their cicerone. He omitted no point of detail; he conducted them throughout the magazines, workshops, through the midst of the engines, and compelled them to visit the whole 1,200 furnaces one after the other. At the end of the twelve-hundredth visit they were pretty well knocked up.

The casting was to take place at twelve o'clock precisely. The previous evening each furnace had been charged with 114,000 pounds weight of metal in bars disposed crossways to each other, so as to allow the hot air to circulate freely between them. At daybreak the 1,200 chimneys vomited their torrents of flame into the air, and the ground was agitated with dull tremblings. As many pounds of metal as there were to cast, so many pounds of coal were there to burn. Thus there were 68,000 tons of coal which projected in the face of the sun a thick curtain of smoke. The heat soon became insupportable within the circle of furnaces, the rumbling of which resembled the rolling of thunder. The powerful ventilators added their continuous blasts and saturated with oxygen the glowing plates. The operation, to be successful, required to be conducted with great rapidity. On a signal given by a cannon-shot each furnace was to give vent to the molten iron and completely to empty itself. These arrangements made, foremen and workmen waited the preconcerted moment with an impatience mingled with a certain amount of emotion. Not a soul remained within the enclosure. Each superintendent took his post by the aperture of the run.

Barbicane and his colleagues, perched on a neighboring eminence, assisted at the operation. In front of them was a piece of artillery ready to give fire on the signal from the engineer. Some minutes before midday the first driblets of metal began to flow; the reservoirs filled little by little; and, by the time that the whole melting was completely accomplished, it was kept in abeyance for a few minutes in order to facilitate the separation of foreign substances.

Twelve o'clock struck! A gunshot suddenly pealed forth and shot its flame into the air. Twelve hundred melting-troughs were simultaneously opened and twelve hundred fiery serpents crept toward the central well, unrolling their incandescent curves. There, down they plunged with a terrific noise into a depth of 900 feet. It was an exciting and a magnificent spectacle. The ground trembled, while these molten waves, launching into the sky their wreaths of smoke, evaporated the moisture of the mould and hurled it upward through the vent-holes of the stone lining in the form of dense vapor-clouds. These artificial clouds unrolled their thick spirals to a height of 1,000 yards into the air. A savage, wandering somewhere beyond the limits of the horizon, might have believed that some new crater was forming in the bosom of Florida, although there was neither any eruption, nor typhoon, nor storm, nor struggle of the elements, nor any of those terrible phenomena which nature is capable of producing. No, it was man alone who had produced these reddish vapors, these gigantic flames worthy of a volcano itself, these tremendous vibrations resembling the shock of an earthquake, these reverberations rivaling those of hurricanes and storms; and it was his hand which precipitated into an abyss, dug by himself, a whole Niagara of molten metal!

CHAPTER XVI THE COLUMBIAD

Had the casting succeeded? They were reduced to mere conjecture. There was indeed every reason to expect success, since the mould has absorbed the entire mass of the molten metal; still some considerable time must elapse before they could arrive at any certainty upon the matter.

The patience of the members of the Gun Club was sorely tried during this period of time. But they could do nothing. J. T. Maston escaped roasting by a miracle. Fifteen days after the casting an immense column of smoke was still rising in the open sky and the ground burned the soles of the feet within a radius of two hundred feet round the summit of Stones Hill. It was impossible to approach nearer. All they could do was to wait with what patience they might.

"Here we are at the 10th of August," exclaimed J. T. Maston one morning, "only four months to the 1st of December! We shall never be ready in time!" Barbicane said nothing, but his silence covered serious irritation.

However, daily observations revealed a certain change going on in the state of the ground. About the 15th of August the vapors ejected had sensibly diminished in intensity and thickness. Some days afterward the earth exhaled only a slight puff of smoke, the last breath of the monster enclosed within its circle of stone. Little by little the belt of heat contracted, until on the 22nd of August, Barbicane, his colleagues, and the engineer were enabled to set foot on the iron sheet which lay level upon the summit of Stones Hill.

"At last!" exclaimed the president of the Gun Club, with an immense sigh of relief.

The work was resumed the same day. They proceeded at once to extract the interior mould, for the purpose of clearing out the boring of the piece. Pickaxes and boring irons were set to work without intermission. The clayey and sandy soils had acquired extreme hardness under the action of the heat; but, by the aid of the machines, the rubbish on being dug out was rapidly carted away on railway wagons; and such was the ardor of the work, so persuasive the arguments of Barbicane's dollars, that by the 3rd of September all traces of the mould had entirely disappeared.

Immediately the operation of boring was commenced; and by the aid of powerful machines, a few weeks later, the inner surface of the immense tube had been rendered perfectly cylindrical, and the bore of the piece had acquired a thorough polish.

At length, on the 22d of September, less than a twelvemonth after Barbicane's original proposition, the enormous weapon, accurately bored, and exactly vertically pointed, was ready for work. There was only the moon now to wait for; and they were pretty sure that she would not fail in the rendezvous.

The ecstasy of J. T. Maston knew no bounds, and he narrowly escaped a frightful fall while staring down the tube. But for the strong hand of Colonel Blomsberry, the worthy secretary, like a modern Erostratus, would have found his death in the depths of the Columbiad.

The cannon was then finished; there was no possible doubt as to its perfect completion. So, on the 6th of October, Captain Nicholl opened an account between himself and President Barbicane, in which he debited himself to the latter in the sum of two thousand dollars. One may believe that the captain's wrath was increased to its highest point, and must have made him seriously ill. However, he had still three bets of three, four, and five thousand dollars, respectively; and if he gained two out of these, his position would not be very bad. But the money question did not enter into his calculations; it was the success of his rival in casting a cannon against which iron plates sixty feet thick would have been ineffectual, that dealt him a terrible blow.

After the 23rd of September the enclosure of Stones hill was thrown open to the public; and it will be easily imagined what was the concourse of visitors to this spot! There was an incessant flow of people to and from Tampa Town and the place, which resembled a procession, or rather, in fact, a pilgrimage.

It was already clear to be seen that, on the day of the experiment itself, the aggregate of spectators would be counted by millions; for they were already arriving from all parts of the earth upon this narrow strip of promontory. Europe was emigrating to America.

Up to that time, however, it must be confessed, the curiosity of the numerous comers was but scantily gratified. Most had counted upon witnessing the spectacle of the casting, and they were treated to nothing but smoke. This was sorry food for hungry eyes; but Barbicane would admit no one to that operation. Then ensued grumbling, discontent, murmurs; they blamed the president, taxed him with dictatorial conduct. His proceedings were declared "un-American." There was very nearly a riot round Stones Hill; but Barbicane remained inflexible. When, however, the Columbiad was entirely finished, this state of closed doors could no longer be maintained; besides it would have been bad taste, and even imprudence, to affront the public feeling. Barbicane, therefore, opened the enclosure to all comers; but, true to his practical disposition, he determined to coin money out of the public curiosity.

It was something, indeed, to be enabled to contemplate this immense Columbiad; but to descend into its depths, this seemed to the Americans the *ne plus ultra* of earthly felicity. Consequently, there was not one curious spectator who was not willing to give himself the treat of visiting the interior of this great metallic abyss. Baskets suspended from steam-cranes permitted them to satisfy their curiosity. There was a perfect mania. Women, children, old men, all made it a point of duty to penetrate the mysteries of the colossal gun. The fare for the descent was fixed at five dollars per head; and despite this high charge, during the two months which preceded the experiment, the influx of visitors enabled the Gun Club to pocket nearly five hundred thousand dollars!

It is needless to say that the first visitors of the Columbiad were the members of the Gun Club. This privilege was justly reserved for that illustrious body. The ceremony took place on the 25th of September. A basket of honor took down the president, J. T. Maston, Major Elphinstone, General Morgan, Colonel Blomsberry, and other members of the club, to the number of ten in all. How hot it was at the bottom of that long tube of metal! They were half suffocated. But what delight! What ecstasy! A table had been laid with six covers on the massive stone which formed the bottom of the Columbiad, and lighted by a jet of electric light resembling that of day itself. Numerous exquisite dishes, which seemed to descend from heaven, were placed successively before the guests, and the richest wines of France flowed in profusion during this splendid repast, served nine hundred feet beneath the surface of the earth!

The festival was animated, not to say somewhat noisy. Toasts flew backward and forward. They drank to the earth and to her satellite, to the Gun Club, the Union, the Moon, Diana, Phoebe, Selene, the "peaceful courier of the night!" All the hurrahs, carried upward upon the sonorous waves of the immense acoustic tube, arrived with the sound of thunder at its mouth; and the multitude ranged round Stones Hill heartily united their shouts with those of the ten revelers hidden from view at the bottom of the gigantic Columbiad.

J. T. Maston was no longer master of himself. Whether he shouted or gesticulated, ate or drank most, would be a difficult matter to determine. At all events, he would not have given his place up for an empire, "not even if the cannon— loaded, primed, and fired at that very moment—were to blow him in pieces into the planetary world."

CHAPTER XVII A TELEGRAPHIC DISPATCH

The great works undertaken by the Gun Club had now virtually come to an end; and two months still remained before the day for the discharge of the shot to the moon. To the general impatience these two months appeared as long as years! Hitherto the smallest details of the operation had been daily chronicled by the journals, which the public devoured with eager eyes.

Just at this moment a circumstance, the most unexpected, the most extraordinary and incredible, occurred to rouse afresh their panting spirits, and to throw every mind into a state of the most violent excitement.

One day, the 30th of September, at 3:47 P.M., a telegram, transmitted by cable from Valentia (Ireland) to Newfoundland and the American Mainland, arrived at the address of President Barbicane.

The president tore open the envelope, read the dispatch, and, despite his remarkable powers of self-control, his lips turned pale and his eyes grew dim, on reading the twenty words of this telegram.

Here is the text of the dispatch, which figures now in the archives of the Gun Club:

FRANCE, PARIS,

30 September, 4 A.M.

Barbicane, Tampa Town, Florida, United States.

Substitute for your spherical shell a cylindro-conical projectile.

I shall go inside. Shall arrive by steamer Atlanta.

MICHEL ARDAN.

CHAPTER XVIII THE PASSENGER OF THE ATLANTA

If this astounding news, instead of flying through the electric wires, had simply arrived by post in the ordinary sealed envelope, Barbicane would not have hesitated a moment. He would have held his tongue about it, both as a measure of prudence, and in order not to have to reconsider his plans. This telegram might be a cover for some jest, especially as it came from a Frenchman. What human being would ever have conceived the idea of such a journey? and, if such a person really existed, he must be an idiot, whom one would shut up in a lunatic ward, rather than within the walls of the projectile.

The contents of the dispatch, however, speedily became known; for the telegraphic officials possessed but little discretion, and Michel Ardan's proposition ran at once throughout the several States of the Union. Barbicane, had, therefore, no further motives for keeping silence. Consequently, he called together such of his colleagues as were at the moment in Tampa Town, and without any expression of his own opinions simply read to them the laconic text itself. It was received with every possible variety of expressions of doubt, incredulity, and derision from every one, with the exception of J. T. Maston, who exclaimed, "It is a grand idea, however!"

When Barbicane originally proposed to send a shot to the moon every one looked upon the enterprise as simple and practicable enough— a mere question of gunnery; but when a person, professing to be a reasonable being, offered to take passage within the projectile, the whole thing became a farce, or, in plainer language a humbug.

One question, however, remained. Did such a being exist? This telegram flashed across the depths of the Atlantic, the designation of the vessel on board which he was to take his passage, the date assigned for his speedy arrival, all combined to impart a certain character of reality to the proposal. They must get some clearer notion of the matter. Scattered groups of inquirers at length condensed themselves into a compact crowd, which made straight for the residence of President Barbicane. That worthy individual was keeping quiet with the intention of watching events as they arose. But he had forgotten to take into account the public impatience; and it was with no pleasant countenance that he watched the population of Tampa Town gathering under his windows. The murmurs and vociferations below presently obliged him to appear. He came forward, therefore, and on silence being procured, a citizen put point-blank to him the following question: "Is the person mentioned in the telegram, under the name of Michel Ardan, on his way here? Yes or no."

"Gentlemen," replied Barbicane, "I know no more than you do."

"We must know," roared the impatient voices.

"Time will show," calmly replied the president.

CHAPTER XVIII THE PASSENGER OF THE ATLANTA

"Time has no business to keep a whole country in suspense," replied the orator. "Have you altered the plans of the projectile according to the request of the telegram?"

"Not yet, gentlemen; but you are right! we must have better information to go by. The telegraph must complete its information."

"To the telegraph!" roared the crowd.

Barbicane descended; and heading the immense assemblage, led the way to the telegraph office. A few minutes later a telegram was dispatched to the secretary of the underwriters at Liverpool, requesting answers to the following queries:

"About the ship Atlanta— when did she leave Europe? Had she on board a Frenchman named Michel Ardan?"

Two hours afterward Barbicane received information too exact to leave room for the smallest remaining doubt.

"The steamer Atlanta from Liverpool put to sea on the 2nd of October, bound for Tampa Town, having on board a Frenchman borne on the list of passengers by the name of Michel Ardan."

That very evening he wrote to the house of Breadwill and Co., requesting them to suspend the casting of the projectile until the receipt of further orders. On the 10th of October, at nine A.M., the semaphores of the Bahama Canal signaled a thick smoke on the horizon. Two hours later a large steamer exchanged signals with them. the name of the Atlanta flew at once over Tampa Town. At four o'clock the English vessel entered the Bay of Espiritu Santo. At five it crossed the passage of Hillisborough Bay at full steam. At six she cast anchor at Port Tampa. The anchor had scarcely caught the sandy bottom when five hundred boats surrounded the Atlanta, and the steamer was taken by assault. Barbicane was the first to set foot on deck, and in a voice of which he vainly tried to conceal the emotion, called "Michel Ardan."

"Here!" replied an individual perched on the poop.

Barbicane, with arms crossed, looked fixedly at the passenger of the Atlanta.

He was a man of about forty-two years of age, of large build, but slightly round-shouldered. His massive head momentarily shook a shock of reddish hair, which resembled a lion's mane. His face was short with a broad forehead, and furnished with a moustache as bristly as a cat's, and little patches of yellowish whiskers upon full cheeks. Round, wildish eyes, slightly near-sighted, completed a physiognomy essentially feline. His nose was firmly shaped, his mouth particularly sweet in expression, high forehead, intelligent and furrowed with wrinkles like a newly-plowed field. The body was powerfully developed and firmly fixed upon long legs. Muscular arms, and a general air of decision gave him the appearance of a hardy, jolly, companion. He was dressed in a suit of ample dimensions, loose neckerchief, open shirtcollar, disclosing a robust neck; his cuffs were invariably unbuttoned, through which appeared a pair of red hands.

On the bridge of the steamer, in the midst of the crowd, he bustled to and fro, never still for a moment, "dragging his anchors," as the sailors say, gesticulating, making free with everybody, biting his nails with nervous avidity. He was one of those originals which nature sometimes invents in the freak of a moment, and of which she then breaks the mould.

Among other peculiarities, this curiosity gave himself out for a sublime ignoramus, "like Shakespeare," and professed supreme contempt for all scientific men. Those "fellows," as he called them, "are only fit to mark the points, while we play the game." He was, in fact, a thorough Bohemian, adventurous, but not an adventurer; a hare-brained fellow, a kind of Icarus, only possessing relays of wings. For the rest, he was ever in scrapes, ending invariably by falling on his feet, like those little figures which they sell for children's toys. In a few words, his motto was "I have my opinions," and the love of the impossible constituted his ruling passion.

Such was the passenger of the Atlanta, always excitable, as if boiling under the action of some internal fire by the character of his physical organization. If ever two individuals offered a striking contrast to each other, these were certainly Michel Ardan and the Yankee Barbicane; both, moreover, being equally enterprising and daring, each in his own way.

The scrutiny which the president of the Gun Club had instituted regarding this new rival was quickly interrupted by the shouts and hurrahs of the crowd. The cries became at last so uproarious, and the popular enthusiasm assumed so personal a form, that Michel Ardan, after having shaken hands some thousands of times, at the imminent risk of leaving his fingers behind him, was fain at last to make a bolt for his cabin.

Barbicane followed him without uttering a word.

"You are Barbicane, I suppose?" said Michel Ardan, in a tone of voice in which he would have addressed a friend of twenty years' standing.

"Yes," replied the president of the Gun Club.

"All right! how d'ye do, Barbicane? how are you getting on— pretty well? that's right."

"So," said Barbicane without further preliminary, "you are quite determined to go."

"Quite decided."

"Nothing will stop you?"

"Nothing. Have you modified your projectile according to my telegram."

"I waited for your arrival. But," asked Barbicane again, "have you carefully reflected?"

"Reflected? have I any time to spare? I find an opportunity of making a tour in the moon, and I mean to profit by it. There is the whole gist of the matter."

Barbicane looked hard at this man who spoke so lightly of his project with such complete absence of anxiety. "But, at least," said he, "you have some plans, some means of carrying your project into execution?"

"Excellent, my dear Barbicane; only permit me to offer one remark: My wish is to tell my story once for all, to everybody, and then have done with it; then there will be no need for recapitulation. So, if you have no objection, assemble your friends, colleagues, the whole town, all Florida, all America if you like, and to-morrow I shall be ready to explain my plans and answer any objections whatever that may be advanced. You may rest assured I shall wait without stirring. Will that suit you?"

"All right," replied Barbicane.

So saying, the president left the cabin and informed the crowd of the proposal of Michel Ardan. His words were received with clappings of hands and shouts of joy. They had removed all difficulties. To-morrow every one would contemplate at his ease this European hero. However, some of the spectators, more infatuated than the rest, would not leave the deck of the Atlanta. They passed the night on board. Among others J. T. Maston got his hook fixed in the combing of the poop, and it pretty nearly required the capstan to get it out again.

"He is a hero! a hero!" he cried, a theme of which he was never tired of ringing the changes; "and we are only like weak, silly women, compared with this European!"

As to the president, after having suggested to the visitors it was time to retire, he re-entered the passenger's cabin, and remained there till the bell of the steamer made it midnight.

But then the two rivals in popularity shook hands heartily and parted on terms of intimate friendship.

CHAPTER XIX A MONSTER MEETING

On the following day Barbicane, fearing that indiscreet questions might be put to Michel Ardan, was desirous of reducing the number of the audience to a few of the initiated, his own colleagues for instance. He might as well have tried to check the Falls of Niagara! he was compelled, therefore, to give up the idea, and let his new friend run the chances of a public conference. The place chosen for this monster meeting was a vast plain situated in the rear of the town. In a few hours, thanks to the help of the shipping in port, an immense roofing of canvas was stretched over the parched prairie, and protected it from the burning rays of the sun. There three hundred thousand people braved for many hours the stifling heat while awaiting the arrival of the Frenchman. Of this crowd of spectators a first set could both see and hear; a second set saw badly and heard nothing at all; and as for the third, it could neither see nor hear anything at all. At three o'clock Michel Ardan made his appearance, accompanied by the principal members of the Gun Club. He was supported on his right by President Barbicane, and on his left by J. T. Maston, more radiant than the midday sun, and nearly as ruddy. Ardan mounted a platform, from the top of which his view extended over a sea of black hats.

He exhibited not the slightest embarrassment; he was just as gay, familiar, and pleasant as if he were at home. To the hurrahs which greeted him he replied by a graceful bow; then, waving his hands to request silence, he spoke in perfectly correct English as follows:

"Gentlemen, despite the very hot weather I request your patience for a short time while I offer some explanations regarding the projects which seem to have so interested you. I am neither an orator nor a man of science, and I had no idea of addressing you in public; but my friend Barbicane has told me that you would like to hear me, and I am quite at your service. Listen to me, therefore, with your six hundred thousand ears, and please excuse the faults of the speaker. Now pray do not forget that you see before you a perfect ignoramus whose ignorance goes so far that he cannot even understand the difficulties! It seemed to him that it was a matter quite simple, natural, and easy to take one's place in a projectile and start for the moon! That journey must be undertaken sooner or later; and, as for the mode of locomotion adopted, it follows simply the law of progress. Man began by walking on all-fours; then, one fine day, on two feet; then in a carriage; then in a stage-coach; and lastly by railway. Well, the projectile is the vehicle of the future, and the planets themselves are nothing else! Now some of you, gentlemen, may imagine that the velocity we propose to impart to it is extravagant. It is nothing of the kind. All the stars exceed it in rapidity, and the earth herself is at this moment carrying us round the sun at three times as rapid a rate, and yet she is a mere lounger on the way compared with many others of the planets! And her velocity is constantly decreasing. Is it not evident, then, I ask you, that there will some day appear velocities far greater than these, of which light or electricity will probably be the mechanical agent?

"Yes, gentlemen," continued the orator, "in spite of the opinions of certain narrow-minded people, who would shut up the human race upon this globe, as within some magic circle which it must never outstep, we shall one day travel to the moon, the planets, and the stars, with the same facility, rapidity, and certainty as we now make the voyage from Liverpool to New York! Distance is but a relative expression, and must end by being reduced to zero."

The assembly, strongly predisposed as they were in favor of the

French hero, were slightly staggered at this bold theory.

Michel Ardan perceived the fact.

"Gentlemen," he continued with a pleasant smile, "you do not seem quite convinced. Very good! Let us reason the matter out. Do you know how long it would take for an express train to reach the moon? Three hundred days; no more! And what is that? The distance is no more than nine times the circumference of the earth; and there are no sailors or travelers, of even moderate activity, who have not made longer journeys than that in their lifetime. And now consider that I shall be only ninety- seven hours on my journey. Ah! I see you are reckoning that the moon is a long way off from the earth, and that one must think twice before making the experiment. What would you say, then, if we were talking of going to Neptune, which revolves at a distance of more than two thousand seven hundred and twenty millions of miles from the sun! And yet what is that compared with the distance of the fixed stars, some of which, such as Arcturus, are billions of miles distant from us? And then you talk of the distance which separates the planets from the sun! And there are people who affirm that such a thing as distance exists. Absurdity, folly, idiotic nonsense! Would you know what I think of our own solar universe? Shall I tell you my theory? It is very simple! In my opinion the solar system is a solid homogeneous body; the planets which compose it are in actual contact with each other; and whatever space exists between them is nothing more than the space which separates the molecules of the densest metal, such as silver, iron, or platinum! I have the right, therefore, to affirm, and I repeat, with the conviction which must penetrate all your minds, `Distance is but an empty name; distance does not really exist!'"

"Hurrah!" cried one voice (need it be said it was that of J. T. Maston). "Distance does not exist!" And overcome by the energy of his movements, he nearly fell from the platform to the ground. He just escaped a severe fall, which would have proved to him that distance was by no means an empty name.

"Gentlemen," resumed the orator, "I repeat that the distance between the earth and her satellite is a mere trifle, and undeserving of serious consideration. I am convinced that before twenty years are over one-half of our earth will have paid a visit to the moon. Now, my worthy friends, if you have any question to put to me, you will, I fear, sadly embarrass a poor man like myself; still I will do my best to answer you."

Up to this point the president of the Gun Club had been satisfied with the turn which the discussion had assumed. It became now, however, desirable to divert Ardan from questions of a practical nature, with which he was doubtless far less conversant. Barbicane, therefore, hastened to get in a word, and began by asking his new friend whether he thought that the moon and the planets were inhabited.

"You put before me a great problem, my worthy president," replied the orator, smiling. "Still, men of great intelligence, such as Plutarch, Swedenborg, Bernardin de St. Pierre, and others have, if I mistake not, pronounced in the affirmative. Looking at the question from the natural philosopher's point of view, I should say that nothing useless existed in the world; and, replying to your question by another, I should venture to assert, that if these worlds are habitable, they either are, have been, or will be inhabited."

"No one could answer more logically or fairly," replied the president. "The question then reverts to this: Are these worlds habitable? For my own part I believe they are."

"For myself, I feel certain of it," said Michel Ardan.

"Nevertheless," retorted one of the audience, "there are many arguments against the habitability of the worlds. The conditions of life must evidently be greatly modified upon the majority of them. To mention only the planets, we should be either broiled alive in some, or frozen to death in others, according as they are more or less removed from the sun."

"I regret," replied Michel Ardan, "that I have not the honor of personally knowing my contradictor, for I would have attempted to answer him. His objection has its merits, I admit; but I think we may successfully combat it, as well as all others which affect the habitability of other worlds. If I were a natural philosopher, I would tell him that if less of caloric were set in motion upon the planets which are nearest to the sun, and more, on the contrary, upon those which are farthest removed from it, this simple fact would alone suffice to equalize the heat, and to render the temperature of those worlds supportable by beings organized like ourselves. If I were a naturalist, I would tell him that, according to some illustrious men of science, nature has furnished us with instances upon the earth of animals existing under very varying conditions of life; that fish respire in a medium fatal to other animals; that amphibious creatures possess a double existence very difficult of explanation; that certain denizens of the seas maintain life at enormous depths, and there support a pressure equal to that of fifty or sixty atmospheres without being crushed; that several aquatic insects, insensible to temperature, are met with equally among boiling springs and in the frozen plains of the Polar Sea; in fine, that we cannot help recognizing in nature a diversity of means of operation oftentimes incomprehensible, but not the less real. If I were a chemist, I would tell him that the aerolites, bodies evidently formed exteriorly of our terrestrial globe, have, upon analysis, revealed indisputable traces of carbon, a substance which owes its origin solely to organized beings, and which, according to the experiments of Reichenbach, must necessarily itself have been endued with animation. And lastly, were I a theologian, I would tell him that the scheme of the Divine Redemption, according to St. Paul, seems to be applicable, not merely to the earth, but to all the celestial worlds. But, unfortunately, I am neither theologian, nor chemist, nor naturalist, nor philosopher; therefore, in my absolute ignorance of the great laws which govern the universe, I confine myself to saying in reply, `I do not know whether the worlds are inhabited or not: and since I do not know, I am going to see!'"

Whether Michel Ardan's antagonist hazarded any further arguments or not it is impossible to say, for the uproarious shouts of the crowd would not allow any expression of opinion to gain a hearing. On silence being restored, the triumphant orator contented himself with adding the following remarks:

"Gentlemen, you will observe that I have but slightly touched upon this great question. There is another altogether different line of argument in favor of the habitability of the stars, which I omit for the present. I only desire to call attention to one point. To those who maintain that the planets are *not* inhabited one may reply: You might be perfectly in the right, if you could only show that the earth is the best possible world, in spite of what Voltaire has said. She has but *one* satellite, while Jupiter, Uranus, Saturn, Neptune have each several, an advantage by no means to be despised. But that which renders our own globe so uncomfortable is the inclination of its axis to the plane of its orbit. Hence the inequality of days and nights; hence the disagreeable diversity of the seasons. On the surface of our unhappy spheroid we are always either too hot or too cold; we are frozen in winter, broiled in summer; it is the planet of rheumatism, coughs, bronchitis; while on the surface of Jupiter, for example, where the axis is but slightly inclined, the inhabitants may enjoy uniform temperatures. It possesses zones of perpetual springs, summers, autumns, and winters; every Jovian may choose for himself what climate he likes, and there spend the whole of his life in security from all variations of temperature. You will, I am sure, readily admit this superiority of Jupiter over our own planet, to say nothing of his years, which each equal twelve of ours! Under such auspices and such marvelous conditions of existence, it appears to me that the inhabitants of so fortunate a world must be in every respect superior to ourselves. All we require, in order to attain such perfection, is the mere trifle of having an axis of rotation less inclined to the plane of its orbit!"

"Hurrah!" roared an energetic voice, "let us unite our efforts, invent the necessary machines, and rectify the earth's axis!"

A thunder of applause followed this proposal, the author of which was, of course, no other than J. T. Maston. And, in all probability, if the truth must be told, if the Yankees could only have found a point of application for it, they would have constructed a lever capable of raising the earth and rectifying its axis. It was just this deficiency which baffled these daring mechanicians.

CHAPTER XX ATTACK AND RIPOSTE

As soon as the excitement had subsided, the following words were heard uttered in a strong and determined voice:

"Now that the speaker has favored us with so much imagination, would he be so good as to return to his subject, and give us a little practical view of the question?"

All eyes were directed toward the person who spoke. He was a little dried-up man, of an active figure, with an American "goatee" beard. Profiting by the different movements in the crowd, he had managed by degrees to gain the front row of spectators. There, with arms crossed and stern gaze, he watched the hero of the meeting. After having put his question he remained silent, and appeared to take no notice of the thousands of looks directed toward himself, nor of the murmur of disapprobation excited by his words. Meeting at first with no reply, he repeated his question with marked emphasis, adding, "We are here to talk about the *moon* and not about the *earth*."

"You are right, sir," replied Michel Ardan; "the discussion has become irregular. We will return to the moon."

"Sir," said the unknown, "you pretend that our satellite is inhabited. Very good, but if Selenites do exist, that race of beings assuredly must live without breathing, for— I warn you for your own sake— there is not the smallest particle of air on the surface of the moon."

At this remark Ardan pushed up his shock of red hair; he saw that he was on the point of being involved in a struggle with this person upon the very gist of the whole question. He looked sternly at him in his turn and said:

"Oh! so there is no air in the moon? And pray, if you are so good, who ventures to affirm that?

"The men of science."

"Really?"

"Really."

"Sir," replied Michel, "pleasantry apart, I have a profound respect for men of science who do possess science, but a profound contempt for men of science who do not."

"Do you know any who belong to the latter category?"

"Decidedly. In France there are some who maintain that, mathematically, a bird cannot possibly fly; and others who demonstrate theoretically that fishes were never made to live in water."

"I have nothing to do with persons of that description, and I can quote, in support of my statement, names which you cannot refuse deference to."

"Then, sir, you will sadly embarrass a poor ignorant, who, besides, asks nothing better than to learn."

"Why, then, do you introduce scientific questions if you have never studied them?" asked the unknown somewhat coarsely.

"For the reason that `he is always brave who never suspects danger.' I know nothing, it is true; but it is precisely my very weakness which constitutes my strength."

"Your weakness amounts to folly," retorted the unknown in a passion.

"All the better," replied our Frenchman, "if it carries me up to the moon."

Barbicane and his colleagues devoured with their eyes the intruder who had so boldly placed himself in antagonism to their enterprise. Nobody knew him, and the president, uneasy as to the result of so free a discussion, watched his new friend with some anxiety. The meeting began to be somewhat fidgety also, for the contest directed their attention to the dangers, if not the actual impossibilities, of the proposed expedition.

"Sir," replied Ardan's antagonist, "there are many and incontrovertible reasons which prove the absence of an atmosphere in the moon. I might say that, *a priori*, if one ever did exist, it must have been absorbed by the earth; but I prefer to bring forward indisputable facts."

"Bring them forward then, sir, as many as you please."

"You know," said the stranger, "that when any luminous rays cross a medium such as the air, they are deflected out of the straight line; in other words, they undergo refraction. Well! When stars are occulted by the moon, their rays, on grazing the edge of her disc, exhibit not the least deviation, nor offer the slightest indication of refraction. It follows, therefore, that the moon cannot be surrounded by an atmosphere.

"In point of fact," replied Ardan, "this is your chief, if not your *only* argument; and a really scientific man might be puzzled to answer it. For myself, I will simply say that it is defective, because it assumes that the angular diameter of the moon has been completely determined, which is not the case. But let us proceed. Tell me, my dear sir, do you admit the existence of volcanoes on the moon's surface?"

"Extinct, yes! In activity, no!"

"These volcanoes, however, were at one time in a state of activity?"

"True, but, as they furnish themselves the oxygen necessary for combustion, the mere fact of their eruption does not prove the presence of an atmosphere."

"Proceed again, then; and let us set aside this class of arguments in order to come to direct observations. In 1715 the astronomers Louville and Halley, watching the eclipse of the 3rd of May, remarked some very extraordinary scintillations. These jets of light, rapid in nature, and of frequent recurrence, they attributed to thunderstorms generated in the lunar atmosphere."

"In 1715," replied the unknown, "the astronomers Louville and Halley mistook for lunar phenomena some which were purely terrestrial, such as meteoric or other bodies which are generated in our own atmosphere. This was the scientific explanation at the time of the facts; and that is my answer now."

"On again, then," replied Ardan; "Herschel, in 1787, observed a great number of luminous points on the moon's surface, did he not?"

"Yes! but without offering any solution of them. Herschel himself never inferred from them the necessity of a lunar atmosphere. And I may add that Baeer and Maedler, the two great authorities upon the moon, are quite agreed as to the entire absence of air on its surface."

A movement was here manifest among the assemblage, who appeared to be growing excited by the arguments of this singular personage.

"Let us proceed," replied Ardan, with perfect coolness, "and come to one important fact. A skillful French astronomer, M. Laussedat, in watching the eclipse of July 18,

1860, probed that the horns of the lunar crescent were rounded and truncated. Now, this appearance could only have been produced by a deviation of the solar rays in traversing the atmosphere of the moon. There is no other possible explanation of the facts."

"But is this established as a fact?"

"Absolutely certain!"

A counter-movement here took place in favor of the hero of the meeting, whose opponent was now reduced to silence. Ardan resumed the conversation; and without exhibiting any exultation at the advantage he had gained, simply said:

"You see, then, my dear sir, we must not pronounce with absolute positiveness against the existence of an atmosphere in the moon. That atmosphere is, probably, of extreme rarity; nevertheless at the present day science generally admits that it exists."

"Not in the mountains, at all events," returned the unknown, unwilling to give in.

"No! but at the bottom of the valleys, and not exceeding a few hundred feet in height."

"In any case you will do well to take every precaution, for the air will be terribly rarified."

"My good sir, there will always be enough for a solitary individual; besides, once arrived up there, I shall do my best to economize, and not to breathe except on grand occasions!"

A tremendous roar of laughter rang in the ears of the mysterious interlocutor, who glared fiercely round upon the assembly.

"Then," continued Ardan, with a careless air, "since we are in accord regarding the presence of a certain atmosphere, we are forced to admit the presence of a certain quantity of water. This is a happy consequence for me. Moreover, my amiable contradictor, permit me to submit to you one further observation. We only know *one* side of the moon's disc; and if there is but little air on the face presented to us, it is possible that there is plenty on the one turned away from us."

"And for what reason?"

"Because the moon, under the action of the earth's attraction, has assumed the form of an egg, which we look at from the smaller end. Hence it follows, by Hausen's calculations, that its center of gravity is situated in the other hemisphere. Hence it results that the great mass of air and water must have been drawn away to the other face of our satellite during the first days of its creation."

"Pure fancies!" cried the unknown.

"No! Pure theories! which are based upon the laws of mechanics, and it seems difficult to me to refute them. I appeal then to this meeting, and I put it to them whether life, such as exists upon the earth, is possible on the surface of the moon?"

Three hundred thousand auditors at once applauded the proposition. Ardan's opponent tried to get in another word, but he could not obtain a hearing. Cries and menaces fell upon him like hail.

"Enough! enough!" cried some.

"Drive the intruder off!" shouted others.

"Turn him out!" roared the exasperated crowd.

But he, holding firmly on to the platform, did not budge an inch, and let the storm pass on, which would soon have assumed formidable proportions, if Michel Ardan had not quieted it by a gesture. He was too chivalrous to abandon his opponent in an apparent extremity.

"You wished to say a few more words?" he asked, in a pleasant voice.

"Yes, a thousand; or rather, no, only one! If you persevere in your enterprise, you must be a——"

"Very rash person! How can you treat me as such? me, who have demanded a cylindro-conical projectile, in order to prevent turning round and round on my way like a squirrel?"

"But, unhappy man, the dreadful recoil will smash you to pieces at your starting."

"My dear contradictor, you have just put your finger upon the true and only difficulty; nevertheless, I have too good an opinion of the industrial genius of the Americans not to believe that they will succeed in overcoming it."

"But the heat developed by the rapidity of the projectile in crossing the strata of air?"

"Oh! the walls are thick, and I shall soon have crossed the atmosphere."

"But victuals and water?"

"I have calculated for a twelvemonth's supply, and I shall be only four days on the journey."

"But for air to breathe on the road?"

"I shall make it by a chemical process."

"But your fall on the moon, supposing you ever reach it?"

"It will be six times less dangerous than a sudden fall upon the earth, because the weight will be only one-sixth as great on the surface of the moon."

"Still it will be enough to smash you like glass!"

"What is to prevent my retarding the shock by means of rockets conveniently placed, and lighted at the right moment?"

"But after all, supposing all difficulties surmounted, all obstacles removed, supposing everything combined to favor you, and granting that you may arrive safe and sound in the moon, how will you come back?"

"I am not coming back!"

At this reply, almost sublime in its very simplicity, the assembly became silent. But its silence was more eloquent than could have been its cries of enthusiasm. The unknown profited by the opportunity and once more protested:

"You will inevitably kill yourself!" he cried; "and your death will be that of a madman, useless even to science!"

"Go on, my dear unknown, for truly your prophecies are most agreeable!"

"It really is too much!" cried Michel Ardan's adversary. "I do not know why I should continue so frivolous a discussion! Please yourself about this insane expedition! We need not trouble ourselves about you!"

"Pray don't stand upon ceremony!"

"No! another person is responsible for your act."

"Who, may I ask?" demanded Michel Ardan in an imperious tone.

"The ignoramus who organized this equally absurd and impossible experiment!"

The attack was direct. Barbicane, ever since the interference of the unknown, had been making fearful efforts of self-control; now, however, seeing himself directly attacked, he could restrain himself no longer. He rose suddenly, and was rushing upon the enemy who thus braved him to the face, when all at once he found himself separated from him.

The platform was lifted by a hundred strong arms, and the president of the Gun Club shared with Michel Ardan triumphal honors. The shield was heavy, but the bearers came in continuous relays, disputing, struggling, even fighting among themselves in their eagerness to lend their shoulders to this demonstration.

However, the unknown had not profited by the tumult to quit his post. Besides he could not have done it in the midst of that compact crowd. There he held on in the front row with crossed arms, glaring at President Barbicane.

CHAPTER XX ATTACK AND RIPOSTE

The shouts of the immense crowd continued at their highest pitch throughout this triumphant march. Michel Ardan took it all with evident pleasure. His face gleamed with delight. Several times the platform seemed seized with pitching and rolling like a weatherbeaten ship. But the two heros of the meeting had good sea-legs. They never stumbled; and their vessel arrived without dues at the port of Tampa Town.

Michel Ardan managed fortunately to escape from the last embraces of his vigorous admirers. He made for the Hotel Franklin, quickly gained his chamber, and slid under the bedclothes, while an army of a hundred thousand men kept watch under his windows.

During this time a scene, short, grave, and decisive, took place between the mysterious personage and the president of the Gun Club.

Barbicane, free at last, had gone straight at his adversary.

"Come!" he said shortly.

The other followed him on the quay; and the two presently found themselves alone at the entrance of an open wharf on Jones' Fall.

The two enemies, still mutually unknown, gazed at each other.

"Who are you?" asked Barbicane.

"Captain Nicholl!"

"So I suspected. Hitherto chance has never thrown you in my way."

"I am come for that purpose."

"You have insulted me."

"Publicly!"

"And you will answer to me for this insult?"

"At this very moment."

"No! I desire that all that passes between us shall be secret. Their is a wood situated three miles from Tampa, the wood of Skersnaw. Do you know it?"

"I know it."

"Will you be so good as to enter it to-morrow morning at five o'clock, on one side?"

"Yes! if you will enter at the other side at the same hour."

"And you will not forget your rifle?" said Barbicane.

"No more than you will forget yours?" replied Nicholl.

These words having been coldly spoken, the president of the Gun Club and the captain parted. Barbicane returned to his lodging; but instead of snatching a few hours of repose, he passed the night in endeavoring to discover a means of evading the recoil of the projectile, and resolving the difficult problem proposed by Michel Ardan during the discussion at the meeting.

CHAPTER XXI HOW A FRENCHMAN MANAGES AN AFFAIR

While the contract of this duel was being discussed by the president and the captain— this dreadful, savage duel, in which each adversary became a man-hunter— Michel Ardan was resting from the fatigues of his triumph. Resting is hardly an appropriate expression, for American beds rival marble or granite tables for hardness.

Ardan was sleeping, then, badly enough, tossing about between the cloths which served him for sheets, and he was dreaming of making a more comfortable couch in his projectile when a frightful noise disturbed his dreams. Thundering blows shook his door. They seemed to be caused by some iron instrument. A great deal of loud talking was distinguishable in this racket, which was rather too early in the morning. "Open the door," some one shrieked, "for heaven's sake!" Ardan saw no reason for complying with a demand so roughly expressed. However, he got up and opened the door just as it was giving way before the blows of this determined visitor. The secretary of the Gun Club burst into the room. A bomb could not have made more noise or have entered the room with less ceremony.

"Last night," cried J. T. Maston, *ex abrupto*, "our president was publicly insulted during the meeting. He provoked his adversary, who is none other than Captain Nicholl! They are fighting this morning in the wood of Skersnaw. I heard all the particulars from the mouth of Barbicane himself. If he is killed, then our scheme is at an end. We must prevent his duel; and one man alone has enough influence over Barbicane to stop him, and that man is Michel Ardan."

While J. T. Maston was speaking, Michel Ardan, without interrupting him, had hastily put on his clothes; and, in less than two minutes, the two friends were making for the suburbs of Tampa Town with rapid strides.

It was during this walk that Maston told Ardan the state of the case. He told him the real causes of the hostility between Barbicane and Nicholl; how it was of old date, and why, thanks to unknown friends, the president and the captain had, as yet, never met face to face. He added that it arose simply from a rivalry between iron plates and shot, and, finally, that the scene at the meeting was only the long-wished-for opportunity for Nicholl to pay off an old grudge.

Nothing is more dreadful than private duels in America. The two adversaries attack each other like wild beasts. Then it is that they might well covet those wonderful properties of the Indians of the prairies— their quick intelligence, their ingenious cunning, their scent of the enemy. A single mistake, a moment's hesitation, a single false step may cause death. On these occasions Yankees are often accompanied by their dogs, and keep up the struggle for hours.

"What demons you are!" cried Michel Ardan, when his companion had depicted this scene to him with much energy.

"Yes, we are," replied J. T. modestly; "but we had better make haste."

Though Michel Ardan and he had crossed the plains still wet with dew, and had taken the shortest route over creeks and ricefields, they could not reach Skersnaw in under five hours and a half.

Barbicane must have passed the border half an hour ago.

There was an old bushman working there, occupied in selling fagots from trees that had been leveled by his axe.

Maston ran toward him, saying, "Have you seen a man go into the wood, armed with a rifle? Barbicane, the president, my best friend?"

The worthy secretary of the Gun Club thought that his president must be known by all the world. But the bushman did not seem to understand him.

"A hunter?" said Ardan.

"A hunter? Yes," replied the bushman.

"Long ago?"

"About an hour."

"Too late!" cried Maston.

"Have you heard any gunshots?" asked Ardan.

"No!"

"Not one?"

"Not one! that hunter did not look as if he knew how to hunt!"

"What is to be done?" said Maston.

"We must go into the wood, at the risk of getting a ball which is not intended for us."

"Ah!" cried Maston, in a tone which could not be mistaken, "I would rather have twenty balls in my own head than one in Barbicane's."

"Forward, then," said Ardan, pressing his companion's hand.

A few moments later the two friends had disappeared in the copse. It was a dense thicket, in which rose huge cypresses, sycamores, tulip-trees, olives, tamarinds, oaks, and magnolias. These different trees had interwoven their branches into an inextricable maze, through which the eye could not penetrate. Michel Ardan and Maston walked side by side in silence through the tall grass, cutting themselves a path through the strong creepers, casting curious glances on the bushes, and momentarily expecting to hear the sound of rifles. As for the traces which Barbicane ought to have left of his passage through the wood, there was not a vestige of them visible: so they followed the barely perceptible paths along which Indians had tracked some enemy, and which the dense foliage darkly overshadowed.

After an hour spent in vain pursuit the two stopped in intensified anxiety.

"It must be all over," said Maston, discouraged. "A man like Barbicane would not dodge with his enemy, or ensnare him, would not even maneuver! He is too open, too brave. He has gone straight ahead, right into the danger, and doubtless far enough from the bushman for the wind to prevent his hearing the report of the rifles."

"But surely," replied Michel Ardan, "since we entered the wood we should have heard!"

"And what if we came too late?" cried Maston in tones of despair.

For once Ardan had no reply to make, he and Maston resuming their walk in silence. From time to time, indeed, they raised great shouts, calling alternately Barbicane and Nicholl, neither of whom, however, answered their cries. Only the birds, awakened by the sound, flew past them and disappeared among the branches, while some frightened deer fled precipitately before them.

For another hour their search was continued. The greater part of the wood had been explored. There was nothing to reveal the presence of the combatants. The information of the bushman was after all doubtful, and Ardan was about to propose their abandoning this useless pursuit, when all at once Maston stopped.

"Hush!" said he, "there is some one down there!"

"Some one?" repeated Michel Ardan.

"Yes; a man! He seems motionless. His rifle is not in his hands.

What can he be doing?"

"But can you recognize him?" asked Ardan, whose short sight was of little use to him in such circumstances.

"Yes! yes! He is turning toward us," answered Maston.

"And it is?"

"Captain Nicholl!"

"Nicholl?" cried Michel Ardan, feeling a terrible pang of grief.

"Nicholl unarmed! He has, then, no longer any fear of his adversary!"

"Let us go to him," said Michel Ardan, "and find out the truth."

But he and his companion had barely taken fifty steps, when they paused to examine the captain more attentively. They expected to find a bloodthirsty man, happy in his revenge.

On seeing him, they remained stupefied.

A net, composed of very fine meshes, hung between two enormous tulip-trees, and in the midst of this snare, with its wings entangled, was a poor little bird, uttering pitiful cries, while it vainly struggled to escape. The bird-catcher who had laid this snare was no human being, but a venomous spider, peculiar to that country, as large as a pigeon's egg, and armed with enormous claws. The hideous creature, instead of rushing on its prey, had beaten a sudden retreat and taken refuge in the upper branches of the tulip-tree, for a formidable enemy menaced its stronghold.

Here, then, was Nicholl, his gun on the ground, forgetful of danger, trying if possible to save the victim from its cobweb prison. At last it was accomplished, and the little bird flew joyfully away and disappeared.

Nicholl lovingly watched its flight, when he heard these words pronounced by a voice full of emotion:

"You are indeed a brave man."

He turned. Michel Ardan was before him, repeating in a different tone:

"And a kindhearted one!"

"Michel Ardan!" cried the captain. "Why are you here?"

"To press your hand, Nicholl, and to prevent you from either killing Barbicane or being killed by him."

"Barbicane!" returned the captain. "I have been looking for him for the last two hours in vain. Where is he hiding?"

"Nicholl!" said Michel Ardan, "this is not courteous! we ought always to treat an adversary with respect; rest assured if Barbicane is still alive we shall find him all the more easily; because if he has not, like you, been amusing himself with freeing oppressed birds, he must be looking for *you*. When we have found him, Michel Ardan tells you this, there will be no duel between you."

"Between President Barbicane and myself," gravely replied

Nicholl, "there is a rivalry which the death of one of us——"

"Pooh, pooh!" said Ardan. "Brave fellows like you indeed! you shall not fight!"

"I will fight, sir!"

"No!"

"Captain," said J. T. Maston, with much feeling, "I am a friend of the president's, his *alter ego*, his second self; if you really must kill some one, *shoot me!* it will do just as well!"

"Sir," Nicholl replied, seizing his rifle convulsively, "these jokes——"

"Our friend Maston is not joking," replied Ardan. "I fully understand his idea of being killed himself in order to save his friend. But neither he nor Barbicane will fall before the balls of Captain Nicholl. Indeed I have so attractive a proposal to make to the two rivals, that both will be eager to accept it."

"What is it?" asked Nicholl with manifest incredulity.

"Patience!" exclaimed Ardan. "I can only reveal it in the presence of Barbicane."

"Let us go in search of him then!" cried the captain.

The three men started off at once; the captain having discharged his rifle threw it over his shoulder, and advanced in silence. Another half hour passed, and the pursuit was still fruitless. Maston was oppressed by sinister forebodings. He looked fiercely at Nicholl, asking himself whether the captain's vengeance had already been satisfied, and the unfortunate Barbicane, shot, was perhaps lying dead on some bloody track. The same thought seemed to occur to Ardan; and both were casting inquiring glances on Nicholl, when suddenly Maston paused.

The motionless figure of a man leaning against a gigantic catalpa twenty feet off appeared, half-veiled by the foliage.

"It is he!" said Maston.

Barbicane never moved. Ardan looked at the captain, but he did not wince. Ardan went forward crying:

"Barbicane! Barbicane!"

No answer! Ardan rushed toward his friend; but in the act of seizing his arms, he stopped short and uttered a cry of surprise.

Barbicane, pencil in hand, was tracing geometrical figures in a memorandum book, while his unloaded rifle lay beside him on the ground.

Absorbed in his studies, Barbicane, in his turn forgetful of the duel, had seen and heard nothing.

When Ardan took his hand, he looked up and stared at his visitor in astonishment.

"Ah, it is you!" he cried at last. "I have found it, my friend,

I have found it!"

"What?"

"My plan!"

"What plan?"

"The plan for countering the effect of the shock at the departure of the projectile!"

"Indeed?" said Michel Ardan, looking at the captain out of the corner of his eye.

"Yes! water! simply water, which will act as a spring— ah!

Maston," cried Barbicane, "you here also?"

"Himself," replied Ardan; "and permit me to introduce to you at the same time the worthy Captain Nicholl!"

"Nicholl!" cried Barbicane, who jumped up at once. "Pardon me, captain, I had quite forgotten— I am ready!"

Michel Ardan interfered, without giving the two enemies time to say anything more.

"Thank heaven!" said he. "It is a happy thing that brave men like you two did not meet sooner! we should now have been mourning for one or other of you. But, thanks to Providence, which has interfered, there is now no further cause for alarm. When one forgets one's anger in mechanics or in cobwebs, it is a sign that the anger is not dangerous."

Michel Ardan then told the president how the captain had been found occupied.

"I put it to you now," said he in conclusion, "are two such good fellows as you are made on purpose to smash each other's skulls with shot?"

There was in "the situation" somewhat of the ridiculous, something quite unexpected; Michel Ardan saw this, and determined to effect a reconciliation.

"My good friends," said he, with his most bewitching smile, "this is nothing but a misunderstanding. Nothing more! well! to prove that it is all over between you, accept frankly the proposal I am going to make to you."

"Make it," said Nicholl.

"Our friend Barbicane believes that his projectile will go straight to the moon?"

"Yes, certainly," replied the president.

"And our friend Nicholl is persuaded it will fall back upon the earth?"

"I am certain of it," cried the captain.

"Good!" said Ardan. "I cannot pretend to make you agree; but I suggest this: Go with me, and so see whether we are stopped on our journey."

"What?" exclaimed J. T. Maston, stupefied.

The two rivals, on this sudden proposal, looked steadily at each other. Barbicane waited for the captain's answer. Nicholl watched for the decision of the president.

"Well?" said Michel. "There is now no fear of the shock!"

"Done!" cried Barbicane.

But quickly as he pronounced the word, he was not before Nicholl.

"Hurrah! bravo! hip! hip! hurrah!" cried Michel, giving a hand to each of the late adversaries. "Now that it is all settled, my friends, allow me to treat you after French fashion. Let us be off to breakfast!"

CHAPTER XXII THE NEW CITIZEN OF THE UNITED STATES

That same day all America heard of the affair of Captain Nicholl and President Barbicane, as well as its singular *denouement*. From that day forth, Michel Ardan had not one moment's rest. Deputations from all corners of the Union harassed him without cessation or intermission. He was compelled to receive them all, whether he would or no. How many hands he shook, how many people he was "hail-fellow-well-met" with, it is impossible to guess! Such a triumphal result would have intoxicated any other man; but he managed to keep himself in a state of delightful *semi*-tipsiness.

Among the deputations of all kinds which assailed him, that of "The Lunatics" were careful not to forget what they owed to the future conqueror of the moon. One day, certain of these poor people, so numerous in America, came to call upon him, and requested permission to return with him to their native country.

"Singular hallucination!" said he to Barbicane, after having dismissed the deputation with promises to convey numbers of messages to friends in the moon. "Do you believe in the influence of the moon upon distempers?"

"Scarcely!"

"No more do I, despite some remarkable recorded facts of history. For instance, during an epidemic in 1693, a large number of persons died at the very moment of an eclipse. The celebrated Bacon always fainted during an eclipse. Charles VI relapsed six times into madness during the year 1399, sometimes during the new, sometimes during the full moon. Gall observed that insane persons underwent an accession of their disorder twice in every month, at the epochs of new and full moon. In fact, numerous observations made upon fevers, somnambulisms, and other human maladies, seem to prove that the moon does exercise some mysterious influence upon man."

"But the how and the wherefore?" asked Barbicane.

"Well, I can only give you the answer which Arago borrowed from Plutarch, which is nineteen centuries old. `Perhaps the stories are not true!'"

In the height of his triumph, Michel Ardan had to encounter all the annoyances incidental to a man of celebrity. Managers of entertainments wanted to exhibit him. Barnum offered him a million dollars to make a tour of the United States in his show. As for his photographs, they were sold of all size, and his portrait taken in every imaginable posture. More than half a million copies were disposed of in an incredibly short space of time.

But it was not only the men who paid him homage, but the women as well. He might have married well a hundred times over, if he had been willing to settle in life. The old maids, in particular, of forty years and upward, and dry in proportion, devoured his photographs day and night. They would have married him by hundreds, even if he had imposed upon them the condition of accompanying him into space. He had, however, no intention of transplanting a race of Franco-Americans upon the surface of the moon.

He therefore declined all offers.

As soon as he could withdraw from these somewhat embarrassing demonstrations, he went, accompanied by his friends, to pay a visit to the Columbiad. He was highly gratified by his inspection, and made the descent to the bottom of the tube of this gigantic machine which was presently to launch him to the regions of the moon. It is necessary here to mention a proposal of J. T. Maston's. When the secretary of the Gun Club found that Barbicane and Nicholl accepted the proposal of Michel Ardan, he determined to join them, and make one of a smug party of four. So one day he determined to be admitted as one of the travelers. Barbicane, pained at having to refuse him, gave him clearly to understand that the projectile could not possibly contain so many passengers. Maston, in despair, went in search of Michel Ardan, who counseled him to resign himself to the situation, adding one or two arguments *ad hominem.*

"You see, old fellow," he said, "you must not take what I say in bad part; but really, between ourselves, you are in too incomplete a condition to appear in the moon!"

"Incomplete?" shrieked the valiant invalid.

"Yes, my dear fellow! imagine our meeting some of the inhabitants up there! Would you like to give them such a melancholy notion of what goes on down here? to teach them what war is, to inform them that we employ our time chiefly in devouring each other, in smashing arms and legs, and that too on a globe which is capable of supporting a hundred billions of inhabitants, and which actually does contain nearly two hundred millions? Why, my worthy friend, we should have to turn you out of doors!"

"But still, if you arrive there in pieces, you will be as incomplete as I am."

"Unquestionably," replied Michel Ardan; "but we shall not."

In fact, a preparatory experiment, tried on the 18th of October, had yielded the best results and caused the most well-grounded hopes of success. Barbicane, desirous of obtaining some notion of the effect of the shock at the moment of the projectile's departure, had procured a 38-inch mortar from the arsenal of Pensacola. He had this placed on the bank of Hillisborough Roads, in order that the shell might fall back into the sea, and the shock be thereby destroyed. His object was to ascertain the extent of the shock of departure, and not that of the return.

A hollow projectile had been prepared for this curious experiment. A thick padding fastened upon a kind of elastic network, made of the best steel, lined the inside of the walls. It was a veritable *nest* most carefully wadded.

"What a pity I can't find room in there," said J. T. Maston, regretting that his height did not allow of his trying the adventure.

Within this shell were shut up a large cat, and a squirrel belonging to J. T. Maston, and of which he was particularly fond. They were desirous, however, of ascertaining how this little animal, least of all others subject to giddiness, would endure this experimental voyage.

The mortar was charged with 160 pounds of powder, and the shell placed in the chamber. On being fired, the projectile rose with great velocity, described a majestic parabola, attained a height of about a thousand feet, and with a graceful curve descended in the midst of the vessels that lay there at anchor.

Without a moment's loss of time a small boat put off in the direction of its fall; some divers plunged into the water and attached ropes to the handles of the shell, which was quickly dragged on board. Five minutes did not elapse between the moment of enclosing the animals and that of unscrewing the coverlid of their prison.

Ardan, Barbicane, Maston, and Nicholl were present on board the boat, and assisted at the operation with an interest which may readily be comprehended. Hardly had the shell been opened when the cat leaped out, slightly bruised, but full of life, and exhibiting no signs whatever of having made an aerial expedition. No trace, however, of the squirrel could be discovered. The truth at last became apparent— the cat had eaten its fellow-traveler!

J. T. Maston grieved much for the loss of his poor squirrel, and proposed to add its case to that of other martyrs to science.

After this experiment all hesitation, all fear disappeared. Besides, Barbicane's plans would ensure greater perfection for his projectile, and go far to annihilate altogether the effects of the shock. Nothing now remained but to go!

Two days later Michel Ardan received a message from the President of the United States, an honor of which he showed himself especially sensible.

After the example of his illustrious fellow-countryman, the Marquis de la Fayette, the government had decreed to him the title of "Citizen of the United States of America."

CHAPTER XXIII THE PROJECTILE-VEHICLE

On the completion of the Columbiad the public interest centered in the projectile itself, the vehicle which was destined to carry the three hardy adventurers into space.

The new plans had been sent to Breadwill and Co., of Albany, with the request for their speedy execution. The projectile was consequently cast on the 2nd of November, and immediately forwarded by the Eastern Railway to Stones Hill, which it reached without accident on the 10th of that month, where Michel Ardan, Barbicane, and Nicholl were waiting impatiently for it.

The projectile had now to be filled to the depth of three feet with a bed of water, intended to support a water-tight wooden disc, which worked easily within the walls of the projectile. It was upon this kind of raft that the travelers were to take their place. This body of water was divided by horizontal partitions, which the shock of the departure would have to break in succession. Then each sheet of the water, from the lowest to the highest, running off into escape tubes toward the top of the projectile, constituted a kind of spring; and the wooden disc, supplied with extremely powerful plugs, could not strike the lowest plate except after breaking successively the different partitions. Undoubtedly the travelers would still have to encounter a violent recoil after the complete escapement of the water; but the first shock would be almost entirely destroyed by this powerful spring. The upper parts of the walls were lined with a thick padding of leather, fastened upon springs of the best steel, behind which the escape tubes were completely concealed; thus all imaginable precautions had been taken for averting the first shock; and if they did get crushed, they must, as Michel Ardan said, be made of very bad materials.

The entrance into this metallic tower was by a narrow aperture contrived in the wall of the cone. This was hermetically closed by a plate of aluminum, fastened internally by powerful screw-pressure. The travelers could therefore quit their prison at pleasure, as soon as they should reach the moon.

Light and view were given by means of four thick lenticular glass scuttles, two pierced in the circular wall itself, the third in the bottom, the fourth in the top. These scuttles then were protected against the shock of departure by plates let into solid grooves, which could easily be opened outward by unscrewing them from the inside. Reservoirs firmly fixed contained water and the necessary provisions; and fire and light were procurable by means of gas, contained in a special reservoir under a pressure of several atmospheres. They had only to turn a tap, and for six hours the gas would light and warm this comfortable vehicle.

There now remained only the question of air; for allowing for the consumption of air by Barbicane, his two companions, and two dogs which he proposed taking with him, it was necessary to renew the air of the projectile. Now air consists principally of twenty-one parts of oxygen and seventy-nine of nitrogen. The lungs absorb the oxygen, which is indispensable for the support of life, and reject the nitrogen. The air expired loses nearly five per cent. of the former and contains nearly an equal volume of carbonic acid, produced by the combustion of the elements of the blood. In an air-tight enclosure, then, after a certain time, all the oxygen of the air will be replaced by the carbonic acid— a gas fatal to life. There were two things to be done then— first, to replace the absorbed oxygen; secondly, to destroy the expired carbonic acid; both easy enough to do, by means of chlorate of potassium and caustic potash. The former is a salt which appears under the form of white crystals; when raised to a temperature of 400 degrees it is transformed into chlorure of potassium, and the oxygen which it contains is entirely liberated. Now twenty-eight pounds of chlorate of potassium produces seven pounds of oxygen, or 2,400 litres— the quantity necessary for the travelers during twenty-four hours.

Caustic potash has a great affinity for carbonic acid; and it is sufficient to shake it in order for it to seize upon the acid and form bicarbonate of potassium. By these two means they would be enabled to restore to the vitiated air its life- supporting properties.

It is necessary, however, to add that the experiments had hitherto been made *in anima vili*. Whatever its scientific accuracy was, they were at present ignorant how it would answer with human beings. The honor of putting it to the proof was energetically claimed by J. T. Maston.

"Since I am not to go," said the brave artillerist, "I may at least live for a week in the projectile."

It would have been hard to refuse him; so they consented to his wish. A sufficient quantity of chlorate of potassium and of caustic potash was placed at his disposal, together with provisions for eight days. And having shaken hands with his friends, on the 12th of November, at six o'clock A.M., after strictly informing them not to open his prison before the 20th, at six o'clock P.M., he slid down the projectile, the plate of which was at once hermetically sealed. What did he do with himself during that week? They could get no information. The thickness of the walls of the projectile prevented any sound reaching from the inside to the outside. On the 20th of November, at six P.M. exactly, the plate was opened. The friends of J. T. Maston had been all along in a state of much anxiety; but they were promptly reassured on hearing a jolly voice shouting a boisterous hurrah.

Presently afterward the secretary of the Gun Club appeared at the top of the cone in a triumphant attitude. He had grown fat!

CHAPTER XXIV THE TELESCOPE OF THE ROCKY MOUNTAINS

On the 20th of October in the preceding year, after the close of the subscription, the president of the Gun Club had credited the Observatory of Cambridge with the necessary sums for the construction of a gigantic optical instrument. This instrument was designed for the purpose of rendering visible on the surface of the moon any object exceeding nine feet in diameter.

At the period when the Gun Club essayed their great experiment, such instruments had reached a high degree of perfection, and produced some magnificent results. Two telescopes in particular, at this time, were possessed of remarkable power and of gigantic dimensions. The first, constructed by Herschel, was thirty-six feet in length, and had an object-glass of four feet six inches; it possessed a magnifying power of 6,000. The second was raised in Ireland, in Parsonstown Park, and belongs to Lord Rosse. The length of this tube is forty-eight feet, and the diameter of its object-glass six feet; it magnifies 6,400 times, and required an immense erection of brick work and masonry for the purpose of working it, its weight being twelve and a half tons.

Still, despite these colossal dimensions, the actual enlargements scarcely exceeded 6,000 times in round numbers; consequently, the moon was brought within no nearer an apparent distance than thirty-nine miles; and objects of less than sixty feet in diameter, unless they were of very considerable length, were still imperceptible.

In the present case, dealing with a projectile nine feet in diameter and fifteen feet long, it became necessary to bring the moon within an apparent distance of five miles at most; and for that purpose to establish a magnifying power of 48,000 times.

Such was the question proposed to the Observatory of Cambridge, There was no lack of funds; the difficulty was purely one of construction.

After considerable discussion as to the best form and principle of the proposed instrument the work was finally commenced. According to the calculations of the Observatory of Cambridge, the tube of the new reflector would require to be 280 feet in length, and the object-glass sixteen feet in diameter. Colossal as these dimensions may appear, they were diminutive in comparison with the 10,000 foot telescope proposed by the astronomer Hooke only a few years ago!

Regarding the choice of locality, that matter was promptly determined. The object was to select some lofty mountain, and there are not many of these in the United States. In fact there are but two chains of moderate elevation, between which runs the magnificent Mississippi, the "king of rivers" as these Republican Yankees delight to call it.

Eastwards rise the Appalachians, the very highest point of which, in New Hampshire, does not exceed the very moderate altitude of 5,600 feet.

CHAPTER XXIV THE TELESCOPE OF THE ROCKY MOUNTAINS

On the west, however, rise the Rocky Mountains, that immense range which, commencing at the Straights of Magellan, follows the western coast of Southern America under the name of the Andes or the Cordilleras, until it crosses the Isthmus of Panama, and runs up the whole of North America to the very borders of the Polar Sea. The highest elevation of this range still does not exceed 10,700 feet. With this elevation, nevertheless, the Gun Club were compelled to be content, inasmuch as they had determined that both telescope and Columbiad should be erected within the limits of the Union. All the necessary apparatus was consequently sent on to the summit of Long's Peak, in the territory of Missouri.

Neither pen nor language can describe the difficulties of all kinds which the American engineers had to surmount, of the prodigies of daring and skill which they accomplished. They had to raise enormous stones, massive pieces of wrought iron, heavy corner-clamps and huge portions of cylinder, with an object-glass weighing nearly 30,000 pounds, above the line of perpetual snow for more than 10,000 feet in height, after crossing desert prairies, impenetrable forests, fearful rapids, far from all centers of population, and in the midst of savage regions, in which every detail of life becomes an almost insoluble problem. And yet, notwithstanding these innumerable obstacles, American genius triumphed. In less than a year after the commencement of the works, toward the close of September, the gigantic reflector rose into the air to a height of 280 feet. It was raised by means of an enormous iron crane; an ingenious mechanism allowed it to be easily worked toward all the points of the heavens, and to follow the stars from the one horizon to the other during their journey through the heavens.

It had cost $400,000. The first time it was directed toward the moon the observers evinced both curiosity and anxiety. What were they about to discover in the field of this telescope which magnified objects 48,000 times? Would they perceive peoples, herds of lunar animals, towns, lakes, seas? No! there was nothing which science had not already discovered! and on all the points of its disc the volcanic nature of the moon became determinable with the utmost precision.

But the telescope of the Rocky Mountains, before doing its duty to the Gun Club, rendered immense services to astronomy. Thanks to its penetrative power, the depths of the heavens were sounded to the utmost extent; the apparent diameter of a great number of stars was accurately measured; and Mr. Clark, of the Cambridge staff, resolved the Crab nebula in Taurus, which the reflector of Lord Rosse had never been able to decompose.

CHAPTER XXV FINAL DETAILS

It was the 22nd of November; the departure was to take place in ten days. One operation alone remained to be accomplished to bring all to a happy termination; an operation delicate and perilous, requiring infinite precautions, and against the success of which Captain Nicholl had laid his third bet. It was, in fact, nothing less than the loading of the Columbiad, and the introduction into it of 400,000 pounds of gun-cotton. Nicholl had thought, not perhaps without reason, that the handling of such formidable quantities of pyroxyle would, in all probability, involve a grave catastrophe; and at any rate, that this immense mass of eminently inflammable matter would inevitably ignite when submitted to the pressure of the projectile.

There were indeed dangers accruing as before from the carelessness of the Americans, but Barbicane had set his heart on success, and took all possible precautions. In the first place, he was very careful as to the transportation of the gun-cotton to Stones Hill. He had it conveyed in small quantities, carefully packed in sealed cases. These were brought by rail from Tampa Town to the camp, and from thence were taken to the Columbiad by barefooted workmen, who deposited them in their places by means of cranes placed at the orifice of the cannon. No steam-engine was permitted to work, and every fire was extinguished within two miles of the works.

Even in November they feared to work by day, lest the sun's rays acting on the gun-cotton might lead to unhappy results. This led to their working at night, by light produced in a vacuum by means of Ruhmkorff's apparatus, which threw an artificial brightness into the depths of the Columbiad. There the cartridges were arranged with the utmost regularity, connected by a metallic thread, destined to communicate to them all simultaneously the electric spark, by which means this mass of gun-cotton was eventually to be ignited.

By the 28th of November eight hundred cartridges had been placed in the bottom of the Columbiad. So far the operation had been successful! But what confusion, what anxieties, what struggles were undergone by President Barbicane! In vain had he refused admission to Stones Hill; every day the inquisitive neighbors scaled the palisades, some even carrying their imprudence to the point of smoking while surrounded by bales of gun-cotton. Barbicane was in a perpetual state of alarm. J. T. Maston seconded him to the best of his ability, by giving vigorous chase to the intruders, and carefully picking up the still lighted cigar ends which the Yankees threw about. A somewhat difficult task! seeing that more than 300,000 persons were gathered round the enclosure. Michel Ardan had volunteered to superintend the transport of the cartridges to the mouth of the Columbiad; but the president, having surprised him with an enormous cigar in his mouth, while he was hunting out the rash spectators to whom he himself offered so dangerous an example, saw that he could not trust this fearless smoker, and was therefore obliged to mount a special guard over him.

At last, Providence being propitious, this wonderful loading came to a happy termination, Captain Nicholl's third bet being thus lost. It remained now to introduce the projectile into the Columbiad, and to place it on its soft bed of gun-cotton.

But before doing this, all those things necessary for the journey had to be carefully arranged in the projectile vehicle. These necessaries were numerous; and had Ardan been allowed to follow his own wishes, there would have been no space remaining for the travelers. It is impossible to conceive of half the things this charming Frenchman wished to convey to the moon. A veritable stock of useless trifles! But Barbicane interfered and refused admission to anything not absolutely needed. Several thermometers, barometers, and telescopes were packed in the instrument case.

The travelers being desirous of examining the moon carefully during their voyage, in order to facilitate their studies, they took with them Boeer and Moeller's excellent *Mappa Selenographica*, a masterpiece of patience and observation, which they hoped would enable them to identify those physical features in the moon, with which they were acquainted. This map reproduced with scrupulous fidelity the smallest details of the lunar surface which faces the earth; the mountains, valleys, craters, peaks, and ridges were all represented, with their exact dimensions, relative positions, and names; from the mountains Doerfel and Leibnitz on the eastern side of the disc, to the *Mare frigoris* of the North Pole.

They took also three rifles and three fowling-pieces, and a large quantity of balls, shot, and powder.

"We cannot tell whom we shall have to deal with," said Michel Ardan. "Men or beasts may possibly object to our visit. It is only wise to take all precautions."

These defensive weapons were accompanied by pickaxes, crowbars, saws, and other useful implements, not to mention clothing adapted to every temperature, from that of polar regions to that of the torrid zone.

Ardan wished to convey a number of animals of different sorts, not indeed a pair of every known species, as he could not see the necessity of acclimatizing serpents, tigers, alligators, or any other noxious beasts in the moon. "Nevertheless," he said to Barbicane, "some valuable and useful beasts, bullocks, cows, horses, and donkeys, would bear the journey very well, and would also be very useful to us."

"I dare say, my dear Ardan," replied the president, "but our projectile-vehicle is no Noah's ark, from which it differs both in dimensions and object. Let us confine ourselves to possibilities."

After a prolonged discussion, it was agreed that the travelers should restrict themselves to a sporting-dog belonging to Nicholl, and to a large Newfoundland. Several packets of seeds were also included among the necessaries. Michel Ardan, indeed, was anxious to add some sacks full of earth to sow them in; as it was, he took a dozen shrubs carefully wrapped up in straw to plant in the moon.

The important question of provisions still remained; it being necessary to provide against the possibility of their finding the moon absolutely barren. Barbicane managed so successfully, that he supplied them with sufficient rations for a year. These consisted of preserved meats and vegetables, reduced by strong hydraulic pressure to the smallest possible dimensions. They were also supplied with brandy, and took water enough for two months, being confident, from astronomical observations, that there was no lack of water on the moon's surface. As to provisions, doubtless the inhabitants of the *earth* would find nourishment somewhere in the *moon*. Ardan never questioned this; indeed, had he done so, he would never have undertaken the journey.

"Besides," he said one day to his friends, "we shall not be completely abandoned by our terrestrial friends; they will take care not to forget us."

"No, indeed!" replied J. T. Maston.

"Nothing would be simpler," replied Ardan; "the Columbiad will be always there. Well! whenever the moon is in a favorable condition as to the zenith, if not to the perigee, that is to say about once a year, could you not send us a shell packed with provisions, which we might expect on some appointed day?"

"Hurrah! hurrah!" cried J. T. Matson; "what an ingenious fellow! what a splendid idea! Indeed, my good friends, we shall not forget you!"

"I shall reckon upon you! Then, you see, we shall receive news regularly from the earth, and we shall indeed be stupid if we hit upon no plan for communicating with our good friends here!"

These words inspired such confidence, that Michel Ardan carried all the Gun Club with him in his enthusiasm. What he said seemed so simple and so easy, so sure of success, that none could be so sordidly attached to this earth as to hesitate to follow the three travelers on their lunar expedition.

All being ready at last, it remained to place the projectile in the Columbiad, an operation abundantly accompanied by dangers and difficulties.

The enormous shell was conveyed to the summit of Stones Hill. There, powerful cranes raised it, and held it suspended over the mouth of the cylinder.

It was a fearful moment! What if the chains should break under its enormous weight? The sudden fall of such a body would inevitably cause the gun-cotton to explode!

Fortunately this did not happen; and some hours later the projectile-vehicle descended gently into the heart of the cannon and rested on its couch of pyroxyle, a veritable bed of explosive eider-down. Its pressure had no result, other than the more effectual ramming down of the charge in the Columbiad.

"I have lost," said the captain, who forthwith paid President

Barbicane the sum of three thousand dollars.

Barbicane did not wish to accept the money from one of his fellow-travelers, but gave way at last before the determination of Nicholl, who wished before leaving the earth to fulfill all his engagements.

"Now," said Michel Ardan, "I have only one thing more to wish for you, my brave captain."

"What is that?" asked Nicholl.

"It is that you may lose your two other bets! Then we shall be sure not to be stopped on our journey!"

CHAPTER XXVI FIRE!

The first of December had arrived! the fatal day! for, if the projectile were not discharged that very night at 10h. 48m. 40s. P.M., more than eighteen years must roll by before the moon would again present herself under the same conditions of zenith and perigee.

The weather was magnificent. Despite the approach of winter, the sun shone brightly, and bathed in its radiant light that earth which three of its denizens were about to abandon for a new world.

How many persons lost their rest on the night which preceded this long-expected day! All hearts beat with disquietude, save only the heart of Michel Ardan. That imperturbable personage came and went with his habitual business-like air, while nothing whatever denoted that any unusual matter preoccupied his mind.

After dawn, an innumerable multitude covered the prairie which extends, as far as the eye can reach, round Stones Hill. Every quarter of an hour the railway brought fresh accessions of sightseers; and, according to the statement of the Tampa Town *Observer*, not less than five millions of spectators thronged the soil of Florida.

For a whole month previously, the mass of these persons had bivouacked round the enclosure, and laid the foundations for a town which was afterward called "Ardan's Town." The whole plain was covered with huts, cottages, and tents. Every nation under the sun was represented there; and every language might be heard spoken at the same time. It was a perfect Babel re-enacted. All the various classes of American society were mingled together in terms of absolute equality. Bankers, farmers, sailors, cotton-planters, brokers, merchants, watermen, magistrates, elbowed each other in the most free-and-easy way. Louisiana Creoles fraternized with farmers from Indiana; Kentucky and Tennessee gentlemen and haughty Virginians conversed with trappers and the half-savages of the lakes and butchers from Cincinnati. Broad-brimmed white hats and Panamas, blue-cotton trousers, light-colored stockings, cambric frills, were all here displayed; while upon shirt-fronts, wristbands, and neckties, upon every finger, even upon the very ears, they wore an assortment of rings, shirt-pins, brooches, and trinkets, of which the value only equaled the execrable taste. Women, children, and servants, in equally expensive dress, surrounded their husbands, fathers, or masters, who resembled the patriarchs of tribes in the midst of their immense households.

At meal-times all fell to work upon the dishes peculiar to the Southern States, and consumed with an appetite that threatened speedy exhaustion of the victualing powers of Florida, fricasseed frogs, stuffed monkey, fish chowder, underdone 'possum, and raccoon steaks. And as for the liquors which accompanied this indigestible repast! The shouts, the vociferations that resounded through the bars and taverns decorated with glasses, tankards, and bottles of marvelous shape, mortars for pounding sugar, and bundles of straws! "Mint-julep" roars one of the barmen; "Claret sangaree!" shouts another; "Cock-tail!" "Brandy-smash!" "Real mint-julep in the new style!" All these cries intermingled produced a bewildering and deafening hubbub.

But on this day, 1st of December, such sounds were rare. No one thought of eating or drinking, and at four P.M. there were vast numbers of spectators who had not even taken their customary lunch! And, a still more significant fact, even the national passion for play seemed quelled for the time under the general excitement of the hour.

Up till nightfall, a dull, noiseless agitation, such as precedes great catastrophes, ran through the anxious multitude. An indescribable uneasiness pervaded all minds, an indefinable sensation which oppressed the heart. Every one wished it was over.

However, about seven o'clock, the heavy silence was dissipated. The moon rose above the horizon. Millions of hurrahs hailed her appearance. She was punctual to the rendezvous, and shouts of welcome greeted her on all sides, as her pale beams shone gracefully in the clear heavens. At this moment the three intrepid travelers appeared. This was the signal for renewed cries of still greater intensity. Instantly the vast assemblage, as with one accord, struck up the national hymn of the United States, and "Yankee Doodle," sung by five million of hearty throats, rose like a roaring tempest to the farthest limits of the atmosphere. Then a profound silence reigned throughout the crowd.

The Frenchman and the two Americans had by this time entered the enclosure reserved in the center of the multitude. They were accompanied by the members of the Gun Club, and by deputations sent from all the European Observatories. Barbicane, cool and collected, was giving his final directions. Nicholl, with compressed lips, his arms crossed behind his back, walked with a firm and measured step. Michel Ardan, always easy, dressed in thorough traveler's costume, leathern gaiters on his legs, pouch by his side, in loose velvet suit, cigar in mouth, was full of inexhaustible gayety, laughing, joking, playing pranks with J. T. Maston. In one word, he was the thorough "Frenchman" (and worse, a "Parisian") to the last moment.

Ten o'clock struck! The moment had arrived for taking their places in the projectile! The necessary operations for the descent, and the subsequent removal of the cranes and scaffolding that inclined over the mouth of the Columbiad, required a certain period of time.

Barbicane had regulated his chronometer to the tenth part of a second by that of Murchison the engineer, who was charged with the duty of firing the gun by means of an electric spark. Thus the travelers enclosed within the projectile were enabled to follow with their eyes the impassive needle which marked the precise moment of their departure.

The moment had arrived for saying "good-by!" The scene was a touching one. Despite his feverish gayety, even Michel Ardan was touched. J. T. Maston had found in his own dry eyes one ancient tear, which he had doubtless reserved for the occasion. He dropped it on the forehead of his dear president.

"Can I not go?" he said, "there is still time!"

"Impossible, old fellow!" replied Barbicane. A few moments later, the three fellow-travelers had ensconced themselves in the projectile, and screwed down the plate which covered the entrance-aperture. The mouth of the Columbiad, now completely disencumbered, was open entirely to the sky.

The moon advanced upward in a heaven of the purest clearness, outshining in her passage the twinkling light of the stars. She passed over the constellation of the Twins, and was now nearing the halfway point between the horizon and the zenith. A terrible silence weighed upon the entire scene! Not a breath of wind upon the earth! not a sound of breathing from the countless chests of the spectators! Their hearts seemed afraid to beat! All eyes were fixed upon the yawning mouth of the Columbiad.

Murchison followed with his eye the hand of his chronometer. It wanted scarce forty seconds to the moment of departure, but each second seemed to last an age! At the twentieth there was a general shudder, as it occurred to the minds of that vast assemblage that the bold travelers shut up within the projectile were also counting those terrible seconds. Some few cries here and there escaped the crowd.

"Thirty-five!— thirty-six!— thirty-seven!— thirty-eight!— thirty-nine!— forty! FIRE!!!"

Instantly Murchison pressed with his finger the key of the electric battery, restored the current of the fluid, and discharged the spark into the breech of the Columbiad.

An appalling unearthly report followed instantly, such as can be compared to nothing whatever known, not even to the roar of thunder, or the blast of volcanic explosions! No words can convey the slightest idea of the terrific sound! An immense spout of fire shot up from the bowels of the earth as from a crater. The earth heaved up, and with great difficulty some few spectators obtained a momentary glimpse of the projectile victoriously cleaving the air in the midst of the fiery vapors!

CHAPTER XXVII FOUL WEATHER

At the moment when that pyramid of fire rose to a prodigious height into the air, the glare of flame lit up the whole of Florida; and for a moment day superseded night over a considerable extent of the country. This immense canopy of fire was perceived at a distance of one hundred miles out at sea, and more than one ship's captain entered in his log the appearance of this gigantic meteor.

The discharge of the Columbiad was accompanied by a perfect earthquake. Florida was shaken to its very depths. The gases of the powder, expanded by heat, forced back the atmospheric strata with tremendous violence, and this artificial hurricane rushed like a water-spout through the air.

Not a single spectator remained on his feet! Men, women children, all lay prostrate like ears of corn under a tempest. There ensued a terrible tumult; a large number of persons were seriously injured. J. T. Maston, who, despite all dictates of prudence, had kept in advance of the mass, was pitched back 120 feet, shooting like a projectile over the heads of his fellow-citizens. Three hundred thousand persons remained deaf for a time, and as though struck stupefied.

As soon as the first effects were over, the injured, the deaf, and lastly, the crowd in general, woke up with frenzied cries. "Hurrah for Ardan! Hurrah for Barbicane! Hurrah for Nicholl!" rose to the skies. Thousands of persons, noses in air, armed with telescopes and race-glasses, were questioning space, forgetting all contusions and emotions in the one idea of watching for the projectile. They looked in vain! It was no longer to be seen, and they were obliged to wait for telegrams from Long's Peak. The director of the Cambridge Observatory was at his post on the Rocky Mountains; and to him, as a skillful and persevering astronomer, all observations had been confided.

But an unforeseen phenomenon came in to subject the public impatience to a severe trial.

The weather, hitherto so fine, suddenly changed; the sky became heavy with clouds. It could not have been otherwise after the terrible derangement of the atmospheric strata, and the dispersion of the enormous quantity of vapor arising from the combustion of 200,000 pounds of pyroxyle!

On the morrow the horizon was covered with clouds— a thick and impenetrable curtain between earth and sky, which unhappily extended as far as the Rocky Mountains. It was a fatality! But since man had chosen so to disturb the atmosphere, he was bound to accept the consequences of his experiment.

Supposing, now, that the experiment had succeeded, the travelers having started on the 1st of December, at 10h. 46m. 40s. P.M., were due on the 4th at 0h. P.M. at their destination. So that up to that time it would have been very difficult after all to have observed, under such conditions, a body so small as the shell. Therefore they waited with what patience they might.

From the 4th to the 6th of December inclusive, the weather remaining much the same in America, the great European instruments of Herschel, Rosse, and Foucault, were constantly directed toward the moon, for the weather was then magnificent; but the comparative weakness of their glasses prevented any trustworthy observations being made.

On the 7th the sky seemed to lighten. They were in hopes now, but their hope was of but short duration, and at night again thick clouds hid the starry vault from all eyes.

Matters were now becoming serious, when on the 9th the sun reappeared for an instant, as if for the purpose of teasing the Americans. It was received with hisses; and wounded, no doubt, by such a reception, showed itself very sparing of its rays.

On the 10th, no change! J. T. Maston went nearly mad, and great fears were entertained regarding the brain of this worthy individual, which had hitherto been so well preserved within his gutta-percha cranium.

But on the 11th one of those inexplicable tempests peculiar to those intertropical regions was let loose in the atmosphere. A terrific east wind swept away the groups of clouds which had been so long gathering, and at night the semi-disc of the orb of night rode majestically amid the soft constellations of the sky.

CHAPTER XXVIII A NEW STAR

That very night, the startling news so impatiently awaited, burst like a thunderbolt over the United States of the Union, and thence, darting across the ocean, ran through all the telegraphic wires of the globe. The projectile had been detected, thanks to the gigantic reflector of Long's Peak! Here is the note received by the director of the Observatory of Cambridge. It contains the scientific conclusion regarding this great experiment of the Gun Club.

LONG'S PEAK, December 12. To the Officers of the Observatory of Cambridge. The projectile discharged by the Columbiad at Stones Hill has been detected by Messrs. Belfast and J. T. Maston, 12th of December, at 8:47 P.M., the moon having entered her last quarter. This projectile has not arrived at its destination. It has passed by the side; but sufficiently near to be retained by the lunar attraction.

The rectilinear movement has thus become changed into a circular motion of extreme velocity, and it is now pursuing an elliptical orbit round the moon, of which it has become a true satellite.

The elements of this new star we have as yet been unable to determine; we do not yet know the velocity of its passage. The distance which separates it from the surface of the moon may be estimated at about 2,833 miles.

However, two hypotheses come here into our consideration.

1. Either the attraction of the moon will end by drawing them into itself, and the travelers will attain their destination; or,

2. The projectile, following an immutable law, will continue to gravitate round the moon till the end of time.

At some future time, our observations will be able to determine this point, but till then the experiment of the Gun Club can have no other result than to have provided our solar system with a new star. J. BELFAST.

To how many questions did this unexpected *denouement* give rise? What mysterious results was the future reserving for the investigation of science? At all events, the names of Nicholl, Barbicane, and Michel Ardan were certain to be immortalized in the annals of astronomy!

When the dispatch from Long's Peak had once become known, there was but one universal feeling of surprise and alarm. Was it possible to go to the aid of these bold travelers? No! for they had placed themselves beyond the pale of humanity, by crossing the limits imposed by the Creator on his earthly creatures. They had air enough for *two* months; they had victuals enough for *twelve;— but after that?* There was only one man who would not admit that the situation was desperate— he alone had confidence; and that was their devoted friend J. T. Maston.

Besides, he never let them get out of sight. His home was henceforth the post at Long's Peak; his horizon, the mirror of that immense reflector. As soon as the moon rose above the horizon, he immediately caught her in the field of the telescope; he never let her go for an instant out of his sight, and followed her assiduously in her course through the stellar spaces. He watched with untiring patience the passage of the projectile across her silvery disc, and really the worthy man remained in perpetual communication with his three friends, whom he did not despair of seeing again some day.

"Those three men," said he, "have carried into space all the resources of art, science, and industry. With that, one can do anything; and you will see that, some day, they will come out all right."

ROUND THE MOON

A SEQUEL TO
FROM THE EARTH TO THE MOON

PRELIMINARY CHAPTER THE FIRST PART OF THIS WORK, AND SERVING AS A PREFACE TO THE SECOND

During the year 186-, the whole world was greatly excited by a scientific experiment unprecedented in the annals of science. The members of the Gun Club, a circle of artillerymen formed at Baltimore after the American war, conceived the idea of putting themselves in communication with the moon!— yes, with the moon— by sending to her a projectile. Their president, Barbicane, the promoter of the enterprise, having consulted the astronomers of the Cambridge Observatory upon the subject, took all necessary means to ensure the success of this extraordinary enterprise, which had been declared practicable by the majority of competent judges. After setting on foot a public subscription, which realized nearly L1,200,000, they began the gigantic work.

According to the advice forwarded from the members of the Observatory, the gun destined to launch the projectile had to be fixed in a country situated between the 0 and 28th degrees of north or south latitude, in order to aim at the moon when at the zenith; and its initiatory velocity was fixed at twelve thousand yards to the second. Launched on the 1st of December, at 10hrs. 46m. 40s. P.M., it ought to reach the moon four days after its departure, that is on the 5th of December, at midnight precisely, at the moment of her attaining her perigee, that is her nearest distance from the earth, which is exactly 86,410 leagues (French), or 238,833 miles mean distance (English).

The principal members of the Gun Club, President Barbicane, Major Elphinstone, the secretary Joseph T. Maston, and other learned men, held several meetings, at which the shape and composition of the projectile were discussed, also the position and nature of the gun, and the quality and quantity of powder to be used. It was decided: First, that the projectile should be a shell made of aluminum with a diameter of 108 inches and a thickness of twelve inches to its walls; and should weigh 19,250 pounds. Second, that the gun should be a Columbiad cast in iron, 900 feet long, and run perpendicularly into the earth. Third, that the charge should contain 400,000 pounds of gun-cotton, which, giving out six billions of litres of gas in rear of the projectile, would easily carry it toward the orb of night.

These questions determined President Barbicane, assisted by Murchison the engineer, to choose a spot situated in Florida, in 27 ° 7' North latitude, and 77 ° 3' West (Greenwich) longitude. It was on this spot, after stupendous labor, that the Columbiad was cast with full success. Things stood thus, when an incident took place which increased the interest attached to this great enterprise a hundredfold.

A Frenchman, an enthusiastic Parisian, as witty as he was bold, asked to be enclosed in the projectile, in order that he might reach the moon, and reconnoiter this terrestrial satellite. The name of this intrepid adventurer was Michel Ardan. He landed in America, was received with enthusiasm, held meetings, saw himself carried in triumph, reconciled President Barbicane to his mortal enemy, Captain Nicholl, and, as a token of reconciliation, persuaded them both to start with him in the projectile. The proposition being accepted, the shape of the projectile was slightly altered. It was made of a cylindro-conical form. This species of aerial car was lined with strong springs and partitions to deaden the shock of departure. It was provided with food for a year, water for some months, and gas for some days. A self-acting apparatus supplied the three travelers with air to breathe. At the same time, on one of the highest points of the Rocky Mountains, the Gun Club had a gigantic telescope erected, in order that they might be able to follow the course of the projectile through space. All was then ready.

On the 30th of November, at the hour fixed upon, from the midst of an extraordinary crowd of spectators, the departure took place, and for the first time, three human beings quitted the terrestrial globe, and launched into inter-planetary space with almost a certainty of reaching their destination. These bold travelers, Michel Ardan, President Barbicane, and Captain Nicholl, ought to make the passage in ninety-seven hours, thirteen minutes, and twenty seconds. Consequently, their arrival on the lunar disc could not take place until the 5th of December at twelve at night, at the exact moment when the moon should be full, and not on the 4th, as some badly informed journalists had announced.

But an unforeseen circumstance, viz., the detonation produced by the Columbiad, had the immediate effect of troubling the terrestrial atmosphere, by accumulating a large quantity of vapor, a phenomenon which excited universal indignation, for the moon was hidden from the eyes of the watchers for several nights.

The worthy Joseph T. Maston, the staunchest friend of the three travelers, started for the Rocky Mountains, accompanied by the Hon. J. Belfast, director of the Cambridge Observatory, and reached the station of Long's Peak, where the telescope was erected which brought the moon within an apparent distance of two leagues. The honorable secretary of the Gun Club wished himself to observe the vehicle of his daring friends.

The accumulation of the clouds in the atmosphere prevented all observation on the 5th, 6th, 7th, 8th, 9th, and 10th of December. Indeed it was thought that all observations would have to be put off to the 3d of January in the following year; for the moon entering its last quarter on the 11th, would then only present an ever-decreasing portion of her disc, insufficient to allow of their following the course of the projectile.

At length, to the general satisfaction, a heavy storm cleared the atmosphere on the night of the 11th and 12th of December, and the moon, with half-illuminated disc, was plainly to be seen upon the black sky.

That very night a telegram was sent from the station of Long's Peak by Joseph T. Maston and Belfast to the gentlemen of the Cambridge Observatory, announcing that on the 11th of December at 8h. 47m. P.M., the projectile launched by the Columbiad of Stones Hill had been detected by Messrs. Belfast and Maston— that it had deviated from its course from some unknown cause, and had not reached its destination; but that it had passed near enough to be retained by the lunar attraction; that its rectilinear movement had been changed to a circular one, and that following an elliptical orbit round the star of night it had become its satellite. The telegram added that the elements of this new star had not yet been calculated; and indeed three observations made upon a star in three different positions are necessary to determine these elements. Then it showed that the distance separating the projectile from the lunar surface "might" be reckoned at about 2,833 miles.

PRELIMINARY CHAPTER THE FIRST PART OF THIS WORK, AND SERVING AS A PREFACE TO THE SECOND

It ended with the double hypothesis: either the attraction of the moon would draw it to herself, and the travelers thus attain their end; or that the projectile, held in one immutable orbit, would gravitate around the lunar disc to all eternity.

With such alternatives, what would be the fate of the travelers? Certainly they had food for some time. But supposing they did succeed in their rash enterprise, how would they return? Could they ever return? Should they hear from them? These questions, debated by the most learned pens of the day, strongly engrossed the public attention.

It is advisable here to make a remark which ought to be well considered by hasty observers. When a purely speculative discovery is announced to the public, it cannot be done with too much prudence. No one is obliged to discover either a planet, a comet, or a satellite; and whoever makes a mistake in such a case exposes himself justly to the derision of the mass. Far better is it to wait; and that is what the impatient Joseph T. Maston should have done before sending this telegram forth to the world, which, according to his idea, told the whole result of the enterprise. Indeed this telegram contained two sorts of errors, as was proved eventually. First, errors of observation, concerning the distance of the projectile from the surface of the moon, for on the 11th of December it was impossible to see it; and what Joseph T. Maston had seen, or thought he saw, could not have been the projectile of the Columbiad. Second, errors of theory on the fate in store for the said projectile; for in making it a satellite of the moon, it was putting it in direct contradiction of all mechanical laws.

One single hypothesis of the observers of Long's Peak could ever be realized, that which foresaw the case of the travelers (if still alive) uniting their efforts with the lunar attraction to attain the surface of the disc.

Now these men, as clever as they were daring, had survived the terrible shock consequent on their departure, and it is their journey in the projectile car which is here related in its most dramatic as well as in its most singular details. This recital will destroy many illusions and surmises; but it will give a true idea of the singular changes in store for such an enterprise; it will bring out the scientific instincts of Barbicane, the industrious resources of Nicholl, and the audacious humor of Michel Ardan. Besides this, it will prove that their worthy friend, Joseph T. Maston, was wasting his time, while leaning over the gigantic telescope he watched the course of the moon through the starry space.

CHAPTER I TWENTY MINUTES PAST TEN TO FORTY-SEVEN MINUTES PAST TEN P. M.

As ten o'clock struck, Michel Ardan, Barbicane, and Nicholl, took leave of the numerous friends they were leaving on the earth. The two dogs, destined to propagate the canine race on the lunar continents, were already shut up in the projectile.

The three travelers approached the orifice of the enormous cast-iron tube, and a crane let them down to the conical top of the projectile. There, an opening made for the purpose gave them access to the aluminum car. The tackle belonging to the crane being hauled from outside, the mouth of the Columbiad was instantly disencumbered of its last supports.

Nicholl, once introduced with his companions inside the projectile, began to close the opening by means of a strong plate, held in position by powerful screws. Other plates, closely fitted, covered the lenticular glasses, and the travelers, hermetically enclosed in their metal prison, were plunged in profound darkness.

"And now, my dear companions," said Michel Ardan, "let us make ourselves at home; I am a domesticated man and strong in housekeeping. We are bound to make the best of our new lodgings, and make ourselves comfortable. And first let us try and see a little. Gas was not invented for moles."

So saying, the thoughtless fellow lit a match by striking it on the sole of his boot; and approached the burner fixed to the receptacle, in which the carbonized hydrogen, stored at high pressure, sufficed for the lighting and warming of the projectile for a hundred and forty-four hours, or six days and six nights. The gas caught fire, and thus lighted the projectile looked like a comfortable room with thickly padded walls, furnished with a circular divan, and a roof rounded in the shape of a dome.

Michel Ardan examined everything, and declared himself satisfied with his installation.

"It is a prison," said he, "but a traveling prison; and, with the right of putting my nose to the window, I could well stand a lease of a hundred years. You smile, Barbicane. Have you any *arriere-pensee*? Do you say to yourself, `This prison may be our tomb?' Tomb, perhaps; still I would not change it for Mahomet's, which floats in space but never advances an inch!"

While Michel Ardan was speaking, Barbicane and Nicholl were making their last preparations.

Nicholl's chronometer marked twenty minutes past ten P.M. when
the three travelers were finally enclosed in their projectile.
This chronometer was set within the tenth of a second by that of
Murchison the engineer. Barbicane consulted it.

CHAPTER I TWENTY MINUTES PAST TEN TO FORTY-SEVEN MINUTES PAST TEN P. M.

"My friends," said he, "it is twenty minutes past ten. At forty- seven minutes past ten Murchison will launch the electric spark on the wire which communicates with the charge of the Columbiad. At that precise moment we shall leave our spheroid. Thus we still have twenty-seven minutes to remain on the earth."

"Twenty-six minutes thirteen seconds," replied the methodical Nicholl.

"Well!" exclaimed Michel Ardan, in a good-humored tone, "much may be done in twenty-six minutes. The gravest questions of morals and politics may be discussed, and even solved. Twenty-six minutes well employed are worth more than twenty-six years in which nothing is done. Some seconds of a Pascal or a Newton are more precious than the whole existence of a crowd of raw simpletons——"

"And you conclude, then, you everlasting talker?" asked Barbicane.

"I conclude that we have twenty-six minutes left," replied Ardan.

"Twenty-four only," said Nicholl.

"Well, twenty-four, if you like, my noble captain," said Ardan; "twenty-four minutes in which to investigate——"

"Michel," said Barbicane, "during the passage we shall have plenty of time to investigate the most difficult questions. For the present we must occupy ourselves with our departure."

"Are we not ready?"

"Doubtless; but there are still some precautions to be taken, to deaden as much as possible the first shock."

"Have we not the water-cushions placed between the partition- breaks, whose elasticity will sufficiently protect us?"

"I hope so, Michel," replied Barbicane gently, "but I am not sure."

"Ah, the joker!" exclaimed Michel Ardan. "He hopes!—He is not sure!— and he waits for the moment when we are encased to make this deplorable admission! I beg to be allowed to get out!"

"And how?" asked Barbicane.

"Humph!" said Michel Ardan, "it is not easy; we are in the train, and the guard's whistle will sound before twenty-four minutes are over."

"Twenty," said Nicholl.

For some moments the three travelers looked at each other.

Then they began to examine the objects imprisoned with them.

"Everything is in its place," said Barbicane. "We have now to decide how we can best place ourselves to resist the shock. Position cannot be an indifferent matter; and we must, as much as possible, prevent the rush of blood to the head."

"Just so," said Nicholl.

"Then," replied Michel Ardan, ready to suit the action to the word, "let us put our heads down and our feet in the air, like the clowns in the grand circus."

"No," said Barbicane, "let us stretch ourselves on our sides; we shall resist the shock better that way. Remember that, when the projectile starts, it matters little whether we are in it or before it; it amounts to much the same thing."

"If it is only `much the same thing,' I may cheer up," said
Michel Ardan.

"Do you approve of my idea, Nicholl?" asked Barbicane.

"Entirely," replied the captain. "We've still thirteen minutes and a half."

"That Nicholl is not a man," exclaimed Michel; "he is a chronometer with seconds, an escape, and eight holes."

But his companions were not listening; they were taking up their last positions with the most perfect coolness. They were like two methodical travelers in a car, seeking to place themselves as comfortably as possible.

We might well ask ourselves of what materials are the hearts of these Americans made, to whom the approach of the most frightful danger added no pulsation.

Three thick and solidly-made couches had been placed in the projectile. Nicholl and Barbicane placed them in the center of the disc forming the floor. There the three travelers were to stretch themselves some moments before their departure.

During this time, Ardan, not being able to keep still, turned in his narrow prison like a wild beast in a cage, chatting with his friends, speaking to the dogs Diana and Satellite, to whom, as may be seen, he had given significant names.

"Ah, Diana! Ah, Satellite!" he exclaimed, teasing them; "so you are going to show the moon-dogs the good habits of the dogs of the earth! That will do honor to the canine race! If ever we do come down again, I will bring a cross type of `moon-dogs,' which will make a stir!"

"If there *are* dogs in the moon," said Barbicane.

"There are," said Michel Ardan, "just as there are horses, cows, donkeys, and chickens. I bet that we shall find chickens."

"A hundred dollars we shall find none!" said Nicholl.

"Done, my captain!" replied Ardan, clasping Nicholl's hand. "But, by the bye, you have already lost three bets with our president, as the necessary funds for the enterprise have been found, as the operation of casting has been successful, and lastly, as the Columbiad has been loaded without accident, six thousand dollars."

"Yes," replied Nicholl. "Thirty-seven minutes six seconds past ten."

"It is understood, captain. Well, before another quarter of an hour you will have to count nine thousand dollars to the president; four thousand because the Columbiad will not burst, and five thousand because the projectile will rise more than six miles in the air."

"I have the dollars," replied Nicholl, slapping the pocket of this coat. "I only ask to be allowed to pay."

"Come, Nicholl. I see that you are a man of method, which I could never be; but indeed you have made a series of bets of very little advantage to yourself, allow me to tell you."

"And why?" asked Nicholl.

"Because, if you gain the first, the Columbiad will have burst, and the projectile with it; and Barbicane will no longer be there to reimburse your dollars."

"My stake is deposited at the bank in Baltimore," replied Barbicane simply; "and if Nicholl is not there, it will go to his heirs."

"Ah, you practical men!" exclaimed Michel Ardan; "I admire you the more for not being able to understand you."

"Forty-two minutes past ten!" said Nicholl.

"Only five minutes more!" answered Barbicane.

"Yes, five little minutes!" replied Michel Ardan; "and we are enclosed in a projectile, at the bottom of a gun 900 feet long! And under this projectile are rammed 400,000 pounds of gun-cotton, which is equal to 1,600,000 pounds of ordinary powder! And friend Murchison, with his chronometer in hand, his eye fixed on the needle, his finger on the electric apparatus, is counting the seconds preparatory to launching us into interplanetary space."

"Enough, Michel, enough!" said Barbicane, in a serious voice; "let us prepare. A few instants alone separate us from an eventful moment. One clasp of the hand, my friends."

CHAPTER I TWENTY MINUTES PAST TEN TO FORTY-SEVEN MINUTES PAST TEN P. M.

"Yes," exclaimed Michel Ardan, more moved than he wished to appear; and the three bold companions were united in a last embrace.

"God preserve us!" said the religious Barbicane.

Michel Ardan and Nicholl stretched themselves on the couches placed in the center of the disc.

"Forty-seven minutes past ten!" murmured the captain.

"Twenty seconds more!" Barbicane quickly put out the gas and lay down by his companions, and the profound silence was only broken by the ticking of the chronometer marking the seconds.

Suddenly a dreadful shock was felt, and the projectile, under the force of six billions of litres of gas, developed by the combustion of pyroxyle, mounted into space.

CHAPTER II THE FIRST HALF-HOUR

What had happened? What effect had this frightful shock produced? Had the ingenuity of the constructors of the projectile obtained any happy result? Had the shock been deadened, thanks to the springs, the four plugs, the water-cushions, and the partition-breaks? Had they been able to subdue the frightful pressure of the initiatory speed of more than 11,000 yards, which was enough to traverse Paris or New York in a second? This was evidently the question suggested to the thousand spectators of this moving scene. They forgot the aim of the journey, and thought only of the travelers. And if one of them— Joseph T. Maston for example— could have cast one glimpse into the projectile, what would he have seen?

Nothing then. The darkness was profound. But its cylindro- conical partitions had resisted wonderfully. Not a rent or a dent anywhere! The wonderful projectile was not even heated under the intense deflagration of the powder, nor liquefied, as they seemed to fear, in a shower of aluminum.

The interior showed but little disorder; indeed, only a few objects had been violently thrown toward the roof; but the most important seemed not to have suffered from the shock at all; their fixtures were intact.

On the movable disc, sunk down to the bottom by the smashing of the partition-breaks and the escape of the water, three bodies lay apparently lifeless. Barbicane, Nicholl, and Michel Ardan— did they still breathe? or was the projectile nothing now but a metal coffin, bearing three corpses into space?

Some minutes after the departure of the projectile, one of the bodies moved, shook its arms, lifted its head, and finally succeeded in getting on its knees. It was Michel Ardan. He felt himself all over, gave a sonorous "Hem!" and then said:

"Michel Ardan is whole. How about the others?"

The courageous Frenchman tried to rise, but could not stand. His head swam, from the rush of blood; he was blind; he was a drunken man.

"Bur-r!" said he. "It produces the same effect as two bottles of Corton, though perhaps less agreeable to swallow." Then, passing his hand several times across his forehead and rubbing his temples, he called in a firm voice:

"Nicholl! Barbicane!"

He waited anxiously. No answer; not even a sigh to show that the hearts of his companions were still beating. He called again. The same silence.

"The devil!" he exclaimed. "They look as if they had fallen from a fifth story on their heads. Bah!" he added, with that imperturbable confidence which nothing could check, "if a Frenchman can get on his knees, two Americans ought to be able to get on their feet. But first let us light up."

CHAPTER II THE FIRST HALF-HOUR

Ardan felt the tide of life return by degrees. His blood became calm, and returned to its accustomed circulation. Another effort restored his equilibrium. He succeeded in rising, drew a match from his pocket, and approaching the burner lighted it. The receiver had not suffered at all. The gas had not escaped. Besides, the smell would have betrayed it; and in that case Michel Ardan could not have carried a lighted match with impunity through the space filled with hydrogen. The gas mixing with the air would have produced a detonating mixture, and the explosion would have finished what the shock had perhaps begun. When the burner was lit, Ardan leaned over the bodies of his companions: they were lying one on the other, an inert mass, Nicholl above, Barbicane underneath.

Ardan lifted the captain, propped him up against the divan, and began to rub vigorously. This means, used with judgment, restored Nicholl, who opened his eyes, and instantly recovering his presence of mind, seized Ardan's hand and looked around him.

"And Barbicane?" said he.

"Each in turn," replied Michel Ardan. "I began with you, Nicholl, because you were on the top. Now let us look to Barbicane." Saying which, Ardan and Nicholl raised the president of the Gun Club and laid him on the divan. He seemed to have suffered more than either of his companions; he was bleeding, but Nicholl was reassured by finding that the hemorrhage came from a slight wound on the shoulder, a mere graze, which he bound up carefully.

Still, Barbicane was a long time coming to himself, which frightened his friends, who did not spare friction.

"He breathes though," said Nicholl, putting his ear to the chest of the wounded man.

"Yes," replied Ardan, "he breathes like a man who has some notion of that daily operation. Rub, Nicholl; let us rub harder." And the two improvised practitioners worked so hard and so well that Barbicane recovered his senses. He opened his eyes, sat up, took his two friends by the hands, and his first words were—

"Nicholl, are we moving?"

Nicholl and Ardan looked at each other; they had not yet troubled themselves about the projectile; their first thought had been for the traveler, not for the car.

"Well, are we really moving?" repeated Michel Ardan.

"Or quietly resting on the soil of Florida?" asked Nicholl.

"Or at the bottom of the Gulf of Mexico?" added Michel Ardan.

"What an idea!" exclaimed the president.

And this double hypothesis suggested by his companions had the effect of recalling him to his senses. In any case they could not decide on the position of the projectile. Its apparent immovability, and the want of communication with the outside, prevented them from solving the question. Perhaps the projectile was unwinding its course through space. Perhaps after a short rise it had fallen upon the earth, or even in the Gulf of Mexico— a fall which the narrowness of the peninsula of Florida would render not impossible.

The case was serious, the problem interesting, and one that must be solved as soon as possible. Thus, highly excited, Barbicane's moral energy triumphed over physical weakness, and he rose to his feet. He listened. Outside was perfect silence; but the thick padding was enough to intercept all sounds coming from the earth. But one circumstance struck Barbicane, viz., that the temperature inside the projectile was singularly high. The president drew a thermometer from its case and consulted it. The instrument showed 81 ° Fahr.

"Yes," he exclaimed, "yes, we are moving! This stifling heat, penetrating through the partitions of the projectile, is produced by its friction on the atmospheric strata. It will soon diminish, because we are already floating in space, and after having nearly stifled, we shall have to suffer intense cold.

"What!" said Michel Ardan. "According to your showing, Barbicane, we are already beyond the limits of the terrestrial atmosphere?"

"Without a doubt, Michel. Listen to me. It is fifty-five minutes past ten; we have been gone about eight minutes; and if our initiatory speed has not been checked by the friction, six seconds would be enough for us to pass through the forty miles of atmosphere which surrounds the globe."

"Just so," replied Nicholl; "but in what proportion do you estimate the diminution of speed by friction?"

"In the proportion of one-third, Nicholl. This diminution is considerable, but according to my calculations it is nothing less. If, then, we had an initiatory speed of 12,000 yards, on leaving the atmosphere this speed would be reduced to 9,165 yards. In any case we have already passed through this interval, and——"

"And then," said Michel Ardan, "friend Nicholl has lost his two bets: four thousand dollars because the Columbiad did not burst; five thousand dollars because the projectile has risen more than six miles. Now, Nicholl, pay up."

"Let us prove it first," said the captain, "and we will pay afterward. It is quite possible that Barbicane's reasoning is correct, and that I have lost my nine thousand dollars. But a new hypothesis presents itself to my mind, and it annuls the wager."

"What is that?" asked Barbicane quickly.

"The hypothesis that, for some reason or other, fire was never set to the powder, and we have not started at all."

"My goodness, captain," exclaimed Michel Ardan, "that hypothesis is not worthy of my brain! It cannot be a serious one. For have we not been half annihilated by the shock? Did I not recall you to life? Is not the president's shoulder still bleeding from the blow it has received?"

"Granted," replied Nicholl; "but one question."

"Well, captain?"

"Did you hear the detonation, which certainly ought to be loud?"

"No," replied Ardan, much surprised; "certainly I did not hear the detonation."

"And you, Barbicane?"

"Nor I, either."

"Very well," said Nicholl.

"Well now," murmured the president "why did we not hear the detonation?"

The three friends looked at each other with a disconcerted air. It was quite an inexplicable phenomenon. The projectile had started, and consequently there must have been a detonation.

"Let us first find out where we are," said Barbicane, "and let down this panel."

This very simple operation was soon accomplished.

The nuts which held the bolts to the outer plates of the right-hand scuttle gave way under the pressure of the English wrench. These bolts were pushed outside, and the buffers covered with India-rubber stopped up the holes which let them through. Immediately the outer plate fell back upon its hinges like a porthole, and the lenticular glass which closed the scuttle appeared. A similar one was let into the thick partition on the opposite side of the projectile, another in the top of the dome, and finally a fourth in the middle of the base. They could, therefore, make observations in four different directions; the firmament by the side and most direct windows, the earth or the moon by the upper and under openings in the projectile.

CHAPTER II THE FIRST HALF-HOUR

Barbicane and his two companions immediately rushed to the uncovered window. But it was lit by no ray of light. Profound darkness surrounded them, which, however, did not prevent the president from exclaiming:

"No, my friends, we have not fallen back upon the earth; no, nor are we submerged in the Gulf of Mexico. Yes! we are mounting into space. See those stars shining in the night, and that impenetrable darkness heaped up between the earth and us!"

"Hurrah! hurrah!" exclaimed Michel Ardan and Nicholl in one voice.

Indeed, this thick darkness proved that the projectile had left the earth, for the soil, brilliantly lit by the moon-beams would have been visible to the travelers, if they had been lying on its surface. This darkness also showed that the projectile had passed the atmospheric strata, for the diffused light spread in the air would have been reflected on the metal walls, which reflection was wanting. This light would have lit the window, and the window was dark. Doubt was no longer possible; the travelers had left the earth.

"I have lost," said Nicholl.

"I congratulate you," replied Ardan.

"Here are the nine thousand dollars," said the captain, drawing a roll of paper dollars from his pocket.

"Will you have a receipt for it?" asked Barbicane, taking the sum.

"If you do not mind," answered Nicholl; "it is more business-like."

And coolly and seriously, as if he had been at his strong-box, the president drew forth his notebook, tore out a blank leaf, wrote a proper receipt in pencil, dated and signed it with the usual flourish[1], and gave it to the captain, who carefully placed it in his pocket-book. Michel Ardan, taking off his hat, bowed to his two companions without speaking. So much formality under such circumstances left him speechless. He had never before seen anything so "American."

This affair settled, Barbicane and Nicholl had returned to the window, and were watching the constellations. The stars looked like bright points on the black sky. But from that side they could not see the orb of night, which, traveling from east to west, would rise by degrees toward the zenith. Its absence drew the following remark from Ardan:

"And the moon; will she perchance fail at our rendezvous?"

"Do not alarm yourself," said Barbicane; "our future globe is at its post, but we cannot see her from this side; let us open the other."

"As Barbicane was about leaving the window to open the opposite scuttle, his attention was attracted by the approach of a brilliant object. It was an enormous disc, whose colossal dimension could not be estimated. Its face, which was turned to the earth, was very bright. One might have thought it a small moon reflecting the light of the large one. She advanced with great speed, and seemed to describe an orbit round the earth, which would intersect the passage of the projectile. This body revolved upon its axis, and exhibited the phenomena of all celestial bodies abandoned in space.

"Ah!" exclaimed Michel Ardan, "What is that? another projectile?"

Barbicane did not answer. The appearance of this enormous body surprised and troubled him. A collision was possible, and might be attended with deplorable results; either the projectile would deviate from its path, or a shock, breaking its impetus, might precipitate it to earth; or, lastly, it might be irresistibly drawn away by the powerful asteroid. The president caught at a glance the consequences of these three hypotheses, either of

---

[1] This is a purcly French habit.

which would, one way or the other, bring their experiment to an unsuccessful and fatal termination. His companions stood silently looking into space. The object grew rapidly as it approached them, and by an optical illusion the projectile seemed to be throwing itself before it.

"By Jove!" exclaimed Michel Ardan, "we shall run into one another!"

Instinctively the travelers drew back. Their dread was great, but it did not last many seconds. The asteroid passed several hundred yards from the projectile and disappeared, not so much from the rapidity of its course, as that its face being opposite the moon, it was suddenly merged into the perfect darkness of space.

"A happy journey to you," exclaimed Michel Ardan, with a sigh of relief. "Surely infinity of space is large enough for a poor little projectile to walk through without fear. Now, what is this portentous globe which nearly struck us?"

"I know," replied Barbicane.

"Oh, indeed! you know everything."

"It is," said Barbicane, "a simple meteorite, but an enormous one, which the attraction of the earth has retained as a satellite."

"Is it possible!" exclaimed Michel Ardan; "the earth then has two moons like Neptune?"

"Yes, my friends, two moons, though it passes generally for having only one; but this second moon is so small, and its speed so great, that the inhabitants of the earth cannot see it. It was by noticing disturbances that a French astronomer, M. Petit, was able to determine the existence of this second satellite and calculate its elements. According to his observations, this meteorite will accomplish its revolution around the earth in three hours and twenty minutes, which implies a wonderful rate of speed."

"Do all astronomers admit the existence of this satellite?" asked Nicholl.

"No," replied Barbicane; "but if, like us, they had met it, they could no longer doubt it. Indeed, I think that this meteorite, which, had it struck the projectile, would have much embarrassed us, will give us the means of deciding what our position in space is."

"How?" said Ardan.

"Because its distance is known, and when we met it, we were exactly four thousand six hundred and fifty miles from the surface of the terrestrial globe."

"More than two thousand French leagues," exclaimed Michel Ardan.

"That beats the express trains of the pitiful globe called the earth."

"I should think so," replied Nicholl, consulting his chronometer; "it is eleven o'clock, and it is only thirteen minutes since we left the American continent."

"Only thirteen minutes?" said Barbicane.

"Yes," said Nicholl; "and if our initiatory speed of twelve thousand yards has been kept up, we shall have made about twenty thousand miles in the hour."

"That is all very well, my friends," said the president, "but the insoluble question still remains. Why did we not hear the detonation of the Columbiad?"

For want of an answer the conversation dropped, and Barbicane began thoughtfully to let down the shutter of the second side. He succeeded; and through the uncovered glass the moon filled the projectile with a brilliant light. Nicholl, as an economical man, put out the gas, now useless, and whose brilliancy prevented any observation of the interplanetary space.

The lunar disc shone with wonderful purity. Her rays, no longer filtered through the vapory atmosphere of the terrestrial globe, shone through the glass, filling the air in the interior of the projectile with silvery reflections. The black curtain of the firmament in reality heightened the moon's brilliancy, which in this void of ether unfavorable to diffusion did not eclipse the neighboring stars. The heavens, thus seen, presented quite a new aspect, and one which the human eye could never dream of. One may conceive the interest with which these bold men watched the orb of night, the great aim of their journey.

In its motion the earth's satellite was insensibly nearing the zenith, the mathematical point which it ought to attain ninety-six hours later. Her mountains, her plains, every projection was as clearly discernible to their eyes as if they were observing it from some spot upon the earth; but its light was developed through space with wonderful intensity. The disc shone like a platinum mirror. Of the earth flying from under their feet, the travelers had lost all recollection.

It was captain Nicholl who first recalled their attention to the vanishing globe.

"Yes," said Michel Ardan, "do not let us be ungrateful to it. Since we are leaving our country, let our last looks be directed to it. I wish to see the earth once more before it is quite hidden from my eyes."

To satisfy his companions, Barbicane began to uncover the window at the bottom of the projectile, which would allow them to observe the earth direct. The disc, which the force of the projection had beaten down to the base, was removed, not without difficulty. Its fragments, placed carefully against a wall, might serve again upon occasion. Then a circular gap appeared, nineteen inches in diameter, hollowed out of the lower part of the projectile. A glass cover, six inches thick and strengthened with upper fastenings, closed it tightly. Beneath was fixed an aluminum plate, held in place by bolts. The screws being undone, and the bolts let go, the plate fell down, and visible communication was established between the interior and the exterior.

Michel Ardan knelt by the glass. It was cloudy, seemingly opaque.

"Well!" he exclaimed, "and the earth?"

"The earth?" said Barbicane. "There it is."

"What! that little thread; that silver crescent?"

"Doubtless, Michel. In four days, when the moon will be full, at the very time we shall reach it, the earth will be new, and will only appear to us as a slender crescent which will soon disappear, and for some days will be enveloped in utter darkness."

"That the earth?" repeated Michel Ardan, looking with all his eyes at the thin slip of his native planet.

The explanation given by President Barbicane was correct. The earth, with respect to the projectile, was entering its last phase. It was in its octant, and showed a crescent finely traced on the dark background of the sky. Its light, rendered bluish by the thick strata of the atmosphere was less intense than that of the crescent moon, but it was of considerable dimensions, and looked like an enormous arch stretched across the firmament. Some parts brilliantly lighted, especially on its concave part, showed the presence of high mountains, often disappearing behind thick spots, which are never seen on the lunar disc. They were rings of clouds placed concentrically round the terrestrial globe.

While the travelers were trying to pierce the profound darkness, a brilliant cluster of shooting stars burst upon their eyes. Hundreds of meteorites, ignited by the friction of the atmosphere, irradiated the shadow of the luminous train, and lined the cloudy parts of the disc with their fire. At this period the earth was in its perihelion, and the month of December is so propitious to these shooting stars, that astronomers have counted as many as twenty-four thousand in an hour. But Michel Ardan, disdaining scientific reasonings, preferred thinking that the earth was thus saluting the departure of her three children with her most brilliant fireworks.

Indeed this was all they saw of the globe lost in the solar world, rising and setting to the great planets like a simple morning or evening star! This globe, where they had left all their affections, was nothing more than a fugitive crescent!

Long did the three friends look without speaking, though united in heart, while the projectile sped onward with an ever-decreasing speed. Then an irresistible drowsiness crept over their brain. Was it weariness of body and mind? No doubt; for after the over-excitement of those last hours passed upon earth, reaction was inevitable.

"Well," said Nicholl, "since we must sleep, let us sleep."

And stretching themselves on their couches, they were all three soon in a profound slumber.

But they had not forgotten themselves more than a quarter of an hour, when Barbicane sat up suddenly, and rousing his companions with a loud voice, exclaimed——

"I have found it!"

"What have you found?" asked Michel Ardan, jumping from his bed.

"The reason why we did not hear the detonation of the Columbiad."

"And it is——?" said Nicholl.

"Because our projectile traveled faster than the sound!"

CHAPTER III THEIR PLACE OF SHELTER

This curious but certainly correct explanation once given, the three friends returned to their slumbers. Could they have found a calmer or more peaceful spot to sleep in? On the earth, houses, towns, cottages, and country feel every shock given to the exterior of the globe. On sea, the vessels rocked by the waves are still in motion; in the air, the balloon oscillates incessantly on the fluid strata of divers densities. This projectile alone, floating in perfect space, in the midst of perfect silence, offered perfect repose.

Thus the sleep of our adventurous travelers might have been indefinitely prolonged, if an unexpected noise had not awakened them at about seven o'clock in the morning of the 2nd of December, eight hours after their departure.

This noise was a very natural barking.

"The dogs! it is the dogs!" exclaimed Michel Ardan, rising at once.

"They are hungry," said Nicholl.

"By Jove!" replied Michel, "we have forgotten them."

"Where are they?" asked Barbicane.

They looked and found one of the animals crouched under the divan. Terrified and shaken by the initiatory shock, it had remained in the corner till its voice returned with the pangs of hunger. It was the amiable Diana, still very confused, who crept out of her retreat, though not without much persuasion, Michel Ardan encouraging her with most gracious words.

"Come, Diana," said he: "come, my girl! thou whose destiny will be marked in the cynegetic annals; thou whom the pagans would have given as companion to the god Anubis, and Christians as friend to St. Roch; thou who art rushing into interplanetary space, and wilt perhaps be the Eve of all Selenite dogs! come, Diana, come here."

Diana, flattered or not, advanced by degrees, uttering plaintive cries.

"Good," said Barbicane: "I see Eve, but where is Adam?"

"Adam?" replied Michel; "Adam cannot be far off; he is there somewhere; we must call him. Satellite! here, Satellite!"

But Satellite did not appear. Diana would not leave off howling. They found, however, that she was not bruised, and they gave her a pie, which silenced her complaints. As to Satellite, he seemed quite lost. They had to hunt a long time before finding him in one of the upper compartments of the projectile, whither some unaccountable shock must have violently hurled him. The poor beast, much hurt, was in a piteous state.

"The devil!" said Michel.

They brought the unfortunate dog down with great care. Its skull had been broken against the roof, and it seemed unlikely that he could recover from such a shock. Meanwhile, he was stretched comfortably on a cushion. Once there, he heaved a sigh.

"We will take care of you," said Michel; "we are responsible for your existence. I would rather lose an arm than a paw of my poor Satellite."

Saying which, he offered some water to the wounded dog, who swallowed it with avidity.

This attention paid, the travelers watched the earth and the moon attentively. The earth was now only discernible by a cloudy disc ending in a crescent, rather more contracted than that of the previous evening; but its expanse was still enormous, compared with that of the moon, which was approaching nearer and nearer to a perfect circle.

"By Jove!" said Michel Ardan, "I am really sorry that we did not start when the earth was full, that is to say, when our globe was in opposition to the sun."

"Why?" said Nicholl.

"Because we should have seen our continents and seas in a new light— the first resplendent under the solar rays, the latter cloudy as represented on some maps of the world. I should like to have seen those poles of the earth on which the eye of man has never yet rested.

"I dare say," replied Barbicane; "but if the earth had been *full*, the moon would have been *new*; that is to say, invisible, because of the rays of the sun. It is better for us to see the destination we wish to reach, than the point of departure."

"You are right, Barbicane," replied Captain Nicholl; "and, besides, when we have reached the moon, we shall have time during the long lunar nights to consider at our leisure the globe on which our likenesses swarm."

"Our likenesses!" exclaimed Michel Ardan; "They are no more our likenesses than the Selenites are! We inhabit a new world, peopled by ourselves— the projectile! I am Barbicane's likeness, and Barbicane is Nicholl's. Beyond us, around us, human nature is at an end, and we are the only population of this microcosm until we become pure Selenites."

"In about eighty-eight hours," replied the captain.

"Which means to say?" asked Michel Ardan.

"That it is half-past eight," replied Nicholl.

"Very well," retorted Michel; "then it is impossible for me to find even the shadow of a reason why we should not go to breakfast."

Indeed the inhabitants of the new star could not live without eating, and their stomachs were suffering from the imperious laws of hunger. Michel Ardan, as a Frenchman, was declared chief cook, an important function, which raised no rival. The gas gave sufficient heat for the culinary apparatus, and the provision box furnished the elements of this first feast.

The breakfast began with three bowls of excellent soup, thanks to the liquefaction in hot water of those precious cakes of Liebig, prepared from the best parts of the ruminants of the Pampas. To the soup succeeded some beefsteaks, compressed by an hydraulic press, as tender and succulent as if brought straight from the kitchen of an English eating-house. Michel, who was imaginative, maintained that they were even "red."

Preserved vegetables ("fresher than nature," said the amiable Michel) succeeded the dish of meat; and was followed by some cups of tea with bread and butter, after the American fashion.

The beverage was declared exquisite, and was due to the infusion of the choicest leaves, of which the emperor of Russia had given some chests for the benefit of the travelers.

And lastly, to crown the repast, Ardan had brought out a fine bottle of Nuits, which was found "by chance" in the provision-box. The three friends drank to the union of the earth and her satellite.

And, as if he had not already done enough for the generous wine which he had distilled on the slopes of Burgundy, the sun chose to be part of the party. At this moment the projectile emerged from the conical shadow cast by the terrestrial globe, and the rays of the radiant orb struck the lower disc of the projectile direct occasioned by the angle which the moon's orbit makes with that of the earth.

"The sun!" exclaimed Michel Ardan.

"No doubt," replied Barbicane; "I expected it."

"But," said Michel, "the conical shadow which the earth leaves in space extends beyond the moon?"

"Far beyond it, if the atmospheric refraction is not taken into consideration," said Barbicane. "But when the moon is enveloped in this shadow, it is because the centers of the three stars, the sun, the earth, and the moon, are all in one and the same straight line. Then the *nodes* coincide with the *phases* of the moon, and there is an eclipse. If we had started when there was an eclipse of the moon, all our passage would have been in the shadow, which would have been a pity."

"Why?"

"Because, though we are floating in space, our projectile, bathed in the solar rays, will receive light and heat. It economizes the gas, which is in every respect a good economy."

Indeed, under these rays which no atmosphere can temper, either in temperature or brilliancy, the projectile grew warm and bright, as if it had passed suddenly from winter to summer. The moon above, the sun beneath, were inundating it with their fire.

"It is pleasant here," said Nicholl.

"I should think so," said Michel Ardan. "With a little earth spread on our aluminum planet we should have green peas in twenty-four hours. I have but one fear, which is that the walls of the projectile might melt."

"Calm yourself, my worthy friend," replied Barbicane; "the projectile withstood a very much higher temperature than this as it slid through the strata of the atmosphere. I should not be surprised if it did not look like a meteor on fire to the eyes of the spectators in Florida."

"But then J. T. Maston will think we are roasted!"

"What astonishes me," said Barbicane, "is that we have not been.

That was a danger we had not provided for."

"I feared it," said Nicholl simply.

"And you never mentioned it, my sublime captain," exclaimed

Michel Ardan, clasping his friend's hand.

Barbicane now began to settle himself in the projectile as if he was never to leave it. One must remember that this aerial car had a base with a *superficies* of fifty-four square feet. Its height to the roof was twelve feet. Carefully laid out in the inside, and little encumbered by instruments and traveling utensils, which each had their particular place, it left the three travelers a certain freedom of movement. The thick window inserted in the bottom could bear any amount of weight, and Barbicane and his companions walked upon it as if it were solid plank; but the sun striking it directly with its rays lit the interior of the projectile from beneath, thus producing singular effects of light.

They began by investigating the state of their store of water and provisions, neither of which had suffered, thanks to the care taken to deaden the shock. Their provisions were abundant, and plentiful enough to last the three travelers for more than a year. Barbicane wished to be cautious, in case the projectile should land on a part of the moon which was utterly barren. As to water and the reserve of brandy, which consisted of fifty gallons, there was only enough for two months; but according to the last observations of astronomers, the moon had a low, dense, and thick atmosphere, at least in the deep valleys, and there springs and streams could not fail. Thus, during their passage, and for the first year of their settlement on the lunar continent, these adventurous explorers would suffer neither hunger nor thirst.

Now about the air in the projectile. There, too, they were secure. Reiset and Regnaut's apparatus, intended for the production of oxygen, was supplied with chlorate of potassium for two months. They necessarily consumed a certain quantity of gas, for they were obliged to keep the producing substance at a temperature of above 400 °. But there again they were all safe. The apparatus only wanted a little care. But it was not enough to renew the oxygen; they must absorb the carbonic acid produced by expiration. During the last twelve hours the atmosphere of the projectile had become charged with this deleterious gas. Nicholl discovered the state of the air by observing Diana panting painfully. The carbonic acid, by a phenomenon similar to that produced in the famous Grotto del Cane, had collected at the bottom of the projectile owing to its weight. Poor Diana, with her head low, would suffer before her masters from the presence of this gas. But Captain Nicholl hastened to remedy this state of things, by placing on the floor several receivers containing caustic potash, which he shook about for a time, and this substance, greedy of carbonic acid, soon completely absorbed it, thus purifying the air.

An inventory of instruments was then begun. The thermometers and barometers had resisted, all but one minimum thermometer, the glass of which was broken. An excellent aneroid was drawn from the wadded box which contained it and hung on the wall. Of course it was only affected by and marked the pressure of the air inside the projectile, but it also showed the quantity of moisture which it contained. At that moment its needle oscillated between 25.24 and 25.08.

It was fine weather.

Barbicane had also brought several compasses, which he found intact. One must understand that under present conditions their needles were acting *wildly*, that is without any *constant* direction. Indeed, at the distance they were from the earth, the magnetic pole could have no perceptible action upon the apparatus; but the box placed on the lunar disc might perhaps exhibit some strange phenomena. In any case it would be interesting to see whether the earth's satellite submitted like herself to its magnetic influence.

A hypsometer to measure the height of the lunar mountains, a sextant to take the height of the sun, glasses which would be useful as they neared the moon, all these instruments were carefully looked over, and pronounced good in spite of the violent shock.

As to the pickaxes and different tools which were Nicholl's especial choice; as to the sacks of different kinds of grain and shrubs which Michel Ardan hoped to transplant into Selenite ground, they were stowed away in the upper part of the projectile. There was a sort of granary there, loaded with things which the extravagant Frenchman had heaped up. What they were no one knew, and the good-tempered fellow did not explain. Now and then he climbed up by cramp-irons riveted to the walls, but kept the inspection to himself. He arranged and rearranged, he plunged his hand rapidly into certain mysterious boxes, singing in one of the falsest of voices an old French refrain to enliven the situation.

Barbicane observed with some interest that his guns and other arms had not been damaged. These were important, because, heavily loaded, they were to help lessen the fall of the projectile, when drawn by the lunar attraction (after having passed the point of neutral attraction) on to the moon's surface; a fall which ought to be six times less rapid than it would have been on the earth's surface, thanks to the difference of bulk. The inspection ended with general satisfaction, when each returned to watch space through the side windows and the lower glass coverlid.

CHAPTER III THEIR PLACE OF SHELTER

There was the same view. The whole extent of the celestial sphere swarmed with stars and constellations of wonderful purity, enough to drive an astronomer out of his mind! On one side the sun, like the mouth of a lighted oven, a dazzling disc without a halo, standing out on the dark background of the sky! On the other, the moon returning its fire by reflection, and apparently motionless in the midst of the starry world. Then, a large spot seemingly nailed to the firmament, bordered by a silvery cord; it was the earth! Here and there nebulous masses like large flakes of starry snow; and from the zenith to the nadir, an immense ring formed by an impalpable dust of stars, the "Milky Way," in the midst of which the sun ranks only as a star of the fourth magnitude. The observers could not take their eyes from this novel spectacle, of which no description could give an adequate idea. What reflections it suggested! What emotions hitherto unknown awoke in their souls! Barbicane wished to begin the relation of his journey while under its first impressions, and hour after hour took notes of all facts happening in the beginning of the enterprise. He wrote quietly, with his large square writing, in a business-like style.

During this time Nicholl, the calculator, looked over the minutes of their passage, and worked out figures with unparalleled dexterity. Michel Ardan chatted first with Barbicane, who did not answer him, and then with Nicholl, who did not hear him, with Diana, who understood none of his theories, and lastly with himself, questioning and answering, going and coming, busy with a thousand details; at one time bent over the lower glass, at another roosting in the heights of the projectile, and always singing. In this microcosm he represented French loquacity and excitability, and we beg you to believe that they were well represented. The day, or rather (for the expression is not correct) the lapse of twelve hours, which forms a day upon the earth, closed with a plentiful supper carefully prepared. No accident of any nature had yet happened to shake the travelers' confidence; so, full of hope, already sure of success, they slept peacefully, while the projectile under an uniformly decreasing speed was crossing the sky.

CHAPTER IV A LITTLE ALGEBRA

The night passed without incident. The word "night," however, is scarcely applicable.

The position of the projectile with regard to the sun did not change. Astronomically, it was daylight on the lower part, and night on the upper; so when during this narrative these words are used, they represent the lapse of time between rising and setting of the sun upon the earth.

The travelers' sleep was rendered more peaceful by the projectile's excessive speed, for it seemed absolutely motionless. Not a motion betrayed its onward course through space. The rate of progress, however rapid it might be, cannot produce any sensible effect on the human frame when it takes place in a vacuum, or when the mass of air circulates with the body which is carried with it. What inhabitant of the earth perceives its speed, which, however, is at the rate of 68,000 miles per hour? Motion under such conditions is "felt" no more than repose; and when a body is in repose it will remain so as long as no strange force displaces it; if moving, it will not stop unless an obstacle comes in its way. This indifference to motion or repose is called inertia.

Barbicane and his companions might have believed themselves perfectly stationary, being shut up in the projectile; indeed, the effect would have been the same if they had been on the outside of it. Had it not been for the moon, which was increasing above them, they might have sworn that they were floating in complete stagnation.

That morning, the 3rd of December, the travelers were awakened by a joyous but unexpected noise; it was the crowing of a cock which sounded through the car. Michel Ardan, who was the first on his feet, climbed to the top of the projectile, and shutting a box, the lid of which was partly open, said in a low voice, "Will you hold your tongue? That creature will spoil my design!"

But Nicholl and Barbicane were awake.

"A cock!" said Nicholl.

"Why no, my friends," Michel answered quickly; "it was I who wished to awake you by this rural sound." So saying, he gave vent to a splendid cock-a-doodledoo, which would have done honor to the proudest of poultry-yards.

The two Americans could not help laughing.

"Fine talent that," said Nicholl, looking suspiciously at his companion.

"Yes," said Michel; "a joke in my country. It is very Gallic; they play the cock so in the best society."

Then turning the conversation:

"Barbicane, do you know what I have been thinking of all night?"

"No," answered the president.

"Of our Cambridge friends. You have already remarked that I am an ignoramus in mathematical subjects; and it is impossible for me to find out how the savants of the observatory were able to calculate what initiatory speed the projectile ought to have on leaving the Columbiad in order to attain the moon."

"You mean to say," replied Barbicane, "to attain that neutral point where the terrestrial and lunar attractions are equal; for, starting from that point, situated about nine-tenths of the distance traveled over, the projectile would simply fall upon the moon, on account of its weight."

"So be it," said Michel; "but, once more; how could they calculate the initiatory speed?"

"Nothing can be easier," replied Barbicane.

"And you knew how to make that calculation?" asked Michel Ardan.

"Perfectly. Nicholl and I would have made it, if the observatory had not saved us the trouble."

"Very well, old Barbicane," replied Michel; "they might have cut off my head, beginning at my feet, before they could have made me solve that problem."

"Because you do not know algebra," answered Barbicane quietly.

"Ah, there you are, you eaters of x^1; you think you have said all when you have said `Algebra.'"

"Michel," said Barbicane, "can you use a forge without a hammer, or a plow without a plowshare?"

"Hardly."

"Well, algebra is a tool, like the plow or the hammer, and a good tool to those who know how to use it."

"Seriously?"

"Quite seriously."

"And can you use that tool in my presence?"

"If it will interest you."

"And show me how they calculated the initiatory speed of our car?"

"Yes, my worthy friend; taking into consideration all the elements of the problem, the distance from the center of the earth to the center of the moon, of the radius of the earth, of its bulk, and of the bulk of the moon, I can tell exactly what ought to be the initiatory speed of the projectile, and that by a simple formula."

"Let us see."

"You shall see it; only I shall not give you the real course drawn by the projectile between the moon and the earth in considering their motion round the sun. No, I shall consider these two orbs as perfectly motionless, which will answer all our purpose."

"And why?"

"Because it will be trying to solve the problem called `the problem of the three bodies,' for which the integral calculus is not yet far enough advanced."

"Then," said Michel Ardan, in his sly tone, "mathematics have not said their last word?"

"Certainly not," replied Barbicane.

"Well, perhaps the Selenites have carried the integral calculus farther than you have; and, by the bye, what is this `integral calculus?'"

"It is a calculation the converse of the differential," replied
Barbicane seriously.

"Much obliged; it is all very clear, no doubt."

"And now," continued Barbicane, "a slip of paper and a bit of pencil, and before a half-hour is over I will have found the required formula."

Half an hour had not elapsed before Barbicane, raising his head, showed Michel Ardan a page covered with algebraical signs, in which the general formula for the solution was contained.

"Well, and does Nicholl understand what that means?"

"Of course, Michel," replied the captain. "All these signs, which seem cabalistic to you, form the plainest, the clearest, and the most logical language to those who know how to read it."

"And you pretend, Nicholl," asked Michel, "that by means of these hieroglyphics, more incomprehensible than the Egyptian Ibis, you can find what initiatory speed it was necessary to give the projectile?"

"Incontestably," replied Nicholl; "and even by this same formula

I can always tell you its speed at any point of its transit."

"On your word?"

"On my word."

"Then you are as cunning as our president."

"No, Michel; the difficult part is what Barbicane has done; that is, to get an equation which shall satisfy all the conditions of the problem. The remainder is only a question of arithmetic, requiring merely the knowledge of the four rules."

"That is something!" replied Michel Ardan, who for his life could not do addition right, and who defined the rule as a Chinese puzzle, which allowed one to obtain all sorts of totals.

"The expression *v* zero, which you see in that equation, is the speed which the projectile will have on leaving the atmosphere."

"Just so," said Nicholl; "it is from that point that we must calculate the velocity, since we know already that the velocity at departure was exactly one and a half times more than on leaving the atmosphere."

"I understand no more," said Michel.

"It is a very simple calculation," said Barbicane.

"Not as simple as I am," retorted Michel.

"That means, that when our projectile reached the limits of the terrestrial atmosphere it had already lost one-third of its initiatory speed."

"As much as that?"

"Yes, my friend; merely by friction against the atmospheric strata. You understand that the faster it goes the more resistance it meets with from the air."

"That I admit," answered Michel; "and I understand it, although your x's and zero's, and algebraic formula, are rattling in my head like nails in a bag."

"First effects of algebra," replied Barbicane; "and now, to finish, we are going to prove the given number of these different expressions, that is, work out their value."

"Finish me!" replied Michel.

Barbicane took the paper, and began to make his calculations with great rapidity. Nicholl looked over and greedily read the work as it proceeded.

"That's it! that's it!" at last he cried.

"Is it clear?" asked Barbicane.

"It is written in letters of fire," said Nicholl.

"Wonderful fellows!" muttered Ardan.

"Do you understand it at last?" asked Barbicane.

"Do I understand it?" cried Ardan; "my head is splitting with it."

CHAPTER IV A LITTLE ALGEBRA

"And now," said Nicholl, "to find out the speed of the projectile when it leaves the atmosphere, we have only to calculate that."

The captain, as a practical man equal to all difficulties, began to write with frightful rapidity. Divisions and multiplications grew under his fingers; the figures were like hail on the white page. Barbicane watched him, while Michel Ardan nursed a growing headache with both hands.

"Very well?" asked Barbicane, after some minutes' silence.

"Well!" replied Nicholl; every calculation made, *v* zero, that is to say, the speed necessary for the projectile on leaving the atmosphere, to enable it to reach the equal point of attraction, ought to be——"

"Yes?" said Barbicane.

"Twelve thousand yards."

"What!" exclaimed Barbicane, starting; "you say——"

"Twelve thousand yards."

"The devil!" cried the president, making a gesture of despair.

"What is the matter?" asked Michel Ardan, much surprised.

"What is the matter! why, if at this moment our speed had already diminished one-third by friction, the initiatory speed ought to have been——"

"Seventeen thousand yards."

"And the Cambridge Observatory declared that twelve thousand yards was enough at starting; and our projectile, which only started with that speed——"

"Well?" asked Nicholl.

"Well, it will not be enough."

"Good."

"We shall not be able to reach the neutral point."

"The deuce!"

"We shall not even get halfway."

"In the name of the projectile!" exclaimed Michel Ardan, jumping as if it was already on the point of striking the terrestrial globe.

"And we shall fall back upon the earth!"

CHAPTER V THE COLD OF SPACE

This revelation came like a thunderbolt. Who could have expected such an error in calculation? Barbicane would not believe it. Nicholl revised his figures: they were exact. As to the formula which had determined them, they could not suspect its truth; it was evident that an initiatory velocity of seventeen thousand yards in the first second was necessary to enable them to reach the neutral point.

The three friends looked at each other silently. There was no thought of breakfast. Barbicane, with clenched teeth, knitted brows, and hands clasped convulsively, was watching through the window. Nicholl had crossed his arms, and was examining his calculations. Michel Ardan was muttering:

"That is just like these scientific men: they never do anything else.
I would give twenty pistoles if we could fall upon the Cambridge
Observatory and crush it, together with the whole lot of dabblers
in figures which it contains."

Suddenly a thought struck the captain, which he at once communicated to Barbicane.

"Ah!" said he; "it is seven o'clock in the morning; we have already been gone thirty-two hours; more than half our passage is over, and we are not falling that I am aware of."

Barbicane did not answer, but after a rapid glance at the captain, took a pair of compasses wherewith to measure the angular distance of the terrestrial globe; then from the lower window he took an exact observation, and noticed that the projectile was apparently stationary. Then rising and wiping his forehead, on which large drops of perspiration were standing, he put some figures on paper. Nicholl understood that the president was deducting from the terrestrial diameter the projectile's distance from the earth. He watched him anxiously.

"No," exclaimed Barbicane, after some moments, "no, we are not falling! no, we are already more than 50,000 leagues from the earth. We have passed the point at which the projectile would have stopped if its speed had only been 12,000 yards at starting. We are still going up."

"That is evident," replied Nicholl; "and we must conclude that our initial speed, under the power of the 400,000 pounds of gun-cotton, must have exceeded the required 12,000 yards. Now I can understand how, after thirteen minutes only, we met the second satellite, which gravitates round the earth at more than 2,000 leagues' distance."

"And this explanation is the more probable," added Barbicane, "Because, in throwing off the water enclosed between its partition-breaks, the projectile found itself lightened of a considerable weight."

"Just so," said Nicholl.

"Ah, my brave Nicholl, we are saved!"

"Very well then," said Michel Ardan quietly; "as we are safe, let us have breakfast."

Nicholl was not mistaken. The initial speed had been, very fortunately, much above that estimated by the Cambridge Observatory; but the Cambridge Observatory had nevertheless made a mistake.

The travelers, recovered from this false alarm, breakfasted merrily. If they ate a good deal, they talked more. Their confidence was greater after than before "the incident of the algebra."

"Why should we not succeed?" said Michel Ardan; "why should we not arrive safely? We are launched; we have no obstacle before us, no stones in the way; the road is open, more so than that of a ship battling with the sea; more open than that of a balloon battling with the wind; and if a ship can reach its destination, a balloon go where it pleases, why cannot our projectile attain its end and aim?"

"It *will* attain it," said Barbicane.

"If only to do honor to the Americans," added Michel Ardan, "the only people who could bring such an enterprise to a happy termination, and the only one which could produce a President Barbicane. Ah, now we are no longer uneasy, I begin to think, What will become of us? We shall get right royally weary."

Barbicane and Nicholl made a gesture of denial.

"But I have provided for the contingency, my friends," replied Michel; "you have only to speak, and I have chess, draughts, cards, and dominoes at your disposal; nothing is wanting but a billiard-table."

"What!" exclaimed Barbicane; "you brought away such trifles?"

"Certainly," replied Michel, "and not only to distract ourselves, but also with the laudable intention of endowing the Selenite smoking divans with them."

"My friend," said Barbicane, "if the moon is inhabited, its inhabitants must have appeared some thousands of years before those of the earth, for we cannot doubt that their star is much older than ours. If then these Selenites have existed their hundreds of thousands of years, and if their brain is of the same organization of the human brain, they have already invented all that we have invented, and even what we may invent in future ages. They have nothing to learn from *us*, and we have everything to learn from *them*."

"What!" said Michel; "you believe that they have artists like
Phidias, Michael Angelo, or Raphael?"

"Yes."

"Poets like Homer, Virgil, Milton, Lamartine, and Hugo?"

"I am sure of it."

"Philosophers like Plato, Aristotle, Descartes, Kant?"

"I have no doubt of it."

"Scientific men like Archimedes, Euclid, Pascal, Newton?"

"I could swear it."

"Comic writers like Arnal, and photographers like— like Nadar?"

"Certain."

"Then, friend Barbicane, if they are as strong as we are, and even stronger— these Selenites— why have they not tried to communicate with the earth? why have they not launched a lunar projectile to our terrestrial regions?"

"Who told you that they have never done so?" said Barbicane seriously.

"Indeed," added Nicholl, "it would be easier for them than for us, for two reasons; first, because the attraction on the moon's surface is six times less than on that of the earth, which would allow a projectile to rise more easily; secondly, because it would be enough to send such a projectile only at 8,000 leagues instead of 80,000, which would require the force of projection to be ten times less strong."

"Then," continued Michel, "I repeat it, why have they not done it?"

"And I repeat," said Barbicane; "who told you that they have not done it?"

"When?"

"Thousands of years before man appeared on earth."

"And the projectile— where is the projectile? I demand to see the projectile."

"My friend," replied Barbicane, "the sea covers five-sixths of our globe. From that we may draw five good reasons for supposing that the lunar projectile, if ever launched, is now at the bottom of the Atlantic or the Pacific, unless it sped into some crevasse at that period when the crust of the earth was not yet hardened."

"Old Barbicane," said Michel, "you have an answer for everything, and I bow before your wisdom. But there is one hypothesis that would suit me better than all the others, which is, the Selenites, being older than we, are wiser, and have not invented gunpowder."

At this moment Diana joined in the conversation by a sonorous barking.

She was asking for her breakfast.

"Ah!" said Michel Ardan, "in our discussion we have forgotten

Diana and Satellite."

Immediately a good-sized pie was given to the dog, which devoured it hungrily.

"Do you see, Barbicane," said Michel, "we should have made a second Noah's ark of this projectile, and borne with us to the moon a couple of every kind of domestic animal."

"I dare say; but room would have failed us."

"Oh!" said Michel, "we might have squeezed a little."

"The fact is," replied Nicholl, "that cows, bulls, and horses, and all ruminants, would have been very useful on the lunar continent, but unfortunately the car could neither have been made a stable nor a shed."

"Well, we might have at least brought a donkey, only a little donkey; that courageous beast which old Silenus loved to mount. I love those old donkeys; they are the least favored animals in creation; they are not only beaten while alive, but even after they are dead."

"How do you make that out?" asked Barbicane. "Why," said

Michel, "they make their skins into drums."

Barbicane and Nicholl could not help laughing at this ridiculous remark. But a cry from their merry companion stopped them. The latter was leaning over the spot where Satellite lay. He rose, saying:

"My good Satellite is no longer ill."

"Ah!" said Nicholl.

"No," answered Michel, "he is dead! There," added he, in a piteous tone, "that is embarrassing. I much fear, my poor Diana, that you will leave no progeny in the lunar regions!"

Indeed the unfortunate Satellite had not survived its wound. It was quite dead. Michel Ardan looked at his friends with a rueful countenance.

"One question presents itself," said Barbicane. "We cannot keep the dead body of this dog with us for the next forty-eight hours."

"No! certainly not," replied Nicholl; "but our scuttles are fixed on hinges; they can be let down. We will open one, and throw the body out into space."

The president thought for some moments, and then said:

"Yes, we must do so, but at the same time taking very great precautions."

"Why?" asked Michel.

CHAPTER V THE COLD OF SPACE

"For two reasons which you will understand," answered Barbicane. "The first relates to the air shut up in the projectile, and of which we must lose as little as possible."

"But we manufacture the air?"

"Only in part. We make only the oxygen, my worthy Michel; and with regard to that, we must watch that the apparatus does not furnish the oxygen in too great a quantity; for an excess would bring us very serious physiological troubles. But if we make the oxygen, we do not make the azote, that medium which the lungs do not absorb, and which ought to remain intact; and that azote will escape rapidly through the open scuttles."

"Oh! the time for throwing out poor Satellite?" said Michel.

"Agreed; but we must act quickly."

"And the second reason?" asked Michel.

"The second reason is that we must not let the outer cold, which is excessive, penetrate the projectile or we shall be frozen to death."

"But the sun?"

"The sun warms our projectile, which absorbs its rays; but it does not warm the vacuum in which we are floating at this moment. Where there is no air, there is no more heat than diffused light; and the same with darkness; it is cold where the sun's rays do not strike direct. This temperature is only the temperature produced by the radiation of the stars; that is to say, what the terrestrial globe would undergo if the sun disappeared one day."

"Which is not to be feared," replied Nicholl.

"Who knows?" said Michel Ardan. "But, in admitting that the sun does not go out, might it not happen that the earth might move away from it?"

"There!" said Barbicane, "there is Michel with his ideas."

"And," continued Michel, "do we not know that in 1861 the earth passed through the tail of a comet? Or let us suppose a comet whose power of attraction is greater than that of the sun. The terrestrial orbit will bend toward the wandering star, and the earth, becoming its satellite, will be drawn such a distance that the rays of the sun will have no action on its surface."

"That *might* happen, indeed," replied Barbicane, "but the consequences of such a displacement need not be so formidable as you suppose."

"And why not?"

"Because the heat and cold would be equalized on our globe. It has been calculated that, had our earth been carried along in its course by the comet of 1861, at its perihelion, that is, its nearest approach to the sun, it would have undergone a heat 28,000 times greater than that of summer. But this heat, which is sufficient to evaporate the waters, would have formed a thick ring of cloud, which would have modified that excessive temperature; hence the compensation between the cold of the aphelion and the heat of the perihelion."

"At how many degrees," asked Nicholl, "is the temperature of the planetary spaces estimated?"

"Formerly," replied Barbicane, "it was greatly exagerated; but now, after the calculations of Fourier, of the French Academy of Science, it is not supposed to exceed 60 ° Centigrade below zero."

"Pooh!" said Michel, "that's nothing!"

"It is very much," replied Barbicane; "the temperature which was observed in the polar regions, at Melville Island and Fort Reliance, that is 76 ° Fahrenheit below zero."

"If I mistake not," said Nicholl, "M. Pouillet, another savant, estimates the temperature of space at 250 ° Fahrenheit below zero. We shall, however, be able to verify these calculations for ourselves."

"Not at present; because the solar rays, beating directly upon our thermometer, would give, on the contrary, a very high temperature. But, when we arrive in the moon, during its fifteen days of night at either face, we shall have leisure to make the experiment, for our satellite lies in a vacuum."

"What do you mean by a vacuum?" asked Michel. "Is it perfectly such?"

"It is absolutely void of air."

"And is the air replaced by nothing whatever?"

"By the ether only," replied Barbicane.

"And pray what is the ether?"

"The ether, my friend, is an agglomeration of imponderable atoms, which, relatively to their dimensions, are as far removed from each other as the celestial bodies are in space. It is these atoms which, by their vibratory motion, produce both light and heat in the universe."

They now proceeded to the burial of Satellite. They had merely to drop him into space, in the same way that sailors drop a body into the sea; but, as President Barbicane suggested, they must act quickly, so as to lose as little as possible of that air whose elasticity would rapidly have spread it into space. The bolts of the right scuttle, the opening of which measured about twelve inches across, were carefully drawn, while Michel, quite grieved, prepared to launch his dog into space. The glass, raised by a powerful lever, which enabled it to overcome the pressure of the inside air on the walls of the projectile, turned rapidly on its hinges, and Satellite was thrown out. Scarcely a particle of air could have escaped, and the operation was so successful that later on Barbicane did not fear to dispose of the rubbish which encumbered the car.

CHAPTER VI QUESTION AND ANSWER

On the 4th of December, when the travelers awoke after fifty-four hours' journey, the chronometer marked five o'clock of the terrestrial morning. In time it was just over five hours and forty minutes, half of that assigned to their sojourn in the projectile; but they had already accomplished nearly seven-tenths of the way. This peculiarity was due to their regularly decreasing speed.

Now when they observed the earth through the lower window, it looked like nothing more than a dark spot, drowned in the solar rays. No more crescent, no more cloudy light! The next day, at midnight, the earth would be *new*, at the very moment when the moon would be full. Above, the orb of night was nearing the line followed by the projectile, so as to meet it at the given hour. All around the black vault was studded with brilliant points, which seemed to move slowly; but, at the great distance they were from them, their relative size did not seem to change. The sun and stars appeared exactly as they do to us upon earth. As to the moon, she was considerably larger; but the travelers' glasses, not very powerful, did not allow them as yet to make any useful observations upon her surface, or reconnoiter her topographically or geologically.

Thus the time passed in never-ending conversations all about the moon. Each one brought forward his own contingent of particular facts; Barbicane and Nicholl always serious, Michel Ardan always enthusiastic. The projectile, its situation, its direction, incidents which might happen, the precautions necessitated by their fall on to the moon, were inexhaustible matters of conjecture.

As they were breakfasting, a question of Michel's, relating to the projectile, provoked rather a curious answer from Barbicane, which is worth repeating. Michel, supposing it to be roughly stopped, while still under its formidable initial speed, wished to know what the consequences of the stoppage would have been.

"But," said Barbicane, "I do not see how it could have been stopped."

"But let us suppose so," said Michel.

"It is an impossible supposition," said the practical Barbicane; "unless that impulsive force had failed; but even then its speed would diminish by degrees, and it would not have stopped suddenly."

"Admit that it had struck a body in space."

"What body?"

"Why that enormous meteor which we met."

"Then," said Nicholl, "the projectile would have been broken into a thousand pieces, and we with it."

"More than that," replied Barbicane; "we should have been burned to death."

"Burned?" exclaimed Michel, "by Jove! I am sorry it did not happen, `just to see.'"

"And you would have seen," replied Barbicane. "It is known now that heat is only a modification of motion. When water is warmed— that is to say, when heat is added to it—its particles are set in motion."

"Well," said michel, "that is an ingenious theory!"

"And a true one, my worthy friend; for it explains every phenomenon of caloric. Heat is but the motion of atoms, a simple oscillation of the particles of a body. When they apply the brake to a train, the train comes to a stop; but what becomes of the motion which it had previously possessed? It is transformed into heat, and the brake becomes hot. Why do they grease the axles of the wheels? To prevent their heating, because this heat would be generated by the motion which is thus lost by transformation."

"Yes, I understand," replied Michel, "perfectly. For example, when I have run a long time, when I am swimming, when I am perspiring in large drops, why am I obliged to stop? Simply because my motion is changed into heat."

Barbicane could not help smiling at Michel's reply; then, returning to his theory, said:

"Thus, in case of a shock, it would have been with our projectile as with a ball which falls in a burning state after having struck the metal plate; it is its motion which is turned into heat. Consequently I affirm that, if our projectile had struck the meteor, its speed thus suddenly checked would have raised a heat great enough to turn it into vapor instantaneously."

"Then," asked Nicholl, "what would happen if the earth's motion were to stop suddenly?"

"Her temperature would be raised to such a pitch," said

Barbicane, "that she would be at once reduced to vapor."

"Well," said Michel, "that is a way of ending the earth which will greatly simplify things."

"And if the earth fell upon the sun?" asked Nicholl.

"According to calculation," replied Barbicane, "the fall would develop a heat equal to that produced by 16,000 globes of coal, each equal in bulk to our terrestrial globe."

"Good additional heat for the sun," replied Michel Ardan, "of which the inhabitants of Uranus or Neptune would doubtless not complain; they must be perished with cold on their planets."

"Thus, my friends," said Barbicane, "all motion suddenly stopped produces heat. And this theory allows us to infer that the heat of the solar disc is fed by a hail of meteors falling incessantly on its surface. They have even calculated——"

"Oh, dear!" murmured Michel, "the figures are coming."

"They have even calculated," continued the imperturbable Barbicane, "that the shock of each meteor on the sun ought to produce a heat equal to that of 4,000 masses of coal of an equal bulk."

"And what is the solar heat?" asked Michel.

"It is equal to that produced by the combustion of a stratum of coal surrounding the sun to a depth of forty-seven miles."

"And that heat——"

"Would be able to boil two billions nine hundred millions of cubic myriameters[1] of water."

"And it does not roast us!" exclaimed Michel.

---

[1] The myriameter is equal to rather more than 10,936 cubic yards English.

"No," replied Barbicane, "because the terrestrial atmosphere absorbs four-tenths of the solar heat; besides, the quantity of heat intercepted by the earth is but a billionth part of the entire radiation."

"I see that all is for the best," said Michel, "and that this atmosphere is a useful invention; for it not only allows us to breathe, but it prevents us from roasting."

"Yes!" said Nicholl, "unfortunately, it will not be the same in the moon."

"Bah!" said Michel, always hopeful. "If there are inhabitants, they must breathe. If there are no longer any, they must have left enough oxygen for three people, if only at the bottom of ravines, where its own weight will cause it to accumulate, and we will not climb the mountains; that is all." And Michel, rising, went to look at the lunar disc, which shone with intolerable brilliancy.

"By Jove!" said he, "it must be hot up there!"

"Without considering," replied Nicholl, "that the day lasts 360 hours!"

"And to compensate that," said Barbicane, "the nights have the same length; and as heat is restored by radiation, their temperature can only be that of the planetary space."

"A pretty country, that!" exclaimed Michel. "Never mind! I wish I was there! Ah! my dear comrades, it will be rather curious to have the earth for our moon, to see it rise on the horizon, to recognize the shape of its continents, and to say to oneself, `There is America, there is Europe;' then to follow it when it is about to lose itself in the sun's rays! By the bye, Barbicane, have the Selenites eclipses?"

"Yes, eclipses of the sun," replied Barbicane, "when the centers of the three orbs are on a line, the earth being in the middle. But they are only partial, during which the earth, cast like a screen upon the solar disc, allows the greater portion to be seen."

"And why," asked Nicholl, "is there no total eclipse? Does not the cone of the shadow cast by the earth extend beyond the moon?"

"Yes, if we do not take into consideration the refraction produced by the terrestrial atmosphere. No, if we take that refraction into consideration. Thus let δ be the horizontal parallel, and p the apparent semidiameter——"

"Oh!" said Michel. "Do speak plainly, you man of algebra!"

"Very well, replied Barbicane; "in popular language the mean distance from the moon to the earth being sixty terrestrial radii, the length of the cone of the shadow, on account of refraction, is reduced to less than forty-two radii. The result is that when there are eclipses, the moon finds itself beyond the cone of pure shadow, and that the sun sends her its rays, not only from its edges, but also from its center."

"Then," said Michel, in a merry tone, "why are there eclipses, when there ought not to be any?"

"Simply because the solar rays are weakened by this refraction, and the atmosphere through which they pass extinguished the greater part of them!"

"That reason satisfies me," replied Michel. "Besides we shall see when we get there. Now, tell me, Barbicane, do you believe that the moon is an old comet?"

"There's an idea!"

"Yes," replied Michel, with an amiable swagger, "I have a few ideas of that sort."

"But that idea does not spring from Michel," answered Nicholl.

"Well, then, I am a plagiarist."

"No doubt about it. According to the ancients, the Arcadians pretend that their ancestors inhabited the earth before the moon became her satellite. Starting from this fact, some scientific men have seen in the moon a comet whose orbit will one day bring it so near to the earth that it will be held there by its attraction."

"Is there any truth in this hypothesis?" asked Michel.

"None whatever," said Barbicane, "and the proof is, that the moon has preserved no trace of the gaseous envelope which always accompanies comets."

"But," continued Nicholl, "Before becoming the earth's satellite, could not the moon, when in her perihelion, pass so near the sun as by evaporation to get rid of all those gaseous substances?"

"It is possible, friend Nicholl, but not probable."

"Why not?"

"Because— Faith I do not know."

"Ah!" exclaimed Michel, "what hundred of volumes we might make of all that we do not know!"

"Ah! indeed. What time is it?" asked Barbicane.

"Three o'clock," answered Nicholl.

"How time goes," said Michel, "in the conversation of scientific men such as we are! Certainly, I feel I know too much! I feel that I am becoming a well!"

Saying which, Michel hoisted himself to the roof of the projectile, "to observe the moon better," he pretended. During this time his companions were watching through the lower glass. Nothing new to note!

When Michel Ardan came down, he went to the side scuttle; and suddenly they heard an exclamation of surprise!

"What is it?" asked Barbicane.

The president approached the window, and saw a sort of flattened sack floating some yards from the projectile. This object seemed as motionless as the projectile, and was consequently animated with the same ascending movement.

"What is that machine?" continued Michel Ardan. "Is it one of the bodies which our projectile keeps within its attraction, and which will accompany it to the moon?"

"What astonishes me," said Nicholl, "is that the specific weight of the body, which is certainly less than that of the projectile, allows it to keep so perfectly on a level with it."

"Nicholl," replied Barbicane, after a moment's reflection, "I do not know what the object it, but I do know why it maintains our level."

"And why?"

"Because we are floating in space, my dear captain, and in space bodies fall or move (which is the same thing) with equal speed whatever be their weight or form; it is the air, which by its resistance creates these differences in weight. When you create a vacuum in a tube, the objects you send through it, grains of dust or grains of lead, fall with the same rapidity. Here in space is the same cause and the same effect."

"Just so," said Nicholl, "and everything we throw out of the projectile will accompany it until it reaches the moon."

"Ah! fools that we are!" exclaimed Michel.

"Why that expletive?" asked Barbicane.

"Because we might have filled the projectile with useful objects, books, instruments, tools, etc. We could have thrown them all out, and all would have followed in our train. But happy thought! Why cannot we walk outside like the meteor? Why cannot we launch into space through the scuttle? What enjoyment it would be to feel oneself thus suspended in ether, more favored than the birds who must use their wings to keep themselves up!"

"Granted," said Barbicane, "but how to breathe?"

"Hang the air, to fail so inopportunely!"

"But if it did not fail, Michel, your density being less than that of the projectile, you would soon be left behind."

"Then we must remain in our car?"

"We must!"

"Ah!" exclaimed Michel, in a load voice.

"What is the matter," asked Nicholl.

"I know, I guess, what this pretended meteor is! It is no asteroid which is accompanying us! It is not a piece of a planet."

"What is it then?" asked Barbicane.

"It is our unfortunate dog! It is Diana's husband!"

Indeed, this deformed, unrecognizable object, reduced to nothing, was the body of Satellite, flattened like a bagpipe without wind, and ever mounting, mounting!

CHAPTER VII A MOMENT OF INTOXICATION

Thus a phenomenon, curious but explicable, was happening under these strange conditions.

Every object thrown from the projectile would follow the same course and never stop until it did. There was a subject for conversation which the whole evening could not exhaust.

Besides, the excitement of the three travelers increased as they drew near the end of their journey. They expected unforseen incidents, and new phenomena; and nothing would have astonished them in the frame of mind they then were in. Their overexcited imagination went faster than the projectile, whose speed was evidently diminishing, though insensibly to themselves. But the moon grew larger to their eyes, and they fancied if they stretched out their hands they could seize it.

The next day, the 5th of November, at five in the morning, all three were on foot. That day was to be the last of their journey, if all calculations were true. That very night, at twelve o'clock, in eighteen hours, exactly at the full moon, they would reach its brilliant disc. The next midnight would see that journey ended, the most extraordinary of ancient or modern times. Thus from the first of the morning, through the scuttles silvered by its rays, they saluted the orb of night with a confident and joyous hurrah.

The moon was advancing majestically along the starry firmament. A few more degrees, and she would reach the exact point where her meeting with the projectile was to take place.

According to his own observations, Barbicane reckoned that they would land on her northern hemisphere, where stretch immense plains, and where mountains are rare. A favorable circumstance if, as they thought, the lunar atmosphere was stored only in its depths.

"Besides," observed Michel Ardan, "a plain is easier to disembark upon than a mountain. A Selenite, deposited in Europe on the summit of Mont Blanc, or in Asia on the top of the Himalayas, would not be quite in the right place."

"And," added Captain Nicholl, "on a flat ground, the projectile will remain motionless when it has once touched; whereas on a declivity it would roll like an avalanche, and not being squirrels we should not come out safe and sound. So it is all for the best."

Indeed, the success of the audacious attempt no longer appeared doubtful. But Barbicane was preoccupied with one thought; but not wishing to make his companions uneasy, he kept silence on this subject.

The direction the projectile was taking toward the moon's northern hemisphere, showed that her course had been slightly altered. The discharge, mathematically calculated, would carry the projectile to the very center of the lunar disc. If it did not land there,

there must have been some deviation. What had caused it? Barbicane could neither imagine nor determine the importance of the deviation, for there were no points to go by.

He hoped, however, that it would have no other result than that of bringing them nearer the upper border of the moon, a region more suitable for landing.

Without imparting his uneasiness to his companions, Barbicane contented himself with constantly observing the moon, in order to see whether the course of the projectile would not be altered; for the situation would have been terrible if it failed in its aim, and being carried beyond the disc should be launched into interplanetary space. At that moment, the moon, instead of appearing flat like a disc, showed its convexity. If the sun's rays had struck it obliquely, the shadow thrown would have brought out the high mountains, which would have been clearly detached. The eye might have gazed into the crater's gaping abysses, and followed the capricious fissures which wound through the immense plains. But all relief was as yet leveled in intense brilliancy. They could scarcely distinguish those large spots which give the moon the appearance of a human face.

"Face, indeed!" said Michel Ardan; "but I am sorry for the amiable sister of Apollo. A very pitted face!"

But the travelers, now so near the end, were incessantly observing this new world. They imagined themselves walking through its unknown countries, climbing its highest peaks, descending into its lowest depths. Here and there they fancied they saw vast seas, scarcely kept together under so rarefied an atmosphere, and water-courses emptying the mountain tributaries. Leaning over the abyss, they hoped to catch some sounds from that orb forever mute in the solitude of space. That last day left them.

They took down the most trifling details. A vague uneasiness took possession of them as they neared the end. This uneasiness would have been doubled had they felt how their speed had decreased. It would have seemed to them quite insufficient to carry them to the end. It was because the projectile then "weighed" almost nothing. Its weight was ever decreasing, and would be entirely annihilated on that line where the lunar and terrestrial attractions would neutralize each other.

But in spite of his preoccupation, Michel Ardan did not forget to prepare the morning repast with his accustomed punctuality. They ate with a good appetite. Nothing was so excellent as the soup liquefied by the heat of the gas; nothing better than the preserved meat. Some glasses of good French wine crowned the repast, causing Michel Ardan to remark that the lunar vines, warmed by that ardent sun, ought to distill even more generous wines; that is, if they existed. In any case, the far-seeing Frenchman had taken care not to forget in his collection some precious cuttings of the Medoc and Cote d'Or, upon which he founded his hopes.

Reiset and Regnaut's apparatus worked with great regularity. Not an atom of carbonic acid resisted the potash; and as to the oxygen, Captain Nicholl said "it was of the first quality." The little watery vapor enclosed in the projectile mixing with the air tempered the dryness; and many apartments in London, Paris, or New York, and many theaters, were certainly not in such a healthy condition.

But that it might act with regularity, the apparatus must be kept in perfect order; so each morning Michel visited the escape regulators, tried the taps, and regulated the heat of the gas by the pyrometer. Everything had gone well up to that time, and the travelers, imitating the worthy Joseph T. Maston, began to acquire a degree of embonpoint which would have rendered them unrecognizable if their imprisonment had been prolonged to some months. In a word, they behaved like chickens in a coop; they were getting fat.

In looking through the scuttle Barbicane saw the specter of the dog, and other divers objects which had been thrown from the projectile, obstinately following them. Diana howled lugubriously on seeing the remains of Satellite, which seemed as motionless as if they reposed on solid earth.

"Do you know, my friends," said Michel Ardan, "that if one of us had succumbed to the shock consequent on departure, we should have had a great deal of trouble to bury him? What am I saying? to *etherize* him, as here ether takes the place of earth. You see the accusing body would have followed us into space like a remorse."

"That would have been sad," said Nicholl.

"Ah!" continued Michel, "what I regret is not being able to take a walk outside. What voluptuousness to float amid this radiant ether, to bathe oneself in it, to wrap oneself in the sun's pure rays. If Barbicane had only thought of furnishing us with a diving apparatus and an air-pump, I could have ventured out and assumed fanciful attitudes of feigned monsters on the top of the projectile."

"Well, old Michel," replied Barbicane, "you would not have made a feigned monster long, for in spite of your diver's dress, swollen by the expansion of air within you, you would have burst like a shell, or rather like a balloon which has risen too high. So do not regret it, and do not forget this— as long as we float in space, all sentimental walks beyond the projectile are forbidden."

Michel Ardan allowed himself to be convinced to a certain extent. He admitted that the thing was difficult but not impossible, a word which he never uttered.

The conversation passed from this subject to another, not failing him for an instant. It seemed to the three friends as though, under present conditions, ideas shot up in their brains as leaves shoot at the first warmth of spring. They felt bewildered. In the middle of the questions and answers which crossed each other, Nicholl put one question which did not find an immediate solution.

"Ah, indeed!" said he; "it is all very well to go to the moon, but how to get back again?"

His two interlocutors looked surprised. One would have thought that this possibility now occurred to them for the first time.

"What do you mean by that, Nicholl?" asked Barbicane gravely.

"To ask for means to leave a country," added Michel, "When we have not yet arrived there, seems to me rather inopportune."

"I do not say that, wishing to draw back," replied Nicholl; "but I repeat my question, and I ask, `How shall we return?'"

"I know nothing about it," answered Barbicane.

"And I," said Michel, "if I had known how to return, I would never have started."

"There's an answer!" cried Nicholl.

"I quite approve of Michel's words," said Barbicane; "and add, that the question has no real interest. Later, when we think it is advisable to return, we will take counsel together. If the Columbiad is not there, the projectile will be."

"That is a step certainly. A ball without a gun!"

"The gun," replied Barbicane, "can be manufactured. The powder can be made. Neither metals, saltpeter, nor coal can fail in the depths of the moon, and we need only go 8,000 leagues in order to fall upon the terrestrial globe by virtue of the mere laws of weight."

"Enough," said Michel with animation. "Let it be no longer a question of returning: we have already entertained it too long. As to communicating with our former earthly colleagues, that will not be difficult."

"And how?"

"By means of meteors launched by lunar volcanoes."

CHAPTER VII A MOMENT OF INTOXICATION

"Well thought of, Michel," said Barbicane in a convinced tone of voice. "Laplace has calculated that a force five times greater than that of our gun would suffice to send a meteor from the moon to the earth, and there is not one volcano which has not a greater pow-power of propulsion than that."

"Hurrah!" exclaimed Michel; "these meteors are handy postmen, and cost nothing. And how we shall be able to laugh at the post-office administration! But now I think of it——"

"What do you think of?"

"A capital idea. Why did we not fasten a thread to our projectile, and we could have exchanged telegrams with the earth?"

"The deuce!" answered Nicholl. "Do you consider the weight of a thread 250,000 miles long nothing?"

"As nothing. They could have trebled the Columbiad's charge; they could have quadrupled or quintupled it!" exclaimed Michel, with whom the verb took a higher intonation each time.

"There is but one little objection to make to your proposition," replied Barbicane, "which is that, during the rotary motion of the globe, our thread would have wound itself round it like a chain on a capstan, and that it would inevitably have brought us to the ground."

"By the thirty-nine stars of the Union!" said Michel, "I have nothing but impracticable ideas to-day; ideas worthy of J. T. Maston. But I have a notion that, if we do not return to earth, J. T. Maston will be able to come to us."

"Yes, he'll come," replied Barbicane; "he is a worthy and a courageous comrade. Besides, what is easier? Is not the Columbiad still buried in the soil of Florida? Is cotton and nitric acid wanted wherewith to manufacture the pyroxyle? Will not the moon pass the zenith of Florida? In eighteen years' time will she not occupy exactly the same place as to-day?"

"Yes," continued Michel, "yes, Maston will come, and with him our friends Elphinstone, Blomsberry, all the members of the Gun Club, and they will be well received. And by and by they will run trains of projectiles between the earth and the moon! Hurrah for J. T. Maston!"

It is probable that, if the Hon. J. T. Maston did not hear the hurrahs uttered in his honor, his ears at least tingled. What was he doing then? Doubtless, posted in the Rocky Mountains, at the station of Long's Peak, he was trying to find the invisible projectile gravitating in space. If he was thinking of his dear companions, we must allow that they were not far behind him; and that, under the influence of a strange excitement, they were devoting to him their best thoughts.

But whence this excitement, which was evidently growing upon the tenants of the projectile? Their sobriety could not be doubted. This strange irritation of the brain, must it be attributed to the peculiar circumstances under which they found themselves, to their proximity to the orb of night, from which only a few hours separated them, to some secret influence of the moon acting upon their nervous system? Their faces were as rosy as if they had been exposed to the roaring flames of an oven; their voices resounded in loud accents; their words escaped like a champagne cork driven out by carbonic acid; their gestures became annoying, they wanted so much room to perform them; and, strange to say, they none of them noticed this great tension of the mind.

"Now," said Nicholl, in a short tone, "now that I do not know whether we shall ever return from the moon, I want to know what we are going to do there?"

"What we are going to do there?" replied Barbicane, stamping with his foot as if he was in a fencing saloon; "I do not know."

"You do not know!" exclaimed Michel, with a bellow which provoked a sonorous echo in the projectile.

"No, I have not even thought about it," retorted Barbicane, in the same loud tone.

"Well, I know," replied Michel.

"Speak, then," cried Nicholl, who could no longer contain the growling of his voice.

"I shall speak if it suits me," exclaimed Michel, seizing his companions' arms with violence.

"*It must* suit you," said Barbicane, with an eye on fire and a threatening hand. "It was you who drew us into this frightful journey, and we want to know what for."

"Yes," said the captain, "now that I do not know *where* I am going, I want to know *why* I am going."

"Why?" exclaimed Michel, jumping a yard high, "why? To take possession of the moon in the name of the United States; to add a fortieth State to the Union; to colonize the lunar regions; to cultivate them, to people them, to transport thither all the prodigies of art, of science, and industry; to civilize the Selenites, unless they are more civilized than we are; and to constitute them a republic, if they are not already one!"

"And if there are no Selenites?" retorted Nicholl, who, under the influence of this unaccountable intoxication, was very contradictory.

"Who said that there were no Selenites?" exclaimed Michel in a threatening tone.

"I do," howled Nicholl.

"Captain," said Michel, "do not repeat that insolence, or I will knock your teeth down your throat!"

The two adversaries were going to fall upon each other, and the incoherent discussion threatened to merge into a fight, when Barbicane intervened with one bound.

"Stop, miserable men," said he, separating his two companions; "if there are no Selenites, we will do without them."

"Yes," exclaimed Michel, who was not particular; "yes, we will do without them. We have only to make Selenites. Down with the Selenites!"

"The empire of the moon belongs to us," said Nicholl.

"Let us three constitute the republic."

"I will be the congress," cried Michel.

"And I the senate," retorted Nicholl.

"And Barbicane, the president," howled Michel.

"Not a president elected by the nation," replied Barbicane.

"Very well, a president elected by the congress," cried Michel; "and as I am the congress, you are unanimously elected!"

"Hurrah! hurrah! hurrah! for President Barbicane," exclaimed Nicholl.

"Hip! hip! hip!" vociferated Michel Ardan.

Then the president and the senate struck up in a tremendous voice the popular song "Yankee Doodle," while from the congress resounded the masculine tones of the "Marseillaise."

Then they struck up a frantic dance, with maniacal gestures, idiotic stampings, and somersaults like those of the boneless clowns in the circus. Diana, joining in the dance, and howling in her turn, jumped to the top of the projectile. An unaccountable flapping of wings was then heard amid most fantastic cock-crows, while five or six hens fluttered like bats against the walls.

CHAPTER VII A MOMENT OF INTOXICATION

Then the three traveling companions, acted upon by some unaccountable influence above that of intoxication, inflamed by the air which had set their respiratory apparatus on fire, fell motionless to the bottom of the projectile.

CHAPTER VIII AT SEVENTY-EIGHT THOUSAND FIVE HUNDRED AND FOURTEEN LEAGUES

What had happened? Whence the cause of this singular intoxication, the consequences of which might have been very disastrous? A simple blunder of Michel's, which, fortunately, Nicholl was able to correct in time.

After a perfect swoon, which lasted some minutes, the captain, recovering first, soon collected his scattered senses. Although he had breakfasted only two hours before, he felt a gnawing hunger, as if he had not eaten anything for several days. Everything about him, stomach and brain, were overexcited to the highest degree. He got up and demanded from Michel a supplementary repast. Michel, utterly done up, did not answer.

Nicholl then tried to prepare some tea destined to help the absorption of a dozen sandwiches. He first tried to get some fire, and struck a match sharply. What was his surprise to see the sulphur shine with so extraordinary a brilliancy as to be almost unbearable to the eye. From the gas-burner which he lit rose a flame equal to a jet of electric light.

A revelation dawned on Nicholl's mind. That intensity of light, the physiological troubles which had arisen in him, the overexcitement of all his moral and quarrelsome faculties— he understood all.

"The oxygen!" he exclaimed.

And leaning over the air apparatus, he saw that the tap was allowing the colorless gas to escape freely, life-giving, but in its pure state producing the gravest disorders in the system. Michel had blunderingly opened the tap of the apparatus to the full.

Nicholl hastened to stop the escape of oxygen with which the atmosphere was saturated, which would have been the death of the travelers, not by suffocation, but by combustion. An hour later, the air less charged with it restored the lungs to their normal condition. By degrees the three friends recovered from their intoxication; but they were obliged to sleep themselves sober over their oxygen as a drunkard does over his wine.

When Michel learned his share of the responsibility of this incident, he was not much disconcerted. This unexpected drunkenness broke the monotony of the journey. Many foolish things had been said while under its influence, but also quickly forgotten.

"And then," added the merry Frenchman, "I am not sorry to have tasted a little of this heady gas. Do you know, my friends, that a curious establishment might be founded with rooms of oxygen, where people whose system is weakened could for a few hours live a more active life. Fancy parties where the room was saturated with this heroic fluid, theaters where it should be kept at high pressure; what passion in the souls of the actors and spectators! what fire, what enthusiasm! And if, instead of an assembly only a whole people could be saturated, what activity in its functions, what a supplement to life it would derive. From an exhausted nation they might make a great and strong one, and I know more than one state in old Europe which ought to put itself under the regime of oxygen for the sake of its health!"

Michel spoke with so much animation that one might have fancied that the tap was still too open. But a few words from Barbicane soon shattered his enthusiasm.

"That is all very well, friend Michel," said he, "but will you inform us where these chickens came from which have mixed themselves up in our concert?"

"Those chickens?"

"Yes."

Indeed, half a dozen chickens and a fine cock were walking about, flapping their wings and chattering.

"Ah, the awkward things!" exclaimed Michel. "The oxygen has made them revolt."

"But what do you want to do with these chickens?" asked Barbicane.

"To acclimatize them in the moon, by Jove!"

"Then why did you hide them?"

"A joke, my worthy president, a simple joke, which has proved a miserable failure. I wanted to set them free on the lunar continent, without saying anything. Oh, what would have been your amazement on seeing these earthly-winged animals pecking in your lunar fields!"

"You rascal, you unmitigated rascal," replied Barbicane, "you do not want oxygen to mount to the head. You are always what we were under the influence of the gas; you are always foolish!"

"Ah, who says that we were not wise then?" replied Michel Ardan.

After this philosophical reflection, the three friends set about restoring the order of the projectile. Chickens and cock were reinstated in their coop. But while proceeding with this operation, Barbicane and his two companions had a most desired perception of a new phenomenon. From the moment of leaving the earth, their own weight, that of the projectile, and the objects it enclosed, had been subject to an increasing diminution. If they could not prove this loss of the projectile, a moment would arrive when it would be sensibly felt upon themselves and the utensils and instruments they used.

It is needless to say that a scale would not show this loss; for the weight destined to weight the object would have lost exactly as much as the object itself; but a spring steelyard for example, the tension of which was independent of the attraction, would have given a just estimate of this loss.

We know that the attraction, otherwise called the weight, is in proportion to the densities of the bodies, and inversely as the squares of the distances. Hence this effect: If the earth had been alone in space, if the other celestial bodies had been suddenly annihilated, the projectile, according to Newton's laws, would weigh less as it got farther from the earth, but without ever losing its weight entirely, for the terrestrial attraction would always have made itself felt, at whatever distance.

But, in reality, a time must come when the projectile would no longer be subject to the law of weight, after allowing for the other celestial bodies whose effect could not be set down as zero. Indeed, the projectile's course was being traced between the earth and the moon. As it distanced the earth, the terrestrial attraction diminished: but the lunar attraction rose in proportion. There must come a point where these two attractions would neutralize each other: the projectile would possess weight no longer. If the moon's and the earth's densities had been equal, this point would have been at an equal distance between the two orbs. But taking the different densities into consideration, it was easy to reckon that this point would be situated at 47/60ths of the whole journey, *i.e.*, at 78,514 leagues from the earth. At this point, a body having no principle of speed or displacement in itself, would remain immovable forever, being attracted equally by both orbs, and not being drawn more toward one than toward the other.

Now if the projectile's impulsive force had been correctly calculated, it would attain this point without speed, having lost all trace of weight, as well as all the objects within it. What would happen then? Three hypotheses presented themselves.

1. Either it would retain a certain amount of motion, and pass the point of equal attraction, and fall upon the moon by virtue of the excess of the lunar attraction over the terrestrial.

2. Or, its speed failing, and unable to reach the point of equal attraction, it would fall upon the moon by virtue of the excess of the lunar attraction over the terrestrial.

3. Or, lastly, animated with sufficient speed to enable it to reach the neutral point, but not sufficient to pass it, it would remain forever suspended in that spot like the pretended tomb of Mahomet, between the zenith and the nadir.

Such was their situation; and Barbicane clearly explained the consequences to his traveling companions, which greatly interested them. But how should they know when the projectile had reached this neutral point situated at that distance, especially when neither themselves, nor the objects enclosed in the projectile, would be any longer subject to the laws of weight?

Up to this time, the travelers, while admitting that this action was constantly decreasing, had not yet become sensible to its total absence.

But that day, about eleven o'clock in the morning, Nicholl having accidentally let a glass slip from his hand, the glass, instead of falling, remained suspended in the air.

"Ah!" exclaimed Michel Ardan, "that is rather an amusing piece of natural philosophy."

And immediately divers other objects, firearms and bottles, abandoned to themselves, held themselves up as by enchantment. Diana too, placed in space by Michel, reproduced, but without any trick, the wonderful suspension practiced by Caston and Robert Houdin. Indeed the dog did not seem to know that she was floating in air.

The three adventurous companions were surprised and stupefied, despite their scientific reasonings. They felt themselves being carried into the domain of wonders! they felt that weight was really wanting to their bodies. If they stretched out their arms, they did not attempt to fall. Their heads shook on their shoulders. Their feet no longer clung to the floor of the projectile. They were like drunken men having no stability in themselves.

Fancy has depicted men without reflection, others without shadow. But here reality, by the neutralizations of attractive forces, produced men in whom nothing had any weight, and who weighed nothing themselves.

Suddenly Michel, taking a spring, left the floor and remained suspended in the air, like Murillo's monk of the *Cusine des Anges*.

The two friends joined him instantly, and all three formed a miraculous "Ascension" in the center of the projectile.

"Is it to be believed? is it probable? is it possible?" exclaimed Michel; "and yet it is so. Ah! if Raphael had seen us thus, what an `Assumption' he would have thrown upon canvas!"

"The `Assumption' cannot last," replied Barbicane. "If the projectile passes the neutral point, the lunar attraction will draw us to the moon."

"Then our feet will be upon the roof," replied Michel.

"No," said Barbicane, "because the projectile's center of gravity is very low; it will only turn by degrees."

CHAPTER VIII AT SEVENTY-EIGHT THOUSAND FIVE HUNDRED AND FOURTEEN LEAGUES

"Then all our portables will be upset from top to bottom, that is a fact."

"Calm yourself, Michel," replied Nicholl; "no upset is to be feared; not a thing will move, for the projectile's evolution will be imperceptible."

"Just so," continued Barbicane; "and when it has passed the point of equal attraction, its base, being the heavier, will draw it perpendicularly to the moon; but, in order that this phenomenon should take place, we must have passed the neutral line."

"Pass the neutral line," cried Michel; "then let us do as the sailors do when they cross the equator."

A slight side movement brought Michel back toward the padded side; thence he took a bottle and glasses, placed them "in space" before his companions, and, drinking merrily, they saluted the line with a triple hurrah. The influence of these attractions scarcely lasted an hour; the travelers felt themselves insensibly drawn toward the floor, and Barbicane fancied that the conical end of the projectile was varying a little from its normal direction toward the moon. By an inverse motion the base was approaching first; the lunar attraction was prevailing over the terrestrial; the fall toward the moon was beginning, almost imperceptibly as yet, but by degrees the attractive force would become stronger, the fall would be more decided, the projectile, drawn by its base, would turn its cone to the earth, and fall with ever-increasing speed on to the surface of the Selenite continent; their destination would then be attained. Now nothing could prevent the success of their enterprise, and Nicholl and Michel Ardan shared Barbicane's joy.

Then they chatted of all the phenomena which had astonished them one after the other, particularly the neutralization of the laws of weight. Michel Ardan, always enthusiastic, drew conclusions which were purely fanciful.

"Ah, my worthy friends," he exclaimed, "what progress we should make if on earth we could throw off some of that weight, some of that chain which binds us to her; it would be the prisoner set at liberty; no more fatigue of either arms or legs. Or, if it is true that in order to fly on the earth's surface, to keep oneself suspended in the air merely by the play of the muscles, there requires a strength a hundred and fifty times greater than that which we possess, a simple act of volition, a caprice, would bear us into space, if attraction did not exist."

"Just so," said Nicholl, smiling; "if we could succeed in suppressing weight as they suppress pain by anaesthesia, that would change the face of modern society!"

"Yes," cried Michel, full of his subject, "destroy weight, and no more burdens!"

"Well said," replied Barbicane; "but if nothing had any weight, nothing would keep in its place, not even your hat on your head, worthy Michel; nor your house, whose stones only adhere by weight; nor a boat, whose stability on the waves is only caused by weight; not even the ocean, whose waves would no longer be equalized by terrestrial attraction; and lastly, not even the atmosphere, whose atoms, being no longer held in their places, would disperse in space!"

"That is tiresome," retorted Michel; "nothing like these matter-of-fact people for bringing one back to the bare reality."

"But console yourself, Michel," continued Barbicane, "for if no orb exists from whence all laws of weight are banished, you are at least going to visit one where it is much less than on the earth."

"The moon?"

"Yes, the moon, on whose surface objects weigh six times less than on the earth, a phenomenon easy to prove."

"And we shall feel it?" asked Michel.

"Evidently, as two hundred pounds will only weigh thirty pounds on the surface of the moon."

"And our muscular strength will not diminish?"

"Not at all; instead of jumping one yard high, you will rise eighteen feet high."

"But we shall be regular Herculeses in the moon!" exclaimed Michel.

"Yes," replied Nicholl; "for if the height of the Selenites is in proportion to the density of their globe, they will be scarcely a foot high."

"Lilliputians!" ejaculated Michel; "I shall play the part of Gulliver. We are going to realize the fable of the giants. This is the advantage of leaving one's own planet and overrunning the solar world."

"One moment, Michel," answered Barbicane; "if you wish to play the part of Gulliver, only visit the inferior planets, such as Mercury, Venus, or Mars, whose density is a little less than that of the earth; but do not venture into the great planets, Jupiter, Saturn, Uranus, Neptune; for there the order will be changed, and you will become Lilliputian."

"And in the sun?"

"In the sun, if its density is thirteen hundred and twenty-four thousand times greater, and the attraction is twenty-seven times greater than on the surface of our globe, keeping everything in proportion, the inhabitants ought to be at least two hundred feet high."

"By Jove!" exclaimed Michel; "I should be nothing more than a pigmy, a shrimp!"

"Gulliver with the giants," said Nicholl.

"Just so," replied Barbicane.

"And it would not be quite useless to carry some pieces of artillery to defend oneself."

"Good," replied Nicholl; "your projectiles would have no effect on the sun; they would fall back upon the earth after some minutes."

"That is a strong remark."

"It is certain," replied Barbicane; "the attraction is so great on this enormous orb, that an object weighing 70,000 pounds on the earth would weigh but 1,920 pounds on the surface of the sun. If you were to fall upon it you would weigh— let me see— about 5,000 pounds, a weight which you would never be able to raise again."

"The devil!" said Michel; "one would want a portable crane. However, we will be satisfied with the moon for the present; there at least we shall cut a great figure. We will see about the sun by and by."

CHAPTER IX THE CONSEQUENCES OF A DEVIATION

Barbicane had now no fear of the issue of the journey, at least as far as the projectile's impulsive force was concerned; its own speed would carry it beyond the neutral line; it would certainly not return to earth; it would certainly not remain motionless on the line of attraction. One single hypothesis remained to be realized, the arrival of the projectile at its destination by the action of the lunar attraction.

It was in reality a fall of 8,296 leagues on an orb, it is true, where weight could only be reckoned at one sixth of terrestrial weight; a formidable fall, nevertheless, and one against which every precaution must be taken without delay.

These precautions were of two sorts, some to deaden the shock when the projectile should touch the lunar soil, others to delay the fall, and consequently make it less violent.

To deaden the shock, it was a pity that Barbicane was no longer able to employ the means which had so ably weakened the shock at departure, that is to say, by water used as springs and the partition breaks.

The partitions still existed, but water failed, for they could not use their reserve, which was precious, in case during the first days the liquid element should be found wanting on lunar soil.

And indeed this reserve would have been quite insufficient for a spring. The layer of water stored in the projectile at the time of starting upon their journey occupied no less than three feet in depth, and spread over a surface of not less than fifty-four square feet. Besides, the cistern did not contain one-fifth part of it; they must therefore give up this efficient means of deadening the shock of arrival. Happily, Barbicane, not content with employing water, had furnished the movable disc with strong spring plugs, destined to lessen the shock against the base after the breaking of the horizontal partitions. These plugs still existed; they had only to readjust them and replace the movable disc; every piece, easy to handle, as their weight was now scarcely felt, was quickly mounted.

The different pieces were fitted without trouble, it being only a matter of bolts and screws; tools were not wanting, and soon the reinstated disc lay on steel plugs, like a table on its legs. One inconvenience resulted from the replacing of the disc, the lower window was blocked up; thus it was impossible for the travelers to observe the moon from that opening while they were being precipitated perpendicularly upon her; but they were obliged to give it up; even by the side openings they could still see vast lunar regions, as an aeronaut sees the earth from his car.

This replacing of the disc was at least an hour's work. It was past twelve when all preparations were finished. Barbicane took fresh observations on the inclination of the projectile, but to his annoyance it had not turned over sufficiently for its fall; it seemed to take a curve parallel to the lunar disc. The orb of night shone splendidly into space, while opposite, the orb of day blazed with fire.

Their situation began to make them uneasy.

"Are we reaching our destination?" said Nicholl.

"Let us act as if we were about reaching it," replied Barbicane.

"You are sceptical," retorted Michel Ardan. "We shall arrive, and that, too, quicker than we like."

This answer brought Barbicane back to his preparations, and he occupied himself with placing the contrivances intended to break their descent. We may remember the scene of the meeting held at Tampa Town, in Florida, when Captain Nicholl came forward as Barbicane's enemy and Michel Ardan's adversary. To Captain Nicholl's maintaining that the projectile would smash like glass, Michel replied that he would break their fall by means of rockets properly placed.

Thus, powerful fireworks, taking their starting-point from the base and bursting outside, could, by producing a recoil, check to a certain degree the projectile's speed. These rockets were to burn in space, it is true; but oxygen would not fail them, for they could supply themselves with it, like the lunar volcanoes, the burning of which has never yet been stopped by the want of atmosphere round the moon.

Barbicane had accordingly supplied himself with these fireworks, enclosed in little steel guns, which could be screwed on to the base of the projectile. Inside, these guns were flush with the bottom; outside, they protruded about eighteen inches. There were twenty of them. An opening left in the disc allowed them to light the match with which each was provided. All the effect was felt outside. The burning mixture had already been rammed into each gun. They had, then, nothing to do but raise the metallic buffers fixed in the base, and replace them by the guns, which fitted closely in their places.

This new work was finished about three o'clock, and after taking all these precautions there remained but to wait. But the projectile was perceptibly nearing the moon, and evidently succumbed to her influence to a certain degree; though its own velocity also drew it in an oblique direction. From these conflicting influences resulted a line which might become a tangent. But it was certain that the projectile would not fall directly on the moon; for its lower part, by reason of its weight, ought to be turned toward her.

Barbicane's uneasiness increased as he saw his projectile resist the influence of gravitation. The Unknown was opening before him, the Unknown in interplanetary space. The man of science thought he had foreseen the only three hypotheses possible— the return to the earth, the return to the moon, or stagnation on the neutral line; and here a fourth hypothesis, big with all the terrors of the Infinite, surged up inopportunely. To face it without flinching, one must be a resolute savant like Barbicane, a phlegmatic being like Nicholl, or an audacious adventurer like Michel Ardan.

Conversation was started upon this subject. Other men would have considered the question from a practical point of view; they would have asked themselves whither their projectile carriage was carrying them. Not so with these; they sought for the cause which produced this effect.

"So we have become diverted from our route," said Michel; "but why?"

"I very much fear," answered Nicholl, "that, in spite of all precautions taken, the Columbiad was not fairly pointed. An error, however small, would be enough to throw us out of the moon's attraction."

"Then they must have aimed badly?" asked Michel.

"I do not think so," replied Barbicane. "The perpendicularity of the gun was exact, its direction to the zenith of the spot incontestible; and the moon passing to the zenith of the spot, we ought to reach it at the full. There is another reason, but it escapes me."

"Are we not arriving too late?" asked Nicholl.

"Too late?" said Barbicane.

"Yes," continued Nicholl. "The Cambridge Observatory's note says that the transit ought to be accomplished in ninety-seven hours thirteen minutes and twenty seconds; which means to say, that *sooner* the moon will *not* be at the point indicated, and *later* it will have passed it."

"True," replied Barbicane. "But we started the 1st of December, at thirteen minutes and twenty-five seconds to eleven at night; and we ought to arrive on the 5th at midnight, at the exact moment when the moon would be full; and we are now at the 5th of December. It is now half-past three in the evening; half-past eight ought to see us at the end of our journey. Why do we not arrive?"

"Might it not be an excess of speed?" answered Nicholl; "for we know now that its initial velocity was greater than they supposed."

"No! a hundred times, no!" replied Barbicane. "An excess of speed, if the direction of the projectile had been right, would not have prevented us reaching the moon. No, there has been a deviation. We have been turned out of our course."

"By whom? by what?" asked Nicholl.

"I cannot say," replied Barbicane.

"Very well, then, Barbicane," said Michel, "do you wish to know my opinion on the subject of finding out this deviation?"

"Speak."

"I would not give half a dollar to know it. That we have deviated is a fact. Where we are going matters little; we shall soon see. Since we are being borne along in space we shall end by falling into some center of attraction or other."

Michel Ardan's indifference did not content Barbicane. Not that he was uneasy about the future, but he wanted to know at any cost *why* his projectile had deviated.

But the projectile continued its course sideways to the moon, and with it the mass of things thrown out. Barbicane could even prove, by the elevations which served as landmarks upon the moon, which was only two thousand leagues distant, that its speed was becoming uniform— fresh proof that there was no fall. Its impulsive force still prevailed over the lunar attraction, but the projectile's course was certainly bringing it nearer to the moon, and they might hope that at a nearer point the weight, predominating, would cause a decided fall.

The three friends, having nothing better to do, continued their observations; but they could not yet determine the topographical position of the satellite; every relief was leveled under the reflection of the solar rays.

They watched thus through the side windows until eight o'clock at night. The moon had grown so large in their eyes that it filled half of the firmament. The sun on one side, and the orb of night on the other, flooded the projectile with light.

At that moment Barbicane thought he could estimate the distance which separated them from their aim at no more than 700 leagues. The speed of the projectile seemed to him to be more than 200 yards, or about 170 leagues a second. Under the centripetal force, the base of the projectile tended toward the moon; but the centrifugal still prevailed; and it was probable that its rectilineal course would be changed to a curve of some sort, the nature of which they could not at present determine.

Barbicane was still seeking the solution of his insoluble problem. Hours passed without any result. The projectile was evidently nearing the moon, but it was also evident that it would never reach her. As to the nearest distance at which it would pass her, that must be the result of two forces, attraction and repulsion, affecting its motion.

"I ask but one thing," said Michel; "that we may pass near enough to penetrate her secrets."

"Cursed be the thing that has caused our projectile to deviate from its course," cried Nicholl.

And, as if a light had suddenly broken in upon his mind, Barbicane answered, "Then cursed be the meteor which crossed our path."

"What?" said Michel Ardan.

"What do you mean?" exclaimed Nicholl.

"I mean," said Barbicane in a decided tone, "I mean that our deviation is owing solely to our meeting with this erring body."

"But it did not even brush us as it passed," said Michel.

"What does that matter? Its mass, compared to that of our projectile, was enormous, and its attraction was enough to influence our course."

"So little?" cried Nicholl.

"Yes, Nicholl; but however little it might be," replied Barbicane, "in a distance of 84,000 leagues, it wanted no more to make us miss the moon."

CHAPTER X THE OBSERVERS OF THE MOON

Barbicane had evidently hit upon the only plausible reason of this deviation. However slight it might have been, it had sufficed to modify the course of the projectile. It was a fatality. The bold attempt had miscarried by a fortuitous circumstance; and unless by some exceptional event, they could now never reach the moon's disc.

Would they pass near enough to be able to solve certain physical and geological questions until then insoluble? This was the question, and the only one, which occupied the minds of these bold travelers. As to the fate in store for themselves, they did not even dream of it.

But what would become of them amid these infinite solitudes, these who would soon want air? A few more days, and they would fall stifled in this wandering projectile. But some days to these intrepid fellows was a century; and they devoted all their time to observe that moon which they no longer hoped to reach.

The distance which had then separated the projectile from the satellite was estimated at about two hundred leagues. Under these conditions, as regards the visibility of the details of the disc, the travelers were farther from the moon than are the inhabitants of earth with their powerful telescopes.

Indeed, we know that the instrument mounted by Lord Rosse at Parsonstown, which magnifies 6,500 times, brings the moon to within an apparent distance of sixteen leagues. And more than that, with the powerful one set up at Long's Peak, the orb of night, magnified 48,000 times, is brought to within less than two leagues, and objects having a diameter of thirty feet are seen very distinctly. So that, at this distance, the topographical details of the moon, observed without glasses, could not be determined with precision. The eye caught the vast outline of those immense depressions inappropriately called "seas," but they could not recognize their nature. The prominence of the mountains disappeared under the splendid irradiation produced by the reflection of the solar rays. The eye, dazzled as if it was leaning over a bath of molten silver, turned from it involuntarily; but the oblong form of the orb was quite clear. It appeared like a gigantic egg, with the small end turned toward the earth. Indeed the moon, liquid and pliable in the first days of its formation, was originally a perfect sphere; but being soon drawn within the attraction of the earth, it became elongated under the influence of gravitation. In becoming a satellite, she lost her native purity of form; her center of gravity was in advance of the center of her figure; and from this fact some savants draw the conclusion that the air and water had taken refuge on the opposite surface of the moon, which is never seen from the earth. This alteration in the primitive form of the satellite was only perceptible for a few moments. The distance of the projectile from the moon diminished very rapidly under its speed, though that was much less than its initial velocity— but eight or nine times greater than that which propels our express trains. The oblique course of the projectile, from its very obliquity, gave Michel Ardan some hopes of striking the lunar disc at some point or other. He could not think that they would never reach it. No! he could not believe it; and this opinion he often repeated. But Barbicane, who was a better judge, always answered him with merciless logic.

"No, Michel, no! We can only reach the moon by a fall, and we are not falling. The centripetal force keeps us under the moon's influence, but the centrifugal force draws us irresistibly away from it."

This was said in a tone which quenched Michel Ardan's last hope.

The portion of the moon which the projectile was nearing was the northern hemisphere, that which the selenographic maps place below; for these maps are generally drawn after the outline given by the glasses, and we know that they reverse the objects. Such was the *Mappa Selenographica* of Boeer and Moedler which Barbicane consulted. This northern hemisphere presented vast plains, dotted with isolated mountains.

At midnight the moon was full. At that precise moment the travelers should have alighted upon it, if the mischievous meteor had not diverted their course. The orb was exactly in the condition determined by the Cambridge Observatory. It was mathematically at its perigee, and at the zenith of the twenty-eighth parallel. An observer placed at the bottom of the enormous Columbiad, pointed perpendicularly to the horizon, would have framed the moon in the mouth of the gun. A straight line drawn through the axis of the piece would have passed through the center of the orb of night. It is needless to say, that during the night of the 5th-6th of December, the travelers took not an instant's rest. Could they close their eyes when so near this new world? No! All their feelings were concentrated in one single thought:— See! Representatives of the earth, of humanity, past and present, all centered in them! It is through their eyes that the human race look at these lunar regions, and penetrate the secrets of their satellite! A strange emotion filled their hearts as they went from one window to the other. Their observations, reproduced by Barbicane, were rigidly determined. To take them, they had glasses; to correct them, maps.

As regards the optical instruments at their disposal, they had excellent marine glasses specially constructed for this journey. They possessed magnifying powers of 100. They would thus have brought the moon to within a distance (apparent) of less than 2,000 leagues from the earth. But then, at a distance which for three hours in the morning did not exceed sixty-five miles, and in a medium free from all atmospheric disturbances, these instruments could reduce the lunar surface to within less than 1,500 yards!

CHAPTER XI FANCY AND REALITY

"Have you ever seen the moon?" asked a professor, ironically, of one of his pupils.

"No, sir!" replied the pupil, still more ironically, "but I must say I have heard it spoken of."

In one sense, the pupil's witty answer might be given by a large majority of sublunary beings. How many people have heard speak of the moon who have never seen it— at least through a glass or a telescope! How many have never examined the map of their satellite!

In looking at a selenographic map, one peculiarity strikes us. Contrary to the arrangement followed for that of the Earth and Mars, the continents occupy more particularly the southern hemisphere of the lunar globe. These continents do not show such decided, clear, and regular boundary lines as South America, Africa, and the Indian peninsula. Their angular, capricious, and deeply indented coasts are rich in gulfs and peninsulas. They remind one of the confusion in the islands of the Sound, where the land is excessively indented. If navigation ever existed on the surface of the moon, it must have been wonderfully difficult and dangerous; and we may well pity the Selenite sailors and hydrographers; the former, when they came upon these perilous coasts, the latter when they took the soundings of its stormy banks.

We may also notice that, on the lunar sphere, the south pole is much more continental than the north pole. On the latter, there is but one slight strip of land separated from other continents by vast seas. Toward the south, continents clothe almost the whole of the hemisphere. It is even possible that the Selenites have already planted the flag on one of their poles, while Franklin, Ross, Kane, Dumont, d'Urville, and Lambert have never yet been able to attain that unknown point of the terrestrial globe.

As to islands, they are numerous on the surface of the moon. Nearly all oblong or circular, and as if traced with the compass, they seem to form one vast archipelago, equal to that charming group lying between Greece and Asia Minor, and which mythology in ancient times adorned with most graceful legends. Involuntarily the names of Naxos, Tenedos, and Carpathos, rise before the mind, and we seek vainly for Ulysses' vessel or the "clipper" of the Argonauts. So at least it was in Michel Ardan's eyes. To him it was a Grecian archipelago that he saw on the map. To the eyes of his matter-of-fact companions, the aspect of these coasts recalled rather the parceled-out land of New Brunswick and Nova Scotia, and where the Frenchman discovered traces of the heroes of fable, these Americans were marking the most favorable points for the establishment of stores in the interests of lunar commerce and industry.

After wandering over these vast continents, the eye is attracted by the still greater seas. Not only their formation, but their situation and aspect remind one of the terrestrial oceans; but again, as on earth, these seas occupy the greater portion of the globe. But in point of fact, these are not liquid spaces, but plains, the nature of which the travelers hoped soon to determine. Astronomers, we must allow, have graced these pretended seas with at least odd names, which science has respected up to the present time. Michel Ardan was right when he compared this map to a "Tendre card," got up by a Scudary or a Cyrano de Bergerac. "Only," said he, "it is no longer the sentimental card of the seventeenth century, it is the card of life, very neatly divided into two parts, one feminine, the other masculine; the right hemisphere for woman, the left for man."

In speaking thus, Michel made his prosaic companions shrug their shoulders. Barbicane and Nicholl looked upon the lunar map from a very different point of view to that of their fantastic friend. Nevertheless, their fantastic friend was a little in the right. Judge for yourselves.

In the left hemisphere stretches the "Sea of Clouds," where human reason is so often shipwrecked. Not far off lies the "Sea of Rains," fed by all the fever of existence. Near this is the "Sea of Storms," where man is ever fighting against his passions, which too often gain the victory. Then, worn out by deceit, treasons, infidelity, and the whole body of terrestrial misery, what does he find at the end of his career? that vast "Sea of Humors," barely softened by some drops of the waters from the "Gulf of Dew!" Clouds, rain, storms, and humors— does the life of man contain aught but these? and is it not summed up in these four words?

The right hemisphere, "dedicated to the ladies," encloses smaller seas, whose significant names contain every incident of a feminine existence. There is the "Sea of Serenity," over which the young girl bends; "The Lake of Dreams," reflecting a joyous future; "The Sea of Nectar," with its waves of tenderness and breezes of love; "The Sea of Fruitfulness;" "The Sea of Crises;" then the "Sea of Vapors," whose dimensions are perhaps a little too confined; and lastly, that vast "Sea of Tranquillity," in which every false passion, every useless dream, every unsatisfied desire is at length absorbed, and whose waves emerge peacefully into the "Lake of Death!"

What a strange succession of names! What a singular division of the moon's two hemispheres, joined to one another like man and woman, and forming that sphere of life carried into space! And was not the fantastic Michel right in thus interpreting the fancies of the ancient astronomers? But while his imagination thus roved over "the seas," his grave companions were considering things more geographically. They were learning this new world by heart. They were measuring angles and diameters.

CHAPTER XII OROGRAPHIC DETAILS

The course taken by the projectile, as we have before remarked, was bearing it toward the moon's northern hemisphere. The travelers were far from the central point which they would have struck, had their course not been subject to an irremediable deviation. It was past midnight; and Barbicane then estimated the distance at seven hundred and fifty miles, which was a little greater than the length of the lunar radius, and which would diminish as it advanced nearer to the North Pole. The projectile was then not at the altitude of the equator; but across the tenth parallel, and from that latitude, carefully taken on the map to the pole, Barbicane and his two companions were able to observe the moon under the most favorable conditions. Indeed, by means of glasses, the above-named distance was reduced to little more than fourteen miles. The telescope of the Rocky Mountains brought the moon much nearer; but the terrestrial atmosphere singularly lessened its power. Thus Barbicane, posted in his projectile, with the glasses to his eyes, could seize upon details which were almost imperceptible to earthly observers.

"My friends," said the president, in a serious voice, "I do not know whither we are going; I do not know if we shall ever see the terrestrial globe again. Nevertheless, let us proceed as if our work would one day by useful to our fellow-men. Let us keep our minds free from every other consideration. We are astronomers; and this projectile is a room in the Cambridge University, carried into space. Let us make our observations!"

This said, work was begun with great exactness; and they faithfully reproduced the different aspects of the moon, at the different distances which the projectile reached.

At the time that the projectile was as high as the tenth parallel, north latitude, it seemed rigidly to follow the twentieth degree, east longitude. We must here make one important remark with regard to the map by which they were taking observations. In the selenographical maps where, on account of the reversing of the objects by the glasses, the south is above and the north below, it would seem natural that, on account of that inversion, the east should be to the left hand, and the west to the right. But it is not so. If the map were turned upside down, showing the moon as we see her, the east would be to the left, and the west to the right, contrary to that which exists on terrestrial maps. The following is the reason of this anomaly. Observers in the northern hemisphere (say in Europe) see the moon in the south— according to them. When they take observations, they turn their backs to the north, the reverse position to that which they occupy when they study a terrestrial map. As they turn their backs to the north, the east is on their left, and the west to their right. To observers in the southern hemisphere (Patagonia for example), the moon's west would be quite to their left, and the east to their right, as the south is behind them. Such is the reason of the apparent reversing of these two cardinal points, and we must bear it in mind in order to be able to follow President Barbicane's observations.

With the help of Boeer and Moedler's *Mappa Selenographica*, the travelers were able at once to recognize that portion of the disc enclosed within the field of their glasses.

"What are we looking at, at this moment?" asked Michel.

"At the northern part of the `Sea of Clouds,'" answered Barbicane. "We are too far off to recognize its nature. Are these plains composed of arid sand, as the first astronomer maintained? Or are they nothing but immense forests, according to M. Warren de la Rue's opinion, who gives the moon an atmosphere, though a very low and a very dense one? That we shall know by and by. We must affirm nothing until we are in a position to do so."

This "Sea of Clouds" is rather doubtfully marked out upon the maps. It is supposed that these vast plains are strewn with blocks of lava from the neighboring volcanoes on its right, Ptolemy, Purbach, Arzachel. But the projectile was advancing, and sensibly nearing it. Soon there appeared the heights which bound this sea at this northern limit. Before them rose a mountain radiant with beauty, the top of which seemed lost in an eruption of solar rays.

"That is—?" asked Michel.

"Copernicus," replied Barbicane.

"Let us see Copernicus."

This mount, situated in 9 ° north latitude and 20 ° east longitude, rose to a height of 10,600 feet above the surface of the moon. It is quite visible from the earth; and astronomers can study it with ease, particularly during the phase between the last quarter and the new moon, because then the shadows are thrown lengthways from east to west, allowing them to measure the heights.

This Copernicus forms the most important of the radiating system, situated in the southern hemisphere, according to Tycho Brahe. It rises isolated like a gigantic lighthouse on that portion of the "Sea of Clouds," which is bounded by the "Sea of Tempests," thus lighting by its splendid rays two oceans at a time. It was a sight without an equal, those long luminous trains, so dazzling in the full moon, and which, passing the boundary chain on the north, extends to the "Sea of Rains." At one o'clock of the terrestrial morning, the projectile, like a balloon borne into space, overlooked the top of this superb mount. Barbicane could recognize perfectly its chief features. Copernicus is comprised in the series of ringed mountains of the first order, in the division of great circles. Like Kepler and Aristarchus, which overlook the "Ocean of Tempests," sometimes it appeared like a brilliant point through the cloudy light, and was taken for a volcano in activity. But it is only an extinct one— like all on that side of the moon. Its circumference showed a diameter of about twenty-two leagues. The glasses discovered traces of stratification produced by successive eruptions, and the neighborhood was strewn with volcanic remains which still choked some of the craters.

"There exist," said Barbicane, "several kinds of circles on the surface of the moon, and it is easy to see that Copernicus belongs to the radiating class. If we were nearer, we should see the cones bristling on the inside, which in former times were so many fiery mouths. A curious arrangement, and one without an exception on the lunar disc, is that the interior surface of these circles is the reverse of the exterior, and contrary to the form taken by terrestrial craters. It follows, then, that the general curve of the bottom of these circles gives a sphere of a smaller diameter than that of the moon."

"And why this peculiar disposition?" asked Nicholl.

"We do not know," replied Barbicane.

CHAPTER XII OROGRAPHIC DETAILS

"What splendid radiation!" said Michel. "One could hardly see a finer spectacle, I think."

"What would you say, then," replied Barbicane, "if chance should bear us toward the southern hemisphere?"

"Well, I should say that it was still more beautiful," retorted

Michel Ardan.

At this moment the projectile hung perpendicularly over the circle. The circumference of Copernicus formed almost a perfect circle, and its steep escarpments were clearly defined. They could even distinguish a second ringed enclosure. Around spread a grayish plain, of a wild aspect, on which every relief was marked in yellow. At the bottom of the circle, as if enclosed in a jewel case, sparkled for one instant two or three eruptive cones, like enormous dazzling gems. Toward the north the escarpments were lowered by a depression which would probably have given access to the interior of the crater.

In passing over the surrounding plains, Barbicane noticed a great number of less important mountains; and among others a little ringed one called Guy Lussac, the breadth of which measured twelve miles.

Toward the south, the plain was very flat, without one elevation, without one projection. Toward the north, on the contrary, till where it was bounded by the "Sea of Storms," it resembled a liquid surface agitated by a storm, of which the hills and hollows formed a succession of waves suddenly congealed. Over the whole of this, and in all directions, lay the luminous lines, all converging to the summit of Copernicus.

The travelers discussed the origin of these strange rays; but they could not determine their nature any more than terrestrial observers.

"But why," said Nicholl, "should not these rays be simply spurs of mountains which reflect more vividly the light of the sun?"

"No," replied Barbicane; "if it was so, under certain conditions of the moon, these ridges would cast shadows, and they do not cast any."

And indeed, these rays only appeared when the orb of day was in opposition to the moon, and disappeared as soon as its rays became oblique.

"But how have they endeavored to explain these lines of light?" asked Michel; "for I cannot believe that savants would ever be stranded for want of an explanation."

"Yes," replied Barbicane; "Herschel has put forward an opinion, but he did not venture to affirm it."

"Never mind. What was the opinion?"

"He thought that these rays might be streams of cooled lava which shone when the sun beat straight upon them. It may be so; but nothing can be less certain. Besides, if we pass nearer to Tycho, we shall be in a better position to find out the cause of this radiation."

"Do you know, my friends, what that plain, seen from the height we are at, resembles?" said Michel.

"No," replied Nicholl.

"Very well; with all those pieces of lava lengthened like rockets, it resembles an immense game of spelikans thrown pellmell. There wants but the hook to pull them out one by one."

"Do be serious," said Barbicane.

"Well, let us be serious," replied Michel quietly; "and instead of spelikans, let us put bones. This plain, would then be nothing but an immense cemetery, on which would repose the mortal remains of thousands of extinct generations. Do you prefer that high-flown comparison?"

"One is as good as the other," retorted Barbicane.

"My word, you are difficult to please," answered Michel.

"My worthy friend," continued the matter-of-fact Barbicane, "it matters but little what it *resembles*, when we do not know what it *is*."

"Well answered," exclaimed Michel. "That will teach me to reason with savants."

But the projectile continued to advance with almost uniform speed around the lunar disc. The travelers, we may easily imagine, did not dream of taking a moment's rest. Every minute changed the landscape which fled from beneath their gaze. About half past one o'clock in the morning, they caught a glimpse of the tops of another mountain. Barbicane, consulting his map, recognized Eratosthenes.

It was a ringed mountain nine thousand feet high, and one of those circles so numerous on this satellite. With regard to this, Barbicane related Kepler's singular opinion on the formation of circles. According to that celebrated mathematician, these crater-like cavities had been dug by the hand of man.

"For what purpose?" asked Nicholl.

"For a very natural one," replied Barbicane. "The Selenites might have undertaken these immense works and dug these enormous holes for a refuge and shield from the solar rays which beat upon them during fifteen consecutive days."

"The Selenites are not fools," said Michel.

"A singular idea," replied Nicholl; "but it is probable that Kepler did not know the true dimensions of these circles, for the digging of them would have been the work of giants quite impossible for the Selenites."

"Why? if weight on the moon's surface is six times less than on the earth?" said Michel.

"But if the Selenites are six times smaller?" retorted Nicholl.

"And if there are *no* Selenites?" added Barbicane.

This put an end to the discussion.

Soon Eratosthenes disappeared under the horizon without the projectile being sufficiently near to allow close observation. This mountain separated the Apennines from the Carpathians. In the lunar orography they have discerned some chains of mountains, which are chiefly distributed over the northern hemisphere. Some, however, occupy certain portions of the southern hemisphere also.

About two o'clock in the morning Barbicane found that they were above the twentieth lunar parallel. The distance of the projectile from the moon was not more than six hundred miles. Barbicane, now perceiving that the projectile was steadily approaching the lunar disc, did not despair; if not of reaching her, at least of discovering the secrets of her configuration.

CHAPTER XIII LUNAR LANDSCAPES

At half-past two in the morning, the projectile was over the thirteenth lunar parallel and at the effective distance of five hundred miles, reduced by the glasses to five. It still seemed impossible, however, that it could ever touch any part of the disc. Its motive speed, comparatively so moderate, was inexplicable to President Barbicane. At that distance from the moon it must have been considerable, to enable it to bear up against her attraction. Here was a phenomenon the cause of which escaped them again. Besides, time failed them to investigate the cause. All lunar relief was defiling under the eyes of the travelers, and they would not lose a single detail.

Under the glasses the disc appeared at the distance of five miles. What would an aeronaut, borne to this distance from the earth, distinguish on its surface? We cannot say, since the greatest ascension has not been more than 25,000 feet.

This, however, is an exact description of what Barbicane and his companions saw at this height. Large patches of different colors appeared on the disc. Selenographers are not agreed upon the nature of these colors. There are several, and rather vividly marked. Julius Schmidt pretends that, if the terrestrial oceans were dried up, a Selenite observer could not distinguish on the globe a greater diversity of shades between the oceans and the continental plains than those on the moon present to a terrestrial observer. According to him, the color common to the vast plains known by the name of "seas" is a dark gray mixed with green and brown. Some of the large craters present the same appearance. Barbicane knew this opinion of the German selenographer, an opinion shared by Boeer and Moedler. Observation has proved that right was on their side, and not on that of some astronomers who admit the existence of only gray on the moon's surface. In some parts green was very distinct, such as springs, according to Julius Schmidt, from the seas of "Serenity and Humors." Barbicane also noticed large craters, without any interior cones, which shed a bluish tint similar to the reflection of a sheet of steel freshly polished. These colors belonged really to the lunar disc, and did not result, as some astronomers say, either from the imperfection in the objective of the glasses or from the interposition of the terrestrial atmosphere.

Not a doubt existed in Barbicane's mind with regard to it, as he observed it through space, and so could not commit any optical error. He considered the establishment of this fact as an acquisition to science. Now, were these shades of green, belonging to tropical vegetation, kept up by a low dense atmosphere? He could not yet say.

Farther on, he noticed a reddish tint, quite defined. The same shade had before been observed at the bottom of an isolated enclosure, known by the name of Lichtenburg's circle, which is situated near the Hercynian mountains, on the borders of the moon; but they could not tell the nature of it.

They were not more fortunate with regard to another peculiarity of the disc, for they could not decide upon the cause of it.

Michel Ardan was watching near the president, when he noticed long white lines, vividly lighted up by the direct rays of the sun. It was a succession of luminous furrows, very different from the radiation of Copernicus not long before; they ran parallel with each other.

Michel, with his usual readiness, hastened to exclaim:

"Look there! cultivated fields!"

"Cultivated fields!" replied Nicholl, shrugging his shoulders.

"Plowed, at all events," retorted Michel Ardan; "but what laborers those Selenites must be, and what giant oxen they must harness to their plow to cut such furrows!"

"They are not furrows," said Barbicane; "they are *rifts*."

"Rifts? stuff!" replied Michel mildly; "but what do you mean by `rifts' in the scientific world?"

Barbicane immediately enlightened his companion as to what he knew about lunar rifts. He knew that they were a kind of furrow found on every part of the disc which was not mountainous; that these furrows, generally isolated, measured from 400 to 500 leagues in length; that their breadth varied from 1,000 to 1,500 yards, and that their borders were strictly parallel; but he knew nothing more either of their formation or their nature.

Barbicane, through his glasses, observed these rifts with great attention. He noticed that their borders were formed of steep declivities; they were long parallel ramparts, and with some small amount of imagination he might have admitted the existence of long lines of fortifications, raised by Selenite engineers. Of these different rifts some were perfectly straight, as if cut by a line; others were slightly curved, though still keeping their borders parallel; some crossed each other, some cut through craters; here they wound through ordinary cavities, such as Posidonius or Petavius; there they wound through the seas, such as the "Sea of Serenity."

These natural accidents naturally excited the imaginations of these terrestrial astronomers. The first observations had not discovered these rifts. Neither Hevelius, Cassin, La Hire, nor Herschel seemed to have known them. It was Schroeter who in 1789 first drew attention to them. Others followed who studied them, as Pastorff, Gruithuysen, Boeer, and Moedler. At this time their number amounts to seventy; but, if they have been counted, their nature has not yet been determined; they are certainly *not* fortifications, any more than they are the ancient beds of dried-up rivers; for, on one side, the waters, so slight on the moon's surface, could never have worn such drains for themselves; and, on the other, they often cross craters of great elevation.

We must, however, allow that Michel Ardan had "an idea," and that, without knowing it, he coincided in that respect with Julius Schmidt.

"Why," said he, "should not these unaccountable appearances be simply phenomena of vegetation?"

"What do you mean?" asked Barbicane quickly.

"Do not excite yourself, my worthy president," replied Michel; "might it not be possible that the dark lines forming that bastion were rows of trees regularly placed?"

"You stick to your vegetation, then?" said Barbicane.

"I like," retorted Michel Ardan, "to explain what you savants cannot explain; at least my hypotheses has the advantage of indicating why these rifts disappear, or seem to disappear, at certain seasons."

"And for what reason?"

"For the reason that the trees become invisible when they lose their leaves, and visible again when they regain them."

"Your explanation is ingenious, my dear companion," replied

Barbicane, "but inadmissible."

"Why?"

"Because, so to speak, there are no seasons on the moon's surface, and that, consequently, the phenomena of vegetation of which you speak cannot occur."

Indeed, the slight obliquity of the lunar axis keeps the sun at an almost equal height in every latitude. Above the equatorial regions the radiant orb almost invariably occupies the zenith, and does not pass the limits of the horizon in the polar regions; thus, according to each region, there reigns a perpetual winter, spring, summer, or autumn, as in the planet Jupiter, whose axis is but little inclined upon its orbit.

What origin do they attribute to these rifts? That is a question difficult to solve. They are certainly anterior to the formation of craters and circles, for several have introduced themselves by breaking through their circular ramparts. Thus it may be that, contemporary with the later geological epochs, they are due to the expansion of natural forces.

But the projectile had now attained the fortieth degree of lunar latitude, at a distance not exceeding 40 miles. Through the glasses objects appeared to be only four miles distant.

At this point, under their feet, rose Mount Helicon, 1,520 feet high, and round about the left rose moderate elevations, enclosing a small portion of the "Sea of Rains," under the name of the Gulf of Iris. The terrestrial atmosphere would have to be one hundred and seventy times more transparent than it is, to allow astronomers to make perfect observations on the moon's surface; but in the void in which the projectile floated no fluid interposed itself between the eye of the observer and the object observed. And more, Barbicane found himself carried to a greater distance than the most powerful telescopes had ever done before, either that of Lord Rosse or that of the Rocky Mountains. He was, therefore, under extremely favorable conditions for solving that great question of the habitability of the moon; but the solution still escaped him; he could distinguish nothing but desert beds, immense plains, and toward the north, arid mountains. Not a work betrayed the hand of man; not a ruin marked his course; not a group of animals was to be seen indicating life, even in an inferior degree. In no part was there life, in no part was there an appearance of vegetation. Of the three kingdoms which share the terrestrial globe between them, one alone was represented on the lunar and that the mineral.

"Ah, indeed!" said Michel Ardan, a little out of countenance; "then you see no one?"

"No," answered Nicholl; "up to this time, not a man, not an animal, not a tree! After all, whether the atmosphere has taken refuge at the bottom of cavities, in the midst of the circles, or even on the opposite face of the moon, we cannot decide."

"Besides," added Barbicane, "even to the most piercing eye a man cannot be distinguished farther than three and a half miles off; so that, if there are any Selenites, they can see our projectile, but we cannot see them."

Toward four in the morning, at the height of the fiftieth parallel, the distance was reduced to 300 miles. To the left ran a line of mountains capriciously shaped, lying in the full light. To the right, on the contrary, lay a black hollow resembling a vast well, unfathomable and gloomy, drilled into the lunar soil.

This hole was the "Black Lake"; it was Pluto, a deep circle which can be conveniently studied from the earth, between the last quarter and the new moon, when the shadows fall from west to east.

This black color is rarely met with on the surface of the satellite. As yet it has only been recognized in the depths of the circle of Endymion, to the east of the "Cold Sea," in the northern hemisphere, and at the bottom of Grimaldi's circle, on the equator, toward the eastern border of the orb.

Pluto is an annular mountain, situated in 51 ° north latitude, and 9 ° east longitude. Its circuit is forty-seven miles long and thirty-two broad.

Barbicane regretted that they were not passing directly above this vast opening. There was an abyss to fathom, perhaps some mysterious phenomenon to surprise; but the projectile's course could not be altered. They must rigidly submit. They could not guide a balloon, still less a projectile, when once enclosed within its walls. Toward five in the morning the northern limits of the "Sea of Rains" was at length passed. The mounts of Condamine and Fontenelle remained— one on the right, the other on the left. That part of the disc beginning with 60 ° was becoming quite mountainous. The glasses brought them to within two miles, less than that separating the summit of Mont Blanc from the level of the sea. The whole region was bristling with spikes and circles. Toward the 60 ° Philolaus stood predominant at a height of 5,550 feet with its elliptical crater, and seen from this distance, the disc showed a very fantastical appearance. Landscapes were presented to the eye under very different conditions from those on the earth, and also very inferior to them.

The moon having no atmosphere, the consequences arising from the absence of this gaseous envelope have already been shown. No twilight on her surface; night following day and day following night with the suddenness of a lamp which is extinguished or lighted amid profound darkness— no transition from cold to heat, the temperature falling in an instant from boiling point to the cold of space.

Another consequence of this want of air is that absolute darkness reigns where the sun's rays do not penetrate. That which on earth is called diffusion of light, that luminous matter which the air holds in suspension, which creates the twilight and the daybreak, which produces the *umbrae* and *penumbrae*, and all the magic of *chiaro-oscuro*, does not exist on the moon. Hence the harshness of contrasts, which only admit of two colors, black and white. If a Selenite were to shade his eyes from the sun's rays, the sky would seem absolutely black, and the stars would shine to him as on the darkest night. Judge of the impression produced on Barbicane and his three friends by this strange scene! Their eyes were confused. They could no longer grasp the respective distances of the different plains. A lunar landscape without the softening of the phenomena of *chiaro-oscuro* could not be rendered by an earthly landscape painter; it would be spots of ink on a white page— nothing more.

This aspect was not altered even when the projectile, at the height of 80 °, was only separated from the moon by a distance of fifty miles; nor even when, at five in the morning, it passed at less than twenty-five miles from the mountain of Gioja, a distance reduced by the glasses to a quarter of a mile. It seemed as if the moon might be touched by the hand! It seemed impossible that, before long, the projectile would not strike her, if only at the north pole, the brilliant arch of which was so distinctly visible on the black sky.

Michel Ardan wanted to open one of the scuttles and throw himself on to the moon's surface! A very useless attempt; for if the projectile could not attain any point whatever of the satellite, Michel, carried along by its motion, could not attain it either.

At that moment, at six o'clock, the lunar pole appeared. The disc only presented to the travelers' gaze one half brilliantly lit up, while the other disappeared in the darkness.

CHAPTER XIII LUNAR LANDSCAPES

Suddenly the projectile passed the line of demarcation between intense light and absolute darkness, and was plunged in profound night!

CHAPTER XIV THE NIGHT OF THREE HUNDRED AND FIFTY-FOUR HOURS AND A HALF

At the moment when this phenomenon took place so rapidly, the projectile was skirting the moon's north pole at less than twenty-five miles distance. Some seconds had sufficed to plunge it into the absolute darkness of space. The transition was so sudden, without shade, without gradation of light, without attenuation of the luminous waves, that the orb seemed to have been extinguished by a powerful blow.

"Melted, disappeared!" Michel Ardan exclaimed, aghast.

Indeed, there was neither reflection nor shadow. Nothing more was to be seen of that disc, formerly so dazzling. The darkness was complete. and rendered even more so by the rays from the stars. It was "that blackness" in which the lunar nights are insteeped, which last three hundred and fifty-four hours and a half at each point of the disc, a long night resulting from the equality of the translatory and rotary movements of the moon. The projectile, immerged in the conical shadow of the satellite, experienced the action of the solar rays no more than any of its invisible points.

In the interior, the obscurity was complete. They could not see each other. Hence the necessity of dispelling the darkness. However desirous Barbicane might be to husband the gas, the reserve of which was small, he was obliged to ask from it a fictitious light, an expensive brilliancy which the sun then refused.

"Devil take the radiant orb!" exclaimed Michel Ardan, "which forces us to expend gas, instead of giving us his rays gratuitously."

"Do not let us accuse the sun," said Nicholl, "it is not his fault, but that of the moon, which has come and placed herself like a screen between us and it."

"It is the sun!" continued Michel.

"It is the moon!" retorted Nicholl.

An idle dispute, which Barbicane put an end to by saying:

"My friends, it is neither the fault of the sun nor of the moon; it is the fault of the *projectile*, which, instead of rigidly following its course, has awkwardly missed it. To be more just, it is the fault of that unfortunate meteor which has so deplorably altered our first direction."

"Well," replied Michel Ardan, "as the matter is settled, let us have breakfast. After a whole night of watching it is fair to build ourselves up a little."

This proposal meeting with no contradiction, Michel prepared the repast in a few minutes. But they ate for eating's sake, they drank without toasts, without hurrahs. The bold travelers being borne away into gloomy space, without their accustomed *cortege* of rays, felt a vague uneasiness in their hearts. The "strange" shadow so dear to Victor Hugo's pen bound them on all sides. But they talked over the interminable night of three hundred and fifty-four hours and a half, nearly fifteen days, which the law of physics has imposed on the inhabitants of the moon.

Barbicane gave his friends some explanation of the causes and the consequences of this curious phenomenon.

"Curious indeed," said they; "for, if each hemisphere of the moon is deprived of solar light for fifteen days, that above which we now float does not even enjoy during its long night any view of the earth so beautifully lit up. In a word she has no moon (applying this designation to our globe) but on one side of her disc. Now if this were the case with the earth— if, for example, Europe never saw the moon, and she was only visible at the antipodes, imagine to yourself the astonishment of a European on arriving in Australia."

"They would make the voyage for nothing but to see the moon!" replied Michel.

"Very well!" continued Barbicane, "that astonishment is reserved for the Selenites who inhabit the face of the moon opposite to the earth, a face which is ever invisible to our countrymen of the terrestrial globe."

"And which we should have seen," added Nicholl, "if we had arrived here when the moon was new, that is to say fifteen days later."

"I will add, to make amends," continued Barbicane, "that the inhabitants of the visible face are singularly favored by nature, to the detriment of their brethren on the invisible face. The latter, as you see, have dark nights of 354 hours, without one single ray to break the darkness. The other, on the contrary, when the sun which has given its light for fifteen days sinks below the horizon, see a splendid orb rise on the opposite horizon. It is the earth, which is thirteen times greater than the diminutive moon that we know— the earth which developes itself at a diameter of two degrees, and which sheds a light thirteen times greater than that qualified by atmospheric strata— the earth which only disappears at the moment when the sun reappears in its turn!"

"Nicely worded!" said Michel, "slightly academical perhaps."

"It follows, then," continued Barbicane, without knitting his brows, "that the visible face of the disc must be very agreeable to inhabit, since it always looks on either the sun when the moon is full, or on the earth when the moon is new."

"But," said Nicholl, "that advantage must be well compensated by the insupportable heat which the light brings with it."

"The inconvenience, in that respect, is the same for the two faces, for the earth's light is evidently deprived of heat. But the invisible face is still more searched by the heat than the visible face. I say that for *you*, Nicholl, because Michel will probably not understand."

"Thank you," said Michel.

"Indeed," continued Barbicane, "when the invisible face receives at the same time light and heat from the sun, it is because the moon is new; that is to say, she is situated between the sun and the earth. It follows, then, considering the position which she occupies in opposition when full, that she is nearer to the sun by twice her distance from the earth; and that distance may be estimated at the two-hundredth part of that which separates the sun from the earth, or in round numbers 400,000 miles. So that invisible face is so much nearer to the sun when she receives its rays."

"Quite right," replied Nicholl.

"On the contrary," continued Barbicane.

"One moment," said Michel, interrupting his grave companion.

"What do you want?"

"I ask to be allowed to continue the explanation."

"And why?"

"To prove that I understand."

"Get along with you," said Barbicane, smiling.

"On the contrary," said Michel, imitating the tone and gestures of the president, "on the contrary, when the visible face of the moon is lit by the sun, it is because the moon is full, that is to say, opposite the sun with regard to the earth. The distance separating it from the radiant orb is then increased in round numbers to 400,000 miles, and the heat which she receives must be a little less."

"Very well said!" exclaimed Barbicane. "Do you know, Michel, that, for an amateur, you are intelligent."

"Yes," replied Michel coolly, "we are all so on the Boulevard des Italiens."

Barbicane gravely grasped the hand of his amiable companion, and continued to enumerate the advantages reserved for the inhabitants of the visible face.

Among others, he mentioned eclipses of the sun, which only take place on this side of the lunar disc; since, in order that they may take place, it is necessary for the moon to be *in opposition.* These eclipses, caused by the interposition of the earth between the moon and the sun, can last *two hours*; during which time, by reason of the rays refracted by its atmosphere, the terrestrial globe can appear as nothing but a black point upon the sun.

"So," said Nicholl, "there is a hemisphere, that invisible hemisphere which is very ill supplied, very ill treated, by nature."

"Never mind," replied Michel; "if we ever become Selenites, we will inhabit the visible face. I like the light."

"Unless, by any chance," answered Nicholl, "the atmosphere should be condensed on the other side, as certain astronomers pretend."

"That would be a consideration," said Michel.

Breakfast over, the observers returned to their post. They tried to see through the darkened scuttles by extinguishing all light in the projectile; but not a luminous spark made its way through the darkness.

One inexplicable fact preoccupied Barbicane. Why, having passed within such a short distance of the moon—about twenty-five miles only— why the projectile had not fallen? If its speed had been enormous, he could have understood that the fall would not have taken place; but, with a relatively moderate speed, that resistance to the moon's attraction could not be explained. Was the projectile under some foreign influence? Did some kind of body retain it in the ether? It was quite evident that it could never reach any point of the moon. Whither was it going? Was it going farther from, or nearing, the disc? Was it being borne in that profound darkness through the infinity of space? How could they learn, how calculate, in the midst of this night? All these questions made Barbicane uneasy, but he could not solve them.

Certainly, the invisible orb was *there*, perhaps only some few miles off; but neither he nor his companions could see it. If there was any noise on its surface, they could not hear it. Air, that medium of sound, was wanting to transmit the groanings of that moon which the Arabic legends call "a man already half granite, and still breathing."

One must allow that that was enough to aggravate the most patient observers. It was just that unknown hemisphere which was stealing from their sight. That face which fifteen days sooner, or fifteen days later, had been, or would be, splendidly illuminated by the solar rays, was then being lost in utter darkness. In fifteen days where would the projectile be? Who could say? Where would the chances of conflicting attractions have drawn it to? The disappointment of the travelers in the midst of this utter darkness may be imagined. All observation of the lunar disc was impossible. The constellations alone claimed all their attention; and we must allow that the astronomers Faye, Charconac, and Secchi, never found themselves in circumstances so favorable for their observation.

Indeed, nothing could equal the splendor of this starry world, bathed in limpid ether. Its diamonds set in the heavenly vault sparkled magnificently. The eye took in the firmament from the Southern Cross to the North Star, those two constellations which in 12,000 years, by reason of the succession of equinoxes, will resign their part of the polar stars, the one to Canopus in the southern hemisphere, the other to Wega in the northern. Imagination loses itself in this sublime Infinity, amid which the projectile was gravitating, like a new star created by the hand of man. From a natural cause, these constellations shone with a soft luster; they did not twinkle, for there was no atmosphere which, by the intervention of its layers unequally dense and of different degrees of humidity, produces this scintillation. These stars were soft eyes, looking out into the dark night, amid the silence of absolute space.

Long did the travelers stand mute, watching the constellated firmament, upon which the moon, like a vast screen, made an enormous black hole. But at length a painful sensation drew them from their watchings. This was an intense cold, which soon covered the inside of the glass of the scuttles with a thick coating of ice. The sun was no longer warming the projectile with its direct rays, and thus it was losing the heat stored up in its walls by degrees. This heat was rapidly evaporating into space by radiation, and a considerably lower temperature was the result. The humidity of the interior was changed into ice upon contact with the glass, preventing all observation.

Nicholl consulted the thermometer, and saw that it had fallen to seventeen degrees (Centigrade) below zero[1]. So that, in spite of the many reasons for economizing, Barbicane, after having begged light from the gas, was also obliged to beg for heat. The projectile's low temperature was no longer endurable. Its tenants would have been frozen to death.

"Well!" observed Michel, "we cannot reasonably complain of the monotony of our journey! What variety we have had, at least in temperature. Now we are blinded with light and saturated with heat, like the Indians of the Pampas! now plunged into profound darkness, amid the cold, like the Esquimaux of the north pole. No, indeed! we have no right to complain; nature does wonders in our honor."

"But," asked Nicholl, "what is the temperature outside?"

"Exactly that of the planetary space," replied Barbicane.

"Then," continued Michel Ardan, "would not this be the time to make the experiment which we dared not attempt when we were drowned in the sun's rays?

"It is now or never," replied Barbicane, "for we are in a good position to verify the temperature of space, and see if Fourier or Pouillet's calculations are exact."

"In any case it is cold," said Michel. "See! the steam of the interior is condensing on the glasses of the scuttles. If the fall continues, the vapor of our breath will fall in snow around us."

"Let us prepare a thermometer," said Barbicane.

We may imagine that an ordinary thermometer would afford no result under the circumstances in which this instrument was to be exposed. The mercury would have been frozen in its ball, as below 42 ° Fahrenheit below zero it is no longer liquid. But Barbicane

---

[1] 1° Fahrenheit.

had furnished himself with a spirit thermometer on Wafferdin's system, which gives the minima of excessively low temperatures.

Before beginning the experiment, this instrument was compared with an ordinary one, and then Barbicane prepared to use it.

"How shall we set about it?" asked Nicholl.

"Nothing is easier," replied Michel Ardan, who was never at a loss. "We open the scuttle rapidly; throw out the instrument; it follows the projectile with exemplary docility; and a quarter of an hour after, draw it in."

"With the hand?" asked Barbicane.

"With the hand," replied Michel.

"Well, then, my friend, do not expose yourself," answered Barbicane, "for the hand that you draw in again will be nothing but a stump frozen and deformed by the frightful cold."

"Really!"

"You will feel as if you had had a terrible burn, like that of iron at a white heat; for whether the heat leaves our bodies briskly or enters briskly, it is exactly the same thing. Besides, I am not at all certain that the objects we have thrown out are still following us."

"Why not?" asked Nicholl.

"Because, if we are passing through an atmosphere of the slightest density, these objects will be retarded. Again, the darkness prevents our seeing if they still float around us. But in order not to expose ourselves to the loss of our thermometer, we will fasten it, and we can then more easily pull it back again."

Barbicane's advice was followed. Through the scuttle rapidly opened, Nicholl threw out the instrument, which was held by a short cord, so that it might be more easily drawn up. The scuttle had not been opened more than a second, but that second had sufficed to let in a most intense cold.

"The devil!" exclaimed Michel Ardan, "it is cold enough to freeze a white bear."

Barbicane waited until half an hour had elapsed, which was more than time enough to allow the instrument to fall to the level of the surrounding temperature. Then it was rapidly pulled in.

Barbicane calculated the quantity of spirits of wine overflowed into the little vial soldered to the lower part of the instrument, and said:

"A hundred and forty degrees Centigrade[1] below zero!"

M. Pouillet was right and Fourier wrong. That was the undoubted temperature of the starry space. Such is, perhaps, that of the lunar continents, when the orb of night has lost by radiation all the heat which fifteen days of sun have poured into her.

---

[1] 218 degrees Fahrenheit below zero.

CHAPTER XV HYPERBOLA OR PARABOLA

We may, perhaps, be astonished to find Barbicane and his companions so little occupied with the future reserved for them in their metal prison which was bearing them through the infinity of space. Instead of asking where they were going, they passed their time making experiments, as if they had been quietly installed in their own study.

We might answer that men so strong-minded were above such anxieties— that they did not trouble themselves about such trifles— and that they had something else to do than to occupy their minds with the future.

The truth was that they were not masters of their projectile; they could neither check its course, nor alter its direction.

A sailor can change the head of his ship as he pleases; an aeronaut can give a vertical motion to his balloon. They, on the contrary, had no power over their vehicle. Every maneuver was forbidden. Hence the inclination to let things alone, or as the sailors say, "let her run."

Where did they find themselves at this moment, at eight o'clock in the morning of the day called upon the earth the 6th of December? Very certainly in the neighborhood of the moon, and even near enough for her to look to them like an enormous black screen upon the firmament. As to the distance which separated them, it was impossible to estimate it. The projectile, held by some unaccountable force, had been within four miles of grazing the satellite's north pole.

But since entering the cone of shadow these last two hours, had the distance increased or diminished? Every point of mark was wanting by which to estimate both the direction and the speed of the projectile.

Perhaps it was rapidly leaving the disc, so that it would soon quit the pure shadow. Perhaps, again, on the other hand, it might be nearing it so much that in a short time it might strike some high point on the invisible hemisphere, which would doubtlessly have ended the journey much to the detriment of the travelers.

A discussion arose on this subject, and Michel Ardan, always ready with an explanation, gave it as his opinion that the projectile, held by the lunar attraction, would end by falling on the surface of the terrestrial globe like an aerolite.

"First of all, my friend," answered Barbicane, "every aerolite does not fall to the earth; it is only a small proportion which do so; and if we had passed into an aerolite, it does not necessarily follow that we should ever reach the surface of the moon."

"But how if we get near enough?" replied Michel.

"Pure mistake," replied Barbicane. "Have you not seen shooting stars rush through the sky by thousands at certain seasons?"

"Yes."

"Well, these stars, or rather corpuscles, only shine when they are heated by gliding over the atmospheric layers. Now, if they enter the atmosphere, they pass at least within forty miles of the earth, but they seldom fall upon it. The same with our projectile. It may approach very near to the moon, and not yet fall upon it."

"But then," asked Michel, "I shall be curious to know how our erring vehicle will act in space?"

"I see but two hypotheses," replied Barbicane, after some moments' reflection.

"What are they?"

"The projectile has the choice between two mathematical curves, and it will follow one or the other according to the speed with which it is animated, and which at this moment I cannot estimate."

"Yes," said Nicholl, "it will follow either a parabola or a hyperbola."

"Just so," replied Barbicane. "With a certain speed it will assume the parabola, and with a greater the hyperbola."

"I like those grand words," exclaimed Michel Ardan; "one knows directly what they mean. And pray what is your parabola, if you please?"

"My friend," answered the captain, "the parabola is a curve of the second order, the result of the section of a cone intersected by a plane parallel to one of the sides."

"Ah! ah!" said Michel, in a satisfied tone.

"It is very nearly," continued Nicholl, "the course described by a bomb launched from a mortar."

"Perfect! And the hyperbola?"

"The hyperbola, Michel, is a curve of the second order, produced by the intersection of a conic surface and a plane parallel to its axis, and constitutes two branches separated one from the other, both tending indefinitely in the two directions."

"Is it possible!" exclaimed Michel Ardan in a serious tone, as if they had told him of some serious event. "What I particularly like in your definition of the hyperbola (I was going to say hyperblague) is that it is still more obscure than the word you pretend to define."

Nicholl and Barbicane cared little for Michel Ardan's fun. They were deep in a scientific discussion. What curve would the projectile follow? was their hobby. One maintained the hyperbola, the other the parabola. They gave each other reasons bristling with x. Their arguments were couched in language which made Michel jump. The discussion was hot, and neither would give up his chosen curve to his adversary.

This scientific dispute lasted so long that it made Michel very impatient.

"Now, gentlemen cosines, will you cease to throw parabolas and hyperbolas at each other's heads? I want to understand the only interesting question in the whole affair. We shall follow one or the other of these curves? Good. But where will they lead us to?"

"Nowhere," replied Nicholl.

"How, nowhere?"

"Evidently," said Barbicane, "they are open curves, which may be prolonged indefinitely."

"Ah, savants!" cried Michel; "and what are either the one or the other to us from the moment we know that they equally lead us into infinite space?"

Barbicane and Nicholl could not forbear smiling. They had just been creating "art for art's sake." Never had so idle a question been raised at such an inopportune moment. The sinister truth remained that, whether hyperbolically or parabolically borne away, the projectile would never again meet either the earth or the moon.

CHAPTER XV HYPERBOLA OR PARABOLA

What would become of these bold travelers in the immediate future? If they did not die of hunger, if they did not die of thirst, in some days, when the gas failed, they would die from want of air, unless the cold had killed them first. Still, important as it was to economize the gas, the excessive lowness of the surrounding temperature obliged them to con-consume a certain quantity. Strictly speaking, they could do without its *light*, but not without its *heat*. Fortunately the caloric generated by Reiset's and Regnaut's apparatus raised the temperature of the interior of the projectile a little, and without much expenditure they were able to keep it bearable.

But observations had now become very difficult. the dampness of the projectile was condensed on the windows and congealed immediately. This cloudiness had to be dispersed continually. In any case they might hope to be able to discover some phenomena of the highest interest.

But up to this time the disc remained dumb and dark. It did not answer the multiplicity of questions put by these ardent minds; a matter which drew this reflection from Michel, apparently a just one:

"If ever we begin this journey over again, we shall do well to choose the time when the moon is at the full."

"Certainly," said Nicholl, "that circumstance will be more favorable. I allow that the moon, immersed in the sun's rays, will not be visible during the transit, but instead we should see the earth, which would be full. And what is more, if we were drawn round the moon, as at this moment, we should at least have the advantage of seeing the invisible part of her disc magnificently lit."

"Well said, Nicholl," replied Michel Ardan. "What do you think, Barbicane?"

"I think this," answered the grave president: "If ever we begin this journey again, we shall start at the same time and under the same conditions. Suppose we had attained our end, would it not have been better to have found continents in broad daylight than a country plunged in utter darkness? Would not our first installation have been made under better circumstances? Yes, evidently. As to the invisible side, we could have visited it in our exploring expeditions on the lunar globe. So that the time of the full moon was well chosen. But we ought to have arrived at the end; and in order to have so arrived, we ought to have suffered no deviation on the road."

"I have nothing to say to that," answered Michel Ardan. "Here is, however, a good opportunity lost of observing the other side of the moon."

But the projectile was now describing in the shadow that incalculable course which no sight-mark would allow them to ascertain. Had its direction been altered, either by the influence of the lunar attraction, or by the action of some unknown star? Barbicane could not say. But a change had taken place in the relative position of the vehicle; and Barbicane verified it about four in the morning.

The change consisted in this, that the base of the projectile had turned toward the moon's surface, and was so held by a perpendicular passing through its axis. The attraction, that is to say the weight, had brought about this alteration. The heaviest part of the projectile inclined toward the invisible disc as if it would fall upon it.

Was it falling? Were the travelers attaining that much desired end? No. And the observation of a sign-point, quite inexplicable in itself, showed Barbicane that his projectile was not nearing the moon, and that it had shifted by following an almost concentric curve.

This point of mark was a luminous brightness, which Nicholl sighted suddenly, on the limit of the horizon formed by the black disc. This point could not be confounded with a star. It was a reddish incandescence which increased by degrees, a decided proof that the projectile was shifting toward it and not falling normally on the surface of the moon.

"A volcano! it is a volcano in action!" cried Nicholl; "a disemboweling of the interior fires of the moon! That world is not quite extinguished."

"Yes, an eruption," replied Barbicane, who was carefully studying the phenomenon through his night glass. "What should it be, if not a volcano?"

"But, then," said Michel Ardan, "in order to maintain that combustion, there must be air. So the atmosphere does surround that part of the moon."

"Perhaps so," replied Barbicane, "but not necessarily.

The volcano, by the decomposition of certain substances, can provide its own oxygen, and thus throw flames into space. It seems to me that the deflagration, by the intense brilliancy of the substances in combustion, is produced in pure oxygen. We must not be in a hurry to proclaim the existence of a lunar atmosphere."

The fiery mountain must have been situated about the 45 ° south latitude on the invisible part of the disc; but, to Barbicane's great displeasure, the curve which the projectile was describing was taking it far from the point indicated by the eruption. Thus he could not determine its nature exactly. Half an hour after being sighted, this luminous point had disappeared behind the dark horizon; but the verification of this phenomenon was of considerable consequence in their selenographic studies. It proved that all heat had not yet disappeared from the bowels of this globe; and where heat exists, who can affirm that the vegetable kingdom, nay, even the animal kingdom itself, has not up to this time resisted all destructive influences? The existence of this volcano in eruption, unmistakably seen by these earthly savants, would doubtless give rise to many theories favorable to the grave question of the habitability of the moon.

Barbicane allowed himself to be carried away by these reflections. He forgot himself in a deep reverie in which the mysterious destiny of the lunar world was uppermost. He was seeking to combine together the facts observed up to that time, when a new incident recalled him briskly to reality. This incident was more than a cosmical phenomenon; it was a threatened danger, the consequence of which might be disastrous in the extreme.

Suddenly, in the midst of the ether, in the profound darkness, an enormous mass appeared. It was like a moon, but an incandescent moon whose brilliancy was all the more intolerable as it cut sharply on the frightful darkness of space. This mass, of a circular form, threw a light which filled the projectile. The forms of Barbicane, Nicholl, and Michel Ardan, bathed in its white sheets, assumed that livid spectral appearance which physicians produce with the fictitious light of alcohol impregnated with salt.

"By Jove!" cried Michel Ardan, "we are hideous. What is that ill-conditioned moon?"

"A meteor," replied Barbicane.

"A meteor burning in space?"

"Yes."

This shooting globe suddenly appearing in shadow at a distance of at most 200 miles, ought, according to Barbicane, to have a diameter of 2,000 yards. It advanced at a speed of about one mile and a half per second. It cut the projectile's path and must reach it in some minutes. As it approached it grew to enormous proportions.

Imagine, if possible, the situation of the travelers! It is impossible to describe it. In spite of their courage, their *sang-froid*, their carelessness of danger, they were mute, motionless with stiffened limbs, a prey to frightful terror. Their projectile, the course of which they could not alter, was rushing straight on this ignited mass, more intense than the open mouth of an oven. It seemed as though they were being precipitated toward an abyss of fire.

Barbicane had seized the hands of his two companions, and all three looked through their half-open eyelids upon that asteroid heated to a white heat. If thought was not destroyed within them, if their brains still worked amid all this awe, they must have given themselves up for lost.

Two minutes after the sudden appearance of the meteor (to them two centuries of anguish) the projectile seemed almost about to strike it, when the globe of fire burst like a bomb, but without making any noise in that void where sound, which is but the agitation of the layers of air, could not be generated.

Nicholl uttered a cry, and he and his companions rushed to the scuttle. What a sight! What pen can describe it? What palette is rich enough in colors to reproduce so magnificent a spectacle?

It was like the opening of a crater, like the scattering of an immense conflagration. Thousands of luminous fragments lit up and irradiated space with their fires. Every size, every color, was there intermingled. There were rays of yellow and pale yellow, red, green, gray— a crown of fireworks of all colors. Of the enormous and much-dreaded globe there remained nothing but these fragments carried in all directions, now become asteroids in their turn, some flaming like a sword, some surrounded by a whitish cloud, and others leaving behind them trains of brilliant cosmical dust.

These incandescent blocks crossed and struck each other, scattering still smaller fragments, some of which struck the projectile. Its left scuttle was even cracked by a violent shock. It seemed to be floating amid a hail of howitzer shells, the smallest of which might destroy it instantly.

The light which saturated the ether was so wonderfully intense, that Michel, drawing Barbicane and Nicholl to his window, exclaimed, "The invisible moon, visible at last!"

And through a luminous emanation, which lasted some seconds, the whole three caught a glimpse of that mysterious disc which the eye of man now saw for the first time. What could they distinguish at a distance which they could not estimate? Some lengthened bands along the disc, real clouds formed in the midst of a very confined atmosphere, from which emerged not only all the mountains, but also projections of less importance; its circles, its yawning craters, as capriciously placed as on the visible surface. Then immense spaces, no longer arid plains, but real seas, oceans, widely distributed, reflecting on their liquid surface all the dazzling magic of the fires of space; and, lastly, on the surface of the continents, large dark masses, looking like immense forests under the rapid illumination of a brilliance.

Was it an illusion, a mistake, an optical illusion? Could they give a scientific assent to an observation so superficially obtained? Dared they pronounce upon the question of its habitability after so slight a glimpse of the invisible disc?

But the lightnings in space subsided by degrees; its accidental brilliancy died away; the asteroids dispersed in different directions and were extinguished in the distance.

The ether returned to its accustomed darkness; the stars, eclipsed for a moment, again twinkled in the firmament, and the disc, so hastily discerned, was again buried in impenetrable night.

CHAPTER XVI THE SOUTHERN HEMISPHERE

The projectile had just escaped a terrible danger, and a very unforseen one. Who would have thought of such an encounter with meteors? These erring bodies might create serious perils for the travelers. They were to them so many sandbanks upon that sea of ether which, less fortunate than sailors, they could not escape. But did these adventurers complain of space? No, not since nature had given them the splendid sight of a cosmical meteor bursting from expansion, since this inimitable firework, which no Ruggieri could imitate, had lit up for some seconds the invisible glory of the moon. In that flash, continents, seas, and forests had become visible to them. Did an atmosphere, then, bring to this unknown face its life-giving atoms? Questions still insoluble, and forever closed against human curiousity!

It was then half-past three in the afternoon. The projectile was following its curvilinear direction round the moon. Had its course again been altered by the meteor? It was to be feared so. But the projectile must describe a curve unalterably determined by the laws of mechanical reasoning. Barbicane was inclined to believe that this curve would be rather a parabola than a hyperbola. But admitting the parabola, the projectile must quickly have passed through the cone of shadow projected into space opposite the sun. This cone, indeed, is very narrow, the angular diameter of the moon being so little when compared with the diameter of the orb of day; and up to this time the projectile had been floating in this deep shadow. Whatever had been its speed (and it could not have been insignificant), its period of occultation continued. That was evident, but perhaps that would not have been the case in a supposedly rigidly parabolical trajectory— a new problem which tormented Barbicane's brain, imprisoned as he was in a circle of unknowns which he could not unravel.

Neither of the travelers thought of taking an instant's repose. Each one watched for an unexpected fact, which might throw some new light on their uranographic studies. About five o'clock, Michel Ardan distributed, under the name of dinner, some pieces of bread and cold meat, which were quickly swallowed without either of them abandoning their scuttle, the glass of which was incessantly encrusted by the condensation of vapor.

About forty-five minutes past five in the evening, Nicholl, armed with his glass, sighted toward the southern border of the moon, and in the direction followed by the projectile, some bright points cut upon the dark shield of the sky. They looked like a succession of sharp points lengthened into a tremulous line. They were very bright. Such appeared the terminal line of the moon when in one of her octants.

They could not be mistaken. It was no longer a simple meteor. This luminous ridge had neither color nor motion. Nor was it a volcano in eruption. And Barbicane did not hesitate to pronounce upon it.

"The sun!" he exclaimed.

"What! the sun?" answered Nicholl and Michel Ardan.

"Yes, my friends, it is the radiant orb itself lighting up the summit of the mountains situated on the southern borders of the moon. We are evidently nearing the south pole."

"After having passed the north pole," replied Michel. "We have made the circuit of our satellite, then?"

"Yes, my good Michel."

"Then, no more hyperbolas, no more parabolas, no more open curves to fear?"

"No, but a closed curve."

"Which is called——"

"An ellipse. Instead of losing itself in interplanetary space, it is probable that the projectile will describe an elliptical orbit around the moon."

"Indeed!"

"And that it will become *her* satellite."

"Moon of the moon!" cried Michel Ardan.

"Only, I would have you observe, my worthy friend," replied

Barbicane, "that we are none the less lost for that."

"Yes, in another manner, and much more pleasantly," answered the careless Frenchman with his most amiable smile.

CHAPTER XVII TYCHO

At six in the evening the projectile passed the south pole at less than forty miles off, a distance equal to that already reached at the north pole. The elliptical curve was being rigidly carried out.

At this moment the travelers once more entered the blessed rays of the sun. They saw once more those stars which move slowly from east to west. The radiant orb was saluted by a triple hurrah. With its light it also sent heat, which soon pierced the metal walls. The glass resumed its accustomed appearance. The layers of ice melted as if by enchantment; and immediately, for economy's sake, the gas was put out, the air apparatus alone consuming its usual quantity.

"Ah!" said Nicholl, "these rays of heat are good. With what impatience must the Selenites wait the reappearance of the orb of day."

"Yes," replied Michel Ardan, "imbibing as it were the brilliant ether, light and heat, all life is contained in them."

At this moment the bottom of the projectile deviated somewhat from the lunar surface, in order to follow the slightly lengthened elliptical orbit. From this point, had the earth been at the full, Barbicane and his companions could have seen it, but immersed in the sun's irradiation she was quite invisible. Another spectacle attracted their attention, that of the southern part of the moon, brought by the glasses to within 450 yards. They did not again leave the scuttles, and noted every detail of this fantastical continent.

Mounts Doerful and Leibnitz formed two separate groups very near the south pole. The first group extended from the pole to the eighty-fourth parallel, on the eastern part of the orb; the second occupied the eastern border, extending from the 65 ° of latitude to the pole.

On their capriciously formed ridge appeared dazzling sheets, as mentioned by Pere Secchi. With more certainty than the illustrious Roman astronomer, Barbicane was enabled to recognize their nature.

"They are snow," he exclaimed.

"Snow?" repeated Nicholl.

"Yes, Nicholl, snow; the surface of which is deeply frozen. See how they reflect the luminous rays. Cooled lava would never give out such intense reflection. There must then be water, there must be air on the moon. As little as you please, but the fact can no longer be contested." No, it could not be. And if ever Barbicane should see the earth again, his notes will bear witness to this great fact in his selenographic observations.

These mountains of Doerful and Leibnitz rose in the midst of plains of a medium extent, which were bounded by an indefinite succession of circles and annular ramparts. These two chains are the only ones met with in this region of circles. Comparatively but slightly marked, they throw up here and there some sharp points, the highest summit of which attains an altitude of 24,600 feet.

But the projectile was high above all this landscape, and the projections disappeared in the intense brilliancy of the disc. And to the eyes of the travelers there reappeared that original aspect of the lunar landscapes, raw in tone, without gradation of colors, and without degrees of shadow, roughly black and white, from the want of diffusion of light.

But the sight of this desolate world did not fail to captivate them by its very strangeness. They were moving over this region as if they had been borne on the breath of some storm, watching heights defile under their feet, piercing the cavities with their eyes, going down into the rifts, climbing the ramparts, sounding these mysterious holes, and leveling all cracks. But no trace of vegetation, no appearance of cities; nothing but stratification, beds of lava, overflowings polished like immense mirrors, reflecting the sun's rays with overpowering brilliancy. Nothing belonging to a *living* world— everything to a dead world, where avalanches, rolling from the summits of the mountains, would disperse noiselessly at the bottom of the abyss, retaining the motion, but wanting the sound. In any case it was the image of death, without its being possible even to say that life had ever existed there.

Michel Ardan, however, thought he recognized a heap of ruins, to which he drew Barbicane's attention. It was about the 80th parallel, in 30 ° longitude. This heap of stones, rather regularly placed, represented a vast fortress, overlooking a long rift, which in former days had served as a bed to the rivers of prehistorical times. Not far from that, rose to a height of 17,400 feet the annular mountain of Short, equal to the Asiatic Caucasus. Michel Ardan, with his accustomed ardor, maintained "the evidences" of his fortress. Beneath it he discerned the dismantled ramparts of a town; here the still intact arch of a portico, there two or three columns lying under their base; farther on, a succession of arches which must have supported the conduit of an aqueduct; in another part the sunken pillars of a gigantic bridge, run into the thickest parts of the rift. He distinguished all this, but with so much imagination in his glance, and through glasses so fantastical, that we must mistrust his observation. But who could affirm, who would dare to say, that the amiable fellow did not really see that which his two companions would not see?

Moments were too precious to be sacrificed in idle discussion. The selenite city, whether imaginary or not, had already disappeared afar off. The distance of the projectile from the lunar disc was on the increase, and the details of the soil were being lost in a confused jumble. The reliefs, the circles, the craters, and the plains alone remained, and still showed their boundary lines distinctly. At this moment, to the left, lay extended one of the finest circles of lunar orography, one of the curiosities of this continent. It was Newton, which Barbicane recognized without trouble, by referring to the *Mappa Selenographica.*

Newton is situated in exactly 77 ° south latitude, and 16 ° east longitude. It forms an annular crater, the ramparts of which, rising to a height of 21,300 feet, seemed to be impassable.

Barbicane made his companions observe that the height of this mountain above the surrounding plain was far from equaling the depth of its crater. This enormous hole was beyond all measurement, and formed a gloomy abyss, the bottom of which the sun's rays could never reach. There, according to Humboldt, reigns utter darkness, which the light of the sun and the earth cannot break. Mythologists could well have made it the mouth of hell.

"Newton," said Barbicane, "is the most perfect type of these annular mountains, of which the earth possesses no sample. They prove that the moon's formation, by means of cooling, is due to violent causes; for while, under the pressure of internal fires the reliefs rise to considerable height, the depths withdraw far below the lunar level."

"I do not dispute the fact," replied Michel Ardan.

Some minutes after passing Newton, the projectile directly overlooked the annular mountains of Moret. It skirted at some distance the summits of Blancanus, and at about half-past seven in the evening reached the circle of Clavius.

This circle, one of the most remarkable of the disc, is situated in 58 ° south latitude, and 15 ° east longitude. Its height is estimated at 22,950 feet. The travelers, at a distance of twenty-four miles (reduced to four by their glasses) could admire this vast crater in its entirety.

"Terrestrial volcanoes," said Barbicane, "are but mole-hills compared with those of the moon. Measuring the old craters formed by the first eruptions of Vesuvius and Etna, we find them little more than three miles in breadth. In France the circle of Cantal measures six miles across; at Ceyland the circle of the island is forty miles, which is considered the largest on the globe. What are these diameters against that of Clavius, which we overlook at this moment?"

"What is its breadth?" asked Nicholl.

"It is 150 miles," replied Barbicane. "This circle is certainly the most important on the moon, but many others measure 150, 100, or 75 miles."

"Ah! my friends," exclaimed Michel, "can you picture to yourselves what this now peaceful orb of night must have been when its craters, filled with thunderings, vomited at the same time smoke and tongues of flame. What a wonderful spectacle then, and now what decay! This moon is nothing more than a thin carcase of fireworks, whose squibs, rockets, serpents, and suns, after a superb brilliancy, have left but sadly broken cases. Who can say the cause, the reason, the motive force of these cataclysms?"

Barbicane was not listening to Michel Ardan; he was contemplating these ramparts of Clavius, formed by large mountains spread over several miles. At the bottom of the immense cavity burrowed hundreds of small extinguished craters, riddling the soil like a colander, and overlooked by a peak 15,000 feet high.

Around the plain appeared desolate. Nothing so arid as these reliefs, nothing so sad as these ruins of mountains, and (if we may so express ourselves) these fragments of peaks and mountains which strewed the soil. The satellite seemed to have burst at this spot.

The projectile was still advancing, and this movement did not subside. Circles, craters, and uprooted mountains succeeded each other incessantly. No more plains; no more seas. A never ending Switzerland and Norway. And lastly, in the canter of this region of crevasses, the most splendid mountain on the lunar disc, the dazzling Tycho, in which posterity will ever preserve the name of the illustrious Danish astronomer.

In observing the full moon in a cloudless sky no one has failed to remark this brilliant point of the southern hemisphere. Michel Ardan used every metaphor that his imagination could supply to designate it by. To him this Tycho was a focus of light, a center of irradiation, a crater vomiting rays. It was the tire of a brilliant wheel, an *asteria* enclosing the disc with its silver tentacles, an enormous eye filled with flames, a glory carved for Pluto's head, a star launched by the Creator's hand, and crushed against the face of the moon!

Tycho forms such a concentration of light that the inhabitants of the earth can see it without glasses, though at a distance of 240,000 miles! Imagine, then, its intensity to the eye of observers placed at a distance of only fifty miles! Seen through this pure ether, its brilliancy was so intolerable that Barbicane and his friends were obliged to blacken their glasses with the gas smoke before they could bear the splendor. Then silent, scarcely uttering an interjection of admiration, they gazed, they contemplated. All their feelings, all their impressions, were concentrated in that look, as under any violent emotion all life is concentrated at the heart.

Tycho belongs to the system of radiating mountains, like Aristarchus and Copernicus; but it is of all the most complete and decided, showing unquestionably the frightful volcanic action to which the formation of the moon is due. Tycho is situated in 43 ° south latitude, and 12 ° east longitude. Its center is occupied by a crater fifty miles broad. It assumes a slightly elliptical form, and is surrounded by an enclosure of annular ramparts, which on the east and west overlook the outer plain from a height of 15,000 feet. It is a group of Mont Blancs, placed round one common center and crowned by radiating beams.

What this incomparable mountain really is, with all the projections converging toward it, and the interior excrescences of its crater, photography itself could never represent. Indeed, it is during the full moon that Tycho is seen in all its splendor. Then all shadows disappear, the foreshortening of perspective disappears, and all proofs become white— a disagreeable fact: for this strange region would have been marvelous if reproduced with photographic exactness. It is but a group of hollows, craters, circles, a network of crests; then, as far as the eye could see, a whole volcanic network cast upon this encrusted soil. One can then understand that the bubbles of this central eruption have kept their first form. Crystallized by cooling, they have stereotyped that aspect which the moon formerly presented when under the Plutonian forces.

The distance which separated the travelers from the annular summits of Tycho was not so great but that they could catch the principal details. Even on the causeway forming the fortifications of Tycho, the mountains hanging on to the interior and exterior sloping flanks rose in stories like gigantic terraces. They appeared to be higher by 300 or 400 feet to the west than to the east. No system of terrestrial encampment could equal these natural fortifications. A town built at the bottom of this circular cavity would have been utterly inaccessible.

Inaccessible and wonderfully extended over this soil covered with picturesque projections! Indeed, nature had not left the bottom of this crater flat and empty. It possessed its own peculiar orography, a mountainous system, making it a world in itself. The travelers could distinguish clearly cones, central hills, remarkable positions of the soil, naturally placed to receive the *chefs-d'oeuvre* of Selenite architecture. There was marked out the place for a temple, here the ground of a forum, on this spot the plan of a palace, in another the plateau for a citadel; the whole overlooked by a central mountain of 1,500 feet. A vast circle, in which ancient Rome could have been held in its entirety ten times over.

"Ah!" exclaimed Michel Ardan, enthusiastic at the sight; "what a grand town might be constructed within that ring of mountains! A quiet city, a peaceful refuge, beyond all human misery. How calm and isolated those misanthropes, those haters of humanity might live there, and all who have a distaste for social life!"

"All! It would be too small for them," replied Barbicane simply.

CHAPTER XVIII GRAVE QUESTIONS

But the projectile had passed the *enceinte* of Tycho, and Barbicane and his two companions watched with scrupulous attention the brilliant rays which the celebrated mountain shed so curiously over the horizon.

What was this radiant glory? What geological phenomenon had designed these ardent beams? This question occupied Barbicane's mind.

Under his eyes ran in all directions luminous furrows, raised at the edges and concave in the center, some twelve miles, others thirty miles broad. These brilliant trains extended in some places to within 600 miles of Tycho, and seemed to cover, particularly toward the east, the northeast and the north, the half of the southern hemisphere. One of these jets extended as far as the circle of Neander, situated on the 40th meridian. Another, by a slight curve, furrowed the "Sea of Nectar," breaking against the chain of Pyrenees, after a circuit of 800 miles. Others, toward the west, covered the "Sea of Clouds" and the "Sea of Humors" with a luminous network. What was the origin of these sparkling rays, which shone on the plains as well as on the reliefs, at whatever height they might be? All started from a common center, the crater of Tycho. They sprang from him. Herschel attributed their brilliancy to currents of lava congealed by the cold; an opinion, however, which has not been generally adopted. Other astronomers have seen in these inexplicable rays a kind of moraines, rows of erratic blocks, which had been thrown up at the period of Tycho's formation.

"And why not?" asked Nicholl of Barbicane, who was relating and rejecting these different opinions.

"Because the regularity of these luminous lines, and the violence necessary to carry volcanic matter to such distances, is inexplicable."

"Eh! by Jove!" replied Michel Ardan, "it seems easy enough to me to explain the origin of these rays."

"Indeed?" said Barbicane.

"Indeed," continued Michel. "It is enough to say that it is a vast star, similar to that produced by a ball or a stone thrown at a square of glass!"

"Well!" replied Barbicane, smiling. "And what hand would be powerful enough to throw a ball to give such a shock as that?"

"The hand is not necessary," answered Nicholl, not at all confounded; "and as to the stone, let us suppose it to be a comet."

"Ah! those much-abused comets!" exclaimed Barbicane. "My brave Michel, your explanation is not bad; but your comet is useless. The shock which produced that rent must have some from the inside of the star. A violent contraction of the lunar crust, while cooling, might suffice to imprint this gigantic star."

"A contraction! something like a lunar stomach-ache." said
Michel Ardan.

"Besides," added Barbicane, "this opinion is that of an English savant, Nasmyth, and it seems to me to sufficiently explain the radiation of these mountains."

"That Nasmyth was no fool!" replied Michel.

Long did the travelers, whom such a sight could never weary, admire the splendors of Tycho. Their projectile, saturated with luminous gleams in the double irradiation of sun and moon, must have appeared like an incandescent globe. They had passed suddenly from excessive cold to intense heat. Nature was thus preparing them to become Selenites. Become Selenites! That idea brought up once more the question of the habitability of the moon. After what they had seen, could the travelers solve it? Would they decide for or against it? Michel Ardan persuaded his two friends to form an opinion, and asked them directly if they thought that men and animals were represented in the lunar world.

"I think that we can answer," said Barbicane; "but according to my idea the question ought not to be put in that form. I ask it to be put differently."

"Put it your own way," replied Michel.

"Here it is," continued Barbicane. "The problem is a double one, and requires a double solution. Is the moon *habitable*? Has the moon ever been *inhabitable*?"

"Good!" replied Nicholl. "First let us see whether the moon is habitable."

"To tell the truth, I know nothing about it," answered Michel.

"And I answer in the negative," continued Barbicane. "In her actual state, with her surrounding atmosphere certainly very much reduced, her seas for the most part dried up, her insufficient supply of water restricted, vegetation, sudden alternations of cold and heat, her days and nights of 354 hours— the moon does not seem habitable to me, nor does she seem propitious to animal development, nor sufficient for the wants of existence as we understand it."

"Agreed," replied Nicholl. "But is not the moon habitable for creatures differently organized from ourselves?"

"That question is more difficult to answer, but I will try; and I ask Nicholl if *motion* appears to him to be a necessary result of *life*, whatever be its organization?"

"Without a doubt!" answered Nicholl.

"Then, my worthy companion, I would answer that we have observed the lunar continent at a distance of 500 yards at most, and that nothing seemed to us to move on the moon's surface. The presence of any kind of life would have been betrayed by its attendant marks, such as divers buildings, and even by ruins. And what have we seen? Everywhere and always the geological works of nature, never the work of man. If, then, there exist representatives of the animal kingdom on the moon, they must have fled to those unfathomable cavities which the eye cannot reach; which I cannot admit, for they must have left traces of their passage on those plains which the atmosphere must cover, however slightly raised it may be. These traces are nowhere visible. There remains but one hypothesis, that of a living race to which motion, which is life, is foreign."

"One might as well say, living creatures which do not live," replied Michel.

"Just so," said Barbicane, "which for us has no meaning."

"Then we may form our opinion?" said Michel.

"Yes," replied Nicholl.

"Very well," continued Michel Ardan, "the Scientific Commission assembled in the projectile of the Gun Club, after having founded their argument on facts recently observed, decide unanimously upon the question of the habitability of the moon— `*No!* the moon is not habitable.'"

This decision was consigned by President Barbicane to his notebook, where the process of the sitting of the 6th of December may be seen.

"Now," said Nicholl, "let us attack the second question, an indispensable complement of the first. I ask the honorable commission, if the moon is not habitable, has she ever been inhabited, Citizen Barbicane?"

"My friends," replied Barbicane, "I did not undertake this journey in order to form an opinion on the past habitability of our satellite; but I will add that our personal observations only confirm me in this opinion. I believe, indeed I affirm, that the moon has been inhabited by a human race organized like our own; that she has produced animals anatomically formed like the terrestrial animals: but I add that these races, human and animal, have had their day, and are now forever extinct!"

"Then," asked Michel, "the moon must be older than the earth?"

"No!" said Barbicane decidedly, "but a world which has grown old quicker, and whose formation and deformation have been more rapid. Relatively, the organizing force of matter has been much more violent in the interior of the moon than in the interior of the terrestrial globe. The actual state of this cracked, twisted, and burst disc abundantly proves this. The moon and the earth were nothing but gaseous masses originally. These gases have passed into a liquid state under different influences, and the solid masses have been formed later. But most certainly our sphere was still gaseous or liquid, when the moon was solidified by cooling, and had become habitable."

"I believe it," said Nicholl.

"Then," continued Barbicane, "an atmosphere surrounded it, the waters contained within this gaseous envelope could not evaporate. Under the influence of air, water, light, solar heat, and central heat, vegetation took possession of the continents prepared to receive it, and certainly life showed itself about this period, for nature does not expend herself in vain; and a world so wonderfully formed for habitation must necessarily be inhabited."

"But," said Nicholl, "many phenomena inherent in our satellite might cramp the expansion of the animal and vegetable kingdom. For example, its days and nights of 354 hours?"

"At the terrestrial poles they last six months," said Michel.

"An argument of little value, since the poles are not inhabited."

"Let us observe, my friends," continued Barbicane, "that if in the actual state of the moon its long nights and long days created differences of temperature insupportable to organization, it was not so at the historical period of time. The atmosphere enveloped the disc with a fluid mantle; vapor deposited itself in the shape of clouds; this natural screen tempered the ardor of the solar rays, and retained the nocturnal radiation. Light, like heat, can diffuse itself in the air; hence an equality between the influences which no longer exists, now that atmosphere has almost entirely disappeared. And now I am going to astonish you."

"Astonish us?" said Michel Ardan.

"I firmly believe that at the period when the moon was inhabited, the nights and days did not last 354 hours!"

"And why?" asked Nicholl quickly.

"Because most probably then the rotary motion of the moon upon her axis was not equal to her revolution, an equality which presents each part of her disc during fifteen days to the action of the solar rays."

"Granted," replied Nicholl, "but why should not these two motions have been equal, as they are really so?"

"Because that equality has only been determined by terrestrial attraction. And who can say that this attraction was powerful enough to alter the motion of the moon at that period when the earth was still fluid?"

"Just so," replied Nicholl; "and who can say that the moon has always been a satellite of the earth?"

"And who can say," exclaimed Michel Ardan, "that the moon did not exist before the earth?"

Their imaginations carried them away into an indefinite field of hypothesis. Barbicane sought to restrain them.

"Those speculations are too high," said he; "problems utterly insoluble. Do not let us enter upon them. Let us only admit the insufficiency of the primordial attraction; and then by the inequality of the two motions of rotation and revolution, the days and nights could have succeeded each other on the moon as they succeed each other on the earth. Besides, even without these conditions, life was possible."

"And so," asked Michel Ardan, "humanity has disappeared from the moon?"

"Yes," replied Barbicane, "after having doubtless remained persistently for millions of centuries; by degrees the atmosphere becoming rarefied, the disc became uninhabitable, as the terrestrial globe will one day become by cooling."

"By cooling?"

"Certainly," replied Barbicane; "as the internal fires became extinguished, and the incandescent matter concentrated itself, the lunar crust cooled. By degrees the consequences of these phenomena showed themselves in the disappearance of organized beings, and by the disappearance of vegetation. Soon the atmosphere was rarefied, probably withdrawn by terrestrial attraction; then aerial departure of respirable air, and disappearance of water by means of evaporation. At this period the moon becoming uninhabitable, was no longer inhabited. It was a dead world, such as we see it to-day."

"And you say that the same fate is in store for the earth?"

"Most probably."

"But when?"

"When the cooling of its crust shall have made it uninhabitable."

"And have they calculated the time which our unfortunate sphere will take to cool?"

"Certainly."

"And you know these calculations?"

"Perfectly."

"But speak, then, my clumsy savant," exclaimed Michel Ardan, "for you make me boil with impatience!"

"Very well, my good Michel," replied Barbicane quietly; "we know what diminution of temperature the earth undergoes in the lapse of a century. And according to certain calculations, this mean temperature will after a period of 400,000 years, be brought down to zero!"

"Four hundred thousand years!" exclaimed Michel. "Ah! I breathe again. Really I was frightened to hear you; I imagined that we had not more than 50,000 years to live."

Barbicane and Nicholl could not help laughing at their companion's uneasiness. Then Nicholl, who wished to end the discussion, put the second question, which had just been considered again.

"Has the moon been inhabited?" he asked.

The answer was unanimously in the affirmative. But during this discussion, fruitful in somewhat hazardous theories, the projectile was rapidly leaving the moon: the lineaments faded away from the travelers' eyes, mountains were confused in the distance; and of all the wonderful, strange, and fantastical form of the earth's satellite, there soon remained nothing but the imperishable remembrance.

CHAPTER XIX A STRUGGLE AGAINST THE IMPOSSIBLE

For a long time Barbicane and his companions looked silently and sadly upon that world which they had only seen from a distance, as Moses saw the land of Canaan, and which they were leaving without a possibility of ever returning to it. The projectile's position with regard to the moon had altered, and the base was now turned to the earth.

This change, which Barbicane verified, did not fail to surprise them. If the projectile was to gravitate round the satellite in an elliptical orbit, why was not its heaviest part turned toward it, as the moon turns hers to the earth? That was a difficult point.

In watching the course of the projectile they could see that on leaving the moon it followed a course analogous to that traced in approaching her. It was describing a very long ellipse, which would most likely extend to the point of equal attraction, where the influences of the earth and its satellite are neutralized.

Such was the conclusion which Barbicane very justly drew from facts already observed, a conviction which his two friends shared with him.

"And when arrived at this dead point, what will become of us?" asked Michel Ardan.

"We don't know," replied Barbicane.

"But one can draw some hypotheses, I suppose?"

"Two," answered Barbicane; "either the projectile's speed will be insufficient, and it will remain forever immovable on this line of double attraction——"

"I prefer the other hypothesis, whatever it may be," interrupted Michel.

"Or," continued Barbicane, "its speed will be sufficient, and it will continue its elliptical course, to gravitate forever around the orb of night."

"A revolution not at all consoling," said Michel, "to pass to the state of humble servants to a moon whom we are accustomed to look upon as our own handmaid. So that is the fate in store for us?"

Neither Barbicane nor Nicholl answered.

"You do not answer," continued Michel impatiently.

"There is nothing to answer," said Nicholl.

"Is there nothing to try?"

"No," answered Barbicane. "Do you pretend to fight against the impossible?"

"Why not? Do one Frenchman and two Americans shrink from such a word?"

"But what would you do?"

"Subdue this motion which is bearing us away."

"Subdue it?"

"Yes," continued Michel, getting animated, "or else alter it, and employ it to the accomplishment of our own ends."

"And how?"

"That is your affair. If artillerymen are not masters of their projectile they are not artillerymen. If the projectile is to command the gunner, we had better ram the gunner into the gun. My faith! fine savants! who do not know what is to become of us after inducing me——"

"Inducing you!" cried Barbicane and Nicholl. "Inducing you!

What do you mean by that?"

"No recrimination," said Michel. "I do not complain, the trip has pleased me, and the projectile agrees with me; but let us do all that is humanly possible to do the fall somewhere, even if only on the moon."

"We ask no better, my worthy Michel," replied Barbicane, "but means fail us."

"We cannot alter the motion of the projectile?"

"No."

"Nor diminish its speed?"

"No."

"Not even by lightening it, as they lighten an overloaded vessel?"

"What would you throw out?" said Nicholl. "We have no ballast on board; and indeed it seems to me that if lightened it would go much quicker."

"Slower."

"Quicker."

"Neither slower nor quicker," said Barbicane, wishing to make his two friends agree; "for we float is space, and must no longer consider specific weight."

"Very well," cried Michel Ardan in a decided voice; "then their remains but one thing to do."

"What is it?" asked Nicholl.

"Breakfast," answered the cool, audacious Frenchman, who always brought up this solution at the most difficult juncture.

In any case, if this operation had no influence on the projectile's course, it could at least be tried without inconvenience, and even with success from a stomachic point of view. Certainly Michel had none but good ideas.

They breakfasted then at two in the morning; the hour mattered little. Michel served his usual repast, crowned by a glorious bottle drawn from his private cellar. If ideas did not crowd on their brains, we must despair of the Chambertin of 1853. The repast finished, observation began again. Around the projectile, at an invariable distance, were the objects which had been thrown out. Evidently, in its translatory motion round the moon, it had not passed through any atmosphere, for the specific weight of these different objects would have checked their relative speed.

On the side of the terrestrial sphere nothing was to be seen. The earth was but a day old, having been new the night before at twelve; and two days must elapse before its crescent, freed from the solar rays, would serve as a clock to the Selenites, as in its rotary movement each of its points after twenty-four hours repasses the same lunar meridian.

On the moon's side the sight was different; the orb shone in all her splendor amid innumerable constellations, whose purity could not be troubled by her rays. On the disc, the plains were already returning to the dark tint which is seen from the earth. The other part of the nimbus remained brilliant, and in the midst of this general brilliancy Tycho shone prominently like a sun.

Barbicane had no means of estimating the projectile's speed, but reasoning showed that it must uniformly decrease, according to the laws of mechanical reasoning. Having admitted that the projectile was describing an orbit around the moon, this orbit must necessarily be elliptical; science proves that it must be so. No motive body circulating round an attracting body fails in this law. Every orbit described in space is elliptical. And why should the projectile of the Gun Club escape this natural arrangement? In elliptical orbits, the attracting body always occupies one of the foci; so that at one moment the satellite is nearer, and at another farther from the orb around which it gravitates. When the earth is nearest the sun she is in her perihelion; and in her aphelion at the farthest point. Speaking of the moon, she is nearest to the earth in her perigee, and farthest from it in her apogee. To use analogous expressions, with which the astronomers' language is enriched, if the projectile remains as a satellite of the moon, we must say that it is in its "aposelene" at its farthest point, and in its "periselene" at its nearest. In the latter case, the projectile would attain its maximum of speed; and in the former its minimum. It was evidently moving toward its aposelenitical point; and Barbicane had reason to think that its speed would decrease up to this point, and then increase by degrees as it neared the moon. This speed would even become *nil*, if this point joined that of equal attraction. Barbicane studied the consequences of these different situations, and thinking what inference he could draw from them, when he was roughly disturbed by a cry from Michel Ardan.

"By Jove!" he exclaimed, "I must admit we are down-right simpletons!"

"I do not say we are not," replied Barbicane; "but why?"

"Because we have a very simple means of checking this speed which is bearing us from the moon, and we do not use it!"

"And what is the means?"

"To use the recoil contained in our rockets."

"Done!" said Nicholl.

"We have not used this force yet," said Barbicane, "it is true, but we will do so."

"When?" asked Michel.

"When the time comes. Observe, my friends, that in the position occupied by the projectile, an oblique position with regard to the lunar disc, our rockets, in slightly altering its direction, might turn it from the moon instead of drawing it nearer?"

"Just so," replied Michel.

"Let us wait, then. By some inexplicable influence, the projectile is turning its base toward the earth. It is probable that at the point of equal attraction, its conical cap will be directed rigidly toward the moon; at that moment we may hope that its speed will be *nil*; then will be the moment to act, and with the influence of our rockets we may perhaps provoke a fall directly on the surface of the lunar disc."

"Bravo!" said Michel. "What we did not do, what we could not do on our first passage at the dead point, because the projectile was then endowed with too great a speed."

"Very well reasoned," said Nicholl.

"Let us wait patiently," continued Barbicane. "Putting every chance on our side, and after having so much despaired, I may say I think we shall gain our end."

This conclusion was a signal for Michel Ardan's hips and hurrahs. And none of the audacious boobies remembered the question that they themselves had solved in the negative. No! the moon is not inhabited; no! the moon is probably not habitable. And yet they were going to try everything to reach her.

One single question remained to be solved. At what precise moment the projectile would reach the point of equal attraction, on which the travelers must play their last card. In order to calculate this to within a few seconds, Barbicane had only to refer to his notes, and to reckon the different heights taken on the lunar parallels. Thus the time necessary to travel over the distance between the dead point and the south pole would be equal to the distance separating the north pole from the dead point. The hours representing the time traveled over were carefully noted, and the calculation was easy. Barbicane found that this point would be reached at one in the morning on the night of the 7th-8th of December. So that, if nothing interfered with its course, it would reach the given point in twenty-two hours.

The rockets had primarily been placed to check the fall of the projectile upon the moon, and now they were going to employ them for a directly contrary purpose. In any case they were ready, and they had only to wait for the moment to set fire to them.

"Since there is nothing else to be done," said Nicholl, "I make a proposition."

"What is it?" asked Barbicane.

"I propose to go to sleep."

"What a motion!" exclaimed Michel Ardan.

"It is forty hours since we closed our eyes," said Nicholl.

"Some hours of sleep will restore our strength."

"Never," interrupted Michel.

"Well," continued Nicholl, "every one to his taste; I shall go to sleep." And stretching himself on the divan, he soon snored like a forty-eight pounder.

"That Nicholl has a good deal of sense," said Barbicane; "presently I shall follow his example." Some moments after his continued bass supported the captain's baritone.

"Certainly," said Michel Ardan, finding himself alone, "these practical people have sometimes most opportune ideas."

And with his long legs stretched out, and his great arms folded under his head, Michel slept in his turn.

But this sleep could be neither peaceful nor lasting, the minds of these three men were too much occupied, and some hours after, about seven in the morning, all three were on foot at the same instant.

The projectile was still leaving the moon, and turning its conical part more and more toward her.

An explicable phenomenon, but one which happily served

Barbicane's ends.

Seventeen hours more, and the moment for action would have arrived.

The day seemed long. However bold the travelers might be, they were greatly impressed by the approach of that moment which would decide all— either precipitate their fall on to the moon, or forever chain them in an immutable orbit. They counted the hours as they passed too slow for their wish; Barbicane and Nicholl were obstinately plunged in their calculations, Michel going and coming between the narrow walls, and watching that impassive moon with a longing eye.

At times recollections of the earth crossed their minds. They saw once more their friends of the Gun Club, and the dearest of all, J. T. Maston. At that moment, the honorable secretary must be filling his post on the Rocky Mountains. If he could see the projectile through the glass of his gigantic telescope, what would he think? After seeing it disappear behind the moon's south pole, he would see them reappear by the north pole! They must therefore be a satellite of a satellite! Had J. T. Maston given this unexpected news to the world? Was this the *denouement* of this great enterprise?

But the day passed without incident. The terrestrial midnight arrived. The 8th of December was beginning. One hour more, and the point of equal attraction would be reached. What speed would then animate the projectile? They could not estimate it. But no error could vitiate Barbicane's calculations. At one in the morning this speed ought to be and would be *nil*.

Besides, another phenomenon would mark the projectile's stopping-point on the neutral line. At that spot the two attractions, lunar and terrestrial, would be annulled. Objects would "weigh" no more. This singular fact, which had surprised Barbicane and his companions so much in going, would be repeated on their return under the very same condiconditions. At this precise moment they must act.

Already the projectile's conical top was sensibly turned toward the lunar disc, presented in such a way as to utilize the whole of the recoil produced by the pressure of the rocket apparatus. The chances were in favor of the travelers. If its speed was utterly annulled on this dead point, a decided movement toward the moon would suffice, however slight, to determine its fall.

"Five minutes to one," said Nicholl.

"All is ready," replied Michel Ardan, directing a lighted match to the flame of the gas.

"Wait!" said Barbicane, holding his chronometer in his hand.

At that moment weight had no effect. The travelers felt in themselves the entire disappearance of it. They were very near the neutral point, if they did not touch it.

"One o'clock," said Barbicane.

Michel Ardan applied the lighted match to a train in communication with the rockets. No detonation was heard in the inside, for there was no air. But, through the scuttles, Barbicane saw a prolonged smoke, the flames of which were immediately extinguished.

The projectile sustained a certain shock, which was sensibly felt in the interior.

The three friends looked and listened without speaking, and scarcely breathing. One might have heard the beating of their hearts amid this perfect silence.

"Are we falling?" asked Michel Ardan, at length.

"No," said Nicholl, "since the bottom of the projectile is not turning to the lunar disc!"

At this moment, Barbicane, quitting his scuttle, turned to his two companions. He was frightfully pale, his forehead wrinkled, and his lips contracted.

"We are falling!" said he.

"Ah!" cried Michel Ardan, "on to the moon?"

"On to the earth!"

"The devil!" exclaimed Michel Ardan, adding philosophically, "well, when we came into this projectile we were very doubtful as to the ease with which we should get out of it!"

And now this fearful fall had begun. The speed retained had borne the projectile beyond the dead point. The explosion of the rockets could not divert its course. This speed in going had carried it over the neutral line, and in returning had done the same thing. The laws of physics condemned it *to pass through every point which it had already gone through.* It was a terrible fall, from a height of 160,000 miles, and no springs to break it. According to the laws of gunnery, the projectile must strike the earth with a speed equal to that with which it left the mouth of the Columbiad, a speed of 16,000 yards in the last second.

But to give some figures of comparison, it has been reckoned that an object thrown from the top of the towers of Notre Dame, the height of which is only 200 feet, will arrive on the pavement at a speed of 240 miles per hour. Here the projectile must strike the earth with a speed of 115,200 miles per hour.

"We are lost!" said Michel coolly.

"Very well! if we die," answered Barbicane, with a sort of religious enthusiasm, "the results of our travels will be magnificently spread. It is His own secret that God will tell us! In the other life the soul will want to know nothing, either of machines or engines! It will be identified with eternal wisdom!"

"In fact," interrupted Michel Ardan, "the whole of the other world may well console us for the loss of that inferior orb called the moon!"

Barbicane crossed his arms on his breast, with a motion of sublime resignation, saying at the same time:

"The will of heaven be done!"

CHAPTER XX THE SOUNDINGS OF THE SUSQUEHANNA

Well, lieutenant, and our soundings?"

"I think, sir, that the operation is nearing its completion," replied Lieutenant Bronsfield. "But who would have thought of finding such a depth so near in shore, and only 200 miles from the American coast?"

"Certainly, Bronsfield, there is a great depression," said Captain Blomsberry. "In this spot there is a submarine valley worn by Humboldt's current, which skirts the coast of America as far as the Straits of Magellan."

"These great depths," continued the lieutenant, "are not favorable for laying telegraphic cables. A level bottom, like that supporting the American cable between Valentia and Newfoundland, is much better."

"I agree with you, Bronsfield. With your permission, lieutenant, where are we now?"

"Sir, at this moment we have 3,508 fathoms of line out, and the ball which draws the sounding lead has not yet touched the bottom; for if so, it would have come up of itself."

"Brook's apparatus is very ingenious," said Captain Blomsberry; "it gives us very exact soundings."

"Touch!" cried at this moment one of the men at the forewheel, who was superintending the operation.

The captain and the lieutenant mounted the quarterdeck.

"What depth have we?" asked the captain.

"Three thousand six hundred and twenty-seven fathoms," replied the lieutenant, entering it in his notebook.

"Well, Bronsfield," said the captain, "I will take down the result. Now haul in the sounding line. It will be the work of some hours. In that time the engineer can light the furnaces, and we shall be ready to start as soon as you have finished. It is ten o'clock, and with your permission, lieutenant, I will turn in."

"Do so, sir; do so!" replied the lieutenant obligingly.

The captain of the Susquehanna, as brave a man as need be, and the humble servant of his officers, returned to his cabin, took a brandy-grog, which earned for the steward no end of praise, and turned in, not without having complimented his servant upon his making beds, and slept a peaceful sleep.

It was then ten at night. The eleventh day of the month of December was drawing to a close in a magnificent night.

The Susquehanna, a corvette of 500 horse-power, of the United States navy, was occupied in taking soundings in the Pacific Ocean about 200 miles off the American coast, following that long peninsula which stretches down the coast of Mexico.

The wind had dropped by degrees. There was no disturbance in the air. The pennant hung motionless from the maintop-gallant- mast truck.

Captain Jonathan Blomsberry (cousin-german of Colonel Blomsberry, one of the most ardent supporters of the Gun Club, who had married an aunt of the captain and daughter of an honorable Kentucky merchant)— Captain Blomsberry could not have wished for finer weather in which to bring to a close his delicate operations of sounding. His corvette had not even felt the great tempest, which by sweeping away the groups of clouds on the Rocky Mountains, had allowed them to observe the course of the famous projectile.

Everything went well, and with all the fervor of a Presbyterian, he did not forget to thank heaven for it. The series of soundings taken by the Susquehanna, had for its aim the finding of a favorable spot for the laying of a submarine cable to connect the Hawaiian Islands with the coast of America.

It was a great undertaking, due to the instigation of a powerful company. Its managing director, the intelligent Cyrus Field, purposed even covering all the islands of Oceanica with a vast electrical network, an immense enterprise, and one worthy of American genius.

To the corvette Susquehanna had been confided the first operations of sounding. It was on the night of the 11th-12th of December, she was in exactly 27 ° 7' north latitude, and 41 ° 37' west longitude, on the meridian of Washington.

The moon, then in her last quarter, was beginning to rise above the horizon.

After the departure of Captain Blomsberry, the lieutenant and some officers were standing together on the poop. On the appearance of the moon, their thoughts turned to that orb which the eyes of a whole hemisphere were contemplating. The best naval glasses could not have discovered the projectile wandering around its hemisphere, and yet all were pointed toward that brilliant disc which millions of eyes were looking at at the same moment.

"They have been gone ten days," said Lieutenant Bronsfield at last. "What has become of them?"

"They have arrived, lieutenant," exclaimed a young midshipman, "and they are doing what all travelers do when they arrive in a new country, taking a walk!"

"Oh! I am sure of that, if you tell me so, my young friend," said Lieutenant Bronsfield, smiling.

"But," continued another officer, "their arrival cannot be doubted. The projectile was to reach the moon when full on the 5th at midnight. We are now at the 11th of December, which makes six days. And in six times twenty-four hours, without darkness, one would have time to settle comfortably. I fancy I see my brave countrymen encamped at the bottom of some valley, on the borders of a Selenite stream, near a projectile half-buried by its fall amid volcanic rubbish, Captain Nicholl beginning his leveling operations, President Barbicane writing out his notes, and Michel Ardan embalming the lunar solitudes with the perfume of his——"

"Yes! it must be so, it is so!" exclaimed the young midshipman, worked up to a pitch of enthusiasm by this ideal description of his superior officer.

"I should like to believe it," replied the lieutenant, who was quite unmoved. "Unfortunately direct news from the lunar world is still wanting."

"Beg pardon, lieutenant," said the midshipman, "but cannot
President Barbicane write?"

A burst of laughter greeted this answer.

"No letters!" continued the young man quickly. "The postal administration has something to see to there."

"Might it not be the telegraphic service that is at fault?" asked one of the officers ironically.

"Not necessarily," replied the midshipman, not at all confused. "But it is very easy to set up a graphic communication with the earth."

"And how?"

"By means of the telescope at Long's Peak. You know it brings the moon to within four miles of the Rocky Mountains, and that it shows objects on its surface of only nine feet in diameter. Very well; let our industrious friends construct a giant alphabet; let them write words three fathoms long, and sentences three miles long, and then they can send us news of themselves."

The young midshipman, who had a certain amount of imagination, was loudly applauded; Lieutenant Bronsfield allowing that the idea was possible, but observing that if by these means they could receive news from the lunar world they could not send any from the terrestrial, unless the Selenites had instruments fit for taking distant observations at their disposal.

"Evidently," said one of the officers; "but what has become of the travelers? what they have done, what they have seen, that above all must interest us. Besides, if the experiment has succeeded (which I do not doubt), they will try it again. The Columbiad is still sunk in the soil of Florida. It is now only a question of powder and shot; and every time the moon is at her zenith a cargo of visitors may be sent to her."

"It is clear," replied Lieutenant Bronsfield, "that J. T. Maston will one day join his friends."

"If he will have me," cried the midshipman, "I am ready!"

"Oh! volunteers will not be wanting," answered Bronsfield; "and if it were allowed, half of the earth's inhabitants would emigrate to the moon!"

This conversation between the officers of the Susquehanna was kept up until nearly one in the morning. We cannot say what blundering systems were broached, what inconsistent theories advanced by these bold spirits. Since Barbicane's attempt, nothing seemed impossible to the Americans. They had already designed an expedition, not only of savants, but of a whole colony toward the Selenite borders, and a complete army, consisting of infantry, artillery, and cavalry, to conquer the lunar world.

At one in the morning, the hauling in of the sounding-line was not yet completed; 1,670 fathoms were still out, which would entail some hours' work. According to the commander's orders, the fires had been lighted, and steam was being got up. The Susquehanna could have started that very instant.

At that moment (it was seventeen minutes past one in the morning) Lieutenant Bronsfield was preparing to leave the watch and return to his cabin, when his attention was attracted by a distant hissing noise. His comrades and himself first thought that this hissing was caused by the letting off of steam; but lifting their heads, they found that the noise was produced in the highest regions of the air. They had not time to question each other before the hissing became frightfully intense, and suddenly there appeared to their dazzled eyes an enormous meteor, ignited by the rapidity of its course and its friction through the atmospheric strata.

This fiery mass grew larger to their eyes, and fell, with the noise of thunder, upon the bowsprit, which it smashed close to the stem, and buried itself in the waves with a deafening roar!

A few feet nearer, and the Susquehanna would have foundered with all on board!

At this instant Captain Blomsberry appeared, half-dressed, and rushing on to the forecastle-deck, whither all the officers had hurried, exclaimed, "With your permission, gentlemen, what has happened?"

And the midshipman, making himself as it were the echo of the body, cried, "Commander, it is `they' come back again!"

CHAPTER XXI J. T. MASTON RECALLED

"It is `they' come back again!" the young midshipman had said, and every one had understood him. No one doubted but that the meteor was the projectile of the Gun Club. As to the travelers which it enclosed, opinions were divided regarding their fate.

"They are dead!" said one.

"They are alive!" said another; "the crater is deep, and the shock was deadened."

"But they must have wanted air," continued a third speaker; "they must have died of suffocation."

"Burned!" replied a fourth; "the projectile was nothing but an incandescent mass as it crossed the atmosphere."

"What does it matter!" they exclaimed unanimously; "living or dead, we must pull them out!"

But Captain Blomsberry had assembled his officers, and "with their permission," was holding a council. They must decide upon something to be done immediately. The more hasty ones were for fishing up the projectile. A difficult operation, though not an impossible one. But the corvette had no proper machinery, which must be both fixed and powerful; so it was resolved that they should put in at the nearest port, and give information to the Gun Club of the projectile's fall.

This determination was unanimous. The choice of the port had to be discussed. The neighboring coast had no anchorage on 27 ° latitude. Higher up, above the peninsula of Monterey, stands the important town from which it takes its name; but, seated on the borders of a perfect desert, it was not connected with the interior by a network of telegraphic wires, and electricity alone could spread these important news fast enough.

Some degrees above opened the bay of San Francisco. Through the capital of the gold country communication would be easy with the heart of the Union. And in less than two days the Susquehanna, by putting on high pressure, could arrive in that port. She must therefore start at once.

The fires were made up; they could set off immediately.

Two thousand fathoms of line were still out, which Captain
Blomsberry, not wishing to lose precious time in hauling in,
resolved to cut.

"we will fasten the end to a buoy," said he, "and that buoy will show us the exact spot where the projectile fell."

"Besides," replied Lieutenant Bronsfield, "we have our situation exact— 27 ° 7' north latitude and 41 ° 37' west longitude."

"Well, Mr. Bronsfield," replied the captain, "now, with your permission, we will have the line cut."

A strong buoy, strengthened by a couple of spars, was thrown into the ocean. The end of the rope was carefully lashed to it; and, left solely to the rise and fall of the billows, the buoy would not sensibly deviate from the spot.

At this moment the engineer sent to inform the captain that steam was up and they could start, for which agreeable communication the captain thanked him. The course was then given north-northeast, and the corvette, wearing, steered at full steam direct for San Francisco. It was three in the morning.

Four hundred and fifty miles to cross; it was nothing for a good vessel like the Susquehanna. In thirty-six hours she had covered that distance; and on the 14th of December, at twenty-seven minutes past one at night, she entered the bay of San Francisco.

At the sight of a ship of the national navy arriving at full speed, with her bowsprit broken, public curiosity was greatly roused. A dense crowd soon assembled on the quay, waiting for them to disembark.

After casting anchor, Captain Blomsberry and Lieutenant Bronsfield entered an eight-pared cutter, which soon brought them to land.

They jumped on to the quay.

"The telegraph?" they asked, without answering one of the thousand questions addressed to them.

The officer of the port conducted them to the telegraph office through a concourse of spectators. Blomsberry and Bronsfield entered, while the crowd crushed each other at the door.

Some minutes later a fourfold telegram was sent out—the first to the Naval Secretary at Washington; the second to the vice-president of the Gun Club, Baltimore; the third to the Hon. J. T. Maston, Long's Peak, Rocky Mountains; and the fourth to the sub-director of the Cambridge Observatory, Massachusetts.

It was worded as follows:

In 20 ° 7' north latitude, and 41 ° 37' west longitude, on the 12th of December, at seventeen minutes past one in the morning, the projectile of the Columbiad fell into the Pacific. Send instructions.— BLOMSBERRY, Commander Susquehanna.

Five minutes afterward the whole town of San Francisco learned the news. Before six in the evening the different States of the Union had heard the great catastrophe; and after midnight, by the cable, the whole of Europe knew the result of the great American experiment. We will not attempt to picture the effect produced on the entire world by that unexpected denouement.

On receipt of the telegram the Naval Secretary telegraphed to the Susquehanna to wait in the bay of San Francisco without extinguishing her fires. Day and night she must be ready to put to sea.

The Cambridge observatory called a special meeting; and, with that composure which distinguishes learned bodies in general, peacefully discussed the scientific bearings of the question. At the Gun Club there was an explosion. All the gunners were assembled. Vice-President the Hon. Wilcome was in the act of reading the premature dispatch, in which J. T. Maston and Belfast announced that the projectile had just been seen in the gigantic reflector of Long's Peak, and also that it was held by lunar attraction, and was playing the part of under satellite to the lunar world.

We know the truth on that point.

But on the arrival of Blomsberry's dispatch, so decidely contradicting J. T. Maston's telegram, two parties were formed in the bosom of the Gun Club. On one side were those who admitted the fall of the projectile, and consequently the return of the travelers; on the other, those who believed in the observations of Long's Peak, concluded that the commander of the Susquehanna had made a mistake. To the latter the pretended projectile was nothing but a meteor! nothing but a meteor, a shooting globe, which in its fall had smashed the bows of the corvette. It was difficult to answer this argument, for the speed with which it was animated must have made observation very difficult. The commander of the Susquehanna and her officers might have made a mistake in all good faith; one argument however, was in their favor, namely, that if the projectile had fallen on the earth, its place of meeting with the terrestrial globe could only take place on this 27 ° north latitude, and (taking into consideration the time that had elapsed, and the rotary motion of the earth) between the 41 ° and the 42 ° of west longitude. In any case, it was decided in the Gun Club that Blomsberry brothers, Bilsby, and Major Elphinstone should go straight to San Francisco, and consult as to the means of raising the projectile from the depths of the ocean.

These devoted men set off at once; and the railroad, which will soon cross the whole of Central America, took them as far as St. Louis, where the swift mail-coaches awaited them. Almost at the same moment in which the Secretary of Marine, the vice-president of the Gun Club, and the sub-director of the Observatory received the dispatch from San Francisco, the Honorable J. T. Maston was undergoing the greatest excitement he had ever experienced in his life, an excitement which even the bursting of his pet gun, which had more than once nearly cost him his life, had not caused him. We may remember that the secretary of the Gun Club had started soon after the projectile (and almost as quickly) for the station on Long's Peak, in the Rocky Mountains, J. Belfast, director of the Cambridge Observatory, accompanying him. Arrived there, the two friends had installed themselves at once, never quitting the summit of their enormous telescope. We know that this gigantic instrument had been set up according to the reflecting system, called by the English "front view." This arrangement subjected all objects to but one reflection, making the view consequently much clearer; the result was that, when they were taking observation, J. T. Maston and Belfast were placed in the *upper* part of the instrument and not in the lower, which they reached by a circular staircase, a masterpiece of lightness, while below them opened a metal well terminated by the metallic mirror, which measured two hundred and eighty feet in depth.

It was on a narrow platform placed above the telescope that the two savants passed their existence, execrating the day which hid the moon from their eyes, and the clouds which obstinately veiled her during the night.

What, then, was their delight when, after some days of waiting, on the night of the 5th of December, they saw the vehicle which was bearing their friends into space! To this delight succeeded a great deception, when, trusting to a cursory observation, they launched their first telegram to the world, erroneously affirming that the projectile had become a satellite of the moon, gravitating in an immutable orbit.

From that moment it had never shown itself to their eyes— a disappearance all the more easily explained, as it was then passing behind the moon's invisible disc; but when it was time for it to reappear on the visible disc, one may imagine the impatience of the fuming J. T. Maston and his not less impatient companion. Each minute of the night they thought they saw the projectile once more, and they did not see it. Hence constant discussions and violent disputes between them, Belfast affirming that the projectile could not be seen, J. T. Maston maintaining that "it had put his eyes out."

"It is the projectile!" repeated J. T. Maston.

"No," answered Belfast; "it is an avalanche detached from a lunar mountain."

"Well, we shall see it to-morrow."

"No, we shall not see it any more. It is carried into space."

"Yes!"

"No!"

And at these moments, when contradictions rained like hail, the well-known irritability of the secretary of the Gun Club constituted a permanent danger for the Honorable Belfast. The existence of these two together would soon have become impossible; but an unforseen event cut short their everlasting discussions.

During the night, from the 14th to the 15th of December, the two irreconcilable friends were busy observing the lunar disc, J. T. Maston abusing the learned Belfast as usual, who was by his side; the secretary of the Gun Club maintaining for the thousandth time that he had just seen the projectile, and adding that he could see Michel Ardan's face looking through one of the scuttles, at the same time enforcing his argument by a series of gestures which his formidable hook rendered very unpleasant.

At this moment Belfast's servant appeared on the platform (it was ten at night) and gave him a dispatch. It was the commander of the Susquehanna's telegram.

Belfast tore the envelope and read, and uttered a cry.

"What!" said J. T. Maston.

"The projectile!"

"Well!"

"Has fallen to the earth!"

Another cry, this time a perfect howl, answered him. He turned toward J. T. Maston. The unfortunate man, imprudently leaning over the metal tube, had disappeared in the immense telescope. A fall of two hundred and eighty feet! Belfast, dismayed, rushed to the orifice of the reflector.

He breathed. J. T. Maston, caught by his metal hook, was holding on by one of the rings which bound the telescope together, uttering fearful cries.

Belfast called. Help was brought, tackle was let down, and they hoisted up, not without some trouble, the imprudent secretary of the Gun Club.

He reappeared at the upper orifice without hurt.

"Ah!" said he, "if I had broken the mirror?"

"You would have paid for it," replied Belfast severely.

"And that cursed projectile has fallen?" asked J. T. Maston.

"Into the Pacific!"

"Let us go!"

A quarter of an hour after the two savants were descending the declivity of the Rocky Mountains; and two days after, at the same time as their friends of the Gun Club, they arrived at San Francisco, having killed five horses on the road.

Elphinstone, the brothers Blomsberry, and Bilsby rushed toward them on their arrival.

"What shall we do?" they exclaimed.

"Fish up the projectile," replied J. T. Maston, "and the sooner the better."

CHAPTER XXII RECOVERED FROM THE SEA

The spot where the projectile sank under the waves was exactly known; but the machinery to grasp it and bring it to the surface of the ocean was still wanting. It must first be invented, then made. American engineers could not be troubled with such trifles. The grappling-irons once fixed, by their help they were sure to raise it in spite of its weight, which was lessened by the density of the liquid in which it was plunged.

But fishing-up the projectile was not the only thing to be thought of. They must act promptly in the interest of the travelers. No one doubted that they were still living.

"Yes," repeated J. T. Maston incessantly, whose confidence gained over everybody, "our friends are clever people, and they cannot have fallen like simpletons. They are alive, quite alive; but we must make haste if we wish to find them so. Food and water do not trouble me; they have enough for a long while. But air, air, that is what they will soon want; so quick, quick!"

And they did go quick. They fitted up the Susquehanna for her new destination. Her powerful machinery was brought to bear upon the hauling-chains. The aluminum projectile only weighed 19,250 pounds, a weight very inferior to that of the transatlantic cable which had been drawn up under similar conditions. The only difficulty was in fishing up a cylindro-conical projectile, the walls of which were so smooth as to offer no hold for the hooks. On that account Engineer Murchison hastened to San Francisco, and had some enormous grappling-irons fixed on an automatic system, which would never let the projectile go if it once succeeded in seizing it in its powerful claws. Diving-dresses were also prepared, which through this impervious covering allowed the divers to observe the bottom of the sea. He also had put on board an apparatus of compressed air very cleverly designed. There were perfect chambers pierced with scuttles, which, with water let into certain compartments, could draw it down into great depths. These apparatuses were at San Francisco, where they had been used in the construction of a submarine breakwater; and very fortunately it was so, for there was no time to construct any. But in spite of the perfection of the machinery, in spite of the ingenuity of the savants entrusted with the use of them, the success of the operation was far from being certain. How great were the chances against them, the projectile being 20,000 feet under the water! And if even it was brought to the surface, how would the travelers have borne the terrible shock which 20,000 feet of water had perhaps not sufficiently broken? At any rate they must act quickly. J. T. Maston hurried the workmen day and night. He was ready to don the diving-dress himself, or try the air apparatus, in order to reconnoiter the situation of his courageous friends.

But in spite of all the diligence displayed in preparing the different engines, in spite of the considerable sum placed at the disposal of the Gun Club by the Government of the

Union, five long days (five centuries!) elapsed before the preparations were complete. During this time public opinion was excited to the highest pitch. Telegrams were exchanged incessantly throughout the entire world by means of wires and electric cables. The saving of Barbicane, Nicholl, and Michel Ardan was an international affair. Every one who had subscribed to the Gun Club was directly interested in the welfare of the travelers.

At length the hauling-chains, the air-chambers, and the automatic grappling-irons were put on board. J. T. Maston, Engineer Murchison, and the delegates of the Gun Club, were already in their cabins. They had but to start, which they did on the 21st of December, at eight o'clock at night, the corvette meeting with a beautiful sea, a northeasterly wind, and rather sharp cold. The whole population of San Francisco was gathered on the quay, greatly excited but silent, reserving their hurrahs for the return. Steam was fully up, and the screw of the Susquehanna carried them briskly out of the bay.

It is needless to relate the conversations on board between the officers, sailors, and passengers. All these men had but one thought. All these hearts beat under the same emotion. While they were hastening to help them, what were Barbicane and his companions doing? What had become of them? Were they able to attempt any bold maneuver to regain their liberty? None could say. The truth is that every attempt must have failed! Immersed nearly four miles under the ocean, this metal prison defied every effort of its prisoners.

On the 23rd inst., at eight in the morning, after a rapid passage, the Susquehanna was due at the fatal spot. They must wait till twelve to take the reckoning exactly. The buoy to which the sounding line had been lashed had not yet been recognized.

At twelve, Captain Blomsberry, assisted by his officers who superintended the observations, took the reckoning in the presence of the delegates of the Gun Club. Then there was a moment of anxiety. Her position decided, the Susquehanna was found to be some minutes westward of the spot where the projectile had disappeared beneath the waves.

The ship's course was then changed so as to reach this exact point.

At forty-seven minutes past twelve they reached the buoy; it was in perfect condition, and must have shifted but little.

"At last!" exclaimed J. T. Maston.

"Shall we begin?" asked Captain Blomsberry.

"Without losing a second."

Every precaution was taken to keep the corvette almost completely motionless. Before trying to seize the projectile, Engineer Murchison wanted to find its exact position at the bottom of the ocean. The submarine apparatus destined for this expedition was supplied with air. The working of these engines was not without danger, for at 20,000 feet below the surface of the water, and under such great pressure, they were exposed to fracture, the consequences of which would be dreadful.

J. T. Maston, the brothers Blomsberry, and Engineer Murchison, without heeding these dangers, took their places in the air-chamber. The commander, posted on his bridge, superintended the operation, ready to stop or haul in the chains on the slightest signal. The screw had been shipped, and the whole power of the machinery collected on the capstan would have quickly drawn the apparatus on board. The descent began at twenty-five minutes past one at night, and the chamber, drawn under by the reservoirs full of water, disappeared from the surface of the ocean.

The emotion of the officers and sailors on board was now divided between the prisoners in the projectile and the prisoners in the submarine apparatus. As to the latter, they forgot themselves, and, glued to the windows of the scuttles, attentively watched the liquid mass through which they were passing.

The descent was rapid. At seventeen minutes past two, J. T. Maston and his companions had reached the bottom of the Pacific; but they saw nothing but an arid desert, no longer animated by either fauna or flora. By the light of their lamps, furnished with powerful reflectors, they could see the dark beds of the ocean for a considerable extent of view, but the projectile was nowhere to be seen.

The impatience of these bold divers cannot be described, and having an electrical communication with the corvette, they made a signal already agreed upon, and for the space of a mile the Susquehanna moved their chamber along some yards above the bottom.

Thus they explored the whole submarine plain, deceived at every turn by optical illusions which almost broke their hearts. Here a rock, there a projection from the ground, seemed to be the much-sought-for projectile; but their mistake was soon discovered, and then they were in despair.

"But where are they? where are they?" cried J. T. Maston. And the poor man called loudly upon Nicholl, Barbicane, and Michel Ardan, as if his unfortunate friends could either hear or answer him through such an impenetrable medium! The search continued under these conditions until the vitiated air compelled the divers to ascend.

The hauling in began about six in the evening, and was not ended before midnight.

"To-morrow," said J. T. Maston, as he set foot on the bridge of the corvette.

"Yes," answered Captain Blomsberry.

"And on another spot?"

"Yes."

J. T. Maston did not doubt of their final success, but his companions, no longer upheld by the excitement of the first hours, understood all the difficulty of the enterprise. What seemed easy at San Francisco, seemed here in the wide ocean almost impossible. The chances of success diminished in rapid proportion; and it was from chance alone that the meeting with the projectile might be expected.

The next day, the 24th, in spite of the fatigue of the previous day, the operation was renewed. The corvette advanced some minutes to westward, and the apparatus, provided with air, bore the same explorers to the depths of the ocean.

The whole day passed in fruitless research; the bed of the sea was a desert. The 25th brought no other result, nor the 26th.

It was disheartening. They thought of those unfortunates shut up in the projectile for twenty-six days. Perhaps at that moment they were experiencing the first approach of suffocation; that is, if they had escaped the dangers of their fall. The air was spent, and doubtless with the air all their *morale*.

"The air, possibly," answered J. T. Maston resolutely, "but their *morale* never!"

On the 28th, after two more days of search, all hope was gone.

This projectile was but an atom in the immensity of the ocean.

They must give up all idea of finding it.

But J. T. Maston would not hear of going away. He would not abandon the place without at least discovering the tomb of his friends. But Commander Blomsberry could no longer persist, and in spite of the exclamations of the worthy secretary, was obliged to give the order to sail.

On the 29th of December, at nine A.M., the Susquehanna, heading northeast, resumed her course to the bay of San Francisco.

It was ten in the morning; the corvette was under half-steam, as it was regretting to leave the spot where the catastrophe had taken place, when a sailor, perched on the main-top-gallant crosstrees, watching the sea, cried suddenly:

"A buoy on the lee bow!"

The officers looked in the direction indicated, and by the help of their glasses saw that the object signalled had the appearance of one of those buoys which are used to mark the passages of bays or rivers. But, singularly to say, a flag floating on the wind surmounted its cone, which emerged five or six feet out of water. This buoy shone under the rays of the sun as if it had been made of plates of silver. Commander Blomsberry, J. T. Maston, and the delegates of the Gun Club were mounted on the bridge, examining this object straying at random on the waves.

All looked with feverish anxiety, but in silence. None dared give expression to the thoughts which came to the minds of all.

The corvette approached to within two cables' lengths of the object.

A shudder ran through the whole crew. That flag was the

American flag!

At this moment a perfect howling was heard; it was the brave J. T. Maston who had just fallen all in a heap. Forgetting on the one hand that his right arm had been replaced by an iron hook, and on the other that a simple gutta-percha cap covered his brain-box, he had given himself a formidable blow.

They hurried toward him, picked him up, restored him to life.

And what were his first words?

"Ah! trebly brutes! quadruply idiots! quintuply boobies that we are!"

"What is it?" exclaimed everyone around him.

"What is it?"

"Come, speak!"

"It is, simpletons," howled the terrible secretary, "it is that the projectile only weighs 19,250 pounds!"

"Well?"

"And that it displaces twenty-eight tons, or in other words 56,000 pounds, and that consequently *it floats*!"

Ah! what stress the worthy man had laid on the verb "float!" And it was true! All, yes! all these savants had forgotten this fundamental law, namely, that on account of its specific lightness, the projectile, after having been drawn by its fall to the greatest depths of the ocean, must naturally return to the surface. And now it was floating quietly at the mercy of the waves.

The boats were put to sea. J. T. Maston and his friends had rushed into them! Excitement was at its height! Every heart beat loudly while they advanced to the projectile. What did it contain? Living or dead?

Living, yes! living, at least unless death had struck

Barbicane and his two friends since they had hoisted the flag.

Profound silence reigned on the boats. All were breathless.

Eyes no longer saw. One of the scuttles of the projectile was open.

Some pieces of glass remained in the frame, showing that it had

been broken. This scuttle was actually five feet above the water.

A boat came alongside, that of J. T. Maston, and J. T. Maston rushed to the broken window.

At that moment they heard a clear and merry voice, the voice of

Michel Ardan, exclaiming in an accent of triumph:

CHAPTER XXII RECOVERED FROM THE SEA

"White all, Barbicane, white all!"
Barbicane, Michel Ardan, and Nicholl were playing at dominoes!

CHAPTER XXIII THE END

We may remember the intense sympathy which had accompanied the travelers on their departure. If at the beginning of the enterprise they had excited such emotion both in the old and new world, with what enthusiasm would they be received on their return! The millions of spectators which had beset the peninsula of Florida, would they not rush to meet these sublime adventurers? Those legions of strangers, hurrying from all parts of the globe toward the American shores, would they leave the Union without having seen Barbicane, Nicholl, and Michel Ardan? No! and the ardent passion of the public was bound to respond worthily to the greatness of the enterprise. Human creatures who had left the terrestrial sphere, and returned after this strange voyage into celestial space, could not fail to be received as the prophet Elias would be if he came back to earth. To see them first, and then to hear them, such was the universal longing.

Barbicane, Michel Ardan, Nicholl, and the delegates of the Gun Club, returning without delay to Baltimore, were received with indescribable enthusiasm. The notes of President Barbicane's voyage were ready to be given to the public. The New York *Herald* bought the manuscript at a price not yet known, but which must have been very high. Indeed, during the publication of "A Journey to the Moon," the sale of this paper amounted to five millions of copies. Three days after the return of the travelers to the earth, the slightest detail of their expedition was known. There remained nothing more but to see the heroes of this superhuman enterprise.

The expedition of Barbicane and his friends round the moon had enabled them to correct the many admitted theories regarding the terrestrial satellite. These savants had observed *de visu*, and under particular circumstances. They knew what systems should be rejected, what retained with regard to the formation of that orb, its origin, its habitability. Its past, present, and future had even given up their last secrets. Who could advance objections against conscientious observers, who at less than twenty-four miles distance had marked that curious mountain of Tycho, the strangest system of lunar orography? How answer those savants whose sight had penetrated the abyss of Pluto's circle? How contradict those bold ones whom the chances of their enterprise had borne over that invisible face of the disc, which no human eye until then had ever seen? It was now their turn to impose some limit on that selenographic science, which had reconstructed the lunar world as Cuvier did the skeleton of a fossil, and say, "The moon *was* this, a habitable world, inhabited before the earth. The moon *is* that, a world uninhabitable, and now uninhabited."

To celebrate the return of its most illustrious member and his two companions, the Gun Club decided upon giving a banquet, but a banquet worthy of the conquerors, worthy of the American people, and under such conditions that all the inhabitants of the Union could directly take part in it.

All the head lines of railroads in the States were joined by flying rails; and on all the platforms, lined with the same flags, and decorated with the same ornaments, were tables laid and all served alike. At certain hours, successively calculated, marked by electric clocks which beat the seconds at the same time, the population were invited to take their places at the banquet tables. For four days, from the 5th to the 9th of January, the trains were stopped as they are on Sundays on the railways of the United States, and every road was open. One engine only at full speed, drawing a triumphal carriage, had the right of traveling for those four days on the railroads of the United States.

The engine was manned by a driver and a stoker, and bore, by special favor, the Hon. J. T. Maston, secretary of the Gun Club. The carriage was reserved for President Barbicane, Colonel Nicholl, and Michel Ardan. At the whistle of the driver, amid the hurrahs, and all the admiring vociferations of the American language, the train left the platform of Baltimore. It traveled at a speed of one hundred and sixty miles in the hour. But what was this speed compared with that which had carried the three heroes from the mouth of the Columbiad?

Thus they sped from one town to the other, finding whole populations at table on their road, saluting them with the same acclamations, lavishing the same bravos! They traveled in this way through the east of the Union, Pennsylvania, Connecticut, Massachusetts, Vermont, Maine, and New Hampshire; the north and west by New York, Ohio, Michigan, and Wisconsin; returning to the south by Illinois, Missouri, Arkansas, Texas, and Louisiana; they went to the southeast by Alabama and Florida, going up by Georgia and the Carolinas, visiting the center by Tennessee, Kentucky, Virginia, and Indiana, and, after quitting the Washington station, re-entered Baltimore, where for four days one would have thought that the United States of America were seated at one immense banquet, saluting them simultaneously with the same hurrahs! The apotheosis was worthy of these three heroes whom fable would have placed in the rank of demigods.

And now will this attempt, unprecedented in the annals of travels, lead to any practical result? Will direct communication with the moon ever be established? Will they ever lay the foundation of a traveling service through the solar world? Will they go from one planet to another, from Jupiter to Mercury, and after awhile from one star to another, from the Polar to Sirius? Will this means of locomotion allow us to visit those suns which swarm in the firmament?

To such questions no answer can be given. But knowing the bold ingenuity of the Anglo-Saxon race, no one would be astonished if the Americans seek to make some use of President Barbicane's attempt.

Thus, some time after the return of the travelers, the public received with marked favor the announcement of a company, limited, with a capital of a hundred million of dollars, divided into a hundred thousand shares of a thousand dollars each, under the name of the "National Company of Interstellary Communication." President, Barbicane; vice-president, Captain Nicholl; secretary, J. T. Maston; director of movements, Michel Ardan.

And as it is part of the American temperament to foresee everything in business, even failure, the Honorable Harry Trolloppe, judge commissioner, and Francis Drayton, magistrate, were nominated beforehand!

THE ENGLISH AT THE NORTH POLE

PART I
OF THE ADVENTURES OF CAPTAIN HATTERAS

CHAPTER I THE "FORWARD"

"To-morrow, at low tide, the brig *Forward*, Captain K. Z——, Richard Shandon mate, will start from New Prince's Docks for an unknown destination."

The foregoing might have been read in the *Liverpool Herald* of April 5th, 1860. The departure of a brig is an event of little importance for the most commercial port in England. Who would notice it in the midst of vessels of all sorts of tonnage and nationality that six miles of docks can hardly contain? However, from daybreak on the 6th of April a considerable crowd covered the wharfs of New Prince's Docks—the innumerable companies of sailors of the town seemed to have met there. Workmen from the neighbouring wharfs had left their work, merchants their dark counting-houses, tradesmen their shops. The different-coloured omnibuses that ran along the exterior wall of the docks brought cargoes of spectators at every moment; the town seemed to have but one pre-occupation, and that was to see the *Forward* go out.

The *Forward* was a vessel of a hundred and seventy tons, charged with a screw and steam-engine of a hundred and twenty horse-power. It might easily have been confounded with the other brigs in the port. But though it offered nothing curious to the eyes of the public, connoisseurs remarked certain peculiarities in it that a sailor cannot mistake. On board the *Nautilus*, anchored at a little distance, a group of sailors were hazarding a thousand conjectures about the destination of the *Forward*.

"I don't know what to think about its masting," said one; "it isn't usual for steamboats to have so much sail."

"That ship," said a quartermaster with a big red face—"that ship will have to depend more on her masts than her engine, and the topsails are the biggest because the others will be often useless. I haven't got the slightest doubt that the *Forward* is destined for the Arctic or Antarctic seas, where the icebergs stop the wind more than is good for a brave and solid ship."

"You must be right, Mr. Cornhill," said a third sailor. "Have you noticed her stern, how straight it falls into the sea?"

"Yes," said the quartermaster, "and it is furnished with a steel cutter as sharp as a razor and capable of cutting a three-decker in two if the *Forward* were thrown across her at top speed."

"That's certain," said a Mersey pilot; "for that 'ere vessel runs her fourteen knots an hour with her screw. It was marvellous to see her cutting the tide when she made her trial trip. I believe you, she's a quick un."

"The canvas isn't intricate either," answered Mr. Cornhill; "it goes straight before the wind, and can be managed by hand. That ship is going to try the Polar seas, or my name isn't what it is. There's something else—do you see the wide helm-port that the head of her helm goes through?"

"It's there, sure enough," answered one; "but what does that prove?"

"That proves, my boys," said Mr. Cornhill with disdainful satisfaction, "that you don't know how to put two and two together and make it four; it proves that they want to be able to take off the helm when they like, and you know it's a manoeuvre that's often necessary when you have ice to deal with."

"That's certain," answered the crew of the *Nautilus*.

"Besides," said one of them, "the way she's loaded confirms Mr. Cornhill's opinion. Clifton told me. The *Forward* is victualled and carries coal enough for five or six years. Coals and victuals are all its cargo, with a stock of woollen garments and sealskins."

"Then," said the quartermaster, "there is no more doubt on the matter; but you, who know Clifton, didn't he tell you anything about her destination?"

"He couldn't tell me; he doesn't know; the crew was engaged without knowing. He'll only know where he's going when he gets there."

"I shouldn't wonder if they were going to the devil," said an unbeliever: "it looks like it."

"And such pay," said Clifton's friend, getting warm—"five times more than the ordinary pay. If it hadn't been for that, Richard Shandon wouldn't have found a soul to go with him. A ship with a queer shape, going nobody knows where, and looking more like not coming back than anything else, it wouldn't have suited this child."

"Whether it would have suited you or not," answered Cornhill, "you couldn't have been one of the crew of the *Forward*."

"And why, pray?"

"Because you don't fulfil the required conditions. I read that all married men were excluded, and you are in the category, so you needn't talk. Even the very name of the ship is a bold one. The *Forward*—where is it to be forwarded to? Besides, nobody knows who the captain is."

"Yes, they do," said a simple-faced young sailor.

"Why, you don't mean to say that you think Shandon is the captain of the *Forward*?" said Cornhill.

"But——" answered the young sailor—

"Why, Shandon is commander, and nothing else; he's a brave and bold sailor, an experienced whaler, and a jolly fellow worthy in every respect to be the captain, but he isn't any more captain than you or I. As to who is going to command after God on board he doesn't know any more than we do. When the moment has come the true captain will appear, no one knows how nor where, for Richard Shandon has not said and hasn't been allowed to say to what quarter of the globe he is going to direct his ship."

"But, Mr. Cornhill," continued the young sailor, "I assure you that there is someone on board who was announced in the letter, and that Mr. Shandon was offered the place of second to."

"What!" said Cornhill, frowning, "do you mean to maintain that the *Forward* has a captain on board?"

"Yes, Mr. Cornhill."

"Where did you get your precious information from?"

"From Johnson, the boatswain."

"From Johnson?"

"Yes, sir."

"Johnson told you so?"

"He not only told me so, but he showed me the captain."

"He showed him to you!" said Cornhill, stupefied. "And who is it, pray?"

"A dog."

"What do you mean by a dog?"

"A dog on four legs."

Stupefaction reigned amongst the crew of the *Nautilus*. Under any other circumstances they would have burst out laughing. A dog captain of a vessel of a hundred and seventy tons burden! It was enough to make them laugh. But really the *Forward* was such an extraordinary ship that they felt it might be no laughing matter, and they must be sure before they denied it. Besides, Cornhill himself didn't laugh.

"So Johnson showed you the new sort of captain, did he?" added he, addressing the young sailor, "and you saw him?"

"Yes, sir, as plainly as I see you now."

"Well, and what do you think about it?" asked the sailors of the quartermaster.

"I don't think anything," he answered shortly. "I don't think anything, except that the *Forward* is a ship belonging to the devil, or madmen fit for nothing but Bedlam."

The sailors continued silently watching the *Forward*, whose preparations for departure were drawing to an end; there was not one of them who pretended that Johnson had only been laughing at the young sailor. The history of the dog had already made the round of the town, and amongst the crowd of spectators many a one looked out for the dog-captain and believed him to be a supernatural animal. Besides, the *Forward* had been attracting public attention for some months past. Everything about her was marvellous; her peculiar shape, the mystery which surrounded her, the incognito kept by the captain, the way Richard Shandon had received the proposition to direct her, the careful selection of the crew, her unknown destination, suspected only by a few—all about her was strange.

To a thinker, dreamer, or philosopher nothing is more affecting than the departure of a ship; his imagination plays round the sails, sees her struggles with the sea and the wind in the adventurous journey which does not always end in port; when in addition to the ordinary incidents of departure there are extraordinary ones, even minds little given to credulity let their imagination run wild.

So it was with the *Forward*, and though the generality of people could not make the knowing remarks of Quartermaster Cornhill, it did not prevent the ship forming the subject of Liverpool gossip for three long months. The ship had been put in dock at Birkenhead, on the opposite side of the Mersey. The builders, Scott and Co., amongst the first in England, had received an estimate and detailed plan from Richard Shandon; it informed them of the exact tonnage, dimensions, and store room that the brig was to have. They saw by the details given that they had to do with a consummate seaman. As Shandon had considerable funds at his disposal, the work advanced rapidly, according to the recommendation of the owner. The brig was constructed of a solidity to withstand all tests; it was evident that she was destined to resist enormous pressure, for her ribs were built of teak-wood, a sort of Indian oak, remarkable for its extreme hardness, and were, besides, plated with iron. Sailors asked why the hull of a vessel made so evidently for resistance was not built of sheet-iron like other steamboats, and were told it was because the mysterious engineer had his own reasons for what he did.

Little by little the brig grew on the stocks, and her qualities of strength and delicacy struck connoisseurs. As the sailors of the *Nautilus* had remarked, her stern formed a right angle with her keel; her steel prow, cast in the workshop of R. Hawthorn, of Newcastle, shone in the sun and gave a peculiar look to the brig, though otherwise she had nothing particularly warlike about her. However, a 16-pounder cannon was installed on the forecastle; it was mounted on a pivot, so that it might easily be turned in any direction; but neither the cannon nor the stern, steel-clad as they were, succeeded in looking warlike.

On the 5th of February, 1860, this strange vessel was launched in the midst of an immense concourse of spectators, and the trial trip was perfectly successful. But if the brig was neither a man-of-war, a merchant vessel, nor a pleasure yacht—for a pleasure trip is not made with six years' provisions in the hold—what was it? Was it a vessel destined for another Franklin expedition? It could not be, because in 1859, the preceding year, Captain McClintock had returned from the Arctic seas, bringing the certain proof of the loss of the unfortunate expedition. Was the *Forward* going to attempt the famous North-West passage? What would be the use? Captain McClure had discovered it in 1853, and his lieutenant, Creswell, was the first who had the honour of rounding the American continent from Behring's Straits to Davis's Straits. Still it was certain to competent judges that the *Forward* was prepared to face the ice regions. Was it going to the South Pole, farther than the whaler Weddell or Captain James Ross? But, if so, what for?

The day after the brig was floated her engine was sent from Hawthorn's foundry at Newcastle. It was of a hundred and twenty horse-power, with oscillating cylinders, taking up little room; its power was considerable for a hundred-and-seventy-ton brig, with so much sail, too, and of such fleetness. Her trial trips had left no doubt on that subject, and even the boatswain, Johnson, had thought right to express his opinion to Clifton's friend—

"When the *Forward* uses her engine and sails at the same time, her sails will make her go the quickest."

Clifton's friend did not understand him, but he thought anything possible of a ship commanded by a dog. After the engine was installed on board, the stowage of provisions began. This was no slight work, for the vessel was to carry enough for six years. They consisted of dry and salted meat, smoked fish, biscuit, and flour; mountains of tea and coffee were thrown down the shafts in perfect avalanches. Richard Shandon presided over the management of this precious cargo like a man who knows what he is about; all was stowed away, ticketed, and numbered in perfect order; a very large provision of the Indian preparation called pemmican, which contains many nutritive elements in a small volume, was also embarked. The nature of the provisions left no doubt about the length of the cruise, and the sight of the barrels of lime-juice, lime-drops, packets of mustard, grains of sorrel and *cochlearia*, all antiscorbutic, confirmed the opinion on the destination of the brig for the ice regions; their influence is so necessary in Polar navigation. Shandon had doubtless received particular instructions about this part of the cargo, which, along with the medicine-chest, he attended to particularly.

Although arms were not numerous on board, the powder-magazine overflowed. The one cannon could not pretend to use the contents. That gave people more to think about. There were also gigantic saws and powerful instruments, such as levers, leaden maces, handsaws, enormous axes, etc., without counting a considerable quantity of blasting cylinders, enough to blow up the Liverpool Customs—all that was strange, not to say fearful, without mentioning rockets, signals, powder-chests, and beacons of a thousand different sorts. The numerous spectators on the wharfs of Prince's Docks admired likewise a long mahogany whaler, a tin *pirogue* covered with gutta-percha, and a certain quantity of halkett-boats, a sort of indiarubber cloaks that can be transformed into canoes by blowing in their lining. Expectation was on the *qui vive*, for the *Forward* was going out with the tide.

CHAPTER II AN UNEXPECTED LETTER

The letter received by Richard Shandon, eight months before, ran as follows:—

"ABERDEEN,

"August 2nd, 1859.

"To Mr. Richard Shandon,

"Liverpool.

"SIR,—I beg to advise you that the sum of sixteen thousand pounds sterling has been placed in the hands of Messrs. Marcuart and Co., bankers, of Liverpool. I join herewith a series of cheques, signed by me, which will allow you to draw upon the said Messrs. Marcuart for the above-mentioned sum. You do not know me, but that is of no consequence. I know you: that is sufficient. I offer you the place of second on board the brig *Forward* for a voyage that may be long and perilous. If you agree to my conditions you will receive a salary of £500, and all through the voyage it will be augmented one-tenth at the end of each year. The *Forward* is not yet in existence. You must have it built so as to be ready for sea at the beginning of April, 1860, at the latest. Herewith is a detailed plan and estimate. You will take care that it is scrupulously followed. The ship is to be built by Messrs. Scott and Co., who will settle with you. I particularly recommend you the choice of the *Forward's* crew; it will be composed of a captain, myself, of a second, you, of a third officer, a boatswain, two engineers, an ice pilot, eight sailors, and two others, eighteen men in all, comprising Dr. Clawbonny, of this town, who will introduce himself to you when necessary. The *Forward's* crew must be composed of Englishmen without incumbrance; they should be all bachelors and sober—for no spirits, nor even beer, will be allowed on board—ready to undertake anything, and to bear with anything. You will give the preference to men of a sanguine constitution, as they carry a greater amount of animal heat. Offer them five times the usual pay, with an increase of one-tenth for each year of service. At the end of the voyage five hundred pounds will be placed at the disposition of each, and two thousand at yours. These funds will be placed with Messrs. Marcuart and Co. The voyage will be long and difficult, but honourable, so you need not hesitate to accept my conditions. Be good enough to send your answer to K. Z., Poste Restante, Goteborg, Sweden.

"P.S.—On the 15th of February next you will receive a large Danish dog, with hanging lips, and tawny coat with black stripes. You will take it on board and have it fed with oaten bread, mixed with tallow grease. You will acknowledge the reception of the said dog to me under the same initials as above, Poste Restante, Leghorn, Italy.

"The captain of the *Forward* will introduce himself to you when necessary. When you are ready to start you will receive further instructions.

"THE CAPTAIN OF THE 'FORWARD,'

THE ENGLISH AT THE NORTH POLE

"K. Z."

CHAPTER III DR. CLAWBONNY

Richard Shandon was a good sailor; he had been commander of whalers in the Arctic seas for many years, and had a wide reputation for skill. He might well be astonished at such a letter, and so he was, but astonished like a man used to astonishments. He fulfilled, too, all the required conditions: he had no wife, children, or relations; he was as free as a man could be. Having no one to consult, he went straight to Messrs. Marcuart's bank.

"If the money is there," he said to himself, "I'll undertake the rest."

He was received by the firm with all the attention due to a man with sixteen thousand pounds in their safes. Sure of that fact, Shandon asked for a sheet of letter-paper, and sent his acceptance in a large sailor's hand to the address indicated. The same day he put himself in communication with the Birkenhead shipbuilders, and twenty-four hours later the keel of the *Forward* lay on the stocks in the dockyard.

Richard Shandon was a bachelor of forty, robust, energetic, and brave, three sailor-like qualities, giving their possessor confidence, vigour, and *sang-froid.* He was reputed jealous and hard to be pleased, so he was more feared than loved by his sailors. But this reputation did not increase the difficulty of finding a crew, for he was known to be a clever commander. He was afraid that the mystery of the enterprise would embarrass his movements, and he said to himself, "The best thing I can do is to say nothing at all; there are sea-dogs who will want to know the why and the wherefore of the business, and as I know nothing myself, I can't tell them. K. Z. is a queer fish, but after all he knows me, and has confidence in me; that's enough. As to the ship, she will be a handsome lass, and my name isn't Richard Shandon if she is not destined for the Frozen Seas. But I shall keep that to myself and my officers."

Upon which Richard Shandon set about recruiting his crew upon the conditions of family and health exacted by the captain. He knew a brave fellow and capital sailor, named James Wall. Wall was about thirty, and had made more than one trip to the North Seas. Shandon offered him the post of third officer, and he accepted blindly; all he cared for was to sail, as he was devoted to his profession. Shandon told him and Johnson (whom he engaged as boatswain) all he knew about the business.

"Just as soon go there as anywhere else," answered Wall. "If it's to seek the North-West passage, many have been and come back."

"Been, yes; but come back I don't answer for," said Johnson; "but that's no reason for not going."

"Besides, if we are not mistaken in our conjectures," said Shandon, "the voyage will be undertaken under good conditions. The *Forward's* a bonny lass, with a good engine, and will stand wear and tear. Eighteen men are all the crew we want."

"Eighteen men?" said Johnson. "That's just the number that the American, Kane, had on board when he made his famous voyage towards the North Pole."

"It's a singular fact that there's always some private individual trying to cross the sea from Davis's Straits to Behring's Straits. The Franklin expeditions have already cost England more than seven hundred and sixty thousand pounds without producing any practical result. Who the devil means to risk his fortune in such an enterprise?"

"We are reasoning now on a simple hypothesis," said Shandon. "I don't know if we are really going to the Northern or Southern Seas. Perhaps we are going on a voyage of discovery. We shall know more when Dr. Clawbonny comes; I daresay he will tell us all about it."

"There's nothing for it but to wait," answered Johnson; "I'll go and hunt up some solid subjects, captain; and as to their animal heat, I guarantee beforehand you can trust me for that."

Johnson was a valuable acquisition; he understood the navigation of these high latitudes. He was quartermaster on board the *Phoenix*, one of the vessels of the Franklin expedition of 1853. He was witness of the death of the French lieutenant Bellot, whom he had accompanied in his expedition across the ice. Johnson knew the maritime population of Liverpool, and started at once on his recruiting expedition. Shandon, Wall, and he did their work so well that the crew was complete in the beginning of December. It had been a difficult task; many, tempted by the high pay, felt frightened at the risk, and more than one enlisted boldly who came afterwards to take back his word and enlistment money, dissuaded by his friends from undertaking such an enterprise. All of them tried to pierce the mystery, and worried Shandon with questions; he sent them to Johnson.

"I can't tell you what I don't know," he answered invariably; "you'll be in good company, that's all I can tell you. You can take it or leave it alone."

And the greater number took it.

"I have only to choose," added the boatswain; "such salary has never been heard of in the memory of sailors, and then the certainty of finding a handsome capital when we come back. Only think: it's tempting enough."

"The fact is," answered the sailor, "it is tempting; enough to live on till the end of one's days."

"I don't hide from you," continued Johnson, "that the cruise will be long, painful, and perilous; that is formally stated in our instructions, and you ought to know what you undertake; you will very likely be required to attempt all that it is possible for human beings to do, and perhaps more. If you are the least bit frightened, if you don't think you may just as well finish yonder as here, you'd better not enlist, but give way to a bolder man."

"But, Mr. Johnson," continued the sailor, for the want of something better to say, "at least you know the captain?"

"The captain is Richard Shandon till another comes."

Richard Shandon, in his secret heart, hoped that the command would remain with him, and that at the last moment he should receive precise instructions as to the destination of the *Forward*. He did all he could to spread the report in his conversations with his officers, or when following the construction of the brig as it grew in the Birkenhead dockyard, looking like the ribs of a whale turned upside down. Shandon and Johnson kept strictly to their instructions touching the health of the sailors who were to form the crew; they all looked hale and hearty, and had enough heat in their bodies to suffice for the engine of the *Forward*; their supple limbs, their clear and florid complexions were fit to react against the action of intense cold. They were confident and resolute men, energetically and solidly constituted. Of course they were not all equally vigorous; Shandon had even hesitated about taking some of them, such as the sailors Gripper and Garry, and the harpooner Simpson, because they looked rather thin; but, on the whole, their build was good; they were a warm-hearted lot, and their engagement was signed.

All the crew belonged to the same sect of the Protestant religion; during these long campaigns prayer in common and the reading of the Bible have a good influence over the men and sustain them in the hour of discouragement; it was therefore important that they should be all of the same way of thinking. Shandon knew by experience the utility of these practices, and their influence on the mind of the crew; they are always employed on board ships that are intended to winter in the Polar Seas. The crew once got together, Shandon and his two officers set about the provisions; they strictly followed the instructions of the captain; these instructions were clear, precise, and detailed, and the least articles were put down with their quality and quantity. Thanks to the cheques at the commander's disposition, every article was paid for at once with a discount of 8 per cent, which Richard carefully placed to the credit of K. Z.

Crew, provisions, and cargo were ready by January, 1860; the *Forward* began to look shipshape, and Shandon went daily to Birkenhead. On the morning of the 23rd of January he was, as usual, on board one of the Mersey ferry-boats with a helm at either end to prevent having to turn it; there was a thick fog, and the sailors of the river were obliged to direct their course by means of the compass, though the passage lasts scarcely ten minutes. But the thickness of the fog did not prevent Shandon seeing a man of short stature, rather fat, with an intelligent and merry face and an amiable look, who came up to him, took him by the two hands, and shook them with an ardour, a petulance, and a familiarity "quite meridional," as a Frenchman would have said. But if this person did not come from the South, he had got his temperament there; he talked and gesticulated with volubility; his thought must come out or the machine would burst. His eyes, small as those of witty men generally are, his mouth, large and mobile, were safety-pipes which allowed him to give passage to his overflowing thoughts; he talked, and talked, and talked so much and so fast that Shandon couldn't understand a word he said. However, this did not prevent the *Forward's* mate from recognising the little man he had never seen before; a lightning flash traversed his mind, and when the other paused to take breath, Shandon made haste to get out the words, "Doctor Clawbonny!"

"Himself in person, commander! I've been at least half a quarter of an hour looking for you, asking everybody everywhere! Just think how impatient I got; five minutes more and I should have lost my head! And so you are the commander Richard? You really exist? You are not a myth? Your hand, your hand! I want to shake it again. It is Richard Shandon's hand, and if there is a commander Shandon, there's a brig *Forward* to command; and if he commands he will start, and if he starts he'll take Dr. Clawbonny on board."

"Well, yes, doctor, I am Richard Shandon; there is a brig *Forward*, and it will start."

"That's logic," answered the doctor, after taking in a large provision of breathing air—"that's logic. And I am ready to jump for joy at having my dearest wishes gratified. I've wanted to undertake such a voyage. Now with you, commander——"

"I don't——" began Shandon.

"With you," continued Clawbonny, without hearing him, "we are sure to go far and not to draw back for a trifle."

"But——" began Shandon again.

"For you have shown what you are made of, commander; I know your deeds of service. You are a fine sailor!"

"If you will allow me——"

"No, I won't have your bravery, audacity, and skill put an instant in doubt, even by you! The captain who chose you for his mate is a man who knows what he's about, I can tell you."

"But that's nothing to do with it," said Shandon, impatient.

"What is it, then? Don't keep me in suspense another minute."

"You don't give me time to speak. Tell me, if you please, doctor, how it comes that you are to take part in the expedition of the *Forward*."

"Read this letter, this worthy letter, the letter of a brave captain—very laconic, but quite sufficient."

Saying which the doctor held out the following letter to Shandon:—

"INVERNESS,

"Jan. 22nd, 1860.

"To Dr. Clawbonny.

"If Dr. Clawbonny wishes to embark on board the *Forward* for a long cruise, he may introduce himself to the commander, Richard Shandon, who has received orders concerning him.

"THE CAPTAIN OF THE 'FORWARD,'

"K. Z."

"This letter reached me this morning, and here I am, ready to embark."

"But, doctor, do you know where we are going to?"

"I haven't the slightest idea, and I do not care so that it is somewhere. They pretend that I am learned; they are mistaken, commander. I know nothing, and if I have published a few books that don't sell badly, I ought not to have done it; the public is silly for buying them. I know nothing, I tell you. I am only an ignorant man. When I have the offer of completing, or rather of going over again, my knowledge of medicine, surgery, history, geography, botany, mineralogy, conchology, geodesy, chemistry, natural philosophy, mechanics, and hydrography, why I accept, of course."

"Then," said Shandon, disappointed, "you do not know where the *Forward* is bound for?"

"Yes, I do; it is bound for where there is something to learn, to discover, and to compare—where we shall meet with other customs, other countries, other nations, to study in the exercise of their functions; it is going, in short, where I have never been."

"But I want to know something more definite than that," cried Shandon.

"Well, I have heard that we are bound for the Northern Seas."

"At least," asked Shandon, "you know the captain?"

"Not the least bit in the world! But he is an honest fellow, you may believe me."

The commander and the doctor disembarked at Birkenhead; the former told the doctor all he knew about the situation of things, and the mystery inflamed the imagination of the doctor. The sight of the brig caused him transports of joy. From that day he stopped with Shandon, and went every day to pay a visit to the shell of the *Forward*. Besides, he was specially appointed to overlook the installation of the ship's medicine-chest. For Dr. Clawbonny was a doctor, and a good one, though practising little. At the age of twenty-five he was an ordinary practitioner; at the age of forty he was a *savant*, well known in the town; he was an influential member of all the literary and scientific institutions of Liverpool. His fortune allowed him to distribute counsels which were none the worse for being gratuitous; beloved as a man eminently lovable must always be, he had never wronged any one, not even himself; lively and talkative, he carried his heart in his hand, and put his hand into that of everybody. When it was known in Liverpool that he was going to embark on board the *Forward* his friends did all they could to dissuade him, and only fixed him more completely in his determination, and when the doctor was determined to do anything no one could prevent him. From that time the suppositions and apprehensions increased, but did not prevent the *Forward* being launched on the 5th of February, 1860. Two months later she was ready to put to sea. On the 15th of March, as the letter of the captain had announced, a dog of Danish breed was sent by railway from Edinburgh to Liverpool, addressed to Richard Shandon. The animal seemed surly, peevish, and even sinister, with quite a singular look in his eyes. The name of the *Forward* was engraved on his brass collar. The commander installed it on board the same day, and acknowledged its reception to K. Z. at Leghorn. Thus, with the exception of the captain, the crew was complete. It was composed as follows:—

1. K. Z., captain; 2. Richard Shandon, commander; 3. James Wall, third officer; 4. Dr. Clawbonny; 5. Johnson, boatswain; 6. Simpson, harpooner; 7. Bell, carpenter; 8. Brunton, chief engineer; 9. Plover, second engineer; 10. Strong (negro), cook; 11. Foker, ice-master; 12. Wolsten, smith; 13. Bolton, sailor; 14. Garry, sailor; 15. Clifton, sailor; 16. Gripper, sailor; 17. Pen, sailor; 18. Warren, stoker.

CHAPTER IV DOG-CAPTAIN

The day of departure arrived with the 5th of April. The admission of the doctor on board had given the crew more confidence. They knew that where the worthy doctor went they could follow. However, the sailors were still uneasy, and Shandon, fearing that some of them would desert, wished to be off. With the coast out of sight, they would make up their mind to the inevitable.

Dr. Clawbonny's cabin was situated at the end of the poop, and occupied all the stern of the vessel. The captain's and mate's cabins gave upon deck. The captain's remained hermetically closed, after being furnished with different instruments, furniture, travelling garments, books, clothes for changing, and utensils, indicated in a detailed list. According to the wish of the captain, the key of the cabin was sent to Lubeck; he alone could enter his room.

This detail vexed Shandon, and took away all chance of the chief command. As to his own cabin, he had perfectly appropriated it to the needs of the presumed voyage, for he thoroughly understood the needs of a Polar expedition. The room of the third officer was placed under the lower deck, which formed a vast sleeping-room for the sailors' use; the men were very comfortably lodged, and would not have found anything like the same convenience on board any other ship; they were cared for like the most priceless cargo: a vast stove occupied all the centre of the common room. Dr. Clawbonny was in his element; he had taken possession of his cabin on the 6th of February, the day after the *Forward* was launched.

"The happiest of animals," he used to say, "is a snail, for it can make a shell exactly to fit it; I shall try to be an intelligent snail."

And considering that the shell was to be his lodging for a considerable time, the cabin began to look like home; the doctor had a *savant's* or a child's pleasure in arranging his scientific traps. His books, his herbals, his set of pigeon-holes, his instruments of precision, his chemical apparatus, his collection of thermometers, barometers, hygrometers, rain-gauges, spectacles, compasses, sextants, maps, plans, flasks, powders, bottles for medicine-chest, were all classed in an order that would have shamed the British Museum. The space of six square feet contained incalculable riches: the doctor had only to stretch out his hand without moving to become instantaneously a doctor, a mathematician, an astronomer, a geographer, a botanist, or a conchologist. It must be acknowledged that he was proud of his management and happy in his floating sanctuary, which three of his thinnest friends would have sufficed to fill. His friends came to it in such numbers that even a man as easy-going as the doctor might have said with Socrates, "My house is small, but may it please Heaven never to fill it with friends!"

CHAPTER IV DOG-CAPTAIN

To complete the description of the *Forward* it is sufficient to say that the kennel of the large Danish dog was constructed under the window of the mysterious cabin but its savage inhabitant preferred wandering between decks and in the hold; it seemed impossible to tame him, and no one had been able to become his master; during the night he howled lamentably, making the hollows of the ship ring in a sinister fashion. Was it regret for his absent master? Was it the instinct of knowing that he was starting for a perilous voyage? Was it a presentiment of dangers to come? The sailors decided that it was for the latter reason, and more than one pretended to joke who believed seriously that the dog was of a diabolical kind. Pen, who was a brutal man, was going to strike him once, when he fell, unfortunately, against the angle of the capstan, and made a frightful wound in his head. Of course this accident was placed to the account of the fantastic animal. Clifton, the most superstitious of the crew, made the singular observation that when the dog was on the poop he always walked on the windward side, and afterwards, when the brig was out at sea, and altered its tack, the surprising animal changed its direction with the wind the same as the captain of the *Forward* would have done in his place. Dr. Clawbonny, whose kindness and caresses would have tamed a tiger, tried in vain to win the good graces of the dog; he lost his time and his pains. The animal did not answer to any name ever written in the dog calendar, and the crew ended by calling him Captain, for he appeared perfectly conversant with ship customs; it was evident that it was not his first trip. From such facts it is easy to understand the boatswain's answer to Clifton's friend, and the credulity of those who heard it; more than one repeated jokingly that he expected one day to see the dog take human shape and command the manoeuvres with a resounding voice.

If Richard Shandon did not feel the same apprehensions he was not without anxiety, and the day before the departure, in the evening of April 5th, he had a conversation on the subject with the doctor, Wall, and Johnson in the poop cabin. These four persons were tasting their tenth grog, and probably their last, for the letter from Aberdeen had ordered that all the crew, from the captain to the stoker, should be teetotallers, and that there should be no wine, beer, nor spirits on board except those given by the doctor's orders. The conversation had been going on about the departure for the last hour. If the instructions of the captain were realised to the end, Shandon would receive his last instructions the next day.

"If the letter," said the commander, "does not tell me the captain's name, it must at least tell me the destination of the brig, or I shall not know where to take her to."

"If I were you," said the impatient doctor, "I should start whether I get a letter or no; they'll know how to send after you, you may depend."

"You are ready for anything, doctor; but if so, to what quarter of the globe should you set sail?"

"To the North Pole, of course; there's not the slightest doubt about that."

"Why should it not be the South Pole?" asked Wall.

"The South Pole is out of the question. No one with any sense would send a brig across the whole of the Atlantic. Just reflect a minute, and you'll see the impossibility."

"The doctor has an answer to everything," said Wall.

"Well, we'll say north," continued Shandon. "But where north? To Spitzbergen or Greenland? Labrador or Hudson's Bay? Although all directions end in insuperable icebergs, I am not less puzzled as to which to take. Have you an answer to that, doctor?"

"No," he answered, vexed at having nothing to say; "but if you don't get a letter what shall you do?"

"I shall do nothing; I shall wait."

"Do you mean to say you won't start?" cried Dr. Clawbonny, agitating his glass in despair.

"Certainly I do."

"And that would be the wisest plan," said Johnson tranquilly, while the doctor began marching round the table, for he could not keep still; "but still, if we wait too long, the consequences may be deplorable; the season is good now if we are really going north, as we ought to profit by the breaking up of the ice to cross Davis's Straits; besides, the crew gets more and more uneasy; the friends and companions of our men do all they can to persuade them to leave the *Forward*, and their influence may be pernicious for us."

"Besides," added Wall, "if one of them deserted they all would, and then I don't know how you would get another crew together."

"But what can I do?" cried Shandon.

"What you said you would do," replied the doctor; "wait and wait till to-morrow before you despair. The captain's promises have all been fulfilled up to now with the greatest regularity, and there's no reason to believe we shan't be made acquainted with our destination when the proper time comes. I haven't the slightest doubt that to-morrow we shall be sailing in the Irish Channel, and I propose we drink a last grog to our pleasant voyage. It begins in an unaccountable fashion, but with sailors like you there are a thousand chances that it will end well."

And all four drank to their safe return.

"Now, commander," continued Johnson, "if you will allow me to advise you, you will prepare everything to start; the crew must think that you know what you are about. If you don't get a letter to-morrow, set sail; do not get up the steam, the wind looks like holding out, and it will be easy enough to sail; let the pilot come on board; go out of the docks with the tide, and anchor below Birkenhead; our men won't be able to communicate with land, and if the devil of a letter comes it will find us as easily there as elsewhere."

"By heavens! you are right, Johnson!" cried the doctor, holding out his hand to the old sailor.

"So be it," answered Shandon.

Then each one entered his cabin, and waited in feverish sleep for the rising of the sun. The next day the first distribution of letters took place in the town, and not one bore the address of the commander, Richard Shandon. Nevertheless, he made his preparations for departure, and the news spread at once all over Liverpool, and, as we have already seen, an extraordinary affluence of spectators crowded the wharfs of New Prince's Docks. Many of them came on board to shake hands for the last time with a comrade, or to try and dissuade a friend, or to take a look at the brig, and to know its destination; they were disappointed at finding the commander more taciturn and reserved than ever. He had his reasons for that.

Ten o'clock struck. Eleven followed. The tide began to go out that day at about one o'clock in the afternoon. Shandon from the top of the poop was looking at the crowd with uneasy eyes, trying to read the secret of his destiny on one of the faces. But in vain. The sailors of the *Forward* executed his orders in silence, looking at him all the time, waiting for orders which did not come. Johnson went on preparing for departure. The weather was cloudy and the sea rough; a south-easter blew with violence, but it was easy to get out of the Mersey.

At twelve o'clock nothing had yet been received. Dr. Clawbonny marched up and down in agitation, looking through his telescope, gesticulating, impatient for the sea, as he said. He felt moved, though he struggled against it. Shandon bit his lips till the blood came. Johnson came up to him and said—

CHAPTER IV DOG-CAPTAIN

"Commander, if we want to profit by the tide, there is no time to be lost; we shall not be clear of the docks for at least an hour."

Shandon looked round him once more and consulted his watch. The twelve o'clock letters had been distributed. In despair he told Johnson to start. The boatswain ordered the deck to be cleared of spectators, and the crowd made a general movement to regain the wharves while the last moorings were unloosed. Amidst the confusion a dog's bark was distinctly heard, and all at once the animal broke through the compact mass, jumped on to the poop, and, as a thousand spectators can testify, dropped a letter at Shandon's feet.

"A letter!" cried Shandon. "*He* is on board, then?"

"He was, that's certain, but he isn't now," said Johnson, pointing to the deserted deck.

Shandon held the letter without opening it in his astonishment.

"But read it, read it, I say," said the doctor.

Shandon looked at it. The envelope had no postmark or date; it was addressed simply to:

"RICHARD SHANDON,

"Commander on board the brig

"Forward."

Shandon opened the letter and read as follows:—

"Sail for Cape Farewell. You will reach it by the 20th of April. If the captain does not appear on board, cross Davis's Straits, and sail up Baffin's Sea to Melville Bay.

"THE CAPTAIN OF THE 'FORWARD,'

"K. Z."

Shandon carefully folded this laconic epistle, put it in his pocket, and gave the order for departure. His voice, which rang above the east wind, had something solemn in it.

Soon the *Forward* had passed the docks, and directed by a Liverpool pilot whose little cutter followed, went down the Mersey with the current. The crowd precipitated itself on to the exterior wharf along the Victoria Docks in order to get a last glimpse of the strange brig. The two topsails, the foresail and the brigantine sail were rapidly set up, and the *Forward*, worthy of its name, after having rounded Birkenhead Point, sailed with extraordinary fleetness into the Irish Sea.

CHAPTER V OUT AT SEA

The wind was favourable, though it blew in April gales. The *Forward* cut through the waves, and towards three o'clock crossed the mail steamer between Liverpool and the Isle of Man. The captain hailed from his deck the last adieu that the *Forward* was destined to hear.

At five o'clock the pilot left the command in the hands of Richard Shandon, the commander of the brig, and regained his cutter, which, turning round, soon disappeared on the south-west. Towards evening the brig doubled the Calf of Man at the southern extremity of the island. During the night the sea was very rough, but the *Forward* behaved well, left the point of Ayr to the north-west, and directed its course for the Northern Channel. Johnson was right; once out at sea the maritime instinct of the sailors gained the upper hand. Life on board went on with regularity.

The doctor breathed in the sea air with delight; he walked about vigorously in the squalls, and for a *savant* he was not a bad sailor.

"The sea is splendid," said he to Johnson, coming up on deck after breakfast. "I have made its acquaintance rather late, but I shall make up for lost time."

"You are right, Mr. Clawbonny. I would give all the continents of the world for a corner of the ocean. They pretend that sailors soon get tired of their profession, but I've been forty years on the sea and I love it as much as the first day."

"It is a great pleasure to feel a good ship under one's feet, and if I'm not a bad judge the *Forward* behaves herself well."

"You judge rightly, doctor," answered Shandon, who had joined the talkers; "she is a good ship, and I acknowledge that a vessel destined for navigation amongst ice has never been better equipped. That reminds me that thirty years ago Captain James Ross, sailing for the North-West passage——"

"In the *Victory*," added the doctor quickly, "a brig about the same tonnage as ours, with a steam-engine too."

"What! you know about that?"

"Judge if I do," answered the doctor. "Machines were then in their infancy, and the *Victory's* kept her back; the captain, James Ross, after having vainly repaired it bit by bit, finished by taking it down, and abandoned it at his first winter quarters."

"The devil!" said Shandon. "You know all about it, I see."

"Yes. I've read the works of Parry, Ross, and Franklin, and the reports of McClure, Kennedy, Kane, and McClintock, and I remember something of what I've read. I can tell you, too, that this same McClintock, on board the *Fox*, a screw brig in the style of ours, went easier to his destination than any of the men who preceded him."

"That's perfectly true," answered Shandon; "he was a bold sailor was McClintock; I saw him at work. You may add that, like him, we shall find ourselves in Davis's Straits in April, and if we succeed in passing the ice our voyage will be considerably advanced."

"Unless," added the doctor, "it happens to us like it did to the *Fox* in 1857, to be caught the very first year by the ice in Baffin's Sea, and have to winter in the midst of the icebergs."

"We must hope for better luck," answered Johnson. "If a ship like the *Forward* can't take us where we want to go, we must renounce all hope for ever."

"Besides," said the doctor, "if the captain is on board he will know better than we do what must be done. We know nothing as yet; his letter says nothing about what our voyage is for."

"It is a good deal to know which way to go," answered Shandon quickly. "We can do without the captain and his instructions for another month at least. Besides, you know what I think about it."

"A short time ago," said the doctor, "I thought like you that the captain would never appear, and that you would remain commander of the ship; but now——"

"Now what?" replied Shandon in an impatient tone.

"Since the arrival of the second letter I have modified that opinion."

"Why, doctor?"

"Because the letter tells you the route to follow, but leaves you ignorant of the *Forward's* destination; and we must know where we are going to. How the deuce are you to get a letter now we are out at sea? On the coast of Greenland the service of the post must leave much to wish for. I believe that our gentleman is waiting for us in some Danish settlement—at Holsteinborg or Uppernawik; he has evidently gone there to complete his cargo of sealskins, buy his sledges and dog, and, in short, get together all the tackle wanted for a voyage in the Arctic Seas. I shouldn't be at all surprised to see him come out of his cabin one of these fine mornings and begin commanding the ship in anything but a supernatural way."

"It's possible," answered Shandon drily; "but in the meantime the wind is getting up, and I can't risk my gallant sails in such weather."

Shandon left the doctor and gave the order to reef the topsails.

"He takes it to heart," said the doctor to the boatswain.

"Yes," answered the latter, "and it's a great pity, for you may be right, Mr. Clawbonny."

In the evening of Saturday the *Forward* doubled the Mull of Galloway, whose lighthouse shone to the north-east; during the night they left the Mull of Cantyre to the north, and Cape Fair, on the coast of Ireland, to the east. Towards three o'clock in the morning, the brig, leaving Rathlin Island on her starboard side, disembogued by the Northern Channel into the ocean. It was Sunday, the 8th of April, and the doctor read some chapters of the Bible to the assembled seamen. The wind then became a perfect hurricane, and tended to throw the brig on to the Irish coast; she pitched, and rolled, and tossed, and if the doctor was not seasick it was because he would not be, for nothing was easier. At noon Cape Malinhead disappeared towards the south; it was the last European ground that these bold sailors were to perceive, and more than one watched it out of sight, destined never to see it again. They were then in 55° 57' latitude and 7° 40' longitude by the Greenwich meridian.

The storm spent itself out about nine o'clock in the evening; the *Forward*, like a good sailor, maintained her route north-west. She showed by her behaviour during the day what her sailing capacities were, and as the Liverpool connoisseurs had remarked, she was above all, a sailing vessel. During the following days the *Forward* gained the north-west with rapidity; the wind veered round south, and the sea had a tremendous swell on; the brig was then going along under full sail. Some petrels and puffins came sailing over the poop; the doctor skilfully shot one of the latter, and it fell, fortunately, on the deck. The harpooner, Simpson, picked it up and brought it to its owner.

"Nasty game that, Mr. Clawbonny," he said.

"It will make an excellent meal, on the contrary," said the doctor.

"You don't mean to say you are going to eat that thing?"

"And so are you, old fellow," said the doctor, laughing.

"Poh!" replied Simpson, "but it's oily and rancid, like all other sea birds."

"Never mind!" answered the doctor, "I have a peculiar way of cooking that game, and if you recognise it for a sea bird I'll consent never to kill another in my life."

"Do you know how to cook, then?"

"A *savant* ought to know how to do a little of everything."

"You'd better take care, Simpson," said the boatswain; "the doctor's a clever man, and he'll make you take this puffin for a grouse."

The fact is that the doctor was quite right about his fowl; he took off all the fat, which all lies under the skin, principally on the thighs, and with it disappeared the rancidity and taste of fish which is so disagreeable in a sea bird. Thus prepared the puffin was declared excellent, and Simpson acknowledged it the first.

During the late storm Richard Shandon had been able to judge of the qualities of his crew; he had watched each man narrowly, and knew how much each was to be depended upon.

James Wall was devoted to Richard, understood quickly and executed well, but he might fail in initiative; he placed him in the third rank. Johnson was used to struggle with the sea; he was an old stager in the Arctic Ocean, and had nothing to learn either in audacity or *sang-froid*. The harpooner, Simpson, and the carpenter, Bell, were sure men, faithful to duty and discipline. The ice-master, Foker, was an experienced sailor, and, like Johnson, was capable of rendering important service. Of the other sailors Garry and Bolton seemed to be the best; Bolton was a gay and talkative fellow; Garry was thirty-five, with an energetic face, but rather pale and sad-looking. The three sailors, Clifton, Gripper, and Pen, seemed less ardent and resolute; they easily grumbled. Gripper wanted to break his engagement even before the departure of the *Forward*; a sort of shame kept him on board. If things went on all right, if there were not too many risks to run, no dangers to encounter, these three men might be depended upon; but they must be well fed, for it might be said that they were led by their stomachs. Although warned beforehand, they grumbled at having to be teetotallers; at their meals they regretted the brandy and gin; it did not, however, make them spare the tea and coffee, which was prodigally given out on board. As to the two engineers, Brunton and Plover, and the stoker, Warren, there had been nothing for them to do as yet, and Shandon could not tell anything about their capabilities.

On the 14th of April the *Forward* got into the grand current of the Gulf Stream, which, after ascending the eastern coast of America to Newfoundland, inclines to the north-east along the coast of Norway. They were then in 57° 37' latitude by 22° 58' longitude, at two hundred miles from the point of Greenland. The weather grew colder, and the thermometer descended to thirty-two degrees, that is to say to freezing point.

The doctor had not yet begun to wear the garments he destined for the Arctic Seas, but he had donned a sailor's dress like the rest; he was a queer sight with his top-boots, in which his legs disappeared, his vast oilcloth hat, his jacket and trousers of the same; when drenched with heavy rains or enormous waves the doctor looked like a sort of sea-animal, and was proud of the comparison.

During two days the sea was extremely rough; the wind veered round to the north-west, and delayed the progress of the *Forward*. From the 14th to the 16th of April the swell was great, but on the Monday there came such a torrent of rain that the sea became calm immediately. Shandon spoke to the doctor about this phenomenon.

"It confirms the curious observations of the whaler Scoresby, who laid it before the Royal Society of Edinburgh, of which I have the honour to be an honorary member. You see that when it rains the waves are not very high, even under the influence of a violent wind, and when the weather is dry the sea is more agitated, even when there is less wind."

"But how is this phenomenon accounted for?"

"Very simply; it is not accounted for at all."

Just then the ice-master, who was keeping watch on the crossbars of the topsails, signalled a floating mass on the starboard, at about fifteen miles distance before the wind.

"An iceberg here!" cried the doctor.

Shandon pointed his telescope in the direction indicated, and confirmed the pilot's announcement.

"That is curious!" said the doctor.

"What! you are astonished at last!" said the commander, laughing.

"I am surprised, but not astonished," answered the doctor, laughing; "for the brig *Ann*, of Poole, from Greenspond, was caught in 1813 in perfect ice-fields, in the forty-fourth degree of north latitude, and her captain, Dayernent, counted them by hundreds!"

"I see you can teach us something, even upon that subject."

"Very little," answered Clawbonny modestly; "it is only that ice has been met with in even lower latitudes."

"I knew that already, doctor, for when I was cabinboy on board the war-sloop *Fly*——"

"In 1818," continued the doctor, "at the end of March, almost in April, you passed between two large islands of floating ice under the forty-second degree of latitude."

"Well, I declare you astonish me!" cried Shandon.

"But the iceberg doesn't astonish me, as we are two degrees further north."

"You are a well, doctor," answered the commander, "and all we have to do is to be water-buckets."

"You will draw me dry sooner than you think for; and now, Shandon, if we could get a nearer look at this phenomenon, I should be the happiest of doctors."

"Just so, Johnson," said Shandon, calling his boatswain. "It seems to me that the breeze is getting up."

"Yes, commander," answered Johnson; "we are making very little way, and the currents of Davis's Straits will soon be against us."

"You are right, Johnson, and if we wish to be in sight of Cape Farewell on the 20th of April we must put the steam on, or we shall be thrown on the coasts of Labrador. Mr. Wall, will you give orders to light the fires?"

The commander's orders were executed, an hour afterwards the steam was up, the sails were furled, and the screw cutting the waves sent the *Forward* against the north-west wind.

CHAPTER VI THE GREAT POLAR CURRENT

A short time after the flights of birds became more and more numerous. Petrels, puffins, and mates, inhabitants of those desolate quarters, signalled the approach of Greenland. The *Forward* was rapidly nearing the north, leaving to her leeward a long line of black smoke.

On Tuesday the 17th of April, about eleven o'clock in the morning, the ice-master signalled the first sight of the ice-blink; it was about twenty miles to the N.N.W. This glaring white strip was brilliantly lighted up, in spite of the presence of thick clouds in the neighbouring parts of the sky. Experienced people on board could make no mistake about this phenomenon, and declared, from its whiteness, that the blink was owing to a large ice-field, situated at about thirty miles out of sight, and that it proceeded from the reflection of luminous rays. Towards evening the wind turned round to the south, and became favourable; Shandon put on all sail, and for economy's sake caused the fires to be put out. The *Forward*, under her topsails and foresails, glided on towards Cape Farewell.

At three o'clock on the 18th they came across the ice-stream, and a white thick line of a glaring colour cut brilliantly the lines of the sea and sky. It was evidently drifting from the eastern coast of Greenland more than from Davis's Straits, for ice generally keeps to the west coast of Baffin's Sea. An hour afterwards the *Forward* passed in the midst of isolated portions of the ice-stream, and in the most compact parts, the icebergs, though welded together, obeyed the movements of the swell. The next day the man at the masthead signalled a vessel. It was the *Valkirien*, a Danish corvette, running alongside the *Forward*, and making for the bank of Newfoundland. The current of the Strait began to make itself felt, and Shandon had to put on sail to go up it. At this moment the commander, the doctor, James Wall, and Johnson were assembled on the poop examining the direction and strength of the current. The doctor wanted to know if the current existed also in Baffin's Sea.

"Without the least doubt," answered Shandon, "and the sailing vessels have much trouble to stem it."

"Besides there," added Wall, "you meet with it on the eastern coast of America, as well as on the western coast of Greenland."

"There," said the doctor, "that is what gives very singular reason to the seekers of the North-West passage! That current runs about five miles an hour, and it is a little difficult to suppose that it springs from the bottom of a gulf."

"It is so much the more probable, doctor," replied Shandon, "that if this current runs from north to south we find in Behring's Straits a contrary current which runs from south to north, and which must be the origin of this one."

CHAPTER VI THE GREAT POLAR CURRENT

"According to that," replied the doctor, "we must admit that America is totally unconnected with the Polar lands, and that the waters of the Pacific run round the coasts of America into the Atlantic. On the other hand, the greater elevation of the waters of the Pacific gives reason to the supposition that they fall into the European seas."

"But," sharply replied Shandon, "there must be facts to establish that theory, and if there are any," added he with irony, "our universally well-informed doctor ought to know them."

"Well," replied the above-mentioned, with amiable satisfaction, "if it interests you, I can tell you that whales, wounded in Davis's Straits, are caught some time afterwards in the neighbourhood of Tartary with the European harpoon still in their flanks."

"And unless they have been able to double Cape Horn or the Cape of Good Hope," replied Shandon, "they must necessarily have rounded the septentrional coasts of America—that's what I call indisputable, doctor."

"However, if you were not convinced, my dear fellow," said the doctor, smiling, "I could still produce other facts, such as drift-wood, of which Davis's Straits are full, larch, aspen, and other tropical trees. Now we know that the Gulf Stream hinders those woods from entering the Straits. If, then, they come out of it they can only get in from Behring's Straits."

"I am convinced, doctor, and I avow that it would be difficult to remain incredulous with you."

"Upon my honour," said Johnson, "there's something that comes just in time to help our discussion. I perceive in the distance a lump of wood of certain dimensions; if the commander permits it we'll haul it in, and ask it the name of its country."

"That's it," said the doctor, "the example after the rule."

Shandon gave the necessary orders; the brig was directed towards the piece of wood signalled, and soon afterwards, not without trouble, the crew hoisted it on deck. It was the trunk of a mahogany tree, gnawed right into the centre by worms, but for which circumstance it would not have floated.

"This is glorious," said the doctor enthusiastically, "for as the currents of the Atlantic could not carry it to Davis's Straits, and as it has not been driven into the Polar basin by the streams of septentrional America, seeing that this tree grew under the Equator, it is evident that it comes in a straight line from Behring; and look here, you see those sea-worms which have eaten it, they belong to a hot-country species."

"It is evident," replied Wall, "that the people who do not believe in the famous passage are wrong."

"Why, this circumstance alone ought to convince them," said the doctor; "I will just trace you out the itinerary of that mahogany; it has been floated towards the Pacific by some river of the Isthmus of Panama or Guatemala, from thence the current has dragged it along the American coast as far as Behring's Straits, and in spite of everything it was obliged to enter the Polar Seas. It is neither so old nor so soaked that we need fear to assign a recent date to its setting out; it has had the good luck to get clear of the obstacles in that long suite of straits which lead out of Baffin's Bay, and quickly seized by the boreal current came by Davis's Straits to be made prisoner by the *Forward* to the great joy of Dr. Clawbonny, who asks the commander's permission to keep a sample of it."

"Do so," said Shandon, "but allow me to tell you that you will not be the only proprietor of such a wreck. The Danish governor of the Isle of Disko——"

"On the coast of Greenland," continued the doctor, "possesses a mahogany table made from a trunk fished up under the same circumstances. I know it, but I don't envy him his table, for if it were not for the bother, I should have enough there for a whole bedroom."

During the night, from Wednesday to Thursday, the wind blew with extreme violence, and driftwood was seen more frequently. Nearing the coast offered many dangers at an epoch in which icebergs were so numerous; the commander caused some of the sails to be furled, and the *Forward* glided away under her foresail and foremast only. The thermometer sank below freezing-point. Shandon distributed suitable clothing to the crew, a woollen jacket and trousers, a flannel shirt, wadmel stockings, the same as those the Norwegian country-people wear, and a pair of perfectly waterproof sea-boots. As to the captain, he contented himself with his natural fur, and appeared little sensible to the change in the temperature; he had, no doubt, gone through more than one trial of this kind, and besides, a Dane had no right to be difficult. He was seen very little, as he kept himself concealed in the darkest parts of the vessel.

Towards evening the coast of Greenland peeped out through an opening in the fog. The doctor, armed with his glass, could distinguish for an instant a line of peaks, ridged with large blocks of ice; but the fog closed rapidly on this vision, like the curtain of a theatre falling in the most interesting moment of the piece.

On the morning of the 20th of April the *Forward* was in sight of an iceberg a hundred and fifty feet high, stranded there from time immemorial; the thaws had taken no effect on it, and had respected its strange forms. Snow saw it; James Ross took an exact sketch of it in 1829; and in 1851 the French lieutenant Bellot saw it from the deck of the *Prince Albert.* Of course the doctor wished to keep a memento of the celebrated mountain, and made a clever sketch of it. It is not surprising that such masses should be stranded and adhere to the land, for to each foot above water they have two feet below, giving, therefore, to this one about eighty fathoms of depth.

At last, under a temperature which at noon was only 12°, under a snowy and foggy sky, Cape Farewell was perceived. The *Forward* arrived on the day fixed; if it pleased the unknown captain to come and occupy his position in such diabolical weather he would have no cause to complain.

"There you are, then," said the doctor to himself, "cape so celebrated and so well named! Many have cleared it like us who were destined never to see it again. Is it, then, an eternal adieu said to one's European friends? You have all passed it. Frobisher, Knight, Barlow, Vaughan, Scroggs, Barentz, Hudson, Blosseville, Franklin, Crozier, Bellot, never to come back to your domestic hearth, and that cape has been really for you the cape of adieus."

It was about the year 970 that some navigators left Iceland and discovered Greenland. Sebastian Cabot forced his way as far as latitude 56° in 1498. Gaspard and Michel Cotreal, in 1500 and 1502, went as far north as 60°; and Martin Frobisher, in 1576, arrived as far as the bay that bears his name. To John Davis belongs the honour of having discovered the Straits in 1585; and two years later, in a third voyage, that bold navigator and great whaler reached the sixty-third parallel, twenty-seven degrees from the Pole.

Barentz in 1596, Weymouth in 1602, James Hall in 1605 and 1607, Hudson, whose name was given to that vast bay which hollows out so profoundly the continent of America, James Poole, in 1611, advanced far into the Strait in search of that North-West passage the discovery of which would have considerably shortened the track of communication between the two worlds. Baffin, in 1616, found the Straits of Lancaster in the sea that bears his own name; he was followed, in 1619, by James Munk, and in 1719 by Knight, Barlow, Vaughan, and Scroggs, of whom no news has ever been heard. In 1776 Lieutenant Pickersgill, sent out to meet Captain Cook, who tried to go up Behring's Straits, reached the sixty-eighth degree; the following year Young, for the same purpose, went as far north as Woman's Island.

Afterwards came Captain James Ross, who, in 1818, rounded the coasts of Baffin's Sea, and corrected the hydrographic errors of his predecessors. Lastly, in 1819 and 1820, the celebrated Parry passed through Lancaster Straits, and penetrated, in spite of unnumbered difficulties, as far as Melville Island, and won the prize of £5,000 promised by Act of Parliament to the English sailors who would reach the hundred and seventeenth meridian by a higher latitude than the seventy-seventh parallel.

In 1826 Beechey touched Chamisso Island; James Ross wintered from 1829 to 1833 in Prince Regent Straits, and amongst other important works discovered the magnetic pole. During this time Franklin, by an overland route, traversed the septentrional coasts of America from the River Mackenzie to Turnagain Point. Captain Back followed in his steps from 1823 to 1835, and these explorations were completed in 1839 by Messrs. Dease and Simpson and Dr. Rae.

Lastly, Sir John Franklin, wishing to discover the North-West passage, left England in 1845 on board the *Erebus* and the *Terror*; he penetrated into Baffin's Sea, and since his passage across Disko Island no news had been heard of his expedition.

That disappearance determined the numerous investigations which have brought about the discovery of the passage, and the survey of these Polar continents, with such indented coast lines. The most daring English, French, and American sailors made voyages towards these terrible countries, and, thanks to their efforts, the maps of that country, so difficult to make, figured in the list of the Royal Geographical Society of London. The curious history of these countries was thus presented to the doctor's imagination as he leaned on the rail, and followed with his eyes the long track left by the brig. Thoughts of the bold navigators weighed upon his mind, and he fancied he could perceive under the frozen arches of the icebergs the pale ghosts of those who were no more.

CHAPTER VII DAVIS'S STRAITS

During that day the *Forward* cut out an easy road amongst the half-broken ice; the wind was good, but the temperature very low; the currents of air blowing across the ice-fields brought with them their penetrating cold. The night required the severest attention; the floating icebergs drew together in that narrow pass; a hundred at once were often counted on the horizon; they broke off from the elevated coasts under the teeth of the grinding waves and the influence of the spring season, in order to go and melt or to be swallowed up in the depths of the ocean. Long rafts of wood, with which it was necessary to escape collision, kept the crew on the alert; the crow's nest was put in its place on the mizenmast; it consisted of a cask, in which the ice-master was partly hidden to protect him from the cold winds while he kept watch over the sea and the icebergs in view, and from which he signalled danger and sometimes gave orders to the crew. The nights were short; the sun had reappeared since the 31st of January in consequence of the refraction, and seemed to get higher and higher above the horizon. But the snow impeded the view, and if it did not cause complete obscurity it rendered navigation laborious.

On the 21st of April Desolation Cape appeared in the midst of thick mists; the crew were tired out with the constant strain on their energies rendered necessary ever since they had got amongst the icebergs; the sailors had not had a minute's rest; it was soon necessary to have recourse to steam to cut a way through the heaped-up blocks. The doctor and Johnson were talking together on the stern, whilst Shandon was snatching a few hours' sleep in his cabin. Clawbonny was getting information from the old sailor, whose numerous voyages had given him an interesting and sensible education. The doctor felt much friendship for him, and the boatswain repaid it with interest.

"You see, Mr. Clawbonny," Johnson used to say, "this country is not like all others; they call it *Green*land, but there are very few weeks in the year when it justifies its name."

"Who knows if in the tenth century this land did not justify its name?" added the doctor. "More than one revolution of this kind has been produced upon our globe, and I daresay I should astonish you if I were to tell you that according to Icelandic chronicles two thousand villages flourished upon this continent about eight or nine hundred years ago."

"You would so much astonish me, Mr. Clawbonny, that I should have some difficulty in believing you, for it is a miserable country."

"However miserable it may be, it still offers a sufficient retreat to its inhabitants, and even to civilised Europeans."

"Without doubt! We met men at Disko and Uppernawik who consented to live in such climates; but my ideas upon the matter were that they lived there by compulsion and not by choice."

"I daresay you are right, though men get accustomed to everything, and the Greenlanders do not appear to me so unfortunate as the workmen of our large towns; they may be unfortunate, but they are certainly not unhappy. I say unhappy, but the word does not translate my thought, for if these people have not the comforts of temperate countries, they are formed for a rude climate, and find pleasures in it which we are not able to conceive."

"I suppose we must think so, as Heaven is just. Many, many voyages have brought me upon these coasts, and my heart always shrinks at the sight of these wretched solitudes; but they ought to have cheered up these capes, promontories, and bays with more engaging names, for Farewell Cape and Desolation Cape are not names made to attract navigators."

"I have also remarked that," replied the doctor, "but these names have a geographical interest that we must not overlook. They describe the adventures of those who gave them those names. Next to the names of Davis, Baffin, Hudson, Ross, Parry, Franklin, and Bellot, if I meet with Cape Desolation I soon find Mercy Bay; Cape Providence is a companion to Port Anxiety; Repulsion Bay brings me back to Cape Eden, and leaving Turnagain Point I take refuge in Refuge Bay. I have there under my eyes an unceasing succession of perils, misfortunes, obstacles, successes, despairs, and issues, mixed with great names of my country, and, like a series of old-fashioned medals, that nomenclature retraces in my mind the whole history of these seas."

"You are quite right, Mr. Clawbonny, and I hope we shall meet with more Success Bays than Despair Capes in our voyage."

"I hope so too, Johnson; but, I say, is the crew come round a little from its terrors?"

"Yes, a little; but since we got into the Straits they have begun to talk about the fantastic captain; more than one of them expected to see him appear at the extremity of Greenland; but between you and me, doctor, doesn't it astonish you a little too?"

"It does indeed, Johnson."

"Do you believe in the captain's existence?"

"Of course I do."

"But what can be his reasons for acting in that manner?"

"If I really must tell you the whole of my thoughts, Johnson, I believe that the captain wished to entice the crew far enough out to prevent them being able to come back. Now if he had been on board when we started they would all have wanted to know our destination, and he might have been embarrassed."

"But why so?"

"Suppose he should wish to attempt some superhuman enterprise, and to penetrate where others have never been able to reach, do you believe if the crew knew it they would ever have enlisted? As it is, having got so far, going farther becomes a necessity."

"That's very probable, Mr. Clawbonny. I have known more than one intrepid adventurer whose name alone was a terror, and who would never have found any one to accompany him in his perilous expeditions——"

"Excepting me," ventured the doctor.

"And me, after you," answered Johnson, "and to follow you; I can venture to affirm that our captain is amongst the number of such adventurers. No matter, we shall soon see; I suppose the unknown will come as captain on board from the coast of Uppernawik or Melville Bay, and will tell us at last where it is his good pleasure to conduct the ship."

"I am of your opinion, Johnson, but the difficulty will be to get as far as Melville Bay. See how the icebergs encircle us from every point! They scarcely leave a passage for the *Forward*. Just examine that immense plain over there."

"The whalers call that in our language an ice-field, that is to say a continued surface of ice the limits of which cannot be perceived."

"And on that side, that broken field, those long pieces of ice more or less joined at their edges?"

"That is a pack; if it was of a circular form we should call it a patch; and, if the form was longer, a stream."

"And there, those floating icebergs?"

"Those are drift-ice; if they were a little higher they would be icebergs or hills; their contact with vessels is dangerous, and must be carefully avoided. Here, look over there: on that ice-field there is a protuberance produced by the pressure of the icebergs; we call that a hummock; if that protuberance was submerged to its base we should call it a calf. It was very necessary to give names to all those forms in order to recognise them."

"It is truly a marvellous spectacle!" exclaimed the doctor, contemplating the wonders of the Boreal Seas; "there is a field for the imagination in such pictures!"

"Yes," answered Johnson, "ice often takes fantastic shapes, and our men are not behindhand in explaining them according to their own notions."

"Isn't that assemblage of ice-blocks admirable? Doesn't it look like a foreign town, an Eastern town, with its minarets and mosques under the pale glare of the moon? Further on there is a long series of Gothic vaults, reminding one of Henry the Seventh's chapel or the Houses of Parliament."

"They would be houses and towns very dangerous to inhabit, and we must not sail too close to them. Some of those minarets yonder totter on their base, and the least of them would crush a vessel like the *Forward*."

"And yet sailors dared to venture into these seas before they had steam at their command! How ever could a sailing vessel be steered amongst these moving rocks?"

"Nevertheless, it has been accomplished, Mr. Clawbonny. When the wind became contrary—and that has happened to me more than once—we quietly anchored to one of those blocks, and we drifted more or less with it and waited for a favourable moment to set sail again. I must acknowledge that such a manner of voyaging required months, whilst with a little good fortune we shall only want a few days."

"It seems to me," said the doctor, "that the temperature has a tendency to get lower."

"That would be a pity," answered Johnson, "for a thaw is necessary to break up these masses and drive them away into the Atlantic; besides, they are more numerous in Davis's Straits, for the sea gets narrower between Capes Walsingham and Holsteinborg; but on the other side of the 67th degree we shall find the seas more navigable during the months of May and June."

"Yes; but first of all we must get to the other side."

"Yes, we must get there, Mr. Clawbonny. In June and July we should have found an open passage, like the whalers do, but our orders were precise; we were to be here in April. I am very much mistaken if our captain has not his reasons for getting us out here so early."

The doctor was right in stating that the temperature was lowering; the thermometer at noon only indicated 6 degrees, and a north-west breeze was getting up, which, although it cleared the sky, assisted the current in precipitating the floating masses of ice into the path of the *Forward*. All of them did not obey the same impulsion, and it was not uncommon to encounter some of the highest masses drifting in an opposite direction, seized at their base by an undercurrent.

It is easy to understand the difficulties of this kind of navigation; the engineers had not a minute's rest; the engines were worked from the deck by means of levers, which opened, stopped, and reversed them according to the orders of the officers on watch. Sometimes the brig had to hasten through an opening in the ice-fields, sometimes to struggle against the swiftness of an iceberg which threatened to close the only practicable issue, or, again, some block, suddenly overthrown, compelled the brig to back quickly so as not to be crushed to pieces. This mass of ice, carried along, broken up and amalgamated by the northern current, crushed up the passage, and if seized by the frost would oppose an impassable barrier to the passage of the *Forward*.

Birds were found in innumerable quantities on these coasts, petrels and other sea-birds fluttered about here and there with deafening cries, a great number of big-headed, short-necked sea-gulls were amongst them; they spread out their long wings and braved in their play the snow whipped by the hurricane. This animation of the winged tribe made the landscape more lively.

Numerous pieces of wood were floating to leeway, clashing with noise; a few enormous, bloated-headed sharks approached the vessel, but there was no question of chasing them, although Simpson, the harpooner, was longing to have a hit at them. Towards evening several seals made their appearance, nose above water, swimming between the blocks.

On the 22nd the temperature again lowered; the *Forward* put on all steam to catch the favourable passes: the wind was decidedly fixed in the north-west; all sails were furled.

During that day, which was Sunday, the sailors had little to do. After the reading of Divine service, which was conducted by Shandon, the crew gave chase to sea-birds, of which they caught a great number. They were suitably prepared according to the doctor's method, and furnished an agreeable increase of provisions to the tables of the officers and crew.

At three o'clock in the afternoon the *Forward* had attained Thin de Sael, Sukkertop Mountain; the sea was very rough; from time to time a vast and inopportune fog fell from the grey sky; however, at noon an exact observation could be taken. The vessel was in 65° 20' latitude by 54° 22' longitude. It was necessary to attain two degrees more in order to meet with freer and more favourable navigation.

During the three following days, the 24th, 25th, and 26th of April, the *Forward* had a continual struggle with the ice; the working of the machines became very fatiguing. The steam was turned off quickly or got up again at a moment's notice, and escaped whistling from its valves. During the thick mist the nearing of icebergs was only known by dull thundering produced by the avalanches; the brig was instantly veered; it ran the risk of being crushed against the heaps of fresh-water ice, remarkable for its crystal transparency, and as hard as a rock.

Richard Shandon never missed completing his provision of water by embarking several tons of ice every day. The doctor could not accustom himself to the optical delusions that refraction produces on these coasts. An iceberg sometimes appeared to him like a small white lump within reach, when it was at least at ten or twelve miles' distance. He endeavoured to accustom his eyesight to this singular phenomenon, so that he might be able to correct its errors rapidly.

At last the crew were completely worn out by their labours in hauling the vessel alongside of the ice-fields and by keeping it free from the most menacing blocks by the aid of long perches. Nevertheless, the *Forward* was still held back in the impassable limits of the Polar Circle on Friday, the 27th of April.

CHAPTER VIII GOSSIP OF THE CREW

However, the *Forward* managed, by cunningly slipping into narrow passages, to gain a few more minutes north; but instead of avoiding the enemy, it was soon necessary to attack it. The ice-fields, several miles in extent, were getting nearer, and as these moving heaps often represent a pressure of more than ten millions of tons, it was necessary to give a wide berth to their embraces. The ice-saws were at once installed in the interior of the vessel, in such a manner as to facilitate immediate use of them. Part of the crew philosophically accepted their hard work, but the other complained of it, if it did not refuse to obey. At the same time that they assisted in the installation of the instruments, Garry, Bolton, Pen and Gripper exchanged their opinions.

"By Jingo!" said Bolton gaily, "I don't know why the thought strikes me that there's a very jolly tavern in Water-street where it's comfortable to be between a glass of gin and a bottle of porter. Can't you imagine it, Gripper?"

"To tell you the truth," quickly answered the questioned sailor, who generally professed to be in a bad temper, "I don't imagine it here."

"It's for the sake of talking, Gripper; it's evident that the snow towns Dr. Clawbonny admires so don't contain the least public where a poor sailor can get a half-pint of brandy."

"That's sure enough, Bolton; and you may as well add that there's nothing worth drinking here. It's a nice idea to deprive men of their grog when they are in the Northern Seas."

"But you know," said Garry, "that the doctor told us it was to prevent us getting the scurvy. It's the only way to make us go far."

"But I don't want to go far, Garry; it's pretty well to have come this far without trying to go where the devil is determined we shan't."

"Well, we shan't go, that's all," replied Pen. "I declare I've almost forgotten the taste of gin."

"But remember what the doctor says," replied Bolton.

"It's all very fine for them to talk. It remains to be seen if it isn't an excuse for being skinny with the drink."

"Pen may be right, after all," said Gripper.

"His nose is too red for that," answered Bolton. "Pen needn't grumble if it loses a little of its colour in the voyage."

"What's my nose got to do with you?" sharply replied the sailor, attacked in the most sensitive place. "My nose doesn't need any of your remarks; take care of your own."

"Now, then, don't get angry, Pen; I didn't know your nose was so touchy. I like a glass of whisky as well as anybody, especially in such a temperature; but if I know it'll do me more harm than good, I go without."

"You go without," said Warren, the stoker; "but everyone don't go without."

"What do you mean, Warren?" asked Garry, looking fixedly at him.

"I mean that for some reason or other there are spirits on board, and I know they don't go without in the stern."

"And how do you know that?" asked Garry.

Warren did not know what to say: he talked for the sake of talking.

"You see Warren don't know anything about it, Garry," said Bolton.

"Well," said Pen, "we'll ask the commander for a ration of gin; we've earned it well and we'll see what he says."

"I wouldn't if I were you," answered Garry.

"Why?" cried Pen and Gripper.

"Because he'll refuse. You knew you weren't to have any when you enlisted; you should have thought of it then."

"Besides," replied Bolton, who took Garry's part because he liked his character, "Richard Shandon isn't master on board; he obeys, like us."

"Who is master if he isn't?"

"The captain."

"Always that unfortunate captain!" exclaimed Pen. "Don't you see that on these ice-banks there's no more a captain than there is a public? It's a polite way of refusing us what we've a right to claim."

"But if there's a captain," replied Bolton, "I'll bet two months' pay we shall see him before long."

"I should like to tell the captain a bit of my mind," said Pen.

"Who's talking about the captain?" said a new-comer. It was Clifton, the sailor, a superstitious and envious man. "Is anything new known about the captain?" he asked.

"No," they all answered at once.

"Well, I believe we shall find him one fine morning installed in his cabin, and no one will know how he got there."

"Get along, do!" replied Bolton. "Why, Clifton, you imagine that he's a hobgoblin—a sort of wild child of the Highlands."

"Laugh as much as you like, Bolton, you won't change my opinion. Every day as I pass his cabin I look through the keyhole. One of these fine mornings I shall come and tell you what he's like."

"Why, he'll be like everyone else," said Pen, "and if he thinks he'll be able to do what he likes with us, he'll find himself mistaken, that's all!"

"Pen don't know him yet," said Bolton, "and he's beginning to quarrel with him already."

"Who doesn't know him?" said Clifton, looking knowing; "I don't know that he don't!"

"What the devil do you mean?" asked Gripper.

"I know very well what I mean."

"But we don't."

"Well, Pen has quarrelled with him before."

"With the captain?"

"Yes, the dog-captain—it's all one."

The sailors looked at one another, afraid to say anything.

"Man or dog," muttered Pen, "I declare that that animal will have his account one of these days."

"Come, Clifton," asked Bolton seriously, "you don't mean to say that you believe the dog is the real captain?"

"Indeed I do," answered Clifton with conviction. "If you noticed things like I do, you would have noticed what a queer beast it is."

"Well, tell us what you've noticed."

"Haven't you noticed the way he walks on the poop with such an air of authority, looking up at the sails as if he were on watch?"

"That's true enough," added Gripper, "and one evening I actually found him with his paws on the paddle-wheel."

"You don't mean it!" said Bolton.

"And now what do you think he does but go for a walk on the ice-fields, minding neither the bears nor the cold?"

"That's true enough," said Bolton.

"Do you ever see that 'ere animal, like an honest dog, seek men's company, sneak about the kitchen, and set his eyes on Mr. Strong when's he taking something good to the commander? Don't you hear him in the night when he goes away two or three miles from the vessel, howling fit to make your blood run cold, as if it weren't easy enough to feel that sensation in such a temperature as this? Again, have you ever seen him feed? He takes nothing from any one. His food is always untouched and unless a secret hand feeds him on board, I may say that he lives without eating, and if he's not unearthly, I'm a fool!"

"Upon my word," said Bell, the carpenter, who had heard all Clifton's reasoning, "I shouldn't be surprised if such was the case." The other sailors were silenced.

"Well, at any rate, where's the *Forward* going to?"

"I don't know anything about it," replied Bell. "Richard Shandon will receive the rest of his instructions in due time."

"But from whom?"

"From whom?"

"Yes, how?" asked Bolton, becoming pressing.

"Now then, answer, Bell!" chimed in all the other sailors.

"By whom? how? Why, I don't know," said the carpenter, embarrassed in his turn.

"Why, by the dog-captain," exclaimed Clifton. "He has written once already; why shouldn't he again? If I only knew half of what that 'ere animal knows, I shouldn't be embarrassed at being First Lord of the Admiralty!"

"So then you stick to your opinion that the dog is the captain?"

"Yes."

"Well," said Pen in a hoarse voice, "if that 'ere animal don't want to turn up his toes in a dog's skin, he's only got to make haste and become a man, or I'm hanged if I don't settle him."

"What for?" asked Garry.

"Because I choose," replied Pen brutally; "besides, it's no business of any one."

"Enough talking, my boys," called out Mr. Johnson, interfering just in time, for the conversation was getting hot. "Get on with your work, and set up your saws quicker than that. We must clear the iceberg."

"What! on a Friday?" replied Clifton, shrugging his shoulders. "You'll see she won't get over the Polar circle as easily as you think."

The efforts of the crew were almost powerless during the whole day. The *Forward* could not separate the ice-fields even by going against them full speed, and they were obliged to anchor for the night. On Saturday the temperature lowered again under the influence of an easterly wind. The weather cleared up, and the eye could sweep over the white plains in the distance, which the reflection of the sun's rays rendered dazzling. At seven in the morning the thermometer marked eight degrees below zero. The doctor was tempted to stay quietly in his cabin, and read the Arctic voyages over again; but, according to his custom, he asked himself what would be the most disagreeable thing he could do, which he settled was to go on deck and assist the men to work in such a temperature. Faithful to the line of conduct he had traced out for himself, he left his well-warmed cabin and came to help in hauling the vessel. His was a pleasant face, in spite of the green spectacles by which he preserved his eyes from the biting of the reflected rays; in his future observations he was always careful in making use of his snow spectacles, in order to avoid ophthalmia, very frequent in these high latitudes.

Towards evening the *Forward* had made several miles further north, thanks to the activity of the men and Shandon's skill, which made him take advantage of every favourable circumstance; at midnight he had got beyond the sixty-sixth parallel, and the fathom line declared twenty-three fathoms of water; Shandon discovered that he was on the shoal where Her Majesty's ship *Victoria* struck, and that land was drawing near, thirty miles to the east. But now the heaps of ice, which up till now had been motionless, divided and began to move; icebergs seemed coming from every point of the horizon; the brig was entangled in a series of moving rocks, the crushing force of which it was impossible to resist. Moving became so difficult that Garry, the best helmsman, took the wheel; the mountains had a tendency to close up behind the brig; it then became essential to cut through the floating ice, and prudence as well as duty ordered them to go ahead. Difficulties became greater from the impossibility that Shandon found in establishing the direction of the vessel amongst such changing points, which kept moving without offering one firm perspective. The crew was divided into two tacks, larboard and starboard; each one, armed with a long perch with an iron point, drove back the two threatening blocks. Soon the *Forward* entered into a pass so narrow, between two high blocks, that the extremity of her yards struck against the walls, hard as rock; by degrees she entangled herself in the midst of a winding valley, filled up with eddies of snow, whilst the floating ice was crashing and splitting with sinister cracklings. But it soon became certain that there was no egress from this gullet. An enormous block, caught in the channel, was driving rapidly on to the *Forward*! It seemed impossible to avoid it, and equally impossible to back out along a road already obstructed.

Shandon and Johnson, standing on the prow, were contemplating the position. Shandon was pointing with his right hand at the direction the helmsman was to take, and with his left was conveying to James Wall, posted near the engineer, his orders for the working of the machine.

"How will this end?" asked the doctor of Johnson.

"As it may please God," replied the boatswain.

The block of ice, at least a hundred feet high, was only about a cable's length from the *Forward*, and threatened to pound her under it.

"Cursed luck!" exclaimed Pen, swearing frightfully.

"Silence!" exclaimed a voice which it was impossible to recognise in the midst of the storm.

The block seemed to be precipitating itself upon the brig; there was a moment of undefinable anguish; the men forsook their poles and flocked to the stern in spite of Shandon's orders.

Suddenly a frightful sound was heard; a genuine waterspout fell upon deck, heaved up by an enormous wave. A cry of terror rang out from the crew whilst Garry, at the helm, held the *Forward* in a straight line in spite of the frightful incumbrance. When their frightened looks were drawn towards the mountain of ice it had disappeared; the pass was free, and further on a long channel, illuminated by the oblique rays of the sun, allowed the brig to pursue her track.

"Well, Mr. Clawbonny," said Johnson, "can you explain to me the cause of that phenomenon?"

"It is a very simple one," answered the doctor, "and happens very often. When those floating bodies are disengaged from each other by the thaw, they sail away separately, maintaining their balance; but by degrees, as they near the south, where the water is relatively warmer, their base, shaken by the collision with other icebergs, begins to melt and weaken; it then happens that their centre of gravity is displaced, and, naturally, they overturn. Only, if that one had turned over two minutes later, it would have crushed our vessel to pieces."

CHAPTER IX NEWS

The Polar circle was cleared at last. On the 30th of April, at midday, the *Forward* passed abreast of Holsteinborg; picturesque mountains rose up on the eastern horizon. The sea appeared almost free from icebergs, and the few there were could easily be avoided. The wind veered round to the south-east, and the brig, under her mizensail, brigantine, topsails, and her topgallant sail, sailed up Baffin's Sea. It had been a particularly calm day, and the crew were able to take a little rest. Numerous birds were swimming and fluttering about round the vessel; amongst others, the doctor observed some *alca-alla*, very much like the teal, with black neck, wings and back, and white breast; they plunged with vivacity, and their immersion often lasted forty seconds.

The day would not have been remarkable if the following fact, however extraordinary it may appear, had not occurred on board. At six o'clock in the morning Richard Shandon, re-entering his cabin after having been relieved, found upon the table a letter with this address:

"To the Commander,
"RICHARD SHANDON,
"On board the 'FORWARD,'
"Baffin's Sea."

Shandon could not believe his own eyes, and before reading such a strange epistle he caused the doctor, James Wall and Johnson to be called, and showed them the letter.

"That grows very strange," said Johnson.

"It's delightful!" thought the doctor.

"At last," cried Shandon, "we shall know the secret."

With a quick hand he tore the envelope and read as follows:

"COMMANDER,—The captain of the *Forward* is pleased with the coolness, skill, and courage that your men, your officers, and yourself have shown on the late occasions, and begs you to give evidence of his gratitude to the crew.

"Have the goodness to take a northerly direction towards Melville Bay, and from thence try and penetrate into Smith's Straits.

"THE CAPTAIN OF THE *Forward*,
"K. Z."

"Monday, April 30th,
"Abreast of Cape Walsingham."

"Is that all?" cried the doctor.

"That's all," replied Shandon, and the letter fell from his hands.

"Well," said Wall, "this chimerical captain doesn't even mention coming on board, so I conclude that he never will come."

"But how did this letter get here?" said Johnson.

Shandon was silent.

"Mr. Wall is right," replied the doctor, after picking up the letter and turning it over in every direction; "the captain won't come on board for an excellent reason——"

"And what's that?" asked Shandon quickly.

"Because he is here already," replied the doctor simply.

"Already!" said Shandon. "What do you mean?"

"How do you explain the arrival of this letter if such is not the case?"

Johnson nodded his head in sign of approbation.

"It is not possible!" said Shandon energetically. "I know every man of the crew. We should have to believe, in that case, that the captain has been with us ever since we set sail. It is not possible, I tell you. There isn't one of them that I haven't seen for more than two years in Liverpool; doctor, your supposition is inadmissible."

"Then what do you admit, Shandon?"

"Everything but that! I admit that the captain, or one of his men, has profited by the darkness, the fog, or anything you like, in order to slip on board; we are not very far from land; there are Esquimaux kaïaks that pass unperceived between the icebergs; someone may have come on board and left the letter; the fog was intense enough to favour their design."

"And to hinder them from seeing the brig," replied the doctor; "if we were not able to perceive an intruder slip on board, how could *he* have discovered the *Forward* in the midst of a fog?"

"That is evident," exclaimed Johnson.

"I come back, then," said the doctor, "to my first hypothesis. What do you think about it, Shandon?"

"I think what you please," replied Shandon fiercely, "with the exception of supposing that this man is on board my vessel."

"Perhaps," added Wall, "there may be amongst the crew a man of his who has received instructions from him."

"That's very likely," added the doctor.

"But which man?" asked Shandon. "I tell you I have known all my men a long time."

"Anyhow," replied Johnson, "if this captain shows himself, let him be man or devil, we'll receive him; but we have another piece of information to draw from this letter."

"What's that?" asked Shandon.

"Why, that we are to direct our path not only towards Melville Bay, but again into Smith's Straits."

"You are right," answered the doctor.

"Smith's Straits?" echoed Shandon mechanically.

"It is evident," replied Johnson, "that the destination of the *Forward* is not to seek a North-West passage, as we shall leave to our left the only track that leads to it—that is to say, Lancaster Straits; that's what forebodes us difficult navigation in unknown seas."

"Yes, Smith's Straits," replied Shandon, "that's the route the American Kane followed in 1853, and at the price of what dangers! For a long time he was thought to be lost in those dreadful latitudes! However, as we must go, go we must. But where? how far? To the Pole?"

"And why not?" cried the doctor.

The idea of such an insane attempt made the boatswain shrug his shoulders.

CHAPTER IX NEWS

"After all," resumed James Wall, "to come back to the captain, if he exists, I see nowhere on the coast of Greenland except Disko or Uppernawik where he can be waiting for us; in a few days we shall know what we may depend upon."

"But," asked the doctor of Shandon, "aren't you going to make known the contents of that letter to the crew?"

"With the commander's permission," replied Johnson, "I should do nothing of the kind."

"And why so?" asked Shandon.

"Because all that mystery tends to discourage the men: they are already very anxious about the fate of our expedition, and if the supernatural side of it is increased it may produce very serious results, and in a critical moment we could not rely upon them. What do you say about it, commander?"

"And you, doctor—what do you think?" asked Shandon.

"I think Johnson's reasoning is just."

"And you, Wall?"

"Unless there's better advice forthcoming, I shall stick to the opinion of these gentlemen."

Shandon reflected seriously during a few minutes, and read the letter over again carefully.

"Gentlemen," said he, "your opinion on this subject is certainly excellent, but I cannot adopt it."

"Why not, Shandon?" asked the doctor.

"Because the instructions of this letter are formal: they command me to give the captain's congratulations to the crew, and up till to-day I have always blindly obeyed his orders in whatever manner they have been transmitted to me, and I cannot——"

"But——" said Johnson, who rightly dreaded the effect of such a communication upon the minds of the sailors.

"My dear Johnson," answered Shandon, "your reasons are excellent, but read—'he begs you to give evidence of his gratitude to the crew.'"

"Act as you think best," replied Johnson, who was besides a very strict observer of discipline. "Are we to muster the crew on deck?"

"Do so," replied Shandon.

The news of a communication having been received from the captain spread like wildfire on deck; the sailors quickly arrived at their post, and the commander read out the contents of the mysterious letter. The reading of it was received in a dead silence; the crew dispersed, a prey to a thousand suppositions. Clifton had heard enough to give himself up to all the wanderings of his superstitious imagination; he attributed a considerable share in this incident to the dog-captain, and when by chance he met him in his passage he never failed to salute him. "I told you the animal could write," he used to say to the sailors. No one said anything in answer to this observation, and even Bell, the carpenter himself, would not have known what to answer.

Nevertheless it was certain to all that, in default of the captain, his spirit or his shadow watched on board; and henceforward the wisest of the crew abstained from exchanging their opinions about him.

On the 1st of May, at noon, they were in 68° latitude and 56° 32' longitude. The temperature was higher and the thermometer marked twenty-five degrees above zero. The doctor was amusing himself with watching the antics of a white bear and two cubs on the brink of a pack that lengthened out the land. Accompanied by Wall and Simpson, he tried to give chase to them by means of the canoe; but the animal, of a rather warlike disposition, rapidly led away its offspring, and consequently the doctor was compelled to renounce following them up.

Chilly Cape was doubled during the night under the influence of a favourable wind, and soon the high mountains of Disko rose in the horizon. Godhavn Bay, the residence of the Governor-General of the Danish Settlements, was left to the right. Shandon did not consider it worth while to stop, and soon outran the Esquimaux pirogues who were endeavouring to reach his ship.

The Island of Disko is also called Whale Island. It was from this point that on the 12th of July, 1845, Sir John Franklin wrote to the Admiralty for the last time. It was also on that island on the 27th of August, 1859, that Captain McClintock set foot on his return, bringing back, alas! proofs too complete of the loss of the expedition. The coincidence of these two facts were noted by the doctor; that melancholy conjunction was prolific in memories, but soon the heights of Disko disappeared from his view.

There were, at that time, numerous icebergs on the coasts, some of those which the strongest thaws are unable to detach; the continual series of ridges showed themselves under the strangest forms.

The next day, towards three o'clock, they were bearing on to Sanderson Hope to the north-east. Land was left on the starboard at a distance of about fifteen miles; the mountains seemed tinged with a red-coloured bistre. During the evening, several whales of the finners species, which have fins on their backs, came playing about in the midst of the ice-trails, throwing out air and water from their blow-holes. It was during the night between the 3rd and 4th of May that the doctor saw for the first time the sun graze the horizon without dipping his luminous disc into it. Since the 31st of January the days had been getting longer and longer till the sun went down no more. To strangers not accustomed to the persistence of this perpetual light it was a constant subject of astonishment, and even of fatigue; it is almost impossible to understand to what extent obscurity is requisite for the well-being of our eyes. The doctor experienced real pain in getting accustomed to this light, rendered still more acute by the reflection of the sun's rays upon the plains of ice.

On May 5th the *Forward* headed the seventy-second parallel; two months later they would have met with numerous whalers under these high latitudes, but at present the straits were not sufficiently open to allow them to penetrate into Baffin's Bay. The following day the brig, after having headed Woman's Island, came in sight of Uppernawik, the most northerly settlement that Denmark possesses on these coasts.

CHAPTER X DANGEROUS NAVIGATION

Shandon, Dr. Clawbonny, Johnson, Foker, and Strong, the cook, went on shore in the small boat. The governor, his wife, and five children, all of the Esquimaux race, came politely to meet the visitors. The doctor knew enough Danish to enable him to establish a very agreeable acquaintance with them; besides, Foker, who was interpreter of the expedition, as well as ice-master, knew about twenty words of the Greenland language, and if not ambitious, twenty words will carry you far. The governor was born on the island, and had never left his native country. He did the honours of the town, which is composed of three wooden huts, for himself and the Lutheran minister, of a school, and magazines stored with the produce of wrecks. The remainder consists of snow-huts, the entrance to which is attained by creeping through a hole.

The greater part of the population came down to greet the *Forward*, and more than one native advanced as far as the middle of the bay in his kaïak, fifteen feet long and scarcely two wide. The doctor knew that the word Esquimaux signified raw-fish-eater, and he likewise knew that the name was considered an insult in the country, for which reason he did not fail to address them by the title of Greenlanders, and nevertheless only by the look of their oily sealskin clothing, their boots of the same material, and all their greasy tainted appearance, it was easy to discover their accustomed food. Like all Ichthyophagans, they were half-eaten up with leprosy; and yet, for all that, were in no worse health.

The Lutheran minister and his wife, with whom the doctor promised himself a private chat, were on a journey towards Proven on the south of Uppernawik; he was therefore reduced to getting information out of the governor. This chief magistrate did not seem to be very learned; a little less and he would have been an ass, a little more and he would have known how to read. The doctor, however, questioned him upon the commercial affairs, the customs and manners of the Esquimaux, and learnt by signs that seals were worth about £40 delivered in Copenhagen, a bearskin forty Danish dollars, a blue foxskin four, and a white one two or three dollars. The doctor also wished, with an eye to completing his personal education, to visit one of the Esquimaux huts; it is almost impossible to imagine of what a learned man who is desirous of knowledge is capable. Happily the opening of those hovels was too narrow, and the enthusiastic fellow was not able to crawl in; it was very lucky for him, for there is nothing more repulsive than that accumulation of things living and dead, seal flesh or Esquimaux flesh, rotten fish and infectious wearing apparel, which constitute a Greenland hovel; no window to revive the unbreathable air, only a hole at the top of the hut, which gives free passage to the smoke, but does not allow the stench to go out.

Foker gave these details to the doctor, who did not curse his corpulence the less for that. He wished to judge for himself about these emanations, *sui generis*.

"I am sure," said he, "one gets used to it in the long run."

In the long run depicts Dr. Clawbonny in a single phrase. During the ethnographical studies of the worthy doctor, Shandon, according to his instructions, was occupied in procuring means of transport to cross the ice. He had to pay £4 for a sledge and six dogs, and even then he had great difficulty in persuading the natives to part with them. Shandon wanted also to engage Hans Christian, the clever dog-driver, who made one of the party of Captain McClintock's expedition; but, unfortunately, Hans was at that time in Southern Greenland. Then came the grand question, the topic of the day, was there in Uppernawik a European waiting for the passage of the *Forward*? Did the governor know if any foreigner, an Englishman probably, had settled in those countries? To what epoch could he trace his last relations with whale or other ships? To these questions the governor replied that not one single foreigner had landed on that side of the coast for more than ten months.

Shandon asked for the names of the last whalers seen there; he knew none of them. He was in despair.

"You must acknowledge, doctor, that all this is quite inconceivable. Nothing at Cape Farewell, nothing at Disko Island, nothing at Uppernawik."

"If when we get there you repeat 'Nothing in Melville Bay,' I shall greet you as the only captain of the *Forward*."

The small boat came back to the brig towards evening, bringing back the visitors. Strong, in order to change the food a little, had procured several dozens of eider-duck eggs, twice as big as hens' eggs, and of greenish colour. It was not much, but the change was refreshing to a crew fed on salted meat. The wind became favourable the next day, but, however, Shandon did not command them to get under sail; he still wished to stay another day, and for conscience' sake to give any human being time to join the *Forward*. He even caused the 16-pounder to be fired from hour to hour; it thundered out with a great crash amidst the icebergs, but the noise only frightened the swarms of molly-mokes and rotches. During the night several rockets were sent up, but in vain. And thus they were obliged to set sail.

On the 8th of May, at six o'clock in the morning, the *Forward* under her topsails, foresails, and topgallant, lost sight of the Uppernawik settlement, and the hideous stakes to which were hung seal-guts and deer-paunches. The wind was blowing from the south-east, and the temperature went up to thirty-two degrees. The sun pierced through the fog, and the ice was getting a little loosened under its dissolving action. But the reflection of the white rays produced a sad effect on the eyesight of several of the crew. Wolsten, the gunsmith, Gripper, Clifton, and Bell were struck with snow blindness, a kind of weakness in the eyes very frequent in spring, and which determines, amongst the Esquimaux, numerous cases of blindness. The doctor advised those who were so afflicted and their companions in general to cover their faces with green gauze, and he was the first to put his own prescription into execution.

The dogs bought by Shandon at Uppernawik were of a rather savage nature, but in the end they became accustomed to the ship; the captain did not take the arrival of these new comrades too much to heart, and he seemed to know their habits. Clifton was not the last to remark the fact that the captain must already have been in communication with his Greenland brethren, as on land they were always famished and reduced by incomplete nourishment; they only thought of recruiting themselves by the diet on board.

On the 9th of May the *Forward* touched within a few cables' length the most westerly of the Baffin Isles. The doctor noticed several rocks in the bay between the islands and the continent, those called Crimson Cliffs; they were covered over with snow as red as carmine, to which Dr. Kane gives a purely vegetable origin. Clawbonny wanted to consider this phenomenon nearer, but the ice prevented them approaching the coast; although the temperature had a tendency to rise, it was easy enough to see that the icebergs and ice-streams were accumulating to the north of Baffin's Sea. The land offered a very different aspect from that of Uppernawik; immense glaciers were outlined on the horizon against a greyish sky. On the 10th the *Forward* left Hingston Bay on the right, near to the seventy-fourth degree of latitude. Several hundred miles westward the Lancaster Channel opened out into the sea.

But afterwards that immense extent of water disappeared under enormous fields of ice, upon which hummocks rose up as regularly as a crystallisation of the same substance. Shandon had the steam put on, and up to the 11th of May the *Forward* wound amongst the sinuous rocks, leaving the print of a track on the sky, caused by the black smoke from her funnels. But new obstacles were soon encountered; the paths were getting closed up in consequence of the incessant displacement of the floating masses; at every minute a failure of water in front of the *Forward's* prow became imminent, and if she had been nipped it would have been difficult to extricate her. They all knew it, and thought about it.

On board this vessel, without aim or known destination, foolishly seeking to advance towards the north, some symptoms of hesitation were manifested amongst those men, accustomed to an existence of danger; many, forgetting the advantages offered, regretted having ventured so far, and already a certain demoralisation prevailed in their minds, still more increased by Clifton's fears, and the idle talk of two or three of the leaders, such as Pen, Gripper, Warren, and Wolston.

To the uneasiness of the crew were joined overwhelming fatigues, for on the 12th of May the brig was closed in on every side; her steam was powerless, and it was necessary to force a road through the ice-fields. The working of the saws was very difficult in the floes, which measured from six to seven feet in thickness. When two parallel grooves divided the ice for the length of a hundred feet, they had to break the interior part with hatchets or handspikes; then took place the elongation of the anchors, fixed in a hole by means of a thick auger; afterwards the working of the capstan began, and in this way the vessel was hauled over. The greatest difficulty consisted in driving the smashed pieces under the floes in order to open up a free passage for the ship, and to thrust them away they were compelled to use long iron-spiked poles.

At last, what with the working of the saws, the hauling, the capstan and poles, incessant, dangerous, and forced work, in the midst of fogs or thick snow, the temperature relatively low, ophthalmic suffering and moral uneasiness, all contributed to discourage the crew, and react on the men's imagination. When sailors have an energetic, audacious, and convinced man to do with, who knows what he wants, where he is bound for, and what end he has in view, confidence sustains them in spite of everything. They make one with their chief, feeling strong in his strength, and quiet in his tranquillity; but on the brig it was felt that the commander was not sure of himself, that he hesitated before his unknown end and destination. In spite of his energetic nature, his weakness showed itself in his changing orders, incomplete manoeuvres, stormy reflections, and a thousand details which could not escape the notice of the crew.

Besides, Shandon was not captain of the ship, a sufficient reason for argument about his orders; from argument to a refusal to obey the step is easy. The discontented soon added to their number the first engineer, who up to now had remained a slave to his duty.

On May 16th, six days after the *Forward's* arrival at the icebergs, Shandon had not gained two miles northward, and the ice threatened to freeze in the brig till the following season. This was becoming dangerous. Towards eight in the evening Shandon and the doctor, accompanied by Garry, went on a voyage of discovery in the midst of the immense plains; they took care not to go too far away from the vessel, as it was difficult to fix any landmarks in those white solitudes, the aspects of which changed constantly.

The refraction produced strange effects; they still astonished the doctor; where he thought he had only one foot to leap he found it was five or six, or the contrary; and in both cases the result was a fall, if not dangerous, at least painful, on the frozen ice as hard as glass.

Shandon and his two companions went in search of a practicable passage. Three miles from the ship they succeeded, not without trouble, in climbing the iceberg, which was perhaps three hundred feet high.

From this point their view extended over that desolated mass which looked like the ruins of a gigantic town with its beaten-down obelisks, its overthrown steeples and palaces turned upside down all in a lump—in fact, a genuine chaos. The sun threw long oblique rays of a light without warmth, as if heat-absorbing substances were placed between it and that gloomy country. The sea seemed to be frozen to the remotest limits of view.

"How shall we get through?" exclaimed the doctor.

"I have not the least idea," replied Shandon; "but we will get through, even if we are obliged to employ powder to blow up those mountains, for I certainly won't let that ice shut me up till next spring."

"Nevertheless, such was the fate of the *Fox*, almost in these same quarters. Never mind," continued the doctor, "we shall get through with a little philosophy. Believe me, that is worth all the engines in the world."

"You must acknowledge," replied Shandon, "that the year doesn't begin under very favourable auspices."

"That is incontestable, and I notice that Baffin's Sea has a tendency to return to the same state in which it was before 1817."

"Then you think, doctor, that the present state of things has not always existed?"

"Yes; from time to time there are vast breakings up which scientific men can scarcely explain; thus, up to 1817 this sea was constantly obstructed, when suddenly an immense cataclysm took place which drove back these icebergs into the ocean, the great part of which were stranded on Newfoundland Bank. From that time Baffin's Bay has been almost free, and has become the haunt of numerous whalers."

"Then, since that epoch, voyages to the north have been easier?"

"Incomparably so; but for the last few years it has been observed that the bay has a tendency to be closed up again, and according to investigations made by navigators, it may probably be so for a long time—a still greater reason for us to go on as far as possible. Just now we look like people who get into unknown galleries, the doors of which are always shut behind them."

"Do you advise me to back out?" asked Shandon, endeavouring to read the answer in the doctor's eyes.

"I! I have never known how to take a step backward, and should we never return, I say 'Go ahead.' However, I should like to make known to you that if we do anything imprudent, we know very well what we are exposed to."

"Well, Garry, what do you think about it?" asked Shandon of the sailor.

"I? Commander, I should go on; I'm of the same opinion as Mr. Clawbonny; but you do as you please; command, and we will obey."

"They don't all speak like you, Garry," replied Shandon. "They aren't all in an obedient humour! Suppose they were to refuse to execute my orders?"

"Commander," replied Garry coldly, "I have given you my advice because you asked me for it; but you are not obliged to act upon it."

CHAPTER X DANGEROUS NAVIGATION

Shandon did not reply; he attentively examined the horizon, and descended with his two companions on to the ice-field.

CHAPTER XI THE DEVIL'S THUMB

During the commander's absence the men had gone through divers works in order to make the ship fit to avoid the pressure of the ice-fields. Pen, Clifton, Gripper, Bolton, and Simpson were occupied in this laborious work; the stoker and the two engineers were even obliged to come to the aid of their comrades, for, from the instant they were not wanted at the engine, they again became sailors, and, as such, they could be employed in all kinds of work on board. But this was not accomplished without a great deal of grumbling.

"I'll tell you what," said Pen, "I've had enough of it, and if in three days the breaking up isn't come, I'll swear to God that I'll chuck up!"

"You'll chuck up?" replied Gripper; "you'd do better to help us to back out. Do you think we are in the humour to winter here till next year?"

"To tell you the truth, it would be a dreary winter," said Plover, "for the ship is exposed from every quarter."

"And who knows," added Brunton, "if even next spring we should find the sea freer than it is now?"

"We aren't talking about next spring," said Pen; "to-day's Thursday; if next Sunday morning the road ain't clear, we'll back out south."

"That's the ticket!" cried Clifton.

"Are you all agreed?" said Pen.

"Yes," answered all his comrades.

"That's right enough," answered Warren, "for if we are obliged to work like this, hauling the ship by the strength of our arms, my advice is to backwater."

"We'll see about that on Sunday," answered Wolsten.

"As soon as I get the order," said Brunton, "I'll soon get my steam up."

"Or we'd manage to get it up ourselves," said Clifton.

"If any of the officers," said Pen, "wants to have the pleasure of wintering here, we'll let him. He can build himself a snow-hut like the Esquimaux."

"Nothing of the kind, Pen," replied Brunton; "we won't leave anybody. You understand that, you others. Besides, I don't think it would be difficult to persuade the commander; he already seems very uncertain, and if we were quietly to propose it——"

"I don't know that," said Plover; "Richard Shandon is a hard, headstrong man, and we should have to sound him carefully."

"When I think," replied Bolton, with a covetous sigh, "that in a month we might be back in Liverpool; we could soon clear the southern ice-line. The pass in Davis's Straits will be open in the beginning of June, and we shall only have to let ourselves drift into the Atlantic."

"Besides," said the prudent Clifton, "if we bring back the commander with us, acting under his responsibility, our pay and bounty money will be sure; whilst if we return alone it won't be so certain."

"That's certain!" said Plover; "that devil of a Clifton speaks like a book. Let us try to have nothing to explain to the Admiralty; it's much safer to leave no one behind us."

"But if the officers refuse to follow us?" replied Pen, who wished to push his comrades to an extremity.

To such a question they were puzzled to reply.

"We shall see about it when the time comes," replied Bolton; "besides, it would be enough to win Richard Shandon over to our side. We shall have no difficulty about that."

"Anyhow," said Pen, swearing, "there's something I'll leave here if I get an arm eaten in the attempt."

"Ah! you mean the dog," said Plover.

"Yes, the dog; and before long I'll settle his hash!"

"The more so," replied Clifton, coming back to his favourite theme, "that the dog is the cause of all our misfortunes."

"He's cast an evil spell over us," said Plover.

"It's through him we're in an iceberg," said Gripper.

"He's the cause that we've had more ice against us than has ever been seen at this time of year," said Wolsten.

"He's the cause of my bad eyes," said Brunton.

"He's cut off the gin and brandy," added Pen.

"He's the cause of everything," said the assembly, getting excited.

"And he's captain into the bargain!" cried Clifton.

"Well, captain of ill-luck," said Pen, whose unreasonable fury grew stronger at every word; "you wanted to come here, and here you'll stay."

"But how are we to nap him?" said Plover.

"We've a good opportunity," replied Clifton; "the commander isn't on deck, the lieutenant is asleep in his cabin, and the fog's thick enough to stop Johnson seeing us."

"But where's the dog?" cried Pen.

"He's asleep near the coalhole," replied Clifton, "and if anybody wants——"

"I'll take charge of him," answered Pen furiously.

"Look out, Pen, he's got teeth that could snap an iron bar in two."

"If he moves I'll cut him open," cried Pen, taking his knife in one hand. He bounced in between decks, followed by Warren, who wanted to help him in his undertaking. They quickly came back, carrying the animal in their arms, strongly muzzled, with his paws bound tightly together. They had taken him by surprise whilst he slept, so that the unfortunate dog could not escape them.

"Hurrah for Pen!" cried Plover.

"What do you mean to do with him now you've got him?" asked Clifton.

"Why, drown him, and if ever he gets over it——" replied Pen, with a fearful smile of satisfaction.

About two hundred steps from the vessel there was a seal-hole, a kind of circular crevice cut out by the teeth of that amphibious animal, hollowed out from underneath, and through which the seal comes up to breathe on to the surface of the ice. To keep this aperture from closing up he has to be very careful because the formation of his jaws would not enable him to bore through the hole again from the outside, and in a moment of danger he would fall a prey to his enemies. Pen and Warren directed their steps towards this crevice, and there, in spite of the dog's energetic efforts, he was unmercifully precipitated into the sea. An enormous lump of ice was then placed over the opening, thus closing all possible issue to the poor animal, walled up in a watery prison.

"Good luck to you, captain," cried the brutal sailor.

Shortly afterwards Pen and Warren returned on deck. Johnson had seen nothing of this performance. The fog thickened round about the ship, and snow began to fall with violence. An hour later, Richard Shandon, the doctor, and Garry rejoined the *Forward.* Shandon had noticed a pass in a north-eastern direction of which he was resolved to take advantage, and gave his orders in consequence. The crew obeyed with a certain activity, not without hinting to Shandon that it was impossible to go further on, and that they only gave him three more days' obedience. During a part of the night and the following day the working of the saws and the hauling were actively kept up; the *Forward* gained about two miles further north. On the 18th she was in sight of land, and at five or six cable-lengths from a peculiar peak, called from its strange shape the Devil's Thumb.

It was there that the *Prince Albert* in 1851, and the *Advance* with Kane, in 1853, were kept prisoners by the ice for several weeks. The odd form of the Devil's Thumb, the dreary deserts in its vicinity, the vast circus of icebergs—some of them more than three hundred feet high—the cracking of the ice, reproduced by the echo in so sinister a manner, rendered the position of the *Forward* horribly dreary. Shandon understood the necessity of getting out of it and going further ahead. Twenty-four hours later, according to his estimation, he had been able to clear the fatal coast for about two miles, but this was not enough. Shandon, overwhelmed with fear, and the false situation in which he was placed, lost both courage and energy; in order to obey his instructions and get further north, he had thrown his vessel into an excessively perilous situation. The men were worn out by the hauling; it required more than three hours to hollow out a channel twenty feet long, through ice that was usually from four to five feet thick. The health of the crew threatened to break down. Shandon was astonished at the silence of his men and their unaccustomed obedience, but he feared that it was the calm before the storm. Who can judge, then, of his painful disappointment, surprise, and despair when he perceived that in consequence of an insensible movement of the ice-field the *Forward* had, during the night from the 18th to the 19th, lost all the advantage she had gained with so much toil? On the Saturday morning they were once more opposite the ever-threatening Devil's Thumb, and in a still more critical position. The icebergs became more numerous, and drifted by in the fog like phantoms. Shandon was in a state of complete demoralisation, for fright had taken possession of the dauntless man and his crew. Shandon had heard the dog's disappearance spoken about, but dared not punish those who were guilty of it. He feared that a rebellion might be the consequence. The weather was fearful during the whole day; the snow rose up in thick whirlpools, wrapping up the *Forward* in an impenetrable cloak. Sometimes, under the action of the storm, the fog was torn asunder, and displayed towards land, raised up like a spectre, the Devil's Thumb.

The *Forward* was anchored to an immense block of ice; it was all that could be done; there was nothing more to attempt; the obscurity became denser, and the man at the helm could not see James Wall, who was on duty in the bow. Shandon withdrew to his cabin, a prey to unremitting uneasiness; the doctor was putting his voyage notes in order; one half the crew remained on deck, the other half stayed in the common cabin. At one moment, when the storm increased in fury, the Devil's Thumb seemed to rise up out of all proportion in the midst of the fog.

"Good God!" cried Simpson, drawing back with fright.

"What the devil's that?" said Foker, and exclamations rose up in every direction.

"It is going to smash us!"

CHAPTER XI THE DEVIL'S THUMB

"We are lost!"

"Mr. Wall! Mr. Wall!"

"It's all over with us!"

"Commander! Commander!"

These cries were simultaneously uttered by the men on watch. Wall fled to the quarter-deck, and Shandon, followed by the doctor, rushed on deck to look. In the midst of the fog the Devil's Thumb seemed to have suddenly neared the brig, and seemed to have grown in a most fantastic manner. At its summit rose up a second cone, turned upside down and spindled on its point; its enormous mass threatened to crush the ship, as it was oscillating and ready to fall. It was a most fearful sight; every one instinctively drew back, and several sailors, leaping on to the ice, abandoned the ship.

"Let no one move!" cried the commander in a severe voice. "Every one to his post!"

"How now, my friends? There's nothing to be frightened at!" said the doctor. "There's no danger! Look, commander, look ahead, Mr. Wall; it's only an effect of the mirage, nothing else."

"You are quite right, Mr. Clawbonny," answered Johnson; "those fools were frightened at a shadow."

After the doctor had spoken most of the sailors drew near, and their fear changed to admiration at the wonderful phenomenon, which shortly disappeared from sight.

"They call that a mirage?" said Clifton. "Well, you may believe me that the devil has something to do with it."

"That's certain!" replied Gripper.

But when the fog cleared away it disclosed to the eyes of the commander an immense free and unexpected passage; it seemed to run away from the coast, and he therefore determined to seize such a favourable hazard. Men were placed on each side of the creek, hawsers were lowered down to them, and they began to tow the vessel in a northerly direction. During long hours this work was actively executed in silence. Shandon caused the steam to be got up, in order to take advantage of the fortunate discovery of this channel.

"This," said he to Johnson, "is a most providential hazard, and if we can only get a few miles ahead, we shall probably get to the end of our misfortunes."

"Brunton! stir up the fires, and as soon as there's enough pressure let me know. In the meantime our men will pluck up their courage—that will be so much gained. They are in a hurry to run away from the Devil's Thumb; we'll take advantage of their good inclinations!"

All at once the progress of the *Forward* was abruptly arrested.

"What's up?" cried Shandon. "I say, Wall! have we broken our tow-ropes?"

"Not at all, commander," answered Wall, looking over the side. "Hallo! Here are the men coming back again. They are climbing the ship's side as if the devil was at their heels."

"What the deuce can it be?" cried Shandon, rushing forward.

"On board! On board!" cried the terrified sailors.

Shandon looked in a northerly direction, and shuddered in spite of himself. A strange animal, with appalling movements, whose foaming tongue emerged from enormous jaws, was leaping about at a cable's length from the ship. In appearance he seemed to be about twenty feet high, with hair like bristles; he was following up the sailors, whilst his formidable tail, ten feet long, was sweeping the snow and throwing it up in thick whirlwinds. The sight of such a monster riveted the most daring to the spot.

"It's a bear!" said one.

"It's the Gevaudan beast!"

"It's the lion of the Apocalypse!"

Shandon ran to his cabin for a gun he always kept loaded. The doctor armed himself, and held himself in readiness to fire upon an animal which, by its dimensions, recalled the antediluvian quadrupeds. He neared the ship in immense leaps; Shandon and the doctor fired at the same time, when, suddenly, the report of their firearms, shaking the atmospheric stratum, produced an unexpected effect. The doctor looked attentively, and burst out laughing.

"It's the refraction!" he exclaimed.

"Only the refraction!" repeated Shandon. But a fearful exclamation from the crew interrupted them.

"The dog!" said Clifton.

"The dog, captain!" repeated all his comrades.

"Himself!" cried Pen; "always that cursed brute."

They were not mistaken—it was the dog. Having got loose from his shackles, he had regained the surface by another crevice. At that instant the refraction, through a phenomenon common to these latitudes, caused him to appear under formidable dimensions, which the shaking of the air had dispersed; but the vexatious effect was none the less produced upon the minds of the sailors, who were very little disposed to admit an explanation of the fact by purely physical reasons. The adventure of the Devil's Thumb, the reappearance of the dog under such fantastic circumstances, gave the finishing touch to their mental faculties, and murmurs broke out on all sides.

CHAPTER XII CAPTAIN HATTERAS

The *Forward*, under steam, rapidly made its way between the ice-mountains and the icebergs. Johnson was at the wheel. Shandon, with his snow spectacles, was examining the horizon, but his joy was of short duration, for he soon discovered that the passage ended in a circus of mountains. However, he preferred going on, in spite of the difficulty, to going back. The dog followed the brig at a long distance, running along the plain, but if he lagged too far behind a singular whistle could be distinguished, which he immediately obeyed. The first time this whistle was heard the sailors looked round about them; they were alone on deck all together, and no stranger was to be seen; and yet the whistle was again heard from time to time. Clifton was the first alarmed.

"Do you hear?" said he. "Just look how that animal answers when he hears the whistle."

"I can scarcely believe my eyes," answered Gripper.

"It's all over!" cried Pen. "I don't go any further."

"Pen's right!" replied Brunton; "it's tempting God!"

"Tempting the devil!" replied Clifton. "I'd sooner lose my bounty money than go a step further."

"We shall never get back!" said Bolton in despair.

The crew had arrived at the highest pitch of insubordination.

"Not a step further!" cried Wolsten. "Are you all of the same mind?"

"Ay! ay!" answered all the sailors.

"Come on, then," said Bolton; "let's go and find the commander; I'll undertake the talking."

The sailors in a tight group swayed away towards the poop. The *Forward* at the time was penetrating into a vast circus, which measured perhaps 800 feet in diameter, and with the exception of one entrance—that by which the vessel had come—was entirely closed up.

Shandon said that he had just imprisoned himself; but what was he to do? How were they to retrace their steps? He felt his responsibility, and his hand grasped the telescope. The doctor, with folded arms, kept silent; he was contemplating the walls of ice, the medium altitude of which was over 300 feet. A foggy dome remained suspended above the gulf. It was at this instant that Bolton addressed his speech to the commander.

"Commander!" said he in a trembling voice, "we can't go any further."

"What do you say?" replied Shandon, whose consciousness of disregarded authority made the blood rise to the roots of his hair.

"Commander," replied Bolton, "we say that we've done enough for that invisible captain, and we are decided to go no further ahead."

"You are decided?" cried Shandon. "You talk thus, Bolton? Take care!"

"Your threats are all the same to us," brutally replied Pen; "we won't go an inch further."

Shandon advanced towards the mutineers; at the same time the mate came up and said in a whisper: "Commander, if you wish to get out of here we haven't a minute to lose; there's an iceberg drifting up the pass, and it is very likely to cork up all issue and keep us prisoners."

Shandon examined the situation.

"You will give an account of your conduct later on, you fellows," said he. "Now heave aboard!"

The sailors rushed to their posts, and the *Forward* quickly veered round; the fires were stuffed with coals; the great question was to outrun the floating mountain. It was a struggle between the brig and the iceberg. The former, in order to get through, was running south; the latter was drifting north, ready to close up every passage.

"Steam up! steam up!" cried Shandon. "Do you hear, Brunton?"

The *Forward* glided like a bird amidst the struggling icebergs, which her prow sent to the right-about; the brig's hull shivered under the action of the screw, and the manometer indicated a prodigious tension of steam, for it whistled with a deafening noise.

"Load the valves!" cried Shandon, and the engineer obeyed at the risk of blowing up the ship; but his despairing efforts were in vain. The iceberg, caught up by an undercurrent, rapidly approached the pass. The brig was still about three cables' length from it, when the mountain, entering like a corner-stone into the open space, strongly adhered to its neighbours and closed up all issue.

"We are lost!" cried Shandon, who could not retain the imprudent words.

"Lost!" repeated the crew.

"Let them escape who can!" said some.

"Lower the shore boats!" said others.

"To the steward's room!" cried Pen and several of his band, "and if we are to be drowned, let's drown ourselves in gin!"

Disorder among the men was at its height. Shandon felt himself overcome; when he wished to command, he stammered and hesitated. His thought was unable to make way through his words. The doctor was walking about in agitation. Johnson stoically folded his arms and said nothing. All at once a strong, imperious, and energetic voice was heard to pronounce these words:

"Every man to his post and tack about!"

Johnson started, and, hardly knowing what he did, turned the wheel rapidly. He was just in time, for the brig, launched at full speed, was about to crush herself against her prison walls. But while Johnson was instinctively obeying, Shandon, Clawbonny, the crew, and all down to the stoker Warren, who had abandoned his fires, even black Strong, who had left his cooking, were all mustered on deck, and saw emerge from that cabin the only man who was in possession of the key, and that man was Garry, the sailor.

"Sir!" cried Shandon, becoming pale. "Garry—you—by what right do you command here?"

"Dick," called out Garry, reproducing that whistle which had so much surprised the crew. The dog, at the sound of his right name, jumped with one bound on to the poop and lay quietly down at his master's feet. The crew did not say a word. The key which the captain of the *Forward* alone possessed, the dog sent by him, and who came thus to verify his identity, that commanding accent which it was impossible to mistake—all this acted strongly on the minds of the sailors, and was sufficient to establish Garry's authority.

Besides, Garry was no longer recognisable; he had cut off the long whiskers which had covered his face, which made it look more energetic and imperious than ever; dressed in the clothes of his rank which had been deposited in the cabin, he appeared in the insignia of commander.

Then immediately, with that mobility which characterised them, the crew of the *Forward* cried out—"Three cheers for the captain!"

"Shandon!" said the latter to his second, "muster the crew; I am going to inspect it!"

Shandon obeyed and gave orders with an altered voice. The captain advanced to meet his officers and men, saying something suitable to each, and treating each according to his past conduct. When he had finished the inspection, he returned on to the poop, and with a calm voice pronounced the following words:

"Officers and sailors, like you, I am English, and my motto is that of Nelson, 'England expects that every man will do his duty.' As an Englishman I am resolved, we are resolved, that no bolder men shall go further than we have been. As an Englishman I will not allow, we will not allow, other people to have the glory of pushing further north themselves. If ever human foot can step upon the land of the North Pole, it shall be the foot of an Englishman. Here is our country's flag. I have equipped this vessel, and consecrated my fortune to this enterprise, and, if necessary, I shall consecrate to it my life and yours; for I am determined that these colours shall float on the North Pole. Take courage. From this day, for every degree we can gain northwards the sum of a thousand pounds will be awarded to you. There are ninety, for we are now in the seventy-second. Count them. Besides, my name is enough. It means energy and patriotism. I am Captain Hatteras!"

"Captain Hatteras!" exclaimed Shandon, and that name, well known to English sailors, was whispered amongst the crew.

"Now," continued Hatteras, "anchor the brig to the ice, put out the fires, and each of you return to your usual work. Shandon, I wish to hold a council with you relative to affairs on board. Join me with the doctor, Wall, and the boatswain in my cabin. Johnson, disperse the men."

Hatteras, calm and haughty, quietly left the poop. In the meantime Shandon was anchoring the brig.

Who, then, was this Hatteras, and for what reason did his name make such a profound impression upon the crew? John Hatteras was the only son of a London brewer, who died in 1852 worth six millions of money. Still young, he embraced the maritime career in spite of the splendid fortune awaiting him. Not that he felt any vocation for commerce, but the instinct of geographical discoveries was dear to him. He had always dreamt of placing his foot where no mortal foot had yet soiled the ground.

At the age of twenty he was already in possession of the vigorous constitution of a thin and sanguine man; an energetic face, with lines geometrically traced; a high and perpendicular forehead; cold but handsome eyes; thin lips, which set off a mouth from which words rarely issued; a middle stature; solidly-jointed limbs, put in motion by iron muscles; the whole forming a man endowed with a temperament fit for anything. When you saw him you felt he was daring; when you heard him you knew he was coldly determined; his was a character that never drew back, ready to stake the lives of others as well as his own. It was well to think twice before following him in his expeditions.

John Hatteras was proud of being an Englishman. A Frenchman once said to him, with what he thought was refined politeness and amiability:

"If I were not a Frenchman I should like to be an Englishman."

"And if I were not an Englishman," answered Hatteras, "I should like to be an Englishman."

That answer revealed the character of the man. It was a great grief to him that Englishmen had not the monopoly of geographical discoveries, and were, in fact, rather behind other nations in that field.

Christopher Columbus, the discoverer of America, was a Genoese; Vasco da Gama, a Portuguese, discovered India; another Portuguese, Fernando de Andrada, China; and a third, Magellan, the Terra del Fuego. Canada was discovered by Jacques Cartier, a Frenchman; Labrador, Brazil, the Cape of Good Hope, the Azores, Madeira, Newfoundland, Guinea, Congo, Mexico, Cape Blanco, Greenland, Iceland, the South Seas, California, Japan, Cambodia, Peru, Kamtchatka, the Philippines, Spitzbergen, Cape Horn, Behring's Straits, Tasmania, New Zealand, New Brittany, New Holland, Louisiana, Jean Mayen Island, were discovered by Icelanders, Scandinavians, French, Russians, Portuguese, Danes, Spaniards, Genoese, and Dutch, but not one by an Englishman. Captain Hatteras could not reconcile himself to the fact that Englishmen were excluded from the glorious list of navigators who made the great discoveries of the 15th and 16th centuries.

Hatteras consoled himself a little when he turned to more modern times. Then Englishmen had the best of it with Sturt, Burke, Wills, King, and Grey in Australia; with Palliser in America; with Cyril Graham, Wadington, and Cummingham in India; with Burton, Speke, Grant, and Livingstone in Africa.

But for a man like Hatteras this was not enough; from his point of view these bold travellers were *improvers* rather than *inventors*; and he was determined to do something better, and he would have invented a country if he could, only to have the honour of discovering it. Now he had noticed that, although Englishmen did not form a majority amongst ancient discoverers, and that he had to go back to Cook in 1774 to obtain New Caledonia and the Sandwich Isles, where the unfortunate captain perished in 1778, yet there existed, nevertheless, a corner of the globe where they seemed to have united all their efforts. This corner was precisely the boreal lands and seas of North America. The list of Polar discoveries may be thus written:

Nova Zembla, discovered by Willoughby, in 1553; Weigatz Island, by Barrough, in 1556; the West Coast of Greenland, by Davis, in 1585; Davis's Straits, by Davis, in 1587; Spitzbergen, by Willoughby, in 1596; Hudson's Bay, by Hudson, in 1610; Baffin's Bay, by Baffin, in 1616.

In more modern times, Hearne, Mackenzie, John Ross, Parry, Franklin, Richardson, Beechey, James Ross, Back, Dease, Simpson, Rae, Inglefield, Belcher, Austin, Kellett, Moore, McClure, Kennedy, and McClintock have continually searched those unknown lands.

The limits of the northern coasts of America had been fixed, and the North-West passage almost discovered, but this was not enough; there was something better still to be done, and John Hatteras had twice attempted it by equipping two ships at his own expense. He wanted to reach the North Pole, and thus crown the series of English discoveries by one of the most illustrious attempts. To attain the Pole was the aim of his life.

After a few successful cruises in the Southern seas, Hatteras endeavoured for the first time, in 1846, to go north by Baffin's Sea; but he could not get beyond the seventy-fourth degree of latitude; he was then commanding the sloop *Halifax*. His crew suffered atrocious torments, and John Hatteras pushed his adventurous rashness so far, that, afterwards, sailors were little tempted to re-commence similar expeditions under such a chief.

However, in 1850 Hatteras succeeded in enrolling on the schooner *Farewell* about twenty determined men, tempted principally by the high prize offered for their audacity. It was upon that occasion that Dr. Clawbonny entered into correspondence with John Hatteras, whom he did not know, requesting to join the expedition, but happily for the doctor the post was already filled up. The *Farewell*, following the track taken in 1817 by the *Neptune* from Aberdeen, got up to the north of Spitzbergen as far as the seventy-sixth degree of latitude. There the expedition was compelled to winter. But the sufferings of the crew from the intense cold were so great that not a single man saw England again, with the exception of Hatteras himself, who was brought back to his own country by a Danish whaler after a walk of more than two hundred miles across the ice.

The sensation produced by the return of this one man was immense. Who in future would dare to follow Hatteras in his mad attempts? However, he did not despair of beginning again. His father, the brewer, died, and he became possessor of a nabob's fortune. Soon after a geographical fact bitterly stirred up John Hatteras. A brig, the *Advance*, manned by seventeen men, equipped by a merchant named Grinnell, under the command of Dr. Kane, and sent in search of Sir John Franklin, advanced in 1853 through Baffin's Sea and Smith's Strait, beyond the eighty-second degree of boreal latitude, much nearer the Pole than any of his predecessors. Now, this vessel was American, Grinnell was American, and Kane was American. The Englishman's disdain for the Yankee will be easily understood; in the heart of Hatteras it changed to hatred; he was resolved to outdo his audacious competitor and reach the Pole itself.

For two years he had been living incognito in Liverpool, passing himself off as a sailor; he recognised in Richard Shandon the man he wanted; he sent him an offer by an anonymous letter, and one to Dr. Clawbonny at the same time. The *Forward* was built, armed, and equipped. Hatteras took great care to conceal his name, for had it been known he would not have found a single man to accompany him. He was determined not to take the command of the brig except in a moment of danger, and when his crew had gone too far to draw back. He had in reserve, as we have seen, such offers of money to make to the men that not one of them would refuse to follow him to the other end of the world; and, in fact, it was right to the other end of the world that he meant to go. Circumstances had become critical, and John Hatteras had made himself known. His dog, the faithful Dick, the companion of his voyages, was the first to recognise him. Luckily for the brave and unfortunately for the timid, it was well and duly established that John Hatteras was the captain of the *Forward*.

CHAPTER XIII THE PROJECTS OF HATTERAS

The appearance of this bold personage was appreciated in different ways by the crew; part of them completely rallied round him, either from love of money or daring; others submitted because they could not help themselves, reserving their right to protest later on; besides, resistance to such a man seemed, for the present, difficult. Each man went back to his post. The 20th of May fell on a Sunday, and was consequently a day of rest for the crew. A council was held by the captain, composed of the officers, Shandon, Wall, Johnson, and the doctor.

"Gentlemen," said the captain in that voice at the same time soft and imperious which characterised him, "you are aware that I intend to go as far as the Pole. I wish to know your opinion about this enterprise. Shandon, what do you think about it?"

"It is not for me to think, captain," coldly replied Shandon; "I have only to obey."

Hatteras was not surprised at the answer.

"Richard Shandon," continued he, not less coldly, "I beg you will say what you think about our chance of success."

"Very well, captain," answered Shandon, "facts are there, and answer for me; attempts of the same kind up till now have always failed; I hope we shall be more fortunate."

"We shall be. What do you think, gentlemen?"

"As far as I am concerned," replied the doctor, "I consider your plan practicable, as it is certain that some day navigators will attain the boreal Pole. I don't see why the honour should not fall to our lot."

"There are many things in our favour," answered Hatteras; "our measures are taken in consequence, and we shall profit by the experience of those who have gone before us. And thereupon, Shandon, accept my thanks for the care you have taken in fitting out this ship; there are a few evil-disposed fellows amongst the crew that I shall have to bring to reason, but on the whole I have only praises to give you."

Shandon bowed coldly. His position on the *Forward*, which he thought to command, was a false one. Hatteras understood this, and did not insist further.

"As to you, gentlemen," he continued, turning to Wall and Johnson, "I could not have secured officers more distinguished for courage and experience."

"Well, captain, I'm your man," answered Johnson, "and although your enterprise seems to me rather daring, you may rely upon me till the end."

"And on me too," said James Wall.

"As to you, doctor, I know what you are worth."

"You know more than I do, then," quickly replied the doctor.

"Now, gentlemen," continued Hatteras, "it is well you should learn upon what undeniable facts my pretension to arrive at the Pole is founded. In 1817 the *Neptune* got up to the north of Spitzbergen, as far as the eighty-second degree. In 1826 the celebrated Parry, after his third voyage to the Polar Seas, started also from Spitzbergen Point, and by the aid of sledge-boats went a hundred and fifty miles northward. In 1852 Captain Inglefield penetrated into Smith's Inlet as far as seventy-eight degrees thirty-five minutes latitude. All these vessels were English, and Englishmen, our countrymen, commanded them." Here Hatteras paused. "I ought to add," he continued, with a constrained look, and as though the words were unable to leave his lips—"I must add that, in 1854, Kane, the American, commanding the brig *Advance*, went still higher, and that his lieutenant, Morton, going across the ice-fields, hoisted the United States standard on the other side of the eighty-second degree. This said, I shall not return to the subject. Now what remains to be known is this, that the captains of the *Neptune*, the *Enterprise*, the *Isabel*, and the *Advance* ascertained that proceeding from the highest latitudes there existed a Polar basin entirely free from ice."

"Free from ice!" exclaimed Shandon, interrupting the captain, "that is impossible!"

"You will notice, Shandon," quietly replied Hatteras, whose eye shone for an instant, "that I quote names and facts as a proof. I may even add that during Captain Parry's station on the border of Wellington Channel, in 1851, his lieutenant, Stewart, also found himself in the presence of open sea, and this peculiarity was confirmed during Sir Edward Beecher's wintering in 1853, in Northumberland Bay, in 76° 52' N. latitude, and 99° 20' longitude. The reports are incontestable, and it would be most unjust not to admit them."

"However, captain," continued Shandon, "those reports are so contradictory."

"You are mistaken, Shandon," cried Dr. Clawbonny. "These reports do not contradict any scientific assertion, the captain will allow me to tell you."

"Go on, doctor," answered Hatteras.

"Well, listen, Shandon; it evidently follows from geographical facts, and from the study of isotherm lines, that the coldest point of the globe is not at the Pole itself; like the magnetic point, it deviates several degrees from the Pole. The calculations of Brewster, Bergham, and several other natural philosophers show us that in our hemisphere there are two cold Poles; one is situated in Asia at 79° 30' N. latitude, and by 120° E. longitude, and the other in America at 78° N. latitude, and 97° W. longitude. It is with the latter that we have to do, and you see, Shandon, we have met with it at more than twelve degrees below the Pole. Well, why should not the Polar Sea be as equally disengaged from ice as the sixty-sixth parallel is in summer—that is to say, the south of Baffin's Bay?"

"That's what I call well pleaded," replied Johnson. "Mr. Clawbonny speaks upon these matters like a professional man."

"It appears very probable," chimed in James Wall.

"All guess-work," answered Shandon obstinately.

"Well, Shandon," said Hatteras, "let us take into consideration either case; either the sea is free from ice or it is not so, and neither of these suppositions can hinder us from attaining the Pole. If the sea is free the *Forward* will take us there without trouble; if it is frozen we will attempt the adventure upon our sledges. This, you will allow, is not impracticable. When once our brig has attained the eighty-third degree we shall only have six hundred miles to traverse before reaching the Pole."

"And what are six hundred miles?" quickly answered the doctor, "when it is known that a Cossack, Alexis Markoff, went over the ice sea along the northern coast of the Russian Empire, in sledges drawn by dogs, for the space of eight hundred miles in twenty-four days?"

"Do you hear that, Shandon?" said Hatteras; "can't Englishmen do as much as a Cossack?"

"Of course they can," cried the impetuous doctor.

"Of course," added the boatswain.

"Well, Shandon?" said the captain.

"I can only repeat what I said before, captain," said Shandon—"I will obey."

"Very good. And now," continued Hatteras, "let us consider our present situation. We are caught by the ice, and it seems to me impossible, for this year at least, to get into Smith's Strait. Well, here, then, this is what I propose."

Hatteras laid open upon the table one of the excellent maps published in 1859 by the order of the Admiralty.

"Be kind enough to follow me. If Smith's Strait is closed up from us, Lancaster Strait, on the west coast of Baffin's Sea, is not. I think we ought to ascend that strait as far as Barrow Strait, and from there sail to Beechey Island; the same track has been gone over a hundred times by sailing vessels; consequently with a screw we can do it easily. Once at Beechey Island we will go north as far as possible, by Wellington Channel, up to the outlet of the creek which joins Wellington's and Queen's Channels, at the very point where the open sea was perceived. It is now only the 20th of May; in a month, if circumstances favour us, we shall have attained that point, and from there we'll drive forward towards the Pole. What do you think about it, gentlemen?"

"It is evidently the only track to follow," replied Johnson.

"Very well, we will take it from to-morrow. I shall let them rest to-day as it is Sunday. Shandon, you will take care that religious service be attended to; it has a beneficial effect on the minds of men, and a sailor above all needs to place confidence in the Almighty."

"It shall be attended to, captain," answered Shandon, who went out with the lieutenant and the boatswain.

"Doctor!" said Hatteras, pointing towards Shandon, "there's a man whose pride is wounded; I can no longer rely upon him."

Early the following day the captain caused the pirogue to be lowered in order to reconnoitre the icebergs in the vicinity, the breadth of which did not exceed 200 yards. He remarked that through a slow pressure of the ice the basin threatened to become narrower. It became urgent, therefore, to make an aperture to prevent the ship being crushed in a vice of the mountains. By the means employed by John Hatteras, it is easy to observe that he was an energetic man.

He first had steps cut out in the walls of ice, and by their means climbed to the summit of an iceberg. From that point he saw that it was easy for him to cut out a road towards the south-west. By his orders a blasting furnace was hollowed nearly in the heart of the mountain. This work, rapidly put into execution, was terminated by noon on Monday. Hatteras could not rely on his eight or ten pound blasting cylinders, which would have had no effect on such masses as those. They were only sufficient to shatter ice-fields. He therefore had a thousand pounds of powder placed in the blasting furnace, of which the diffusive direction was carefully calculated. This mine was provided with a long wick, bound in gutta-percha, the end of which was outside. The gallery conducting to the mine was filled up with snow and lumps of ice, which the cold of the following night made as hard as granite. The temperature, under the influence of an easterly wind, came down to twelve degrees.

At seven the next morning the *Forward* was held under steam, ready to profit by the smallest issue. Johnson was charged with setting fire to the wick, which, according to calculation, would burn for half an hour before setting fire to the mine. Johnson had, therefore, plenty of time to regain the brig; ten minutes after having executed Hatteras's order he was again at his post. The crew remained on deck, for the weather was dry and bright; it had left off snowing.

Hatteras was on the poop, chronometer in hand, counting the minutes; Shandon and the doctor were with him. At eight thirty-five a dull explosion was heard, much less loud than any one would have supposed. The outline of the mountains was changed all at once as if by an earthquake; thick white smoke rose up to a considerable height in the sky, leaving long crevices in the iceberg, the top part of which fell in pieces all round the *Forward*. But the path was not yet free; large blocks of ice remained suspended above the pass on the adjacent mountains, and there was every reason to fear that they would fall and close up the passage. Hatteras took in the situation at one glance.

"Wolsten!" cried he.

The gunsmith hastened up.

"Yes, captain?" cried he.

"Load the gun in the bow with a triple charge," said Hatteras, "and wad it as hard as possible."

"Are we going to attack the mountain with cannon-balls?" asked the doctor.

"No," answered Hatteras, "that would be useless. No bullet, Wolsten, but a triple charge of powder. Look sharp!"

A few minutes after the gun was loaded.

"What does he mean to do without a bullet?" muttered Shandon between his teeth.

"We shall soon see," answered the doctor.

"Ready, captain!" called out Wolsten.

"All right!" replied Hatteras.

"Brunton!" he called out to the engineer, "a few turns ahead."

Brunton opened the sliders, and the screw being put in movement, the *Forward* neared the mined mountain.

"Aim at the pass!" cried the captain to the gunsmith. The latter obeyed, and when the brig was only half a cable's length from it, Hatteras called out:

"Fire!"

A formidable report followed his order, and the blocks, shaken by the atmospheric commotion, were suddenly precipitated into the sea; the disturbance amongst the strata of the air had been sufficient to accomplish this.

"All steam on, Brunton! Straight for the pass, Johnson!"

The latter was at the helm; the brig, driven along by her screw, which turned in the foaming waves, dashed into the middle of the then opened pass; it was time, for scarcely had the *Forward* cleared the opening than her prison closed up again behind her. It was a thrilling moment, and on board there was only one stout and undisturbed heart—that of the captain. The crew, astonished at the manoeuvre, cried out:

"Hurrah for the captain!"

CHAPTER XIV EXPEDITION IN SEARCH OF FRANKLIN

On Wednesday, the 23rd of May, the *Forward* had again taken up her adventurous navigation, cleverly tacking amongst the packs and icebergs. Thanks to steam, that obedient force which so many of our Polar sea navigators have had to do without, she appeared to be playing in the midst of the moving rocks. She seemed to recognise the hand of an experienced master, and like a horse under an able rider, she obeyed the thought of her captain. The temperature rose. At six o'clock in the morning the thermometer marked twenty-six degrees, at six in the evening twenty-nine degrees, and at midnight twenty-five degrees; the wind was lightly blowing from the south-east.

On Thursday, towards three in the morning, the *Forward* was in sight of Possession Bay, on the coast of America. At the entrance to Lancaster Strait, shortly after, the crew caught a glimpse of Burney Cape. A few Esquimaux pulled off towards the vessel, but Hatteras did not take the trouble to wait for them. The Byam-Martin peaks, which overlook Cape Liverpool, were sighted to the left, and soon disappeared in the evening mists, which also prevented any observation being taken from Cape Hay. This cape is so low that it gets confounded with the ice on the coast, a circumstance which often renders the hydrographic determination of the Polar seas extremely difficult.

Puffins, ducks, and white sea-gulls showed up in very great numbers. The *Forward* was then in latitude 74° 1', and in longitude 77° 15'. The snowy hoods of the two mountains, Catherine and Elizabeth, rose up above the clouds.

On Friday, at six o'clock, Cape Warender was passed on the right side of the strait, and on the left Admiralty Inlet, a bay that has been little explored by navigators, who are generally in a hurry to sail away west. The sea became rather rough, and the waves often swept the deck of the brig, throwing up pieces of ice. The land on the north coast, with its high table lands almost level, and which reverberated the sun's rays, offered a very curious appearance.

Hatteras wanted to run along the north coast, in order to reach Beechey Island and the entrance to Wellington Channel sooner; but continual icebergs compelled him, to his great annoyance, to follow the southern passes. That was why, on the 26th of May, the *Forward* was abreast of Cape York in a thick fog interspersed with snow; a very high mountain, almost perpendicular, caused it to be recognised. The weather cleared up a little, and the sun, towards noon, appeared for an instant, allowing a tolerably good observation to be taken; 74° 4' latitude and 84° 23' longitude. The *Forward* was then at the extremity of Lancaster Strait.

Hatteras pointed out to the doctor on his map the route already taken, and the one he meant to follow. The position of the brig at the time was very interesting.

"I should like to have been further north," said he, "but no one can do the impossible; see, this is our exact situation."

And the captain pricked his map at a short distance from Cape York.

"We are in the centre of this four-road way, open to every wind, fenced by the outlets of Lancaster Strait, Barrow Strait, Wellington Channel, and Regent's Passage; it is a point that all navigators in these seas have been obliged to come to."

"Well," replied the doctor, "it must have puzzled them greatly; four cross-roads with no sign-posts to tell them which to take. How did Parry, Ross, and Franklin manage?"

"They did not manage at all, they were managed; they had no choice, I can assure you; sometimes Barrow Strait was closed to one of them, and the next year another found it open; sometimes the vessel was irresistibly drawn towards Regent's Passage, so that we have ended by becoming acquainted with these inextricable seas."

"What a singular country!" said the doctor, examining the map. "It is all in pieces, and they seem to have no logical connection. It seems as if the land in the vicinity of the North Pole had been cut up like this on purpose to make access to it more difficult, whilst that in the other hemisphere quietly terminates in tapered-out points like those of Cape Horn, the Cape of Good Hope, and the Indian Peninsula. Is it the greater rapidity of the equator which has thus modified matters, whilst the land at the extremities, yet fluid from the creation, has not been able to get condensed or agglomerated together, for want of a sufficiently rapid rotation?"

"That must be the case, for everything on earth is logical, and 'nothing is that errs from law,' and God often allows men to discover His laws; make use of His permission, doctor."

"Unfortunately, I shall not be able to take much advantage of it," said the doctor, "but the wind here is something dreadful," added he, muffling himself up as well as he could.

"Yes, we are quite exposed to the north wind, and it is turning us out of our road."

"Anyhow it ought to drive the ice down south, and level a clear road."

"It ought to do so, doctor, but the wind does not always do what it ought. Look, that ice-bank seems impenetrable. Never mind, we will try to reach Griffith Island, sail round Cornwallis Island, and get into Queen's Channel without going by Wellington Channel. Nevertheless I positively desire to touch at Beechey Island in order to renew my coal provision."

"What do you mean?" asked the astonished doctor.

"I mean that, according to orders from the Admiralty, large provisions have been deposited on that island in order to provide for future expeditions, and although Captain McClintock took some in 1859, I assure you that there will be some left for us."

"By-the-bye," said the doctor, "these parts have been explored for the last fifteen years, and since the day when the proof of the loss of Franklin was acquired, the Admiralty has always kept five or six cruisers in these seas. If I am not mistaken, Griffith Island, which I see there on the map, almost in the middle of the cross-roads, has become a general meeting-place for navigators."

"It is so, doctor; and Franklin's unfortunate expedition resulted in making known these distant countries to us."

"That is true, captain, for since 1845 expeditions have been very numerous. It was not until 1848 that we began to be uneasy about the disappearance of the *Erebus* and the *Terror*, Franklin's two vessels. It was then that we saw the admiral's old friend, Dr. Richardson, at the age of seventy, go to Canada, and ascend Coppermine River as far as the Polar Sea; and James Ross, commanding the *Enterprise* and *Investigation*, set out from Uppernawik in 1848 and arrived at Cape York, where we now are. Every day he threw a tub containing papers into the sea, for the purpose of making known his whereabouts. During the mists he caused the cannon to be fired, and had sky-rockets sent up at night along with Bengal lights, and kept under sail continually. He wintered in Port Leopold from 1848 to 1849, where he took possession of a great number of white foxes, and caused brass collars, upon which was engraved the indication of the whereabouts of ships and the store depots, to be riveted on their necks. Afterwards they were dispersed in all directions; in the following spring he began to search the coasts of North Somerset on sledges in the midst of dangers and privations from which almost all his men fell ill or lame. He built up cairns in which he inclosed brass cylinders with the necessary memoranda for rallying the lost expedition. While he was away his lieutenant McClure explored the northern coasts of Barrow Strait, but without result. James Ross had under his orders two officers who, later on, were destined to become celebrities—McClure, who cleared the North-West passage, and McClintock, who discovered the remains of Sir John Franklin."

"Yes; they are now two good and brave English captains. You know the history of these seas well, doctor, and you will benefit us by telling us about it. There is always something to be gained by hearing about such daring attempts."

"Well, to finish all I know about James Ross: he tried to reach Melville Island by a more westerly direction, but he nearly lost his two vessels, for he was caught by the ice and driven back into Baffin's Sea."

"Driven back?" repeated Hatteras, contracting his brows; "forced back in spite of himself?"

"Yes, and without having discovered anything," continued the doctor; "and ever since that year, 1850, English vessels have never ceased to plough these seas, and a reward of twenty thousand pounds was offered to any one who might find the crews of the *Erebus* and *Terror*. Captains Kellett and Moore had already, in 1848, attempted to get through Behring's Strait. In 1850 and 1851 Captain Austin wintered in Cornwallis Island; Captain Parry, on board the *Assistance* and the *Resolute*, explored Wellington Channel; John Ross, the venerable hero of the magnetic pole, set out again with his yacht, the *Felix*, in search of his friend; the brig *Prince Albert* went on a first cruise at the expense of Lady Franklin; and, lastly, two American ships, sent out by Grinnell with Captain Haven, were drifted out of Wellington Channel and thrown back into Lancaster Strait. It was during this year that McClintock, who was then Austin's lieutenant, pushed on as far as Melville Island and Cape Dundas, the extreme points attained by Parry in 1819; it was then that he found traces of Franklin's wintering on Beechey Island in 1845."

"Yes," answered Hatteras, "three of his sailors had been buried there—three men more fortunate than the others!"

The doctor nodded in approval of Hatteras's remark, and continued:

"During 1851 and 1852 the *Prince Albert* went on a second voyage under the French lieutenant, Bellot; he wintered at Batty Bay, in Prince Regent Strait, explored the south-west of Somerset, and reconnoitred the coast as far as Cape Walker. During that time the *Enterprise* and the *Investigator* returned to England and passed under the command of Collinson and McClure for the purpose of rejoining Kellett and Moore in Behring's Straits; whilst Collinson came back to winter at Hong-Kong, McClure made the best of his way onward, and after being obliged to winter three times—from 1850 to '51; from 1851 to '52; and from 1852 to '53—he discovered the North-West passage without learning anything of Franklin's fate. During 1852 and '53 a new expedition composed of three sailing vessels, the *Resolute*, the *Assistance*, the *North Star*, and two steamers, the *Pioneer* and *Intrepid*, set sail under the command of Sir Edward Belcher, with Captain Kellett under him; Sir Edward visited Wellington Channel, wintered in Northumberland Bay, and went over the coast, whilst Kellett, pushing on to Bridport in Melville Island, explored, without success, that part of the boreal land. It was at this time that news was spread in England that two ships, abandoned in the midst of icebergs, had been descried near the coast of New Scotland. Lady Franklin immediately had prepared the little screw *Isabelle*, and Captain Inglefield, after having steamed up Baffin's Bay as far as Victoria Point on the eightieth parallel, came back to Beechey Island no more successful than his predecessors. At the beginning of 1855, Grinnell, an American, fitted up a fresh expedition, and Captain Kane tried to penetrate to the Pole——"

"But he didn't do it," cried Hatteras violently; "and what he didn't do we will, with God's help!"

"I know, captain," answered the doctor, "and I mention it because this expedition is of necessity connected with the search for Franklin. But it had no result. I was almost forgetting to tell you that the Admiralty, considering Beechey Island as the general rendezvous of expeditions, charged Captain Inglefield, who then commanded the steamer *Phoenix*, to transport provisions there in 1853; Inglefield set out with Lieutenant Bellot, and lost the brave officer who for the second time had devoted his services to England; we can have more precise details upon this catastrophe, as our boatswain, Johnson, was witness to the misfortune."

"Lieutenant Bellot was a brave Frenchman," said Hatteras, "and his memory is honoured in England."

"By that time," continued the doctor, "Belcher's fleet began to come back little by little; not all of it, for Sir Edward had been obliged to abandon the *Assistance* in 1854, as McClure had done with the *Investigator* in 1853. In the meantime, Dr. Rae, in a letter dated the 29th of July, 1854, and addressed from Repulse Bay, which he had succeeded in reaching through America, sent word that the Esquimaux of King William's Land were in possession of different objects taken from the wrecks of the *Erebus* and *Terror*; there was then not the least doubt about the fate of the expedition; the *Phoenix*, the *North Star*, and Collinson's vessel then came back to England, leaving the Arctic Seas completely abandoned by English ships. But if the Government seemed to have lost all hope it was not so with Lady Franklin, and with the remnants of her fortune she fitted out the *Fox*, commanded by McClintock, who set sail in 1857, and wintered in the quarters where you made your apparition; he reached Beechey Island on the 11th of August, 1858, wintered a second time in Bellot's Strait, began his search again in February, 1859, and on the 6th of May found the document which cleared away all doubt about the fate of the *Erebus* and the *Terror*, and returned to England at the end of the year. That is all that has happened for fifteen years in these fateful countries, and since the return of the *Fox* not a single vessel has returned to attempt success in the midst of these dangerous seas."

"Well," replied Hatteras, "we will attempt it."

CHAPTER XV THE "FORWARD" DRIVEN BACK SOUTH

The weather cleared up towards evening, and land was clearly distinguished between Cape Sepping and Cape Clarence, which runs east, then south, and is joined to the coast on the west by a rather low neck of land. The sea at the entrance to Regent Strait was free from ice, with the exception of an impenetrable ice-bank, a little further than Port Leopold, which threatened to stop the *Forward* in her north-westerly course. Hatteras was greatly vexed, but he did not show it; he was obliged to have recourse to petards in order to force an entrance to Port Leopold; he reached it on Sunday, the 27th of May; the brig was solidly anchored to the enormous icebergs, which were as upright, hard, and solid as rocks.

The captain, followed by the doctor, Johnson, and his dog Dick, immediately leaped upon the ice, and soon reached land. Dick leaped with joy, for since he had recognised the captain he had become more sociable, keeping his grudge against certain men of the crew for whom his master had no more friendship than he. The port was not then blocked up with ice that the east winds generally heaped up there; the earth, intersected with peaks, offered at their summits graceful undulations of snow. The house and lantern erected by James Ross were still in a tolerable state of preservation; but the provisions seemed to have been ransacked by foxes and bears, the recent traces of which were easily distinguished. Men, too, had had something to do with the devastation, for a few remains of Esquimaux huts remained upon the shores of the Bay. The six graves inclosing the remains of the six sailors of the *Enterprise* and the *Investigator* were recognisable by a slight swelling of the ground; they had been respected both by men and animals. In placing his foot for the first time on boreal land, the doctor experienced much emotion. It is impossible to imagine the feelings with which the heart is assailed at the sight of the remains of houses, tents, huts, and magazines that Nature so marvellously preserves in those cold countries.

"There is that residence," he said to his companions, "which James Ross himself called the Camp of Refuge; if Franklin's expedition had reached this spot, it would have been saved. There is the engine which was abandoned here, and the stove at which the crew of the *Prince Albert* warmed themselves in 1851. Things have remained just as they were, and any one would think that Captain Kennedy had only left yesterday. Here is the long boat which sheltered him and his for a few days, for this Kennedy, separated from his ship, was in reality saved by Lieutenant Bellot, who braved the October temperature in order to go to his assistance."

"I knew that brave and worthy officer," said Johnson.

CHAPTER XV THE "FORWARD" DRIVEN BACK SOUTH

Whilst the doctor was examining with all an antiquarian's enthusiasm the vestiges of previous winterings, Hatteras was occupied in piling together the various provisions and articles of fuel, which were only to be found in very small quantities. The following day was employed in transporting them on board. The doctor, without going too far from the ship, surveyed the country, and took sketches of the most remarkable points of view. The temperature rose by degrees, and the heaped-up snow began to melt. The doctor made an almost complete collection of northern birds, such as gulls, divers, eider-down ducks, which are very much like common ducks, with white breasts and backs, blue bellies, the top of the head blue, and the remainder of the plumage white, shaded with green; several of them had already their breasts stripped of that beautiful down with which the male and female line their nests. The doctor also perceived large seals taking breath on the surface of the ice, but could not shoot one. In his excursions he discovered the high water mark, a stone upon which the following signs are engraved:

(E. I.)

1849,

and which indicate the passage of the *Enterprise* and *Investigator*; he pushed forward as far as Cape Clarence to the spot where John and James Ross, in 1833, waited with so much impatience for the breaking up of the ice. The land was strewn with skulls and bones of animals, and traces of Esquimaux habitations could be still distinguished.

The doctor wanted to raise up a cairn on Port Leopold, and deposit in it a note indicating the passage of the *Forward*, and the aim of the expedition. But Hatteras would not hear of it; he did not want to leave traces behind of which a competitor might take advantage. In spite of his good motives the doctor was forced to yield to the captain's will. Shandon blamed the captain's obstinacy, which prevented any ships following the trace of the *Forward* in case of accident. Hatteras would not give way. His lading was finished on Monday night, and he attempted once more to gain the north by breaking open the ice-bank; but after dangerous efforts he was forced to resign himself, and to go down Regent's Channel again; he would not stop at Port Leopold, which, open to-day, might be closed again to-morrow by an unexpected displacement of ice-fields, a very frequent phenomenon in these seas, and which navigators ought particularly to take into consideration.

If Hatteras did not allow his uneasiness to be outwardly perceived, it did not prevent him feeling it inwardly. His desire was to push northward, whilst, on the contrary, he found himself constrained to put back southward. Where should he get to in that case? Should he be obliged to put back to Victoria Harbour, in Boothia Gulf, where Sir John Ross wintered in 1833? Would he find Bellot Strait open at that epoch, and could he ascend Peel Strait by rounding North Somerset? Or, again, should he, like his predecessors, find himself captured during several winters, and be compelled to exhaust his strength and provisions? These fears were fermenting in his brain; he must decide one way or other. He heaved about, and struck out south. The width of Prince Regent's Channel is about the same from Port Leopold to Adelaide Bay. The *Forward*, more favoured than the ships which had preceded her, and of which the greater number had required more than a month to descend the channel, even in a more favourable season, made her way rapidly amongst the icebergs; it is true that other ships, with the exception of the *Fox*, had no steam at their disposal, and had to endure the caprices of an uncertain and often foul wind.

In general the crew showed little wish to push on with the enterprising Hatteras; the men were only too glad to perceive that the vessel was taking a southerly direction. Hatteras would have liked to go on regardless of consequences.

The *Forward* rushed along under the pressure of her engines, the smoke from which twisted round the shining points of the icebergs; the weather was constantly changing from dry cold to snowy fogs. The brig, which drew little water, sailed along the west coast; Hatteras did not wish to miss the entrance to Bellot Strait, as the only outlet to the Gulf of Boothia on the south was the strait, only partially known to the *Fury* and the *Hecla*; if he missed the Bellot Strait, he might be shut up without possibility of egress.

In the evening the *Forward* was in sight of Elwin Bay, known by its high perpendicular rocks; on the Tuesday morning Batty Bay was sighted, where the *Prince Albert* anchored for its long wintering on the 10th of September, 1851. The doctor swept the whole coast with his telescope. It was from this point that the expeditions radiated that established the geographical configuration of North Somerset. The weather was clear, and the profound ravines by which the bay is surrounded could be clearly distinguished.

The doctor and Johnson were perhaps the only beings on board who took any interest in these deserted countries. Hatteras was always intent upon his maps, and said little; his taciturnity increased as the brig got more and more south; he often mounted the poop, and there with folded arms, and eyes lost in vacancy, he stood for hours. His orders, when he gave any, were curt and rough. Shandon kept a cold silence, and kept himself so much aloof by degrees that at last he had no relations with Hatteras except those exacted by the service; James Wall remained devoted to Shandon, and regulated his conduct accordingly. The remainder of the crew waited for something to turn up, ready to take any advantage in their own interest. There was no longer that unity of thought and communion of ideas on board which are so necessary for the accomplishment of anything great, and this Hatteras knew to his sorrow.

During the day two whales were perceived rushing towards the south; a white bear was also seen, and was shot at without any apparent success. The captain knew the value of an hour under the circumstances, and would not allow the animal to be chased.

On Wednesday morning the extremity of Regent's Channel was passed; the angle on the west coast was followed by a deep curve in the land. By consulting his map the doctor recognised the point of Somerset House, or Fury Point.

"There," said he to his habitual companion—"there is the very spot where the first English ship, sent into these seas in 1815, was lost, during the third of Parry's voyages to the Pole; the *Fury* was so damaged by the ice on her second wintering, that her crew were obliged to desert her and return to England on board her companion ship the *Hecla*."

"That shows the advantage of having a second ship," answered Johnson. "It is a precaution that Polar navigators ought not to neglect, but Captain Hatteras wasn't the sort of man to trouble himself with another ship."

"Do you think he is imprudent, Johnson?" asked the doctor.

"I? I think nothing, Mr. Clawbonny. Do you see those stakes over there with some rotten tent-rags still hanging to them?"

"Yes; that's where Parry disembarked his provisions from his ship, and, if I remember rightly, the roof of his tent was a topsail."

"Everything must be greatly changed since 1825!"

"Not so much as any one might think. John Ross owed the health and safety of his crew to that fragile habitation in 1829. When the *Prince Albert* sent an expedition there in 1851, it was still existing; Captain Kennedy had it repaired, nine years ago now. It would be interesting to visit it, but Hatteras isn't in the humour to stop!"

"I daresay he is right, Mr. Clawbonny; if time is money in England, here it is life, and a day's or even an hour's delay might make all the difference."

CHAPTER XV THE "FORWARD" DRIVEN BACK SOUTH

During the day of Thursday, the 1st of June, the *Forward* cut across Creswell Bay; from Fury Point the coast rose towards the north in perpendicular rocks three hundred feet high; it began to get lower towards the south; some snow summits looked like neatly-cut tables, whilst others were shaped like pyramids, and had other strange forms.

The weather grew milder during that day, but was not so clear; land was lost to sight, and the thermometer went up to thirty-two degrees; seafowl fluttered about, the flocks of wild ducks were seen flying north; the crew could divest themselves of some of their garments, and the influence of the Arctic summer began to be felt. Towards evening the *Forward* doubled Cape Garry at a quarter of a mile from the shore, where the soundings gave from ten to twelve fathoms; from thence she kept near the coast as far as Brentford Bay. It was under this latitude that Bellot Strait was to be met with; a strait the existence of which Sir John Ross did not even guess at during his expedition in 1828; his maps indicated an uninterrupted coast-line, whose irregularities he noted with the utmost care; the entrance to the strait must therefore have been blocked up by ice at the time. It was really discovered by Kennedy in April, 1852, and he gave it the name of his lieutenant, Bellot, as "a just tribute," he said, "to the important services rendered to our expedition by the French officer."

CHAPTER XVI THE MAGNETIC POLE

Hatteras felt his anxiety increase as he neared the strait; the fate of his voyage depended upon it; up till now he had done more than his predecessors, the most fortunate of whom, McClintock, had taken fifteen months to reach this part of the Polar Seas; but it was little or nothing if he did not succeed in clearing Bellot Strait; he could not retrace his steps, and would be blocked up till the following year.

He trusted the care of examining the coast to no one but himself; he mounted the crow's nest and passed several hours there during the morning of Saturday. The crew perfectly understood the ship's position; profound silence reigned on board; the engine slackened steam, and the *Forward* kept as near land as possible; the coast bristled with icebergs, which the warmest summers do not melt; an experienced eye alone could distinguish an opening between them. Hatteras compared his maps with the land. As the sun showed himself for an instant towards noon, he caused Shandon and Wall to take a pretty exact observation, which was shouted to him. All the crew suffered the tortures of anxiety for half the day, but towards two o'clock these words were shouted from the top of the mizenmast:

"Veer to the west, all steam on."

The brig instantly obeyed; her prow was directed towards the point indicated; the sea foamed under the screws, and the *Forward*, with all speed on, entered between two ice-streams. The road was found, Hatteras descended upon deck, and the ice-master took his place.

"Well, captain," said the doctor, "we are in the famous strait at last."

"Yes," answered Hatteras, lowering his voice; "but getting in isn't everything; we must get out too," and so saying he regained his cabin.

"He's right," said the doctor; "we are here in a sort of mousetrap, with scarcely enough space for working the brig, and if we are forced to winter in the strait!... Well, we shan't be the first that have had to do it, and they got over it, and so shall we."

The doctor was not mistaken. It was in that very place, in a little sheltered harbour called Kennedy Harbour by McClintock himself, that the *Fox* wintered in 1858. The high granite chain and the steep cliffs of the two banks were clearly discernible.

Bellot Strait is seventeen miles long and a mile wide, and about six or seven fathoms deep. It lies between mountains whose height is estimated at 1,600 feet. It separates North Somerset from Boothia Land.

It is easy to understand that there is not much elbow-room for vessels in such a strait. The *Forward* advanced slowly, but it did advance; tempests are frequent in the strait, and the brig did not escape them; by Hatteras's order all sails were furled; but, notwithstanding all precautions, the brig was much knocked about; the waves dashed over her, and her smoke fled towards the east with astonishing rapidity; her course was not certain amongst the moving ice; the barometer fell; it was difficult to stop on deck, and most of the men stayed below to avoid useless suffering.

Hatteras, Johnson, and Shandon remained on the poop in spite of the gales of snow and rain; as usual the doctor had asked himself what would be the most disagreeable thing he could do, and answered himself by going on deck at once; it was impossible to hear and difficult to see one another, so that he kept his reflections to himself. Hatteras tried to see through the fog; he calculated that they would be at the mouth of the strait at six o'clock, but when the time came all issue seemed closed up; he was obliged to wait and anchor the brig to an iceberg; but he stopped under pressure all night.

The weather was frightful. The *Forward* threatened to break her chains at every instant; it was feared that the iceberg to which they were anchored, torn away at its base under the violent west wind, would float away with the brig. The officers were constantly on the look-out and under extreme apprehension; along with the snow there fell a perfect hail of ice torn off from the surface of the icebergs by the strength of the wind; it was like a shower of arrows bristling in the atmosphere. The temperature rose singularly during this terrible night; the thermometer marked fifty-seven degrees, and the doctor, to his great astonishment, thought he saw flashes of lightning in the south, followed by the roar of far-off thunder that seemed to corroborate the testimony of the whaler Scoresby, who observed a similar phenomenon above the sixty-fifth parallel. Captain Parry was also witness to a similar meteorological wonder in 1821.

Towards five o'clock in the morning the weather changed with astonishing rapidity; the temperature went down to freezing point, the wind turned north, and became calmer. The western opening to the strait was in sight, but entirely obstructed. Hatteras looked eagerly at the coast, asking himself if the passage really existed. However, the brig got under way, and glided slowly amongst the ice-streams, whilst the icebergs pressed noisily against her planks, the packs at that epoch were still from six to seven feet thick; they were obliged carefully to avoid their pressure, for if the brig had resisted them she would have run the risk of being lifted up and turned over on her side. At noon, for the first time, they could admire a magnificent solar phenomenon, a halo with two parhelia; the doctor observed it, and took its exact dimensions; the exterior bow was only visible over an extent of thirty degrees on each side of its horizontal diameter; the two images of the sun were remarkably clear; the colours of the luminous bows proceeded from inside to outside, and were red, yellow, green, and very light blue—in short, white light without any assignable exterior limit. The doctor remembered the ingenious theory of Thomas Young about these meteors; this natural philosopher supposed that certain clouds composed of prisms of ice are suspended in the atmosphere; the rays of the sun that fall on the prisms are decomposed at angles of sixty and ninety degrees. Halos cannot, therefore, exist in a calm atmosphere. The doctor thought this theory very probable. Sailors accustomed to the boreal seas generally consider this phenomenon as the precursor of abundant snow. If their observation was just, the position of the *Forward* became very difficult. Hatteras, therefore, resolved to go on fast; during the remainder of the day and following night he did not take a minute's rest, sweeping the horizon with his telescope, taking advantage of the least opening, and losing no occasion of getting out of the strait.

But in the morning he was obliged to stop before the insuperable ice-bank. The doctor joined him on the poop. Hatteras went with him apart where they could talk without fear of being overheard.

"We are in for it," began Hatteras; "it is impossible to go any further."

"Is there no means of getting out?" asked the doctor.

"None. All the powder in the *Forward* would not make us gain half a mile!"

"What shall we do, then?" said the doctor.

"I don't know. This cursed year has been unfavourable from the beginning."

"Well," answered the doctor, "if we must winter here, we must. One place is as good as another."

"But," said Hatteras, lowering his voice, "we must not winter here, especially in the month of June. Wintering is full of physical and moral danger. The crew would be unmanageable during a long inaction in the midst of real suffering. I thought I should be able to stop much nearer the Pole than this!"

"Luck would have it so, or Baffin's Bay wouldn't have been closed."

"It was open enough for that American!" cried Hatteras in a rage.

"Come, Hatteras," said the doctor, interrupting him on purpose, "to-day is only the 5th of June; don't despair; a passage may suddenly open up before us; you know that the ice has a tendency to break up into several blocks, even in the calmest weather, as if a force of repulsion acted upon the different parts of it; we may find the sea free at any minute."

"If that minute comes we shall take advantage of it. It is quite possible that, once out of Bellot Strait, we shall be able to go north by Peel Strait or McClintock Channel, and then——"

"Captain," said James Wall, who had come up while Hatteras was speaking, "the ice nearly carries off our rudder."

"Well," answered Hatteras, "we must risk it. We must be ready day and night. You must do all you can to protect it, Mr. Wall, but I can't have it removed."

"But——" added Wall.

"That is my business," said Hatteras severely, and Wall went back to his post.

"I would give five years of my life," said Hatteras, in a rage, "to be up north. I know no more dangerous passage. To add to the difficulty, the compass is no guide at this distance from the magnetic pole: the needle is constantly shifting its direction."

"I acknowledge," answered the doctor, "that navigation is difficult, but we knew what we had to expect when we began our enterprise, and we ought not to be surprised at it."

"Ah, doctor, my crew is no longer what it was; the officers are spoiling the men. I could make them do what I want by offering them a pecuniary reward, but I am not seconded by my officers, but they shall pay dearly for it!"

"You are exaggerating, Hatteras."

"No, I am not. Do you think the crew is sorry for the obstacles that I meet with? On the contrary, they hope they will make me abandon my projects. They do not complain now, and they won't as long as the *Forward* is making for the south. The fools! They think they are getting nearer England! But once let me go north and you'll see how they'll change! I swear, though, that no living being will make me deviate from my line of conduct. Only let me find a passage, that's all!"

One of the captain's wishes was fulfilled soon enough. There was a sudden change during the evening; under some influence of the wind, the current, or the temperature, the ice-fields were separated; the *Forward* went along boldly, breaking up the ice with her steel prow; she sailed along all night, and the next morning about six cleared Bellot Strait. But that was all; the northern passage was completely obstructed—to the great disgust of Hatteras. However, he had sufficient strength of character to hide his disappointment, and as if the only passage open was the one he preferred, he let the *Forward* sail down Franklin Strait again; not being able to get up Peel Strait, he resolved to go round Prince of Wales's Land to get into McClintock Channel. But he felt he could not deceive Shandon and Wall as to the extent of his disappointment. The day of the 6th of June was uneventful; the sky was full of snow, and the prognostics of the halo were fulfilled.

During thirty-six hours the *Forward* followed the windings of Boothia Land, unable to approach Prince of Wales's Land; the captain counted upon getting supplies at Beechey Island; he arrived on the Thursday at the extremity of Franklin Strait, where he again found the road to the north blocked up. It was enough to make him despair; he could not even retrace his steps; the icebergs pushed him onwards, and he saw the passages close up behind him as if there never had existed open sea where he had passed an hour before. The *Forward* was, therefore, not only prevented from going northwards, but could not stop still an instant for fear of being caught, and she fled before the ice as a ship flies before a storm.

On Friday, the 8th of June, they arrived near the shore of Boothia, at the entrance to James Ross Strait, which they were obliged to avoid, as its only issue is on the west, near the American coasts.

Observations taken at noon from this point gave 70° 5' 17" latitude, and 96° 46' 45" longitude; when the doctor heard that he consulted his map, and saw they were at the magnetic pole, at the very place where James Ross, the nephew of Sir John, had fixed it. The land was low near the coast, and at about a mile's distance became slightly elevated, sixty feet only. The *Forward's* boiler wanted cleaning, and the captain caused the brig to be anchored to an ice-field, and allowed the doctor and the boatswain to land. He himself cared for nothing but his pet project, and stayed in his cabin, consulting his map of the Pole.

The doctor and his companion easily succeeded in reaching land; the doctor took a compass to make experiments with. He wished to try if James Ross's conclusions hold good. He easily discovered the limestone heap raised by Ross; he ran to it; an opening allowed him to see, in the interior, the tin case in which James Ross had placed the official report of his discoveries. No living being seemed to have visited this desolate coast for the last thirty years. In this spot a loadstone needle, suspended as delicately as possible, immediately moved into an almost vertical position under the magnetic influence; if the centre of attraction was not immediately under the needle, it could only be at a trifling distance. The doctor made the experiment carefully, and found that the imperfect instruments of James Ross had given his vertical needle an inclination of 89° 59', making the real magnetic point at a minute's distance from the spot, but that his own at a little distance gave him an inclination of 90°.

"Here is the exact spot of the world's magnetic pole," said the doctor, rapping the earth.

"Then," said the boatswain, "there's no loadstone mountain, after all."

"Of course not; that mountain was only a credulous hypothesis. As you see, there isn't the least mountain capable of attracting ships, of attracting their iron anchor after anchor and nail after nail, and you see it respects your shoes as much as any other land on the globe."

"Then how do you explain——"

"Nothing is explained, Johnson; we don't know enough for that yet. But it is certain, exact, mathematical, that the magnetic pole is in this very spot!"

"Ah, Mr. Clawbonny! how happy the captain would be to say as much of the boreal pole!"

"He will some day, Johnson, you will see."

"I hope he will," answered the boatswain.

He and the doctor elevated a cairn on the exact spot where the experiment had been made, and returned on board at five o'clock in the evening.

CHAPTER XVII THE FATE OF SIR JOHN FRANKLIN

The *Forward* succeeded in cutting straight across James Ross Strait, but not without difficulty; the crew were obliged to work the saws and use petards, and they were worn out with fatigue. Happily the temperature was bearable, and thirty degrees higher than that experienced by James Ross at the same epoch. The thermometer marked thirty-four degrees.

On Saturday they doubled Cape Felix at the northern extremity of King William's Land, one of the middle-sized isles of the northern seas. The crew there experienced a strong and painful sensation, and many a sad look was turned towards the island as they sailed by the coast. This island had been the theatre of the most terrible tragedy of modern times. Some miles to the west the *Erebus* and the *Terror* had been lost for ever. The sailors knew about the attempts made to find Admiral Franklin and the results, but they were ignorant of the affecting details of the catastrophe. While the doctor was following the progress of the ship on his map, several of them, Bell, Bolton, and Simpson, approached and entered into conversation with him. Their comrades, animated by curiosity, soon followed them; while the brig flew along with extreme rapidity, and the coast with its bays, capes, and promontories passed before their eyes like a gigantic panorama.

Hatteras was marching up and down the poop with quick steps. The doctor, on the deck, looked round, and saw himself surrounded by almost the whole crew. He saw how powerful a recital would be in such a situation, and he continued the conversation begun with Johnson as follows:—

"You know how Franklin began, my friends; he was a cabin-boy like Cook and Nelson; after having employed his youth in great maritime expeditions, he resolved in 1845 to launch out in search of the North-West passage; he commanded the *Erebus* and the *Terror*, two vessels, already famous, that had just made an Antarctic campaign under James Ross, in 1840. The *Erebus*, equipped by Franklin, carried a crew of seventy men, officers and sailors, with Fitz-James as captain; Gore and Le Vesconte, lieutenants; Des Voeux, Sargent, and Couch, boatswains; and Stanley as surgeon. The *Terror* had sixty-eight men, Captain Crozier; Lieutenants Little, Hodgson, and Irving; Horesby and Thomas were the boatswains, and Peddie the surgeon. In the names on the map of the capes, straits, points, and channels, you may read those of these unfortunate men, not one of whom was destined ever again to see his native land. There were a hundred and thirty-eight men in all! We know that Franklin's last letters were addressed from Disko Island, and were dated July 12th, 1845. 'I hope,' he said, 'to get under way to-night for Lancaster Strait.' What happened after his departure from Disko Bay? The captains of two whalers, the *Prince of Wales* and the *Enterprise*, perceived the two ships in Melville Bay for the last time, and after that day nothing was heard of them. However, we can follow Franklin in his westerly course: he passed through Lancaster and Barrow Straits, and arrived at Beechey Island, where he passed the winter of 1845 and '46."

"But how do you know all this?" asked Bell, the carpenter.

"By three tombs which Austin discovered on that island in 1850. Three of Franklin's sailors were buried there, and by a document which was found by Lieutenant Hobson, of the *Fox*, which bears the date of April 25th, 1848, we know that after their wintering the *Erebus* and the *Terror* went up Wellington Strait as far as the seventy-seventh parallel; but instead of continuing their route northwards, which was, probably, not practicable, they returned south."

"And that was their ruin!" said a grave voice. "Safety lay to the north."

Every one turned round. Hatteras, leaning on the rail of the poop, had just uttered that terrible observation.

"There is not a doubt," continued the doctor, "that Franklin's intention was to get back to the American coast; but tempests stopped him, and on the 12th September, 1846, the two ships were seized by the ice, at a few miles from here, to the north-west of Cape Felix; they were dragged along N.N.W. to Victoria Point over there," said the doctor, pointing to a part of the sea. "Now," he continued, "the ships were not abandoned till the 22nd of April, 1848. What happened during these nineteen months? What did the poor unfortunate men do? They, doubtless, explored the surrounding land, attempting any chance of safety, for the admiral was an energetic man, and if he did not succeed——"

"Very likely his crew betrayed him," added Hatteras.

The sailors dared not raise their eyes; these words pricked their conscience.

"To end my tale, the fatal document informs us also that John Franklin succumbed to fatigue on the 11th of June, 1847. Honour to his memory!" said the doctor, taking off his hat. His audience imitated him in silence.

"What became of the poor fellows for the next ten months after they had lost their chief? They remained on board their vessels, and only resolved to abandon them in April, 1848; a hundred and five men out of a hundred and thirty-eight were still living; thirty-three were dead! Then Captain Crozier and Captain Fitz-James raised a cairn on Victory Point, and there deposited their last document. See, my friends, we are passing the point now! You can still see the remains of the cairn placed on the extreme point, reached by John Ross in 1831. There is Jane Franklin Cape. There is Franklin Point. There is Le Vesconte Point. There is Erebus Bay, where the boat made out of the *débris* of one of the vessels was found on a sledge. Silver spoons, provisions in abundance, chocolate, tea, and religious books were found there too. The hundred and five survivors, under Captain Crozier, started for Great Fish River. Where did they get to? Did they succeed in reaching Hudson's Bay? Did any survive? What became of them after this last departure?"

"I will tell you what became of them," said John Hatteras in a firm voice. "Yes, they did try to reach Hudson's Bay, and they split up into several parties! Yes, they did make for the south! A letter from Dr. Rae in 1854 contained the information that in 1850 the Esquimaux had met on King William's Land a detachment of forty men travelling on the ice, and dragging a boat, thin, emaciated, worn out by fatigue and suffering! Later on they discovered thirty corpses on the continent and five on a neighbouring island, some half-buried, some left without burial, some under a boat turned upside down, others under the remains of a tent; here an officer with his telescope on his shoulder and a loaded gun at his side, further on a boiler with the remnants of a horrible meal! When the Admiralty received these tidings it begged the Hudson's Bay Company to send its most experienced agents to the scene. They descended Back River to its mouth. They visited the islands of Montreal, Maconochie, and Ogle Point. But they discovered nothing. All the poor wretches had died from misery, suffering, and hunger, whilst trying to prolong their existence by the dreadful resource of cannibalism. That is what became of them on the southern route. Well! Do you still wish to march in their footsteps?"

His trembling voice, his passionate gestures and beaming face, produced an indescribable effect. The crew, excited by its emotion before this fatal land, cried out with one voice: "To the north! To the north!"

"Yes, to the north! Safety and glory lie to the north. Heaven is for us! The wind is changing; the pass is free!"

So saying, Hatteras gave orders to turn the vessel; the sailors went to work with alacrity; the ice streams got clear little by little; the *Forward*, with all steam on, made for McClintock Channel. Hatteras was right when he counted upon a more open sea; he followed up the supposed route taken by Franklin, sailing along the western coast of Prince of Wales's Land, then pretty well known, whilst the opposite shore is still unknown. It was evident that the breaking up of the ice had taken place in the eastern locks, for this strait appeared entirely free; the *Forward* made up for lost time; she fled along so quickly that she passed Osborne Bay on the 14th of June, and the extreme points attained by the expeditions of 1851. Icebergs were still numerous, but the sea did not threaten to quit the keel of the *Forward*.

CHAPTER XVIII THE NORTHERN ROUTE

The crew seemed to have returned to its habits of discipline and obedience. There was little fatiguing work to do, and they had a good deal of leisure. The temperature kept above freezing point, and it seemed as if the thaw had removed the great obstacles to navigation.

Dick, now sociable and familiar, had made great friends with Dr. Clawbonny. But as in most friendships one friend has to give way to the other, it must be acknowledged it was not the dog. Dick did what he liked with the doctor, who obeyed him as if he were the dog. He was amiable with most of the sailors and officers on board, only by instinct, doubtless, he shunned Shandon's society; he also kept up a grudge against Pen and Foker; he vented his hatred of them by growling at their approach. But they dare not now attack the captain's dog—his "familiar," as Clifton called him. On the whole the crew had plucked up courage again and worked well.

"It seems to me," said James Wall one day to Richard Shandon, "that our men took the captain's speech seriously; they no longer seem to be doubtful of success."

"The more fools they!" answered Shandon. "If they reflected, if they examined the situation, they would see that we are going out of one imprudence into another."

"But," continued Wall, "the sea is open now, and we are getting back into well-known tracks; aren't you exaggerating a bit, Shandon?"

"No, I am not exaggerating; the dislike I feel to Hatteras is not blinding me. Have you seen the coal-holes lately?"

"No," answered Wall.

"Well, then, go and examine them: you will see how much there's left. He ought to have navigated under sail, and have kept the engine for currents and contrary winds; he ought only to have used his coal where he was obliged; who can tell where we shall be kept, and for how many years? But Hatteras only thinks about getting north. Whether the wind is contrary or not, he goes along at full steam, and if things go on as they are doing now, we shall soon be in a pretty pickle."

"If what you say is true, it is very serious."

"Yes, it is, because of the wintering. What shall we do without coal in a country where even the thermometer freezes?"

"But, if I am not mistaken, the captain counts upon renewing his stock of coal at Beechey Island. It appears there is a large provision there."

"And suppose we can't reach Beechey Island, what will become of us then?"

"You are right, Shandon; Hatteras seems to me very imprudent; but why don't you expostulate with him on the subject?"

"No," said Shandon, with ill-concealed bitterness, "I won't say a word. It is nothing to do with me now. I shall wait to see what turns up; I shall obey orders, and not give my opinion where it isn't wanted."

"Allow me to tell you that you are in the wrong, Shandon; you have as much interest in setting yourself against the captain's imprudence as we have."

"He wouldn't listen to me if I were to speak; do you think he would?"

Wall dared not answer in the affirmative, and he added—

"But perhaps he would listen to the crew."

"The crew!" answered Shandon, shrugging his shoulders; "you don't know the crew. The men know they are nearing the 72nd parallel, and that they will earn a thousand pounds for every degree above that."

"The captain knew what he was doing when he offered them that."

"Of course he did, and for the present he can do what he likes with them."

"What do you mean?"

"I mean that while they have nothing to do, and there is an open sea, they will go on right enough; but wait till difficulty and danger come, and you will see how much they'll think about the money!"

"Then you don't think Hatteras will succeed?"

"No, he will not; to succeed in such an enterprise there must be a good understanding between him and his officers, and that does not exist. Hatteras is a madman; all his past career proves it. Well, we shall see; perhaps circumstances will force them to give the command to a less adventurous captain."

"Still," said Wall, shaking his head, "he will always have on his side——"

"Dr. Clawbonny, a man who only cares for science, and Johnson, a sailor who only cares to obey, and perhaps two more men like Bell, the carpenter; four at the most, and we are eighteen on board! No, Wall, Hatteras has not got the confidence of his men, and he knows it, so he bribes them; he profited cleverly by the Franklin affair, but that won't last, I tell you, and if he doesn't reach Beechey Island he's a lost man!"

"Suppose the crew should take it into its head——"

"Don't tell the crew what I think," answered Shandon quickly; "the men will soon see for themselves. Besides, just now we must go north. Who knows if Hatteras won't find that way will bring us back sooner? At the end of McClintock Channel lies Melville Bay, and from thence go the straits that lead to Baffin's Bay. Hatteras must take care! The way to the east is easier than the road to the north!"

Hatteras was not mistaken in his opinion that Shandon would betray him if he could. Besides, Shandon was right in attributing the contentment of the men to the hope of gain. Clifton had counted exactly how much each man would have. Without reckoning the captain and the doctor, who would not expect a share in the bounty-money, there remained sixteen men to divide it amongst. If ever they succeeded in reaching the Pole, each man would have £1,125—that is to say, a fortune. It would cost the captain £18,000, but he could afford it. The thoughts of the money inflamed the minds of the crew, and they were now as anxious to go north as before they had been eager to turn south. The *Forward* during the day of June 16th passed Cape Aworth. Mount Rawlinson raised its white peaks towards the sky; the snow and fog made it appear colossal, as they exaggerated its distance; the temperature still kept some degrees above freezing point; improvised cascades and cataracts showed themselves on the sides of the mountains, and avalanches roared down with the noise of artillery discharges. The glaciers, spread out in long white sheets, projected an immense reverberation into space. Boreal nature, in its struggle with the frost, presented a splendid spectacle. The brig went very near the coast; on some sheltered rocks rare heaths were to be seen, the pink flowers lifting their heads timidly out of the snows, and some meagre lichens of a reddish colour and the shoots of a dwarf willow.

At last, on the 19th of June, at the famous seventy-third parallel, they doubled Cape Minto, which forms one of the extremities of Ommaney Bay; the brig entered Melville Bay, surnamed by Bolton Money Bay; the merry sailors joked about the name, and made Dr. Clawbonny laugh heartily. Notwithstanding a strong breeze from the northeast, the *Forward* made considerable progress, and on the 23rd of June she passed the 74th degree of latitude. She was in the midst of Melville Bay, one of the most considerable seas in these regions. This sea was crossed for the first time by Captain Parry in his great expedition of 1819, and it was then that his crew earned the prize of £5,000 promised by Act of Parliament. Clifton remarked that there were two degrees from the 72nd to the 74th; that already placed £125 to his credit. But they told him that a fortune was not worth much there, and that it was of no use being rich if he could not drink his riches, and he had better wait till he could roll under a Liverpool table before he rejoiced and rubbed his hands.

CHAPTER XIX A WHALE IN SIGHT

Melville Bay, though easily navigable, was not free from ice; ice-fields lay as far as the utmost limits of the horizon; a few icebergs appeared here and there, but they were immovable, as if anchored in the midst of the frozen fields. The *Forward*, with all steam on, followed the wide passes where it was easy to work her. The wind changed frequently from one point of the compass to another. The variability of the wind in the Arctic Seas is a remarkable fact; sometimes a dead calm is followed in a few minutes by a violent tempest, as the *Forward* found to her cost on the 23rd of June in the midst of the immense bay. The more constant winds blow from off the ice-bank on to the open sea, and are intensely cold. On that day the thermometer fell several degrees; the wind veered round to the south, and violent gusts, sweeping over the ice-fields, brought a thick snow along with them. Hatteras immediately caused the sails that helped the screw to be furled, but not quickly enough to prevent his little foresail being carried away in the twinkling of an eye. Hatteras worked his ship with the greatest composure, and did not leave the deck during the tempest; he was obliged to fly before the weather and to turn westward. The wind raised up enormous waves, in the midst of which blocks of ice balanced themselves; these blocks were of all sizes and shapes, and had been struck off the surrounding ice-fields; the brig was tossed about like a child's plaything, and morsels of the packs were thrown over her hull; at one instant she was lying perpendicularly along the side of a liquid mountain; her steel prow concentrated the light, and shone like a melting metal bar; at another she was down an abyss, plunging her head into whirlwinds of snow, whilst her screws, out of the water, turned in space with a sinister noise, striking the air with their paddles. Rain mixed with the snow and fell in torrents.

The doctor could not miss such an occasion of getting wet to the skin; he remained on deck, a prey to that emotional admiration which a scientific man must necessarily feel during such a spectacle. His nearest neighbour could not have heard him speak, so he said nothing and watched; but whilst watching he was witness to an odd phenomenon, peculiar to hyperborean regions. The tempest was confined to a restricted area, and only extended for about three or four miles; the wind that passes over ice-fields loses much of its strength and cannot carry its violence far out; the doctor perceived from time to time, through an opening in the tempest, a calm sky and a quiet sea beyond some ice-fields. The *Forward* would therefore only have to take advantage of some channels left by the ice to find a peaceful navigation again, but she ran the risk of being thrown on to one of the moving banks which followed the movement of the swell. However, in a few hours Hatteras succeeded in getting his ship into a calm sea, whilst the violence of the hurricane spent itself at a few cables' length from the *Forward*. Melville Bay no longer presented the same aspect; under the influence of the winds and the waves a great number of icebergs, detached from the coast, floated northward, running against one another in every direction. There were several hundreds of them, but the bay is very wide, and the brig easily avoided them. The spectacle of these floating masses was magnificent; they seemed to be having a grand race for it on the open sea. The doctor was getting quite excited with watching them, when the harpooner, Simpson, came up and made him look at the changing tints in the sea; they varied from a deep blue to olive green; long stripes stretched north and south in such decided lines that the eye could follow each shade out of sight. Sometimes a transparent sheet of water would follow a perfectly opaque sheet.

"Well, Mr. Clawbonny, what do you think of that?" said Simpson.

"I am of the same opinion as the whaler Scoresby on the nature of the different coloured waters; blue water has no animalculæ, and green water is full of them. Scoresby has made several experiments on this subject, and I think he is right."

"Well, sir, I know something else about the colours in the sea, and if I were a whaler I should be precious glad to see them."

"But I don't see any whales," answered the doctor.

"You won't be long before you do, though, I can tell you. A whaler is lucky when he meets with those green stripes under this latitude."

"Why?" asked the doctor, who always liked to get information from anybody who understood what they were talking about.

"Because whales are always found in great quantities in green water."

"What's the reason of that?"

"Because they find plenty of food in them."

"Are you sure of that?"

"I've seen it a hundred times, at least, in Baffin Sea; why shouldn't it be the same in Melville Bay? Besides, look there, Mr. Clawbonny," added Simpson, leaning over the barricading.

"Why any one would think it was the wake of a ship!"

"It is an oily substance that the whale leaves behind. The animal can't be far off!"

The atmosphere was impregnated with a strong oily odour, and the doctor attentively watched the surface of the water. The prediction of the harpooner was soon accomplished. Foker called out from the masthead—

"A whale alee!"

All looks turned to the direction indicated. A small spout was perceived coming up out of the sea about a mile from the brig.

"There she spouts!" cried Simpson, who knew what that meant.

"She has disappeared!" answered the doctor.

"Oh, we could find her again easily enough if necessary!" said Simpson, with an accent of regret. To his great astonishment, and although no one dared ask for it, Hatteras gave orders to man the whaler. Johnson went aft to the stern, while Simpson, harpoon in hand, stood in the bow. They could not prevent the doctor joining the expedition. The sea was pretty calm. The whaler soon got off, and in ten minutes was a mile from the brig. The whale had taken in another provision of air, and had plunged again; but she soon returned to the surface and spouted out that mixture of gas and mucus that escapes from her air-holes.

"There! There!" said Simpson, pointing to a spot about eight hundred yards from the boat. It was soon alongside the animal, and as they had seen her from the brig too, she came nearer, keeping little steam on. The enormous cetacean disappeared and reappeared as the waves rose and fell, showing its black back like a rock in open sea. Whales do not swim quickly unless they are pursued, and this one only rocked itself in the waves. The boat silently approached along the green water; its opacity prevented the animal seeing the enemy. It is always an agitating spectacle when a fragile boat attacks one of these monsters; this one was about 130 feet long, and it is not rare, between the 72nd and the 80th degree, to meet with whales more than 180 feet long. Ancient writers have described animals more than 700 feet long, but they drew upon their imagination for their facts. The boat soon neared the whale; on a sign from Simpson the men rested on their oars, and brandishing his harpoon, the experienced sailor threw it with all his strength; it went deep into the thick covering of fat. The wounded whale struck the sea with its tail and plunged. The four oars were immediately raised perpendicularly; the cord fastened to the harpoon, and attached to the bow, rolled rapidly out and dragged the boat along, steered cleverly by Johnson.

The whale got away from the brig and made for the moving icebergs; she kept on for more than half-an-hour; they were obliged to wet the cord fastened to the harpoon to prevent it catching fire by rubbing against the boat. When the whale seemed to be going along a little more slowly, the cord was pulled in little by little and rolled up; the whale soon reappeared on the surface of the sea, which she beat with her formidable tail: veritable waterspouts fell in a violent rain on to the boat. It was getting nearer. Simpson had seized a long lance, and was preparing to give close battle to the animal, when all at once the whale glided into a pass between two mountainous icebergs. The pursuit then became really dangerous.

"The devil!" said Johnson.

"Go ahead," cried Simpson; "we've got her!"

"But we can't follow her into the icebergs!" said Johnson, steering steadily.

"Yes we can!" cried Simpson.

"No, no!" cried some of the sailors.

"Yes, yes!" said others.

During the discussion the whale had got between two floating mountains which the swell was bringing close together. The boat was being dragged into this dangerous part when Johnson rushed to the fore, an axe in his hand, and cut the cord. He was just in time; the two mountains came together with a tremendous crash, crushing the unfortunate animal.

"The whale's lost!" cried Simpson.

"But we are saved!" answered Johnson.

"Well," said the doctor, who had not moved, "that was worth seeing!"

The crushing force of these ice-mountains is enormous. The whale was victim to an accident that often happens in these seas. Scoresby relates that in the course of a single summer thirty whales perished in the same way in Baffin's Sea; he saw a three-master flattened in a minute between two immense walls of ice. Other vessels were split through, as if with a lance, by pointed icicles a hundred feet long, meeting through the planks. A few minutes afterwards the boat hailed the brig, and was soon in its accustomed place on deck.

"It is a lesson for those who are imprudent enough to adventure into the channels amongst the ice!" said Shandon in a loud voice.

CHAPTER XX BEECHEY ISLAND

On the 25th of June the *Forward* arrived in sight of Cape Dundas at the north-western extremity of Prince of Wales's Land. There the difficulty of navigating amongst the ice grew greater. The sea is narrower there, and the line made by Crozier, Young, Day, Lowther, and Garret Islands, like a chain of forts before a roadstead, forced the ice-streams to accumulate in this strait. The brig took from the 25th to the 30th of June to make as much way as she would have done in one day under any other circumstances; she stopped, retraced her steps, waiting for a favourable occasion so as not to miss Beechey Island, using a great deal of coal, as the fires were only moderated when she had to halt, but were never put out, so that she might be under pressure day and night. Hatteras knew the extent of his coal provision as well as Shandon, but as he was certain of getting his provision renewed at Beechey Island he would not lose a minute for the sake of economy; he had been much delayed by his forced march southward, and although he had taken the precaution of leaving England before the month of April, he did not find himself more advanced than preceding expeditions had been at the same epoch. On the 30th they sighted Cape Walker at the north-eastern extremity of Prince of Wales's Land; it was the extreme point that Kennedy and Bellot perceived on the 3rd of May, 1852, after an excursion across the whole of North Somerset. Before that, in 1851, Captain Ommaney, of the Austin expedition, had the good luck to revictual his detachments there. This cape is very high, and remarkable for its reddish-brown colour; from there, when the weather is clear, the view stretches as far as the entrance to Wellington Channel. Towards evening they saw Cape Bellot, separated from Cape Walker by McLeon Bay. Cape Bellot was so named in the presence of the young French officer, for whom the English expedition gave three cheers. At this spot the coast is made of yellowish limestone, presenting a very rugged outline; it is defended by enormous icebergs which the north winds pile up there in a most imposing way. It was soon lost to sight by the *Forward* as she opened a passage amongst the ice to get to Beechey Island through Barrow Strait. Hatteras resolved to go straight on, and, so as not to be drifted further than the island, scarcely quitted his post during the following days; he often went to the masthead to look out for the most advantageous channels. All that pluck, skill, and genius could do he did while they were crossing the strait. Fortune did not favour him, for the sea is generally more open at this epoch. But at last, by dint of sparing neither his steam, his crew, nor himself, he attained his end.

On the 3rd of July, at 11 o'clock in the morning, the ice-master signalled land to the north. After taking an observation Hatteras recognised Beechey Island, that general meeting-place of Arctic navigators. Almost all ships that adventure in these seas stop there. Franklin wintered there for the first time before getting into Wellington Strait, and Creswell, with Lieutenant McClure, after having cleared 170 miles on the ice, rejoined the *Phoenix* and returned to England. The last ship which anchored at Beechey Island before the *Forward* was the *Fox*; McClintock revictualled there the 11th of August, 1858, and repaired the habitations and magazines; only two years had elapsed since then, and Hatteras knew all these details. The boatswain's heart beat with emotion at the sight of this island; when he had visited it he was quartermaster on board the *Phoenix*; Hatteras questioned him about the coast line, the facilities for anchoring, how far they could go inland, &c.; the weather was magnificent, and the temperature kept at 57°.

"Well, Johnson," said the captain, "do you know where you are?"

"Yes, sir, that is Beechey Island; only you must let us get further north—the coast is more easy of access."

"But where are the habitations and the magazines?" said Hatteras.

"Oh, you can't see them till you land; they are sheltered behind those little hills you see yonder."

"And is that where you transported a considerable quantity of provisions?"

"Yes, sir; the Admiralty sent us here in 1853, under the command of Captain Inglefield, with the steamer *Phoenix* and a transport ship, the *Breadalbane*, loaded with provisions; we brought enough with us to revictual a whole expedition."

"But the commander of the *Fox* took a lot of them in 1858," said Hatteras.

"That doesn't matter, sir; there'll be plenty left for you; the cold preserves them wonderfully, and we shall find them as fresh and in as good a state of preservation as the first day."

"What I want is coal," said Hatteras; "I have enough provisions for several years."

"We left more than a thousand tons there, so you can make your mind easy."

"Are we getting near?" said Hatteras, who, telescope in hand, was watching the coast.

"You see that point?" continued Johnson. "When we have doubled it we shall be very near where we drop anchor. It was from that place that we started for England with Lieutenant Creswell and the twelve invalids from the *Investigator*. We were fortunate enough to bring back McClure's lieutenant, but the officer Bellot, who accompanied us on board the *Phoenix*, never saw his country again! It is a painful thing to think about. But, captain, I think we ought to drop anchor here."

"Very well," answered Hatteras, and he gave his orders in consequence. The *Forward* was in a little bay naturally sheltered on the north, east, and south, and at about a cable's length from the coast.

"Mr. Wall," said Hatteras, "have the long boat got ready to transport the coal on board. I shall land in the pirogue with the doctor and the boatswain. Will you accompany us, Mr. Shandon?"

"As you please," answered Shandon.

A few minutes later the doctor, armed as a sportsman and a *savant*, took his place in the pirogue along with his companions; in ten minutes they landed on a low and rocky coast.

"Lead the way, Johnson," said Hatteras. "You know it, I suppose?"

"Perfectly, sir; only there's a monument here that I did not expect to find!"

"That!" cried the doctor; "I know what it is; let us go up to it; the stone itself will tell us."

The four men advanced, and the doctor said, after taking off his hat—

"This, my friends, is a monument in memory of Franklin and his companions."

Lady Franklin had, in 1855, confided a black marble tablet to Doctor Kane, and in 1858 she gave a second to McClintock to be raised on Beechey Island. McClintock accomplished this duty religiously, and placed the stone near a funeral monument erected to the memory of Bellot by Sir John Barrow.

The tablet bore the following inscription:

"TO THE MEMORY OF
FRANKLIN, CROZIER, FITZ-JAMES,
AND ALL THEIR VALIANT BRETHREN
OFFICERS AND FAITHFUL COMPANIONS

who suffered for the cause of science and for their country's glory. "This stone is erected near the place where they passed their first Arctic winter, and from whence they departed to conquer obstacles or to die.

"It perpetuates the regret of their countrymen and friends who admire them, and the anguish, conquered by Faith, of her who lost in the chief of the expedition the most devoted and most affectionate of husbands.

"It is thus that He led them to the supreme haven where all men take their rest.

"1855."

This stone, on a forlorn coast of these far-off regions, appealed mournfully to the heart; the doctor, in presence of these touching regrets, felt his eyes fill with tears. At the very same place which Franklin and his companions passed full of energy and hope, there only remained a block of marble in remembrance! And notwithstanding this sombre warning of destiny, the *Forward* was going to follow in the track of the *Erebus* and the *Terror*. Hatteras was the first to rouse himself from the perilous contemplation, and quickly climbed a rather steep hill, almost entirely bare of snow.

"Captain," said Johnson, following him, "we shall see the magazines from here."

Shandon and the doctor joined them on the summit. But from there the eye contemplated the vast plains, on which there remained no vestige of a habitation.

"That is singular!" cried the boatswain.

"Well, and where are the magazines?" said Hatteras quickly.

"I don't know—I don't see——" stammered Johnson.

"You have mistaken the way," said the doctor.

"It seemed to me that this was the very place," continued Johnson.

"Well," said Hatteras, impatiently "where are we to go now?"

"We had better go down, for I may be mistaken. I may have forgotten the exact locality in seven years!"

"Especially when the country is so uniformly monotonous!" added the doctor.

"And yet——" murmured Johnson.

Shandon had not spoken a word. After walking for a few minutes, Johnson stopped.

"But no," he cried, "I am not mistaken!"

"Well?" said Hatteras, looking round him.

"Do you see that swell of the ground?" asked the boatswain, pointing to a sort of mound with three distinct swells on it.

"What do you conclude from that?" asked the doctor.

"Those are the three graves of Franklin's sailors. I am sure now that I am not mistaken; the habitations ought to be about a hundred feet from here, and if they are not, they——"

He dared not finish his sentence; Hatteras had rushed forward, a prey to violent despair. There, where the wished-for stores on which he had counted ought to have been, there ruin, pillage and destruction had been before him. Who had done it? Animals would only have attacked the provisions, and there did not remain a single rag from the tent, a piece of wood or iron, and, more terrible still, not a fragment of coal! It was evident that the Esquimaux had learnt the value of these objects from their frequent relations with Europeans; since the departure of the *Fox* they had fetched everything away, and had not left a trace even of their passage. A slight coating of snow covered the ground. Hatteras was confounded. The doctor looked and shook his head. Shandon still said nothing, but an attentive observer would have noticed his lips curl with a cruel smile. At this moment the men sent by Lieutenant Wall came up; they soon saw the state of affairs. Shandon advanced towards the captain, and said:

"Mr. Hatteras, we need not despair; happily we are near the entrance to Barrow Strait, which will take us back to Baffin's Sea!"

"Mr. Shandon," answered Hatteras, "happily we are near the entrance to Wellington Strait, and that will take us north!"

"But how shall we get along, captain?"

"With the sails, sir. We have two months' firing left, and that is enough for our wintering."

"But allow me to tell you——" added Shandon.

"I will allow you to follow me on board my ship, sir," answered Hatteras, and turning his back on his second, he returned to the brig and shut himself up in his cabin. For the next two days the wind was contrary, and the captain did not show up on deck. The doctor profited by the forced sojourn to go over Beechey Island; he gathered some plants, which the temperature, relatively high, allowed to grow here and there on the rocks that the snow had left, some heaths, a few lichens, a sort of yellow ranunculus, a sort of plant something like sorrel, with wider leaves and more veins, and some pretty vigorous saxifrages. He found the fauna of this country much richer than the flora; he perceived long flocks of geese and cranes going northward, partridges, eider ducks of a bluish black, sandpipers, a sort of wading bird of the scolopax class, northern divers, plungers with very long bodies, numerous ptarmites, a sort of bird very good to eat, dovekies with black bodies, wings spotted with white, feet and beak red as coral; noisy bands of kittywakes and fat loons with white breasts, represented the ornithology of the island. The doctor was fortunate enough to kill a few grey hares, which had not yet put on their white winter fur, and a blue fox which Dick ran down skilfully. Some bears, evidently accustomed to dread the presence of men, would not allow themselves to be got at, and the seals were extremely timid, doubtless for the same reason as their enemies the bears. The class of articulated animals was represented by a single mosquito, which the doctor caught to his great delight, though not till it had stung him. As a conchologist he was less favoured, and only found a sort of mussel and some bivalve shells.

CHAPTER XXI THE DEATH OF BELLOT

The temperature during the days of the 3rd and 4th of July kept up to 57°; this was the highest thermometric point observed during the campaign. But on Thursday, the 5th, the wind turned to the south-east, and was accompanied by violent snow-storms. The thermometer fell during the preceding night to 23°. Hatteras took no notice of the murmurs of the crew, and gave orders to get under way. For the last thirteen days, from Cape Dundas, the *Forward* had not been able to gain one more degree north, so the party represented by Clifton was no longer satisfied, but wished like Hatteras to get into Wellington Channel, and worked away with a will. The brig had some difficulty in getting under sail; but Hatteras having set his mizensail, his topsails, and his gallantsails during the night, advanced boldly in the midst of fields of ice which the current was drifting south. The crew were tired out with this winding navigation, which kept them constantly at work at the sails. Wellington Channel is not very wide; it is bounded by North Devon on the east and Cornwallis Island on the west; this island was long believed to be a peninsula. It was Sir John Franklin who first sailed round it in 1846, starting west, and coming back to the same point to the north of the channel. The exploration of Wellington Channel was made in 1851 by Captain Penny in the whalers *Lady Franklin* and *Sophia*; one of his lieutenants, Stewart, reached Cape Beecher in latitude 76° 20', and discovered the open sea—that open sea which was Hatteras's dream!

"What Stewart found I shall find," said he to the doctor; "then I shall be able to set sail to the Pole."

"But aren't you afraid that your crew——"

"My crew!" said Hatteras severely. Then in a low tone—"Poor fellows!" murmured he, to the great astonishment of the doctor. It was the first expression of feeling he had heard the captain deliver.

"No," he repeated with energy, "they must follow me! They shall follow me!"

However, although the *Forward* had nothing to fear from the collision of the ice-streams, which were still pretty far apart, they made very little progress northward, for contrary winds often forced them to stop. They passed Capes Spencer and Innis slowly, and on Tuesday, the 10th, cleared 75° to the great delight of Clifton. The *Forward* was then at the very place where the American ships, the *Rescue* and the *Advance*, encountered such terrible dangers. Doctor Kane formed part of this expedition; towards the end of September, 1850, these ships got caught in an ice-bank, and were forcibly driven into Lancaster Strait. It was Shandon who related this catastrophe to James Wall before some of the brig's crew.

"The *Advance* and the *Rescue*," he said to them, "were so knocked about by the ice, that they were obliged to leave off fires on board; but that did not prevent the temperature sinking 18° below zero. During the whole winter the unfortunate crews were kept prisoners in the ice-bank, ready to abandon their ships at any moment; for three weeks they did not even change their clothes. They floated along in that dreadful situation for more than a thousand miles, when at last they were thrown into the middle of Baffin's Sea."

The effect of this speech upon a crew already badly disposed can be well imagined. During this conversation Johnson was talking to the doctor about an event that had taken place in those very quarters; he asked the doctor to tell him when the brig was in latitude 75° 30', and when they passed it he cried:

"Yes, it was just there!" in saying which tears filled his eyes.

"You mean that Lieutenant Bellot died there?" said the doctor.

"Yes, Mr. Clawbonny. He was as good and brave a fellow as ever lived! It was upon this very North Devon coast! It was to be, I suppose, but if Captain Pullen had returned on board sooner it would not have happened."

"What do you mean, Johnson?"

"Listen to me, Mr. Clawbonny, and you will see on what a slight thread existence often hangs. You know that Lieutenant Bellot went his first campaign in search of Franklin in 1850?"

"Yes, on the *Prince Albert*."

"Well, when he got back to France he obtained permission to embark on board the *Phoenix* under Captain Inglefield; I was a sailor on board. We came with the *Breadalbane* to transport provisions to Beechey Island!"

"Those provisions we, unfortunately, did not find. Well?"

"We reached Beechey Island in the beginning of August; on the 10th Captain Inglefield left the *Phoenix* to rejoin Captain Pullen, who had been separated from his ship, the *North Star*, for a month. When he came back he thought of sending his Admiralty despatches to Sir Edward Belcher, who was wintering in Wellington Channel. A little while after the departure of our captain, Captain Pullen got back to his ship. Why did he not arrive before the departure of Captain Inglefield? Lieutenant Bellot, fearing that our captain would be long away, and knowing that the Admiralty despatches ought to be sent at once, offered to take them himself. He left the command of the two ships to Captain Pullen, and set out on the 12th of August with a sledge and an indiarubber boat. He took the boatswain of the *North Star* (Harvey) with him, and three sailors, Madden, David Hook, and me. We supposed that Sir Edward Belcher was to be found in the neighbourhood of Beecher Cape, to the north of the channel; we made for it with our sledge along the eastern coast. The first day we encamped about three miles from Cape Innis; the next day we stopped on a block of ice about three miles from Cape Bowden. As land lay at about three miles' distance, Lieutenant Bellot resolved to go and encamp there during the night, which was as light as the day; he tried to get to it in his indiarubber canoe; he was twice repulsed by a violent breeze from the south-east; Harvey and Madden attempted the passage in their turn, and were more fortunate; they took a cord with them, and established a communication between the coast and the sledge; three objects were transported by means of the cord, but at the fourth attempt we felt our block of ice move; Mr. Bellot called out to his companions to drop the cord, and we were dragged to a great distance from the coast. The wind blew from the south-east, and it was snowing; but we were not in much danger, and the lieutenant might have come back as we did."

Here Johnson stopped an instant to take a glance at the fatal coast, and continued:

"After our companions were lost to sight we tried to shelter ourselves under the tent of our sledge, but in vain; then, with our knives, we began to cut out a house in the ice. Mr. Bellot helped us for half an hour, and talked to us about the danger of our situation. I told him I was not afraid. 'By God's help,' he answered, 'we shall not lose a hair of our heads.' I asked him what o'clock it was, and he answered, 'About a quarter-past six.' It was a quarter-past six in the morning of Thursday, August 18th. Then Mr. Bellot tied up his books, and said he would go and see how the ice floated; he had only been gone four minutes when I went round the block of ice to look for him; I saw his stick on the opposite side of a crevice, about five fathoms wide, where the ice was broken, but I could not see him anywhere. I called out, but no one answered. The wind was blowing great guns. I looked all round the block of ice, but found no trace of the poor lieutenant."

"What do you think had become of him?" said the doctor, much moved.

"I think that when Mr. Bellot got out of shelter the wind blew him into the crevice, and, as his greatcoat was buttoned up he could not swim. Oh! Mr. Clawbonny, I never was more grieved in my life! I could not believe it! He was a victim to duty, for it was in order to obey Captain Pullen's instructions that he tried to get to land. He was a good fellow, everybody liked him; even the Esquimaux, when they learnt his fate from Captain Inglefield on his return from Pound Bay, cried while they wept, as I am doing now, 'Poor Bellot! poor Bellot!'"

"But you and your companion, Johnson," said the doctor, "how did you manage to reach land?"

"Oh! we stayed twenty-four hours more on the block of ice, without food or firing; but at last we met with an ice-field; we jumped on to it, and with the help of an oar we fastened ourselves to an iceberg that we could guide like a raft, and we got to land, but without our brave officer."

By the time Johnson had finished his story the *Forward* had passed the fatal coast, and Johnson lost sight of the place of the painful catastrophe. The next day they left Griffin Bay to the starboard, and, two days after, Capes Grinnell and Helpmann; at last, on the 14th of July, they doubled Osborn Point, and on the 15th the brig anchored in Baring Bay, at the extremity of the channel. Navigation had not been very difficult; Hatteras met with a sea almost as free as that of which Belcher profited to go and winter with the *Pioneer* and the *Assistance* as far north as 77°. It was in 1852 and 1853, during his first wintering, for he passed the winter of 1853 to 1854 in Baring Bay, where the *Forward* was now at anchor. He suffered so much that he was obliged to leave the *Assistance* in the midst of the ice. Shandon told all these details to the already discontented sailors. Did Hatteras know how he was betrayed by his first officer? It is impossible to say; if he did, he said nothing about it.

At the top of Baring Bay there is a narrow channel which puts Wellington and Queen's Channel into communication with each other. There the rafts of ice lie closely packed. Hatteras tried, in vain, to clear the passes to the north of Hamilton Island; the wind was contrary; five precious days were lost in useless efforts. The temperature still lowered, and, on the 19th of July, fell to 26°; it got higher the following day; but this foretaste of winter made Hatteras afraid of waiting any longer. The wind seemed to be going to keep in the west, and to stop the progress of the ship. However, he was in a hurry to gain the point where Stewart had met with the open sea. On the 19th he resolved to get into the Channel at any price; the wind blew right on the brig, which might, with her screw, have stood against it, had not Hatteras been obliged to economise his fuel; on the other hand, the Channel was too wide to allow the men to haul the brig along. Hatteras, not considering the men's fatigue, resolved to have recourse to means often employed by whalers under similar circumstances. The men took it in turns to row, so as to push the brig on against the wind. The *Forward* advanced slowly up the Channel. The men were worn out and murmured loudly. They went on in that manner till the 23rd of July, when they reached Baring Island in Queen's Channel. The wind was still against them. The doctor thought the health of the men much shaken, and perceived the first symptoms of scurvy amongst them; he did all he could to prevent the spread of the wretched malady, and distributed lime-juice to the men.

Hatteras saw that he could no longer count upon his crew; reasoning and kindness were ineffectual, so he resolved to employ severity for the future; he suspected Shandon and Wall, though they dare not speak out openly. Hatteras had the doctor, Johnson, Bell, and Simpson for him; they were devoted to him body and soul; amongst the undecided were Foker, Bolton, Wolsten the gunsmith, and Brunton the first engineer; and they might turn against the captain at any moment; as to Pen, Gripper, Clifton, and Warren, they were in open revolt; they wished to persuade their comrades to force the captain to return to England. Hatteras soon saw that he could not continue to work his ship with such a crew. He remained twenty-four hours at Baring Island without taking a step forward. The weather grew cooler still, for winter begins to be felt in July in these high latitudes. On the 24th the thermometer fell to 22°. Young ice formed during the night, and if snow fell it would soon be thick enough to bear the weight of a man. The sea began already to have that dirty colour which precedes the formation of the first crystals. Hatteras could not mistake these alarming symptoms; if the channels got blocked up, he should be obliged to winter there at a great distance from the point he had undertaken the voyage in order to reach, without having caught a glimpse of that open sea which his predecessors made out was so near. He resolved, then, to gain several degrees further north, at whatever cost; seeing that he could not employ oars without the rowers were willing, nor sail in a contrary wind, he gave orders to put steam on again.

CHAPTER XXII BEGINNING OF REVOLT

At this unexpected command, the surprise was great on board the *Forward*.

"Light the fires!" exclaimed some.

"What with?" asked others.

"When we've only two months' coal in the hold!" said Pen.

"What shall we warm ourselves with in the winter?" asked Clifton.

"We shall be obliged to burn the brig down to her water-line," answered Gripper.

"And stuff the stove with the masts," added Warren. Shandon looked at Wall. The stupefied engineers hesitated to go down to the machine-room.

"Did you hear me?" cried the captain in an irritated tone.

Brunton made for the hatchway, but before going down he stopped.

"Don't go, Brunton!" called out a voice.

"Who spoke?" cried Hatteras.

"I did," said Pen, advancing towards the captain.

"And what did you say?" asked Hatteras.

"I say," answered Pen with an oath—"I say, we've had enough of it, and we won't go any further. You shan't kill us with hunger and work in the winter, and they shan't light the fires!"

"Mr. Shandon," answered Hatteras calmly, "have that man put in irons!"

"But, captain," replied Shandon, "what the man says——"

"If you repeat what the man says," answered Hatteras, "I'll have you shut up in your cabin and guarded! Seize that man! Do you hear?" Johnson, Bell, and Simpson advanced towards the sailor, who was in a terrible passion.

"The first who touches me——" he said, brandishing a handspike. Hatteras approached him.

"Pen," said he tranquilly, "if you move, I shall blow out your brains!" So speaking, he cocked a pistol and aimed it at the sailor. A murmur was heard.

"Not a word, men," said Hatteras, "or that man falls dead!" Johnson and Bell disarmed Pen, who no longer made any resistance, and placed him in the hold.

"Go, Brunton," said Hatteras. The engineer, followed by Plover and Warren, went down to his post. Hatteras returned to the poop.

"That Pen is a wretched fellow!" said the doctor.

"No man has ever been nearer death!" answered the captain, simply.

The steam was soon got up, the anchors were weighed, and the *Forward* veered away east, cutting the young ice with her steel prow. Between Baring Island and Beecher Point there are a considerable quantity of islands in the midst of ice-fields; the streams crowd together in the little channels which cut up this part of the sea; they had a tendency to agglomerate under the relatively low temperature; hummocks were formed here and there, and these masses, already more compact, denser, and closer together, would soon form an impenetrable mass. The *Forward* made its way with great difficulty amidst the snowstorms. However, with the mobility that characterises the climate of these regions, the sun appeared from time to time, the temperature went up several degrees, obstacles melted as if by magic, and a fine sheet of water lay where icebergs bristled all the passes. The horizon glowed with those magnificent orange shades which rest the eye, tired with the eternal white of the snow.

On the 26th of July the *Forward* passed Dundas Island, and veered afterwards more to the north; but there Hatteras found himself opposite an ice-bank eight or nine feet high, formed of little icebergs detached from the coast; he was obliged to turn west. The uninterrupted cracking of the ice, added to the noise of the steamer, was like sighs or groans. At last the brig found a channel, and advanced painfully along it; often an enormous iceberg hindered her course for hours; the fog hindered the pilot's look-out; as long as he can see for a mile in front of him, he can easily avoid obstacles; but in the midst of the fog it was often impossible to see a cable's length, and the swell was very strong. Sometimes the clouds looked smooth and white as though they were reflections of the ice-banks; but there were entire days when the yellow rays of the sun could not pierce the tenacious fog. Birds were still very numerous, and their cries were deafening; seals, lying idle on the floating ice, raised their heads, very little frightened, and moved their long necks as the brig passed. Pieces from the ship's sheathing were often rubbed off in her contact with the ice. At last, after six days of slow navigation, Point Beecher was sighted to the north on the 1st of August. Hatteras passed the last few hours at his masthead; the open sea that Stewart had perceived on May 30th, 1851, about latitude 76° 20', could not be far off; but as far as the eye could reach, Hatteras saw no indication of it. He came down without saying a word.

"Do you believe in an open sea?" asked Shandon of the lieutenant.

"I am beginning not to," answered Wall.

"Wasn't I right to say the pretended discovery was purely imagination? But they would not believe me, and even you were against me, Wall."

"We shall believe in you for the future, Shandon."

"Yes," said he, "when it's too late," and so saying he went back to his cabin, where he had stopped almost ever since his dispute with the captain. The wind veered round south towards evening; Hatteras ordered the brig to be put under sail and the fires to be put out; the crew had to work very hard for the next few days; they were more than a week getting to Barrow Point. The *Forward* had only made thirty miles in ten days. There the wind turned north again, and the screw was set to work. Hatteras still hoped to find an open sea beyond the 77th parallel, as Sir Edward Belcher had done. Ought he to treat these accounts as apocryphal? or had the winter come upon him earlier? On the 15th of August Mount Percy raised its peak, covered with eternal snow, through the mist. The next day the sun set for the first time, ending thus the long series of days with twenty-four hours in them. The men had ended by getting accustomed to the continual daylight, but it had never made any difference to the animals; the Greenland dogs went to their rest at their accustomed hour, and Dick slept as regularly every evening as though darkness had covered the sky. Still, during the nights which followed the 15th of August, darkness was never profound; although the sun set, he still gave sufficient light by refraction. On the 19th of August, after a pretty good observation, they sighted Cape Franklin on the east coast and Cape Lady Franklin on the west coast; the gratitude of the English people had given these names to the two opposite points—probably the last reached by Franklin: the name of the devoted wife, opposite to that of her husband, is a touching emblem of the sympathy which always united them.

The doctor, by following Johnson's advice, accustomed himself to support the low temperature; he almost always stayed on deck braving the cold, the wind, and the snow. He got rather thinner, but his constitution did not suffer. Besides, he expected to be much worse off, and joyfully prepared for the approaching winter.

"Look at those birds," he said to Johnson one day; "they are emigrating south in flocks! They are shrieking out their good-byes!"

"Yes, Mr. Clawbonny, some instinct tells them they must go, and they set out."

"There's more than one amongst us who would like to imitate them, I think."

"They are cowards, Mr. Clawbonny; those animals have no provisions as we have, and are obliged to seek their food where it is to be found. But sailors, with a good ship under their feet, ought to go to the world's end."

"You hope that Hatteras will succeed, then?"

"He certainly will, Mr. Clawbonny."

"I am of the same opinion as you, Johnson, and if he only wanted one faithful companion——"

"He'll have two!"

"Yes, Johnson," answered the doctor, shaking hands with the brave sailor.

Prince Albert Land, which the *Forward* was then coasting, bears also the name of Grinnell Land, and though Hatteras, from his hatred to the Yankees, would never call it by its American name, it is the one it generally goes by. It owes its double appellation to the following circumstances: At the same time that Penny, an Englishman, gave it the name of Prince Albert, Lieutenant Haven, commander of the *Rescue*, called it Grinnell Land in honour of the American merchant who had fitted out the expedition from New York at his own expense. Whilst the brig was coasting it, she experienced a series of unheard-of difficulties, navigating sometimes under sail, sometimes by steam. On the 18th of August they sighted Britannia Mountain, scarcely visible through the mist, and the *Forward* weighed anchor the next day in Northumberland Bay. She was hemmed in on all sides.

CHAPTER XXIII ATTACKED BY ICEBERGS

Hatteras, after seeing to the anchoring of his ship, re-entered his cabin and examined his map attentively. He found himself in latitude 76° 57' and longitude 99° 20'—that is to say, at only three minutes from the 77th parallel. It was at this very spot that Sir Edward Belcher passed his first winter with the *Pioneer* and the *Assistance*. It was thence that he organised his sledge and boat excursions. He discovered Table Isle, North Cornwall, Victoria Archipelago, and Belcher Channel. He reached the 78th parallel, and saw that the coast was depressed on the south-east. It seemed to go down to Jones's Strait, the entrance to which lies in Baffin's Bay. But to the north-west, on the contrary, says his report, an open sea lay as far as the eye could reach.

Hatteras considered attentively the white part of the map, which represented the Polar basin free from ice.

"After such testimony as that of Stewart, Penny, and Belcher, I can't have a doubt about it," he said to himself. "They saw it with their own eyes. But if the winter has already frozen it! But no; they made their discoveries at intervals of several years. It exists, and I shall find it! I shall see it."

Hatteras went on to the poop. An intense fog enveloped the *Forward*; the masthead could scarcely be distinguished from the deck. However, Hatteras called down the ice-master from his crow's nest, and took his place. He wished to profit by the shortest clear interval to examine the north-western horizon. Shandon did not let the occasion slip for saying to the lieutenant:

"Well, Wall, where is the open sea?"

"You were right, Shandon, and we have only six weeks' coal in the hold."

"Perhaps the doctor will find us some scientific fuel to warm us in the place of coal," answered Shandon. "I have heard say you can turn fire to ice; perhaps he'll turn ice to fire." And he entered his cabin, shrugging his shoulders. The next day was the 20th of August, and the fog cleared away for several minutes. They saw Hatteras look eagerly at the horizon, and then come down without speaking; but it was easy to see that his hopes had again been crushed. The *Forward* weighed anchor, and took up her uncertain march northward. As the *Forward* began to be weather-worn, the masts were unreeved, for they could no longer rely on the variable wind, and the sails were nearly useless in the winding channels. Large white marks appeared here and there on the sea like oil spots; they presaged an approaching frost; as soon as the breeze dropped the sea began to freeze immediately; but as soon as the wind got up again, the young ice was broken up and dispersed. Towards evening the thermometer went down to 17°.

When the brig came to a closed-up pass she acted as a battering ram, and ran at full steam against the obstacle, which she sunk. Sometimes they thought she was stopped for good; but an unexpected movement of the streams opened her a new passage, and she took advantage of it boldly. When the brig stopped, the steam which escaped from the safety-pipes was condensed by the cold air and fell in snow on to the deck. Another impediment came in the way; the ice-blocks sometimes got entangled in the paddles, and they were so hard that all the strength of the machine was not sufficient to break them; it was then necessary to back the engine and send men to clear the screws with their hand-spikes. All this delayed the brig; it lasted thirteen days. The *Forward* dragged herself painfully along Penny Strait; the crew grumbled, but obeyed: the men saw now that it was impossible to go back. Keeping north was less dangerous than retreating south. They were obliged to think about wintering. The sailors talked together about their present position, and one day they mentioned it to Richard Shandon, who, they knew, was on their side. The second officer forgot his duty as an officer, and allowed them to discuss the authority of the captain before him.

"You say, then, Mr. Shandon, that we can't go back now?" said Gripper.

"No, it's too late now," answered Shandon.

"Then we must think about wintering," said another sailor.

"It's the only thing we can do. They wouldn't believe me."

"Another time," said Pen, who had been released, "we shall believe you."

"But as I am not the master——" replied Shandon.

"Who says you mayn't be?" answered Pen. "John Hatteras may go as far as he likes, but we aren't obliged to follow him."

"You all know what became of the crew that did follow him in his first cruise to Baffin's Sea?" said Gripper.

"And the cruise of the *Farewell* under him that got lost in the Spitzbergen seas!" said Clifton.

"He was the only man that came back," continued Gripper.

"He and his dog," answered Clifton.

"We won't die for his pleasure," added Pen.

"Nor lose the bounty we've been at so much trouble to earn," cried Clifton. "When we've passed the 78th degree—and we aren't far off it, I know—that will make just the £375 each."

"But," answered Gripper, "shan't we lose it if we go back without the captain?"

"Not if we prove that we were obliged to," answered Clifton.

"But it's the captain——"

"You never mind, Gripper," answered Pen; "we'll have a captain and a good one—that Mr. Shandon knows. When one commander goes mad, folks have done with him, and they take another; don't they, Mr. Shandon?"

Shandon answered evasively that they could reckon upon him, but that they must wait to see what turned up. Difficulties were getting thick round Hatteras, but he was as firm, calm, energetic, and confident as ever. After all, he had done in five months what other navigators had taken two or three years to do! He should be obliged to winter now, but there was nothing to frighten brave sailors in that. Sir John Ross and McClure had passed three successive winters in the Arctic regions. What they had done he could do too!

"If I had only been able to get up Smith Strait at the north of Baffin's Sea, I should be at the Pole by now!" he said to the doctor regretfully.

"Never mind, captain!" answered the doctor, "we shall get at it by the 99th meridian instead of by the 75th; if all roads lead to Rome, it's more certain still that all meridians lead to the Pole."

CHAPTER XXIII ATTACKED BY ICEBERGS

On the 31st of August the thermometer marked 13°. The end of the navigable season was approaching; the *Forward* left Exmouth Island to the starboard, and three days after passed Table Island in the middle of Belcher Channel. At an earlier period it would perhaps have been possible to regain Baffin's Sea by this channel, but it was not to be dreamt of then; this arm of the sea was entirely barricaded by ice; ice-fields extended as far as the eye could reach, and would do so for eight months longer. Happily they could still gain a few minutes further north on the condition of breaking up the ice with huge clubs and petards. Now the temperature was so low, any wind, even a contrary one, was welcome, for in a calm the sea froze in a single night. The *Forward* could not winter in her present situation, exposed to winds, icebergs, and the drift from the channel; a shelter was the first thing to find; Hatteras hoped to gain the coast of New Cornwall, and to find above Albert Point a bay of refuge sufficiently sheltered. He therefore pursued his course northward with perseverance. But on the 8th an impenetrable ice-bank lay in front of him, and the temperature was at 10°. Hatteras did all he could to force a passage, continually risking his ship and getting out of danger by force of skill. He could be accused of imprudence, want of reflection, folly, blindness, but he was a good sailor, and one of the best! The situation of the *Forward* became really dangerous; the sea closed up behind her, and in a few hours the ice got so hard that the men could run along it and tow the ship in all security.

Hatteras found he could not get round the obstacle, so he resolved to attack it in front; he used his strongest blasting cylinders of eight to ten pounds of powder; they began by making a hole in the thick of the ice, and filled it with snow, taking care to place the cylinder in a horizontal position, so that a greater portion of the ice might be submitted to the explosion; lastly, they lighted the wick, which was protected by a gutta-percha tube. They worked at the blasting, as they could not saw, for the saws stuck immediately in the ice. Hatteras hoped to pass the next day. But during the night a violent wind raged, and the sea rose under her crust of ice as if shaken by some submarine commotion, and the terrified voice of the pilot was heard crying:

"Look out aft!"

Hatteras turned to the direction indicated, and what he saw by the dim twilight was frightful. A high iceberg, driven back north, was rushing on to the ship with the rapidity of an avalanche.

"All hands on deck!" cried the captain.

The rolling mountain was hardly half a mile off; the blocks of ice were driven about like so many huge grains of sand; the tempest raged with fury.

"There, Mr. Clawbonny," said Johnson to the doctor, "we are in something like danger now."

"Yes," answered the doctor tranquilly, "it looks frightful enough."

"It's an assault we shall have to repulse," replied the boatswain.

"It looks like a troop of antediluvian animals, those that were supposed to inhabit the Pole. They are trying which shall get here first!"

"Well," added Johnson, "I hope we shan't get one of their spikes into us!"

"It's a siege—let's run to the ramparts!"

And they made haste aft, where the crew, armed with poles, bars of iron, and handspikes, were getting ready to repulse the formidable enemy. The avalanche came nearer, and got bigger by the addition of the blocks of ice which it caught in its passage; Hatteras gave orders to fire the cannon in the bow to break the threatening line. But it arrived and rushed on to the brig; a great crackling noise was heard, and as it struck on the brig's starboard a part of her barricading was broken. Hatteras gave his men orders to keep steady and prepare for the ice. It came along in blocks; some of them weighing several hundred-weight came over the ship's side; the smaller ones, thrown up as high as the topsails, fell in little spikes, breaking the shrouds and cutting the rigging. The ship was boarded by these innumerable enemies, which in a block would have crushed a hundred ships like the *Forward.* Some of the sailors were badly wounded whilst trying to keep off the ice, and Bolton had his left shoulder torn open. The noise was deafening. Dick barked with rage at this new kind of enemy. The obscurity of the night came to add to the horror of the situation, but did not hide the threatening blocks, their white surface reflected the last gleams of light. Hatteras's orders were heard in the midst of the crew's strange struggle with the icebergs. The ship giving way to the tremendous pressure, bent to the larboard, and the extremity of her mainyard leaned like a buttress against the iceberg and threatened to break her mast.

Hatteras saw the danger; it was a terrible moment; the brig threatened to turn completely over, and the masting might be carried away. An enormous block, as big as the steamer itself, came up alongside her hull; it rose higher and higher on the waves; it was already above the poop; it fell over the *Forward.* All was lost; it was now upright, higher than the gallant yards, and it shook on its foundation. A cry of terror escaped the crew. Everyone fled to starboard. But at this moment the steamer was lifted completely up, and for a little while she seemed to be suspended in the air, and fell again on to the ice-blocks; then she rolled over till her planks cracked again. After a minute, which appeared a century, she found herself again in her natural element, having been turned over the ice-bank that blocked her passage by the rising of the sea.

"She's cleared the ice-bank!" shouted Johnson, who had rushed to the fore of the brig.

"Thank God!" answered Hatteras.

The brig was now in the midst of a pond of ice, which hemmed her in on every side, and though her keel was in the water, she could not move; she was immovable, but the ice-field moved for her.

"We are drifting, captain!" cried Johnson.

"We must drift," answered Hatteras; "we can't help ourselves."

When daylight came, it was seen that the brig was drifting rapidly northward, along with a submarine current. The floating mass carried the *Forward* along with it. In case of accident, when the brig might be thrown on her side, or crushed by the pressure of the ice, Hatteras had a quantity of provisions brought up on deck, along with materials for encamping, the clothes and blankets of the crew. Taking example from Captain McClure under similar circumstances, he caused the brig to be surrounded by a belt of hammocks, filled with air, so as to shield her from the thick of the damage; the ice soon accumulated under a temperature of 7°, and the ship was surrounded by a wall of ice, above which her masts only were to be seen. They navigated thus for seven days; Point Albert, the western extremity of New Cornwall, was sighted on the 10th of September, but soon disappeared; from thence the ice-field drifted east. Where would it take them to? Where should they stop? Who could tell? The crew waited, and the men folded their arms. At last, on the 15th of September, about three o'clock in the afternoon, the ice-field, stopped, probably, by collision with another field, gave a violent shake to the brig, and stood still. Hatteras found himself out of sight of land in latitude 78° 15' and longitude 95° 35' in the midst of the unknown sea, where geographers have placed the Frozen Pole.

CHAPTER XXIV PREPARATIONS FOR WINTERING

The southern hemisphere is colder in parallel latitudes than the northern hemisphere; but the temperature of the new continent is still 15° below that of the other parts of the world; and in America the countries known under the name of the Frozen Pole are the most formidable. The average temperature of the year is 2° below zero. Scientific men, and Dr. Clawbonny amongst them, explain the fact in the following way. According to them, the prevailing winds of the northern regions of America blow from the south-west; they come from the Pacific Ocean with an equal and bearable temperature; but in order to reach the Arctic Seas they have to cross the immense American territory, covered with snow, they get cold by contact with it, and then cover the hyperborean regions with their frigid violence. Hatteras found himself at the Frozen Pole beyond the countries seen by his predecessors; he, therefore, expected a terrible winter on a ship lost in the midst of the ice with a crew nearly in revolt. He resolved to face these dangers with his accustomed energy. He began by taking, with the help of Johnson's experience, all the measures necessary for wintering. According to his calculations he had been dragged two hundred and fifty miles beyond New Cornwall, the last country discovered; he was clasped in an ice-field as securely as in a bed of granite, and no power on earth could extricate him.

There no longer existed a drop of water in the vast seas over which the Arctic winter reigned. Ice-fields extended as far as the eye could reach, bristling with icebergs, and the *Forward* was sheltered by three of the highest on three points of the compass; the south-east wind alone could reach her. If instead of icebergs there had been rocks, verdure instead of snow, and the sea in its liquid state again, the brig would have been safely anchored in a pretty bay sheltered from the worst winds. But in such a latitude it was a miserable state of things. They were obliged to fasten the brig by means of her anchors, notwithstanding her immovability; they were obliged to prepare for the submarine currents and the breaking up of the ice. When Johnson heard where they were, he took the greatest precautions in getting everything ready for wintering.

"It's the captain's usual luck," said he to the doctor; "we've got nipped in the most disagreeable point of the whole glove! Never mind; we'll get out of it!"

As to the doctor, he was delighted at the situation. He would not have changed it for any other! A winter at the Frozen Pole seemed to him desirable. The crew were set to work at the sails, which were not taken down, and put into the hold, as the first people who wintered in these regions had thought prudent; they were folded up in their cases, and the ice soon made them an impervious envelope. The crow's nest, too, remained in its place, serving as a nautical observatory; the rigging alone was taken away. It became necessary to cut away the part of the field that surrounded the brig, which began to suffer from the pressure. It was a long and painful work. In a few days the keel was cleared, and on examination was found to have suffered little, thanks to the solidity of its construction, only its copper plating was almost all torn off. When the ship was once liberated she rose at least nine inches; the crew then bevelled the ice in the shape of the keel, and the field formed again under the brig, and offered sufficient opposition to pressure from without. The doctor helped in all this work; he used the ice-knife skilfully; he incited the sailors by his happy disposition. He instructed himself and others, and was delighted to find the ice under the ship.

"It's a very good precaution!" said he.

"We couldn't do without it, Mr. Clawbonny," said Johnson. "Now we can raise a snow-wall as high as the gunwale, and if we like we can make it ten feet thick, for we've plenty of materials."

"That's an excellent idea," answered the doctor. "Snow is a bad conductor of heat; it reflects it instead of absorbing it, and the heat of the interior does not escape."

"That's true," said Johnson. "We shall raise a fortification against the cold, and against animals too, if they take it into their heads to pay us a visit; when the work is done it will answer, I can tell you. We shall make two flights of steps in the snow, one from the ship and the other from outside; when once we've cut out the steps we shall pour water over them, and it will make them as hard as rock. We shall have a royal staircase."

"It's a good thing that cold makes ice and snow, and so gives us the means of protecting ourselves against it. I don't know what we should do if it did not."

A roofing of tarred cloth was spread over the deck and descended to the sides of the brig. It was thus sheltered from all outside impression, and made a capital promenade; it was covered with two feet and a-half of snow, which was beaten down till it became very hard, and above that they put a layer of sand, completely macadamising it.

"With a few trees I should imagine myself in Hyde Park," said the doctor, "or in one of the hanging gardens of Babylon."

They made a hole at a short distance from the brig; it was round, like a well; they broke the ice every morning. This well was useful in case of fire or for the frequent baths ordered to keep the crew in health. In order to spare their fuel, they drew the water from a greater depth by means of an apparatus invented by a Frenchman, François Arago. Generally, when a ship is wintering, all the objects which encumber her are placed in magazines on the coast, but it was impossible to do this in the midst of an ice-field. Every precaution was taken against cold and damp; men have been known to resist the cold and succumb to damp; therefore both had to be guarded against. The *Forward* had been built expressly for these regions, and the common room was wisely arranged. They had made war on the corners, where damp takes refuge at first. If it had been quite circular it would have done better, but warmed by a vast stove and well ventilated, it was very comfortable; the walls were lined with buckskins and not with woollen materials, for wool condenses the vapours and impregnates the atmosphere with damp. The partitions were taken down in the poop, and the officers had a large comfortable room, warmed by a stove. Both this room and that of the crew had a sort of antechamber, which prevented all direct communication with the exterior, and prevented the heat going out; it also made the crew pass more gradually from one temperature to another. They left their snow-covered garments in these antechambers, and scraped their feet on scrapers put there on purpose to prevent any unhealthy element getting in.

Canvas hose let in the air necessary to make the stoves draw; other hose served for escape-pipes for the steam. Two condensers were fixed in the two rooms; they gathered the vapour instead of letting it escape, and were emptied twice a week; sometimes they contained several bushels of ice. By means of the air-pipes the fires could be easily regulated, and it was found that very little fuel was necessary to keep up a temperature of 50 degrees in the rooms. But Hatteras saw with grief that he had only enough coal left for two months' firing. A drying-room was prepared for the garments that were obliged to be washed, as they could not be hung in the air or they would have been frozen and spoiled. The delicate parts of the machine were taken to pieces carefully, and the room where they were placed was closed up hermetically. The rules for life on board were drawn up by Hatteras and hung up in the common room. The men got up at six in the morning, and their hammocks were exposed to the air three times a week; the floors of the two rooms were rubbed with warm sand every morning; boiling tea was served out at every meal, and the food varied as much as possible, according to the different days of the week; it consisted of bread, flour, beef suet and raisins for puddings, sugar, cocoa, tea, rice, lemon-juice, preserved meat, salted beef and pork, pickled cabbage and other vegetables; the kitchen was outside the common rooms, and the men were thus deprived of its heat, but cooking is a constant source of evaporation and humidity.

The health of men depends a great deal on the food they eat; under these high latitudes it is of great importance to consume as much animal food as possible. The doctor presided at the drawing up of the bill of fare.

"We must take example from the Esquimaux," said he; "they have received their lessons from nature, and are our teachers here; although Arabians and Africans can live on a few dates and a handful of rice, it is very different here, where we must eat a great deal and often. The Esquimaux absorb as much as ten and fifteen pounds of oil in a day. If you do not like oil, you must have recourse to things rich in sugar and fat. In a word, you want carbon in the stove inside you as much as the stove there wants coal."

Every man was forced to take a bath in the half-frozen water condensed from the fire. The doctor set the example; he did it at first as we do all disagreeable things that we feel obliged to do, but he soon began to take extreme pleasure in it. When the men had to go out either to hunt or work they had to take great care not to get frost-bitten; and if by accident it happened, they made haste to rub the part attacked with snow to bring back the circulation of the blood. Besides being carefully clothed in wool from head to foot, the men wore hoods of buckskin and sealskin trousers, through which it is impossible for the wind to penetrate. All these preparations took about three weeks, and the 10th of October came round without anything remarkable happening.

CHAPTER XXV AN OLD FOX

That day the thermometer went down to 3° below zero. The weather was pretty calm, and the cold without breeze was bearable. Hatteras profited by the clearness of the atmosphere to reconnoitre the surrounding plains; he climbed one of the highest icebergs to the north, and could see nothing, as far as his telescope would let him, but ice-fields and icebergs. No land anywhere, but the image of chaos in its saddest aspect. He came back on board trying to calculate the probable duration of his captivity. The hunters, and amongst them the doctor, James Wall, Simpson, Johnson, and Bell, did not fail to supply the ship with fresh meat. Birds had disappeared; they were gone to less rigorous southern climates. The ptarmigans, a sort of partridge, alone stay the winter in these latitudes; they are easily killed, and their great number promised an abundant supply of game. There were plenty of hares, foxes, wolves, ermine, and bears; there were enough for any sportsman, English, French, or Norwegian; but they were difficult to get at, and difficult to distinguish on the white plains from the whiteness of their fur; when the intense cold comes their fur changes colour, and white is their winter colour. The doctor found that this change of fur is not caused by the change of temperature, for it takes place in the month of October, and is simply a precaution of Providence to guard them from the rigour of a boreal winter.

Seals were abundant in all their varieties, and were particularly sought after by the hunters for the sake, not only of their skins, but their fat, which is very warming; besides which, the liver of these animals makes excellent fuel: hundreds of them were to be seen, and two or three miles to the north of the brig the ice was literally perforated all over with the holes these enormous amphibians make; only they smelt the hunters from afar, and many were wounded that escaped by plunging under the ice. However, on the 19th, Simpson managed to catch one at about a hundred yards from the ship; he had taken the precaution to block up its hole of refuge so that it was at the mercy of the hunters. It took several bullets to kill the animal, which measured nine feet in length; its bulldog head, the sixteen teeth in its jaws, its large pectoral fins in the shape of pinions, and its little tail, furnished with another pair of fins, made it a good specimen of the family of dog-hound fish. The doctor, wishing to preserve the head for his natural history collection, and its skin for his future use, had them prepared by a rapid and inexpensive process. He plunged the body of the animal into the hole in the ice, and thousands of little prawns soon ate off all the flesh; in half a day the work was accomplished, and the most skilful of the honourable corporation of Liverpool tanners could not have succeeded better.

As soon as the sun had passed the autumnal equinox—that is to say, on the 23rd of September—winter may be said to begin in the Arctic regions. The sun disappears entirely on the 23rd of October, lighting up with its oblique rays the summits of the frozen mountains. The doctor wished him a traveller's farewell; he was not going to see him again till

February. But obscurity is not complete during this long absence of the sun; the moon comes each month to take its place as well as she can; starlight is very bright, and there is besides frequent aurora borealis, and a refraction peculiar to the snowy horizons; besides, the sun at the very moment of his greatest austral declination, the 21st of December, is still only 13° from the Polar horizon, so that there is twilight for a few hours; only fogs, mists, and snowstorms often plunge these regions into complete obscurity. However, at this epoch the weather was pretty favourable; the partridges and the hares were the only animals that had a right to complain, for the sportsmen did not give them a moment's peace; they set several fox-traps, but the suspicious animals did not let themselves be caught so easily; they would often come and eat the snare by scratching out the snow from under the trap; the doctor wished them at the devil, as he could not get them himself. On the 25th of October the thermometer marked more than 4° below zero. A violent tempest set in; the air was thick with snow, which prevented a ray of light reaching the *Forward*. During several hours they were very uneasy about Bell and Simpson, who had gone too far whilst hunting; they did not reach the ship till the next day, after having lain for a whole day in their buckskins, whilst the tempest swept the air about them, and buried them under five feet of snow. They were nearly frozen, and the doctor had some trouble to restore their circulation.

The tempest lasted a week without interruption. It was impossible to stir out. In a single day the temperature varied fifteen and twenty degrees. During their forced idleness each one lived to himself; some slept, others smoked, or talked in whispers, stopping when they saw the doctor or Johnson approach; there was no moral union between the men; they only met for evening prayers, and on Sunday for Divine service. Clifton had counted that once the 78th parallel cleared, his share in the bounty would amount to £375; he thought that enough, and his ambition did not go beyond. The others were of the same opinion, and only thought of enjoying the fortune acquired at such a price. Hatteras was hardly ever seen. He neither took part in the hunting nor other excursions. He felt no interest in the meteorological phenomena which excited the doctor's admiration. He lived for one idea; it was comprehended in three words—the North Pole. He was constantly looking forward to the moment when the *Forward*, once more free, would begin her adventurous voyage again.

In short, it was a melancholy life; the brig, made for movement, seemed quite out of place as a stationary dwelling; her original form could not be distinguished amidst the ice and snow that covered her, and she was anything but a lively spectacle. During these unoccupied hours the doctor put his travelling notes in order—the notes from which this history is taken; he was never idle, and the evenness of his humour remained the same, only he was very glad to see the tempest clearing off so as to allow him to set off hunting once more. On the 3rd of November, at six in the morning, with a temperature at 5° below zero, he started, accompanied by Johnson and Bell; the plains of ice were level; the snow, which covered the ground thickly, solidified by the frost, made the ground good for walking; a dry and keen cold lightened the atmosphere; the moon shone in all her splendour, and threw an astonishing light on all the asperities of the field; their footsteps left marks on the snow, and the moon lighted up their edges, so that they looked like a luminous track behind the hunters whose shadows fell on the ice with astonishing outlines.

The doctor had taken his friend Dick with him; he preferred him to the Greenland dogs to run down the game for a good reason; the latter do not seem to have the scent of their brethren of more temperate climates. Dick ran on and often pointed out the track of a bear, but in spite of his skill the hunters had not even killed a hare after two hours' walking.

"Do you think the game has gone south too?" asked the doctor, halting at the foot of a hummock.

"It looks like it, Mr. Clawbonny," answered the carpenter.

"I don't think so," answered Johnson; "hares, foxes, and bears are accustomed to the climate; I believe the late tempest is the cause of their disappearance; but with the south winds they'll soon come back. Ah! if you said reindeers or musk-oxen it would be a different thing."

"But it appears those, too, are found in troops in Melville Island," replied the doctor; "that is much further south, I grant you; when Parry wintered there he always had as much game as he wanted."

"We are not so well off," said Bell; "if we could only get plenty of bear's flesh I should not complain."

"Bears are very difficult to get at," answered the doctor; "it seems to me they want civilising."

"Bell talks about the bear's flesh, but we want its fat more than its flesh or its skin," said Johnson.

"You are right, Johnson; you are always thinking about the fuel."

"How can I help thinking about it? I know if we are ever so careful of it we've only enough left for three weeks."

"Yes," replied the doctor, "that is our greatest danger, for we are only at the beginning of November, and February is the coldest month of the year in the Frozen Zone; however, if we can't get bear's grease we can rely on that of the seals."

"Not for long, Mr. Clawbonny," answered Johnson. "They'll soon desert us too; either through cold or fright, they'll soon leave off coming on to the surface of the ice."

"Then we must get at the bears," said the doctor; "they are the most useful animals in these countries: they furnish food, clothes, light, and fuel. Do you hear, Dick?" continued he, caressing his friend; "we must have a bear, so look out."

Dick, who was smelling the ice as the doctor spoke, started off all at once, quick as an arrow. He barked loudly, and, notwithstanding his distance, the sportsmen heard him distinctly. The extreme distance to which sound is carried in these low temperatures is astonishing; it is only equalled by the brilliancy of the constellations in the boreal sky.

The sportsmen, guided by Dick's barking, rushed on his traces; they had to run about a mile, and arrived quite out of breath, for the lungs are rapidly suffocated in such an atmosphere. Dick was pointing at about fifty paces from an enormous mass at the top of a mound of ice.

"We've got him," said the doctor, taking aim.

"And a fine one," added Bell, imitating the doctor.

"It's a queer bear," said Johnson, waiting to fire after his two companions.

Dick barked furiously. Bell advanced to within twenty feet and fired, but the animal did not seem to be touched. Johnson advanced in his turn, and after taking a careful aim, pulled the trigger.

"What," cried the doctor, "not touched yet? Why, it's that cursed refraction. The bear is at least a thousand paces off."

The three sportsmen ran rapidly towards the animal, whom the firing had not disturbed; he seemed to be enormous, and without calculating the dangers of the attack, they began to rejoice in their conquest. Arrived within reasonable distance they fired again; the bear, mortally wounded, gave a great jump and fell at the foot of the mound. Dick threw himself upon it.

"That bear wasn't difficult to kill," said the doctor.

"Only three shots," added Bell in a tone of disdain, "and he's down."

"It's very singular," said Johnson.

"Unless we arrived at the very moment when it was dying of old age," said the doctor, laughing.

So speaking, the sportsmen reached the foot of the mound, and, to their great stupefaction, they found Dick with his fangs in the body of a white fox.

"Well, I never!" cried Bell.

"We kill a bear and a fox falls," added the doctor.

Johnson did not know what to say.

"Why!" said the doctor, with a roar of laughter, "it's the refraction again!"

"What do you mean, Mr. Clawbonny?" asked the carpenter.

"Why, it deceived us about the size as it did about the distance. It made us see a bear in a fox's skin."

"Well," answered Johnson, "now we've got him, we'll eat him."

Johnson was going to lift the fox on to his shoulders, when he cried like Bell—"Well, I never!"

"What is it?" asked the doctor.

"Look, Mr. Clawbonny—look what the animal's got on its neck; it's a collar, sure enough."

"A collar?" echoed the doctor, leaning over the animal. A half worn-out collar encircled the fox's neck, and the doctor thought he saw something engraved on it; he took it off and examined it.

"That bear is more than twelve years old, my friends," said the doctor; "it's one of James Ross's foxes, and the collar has been round its neck ever since 1848."

"Is it possible?" cried Bell.

"There isn't a doubt about it, and I'm sorry we've shot the poor animal. During his wintering James Ross took a lot of white foxes in his traps, and had brass collars put round their necks on which were engraved the whereabouts of his ships, the *Enterprise* and the *Investigator*, and the store magazines. He hoped one of them might fall into the hands of some of the men belonging to Franklin's expedition. The poor animal might have saved the lives of the ship's crews, and it has fallen under our balls."

"Well, we won't eat him," said Johnson, "especially as he's twelve years old. Anyway, we'll keep his skin for curiosity sake." So saying he lifted the animal on his shoulders, and they made their way to the ship, guided by the stars; still their expedition was not quite fruitless: they bagged several brace of ptarmigans. An hour before they reached the *Forward*, a phenomenon occurred which excited the astonishment of the doctor; it was a very rain of shooting stars; they could be counted by thousands, like rockets in a display of fireworks. They paled the light of the moon, and the admirable spectacle lasted several hours. A like meteor was observed at Greenland by the Moravian brothers in 1799. The doctor passed the whole night watching it, till it ceased, at seven in the morning, amidst the profound silence of the atmosphere.

CHAPTER XXVI THE LAST LUMP OF COAL

It seemed certain that no bears were to be had; several seals were killed during the days of the 4th, 5th, and 6th of November; then the wind changed, and the thermometer went up several degrees; but the snow-drifts began again with great violence. It became impossible to leave the vessel, and the greatest precaution was needed to keep out the damp. At the end of the week there were several bushels of ice in the condensers. The weather changed again on the 15th of November, and the thermometer, under the influence of certain atmospherical conditions, went down to 24° below zero. It was the lowest temperature observed up till then. This cold would have been bearable in a quiet atmosphere, but there was a strong wind which seemed to fill the atmosphere with sharp blades. The doctor was vexed at being kept prisoner, for the ground was covered with snow, made hard by the wind, and was easy to walk upon; he wanted to attempt some long excursion.

It is very difficult to work when it is so cold, because of the shortness of breath it causes. A man can only do a quarter of his accustomed work; iron implements become impossible to touch; if one is taken up without precaution, it causes a pain as bad as a burn, and pieces of skin are left on it. The crew, confined to the ship, were obliged to walk for two hours on the covered deck, where they were allowed to smoke, which was not allowed in the common room. There, directly the fire got low, the ice invaded the walls and the joins in the flooring; every bolt, nail, or metal plate became immediately covered with a layer of ice. The doctor was amazed at the instantaneity of the phenomenon. The breath of the men condensed in the air, and passing quickly from a fluid to a solid state, fell round them in snow. At a few feet only from the stoves the cold was intense, and the men stood near the fire in a compact group. The doctor advised them to accustom their skin to the temperature, which would certainly get worse, and he himself set the example; but most of them were too idle or too benumbed to follow his advice, and preferred remaining in the unhealthy heat. However, according to the doctor, there was no danger in the abrupt changes of temperature in going from the warm room into the cold. It is only dangerous for people in perspiration; but the doctor's lessons were thrown away on the greater part of the crew.

As to Hatteras, he did not seem to feel the influence of the temperature. He walked silently about at his ordinary pace. Had the cold no empire over his strong constitution, or did he possess in a supreme degree the natural heat he wished his sailors to have? Was he so armed in his one idea as to be insensible to exterior impressions? His men were profoundly astonished at seeing him facing the 24° below zero; he left the ship for hours, and came back without his face betraying the slightest mark of cold.

"He is a strange man," said the doctor to Johnson; "he even astonishes me. He is one of the most powerful natures I have ever studied in my life."

"The fact is," answered Johnson, "that he comes and goes in the open air without clothing himself more warmly than in the month of June."

"Oh! the question of clothes is not of much consequence," replied the doctor; "it is of no use clothing people who do not produce heat naturally. It is the same as if we tried to warm a piece of ice by wrapping it up in a blanket! Hatteras does not want that; he is constituted so, and I should not be surprised if being by his side were as good as being beside a stove."

Johnson had the job of clearing the water-hole the next day, and remarked that the ice was more than ten feet thick. The doctor could observe magnificent aurora borealis almost every night; from four till eight p.m. the sky became slightly coloured in the north; then this colouring took the regular form of a pale yellow border, whose extremities seemed to buttress on to the ice-field. Little by little the brilliant zone rose in the sky, following the magnetic meridian, and appeared striated with blackish bands; jets of some luminous matter, augmenting and diminishing, shot out lengthways; the meteor, arrived at its zenith, was often composed of several bows, bathed in floods of red, yellow, or green light. It was a dazzling spectacle. Soon the different curves all joined in one point, and formed boreal crowns of a heavenly richness. At last the bows joined, the splendid aurora faded, the intense rays melted into pale, vague, undetermined shades, and the marvellous phenomenon, feeble, and almost extinguished, fainted insensibly into the dark southern clouds. Nothing can equal the wonders of such a spectacle under the high latitudes less than eight degrees from the Pole; the aurora borealis perceived in temperate regions gives no idea of them—not even a feeble one; it seems as if Providence wished to reserve its most astonishing marvels for these climates.

During the duration of the moon several images of her are seen in the sky, increasing her brilliancy; often simple lunar halos surround her, and she shines from the centre of her luminous circle with a splendid intensity.

On the 26th of November there was a high tide, and the water escaped with violence from the water-hole; the thick layer of ice was shaken by the rising of the sea, and sinister crackings announced the submarine struggle; happily the ship kept firm in her bed, and her chains only were disturbed. Hatteras had had them fastened in anticipation of the event. The following days were still colder; there was a penetrating fog, and the wind scattered the piled-up snow; it became difficult to see whether the whirlwinds began in the air or on the ice-fields; confusion reigned.

The crew were occupied in different works on board, the principal of which consisted in preparing the grease and oil produced by the seals; they had become blocks of ice, which had to be broken with axes into little bits, and ten barrels were thus preserved.

All sorts of vessels were useless, and the liquid they contained would only have broken them when the temperature changed. On the 28th the thermometer went down to 32° below zero; there was only coal enough left for ten days, and everyone looked forward to its disappearance with dread. Hatteras had the poop stove put out for economy's sake, and from that time Shandon, the doctor, and he stayed in the common room. Hatteras was thus brought into closer contact with the men, who threw ferocious and stupefied looks at him. He heard their reproaches, their recriminations, and even their threats, and he could not punish them. But he seemed to be deaf to everything. He did not claim the place nearest the fire, but stopped in a corner, his arms folded, never speaking.

In spite of the doctor's recommendations, Pen and his friends refused to take the least exercise; they passed whole days leaning against the stove or lying under the blankets of their hammocks. Their health soon began to suffer; they could not bear up against the fatal influence of the climate, and the terrible scurvy made its appearance on board. The doctor had, however, begun, some time ago, to distribute limejuice and lime pastilles every morning; but these preservatives, generally so efficacious, had very little effect on the malady, which soon presented the most horrible symptoms. The sight of the poor fellows, whose nerves and muscles contracted with pain, was pitiable. Their legs swelled in an extraordinary fashion, and were covered with large blackish blue spots; their bloody gums and ulcerated lips only gave passage to inarticulate sounds; the vitiated blood no longer went to the extremities.

Clifton was the first attacked; then Gripper, Brunton, and Strong took to their hammocks. Those that the malady still spared could not lose sight of their sufferings; they were obliged to stay there, and it was soon transformed into a hospital, for out of eighteen sailors of the *Forward*, thirteen were attacked in a few days. Pen seemed destined to escape contagion; his vigorous nature preserved him from it. Shandon felt the first symptoms, but they did not go further, and exercise kept the two in pretty good health.

The doctor nursed the invalids with the greatest care, and it made him miserable to see the sufferings he could not alleviate. He did all he could to keep his companions in good spirits; he talked to them, read to them, and told them tales, which his astonishing memory made it easy for him to do. He was often interrupted by the complaints and groans of the invalids, and he stopped his talk to become once more the attentive and devoted doctor. His health kept up well; he did not get thinner, and he used to say that it was a good thing for him that he was dressed like a seal or a whale, who, thanks to its thick layer of fat, easily supports the Arctic atmosphere. Hatteras felt nothing, either physically or morally. Even the sufferings of his crew did not seem to touch him. Perhaps it was because he would not let his face betray his emotions; but an attentive observer would have remarked that a man's heart beat beneath the iron envelope. The doctor analysed him, studied him, but did not succeed in classifying so strange an organisation, a temperament so supernatural. The thermometer lowered again; the walk on deck was deserted; the Esquimaux dogs alone frequented it, howling lamentably.

There was always one man on guard near the stove to keep up the fire; it was important not to let it go out. As soon as the fire got lower, the cold glided into the room; ice covered the walls, and the humidity, rapidly condensed, fell in snow on the unfortunate inhabitants of the brig. It was in the midst of these unutterable tortures that the 8th of December was reached. That morning the doctor went as usual to consult the exterior thermometer. He found the mercury completely frozen.

"Forty-four degrees below zero!" he cried with terror. And that day they threw the last lump of coal into the stove.

CHAPTER XXVII CHRISTMAS

There was then a movement of despair. The thought of death, and death from cold, appeared in all its horror; the last piece of coal burnt away as quickly as the rest, and the temperature of the room lowered sensibly. But Johnson went to fetch some lumps of the new fuel which the marine animals had furnished him with, and he stuffed it into the stove; he added some oakum, impregnated with frozen oil, and soon obtained enough heat. The smell of the grease was abominable, but how could they get rid of it? They were obliged to get used to it. Johnson agreed that his expedient left much to wish for, and would have no success in a Liverpool house.

"However," added he, "the smell may have one good result."

"What's that?" asked the carpenter.

"It will attract the bears; they are very fond of the stink."

"And what do we want with bears?" added Bell.

"You know, Bell, we can't depend on the seals; they've disappeared for a good while to come; if the bears don't come to be turned into fuel too, I don't know what will become of us."

"There would be only one thing left; but I don't see how——"

"The captain would never consent; but perhaps we shall be obliged."

Johnson shook his head sadly, and fell into a silent reverie, which Bell did not interrupt. He knew that their stock of grease would not last more than a week with the strictest economy.

The boatswain was not mistaken. Several bears, attracted by the fetid exhalations, were signalled to the windward; the healthy men gave chase to them, but they are extraordinarily quick, and did not allow themselves to be approached, and the most skilful shots could not touch them. The ship's crew was seriously menaced with death from cold; it was impossible to resist such a temperature more than forty-eight hours, and every one feared the end of the fuel. The dreaded moment arrived at three o'clock p.m. on the 20th of December. The fire went out; the sailors looked at each other with haggard eyes. Hatteras remained immovable in his corner. The doctor as usual marched up and down in agitation; he was at his wits' end. The temperature of the room fell suddenly to 7° below zero. But if the doctor did not know what to do, some of the others did. Shandon, calm and resolute, and Pen with anger in his eyes, and two or three of their comrades, who could still walk, went up to Hatteras.

"Captain!" said Shandon.

Hatteras, absorbed in thought, did not hear him.

"Captain!" repeated Shandon, touching his hand.

Hatteras drew himself up.

"What is it?" he said.

"Our fire is out!"

"What then?" answered Hatteras.

"If you mean to kill us with cold, you had better say so," said Shandon ironically.

"I mean," said Hatteras gravely, "to require every man to do his duty to the end."

"There's something higher than duty, captain—there's the right to one's own preservation. I repeat that the fire is out, and if it is not relighted, not one of us will be alive in two days."

"I have no fuel," answered Hatteras, with a hollow voice.

"Very well," cried Pen violently, "if you have no fuel, we must take it where we can!"

Hatteras grew pale with anger.

"Where?" said he.

"On board," answered the sailor insolently.

"On board!" echoed the captain, his fists closed, his eyes sparkling.

He had seized an axe, and he now raised it over Pen's head.

"Wretch!" he cried.

The doctor rushed between the captain and Pen; the axe fell to the ground, its sharp edge sinking into the flooring. Johnson, Bell, and Simpson were grouped round Hatteras, and appeared determined to give him their support. But lamentable and plaintive voices came from the beds.

"Some fire! Give us some fire!" cried the poor fellows.

Hatteras made an effort, and said calmly:

"If we destroy the brig, how shall we get back to England?"

"We might burn some of the rigging and the gunwale, sir," said Johnson.

"Besides, we should still have the boats left," answered Shandon; "and we could build a smaller vessel with the remains of the old one!"

"Never!" answered Hatteras.

"But——" began several sailors, raising their voices.

"We have a great quantity of spirits of wine," answered Hatteras; "burn that to the last drop."

"Ah, we didn't think of that!" said Johnson, with affected cheerfulness, and by the help of large wicks steeped in spirits he succeeded in raising the temperature a few degrees.

During the days that followed this melancholy scene the wind went round to the south, and the thermometer went up. Some of the men could leave the vessel during the least damp part of the day; but ophthalmia and scurvy kept the greater number on board; besides, neither fishing nor hunting was practicable. But it was only a short respite from the dreadful cold, and on the 25th, after an unexpected change in the wind, the mercury again froze; they were then obliged to have recourse to the spirits of wine thermometer, which never freezes. The doctor found, to his horror, that it marked 66° below zero; men had never been able to support such a temperature. The ice spread itself in long tarnished mirrors on the floor; a thick fog invaded the common room; the damp fell in thick snow; they could no longer see one another; the extremities became blue as the heat of the body left them; a circle of iron seemed to be clasping their heads, and made them nearly delirious. A still more fearful symptom was that their tongues could no longer articulate a word.

From the day they had threatened to burn his ship, Hatteras paced the deck for hours. He was guarding his treasures; the wood of the ship was his own flesh, and whoever cut a piece off cut off one of his limbs. He was armed, and mounted guard, insensible to the cold, the snow, and the ice, which stiffened his garments and enveloped him in granite armour. His faithful Dick accompanied him, and seemed to understand why he was there.

However, on Christmas Day he went down to the common room. The doctor, taking advantage of what energy he had left, went straight to him, and said—

"Hatteras, we shall all die if we get no fuel."

"Never!" said Hatteras, knowing what was coming.

"We must," said the doctor gently.

"Never!" repeated Hatteras with more emphasis still. "I will never consent! They can disobey me if they like!"

Johnson and Bell took advantage of the half-permission, and rushed on deck. Hatteras heard the wood crack under the axe. He wept. What a Christmas Day for Englishmen was that on board the *Forward*! The thought of the great difference between their position and that of the happy English families who rejoiced in their roast beef, plum pudding, and mince pies added another pang to the miseries of the unfortunate crew. However, the fire put a little hope and confidence into the men; the boiling of coffee and tea did them good, and the next week passed less miserably, ending the dreadful year 1860; its early winter had defeated all Hatteras's plans.

On the 1st of January, 1861, the doctor made a discovery. It was not quite so cold, and he had resumed his interrupted studies; he was reading Sir Edward Belcher's account of his expedition to the Polar Seas; all at once a passage struck him; he read it again and again. It was where Sir Edward Belcher relates that after reaching the extremity of Queen's Channel he had discovered important traces of the passage and residence of men. "They were," said he, "very superior habitations to those which might be attributed to the wandering Esquimaux. The walls had foundations, the floors of the interior had been covered with a thick layer of fine gravel, and were paved. Reindeer, seal, and walrus bones were seen in great quantities. *We found some coal.*" At the last words the doctor was struck with an idea; he carried the book to Hatteras and showed him the passage.

"They could not have found coal on this deserted coast," said Hatteras; "it is not possible!"

"Why should we doubt what Belcher says? He would not have recorded such a fact unless he had been certain and had seen it with his own eyes."

"And what then, doctor?"

"We aren't a hundred miles from the coast where Belcher saw the coal, and what is a hundred miles' excursion? Nothing. Longer ones than that have often been made across the ice."

"We will go," said Hatteras.

Johnson was immediately told of their resolution, of which he strongly approved; he told his companions about it: some were glad, others indifferent.

"Coal on these coasts!" said Wall, stretched on his bed of pain.

"Let them go," answered Shandon mysteriously.

But before Hatteras began his preparations for the journey, he wished to be exactly certain of the *Forward's* position. He was obliged to be mathematically accurate as to her whereabouts, because of finding her again. His task was very difficult; he went upon deck and took at different moments several lunar distances and the meridian heights of the principal stars. These observations were hard to make, for the glass and mirrors of the instrument were covered with ice from Hatteras's breath; he burnt his eyelashes more than once by touching the brass of the glasses. However, he obtained exact bases for his calculations, and came down to make them in the room. When his work was over, he raised his head in astonishment, took his map, pricked it, and looked at the doctor.

"What is it?" asked the latter.

"In what latitude were we at the beginning of our wintering?"

"We were in latitude 78° 15', by longitude 95° 35'; exactly at the Frozen Pole."

"Well," said Hatteras, in a low tone, "our ice-field has been drifting! We are two degrees farther north and farther west, and three hundred miles at least from your store of coal!"

"And those poor fellows don't know," said the doctor.

"Hush!" said Hatteras, putting his finger on his lips.

CHAPTER XXVIII PREPARATIONS FOR DEPARTURE

Hatteras would not inform his crew of their situation, for if they had known that they had been dragged farther north they would very likely have given themselves up to the madness of despair. The captain had hidden his own emotions at his discovery. It was his first happy moment during the long months passed in struggling with the elements. He was a hundred and fifty miles farther north, scarcely eight degrees from the Pole! But he hid his delight so profoundly that even the doctor did not suspect it; he wondered at seeing an unwonted brilliancy in the captain's eyes; but that was all, and he never once thought of the reason.

The *Forward*, by getting nearer the Pole, had got farther away from the coal repository observed by Sir Edward Belcher; instead of one hundred, it lay at two hundred and fifty miles farther south. However, after a short discussion about it between Hatteras and Clawbonny, the journey was persisted in. If Belcher had written the truth—and there was no reason for doubting his veracity—they should find things exactly in the same state as he had left them, for no new expedition had gone to these extreme continents since 1853. There were few or no Esquimaux to be met with in that latitude. They could not be disappointed on the coast of New Cornwall as they had been on Beechey Island. The low temperature preserves the objects abandoned to its influence for any length of time. All probabilities were therefore in favour of this excursion across the ice. It was calculated that the expedition would take, at the most, forty days, and Johnson's preparations were made in consequence.

The sledge was his first care; it was in the Greenland style, thirty-five inches wide and twenty-four feet long. The Esquimaux often make them more than fifty feet long. This one was made of long planks, bent up front and back, and kept bent like a bow by two thick cords; the form thus given to it gave it increased resistance to shocks; it ran easily on the ice, but when the snow was soft on the ground it was put upon a frame; to make it glide more easily it was rubbed, Esquimaux fashion, with sulphur and snow. Six dogs drew it; notwithstanding their leanness these animals did not appear to suffer from the cold; their buckskin harness was in good condition, and they could draw a weight of two thousand pounds without fatigue. The materials for encampment consisted of a tent, should the construction of a snow-house be impossible, a large piece of mackintosh to spread over the snow, to prevent it melting in contact with the human body, and lastly, several blankets and buffalo-skins. They took the halkett boat too.

The provisions consisted of five cases of pemmican, weighing about four hundred and fifty pounds; they counted one pound of pemmican for each man and each dog; there were seven dogs including Dick, and four men. They also took twelve gallons of spirits of wine—that is to say, about one hundred fifty pounds weight—a sufficient quantity of tea and biscuit, a portable kitchen with plenty of wicks, oakum, powder, ammunition, and two double-barrelled guns. They also used Captain Parry's invention of indiarubber belts, in which the warmth of the body and the movement of walking keeps coffee, tea, and water in a liquid state. Johnson was very careful about the snow-shoes; they are a sort of wooden patten, fastened on with leather straps; when the ground was quite hard and frozen they could be replaced by buckskin moccasins; each traveller had two pairs of both.

These preparations were important, for any detail omitted might occasion the loss of an expedition; they took four whole days. Each day at noon Hatteras took care to set the position of his ship; they had ceased to drift; he was obliged to be certain in order to get back. He next set about choosing the men he should take with him; some of them were not fit either to take or leave, but the captain decided to take none but sure companions, as the common safety depended upon the success of the excursion. Shandon was, therefore, excluded, which he did not seem to regret. James Wall was ill in bed. The state of the sick got no worse, however, and as the only thing to do for them was to rub them with lime-juice, and give them doses of it, the doctor was not obliged to stop, and he made one of the travellers. Johnson very much wished to accompany the captain in his perilous enterprise, but Hatteras took him aside, and said, in an affectionate tone:

"Johnson, I have confidence in you alone. You are the only officer in whose hands I can leave my ship. I must know that you are there to overlook Shandon and the others. They are kept prisoners here by the winter, but I believe them capable of anything. You will be furnished with my formal instructions, which, in case of need, will give you the command. You will take my place entirely. Our absence will last four or five weeks at the most. I shall not be anxious, knowing you are where I cannot be. You must have wood, Johnson, I know, but, as far as possible, spare my poor ship. Do you understand me, Johnson?"

"Yes, sir," answered the old sailor, "I'll stop if you wish."

"Thank you," said Hatteras, shaking his boatswain's hand; "and if we don't come back, wait for the next breaking-up time, and try to push forward towards the Pole. But if the others won't go, don't mind us, and take the *Forward* back to England."

"Are those your last commands, captain?"

"Yes, my express commands," answered Hatteras.

"Very well, sir, they shall be carried out," said Johnson simply.

The doctor regretted his friend, but he thought Hatteras had acted wisely in leaving him. Their other two travelling companions were Bell the carpenter and Simpson. The former was in good health, brave and devoted, and was the right man to render service during the encampments on the snow; Simpson was not so sure, but he accepted a share in the expedition, and his hunting and fishing capabilities might be of the greatest use. The expedition consisted, therefore, of four men, Hatteras, Clawbonny, Bell, and Simpson, and seven dogs. The provisions had been calculated in consequence. During the first days of January the temperature kept at an average of 33° below zero. Hatteras was very anxious for the weather to change; he often consulted the barometer, but it is of little use in such high latitudes. A clear sky in these regions does not always bring cold, and the snow does not make the temperature rise; the barometer is uncertain; it goes down with the north and east winds; low, it brought fine weather; high, snow or rain. Its indications could not, therefore, be relied upon.

At last, on January 5th, the mercury rose to 18° below zero, and Hatteras resolved to start the next day; he could not bear to see his ship burnt piece by piece before his eyes; all the poop had gone into the stove. On the 6th, then, in the midst of whirlwinds of snow, the order for departure was given. The doctor gave his last orders about the sick; Bell and

Simpson shook hands silently with their companions. Hatteras wished to say his good-byes aloud, but he saw himself surrounded by evil looks and thought he saw Shandon smile ironically. He was silent, and perhaps hesitated for an instant about leaving the *Forward*, but it was too late to turn back; the loaded sledge, with the dogs harnessed to it, awaited him on the ice-field. Bell started the first; the others followed.

Johnson accompanied the travellers for a quarter of a mile, then Hatteras begged him to return on board, and the old sailor went back after making a long farewell gesture. At that moment Hatteras turned a last look towards the brig, and saw the extremity of her masts disappear in the dark clouds of the sky.

CHAPTER XXIX ACROSS THE ICE

The little troop descended towards the south-east. Simpson drove the sledge. Dick helped him with zeal, and did not seem astonished at the new occupation of his companions. Hatteras and the doctor walked behind, whilst Bell went on in front, sounding the ice with his iron-tipped stick. The rising of the thermometer indicated approaching snow; it soon fell in thick flakes, and made the journey difficult for the travellers; it made them deviate from the straight line, and obliged them to walk slower; but, on an average, they made three miles an hour. The surface of the ice was unequal, and the sledge was often in danger of being overturned, but by great care it was kept upright.

Hatteras and his companions were clothed in skins more useful than elegant. Their heads and faces were covered with hoods, their mouths, eyes, and noses alone coming into contact with the air. If they had not been exposed the breath would have frozen their coverings, and they would have been obliged to take them off with the help of an axe—an awkward way of undressing. The interminable plain kept on with fatiguing monotony; icebergs of uniform aspect and hummocks whose irregularity ended by seeming always the same; blocks cast in the same mould, and icebergs between which tortuous valleys wound. The travellers spoke little, and marched on, compass in hand. It is painful to open one's mouth in such an atmosphere; sharp icicles form immediately between one's lips, and the breath is not warm enough to melt them. Bell's steps were marked in the soft ground, and they followed them attentively, certain of being able to go where he had been before.

Numerous traces of bears and foxes crossed their path, but not an animal was seen that day. It would have been dangerous and useless to hunt them, as the sledge was sufficiently freighted. Generally in this sort of excursion travellers leave provision-stores along their route; they place them in hiding-places of snow, out of reach of animals; unload during the journey, and take up the provisions on their return. But Hatteras could not venture to do this on moveable ice-fields, and the uncertainty of the route made the return the same way exceedingly problematic. At noon Hatteras caused his little troop to halt under shelter of an ice-wall. Their breakfast consisted of pemmican and boiling tea; the latter beverage comforted the cold wayfarers. They set out again after an hour's rest. The first day they walked about twenty miles, and in the evening both men and dogs were exhausted. However, notwithstanding their fatigue, they were obliged to construct a snow-house in which to pass the night. It took about an hour and a half to build. Bell showed himself very skilful. The ice-blocks were cut out and placed above one another in the form of a dome; a large block at the top made the vault. Snow served for mortar and filled up the chinks. It soon hardened and made a single block of the entire structure. It was reached by a narrow opening, through which the doctor squeezed himself painfully, and the others followed him. The supper was rapidly prepared with spirits of wine. The interior temperature of the snow-house was bearable, as the wind which raged outside could not penetrate. When their repast, which was always the same, was over, they began to think of sleep. A mackintosh was spread over the floor and kept them from the damp. Their stockings and shoes were dried by the portable grate, and then three of the travellers wrapped themselves up in their blankets, leaving the fourth to keep watch; he watched over the common safety, and prevented the opening getting blocked up, for if it did they would be buried alive.

Dick shared the snow-house; the other dogs remained outside, and after their supper they squatted down in the snow, which made them a blanket. The men were tired out with their day's walk, and soon slept. The doctor took his turn on guard at three o'clock in the morning. There was a tempest during the night, the gusts of which thickened the walls of the snow-house. The next day, at six o'clock, they set out again on their monotonous march. The temperature lowered several degrees, and hardened the ground so that walking was easier. They often met with mounds or cairns something like the Esquimaux hiding-places. The doctor had one demolished, and found nothing but a block of ice.

"What did you expect, Clawbonny?" said Hatteras. "Are we not the first men who have set foot here?"

"It's very likely we are, but who knows?" answered the doctor.

"I do not want to lose my time in useless search," continued the captain; "I want to be quick back to my ship, even if we don't find the fuel."

"I believe we are certain of doing that," said the doctor.

"I often wish I had not left the *Forward*," said Hatteras; "a captain's place is on board."

"Johnson is there."

"Yes; but—well, we must make haste, that's all."

The procession marched along rapidly; Simpson excited the dogs by calling to them; in consequence of a phosphorescent phenomenon they seemed to be running on a ground in flames, and the sledges seemed to raise a dust of sparks. The doctor went on in front to examine the state of the snow, but all at once he disappeared. Bell, who was nearest to him, ran up.

"Well, Mr. Clawbonny," he called out in anxiety, "where are you?"

"Doctor!" called the captain.

"Here, in a hole," answered a reassuring voice; "throw me a cord, and I shall soon be on the surface of the globe again."

They threw a cord to the doctor, who was at the bottom of a hole about ten feet deep; he fastened it round his waist, and his companions hauled him up with difficulty.

"Are you hurt?" asked Hatteras.

"Not a bit," answered the doctor, shaking his kind face, all covered with snow.

"But how did you tumble down there?"

"Oh, it was the refraction's fault," he answered laughing. "I thought I was stepping across about a foot's distance, and I fell into a hole ten feet deep! I never shall get used to it. It will teach us to sound every step before we advance. Ears hear and eyes see all topsy-turvy in this enchanted spot."

"Can you go on?" asked the captain.

"Oh, yes; the little fall has done me more good than harm."

In the evening the travellers had marched twenty-five miles; they were worn out, but it did not prevent the doctor climbing up an iceberg while the snow-house was being built. The full moon shone with extraordinary brilliancy in the clearest sky; the stars were singularly bright; from the top of the iceberg the view stretched over an immense plain, bristling with icebergs; they were of all sizes and shapes, and made the field look like a vast cemetery, in which twenty generations slept the sleep of death. Notwithstanding the cold, the doctor remained a long time in contemplation of the spectacle, and his companions had much trouble to get him away; but they were obliged to think of rest; the snow-hut was ready; the four companions burrowed into it like moles, and soon slept the sleep of the just.

The next day and the following ones passed without any particular incident; the journey was easy or difficult according to the weather; when it was cold and clear they wore their moccasins and advanced rapidly, when damp and penetrating, their snow-shoes, and made little way. They reached thus the 15th of January; the moon was in her last quarter, and was only visible for a short time; the sun, though still hidden below the horizon, gave six hours of a sort of twilight, not sufficient to see the way by; they were obliged to stake it out according to the direction given by the compass. Bell led the way; Hatteras marched in a straight line behind him; then Simpson and the doctor, taking it in turns, so as only to see Hatteras, and keep in a straight line. But notwithstanding all their precautions, they deviated sometimes thirty or forty degrees; they were then obliged to stake it out again. On Sunday, the 15th of January, Hatteras considered he had made a hundred miles to the south; the morning was consecrated to the mending of different articles of clothing and encampment; divine service was not forgotten. They set out again at noon; the temperature was cold, the thermometer marked only 32° below zero in a very clear atmosphere.

All at once, without warning of any kind, a vapour rose from the ground in a complete state of congelation, reaching a height of about ninety feet, and remaining stationary; they could not see a foot before them; it clung to their clothing, and bristled it with ice. Our travellers, surprised by the frost-rime, had all the same idea—that of getting near one another. They called out, "Bell!" "Simpson!" "This way, doctor!" "Where are you, captain?" But no answers were heard; the vapour did not conduct sound. They all fired as a sign of rallying. But if the sound of the voice appeared too weak, the detonation of the firearms was too strong, for it was echoed in all directions, and produced a confused rumble without appreciable direction. Each acted then according to his instincts. Hatteras stopped, folded his arms, and waited. Simpson contented himself with stopping his sledge. Bell retraced his steps, feeling the traces with his hands. The doctor ran hither and thither, bumping against the icebergs, falling down, getting up, and losing himself more and more. At the end of five minutes he said:

"I can't go on like this! What a queer climate! It changes too suddenly, and the icicles are cutting my face. Captain! I say, captain!"

But he obtained no answer; he discharged his gun, and notwithstanding his thick gloves, burnt his hand with the trigger. During this operation he thought he saw a confused mass moving at a few steps from him.

"At last!" said he. "Hatteras! Bell! Simpson! Is it you? Answer, do!"

A hollow growl was the only answer.

"Whatever is that?" thought the doctor. The mass approached, and its outline was more distinctly seen. "Why, it's a bear!" thought the terrified doctor. It was a bear, lost too in the frost-rime, passing within a few steps of the men of whose existence it was ignorant. The doctor saw its enormous paws beating the air, and did not like the situation. He jumped back and the mass disappeared like a phantom. The doctor felt the ground rising under his feet; climbing on all-fours he got to the top of a block, then another, feeling the end with his stick. "It's an iceberg!" he said to himself: "if I get to the top I shall be saved." So saying he climbed to a height of about eighty feet; his head was higher than the frozen fog, of which he could clearly see the top. As he looked round he saw the heads of his three companions emerging from the dense fluid.

CHAPTER XXIX ACROSS THE ICE

"Hatteras!"

"Doctor!"

"Bell!"

"Simpson!"

The four names were all shouted at the same time; the sky, lightened by a magnificent halo, threw pale rays which coloured the frost-rime like clouds, and the summits of the icebergs seemed to emerge from liquid silver. The travellers found themselves circumscribed by a circle less than a hundred feet in diameter. Thanks to the purity of the upper layers of air, they could hear each other distinctly, and could talk from the top of their icebergs. After the first shots they had all thought the best thing they could do was to climb.

"The sledge!" cried the captain.

"It's eighty feet below us," answered Simpson.

"In what condition?"

"In good condition."

"What about the bear?" asked the doctor.

"What bear?" asked Bell.

"The bear that nearly broke my head," answered the doctor.

"If there is a bear we must go down," said Hatteras.

"If we do we shall get lost again," said the doctor.

"And our dogs?" said Hatteras.

At this moment Dick's bark was heard through the fog.

"That's Dick," said Hatteras; "there's something up; I shall go down."

Growls and barks were heard in a fearful chorus. In the fog it sounded like an immense humming in a wadded room. Some struggle was evidently going on.

"Dick! Dick!" cried the captain, re-entering the frost-rime.

"Wait a minute, Hatteras; I believe the fog is clearing off," called out the doctor. So it was, but lowering like the waters of a pond that is being emptied; it seemed to enter the ground from whence it sprang; the shining summits of the icebergs grew above it; others, submerged till then, came out like new islands; by an optical illusion the travellers seemed to be mounting with their icebergs above the fog. Soon the top of the sledge appeared, then the dogs, then about thirty other animals, then enormous moving masses, and Dick jumping about in and out of the fog.

"Foxes!" cried Bell.

"Bears!" shouted the doctor. "Five!"

"Our dogs! Our provisions!" cried Simpson. A band of foxes and bears had attacked the sledge, and were making havoc with the provisions. The instinct of pillage made them agree; the dogs barked furiously, but the herd took no notice, and the scene of destruction was lamentable.

"Fire!" cried the captain, discharging his gun. His companions imitated him. Upon hearing the quadruple detonation the bears raised their heads, and with a comical growl gave the signal for departure; they went faster than a horse could gallop, and, followed by the herd of foxes, soon disappeared amongst the northern icebergs.

CHAPTER XXX THE CAIRN

The frost-rime had lasted about three-quarters of an hour; quite long enough for the bears and foxes to make away with a considerable quantity of provisions which they attacked all the more greedily, arriving, as they did, when the animals were perishing with hunger from the long winter. They had torn open the covering of the sledge with their enormous paws; the cases of pemmican were open, and half-empty; the biscuit-bags pillaged, the provisions of tea spilt over the snow, a barrel of spirits of wine broken up, and its precious contents run out; the camping materials lying all about. The wild animals had done their work.

"The devils have done for us!" said Bell.

"What shall we do now?" said Simpson.

"Let us first see how much we've lost," said the doctor; "we can talk after."

Hatteras said nothing, but began picking up the scattered objects. They picked up all the pemmican and biscuit that was still eatable. The loss of so much spirits of wine was deplorable, as without it it was impossible to get any hot drinks—no tea nor coffee.

The doctor made an inventory of the provisions that were left, and found that the animals had eaten two hundred pounds of pemmican and a hundred and fifty pounds of biscuit; if the travellers continued their journey they would be obliged to put themselves on half-rations. They deliberated about what was to be done under the circumstances. Should they return to the brig and begin their expedition again? But how could they resolve to lose the hundred and fifty miles already cleared? and coming back without the fuel, how would they be received by the crew? and which of them would begin the excursion again? It was evident that the best thing to do was to go on, even at the price of the worst privations. The doctor, Hatteras, and Bell were for going on, but Simpson wanted to go back; his health had severely suffered from the fatigues of the journey, and he grew visibly weaker; but at last, seeing he was alone in his opinion, he took his place at the head of the sledge, and the little caravan continued its route. During the three following days, from the 15th to the 17th of January, the monotonous incidents of the journey took place again. They went on more slowly; the travellers were soon tired; their legs ached with fatigue, and the dogs drew with difficulty. Their insufficient food told upon them. The weather changed with its usual quickness, going suddenly from intense cold to damp and penetrating fogs.

On the 18th of January the aspect of the ice-field changed all at once. A great number of peaks, like pyramids, ending in a sharp point at a great elevation, showed themselves on the horizon. The soil in certain places was seen through the layer of snow; it seemed to consist of schist and quartz, with some appearance of calcareous rock. At last the travellers had reached *terra firma*, and, according to their estimation, the continent must be

New Cornwall. The doctor was delighted to tread on solid ground once more; the travellers had only a hundred more miles to go before reaching Belcher Cape; but the trouble of walking increased on this rocky soil, full of inequalities, crevices, and precipices; they were obliged to plunge into the interior of the land and climb the high cliffs on the coast, across narrow gorges, in which the snow was piled up to a height of thirty or forty feet. The travellers soon had cause to regret the levels they had left, on which the sledge rolled so easily. Now they were obliged to drag it with all their strength. The dogs were worn out, and had to be helped; the men harnessed themselves along with them, and wore themselves out too. They were often obliged to unload the provisions in order to get over a steep hill, whose frozen surface gave no hold. Some passages ten feet long took hours to clear. During the first day they only made about five miles on that land, so well named Cornwall. The next day the sledge attained the upper part of the cliffs; the travellers were too exhausted to construct their snow-house, and were obliged to pass the night under the tent, enveloped in their buffalo-skins, and drying their stockings by placing them on their chests. The consequences of such a state of things may be readily imagined; during the night the thermometer went down to 44° below zero, and the mercury froze.

The health of Simpson became alarming; an obstinate cold, violent rheumatism, and intolerable pain forced him to lie down on the sledge, which he could no longer guide. Bell took his place; he was not well, but was obliged not to give in. The doctor also felt the influence of his terrible winter excursion, but he did not utter a complaint; he marched on in front, leaning on his stick; he lighted the way; he helped in everything. Hatteras, impassive, impenetrable, insensible, in as good health as the first day, with his iron constitution, followed the sledge in silence. On the 20th of January the weather was so bad that the least effort caused immediate prostration; but the difficulties of the ground became so great that Hatteras and Bell harnessed themselves along with the dogs; the front of the sledge was broken by an unexpected shock, and they were forced to stop and mend it. Such delays occurred several times a day. The travellers were journeying along a deep ravine up to their waists in snow, and perspiring, notwithstanding the violent cold. No one spoke. All at once Bell looked at the doctor in alarm, picked up a handful of snow, and began to rub his companion's face with all his might.

"What the deuce, Bell?" said the doctor, struggling.

But Bell went on rubbing.

"Are you mad? You've filled my eyes, nose, and mouth with snow. What is it?"

"Why," answered Bell, "if you've got a nose left, you owe it to me."

"A nose?" said the doctor, putting his hand to his face.

"Yes, Mr. Clawbonny, you were quite frostbitten; your nose was quite white when I looked at you, and without my bit of rubbing you would be minus nose."

"Thanks, Bell," said the doctor; "I'll do the same for you in case of need."

"I hope you will, Mr. Clawbonny, and I only wish we had nothing worse to look forward to!"

"You mean Simpson! Poor fellow, he is suffering dreadfully!"

"Do you fear for him?" asked Hatteras quickly.

"Yes, captain," answered the doctor.

"What do you fear?"

"A violent attack of scurvy. His legs swell already, and his gums are attacked; the poor fellow is lying under his blankets on the sledge, and every shock increases his pain. I pity him, but I can't do anything for him!"

"Poor Simpson!" said Bell.

"Perhaps we had better stop a day or two," said the doctor.

"Stop!" cried Hatteras, "when the lives of eighteen men depend upon our return! You know we have only enough provisions left for twenty days."

Neither the doctor nor Bell could answer that, and the sledge went on its way. In the evening they stopped at the foot of an ice-hill, out of which Bell soon cut a cavern; the travellers took refuge in it, and the doctor passed the night in nursing Simpson; he was a prey to the scurvy, and constant groans issued from his terrified lips.

"Ah, Mr. Clawbonny, I shall never get over it. I wish I was dead already."

"Take courage, my poor fellow!" answered the doctor, with pity in his tone, and he answered Simpson's complaints by incessant attention. Though half-dead with fatigue, he employed a part of the night in making the sick man a soothing draught, and rubbed him with lime-juice. Unfortunately it had little effect, and did not prevent the terrible malady spreading. The next day they were obliged to lift the poor fellow on to the sledge, although he begged and prayed them to leave him to die in peace, and begin their painful march again.

The freezing mists wet the three men to the skin; the snow and sleet beat in their faces; they did the work of beasts of burden, and had not even sufficient food. Dick ran hither and thither, discovering by instinct the best route to follow. During the morning of the 23rd of January, when it was nearly dark, for the new moon had not yet made her appearance, Dick ran on first; he was lost to sight for several hours. Hatteras became anxious, as there were many bear-marks on the ground; he was considering what had better be done, when a loud barking was heard in front. The little procession moved on quicker, and soon came upon the faithful animal in the depth of a ravine. Dick was set as if he had been petrified in front of a sort of cairn, made of limestone, and covered with a cement of ice.

"This time," said the doctor, disengaging himself from the traces, "it's really a cairn; we can't be mistaken."

"What does it matter to us?" said Hatteras.

"Why, if it is a cairn, it may inclose something that would be useful to us—some provisions perhaps."

"As if Europeans had ever been here!" said Hatteras, shrugging his shoulders.

"But if not Europeans, it may be that the Esquimaux have hidden some product of their hunting here. They are accustomed to doing it, I think."

"Well, look if you like, Clawbonny, but I don't think it is worth your while."

Clawbonny and Bell, armed with their pickaxes made for the cairn. Dick kept on barking furiously. The cairn was soon demolished, and the doctor took out a damp paper. Hatteras took the document and read:

"Altam..., *Porpoise*, Dec... 13th, 1860,

12..° long... 8..° 35' lat..." "The *Porpoise*!" said the doctor.

"I don't know any ship of that name frequenting these seas," said Hatteras.

"It is evident," continued the doctor, "that some sailors, or perhaps some shipwrecked fellows, have passed here within the last two months."

"That's certain," said Bell.

"What shall we do?" asked the doctor.

"Continue our route," said Hatteras coldly. "I don't know anything about the *Porpoise*, but I do know that the *Forward* is waiting for our return."

CHAPTER XXXI THE DEATH OF SIMPSON

The travellers went on their weary way, each thinking of the discovery they had just made. Hatteras frowned with uneasiness.

"What can the *Porpoise* be?" he asked himself. "Is it a ship? and if so, what was it doing so near the Pole?"

At this thought he shivered, but not from the cold. The doctor and Bell only thought of the result their discovery might have for others or for themselves. But the difficulties and obstacles in their way soon made them oblivious to everything but their own preservation.

Simpson's condition grew worse; the doctor saw that death was near. He could do nothing, and was suffering cruelly on his own account from a painful ophthalmia which might bring on blindness if neglected. The twilight gave them enough light to hurt the eyes when reflected by the snow; it was difficult to guard against the reflection, for the spectacle-glasses got covered with a layer of opaque ice which obstructed the view, and when so much care was necessary for the dangers of the route, it was important to see clearly; however, the doctor and Bell took it in turns to cover their eyes or to guide the sledge. The soil was volcanic, and by its inequalities made it very difficult to draw the sledge, the frame of which was getting worn out. Another difficulty was the effect of the uniform brilliancy of the snow; the ground seemed to fall beneath the feet of the travellers, and they experienced the same sensation as that of the rolling of a ship; they could not get accustomed to it, and it made them sleepy, and they often walked on half in a dream. Then some unexpected shock, fall, or obstacle would wake them up from their inertia, which afterwards took possession of them again.

On the 25th of January they began to descend, and their dangers increased. The least slip might send them down a precipice, and there they would have been infallibly lost. Towards evening an extremely violent tempest swept the snow-clad summits; they were obliged to lie down on the ground, and the temperature was so low that they were in danger of being frozen to death. Bell, with the help of Hatteras, built a snow-house, in which the poor fellows took shelter; there they partook of a little pemmican and warm tea; there were only a few gallons of spirits of wine left, and they were obliged to use them to quench their thirst, as they could not take snow in its natural state; it must be melted. In temperate countries, where the temperature scarcely falls below freezing point, it is not injurious; but above the Polar circle it gets so cold that it cannot be touched more than a red-hot iron; there is such a difference of temperature that its absorption produces suffocation. The Esquimaux would rather suffer the greatest torments than slake their thirst with snow.

The doctor took his turn to watch at three o'clock in the morning, when the tempest was at its height; he was leaning in a corner of the snow-house, when a lamentable groan from Simpson drew his attention; he rose to go to him, and struck his head against the roof; without thinking of the accident he began to rub Simpson's swollen limbs; after about a quarter of an hour he got up again, and bumped his head again, although he was kneeling then.

"That's very queer," he said to himself.

He lifted his hand above his head, and felt that the roof was lowering.

"Good God!" he cried; "Hatteras! Bell!"

His cries awoke his companions, who got up quickly, and bumped themselves too; the darkness was thick.

"The roof is falling in!" cried the doctor.

They all rushed out, dragging Simpson with them; they had no sooner left their dangerous retreat, than it fell in with a great noise. The poor fellows were obliged to take refuge under the tent covering, which was soon covered with a thick layer of snow, which, as a bad conductor, prevented the travellers being frozen alive. The tempest continued all through the night. When Bell harnessed the dogs the next morning he found that some of them had begun to eat their leather harness, and that two of them were very ill, and could not go much further. However, the caravan set out again; there only remained sixty miles to go. On the 26th, Bell, who went on in front, called out suddenly to his companions. They ran up to him, and he pointed to a gun leaning against an iceberg.

"A gun!" cried the doctor.

Hatteras took it; it was loaded and in good condition.

"The men from the *Porpoise* can't be far off," said the doctor.

Hatteras remarked that the gun was of American manufacture, and his hands crisped the frozen barrel. He gave orders to continue the march, and they kept on down the mountain slope. Simpson seemed deprived of all feeling; he had no longer the strength to complain. The tempest kept on, and the sledge proceeded more and more slowly; they scarcely made a few miles in twenty-four hours, and in spite of the strictest economy, the provisions rapidly diminished; but as long as they had enough for the return journey, Hatteras kept on.

On the 27th they found a sextant half-buried in the snow, then a leather bottle; the latter contained brandy, or rather a lump of ice, with a ball of snow in the middle, which represented the spirit; it could not be used. It was evident that they were following in the steps of some poor shipwrecked fellows who, like them, had taken the only practicable route. The doctor looked carefully round for other cairns, but in vain. Sad thoughts came into his mind; he could not help thinking that it would be a good thing not to meet with their predecessors; what could he and his companions do for them? They wanted help themselves; their clothes were in rags, and they had not enough to eat. If their predecessors were numerous they would all die of hunger. Hatteras seemed to wish to avoid them, and could he be blamed? But these men might be their fellow-countrymen, and, however slight might be the chance of saving them, ought they not to try it? He asked Bell what he thought about it, but the poor fellow's heart was hardened by his own suffering, and he did not answer. Clawbonny dared not question Hatteras, so he left it to Providence.

In the evening of the 27th, Simpson appeared to be at the last extremity; his limbs were already stiff and frozen; his difficult breathing formed a sort of mist round his head, and convulsive movements announced that his last hour was come. The expression of his face was terrible, desperate, and he threw looks of powerless anger towards the captain. He accused him silently, and Hatteras avoided him and became more taciturn and wrapped up in himself than ever. The following night was frightful; the tempest redoubled in violence; the tent was thrown down three times, and the snowdrifts buried the poor fellows, blinded them, froze them, and wounded them with the sharp icicles struck off the surrounding icebergs. The dogs howled lamentably. Simpson lay exposed to the cruel atmosphere. Bell succeeded in getting up the tent again, which, though it did not protect them from the cold, kept out the snow. But a more violent gust blew it down a fourth time, and dragged it along in its fury.

"Oh, we can't bear it any longer!" cried Bell.

"Courage, man, courage!" answered the doctor, clinging to him in order to prevent themselves rolling down a ravine. Simpson's death-rattle was heard. All at once, with a last effort, he raised himself up and shook his fist at Hatteras, who was looking at him fixedly, then gave a fearful cry, and fell back dead in the midst of his unfinished threat.

"He is dead!" cried the doctor.

"Dead!" repeated Bell.

Hatteras advanced towards the corpse, but was driven back by a gust of wind.

Poor Simpson was the first victim to the murderous climate, the first to pay with his life the unreasonable obstinacy of the captain. The dead man had called Hatteras an assassin, but he did not bend beneath the accusation. A single tear escaped from his eyes and froze on his pale cheek. The doctor and Bell looked at him with a sort of terror. Leaning on his stick, he looked like the genius of the North, upright in the midst of the whirlwind, and frightful in his immobility.

He remained standing thus till the first dawn of twilight, bold, tenacious, indomitable, and seemed to defy the tempest that roared round him.

CHAPTER XXXII THE RETURN

The wind went down about six in the morning, and turning suddenly north cleared the clouds from the sky; the thermometer marked 33° below zero. The first rays of the sun reached the horizon which they would gild a few days later. Hatteras came up to his two dejected companions, and said to them, in a low, sad voice:

"We are still more than sixty miles from the spot indicated by Sir Edward Belcher. We have just enough provisions to allow us to get back to the brig. If we go on any further we shall meet with certain death, and that will do good to no one. We had better retrace our steps."

"That is a sensible resolution, Hatteras," answered the doctor; "I would have followed you as far as you led us, but our health gets daily weaker; we can scarcely put one foot before the other; we ought to go back."

"Is that your opinion too, Bell?" asked Hatteras.

"Yes, captain," answered the carpenter.

"Very well," said Hatteras; "we will take two days' rest. We want it. The sledge wants mending. I think we had better build ourselves a snow-house, and try to regain a little strength."

After this was settled, our three men set to work with vigour. Bell took the necessary precautions to assure the solidity of the construction, and they soon had a good shelter at the bottom of the ravine where the last halt had taken place. It had cost Hatteras a great effort to interrupt his journey. All their trouble and pain lost! A useless excursion, which one man had paid for with his life. What would become of the crew now that all hope of coal was over? What would Shandon think? Notwithstanding all these painful thoughts, he felt it impossible to go on any further. They began their preparations for the return journey at once. The sledge was mended; it had now only two hundred pounds weight to carry. They mended their clothes, worn-out, torn, soaked with snow, and hardened by the frost; new moccasins and snow-shoes replaced those that were worn out. This work took the whole day of the 29th and the morning of the 30th; the three travellers rested and comforted themselves as well as they could.

During the thirty-six hours passed in the snow-house and on the icebergs of the ravine, the doctor had noticed that Dick's conduct was very strange; he crept smelling about a sort of rising in the ground made by several layers of ice; he kept wagging his tail with impatience, and trying to draw the attention of his master to the spot. The doctor thought that the dog's uneasiness might be caused by the presence of Simpson's body, which he and his companions had not yet had time to bury. He resolved to put it off no longer, especially as they intended starting early the next morning. Bell and the doctor took their pickaxes and directed their steps towards the lowest part of the ravine; the mound indicated by Dick seemed to be a good spot to place the corpse in; they were obliged to bury it deep to keep it from the bears. They began by removing the layer of soft snow, and then attacked the ice. At the third blow of his pickaxe the doctor broke some hard obstacle; he took out the pieces and saw that it was a glass bottle; Bell discovered a small biscuit-sack with a few crumbs at the bottom.

"Whatever does this mean?" said the doctor.

"I can't think," answered Bell, suspending his work.

They called Hatteras, who came immediately. Dick barked loudly, and began scratching at the ice.

"Perhaps we have found a provision-store," said the doctor.

"It is possible," said Bell.

"Go on," said Hatteras.

Some remains of food were drawn out, and a case a quarter full of pemmican.

"If it is a hiding-place," said Hatteras, "the bears have been before us. See, the provisions are not intact."

"I am afraid so," answered the doctor; "for——"

He was interrupted by a cry from Bell, who had come upon a man's leg, stiffened and frozen.

"A corpse," cried the doctor.

"It is a tomb," answered Hatteras.

When the corpse was disinterred it turned out to be that of a sailor, about thirty years old, perfectly preserved. He wore the clothes of an Arctic navigator. The doctor could not tell how long he had been dead. But after this corpse, Bell discovered a second, that of a man of fifty, bearing the mark of the suffering that had killed him on his face.

"These are not buried bodies," cried the doctor, "the poor fellows were surprised by death just as we find them."

"You are right, Mr. Clawbonny," answered Bell.

"Go on! go on!" said Hatteras.

Bell obeyed tremblingly; for who knew how many human bodies the mound contained?

"These men have been the victims of the same accident that almost happened to us," said the doctor. "Their snow-house tumbled in. Let us see if any one of them is still alive."

The place was soon cleared, and Bell dug out a third body, that of a man of forty, who had not the cadaverous look of the others. The doctor examined him and thought he recognised some symptoms of existence.

"He is alive!" he cried.

Bell and he carried the body into the snow-house whilst Hatteras, unmoved, contemplated their late habitation. The doctor stripped the resuscitated man and found no trace of a wound on him. He and Bell rubbed him vigorously with oakum steeped in spirits of wine, and they saw signs of returning consciousness; but the unfortunate man was in a state of complete prostration, and could not speak a word. His tongue stuck to his palate as if frozen. The doctor searched his pockets, but they were empty. He left Bell to continue the friction, and rejoined Hatteras. The captain had been down into the depths of the snow-house, and had searched about carefully. He came up holding a half-burnt fragment of a letter. These words were on it:

... tamont

... orpoise

... w York. "Altamont!" cried the doctor, of the ship *Porpoise*, of New York."

"An American," said Hatteras.

"I'll save him," said the doctor, "and then we shall know all about it."

He went back to Altamont whilst Hatteras remained pensive. Thanks to his attentions, the doctor succeeded in recalling the unfortunate man to life, but not to feeling; he neither saw, heard, nor spoke, but he lived. The next day Hatteras said to the doctor:

"We must start at once."

"Yes. The sledge is not loaded; we'll put the poor fellow on it and take him to the brig."

"Very well; but we must bury these bodies first."

The two unknown sailors were placed under the ruins of the snow-house again, and Simpson's corpse took Altamont's place. The three travellers buried their companion, and at seven o'clock in the morning they set out again. Two of the Greenland dogs were dead, and Dick offered himself in their place. He pulled with energy.

During the next twenty days the travellers experienced the same incidents as before. But as it was in the month of February they did not meet with the same difficulty from the ice. It was horribly cold, but there was not much wind. The sun reappeared for the first time on the 31st of January, and every day he stopped longer above the horizon. Bell and the doctor were almost blinded and half-lame; the carpenter was obliged to walk upon crutches. Altamont still lived, but he was in a state of complete insensibility. The doctor took great care of him, although he wanted attention himself; he was getting ill with fatigue. Hatteras thought of nothing but his ship. What state should he find it in?

On the 24th of February he stopped all of a sudden. A red light appeared about 300 paces in front, and a column of black smoke went up to the sky.

"Look at that smoke! my ship is burning," said he with a beating heart.

"We are three miles off yet," said Bell; "it can't be the *Forward*."

"Yes it is," said the doctor; "the mirage makes it seem nearer."

The three men, leaving the sledge to the care of Dick, ran on, and in an hour's time were in sight of the ship. She was burning in the midst of the ice, which melted around her. A hundred steps farther a man met them, wringing his hands before the *Forward* in flames. It was Johnson. Hatteras ran to him.

"My ship! My ship!" cried he.

"Is that you, captain? Oh, don't come any nearer," said Johnson.

"What is it?" said Hatteras.

"The wretches left forty-eight hours ago, after setting fire to the ship."

"Curse them!" cried Hatteras.

A loud explosion was then heard; the ground trembled; the icebergs fell upon the ice-field; a column of smoke went up into the clouds, and the *Forward* blew up. The doctor and Bell reached Hatteras, who out of the depths of despair cried:

"The cowards have fled! The strong will succeed! Johnson and Bell, you are courageous. Doctor, you have science. I have faith. To the North Pole! To the North Pole!"

His companions heard these energetic words, and they did them good; but it was a terrible situation for these four men, alone, under the 80th degree of latitude, in the midst of the Polar Regions!

THE FIELD OF ICE

PART II
OF THE ADVENTURES OF CAPTAIN HATTERAS

CHAPTER I. THE DOCTOR'S INVENTORY.

It was a bold project of Hatteras to push his way to the North Pole, and gain for his country the honour and glory of its discovery. But he had done all that lay in human power now, and, after having struggled for nine months against currents and tempests, shattering icebergs and breaking through almost insurmountable barriers, amid the cold of an unprecedented winter, after having outdistanced all his predecessors and accomplished half his task, he suddenly saw all his hopes blasted. The treachery, or rather the despondency, of his worn-out crew, and the criminal folly of one or two leading spirits among them had left him and his little band of men in a terrible situation—helpless in an icy desert, two thousand five hundred miles away from their native land, and without even a ship to shelter them.

However, the courage of Hatteras was still undaunted. The three men which were left him were the

best on board his brig, and while they remained he might venture to hope.

After the cheerful, manly words of the captain, the Doctor felt the best thing to be done was to look their prospects fairly in the face, and know the exact state of things. Accordingly, leaving his companions, he stole away alone down to the scene of the explosion.

Of the *Forward*, the brig that had been so carefully built and had become so dear, not a vestige remained. Shapeless blackened fragments, twisted bars of iron,

cable ends still smouldering, and here and there in the distance spiral wreaths of smoke, met his eye on all sides. His cabin and all his precious treasures were gone, his books, and instruments, and collections reduced to ashes. As he stood thinking mournfully of his irreparable loss, he was joined by Johnson, who grasped his offered hand in speechless sorrow.

"What's to become of us?" asked the Doctor.

"Who can tell!" was the old sailor's reply.

"Anyhow," said Clawbonny, "do not let us despair! Let us be men!"

"Yes, Mr. Clawbonny, you are right. Now is the time to show our mettle. We are in a bad plight, and how to get out of it, that is the question."

"Poor old brig!" exclaimed the Doctor. "I had grown so attached to her. I loved her as one loves a house where he has spent a life-time."

"Ay! it's strange what a hold those planks and beams get on a fellow's heart."

"And the long-boat—is that burnt?" asked the Doctor.

"No, Mr. Clawbonny. Shandon and his gang have carried it off."

"And the pirogue?"

"Shivered into a thousand pieces? Stop. Do you see those bits of sheet-iron? That is all that remains of it."

"Then we have nothing but the Halkett-boat?"

"Yes, we have that still, thanks to your idea of taking it with you."

"That isn't much," said the Doctor.

"Oh, those base traitors!" exclaimed Johnson. "Heaven punish them as they deserve!"

"Johnson," returned the Doctor, gently, "we must not forget how sorely they have been tried. Only the best remain good in the evil day; few can stand trouble. Let us pity our fellow-sufferers, and not curse them."

For the next few minutes both were silent, and then Johnson asked what had become of the sledge.

"We left it about a mile off," was the reply.

"In charge of Simpson?"

"No, Simpson is dead, poor fellow!"

"Simpson dead!"

"Yes, his strength gave way entirely, and he first sank."

"Poor Simpson! And yet who knows if he isn't rather to be envied?"

"But, for the dead man we have left behind, we have brought back a dying one."

"A dying man?"

"Yes, Captain Altamont."

And in a few words he informed Johnson of their discovery.

"An American!" said Johnson, as the recital was ended.

"Yes, everything goes to prove that. But I wonder what the *Porpoise* was, and what brought her in these seas?"

"She rushed on to her ruin like the rest of foolhardy adventurers; but, tell me, did you find the coal?"

The Doctor shook his head sadly.

"No coal! not a vestige! No, we did not even get as far as the place mentioned by Sir Edward Belcher."

"Then we have no fuel whatever?" said the old sailor.

"No."

"And no provisions?"

"No."

"And no ship to make our way back to England?"

It required courage indeed to face these gloomy realities, but, after a moment's silence, Johnson said again—

"Well, at any rate we know exactly how we stand. The first thing to be done now is to make a hut, for we can't stay long exposed to this temperature."

"Yes, we'll soon manage that with Bell's help," replied the Doctor. "Then we must go and find the sledge, and bring back the American, and have a consultation with Hatteras."

"Poor captain," said Johnson, always forgetting his own troubles, "how he must feel it!"

Clawbonny and Bell found Hatteras standing motionless, his arms folded in his usual fashion. He seemed gazing into space, but his face had recovered its calm, self-possessed expression. His faithful dog stood beside him, like his master, apparently insensible to the biting cold, though the temperature was 32 degrees below zero.

Bell lay on the ice in an almost inanimate condition. Johnson had to take vigorous measures to rouse him, but at last, by dint of shaking and rubbing him with snow, he succeeded.

CHAPTER I. THE DOCTOR'S INVENTORY.

"Come, Bell," he cried, "don't give way like this. Exert yourself, my man; we must have a talk about our situation, and we need a place to put our heads in. Come and help me, Bell. You haven't forgotten how to make a snow hut, have you? There is an iceberg all ready to hand; we've only got to hollow it out. Let's set to work; we shall find that is the best remedy for us."

Bell tried to shake off his torpor and help his comrade, while Mr. Clawbonny undertook to go and fetch the sledge and the dogs.

"Will you go with him, captain?" asked Johnson.

"No, my friend," said Hatteras, in a gentle tone, "if the Doctor will kindly undertake the task. Before the day ends I must come to some resolution, and I need to be alone to think. Go. Do meantime whatever you think best. I will deal with the future."

Johnson went back to the Doctor, and said—

"It's very strange, but the captain seems quite to have got over his anger. I never heard him speak so gently before."

"So much the better," said Clawbonny. "Believe me, Johnson, that man can save us yet."

And drawing his hood as closely round his head as possible, the Doctor seized his iron-tipped staff, and set out without further delay.

Johnson and Bell commenced operations immediately. They had simply to dig a hole in the heart of a great block of ice; but it was not easy work, owing to the extreme hardness of the material. However, this very hardness guaranteed the solidity of the dwelling, and the further their labours advanced the more they became sheltered.

Hatteras alternately paced up and down, and stood motionless, evidently shrinking from any approach to the scene of explosion.

In about an hour the Doctor returned, bringing with him Altamont lying on the sledge, wrapped up in the folds of the tent. The poor dogs were so exhausted from starvation that they could scarcely draw it along, and they had begun to gnaw their harness. It was, indeed, high time for feasts and men to take food and rest.

While the hut was being still further dug out, the Doctor went foraging about, and had the good fortune to find a little stove, almost undamaged by the explosion. He soon restored it to working trim, and, by the time the hut was completed, had filled it with wood and got it lighted. Before long it was roaring, and diffusing a genial warmth on all sides. The American was brought in and laid on blankets, and the four Englishmen seated themselves round the fire to enjoy their scanty meal of biscuit and hot tea, the last remains of the provisions on the sledge. Not a word was spoken by Hatteras, and the others respected his silence.

When the meal was over, the Doctor rose and went out, making a sign to Johnson to follow.

"Come, Johnson," he said, "we will take an inventory of all we have left. We must know exactly how we are off, and our treasures are scattered in all directions; so we had better begin, and pick them up as fast as possible, for the snow may fall at any moment, and then it would be quite useless to look for anything."

"Don't let us lose a minute, then," replied Johnson. "Fire and food— those are our chief wants."

"Very well, you take one side and I'll take the other, and we'll search from the centre to the circumference."

This task occupied two hours, and all they discovered was a little salt meat, about 50 lbs. of pemmican, three sacks of biscuits, a small stock of chocolate, five or six pints of brandy, and about 2 lbs. of coffee, picked up bean by bean off the ice.

Neither blankets, nor hammocks, nor clothing—all had been consumed in the devouring flame.

This slender store of provisions would hardly last three weeks, and they had wood enough to supply the stove for about the same time.

Now that the inventory was made, the next business was to fetch the sledge. The tired-out dogs were harnessed sorely against their will, and before long returned bringing the few but precious treasures found among the *débris* of the brig. These were safely deposited in the hut, and then Johnson and Clawbonny, half-frozen with their work, resumed their places beside their companions in misfortune.

CHAPTER II. FIRST WORDS OF ALTAMONT.

About eight o'clock in the evening, the grey snow clouds cleared away for a little, and the stars shone out brilliantly in the sky.

Hatteras seized the opportunity and went out silently to take the altitude of some of the principal constellations. He wished to ascertain if the ice-field was still drifting.

In half an hour he returned and sat down in a corner of the hut, where he remained without stirring all night, motionless as if asleep, but in reality buried in deepest thought.

The next day the snow fell heavily, and the Doctor congratulated himself on his wise forethought, when he saw the white sheet lying three feet thick over the scene of the explosion, completely obliterating all traces of the *Forward.*

It was impossible to venture outside in such weather, but the stove drew capitally, and made the hut quite comfortable, or at any rate it seemed so to the weary, worn out adventurers.

The American was in less pain, and was evidently gradually coming back to life. He opened his eyes, but could not yet speak, for his lips were so affected by the scurvy that articulation was impossible, but he could hear and understand all that was said to him. On learning what had passed, and the circumstances of his discovery, he expressed his thanks by gestures, and the Doctor was too wise to let him know how brief his respite from death would prove. In three weeks at most every vestige of food would be gone.

About noon Hatteras roused himself, and going up to his friends, said—

"We must make up our minds what to do, but I must request Johnson to tell me first all the particulars of the mutiny on the brig, and how this final act of baseness came about."

"What good will that do?" said the Doctor. "The fact is certain, and it is no use thinking over it."

"I differ from your opinion," rejoined Hatteras. "Let me hear the whole affair from Johnson, and then I will banish it from my thoughts."

"Well," said the boatswain, "this was how it happened. I did all in my power to prevent, but——"

"I am sure of that, Johnson; and what's more, I have no doubt the ringleaders had been hatching their plans for some time."

"That's my belief too," said the Doctor.

"And so it is mine," resumed Johnson; "for almost immediately after your departure Shandon, supported by the others, took the command of the ship.

I could not resist him, and from that moment everybody did pretty much as they pleased. Shandon made no attempt to restrain them: it was his policy to make them believe that their privations and toils were at an end. Economy was entirely disregarded. A blazing fire was kept up in the stove, and the men were allowed to eat and drink at discretion; not only tea and coffee was at their disposal, but all the spirits on board, and on men who had been so long deprived of ardent liquors, you may guess the result. They went on in this manner from the 7th to the 15th of January."

"And this was Shandon's doing?" asked Hatteras.

"Yes, captain."

"Never mention his name to me again! Go on, Johnson."

"It was about the 24th or 25th of January, that they resolved to abandon the ship. Their plan was to reach the west coast of Baffin's Bay, and from thence to embark in the boat and follow the track of the whalers, or to get to some of the Greenland settlements on the eastern side. Provisions were abundant, and the sick men were so excited by the hope of return that they were almost well. They began their preparations for departure by making a sledge which they were to draw themselves, as they had no dogs. This was not ready till the 15th of February, and I was always hoping for your arrival, though I half dreaded it too, for you could have done nothing with the men, and they would have massacred you rather than remain on board. I tried my influence on each one separately, remonstrating and reasoning with them, and pointing out the dangers they would encounter, and also the cowardice of leaving you, but it was a mere waste of words; not even the best among them would listen to me. Shandon was impatient to be off, and fixed the 22nd of February for starting. The sledge and the boat were packed as closely as possible with provisions and spirits, and heaps of wood, to obtain which they had hewed the brig down to her water-line. The last day the men ran riot. They completely sacked the ship, and in a drunken paroxysm Pen and two or three others set it on fire. I fought and struggled against them, but they threw me down and assailed me with blows, and then the wretches, headed by Shandon, went off towards the east and were soon out of sight. I found myself alone on the burning ship, and what could I do? The fire- hole was completely blocked up with ice. I had not a single drop of water! For two days the *Forward* struggled with the flames, and you know the rest."

A long silence followed the gloomy recital, broken at length by Hatteras, who said—

"Johnson, I thank you; you did all you could to save my ship, but single-handed you could not resist. Again I thank you, and now let the subject be dropped. Let us unite efforts for our common salvation. There are four of us, four companions, four friends, and all our lives are equally precious. Let each give his opinion on the best course for us to pursue."

"You ask us then, Hatteras," said the Doctor, "we are all devoted to you, and our words come from our hearts. But will you not state you own views first?"

"That would be little use," said Hatteras, sadly; "my opinion might appear interested; let me hear all yours first."

"Captain," said Johnson, "before pronouncing on such an important matter, I wish to ask you a question."

"Ask it, then, Johnson."

"You went out yesterday to ascertain our exact position; well, is the field drifting or stationary?"

"Perfectly stationary. It had not moved since the last reckoning was made. I find we are just where we were before we left, in 80° 15" lat. and 97° 35" long."

"And what distance are we from the nearest sea to the west?"

"About six hundred miles."

"And that sea is——?"

"Smith's Sound," was the reply.

"The same that we could not get through last April?"

"The same."

"Well, captain, now we know our actual situation, we are in a better position to determine our course of action."

"Speak your minds, then," said Hatteras, again burying his head in his hands.

"What do you say, Bell?" asked the Doctor.

"It strikes me the case doesn't need long thinking over," said the carpenter. "We must get back at once without losing a single day or even a single hour, either to the south or west, and make our way to the nearest coast, even if we are two months doing it!"

"We have only food for three weeks," replied Hatteras, without raising his head.

"Very well," said Johnson, "we must make the journey in three weeks, since it is our last chance. Even if we can only crawl on our knees before we get to our destination, we must be there in twenty-five days."

"This part of the Arctic Continent is unexplored. We may have to encounter difficulties. Mountains and glaciers may bar our progress," objected Hatteras.

"I don't see that's any sufficient reason for not attempting it. We shall have to endure sufferings, no doubt, and perhaps many. We shall have to limit ourselves to the barest quantities of food, unless our guns should procure us anything."

"There is only about half a pound of powder left," said Hatteras.

"Come now, Hatteras, I know the full weight of your objections, and I am not deluding myself with vain hopes. But I think I can read your motive. Have you any practical suggestion to offer?"

"No," said Hatteras, after a little hesitation.

"You don't doubt our courage," continued the Doctor. "We would follow you to the last—you know that. But must we not, meantime, give up all hope of reaching the Pole? Your plans have been defeated by treachery. Natural difficulties you might have overcome, but you have been outmatched by perfidy and human weakness. You have done all that man could do, and you would have succeeded I am certain; but situated as we are now, are you not obliged to relinquish your projects for the present, and is not a return to England even positively necessary before you could continue them?"

"Well, captain?" asked Johnson after waiting a considerable time for Hatteras to reply.

Thus interrogated, he raised his head, and said in a constrained tone—

"You think yourselves quite certain then of reaching the Sound, exhausted though you are, and almost without food?"

"No," replied the Doctor, "but there is one thing certain, the Sound won't come to us, we must go to it. We may chance to find some Esquimaux tribes further south."

"Besides, isn't there the chance of falling in with some ship that is wintering here?" asked Johnson.

"Even supposing the Sound is blocked up, couldn't we get across to some Greenland or Danish settlement? At any rate, Hatteras, we can get nothing by remaining here. The route to England is towards the south, not the north."

"Yes," said Bell, "Mr. Clawbonny is right. We must start, and start at once. We have been forgetting our country too long already."

"Is this your advice, Johnson?" asked Hatteras again.

"Yes, captain."

"And yours, Doctor?"

"Yes, Hatteras."

Hatteras remained silent, but his face, in spite of himself, betrayed his inward agitation. The issue of his whole life hung on the decision he had to make, for he felt that to return to England was to lose all! He could not venture on a fourth expedition.

The Doctor finding he did not reply, added—

"I ought also to have said, that there is not a moment to lose. The sledge must be loaded with the provisions at once, and as much wood as possible. I must confess six hundred miles is a long journey, but we can, or rather we must make twenty miles a day, which will bring us to the coast about the 26th of March."

"But cannot we wait a few days yet?" said Hatteras.

"What are you hoping for?" asked Johnson.

"I don't know. Who can tell the future? It is necessary, too, that you should get your strength a little recruited. You might sink down on the road with fatigue, without even a snow hut to shelter you."

"But think of the terrible death that awaits us here," replied the carpenter.

"My friends," said Hatteras, in almost supplicating tones; "you are despairing too soon. I should propose that we should seek our deliverance towards the north, but you would refuse to follow me, and yet why should there not be Esquimaux tribes round about the Pole as well as towards the south? The open sea, of the existence of which we are certified, must wash the shores of continents. Nature is logical in all her doings. Consequently vegetation must be found there when the earth is no longer ice-bound. Is there not a promised land awaiting us in the north from which you would flee?"

Hatteras became animated as he spoke, and Doctor Clawbonny's excitable nature was so wrought upon that his decision began to waver. He was on the point of yielding, when Johnson, with his wiser head and calmer temperament, recalled him to reason and duty by calling out—

"Come, Bell, let us be off to the sledge."

"All right," said Bell, and the two had risen to leave the hut, when Hatteras exclaimed—

"Oh, Johnson! You! you! Well, go! I shall stay, I shall stay!"

"Captain!" said Johnson, stopping in spite of himself.

"I shall stay, I tell you. Go! Leave me like the rest! Come, Duk, you and I will stay together."

The faithful dog barked as if he understood, and settled himself down beside his master. Johnson looked at the Doctor, who seemed at a loss to know what to do, but came to the conclusion at last that the best way, meantime, was to calm Hatteras, even at the sacrifice of a day. He was just about to try the force of his eloquence in this direction, when he felt a light touch on his arm, and turning round saw Altamont who had crawled out of bed and managed to get on his knees. He was trying to speak, but his swollen lips could scarcely make a sound. Hatteras went towards him, and watched his efforts to articulate so attentively that in a few minutes he made out a word that sounded like *Porpoise*, and stooping over him he asked—

"Is it the *Porpoise*?"

Altamont made a sign in the affirmative, and Hatteras went on with his queries, now that he had found a clue.

"In these seas?"

The affirmative gesture was repeated.

"Is she in the north?"

"Yes."

"Do you know her position?"

"Yes."

"Exactly?"

"Yes."

CHAPTER II. FIRST WORDS OF ALTAMONT.

For a minute or so, nothing more was said, and the onlookers waited with palpitating hearts.

Then Hatteras spoke again and said—

"Listen to me. We must know the exact position of your vessel. I will count the degrees aloud, and you; will stop me when I come to the right one."

The American assented by a motion of the head, and Hatteras began—

"We'll take the longitude first. 105°, No? 106°, 107°? It is to the west, I suppose?"

"Yes," replied Altamont.

"Let us go on, then: 109°, 110°, 112°, 114°, 116°, 118°, 120°."

"Yes," interrupted the sick man.

"120° of longitude, and how many minutes? I will count."

Hatteras began at number one, and when he got to fifteen, Altamont made a sign to stop.

"Very good," said Hatteras; "now for the latitude. Are you listening? 80°, 81°, 82°, 83°."

Again the sign to stop was made.

"Now for the minutes: 5', 10', 15', 20', 25', 30', 35'."

Altamont stopped him once more, and smiled feebly.

"You say, then, that the *Porpoise* is in longitude 120° 15', and latitude 83° 35'?"

"Yes," sighed the American, and fell back motionless in the Doctor's arms, completely overpowered by the effort he had made.

"Friends!" exclaimed Hatteras; "you see I was right. Our salvation lies indeed in the north, always in the north. We shall be saved!"

But the joyous, exulting words had hardly escaped his lips before a sudden thought made his countenance change. The serpent of jealousy had stung him, for this stranger was an American, and he had reached three degrees nearer the Pole than the ill-fated *Forward.*

CHAPTER III. A SEVENTEEN DAYS' MARCH.

These first words of Altamont had completely changed the whole aspect of affairs, but his communication was still incomplete, and, after giving him a little time to rest, the Doctor undertook the task of conversing again with him, putting his questions in such a form that a movement of the head or eyes would be a sufficient answer.

He soon ascertained that the *Porpoise* was a three-mast American ship, from New York, wrecked on the ice, with provisions and combustibles in abundance still on board, and that, though she had been thrown on her side, she had not gone to pieces, and there was every chance of saving her cargo.

Altamont and his crew had left her two months previously, taking the long boat with them on a sledge. They intended to get to Smith's Sound, and reach some whaler that would take them back to America; but one after another succumbed to fatigue and illness, till at last Altamont and two men were all that remained out of thirty; and truly he had survived by a providential miracle, while his two companions already lay beside him in the sleep of death.

Hatteras wished to know why the *Porpoise* had come so far north, and learned in reply that she had been irresistibly driven there by the ice. But his anxious fears were not satisfied with this explanation, and he asked further what was the purpose of his voyage. Altamont said he wanted to make the north-west passage, and this appeared to content the jealous Englishman, for he made no more reference to the subject. "Well," said the Doctor, "it strikes me that, instead of trying to get to Baffin's Bay, our best plan would be to go in search of the *Porpoise*, for here lies a ship a full third of the distance nearer, and, more than that, stocked with everything necessary for winter quarters."

"I see no other course open to us," replied Bell.

"And the sooner we go the better," added Johnson, "for the time we allow ourselves must depend on our provisions."

"You are right, Johnson," returned the Doctor. "If we start to- morrow, we must reach the *Porpoise* by the 15th of March, unless we mean to die of starvation. What do you say, Hatteras?"

"Let us make preparations immediately, but perhaps the route may be longer than we suppose."

"How can that be, captain? The man seems quite sure of the position of his ship," said the Doctor.

"But suppose the ice-field should have drifted like ours?"

Here Altamont, who was listening attentively, made a sign that he wished to speak, and, after much difficulty, he succeeded in telling the Doctor that the *Porpoise* had struck on rocks near the coast, and that it was impossible for her to move.

CHAPTER III. A SEVENTEEN DAYS' MARCH.

This was re-assuring information, though it cut off all hope of returning to Europe, unless Bell could construct a smaller ship out of the wreck.

No time was lost in getting ready to start. The sledge was the principal thing, as it needed thorough repair. There was plenty of wood, and, profiting by the experience they had recently had of this mode of transit, several improvements were made by Bell.

Inside, a sort of couch was laid for the American, and covered over with the tent. The small stock of provisions did not add much to the weight, but, to make up the deficiency, as much wood was piled up on it as it could hold.

The Doctor did the packing, and made an exact calculation of how long their stores would last. He found that, by allowing three-quarter rations to each man and full rations to the dogs, they might hold out for three weeks.

Towards seven in the evening, they felt so worn out that they were obliged to give up work for the night; but, before lying down to sleep, they heaped up the wood in the stove, and made a roaring fire, determined to allow themselves this parting luxury. As they gathered round it, basking in the unaccustomed heat, and enjoying their hot coffee and biscuits and pemmican, they became quite cheerful, and forgot all their sufferings.

About seven in the morning they set to work again and by three in the afternoon everything was ready.

It was almost dark, for, though the sun had reappeared above the horizon since the 31st of January, his light was feeble and of short duration. Happily the moon would rise about half-past six, and her soft beams would give sufficient light to show the road.

The parting moment came. Altamont was overjoyed at the idea of starting, though the jolting would necessarily increase his sufferings, for the Doctor would find on board the medicines he required for his cure.

They lifted him on to the sledge, and laid him as comfortably as possible, and then harnessed the dogs, including Duk. One final look towards the icy bed where the *Forward* had been, and the little party set out for the *Porpoise*. Bell was scout, as before; the Doctor and Johnson took each a side of the sledge, and lent a helping hand when necessary; while Hatteras walked behind to keep all in the right track.

They got on pretty quickly, for the weather was good, and the ice smooth and hard, allowing the sledge to glide easily along, yet the temperature was so low that men and dogs were soon panting, and had often to stop and take breath. About seven the moon shone out, and irradiated the whole horizon. Far as the eye could see, there was nothing visible but a wide- stretching level plain of ice, without a solitary hummock or patch to relieve the uniformity.

As the Doctor remarked to his companion, it looked like some vast, monotonous desert.

"Ay! Mr. Clawbonny, it is a desert, but we shan't die of thirst in it at any rate."

"That's a comfort, certainly, but I'll tell you one thing: it proves, Johnson, we must be a great distance from any coast. The nearer the coast, the more numerous the icebergs in general, and you see there is not one in sight."

"The horizon is rather misty, though."

"So it is, but ever since we started, we have been on this same interminable ice-field."

"Do you know, Mr. Clawbonny, that smooth as this ice is, we are going over most dangerous ground? Fathomless abysses lie beneath our feet."

"That's true enough, but they won't engulph us. This white sheet over them is pretty tough, I can tell you. It is always getting thicker too; for in these latitudes, it snows nine days out of ten even in April and May; ay, and in June as well. The ice here, in some parts, cannot be less than between thirty and forty feet thick."

"That sounds reassuring, at all events." said Johnson.

"Yes, we're not like the skaters on the Serpentine—always in danger of falling through. This ice is strong enough to bear the weight of the Custom House in Liverpool, or the Houses of Parliament in Westminster."

"Can they reckon pretty nearly what ice will bear, Mr. Clawbonny?" asked the old sailor, always eager for information.

"What can't be reckoned now-a-days? Yes, ice two inches thick will bear a man; three and a half inches, a man on horse-back; five inches, an eight pounder; eight inches, field artillery; and ten inches, a whole army."

"It is difficult to conceive of such a power of resistance, but you were speaking of the incessant snow just now, and I cannot help wondering where it comes from, for the water all round is frozen, and what makes the clouds?"

"That's a natural enough question, but my notion is that nearly all the snow or rain that we get here comes from the temperate zones. I fancy each of those snowflakes was originally a drop of water in some river, caught up by evaporation into the air, and wafted over here in the shape of clouds; so that it is not impossible that when we quench our thirst with the melted snow, we are actually drinking from the very rivers of our own native land."

Just at this moment the conversation was interrupted by Hatteras, who called out that they were getting out of the straight line. The increasing mist made it difficult to keep together, and at last, about eight o'clock, they determined to come to a halt, as they had gone fifteen miles. The tent was put up and the stove lighted, and after their usual supper they lay down and slept comfortably till morning.

The calm atmosphere was highly favourable, for though the cold became intense, and the mercury was always frozen in the thermometer, they found no difficulty in continuing their route, confirming the truth of Parry's assertion that any man suitably clad may walk abroad with impunity in the lowest temperature, provided there is no wind; while, on the other hand, the least breeze would make the skin smart acutely, and bring on violent headache, which would soon end in death.

On the 5th of March a peculiar phenomenon occurred. The sky was perfectly clear and glittering with stars, when suddenly snow began to fall thick and fast, though there was not a cloud in the heavens and through the white flakes the constellations could be seen shining. This curious display lasted two hours, and ceased before the Doctor could arrive at any satisfactory conclusion as to its cause.

The moon had ended her last quarter, and complete darkness prevailed now for seventeen hours out of the twenty-four. The travellers had to fasten themselves together with a long rope to avoid getting separated, and it was all but impossible to pursue the right course. Moreover, the brave fellows, in spite of their iron will, began to show signs of fatigue. Halts became more frequent, and yet every hour was precious, for the provisions were rapidly coming to an end.

Hatteras hardly knew what to think as day after day went on without apparent result, and he asked himself sometimes whether the *Porpoise* had any actual existence except in Altamont's fevered brain, and more than once the idea even came into his head that perhaps national hatred might have induced the American to drag them along with himself to certain death.

He told the Doctor his suppositions, who rejected them absolutely, and laid them down to the score of the unhappy rivalry that had arisen already between the two captains.

On the 14th of March, after sixteen days' march the little party found themselves only yet in the 82° latitude. Their strength was exhausted, and they had a hundred miles more to go. To increase their sufferings, rations had to be still further reduced. Each man must be content with a fourth part to allow the dogs their full quantity.

Unfortunately they could not rely at all on their guns, for only seven charges of powder were left, and six balls. They had fired at several hares and foxes on the road already, but unsuccessfully.

However, on the 15th, the Doctor was fortunate enough to surprise a seal basking on the ice, and, after several shots, the animal was captured and killed.

Johnson soon had it skinned and cut in pieces, but it was so lean that it was worthless as food, unless its captors would drink the oil like the Esquimaux.

The Doctor was bold enough to make the attempt, but failed in spite of himself.

Next day several icebergs and hummocks were noticed on the horizon. Was this a sign that land was near, or was it some ice-field that had broken up? It was difficult to know what to surmise.

On arriving at the first of these hummocks, the travellers set to work to make a cave in it where they could rest more comfortably than in the tent, and after three hours' persevering toil, were able to light their stove and lie down beside it to stretch their weary limbs.

CHAPTER IV. THE LAST CHARGE OF POWDER

Johnson was obliged to take the dogs inside the hut, for they would have been soon frozen outside in such dry weather. Had it been snowing they would have been safe enough, for the snow served as a covering, and kept in the natural heat of the animals.

The old sailor, who made a first-rate dog-driver, tried his beasts with the oily flesh of the seal; and found, to his joyful surprise, that they ate it greedily. The Doctor said he was not astonished at this, as in North America the horses were chiefly fed on fish; and he thought that what would satisfy an herbivorous horse might surely content an omnivorous dog.

The whole party were soon buried in deep sleep, for they were fairly overcome with fatigue. Johnson awoke his companions early next morning, and the march was resumed in haste. Their lives depended now on their speed, for provisions would only hold out three days longer.

The sky was magnificent; the atmosphere extremely clear, and the temperature very low. The sun rose in the form of a long ellipse, owing to refraction, which made his horizontal diameter appear twice the length of his vertical.

The Doctor, gun in hand, wandered away from the others, braving the solitude and the cold in the hope of discovering game. He had only sufficient powder left to load three times, and he had just three balls. That was little enough should he encounter a bear, for it often takes ten or twelve shots to have any effect on these enormous animals.

But the brave Doctor would have been satisfied with humbler game. A few hares or foxes would be a welcome addition to their scanty food; but all that day, if even he chanced to see one, either he was too far away, or he was deceived by refraction, and took a wrong aim. He came back to his companions at night with crestfallen looks, having wasted one ball and one charge of powder.

Next day the route appeared more difficult, and the weary men could hardly drag themselves along. The dogs had devoured even the entrails of the seal, and began to gnaw their traces.

A few foxes passed in the distance, and the Doctor lost another ball in attempting to shoot them.

They were forced to come to a halt early in the evening, though the road was illumined by a splendid Aurora Borealis; for they could not put one foot before the other.

Their last meal, on the Sunday evening, was a very sad one—if no providential help came, their doom was sealed.

Johnson set a few traps before going to sleep, though he had no baits to put inside them. He was very disappointed to find them all empty in the morning, and was returning gloomily to the hut, when he perceived a bear of huge dimensions. The old sailor took it into his head that Heaven had sent this beast specially for him to kill; and without waking his comrades, he seized the Doctor's gun, and was soon in pursuit of his prey. On reaching the right distance, he took aim; but, just as his finger touched the trigger, he felt his arm tremble. His thick gloves hampered him, and, flinging them hastily off, he took up the gun with a firmer grasp. But what a cry of agony escaped him! The skin of his fingers stuck to the gun as if it had been red-hot, and he was forced to let it drop. The sudden fall made it go off, and the last ball was discharged in the air.

The Doctor ran out at the noise of the report, and understood all at a glance. He saw the animal walking quietly off, and poor Johnson forgetting his sufferings in his despair.

"I am a regular milksop!" he exclaimed, "a cry-baby, that can't stand the least pain! And at my age, too!"

"Come, Johnson; go in at once, or you will be frost-bitten. Look at your hands—they are white already! Come, come this minute."

"I am not worth troubling about, Mr. Clawbonny," said the old boatswain. "Never mind me!"

"But you must come in, you obstinate fellow. Come, now, I tell you; it will be too late presently."

At last he succeeded in dragging the poor fellow into the tent, where he made him plunge his hands into a bowl of water, which the heat of the stove kept in a liquid state, though still cold. Johnson's hands had hardy touched it before it froze immediately.

"You see it was high time you came in; I should have been forced to amputate soon," said the Doctor.

Thanks to his endeavours, all danger was over in about an hour, but he was advised to keep his hands at a good distance from the stove for some time still.

That morning they had no breakfast. Pemmican and salt beef were both done. Not a crumb of biscuit remained. They were obliged to content themselves with half a cup of hot coffee, and start off again.

They scarcely went three miles before they were compelled to give up for the day. They had no supper but coffee, and the dogs were so ravenous that they were almost devouring each other.

Johnson fancied he could see the bear following them in the distance, but he made no remark to his companions. Sleep forsook the unfortunate men, and their eyes grew wild and haggard.

Tuesday morning came, and it was thirty-four hours since they had tasted a morsel of food. Yet these brave, stout-hearted men continued their march, sustained by their superhuman energy of purpose. They pushed the sledge themselves, for the dogs could no longer draw it.

At the end of two hours, they sank exhausted. Hatteras urged them to make a fresh attempt, but his entreaties and supplications were powerless; they could not do impossibilities.

"Well, at any rate," he said, "I won't die of cold if I must of hunger." He set to work to hew out a hut in an iceberg, aided by Johnson, and really they looked like men digging their own tomb.

It was hard labour, but at length the task was accomplished. The little house was ready, and the miserable men took up their abode in it.

In the evening, while the others lay motionless, a sort of hallucination came over Johnson, and he began raving about bears.

The Doctor roused himself from his torpor, and asked the old man what he meant, and what bear he was talking about.

"The bear that is following us," replied Johnson.

"A bear following us?"

"Yes, for the last two days!"

"For the last two days! You have seen him?"

"Yes, about a mile to leeward."

"And you never told me, Johnson!"

"What was the good!"

"True enough," said the Doctor; "we have not a single bail to send after him!"

"No, not even a bit of iron!"

The Doctor was silent for a minute, as if thinking. Then he said—

"Are you quite certain the animal is following us?"

"Yes, Mr. Clawbonny, he is reckoning on a good feed of human flesh!"

"Johnson!" exclaimed the Doctor, grieved at the despairing mood of his companion.

"He is sure enough of his meal!" continued the

"You have no ball!"

"I'll make one."

"You have no lead!"

"No, but I have mercury."

So saying, he took the thermometer, which stood at 50° above zero, and went outside and laid it on a block of ice. Then he came in again, and said, "Tomorrow! Go to sleep, and wait till the sun rises."

With the first streak of dawn next day, the Doctor and Johnson rushed out to look at the thermometer. All the mercury had frozen into a compact cylindrical mass. The Doctor broke the tube and took it out. Here was a hard piece of metal ready for use.

"It is wonderful, Mr. Clawbonny; you ought to be a proud man."

"Not at all, my friend, I am only gifted with a good memory, and I have read a great deal."

"How did that help you?"

"Why, I just happened to recollect a fact related by Captain Ross in his voyages. He states that they pierced a plank, an inch thick, with a bullet made of mercury. Oil would even have suited my purpose, for, he adds, that a ball of frozen almond oil splits through a post without breaking in pieces."

"It is quite incredible!"

"But it is a fact, Johnson. Well, come now, this bit of metal may save our lives. We'll leave it exposed to the air a little while, and go and have a look for the bear."

Just then Hatteras made his appearance, and the

Doctor told him his project, and showed him the mercury.

The captain grasped his hand silently, and the three hunters went off in quest of their game.

The weather was very clear, and Hatteras, who was a little ahead of the others, speedily discovered the bear about three hundred yards distant, sitting on his hind quarters sniffing the air, evidently scenting the intruders on his domains.

"There he is!" he exclaimed.

"Hush!" cried the Doctor.

CHAPTER IV. THE LAST CHARGE OF POWDER

But the enormous quadruped, even when he perceived his antagonists, never stirred, and displayed neither fear nor anger. It would not be easy to get near him, however, and Hatteras said—

"Friends, this is no idle sport, our very existence is at stake; we must act prudently."

"Yes," replied the Doctor, "for we have but the one shot to depend upon. We must not miss, for if Away they went, while the old boatswain slipped behind a hummock, which completely hid him from the bear, who continued still in the same place and in the same position.

CHAPTER V. THE SEAL AND THE BEAR.

"You know, Doctor," said Hatteras, as they returned to the hut, "the polar bears subsist almost entirely on seals. They'll lie in wait for them beside the crevasses for whole days, ready to strangle them the moment their heads appear above the surface. It is not likely, then, that a bear will be frightened of a seal."

"I think I see what you are after, but it is dangerous."

"Yes, but there is more chance of success than in trying any other plan, so I mean to risk it. I am going to dress myself in the seal's skin, and creep along the ice. Come, don't let us lose time. Load the gun and give it me."

The Doctor could not say anything, for he would have done the same himself, so he followed Hatteras silently to the sledge, taking with him a couple of hatchets for his own and Johnson's use.

Hatteras soon made his *toilette*, and slipped into the skin, which was big enough to cover him almost entirely.

"Now, then, give me the gun," he said, "and you be off to Johnson. I must try and steal a march on my adversary."

"Courage, Hatteras!" said the Doctor, handing him the weapon, which he had carefully loaded meanwhile.

"Never fear! but be sure you don't show yourselves till I fire."

The Doctor soon joined the old boatswain behind the hummock, and told him what they had been doing. The bear was still there, but moving restlessly about, as if he felt the approach of danger.

In a quarter of an hour or so the seal made his appearance on the ice. He had gone a good way round, so as to come on the bear by surprise, and every movement was so perfect an imitation of a seal, that even the Doctor would have been deceived if he had not known it was Hatteras.

"It is capital!" said Johnson, in a low voice. The bear had instantly caught sight of the supposed seal, for he gathered himself up, preparing to make a spring as the animal came nearer, apparently seeking to return to his native element, and unaware of the enemy's proximity. Bruin went to work with extreme prudence, though his eyes glared with greedy desire to clutch the coveted prey, for he had probably been fasting a month, if not two. He allowed his victim to get within ten paces of him, and then sprang forward with a tremendous bound, but stopped short, stupefied and frightened, within three steps of Hatteras, who started up that moment, and, throwing off his disguise, knelt on one knee, and aimed straight at the bear's heart. He fired, and the huge monster rolled back on the ice.

CHAPTER V. THE SEAL AND THE BEAR.

"Forward! Forward!" shouted the Doctor, hurrying towards Hatteras, for the bear had reared on his hind legs, and was striking the air with one paw and tearing up the snow to stanch his wound with the other.

Hatteras never moved, but waited, knife in hand. He had aimed well, and fired with a sure and steady aim. Before either of his companions came up he had plunged the knife in the animal's throat, and made an end of him, for he fell down at once to rise no more.

"Hurrah! Bravo!" shouted Johnson and the Doctor, but Hatteras was as cool and unexcited as possible, and stood with folded arms gazing at his prostrate foe.

"It is my turn now," said Johnson. "It is a good thing the bear is killed, but if we leave him out here much longer, he will get as hard as a stone, and we shall be able to do nothing with him."

He began forthwith to strip the skin off, and a fine business it was, for the enormous quadruped was almost as large as an ox. It measured nearly nine feet long, and four round, and the great tusks in his jaws were three inches long.

On cutting the carcase open, Johnson found nothing but water in the stomach. The beast had evidently had no food for a long time, yet it was very fat, and weighed fifteen hundred pounds. The hunters were so famished that they had hardly patience to carry home the flesh to be cooked, and it needed all the Doctor's persuasion to prevent them eating it raw.

On entering the hut, each man with a load on his back, Clawbonny was struck with the coldness that pervaded the atmosphere. On going up to the stove he found the fire black out. The exciting business of the morning had made Johnson neglect his accustomed duty of replenishing the stove.

The Doctor tried to blow the embers into a flame, but finding he could not even get a red spark, he went out to the sledge to fetch tinder, and get the steel from Johnson.

The old sailor put his hand into his pocket, but was surprised to find the steel missing. He felt in the other pockets, but it was not there. Then he went into the hut again, and shook the blanket he had slept in all night, but his search was still unsuccessful.

He went back to his companions and said—

"Are you sure, Doctor, you haven't the steel?"

"Quite, Johnson."

"And you haven't it either, captain?"

"Not I!" replied Hatteras.

"It has always been in your keeping," said the Doctor.

"Well, I have not got it now!" exclaimed Johnson, turning pale.

"Not got the steel!" repeated the Doctor, shuddering involuntarily at the bare idea of its loss, for it was all the means they had of procuring a fire.

"Look again, Johnson," he said.

The boatswain hurried to the only remaining place he could think of, the hummock where he had stood to watch the bear. But the missing treasure was nowhere to be found, and the old sailor returned in despair.

Hatteras looked at him, but no word of reproach escaped his lips. He only said—

"This is a serious business, Doctor."

"It is, indeed!" said Clawbonny.

"We have not even an instrument, some glass that we might take the lens out of, and use like a burning glass."

"No, and it is a great pity, for the sun's rays are quite strong enough just now to light our tinder."

"Well," said Hatteras, "we must just appease our hunger with the raw meat, and set off again as soon as we can, to try to discover the ship."

"Yes!" replied Clawbonny, speaking to himself, absorbed in his own reflections. "Yes, that might do at a pinch! Why not? We might try."

"What are you dreaming about?" asked Hatteras.

"An idea has just occurred to me."

"An idea come into your head, Doctor," exclaimed Johnson; "then we are saved!"

"Will it succeed? that's the question."

"What's your project?" said Hatteras.

"We want a lens; well, let us make one."

"How?" asked Johnson.

"With a piece of ice."

"What? Do you think that would do?"

"Why not? All that is needed is to collect the sun's rays into one common focus, and ice will serve that purpose as well as the finest crystal."

"Is it possible?" said Johnson.

"Yes, only I should like fresh water ice, it is harder and more transparent than the other."

"There it is to your hand, if I am not much mistaken," said Johnson, pointing to a hummock close by.

"I fancy that is fresh water, from the dark look of it, and the green tinge."

"You are right. Bring your hatchet, Johnson."

A good-sized piece was soon cut off, about a foot in diameter, and the Doctor set to work. He began by chopping it into rough shape with the hatchet; then he operated upon it more carefully with his knife, making as smooth a surface as possible, and finished the polishing process with his fingers, rubbing away until he had obtained as transparent a lens as if it had been made of magnificent crystal.

The sun was shining brilliantly enough for the Doctor's experiment. The tinder was fetched, and held beneath the lens so as to catch the rays in full power. In a few seconds it took fire, to Johnson's rapturous delight.

He danced about like an idiot, almost beside himself with joy, and shouted, "Hurrah! hurrah!" while Clawbonny hurried back into the hut and rekindled the fire. The stove was soon roaring, and it was not many minutes before the savoury odour of broiled bear-steaks roused Bell from his torpor.

What a feast this meal was to the poor starving men may be imagined. The Doctor, however, counselled moderation in eating, and set the example himself.

"This is a glad day for us," he said, "and we have no fear of wanting food all the rest of our journey. Still we must not forget we have further to go yet, and I think the sooner we start the better."

"We cannot be far off now," said Altamont, who could almost articulate perfectly again; "we must be within forty-eight hours' march of the *Porpoise*."

"I hope we'll find something there to make a fire with," said the Doctor, smiling. "My lens does well enough at present; but it needs the sun, and there are plenty of days when he does not make his appearance here, within less than four degrees of the pole."

"Less than four degrees!" repeated Altamont, with a sigh; "yes, my ship went further than any other has ever ventured."

"It is time we started," said Hatteras, abruptly.

"Yes," replied the Doctor, glancing uneasily at the two captains.

The dogs were speedily harnessed to the sledge, and the march resumed.

CHAPTER V. THE SEAL AND THE BEAR.

As they went along, the Doctor tried to get out of Altamont the real motive that had brought him so far north. But the American made only evasive replies, and Clawbonny whispered in old Johnson's ear—

"Two men we've got that need looking after."

"You are right," said Johnson.

"Hatteras never says a word to this American, and I must say the man has not shown himself very grateful. I am here, fortunately."

"Mr. Clawbonny," said Johnson, "now this Yankee has come back to life again, I must confess I don't much like the expression of his face."

"I am much mistaken if he does not suspect the projects of Hatteras."

"Do you think his own were similar?"

"Who knows? These Americans, Johnson, are bold, daring fellows. It is likely enough an American would try to do as much as an Englishman."

"Then you think that Altamont—"

"I think nothing about it, but his ship is certainly on the road to the North Pole."

"But didn't Altamont say that he had been caught among the ice, and dragged there irresistibly?"

"He said so, but I fancied there was a peculiar smile on his lips while he spoke."

"Hang it! It would be a bad job, Mr. Clawbonny, if any feeling of rivalry came between two men of their stamp."

"Heaven forfend! for it might involve the most serious consequences, Johnson."

"I hope Altamont will remember he owes his life to us?"

"But do we not owe ours to him now? I grant, without us, he would not be alive at this moment, but without him and his ship, what would become of us?"

"Well, Mr. Clawbonny, you are here to keep things straight anyhow, and that is a blessing."

"I hope I may manage it, Johnson."

The journey proceeded without any fresh incident, but on the Saturday morning the travellers found themselves in a region of quite an altered character. Instead of the wide smooth plain of ice that had hitherto stretched before them, overturned icebergs and broken hummocks covered the horizon; while the frequent blocks of fresh-water ice showed that some coast was near.

Next day, after a hearty breakfast off the bear's paws, the little party continued their route; but the road became toilsome and fatiguing. Altamont lay watching the horizon with feverish anxiety—an anxiety shared by all his companions, for, according to the last reckoning made by Hatteras, they were now exactly in latitude 83° 35" and longitude 120° 15", and the question of life or death would be decided before the day was over.

At last, about two o'clock in the afternoon, Altamont started up with a shout that arrested the whole party, and pointing to a white mass that no eye but his could have distinguished from the surrounding icebergs, exclaimed in a loud, ringing voice, "The *Porpoise*."

CHAPTER VI. THE *PORPOISE*

It was the 24th of March, and Palm Sunday, a bright, joyous day in many a town and village of the Old World, but in this desolate region what mournful silence prevailed! No willow branches here with their silvery blossom — not even a single withered leaf to be seen — not a blade of grass!

Yet this was a glad day to the travellers, for it promised them speedy deliverance from the death that had seemed so inevitable.

They hastened onward, the dogs put forth renewed energy, and Duk barked his loudest, till, before long, they arrived at the ship. The *Porpoise* was completely buried under the snow. All her masts and rigging had been destroyed in the shipwreck, and she was lying on a bed of rocks so entirely on her side that her hull was uppermost.

They had to knock away fifteen feet of ice before they could even catch a glimpse of her, and it was not without great difficulty that they managed to get on board, and made the welcome discovery that the provision stores had not been visited by any four-footed marauders. It was quite evident, however, that the ship was not habitable.

"Never mind!" said Hatteras, "we must build a snow-house, and make ourselves comfortable on land."

"Yes, but we need not hurry over it," said the Doctor; "let us do it well while we're about it, and for a time we can make shift on board; for we must build a good, substantial house, that will protect us from the bears as well as the cold. I'll undertake to be the architect, and you shall see what a first-rate job I'll make of it."

"I don't doubt your talents, Mr. Clawbonny," replied Johnson; "but, meantime, let us see about taking up our abode here, and making an inventory of the stores we find. There does not seem a boat visible of any description, and I fear these timbers are in too bad a condition to build a new ship out of them."

"I don't know that," returned Clawbonny, "time and thought do wonders; but our first business is to build a house, and not a ship; one thing at a time, I propose."

"And quite right too," said Hatteras; "so we'll go ashore again."

They returned to the sledge, to communicate the result of their investigation to Bell and Altamont; and about four in the afternoon the five men installed themselves as well as they could on the wreck. Bell had managed to make a tolerably level floor with planks and spars; the stiffened cushions and hammocks were placed round the stove to thaw, and were soon fit for use. Altamont, with the Doctor's assistance, got on board without much trouble, and a sigh of satisfaction escaped him as if he felt himself once more at home—a sigh which to Johnson's ear boded no good.

The rest of the day was given to repose, and they wound up with a good supper off the remains of the bear, backed by a plentiful supply of biscuit and hot tea.

CHAPTER VI. THE PORPOISE

It was late next morning before Hatteras and his companions woke, for their minds were not burdened now with any solicitudes about the morrow, and they might sleep as long as they pleased. The poor fellows felt like colonists safely arrived at their destination, who had forgotten all the sufferings of the voyage, and thought only of the new life that lay before them.

"Well, it is something at all events," said the Doctor, rousing himself and stretching his arms, "for a fellow not to need to ask where he is going to find his next bed and breakfast."

"Let us see what there is on board before we say much," said Johnson.

The *Porpoise* has been thoroughly equipped and provisioned for a long voyage, and, on making an inventory of what stores remained, they found 6150 lbs. of flour, fat, and raisins; 2000 lbs. of salt beef and pork, 1500 lbs. of pemmican; 700 lbs. of sugar, and the same of chocolate; a chest and a half of tea, weighing 96 lbs.; 500 lbs. of rice; several barrels of preserved fruits and vegetables; a quantity of lime-juice, with all sorts of medicines, and 300 gallons of rum and brandy. There was also a large supply of gunpowder, ball, and shot, and coal and wood in abundance.

Altogether, there was enough to last those five men for more than two years, and all fear of death from starvation or cold was at an end.

"Well, Hatteras, we're sure of enough to live on now," said the Doctor, "and there is nothing to hinder us reaching the Pole."

"The Pole!" echoed Hatteras.

"Yes, why not? Can't we push our way overland in the summer months?"

"We might overland; but how could we cross water?"

"Perhaps we may be able to build a boat out of some of the ship's planks."

"Out of an American ship!" exclaimed the captain, contemptuously.

Clawbonny was prudent enough to make no reply, and presently changed the conversation by saying—

"Well, now we have seen what we have to depend upon, we must begin our house and store-rooms. We have materials enough at hand; and, Bell, I hope you are going to distinguish yourself," he added.

"I am ready, Mr. Clawbonny," replied Bell; "and, as for material, there is enough for a town here with houses and streets."

"We don't require that; we'll content ourselves with imitating the Hudson's Bay Company. They entrench themselves in fortresses against the Indians and wild beasts. That's all we need—a house one side and stores the other, with a wall and two bastions. I must try to make a plan."

"Ah! Doctor, if you undertake it," said Johnson, "I am sure you'll make a good thing of it."

"Well, the first part of the business is to go and choose the ground. Will you come with us Hatteras?"

"I'll trust all that to you, Doctor," replied the captain. "I'm going to look along the coast."

Altamont was too feeble yet to take part in any work, so he remained on the ship, while the others commenced to explore the unknown continent.

On examining the coast, they found that the *Porpoise* was in a sort of bay bristling with dangerous rocks, and that to the west, far as the eye could reach, the sea extended, entirely frozen now, though if Belcher and Penny were to be believed, open during the summer months. Towards the north, a promontory stretched out into the sea, and about three miles away was an island of moderate size. The roadstead thus formed would have afforded safe anchorage to ships, but for the difficulty of entering it. A considerable distance inland there was a solitary mountain, about 3000 feet high, by the Doctor's reckoning; and half-way up the steep rocky cliffs that rose from the shore, they noticed a circular plateau, open on three sides to the bay and sheltered on the fourth by a precipitous wall, 120 feet high.

This seemed to the Doctor the very place for this house, from its naturally fortified situation. By cutting steps in the ice, they managed to climb up and examine it more closely.

They were soon convinced they could not have a better foundation, and resolved to commence operations forthwith, by removing the hard snow more than ten feet deep, which covered the ground, as both dwelling and storehouses must have a solid foundation.

This preparatory work occupied the whole of Monday, Tuesday, and Wednesday. At last they came to hard granite close in grain, and containing garnets and felspar crystals, which flew out with every stroke of the pickaxe.

The dimensions and plan of the snow-house were then settled by the Doctor. It was to be divided into three rooms, as all they needed was a bed-room, sitting-room and kitchen. The sitting-room was to be in the middle, the kitchen to the left, and the bed-room to the right.

For five days they toiled unremittingly. There was plenty of material, and the walls required to be thick enough to resist summer thaws. Already the house began to present an imposing appearance. There were four windows in front, made of splendid sheets of ice, in Esquimaux fashion, through which the light came softly in as if through frosted glass.

Outside there was a long covered passage between the two windows of the sitting-room. This was the entrance hall, and it was shut in by a strong door taken from the cabin of the *Porpoise*. The Doctor was highly delighted with his performance when all was finished, for though it would have been difficult to say to what style of architecture it belonged, it was strong, and that was the chief thing.

The next business was to move in all the furniture of the *Porpoise*. The beds were brought first and laid down round the large stove in the sleeping room; then came chairs, tables, arm-chairs, cupboards, and benches for the sitting-room, and finally the ship furnaces and cooking utensils for the kitchen. Sails spread on the ground did duty for carpets, and also served for inner doors.

The walls of the house were over five feet thick, and the windows resembled port-holes for cannon. Every part was as solid as possible, and what more was wanted? Yet if the Doctor could have had his way, he would have made all manner of ornamental additions, in humble imitation of the Ice Palace built in St. Petersburgh in January, 1740, of which he had read an account. He amused his companions after work in the evening by describing its grandeur, the cannons in front, and statues of exquisite beauty, and the wonderful elephant that spouted water out of his trunk by day and flaming naphtha by night—all cut out of ice. He also depicted the interior, with tables, and toilette tables, mirrors, candelabra, tapers, beds, mattresses, pillows, curtains, time-pieces, chairs, playing-cards, wardrobes, completely fitted up—in fact, everything in the way of furniture that could be mentioned, and the whole entirely composed of ice.

It was on Easter Sunday, the 31st of March, when the travellers installed themselves in their new abode and after holding divine service in the sitting-room, they devoted the remainder of the day to rest.

Next morning they set about building the storehouses and powder magazine. This took a whole week longer, including the time spent in unloading the vessel, which was a task of considerable difficulty, as the temperature was so low, that they could not work for many hours at a time. At length on the 8th of April, provisions, fuel, and ammunition were all safe on *terra firma,* and deposited in their respective places. A sort of kennel was constructed a little distance from the house for the Greenland dogs, which the Doctor dignified by the name of "Dog Palace." Duk shared his master's quarters.

All that now remained to be done was to put a parapet right round the plateau by way of fortification.

By the 15th this was also completed, and the snow-house might bid defiance to a whole tribe of Esquimaux, or any other hostile invaders, if indeed any human beings whatever were to be found on this unknown continent, for Hatteras, who had minutely examined the bay and the surrounding coast, had not been able to discover the least vestiges of the huts that are generally met with on shores frequented by Greenland tribes. The shipwrecked sailors of the *Porpoise* and *Forward* seemed to be the first whose feet had ever trod this lone region.

CHAPTER VII. AN IMPORTANT DISCUSSION.

While all these preparations for winter were going on Altamont was fast regaining strength. His vigorous constitution triumphed, and he was even able to lend a helping hand in the unlading of the ship. He was a true type of the American, a shrewd, intelligent man, full of energy and resolution, enterprising, bold, and ready for anything. He was a native of New York, he informed his companions, and had been a sailor from his boyhood.

The *Porpoise* had been equipped and sent out by a company of wealthy merchants belonging to the States, at the head of which was the famous Grinnell.

There were many points of resemblance between Altamont and Hatteras, but no affinities. Indeed, any similarity that there was between them, tended rather to create discord than to make the men friends. With a greater show of frankness, he was in reality far more deep and crafty than Hatteras. He was more free and easy, but not so true-hearted, and somehow his apparent openness did not inspire such confidence as the Englishman's gloomy reserve.

The Doctor was in constant dread of a collision between the rival captains, and yet one must command inevitably, and which should it be! Hatteras had the men, but Altamont had the ship, and it was hard to say whose was the better right.

It required all the Doctor's tact to keep things smooth, for the simplest conversation threatened to lead to strife.

At last, in spite of all his endeavours, an outbreak occurred on the occasion of a grand banquet by way of "house-warming," when the new habitation was completed.

This banquet was Dr Clawbonny's idea. He was head-cook, and distinguished himself by the concoction of a wonderful pudding, which would positively have done no dishonour to the *cuisine* of the Lord Chancellor of England.

Bell most opportunely chanced to shoot a white hare and several ptarmigans, which made an agreeable variety from the pemmican and salt meat.

Clawbonny was master of the ceremonies, and brought in his pudding, adorning himself with the insignia of his office—a big apron, and a knife dangling at his belt.

As Altamont did not conform to the teetotal *régime* of his English companions, gin and brandy were set on the table after dinner, and the others, by the Doctor's orders, joined him in a glass for once, that the festive occasion might be duly honoured. When the different toasts were being drunk, one was given to the United States, to which Hatteras made no response.

This important business over, the Doctor introduced an interesting subject of conversation by saying—

CHAPTER VII. AN IMPORTANT DISCUSSION.

"My friends, it is not enough to have come thus far in spite of so many difficulties; we have something more yet to do. I propose we should bestow a name on this continent, where we have found friendly shelter and rest, and not only on the continent, but on the several bays, peaks, and promontories that we meet with. This has been invariably done by navigators and is a most necessary proceeding."

"Quite right," said Johnson, "when once a place is named, it takes away the feeling of being castaways on an unknown shore."

"Yes," added Bell, "and we might be going on some expedition and obliged to separate, or go out hunting, and it would make it much easier to find one another if each locality had a definite name."

"Very well; then," said the Doctor, "since we are all agreed, let us go steadily to work."

Hatteras had taken no part in the conversation as yet, but seeing all eyes fixed on him, he rose at last, and said—

"If no one objects, I think the most suitable name we can give our house is that of its skilful architect, the best man among us. Let us call it 'Doctor's House.' "

"Just the thing!" said Bell.

"First rate!" exclaimed Johnson, " 'Doctor's House!' "

"We cannot do better," chimed in Altamont. "Hurrah for Doctor Clawbonny."

Three hearty cheers were given, in which Duk joined lustily, barking his loudest.

"It is agreed then," said Hatteras, "that this house is to be called 'Doctor's House.' "

The Doctor, almost overcome by his feelings, modestly protested against the honour; but he was obliged to yield to the wishes of his friends, and the new habitation was formally named "Doctor's House."

"Now, then," said the Doctor, "let us go onto name the most important of our discoveries."

"There is that immense sea which surrounds us, unfurrowed as yet by a single ship."

"A single ship!" repeated Altamont. "I think you have forgotten the *Porpoise*, and yet she certainly did not get here overland,"

"Well, it would not be difficult to believe she had," replied Hatteras, "to see on what she lies at present."

"True, enough, Hatteras," said Altamont, in a piqued tone; "but, after all, is not that better than being blown to atoms like the *Forward*?"

Hatteras was about to make some sharp retort, but Clawbonny interposed.

"It is not a question of ships, my friends," he said, "but of a fresh sea."

"It is no new sea," returned Altamont; "it is in every Polar chart, and has a name already. It is called the Arctic Ocean, and I think it would be very inconvenient to alter its designation. Should we find out by and by, that, instead of being an ocean it is only a strait or gulf, it will be time enough to alter it then."

"So be it," said Hatteras.

"Very well, that is an understood thing, then," said the Doctor, almost regretting that he had started a discussion so pregnant with national rivalries.

"Let us proceed with the continent where we find ourselves at present," resumed Hatteras. "I am not aware that any name whatever has been affixed to it, even in the most recent charts."

He looked at Altamont as he spoke, who met his gaze steadily, and said—

"Possibly you may be mistaken again, Hatteras."

"Mistaken! What! This unknown continent, this virgin soil——"

"Has already a name," replied Altamont, coolly.

Hatteras was silent, but his lip quivered.

"And what name has it, then?" asked the Doctor, rather astonished at Altamont's affirmation.

"My dear Clawbonny," replied the American, "it is the custom, not to say the right, of every navigator to christen the soil on which he is the first to set foot. It appears to me, therefore, that it is my privilege and duty on this occasion to exercise my prerogative, and—"

"But, sir," interrupted Johnson, rather nettled at his *sang froid.*

"It would be a difficult matter to prove that the *Porpoise* did not come here, even supposing she reached this coast by land," continued Altamont, without noticing Johnson's protest. "The fact is indisputable," he added looking at Hatteras.

"I dispute the claim," said the Englishman, restraining himself by a powerful effort. "To name a country, you must first discover it, I suppose, and that you certainly did not do. Besides, but for us, where would you have been, sir, at this moment, pray? Lying twenty feet deep under the snow."

"And without me, sir," retorted Altamont, hotly, "without me and my ship, where would you all be at this moment? Dead, from cold and hunger."

"Come, come, friends," said the Doctor, "don't get to words, all that can be easily settled. Listen to me."

"Mr. Hatteras," said Altamont, "is welcome to name whatever territories he may discover, should he succeed in discovering any; but this continent belongs to me. I should not even consent to its having two names like Grinnell's Land, which is also called Prince Albert's Land, because it was discovered almost simultaneously by an Englishman and an American. This is quite another matter; my right of priority is incontestable. No ship before mine ever touched this shore, no foot before mine ever trod this soil. I have given it a name, and that name it shall keep."

"And what is that name?" inquired the Doctor.

"New America," replied Altamont.

Hatteras trembled with suppressed passion, but by a violent effort restrained himself.

"Can you prove to me," said Altamont, "that an Englishman has set foot here before an American?"

Johnson and Bell said nothing, though quite as much offended as the captain by Altamont's imperious tone. They felt that reply was impossible.

For a few minutes there was an awkward silence, which the Doctor broke by saying—

"My friends, the highest human law is justice. It includes all others. Let us be just, then, and don't let any bad feeling get in among us. The priority of Altamont seems to me indisputable. We will take our revenge by and by, and England will get her full share in our future discoveries. Let the name New America stand for the continent itself, but I suppose Altamont has not yet disposed of all the bays, and capes, and headlands it contains, and I imagine there will be nothing to prevent us calling this bay Victoria Bay?"

"Nothing whatever, provided that yonder cape is called Cape Washington," replied Altamont.

"You might choose a name, sir," exclaimed Hatteras, almost beside himself with passion, "that is less offensive to an Englishman."

"But not one which sounds so sweet to an American," retorted Altamont, proudly.

"Come, come," said the Doctor, "no discussion on that subject. An American has a perfect right to be proud of his great countryman! Let us honour genius wherever it is met with; and since Altamont has made his choice, let us take our turn next; let the captain——"

"Doctor!" interrupted Hatteras, "I have no wish that my name should figure anywhere on this continent, seeing that it belongs to America."

"Is this your unalterable determination?" asked Clawbonny.

"It is."

The Doctor did not insist further.

"Very well, we'll have it to ourselves then," he continued, turning to Johnson and Bell. "We'll leave our traces behind us. I propose that the island we see out there, about three miles away from the shore, should be called Isle Johnson, in honour of our boatswain,''

"Oh, Mr. Clawbonny," began Johnson, in no little confusion.

"And that mountain that we discovered in the west we will call Bell Mount, if our carpenter is willing."

"It is doing me too much honour," replied Bell.

"It is simple justice," returned the Doctor.

"Nothing could be better," said Altamont.

"Now then, all we have to do is to christen our fort," said the Doctor, "about that there will be no discussion, I hope, for it is neither to our gracious sovereign Queen Victoria, nor to Washington, that we owe our safety and shelter here, but to God, who brought about our meeting, and by so doing saved us all. Let our little fort be called Fort Providence."

"Your remarks are just," said Altamont; "no name could be more suitable."

"Fort Providence," added Johnson, "sounds well too. In our future excursions, then, we shall go by Cape Washington to Victoria Bay, and from thence to Fort Providence, where we shall find food and rest at Doctor's House!"

"The business is settled then so far," resumed the Doctor. "As our discoveries multiply we shall have other names to give; but I trust, friends, we shall have no disputes about them, for placed as we are, we need all the help and love we can give each other. Let us be strong by being united. Who knows what dangers yet we may have to brave, and what sufferings to endure before we see our native land once more. Let us be one in heart though five in number, and let us lay aside all feelings of rivalry. Such feelings are bad enough at all times, but among us they would be doubly wrong. You understand me, Altamont, and you, Hatteras?"

Neither of the captains replied, but the Doctor took no notice of their silence, and went on to speak of other things. Sundry expeditions were planned to forage for fresh food. It would soon be spring, and hares and partridges, foxes and bears would re-appear. So it was determined that part of every day should be spent in hunting and exploring this unknown continent of New America.

CHAPTER VIII. AN EXCURSION TO THE NORTH OF VICTORIA BAY

Next morning Clawbonny was out by dawn of day. Clambering up the steep, rocky wall, against which the Doctor's House leaned, he succeeded, though with considerable difficulty, in reaching the top, which he found terminated abruptly in a sort of truncated cone. From this elevation there was an extensive view over a vast tract of country, which was all disordered and convulsed as if it had undergone some volcanic commotion. Sea and land, as far as it was possible to distinguish one from the other, were covered with a sheet of ice.

A new project struck the Doctor's mind, which was soon matured and ripe for execution. He lost no time in going back to the snow house, and consulting over it with his companions.

"I have got an idea," he said; "I think of constructing a lighthouse on the top of that cone above our heads."

"A lighthouse!" they all exclaimed.

"Yes, a lighthouse. It would be a double advantage. It would be a beacon to guide us in distant excursions, and also serve to illumine our *plateau* in the long dreary winter months."

"There is no doubt," replied Altamont, "of its utility; but how would you contrive to make it?"

"With one of the lanterns out of the *Porpoise*."

"All right; but how will you feed your lamp? With seal oil?"

"No, seal oil would not give nearly sufficient light. It would scarcely be visible through the fog."

"Are you going to try to make gas out of our coal then?"

"No, not that either, for gas would not be strong enough; and, worse still, it would waste our combustibles."

"Well," replied Altamont; "I'm at a loss to see how you—"

"Oh, I'm prepared for everything after the mercury bullet, and the ice lens, and Fort Providence. I believe Mr. Clawbonny can do anything," exclaimed Johnson.

"Come, Clawbonny, tell us what your light is to be, then," said Altamont.

"That's soon told," replied Clawbonny. "I mean to have an electric light."

"An electric light?"

"Yes, why not? Haven't you a galvanic battery on board your ship?"

"Yes."

"Well, there will be no difficulty then in producing an electric light, and that will cost nothing, and be far brighter."

"First-rate?" said Johnson; "let us set to work at once."

"By all means. There is plenty of material. In an hour we can raise a pillar of ice ten feet high, and that is quite enough.

Away went the Doctor, followed by his companions, and the column was soon erected and crowned with a ship lantern. The conducting wires were properly adjusted within it, and the pile with which they communicated fixed up in the sitting-room, where the warmth of the stove would protect it from the action of the frost.

As soon as it grew dark the experiment was made, and proved a complete success. An intense brilliant light streamed from the lantern and illumined the entire plateau and the plains beneath.

Johnson could not help clapping his hands, half beside himself with delight.

"Well, I declare, Mr. Clawbonny," he exclaimed, "you're our sun now."

"One must be a little of everything, you know," was Clawbonny's modest reply.

It was too cold. however, even to stand admiring more than a minute, and the whole party were glad enough to get indoors again, and tuck themselves up in their warm blankets.

A regular course of life commenced now, though uncertain weather and frequent changes of temperature made it sometimes impracticable to venture outside the hut at all, and it was not till the Saturday after the installation, that a day came that was favourable enough for a hunting excursion; when Bell, and Altamont, and the Doctor determined to take advantage of it, and try to replenish their stock of provisions.

They started very early in the morning, each armed with a double- barrelled gun and plenty of powder and shot, a hatchet, and a snow knife.

The weather was cloudy, but Clawbonny put the galvanic battery in action before he left, and the bright rays of the electric light did duty for the glorious orb of day, and in truth was no bad substitute, for the light was equal to three thousand candles, or three hundred gas burners.

It was intensely cold, but dry, and there was little or no wind. The hunters set off in the direction of Cape Washington, and the hard snow so favoured their march, that in three hours they had gone fifteen miles, Duk jumping and barking beside them all the way. They kept as close to the coast as possible, but found no trace of human habitation and indeed scarcely a sign of animal life. A few snow birds, however, darting to and fro announced the approach of spring and the return of the animal creation. The sea was still entirely frozen over, but it was evident from the open breathing holes in the ice, that the seals had been quite recently on the surface. In one part the holes were so numerous, that the Doctor said to his companions that he had no doubt that when summer came, they would be seen there in hundreds, and would be easily captured, for on unfrequented shores they were not so difficult of approach. But once frighten them and they all vanish as if by enchantment, and never return to the spot again. "Inexperienced hunters," he said, "have often lost a whole shoal by attacking them, *en masse*, with noisy shouts instead of singly and silently."

"Is it for the oil or skin that they are mostly hunted?"

"Europeans hunt them for the skin, but the Esquimaux eat them. They live on seals, and nothing is so delicious to them as a piece of the flesh, dipped in the blood and oil. After all, cooking has a good deal to do with it, and I'll bet you something I could dress you cutlets you would not turn up your nose at, unless for their black appearance."

"We'll set you to work on it," said Bell, "and I'll eat as much as you like to please you."

"My good Bell, you mean to say to please yourself, but your voracity would never equal the Green-landers', for they devour from ten to fifteen pounds of meat a day."

"Fifteen pounds!" said Bell. "What stomachs!"

"Arctic stomachs," replied the Doctor, "are prodigious; they can expand at will, and, I may add, contract at will; so that they can endure starvation quite as well as abundance. When an Esquimaux sits down to dinner he is quite thin, and by the time he has finished, he is so corpulent you would hardly recognize him. But then we must remember that one meal sometimes has to last a whole day."

"This voracity must be peculiar to the inhabitants of cold countries," said Altamont.

"I think it is," replied the Doctor. "In the Arctic regions people must eat enormously: it is not only one of the conditions of strength, but of existence. The Hudson's Bay Company always reckoned on this account 8 lbs. of meat to each man a day, or 12 lbs. of fish, or 2 lbs. of pemmican."

"Invigorating regimen, certainly!" said Bell.

"Not so much as you imagine, my friend. An Indian who guzzles like that can't do a whit better day's work than an Englishman, who has his pound of beef and pint of beer."

"Things are best as they are, then, Mr. Clawbonny."

"No doubt of it; and yet an Esquimaux meal may well astonish us. In Sir John Ross's narrative, he states his surprise at the appetites of his guides. He tells us that two of them—just two mind—devoured a quarter of a buffalo in one morning. They cut the meat in long narrow strips, and the mode of eating was either for the one to bite off as much as his mouth could hold, and then pass it on to the other, or to leave the long ribbons of meat dangling from the mouth and devour them gradually like boa-constrictors, lying at full length on the ground."

"Faugh!" exclaimed Bell, "what disgusting brutes!"

"Every man has his own fashion of dining," remarked the philosophical American.

"Happily," said the Doctor.

"Well, if eating is such an imperative necessity in these latitudes, it quite accounts for all the journals of Arctic travellers being so full of eating and drinking."

"You are right," returned the Doctor. "I have been struck by the same fact; but I think it arises not only from the necessity of full diet, but from the extreme difficulty sometimes in procuring it. The thought of food is always uppermost in the mind, and naturally finds mention in the narrative."

"And yet," said Altamont, "if my memory serves me right, in the coldest parts of Norway the peasants do not seem to need such substantial fare. Milk diet is their staple food, with eggs, and bread made of the bark of the birch-tree; a little salmon occasionally, but never meat; and still they are fine hardy fellows."

"It is an affair of organization out of my power to explain," replied Clawbonny; "but I have no doubt that if these same Norwegians were transplanted to Greenland, they would learn to eat like the Esquimaux by the second or third generation. Even if we ourselves were to remain in this blessed country long, we should be as bad as the Esquimaux, even if we escaped becoming regular gluttons."

"I declare, Mr. Clawbonny, you make me feel hungry with talking so much about eating," exclaimed Bell.

"Not I!" said Altamont. "It rather sickens me, and makes me loathe the sight of a seal. But, stop, I do believe we are going to have the chance of a dinner off one, for I am much mistaken if that's not something alive lying on those lumps of ice yonder!"

"It is a walrus!" exclaimed the Doctor. "Be quiet, and let us get up to him."

Clawbonny was right, it was a walrus of huge dimensions, disporting himself not more than two hundred yards away. The hunters separated, going in different directions, so as to surround the animal and cut off all retreat. They crept along cautiously behind the hummocks, and managed to get within a few paces of him unperceived, when they fired simul-simultaneously.

The walrus rolled over, but speedily got up again, and tried to make his escape, but Altamont fell upon him with his hatchet, and cut off his dorsal fins. He made a desperate resistance, but was overpowered by his enemies, and soon lay dead, reddening the ice-field with his blood.

It was a fine animal, measuring more than fifteen feet in length, and would have been worth a good deal for the oil; but the hunters contented themselves with cutting off the most savoury parts, and left the rest to the ravens, which had just begun to make their appearance.

Night was drawing on, and it was time to think of returning to Fort Providence. The moon had not yet risen, but the sky was serene and cloudless, and already glittering with stars—magnificent stars.

"Come," said the Doctor, "let us be off, for it is getting late. Our hunting has not been very successful; but still, if a man has found something for his supper, he need not grumble. Let us go the shortest road, however, and get quickly home without losing our way. The stars will guide us."

They resolved to try a more direct route back by going further inland, and avoiding the windings of the coast; but, after some hours' walking, they found themselves no nearer Doctor's House, and it was evident that they must have lost their way. The question was raised whether to construct a hut and rest till morning, or proceed; but Clawbonny insisted on going on, as Hatteras and Johnson would be so uneasy.

"Duk will guide us," he said; "he won't go wrong. His instinct can dispense with star and compass. Just let us keep close behind him."

They did well to trust to Duk, for very speedily a faint light appeared in the horizon almost like a star glimmering through the mist, which hung low above the ground.

"There's our lighthouse!" exclaimed the Doctor.

"Do you think it is, Mr. Clawbonny?" said Bell.

"I'm certain of it! Come on faster." The light became stronger the nearer they approached, and soon they were walking in a bright luminous track, leaving their long shadows behind them on the spotless snow.

Quickening their steps, they hastened forward, and in another half hour they were climbing the ascent to Fort Providence.

CHAPTER IX. COLD AND HEAT.

Hatteras and Johnson had been getting somewhat uneasy at the prolonged absence of their companions, and were delighted to see them back safe and sound. The hunters were no less glad to find themselves once more in a warm shelter, for the temperature had fallen considerably as night drew on, and the thermometer outside was 73° below zero.

The poor hunters were half frozen, and so worn out that they could hardly drag their limbs along; but the stoves were roaring and crackling cheerily, and the big kitchen fire waiting to cook such game as might be brought in. Clawbonny donned his official apron again, and soon had his seal cutlets dressed and smoking on the table. By nine o'clock the whole party were enjoying a good supper, and Bell couldn't help exclaiming—

"Well, even at the risk of being taken for an Esquimaux, I must confess eating is the most important business if one has to winter in these regions. A good meal isn't to be sneezed at."

They all had their mouths crammed too full to speak, but the Doctor signified his agreement with Bell's views by an approving nod.

The cutlets were pronounced first-rate, and it seemed as if they were, for they were all eaten, to the very last morsel.

For dessert they had coffee, which the Doctor brewed himself in a French coffee-pot over spirits-of-wine. He never allowed anybody but himself to concoct this precious beverage; for he made a point of serving it boiling hot, always declaring it was not fit to drink unless it burnt his tongue. This evening he took it so scalding that Altamont exclaimed—

"You'll skin your throat!"

"Not a bit of it," was the Doctor's reply.

"Then your palate must be copper-sheathed," said Johnson.

"Not at all, friends. I advise you to copy my example. Many persons, and I am one, can drink coffee at a temperature of 131°."

"131°?" said Altamont; "why, that is hotter than the hand could bear!"

"Of course it is, Altamont, for the hand could not bear more than 122°, but the palate and tongue are less sensitive."

"You surprise me."

"Well, I will convince you it is fact," returned Clawbonny, and taking up a thermometer, he plunged it into the steaming coffee. He waited till the mercury rose as high as 131° and then withdrew it, and swallowed the liquid with evident gusto.

Bell tried to follow his example, but burnt his mouth severely.

"You are not used to it," said the Doctor, coolly.

"Can you tell us, Clawbonny," asked Altamont, "what is the highest temperature that the human body can bear."

"Yes, several curious experiments have been made in that respect. I remember reading of some servant girls, in the town of Rochefoucauld, in France, who could stay ten minutes in a baker's large oven when the temperature was 300°, while potatoes and meat were cooking all round them."

"What girls!" exclaimed Altamont.

"Well, there is another case, where eight of our own countrymen— Fordyce, Banks, Solander, Blagdin, Home, Nooth, Lord Seaforth, and Captain Phillips—went into one as hot as 200°, where eggs and beef were frizzling."

"And they were Englishmen!" said Bell, with a touch of national pride.

"Oh, the Americans could have done better than that," said Altamont.

"They would have roasted," returned the Doctor, laughing. " At all events they have never tried it, so I shall stand up for my countrymen. There is one more instance I recollect, and really it is so incredible, that it would be impossible to believe it, if it were not attested by unimpeachable evidence. The Duke of Ragusa and

Dr. Jung, a Frenchman and an Austrian, saw a Turk plunge into a bath at 170°."

"But that is not so astonishing as those servant girls, or our own countrymen," said Johnson.

"I beg your pardon," replied Clawbonny; "there is a great difference between plunging into hot air and hot water. Hot air produces perspiration, which protects the skin, but boiling water scalds. The *maximum* heat of baths is 107°, so that this Turk must have been an extraordinary fellow to endure such temperature."

"What is the mean temperature, Mr. Clawbonny, of animated beings?" asked Johnson.

"That varies with the species," replied the Doctor. "Birds have the highest, especially the duck and the hen. The mammalia come next, and human beings. The temperature of Englishmen averages 101°."

"I am sure Mr. Altamont is going to claim a higher rate for his countrymen," said Johnson, smiling.

"Well, sure enough, we've some precious hot ones among us, but as I never have put a thermometer down their throats to ascertain, I can't give you statistics."

"There is no sensible difference," said the Doctor, "between men of different races when they are placed under the same conditions, whatever their food may be. I may almost say their temperature would be the same at the Equator as the Pole."

"Then the heat of our bodies is the same here as in England," replied Altamont.

"Just about it. The other species of mammalia are generally hotter than human beings. The horse, the hare, the elephant, the porpoise, and the tiger are nearly the same; but the cat, the squirrel, the rat, the panther, the sheep, the ox, the dog, the monkey, and the goat, are as high as 103°; and the pig is 104°."

"Rather humiliating to us," put in Altamont.

"Then come the amphibia and the fish," resumed the Doctor, " whose temperature varies with that of the water. The serpent has a temperature of 86°, the frog 70°, and the shark several degrees less. Insects appear to have the temperature of air and water."

"All this is very well," interrupted Hatteras, who had hitherto taken no part in the conversation, "and we are obliged to the Doctor for his scientific information; but we are really talking as if we were going to brave the heat of the torrid zone. I think it would be far more seasonable to speak of cold, if the Doctor could tell us what is the lowest temperature on record."

"I can enlighten you on that too," replied the Doctor. "There are a great number of memorable winters, which appear to have come at intervals of about forty-one years. In 1364, the Rhone was frozen over as far as Arles; in 1408, the Danube was frozen throughout its entire extent, and the wolves crossed the Cattigut on firm ground; in 1509, the Adriatic and the Mediterranean were frozen at Venice and Marseilles, and the Baltic on the 10th of April; in 1608, all the cattle died in England from the cold; in 1789, the Thames was frozen as far as Gravesend; and the frightful winter of 1813 will long be remembered in France. The earliest and longest ever known in the present century was in 1829. So much for Europe."

"But here, within the Polar circle, what is the lowest degree?" asked Altamont.

"My word!" said the Doctor. "I think we have experienced the lowest ourselves, for one day the thermometer was 72° below zero, and, if my memory serves me right, the lowest temperature mentioned hitherto by Arctic voyagers has been 61° at Melville Island, 65° at Port Felix, and 70° at Fort Reliance."

"Yes," said Hatteras, "it was the unusual severity of the winter that barred our progress, for it came on just at the worst time possible."

"You were stopped, you say?" asked Altamont, looking fixedly at the captain.

"Yes, in our voyage west," the Doctor hastened to reply.

"Then the maximum and minimum temperatures," said Altamont, resuming the conversation, "are about 200° apart. So you see, my friends, we may make ourselves easy."

"But if the sun were suddenly extinguished," suggested Johnson, "would not the earth's temperature be far lower?"

"There is no fear of such a catastrophe; but, even should it happen, the temperature would be scarcely any different."

"That's curious."

"It is; but Fourrier, a learned Frenchman, has proved the fact incontestably. If it were not the case, the difference between day and night would be far greater, as also the degree of cold at the Poles. But now I think, friends, we should be the better of a few hours' sleep. Who has charge of the stove?"

"It is my turn to-night," said Bell.

"Well, pray keep up a good fire, for it is a perishing night."

"Trust me for that," said Bell. "But do look out, the sky is all in a blaze."

"Ay! it is a magnificent aurora," replied the Doctor, going up to the window. "How beautiful! I never tire gazing at it."

No more he ever did, though his companions had become so used to such displays that they hardly noticed them now. He soon followed the example of the others, however, and lay down on his bed beside the fire, leaving Bell to mount guard.

CHAPTER X. WINTER PLEASURES

It is a dreary affair to live at the Pole, for there is no going out for many long months, and nothing to break the weary monotony.

The day after the hunting excursion was dark and snowy, and Clawbonny could find no occupation except polishing up the ice walls of the hut as they became damp with the heat inside, and emptying out the snow which drifted into the long passage leading to the inner door. The "Snow- House" stood out well, defying storm and tempest, and the snow only seemed to increase the thickness of the walls.

The storehouses, too, did not give way the least; but though they were only a few yards off, it was found necessary to lay in enough provisions for the day, as very often the weather made it almost impossible to venture that short distance.

The unloading of the *Porpoise* turned out to have been a wise precaution, for she was slowly but surely being crashed to pieces by the silent, irresistible pressure around her. Still the Doctor was always hoping enough planks might be sufficiently sound to construct a small vessel to convey them back to England, but the right time to build had not come.

The five men were consequently compelled to spend the greater part of the day in complete idleness. Hatteras lolled on his bed absorbed in thought. Altamont smoked or dozed, and the Doctor took care not to disturb either of them, for he was in perpetual fear of a quarrel between them.

At meal times he always led the conversation away from irritating topics and sought, as far as possible, to instruct and interest all parties. Whenever he was not engaged with the preparation of his notes, he gave them dissertations on history, geography, or meteorology, handling his subject in an easy, though philosophical manner, drawing lessons from the most trivial incidents. His inexhaustible memory was never at a loss for fact or illustration when his good humour and geniality made him the life and soul of the little company. He was implicitly trusted by all, even by Hatteras, who cherished a deep affection for him.

Yet no man felt the compulsory confinement more painfully than Clawbonny. He longed ardently for the breaking up of the frost to resume his excursions though he dreaded the rivalry that might ensue between the two captains.

Yet things must come to a crisis soon or late, and meantime he resolved to use his best endeavors to bring both parties to a better mind, but to reconcile an American and an Englishman was no easy task. He and Johnson had many a talk on the subject, for the old sailor's views quite coincided with his own as to the difficult complications which awaited them in the future.

However, the bad weather continued, and leaving Fort Providence, even for an hour, was out of the question. Day and night they were pent up in these glittering ice-walls, and time hung heavily on their hands, at least on all but the Doctor's, and he always managed to find some occupation for himself.

"I declare," said Altamont, one evening; "life like this is not worth having. We might as well be some of those reptiles that sleep all the winter. But I suppose there is no help for it."

"I am afraid not," said the Doctor; "unfortunately we are too few in number to get up any amusement."

"Then you think if there were more of us, we should find more to do?"

"Of course: when whole ships' crews have wintered here, they have managed to while away the time famously."

"Well, I must say I should like to know how. It would need a vast amount of ingenuity to extract anything amusing out of our circumstances. I suppose they did not play at charades?"

"No, but they introduced the press and the theatre."

"What? They had a newspaper?" exclaimed the American.

"They acted a comedy?" said Bell.

"That they did," said the Doctor. "When Parry wintered at Melville Island, he started both amusements among his men, and they met with great success."

"Well, I must confess, I should like to have been there," returned Johnson; "for it must have been rather curious work."

"Curious and amusing too, my good Johnson. Lieutenant Beechey was the theatre manager, and Captain Sabina chief editor of the newspaper called 'The Winter Chronicle, or the Gazette of Northern Georgia.' "

"Good titles," said Altamont.

"The newspaper appeared daily from the 1st of November, 1819, to the 20th of March, 1820. It reported the different excursions, and hunting parties, and accidents, and adventures, and published amusing stories. No doubt the articles were not up to the 'Spectator' or the 'Daily Telegraph,' but the readers were neither critical nor *blasé*, and found great pleasure in their perusal."

"My word!" said Altamont. "I should like to read some of the articles."

"Would you? Well, you shall judge for yourself."

"What! can you repeat them from memory?"

"No; but you had Parry's Voyages on board the *Porpoise*, and I can read you his own narrative if you like."

This proposition was so eagerly welcomed that the Doctor fetched the book forthwith, and soon found the passage in question.

"Here is a letter," he said, "addressed to the editor."

" 'Your proposition to establish a journal has been received by us with the greatest satisfaction. I am convinced that, under your direction, it will be a great source of amusement, and go a long way to lighten our hundred days of darkness.

" 'The interest I take in the matter myself has led me to study the effect of your announcement on my comrades, and I can testify, to use reporter's language, that the thing has produced an immense sensation.

" 'The day after your prospectus appeared, there was an unusual and unprecedented demand for ink among us, and our green tablecloth was deluged with snippings and parings of quill-pens, to the injury of one of our servants, who got a piece driven right under his nail. I know for a fact that Sergeant Martin had no less than nine pen-knives to sharpen.

" 'It was quite a novel sight to see all the writing-desks brought out, which had not made their appearance for a couple of months, and judging by the reams of paper visible, more than one visit must have been made to the depths of the hold.

" 'I must not forget to tell you, that I believe attempts will be made to slip into your box sundry articles which are not altogether original, as they have been published already. I can declare that, no later than last night, I saw an author bending over his desk, holding a volume of the "Spectator" open with one hand, and thawing the frozen ink in his pen at the lamp with the other. I need not warn you to be on your guard against such tricks, for it would never do for us to have articles in our "Winter Chronicle" which our great-grandfathers read over their breakfast-tables a century ago.' "

"Well, well," said Altamont, "there is a good deal of clever humour in that writer. He must have been a sharp fellow."

"You're right. Here is an amusing catalogue of Arctic tribulations:—

" 'To go out in the morning for a walk, and the moment you put your foot outside the ship, find yourself immersed in the cook's water-hole.

" 'To go out hunting, and fall in with a splendid reindeer, take aim, and find your gun has gone off with a flash in the pan, owing to damp powder.

" 'To set out on a march with a good supply of soft new bread in your pocket, and discover, when you want to eat, that it has frozen so hard that you would break your teeth if you attempted to bite it through.

" 'To rush from the table when it is reported that a wolf is in sight, and on coming back to find the cat has eaten your dinner.

" 'To be returning quietly home from a walk, absorbed in profitable meditation, and suddenly find yourself in the embrace of a bear.'

"We might supplement this list ourselves," said the Doctor, "to almost any amount, for there is a sort of pleasure in enumerating troubles when one has got the better of them."

"I declare," said Altamont, "this 'Winter Journal' is an amusing affair. I wish we could subscribe to it."

"Suppose we start one," said Johnson.

"For us five!" exclaimed Clawbonny; "we might do for editors, but there would not be readers enough."

"No, nor spectators enough, if we tried to get up a comedy," added Altamont.

"Tell us some more about Captain Parry's theatre," said Johnson; "did they play new pieces?"

"Certainly. At first two volumes on board the 'Hecla' were gone through, but as there was a performance once a fortnight, this *repertoire* was soon exhausted. Then they had to improvise fresh plays; Parry himself composed one which had immense success. It was called 'The North-West Passage, or the End of the Voyage.' "

"A famous title," said Altamont; "but I must confess, if I had chosen such a subject, I should have been at a loss for the *dénouement*."

"You are right," said Bell; "who can say what the end will be?"

"What does that matter?" replied Mr. Clawbonny. "Why should we trouble about the last act, while the first ones are going on well. Leave all that to Providence, friends; let us each play our own *rôle* as perfectly as we can, and since the *dénouement* belongs to the Great Author of all things, we will trust his skill. He will manage our affairs for us, never fear."

"Well, we'd better go and dream about it," said Johnson, "for it's getting late, and it is time we went to bed," said Johnson.

"You're in a great hurry, old fellow," replied the Doctor.

"Why would you sit up, Mr. Clawbonny? I am so comfortable in my bed, and then I always have such good dreams. I dream invariably of hot countries, so that I might almost say, half my life is spent in the tropics, and half at the North Pole."

"You're a happy man, Johnson," said Altamont, "to be blessed with such a fortunate organization."

"Indeed I am," replied Johnson.

"Well, come, after that it would be positive cruelty to keep our good friend pining here," said the Doctor, "his tropical sun awaits him, so let's all go to bed."

CHAPTER XI TRACES OF BEARS

On the 26th of April during the night there was a sudden change in the weather. The thermometer fell several degrees, and the inmates of Doctor's House could hardly keep themselves warm even in their beds. Altamont had charge of the stove, and he found it needed careful replenishing to preserve the temperature at 50° above zero.

This increase of cold betokened the cessation of the stormy weather, and the Doctor hailed it gladly as the harbinger of his favourite hunting and exploring expeditions.

He rose early next morning, and climbed up to the top of the cone. The wind had shifted north, the air was clear, and the snow firm and smooth to the tread.

Before long the five companions had left Doctor's House, and were busily engaged in clearing the heavy masses of snow off the roof and sides, for the house was no longer distinguishable from the plateau, as the snow had drifted to a depth of full fifteen feet. It took two hours to remove the frozen snow, and restore the architectural form of the dwelling. At length the granite foundations appeared, and the storehouses and powder magazines were once more accessible.

But as, in so uncertain a climate, a storm might cut off their supplies any day, they wisely resolved to provide for any such emergency by carrying over a good stock of provisions to the kitchen; and then Clawbonny, Altamont, and Bell started off with their guns in search of gamc, for the want of fresh food began to be urgently felt.

The three companions went across the east side of the cone, right down into the centre of the far-stretching, snow-covered plain beneath, but they did not need to go far, for numerous traces of animals appeared on all sides within a circle of two miles round Fort Providence.

After gazing attentively at these traces for some minutes, the hunters looked at each other silently, and then the Doctor exclaimed:—

"Well, these are plain enough, I think!"

"Ay, only too plain," added Bell, "bears have been here!"

"First rate game!" said Altamont. "There's only one fault about it."

"And what is that?" asked Bell.

"What do you mean?"

"I mean this—there are distinct traces of five bears, and five bears are rather too much for five men."

"Are you sure there are five?" said Clawbonny.

"Look and see for yourself. Here is one footprint, and there is another quite different. These claws are far wider apart than those; and see here, again, that paw belongs to a much smaller bear. I tell you, if you look carefully, you will see the marks of all five different bears distinctly."

"You're right," said Bell, after a close inspection.

"If that's the case, then," said the Doctor, "we must take care what we're about, and not be foolhardy, for these animals are starving after the severe winter, and they might be extremely dangerous to encounter and, since we are sure of their number——"

"And of their intentions, too," put in Altamont.

"You think they have discovered our presence here?"

"No doubt of it, unless we have got into a bear-pass, but then, why should these footprints be in a circle round our fort? Look, these animals have come from the south-east, and stopped at this place, and commenced to reconnoitre the coast."

"You're right," said the Doctor, "and, what's more, it is certain that they have been here last night."

"And other nights before that," replied Altamont.

"I don't think so," rejoined Clawbonny. "It is more likely that they waited till the cessation of the tempest, and were on their way down to the bay, intending to catch seals, when they scented us."

"Well, we can easily find out if they come tonight," said Altamont.

"How?"

"By effacing all the marks in a given place, and if to-morrow, we find fresh ones, it will be evident that Fort Providence is the goal for which the bears are bound."

"Very good, at any rate we shall know, then, what we have to expect."

The three hunters set to work, and scraped the snow over till all the footprints were obliterated for a considerable distance.

"It is singular, though," said Bell, "that bears could scent us all that way off; we have not been burning anything fat which might have attracted them."

"Oh!" replied the Doctor, "bears are endowed with a wonderfully keen sense of smell, and a piercing sight; and, more than that, they are extremely intelligent, almost more so than any other animal. They have smelt something unusual; and, besides, who can tell whether they have not even found their way as far as our plateau during the tempest?"

"But then, why did they stop here last night?" asked Altamont.

"Well, that's a question I can't answer, but there is no doubt they will continue narrowing their circles, till they reach Fort Providence."

"We shall soon see," said Altamont.

"And, meantime, we had best go on," added the Doctor, "and keep a sharp look out."

But not a sign of anything living was visible, and after a time they returned to the snow-house.

Hatteras and Johnson were informed how matters stood, and it was resolved to maintain a vigilant watch. Night came, but nothing disturbed its calm splendour—nothing was heard to indicate approaching danger.

Next morning at early dawn, Hatteras and his companions, well armed, went out to reconnoitre the state of the snow. They found the same identical footmarks, but somewhat nearer. Evidently the enemy was bent on the siege of Fort Providence.

"But where can the bears be?" said Bell.

"Behind the icebergs watching us," replied the Doctor. "Don't let us expose ourselves imprudently."

"What about going hunting, then?" asked Altamont.

"We must put it off for a day or two, I think, and rub out the marks again, and see if they are renewed to-morrow."

CHAPTER XI TRACES OF BEARS

The Doctor's advice was followed, and they entrenched themselves for the present in the fort. The lighthouse was taken down, as it was not of actual use meantime, and might help to attract the bears. Each took it in turn to keep watch on the upper plateau.

The day passed without a sign of the enemy's existence, and next morning, when they hurried eagerly out to examine the snow, judge their astonishment to find it wholly untouched!

"Capital!" exclaimed Altamont. "The bears are put off the scent; they have no perseverance, and have grown tired waiting for us. They are off, and a good riddance. Now let us start for a day's hunting."

"Softly, softly," said the Doctor; "I'm not so sure they have gone. I think we had better wait one day more. It is evident the bears have not been here last night, at least on this side; but still—"

"Well, let us go right round the plateau, and see how things stand," said the impatient Altamont.

"All right," said Clawbonny. "Come along."

Away they went, but it was impossible to scrutinize carefully a track of two miles, and no trace of the enemy was discoverable.

"Now, then, can't we go hunting?" said Altamont.

"Wait till to-morrow," urged the Doctor again.

His friend was very unwilling to delay, but yielded the point at last, and returned to the fort.

As on the preceding night, each man took his hour's watch on the upper plateau. When it came to Altamont's turn, and he had gone out to relieve Bell, Hatteras called his old companions round him. The Doctor left his desk and Johnson his cooking, and hastened to their captain's side, supposing he wanted to talk over their perilous situation; but Hatteras never gave it a thought.

"My friends," he said, "let us take advantage of the American's absence to speak of business. There are things which cannot concern him, and with which I do not choose him to meddle."

Johnson and Clawbonny looked at each other, wondering what the captain was driving at.

"I wish," he continued, "to talk with you about our plans for the future."

"All right! talk away while we are alone," said the Doctor.

"In a month, or six weeks at the outside, the time for making distant excursions will come again. Have you thought of what we had better undertake in summer?"

"Have you, captain?" asked Johnson.

"Have I? I may say that not an hour of my life passes without revolving in my mind my one cherished purpose. I suppose not a man among you intends to retrace his steps?"

No one replied, and Hatteras went on to say—

"For my own part, even if I must go alone, I will push on to the North Pole. Never were men so near it before, for we are not more than 360 miles distant at most, and I will not lose such an opportunity without making every attempt to reach it, even though it be an impossibility. What are your views, Doctor?"

"Your own, Hatteras."

"And yours, Johnson?"

"Like the Doctor's."

"And yours, Bell?"

"Captain," replied the carpenter, "it is true we have neither wives nor children waiting us in England, but, after all, it is one's country— one's native land! Have you no thoughts of returning home?"

"We can return after we have discovered the Pole quite as well as before, and even better. Our difficulties will not increase, for as we near the Pole we get away from the point of greatest cold. We have fuel and provisions enough. There is nothing to stop us, and we should be culpable, in my opinion, if we allowed ourselves to abandon the project."

"Very well, captain, I'll go along with you."

"That's right; I never doubted you," said Hatteras. "We shall succeed, and England will have all the glory."

"But there is an American among us!" said Johnson.

Hatteras could not repress an impatient exclamation.

"I know it!" he said, in a stern voice.

"We cannot leave him behind," added the Doctor.

"No, we can't," repeated Hatteras, almost mechanically.

"And he will be sure to go too."

"Yes, he will go too; but who will command?"

"You, captain."

"And if you all obey my orders, will the Yankee refuse?"

"I shouldn't think so; but suppose he should, what can be done?"

"He and I must fight it out, then."

The three Englishmen looked at Hatteras, but said nothing. Then the Doctor asked how they were to go.

"By the coast, as far as possible," was the reply.

"But what if we find open water, as is likely enough?"

"Well, we'll go across it."

"But we have no boat."

Hatteras did not answer, and looked embarrassed.

"Perhaps," suggested Bell, "we might make a ship out of some of the planks of the *Porpoise*."

"Never!" exclaimed Hatteras, vehemently.

"Never!" said Johnson.

The Doctor shook his head. He understood the feeling of the captain.

"Never!" reiterated Hatteras. "A boat made out of an American ship would be an American!"

"But, captain——" began Johnson.

The Doctor made a sign to the old boatswain not to press the subject further, and resolved in his own mind to reserve the question for discussion at a more opportune moment. He managed to turn the conversation to other matters, till it abruptly terminated by the entrance of Altamont.

This ended the day, and the night passed quietly without the least disturbance. The bears had evidently disappeared.

CHAPTER XII IMPRISONED IN DOCTOR'S HOUSE

The first business next day was to arrange for a hunt. It was settled that Altamont, Bell, and Hatteras should form the party, while Clawbonny should go and explore as far as Isle Johnson, and make some hydrographic notes and Johnson should remain behind to keep house.

The three hunters soon completed their preparations. They armed themselves each with a double barrelled revolver and a rifle, and took plenty of powder and shot. Each man also carried in his belt his indispensable snow knife and hatchet, and a small supply of pemmican in case night should surprise them before their return.

Thus equipped, they could go far, and might count on a good supply of game.

At eight o'clock they started, accompanied by Duk, who frisked and gambolled with delight. They went up the hill to the east, across the cone, and down into the plain below.

The Doctor next took his departure, after agreeing with Johnson on a signal of alarm in case of danger.

The old boatswain was left alone, but he had plenty to do. He began by unfastening the Greenland dogs, and letting them out for a run after their long, wearisome confinement. Then he attended to divers housekeeping matters. He had to replenish the stock of combustibles and provisions, to arrange the store-houses, to mend several broken utensils, to repair the rents in coverlets, and get new shoes ready for summer excursions. There was no lack of work, and the old sailor's nimble clever fingers could do anything.

While his hands were busy, his mind was occupied with the conversation of the preceding evening. He thought with regret over the captain's obstinacy, and yet he felt that there was something grand and even heroic in his determination that neither an American nor an American ship should first touch the Pole.

The hunters had been gone about an hour when Johnson suddenly heard the report of a gun.

"Capital!" he exclaimed. "They have found something, and pretty quickly too, for me to hear their guns so distinctly. The atmosphere must be very clear."

A second and a third shot followed.

"Bravo!" again exclaimed the boatswain; "they must have fallen in luck's way!"

But when three more shots came in rapid succession, the old man turned pale, and a horrible thought crossed his mind, which made him rush out and climb hastily to the top of the cone. He shuddered at the sight which met his eyes. The three hunters, followed by Duk, were tearing home at full speed, followed by the five huge bears! Their six balls had evidently taken no effect, and the terrible monsters were close on their heels. Hatteras, who brought up the rear, could only manage to keep off his pursuers by flinging down one article after another—first his cap, then his hatchet, and, finally, his gun. He knew that the inquisitive bears would stop and examine every object, sniffing all round it, and this gave him a little time, otherwise he could not have escaped, for these animals outstrip the fleetest horse, and one monster was so near that Hatteras had to brandish his knife vigorously, to ward off a tremendous blow of his paw.

At last, though panting and out of breath, the three men reached Johnson safely, and slid down the rock with him into the snow-house. The bears stopped short on the upper plateau, and Hatteras and his companions lost no time in barring and barricading them out.

"Here we are at last!" exclaimed Hatteras; "we can defend ourselves better now. It is five against five."

"Four!" said Johnson in a frightened voice.

"How?"

"The Doctor!" replied Johnson, pointing to the empty sitting-room.

"Well, he is in Isle Johnson."

"A bad job for him," said Bell.

"But we can't leave him to his fate, in this fashion," said Altamont.

"No, let's be off to find him at once," replied Hatteras.

He opened the door, but soon shut it, narrowly escaping a bear's hug.

"They are there!" he exclaimed.

"All?" asked Bell.

"The whole pack."

Altamont rushed to the windows, and began to fill up the deep embrasure with blocks of ice, which he broke off the walls of the house.

His companions followed his example silently. Not a sound was heard but the low, deep growl of Duk.

To tell the simple truth, however, it was not their own danger that occupied their thoughts, but their absent friend, the Doctor's. It was for him they trembled, not for themselves. Poor Clawbonny, so good and devoted as he had been to every member of the little colony! This was the first time they had been separated from him. Extreme peril, and most likely a frightful death awaited him, for he might return unsuspectingly to Fort Providence, and find himself in the power of these ferocious animals.

"And yet," said Johnson, "unless I am much mistaken, he must be on guard. Your repeated shots cannot but have warned him. He must surely be aware that something unusual has happened."

"But suppose he was too far away to hear them," replied Altamont, "or has not understood the cause of them? It is ten chances to one but he'll come quickly back, never imagining the danger. The bears are screened from sight by the crag completely."

"We must get rid of them before he comes," said Hatteras.

"But how?" asked Bell.

It was difficult to reply to this, for a sortie was out of the question. They had taken care to barricade the entrance passage, but the bears could easily find a way in if they chose. So it was thought advisable to keep a close watch on their movements outside, by listening attentively in each room, so as to be able to resist all attempts at invasion. They could hear them distinctly prowling about, growling and scraping the walls with their enormous paws.

However, some action must be taken speedily, for time was passing. Altamont resolved to try a port-hole through which he might fire on his assailants. He had soon scooped out a hole in the wall, but his gun was hardly pushed through, when it was seized with irresistible force, and wrested from his grasp before he could even fire.

"Confound it!" he exclaimed, "we're no match for them."

And he hastened to stop up the breach as fast as possible.

This state of things had lasted upwards of an hour, and there seemed no prospect of a termination. The question of a *sortie* began now to be seriously discussed. There was little chance of success, as the bears could not be attacked separately, but Hatteras and his companions had grown so impatient, and it must be confessed were also so much ashamed of being kept in prison by beasts, that they would even have dared the risk if the captain had not suddenly thought of a new mode of defence.

He took Johnson's furnace-poker, and thrust it into the stove while he made an opening in the snow wall, or rather a partial opening, for he left a thin sheet of ice on the outer side. As soon as the poker was red hot, he said to his comrades who stood eagerly watching him, wondering what he was going to do—

"This red-hot bar will keep off the bears when they try to get hold of it, and we shall be able easily to fire across it without letting them snatch away our guns."

"A good idea," said Bell, posting himself beside Altamont.

Hatteras withdrew the poker, and instantly plunged it in the wall. The melting snow made a loud hissing noise, and two bears ran and made a snatch at the glowing bar; but they fell back with a terrible howl, and at the same moment four shots resounded, one after the other.

"Hit!" exclaimed Altamont.

"Hit!" echoed Bell.

"Let us repeat the dose," said Hatteras, carefully stopping up the opening meantime.

The poker was again thrust into the fire, and in a few minutes was ready for Hatteras to recommence operations.

Altamont and Bell reloaded their guns, and took their places; but this time the poker would not pass through.

"Confound the beasts!" exclaimed the impetuous American.

"What's the matter?" asked Johnson.

"What's the matter? Why, those plaguey animals are piling up block after block, intending to bury us alive!"

"Impossible!"

"Look for yourself; the poker can't get through. I declare it is getting absurd now."

It was worse than absurd, it was alarming. Things grew worse. It was evident that the bears meant to stifle their prey, for the sagacious animals were heaping up huge masses, which would make escape impossible.

"It is too bad," said old Johnson, with a mortified look. "One might put up with men, but bears!"

Two hours elapsed without bringing any relief to the prisoners; to go out was impossible, and the thick walls excluded all sound. Altamont walked impatiently up and down full of exasperation and excitement at finding himself worsted for once. Hatteras could think of nothing but the Doctor, and of the serious peril which threatened him.

"Oh, if Mr. Clawbonny were only here!" said Johnson.

"What could he do?" asked Altamont.

"Oh, he'd manage to get us out somehow."

"How, pray?" said the American, crossly.

"If I knew that I should not need him. However, I know what his advice just now would be."

"What?"

"To take some food; that can't hurt us. What do you say, Mr. Altamont?"

"Oh, let's eat, by all means, if that will please you, though we're in a ridiculous, not to say humiliating, plight."

"I'll bet you we'll find a way out after dinner."

No one replied, but they seated themselves round the table.

Johnson, trained in Clawbonny's school, tried to be brave and unconcerned about the danger, but he could scarcely manage it. His jokes stuck in his throat. Moreover, the whole party began to feel uncomfortable. The atmosphere was getting dense, for every opening was hermetically sealed. The stoves would hardly draw, and it was evident would soon go out altogether for want of oxygen.

Hatteras was the first to see their fresh danger, and he made no attempt to hide it from his companions.

"If that is the case," said Altamont, "we must get out at all risks."

"Yes," replied Hatteras; "but let us wait till night. We will make a hole in the roof, and let in a provision of air, and then one of us can fire out of it on the bears."

"It is the only thing we can do, I suppose," said Altamont.

So it was agreed; but waiting was hard work, and Altamont could not refrain from giving vent to his impatience by thundering maledictions on the bears, and abusing the ill fate which had placed them in such an awkward and humbling predicament. "It was beasts versus men," he said, "and certainly the men cut a pretty figure."

CHAPTER XIII. THE MINE.

Night drew on, and the lamp in the sitting-room already began to burn dim for want of oxygen.

At eight o'clock the final arrangements were completed, and all that remained to do was to make an opening in the roof.

They had been working away at this for some minutes, and Bell was showing himself quite an adept in the business, when Johnson, who had been keeping watch in the sleeping room, came hurriedly in to his companions, pulling such a long face, that the captain asked immediately what was the matter?

"Nothing exactly," said the old sailor, "and yet—"

"Come, out with it!" exclaimed Altamont.

"Hush! don't you hear a peculiar noise?"

"Where?"

"Here, on this side, on the wall of the room."

Bell stopped working, and listened attentively like the rest. Johnson was right; a noise there certainly was on the side wall, as if some one were cutting the ice.

"Don't you hear it?" repeated Johnson.

"Hear it? Yes, plain enough," replied Altamont.

"Is it the bears?" asked Bell.

"Most assuredly."

"Well; they have changed their tactics," said old Johnson, "and given up the idea of suffocating us."

"Or may be they suppose we are suffocated by now," suggested the American, getting furious at his invisible enemies.

"They are going to attack us," said Bell.

"Well, what of it?" returned Hatteras.

"We shall have a hand-to-hand struggle, that's all."

"And so much the better," added Altamont; "that's far more to my taste; I have had enough of invisible foes—let me see my antagonist, and then I can fight him."

"Ay," said Johnson; "but not with guns. They would be useless here."

"With knife and hatchet then," returned the American.

The noise increased, and it was evident that the point of attack was the angle of the wall formed by its junction with the cliff.

"They are hardly six feet off now," said the boatswain.

"Right, Johnson!" replied Altamont; "but we have time enough to be ready for them."

And seizing a hatchet, he placed himself in fighting attitude, planting his right foot firmly forward and throwing himself back.

Hatteras and the others followed his example, and Johnson took care to load a gun in case of necessity.

Every minute the sound came nearer, till at last only a thin coating separated them from their assailants.

Presently this gave way with a loud crack, and a huge dark mass rolled over into the room.

Altamont had already swung his hatchet to strike, when he was arrested by a well-known voice, exclaiming—

"For Heaven's sake, stop!"

"The Doctor! the Doctor!" cried Johnson.

And the Doctor it actually was who had tumbled in among them in such undignified fashion.

"How do ye do, good friends?" he said, picking himself smartly up.

His companions stood stupefied for a moment, but joy soon loosened their tongues, and each rushed eagerly forward to welcome his old comrade with a loving embrace. Hatteras was for once fairly overcome with emotion, and positively hugged him like a child.

"And is it really you, Mr. Clawbonny?" said Johnson.

"Myself and nobody else, my old fellow. I assure you I have been far more uneasy about you than you could have been about me."

"But how did you know we had been attacked by a troop of bears?" asked Altamont. "What we were most afraid of was that you would come quickly back to Fort Providence, never dreaming of danger."

"Oh, I saw it all. Your repeated shots gave me the alarm. When you commenced firing I was beside the wreck of the *Porpoise*, but I climbed up a hummock, and discovered five bears close on your heels. Oh, how anxious I was for you! But when I saw you disappear down the cliff, while the bears stood hesitating on the edge, as if uncertain what to do, I felt sure that you had managed to get safely inside the house and barricade it. I crept cautiously nearer, sometimes going on all-fours, sometimes slipping between great blocks of ice, till I came at last quite close to our fort, and then I found the bears working away like beavers. They were prowling about the snow, and dragging enormous blocks of ice towards the house, piling them up like a wall, evidently intending to bury you alive. It is a lucky thing they did not take it into their heads to dash down the blocks from the summit of the cone, for you must have been crushed inevitably."

"But what danger you were in, Mr. Clawbonny," said Bell. "Any moment they might have turned round and attacked you."

"They never thought of it even. Johnson's Greenland dogs came in sight several times, but they did not take the trouble to go after them. No, they imagined themselves sure of a more savoury supper!"

"Thanks for the compliment!" said Altamont, laughing.

"Oh, there is nothing to be proud of. When I saw what the bears were up to, I determined to get back to you by some means or other. I waited till night, but as soon as it got dark I glided noiselessly along towards the powder-magazine. I had my reasons for choosing that point from which to work my way hither, and I speedily commenced operations with my snow-knife. A famous tool it is. For three mortal hours I have been hacking and heaving away, but here I am at last tired enough and starving, but still safe here."

"To share our fate!" said Altamont.

"No, to save you all; but, for any sake, give me a biscuit and a bit of meat, for I feel sinking for want of food."

CHAPTER XIII. THE MINE.

A substantial meal was soon before him, but the vivacious little man could talk all the while he was eating, and was quite ready to answer any questions.

"Did you say *to save us*?" asked Bell.

"Most assuredly!" was the reply.

"Well, certainly, if you found your way in, we can find our way out by the same road."

"A likely story, and leave the field clear for the whole pack to come in and find out our stores. Pretty havoc they would make!"

"No, we must stay here," said Hatteras.

"Of course we must," replied Clawbonny, "but we'll get rid of the bears for all that."

"I told you so," said Johnson, rubbing his hands. "I knew nothing was hopeless if Mr. Clawbonny was here; he has always some expedient in his wise head."

"My poor head is very empty, I fear, but by dint of rummaging perhaps I——"

"Doctor," interrupted Altamont, "I suppose there is no fear of the bears getting in by the passage you have made?"

"No, I took care to stop up the opening thoroughly, and now we can reach the powder-magazine without letting them see us."

"All right; and now will you let us have your plan of getting rid of these comical assailants?"

"My plan is quite simple, and part of the work is done already."

"What do you mean?"

"You shall see. But I am forgetting that I brought a companion with me."

"What do you say?" said Johnson.

"I have a companion to introduce to you," replied the Doctor, going out again into the passage, and bringing back a dead fox, newly killed.

"I shot it this morning," he continued, "and never did fox come more opportunely."

"What on earth do you mean?" asked Altamont.

"I mean to blow up the bears *en masse* with 100 lbs of powder."

"But where is the powder?" exclaimed his friend.

"In the magazine. This passage will lead to it. I made it purposely."

"And where is the mine to be?" inquired Altamont.

"At the furthest point from the house and stores."

"And how will you manage to entice the bears there, all to one spot?"

"I'll undertake that business; but we have talked enough, let us set to work. We have a hundred feet more to add to our passage to-night, and that is no easy matter, but as there are five of us, we can take turns at it. Bell will begin, and we will lie down and sleep meantime."

"Well, really," said Johnson, "the more I think of it, the more feasible seems the Doctor's plan."

"It is a sure one, anyway," said Clawbonny.

"So sure that I can feel the bear's fur already on my shoulder. Well, come, let's begin then."

Away he went into the gloomy passage, followed by Bell, and in a few moments they had reached the powder-magazine, and stood among the well- arranged barrels. The Doctor pointed out to his companion the exact spot where he began excavating, and then left him to his task, at which he laboured diligently for about an hour, when Altamont came to relieve him. All the snow he had dug out was taken to the kitchen and melted, to prevent its taking up room.

The captain succeeded Altamont, and was followed by Johnson. In ten hours—that is to say, about eight in the morning—the gallery was entirely open.

With the first streak of day, the Doctor was up to reconnoitre the position of the enemy. The patient animals were still occupying their old position, prowling up and down and growling. The house had already almost disappeared beneath the piled-up blocks of ice, but even while he gazed a council of war seemed being held, which evidently resulted in the determination to alter the plan of action, for suddenly all the five bears began vigorously to pull down these same heaped-up blocks.

"What are they about?" asked Hatteras, who was standing beside him.

"Well, they look to me to be bent on demolishing their own work, and getting right down to us as fast as possible; but wait a bit, my gentlemen, we'll demolish you first. However, we have not a minute to lose."

Hastening away to the mine, he had the chamber where the powder was to be lodged enlarged the whole breadth and height of the sloping rock against which the wall leaned, till the upper part was about a foot thick, and had to be propped up to prevent its falling in. A strong stake was fixed firmly on the granite foundation, on the top of which the dead fox was fastened. A rope was attached to the lower part of the stake, sufficiently long to reach the powder stores.

"This is the bait," he said, pointing to the dead fox, "and here is the mine," he added, rolling in a keg of powder containing about 100 lbs.

"But, Doctor," said Hatteras, "won't that blow us up too, as well as the bears?"

"No, we shall be too far from the scene of explosion. Besides, our house is solid, and we can soon repair the walls even if they should get a bit shaken."

"And how do you propose to manage?" asked Altamont.

"See! By hauling in this rope we lower the post which props up the roof, and make it give way, and bring up the dead fox to light, and I think you will agree with me that the bears are so famished with their long fasting, that they won't lose much time in rushing towards their unexpected meal. Well, just at that very moment, I shall set fire to the mine, and blow up both the guests and the meal."

"Capital! Capital!" shouted Johnson, who had been listening with intense interest.

Hatteras said nothing, for he had such absolute confidence in his friend that he wanted no further explanation. But Altamont must know the why and wherefore of everything.

"But Doctor," he said, "can you reckon on your match so exactly that you can be quite sure it will fire the mine at the right moment?"

"I don't need to reckon at all; that's a difficulty easily got over."

"Then you have a match a hundred feet long?"

"No."

"You are simply going to lay a train of powder."

"No, that might miss fire."

"Well, there is no way then but for one of us to devote his life to the others, and go and light the powder himself."

"I'm ready," said Johnson, eagerly, "ready and willing."

"Quite useless my brave fellow," replied the Doctor, holding out his hand. "All our lives are precious, and they will be all spared, thank God!"

"Well, I give it up!" said the American. "I'll make no more guesses."

"I should like to know what is the good of learning physics," said the Doctor, smiling, "if they can't help a man at a pinch like this. Haven't we an electric battery, and long enough lines attached to it to serve our purpose? We can fire our mine whenever we please in an instant, and without the slightest danger."

"Hurrah!" exclaimed Johnson.

"Hurrah!" echoed the others, without heeding whether the enemy heard them or not.

CHAPTER XIII. THE MINE.

The Doctor's idea was immediately carried out, and the connecting lines uncoiled and laid down from the house to the chamber of the mine, one end of each remaining attached to the electric pile, and the other inserted into the keg of powder.

By nine o'clock everything was ready. It was high time, for the bears were furiously engaged in the work of demolition. Johnson was stationed in the powder-magazine, in charge of the cord which held the bait.

"Now," said Clawbonny to his companions, "load your guns, in case our assailants are not killed. Stand beside Johnson, and the moment the explosion is over rush out."

"All right," said Altamont.

"And now we have done all we can to help ourselves. So may Heaven help us!"

Hatteras, Altamont, and Bell repaired to the powder-magazine, while the Doctor remained alone beside the pile.

Soon he heard Johnson's voice in the distance calling out "Ready."

"All right," was the reply.

Johnson pulled his rope vigorously, and then rushed to the loop-hole to see the effect. The thin shell of ice had given way, and the body of the fox lay among the ruins. The bears were somewhat scared at first, but the next minute had eagerly rushed to seize the booty.

"Fire!" called out Johnson, and at once the electric spark was sent along the lines right into the keg of powder. A formidable explosion ensued; the house was shaken as if by an earthquake, and the walls cracked asunder. Hatteras, Altamont, and Bell hurried out with the guns, but they might spare their shot, for four of the bears lay dead, and the fifth, half roasted, though alive, was scampering away in terror as fast as his legs could carry him.

"Hurrah! Three cheers for Clawbonny," they shouted and overwhelmed the Doctor with plaudits and thanks.

CHAPTER XIV. AN ARCTIC SPRING.

The prisoners were free, and their joy found vent in the noisiest demonstrations. They employed the rest of the day in repairing the house, which had suffered greatly by the explosion. They cleared away the blocks piled up by the animals, and filled up the rents in the walls, working with might and main, enlivened by the many songs of old Johnson.

Next morning there was a singular rise in the temperature, the thermometer going up to 15° above zero.

This comparative heat lasted several days. In sheltered spots the glass rose as high as 31°, and symptoms of a thaw appeared.

The ice began to crack here and there, and jets of salt water were thrown up, like fountains in an English park. A few days later, the rain fell in torrents.

Thick vapour rose from the snow, giving promise of the speedy disappearance of these immense masses. The sun's pale disc became deeper in colour, and remained longer above the horizon. The night was scarcely longer than three hours.

Other tokens of spring's approach were manifest of equal significance, the birds were returning in flocks, and the air resounded with their deafening cries. Hares were seen on the shores of the bay, and mice in such abundance that their burrows completely honeycombed the ground.

The Doctor drew the attention of his companions to the fact, that almost all these animals were beginning to lose their white winter dress, and would soon put on summer attire, while nature was already providing mosses, and poppies, and saxifragas, and short grass for their sustenance. A new world lay beneath that melting snow.

But with these inoffensive animals came back their natural enemies. Foxes and wolves arrived in search of their prey, and dismal howls broke the silence of the short night.

Arctic wolves closely resemble dogs, and their barking would deceive the most practised ears; even the canine race themselves have been deceived by it. Indeed, it seems as if the wily animals employed this ruse to attract the dogs, and make them their prey. Several navigators have mentioned the fact, and the Doctor's own experience confirmed it. Johnson took care not to let his Greenlanders loose; of Duk there was little fear; nothing could take him in.

For about a fortnight hunting was the principal occupation. There was an abundant supply of fresh meat to be had. They shot partridges, ptarmigans, and snow ortolans, which are delicious eating. The hunters never went far from Fort Providence, for game was so plentiful that it seemed waiting their guns, and the whole bay presented an animated appearance.

The thaw, meanwhile, was making rapid progress. The thermometer stood steadily at 32° above zero, and the water ran down the mountain sides in cataracts, and dashed in torrents through the ravines.

The Doctor lost no time in clearing about an acre of ground, in which he sowed the seeds of anti-scorbutic plants. He just had the pleasure of seeing tiny little green leaves begin to sprout, when the cold returned in full force.

In a single night, the thermometer lost nearly 40°; it went down to 8° below zero. Everything was frozen—birds, quadrupeds, amphibia disappeared as if by magic; seal-holes reclosed, and the ice once more became hard as granite.

The change was most striking; it occurred on the 18th of May, during the night. The Doctor was rather disappointed at having all his work to do again, but Hatteras bore the grievance most unphilosophically, as it interfered with all his plans of speedy departure.

"Do you think we shall have a long spell of this weather, Mr. Clawbonny?" asked Johnson.

"No, my friend, I don't; it is a last blow from the cold. You see these are his dominions, and he won't be driven out without making some resistance."

"He can defend himself pretty well," said Bell, rubbing his face.

"Yes; but I ought to have waited, and not have wasted my seed like an ignoramus; and all the more as I could, if necessary, have made them sprout by the kitchen stoves."

"But do you mean to say," asked Altamont, "that you might have anticipated the sudden change?"

"Of course, and without being a wizard. I ought to have put my seed under the protection of Saint Paucratius and the other two saints, whose fête days fall this month."

"Absurd! Pray tell me what they have to do with it? What influence can they possibly have on the temperature?"

"An immense one, if we are to believe horticulturists, who call them the patron saints of the frost."

"And for what reason?"

"Because generally there is a periodical frost in the month of May, and it is coldest from the 11th to the 13th. That is the fact."

"And how is it explained?"

"In two ways. Some say that a larger number of asteroids come between the earth and the sun at this time of year, and others that the mere melting of the snow necessarily absorbs a large amount of heat, and accounts for the low temperature. Both theories are plausible enough, but the fact remains whichever we accept, and I ought to have remembered it."

The Doctor was right, for the cold lasted till the end of the month, and put an end to all their hunting expeditions. The old monotonous life in-doors recommenced, and was unmarked by any incident except a serious illness which suddenly attacked Bell. This was violent quinsy, but, under the Doctor's skilful treatment, it was soon cured. Ice was the only remedy he employed, administered in small pieces, and in twenty- four hours Bell was himself again.

During this compulsory leisure, Clawbonny determined to have a talk with the captain on an important subject—the building of a sloop out of the planks of the *Porpoise*.

The Doctor hardly knew how to begin, as Hatteras had declared so vehemently that he would never consent to use a morsel of American wood; yet it was high time he were brought to reason, as June was at hand, the only season for distant expeditions, and they could not start without a ship.

He thought over it a long while, and at last drew the captain aside, and said in the kindest, gentlest way—

"Hatteras, do you believe I'm your friend?"

"Most certainly I do," replied the captain, earnestly; "my best, indeed my only friend."

"And if I give you a piece of advice without your asking, will you consider my motive is perfectly disinterested?"

"Yes, for I know you have never been actuated by self-interest. But what are you driving at?"

"Wait, Hatteras, I have one thing more to ask. Do you look on me as a true-hearted Englishman like yourself, anxious for his country's glory?"

Hatteras looked surprised, but simply said—

"I do."

"You desire to reach the North Pole," the Doctor went on; "and I understand and share your ambition, but to achieve your object you must employ the right means."

"Well, and have I not sacrificed everything for it?"

"No, Hatteras, you have not sacrificed your personal antipathies. Even at this very moment I know you are in the mood to refuse the indispensable conditions of reaching the pole."

"Ah! it is the boat you want to talk about, and that man——"

"Hatteras, let us discuss the question calmly, and examine the case on all sides. The coast on which we find ourselves at present may terminate abruptly; we have no proof that it stretches right away to the pole; indeed, if your present information prove correct, we ought to come to an open sea during the summer months. Well, supposing we reach this Arctic Ocean and find it free from ice and easy to navigate, what shall we do if we have no ship?"

Hatteras made no reply.

"Tell me, now, would you like to find yourself only a few miles from the pole and not be able to get to it?"

Hatteras still said nothing, but buried his head in his hands.

"Besides," continued the Doctor, "look at the question in its moral aspect. Here is an Englishman who sacrifices his fortune, and even his life, to win fresh glory for his country, but because the boat which bears him across an unknown ocean, or touches the new shore, happens to be made of the planks of an American vessel—a cast-away wreck of no use to anyone—will that lessen the honour of the discovery? If you yourself had found the hull of some wrecked vessel lying deserted on the shore, would you have hesitated to make use of it; and must not a sloop built by four Englishmen and manned by four Englishmen be English from keel to gunwale?"

Hatteras was still silent.

"No," continued Clawbonny; "the real truth is, it is not the sloop you care about: it is the man."

"Yes, Doctor, yes," replied the captain. "It is this American I detest; I hate him with a thorough English hatred. Fate has thrown him in my path."

"To save you!"

"To ruin me. He seems to defy me, and speaks as if he were lord and master. He thinks he has my destiny in his hands, and knows all my projects. Didn't we see the man in his true colours when we were giving names to the different coasts? Has he ever avowed his object in coming so far north? You will never get out of my head that this man is not the leader of some expedition sent out by the American government."

"Well, Hatteras, suppose it is so, does it follow that this expedition is to search for the North Pole? May it not be to find the North-West Passage? But anyway, Altamont is in complete ignorance of our object, for neither Johnson, nor Bell, nor myself, have ever breathed a word to him about it, and I am sure you have not."

"Well, let him always remain so."

"He must be told in the end, for we can't leave him here alone."

"Why not? Can't he stay here in Fort Providence?"

"He would never consent to that, Hatteras; and, moreover, to leave a man in that way, and not know whether we might find him safe when we came back, would be worse than imprudent: it would be inhuman. Altamont will come with us; he must come. But we need not disclose our projects; let us tell him nothing, but simply build a sloop for the ostensible purpose of making a survey of the coast."

Hatteras could not bring himself to consent, but said—

"And suppose the man won't allow his ship to be cut up?"

"In that case, you must take the law in your own hands, and build a vessel in spite of him."

"I wish to goodness he would refuse, then!"

"He must be asked before he can refuse. I'll undertake the asking," said Clawbonny.

He kept his word, for that very same night, at supper, he managed to turn the conversation towards the subject of making excursions during summer for hydrographical purposes.

"You will join us, I suppose, Altamont," he said.

"Of course," replied the American. "We must know how far New America extends."

Hatteras looked fixedly at his rival, but said nothing.

"And for that purpose," continued Altamont, "we had better build a little ship out of the remains of the *Porpoise*. It is the best possible use we can make of her."

"You hear, Bell," said the Doctor, eagerly. "We'll all set to work to-morrow morning."

CHAPTER XV. THE NORTH-WEST PASSAGE.

Next morning, Altamont Bell and the Doctor repaired to the *Porpoise*. There was no lack of wood, for, shattered as the old "three-master" had been by the icebergs, she could still supply the principal parts of a new ship, and the carpenter began his task immediately.

In the end of May, the temperature again rose, and spring returned for good and all. Rain fell copiously, and before long the melting snow was running down every little slope in falls and cascades.

Hatteras could not contain his delight at these signs of a general thaw among the ice-fields, for an open sea would bring him liberty. At last he might hope to ascertain for himself whether his predecessors were correct in their assertions about a polar basin.

This was a frequent topic of thought and conversation with him, and one evening when he was going over all the old familiar arguments in support of his theory, Altamont took up the subject, and declared his opinion that the polar basin extended west as well as east. But it was impossible for the American and Englishman, to talk long about anything without coming to words, so intensely national were both. Dr. Kane was the first bone of contention on this occasion, for the jealous Englishman was unwilling to grant his rival the glory of being a discoverer, alleging his belief that though the brave adventurer had gone far north, it was by mere chance he had made a discovery.

"Chance!" interrupted Altamont, hotly. "Do you mean to assert that it is not to Kane's energy and science that we owe his great discovery?"

"I mean to say that Dr. Kane's name is not worth mentioning in a country made illustrious by such names as Parry, and Franklin, and Ross, and Belcher, and Penny; in a country where the seas opened the North- West Passage to an Englishman—McClure!"

"McClure!" exclaimed the American. "Well, if ever chance favoured anyone it was that McClure. Do you pretend to deny it?"

"I do," said Hatteras, becoming quite excited. "It was his courage and perseverance in remaining four whole winters among the ice."

"I believe that, don't I?" said Altamont, sneeringly. "He was caught among the bergs and could not get away; but didn't he after all abandon his ship, the *Investigator*, and try to get back home? Besides, putting the man aside, what is the value of his discovery? I maintain that the North-West Passage is still undiscovered, for not a single ship to this day has ever sailed from Behring's Straits to Baffin's Bay!"

The fact was indisputable, but Hatteras started to his feet, and said—

"I will not permit the honour of an English captain to be attacked in my presence any longer!"

"You will not permit!" echoed Altamont, also springing erect. "But these are facts, and it is out of your power to destroy them!"

"Sir!" shouted Hatteras, pale with rage.

"My friends!" interposed the Doctor; "pray be calm. This is a scientific point we are discussing."

But Hatteras was deaf to reason now, and said angrily—

"I'll tell you the facts, sir."

"And I'll tell you," retorted the irate American.

"Gentlemen," said Clawbonny, in a firm tone; "allow me to speak, for I know the facts of the case as well as and perhaps better than you, and I can state them impartially."

"Yes, yes!" cried Bell and Johnson, who had been anxiously watching the strife.

"Well, go on," said Altamont, finding himself in the minority, while Hatteras simply made a sign of acquiescence, and resumed his seat.

The Doctor brought a chart and spread it out on the table, that his auditors might follow his narration intelligibly, and be able to judge the merits of McClure for themselves.

"It was in 1848," he said, "that two vessels, the *Herald* and the *Plover*, were sent out in search of Franklin, but their efforts proving ineffectual, two others were despatched to assist them— the *Investigator*, in command of McClure, and the *Enterprise*, in command of Captain Collison. The *Investigator* arrived first in Behring's Straits, and without waiting for her consort, set out with the declared purpose to find Franklin or the North-West Passage. The gallant young officer hoped to push north as far as Melville Sound, but just at the extremity of the Strait, he was stopped by an insurmountable barrier of ice, and forced to winter there. During the long, dreary months, however, he and his officers undertook a journey over the ice-field, to make sure of its communicating with Melville Sound."

"Yes, but he did not get through," said Altamont.

"Stop a bit," replied Clawbonny; "as soon as a thaw set in, McClure renewed his attempt to bring his ship into Melville Sound, and had succeeded in getting within twenty miles, when contrary winds set in, and dragged her south with irresistible violence. This decided the captain to alter his course. He determined to go in a westerly direction; but after a fearful struggle with icebergs, he stuck fast in the first of the series of straits

which end in Baffin's Bay, and was obliged to winter in Mercy Bay. His provisions would only hold out eighteen months longer, but he would not give up. He set out on a sledge, and reached Melville Island, hoping to fall in with some ship or other, but all he found in Winter Harbour was a cairn, which contained a document, stating that Captain Austin's lieutenant, McClintock, had been there the preceding year. McClure replaced this document by another, which stated his intention of returning to England by the North-West Passage he had discovered, by Lancaster Sound and Baffin's Bay, and that in the event of his not being heard of, he might be looked for north or west of Melville Island. Then he went back to Mercy Bay with undaunted courage, to pass a third winter. By the beginning of March his stock of provisions was so reduced in consequence of the utter scarcity of game through the severity of the season, that McClure resolved to send half his men to England, either by Baffin's Bay or by McKenzie River and Hudson's Bay. The other half would manage to work the vessel to Europe. He kept all his best sailors, and selected for departure only those to whom a fourth winter would have been fatal. Everything was arranged for their leaving, and the day fixed, when McClure, who was out walking with Lieutenant Craswell, observed a man running towards them, flinging up his arms and gesticulating frantically, and on getting nearer recognized him as Lieutenant

Prim, officer on board the *Herald*, one of the ships he had parted with in Behring's Straits two years before.

Captain Kellett, the Commander, had reached Winter Harbour, and finding McClure's document in the cairn, had dispatched his lieutenant in search of him. McClure accompanied him back, and arranged with the captain to send him his batch of invalids. Lieutenant Craswell took charge of these and conveyed them safely to Winter Harbour. Leaving them there he went across the ice four hundred and seventy miles, and arrived at Isle Beechy, where, a few days afterwards, he took passage with twelve men on board the *Phoenix*, and reached London safely on the 7th of October, 1853, having traversed the whole extent between Behring's Straits and Cape Farewell."

"Well, if arriving on one side and leaving at the other is not going through, I don't know what is!" said Hatteras.

"Yes, but he went four hundred and seventy miles over ice-fields," objected Altamont.

"What of that?"

"Everything; that is the gist of the whole argument. It was not the *Investigator* that went through."

"No," replied Clawbonny, "for, at the close of the fourth winter, McClure was obliged to leave her among the ice."

"Well, in maritime expeditions the vessel has to get through, and not the man; and if ever the Northwest Passage is practicable, it will be for ships and not sledges. If a ship cannot go, a sloop must."

"A sloop!" exclaimed Hatteras, discovering a hidden meaning in the words.

"Altamont," said the Doctor, "your distinction is simply puerile, and in that respect we all consider that you are in the wrong."

"You may easily do that," returned the American. "It is four against one, but that will not prevent me from holding my own opinion."

"Keep it and welcome, but keep it to yourself, if you please, for the future," exclaimed Hatteras.

"And pray what right have you to speak to me like this, sir?" shouted Altamont, in a fury.

"My right as captain," returned Hatteras, equally angry.

"Am I to submit to your orders, then?"

"Most assuredly, and woe to you if——"

The Doctor did not allow him to proceed, for he really feared the two antagonists might come to blows. Bell and Johnson seconded his endeavours to make peace, and, after a few conciliatory words, Altamont turned on his heel, and walked carelessly away, whistling "Yankee Doodle." Hatteras went outside, and paced up and down with rapid strides. In about an hour he came back, and retired to bed without saying another word.

CHAPTER XVI. ARCTIC ARCADIA

On the 29th of May, for the first time, the sun never set. His glowing disc just touched the boundary line of the horizon, and rose again immediately. The period was now entered when the day lasts twenty- four hours.

Next morning there was a magnificent halo; the monarch of day appeared surrounded by a luminous circle, radiant with all the prismatic colours. This phenomenon never lost its charm, for the Doctor, however frequently it occurred, and he always noted carefully down all particulars respecting it.

Before long the feathered tribes began to return, filling the air with their discordant cries. Flocks of bustards and Canadian geese from Florida or Arkansas came flying north with marvellous rapidity, bringing spring beneath their wings. The Doctor shot several, and among them one or two cranes and a solitary stork.

The snow was now fast melting, and the ice-fields were covered with "slush." All round the bay large pools had formed, between which the soil appeared as if some product of spring.

The Doctor recommenced his sowing, for he had plenty of seed; but he was surprised to find sorrel growing already between the half-dried stones, and even pale sickly heaths, trying to show their delicate pink blossoms.

At last it began to be really hot weather. On the 15th of June, the thermometer stood at 57° above zero. The Doctor scarcely believed his eyes, but it was a positive fact, and it was soon confirmed by the changed appearance of the country.

An excursion was made to Isle Johnson, but it turned out to be a barren little islet of no importance whatever, though it gave the old boatswain infinite pleasure to know that those sea girt rocks bore his name.

There was some danger of both house and stores melting, but happily this high temperature proved exceptional, the thermometer seldom averaging much above freezing point.

By the middle of June, the sloop had made good progress, and already presented a shapely appearance. As Bell and Johnson took the work of construction entirely on themselves, the others went hunting, and succeeded in killing several deer, in spite of its being difficult game to approach. Altamont adopted the Indian practice of crawling on all fours, and adjusting his gun and arms so as to simulate horns and deceive the timid animal, till he could get near enough to take good aim.

Their principal object of pursuit, however, was the musk-ox, which Parry had met with in such numbers in Melville Island; but not a solitary specimen was to be seen anywhere about Victoria Bay, and a distant excursion was, therefore, resolved upon, which would serve the double purpose of hunting and surveying the eastern coast.

The three hunters, accompanied by Duk, set out on Monday, the 17th of June, at six in the morning, each man armed with a double-barrelled gun, a hatchet and snow-knife, and provisions for several days.

It was a fine bright morning, and by ten o'clock they had gone twelve miles; but not a living thing had crossed their path, and the hunt threatened to turn out a mere excursion.

However, they went on in hope, after a good breakfast and half-an- hour's rest.

The ground was getting gradually lower, and presented a peculiar appearance from the snow, which lay here and there in ridges unmelted. At a distance it looked like the sea when a strong wind is lashing up the waves, and cresting them with a white foam.

Before long they reached a sort of glen, at the bottom of which was a winding river. It was almost completely thawed, and already the banks were clothed with a species of vegetation, as if the sun had done his best to fertilise the soil.

"I tell you what," said the Doctor, "a few enterprising colonists might make a fine settlement here. With a little industry and perseverance wonders might be done in this country. Ah! if I am not much mistaken, it has some four-footed inhabitants already. Those frisky little fellows know the best spots to choose."

"Hares! I declare. That's jolly! " said Altamont, loading his gun.

"Stop!" cried the Doctor; "stop, you furious hunter. Let the poor little things alone; they are not thinking of running away. Look, they are actually coming to us, I do believe!"

He was right, for presently three or four young hares, gambolling away among the fresh moss and tiny heaths, came running about their legs so fearlessly and trustfully, that even Altamont was disarmed. They

rubbed against the Doctor's knees, and let him stroke them till the kind-hearted man could not help saying to Altamont—

"Why give shot to those who come for caresses? The death of these little beasts could do us no good."

"You say what's true, Clawbonny. Let them live!" replied Hatteras.

"And these ptarmigans too, I suppose, and these long-legged plovers," added Altamont, as a whole covey of birds flew down among the hunters, never suspecting their danger. Duk could not tell what to make of it, and stood stupefied.

It was a strange and touching spectacle to see the pretty creatures; they flew on Clawbonny's shoulders, and lay down at his feet as if inviting friendly caresses, and doing their utmost to welcome the strangers. The whole glen echoed with their joyous cries as they darted to and fro from all parts. The good Doctor seemed some mighty enchanter.

The hunters had continued their course along the banks of the river, when a sudden bend in the valley revealed a herd of deer, eight or ten in number, peacefully browsing on some lichens that lay half-buried in the snow. They were charming creatures, so graceful and gentle, male and female, both adorned with noble antlers, wide-spreading and deeply-notched. Their skin had already lost its winter whiteness, and began to assume the brown tint of summer. Strange to say, they appeared not a whit more afraid than the birds or hares.

The three men were now right in the centre of the herd, but not one made the least movement to run away. This time the worthy Doctor had far more difficulty in restraining Altamont's impatience, for the mere sight of such magnificent animals roused his hunting instincts, and he became quite excited; while Hatteras, on the contrary, seemed really touched to see the splendid creatures rubbing their heads so affectionately and trustfully against the good Clawbonny, the friend of every living thing.

"But, I say," exclaimed Altamont, "didn't we come out expressly to hunt?"

"To hunt the musk-ox, and nothing else," replied Clawbonny. "Besides, we shouldn't know what to do with this game, even if we killed it; we have provisions enough. Let us for once enjoy the sight of men and animals in perfect amity."

"It proves no human beings have been here before," said Hatteras.

"True, and that proves something more, these animals are not of American origin."

"How do you make that out?" said Altamont.

"Why, if they had been born in North America they would have known how to treat that mammiferous biped called man, and would have fled at the first glimpse of us. No, they are from the north, most likely from the untrodden wilds of Asia, so Altamont, you have no right to claim them as fellow-countrymen."

"Oh! a hunter doesn't examine his game so closely as all that. Everything is grist that comes to his mill."

"All right. Calm yourself, my brave Nimrod! For my own part, I would rather never fire another shot than make one of these beautiful creatures afraid of me. See, even Duk fraternizes with them. Believe me, it is well to be kind where we can. Kindness is power."

"Well, well, so be it," said Altamont, not at all understanding such scruples. "But I should like to see what you would do if you had no weapon but kindness among a pack of bears or wolves! You wouldn't make much of it."

"I make no pretensions to charm wild beasts. I don't believe much in Orpheus and his enchantments. Besides, bears and wolves would not come to us like these hares, and partridges, and deer."

"Why not? They have never seen human beings either."

"No but they are savage by nature," said Clawbonny, "and ferocity, like wickedness, engenders suspicion. This is true of men as well as animals."

They spent the whole day in the glen, which the Doctor christened "Arctic Arcadia," and when evening came they lay down to rest in the hollow of a rock, which seemed as if expressly prepared for their accommodation.

CHAPTER XVII. ALTAMONT'S REVENGE.

Next morning, as the fine weather still continued, the hunters determined to have another search for the musk ox. It was only fair to give Altamont a chance, with the distinct understanding that he should have the right of firing, however fascinating the game they might meet. Besides, the flesh of the musk ox, though a little too highly impregnated with the smell, is savoury food, and the hunters would gladly carry back a few pounds of it to Fort Providence.

During the first part of the day, nothing occurred worth mentioning, but they noticed a considerable change in the aspect of the country, and appearances seemed to indicate that they were approaching a hilly region. This New America was evidently either a continent or an island of considerable extent.

Duk was running far ahead of his party when he stopped suddenly short, and began sniffing the ground as if he had caught scent of game. Next minute he rushed forward again with extreme rapidity, and was speedily out of sight. But loud distinct barking convinced the hunters that the faithful fellow had at last discovered the desired object.

They hurried onwards, and after an hour and a half's quick walking, found him standing in front of two formidable looking animals, and barking furiously. The Doctor recognized them at once as belonging to the musk ox, or *Ovibos* genus, as naturalists call it, by the very wide horns touching each other at their base, by the absence of muzzle, by the narrow square chanfrin resembling that of a sheep, and by the very short tail. Their hair was long and thickly matted, and mixed with fine brown, silky wool.

These singular-looking quadrupeds were not the least afraid of Duk, though extremely surprised; but at the first glimpse of the hunters they took flight, and it was no easy task to go after them, for half an hour's swift running brought them no nearer, and made the whole party so out of breath, that they were forced to come to a halt.

"Confound the beasts!" said Altamont.

"Yes, Altamont, I'll make them over to you," replied Clawbonny; "they are true Americans, and they don't appear to have a very favourable idea of their fellow countrymen."

"That proves our hunting prowess," rejoined Altamont.

Meantime the oxen finding themselves no longer pursued, had stopped short. Further pursuit was evidently useless. If they were to be captured at all they must be surrounded, and the plateau which they first happened to have reached, was very favourable for the purpose. Leaving Duk to worry them, they went down by the neighbouring ravines; and got to the one end of the plateau, where Altamont and the Doctor hid themselves behind projecting rocks, while Hatteras went on to the other end, intending to startle the animals by his sudden appearance, and drive them back towards his companions.

"I suppose you have no objection this time to bestow a few bullets on these gentry?" said Altamont.

"Oh, no, it is 'a fair field now and no favour,'" returned Clawbonny.

The oxen had begun to shake themselves impatiently at Duk, trying to kick him off, when Hatteras started up right in front of them, shouting and chasing them back. This was the signal for Altamont and the Doctor to rush forward and fire, but at the sight of two assailants, the terrified animals wheeled round and attacked Hatteras. He met their onset with a firm, steady foot, and fired straight at their heads. But both his balls were powerless, and only served still further to madden the enraged beasts. They rushed upon the unfortunate man like furies, and threw him on the ground in an instant.

"He is a dead man!" exclaimed the Doctor, in despairing accents.

A tremendous struggle was going on in Altamont's breast at the sight of his prostrate foe, and though his first impulse was to hasten to his help, he stopped short, battling with himself and his prejudices. But his hesitation scarcely lasted half a second, his better self conquered, and exclaiming,

"No, it would be cowardly!" he rushed forward with Clawbonny.

Hatteras full well understood how his rival felt, but would rather have died than have begged his intervention. However, he had hardly time to think about it, before Altamont was at his side.

He could not have held out much longer, for it was impossible to ward off the blows of horns and hoofs of two such powerful antagonists, and in a few minutes more he must have been torn to pieces. But suddenly two shots resounded, and Hatteras felt the balls graze his head.

"Courage!" shouted Altamont, flinging away his discharged weapon, and throwing himself right in front of the raging animals. One of them, shot to the heart, fell dead as he reached the spot, while the other dashed madly on Hatteras, and was about to gore the unfortunate captain with his horns, when Altamont plunged his snow knife far into the beast's wide open jaws with one hand, with the other dealt him such a tremendous blow on the head with his hatchet, that the skull was completely split open.

It was done so quickly that it seemed like a flash of lightning, and all was over. The second ox lay dead, and Clawbonny shouted "Hurrah! hurrah!" Hatteras was saved.

He owed his life to the man he hated the most. What a storm of conflicting passions this must have roused in his soul! But where was the emotion he could not master?

However, his action was prompt, whatever his feeling might be. Without a moment's hesitancy, he went up to his rival, and said in a grave voice—

"Altamont, you have saved my life!"

"You saved mine," replied the American.

There was a moment's silence, and then Altamont added—

"We're quits, Hatteras."

"No, Altamont," said the captain; "when the Doctor dragged you out of your icy tomb, I did not know who you were; but you saved me at the peril of your own life, knowing quite well who I was."

"Why, you are a fellow-creature at any rate, and whatever faults an American may have, he is no coward."

"No, indeed," said the Doctor. "He is a man, every inch as much as yourself, Hatteras."

"And like me, he shall have part in the glory that awaits us."

"The glory of reaching the North Pole?" asked Altamont.

"Yes," replied Hatteras, proudly.

"I guessed right, then," said Altamont.

"And you have actually dared to conceive such a project? Oh! it is grand; I tell you it is sublime even to think of it?"

"But tell me," said Hatteras in a hurried manner; "you were not bound for the Pole then yourself?"

Altamont hesitated.

"Come, speak out, man," urged the Doctor.

"Well, to tell the truth, I was not, and the truth is better than self-love. No, I had no such grand purpose in view. I was trying to clear the North-West Passage, and that was all."

"Altamont," said Hatteras, holding out his hand; "be our companion to glory, come with us and find the North Pole."

The two men clasped hands in a warm, hearty grasp, and the bond of friendship between them was sealed.

When they turned to look for the Doctor they found him in tears.

"Ah! friends," he said, wiping his eyes; "you have made me so happy, it is almost more than I can bear' You have sacrificed this miserable nationality for the sake of the common cause. You have said, 'What does it matter if only the Pole is discovered, whether it is by an Englishman or an American?' Why should we brag of being American or English, when we can boast that we are men?"

The good little man was beside himself with joy He hugged the reconciled enemies to his bosom, and cemented their friendship by his own affection to both.

At last he grew calm after at least a twentieth embrace, and said—

"It is time I went to work now. Since I am no hunter, I must use my talents in another direction"

And he began to cut up the oxen so skilfully, that he seemed like a surgeon making a delicate autopsy.

His two companions looked on smiling. In a few minutes the adroit operator had cut off more than a hundred pounds of flesh. This he divided into three parts. Each man took one, and they retraced their steps to Fort Providence.

At ten o'clock they arrived at Doctor's House, where Johnson and Bell had a good supper prepared for them.

But before sitting down to enjoy it, the Doctor exclaimed in a jubilant tone, and pointing to his two companions—

"My dear old Johnson, I took out an American and an Englishman with me, didn't I?"

"Yes, Mr. Clawbonny."

"Well, I bring back two brothers."

This was joyous news to the sailors, and they shook hands warmly with Altamont; while the Doctor recounted all that had passed, and how the American captain had saved the English captain's life. That night no five happier men could have been found than those that lay sleeping in the little snow house.

CHAPTER XVIII. FINAL PREPARATIONS

Next day the weather changed, the cold returned. Snow, and rain, and tempest came in quick succession for several days.

Bell had completed the sloop, and done his work well, for the little vessel was admirably adapted for the purpose contemplated, being high at the sides and partly decked so as to be able to stand a heavy sea, and yet light enough to be drawn on the sledge without overburdening the dogs.

At last a change of the greatest importance took place. The ice began to tremble in the centre of the bay, and the highest masses became loosened at their base ready to form icebergs, and drift away before the first gale; but Hatteras would not wait for the ice-fields to break up before he started. Since the journey must be made on land, he did not care whether the sea was open or not; and the day of departure was fixed for the 25th of June—Johnson and Bell undertaking the necessary repairs of the sledge.

On the 20th, finding there was space enough between the broken ice to allow the sloop to get through, it was determined to take her a trial trip to Cape Washington.

The sea was not quite open but it would have been impossible to go across on foot.

This short sail of six hours sufficiently tested the powers of the sloop, and proved her excellent qualities. In coming back they witnessed a curious sight; it was the chase of a seal by a gigantic bear. Mr. Bruin was too busily engaged to notice the vessel, or he would have pursued; he was intently watching beside a seal hole with the patience of a true hunter, or rather angler, for he was certainly fishing just then. He watched in absolute silence, without stirring or giving the least sign of life.

But all of a sudden there was a slight disturbance on the surface of the water in the hole, which announced the coming up of the amphibious animal to breathe. Instantly the bear lay flat on his belly with his two paws stretched round the opening.

Next minute up came the seal, but his head no sooner appeared above the water than the bear's paws closed about him like a vice, and dragged him right out. The poor seal struggled desperately, but could not free himself from the iron grasp of his enemy, who hugged him closer and closer till suffocation was complete. Then he carried him off to his den as if the weight were nothing, leaping lightly from pack to pack till he gained *terra firma* safely.

On the 22nd of June, Hatteras began to load the sledge. They put in 200 lbs. of salt meat, three cases of vegetables and preserved meat, besides lime-juice, and flour, and medicines. They also took 200 lbs. of powder and a stock of fire-arms. Including the sloop and the Halkett- boat, there was about 1500 lbs. weight, a heavy

load for four dogs, and all the more as they would have to drag it every day, instead of only four days successively, like the dogs employed by the Esquimaux, who always keep a relay for their sledges. However, the distance to the Pole was not 150 miles at the outside, and they did not intend to go more than twelve miles a day, as they could do it comfortably in a month. Even if land failed them, they could always fall back on the sloop, and finish the journey without fatigue to men or dogs.

All the party were in excellent health, though they had lost flesh a little; but, by attending to the Doctor's wise counsels, they had weathered the winter without being attacked by any of the maladies incident to the climate.

Now, they were almost at their journey's end, and not one doubted of success, for a common bond of sympathy bound fast the five men, and made them strong to persevere.

On Sunday, the 23rd, all was ready, and it was resolved to devote the entire day to rest.

The dwellers on Fort Providence could not see the last day dawn without some emotion. It cost them a pang to leave the snow-hut which had served them in such good stead, and this hospitable shore where they had passed the winter. Take it altogether, they had spent very happy hours there, and the Doctor made a touching reference to the subject as they sat round the table at the evening meal, and did not forget to thank God for his manifest protection.

They retired early to rest, for they needed to be up betimes. So passed the last night in Fort Providence.

CHAPTER XIX. MARCH TO THE NORTH

Next day at early dawn, Hatteras gave the signal for departure. The well-fed and well-rested dogs were harnessed to the sledge. They had been having a good time of it all the winter, and might be expected to do good service during the summer.

It was six in the morning when the expedition started. After following the windings of the bay and going past Cape Washington, they struck into the direct route for the north, and by seven o'clock had lost sight of the lighthouse and Fort Providence.

During the first two days they made twenty miles in twelve hours, devoting the remainder of the time to rest and meals. The tent was quite sufficient protection during sleep.

The temperature began to rise. In many places the snow melted entirely away, and great patches of water appeared; here and there complete ponds, which a little stretch of imagination might easily convert into lakes. The travellers were often up to their knees, but they only laughed over it; and, indeed, the Doctor was rather glad of such unexpected baths.

"But for all that," he said, "the water has no business to wet us here. It is an element which has no right to this country, except in a solid or vaporous state. Ice or vapour is all very well, but water— never!"

Hunting was not forgotten during the march, for fresh meat was a necessity. Altamont and Bell kept their guns loaded, and shot ptarmigans, guillemots, geese, and a few young hares; but, by degrees, birds and animals had been changing from trustfulness to fear, and had become so shy and difficult to approach, that very often, but for Duk, the hunters would have wasted their powder.

Hatteras advised them not to go more than a mile away, as there was not a day, nor even an hour, to lose, for three months of fine weather was the utmost they could count upon. Besides, the sledge was often coming to difficult places, when each man was needed to lend a helping hand.

On the third day they came to a lake, several acres in extent, and still entirely frozen over. The sun's rays had little access to it, owing to its situation, and the ice was so strong that it must have dated from some remote winter. It was strong enough to bear both the travellers and their sledge, and was covered with dry snow.

From this point the country became gradually lower, from which the Doctor concluded that it did not extend to the Pole, but that most probably this New America was an island.

Up to this time the expedition had been attended with no fatigue. The travellers had only suffered from the intense glare of the sun on the snow, which threatened them with snow-blindness. At another time of the year they might have avoided this by walking during the night, but at present there was no night at all. Happily the snow was beginning to melt, and the brilliancy would diminish as the process of dissolution advanced.

On the 28th of June the thermometer rose to 45°, and the rain fell in torrents. Hatteras and his companions, however, marched stoically on, and even hailed the downpour with delight, knowing that it would hasten the disappearance of the snow.

As they went along, the Doctor often picked up stones, both round ones and flat pebbles, as if worn away by the tide. He thought from this they must be near the Polar Basin, and yet far as the eye could reach was one interminable plain.

There was not a trace of houses, or huts, or cairns visible. It was evident that the Greenlanders had not pushed their way so far north, and yet the famished tribes would have found their account in coming, for the country abounded in game. Bears were frequently seen, and numerous herds of musk-oxen and deer.

On the 29th, Bell killed a fox and Altamont a musk-ox. These supplies of fresh food were very acceptable, and even the Doctor surveyed, with considerable satisfaction, the haunches of meat they managed to procure from time to time.

"Don't let us stint ourselves," he used to say on these occasions; "food is no unimportant matter in expeditions like ours."

"Especially," said Johnson, "when a meal depends on a lucky shot."

"You're right, Johnson; a man does not think so much about dinner when he knows the soup-pot is simmering by the kitchen-fire."

On the 30th, they came to a district which seemed

to have been upturned by some volcanic convulsion, so covered was it with cones and sharp lofty peaks.

A strong breeze from the south-east was blowing, which soon increased to a hurricane, sweeping over the rocks covered with snow and the huge masses, of ice, which took the forms of icebergs and hummocks, though on dry land.

The tempest was followed by damp, warm weather, which caused a regular thaw.

On all sides nothing could be heard but the noise of cracking ice and falling avalanches.

The travellers had to be very careful in avoiding hills, and even in speaking aloud, for the slightest agitation in the air might have caused a catastrophe. Indeed, the suddenness is the peculiar feature in Arctic

avalanches, distinguishing them from those of Switzerland and Norway. Often the dislodgment of a block of ice is instantaneous, and not even a cannon-ball or thunderbolt could be more rapid in its descent. The loosening, the fall, and the crash happen almost simultaneously.

Happily, however, no accident befel any of the party, and three days afterwards they came to smooth, level ground again.

But here a new phenomenon met their gaze—a phenomenon which was long a subject of patient inquiry among the learned of both hemispheres. They came to a long chain of low hills which seemed to extend for miles, and were all covered on the eastern side with bright red snow.

It is easy to imagine the surprise and half-terrified exclamations of the little company at the sight of this long red curtain; but the Doctor hastened to reassure them, or rather to instruct them, as to the nature of this peculiar snow. He told them that this same red substance had been found in Switzerland, in the heart of the Alps, and that the colour proceeded solely from the presence of certain corpuscles, about the nature of which for a long time chemists could not agree. They could not decide whether these corpuscles were of animal or vegetable origin, but at last it was settled that they belonged to the family of fungi, being a sort of microscopic champignon of the species *Uredo*.

Turning the snow over with his iron-tipped staff, the Doctor found that the colouring matter measured nine feet deep. He pointed this out to his companions, that they might have some idea of the enormous number of these tiny mushrooms in a layer extending so many miles.

This phenomenon was none the less strange for being explained, for red is a colour seldom seen in nature over any considerable area. The reflection of the sun's rays upon it produced the most peculiar effect, lighting up men, and animals, and rocks with a fiery glow, as if proceeding from some flame within. When the snow melted it looked like blood, as the red particles do not decompose. It seemed to the travellers as if rivulets of blood were running among their feet.

The Doctor filled several bottles with this precious substance to examine at leisure, as he had only had a glimpse of the Crimson Cliffs in Baffin's Bay.

This Field of Blood, as he called it, took three hours to get over, and then the country resumed its usual aspect.

CHAPTER XX. FOOTPRINTS IN THE SNOW.

On the fourth of July there was such an exceedingly dense fog, that it was very difficult to keep the straight course for the north. No misadventure, however, befel the party during the darkness, except the loss of Bell's snow-shoes. At Bell's suggestion, which fired the Doctor's inventive genius, torches were contrived, made of tow steeped in spirits-of-wine and fastened on the end of a stick, and these served somewhat to help them on, though they made but small progress; for, on the sixth, after the fog had cleared off, the Doctor took their bearings, and found that they had only been marching at the rate of eight miles a day.

Determined to make up for lost time, they rose next morning very early and started off, Bell and Altamont as usual going ahead of the rest and acting as scouts. Johnson and the others kept beside the sledge, and were soon nearly two miles behind the guides; but the weather was so dry and clear that all their movements could be distinctly observed.

"What now? " said Clawbonny, as he saw them make a sudden halt, and stoop down as if examining the ground.

"I was just wondering what they are about, myself," replied old Johnson.

"Perhaps they have come on the tracks of animals," suggested Hatteras.

"No," said Clawbonny, "it can't be that."

"Why not?"

"Because Duk would bark."

"Well, it is quite evident they are examining some sort of marks."

"Let's get on, then," said Hatteras; and, urging forward the dogs, they rejoined their companions in about twenty minutes, and shared their surprise at finding unmistakable fresh footprints of human beings in the snow, as plain as if only made the preceding day.

"They are Esquimaux footprints," said Hatteras.

"Do you think so?" asked Altamont.

"There is no doubt of it."

"But what do you make of this, then?" returned Altamont, pointing to another footmark repeated in

several places. "Do you believe for a minute that was made by an Esquimaux?"

It was incontestably the print of a European boot—nails, sole, and heel clearly stamped in the snow. There was no room for doubt, and Hatteras exclaimed in amazement—

"Europeans here!"

"Evidently," said Johnson.

"And yet it is so improbable that we must take a second look before pronouncing an opinion," said Clawbonny.

CHAPTER XX. FOOTPRINTS IN THE SNOW.

But the longer he looked, the more apparent became the fact. Hatteras was chagrined beyond measure. A European here, so near the Pole!

The footprints extended for about a quarter of a mile, and then diverged to the west. Should the travellers follow them further?

"No," said Hatteras, "let us go on."

He was interrupted by an exclamation from the Doctor, who had just picked up an object that gave still more convincing proof of European origin. It was part of a pocket spyglass!

"Well, if we still had any doubts about the footmarks, this settles the case at once, at any rate," said Clawbonny.

"Forward!" exclaimed Hatteras so energetically, that instinctively each one obeyed, and the march was resumed forthwith.

The day wore away, but no further sign of the presence of suspected rivals was discovered, and they prepared to encamp for the night.

The tent was pitched in a ravine for shelter, as the sky was dark and threatening, and a violent north wind was blowing.

"I'm afraid we'll have a bad night," said Johnson.

" A pretty noisy one, I expect," replied the Doctor, "but not cold. We had better take every precaution, and fasten down our tent with good big stones."

"You are right, Mr. Clawbonny. If the hurricane swept away our tent, I don't know where we should find it again."

The tent held fast, but sleep was impossible, for the tempest was let loose and raged with tremendous violence.

"It seems to me," said the Doctor, during a brief lull in the deafening roar," as if I could hear the sound of collisions between icebergs and ice-fields. If we were near the sea, I could really believe there was a general break-up in the ice."

"I can't explain the noises any other way," said Johnson.

"Can we have reached the coast, I wonder?" asked Hatteras.

"It is not impossible," replied Clawbonny. "Listen! Do you hear that crash? That is certainly the sound of icebergs falling. We cannot be very far from the ocean."

"Well, if it turn out to be so, I shall push right on over the ice- fields."

"Oh, they'll be all broken up after such a storm as this. We shall see what to-morrow, brings; but all I can say is, if any poor fellows are wandering about in a night like this, I pity them.

The storm lasted for ten hours, and the weary travellers anxiously watched for the morning. About daybreak its fury seemed to have spent itself, and Hatteras, accompanied by Bell and Altamont, ventured to leave the tent. They climbed a hill about three hundred feet high, which commanded a wide view. But what a metamorphosed region met their gaze! All the ice had completely vanished, the storm had chased away the winter, and stripped the soil everywhere of its snow covering.

But Hatteras scarcely bestowed a glance on surrounding objects; his eager gaze was bent on the northern horizon, which appeared shrouded in black mist.

"That may very likely be caused by the ocean," suggested Clawbonny.

"You are right. The sea must be there," was the reply.

"That tint is what we call the *blink* of open water," said Johnson.

"Come on, then, to the sledge at once, and let us get to this unknown ocean," exclaimed Hatteras.

Their few preparations were soon made, and the march resumed. Three hours afterwards they arrived at the coast, and shouted simultaneously, "The sea! the sea!"

"Ay, and open sea!" added Hatteras.

And so it was. The storm had opened wide the Polar Basin, and the loosened packs were drifting in all directions. The icebergs had weighed anchor, and were sailing out into the open sea.

This new ocean stretched far away out of sight, and not a single island or continent was visible.

On the east and west the coast formed two capes or headlands, which sloped gently down to the sea. In the centre, a projecting rock formed a small natural bay, sheltered on three sides, into which a wide river fell, bearing in its bosom the melted snows of winter.

After a careful survey of the coast, Hatteras determined to launch the sloop that very day, and to unpack the sledge, and get everything on board. The tent was soon put up, and a comfortable repast prepared. This important business despatched, work commenced; and all hands were so expeditious and willing, that by five

o'clock nothing more remained to be done. The sloop lay rocking gracefully in the little bay, and all the cargo was on board except the tent, and what was required for the night's encampment.

The sight of the sloop suggested to Clawbonny the propriety of giving Altamont's name to the little bay. His proposition to that effect met with unanimous approval, and the port was forthwith dignified by the title of Altamont Harbour.

According to the Doctor's calculations the travellers were now only 9° distant from the Pole. They had gone over two hundred miles from Victoria Bay to Altamont Harbour, and were in latitude 87° 5' and longitude 118° 35'.

CHAPTER XXI. THE OPEN SEA.

Next morning by eight o'clock all the remaining effects were on board, and the preparations for departure completed. But before starting the Doctor thought he would like to take a last look at the country and see if any further traces of the presence of strangers could be discovered, for the mysterious footmarks they had met with were never out of his thoughts. He climbed to the top of a height which commanded a view of the whole southern horizon, and took out his pocket telescope. But what was his astonishment, to find he could see nothing through it, not even neighbouring objects. He rubbed his eyes and looked again, but with no better result. Then he began to examine the telescope, the object glass was gone!

The object glass! This explained the whole mystery, foot-prints and all; and with a shout of surprise he hurried down the hill to impart his discovery to the wondering companions, who came running towards him, startled by his loud exclamation, and full of anxiety at his precipitate descent.

"Well, what is the matter now?" said Johnson.

The Doctor could hardly speak, he was so out of breath. At last he managed to gasp out—

"The tracks, footmarks, strangers."

"What?" said Hatteras, "strangers here?"

"No, no, the object glass; the object glass out of my telescope."

And he held out his spy-glass for them to look at.

"Ah! I see," said Altamont; "it is wanting."

"Yes."

"But then the footmarks?"

"They were ours, friends, just ours," exclaimed the Doctor. "We had lost ourselves in the fog, and been wandering in a circle."

"But the boot-marks," objected Hatteras.

"Bell's. He walked about a whole day after he had lost his snow shoes."

"So I did," said Bell.

The mistake was so evident, that they all laughed heartily, except Hatteras, though no one was more glad than he at the discovery.

A quarter of an hour afterwards the little sloop sailed out of Altamont Harbour, and commenced her voyage of discovery. The wind was favourable, but there was little of it, and the weather was positively warm.

The sloop was none the worse for the sledge journey. She was in first-rate trim, and easily managed. Johnson steered, the Doctor, Bell, and the American leaned back against the cargo, and Hatteras stood at the prow, his fixed, eager gaze bent steadily on that mysterious point towards which he felt drawn with irresistible power, like the magnetic needle to the Pole. He wished to be the first to descry any shore that might come in sight, and he had every right to the honour.

The water of this Polar Sea presented some peculiar features worth mentioning. In colour it was a faint ultramarine blue, and possessed such wonderful transparency that one seemed to gaze down into fathomless depths. These depths were lighted up, no doubt, by some electrical phenomenon, and so many varieties of living creatures were visible that the vessel seemed to be sailing over a vast aquarium.

Innumerable flocks of birds were flying over the surface of this marvellous ocean, darkening the sky like thick heavy storm-clouds. Water-fowl of every description were among them, from the albatross to the penguin, and all of gigantic proportions. Their cries were absolutely deafening, and some of them had such immense, wide-spreading wings, that they covered the sloop completely as they flew over. The Doctor thought himself a good naturalist, but he found his science greatly at fault, for many a species here was wholly unknown to any ornithological society.

The good little man was equally nonplussed when he looked at the water, for he saw the most wonderful medusæ, some so large that they looked like little islands floating about among Brobdignagian sea-weeds. And below the surface, what a spectacle met the eye! Myriads of fish of every species; young manati at play with each other; narwhals with their one strong weapon of defence, like the horn of a unicorn, chasing the timid seals; whales of every tribe, spouting out columns of water and mucilage, and filling the air with a peculiar whizzing noise; dolphins, seals, and walruses; sea-dogs and sea-horses, sea-bears and sea-elephants, quietly browsing on submarine pastures; and the Doctor could gaze at them all as easily and clearly as if they were in glass tanks in the Zoological Gardens.

There was a strange supernatural purity about the atmosphere. It seemed charged to overflowing with oxygen, and had a marvellous power of exhilaration, producing an almost intoxicating effect on the brain.

Towards evening, Hatteras and his companions lost sight of the coast. Night came on, though the sun remained just above the horizon; but it had the same influence on animated nature as in temperate zones. Birds, fish, and all the cetacea disappeared and perfect silence prevailed.

Since the departure from Altamont Harbour, the sloop had made one degree further north. The next day brought no signs of land; there was not even a speck on the horizon. The wind was still favourable, and the sea pretty calm. The birds and fishes returned as numerously as on the preceding day, and the Doctor leaning over the side of the vessel, could see the whales and the dolphins, and all the rest of the monsters of the deep, gradually coming up from the clear depths below. On the surface, far as the eye could reach, nothing was visible except a solitary iceberg here and there, and a few scattered floes.

Indeed, but little ice was met with anywhere. The sloop was ten degrees above the point of greatest cold, and consequently in the same temperature as Baffin's Bay and Disko. It was therefore not astonishing that the sea should be open in these summer months.

This is a fact of great practical value, for if ever the whalers can penetrate north as far as the Polar basin, they may be sure of an immediate cargo, as this part of the ocean seems the general reservoir of whales and seals, and every marine species.

The day wore on, but still nothing appeared on the horizon. Hatteras never left the prow of the ship, but stood, glass in hand, eagerly gazing into the distance with anxious, questioning eyes, and seeking to discover, in the colour of the water, the shape of the waves, and the breath of the wind, indications of approaching land.

CHAPTER XXII. GETTING NEAR THE POLE.

Hour after hour passed away, and still Hatteras persevered in his weary watch, though his hopes appeared doomed to disappointment.

At length, about six in the evening, a dim, hazy, shapeless sort of mist seemed to rise far away between sea and sky. It was not a cloud, for it was constantly vanishing, and then reappearing next minute.

Hatteras was the first to notice this peculiar phenomenon; but after an hour's scrutiny through his telescope, he could make nothing of it.

All at once, however, some sure indication met his eye, and stretching out his arm to the horizon, he shouted, in a clear ringing voice—-

"Land! land!"

His words produced an electrical effect on his companions, and every man rushed to his side.

"I see it, I see it," said Clawbonny.

"Yes, yes, so do I! " exclaimed Johnson.

"It is a cloud," said Altamont.

"Land! land!" repeated Hatteras, in tones of absolute conviction.

Even while he spoke the appearance vanished, and when it returned again the Doctor fancied he caught a gleam of light about the smoke for an instant.

"It is a volcano!" he exclaimed.

"A volcano?" repeated Altamont.

"Undoubtedly."

"In so high a latitude?"

"Why not? Is not Iceland a volcanic island—indeed, almost made of volcanoes, one might say?"

"Well, has not our famous countryman, James Ross, affirmed the existence of two active volcanoes, the Erebus and the Terror, on the Southern Continent, in longitude 170° and latitude 78°? Why, then, should not volcanoes be found near the North Pole?"

"It is possible, certainly," replied Altamont.

"Ah, now I see it distinctly," exclaimed the Doctor." It is a volcano!"

"Let us make right for it then," said Hatteras.

It was impossible longer to doubt the proximity of the coast. In twenty-four hours, probably, the bold navigators might hope to set foot on its untrodden soil. But strange as it was, now that they were so near the goal of their voyage, no one showed the joy which might have been expected. Each man sat silent, absorbed in his own thoughts, wondering what sort of place this Pole must be. The birds seemed to shun it, for though it was evening, they were all flying towards the south with outspread wings. Was it, then, so inhospitable, that not so much as a sea-gull or a ptarmigan could find a shelter? The fish, too, even the large cetacea, were hastening away through the transparent waters. What could cause this feeling either of repulsion or terror?

At last sleep overcame the tired men, and one after another dropped off, leaving Hatteras to keep watch.

He took the helm, and tried his best not to close his eyes, for he grudged losing precious time; but the slow motion of the vessel rocked him into a state of such irresistible somnolence that, in spite of himself, he was soon, like his companions, locked fast in deep slumber. He began to dream, and imagination brought back all the scenes of his past life. He dreamt of his ship, the *Forward*, and of the traitors that had burnt it. Again he felt all the agonies of disappointment and failure, and forgot his actual situation. Then the scene changed, and he saw himself at the Pole unfurling the Union Jack!

While memory and fancy were thus busied, an enormous cloud of an olive tinge had begun to darken sea and sky. A hurricane was at hand. The first blast of the tempest roused the captain and his companions, and they were on their feet in an instant, ready to meet it. The sea had risen tremendously, and the ship was tossing violently up and down on the billows. Hatteras took the helm again, and kept a firm hold of it, while Johnson and Bell baled out the water which was constantly dashing over the ship.

It was a difficult matter to preserve the right course, for the thick fog made it impossible to see more than a few yards off.

This sudden tempest might well seem to such excited men, a stern prohibition against further approach to the Pole; but it needed but a glance at their resolute faces to know that they would neither yield to winds nor waves, but go right on to the end.

For a whole day the struggle lasted, death threatening them each moment; but about six in the evening, just as the fury of the waves seemed at its highest pitch, there came a sudden calm. The wind was stilled as if miraculously, and the sea became smooth as glass.

Then came a most extraordinary inexplicable phenomenon.

The fog, without dispersing, became strangely luminous, and the sloop sailed along in a zone of electric light. Mast, sail, and rigging appeared pencilled in black against the phosphorescent sky with wondrous distinctness. The men were bathed in light, and their faces shone with a fiery glow.

"The volcano!" exclaimed Hatteras.

"Is it possible?" said Bell.

"No, no!" replied Clawbonny. "We should be suffocated with its flames so near."

"Perhaps it is the reflection," suggested Altamont.

"Not that much even, for then we must be near land, and in that case we should hear the noise of the eruption."

"What is it, then?" asked the captain.

"It is a cosmical phenomenon," replied the Doctor, "seldom met hitherto. If we go on, we shall soon get out of our luminous sphere and be back in the darkness and tempest again."

"Well, let's go on, come what may," said Hatteras.

The Doctor was right. Gradually the fog began to lose its light, and then its transparency, and the howling wind was heard not far off. A few minutes more, and the little vessel was caught in a violent squall, and swept back into the cyclone.

But the hurricane had fortunately turned a point towards the south, and left the vessel free to run before the wind straight towards the Pole. There was imminent danger of her sinking, for she sped along at frenzied speed, and any sudden collision with rock or iceberg must have inevitably dashed her to pieces.

CHAPTER XXII. GETTING NEAR THE POLE.

But not a man on board counselled prudence. They were intoxicated with the danger, and no speed could be quick enough to satisfy their longing impatience to reach the unknown.

At last they began evidently to near the coast. Strange symptoms were manifest in the air; the fog suddenly rent like a curtain torn by the wind; and for an instant, like a flash of lightning, an immense column of flame was seen on the horizon.

"The volcano! the volcano!" was the simultaneous exclamation.

But the words had hardly passed their lips before the fantastic vision had vanished. The wind suddenly changed to south-east, and drove the ship back again from the land.

"Confound it!" said Hatteras; "we weren't three miles from the coast."

However, resistance was impossible. All that could be done was to keep tacking; but every few minutes the little sloop would be thrown on her side, though she righted herself again immediately obedient to the helm.

As Hatteras stood with dishevelled hair, grasping the helm as if welded to his hand, he seemed the animating soul of the ship.

All at once, a fearful sight met his gaze.

Scarcely twenty yards in front was a great block of ice coming right towards them, mounting and falling on the stormy billows, ready to overturn at any moment and crush them in its descent.

But this was not the only danger that threatened the bold navigators. The iceberg was packed with white bears, huddling close together, and evidently beside themselves with terror.

The iceberg made frightful lurches, sometimes inclining at such a sharp angle that the animals rolled pell-mell over each other and set up a loud growling, which mingled with the roar of the elements and made a terrible concert.

For a quarter of an hour, which seemed a whole century, the sloop sailed on in this formidable company, sometimes a few yards distant and sometimes near enough to touch. The Greenland dogs trembled for fear, but Duk was quite imperturbable. At last the iceberg lost ground, and got driven by the wind further and further away till it disappeared in the fog, only at intervals betraying its presence by the ominous growls of its equipage.

The storm now burst forth with redoubled fury. The little barque was lifted bodily out of the water, and whirled round and round with the most frightful rapidity. Mast and sail were torn off, and went flying away through the darkness like some large white bird. A whirlpool began to form among the waves, drawing down the ship gradually by its irresistible suction.

Deeper and deeper she sank, whizzing round at such tremendous speed that to the poor fellows on board, the water seemed motionless. All five men stood erect, gazing at each other in speechless terror. But suddenly the ship rose perpendicularly, her prow went above the edge of the vortex, and getting out of the centre of attraction by her own velocity, she escaped at a tangent from the circumference, and was thrown far beyond, swift as a ball from a cannon's mouth.

Altamont, the Doctor, Johnson, and Bell were pitched flat on the planks. When they got up, Hatteras had disappeared!

It was two o'clock in the morning.

CHAPTER XXIII. THE ENGLISH FLAG

For a few seconds they seemed stupefied, and then a cry of "Hatteras!" broke from every lip.

On all sides, nothing was visible but the tempestuous ocean. Duk barked desperately, and Bell could hardly keep him from leaping into the waves.

"Take the helm, Altamont," said the Doctor, "and let us try our utmost to find our poor captain."

Johnson and Bell seized the oars, and rowed about for more than an hour; but their search was vain— Hatteras was lost!

Lost! and so near the Pole, just as he had caught sight of the goal!

The Doctor called, and shouted, and fired signals, and Duk made piteous lamentations; but there was no response. Clawbonny could bear up no longer; he buried his head in his hands, and fairly wept aloud.

At such a distance from the coast, it was impossible Hatteras could reach it alive, without an oar or even so much as a spar to help him; if ever he touched the haven of his desire, it would be as a swollen, mutilated corpse!

Longer search was useless, and nothing remained but to resume the route north. The tempest was dying out, and about five in the morning on the 11th of July, the wind fell, and the sea gradually became calm. The sky recovered its polar clearness, and less than three miles away the land appeared in all its grandeur.

The new continent was only an island, or rather a volcano, fixed like a lighthouse on the North Pole of the world.

The mountain was in full activity, pouring out a mass of burning stones and glowing rock. At every fresh eruption there was a convulsive heaving within, as if some mighty giant were respiring, and the masses ejected were thrown up high into the air amidst jets of bright flame, streams of lava rolling down the sides in impetuous torrents. In one part, serpents of fire seemed writhing and wriggling amongst smoking rocks, and in another the glowing liquid fell in cascades, in the midst of purple vapour, into a river of fire below, formed of a thousand igneous streams, which emptied itself into the sea, the waters hissing and seething like a boiling cauldron.

Apparently there was only one crater to the volcano, out of which the columns of fire issued, streaked with forked lightning. Electricity seemed to have something to do with this magnificent panorama.

Above the panting flames waved an immense plume-shaped cloud of smoke, red at its base and black at its summit. It rose with incomparable majesty, and unrolled in thick volumes.

CHAPTER XXIII. THE ENGLISH FLAG

The sky was ash-colour to a great height, and it was evident that the darkness that had prevailed while the tempest lasted, which had seemed quite inexplicable to the Doctor, was owing to the columns of cinders overspreading the sun like a thick curtain. He remembered a similar phenomenon which occurred in the Barbadoes, where the whole island was plunged in profound obscurity by the mass of cinders ejected from the crater of Isle St. Vincent.

This enormous ignivomous rock in the middle of the sea was six thousand feet high, just about the altitude of Hecla.

It seemed to rise gradually out of the water as the boat got nearer. There was no trace of vegetation, indeed there was no shore; the rock ran straight down to the sea.

"Can we land?" said the Doctor.

"The wind is carrying us right to it," said Altamont. "But I don't see an inch of land to set our foot upon."

"It seems so at this distance," said Johnson; "but we shall be sure to find some place to run in our boat at, and that is all we want."

"Let us go on, then," said Clawbonny, dejectedly.

He had no heart now for anything. The North Pole was indeed before his eyes, but not the man who had discovered it.

As they got nearer the island, which was not more than eight or ten miles in circumference, the navigators noticed a tiny fiord, just large enough to harbour their boat, and made towards it immediately. They feared their captain's dead body would meet their eyes on the coast, and yet it seemed difficult for a corpse to lie on it, for there was no shore, and the sea broke on steep rocks, which were covered with cinders above watermark.

At last the little sloop glided gently into the narrow opening between two sandbanks just visible above the water, where she would be safe from the violence of the breakers; but before she could be moored, Duk began howling and barking again in the most piteous manner, as if calling on the cruel sea and stony rocks to yield up his lost master. The Doctor tried to calm him by caresses, but in vain. The faithful beast, as if he would represent the captain, sprang on shore with a tremendous bound, sending a cloud of cinders after him.

"Duk! Duk!" called Clawbonny.

But Duk had already disappeared.

After the sloop was made fast, they all got out and went after him. Altamont was just going to climb to the top of a pile of stones, when the Doctor exclaimed, "Listen!"

Duk was barking vehemently some distance off, but his bark seemed full of grief rather than fury.

"Has he come on the track of some animal, do you think? " asked Johnson.

"No, no!" said Clawbonny, shuddering. "His bark is too sorrowful; it is the dog's tear. He has found the body of Hatteras."

They all four rushed forward, in spite of the blinding cinder-dust, and came to the far-end of a fiord, where they discovered the dog barking round a corpse wrapped in the British flag!

"Hatteras! Hatteras!" cried the Doctor, throwing himself on the body of his friend. But next minute he started up with an indescribable cry, and shouted, "Alive! alive!"

"Yes!" said a feeble voice; "yes, alive at the North Pole, on *Queen's Island*."

"Hurrah for England!" shouted all with one accord.

"And for America!" added Clawbonny, holding out one hand to Hatteras and the other to Altamont.

Duk was not behind with his hurrah, which was worth quite as much as the others.

For a few minutes the joy of recovery of their captain filled all their hearts, and the poor fellows could not restrain their tears.

The Doctor found, on examination, that he was not seriously hurt. The wind threw him on the coast where landing was perilous work, but, after being driven back more than once into the sea, the hardy sailor had managed to scramble on to a rock, and gradually to hoist himself above the waves.

Then he must have become insensible, for he remembered nothing more except rolling himself in his flag. He only awoke to consciousness with the loud barking and caresses of his faithful Duk.

After a little, Hatteras was able to stand up supported by the Doctor, and tried to get back to the sloop.

He kept exclaiming, "The Pole! the North Pole!"

"You are happy now?" said his friend.

"Yes, happy! And are not you? Isn't it joy to find yourself here! The ground we tread is round the Pole! The air we breathe is the air that blows round the Pole! The sea we have crossed is the sea which washes the Pole! Oh! the North Pole! the North Pole!"

He had become quite delirious with excitement, and fever burned in his veins. His eyes shone with unnatural brilliancy, and his brain seemed on fire. Perfect rest was what he most needed, for the Doctor found it impossible to quiet him.

A place of encampment must therefore be fixed upon immediately.

Altamont speedily discovered a grotto composed of rocks, which had so fallen as to form a sort of cave. Johnson and Bell carried in provisions, and gave the dogs their liberty.

About eleven o'clock, breakfast, or rather dinner, was ready, consisting of pemmican, salt meat, and smoking-hot tea and coffee.

But Hatteras would do nothing till the exact position of the island was ascertained; so the Doctor and Altamont set to work with their instruments, and found that the exact latitude of the grotto was 89° 59' 15". The longitude was of little importance, for all the meridians blended a few hundred feet higher.

The 90° of lat. was then only about three quarters of a mile off, or just about the summit of the volcano.

When the result was communicated to Hatteras, he desired that a formal document might be drawn up to attest the fact, and two copies made, one of which should be deposited on a cairn on the island.

Clawbonny was the scribe, and indited the following document, a copy of which is now among the archives of the Royal Geographical Society of London:—

"On this 11th day of July, 1861, in North latitude 89° 59' 15" was discovered *Queen's* Island at the North Pole, by Captain Hatteras, Commander of the brig *Forward* of Liverpool, who signs this, as also all his companions.

"Whoever may find this document is requested to forward it to the Admiralty.

"(Signed) JOHN HATTERAS, Commander
of the *Forward*
"DR. CLAWBONNY
"ALTAMONT, Commander of the *Porpoise*
"JOHNSON, Boatswain
"BELL, Carpenter."

"And now, friends, come to table," said the Doctor, merrily.

Coming to table was just squatting on the ground.

"But who," said Clawbonny, "would not give all the tables and dining-rooms in the world to dine at 89" 59' and 15" N. lat.?"

It was an exciting occasion this first meal at the Pole! What neither ancients nor moderns, neither Europeans, nor Americans, nor Asiatics had been able to accomplish was now achieved, and all past sufferings and perils were forgotten in the glow of success.

"But, after all," said Johnson, after toasts to Hatteras and the North Pole had been enthusiastically drunk, "what is there so very special about the North Pole? Will you tell me, Mr. Clawbonny?"

"Just this, my good Johnson. It is the only point of the globe that is motionless; all the other points are revolving with extreme rapidity."

"But I don't see that we are any more motionless here than at Liverpool."

"Because in both cases you are a party concerned, both in the motion and the rest; but the fact is certain."

Clawbonny then went on to describe the diurnal and annual motions of the earth—the one round its own axis, the extremities of which are the poles, which is accomplished in twenty-four hours, and the other round the sun, which takes a whole year.

Bell and Johnson listened half incredulously, and

couldn't see why the earth could not have been allowed to keep still, till Altamont informed them that they would then have had neither day nor night, nor spring, summer, autumn, and winter.

"Ay, and worse still," said Clawbonny, "if the motion chanced to be interrupted, we should fall right into the sun in sixty-four and a half days."

"What! take sixty-four and a half days, to fall?" exclaimed Johnson.

"Yes, we are ninety-five millions of miles off. But when I say the Pole is motionless, it is not strictly true; it is only so in comparison with the rest of the globe, for it has a certain movement of its own, and completes a circle in about twenty-six thousand years. This comes from the precession of the equinoxes."

A long and learned talk was started on this subject between Altamont and the Doctor, simplified, however, as much as possible for the benefit of Bell and Johnson.

Hatteras took no part in it, and even when they went on to speculate about the earth's centre, and discussed several of the theories that had been advanced respecting it, he seemed not to hear; it was evident his thoughts were far away.

Among other opinions put forth was one in our own days, which greatly excited Altamont's surprise. It was held that there was an immense opening at the poles which led into the heart of the earth, and that it was out of the opening that the light of the *Aurora Borealis* streamed. This was gravely stated, and Captain Synness, a countryman of our own, actually proposed that Sir Humphrey Davy, Humboldt, and Arago should undertake an expedition through it, but they refused."

"And quite right too," said Altamont.

"So say I; but you see, my friends, what absurdities imagination has conjured up about these regions, and how, sooner or later, the simple reality comes to light."

CHAPTER XXIV. MOUNT HATTERAS.

After this conversation they all made themselves as comfortable as they could, and lay down to sleep.

All, except Hatteras; and why could this extraordinary man not sleep like the others?

Was not the purpose of his life attained now? Had he not realized his most daring project? Why could he not rest? Indeed, might not one have supposed that, after the strain his nervous system had undergone, he would long for rest?

But no, he grew more and more excited, and it was not the thought of returning that so affected him. Was he bent on going farther still? Had his passion for travel no limits? Was the world too small for him now he had circumnavigated it.

Whatever might be the cause, he could not sleep; yet this first night at the Pole was clear and calm. The isle was absolutely uninhabited—not a bird was to be seen in this burning atmosphere, not an animal on these scoriae-covered rocks, not a fish in these seething waters. Next morning, when Altamont, and the others awoke, Hatteras was gone. Feeling uneasy at his absence, they hurried out of the grotto in search of him.

There he was standing on a rock, gazing fixedly at the top of the mountain. His instruments were in his hand, and he was evidently calculating the exact longitude and latitude.

The Doctor went towards him and spoke, but it was long before he could rouse him from his absorbing contemplations. At last the captain seemed to understand, and Clawbonny said, while he examined him with a keen scrutinizing glance—

"Let us go round the island. Here we are, all ready for our last excursion."

"The last!" repeated Hatteras, as if in a dream. "Yes!, the last truly, but," he added, with more animation, "the most wonderful."

He pressed both hands on his brow as he spoke, as if to calm the inward tumult.

Just then Altamont and the others came up, and their appearance seemed to dispel the hallucinations under which he was labouring.

"My friends," he said, in a voice full of emotion, "thanks for your courage, thanks for your perseverance, thanks for your superhuman efforts, through which we are permitted to set our feet on this soil."

"Captain," said Johnson, "we have only obeyed orders to you alone belongs the honour."

"No, no!" exclaimed Hatteras, with a violent outburst of emotion, "to all of you as much as to me! To Altamont as much as any of us, as much as the Doctor himself! Oh, let my heart break in your hands, it cannot contain its joy and gratitude any longer."

He grasped the hands of his brave companions as he spoke, and paced up and down as if he had lost all self-control.

"We have only done our duty as Englishmen," said Bell.

"And as friends," added Clawbonny.

"Yes, but all did not do it," replied Hatteras "some gave way. However, we must pardon them—pardon both the traitors and those who were led away by them. Poor fellows! I forgive them. You hear me, Doctor?"

"Yes," replied Clawbonny, beginning to be seriously uneasy at his friend's excitement.

"I have no wish, therefore," continued the captain, "that they should lose the little fortune they came so far to seek. No, the original agreement is to remain unaltered, and they shall be rich—if they ever see England again."

It would have been difficult not to have been touched by the pathetic tone of voice in which Hatteras said this.

"But, captain," interrupted Johnson, trying to joke, "one would think you were making your will!"

"Perhaps I am," said Hatteras, gravely.

"And yet you have a long bright career of glory before you!"

"Who knows?" was the reply.

No one answered, and the Doctor did not dare to guess his meaning; but Hatteras soon made them understand it, for presently he said, in a hurried, agitated manner, as if he could scarcely command himself—

"Friends, listen to me. We have done much already, but much yet remains to be done."

His companions heard him with profound astonishment.

"Yes," he resumed, "we are close to the Pole, but we are not on it."

"How do you make that out," said Altamont.

"Yes," replied Hatteras, with vehemence, "I said an Englishman should plant his foot on the Pole of the world! I said it, and an Englishman shall."

"What!" cried Clawbonny.

"We are still 45" from the unknown point," resumed Hatteras, with increasing animation, "and to that point I shall go."

"But it is on the summit of the volcano," said the Doctor.

"I shall go."

"It is an inaccessible cone!"

"I shall go."

"But it is a yawning fiery crater!"

"I shall go."

The tone of absolute determination in which Hatteras pronounced these words it is impossible to describe.

His friends were stupefied, and gazed in terror at the blazing mountain.

At last the Doctor recovered himself, and began to urge and entreat Hatteras to renounce his project. He tried every means his heart dictated, from humble supplications to friendly threats; but he could gain nothing—a sort of frenzy had come over the captain, an absolute monomania about the Pole.

Nothing but violent measures would keep him back from destruction, but the Doctor was unwilling to employ these unless driven to extremity.

He trusted, moreover, that physical impossibilities, insuperable obstacles would bar his further progress, and meantime finding all protestations were useless, he simply said—

"Very well, since you are bent on it, we'll go too."

"Yes," replied Hatteras, "half-way up the mountain, but not a step beyond. You know you have to carry back to England the duplicate of the document in the cairn——"

"Yes; but——"

"It is settled," said Hatteras, in an imperious tone; "and since the prayers of a friend will not suffice, the captain commands."

The Doctor did not insist longer, and a few minutes after the little band set out, accompanied by Duk.

It was about eight o'clock when they commenced their difficult ascent; the sky was splendid, and the thermometer stood at 52°.

Hatteras and his dog went first, closely followed by the others.

"I am afraid," said Johnson to the Doctor.

"No, no, there's nothing to be afraid of; we are here."

This singular little island appeared to be of recent formation, and was evidently the product of successive volcanic eruptions. The rocks were all lying loose on the top of each other, and it was a marvel how they preserved their equilibrium. Strictly speaking, the mountain was only a heap of stones thrown down from a height, and the mass of rocks which composed the island had evidently come out of the bowels of the earth.

The earth, indeed, may be compared to a vast cauldron of spherical form, in which, under the influence of a central fire, immense quantities of vapours are generated, which would explode the globe but for the safety-valves outside.

These safety-valves are volcanoes, when one closes another opens; and at the Poles where the crust of the earth is thinner, owing to its being flattened, it is not surprising that a volcano should be suddenly formed by the upheaving of some part of the ocean-bed.

The Doctor, while following Hatteras, was closely following all the peculiarities of the island, and he was further confirmed in his opinion as to its recent formation by the absence of water. Had it existed for centuries, the thermal springs would have flowed from its bosom.

As they got higher, the ascent became more and more difficult, for the flanks of the mountain were almost perpendicular, and it required the utmost care to keep them from falling. Clouds of scoriæ and ashes would whirl round them repeatedly, threatening them with asphyxia, or torrents of lava would bar their passage. In parts where these torrents ran horizontally, the outside had become hardened; while underneath was the boiling lava, and every step the travellers took had first to be tested with the iron-tipped staff to avoid being suddenly plunged into the scalding liquid.

At intervals large fragments of red-hot rock were thrown up from the crater, and burst in the air like bomb-shells, scattering the debris to enormous distances in all directions.

Hatteras, however, climbed up the steepest ascents with surprising agility, disdaining the help of his staff.

He arrived before long at a circular rock, a sort of plateau about ten feet wide. A river of boiling lava surrounded it, except in one part, where it forked away to a higher rock, leaving a narrow passage, through which Hatteras fearlessly passed.

Here he stopped, and his companions managed to rejoin him. He seemed to be measuring with his eye the distance he had yet to get over. Horizontally, he was not more than two hundred yards from the top of the crater, but vertically he had nearly three times that distance to traverse.

The ascent had occupied three hours already. Hatteras showed no signs of fatigue, while the others were almost spent.

The summit of the volcano appeared inaccessible, and the Doctor determined at any price to prevent Hatteras from attempting to proceed. He tried gentle means first, but the captain's excitement was fast becoming delirium. During their ascent, symptoms of insanity had become more and more marked, and no one could be surprised who knew anything of his previous history.

"Hatteras," said the Doctor, "it is enough! we cannot go further!"

"Stop, then," he replied, in a strangely altered voice; "I am going higher."

"No, it is useless; you are at the Pole already."

"No, no! higher, higher!"

"My friend, do you know who is speaking to you? It is I, Doctor Clawbonny."

"Higher, higher!" repeated the madman.

"Very well, we shall not allow it—that is all."

He had hardly uttered the words before Hatteras, by a superhuman effort, sprang over the boiling lava, and was beyond the reach of his companions.

A cry of horror burst from every lip, for they thought the poor captain must have perished in that fiery gulf; but there he was safe on the other side, accompanied by his faithful Duk, who would not leave him.

He speedily disappeared behind a curtain of smoke, and they heard his voice growing fainter in the distance, shouting—

"To the north! to the north! to the top of Mount Hatteras! Remember Mount Hatteras!"

All pursuit of him was out of the question; it was impossible to leap across the fiery torrent, and equally impossible to get round it. Altamont, indeed, was mad enough to make an attempt, and would certainly have lost his life if the others had not held him back by main force.

"Hatteras! Hatteras!" shouted the Doctor, but no response was heard save the faint bark of Duk.

At intervals, however, a glimpse of him could be caught through the clouds of smoke and showers of ashes. Sometimes his head, sometimes his arm appeared; then he was out of sight again, and a few minutes later was seen higher up clinging to the rocks. His size constantly decreased with the fantastic rapidity of objects rising upwards in the air. In half-an-hour he was only half his size.

The air was full of the deep rumbling noise of the volcano, and the mountain shook and trembled. From time to time a loud fail was heard behind, and the travellers would see some enormous rock rebounding from the heights to engulph itself in the polar basin below.

Hatteras did not even turn once to look back, but marched straight on, carrying his country's flag attached to his staff. His terrified friends watched every movement, and saw him gradually decrease to microscopic dimensions, while Duk looked no larger than a big rat.

Then came a moment of intense anxiety, for the wind beat down on them an immense sheet of flame, and they could see nothing but the red glare. A cry of agony escaped the Doctor; but an instant afterwards Hatteras reappeared, waving his flag.

For a whole hour this fearful spectacle went on—an hour of battle with unsteady loose rocks and quagmires of ashes, where the foolhardy climber sank up to his waist. Sometimes they saw him hoist himself up by leaning knees and loins against the rocks in narrow, intricate winding paths, and sometimes he would be hanging on by both hands to some sharp crag, swinging to and fro like a withered tuft.

At last he reached the summit of the mountain, the mouth of the crater. Here the Doctor hoped the infatuated man would stop, at any rate, and would, perhaps, recover his senses, and expose himself to no more danger than the descent involved.

Once more he shouted—

"Hatteras! Hatteras!"

There was such a pathos of entreaty in his tone that Altamont felt moved to his inmost soul.

"I'll save him yet!" he exclaimed; and before Clawbonny could hinder him, he had cleared with a bound the torrent of fire, and was out of sight among the rocks.

Meantime, Hatteras had mounted a rock which overhung the crater, and stood waving his flag amidst showers of stones which rained down on him. Duk was by his side; but the poor beast was growing dizzy in such close proximity to the abyss.

Hatteras balanced his staff in one hand, and with the other sought to find the precise mathematical point where all the meridians of the globe meet, the point on which it was his sublime purpose to plant his foot.

All at once the rock gave way, and he disappeared. A cry of horror broke from his companions, and rang to the top of the mountain. Clawbonny thought his friend had perished, and lay buried for ever in the depths of the volcano. A second—only a second, though it seemed an age—elapsed, and there was Altamont and the dog holding the ill-fated Hatteras! Man and dog had caught him at the very moment when he disappeared in the abyss.

Hatteras was saved! Saved in spite of himself; and half-an-hour later be lay unconscious in the arms of his despairing companions.

When he came to himself, the Doctor looked at him in speechless anguish, for there was no glance of recognition in his eye. It was the eye of a blind man, who gazes without seeing.

"Good heavens!" exclaimed Johnson; "he is blind!"

"No," replied Clawbonny, "no! My poor friends, we have only saved the body of Hatteras; his soul is left behind on the top of the volcano. His reason is gone!"

"Insane!" exclaimed Johnson and Altamont, in consternation.

"Insane!" replied the Doctor, and the big tears ran down his cheeks.

CHAPTER XXV. RETURN SOUTH.

Three hours after this sad *dénouement* of the adventures of Captain Hatteras, the whole party were back once more in the grotto.

Clawbonny was asked his opinion as to what was best to be done.

"Well, friends," he said, "we cannot stay longer in this island; the sea is open, and we have enough provisions. We ought to start at once, and get back without the least delay to Fort Providence, where we must winter."

"That is my opinion, too," said Altamont. "The wind is favourable, so to-morrow we will get to sea."

The day passed in profound dejection. The insanity of the captain was a bad omen and when they began to talk over the return voyage, their hearts failed them for fear. They missed the intrepid spirit of their leader.

However, like brave men, they prepared to battle anew with the elements and with themselves, if ever they felt inclined to give way.

Next morning they made all ready to sail, and brought the tent and all its belongings on board.

But before leaving these rocks, never to return, the Doctor carrying out the intentions of Hatteras, had a cairn erected on the very spot where the poor fellow had jumped ashore. It was made of great blocks placed one on the top of the other, so as to be a landmark perfectly visible while the eruptions of the volcano left it undisturbed. On one of the side stones, Bell chiselled the simple inscription—

JOHN HATTERAS.

The duplicate of the document attesting the discovery of the North Pole was enclosed in a tinned iron cylinder, and deposited in the cairn, to remain as a silent witness among those desert rocks.

This done, the four men and the captain, a poor body without a soul, set out on the return voyage, accompanied by the faithful Duk, who had become sad and downcast. A new sail was manufactured out of the tent, and about ten o'clock, the little sloop sailed out before the wind.

She made a quick passage, finding abundance of open water. It was certainly easier to get away from the Pole than to get to it.

But Hatteras knew nothing that was passing around him. He lay full length in the boat, perfectly silent, with lifeless eye and folded arms, and Duk lying at his feet. Clawbonny frequently addressed him, but could elicit no reply.

On the 15th they sighted Altamont Harbour, but as the sea was open all along the coast, they determined to go round to Victoria Bay by water, instead of crossing New America in the sledge.

The voyage was easy and rapid. In a week they accomplished what had taken a fortnight in the sledge, and on the 23rd they cast anchor in Victoria Bay.

As soon as the sloop was made fast, they all hastened to Fort Providence. But what a scene of devastation met their eyes! Doctor's House, stores, powder-magazine, fortifications, all had melted away, and the provisions had been ransacked by devouring animals.

The navigators had almost come to the end of their supplies, and had been reckoning on replenishing their stores at Fort Providence. The impossibility of wintering there now was evident, and they decided to get to Baffin's Bay by the shortest route.

"We have no alternative," said Clawbonny; "Baffin's Bay is not more than six hundred miles distant. We can sail as long as there is water enough under our sloop, and get to Jones' Sound, and then on to the Danish settlements."

"Yes," said Altamont; "let us collect what food remains, and be off at once."

After a thorough search, a few cases of pemmican were found scattered here and there, and two barrels of preserved meat, altogether enough for six weeks, and a good supply of powder. It was soon collected and brought on board, and the remainder of the day was employed in caulking the sloop and putting her in good trim.

Next morning they put out once more to sea. The voyage presented no great difficulties, the drift-ice being easily avoided; but still the Doctor thought it advisable, in case of possible delays, to limit the rations to one-half. This was no great hardship, as there was not much work for anyone to do, and all were in perfect health.

Besides, they found a little shooting, and brought down ducks, and geese, and guillemots, or sea turtledoves. Water they were able to supply themselves with in abundance, from the fresh-water icebergs they constantly fell in with as they kept near the coast, not daring to venture out to the open sea in so frail a barque.

At that time of the year, the thermometer was already constantly below freezing point. The frequent rains changed to snow, and the weather became gloomy. Each day the sun dipped lower below the horizon, and on the 30th, for a few minutes, he was out of sight altogether.

However, the little sloop sailed steadily on without stopping an instant. They knew what fatigues and obstacles a land journey involved, if they should be forced to adopt it, and no time was to be lost, for soon the open water would harden to firm ground; already the young ice had begun to form. In these high latitudes there is neither spring nor autumn; winter follows close on the heels of summer.

On the 31st the first stars glimmered overhead, and from that time forwards there was continual fog, which considerably impeded navigation.

The Doctor became very uneasy at these multiplied indications of approaching winter. He knew the difficulties Sir John Ross had to contend with after he left his ship to try and reach Baffin's Bay, and how, after all, he was compelled to return and pass a fourth winter on board. It was bad enough with shelter and food and fuel, but if any such calamity befell the survivors of the *Forward*, if they were obliged to stop or return, they were lost.

The Doctor said nothing of his anxieties to his companions, but only urged them to get as far east as possible.

At last, after thirty days' tolerably quick sailing, and after battling for forty-eight hours against the increasing drift ice, and risking the frail sloop a hundred times, the navigators saw themselves blocked in on all sides. Further progress was impossible, for the sea was frozen in every direction, and the thermometer was only 15° above zero.

Altamont made a reckoning with scrupulous precision, and found they were in 77°15' latitude, and 85° 2' longitude.

"This is our exact position then," said the Doctor. "We are in South Lincoln, just at Cape Eden, and are entering Jones' Sound. With a little more good luck, we should have found open water right to Baffin's Bay. But we must not grumble. If my poor Hatteras had found as navigable a sea at first, he would have soon reached the Pole. His men would not have deserted him, and his brain would not have given way under the pressure of terrible trial."

"I suppose, then," said Altamont, "our only course is to leave the sloop, and get by sledge to the east coast of Lincoln."

"Yes; but I think we should go through Jones' Sound, and get to South Devon instead of crossing Lincoln."

"Why?"

"Because the nearer we get to Lancaster Sound, the more chance we have of meeting whalers."

"You are right; but I question whether the ice is firm enough to make it practicable."

"We'll try," replied Clawbonny.

The little vessel was unloaded, and the sledge put together again. All the parts were in good condition, so the next day the dogs were harnessed, and they started off along the coast to reach the ice-field; but Altamont's opinion proved right. They could not get through Jones' Sound, and were obliged to follow the coast to Lincoln.

At last, on the 24th, they set foot on North Devon.

"Now," said Clawbonny, "we have only to cross this, and get to Cape Warender at the entrance to Lancaster Sound."

But the weather became frightful, and very cold. The snow-storms and tempests returned with winter violence, and the travellers felt too weak to contend with them. Their stock of provisions was almost exhausted, and rations had to be reduced now to a third, that the dogs might have food enough to keep them in working condition.

The nature of the ground added greatly to the fatigue. North Devon is extremely wild and rugged, and the path across the Trauter mountains is through difficult gorges. The whole party—men, and dogs, and sledge alike—were frequently forced to stop, for they could not struggle on against the fury of the elements. More than once despair crept over the brave little band, hardy as they were, and used to Polar sufferings. Though scarcely aware of it themselves, they were completely worn out, physically and mentally.

It was not till the 30th of August that they emerged from these wild mountains into a plain, which seemed to have been upturned and convulsed by volcanic action at some distant period.

Here it was absolutely necessary to take a few days' rest, for the travellers could not drag one foot after the other, and two of the dogs had died from exhaustion. None of the party felt equal to put up the tent, so they took shelter behind an iceberg.

Provisions were now so reduced, that, notwithstanding their scanty rations, there was only enough left for one week. Starvation stared the poor fellows in the face.

Altamont, who had displayed great unselfishness and devotion to the others, roused his sinking energies, and determined to go out and find food for his comrades.

He took his gun, called Duk, and went off almost unnoticed by the rest.

He had been absent about an hour, and only once during that time had they heard the report of his gun; and now he was coming back empty- handed, but running as if terrified.

"What is the matter?" asked the Doctor.

"Down there, under the snow!" said Altamont, speaking as if scared, and pointing in a particular direction.

"What?"

"A whole party of men!"

"Alive?"

"Dead—frozen—and even—"

He did not finish the sentence, but a look of unspeakable horror came over his face.

The Doctor and the others were so roused by this incident, that they managed to get up and drag themselves after Altamont towards the place he indicated.

They soon arrived, at a narrow part at the bottom of a ravine, and what a spectacle met their gaze! Dead bodies, already stiff, lay half- buried in a winding-sheet of snow. A leg visible here, an arm there, and yonder shrunken hands and rigid faces, stamped with the expression of rage and despair.

The Doctor stooped down to look at them more closely, but instantly started back pale and agitated, while Duk barked ominously.

"Horrible, horrible!" he said.

"What is it?" asked Johnson.

"Don't you recognize them?"

"What do you mean?"

"Look and see!"

It was evident this ravine had been but recently the scene of a fearful straggle with cold, and despair, and starvation, for by certain horrible remains it was manifest that the poor wretches had been feeding on human flesh, perhaps while still warm and palpitating; and among them the Doctor recognized Shandon, Pen, and the ill-fated crew of the *Forward!* Their strength had failed; provisions had come to an end; their boat had been broken, perhaps by an avalanche or engulphed in some abyss, and they could not take advantage of the open sea; or perhaps they had lost their way in wandering over these unknown continents. Moreover, men who set out under the excitement of a revolt were not likely to remain long united. The leader of a rebellion has but a doubtful power, and no doubt Shandon's authority had been soon cast off.

Be that as it might, it was evident the crew had come through agonies of suffering and despair before this last terrible catastrophe, but the secret of their miseries is buried with them beneath the polar snows.

"Come away! come away!" said the Doctor, dragging his companions from the scene. Horror gave them momentary strength, and they resumed their march without stopping a minute longer.

CHAPTER XXVI. CONCLUSION.

It would be useless to enumerate all the misfortunes which befell the survivors of the expedition. Even the men themselves were never able to give any detailed narrative of the events which occurred during the week subsequent to the horrible discovery related in the last chapter. However, on the 9th of September, by superhuman exertions, they arrived at last at Cape Horsburg, the extreme point of North Devon.

They were absolutely starving. For forty-eight hours they had tasted nothing, and their last meal had been off the flesh of their last Esquimaux dog. Bell could go no further, and Johnson felt himself dying.

They were on the shore of Baffin's Bay, now half-frozen over; that is to say, on the road to Europe, and three miles off the waves were dashing noiselessly on the sharp edges of the ice-field.

Here they must wait their chance of a whaler appearing; and for how long?

But Heaven pitied the poor fellows, for the very next day Altamont distinctly perceived a sail on the horizon. Every one knows the torturing suspense that follows such an appearance, and the agonizing dread lest it should prove a false hope. The vessel seems alternately to approach and recede, and too often just at the very moment when the poor castaways think they are saved, the sail begins to disappear, and is soon out of sight.

The Doctor and his companions went through all these experiences. They had succeeded in reaching the western boundary of the ice-field by carrying and pushing each other along, and they watched the ship gradually fade away from view without observing them, in spite of their loud cries for help.

Just then a happy inspiration came to the Doctor. His fertile genius, which had served him many a time in such good stead, supplied him with one last idea!

A floe driven by the current struck against the icefield, and Clawbonny exclaimed, pointing to it—

"This floe!"

His companions could not understand what he meant.

"Let us embark on it! let us embark on it!"

"Oh! Mr. Clawbonny, Mr. Clawbonny," said Johnson, pressing his hand.

Bell, assisted by Altamont, hurried to the sledge, and brought back one of the poles, which he stuck fast on the ice like a mast, and fastened it with ropes. The tent was torn up to furnish a sail, and as soon as the frail raft was ready the poor fellows jumped upon it, and sailed out to the open sea.

Two hours later, after unheard-of exertions, the survivors of the *Forward* were picked up by the *Hans Christian*, a Danish whaler, on her way to Davis' Straits. They were more like spectres than human beings, and the sight of their sufferings was enough. It told its own tale; but the captain received them with such hearty sympathy, and lavished on them such care and kindness, that he succeeded in keeping them alive.

Ten days afterwards, Clawbonny, Johnson, Bell, Altamont, and Captain Hatteras landed at Korsam, in Zealand, an island belonging to Denmark. They took the steamer to Kiel, and from there proceeded by Altona and Hamburg to London, where they arrived on the 13th of the same month, scarcely recovered after their long sufferings.

The first care of Clawbonny was to request the Royal Geographical Society to receive a communication from him. He was accordingly admitted to the next *séance*, and one can imagine the astonishment of the learned assembly and the enthusiastic applause produced by the reading of Hatteras' document.

The English have a passion for geographical discovery, from the lord to the cockney, from the merchant down to the dock labourer, and the news of this grand discovery speedily flashed along the telegraph wires, throughout the length and breadth of the kingdom. Hatteras was lauded as a martyr by all the newspapers, and every Englishman felt proud of him.

The Doctor and his companions had the honour of being presented to the Queen by the Lord Chancellor, and they were feted and "lionized" in all quarters.

The Government confirmed the names of "Queen's Island," "Mount Hatteras," and "Altamont Harbour."

Altamont would not part from his companions in misery and glory, but followed them to Liverpool, where they were joyously welcomed back, after being so long supposed dead and buried beneath the eternal snows.

But Dr. Clawbonny would never allow that any honour was due to himself. He claimed all the merit of the discovery for his unfortunate captain, and in the narrative of his voyage, published the next year under the auspices of the Royal Geographical Society, he places John Hatteras on a level with the most illustrious navigators, and makes him the compeer of all the brave, daring men who have sacrificed themselves for the progress of science.

The insanity of this poor victim of a sublime passion was of a mild type, and he lived quietly at Sten Cottage, a private asylum near Liverpool, where the Doctor himself had placed him. He never spoke, and understood nothing that was said to him; reason and speech had fled together. The only tie that connected him with the outside world was his friendship for Duk, who was allowed to remain with him.

For a considerable time the captain had been in the habit of walking in the garden for hours, accompanied by his faithful dog, who watched him with sad, wistful eyes, but his promenade was always in one direction in a particular part of the garden. When he got to the end of this path, he would stop and begin to walk backwards. If anyone stopped him he would point with his finger towards a certain part of the sky, but let anyone attempt to turn him round, and he became angry, while Duk, as if sharing his master's sentiments, would bark furiously.

The Doctor, who often visited his afflicted friend, noticed this strange proceeding one day, and soon understood the reason of it. He saw how it was that he paced so constantly in a given direction, as if under the influence of some magnetic force.

This was the secret: John Hatteras invariably walked towards the North.

IN SEARCH OF THE CASTAWAYS

OR THE CHILDREN OF CAPTAIN GRANT

SOUTH AMERICA

CHAPTER I THE SHARK

ON the 26th of July, 1864, a magnificent yacht was steaming along the North Channel at full speed, with a strong breeze blowing from the N. E. The Union Jack was flying at the mizzen-mast, and a blue standard bearing the initials E. G., embroidered in gold, and surmounted by a ducal coronet, floated from the topgallant head of the main-mast. The name of the yacht was the DUNCAN, and the owner was Lord Glenarvan, one of the sixteen Scotch peers who sit in the Upper House, and the most distinguished member of the Royal Thames Yacht Club, so famous throughout the United Kingdom.

Lord Edward Glenarvan was on board with his young wife, Lady Helena, and one of his cousins, Major McNabbs.

The DUNCAN was newly built, and had been making a trial trip a few miles outside the Firth of Clyde. She was returning to Glasgow, and the Isle of Arran already loomed in the distance, when the sailor on watch caught sight of an enormous fish sporting in the wake of the ship. Lord Edward, who was immediately apprised of the fact, came up on the poop a few minutes after with his cousin, and asked John Mangles, the captain, what sort of an animal he thought it was.

"Well, since your Lordship asks my opinion," said Mangles, "I think it is a shark, and a fine large one too."

"A shark on these shores!"

"There is nothing at all improbable in that," returned the captain. "This fish belongs to a species that is found in all latitudes and in all seas. It is the 'balance-fish,' or hammer-headed shark, if I am not much mistaken. But if your Lordship has no objections, and it would give the smallest pleasure to Lady Helena to see a novelty in the way of fishing, we'll soon haul up the monster and find out what it really is."

"What do you say, McNabbs? Shall we try to catch it?" asked Lord Glenarvan.

"If you like; it's all one to me," was his cousin's cool reply.

"The more of those terrible creatures that are killed the better, at all events," said John Mangles, "so let's seize the chance, and it will not only give us a little diversion, but be doing a good action."

"Very well, set to work, then," said Glenarvan.

Lady Helena soon joined her husband on deck, quite charmed at the prospect of such exciting sport. The sea was splendid, and every movement of the shark was distinctly visible. In obedience to the captain's orders, the sailors threw a strong rope over the starboard side of the yacht, with a big hook at the end of it, concealed in a thick lump of bacon. The bait took at once, though the shark was full fifty yards distant. He began to make rapidly for the yacht, beating the waves violently with his fins, and keeping his tail in a perfectly straight line. As he got nearer, his great projecting eyes could be seen inflamed with greed, and his gaping jaws with their quadruple row of teeth. His head was large, and shaped like a double hammer at the end of a handle. John Mangles was right. This was evidently a balance-fish— the most voracious of all the SQUALIDAE species.

The passengers and sailors on the yacht were watching all the animal's movements with the liveliest interest. He soon came within reach of the bait, turned over on his back to make a good dart at it, and in a second bacon and contents had disappeared. He had hooked himself now, as the tremendous jerk he gave the cable proved, and the sailors began to haul in the monster by means of tackle attached to the mainyard. He struggled desperately, but his captors were prepared for his violence, and had a long rope ready with a slip knot, which caught his tail and rendered him powerless at once. In a few minutes more he was hoisted up over the side of the yacht and thrown on the deck. A man came forward immediately, hatchet in hand, and approaching him cautiously, with one powerful stroke cut off his tail.

This ended the business, for there was no longer any fear of the shark. But, though the sailors' vengeance was satisfied, their curiosity was not; they knew the brute had no very delicate appetite, and the contents of his stomach might be worth investigation. This is the common practice on all ships when a shark is captured, but Lady Glenarvan declined to be present at such a disgusting exploration, and withdrew to the cabin again. The fish was still breathing; it measured ten feet in length, and weighed more than six hundred pounds. This was nothing extraordinary, for though the hammer-headed shark is not classed among the most gigantic of the species, it is always reckoned among the most formidable.

The huge brute was soon ripped up in a very unceremonious fashion. The hook had fixed right in the stomach, which was found to be absolutely empty, and the disappointed sailors were just going to throw the remains overboard, when the boatswain's attention was attracted by some large object sticking fast in one of the viscera.

"I say! what's this?" he exclaimed.

"That!" replied one of the sailors, "why, it's a piece of rock the beast swallowed by way of ballast."

"It's just a bottle, neither more nor less, that the fellow has got in his inside, and couldn't digest," said another of the crew.

"Hold your tongues, all of you!" said Tom Austin, the mate of the DUNCAN. "Don't you see the animal has been such an inveterate tippler that he has not only drunk the wine, but swallowed the bottle?"

"What!" said Lord Glenarvan. "Do you mean to say it is a bottle that the shark has got in his stomach."

"Ay, it is a bottle, most certainly," replied the boatswain, "but not just from the cellar."

"Well, Tom, be careful how you take it out," said Lord Glenarvan, "for bottles found in the sea often contain precious documents."

"Do you think this does?" said Major McNabbs, incredulously.

"It possibly may, at any rate."

"Oh! I'm not saying it doesn't. There may perhaps be some secret in it," returned the Major.

"That's just what we're to see," said his cousin. "Well, Tom."

"Here it is," said the mate, holding up a shapeless lump he had managed to pull out, though with some difficulty.

"Get the filthy thing washed then, and bring it to the cabin."

Tom obeyed, and in a few minutes brought in the bottle and laid it on the table, at which Lord Glenarvan and the Major were sitting ready with the captain, and, of course Lady Helena, for women, they say, are always a little curious. Everything is an event at sea. For a moment they all sat silent, gazing at this frail relic, wondering if it told the tale of sad disaster, or brought some trifling message from a frolic-loving sailor, who had flung it into the sea to amuse himself when he had nothing better to do.

However, the only way to know was to examine the bottle, and Glenarvan set to work without further delay, so carefully and minutely, that he might have been taken for a coroner making an inquest.

He commenced by a close inspection of the outside.

The neck was long and slender, and round the thick rim there

was still an end of wire hanging, though eaten away with rust.

The sides were very thick, and strong enough to bear great pressure.

It was evidently of Champagne origin, and the Major said immediately,

"That's one of our Clicquot's bottles."

Nobody contradicted him, as he was supposed to know; but Lady Helena exclaimed, "What does it matter about the bottle, if we don't know where it comes from?"

"We shall know that, too, presently, and we may affirm this much already— it comes from a long way off. Look at those petrifactions all over it, these different substances almost turned to mineral, we might say, through the action of the salt water! This waif had been tossing about in the ocean a long time before the shark swallowed it."

"I quite agree with you," said McNabbs. "I dare say this frail concern has made a long voyage, protected by this strong covering."

"But I want to know where from?" said Lady Glenarvan.

"Wait a little, dear Helena, wait; we must have patience with bottles; but if I am not much mistaken, this one will answer all our questions," replied her husband, beginning to scrape away the hard substances round the neck. Soon the cork made its appearance, but much damaged by the water.

"That's vexing," said Lord Edward, "for if papers are inside, they'll be in a pretty state!"

"It's to be feared they will," said the Major.

"But it is a lucky thing the shark swallowed them, I must say," added Glenarvan, "for the bottle would have sunk to the bottom before long with such a cork as this."

"That's true enough," replied John Mangles, "and yet it would have been better to have fished them up in the open sea. Then we might have found out the road they had come by taking the exact latitude and longitude, and studying the atmospheric and submarine currents; but with such a postman as a shark, that goes against wind and tide, there's no clew whatever to the starting-point."

"We shall see," said Glenarvan, gently taking out the cork. A strong odor of salt water pervaded the whole saloon, and Lady Helena asked impatiently: "Well, what is there?"

"I was right!" exclaimed Glenarvan. "I see papers inside. But I fear it will be impossible to remove them," he added, "for they appear to have rotted with the damp, and are sticking to the sides of the bottle."

"Break it," said the Major.

"I would rather preserve the whole if I could."

"No doubt you would," said Lady Helena; "but the contents are more valuable than the bottle, and we had better sacrifice the one than the other."

"If your Lordship would simply break off the neck, I think we might easily withdraw the papers," suggested John Mangles.

"Try it, Edward, try it," said Lady Helena.

Lord Glenarvan was very unwilling, but he found there was no alternative; the precious bottle must be broken. They had to get a hammer before this could be done, though, for the stony material had acquired the hardness of granite. A few sharp strokes, however, soon shivered it to fragments, many of which had pieces of paper sticking to them. These were carefully removed by Lord Glenarvan, and separated and spread out on the table before the eager gaze of his wife and friends.

CHAPTER II THE THREE DOCUMENTS

ALL that could be discovered, however, on these pieces of paper was a few words here and there, the remainder of the lines being almost completely obliterated by the action of the water. Lord Glenarvan examined them attentively for a few minutes, turning them over on all sides, holding them up to the light, and trying to decipher the least scrap of writing, while the others looked on with anxious eyes. At last he said: "There are three distinct documents here, apparently copies of the same document in three different languages. Here is one in English, one in French, and one in German."

"But can you make any sense out of them?" asked Lady Helena.

"That's hard to say, my dear Helena, the words are quite incomplete."

"Perhaps the one may supplement the other," suggested Major McNabbs.

"Very likely they will," said the captain. "It is impossible that the very same words should have been effaced in each document, and by putting the scraps together we might gather some intelligible meaning out of them."

"That's what we will do," rejoined Lord Glenarvan; "but let us proceed methodically. Here is the English document first."

All that remained of it was the following:

62 *Bri gow*
sink stra
aland
skipp Gr
that monit of long
and ssistance
lost

"There's not much to be made out of that," said the Major, looking disappointed.

"No, but it is good English anyhow," returned the captain.

"There's no doubt of it," said Glenarvan. "The words SINK, ALAND, LOST are entire; SKIPP is evidently part of the word SKIPPER, and that's what they call ship captains often in England. There seems a Mr. Gr. mentioned, and that most likely is the captain of the shipwrecked vessel."

"Well, come, we have made out a good deal already," said Lady Helena.

"Yes, but unfortunately there are whole lines wanting," said the Major, "and we have neither the name of the ship nor the place where she was shipwrecked."

"We'll get that by and by," said Edward.

"Oh, yes; there is no doubt of it," replied the Major, who always echoed his neighbor's opinion. "But how?"

"By comparing one document with the other."

"Let us try them," said his wife.

The second piece of paper was even more destroyed than the first; only a few scattered words remained here and there.

It ran as follows:

7 Juni Glas

zwei atrosen

graus

bringt ihnen

"This is written in German," said John Mangles the moment he looked at it.

"And you understand that language, don't you?" asked Lord Glenarvan.

"Perfectly."

"Come, then, tell us the meaning of these words."

The captain examined the document carefully, and said:

"Well, here's the date of the occurrence first: 7 Juni means June 7; and if we put that before the figures 62 we have in the other document, it gives us the exact date, 7th of June, 1862."

"Capital!" exclaimed Lady Helena. "Go on, John!"

"On the same line," resumed the young captain, "there is the syllable GLAS and if we add that to the GOW we found in the English paper, we get the whole word GLASGOW at once. The documents evidently refer to some ship that sailed out of the port of Glasgow." "That is my opinion, too," said the Major.

"The second line is completely effaced," continued the Captain; "but here are two important words on the third. There is ZWEI, which means TWO, and ATROSEN or MATROSEN, the German for SAILORS."

"Then I suppose it is about a captain and two sailors," said Lady Helena.

"It seems so," replied Lord Glenarvan.

"I must confess, your Lordship, that the next word puzzles me. I can make nothing of it. Perhaps the third document may throw some light on it. The last two words are plain enough. BRINGT IHNEN means BRING THEM; and, if you recollect, in the English paper we had SSISTANCE, so by putting the parts together, it reads thus, I think: 'BRING THEM ASSISTANCE.'"

"Yes, that must be it," replied Lord Glenarvan. "But where are the poor fellows? We have not the slightest indication of the place, meantime, nor of where the catastrophe happened."

"Perhaps the French copy will be more explicit," suggested Lady Helena.

"Here it is, then," said Lord Glenarvan, "and that is in a language we all know."

The words it contained were these:

troi ats tannia

gonie austral

abor

contin pr cruel indi

jete ongit

et 37 degrees 11" LAT

"There are figures!" exclaimed Lady Helena. "Look!"

"Let us go steadily to work," said Lord Glenarvan, "and begin at the beginning. I think we can make out from the incomplete words in the first line that a three-mast vessel is in question, and there is little doubt about the name; we get that from the fragments of the other papers; it is the BRITANNIA. As to the next two words, GONIE and AUSTRAL, it is only AUSTRAL that has any meaning to us."

"But that is a valuable scrap of information," said John Mangles.

"The shipwreck occurred in the southern hemisphere."

"That's a wide world," said the Major.

"Well, we'll go on," resumed Glenarvan. "Here is the word ABOR; that is clearly the root of the verb ABORDER. The poor men have landed somewhere; but where? CONTIN—does that mean continent? CRUEL!"

"CRUEL!" interrupted John Mangles. "I see now what GRAUS is part of in the second document. It is GRAUSAM, the word in German for CRUEL!"

"Let's go on," said Lord Glenarvan, becoming quite excited over his task, as the incomplete words began to fill up and develop their meaning. "INDI,—is it India where they have been shipwrecked? And what can this word ONGIT be part of? Ah! I see—it is LONGITUDE; and here is the latitude, 37 degrees 11". That is the precise indication at last, then!"

"But we haven't the longitude," objected McNabbs.

"But we can't get everything, my dear Major; and it is something at all events, to have the exact latitude. The French document is decidedly the most complete of the three; but it is plain enough that each is the literal translation of the other, for they all contain exactly the same number of lines. What we have to do now is to put together all the words we have found, and translate them into one language, and try to ascertain their most probable and logical sense."

"Well, what language shall we choose?" asked the Major.

"I think we had better keep to the French, since that was the most complete document of the three."

"Your Lordship is right," said John Mangles, "and besides, we're all familiar with the language."

"Very well, then, I'll set to work."

In a few minutes he had written as follows:

7 Juin 1862 trois-mats Britannia Glasgow
sombre gonie austral
a terre deux matelots
capitaine Gr abor
contin pr cruel indi
jete ce document de longitude
et 37 degrees 11" de latitude Portez-leur secours
perdus.

[7th of June, 1862 three-mast BRITANNIA Glasgow] foundered gonie southern on the coast two sailors Gr Captain landed contin pr cruel indi thrown this document in longitude and 37 degrees 11" latitude Bring them assistance lost

Just at that moment one of the sailors came to inform the captain that they were about entering the Firth of Clyde, and to ask what were his orders.

"What are your Lordship's intentions?" said John Mangles, addressing Lord Glenarvan.

"To get to Dunbarton as quickly as possible, John; and Lady Helena will return to Malcolm Castle, while I go on to London and lay this document before the Admiralty."

The sailor received orders accordingly, and went out to deliver them to the mate.

"Now, friends," said Lord Glenarvan, "let us go on with our investigations, for we are on the track of a great catastrophe, and the lives of several human beings depend on our sagacity. We must give our whole minds to the solution of this enigma."

"First of all, there are three very distinct things to be considered in this document—the things we know, the things we may conjecture, the things we do not know."

"What are those we know? We know that on the 7th of June a three-mast vessel, the BRITANNIA of Glasgow, foundered; that two sailors and the captain threw this document into the sea in 37 degrees 11" latitude, and they entreat help."

"Exactly so," said the Major.

"What are those now we may conjecture?" continued Glenarvan. "That the shipwreck occurred in the southern seas; and here I would draw your attention at once to the incomplete word GONIE. Doesn't the name of the country strike you even in the mere mention of it?"

"Patagonia!" exclaimed Lady Helena.

"Undoubtedly."

"But is Patagonia crossed by the 37th parallel?" asked the Major.

"That is easily ascertained," said the captain, opening a map of
South America. "Yes, it is; Patagonia just touches the 37th parallel.
It cuts through Araucania, goes along over the Pampas to the north,
and loses itself in the Atlantic."

"Well, let us proceed then with our conjectures. The two sailors and the captain LAND—land where? CONTIN—on a continent; on a continent, mark you, not an island. What becomes of them? There are two letters here providentially which give a clew to their fate—PR, that must mean prisoners, and CRUEL INDIAN is evidently the meaning of the next two words. These unfortunate men are captives in the hands of cruel Indians. Don't you see it? Don't the words seem to come of themselves, and fill up the blanks? Isn't the document quite clear now? Isn't the sense self-evident?"

Glenarvan spoke in a tone of absolute conviction, and his enthusiastic confidence appeared contagious, for the others all exclaimed, too, "Yes, it is evident, quite evident!"

After an instant, Lord Edward said again, "To my own mind the hypothesis is so plausible, that I have no doubt whatever the event occurred on the coast of Patagonia, but still I will have inquiries made in Glasgow, as to the destination of the BRITANNIA, and we shall know if it is possible she could have been wrecked on those shores."

"Oh, there's no need to send so far to find out that," said John Mangles. "I have the *Mercantile and Shipping Gazette* here, and we'll see the name on the list, and all about it."

"Do look at once, then," said Lord Glenarvan.

The file of papers for the year 1862 was soon brought, and John began to turn over the leaves rapidly, running down each page with his eye in search of the name required. But his quest was not long, for in a few minutes he called out: "I've got it! 'May 30, 1862, Peru-Callao, with cargo for Glasgow, the BRITANNIA, Captain Grant.'"

"Grant!" exclaimed Lord Glenarvan. "That is the adventurous Scotchman that attempted to found a new Scotland on the shores of the Pacific."

"Yes," rejoined John Mangles, "it is the very man. He sailed from Glasgow in the BRITANNIA in 1861, and has not been heard of since."

"There isn't a doubt of it, not a shadow of doubt," repeated Lord Glenarvan. "It is just that same Captain Grant. The BRITANNIA left Callao on the 30th of May, and on the 7th of June, a week afterward, she is lost on the coast of Patagonia. The few broken disjointed words we find in these documents tell us the whole story. You see, friends, our conjectures hit the mark very well; we know all now except one thing, and that is the longitude."

"That is not needed now, we know the country. With the latitude alone,
I would engage to go right to the place where the wreck happened."

CHAPTER II THE THREE DOCUMENTS

"Then have we really all the particulars now?" asked Lady Helena.

"All, dear Helena; I can fill up every one of these blanks the sea has made in the document as easily as if Captain Grant were dictating to me."

And he took up the pen, and dashed off the following lines immediately: "On the 7th of June, 1862, the three-mast vessel, BRITANNIA, of Glasgow, has sunk on the coast of Patagonia, in the southern hemisphere. Making for the shore, two sailors and Captain Grant are about to land on the continent, where they will be taken prisoners by cruel Indians. They have thrown this document into the sea, in longitude and latitude 37 degrees 11". Bring them assistance, or they are lost."

"Capital! capital! dear Edward," said Lady Helena. "If those poor creatures ever see their native land again, it is you they will have to thank for it."

"And they will see it again," returned Lord Glenarvan; "the statement is too explicit, and clear, and certain for England to hesitate about going to the aid of her three sons cast away on a desert coast. What she has done for Franklin and so many others, she will do to-day for these poor shipwrecked fellows of the BRITANNIA."

"Most likely the unfortunate men have families who mourn their loss. Perhaps this ill-fated Captain Grant had a wife and children," suggested Lady Helena.

"Very true, my dear, and I'll not forget to let them know that there is still hope. But now, friends, we had better go up on deck, as the boat must be getting near the harbor."

A carriage and post-horses waited there, in readiness to convey Lady Helena and Major McNabbs to Malcolm Castle, and Lord Glenarvan bade adieu to his young wife, and jumped into the express train for Glasgow.

But before starting he confided an important missive to a swifter agent than himself, and a few minutes afterward it flashed along the electric wire to London, to appear next day in the *Times and Morning Chronicle* in the following words: "For information respecting the fate of the three-mast vessel BRITANNIA, of Glasgow, Captain Grant, apply to Lord Glenarvan, Malcolm Castle, Luss, Dumbartonshire, Scotland."

CHAPTER III THE CAPTAIN'S CHILDREN

LORD GLENARVAN'S fortune was enormous, and he spent it entirely in doing good. His kindheartedness was even greater than his generosity, for the one knew no bounds, while the other, of necessity, had its limits. As Lord of Luss and "laird" of Malcolm, he represented his county in the House of Lords; but, with his Jacobite ideas, he did not care much for the favor of the House of Hanover, and he was looked upon coldly by the State party in England, because of the tenacity with which he clung to the traditions of his forefathers, and his energetic resistance to the political encroachments of Southerners. And yet he was not a man behind the times, and there was nothing little or narrow-minded about him; but while always keeping open his ancestral county to progress, he was a true Scotchman at heart, and it was for the honor of Scotland that he competed in the yacht races of the Royal Thames Yacht Club.

Edward Glenarvan was thirty-two years of age. He was tall in person, and had rather stern features; but there was an exceeding sweetness in his look, and a stamp of Highland poetry about his whole bearing. He was known to be brave to excess, and full of daring and chivalry— a Fergus of the nineteenth century; but his goodness excelled every other quality, and he was more charitable than St. Martin himself, for he would have given the whole of his cloak to any of the poor Highlanders.

He had scarcely been married three months, and his bride was Miss Helena Tuffnell, the daughter of William Tuffnell, the great traveler, one of the many victims of geographical science and of the passion for discovery. Miss Helena did not belong to a noble family, but she was Scotch, and that was better than all nobility in the eyes of Lord Glenarvan; and she was, moreover, a charming, high-souled, religious young woman.

Lord Glenarvan did not forget that his wife was the daughter of a great traveler, and he thought it likely that she would inherit her father's predilections. He had the DUNCAN built expressly that he might take his bride to the most beautiful lands in the world, and complete their honeymoon by sailing up the Mediterranean, and through the clustering islands of the Archipelago.

However, Lord Glenarvan had gone now to London. The lives of the shipwrecked men were at stake, and Lady Helena was too much concerned herself about them to grudge her husband's temporary absence. A telegram next day gave hope of his speedy return, but in the evening a letter apprised her of the difficulties his proposition had met with, and the morning after brought another, in which he openly expressed his dissatisfaction with the Admiralty.

Lady Helena began to get anxious as the day wore on. In the evening, when she was sitting alone in her room, Mr. Halbert, the house steward, came in and asked if she would see a young girl and boy that wanted to speak to Lord Glenarvan.

"Some of the country people?" asked Lady Helena.

"No, madame," replied the steward, "I do not know them at all.

They came by rail to Balloch, and walked the rest of the way to Luss."

"Tell them to come up, Halbert."

In a few minutes a girl and boy were shown in. They were evidently brother and sister, for the resemblance was unmistakable. The girl was about sixteen years of age; her tired pretty face, and sorrowful eyes, and resigned but courageous look, as well as her neat though poor attire, made a favorable impression. The boy she held by the hand was about twelve, but his face expressed such determination, that he appeared quite his sister's protector.

The girl seemed too shy to utter a word at first, but Lady Helena quickly relieved her embarrassment by saying, with an encouraging smile: "You wish to speak to me, I think?"

"No," replied the boy, in a decided tone; "not to you, but to Lord Glenarvan."

"Excuse him, ma'am," said the girl, with a look at her brother.

"Lord Glenarvan is not at the castle just now," returned Lady Helena; "but I am his wife, and if I can do anything for you—"

"You are Lady Glenarvan?" interrupted the girl.

"I am."

"The wife of Lord Glenarvan, of Malcolm Castle, that put an announcement in the TIMES about the shipwreck of the BRITANNIA?"

"Yes, yes," said Lady Helena, eagerly; "and you?"

"I am Miss Grant, ma'am, and this is my brother."

"Miss Grant, Miss Grant!" exclaimed Lady Helena, drawing the young girl toward her, and taking both her hands and kissing the boy's rosy cheeks.

"What is it you know, ma'am, about the shipwreck? Tell me, is my father living? Shall we ever see him again? Oh, tell me," said the girl, earnestly.

"My dear child," replied Lady Helena. "Heaven forbid that I should answer you lightly such a question; I would not delude you with vain hopes."

"Oh, tell me all, tell me all, ma'am. I'm proof against sorrow.

I can bear to hear anything."

"My poor child, there is but a faint hope; but with the help of almighty Heaven it is just possible you may one day see your father once more."

The girl burst into tears, and Robert seized Lady Glenarvan's hand and covered it with kisses.

As soon as they grew calmer they asked a complete string of questions, and Lady Helena recounted the whole story of the document, telling them that their father had been wrecked on the coast of Patagonia, and that he and two sailors, the sole survivors, appeared to have reached the shore, and had written an appeal for help in three languages and committed it to the care of the waves.

During the recital, Robert Grant was devouring the speaker with his eyes, and hanging on her lips. His childish imagination evidently retraced all the scenes of his father's shipwreck. He saw him on the deck of the BRITANNIA, and then struggling with the billows, then clinging to the rocks, and lying at length exhausted on the beach.

More than once he cried out, "Oh, papa! my poor papa!" and pressed close to his sister.

Miss Grant sat silent and motionless, with clasped hands, and all she said when the narration ended, was: "Oh, ma'am, the paper, please!"

"I have not it now, my dear child," replied Lady Helena.

"You haven't it?"

"No. Lord Glenarvan was obliged to take it to London, for the sake of your father; but I have told you all it contained, word for word, and how we managed to make out the complete sense from the fragments of words left—all except the longitude, unfortunately."

"We can do without that," said the boy.

"Yes, Mr. Robert," rejoined Lady Helena, smiling at the child's decided tone. "And so you see, Miss Grant, you know the smallest details now just as well as I do."

"Yes, ma'am, but I should like to have seen my father's writing."

"Well, to-morrow, perhaps, to-morrow, Lord Glenarvan will be back. My husband determined to lay the document before the Lords of the Admiralty, to induce them to send out a ship immediately in search of Captain Grant."

"Is it possible, ma'am," exclaimed the girl, "that you have done that for us?"

"Yes, my dear Miss Grant, and I am expecting Lord Glenarvan back every minute now."

"Oh, ma'am! Heaven bless you and Lord Glenarvan," said the young girl, fervently, overcome with grateful emotion."

"My dear girl, we deserve no thanks; anyone in our place would have done the same. I only trust the hopes we are leading you to entertain may be realized, but till my husband returns, you will remain at the Castle."

"Oh, no, ma'am. I could not abuse the sympathy you show to strangers."

"Strangers, dear child!" interrupted Lady Helena; "you and your brother are not strangers in this house, and I should like Lord Glenarvan to be able on his arrival to tell the children of Captain Grant himself, what is going to be done to rescue their father."

It was impossible to refuse an invitation given with such heart, and Miss Grant and her brother consented to stay till Lord Glenarvan returned.

CHAPTER IV LADY GLENARVAN'S PROPOSAL

LADY HELENA thought it best to say nothing to the children about the fears Lord Glenarvan had expressed in his letters respecting the decisions of the Lords of the Admiralty with regard to the document. Nor did she mention the probable captivity of Captain Grant among the Indians of South America. Why sadden the poor children, and damp their newly cherished hopes? It would not in the least alter the actual state of the case; so not a word was said, and after answering all Miss Grant's questions, Lady Helena began to interrogate in her turn, asking her about her past life and her present circumstances.

It was a touching, simple story she heard in reply, and one which increased her sympathy for the young girl.

Mary and Robert were the captain's only children. Harry Grant lost his wife when Robert was born, and during his long voyages he left his little ones in charge of his cousin, a good old lady. Captain Grant was a fearless sailor. He not only thoroughly understood navigation, but commerce also—a two-fold qualification eminently useful to skippers in the merchant service. He lived in Dundee, in Perthshire, Scotland. His father, a minister of St. Katrine's Church, had given him a thorough education, as he believed that could never hurt anybody.

Harry's voyages were prosperous from the first, and a few years after

Robert was born, he found himself possessed of a considerable fortune.

It was then that he projected the grand scheme which made him popular in Scotland. Like Glenarvan, and a few noble families in the Lowlands, he had no heart for the union with England. In his eyes the interests of his country were not identified with those of the Anglo-Saxons, and to give scope for personal development, he resolved to found an immense Scotch colony on one of the ocean continents. Possibly he might have thought that some day they would achieve their independence, as the United States did—an example doubtless to be followed eventually by Australia and India. But whatever might be his secret motives, such was his dream of colonization. But, as is easily understood, the Government opposed his plans, and put difficulties enough in his way to have killed an ordinary man. But Harry would not be beaten. He appealed to the patriotism of his countrymen, placed his fortune at the service of the cause, built a ship, and manned it with a picked crew, and leaving his children to the care of his old cousin set off to explore the great islands of the Pacific. This was in 1861, and for twelve months, or up to May, 1862, letters were regularly received from him, but no tidings whatever had come since his departure from Callao, in June, and the name of the BRITANNIA never appeared in the Shipping List.

Just at this juncture the old cousin died, and Harry Grant's two children were left alone in the world.

Mary Grant was then only fourteen, but she resolved to face her situation bravely, and to devote herself entirely to her little brother, who was still a mere child. By dint of close economy, combined with tact and prudence, she managed to support and educate him, working day and night, denying herself everything, that she might give him all he needed, watching over him and caring for him like a mother.

The two children were living in this touching manner in Dundee, struggling patiently and courageously with their poverty. Mary thought only of her brother, and indulged in dreams of a prosperous future for him. She had long given up all hope of the BRITANNIA, and was fully persuaded that her father was dead. What, then, was her emotion when she accidentally saw the notice in the TIMES!

She never hesitated for an instant as to the course she should adopt, but determined to go to Dumbartonshire immediately, to learn the best and worst. Even if she were to be told that her father's lifeless body had been found on a distant shore, or in the bottom of some abandoned ship, it would be a relief from incessant doubt and torturing suspense.

She told her brother about the advertisement, and the two children started off together that same day for Perth, where they took the train, and arrived in the evening at Malcolm Castle.

Such was Mary Grant's sorrowful story, and she recounted it in so simple and unaffected a manner, that it was evident she never thought her conduct had been that of a heroine through those long trying years. But Lady Helena thought it for her, and more than once she put her arms round both the children, and could not restrain her tears.

As for Robert, he seemed to have heard these particulars for the first time. All the while his sister was speaking, he gazed at her with wide-open eyes, only knowing now how much she had done and suffered for him; and, as she ended, he flung himself on her neck, and exclaimed, "Oh, mamma! My dear little mamma!"

It was quite dark by this time, and Lady Helena made the children go to bed, for she knew they must be tired after their journey. They were soon both sound asleep, dreaming of happy days.

After they had retired. Lady Helena sent for Major McNabbs, and told him the incidents of the evening.

"That Mary Grant must be a brave girl," said the Major.

"I only hope my husband will succeed, for the poor children's sake," said his cousin. "It would be terrible for them if he did not."

"He will be sure to succeed, or the Lords of the Admiralty must have hearts harder than Portland stone."

But, notwithstanding McNabbs's assurance, Lady Helena passed the night in great anxiety, and could not close her eyes.

Mary Grant and her brother were up very early next morning, and were walking about in the courtyard when they heard the sound of a carriage approaching. It was Lord Glenarvan; and, almost immediately, Lady Helena and the Major came out to meet him.

Lady Helena flew toward her husband the moment he alighted; but he embraced her silently, and looked gloomy and disappointed— indeed, even furious.

"Well, Edward?" she said; "tell me."

"Well, Helena, dear; those people have no heart!"

"They have refused?"

"Yes. They have refused me a ship! They talked of the millions that had been wasted in search for Franklin, and declared the document was obscure and unintelligible. And, then, they said it was two years now since they were cast away, and there was little chance of finding them. Besides, they would have it that the Indians, who made them prisoners, would have dragged them into the interior, and it was impossible, they said, to hunt all through Patagonia for three men—three Scotchmen; that the search would be vain and perilous, and cost more lives than it saved. In short, they assigned all the reasons that people invent who have made up their minds to refuse. The truth is, they remembered Captain Grant's projects, and that is the secret of the whole affair. So the poor fellow is lost for ever."

"My father! my poor father!" cried Mary Grant, throwing herself on her knees before Lord Glenarvan, who exclaimed in amazement:

"Your father? What? Is this Miss—"

"Yes, Edward," said Lady Helena; "this is Miss Mary Grant and her brother, the two children condemned to orphanage by the cruel Admiralty!"

"Oh! Miss Grant," said Lord Glenarvan, raising the young girl, "if I had known of your presence—"

He said no more, and there was a painful silence in the courtyard, broken only by sobs. No one spoke, but the very attitude of both servants and masters spoke their indignation at the conduct of the English Government.

At last the Major said, addressing Lord Glenarvan: "Then you have no hope whatever?"

"None," was the reply.

"Very well, then," exclaimed little Robert, "I'll go and speak to those people myself, and we'll see if they—" He did not complete his sentence, for his sister stopped him; but his clenched fists showed his intentions were the reverse of pacific.

"No, Robert," said Mary Grant, "we will thank this noble lord and lady for what they have done for us, and never cease to think of them with gratitude; and then we'll both go together."

"Mary!" said Lady Helena, in a tone of surprise.

"Go where?" asked Lord Glenarvan.

"I am going to throw myself at the Queen's feet, and we shall see if she will turn a deaf ear to the prayers of two children, who implore their father's life."

Lord Glenarvan shook his head; not that he doubted the kind heart of her Majesty, but he knew Mary would never gain access to her. Suppliants but too rarely reach the steps of a throne; it seems as if royal palaces had the same inscription on their doors that the English have on their ships: *Passengers are requested not to speak to the man at the wheel.*

Lady Glenarvan understood what was passing in her husband's mind, and she felt the young girl's attempt would be useless, and only plunge the poor children in deeper despair. Suddenly, a grand, generous purpose fired her soul, and she called out: "Mary Grant! wait, my child, and listen to what I'm going to say."

Mary had just taken her brother by the hand, and turned to go away; but she stepped back at Lady Helena's bidding.

The young wife went up to her husband, and said, with tears in her eyes, though her voice was firm, and her face beamed with animation: "Edward, when Captain Grant wrote that letter and threw it into the sea, he committed it to the care of God. God has sent it to us—to us! Undoubtedly God intends us to undertake the rescue of these poor men."

"What do you mean, Helena?"

"I mean this, that we ought to think ourselves fortunate if we can begin our married life with a good action. Well, you know, Edward, that to please me you planned a pleasure trip; but what could give us such genuine pleasure, or be so useful, as to save those unfortunate fellows, cast off by their country?"

"Helena!" exclaimed Lord Glenarvan.

"Yes, Edward, you understand me. The DUNCAN is a good strong ship, she can venture in the Southern Seas, or go round the world if necessary. Let us go, Edward; let us start off and search for Captain Grant!"

Lord Glenarvan made no reply to this bold proposition, but smiled, and, holding out his arms, drew his wife into a close, fond embrace. Mary and Robert seized her hands, and covered them with kisses; and the servants who thronged the courtyard, and had been witnesses of this touching scene, shouted with one voice, "Hurrah for the Lady of Luss. Three cheers for Lord and Lady Glenarvan!"

CHAPTER V THE DEPARTURE OF THE "DUNCAN"

WE have said already that Lady Helena was a brave, generous woman, and what she had just done proved it in-disputably. Her husband had good reason to be proud of such a wife, one who could understand and enter into all his views. The idea of going to Captain Grant's rescue had occurred to him in London when his request was refused, and he would have anticipated Lady Helena, only he could not bear the thought of parting from her. But now that she herself proposed to go, all hesitation was at an end. The servants of the Castle had hailed the project with loud acclamations— for it was to save their brothers— Scotchmen, like themselves— and Lord Glenarvan cordially joined his cheers with theirs, for the Lady of Luss.

The departure once resolved upon, there was not an hour to be lost. A telegram was dispatched to John Mangles the very same day, conveying Lord Glenarvan's orders to take the DUNCAN immediately to Glasgow, and to make preparations for a voyage to the Southern Seas, and possibly round the world, for Lady Helena was right in her opinion that the yacht might safely attempt the circumnavigation of the globe, if necessary.

The DUNCAN was a steam yacht of the finest description. She was 210 tons burden— much larger than any of the first vessels that touched the shores of the New World, for the largest of the four ships that sailed with Columbus was only 70 tons. She had two masts and all the sails and rigging of an ordinary clipper, which would enable her to take advantage of every favorable wind, though her chief reliance was on her mechanical power. The engine, which was constructed on a new system, was a high-pressure one, of 160-horse power, and put in motion a double screw. This gave the yacht such swiftness that during her trial trip in the Firth of Clyde, she made seventeen miles an hour, a higher speed than any vessel had yet attained. No alterations were consequently needed in the DUNCAN herself; John Mangles had only to attend to her interior arrangements.

His first care was to enlarge the bunkers to carry as much coal as possible, for it is difficult to get fresh supplies *en route*. He had to do the same with the store-rooms, and managed so well that he succeeded in laying in provisions enough for two years. There was abundance of money at his command, and enough remained to buy a cannon, on a pivot carriage, which he mounted on the forecastle. There was no knowing what might happen, and it is always well to be able to send a good round bullet flying four miles off.

John Mangles understood his business. Though he was only the captain of a pleasure yacht, he was one of the best skippers in Glasgow. He was thirty years of age, and his countenance expressed both courage and goodness, if the features were somewhat coarse. He had been brought up at the castle by the Glenarvan family, and had turned out a capital sailor, having already given proof, in some of his long voyages, of his skill and energy and *sang-froid*. When Lord Glenarvan offered him the command of the DUNCAN, he accepted it with right good will, for he loved the master of Malcolm Castle, like a brother, and had hitherto vainly sought some opportunity of showing his devotion.

Tom Austin, the mate, was an old sailor, worthy of all confidence. The crew, consisting of twenty-five men, including the captain and chief officer, were all from Dumbartonshire, experienced sailors, and all belonging to the Glenarvan estate; in fact, it was a regular clan, and they did not forget to carry with them the traditional bagpipes. Lord Glenarvan had in them a band of trusty fellows, skilled in their calling, devoted to himself, full of courage, and as practiced in handling fire-arms as in the maneuvering of a ship; a valiant little troop, ready to follow him any where, even in the most dangerous expeditions. When the crew heard whither they were bound, they could not restrain their enthusiasm, and the rocks of Dumbarton rang again with their joyous outbursts of cheers.

But while John Mangles made the stowage and provisioning of the yacht his chief business, he did not forget to fit up the rooms of Lord and Lady Glenarvan for a long voyage. He had also to get cabins ready for the children of Captain Grant, as Lady Helena could not refuse Mary's request to accompany her.

As for young Robert, he would have smuggled himself in somewhere in the hold of the DUNCAN rather than be left behind. He would willingly have gone as cabin-boy, like Nelson. It was impossible to resist a little fellow like that, and, indeed, no one tried. He would not even go as a passenger, but must serve in some capacity, as cabin-boy, apprentice or sailor, he did not care which, so he was put in charge of John Mangles, to be properly trained for his vocation.

"And I hope he won't spare me the 'cat-o-nine-tails' if I don't do properly," said Robert.

"Rest easy on that score, my boy," said Lord Glenarvan, gravely; he did not add, that this mode of punishment was forbidden on board the DUNCAN, and moreover, was quite unnecessary.

To complete the roll of passengers, we must name Major McNabbs. The Major was about fifty years of age, with a calm face and regular features—a man who did whatever he was told, of an excellent, indeed, a perfect temper; modest, silent, peaceable, and amiable, agreeing with everybody on every subject, never discussing, never disputing, never getting angry. He wouldn't move a step quicker, or slower, whether he walked upstairs to bed or mounted a breach. Nothing could excite him, nothing could disturb him, not even a cannon ball, and no doubt he will die without ever having known even a passing feeling of irritation.

This man was endowed in an eminent degree, not only with ordinary animal courage, that physical bravery of the battle-field, which is solely due to muscular energy, but he had what is far nobler— moral courage, firmness of soul. If he had any fault it was his being so intensely Scotch from top to toe, a Caledonian of the Caledonians, an obstinate stickler for all the ancient customs of his country. This was the reason he would never serve in England, and he gained his rank of Major in the 42nd regiment, the Highland Black Watch, composed entirely of Scotch noblemen.

As a cousin of Glenarvan, he lived in Malcolm Castle, and as a major he went as a matter of course with the DUNCAN.

Such, then, was the PERSONNEL of this yacht, so unexpectedly called to make one of the most wonderful voyages of modern times. From the hour she reached the steamboat quay at Glasgow, she completely monopolized the public attention. A considerable crowd visited her every day, and the DUNCAN was the one topic of interest and conversation, to the great vexation of the different captains in the port, among others of Captain Burton, in command of the SCOTIA, a magnificent steamer lying close beside her, and bound for Calcutta. Considering her size, the SCOTIA might justly look upon the DUNCAN as a mere fly-boat, and yet this pleasure yacht of Lord Glenarvan was quite the center of attraction, and the excitement about her daily increased.

The DUNCAN was to sail out with the tide at three o'clock on the morning of the 25th of August. But before starting, a touching ceremony was witnessed by the good people of Glasgow. At eight o'clock the night before, Lord Glenarvan and his friends, and the entire crew, from the stokers to the captain, all who were to take part in this self-sacrificing voyage, left the yacht and repaired to St. Mungo's, the ancient cathedral of the city. This venerable edifice, so marvelously described by Walter Scott, remains intact amid the ruins made by the Reformation; and it was there, beneath its lofty arches, in the grand nave, in the presence of an immense crowd, and surrounded by tombs as thickly set as in a cemetery, that they all assembled to implore the blessing of Heaven on their expedition, and to put themselves under the protection of Providence. The Rev. Mr. Morton conducted the service, and when he had ended and pronounced the benediction, a young girl's voice broke the solemn silence that followed. It was Mary Grant who poured out her heart to God in prayer for her benefactors, while grateful happy tears streamed down her cheeks, and almost choked her utterance. The vast assembly dispersed under the influence of deep emotion, and at ten o'clock the passengers and crew returned on board the vessel.

CHAPTER VI AN UNEXPECTED PASSENGER

THE ladies passed the whole of the first day of the voyage in their berths, for there was a heavy swell in the sea, and toward evening the wind blew pretty fresh, and the DUNCAN tossed and pitched considerably.

But the morning after, the wind changed, and the captain ordered the men to put up the foresail, and brigantine and foretopsail, which greatly lessened the rolling of the vessel. Lady Helena and Mary Grant were able to come on deck at daybreak, where they found Lord Glenarvan, Major McNabbs and the captain.

"And how do you stand the sea, Miss Mary?" said Lord Glenarvan.

"Pretty well, my Lord. I am not very much inconvenienced by it.

Besides I shall get used to it."

"And our young Robert!"

"Oh, as for Robert," said the captain, "whenever he is not poking about down below in the engine-room, he is perched somewhere aloft among the rigging. A youngster like that laughs at sea-sickness. Why, look at him this very moment! Do you see him?"

The captain pointed toward the foremast, and sure enough there was Robert, hanging on the yards of the topgallant mast, a hundred feet above in the air. Mary involuntarily gave a start, but the captain said:

"Oh, don't be afraid, Miss Mary; he is all right, take my word for it; I'll have a capital sailor to present to Captain Grant before long, for we'll find the worthy captain, depend upon it."

"Heaven grant it, Mr. John," replied the young girl.

"My dear child," said Lord Glenarvan, "there is something so providential in the whole affair, that we have every reason to hope. We are not going, we are led; we are not searching, we are guided. And then see all the brave men that have enlisted in the service of the good cause. We shall not only succeed in our enterprise, but there will be little difficulty in it. I promised Lady Helena a pleasure trip, and I am much mistaken if I don't keep my word."

"Edward," said his wife, "you are the best of men."

"Not at all," was the reply; "but I have the best of crews and the best of ships. You don't admire the DUNCAN, I suppose, Miss Mary?"

"On the contrary, my lord, I do admire her, and I'm a connoisseur in ships," returned the young girl.

"Indeed!"

"Yes. I have played all my life on my father's ships.

He should have made me a sailor, for I dare say, at a push,

I could reef a sail or plait a gasket easily enough."

"Do you say so, miss?" exclaimed John Mangles.

"If you talk like that you and John will be great friends, for he can't think any calling is equal to that of a seaman; he can't fancy any other, even for a woman. Isn't it true, John?"

"Quite so," said the captain, "and yet, your Lordship, I must confess that Miss Grant is more in her place on the poop than reefing a topsail. But for all that, I am quite flattered by her remarks."

"And especially when she admires the DUNCAN," replied Glenarvan.

"Well, really," said Lady Glenarvan, "you are so proud of your yacht that you make me wish to look all over it; and I should like to go down and see how our brave men are lodged."

"Their quarters are first-rate," replied John, "they are as comfortable as if they were at home."

"And they really are at home, my dear Helena," said Lord Glenarvan. "This yacht is a portion of our old Caledonia, a fragment of Dumbartonshire, making a voyage by special favor, so that in a manner we are still in our own country. The DUNCAN is Malcolm Castle, and the ocean is Loch Lomond."

"Very well, dear Edward, do the honors of the Castle then."

"At your service, madam; but let me tell Olbinett first."

The steward of the yacht was an excellent *maitre d'hotel*, and might have been French for his airs of importance, but for all that he discharged his functions with zeal and intelligence.

"Olbinett," said his master, as he appeared in answer to his summons, "we are going to have a turn before breakfast. I hope we shall find it ready when we come back."

He said this just as if it had been a walk to Tarbert or Loch Katrine they were going, and the steward bowed with perfect gravity in reply.

"Are you coming with us, Major?" asked Lady Helena.

"If you command me," replied McNabbs.

"Oh!" said Lord Glenarvan; "the Major is absorbed in his cigar; "you mustn't tear him from it. He is an inveterate smoker, Miss Mary, I can tell you. He is always smoking, even while he sleeps."

The Major gave an assenting nod, and Lord Glenarvan and his party went below.

McNabbs remained alone, talking to himself, as was his habit, and was soon enveloped in still thicker clouds of smoke. He stood motionless, watching the track of the yacht. After some minutes of this silent contemplation he turned round, and suddenly found himself face to face with a new comer. Certainly, if any thing could have surprised him, this RENCONTRE would, for he had never seen the stranger in his life before.

He was a tall, thin, withered-looking man, about forty years of age, and resembled a long nail with a big head. His head was large and massive, his forehead high, his chin very marked. His eyes were concealed by enormous round spectacles, and in his look was that peculiar indecision which is common to nyctalopes, or people who have a peculiar construction of the eye, which makes the sight imperfect in the day and better at night. It was evident from his physiognomy that he was a lively, intelligent man; he had not the crabbed expression of those grave individuals who never laugh on principle, and cover their emptiness with a mask of seriousness. He looked far from that. His careless, good-humored air, and easy, unceremonious manners, showed plainly that he knew how to take men and things on their bright side. But though he had not yet opened his mouth, he gave one the impression of being a great talker, and moreover, one of those absent folks who neither see though they are looking, nor hear though they are listening. He wore a traveling cap, and strong, low, yellow boots with leather gaiters. His pantaloons and jacket were of brown velvet, and their innumerable pockets were stuffed with note-books, memorandum-books, account-books, pocket-books, and a thousand other things equally cumbersome and useless, not to mention a telescope in addition, which he carried in a shoulder-belt.

The stranger's excitement was a strong contrast to the Major's placidity. He walked round McNabbs, looking at him and questioning him with his eyes without eliciting one remark from the imperturbable Scotchman, or awakening his curiosity in the least, to know where he came from, and where he was going, and how he had got on board the DUNCAN.

Finding all his efforts baffled by the Major's indifference, the mysterious passenger seized his telescope, drew it out to its fullest extent, about four feet, and began gazing at the horizon, standing motionless with his legs wide apart. His examination lasted some few minutes, and then he lowered the glass, set it up on deck, and leaned on it as if it had been a walking-stick. Of course, his weight shut up the instrument immediately by pushing the different parts one into the other, and so suddenly, that he fell full length on deck, and lay sprawling at the foot of the mainmast.

Any one else but the Major would have smiled, at least, at such a ludicrous sight; but McNabbs never moved a muscle of his face.

This was too much for the stranger, and he called out, with an unmistakably foreign accent:

"Steward!"

He waited a minute, but nobody appeared, and he called again, still louder, "Steward!"

Mr. Olbinett chanced to be passing that minute on his way from the galley, and what was his astonishment at hearing himself addressed like this by a lanky individual of whom he had no knowledge whatever.

"Where can he have come from? Who is he?" he thought to himself.

"He can not possibly be one of Lord Glenarvan's friends?"

However, he went up on the poop, and approached the unknown personage, who accosted him with the inquiry, "Are you the steward of this vessel? "

"Yes, sir," replied Olbinett; "but I have not the honor of—"

"I am the passenger in cabin Number 6."

"Number 6!" repeated the steward.

"Certainly; and your name, what is it?"

"Olbinett."

"Well, Olbinett, my friend, we must think of breakfast, and that pretty quickly. It is thirty-six hours since I have had anything to eat, or rather thirty-six hours that I have been asleep— pardonable enough in a man who came all the way, without stopping, from Paris to Glasgow. What is the breakfast hour?"

"Nine o'clock," replied Olbinett, mechanically.

The stranger tried to pull out his watch to see the time; but it was not till he had rummaged through the ninth pocket that he found it.

"Ah, well," he said, "it is only eight o'clock at present. Fetch me a glass of sherry and a biscuit while I am waiting, for I am actually falling through sheer inanition."

Olbinett heard him without understanding what he meant for the voluble stranger kept on talking incessantly, flying from one subject to another.

"The captain? Isn't the captain up yet? And the chief officer? What is he doing? Is he asleep still? It is fine weather, fortunately, and the wind is favorable, and the ship goes all alone."

Just at that moment John Mangles appeared at the top of the stairs.

"Here is the captain!" said Olbinett.

"Ah! delighted, Captain Burton, delighted to make your acquaintance," exclaimed the unknown.

John Mangles stood stupefied, as much at seeing the stranger on board as at hearing himself called "Captain Burton."

But the new comer went on in the most affable manner.

"Allow me to shake hands with you, sir; and if I did not do so yesterday evening, it was only because I did not wish to be troublesome when you were starting. But to-day, captain, it gives me great pleasure to begin my intercourse with you."

John Mangles opened his eyes as wide as possible, and stood staring at Olbinett and the stranger alternately.

But without waiting for a reply, the rattling fellow continued:

"Now the introduction is made, my dear captain, we are old friends.

Let's have a little talk, and tell me how you like the SCOTIA?"

"What do you mean by the SCOTIA?" put in John Mangles at last.

"By the SCOTIA? Why, the ship we're on, of course—a good ship that has been commended to me, not only for its physical qualities, but also for the moral qualities of its commander, the brave Captain Burton. You will be some relation of the famous African traveler of that name. A daring man he was, sir. I offer you my congratulations."

"Sir," interrupted John. "I am not only no relation of Burton the great traveler, but I am not even Captain Burton."

"Ah, is that so? It is Mr. Burdness, the chief officer, that I am talking to at present."

"Mr. Burdness!" repeated John Mangles, beginning to suspect how the matter stood. Only he asked himself whether the man was mad, or some heedless rattle pate? He was beginning to explain the case in a categorical manner, when Lord Glenarvan and his party came up on the poop. The stranger caught sight of them directly, and exclaimed:

"Ah! the passengers, the passengers! I hope you are going to introduce me to them, Mr. Burdness!"

But he could not wait for any one's intervention, and going up to them with perfect ease and grace, said, bowing to Miss Grant, "Madame;" then to Lady Helena, with another bow, "Miss;" and to Lord Glenarvan, "Sir."

Here John Mangles interrupted him, and said, "Lord Glenarvan."

"My Lord," continued the unknown, "I beg pardon for presenting myself to you, but at sea it is well to relax the strict rules of etiquette a little. I hope we shall soon become acquainted with each other, and that the company of these ladies will make our voyage in the SCOTIA appear as short as agreeable."

Lady Helena and Miss Grant were too astonished to be able to utter a single word. The presence of this intruder on the poop of the DUNCAN was perfectly inexplicable.

Lord Glenarvan was more collected, and said, "Sir, to whom have I the honor of speaking?"

"To Jacques Eliacin Francois Marie Paganel, Secretary of the Geographical Society of Paris, Corresponding Member of the Societies of Berlin, Bombay, Darmstadt, Leipsic, London, St. Petersburg, Vienna, and New York; Honorary Member of the Royal Geographical and Ethnographical Institute of the East Indies; who, after having spent twenty years of his life in geographical work in the study, wishes to see active service, and is on his way to India to gain for the science what information he can by following up the footsteps of great travelers."

CHAPTER VII JACQUES PAGANEL IS UNDECEIVED

THE Secretary of the Geographical Society was evidently an amiable personage, for all this was said in a most charming manner. Lord Glenarvan knew quite well who he was now, for he had often heard Paganel spoken of, and was aware of his merits. His geographical works, his papers on modern discoveries, inserted in the reports of the Society, and his world-wide correspondence, gave him a most distinguished place among the LITERATI of France.

Lord Glenarvan could not but welcome such a guest, and shook hands cordially.

"And now that our introductions are over," he added, "you will allow me,

Monsieur Paganel, to ask you a question?"

"Twenty, my Lord, " replied Paganel; "it will always be a pleasure to converse with you."

"Was it last evening that you came on board this vessel?"

"Yes, my Lord, about 8 o'clock. I jumped into a cab at the Caledonian Railway, and from the cab into the SCOTIA, where I had booked my cabin before I left Paris. It was a dark night, and I saw no one on board, so I found cabin No. 6, and went to my berth immediately, for I had heard that the best way to prevent sea-sickness is to go to bed as soon as you start, and not to stir for the first few days; and, moreover, I had been traveling for thirty hours. So I tucked myself in, and slept conscientiously, I assure you, for thirty-six hours."

Paganel's listeners understood the whole mystery, now, of his presence on the DUNCAN. The French traveler had mistaken his vessel, and gone on board while the crew were attending the service at St. Mungo's. All was explained. But what would the learned geographer say, when he heard the name and destination of the ship, in which he had taken passage?

"Then it is Calcutta, M. Paganel, that you have chosen as your point of departure on your travels?"

"Yes, my Lord, to see India has been a cherished purpose with me all my life. It will be the realization of my fondest dreams, to find myself in the country of elephants and Thugs."

"Then it would be by no means a matter of indifference to you, to visit another country instead."

"No, my Lord; indeed it would be very disagreeable, for I have letters from Lord Somerset, the Governor-General, and also a commission to execute for the Geographical Society."

"Ah, you have a commission."

CHAPTER VII JACQUES PAGANEL IS UNDECEIVED

"Yes, I have to attempt a curious and important journey, the plan of which has been drawn up by my learned friend and colleague, M. Vivien de Saint Martin. I am to pursue the track of the Schlaginweit Brothers; and Colonels Waugh and Webb, and Hodgson; and Huc and Gabet, the missionaries; and Moorecroft and M. Jules Remy, and so many celebrated travelers. I mean to try and succeed where Krick, the missionary so unfortunately failed in 1846; in a word, I want to follow the course of the river Yarou-Dzangbo-Tchou, which waters Thibet for a distance of 1500 kilometres, flowing along the northern base of the Himalayas, and to find out at last whether this river does not join itself to the Brahmapoutre in the northeast of Assam. The gold medal, my Lord, is promised to the traveler who will succeed in ascertaining a fact which is one of the greatest DESIDERATA to the geography of India."

Paganel was magnificent. He spoke with superb animation, soaring away on the wings of imagination. It would have been as impossible to stop him as to stop the Rhine at the Falls of Schaffhausen.

"Monsieur Jacques Paganel," said Lord Glenarvan, after a brief pause, "that would certainly be a grand achievement, and you would confer a great boon on science, but I should not like to allow you to be laboring under a mistake any longer, and I must tell you, therefore, that for the present at least, you must give up the pleasure of a visit to India."

"Give it up. And why?"

"Because you are turning your back on the Indian peninsula."

"What! Captain Burton."

"I am not Captain Burton," said John Mangles.

"But the SCOTIA."

"This vessel is not the SCOTIA."

It would be impossible to depict the astonishment of Paganel. He stared first at one and then at another in the utmost bewilderment.

Lord Glenarvan was perfectly grave, and Lady Helena and Mary showed their sympathy for his vexation by their looks. As for John Mangles, he could not suppress a smile; but the Major appeared as unconcerned as usual. At last the poor fellow shrugged his shoulders, pushed down his spectacles over his nose and said:

"You are joking."

But just at that very moment his eye fell on the wheel of the ship,

and he saw the two words on it:

Duncan.

Glasgow.

"The DUNCAN! the DUNCAN!" he exclaimed, with a cry of despair, and forthwith rushed down the stairs, and away to his cabin.

As soon as the unfortunate SAVANT had disappeared, every one, except the Major, broke out into such peals of laughter that the sound reached the ears of the sailors in the forecastle. To mistake a railway or to take the train to Edinburgh when you want to go to Dumbarton might happen; but to mistake a ship and be sailing for Chili when you meant to go to India— that is a blunder indeed!

"However," said Lord Glenarvan, "I am not much astonished at it in Paganel. He is quite famous for such misadventures. One day he published a celebrated map of America, and put Japan in it! But for all that, he is distinguished for his learning, and he is one of the best geographers in France."

"But what shall we do with the poor gentleman?" said Lady Helena; "we can't take him with us to Patagonia."

"Why not?" replied McNabbs, gravely. "We are not responsible for his heedless mistakes. Suppose he were in a railway train, would they stop it for him?"

"No, but he would get out at the first station."

"Well, that is just what he can do here, too, if he likes; he can disembark at the first place where we touch."

While they were talking, Paganel came up again on the poop, looking very woebegone and crestfallen. He had been making inquiry about his luggage, to assure himself that it was all on board, and kept repeating incessantly the unlucky words, "The DUNCAN! the DUNCAN!"

He could find no others in his vocabulary. He paced restlessly up and down; sometimes stopping to examine the sails, or gaze inquiringly over the wide ocean, at the far horizon. At length he accosted Lord Glenarvan once more, and said—

"And this DUNCAN—where is she going?"

"To America, Monsieur Paganel," was the reply.

"And to what particular part?"

"To Concepcion."

"To Chili! to Chili!" cried the unfortunate geographer. "And my mission to India. But what will M. de Quatre-fages, the President of the Central Commission, say? And M. d' Avezac? And M. Cortanbert? And M. Vivien de Saint Martin? How shall I show my face at the SEANCES of the Society?"

"Come, Monsieur Paganel, don't despair. It can all be managed; you will only have to put up with a little delay, which is relatively of not much importance. The Yarou-Dzangbo-Tchou will wait for you still in the mountains of Thibet. We shall soon put in at Madeira, and you will get a ship there to take you back to Europe."

"Thanks, my Lord. I suppose I must resign myself to it; but people will say it is a most extraordinary adventure, and it is only to me such things happen. And then, too, there is a cabin taken for me on board the SCOTIA."

"Oh, as to the SCOTIA, you'll have to give that up meantime."

"But the DUNCAN is a pleasure yacht, is it not?" began Paganel again, after a fresh examination of the vessel.

"Yes, sir," said John Mangles, "and belongs to Lord Glenarvan."

"Who begs you will draw freely on his hospitality," said Lord Glenarvan.

"A thousand thanks, my Lord! I deeply feel your courtesy, but allow me to make one observation: India is a fine country, and can offer many a surprising marvel to travelers. These ladies, I suppose, have never seen it. Well now, the man at the helm has only to give a turn at the wheel, and the DUNCAN will sail as easily to Calcutta as to Concepcion; and since it is only a pleasure trip that you are—"

His proposal was met by such grave, disapproving shakes of the head, that he stopped short before the sentence was completed; and Lady Helena said:

"Monsieur Paganel, if we were only on a pleasure trip, I should reply, 'Let us all go to India together,' and I am sure Lord Glenarvan would not object; but the DUNCAN is going to bring back shipwrecked mariners who were cast away on the shores of Patagonia, and we could not alter such a destination."

The Frenchman was soon put in possession of all the circumstances of the case. He was no unmoved auditor, and when he heard of Lady Helena's generous proposition, he could not help saying,

"Madame, permit me to express my admiration of your conduct throughout— my unreserved admiration. Let your yacht continue her course. I should reproach myself were I to cause a single day's delay."

"Will you join us in our search, then?" asked Lady Helena.

"It is impossible, madame. I must fulfill my mission. I shall disembark at the first place you touch at, wherever it may be."

"That will be Madeira," said John Mangles.

"Madeira be it then. I shall only be 180 leagues from Lisbon, and I shall wait there for some means of transport."

"Very well, Monsieur Paganel, it shall be as you wish; and, for my own part, I am very glad to be able to offer you, meantime, a few days' hospitality. I only hope you will not find our company too dull."

"Oh, my Lord," exclaimed Paganel, "I am but too happy to have made a mistake which has turned out so agreeably. Still, it is a very ridiculous plight for a man to be in, to find himself sailing to America when he set out to go to the East Indies!"

But in spite of this melancholy reflection, the Frenchman submitted gracefully to the compulsory delay. He made himself amiable and merry, and even diverting, and enchanted the ladies with his good humor. Before the end of the day he was friends with everybody. At his request, the famous document was brought out. He studied it carefully and minutely for a long time, and finally declared his opinion that no other interpretation of it was possible. Mary Grant and her brother inspired him with the most lively interest. He gave them great hope; indeed, the young girl could not help smiling at his sanguine prediction of success, and this odd way of foreseeing future events. But for his mission he would have made one of the search party for Captain Grant, undoubtedly.

As for Lady Helena, when he heard that she was a daughter of William Tuffnell, there was a perfect explosion of admiring epithets. He had known her father, and what letters had passed between them when William Tuffnell was a corresponding member of the Society! It was he himself that had introduced him and M. Malte Brun. What a *rencontre* this was, and what a pleasure to travel with the daughter of Tuffnell.

He wound up by asking permission to kiss her, which Lady Helena granted, though it was, perhaps, a little improper.

CHAPTER VIII THE GEOGRAPHER'S RESOLUTION

MEANTIME the yacht, favored by the currents from the north of Africa, was making rapid progress toward the equator. On the 30th of August they sighted the Madeira group of islands, and Glenarvan, true to his promise, offered to put in there, and land his new guest.

But Paganel said:

"My dear Lord, I won't stand on ceremony with you. Tell me, did you intend to stop at Madeira before I came on board?"

"No," replied Glenarvan.

"Well, then, allow me to profit by my unlucky mistake. Madeira is an island too well known to be of much interest now to a geographer. Every thing about this group has been said and written already. Besides, it is completely going down as far as wine growing is concerned. Just imagine no vines to speak of being in Madeira! In 1813, 22,000 pipes of wine were made there, and in 1845 the number fell to 2,669. It is a grievous spectacle! If it is all the same to you, we might go on to the Canary Isles instead."

"Certainly. It will not the least interfere with our route."

"I know it will not, my dear Lord. In the Canary Islands, you see, there are three groups to study, besides the Peak of Teneriffe, which I always wished to visit. This is an opportunity, and I should like to avail myself of it, and make the ascent of the famous mountain while I am waiting for a ship to take me back to Europe."

"As you please, my dear Paganel," said Lord Glenarvan, though he could not help smiling; and no wonder, for these islands are scarcely 250 miles from Madeira, a trifling distance for such a quick sailer as the DUNCAN.

Next day, about 2 P. M., John Mangles and Paganel were walking on the poop. The Frenchman was assailing his companion with all sorts of questions about Chili, when all at once the captain interrupted him, and pointing toward the southern horizon, said:

"Monsieur Paganel?"

"Yes, my dear Captain."

"Be so good as to look in this direction. Don't you see anything?"

"Nothing."

"You're not looking in the right place. It is not on the horizon, but above it in the clouds."

"In the clouds? I might well not see."

"There, there, by the upper end of the bowsprit."

"I see nothing."

"Then you don't want to see. Anyway, though we are forty miles off, yet I tell you the Peak of Teneriffe is quite visible yonder above the horizon."

CHAPTER VIII THE GEOGRAPHER'S RESOLUTION

But whether Paganel could not or would not see it then, two hours later he was forced to yield to ocular evidence or own himself blind.

"You do see it at last, then," said John Mangles.

"Yes, yes, distinctly," replied Paganel, adding in a disdainful tone, "and that's what they call the Peak of Teneriffe!"

"That's the Peak."

"It doesn't look much of a height."

"It is 11,000 feet, though, above the level of the sea."

"That is not equal to Mont Blanc."

"Likely enough, but when you come to ascend it, probably you'll think it high enough."

"Oh, ascend it! ascend it, my dear captain! What would be the good after Humboldt and Bonplan? That Humboldt was a great genius. He made the ascent of this mountain, and has given a description of it which leaves nothing unsaid. He tells us that it comprises five different zones—the zone of the vines, the zone of the laurels, the zone of the pines, the zone of the Alpine heaths, and, lastly, the zone of sterility. He set his foot on the very summit, and found that there was not even room enough to sit down. The view from the summit was very extensive, stretching over an area equal to Spain. Then he went right down into the volcano, and examined the extinct crater. What could I do, I should like you to tell me, after that great man?"

"Well, certainly, there isn't much left to glean. That is vexing, too, for you would find it dull work waiting for a vessel in the Peak of Teneriffe."

"But, I say, Mangles, my dear fellow, are there no ports in the Cape Verde Islands that we might touch at?"

"Oh, yes, nothing would be easier than putting you off at Villa Praya."

"And then I should have one advantage, which is by no means inconsiderable—I should find fellow-countrymen at Senegal, and that is not far away from those islands. I am quite aware that the group is said to be devoid of much interest, and wild, and unhealthy; but everything is curious in the eyes of a geographer. Seeing is a science. There are people who do not know how to use their eyes, and who travel about with as much intelligence as a shell-fish. But that's not in my line, I assure you."

"Please yourself, Monsieur Paganel. I have no doubt geographical science will be a gainer by your sojourn in the Cape Verde Islands. We must go in there anyhow for coal, so your disembarkation will not occasion the least delay."

The captain gave immediate orders for the yacht to continue her route, steering to the west of the Canary group, and leaving Teneriffe on her larboard. She made rapid progress, and passed the Tropic of Cancer on the second of September at 5 A. M.

The weather now began to change, and the atmosphere became damp and heavy. It was the rainy season, "*le tempo das aguas*," as the Spanish call it, a trying season to travelers, but useful to the inhabitants of the African Islands, who lack trees and consequently water. The rough weather prevented the passengers from going on deck, but did not make the conversation any less animated in the saloon.

On the 3d of September Paganel began to collect his luggage to go on shore. The DUNCAN was already steaming among the Islands. She passed Sal, a complete tomb of sand lying barren and desolate, and went on among the vast coral reefs and athwart the Isle of St. Jacques, with its long chain of basaltic mountains, till she entered the port of Villa Praya and anchored in eight fathoms of water before the town. The weather was frightful, and the surf excessively violent, though the bay was sheltered from the sea winds. The rain fell in such torrents that the town was scarcely visible through it. It rose on a plain in the form of a terrace, buttressed on volcanic rocks three hundred feet high. The appearance of the island through the thick veil of rain was mournful in the extreme.

Lady Helena could not go on shore as she had purposed; indeed, even coaling was a difficult business, and the passengers had to content themselves below the poop as best they might. Naturally enough, the main topic of conversation was the weather. Everybody had something to say about it except the Major, who surveyed the universal deluge with the utmost indifference. Paganel walked up and down shaking his head.

"It is clear enough, Paganel," said Lord Glenarvan, "that the elements are against you."

"I'll be even with them for all that," replied the Frenchman.

"You could not face rain like that, Monsieur Paganel," said Lady Helena.

"Oh, quite well, madam, as far as I myself am concerned.

It is for my luggage and instruments that I am afraid.

Everything will be ruined."

"The disembarking is the worst part of the business. Once at Villa Praya you might manage to find pretty good quarters. They wouldn't be over clean, and you might find the monkeys and pigs not always the most agreeable companions. But travelers are not too particular, and, moreover, in seven or eight months you would get a ship, I dare say, to take you back to Europe."

"Seven or eight months!" exclaimed Paganel.

"At least. The Cape Verde Islands are not much frequented by ships during the rainy season. But you can employ your time usefully. This archipelago is still but little known."

"You can go up the large rivers," suggested Lady Helena.

"There are none, madam."

"Well, then, the small ones."

"There are none, madam."

"The running brooks, then."

"There are no brooks, either."

"You can console yourself with the forests if that's the case," put in the Major.

"You can't make forests without trees, and there are no trees."

"A charming country!" said the Major.

"Comfort yourself, my dear Paganel, you'll have the mountains at any rate," said Glenarvan.

"Oh, they are neither lofty nor interesting, my Lord, and, beside, they have been described already."

"Already!" said Lord Glenarvan.

"Yes, that is always my luck. At the Canary Islands, I saw myself anticipated by Humboldt, and here by M. Charles Sainte-Claire Deville, a geologist."

"Impossible!"

"It is too true," replied Paganel, in a doleful voice. "Monsieur Deville was on board the government corvette, La Decidee, when she touched at the Cape Verde Islands, and he explored the most interesting of the group, and went to the top of the volcano in Isle Fogo. What is left for me to do after him?"

"It is really a great pity," said Helena. "What will become of you, Monsieur Paganel?"

Paganel remained silent.

"You would certainly have done much better to have landed at Madeira, even though there had been no wine," said Glenarvan.

Still the learned secretary was silent.

"I should wait," said the Major, just as if he had said,

"I should not wait."

CHAPTER VIII THE GEOGRAPHER'S RESOLUTION

Paganel spoke again at length, and said:

"My dear Glenarvan, where do you mean to touch next?"

"At Concepcion."

"Plague it! That is a long way out of the road to India."

"Not it! From the moment you pass Cape Horn, you are getting nearer to it."

"I doubt it much."

"Beside," resumed Lord Glenarvan, with perfect gravity, "when people are going to the Indies it doesn't matter much whether it is to the East or West."

"What! it does not matter much?"

"Without taking into account the fact that the inhabitants of the Pampas in Patagonia are as much Indians as the natives of the Punjaub."

"Well done, my Lord. That's a reason that would never have entered my head!"

"And then, my dear Paganel, you can gain the gold medal anyway. There is as much to be done, and sought, and investigated, and discovered in the Cordilleras as in the mountains of Thibet."

"But the course of the Yarou-Dzangbo-Tchou—what about that?"

"Go up the Rio Colorado instead. It is a river but little known, and its course on the map is marked out too much according to the fancy of geographers."

"I know it is, my dear Lord; they have made grave mistakes. Oh, I make no question that the Geographical Society would have sent me to Patagonia as soon as to India, if I had sent in a request to that effect. But I never thought of it."

"Just like you."

"Come, Monsieur Paganel, will you go with us?" asked Lady Helena, in her most winning tone.

"Madam, my mission?"

"We shall pass through the Straits of Magellan, I must tell you," said Lord Glenarvan.

"My Lord, you are a tempter."

"Let me add, that we shall visit Port Famine."

"Port Famine!" exclaimed the Frenchman, besieged on all sides.

"That famous port in French annals!"

"Think, too, Monsieur Paganel, that by taking part in our enterprise, you will be linking France with Scotland."

"Undoubtedly."

"A geographer would be of much use to our expedition, and what can be nobler than to bring science to the service of humanity?"

"That's well said, madam."

"Take my advice, then, and yield to chance, or rather providence. Follow our example. It was providence that sent us the document, and we set out in consequence. The same providence brought you on board the DUNCAN. Don't leave her."

"Shall I say yes, my good friends? Come, now, tell me, you want me very much to stay, don't you?" said Paganel.

"And you're dying to stay, now, aren't you, Paganel?" returned Glenarvan.

"That's about it," confessed the learned geographer; "but I was afraid it would be inconsiderate."

CHAPTER IX THROUGH THE STRAITS OF MAGELLAN

THE joy on board was universal when Paganel's resolution was made known.

Little Robert flung himself on his neck in such tumultuous delight that he nearly threw the worthy secretary down, and made him say, "Rude *petit bonhomme.* I'll teach him geography."

Robert bade fair to be an accomplished gentleman some day, for John Mangles was to make a sailor of him, and the Major was to teach him *sang-froid*, and Glenarvan and Lady Helena were to instil into him courage and goodness and generosity, while Mary was to inspire him with gratitude toward such instructors.

The DUNCAN soon finished taking in coal, and turned her back on the dismal region. She fell in before long with the current from the coast of Brazil, and on the 7th of September entered the Southern hemisphere.

So far, then, the voyage had been made without difficulty. Everybody was full of hope, for in this search for Captain Grant, each day seemed to increase the probability of finding him. The captain was among the most confident on board, but his confidence mainly arose from the longing desire he had to see Miss Mary happy. He was smitten with quite a peculiar interest for this young girl, and managed to conceal his sentiments so well that everyone on board saw it except himself and Mary Grant.

As for the learned geographer, he was probably the happiest man in all the southern hemisphere. He spent the whole day in studying maps, which were spread out on the saloon table, to the great annoyance of M. Olbinett, who could never get the cloth laid for meals, without disputes on the subject. But all the passengers took his part except the Major, who was perfectly indifferent about geographical questions, especially at dinner-time. Paganel also came across a regular cargo of old books in the chief officer's chest. They were in a very damaged condition, but among them he raked out a few Spanish volumes, and determined forthwith to set to work to master the language of Cervantes, as no one on board understood it, and it would be helpful in their search along the Chilian coast. Thanks to his taste for languages, he did not despair of being able to speak the language fluently when they arrived at Concepcion. He studied it furiously, and kept constantly muttering heterogeneous syllables.

He spent his leisure hours in teaching young Robert, and instructed him in the history of the country they were so rapidly approaching.

On the 25th of September, the yacht arrived off the Straits of Magellan, and entered them without delay. This route is generally preferred by steamers on their way to the Pacific Ocean. The exact length of the straits is 372 miles. Ships of the largest tonnage find, throughout, sufficient depth of water, even close to the shore, and there is a good bottom everywhere, and abundance of fresh water, and rivers abounding in fish, and forests in game, and plenty of safe and accessible harbors; in fact a thousand things which arc lacking in Strait Lemaire and Cape Horn, with its terrible rocks, incessantly visited by hurricane and tempest.

For the first three or four hours—that is to say, for about sixty to eighty miles, as far as Cape Gregory—the coast on either side was low and sandy. Jacques Paganel would not lose a single point of view, nor a single detail of the straits. It would scarcely take thirty-six hours to go through them, and the moving panorama on both sides, seen in all the clearness and glory of the light of a southern sun, was well worth the trouble of looking at and admiring. On the Terra del Fuego side, a few wretched-looking creatures were wandering about on the rocks, but on the other side not a solitary inhabitant was visible.

Paganel was so vexed at not being able to catch a glimpse of
any Patagonians, that his companions were quite amused at him.
He would insist that Patagonia without Patagonians was not
Patagonia at all.

But Glenarvan replied:

"Patience, my worthy geographer. We shall see the Patagonians yet."

"I am not sure of it."

"But there is such a people, anyhow," said Lady Helena.

"I doubt it much, madam, since I don't see them."

"But surely the very name Patagonia, which means 'great feet' in Spanish, would not have been given to imaginary beings." "Oh, the name is nothing," said Paganel, who was arguing simply for the sake of arguing. "And besides, to speak the truth, we are not sure if that is their name."

"What an idea!" exclaimed Glenarvan. "Did you know that, Major?"

"No," replied McNabbs, "and wouldn't give a Scotch pound-note for the information."

"You shall hear it, however, Major Indifferent. Though Magellan called the natives Patagonians, the Fuegians called them Tiremenen, the Chilians Caucalhues, the colonists of Carmen Tehuelches, the Araucans Huiliches; Bougainville gives them the name of Chauha, and Falkner that of Tehuelhets. The name they give themselves is Inaken. Now, tell me then, how would you recognize them? Indeed, is it likely that a people with so many names has any actual existence?"

"That's a queer argument, certainly," said Lady Helena.

"Well, let us admit it," said her husband, "but our friend Paganel must own that even if there are doubts about the name of the race there is none about their size."

"Indeed, I will never own anything so outrageous as that," replied Paganel.

"They are tall," said Glenarvan.

"I don't know that."

"Are they little, then?" asked Lady Helena.

"No one can affirm that they are."

"About the average, then?" said McNabbs.

"I don't know that either."

"That's going a little too far," said Glenarvan. "Travelers who have seen them tell us."

"Travelers who have seen them," interrupted Paganel, "don't agree at all in their accounts. Magellan said that his head scarcely reached to their waist."

"Well, then, that provcs."

"Yes, but Drake declares that the English are taller than the tallest Patagonian?"

"Oh, the English—that may be," replied the Major, disdainfully, "but we are talking of the Scotch."

"Cavendish assures us that they are tall and robust," continued Paganel. "Hawkins makes out they are giants. Lemaire and Shouten declare that they are eleven feet high."

"These are all credible witnesses," said Glenarvan.

"Yes, quite as much as Wood, Narborough, and Falkner, who say they are of medium stature. Again, Byron, Giraudais, Bougainville, Wallis, and Carteret, declared that the Patagonians are six feet six inches tall."

"But what is the truth, then, among all these contradictions?" asked Lady Helena.

"Just this, madame; the Patagonians have short legs, and a large bust; or by way of a joke we might say that these natives are six feet high when they are sitting, and only five when they are standing."

"Bravo! my dear geographer," said Glenarvan. "That is very well put."

"Unless the race has no existence, that would reconcile all statements," returned Paganel. "But here is one consolation, at all events: the Straits of Magellan are very magnificent, even without Patagonians."

Just at this moment the DUNCAN was rounding the peninsula of Brunswick between splendid panoramas.

Seventy miles after doubling Cape Gregory, she left on her starboard the penitentiary of Punta Arena. The church steeple and the Chilian flag gleamed for an instant among the trees, and then the strait wound on between huge granitic masses which had an imposing effect. Cloud-capped mountains appeared, their heads white with eternal snows, and their feet hid in immense forests. Toward the southwest, Mount Tarn rose 6,500 feet high. Night came on after a long lingering twilight, the light insensibly melting away into soft shades. These brilliant constellations began to bestud the sky, and the Southern Cross shone out. There were numerous bays along the shore, easy of access, but the yacht did not drop anchor in any; she continued her course fearlessly through the luminous darkness. Presently ruins came in sight, crumbling buildings, which the night invested with grandeur, the sad remains of a deserted settlement, whose name will be an eternal protest against these fertile shores and forests full of game. The DUNCAN was passing Fort Famine.

It was in that very spot that Sarmiento, a Spaniard, came in 1581, with four hundred emigrants, to establish a colony. He founded the city of St. Philip, but the extreme severity of winter decimated the inhabitants, and those who had struggled through the cold died subsequently of starvation. Cavendish the Corsair discovered the last survivor dying of hunger in the ruins.

After sailing along these deserted shores, the DUNCAN went through a series of narrow passes, between forests of beech and ash and birch, and at length doubled Cape Froward, still bristling with the ice of the last winter. On the other side of the strait, in Terra del Fuego, stood Mount Sarmiento, towering to a height of 6,000 feet, an enormous accumulation of rocks, separated by bands of cloud, forming a sort of aerial archipelago in the sky.

It is at Cape Froward that the American continent actually terminates, for Cape Horn is nothing but a rock sunk in the sea in latitude 52 degrees. At Cape Momax the straits widened, and she was able to get round Narborough Isles and advance in a more southerly direction, till at length the rock of Cape Pilares, the extreme point of Desolation Island, came in sight, thirty-six hours after entering the straits. Before her stem lay a broad, open, sparkling ocean, which Jacques Paganel greeted with enthusiastic gestures, feeling kindred emotions with those which stirred the bosom of Ferdinand de Magellan himself, when the sails of his ship, the TRINIDAD, first bent before the breeze from the great Pacific.

CHAPTER X THE COURSE DECIDED

A WEEK after they had doubled the Cape Pilares, the DUNCAN steamed into the bay of Talcahuano, a magnificent estuary, twelve miles long and nine broad. The weather was splendid. From November to March the sky is always cloudless, and a constant south wind prevails, as the coast is sheltered by the mountain range of the Andes. In obedience to Lord Glenarvan's order, John Mangles had sailed as near the archipelago of Chiloe as possible, and examined all the creeks and windings of the coast, hoping to discover some traces of the shipwreck. A broken spar, or any fragment of the vessel, would have put them in the right track; but nothing whatever was visible, and the yacht continued her route, till she dropped anchor at the port of Talcahuano, forty-two days from the time she had sailed out of the fogs of the Clyde.

Glenarvan had a boat lowered immediately, and went on shore, accompanied by Paganel. The learned geographer gladly availed himself of the opportunity of making use of the language he had been studying so conscientiously, but to his great amazement, found he could not make himself understood by the people. "It is the accent I've not got," he said.

"Let us go to the Custom-house," replied Glenarvan.

They were informed on arriving there, by means of a few English words, aided by expressive gestures, that the British Consul lived at Concepcion, an hour's ride distant. Glenarvan found no difficulty in procuring two fleet horses, and he and Paganel were soon within the walls of the great city, due to the enterprising genius of Valdivia, the valiant comrade of the Pizarros.

How it was shorn of its ancient splendor! Often pillaged by the natives, burned in 1819, it lay in desolation and ruins, its walls still blackened by the flames, scarcely numbering 8,000 inhabitants, and already eclipsed by Talcahuano. The grass was growing in the streets, beneath the lazy feet of the citizens, and all trade and business, indeed any description of activity, was impossible. The notes of the mandolin resounded from every balcony, and languishing songs floated on the breeze. Concepcion, the ancient city of brave men, had become a village of women and children. Lord Glenarvan felt no great desire to inquire into the causes of this decay, though Paganel tried to draw him into a discussion on the subject. He would not delay an instant, but went straight on to the house of Mr. Bentic, her Majesty's Consul, who received them very courteously, and, on learning their errand, undertook to make inquiries all along the coast.

But to the question whether a three-mast vessel, called the BRITANNIA, had gone ashore either on the Chilian or Araucanian coast, he gave a decided negative. No report of such an event had been made to him, or any of the other consuls. Glenarvan, however, would not allow himself to be disheartened; he went back to Talcahuano, and spared neither pains nor expense to make a thorough investigation of the whole seaboard. But it was all in vain. The most minute inquiries were fruitless, and Lord Glenarvan returned to the yacht to report his ill success. Mary Grant and her brother could not restrain their grief. Lady Helena did her best to comfort them by loving caresses, while Jacques Paganel took up the document and began studying it again. He had been poring over it for more than an hour when Glenarvan interrupted him and said:

"Paganel! I appeal to your sagacity. Have we made an erroneous interpretation of the document? Is there anything illogical about the meaning?"

Paganel was silent, absorbed in reflection.

"Have we mistaken the place where the catastrophe occurred?" continued Glenarvan. "Does not the name Patagonia seem apparent even to the least clear-sighted individual?"

Paganel was still silent.

"Besides," said Glenarvan, "does not the word INDIEN prove we are right?"

"Perfectly so," replied McNabbs.

"And is it not evident, then, that at the moment of writing the words, the shipwrecked men were expecting to be made prisoners by the Indians?"

"I take exception to that, my Lord," said Paganel; "and even if your other conclusions are right, this, at least, seemed to me irrational."

"What do you mean?" asked Lady Helena, while all eyes were fixed on the geographer.

"I mean this," replied Paganel, "that Captain Grant is *now a prisoner among the Indians*, and I further add that the document states it unmistakably."

"Explain yourself, sir," said Mary Grant.

"Nothing is plainer, dear Mary. Instead of reading the document *seront prisonniers*, read *sont prisonniers*, and the whole thing is clear."

"But that is impossible," replied Lord Glenarvan.

"Impossible! and why, my noble friend?" asked Paganel, smiling.

"Because the bottle could only have been thrown into the sea just when the vessel went to pieces on the rocks, and consequently the latitude and longitude given refer to the actual place of the shipwreck."

"There is no proof of that," replied Paganel, "and I see nothing to preclude the supposition that the poor fellows were dragged into the interior by the Indians, and sought to make known the place of their captivity by means of this bottle."

"Except this fact, my dear Paganel, that there was no sea, and therefore they could not have flung the bottle into it."

"Unless they flung it into rivers which ran into the sea," returned Paganel.

This reply was so unexpected, and yet so admissible, that it made them all completely silent for a minute, though their beaming eyes betrayed the rekindling of hope in their hearts. Lady Helena was the first to speak.

"What an idea!" she exclaimed.

"And what a good idea," was Paganel's naive rejoinder to her exclamation.

"What would you advise, then?" said Glenarvan.

"My advice is to follow the 37th parallel from the point where it touches the American continent to where it dips into the Atlantic, without deviating from it half a degree, and possibly in some part of its course we shall fall in with the shipwrecked party."

"There is a poor chance of that," said the Major.

"Poor as it is," returned Paganel, "we ought not to lose it. If I am right in my conjecture, that the bottle has been carried into the sea on the bosom of some river, we cannot fail to find the track of the prisoners. You can easily convince yourselves of this by looking at this map of the country."

He unrolled a map of Chili and the Argentine provinces as he spoke, and spread it out on the table.

"Just follow me for a moment," he said, "across the American continent. Let us make a stride across the narrow strip of Chili, and over the Cordilleras of the Andes, and get into the heart of the Pampas. Shall we find any lack of rivers and streams and currents? No, for here are the Rio Negro and Rio Colorado, and their tributaries intersected by the 37th parallel, and any of them might have carried the bottle on its waters. Then, perhaps, in the midst of a tribe in some Indian settlement on the shores of these almost unknown rivers, those whom I may call my friends await some providential intervention. Ought we to disappoint their hopes? Do you not all agree with me that it is our duty to go along the line my finger is pointing out at this moment on the map, and if after all we find I have been mistaken, still to keep straight on and follow the 37th parallel till we find those we seek, if even we go right round the world?"

His generous enthusiasm so touched his auditors that, involuntarily, they rose to their feet and grasped his hands, while Robert exclaimed as he devoured the map with his eyes:

"Yes, my father is there!"

"And where he is," replied Glenarvan, "we'll manage to go, my boy, and find him. Nothing can be more logical than Paganel's theory, and we must follow the course he points out without the least hesitation. Captain Grant may have fallen into the hands of a numerous tribe, or his captors may be but a handful. In the latter case we shall carry him off at once, but in the event of the former, after we have reconnoitered the situation, we must go back to the DUNCAN on the eastern coast and get to Buenos Ayres, where we can soon organize a detachment of men, with Major McNabbs at their head, strong enough to tackle all the Indians in the Argentine provinces."

"That's capital, my Lord," said John Mangles, "and I may add, that there is no danger whatever crossing the continent."

"Monsieur Paganel," asked Lady Helena, "you have no fear then that if the poor fellows have fallen into the hands of the Indians their lives at least have been spared."

"What a question? Why, madam, the Indians are not anthropophagi! Far from it. One of my own countrymen, M. Guinnard, associated with me in the Geographical Society, was three years a prisoner among the Indians in the Pampas. He had to endure sufferings and ill-treatment, but came off victorious at last. A European is a useful being in these countries. The Indians know his value, and take care of him as if he were some costly animal."

"There is not the least room then for hesitation," said Lord Glenarvan. "Go we must, and as soon as possible. What route must we take?"

"One that is both easy and agreeable," replied Paganel. "Rather mountainous at first, and then sloping gently down the eastern side of the Andes into a smooth plain, turfed and graveled quite like a garden."

"Let us see the map?" said the Major.

"Here it is, my dear McNabbs. We shall go through the capital of Araucania, and cut the Cordilleras by the pass of Antuco, leaving the volcano on the south, and gliding gently down the mountain sides, past the Neuquem and the Rio Colorado on to the Pampas, till we reach the Sierra Tapalquen, from whence we shall see the frontier of the province of Buenos Ayres. These we shall pass by, and cross over the Sierra Tandil, pursuing our search to the very shores of the Atlantic, as far as Point Medano."

Paganel went through this programme of the expedition without so much as a glance at the map. He was so posted up in the travels of Frezier, Molina, Humboldt, Miers, and Orbigny, that he had the geographical nomenclature at his fingers' ends, and could trust implicitly to his never-failing memory.

"You see then, friend," he added, "that it is a straight course. In thirty days we shall have gone over it, and gained the eastern side before the DUNCAN, however little she may be delayed by the westerly winds."

"Then the DUNCAN is to cruise between Corrientes and Cape Saint Antonie," said John Mangles.

"Just so."

"And how is the expedition to be organized?" asked Glenarvan.

"As simply as possible. All there is to be done is to reconnoiter the situation of Captain Grant and not to come to gunshot with the Indians. I think that Lord Glenarvan, our natural leader; the Major, who would not yield his place to anybody; and your humble servant, Jacques Paganel."

"And me," interrupted Robert.

"Robert, Robert!" exclaimed Mary.

"And why not?" returned Paganel. "Travels form the youthful mind.

Yes, Robert, we four and three of the sailors."

"And does your Lordship mean to pass me by?" said John Mangles, addressing his master.

"My dear John," replied Glenarvan, "we leave passengers on board, those dearer to us than life, and who is to watch over them but the devoted captain?"

"Then we can't accompany you?" said Lady Helena, while a shade of sadness beclouded her eyes.

"My dear Helena, the journey will so soon be accomplished that it will be but a brief separation, and—"

"Yes, dear, I understand, it is all right; and I do hope you may succeed."

"Besides, you can hardly call it a journey," added Paganel.

"What is it, then?"

"It is just making a flying passage across the continent, the way a good man goes through the world, doing all the good he can. *Transire beneficiendo*—that is our motto."

This ended the discussion, if a conversation can be so called, where all who take part in it are of the same opinion. Preparations commenced the same day, but as secretly as possible to prevent the Indians getting scent of it.

The day of departure was fixed for the 14th of October. The sailors were all so eager to join the expedition that Glenarvan found the only way to prevent jealousy among them was to draw lots who should go. This was accordingly done, and fortune favored the chief officer, Tom Austin, Wilson, a strong, jovial young fellow, and Mulrady, so good a boxer that he might have entered the lists with Tom Sayers himself.

Glenarvan displayed the greatest activity about the preparations, for he was anxious to be ready by the appointed day. John Mangles was equally busy in coaling the vessel, that she might weigh anchor at the same time. There was quite a rivalry between Glenarvan and the young captain about getting first to the Argentine coast.

Both were ready on the 14th. The whole search party assembled in the saloon to bid farewell to those who remained behind. The DUNCAN was just about to get under way, and already the vibration of the screw began to agitate the limpid waters of Talcahuano, Glenarvan, Paganel, McNabbs, Robert Grant, Tom Austin, Wilson, and Mulrady, stood armed with carbines and Colt's revolvers. Guides and mules awaited them at the landing stairs of the harbor.

"It is time," said Lord Glenarvan at last.

"Go then, dear Edward," said Lady Helena, restraining her emotion.

Lord Glenarvan clasped her closely to his breast for an instant, and then turned away, while Robert flung his arms round Mary's neck.

"And now, friends," said Paganel, "let's have one good hearty shake of the hand all round, to last us till we get to the shores of the Atlantic."

This was not much to ask, but he certainly got strong enough grips to go some way towards satisfying his desire.

All went on deck now, and the seven explorers left the vessel. They were soon on the quay, and as the yacht turned round to pursue her course, she came so near where they stood, that Lady Helena could exchange farewells once more.

"God help you!" she called out.

"Heaven will help us, madam," shouted Paganel, in reply, "for you may be sure we'll help ourselves."

"Go on," sung out the captain to his engineer.

At the same moment Lord Glenarvan gave the signal to start, and away went the mules along the coast, while the DUNCAN steamed out at full speed toward the broad ocean.

CHAPTER XI TRAVELING IN CHILI

THE native troops organized by Lord Glenarvan consisted of three men and a boy. The captain of the muleteers was an Englishman, who had become naturalized through twenty years' residence in the country. He made a livelihood by letting out mules to travelers, and leading them over the difficult passes of the Cordilleras, after which he gave them in charge of a BAQUEANO, or Argentine guide, to whom the route through the Pampas was perfectly familiar. This Englishman had not so far forgotten his mother tongue among mules and Indians that he could not converse with his countrymen, and a lucky thing it was for them, as Lord Glenarvan found it far easier to give orders than to see them executed, Paganel was still unsuccessful in making himself understood.

The CATAPEZ, as he was called in Chilian, had two natives called PEONS, and a boy about twelve years of age under him. The PEONS took care of the baggage mules, and the boy led the MADRINA, a young mare adorned with rattle and bells, which walked in front, followed by ten mules. The travelers rode seven of these, and the CATAPEZ another. The remaining two carried provisions and a few bales of goods, intended to secure the goodwill of the Caciques of the plain. The PEONS walked, according to their usual habit.

Every arrangement had been made to insure safety and speed, for crossing the Andes is something more than an ordinary journey. It could not be accomplished without the help of the hardy mules of the far-famed Argentine breed. Those reared in the country are much superior to their progenitors. They are not particular about their food, and only drink once a day, and they can go with ease ten leagues in eight hours.

There are no inns along this road from one ocean to another. The only viands on which travelers can regale themselves are dried meat, rice seasoned with pimento, and such game as may be shot *en route*. The torrents provide them with water in the mountains, and the rivulets in the plains, which they improve by the addition of a few drops of rum, and each man carries a supply of this in a bullock's horn, called CHIFFLE. They have to be careful, however, not to indulge too freely in alcoholic drinks, as the climate itself has a peculiarly exhilarating effect on the nervous system. As for bedding, it is all contained in the saddle used by the natives, called RECADO. This saddle is made of sheepskins, tanned on one side and woolly on the other, fastened by gorgeous embroidered straps. Wrapped in these warm coverings a traveler may sleep soundly, and brave exposure to the damp nights.

Glenarvan, an experienced traveler, who knew how to adapt himself to the customs of other countries, adopted the Chilian costume for himself and his whole party. Paganel and Robert, both alike children, though of different growth, were wild with delight as they inserted their heads in the national PONCHO, an immense plaid with a hole in center, and their legs in high leather boots. The mules were richly caparisoned, with the Arab bit in their mouths, and long reins of plaited leather, which served as a whip; the headstall of the bridle was decorated with metal ornaments, and the ALFORJAS, double sacks of gay colored linen, containing the day's provisions. Paganel, DISTRAIT as usual, was flung several times before he succeeded in bestriding his good steed, but once in the saddle, his inseparable telescope on his shoulder-belt, he held on well enough, keeping his feet fast in the stirrups, and trusting entirely to the sagacity of his beast. As for Robert, his first attempt at mounting was successful, and proved that he had the making in him of an excellent horseman.

The weather was splendid when they started, the sky a deep cloudless blue, and yet the atmosphere so tempered by the sea breezes as to prevent any feeling of oppressive heat. They marched rapidly along the winding shore of the bay of Talcahuano, in order to gain the extremity of the parallel, thirty miles south. No one spoke much the first day, for the smoke of the DUNCAN was still visible on the horizon, and the pain of parting too keenly felt. Paganel talked to himself in Spanish, asking and answering questions.

The CATAPEZ, moreover, was a taciturn man naturally, and had not been rendered loquacious by his calling. He hardly spoke to his PEONS. They understood their duties perfectly. If one of the mules stopped, they urged it on with a guttural cry, and if that proved unavailing, a good-sized pebble, thrown with unerring aim, soon cured the animal's obstinacy. If a strap got loose, or a rein fell, a PEON came forward instantly, and throwing off his poncho, flung it over his beast's head till the accident was repaired and the march resumed.

The custom of the muleteers is to start immediately after breakfast, about eight o'clock, and not to stop till they camp for the night, about 4 P. M. Glenarvan fell in with the practice, and the first halt was just as they arrived at Arauco, situated at the very extremity of the bay. To find the extremity of the 37th degree of latitude, they would have required to proceed as far as the Bay of Carnero, twenty miles further. But the agents of Glenarvan had already scoured that part of the coast, and to repeat the exploration would have been useless. It was, therefore, decided that Arauco should be the point of departure, and they should keep on from there toward the east in a straight line.

Since the weather was so favorable, and the whole party, even Robert, were in perfect health, and altogether the journey had commenced under such favorable auspices, it was deemed advisable to push forward as quickly as possible. Accordingly, the next day they marched 35 miles or more, and encamped at nightfall on the banks of Rio Biobio. The country still presented the same fertile aspect, and abounded in flowers, but animals of any sort only came in sight occasionally, and there were no birds visible, except a solitary heron or owl, and a thrush or grebe, flying from the falcon. Human beings there were none, not a native appeared; not even one of the GUASSOS, the degenerate offspring of Indians and Spaniards, dashed across the plain like a shadow, his flying steed dripping with blood from the cruel thrusts inflicted by the gigantic spurs of his master's naked feet. It was absolutely impossible to make inquiries when there was no one to address, and Lord Glenarvan came to the conclusion that Captain Grant must have been dragged right over the Andes into the Pampas, and that it would be useless to search for him elsewhere. The only thing to be done was to wait patiently and press forward with all the speed in their power.

On the 17th they set out in the usual line of march, a line which it was hard work for Robert to keep, his ardor constantly compelled him to get ahead of the MADRINA, to the great despair of his mule. Nothing but a sharp recall from Glenarvan kept the boy in proper order.

The country now became more diversified, and the rising ground indicated their approach to a mountainous district. Rivers were more numerous, and came rushing noisily down the slopes. Paganel consulted his maps, and when he found any of those streams not marked, which often happened, all the fire of a geographer burned in his veins, and he would exclaim, with a charming air of vexation:

"A river which hasn't a name is like having no civil standing.

It has no existence in the eye of geographical law."

He christened them forthwith, without the least hesitation, and marked them down on the map, qualifying them with the most high-sounding adjectives he could find in the Spanish language.

"What a language!" he said. "How full and sonorous it is! It is like the metal church bells are made of—composed of seventy-eight parts of copper and twenty-two of tin."

"But, I say, do you make any progress in it?" asked Glenarvan.

"Most certainly, my dear Lord. Ah, if it wasn't the accent, that wretched accent!"

And for want of better work, Paganel whiled away the time along the road by practising the difficulties in pronunciation, repeating all the break-jaw words he could, though still making geographical observations. Any question about the country that Glenarvan might ask the CATAPEZ was sure to be answered by the learned Frenchman before he could reply, to the great astonishment of the guide, who gazed at him in bewilderment.

About two o'clock that same day they came to a cross road, and naturally enough Glenarvan inquired the name of it.

"It is the route from Yumbel to Los Angeles," said Paganel.

Glenarvan looked at the CATAPEZ, who replied:

"Quite right."

And then, turning toward the geographer, he added:

"You have traveled in these parts before, sir?"

"Oh, yes," said Paganel, quite gravely.

"On a mule?"

"No, in an easy chair."

The CATAPEZ could not make him out, but shrugged his shoulders and resumed his post at the head of the party.

At five in the evening they stopped in a gorge of no great depth, some miles above the little town of Loja, and encamped for the night at the foot of the Sierras, the first steppes of the great Cordilleras.

CHAPTER XII ELEVEN THOUSAND FEET ALOFT

NOTHING of importance had occurred hitherto in the passage through Chili; but all the obstacles and difficulties incident to a mountain journey were about to crowd on the travelers now.

One important question had first to be settled. Which pass would take them over the Andes, and yet not be out of their fixed route?

On questioning the CATAPEZ on the subject, he replied:

"There are only two practicable passes that I know of in this part of the Cordilleras."

"The pass of Arica is one undoubtedly discovered by Valdivia Mendoze," said Paganel.

"Just so."

"And that of Villarica is the other."

"Precisely."

"Well, my good fellow, both these passes have only one fault; they take us too far out of our route, either north or south."

"Have you no other to propose?" asked the Major.

"Certainly," replied Paganel. "There is the pass of Antuco, on the slope of the volcano, in latitude, 37 degrees 30' , or, in other words, only half a degree out of our way."

"That would do, but are you acquainted with this pass of Antuco, CATAPEZ?" said Glenarvan.

"Yes, your Lordship, I have been through it, but I did not mention it, as no one goes that way but the Indian shepherds with the herds of cattle."

"Oh, very well; if mares and sheep and oxen can go that way, we can, so let's start at once."

The signal for departure was given immediately, and they struck into the heart of the valley of Las Lejas, between great masses of chalk crystal. From this point the pass began to be difficult, and even dangerous. The angles of the declivities widened and the ledges narrowed, and frightful precipices met their gaze. The mules went cautiously along, keeping their heads near the ground, as if scenting the track. They marched in file. Sometimes at a sudden bend of the road, the MADRINA would disappear, and the little caravan had to guide themselves by the distant tinkle of her bell. Often some capricious winding would bring the column in two parallel lines, and the CATAPEZ could speak to his PEONS across a crevasse not two fathoms wide, though two hundred deep, which made between them an inseparable gulf.

Glenarvan followed his guide step by step. He saw that his perplexity was increasing as the way became more difficult, but did not dare to interrogate him, rightly enough, perhaps, thinking that both mules and muleteers were very much governed by instinct, and it was best to trust to them.

For about an hour longer the CATAPEZ kept wandering about almost at haphazard, though always getting higher up the mountains. At last he was obliged to stop short. They were in a narrow valley, one of those gorges called by the Indians "quebrads," and on reaching the end, a wall of porphyry rose perpendicularly before them, and barred further passage. The CATAPEZ, after vain attempts at finding an opening, dismounted, crossed his arms, and waited. Glenarvan went up to him and asked if he had lost his way.

"No, your Lordship," was the reply.

"But you are not in the pass of Antuco."

"We are."

"You are sure you are not mistaken?"

"I am not mistaken. See! there are the remains of a fire left by the Indians, and there are the marks of the mares and the sheep."

"They must have gone on then."

"Yes, but no more will go; the last earthquake has made the route impassable."

"To mules," said the Major, "but not to men."

"Ah, that's your concern; I have done all I could. My mules and myself are at your service to try the other passes of the Cordilleras."

"And that would delay us?"

"Three days at least."

Glenarvan listened silently. He saw the CATAPEZ was right. His mules could not go farther. When he talked of returning, however, Glenarvan appealed to his companions and said:

"Will you go on in spite of all the difficulty?"

"We will follow your Lordship," replied Tom Austin.

"And even precede you," added Paganel. "What is it after all? We have only to cross the top of the mountain chain, and once over, nothing can be easier of descent than the slopes we shall find there. When we get below, we shall find BAQUEANOS, Argentine shepherds, who will guide us through the Pampas, and swift horses accustomed to gallop over the plains. Let's go forward then, I say, and without a moment's hesitation."

"Forward!" they all exclaimed. "You will not go with us, then?" said Glenarvan to the CATAPEZ.

"I am the muleteer," was the reply.

"As you please," said Glenarvan.

"We can do without him," said Paganel. "On the other side we shall get back into the road to Antuco, and I'm quite sure I'll lead you to the foot of the mountain as straight as the best guide in the Cordilleras."

Accordingly, Glenarvan settled accounts with the CATAPEZ, and bade farewell to him and his PEONS and mules. The arms and instruments, and a small stock of provisions were divided among the seven travelers, and it was unanimously agreed that the ascent should recommence at once, and, if necessary, should continue part of the night. There was a very steep winding path on the left, which the mules never would have attempted. It was toilsome work, but after two hours' exertion, and a great deal of roundabout climbing, the little party found themselves once more in the pass of Antuco.

They were not far now from the highest peak of the Cordilleras, but there was not the slightest trace of any beaten path. The entire region had been overturned by recent shocks of earthquake, and all they could do was to keep on climbing higher and higher. Paganel was rather disconcerted at finding no way out to the other side of the chain, and laid his account with having to undergo great fatigue before the topmost peaks of the Andes could be reached, for their mean height is between eleven and twelve thousand six hundred feet. Fortunately the weather was calm and the sky clear, in addition to the season being favorable, but in Winter, from May to October, such an ascent would have been impracticable. The intense cold quickly kills travelers, and those who even manage to hold out against it fall victims to the violence of the TEMPORALES, a sort of hurricane peculiar to those regions, which yearly fills the abysses of the Cordilleras with dead bodies.

They went on toiling steadily upward all night, hoisting themselves up to almost inaccessible plateaux, and leaping over broad, deep crevasses. They had no ropes, but arms linked in arms supplied the lack, and shoulders served for ladders. The strength of Mulrady and the dexterity of Wilson were taxed heavily now. These two brave Scots multiplied themselves, so to speak. Many a time, but for their devotion and courage the small band could not have gone on. Glenarvan never lost sight of young Robert, for his age and vivacity made him imprudent. Paganel was a true Frenchman in his impetuous ardor, and hurried furiously along. The Major, on the contrary, only went as quick as was necessary, neither more nor less, climbing without the least apparent exertion. Perhaps he hardly knew, indeed, that he was climbing at all, or perhaps he fancied he was descending.

The whole aspect of the region had now completely changed. Huge blocks of glittering ice, of a bluish tint on some of the declivities, stood up on all sides, reflecting the early light of morn. The ascent became very perilous. They were obliged to reconnoiter carefully before making a single step, on account of the crevasses. Wilson took the lead, and tried the ground with his feet. His companions followed exactly in his footprints, lowering their voices to a whisper, as the least sound would disturb the currents of air, and might cause the fall of the masses of snow suspended in the air seven or eight hundred feet above their heads.

They had come now to the region of shrubs and bushes, which, higher still, gave place to grasses and cacti. At 11,000 feet all trace of vegetation had disappeared. They had only stopped once, to rest and snatch a hurried meal to recruit their strength. With superhuman courage, the ascent was then resumed amid increasing dangers and difficulties. They were forced to bestride sharp peaks and leap over chasms so deep that they did not dare to look down them. In many places wooden crosses marked the scene of some great catastrophes.

About two o'clock they came to an immense barren plain, without a sign of vegetation. The air was dry and the sky unclouded blue. At this elevation rain is unknown, and vapors only condense into snow or hail. Here and there peaks of porphyry or basalt pierced through the white winding-sheet like the bones of a skeleton; and at intervals fragments of quartz or gneiss, loosened by the action of the air, fell down with a faint, dull sound, which in a denser atmosphere would have been almost imperceptible.

However, in spite of their courage, the strength of the little band was giving way. Glenarvan regretted they had gone so far into the interior of the mountain when he saw how exhausted his men had become. Young Robert held out manfully, but he could not go much farther.

At three o'clock Glenarvan stopped and said:

"We must rest."

He knew if he did not himself propose it, no one else would.

"Rest?" rejoined Paganel; "we have no place of shelter."

"It is absolutely necessary, however, if it were only for Robert."

"No, no," said the courageous lad; "I can still walk; don't stop."

"You shall be carried, my boy; but we must get to the other side of the Cordilleras, cost what it may. There we may perhaps find some hut to cover us. All I ask is a two hours' longer march."

"Are you all of the same opinion?" said Glenarvan.

"Yes," was the unanimous reply: and Mulrady added, "I'll carry the boy."

The march eastward was forthwith resumed. They had a frightful height to climb yet to gain the topmost peaks. The rarefaction of the atmosphere produced that painful oppression known by the name of PUNA. Drops of blood stood on the gums and lips, and respiration became hurried and difficult. However strong the will of these brave men might be, the time came at last when their physical powers failed, and vertigo, that terrible malady in the mountains, destroyed not only their bodily strength but their moral energy. Falls became frequent, and those who fell could not rise again, but dragged themselves along on their knees.

But just as exhaustion was about to make short work of any further ascent, and Glenarvan's heart began to sink as he thought of the snow lying far as the eye could reach, and of the intense cold, and saw the shadow of night fast overspreading the desolate peaks, and knew they had not a roof to shelter them, suddenly the Major stopped and said, in a calm voice, "A hut!"

CHAPTER XIII A SUDDEN DESCENT

ANYONE else but McNabbs might have passed the hut a hundred times, and gone all round it, and even over it without suspecting its existence. It was covered with snow, and scarcely distinguishable from the surrounding rocks; but Wilson and Mulrady succeeded in digging it out and clearing the opening after half an hour's hard work, to the great joy of the whole party, who eagerly took possession of it.

They found it was a CASUCHA, constructed by the Indians, made of ADOBES, a species of bricks baked in the sun. Its form was that of a cube, 12 feet on each side, and it stood on a block of basalt. A stone stair led up to the door, the only opening; and narrow as this door was, the hurricane, and snow, and hail found their way in when the TEMPORALES were unchained in the mountains.

Ten people could easily find room in it, and though the walls might be none too water-tight in the rainy season, at this time of the year, at any rate, it was sufficient protection against the intense cold, which, according to the thermometer, was ten degrees below zero. Besides, there was a sort of fireplace in it, with a chimney of bricks, badly enough put together, certainly, but still it allowed of a fire being lighted.

"This will shelter us, at any rate," said Glenarvan, "even if it is not very comfortable. Providence has led us to it, and we can only be thankful."

"Why, it is a perfect palace, I call it," said Paganel; "we only want flunkeys and courtiers. We shall do capital here."

"Especially when there is a good fire blazing on the hearth, for we are quite as cold as we are hungry. For my part, I would rather see a good faggot just now than a slice of venison."

"Well, Tom, we'll try and get some combustible or other," said Paganel.

"Combustibles on the top of the Cordilleras!" exclaimed Mulrady, in a dubious tone.

"Since there is a chimney in the CASUCHA," said the Major, "the probability is that we shall find something to burn in it."

"Our friend McNabbs is right," said Glenarvan. "Get everything in readiness for supper, and I'll go out and turn woodcutter."

"Wilson and I will go with you," said Paganel.

"Do you want me?" asked Robert, getting up.

"No, my brave boy, rest yourself. You'll be a man, when others are only children at your age," replied Glenarvan.

On reaching the little mound of porphyry, Glenarvan and his two companions left the CASUCHA. In spite of the perfect calmness of the atmosphere, the cold was stinging. Paganel consulted his barometer, and found that the depression of the mercury corresponded to an elevation of 11,000 feet, only 910 meters lower than Mont Blanc. But if these mountains had presented the difficulties of the giant of the Swiss Alps, not one of the travelers could have crossed the great chain of the New World.

On reaching a little mound of porphyry, Glenarvan and Paganel stopped to gaze about them and scan the horizon on all sides. They were now on the summit of the Nevadas of the Cordilleras, and could see over an area of forty miles. The valley of the Colorado was already sunk in shadow, and night was fast drawing her mantle over the eastern slopes of the Andes. The western side was illumined by the rays of the setting sun, and peaks and glaciers flashed back his golden beams with dazzling radiance. On the south the view was magnificent. Across the wild valley of the Torbido, about two miles distant, rose the volcano of Antuco. The mountain roared like some enormous monster, and vomited red smoke, mingled with torrents of sooty flame. The surrounding peaks appeared on fire. Showers of red-hot stones, clouds of reddish vapor and rockets of lava, all combined, presented the appearance of glowing sparkling streams. The splendor of the spectacle increased every instant as night deepened, and the whole sky became lighted up with a dazzling reflection of the blazing crater, while the sun, gradually becoming shorn of his sunset glories, disappeared like a star lost in the distant darkness of the horizon.

Paganel and Glenarvan would have remained long enough gazing at the sublime struggle between the fires of earth and heaven, if the more practical Wilson had not reminded them of the business on hand. There was no wood to be found, however, but fortunately the rocks were covered with a poor, dry species of lichen. Of this they made an ample provision, as well as of a plant called LLARETTA, the root of which burns tolerably well. This precious combustible was carried back to the CASUCHA and heaped up on the hearth. It was a difficult matter to kindle it, though, and still more to keep it alight. The air was so rarefied that there was scarcely oxygen enough in it to support combustion. At least, this was the reason assigned by the Major.

"By way of compensation, however," he added, "water will boil at less than 100 degrees heat. It will come to the point of ebullition before 99 degrees."

McNabbs was right, as the thermometer proved, for it was plunged into the
kettle when the water boiled, and the mercury only rose to 99 degrees.

Coffee was soon ready, and eagerly gulped down by everybody.

The dry meat certainly seemed poor fare, and Paganel couldn't help saying:

"I tell you what, some grilled llama wouldn't be bad with this, would it? They say that the llama is substitute for the ox and the sheep, and I should like to know if it is, in an alimentary respect."

"What!" replied the Major. "You're not content with your supper, most learned Paganel."

"Enchanted with it, my brave Major; still I must confess I should not say no to a dish of llama."

"You are a Sybarite."

"I plead guilty to the charge. But come, now, though you call me that, you wouldn't sulk at a beefsteak yourself, would you?"

"Probably not."

"And if you were asked to lie in wait for a llama, notwithstanding the cold and the darkness, you would do it without the least hesitation?"

"Of course; and if it will give you the slightest pleasure—"

His companions had hardly time to thank him for his obliging good nature, when distant and prolonged howls broke on their ear, plainly not proceeding from one or two solitary animals, but from a whole troop, and one, moreover, that was rapidly approaching.

Providence had sent them a supper, as well as led them to a hut. This was the geographer's conclusion; but Glenarvan damped his joy somewhat by remarking that the quadrupeds of the Cordilleras are never met with in such a high latitude.

"Then where can these animals come from?" asked Tom Austin. "Don't you hear them getting nearer!"

"An avalanche," suggested Mulrady.

"Impossible," returned Paganel. "That is regular howling."

"Let us go out and see," said Glenarvan.

"Yes, and be ready for hunting," replied McNabbs, arming himself with his carbine.

They all rushed forthwith out of the CASUCHA. Night had completely set in, dark and starry. The moon, now in her last quarter, had not yet risen. The peaks on the north and east had disappeared from view, and nothing was visible save the fantastic SILHOUETTE of some towering rocks here and there. The howls, and clearly the howls of terrified animals, were redoubled. They proceeded from that part of the Cordilleras which lay in darkness. What could be going on there? Suddenly a furious avalanche came down, an avalanche of living animals mad with fear. The whole plateau seemed to tremble. There were hundreds, perhaps thousands, of these animals, and in spite of the rarefied atmosphere, their noise was deafening. Were they wild beasts from the Pampas, or herds of llamas and vicunas? Glenarvan, McNabbs, Robert, Austin, and the two sailors, had just time to throw themselves flat on the ground before they swept past like a whirlwind, only a few paces distant. Paganel, who had remained standing, to take advantage of his peculiar powers of sight, was knocked down in a twinkling. At the same moment the report of firearms was heard. The Major had fired, and it seemed to him that an animal had fallen close by, and that the whole herd, yelling louder than ever, had rushed down and disappeared among the declivities lighted up by the reflection of the volcano.

"Ah, I've got them," said a voice, the voice of Paganel.

"Got what?" asked Glenarvan.

"My spectacles," was the reply. "One might expect to lose that much in such a tumult as this."

"You are not wounded, I hope?"

"No, only knocked down; but by what?"

"By this," replied the Major, holding up the animal he had killed.

They all hastened eagerly into the hut, to examine McNabbs' prize by the light of the fire.

It was a pretty creature, like a small camel without a hump. The head was small and the body flattened, the legs were long and slender, the skin fine, and the hair the color of *cafe au lait*.

Paganel had scarcely looked at it before he exclaimed, "A guanaco!"

"What sort of an animal is that?" asked Glenarvan.

"One you can eat."

"And it is good savory meat, I assure you; a dish of Olympus! I knew we should have fresh meat for supper, and such meat! But who is going to cut up the beast?"

"I will," said Wilson.

"Well, I'll undertake to cook it," said Paganel.

"Can you cook, then, Monsieur Paganel?" asked Robert.

"I should think so, my boy. I'm a Frenchman, and in every Frenchman there is a cook."

Five minutes afterward Paganel began to grill large slices of venison on the embers made by the use of the LLARETTAS, and in about ten minutes a dish was ready, which he served up to his companions by the tempting name of guanaco cutlets. No one stood on ceremony, but fell to with a hearty good will.

To the absolute stupefaction of the geographer, however, the first mouthful was greeted with a general grimace, and such exclamations as—"Tough!" "It is horrible." "It is not eatable."

The poor SAVANT was obliged to own that his cutlets could not be relished, even by hungry men. They began to banter him about his "Olympian dish," and indulge in jokes at his expense; but all he cared about was to find out how it happened that the flesh of the guanaco, which was certainly good and eatable food, had turned out so badly in his hands. At last light broke in on him, and he called out:

"I see through it now! Yes, I see through it. I have found out the secret now."

"The meat was too long kept, was it?" asked McNabbs, quietly.

"No, but the meat had walked too much. How could I have forgotten that?"

"What do you mean?" asked Tom Austin.

"I mean this: the guanaco is only good for eating when it is killed in a state of rest. If it has been long hunted, and gone over much ground before it is captured, it is no longer eatable. I can affirm the fact by the mere taste, that this animal has come a great distance, and consequently the whole herd has."

"You are certain of this?" asked Glenarvan.

"Absolutely certain."

"But what could have frightened the creatures so, and driven them from their haunts, when they ought to have been quietly sleeping?"

"That's a question, my dear Glenarvan, I could not possibly answer. Take my advice, and let us go to sleep without troubling our heads about it. I say, Major, shall we go to sleep?"

"Yes, we'll go to sleep, Paganel."

Each one, thereupon, wrapped himself up in his poncho, and the fire was made up for the night.

Loud snores in every tune and key soon resounded from all sides of the hut, the deep bass contribution of Paganel completing the harmony.

But Glenarvan could not sleep. Secret uneasiness kept him in a continual state of wakefulness. His thoughts reverted involuntarily to those frightened animals flying in one common direction, impelled by one common terror. They could not be pursued by wild beasts, for at such an elevation there were almost none to be met with, and of hunters still fewer. What terror then could have driven them among the precipices of the Andes? Glenarvan felt a presentiment of approaching danger.

But gradually he fell into a half-drowsy state, and his apprehensions were lulled. Hope took the place of fear. He saw himself on the morrow on the plains of the Andes, where the search would actually commence, and perhaps success was close at hand. He thought of Captain Grant and his two sailors, and their deliverance from cruel bondage. As these visions passed rapidly through his mind, every now and then he was roused by the crackling of the fire, or sparks flying out, or some little jet of flame would suddenly flare up and illumine the faces of his slumbering companions.

Then his presentiments returned in greater strength than before, and he listened anxiously to the sounds outside the hut.

At certain intervals he fancied he could hear rumbling noises in the distance, dull and threatening like the mutterings of thunder before a storm. There surely must be a storm raging down below at the foot of the mountains. He got up and went out to see.

CHAPTER XIII A SUDDEN DESCENT

The moon was rising. The atmosphere was pure and calm. Not a cloud visible either above or below. Here and there was a passing reflection from thc flames of Antuco, but neither storm nor lightning, and myriads of bright stars studded the zenith. Still the rumbling noises continued. They seemed to meet together and cross the chain of the Andes. Glenarvan returned to the CASUCHA more uneasy than ever, questioning within himself as to the connection between these sounds and the flight of the guanacos. He looked at his watch and found the time was about two in the morning. As he had no certainty, however, of any immediate danger, he did not wake his companions, who were sleeping soundly after their fatigue, and after a little dozed off himself, and slumbered heavily for some hours.

All of a sudden a violent crash made him start to his feet.

A deafening noise fell on his ear like the roar of artillery.

He felt the ground giving way beneath him, and the CASUCHA

rocked to and fro, and opened.

He shouted to his companions, but they were already awake, and tumbling pell-mell over each other. They were being rapidly dragged down a steep declivity. Day dawned and revealed a terrible scene. The form of the mountains changed in an instant. Cones were cut off. Tottering peaks disappeared as if some trap had opened at their base. Owing to a peculiar phenomenon of the Cordilleras, an enormous mass, many miles in extent, had been displaced entirely, and was speeding down toward the plain.

"An earthquake!" exclaimed Paganel. He was not mistaken. It was one of those cataclysms frequent in Chili, and in this very region where Copiapo had been twice destroyed, and Santiago four times laid in ruins in fourteen years. This region of the globe is so underlaid with volcanic fires and the volcanoes of recent origin are such insufficient safety valves for the subterranean vapors, that shocks are of frequent occurrence, and are called by the people TREMBLORES.

The plateau to which the seven men were clinging, holding on by tufts of lichen, and giddy and terrified in the extreme, was rushing down the declivity with the swiftness of an express, at the rate of fifty miles an hour. Not a cry was possible, nor an attempt to get off or stop. They could not even have heard themselves speak. The internal rumblings, the crash of the avalanches, the fall of masses of granite and basalt, and the whirlwind of pulverized snow, made all communication impossible. Sometimes they went perfectly smoothly along without jolts or jerks, and sometimes on the contrary, the plateau would reel and roll like a ship in a storm, coasting past abysses in which fragments of the mountain were falling, tearing up trees by the roots, and leveling, as if with the keen edge of an immense scythe, every projection of the declivity.

How long this indescribable descent would last, no one could calculate, nor what it would end in ultimately. None of the party knew whether the rest were still alive, whether one or another were not already lying in the depths of some abyss. Almost breathless with the swift motion, frozen with the cold air, which pierced them through, and blinded with the whirling snow, they gasped for breath, and became exhausted and nearly inanimate, only retaining their hold of the rocks by a powerful instinct of self-preservation. Suddenly a tremendous shock pitched them right off, and sent them rolling to the very foot of the mountain. The plateau had stopped.

For some minutes no one stirred. At last one of the party picked himself up, and stood on his feet, stunned by the shock, but still firm on his legs. This was the Major. He shook off the blinding snow and looked around him. His companions lay in a close circle like the shots from a gun that has just been discharged, piled one on top of another.

The Major counted them. All were there except one—that one was Robert Grant.

CHAPTER XIV PROVIDENTIALLY RESCUED

THE eastern side of the Cordilleras of the Andes consists of a succession of lengthened declivities, which slope down almost insensibly to the plain. The soil is carpeted with rich herbage, and adorned with magnificent trees, among which, in great numbers, were apple-trees, planted at the time of the conquest, and golden with fruit. There were literally, perfect forests of these. This district was, in fact, just a corner of fertile Normandy.

The sudden transition from a desert to an oasis, from snowy peaks to verdant plains, from Winter to Summer, can not fail to strike the traveler's eye.

The ground, moreover, had recovered its immobility. The trembling had ceased, though there was little doubt the forces below the surface were carrying on their devastating work further on, for shocks of earthquake are always occurring in some part or other of the Andes. This time the shock had been one of extreme violence. The outline of the mountains was wholly altered, and the Pampas guides would have sought vainly for the accustomed landmarks.

A magnificent day had dawned. The sun was just rising from his ocean bed, and his bright rays streamed already over the Argentine plains, and ran across to the Atlantic. It was about eight o'clock.

Lord Glenarvan and his companions were gradually restored to animation by the Major's efforts. They had been completely stunned, but had sustained no injury whatever. The descent of the Cordilleras was accomplished; and as Dame Nature had conveyed them at her own expense, they could only have praised her method of locomotion if one of their number, and that one the feeblest and youngest, the child of the party, had not been missing at the roll call.

The brave boy was beloved by everybody. Paganel was particularly attached to him, and so was the Major, with all his apparent coldness. As for Glenarvan, he was in absolute despair when he heard of his disappearance, and pictured to himself the child lying in some deep abyss, wildly crying for succor.

"We must go and look for him, and look till we find him," he exclaimed, almost unable to keep back his tears. "We cannot leave him to his fate. Every valley and precipice and abyss must be searched through and through. I will have a rope fastened round my waist, and go down myself. I insist upon it; you understand; I insist upon it. Heaven grant Robert may be still alive! If we lose the boy, how could we ever dare to meet the father? What right have we to save the captain at the cost of his son's life?"

Glenarvan's companions heard him in silence. He sought to read hope in their eyes, but they did not venture to meet his gaze.

At last he said,

"Well, you hear what I say, but you make no response.

Do you mean to tell me that you have no hope—not the slightest?"

Again there was silence, till McNabbs asked:

"Which of you can recollect when Robert disappeared?"

No one could say.

"Well, then," resumed the Major, "you know this at any rate.

Who was the child beside during our descent of the Cordilleras?"

"Beside me," replied Wilson.

"Very well. Up to what moment did you see him beside you?

Try if you can remember."

"All that I can recollect is that Robert Grant was still by my side, holding fast by a tuft of lichen, less than two minutes before the shock which finished our descent."

"Less than two minutes? Mind what you are saying;

I dare say a minute seemed a very long time to you.

Are you sure you are not making a mistake?"

"I don't think I am. No; it was just about two minutes, as I tell you."

"Very well, then; and was Robert on your right or left?"

"On my left. I remember that his poncho brushed past my face."

"And with regard to us, how were you placed?"

"On the left also."

"Then Robert must have disappeared on this side," said the Major, turning toward the mountain and pointing toward the right: "and I should judge," he added, "considering the time that has elapsed, that the spot where he fell is about two miles up. Between that height and the ground is where we must search, dividing the different zones among us, and it is there we shall find him."

Not another word was spoken. The six men commenced their explorations, keeping constantly to the line they had made in their descent, examining closely every fissure, and going into the very depths of the abysses, choked up though they partly were with fragments of the plateau; and more than one came out again with garments torn to rags, and feet and hands bleeding. For many long hours these brave fellows continued their search without dreaming of taking rest. But all in vain. The child had not only met his death on the mountain, but found a grave which some enormous rock had sealed forever.

About one o'clock, Glenarvan and his companions met again in the valley.

Glenarvan was completely crushed with grief. He scarcely spoke.

The only words that escaped his lips amid his sighs were,

"I shall not go away! I shall not go away!"

No one of the party but could enter into his feeling, and respect it.

"Let us wait," said Paganel to the Major and Tom Austin. "We will take a little rest, and recruit our strength. We need it anyway, either to prolong our search or continue our route."

"Yes; and, as Edward wishes it, we will rest. He has still hope, but what is it he hopes?"

"Who knows!" said Tom Austin.

"Poor Robert!" replied Paganel, brushing away a tear.

The valley was thickly wooded, and the Major had no difficulty in finding a suitable place of encampment. He chose a clump of tall carob trees, under which they arranged their few belongings—few indeed, for all they had were sundry wraps and fire-arms, and a little dried meat and rice. Not far off there was a RIO, which supplied them with water, though it was still somewhat muddy after the disturbance of the avalanche. Mulrady soon had a fire lighted on the grass, and a warm refreshing beverage to offer his master. But Glenarvan refused to touch it, and lay stretched on his poncho in a state of absolute prostration.

So the day passed, and night came on, calm and peaceful as the preceding had been. While his companions were lying motionless, though wide awake, Glenarvan betook himself once more to the slopes of the Cordilleras, listening intently in hope that some cry for help would fall upon his ear. He ventured far up in spite of his being alone, straining his ear with painful eagerness to catch the faintest sound, and calling aloud in an agony of despair.

But he heard nothing save the beatings of his own heart, though he wandered all night on the mountain. Sometimes the Major followed him, and sometimes Paganel, ready to lend a helping hand among the slippery peaks and dangerous precipices among which he was dragged by his rash and useless imprudence. All his efforts were in vain, however, and to his repeated cries of "Robert, Robert!" echo was the only response.

Day dawned, and it now became a matter of necessity to go and bring back the poor Lord from the distant plateau, even against his will. His despair was terrible. Who could dare to speak of quitting this fatal valley? Yet provisions were done, and Argentine guides and horses were not far off to lead them to the Pampas. To go back would be more difficult than to go forward. Besides, the Atlantic Ocean was the appointed meeting place with the DUNCAN. These were strong reasons against any long delay; indeed it was best for all parties to continue the route as soon as possible.

McNabbs undertook the task of rousing Lord Glenarvan from his grief. For a long time his cousin seemed not to hear him. At last he shook his head, and said, almost in-audibly:

"Did you say we must start?"

"Yes, we must start."

"Wait one hour longer."

"Yes, we'll wait another," replied the Major.

The hour slipped away, and again Glenarvan begged for longer grace. To hear his imploring tones, one might have thought him a criminal begging a respite. So the day passed on till it was almost noon. McNabbs hesitated now no longer, but, acting on the advice of the rest, told his cousin that start they must, for all their lives depended on prompt action.

"Yes, yes!" replied Glenarvan. "Let us start, let us start!"

But he spoke without looking at McNabbs. His gaze was fixed intently on a certain dark speck in the heavens. Suddenly he exclaimed, extending his arm, and keeping it motionless, as if petrified:

"There! there! Look! look!"

All eyes turned immediately in the direction indicated so imperiously. The dark speck was increasing visibly. It was evidently some bird hovering above them.

"A condor," said Paganel.

"Yes, a condor," replied Glenarvan. "Who knows? He is coming down— he is gradually getting lower! Let us wait."

Paganel was not mistaken, it was assuredly a condor. This magnificent bird is the king of the Southern Andes, and was formerly worshiped by the Incas. It attains an extraordinary development in those regions. Its strength is prodigious. It has frequently driven oxen over the edge of precipices down into the depths of abysses. It seizes sheep, and kids, and young calves, browsing on the plains, and carries them off to inaccessible heights. It hovers in the air far beyond the utmost limits of human sight, and its powers of vision are so great that it can discern the smallest objects on the earth beneath.

CHAPTER XIV PROVIDENTIALLY RESCUED

What had this condor discovered then? Could it be the corpse of Robert Grant? "Who knows?" repeated Glenarvan, keeping his eye immovably fixed on the bird. The enormous creature was fast approaching, sometimes hovering for awhile with outspread wings, and sometimes falling with the swiftness of inert bodies in space. Presently he began to wheel round in wide circles. They could see him distinctly. He measured more than fifteen feet, and his powerful wings bore him along with scarcely the slightest effort, for it is the prerogative of large birds to fly with calm majesty, while insects have to beat their wings a thousand times a second.

The Major and Wilson had seized their carbines, but Glenarvan stopped them by a gesture. The condor was encircling in his flight a sort of inaccessible plateau about a quarter of a mile up the side of the mountain. He wheeled round and round with dazzling rapidity, opening and shutting his formidable claws, and shaking his cartilaginous carbuncle, or comb.

"It is there, there!" exclaimed Glenarvan.

A sudden thought flashed across his mind, and with a terrible cry, he called out, "Fire! fire! Oh, suppose Robert were still alive! That bird."

But it was too late. The condor had dropped out of sight behind the crags. Only a second passed, a second that seemed an age, and the enormous bird reappeared, carrying a heavy load and flying at a slow rate.

A cry of horror rose on all sides. It was a human body the condor had in his claws, dangling in the air, and apparently lifeless— it was Robert Grant. The bird had seized him by his clothes, and had him hanging already at least one hundred and fifty feet in the air. He had caught sight of the travelers, and was flapping his wings violently, endeavoring to escape with his heavy prey.

"Oh! would that Robert were dashed to pieces against the rocks, rather than be a—"

He did not finish his sentence, but seizing Wilson's carbine, took aim at the condor. His arm was too trembling, however, to keep the weapon steady.

"Let me do it," said the Major. And with a calm eye, and sure hands and motionless body, he aimed at the bird, now three hundred feet above him in the air.

But before he had pulled the trigger the report of a gun resounded from the bottom of the valley. A white smoke rose from between two masses of basalt, and the condor, shot in the head, gradually turned over and began to fall, supported by his great wings spread out like a parachute. He had not let go his prey, but gently sank down with it on the ground, about ten paces from the stream.

"We've got him, we've got him," shouted Glenarvan; and without waiting to see where the shot so providentially came from, he rushed toward the condor, followed by his companions.

When they reached the spot the bird was dead, and the body of Robert was quite concealed beneath his mighty wings. Glenarvan flung himself on the corpse, and dragging it from the condor's grasp, placed it flat on the grass, and knelt down and put his ear to the heart.

But a wilder cry of joy never broke from human lips, than Glenarvan uttered the next moment, as he started to his feet and exclaimed:

"He is alive! He is still alive!"

The boy's clothes were stripped off in an instant, and his face bathed with cold water. He moved slightly, opened his eyes, looked round and murmured, "Oh, my Lord! Is it you!" he said; "my father!"

Glenarvan could not reply. He was speechless with emotion, and kneeling down by the side of the child so miraculously saved, burst into tears.

CHAPTER XV THALCAVE

ROBERT had no sooner escaped one terrible danger than he ran the risk of another scarcely less formidable. He was almost torn to pieces by his friends, for the brave fellows were so overjoyed at the sight of him, that in spite of his weak state, none of them would be satisfied without giving him a hug. However, it seemed as if good rough hugging did not hurt sick people; at any rate it did not hurt Robert, but quite the contrary.

But the first joy of deliverance over, the next thought was who was the deliverer? Of course it was the Major who suggested looking for him, and he was not far off, for about fifty paces from the RIO a man of very tall stature was seen standing motionless on the lowest crags at the foot of the mountain. A long gun was lying at his feet.

He had broad shoulders, and long hair bound together with leather thongs. He was over six feet in height. His bronzed face was red between the eyes and mouth, black by the lower eyelids, and white on the forehead. He wore the costume of the Patagonians on the frontiers, consisting of a splendid cloak, ornamented with scarlet arabesques, made of the skins of the guanaco, sewed together with ostrich tendons, and with the silky wool turned up on the edge. Under this mantle was a garment of fox-skin, fastened round the waist, and coming down to a point in front. A little bag hung from his belt, containing colors for painting his face. His boots were pieces of ox hide, fastened round the ankles by straps, across.

This Patagonian had a splendid face, indicating real intelligence, notwithstanding the medley of colors by which it was disfigured. His waiting attitude was full of dignity; indeed, to see him standing grave and motionless on his pedestal of rocks, one might have taken him for a statue of *sang-froid*.

As soon as the Major perceived him, he pointed him out to Glenarvan, who ran toward him immediately. The Patagonian came two steps forward to meet him, and Glenarvan caught hold of his hand and pressed it in his own. It was impossible to mistake the meaning of the action, for the noble face of the Scotch lord so beamed with gratitude that no words were needed. The stranger bowed slightly in return, and said a few words that neither Glenarvan nor the Major could understand.

The Patagonian surveyed them attentively for a few minutes, and spoke again in another language. But this second idiom was no more intelligible than the first. Certain words, however, caught Glenarvan's ear as sounding like Spanish, a few sentences of which he could speak.

ESPANOL?" he asked.

The Patagonian nodded in reply, a movement of the head which has an affirmative significance among all nations.

"That's good!" said the Major. "Our friend Paganel will be the very man for him. It is lucky for us that he took it into his head to learn Spanish."

Paganel was called forthwith. He came at once, and saluted the stranger with all the grace of a Frenchman. But his compliments were lost on the Patagonian, for he did not understand a single syllable.

However, on being told how things stood, he began in Spanish, and opening his mouth as wide as he could, the better to articulate, said:

"*Vos sois um homen de bem.*" (You are a brave man.)

The native listened, but made no reply.

"He doesn't understand," said the geographer.

"Perhaps you haven't the right accent," suggested the Major.

"That's just it! Confound the accent!"

Once more Paganel repeated his compliment, but with no better success.

"I'll change the phrase," he said; and in slow, deliberate tones he went on, "*Sam duvida um Patagao*" (A Patagonian, undoubtedly).

No response still.

"DIZEIME!" said Paganel (Answer me).

But no answer came.

"*Vos compriendeis?*" (Do you understand?) shouted Paganel, at the very top of his voice, as if he would burst his throat.

Evidently the Indian did not understand, for he replied in Spanish,

"*No comprendo*" (I do not understand).

It was Paganel's turn now to be amazed. He pushed his spectacles right down over his nose, as if greatly irritated, and said,

"I'll be hanged if I can make out one word of his infernal patois.

It is Araucanian, that's certain!"

"Not a bit of it!" said Glenarvan. "It was Spanish he spoke."

And addressing the Patagonian, he repeated the word, "ESPANOL?"

(Spanish?).

"*Si, si*" (yes, yes) replied the Indian.

Paganel's surprise became absolute stupefaction. The Major and his cousin exchanged sly glances, and McNabbs said, mischievously, with a look of fun on his face, "Ah, ah, my worthy friend; is this another of your misadventures? You seem to have quite a monopoly of them."

"What!" said Paganel, pricking up his ear.

"Yes, it's clear enough the man speaks Spanish."

"He!"

"Yes, he certainly speaks Spanish. Perhaps it is some other language you have been studying all this time instead of—"

But Paganel would not allow him to proceed. He shrugged his shoulders, and said stiffly,

"You go a little too far, Major."

"Well, how is it that you don't understand him then?"

"Why, of course, because the man speaks badly," replied the learned geographer, getting impatient.

"He speaks badly; that is to say, because you can't understand him," returned the Major coolly.

"Come, come, McNabbs," put in Glenarvan, "your supposition is quite inadmissable. However DISTRAIT our friend Paganel is, it is hardly likely he would study one language for another."

"Well, Edward—or rather you, my good Paganel—explain it then."

"I explain nothing. I give proof. Here is the book I use daily, to practice myself in the difficulties of the Spanish language. Examine it for yourself, Major," he said, handing him a volume in a very ragged condition, which he had brought up, after a long rummage, from the depths of one of his numerous pockets. "Now you can see whether I am imposing on you," he continued, indignantly.

"And what's the name of this book?" asked the Major, as he took it from his hand.

"The LUSIADES, an admirable epic, which—"

"The LUSIADES!" exclaimed Glenarvan.

"Yes, my friend, the LUSIADES of the great Camoens, neither more nor less."

"Camoens!" repeated Glenarvan; "but Paganel, my unfortunate fellow, Camoens was a Portuguese! It is Portuguese you have been learning for the last six weeks!"

"Camoens! LUISADES! Portuguese!" Paganel could not say more. He looked vexed, while his companions, who had all gathered round, broke out in a furious burst of laughter.

The Indian never moved a muscle of his face. He quietly awaited the explanation of this incomprehensible mirth.

"Fool, idiot, that I am!" at last uttered Paganel. "Is it really a fact? You are not joking with me? It is what I have actually been doing? Why, it is a second confusion of tongues, like Babel. Ah me! alack-a-day! my friends, what is to become of me? To start for India and arrive at Chili! To learn Spanish and talk Portuguese! Why, if I go on like this, some day I shall be throwing myself out of the window instead of my cigar!"

To hear Paganel bemoan his misadventures and see his comical discomfiture, would have upset anyone's gravity. Besides, he set the example himself, and said:

"Laugh away, my friends, laugh as loud as you like; you can't laugh at me half as much as I laugh at myself!"

"But, I say," said the Major, after a minute, "this doesn't alter the fact that we have no interpreter."

"Oh, don't distress yourself about that," replied Paganel, "Portuguese and Spanish are so much alike that I made a mistake; but this very resemblance will be a great help toward rectifying it. In a very short time I shall be able to thank the Patagonian in the language he speaks so well."

Paganel was right. He soon managed to exchange a few words with the stranger, and found out even that his name was Thalcave, a word that signified in Araucanian, "The Thunderer." This surname had, no doubt, come from his skill in handling fire-arms.

But what rejoiced Glenarvan most was to learn that he was a guide by occupation, and, moreover, a guide across the Pampas. To his mind, the meeting with him was so providential, that he could not doubt now of the success of their enterprise. The deliverance of Captain Grant seemed an accomplished fact.

When the party went back to Robert, the boy held out his arms to the Patagonian, who silently laid his hand on his head, and proceeded to examine him with the greatest care, gently feeling each of his aching limbs. Then he went down to the RIO, and gathered a few handfuls of wild celery, which grew on the banks, with which he rubbed the child's body all over. He handled him with the most exquisite delicacy, and his treatment so revived the lad's strength, that it was soon evident that a few hours' rest would set him all right.

CHAPTER XV THALCAVE

It was accordingly decided that they should encamp for the rest of the day and the ensuing night. Two grave questions, moreover, had to be settled: where to get food, and means of transport. Provisions and mules were both lacking. Happily, they had Thalcave, however, a practised guide, and one of the most intelligent of his class. He undertook to find all that was needed, and offered to take him to a TOLDERIA of Indians, not further than four miles off at most, where he could get supplies of all he wanted. This proposition was partly made by gestures, and partly by a few Spanish words which Paganel managed to make out. His offer was accepted, and Glenarvan and his learned friend started off with him at once.

They walked at a good pace for an hour and a half, and had to make great strides to keep up with the giant Thalcave. The road lay through a beautiful fertile region, abounding in rich pasturages; where a hundred thousand cattle might have fed comfortably. Large ponds, connected by an inextricable labyrinth of RIOS, amply watered these plains and produced their greenness. Swans with black heads were disporting in the water, disputing possession with the numerous intruders which gamboled over the LLANOS. The feathered tribes were of most brilliant plumage, and of marvelous variety and deafening noise. The isacus, a graceful sort of dove with gray feathers streaked with white, and the yellow cardinals, were flitting about in the trees like moving flowers; while overhead pigeons, sparrows, chingolos, bulgueros, and mongitas, were flying swiftly along, rending the air with their piercing cries.

Paganel's admiration increased with every step, and he had nearly exhausted his vocabulary of adjectives by his loud exclamations, to the astonishment of the Patagonian, to whom the birds, and the swans, and the prairies were every day things. The learned geographer was so lost in delight, that he seemed hardly to have started before they came in sight of the Indian camp, or TOLDERIA, situated in the heart of a valley.

About thirty nomadic Indians were living there in rude cabins made of branches, pasturing immense herds of milch cows, sheep, oxen, and horses. They went from one prairie to another, always finding a well-spread table for their four-footed guests.

These nomads were a hybrid type of Araucans, Pehu-enches, and Aucas. They were Ando-Peruvians, of an olive tint, of medium stature and massive form, with a low forehead, almost circular face, thin lips, high cheekbones, effeminate features, and cold expression. As a whole, they arc about the least interesting of the Indians. However, it was their herds Glenarvan wanted, not themselves. As long as he could get beef and horses, he cared for nothing else.

Thalcave did the bargaining. It did not take long. In exchange for seven ready saddled horses of the Argentine breed, 100 pounds of CHARQUI, or dried meat, several measures of rice, and leather bottles for water, the Indians agreed to take twenty ounces of gold as they could not get wine or rum, which they would have preferred, though they were perfectly acquainted with the value of gold. Glenarvan wished to purchase an eighth horse for the Patagonian, but he gave him to understand that it would be useless.

They got back to the camp in less than half an hour, and were hailed with acclamations by the whole party or rather the provisions and horses were. They were all hungry, and ate heartily of the welcome viands. Robert took a little food with the rest. He was fast recovering strength. The close of the day was spent in complete repose and pleasant talk about the dear absent ones.

Paganel never quitted the Indian's side. It was not that he was so glad to see a real Patagonian, by whom he looked a perfect pigmy— a Patagonian who might have almost rivaled the Emperor Maximii, and that Congo negro seen by the learned Van der Brock, both eight feet high; but he caught up Spanish phrases from the Indian and studied the language without a book this time, gesticulating at a great rate all the grand sonorous words that fell on his ear.

"If I don't catch the accent," he said to the Major, "it won't be my fault; but who would have said to me that it was a Patagonian who would teach me Spanish one day?"

CHAPTER XVI THE NEWS OF THE LOST CAPTAIN

NEXT day, the 22d of October, at eight o'clock in the morning, Thalcave gave the signal for departure. Between the 22d and 42d degrees the Argentine soil slopes eastward, and all the travelers had to do was to follow the slope right down to the sea.

Glenarvan had supposed Thalcave's refusal of a horse was that he preferred walking, as some guides do, but he was mistaken, for just as they were ready, the Patagonian gave a peculiar whistle, and immediately a magnificent steed of the pure Argentine breed came bounding out of a grove close by, at his master's call. Both in form and color the animal was of perfect beauty. The Major, who was a thorough judge of all the good points of a horse, was loud in admiration of this sample of the Pampas breed, and considered that, in many respects, he greatly resembled an English hunter. This splendid creature was called "Thaouka," a word in Patagonia which means bird, and he well deserved the name.

Thalcave was a consummate horseman, and to see him on his prancing steed was a sight worth looking at. The saddle was adapted to the two hunting weapons in common use on the Argentine plains—the BOLAS and the LAZO. The BOLAS consists of three balls fastened together by a strap of leather, attached to the front of the RECADO. The Indians fling them often at the distance of a hundred feet from the animal or enemy of which they are in pursuit, and with such precision that they catch round their legs and throw them down in an instant. It is a formidable weapon in their hands, and one they handle with surprising skill. The LAZO is always retained in the hand. It is simply a rope, thirty feet long, made of tightly twisted leather, with a slip knot at the end, which passes through an iron ring. This noose was thrown by the right hand, while the left keeps fast hold of the rope, the other end of which is fastened to the saddle. A long carbine, in the shoulder belt completed the accouterments of the Patagonian.

He took his place at the head of the party, quite unconscious of the admiration he was exciting, and they set off, going alternately at a gallop and walking pace, for the "trot" seemed altogether unknown to them. Robert proved to be a bold rider, and completely reassured Glenarvan as to his ability to keep his seat.

The Pampas commenced at the very foot of the Cordilleras. They may be divided into three parts. The first extends from the chain of the Andes, and stretches over an extent of 250 miles covered with stunted trees and bushes; the second 450 miles is clothed with magnificent herbage, and stops about 180 miles from Buenos Ayres; from this point to the sea, the foot of the traveler treads over immense prairies of lucerne and thistles, which constitute the third division of the Pampas.

On issuing from the gorges of the Cordilleras, Glenarvan and his band came first to plains of sand, called MEDANOS, lying in ridges like waves of the sea, and so extremely fine that the least breath of wind agitated the light particles, and sent them flying in clouds, which rose and fell like water-spouts. It was a spectacle which caused both pleasure and pain, for nothing could be more curious than to see the said water-spouts wandering over the plain, coming in contact and mingling with each other, and falling and rising in wild confusion; but, on the other hand, nothing could be more disagreeable than the dust which was thrown off by these innumerable MEDANOS, which was so impalpable that close one's eyes as they might, it found its way through the lids.

This phenomenon lasted the greater part of the day. The travelers made good progress, however, and about four o'clock the Cordilleras lay full forty miles behind them, the dark outlines being already almost lost in the evening mists. They were all somewhat fatigued with the journey, and glad enough to halt for the night on the banks of the Neuquem, called Ramid, or Comoe by certain geographers, a troubled, turbulent rapid flowing between high red banks.

No incident of any importance occurred that night or the following day. They rode well and fast, finding the ground firm, and the temperature bearable. Toward noon, however, the sun's rays were extremely scorching, and when evening came, a bar of clouds streaked the southwest horizon—a sure sign of a change in the weather. The Patagonian pointed it out to the geographer, who replied:

"Yes, I know;" and turning to his companions, added, "see, a change of weather is coming! We are going to have a taste of PAMPERO."

And he went on to explain that this PAMPERO is very common in the Argentine plains. It is an extremely dry wind which blows from the southwest. Thalcave was not mistaken, for the PAMPERO blew violently all night, and was sufficiently trying to poor fellows only sheltered by their ponchos. The horses lay down on the ground, and the men stretched themselves beside them in a close group. Glenarvan was afraid they would be delayed by the continuance of the hurricane, but Paganel was able to reassure him on that score, after consulting his barometer.

"The PAMPERO generally brings a tempest which lasts three days, and may be always foretold by the depression of the mercury," he said. "But when the barometer rises, on the contrary, which is the case now, all we need expect is a few violent blasts. So you can make your mind easy, my good friend; by sunrise the sky will be quite clear again."

"You talk like a book, Paganel," replied Glenarvan.

"And I am one; and what's more, you are welcome to turn over my leaves whenever you like."

The book was right. At one o'clock the wind suddenly lulled, and the weary men fell asleep and woke at daybreak, refreshed and invigorated.

It was the 20th of October, and the tenth day since they had left Talcahuano. They were still ninety miles from the point where the Rio Colorado crosses the thirty-seventh parallel, that is to say, about two days' journey. Glenarvan kept a sharp lookout for the appearance of any Indians, intending to question them, through Thalcave, about Captain Grant, as Paganel could not speak to him well enough for this. But the track they were following was one little frequented by the natives, for the ordinary routes across the Pampas lie further north. If by chance some nomadic horseman came in sight far away, he was off again like a dart, not caring to enter into conversation with strangers. To a solitary individual, a little troop of eight men, all mounted and well armed, wore a suspicious aspect, so that any intercourse either with honest men or even banditti, was almost impossible.

Glenarvan was regretting this exceedingly, when he unexpectedly met with a singular justification of his rendering of the eventful document.

CHAPTER XVI THE NEWS OF THE LOST CAPTAIN

In pursuing the course the travelers had laid down for themselves, they had several times crossed the routes over the plains in common use, but had struck into none of them. Hitherto Thalcave had made no remark about this. He understood quite well, however, that they were not bound for any particular town, or village, or settlement. Every morning they set out in a straight line toward the rising sun, and went on without the least deviation. Moreover, it must have struck Thalcave that instead of being the guide he was guided; yet, with true Indian reserve, he maintained absolute silence. But on reaching a particular point, he checked his horse suddenly, and said to Paganel:

"The Carmen route."

"Yes, my good Patagonian," replied Paganel in his best Spanish; "the route from Carmen to Mendoza."

"We are not going to take it?"

"No," replied Paganel.

"Where are we going then?"

"Always to the east."

"That's going nowhere."

"Who knows?"

Thalcave was silent, and gazed at the geographer with an air of profound surprise. He had no suspicion that Paganel was joking, for an Indian is always grave.

"You are not going to Carmen, then?" he added, after a moment's pause.

"No."

"Nor to Mendoza?"

"No, nor to Mendoza."

Just then Glenarvan came up to ask the reason of the stoppage, and what he and Thalcave were discussing.

"He wanted to know whether we were going to Carmen or Mendoza, and was very much surprised at my negative reply to both questions."

"Well, certainly, it must seem strange to him."

"I think so. He says we are going nowhere."

"Well, Paganel, I wonder if it is possible to make him understand the object of our expedition, and what our motive is for always going east."

"That would be a difficult matter, for an Indian knows nothing about degrees, and the finding of the document would appear to him a mere fantastic story."

"Is it the story he would not understand, or the storyteller?" said McNabbs, quietly

"Ah, McNabbs, I see you have small faith in my Spanish yet."

"Well, try it, my good friend."

"So I will."

And turning round to the Patagonian he began his narrative, breaking down frequently for the want of a word, and the difficulty of making certain details intelligible to a half-civilized Indian. It was quite a sight to see the learned geographer. He gesticulated and articulated, and so worked himself up over it, that the big drops of sweat fell in a cascade down his forehead on to his chest. When his tongue failed, his arms were called to aid. Paganel got down on the ground and traced a geographical map on the sand, showing where the lines of latitude and longitude cross and where the two oceans were, along which the Carmen route led. Thalcave looked on composedly, without giving any indication of comprehending or not comprehending.

The lesson had lasted half an hour, when the geographer left off, wiped his streaming face, and waited for the Patagonian to speak.

"Does he understand?" said Glenarvan.

"That remains to be seen; but if he doesn't, I give it up," replied Paganel.

Thalcave neither stirred nor spoke. His eyes remained fixed on the lines drawn on the sand, now becoming fast effaced by the wind.

"Well?" said Paganel to him at length.

The Patagonian seemed not to hear. Paganel fancied he could detect an ironical smile already on the lips of the Major, and determined to carry the day, was about to recommence his geographical illustrations, when the Indian stopped him by a gesture, and said:

"You are in search of a prisoner?"

"Yes," replied Paganel.

"And just on this line between the setting and rising sun?" added Thalcave, speaking in Indian fashion of the route from west to east.

"Yes, yes, that's it."

"And it's your God," continued the guide, "that has sent you the secret of this prisoner on the waves."

"God himself."

"His will be accomplished then," replied the native almost solemnly.

"We will march east, and if it needs be, to the sun."

Paganel, triumphing in his pupil, immediately translated his replies to his companions, and exclaimed:

"What an intelligent race! All my explanations would have been lost on nineteen in every twenty of the peasants in my own country."

Glenarvan requested him to ask the Patagonian if he had heard of any foreigners who had fallen into the hands of the Indians of the Pampas.

Paganel did so, and waited an answer.

"Perhaps I have."

The reply was no sooner translated than the Patagonian found himself surrounded by the seven men questioning him with eager glances. Paganel was so excited, he could hardly find words, and he gazed at the grave Indian as if he could read the reply on his lips.

Each word spoken by Thalcave was instantly translated, so that the whole party seemed to hear him speak in their mother tongue.

"And what about the prisoner?" asked Paganel.

"He was a foreigner."

"You have seen him?"

"No; but I have heard the Indian speak of him. He is brave; he has the heart of a bull."

"The heart of a bull!" said Paganel. "Ah, this magnificent Patagonian language. You understand him, my friends, he means a courageous man."

"My father!" exclaimed Robert Grant, and, turning to Paganel, he asked what the Spanish was for, "Is it my father."

"*Es mio padre*," replied the geographer.

Immediately taking Thalcave's hands in his own, the boy said, in a soft tone:

"*Es mio padre*."

"*Suo padre*," replied the Patagonian, his face lighting up.

He took the child in his arms, lifted him up on his horse, and gazed at him with peculiar sympathy. His intelligent face was full of quiet feeling.

But Paganel had not completed his interrogations. "This prisoner, who was he? What was he doing? When had Thalcave heard of him?" All these questions poured upon him at once.

He had not long to wait for an answer, and learned that the European was a slave in one of the tribes that roamed the country between the Colorado and the Rio Negro.

"But where was the last place he was in?"

"With the Cacique Calfoucoura."

"In the line we have been following?"

"Yes."

"And who is this Cacique?"

"The chief of the Poyuches Indians, a man with two tongues and two hearts."

"That's to say false in speech and false in action," said Paganel, after he had translated this beautiful figure of the Patagonian language.

"And can we deliver our friend?" he added.

"You may if he is still in the hands of the Indians."

"And when did you last hear of him?"

"A long while ago; the sun has brought two summers since then to the Pampas."

The joy of Glenarvan can not be described. This reply agreed perfectly with the date of the document. But one question still remained for him to put to Thalcave.

"You spoke of a prisoner," he said; "but were there not three?"

"I don't know," said Thalcave.

"And you know nothing of his present situation?"

"Nothing."

This ended the conversation. It was quite possible that the three men had become separated long ago; but still this much was certain, that the Indians had spoken of a European that was in their power; and the date of the captivity, and even the descriptive phrase about the captive, evidently pointed to Harry Grant.

CHAPTER XVII A SERIOUS NECESSITY

THE Argentine Pampas extend from the thirty-fourth to the fortieth degree of southern latitude. The word PAMPA, of Araucanian origin, signifies *grass plain*, and justly applies to the whole region. The mimosas growing on the western part, and the substantial herbage on the eastern, give those plains a peculiar appearance. The soil is composed of sand and red or yellow clay, and this is covered by a layer of earth, in which the vegetation takes root. The geologist would find rich treasures in the tertiary strata here, for it is full of antediluvian remains—enormous bones, which the Indians attribute to some gigantic race that lived in a past age.

The horses went on at a good pace through the thick PAJA-BRAVA, the grass of the Pampas, *par excellence*, so high and thick that the Indians find shelter in it from storms. At certain distances, but increasingly seldom, there were wet, marshy spots, almost entirely under water, where the willows grew, and a plant called the *Gygnerium argenteum*. Here the horses drank their fill greedily, as if bent on quenching their thirst for past, present and future. Thalcave went first to beat the bushes and frighten away the cholinas, a most dangerous species of viper, the bite of which kills an ox in less than an hour.

For two days they plodded steadily across this arid and deserted plain.

The dry heat became severe. There were not only no RIOS,

but even the ponds dug out by the Indians were dried up.

As the drought seemed to increase with every mile, Paganel asked

Thalcave when he expected to come to water.

"At Lake Salinas," replied the Indian.

"And when shall we get there?"

"To-morrow evening."

When the Argentines travel in the Pampas they generally dig wells, and find water a few feet below the surface. But the travelers could not fall back on this resource, not having the necessary implements. They were therefore obliged to husband the small provision of water they had still left, and deal it out in rations, so that if no one had enough to satisfy his thirst no one felt it too painful.

They halted at evening after a course of thirty miles and eagerly looked forward to a good night's rest to compensate for the fatigue of day. But their slumbers were invaded by a swarm of mosquitoes, which allowed them no peace. Their presence indicated a change of wind which shifted to the north. A south or southwest wind generally puts to flight these little pests.

Even these petty ills of life could not ruffle the Major's equanimity; but Paganel, on the contrary, was perfectly exasperated by such trifling annoyances. He abused the poor mosquitoes desperately, and deplored the lack of some acid lotion which would have eased the pain of their stings. The Major did his best to console him by reminding him of the fact that they had only to do with one species of insect, among the 300,000 naturalists reckon. He would listen to nothing, and got up in a very bad temper.

He was quite willing to start at daybreak, however, for they had to get to Lake Salinas before sundown. The horses were tired out and dying for water, and though their riders had stinted themselves for their sakes, still their ration was very insufficient. The drought was constantly increasing, and the heat none the less for the wind being north, this wind being the simoom of the Pampas.

There was a brief interruption this day to the monotony of the journey. Mulrady, who was in front of the others, rode hastily back to report the approach of a troop of Indians. The news was received with very different feelings by Glenarvan and Thalcave. The Scotchman was glad of the chance of gleaning some information about his shipwrecked countryman, while the Patagonian hardly cared to encounter the nomadic Indians of the prairie, knowing their bandit propensities. He rather sought to avoid them, and gave orders to his party to have their arms in readiness for any trouble.

Presently the nomads came in sight, and the Patagonian was reassured at finding they were only ten in number. They came within a hundred yards of them, and stopped. This was near enough to observe them distinctly. They were fine specimens of the native races, which had been almost entirely swept away in 1833 by General Rosas, tall in stature, with arched forehead and olive complexion. They were dressed in guanaco skins, and carried lances twenty feet long, knives, slings, bolas, and lassos, and, by their dexterity in the management of their horses, showed themselves to be accomplished riders.

They appeared to have stopped for the purpose of holding a council with each other, for they shouted and gesticulated at a great rate. Glenarvan determined to go up to them; but he had no sooner moved forward than the whole band wheeled round, and disappeared with incredible speed. It would have been useless for the travelers to attempt to overtake them with such wornout horses.

"The cowards!" exclaimed Paganel.

"They scampered off too quick for honest folks," said McNabbs.

"Who are these Indians, Thalcave?" asked Paganel.

"Gauchos."

"The Gauchos!" cried Paganel; and, turning to his companions, he added, "we need not have been so much on our guard; there was nothing to fear."

"How is that?" asked McNabbs.

"Because the Gauchos are inoffensive peasants."

"You believe that, Paganel?"

"Certainly I do. They took us for robbers, and fled in terror."

"I rather think they did not dare to attack us," replied Glenarvan, much vexed at not being able to enter into some sort of communication with those Indians, whatever they were.

"That's my opinion too," said the Major, "for if I am not mistaken, instead of being harmless, the Gauchos are formidable out-and-out bandits."

"The idea!" exclaimed Paganel.

And forthwith commenced a lively discussion of this ethnological thesis— so lively that the Major became excited, and, quite contrary to his usual suavity, said bluntly:

"I believe you are wrong, Paganel."

"Wrong?" replied Paganel.

"Yes. Thalcave took them for robbers, and he knows what he is talking about."

"Well, Thalcave was mistaken this time," retorted Paganel, somewhat sharply. "The Gauchos are agriculturists and shepherds, and nothing else, as I have stated in a pamphlet on the natives of the Pampas, written by me, which has attracted some notice."

"Well, well, you have committed an error, that's all, Monsieur Paganel."

"What, Monsieur McNabbs! you tell me I have committed an error?"

"An inadvertence, if you like, which you can put among the ERRATA in the next edition."

Paganel, highly incensed at his geographical knowledge being brought in question, and even jested about, allowed his ill-humor to get the better of him, and said:

"Know, sir, that my books have no need of such ERRATA."

"Indeed! Well, on this occasion they have, at any rate," retorted McNabbs, quite as obstinate as his opponent.

"Sir, I think you are very annoying to-day."

"And I think you are very crabbed."

Glenarvan thought it was high time to interfere, for the discussion was getting too hot, so he said:

"Come, now, there is no doubt one of you is very teasing and the other is very crabbed, and I must say I am surprised at both of you."

The Patagonian, without understanding the cause, could see that the two friends were quarreling. He began to smile, and said quietly:

"It's the north wind."

"The north wind," exclaimed Paganel; "what's the north wind to do with it?"

"Ah, it is just that," said Glenarvan. "It's the north wind that has put you in a bad temper. I have heard that, in South America, the wind greatly irritates the nervous system."

"By St. Patrick, Edward you are right," said the Major, laughing heartily.

But Paganel, in a towering rage, would not give up the contest, and turned upon Glenarvan, whose intervention in this jesting manner he resented.

"And so, my Lord, my nervous system is irritated?" he said.

"Yes, Paganel, it is the north wind—a wind which causes many a crime in the Pampas, as the TRAMONTANE does in the Campagna of Rome."

"Crimes!" returned the geographer. "Do I look like a man that would commit crimes?"

"That's not exactly what I said."

"Tell me at once that I want to assassinate you?"

"Well, I am really afraid," replied Glenarvan, bursting into an uncontrollable fit of laughter, in which all others joined.

Paganel said no more, but went off in front alone, and came back in a few minutes quite himself, as if he had completely forgotten his grievance.

At eight o'clock in the evening, Thalcave, who was considerably in advance of the rest, descried in the distance the much-desired lake, and in less than a quarter of an hour they reached its banks; but a grievous disappointment awaited them—the lake was dried up.

CHAPTER XVIII IN SEARCH OF WATER

LAKE SALINAS ends the string of lagoons connected with the Sierras Ventana and Guamini. Numerous expeditions were formerly made there from Buenos Ayres, to collect the salt deposited on its banks, as the waters contain great quantities of chloride of sodium.

But when Thalcave spoke of the lake as supplying drinkable water he was thinking of the RIOS of fresh water which run into it. Those streams, however, were all dried up also; the burning sun had drunk up every thing liquid, and the consternation of the travelers may be imagined at the discovery.

Some action must be taken immediately, however; for what little water still remained was almost bad, and could not quench thirst. Hunger and fatigue were forgotten in the face of this imperious necessity. A sort of leather tent, called a ROUKAH, which had been left by the natives, afforded the party a temporary resting-place, and the weary horses stretched themselves along the muddy banks, and tried to browse on the marine plants and dry reeds they found there— nauseous to the taste as they must have been.

As soon as the whole party were ensconced in the ROUKAH, Paganel asked Thalcave what he thought was best to be done. A rapid conversation followed, a few words of which were intelligible to Glenarvan. Thalcave spoke calmly, but the lively Frenchman gesticulated enough for both. After a little, Thalcave sat silent and folded his arms.

"What does he say?" asked Glenarvan. "I fancied he was advising us to separate."

"Yes, into two parties. Those of us whose horses are so done out with fatigue and thirst that they can scarcely drag one leg after the other, are to continue the route as they best can, while the others, whose steeds are fresher, are to push on in advance toward the river Guamini, which throws itself into Lake San Lucas about thirty-one miles off. If there should be water enough in the river, they are to wait on the banks till their companions reach them; but should it be dried up, they will hasten back and spare them a useless journey."

"And what will we do then?" asked Austin.

"Then we shall have to make up our minds to go seventy-two miles south, as far as the commencement of the Sierra Ventana, where rivers abound."

"It is wise counsel, and we will act upon it without loss of time. My horse is in tolerable good trim, and I volunteer to accompany Thalcave."

"Oh, my Lord, take me," said Robert, as if it were a question of some pleasure party.

"But would you be able for it, my boy?"

"Oh, I have a fine beast, which just wants to have a gallop.

Please, my Lord, to take me."

"Come, then, my boy," said Glenarvan, delighted not to leave Robert behind. "If we three don't manage to find out fresh water somewhere," he added, "we must be very stupid."

"Well, well, and what about me?" said Paganel.

"Oh, my dear Paganel, you must stay with the reserve corps," replied the Major. "You are too well acquainted with the 37th parallel and the river Guamini and the whole Pampas for us to let you go. Neither Mulrady, nor Wilson, nor myself would be able to rejoin Thalcave at the given rendezvous, but we will put ourselves under the banner of the brave Jacques Paganel with perfect confidence."

"I resign myself," said the geographer, much flattered at having supreme command.

"But mind, Paganel, no distractions," added the Major. "Don't you take us to the wrong place—to the borders of the Pacific, for instance."

"Oh, you insufferable Major; it would serve you right," replied Paganel, laughing. "But how will you manage to understand what Thalcave says, Glenarvan?" he continued.

"I suppose," replied Glenarvan, "the Patagonian and I won't have much to talk about; besides, I know a few Spanish words, and, at a pinch, I should not fear either making him understand me, or my understanding him."

"Go, then, my worthy friend," said Paganel.

"We'll have supper first," rejoined Glenarvan, "and then sleep, if we can, till it is starting time."

The supper was not very reviving without drink of any kind, and they tried to make up for the lack of it by a good sleep. But Paganel dreamed of water all night, of torrents and cascades, and rivers and ponds, and streams and brooks—in fact, he had a complete nightmare.

Next morning, at six o'clock, the horses of Thalcave, Glenarvan and Robert were got ready. Their last ration of water was given them, and drunk with more avidity than satisfaction, for it was filthy, disgusting stuff. The three travelers then jumped into their saddles, and set off, shouting "*Au revoir!*" to their companions.

"Don't come back whatever you do," called Paganel after them.

The *Desertio de las Salinas*, which they had to traverse, is a dry plain, covered with stunted trees not above ten feet high, and small mimosas, which the Indians call *curra-mammel;* and JUMES, a bushy shrub, rich in soda. Here and there large spaces were covered with salt, which sparkled in the sunlight with astonishing brilliancy. These might easily have been taken for sheets of ice, had not the intense heat forbidden the illusion; and the contrast these dazzling white sheets presented to the dry, burned-up ground gave the desert a most peculiar character. Eighty miles south, on the contrary, the Sierra Ventana, toward which the travelers might possibly have to betake themselves should the Guamini disappoint their hopes, the landscape was totally different. There the fertility is splendid; the pasturage is incomparable. Unfortunately, to reach them would necessitate a march of one hundred and thirty miles south; and this was why Thalcave thought it best to go first to Guamini, as it was not only much nearer, but also on the direct line of route.

The three horses went forward might and main, as if instinctively knowing whither they were bound. Thaouka especially displayed a courage that neither fatigue nor hunger could damp. He bounded like a bird over the dried-up CANADAS and the bushes of CURRA-MAMMEL, his loud, joyous neighing seeming to bode success to the search. The horses of Glenarvan and Robert, though not so light-footed, felt the spur of his example, and followed him bravely. Thalcave inspirited his companions as much as Thaouka did his four-footed brethren. He sat motionless in the saddle, but often turned his head to look at Robert, and ever and anon gave him a shout of encouragement and approval, as he saw how well he rode. Certainly the boy deserved praise, for he was fast becoming an excellent cavalier.

"Bravo! Robert," said Glenarvan. "Thalcave is evidently congratulating you, my boy, and paying you compliments."

"What for, my Lord?"

"For your good horsemanship."

"I can hold firm on, that's all," replied Robert blushing with pleasure at such an encomium.

"That is the principal thing, Robert; but you are too modest.

I tell you that some day you will turn out an accomplished horseman."

"What would papa say to that?" said Robert, laughing.

"He wants me to be a sailor."

"The one won't hinder the other. If all cavaliers wouldn't make good sailors, there is no reason why all sailors should not make good horsemen. To keep one's footing on the yards must teach a man to hold on firm; and as to managing the reins, and making a horse go through all sorts of movements, that's easily acquired. Indeed, it comes naturally."

"Poor father," said Robert; "how he will thank you for saving his life."

"You love him very much, Robert?"

"Yes, my Lord, dearly. He was so good to me and my sister. We were his only thought: and whenever he came home from his voyages, we were sure of some SOUVENIR from all the places he had been to; and, better still, of loving words and caresses. Ah! if you knew him you would love him, too. Mary is most like him. He has a soft voice, like hers. That's strange for a sailor, isn't it?"

"Yes, Robert, very strange."

"I see him still," the boy went on, as if speaking to himself. "Good, brave papa. He put me to sleep on his knee, crooning an old Scotch ballad about the lochs of our country. The time sometimes comes back to me, but very confused like. So it does to Mary, too. Ah, my Lord, how we loved him. Well, I do think one needs to be little to love one's father like that."

"Yes, and to be grown up, my child, to venerate him," replied Glenarvan, deeply touched by the boy's genuine affection.

During this conversation the horses had been slackening speed, and were only walking now.

"You will find him?" said Robert again, after a few minutes' silence.

"Yes, we'll find him," was Glenarvan's reply, "Thalcave has set us on the track, and I have great confidence in him."

"Thalcave is a brave Indian, isn't he?" said the boy.

"That indeed he is."

"Do you know something, my Lord?"

"What is it, and then I will tell you?"

"That all the people you have with you are brave. Lady Helena, whom I love so, and the Major, with his calm manner, and Captain Mangles, and Monsieur Paganel, and all the sailors on the DUNCAN. How courageous and devoted they are."

"Yes, my boy, I know that," replied Glenarvan.

"And do you know that you are the best of all."

"No, most certainly I don't know that."

"Well, it is time you did, my Lord," said the boy, seizing his lordship's hand, and covering it with kisses.

Glenarvan shook his head, but said no more, as a gesture from Thalcave made them spur on their horses and hurry forward.

But it was soon evident that, with the exception of Thaouka, the wearied animals could not go quicker than a walking pace. At noon they were obliged to let them rest for an hour. They could not go on at all, and refused to eat the ALFAFARES, a poor, burnt-up sort of lucerne that grew there.

Glenarvan began to be uneasy. Tokens of sterility were not the least on the decrease, and the want of water might involve serious calamities. Thalcave said nothing, thinking probably, that it would be time enough to despair if the Guamini should be dried up—if, indeed, the heart of an Indian can ever despair.

Spur and whip had both to be employed to induce the poor animals to resume the route, and then they only crept along, for their strength was gone.

Thaouka, indeed, could have galloped swiftly enough, and reached the RIO in a few hours, but Thalcave would not leave his companions behind, alone in the midst of a desert.

It was hard work, however, to get the animal to consent to walk quietly. He kicked, and reared, and neighed violently, and was subdued at last more by his master's voice than hand. Thalcave positively talked to the beast, and Thaouka understood perfectly, though unable to reply, for, after a great deal of arguing, the noble creature yielded, though he still champed the bit.

Thalcave did not understand Thaouka, it turned out, though Thaouka understood him. The intelligent animal felt humidity in the atmosphere and drank it in with frenzy, moving and making a noise with his tongue, as if taking deep draughts of some cool refreshing liquid. The Patagonian could not mistake him now—water was not far off.

The two other horses seemed to catch their comrade's meaning, and, inspired by his example, made a last effort, and galloped forward after the Indian.

About three o'clock a white line appeared in a dip of the road, and seemed to tremble in the sunlight.

"Water!" exclaimed Glenarvan.

"Yes, yes! it is water!" shouted Robert.

They were right; and the horses knew it too, for there was no need now to urge them on; they tore over the ground as if mad, and in a few minutes had reached the river, and plunged in up to their chests.

Their masters had to go on too, whether they would or not but they were so rejoiced at being able to quench their thirst, that this compulsory bath was no grievance.

"Oh, how delicious this is!" exclaimed Robert, taking a deep draught.

"Drink moderately, my boy," said Glenarvan; but he did not set the example.

Thalcave drank very quietly, without hurrying himself, taking small gulps, but "as long as a lazo," as the Patagonians say. He seemed as if he were never going to leave off, and really there was some danger of his swallowing up the whole river.

At last Glenarvan said:

"Well, our friends won't be disappointed this time; they will be sure of finding clear, cool water when they get here— that is to say, if Thalcave leaves any for them."

"But couldn't we go to meet them? It would spare them several hours' suffering and anxiety."

"You're right my boy; but how could we carry them this water? The leather bottles were left with Wilson. No; it is better for us to wait for them as we agreed. They can't be here till about the middle of the night, so the best thing we can do is to get a good bed and a good supper ready for them."

CHAPTER XVIII IN SEARCH OF WATER

Thalcave had not waited for Glenarvan's proposition to prepare an encampment. He had been fortunate enough to discover on the banks of the *rio a ramada*, a sort of enclosure, which had served as a fold for flocks, and was shut in on three sides. A more suitasuitable place could not be found for their night's lodging, provided they had no fear of sleeping in the open air beneath the star-lit heavens; and none of Thalcave's companions had much solicitude on that score. Accordingly they took possession at once, and stretched themselves at full length on the ground in the bright sunshine, to dry their dripping garments.

"Well, now we've secured a lodging, we must think of supper," said Glenarvan. "Our friends must not have reason to complain of the couriers they sent to precede them; and if I am not much mistaken, they will be very satisfied. It strikes me that an hour's shooting won't be lost time. Are you ready, Robert?"

"Yes, my Lord," replied the boy, standing up, gun in hand.

Why Glenarvan proposed this was, that the banks of the Guamini seemed to be the general rendezvous of all the game in the surrounding plains. A sort of partridge peculiar to the Pampas, called TINAMOUS; black wood-hens; a species of plover, called TERU-TERU; yellow rays, and waterfowl with magnificent green plumage, rose in coveys. No quadrupeds, however, were visible, but Thalcave pointed to the long grass and thick brushwood, and gave his friends to understand they were lying there in concealment.

Disdaining the feathered tribes when more substantial game was at hand, the hunters' first shots were fired into the underwood. Instantly there rose by the hundred roebucks and guanacos, like those that had swept over them that terrible night on the Cordilleras, but the timid creatures were so frightened that they were all out of gunshot in a twinkling. The hunters were obliged to content themselves with humbler game, though in an alimentary point of view nothing better could be wished. A dozen of red partridges and rays were speedily brought down, and Glenarvan also managed very cleverly to kill a TAY-TETRE, or peccary, a pachydermatous animal, the flesh of which is excellent eating.

In less than half an hour the hunters had all the game they required. Robert had killed a curious animal belonging to the order EDENTATA, an armadillo, a sort of tatou, covered with a hard bony shell, in movable pieces, and measuring a foot and a half long. It was very fat and would make an excellent dish, the Patagonian said. Robert was very proud of his success.

Thalcave did his part by capturing a NANDOU, a species of ostrich, remarkable for its extreme swiftness.

There could be no entrapping such an animal, and the Indian did not attempt it. He urged Thaouka to a gallop, and made a direct attack, knowing that if the first aim missed the NANDOU would soon tire out horse and rider by involving them in an inextricable labyrinth of windings. The moment, therefore, that Thalcave got to a right distance, he flung his BOLAS with such a powerful hand, and so skillfully, that he caught the bird round the legs and paralyzed his efforts at once. In a few seconds it lay flat on the ground.

The Indian had not made his capture for the mere pleasure and glory of such a novel chase. The flesh of the NANDOU is highly esteemed, and Thalcave felt bound to contribute his share of the common repast.

They returned to the RAMADA, bringing back the string of partridges, the ostrich, the peccary, and the armadillo. The ostrich and the peccary were prepared for cooking by divesting them of their tough skins, and cutting them up into thin slices. As to the armadillo, he carries his cooking apparatus with him, and all that had to be done was to place him in his own shell over the glowing embers.

The substantial dishes were reserved for the night-comers, and the three hunters contented themselves with devouring the partridges, and washed down their meal with clear, fresh water, which was pronounced superior to all the porter in the world, even to the famous Highland USQUEBAUGH, or whisky.

The horses had not been overlooked. A large quantity of dry fodder was discovered lying heaped up in the RAMADA, and this supplied them amply with both food and bedding.

When all was ready the three companions wrapped themselves in the ponchos, and stretched themselves on an eiderdown of ALFAFARES, the usual bed of hunters on the Pampas.

CHAPTER XIX THE RED WOLVES

NIGHT came, but the orb of night was invisible to the inhabitants of the earth, for she was just in her first quarter. The dim light of the stars was all that illumined the plain. The waters of the Guamini ran silently, like a sheet of oil over a surface of marble. Birds, quadrupeds, and reptiles were resting motionless after the fatigues of the day, and the silence of the desert brooded over the far-spreading Pampas.

Glenarvan, Robert, and Thalcave, had followed the common example, and lay in profound slumber on their soft couch of lucerne. The worn-out horses had stretched themselves full length on the ground, except Thaouka, who slept standing, true to his high blood, proud in repose as in action, and ready to start at his master's call. Absolute silence reigned within the inclosure, over which the dying embers of the fire shed a fitful light.

However, the Indian's sleep did not last long; for about ten o'clock he woke, sat up, and turned his ear toward the plain, listening intently, with half-closed eyes. An uneasy look began to depict itself on his usually impassive face. Had he caught scent of some party of Indian marauders, or of jaguars, water tigers, and other terrible animals that haunt the neighborhood of rivers? Apparently it was the latter, for he threw a rapid glance on the combustible materials heaped up in the inclosure, and the expression of anxiety on his countenance seemed to deepen. This was not surprising, as the whole pile of ALFAFARES would soon burn out and could only ward off the attacks of wild beasts for a brief interval.

There was nothing to be done in the circumstances but wait; and wait he did, in a half-recumbent posture, his head leaning on his hands, and his elbows on his knees, like a man roused suddenly from his night's sleep.

A whole hour passed, and anyone except Thalcave would have lain down again on his couch, reassured by the silence round him. But where a stranger would have suspected nothing, the sharpened senses of the Indian detected the approach of danger.

As he was thus watching and listening, Thaouka gave a low neigh, and stretched his nostrils toward the entrance of the RAMADA.

This startled the Patagonian, and made him rise to his feet at once.

"Thaouka scents an enemy," he said to himself, going toward the opening, to make careful survey of the plains.

Silence still prevailed, but not tranquillity; for Thalcave caught a glimpse of shadows moving noiselessly over the tufts of CURRA-MAMMEL. Here and there luminous spots appeared, dying out and rekindling constantly, in all directions, like fantastic lights dancing over the surface of an immense lagoon. An inexperienced eye might have mistaken them for fireflies, which shine at night in many parts of the Pampas; but Thalcave was not deceived; he knew the enemies he had to deal with, and lost no time in loading his carbine and taking up his post in front of the fence.

He did not wait long, for a strange cry—a confused sound of barking and howling—broke over the Pampas, followed next instant by the report of the carbine, which made the uproar a hundred times worse.

Glenarvan and Robert woke in alarm, and started to their feet instantly.

"What is it?" exclaimed Robert.

"Is it the Indians?" asked Glenarvan.

"No," replied Thalcave, "the AGUARAS."

"AGUARAS?" said Robert, looking inquiringly at Glenarvan.

"Yes," replied Glenarvan, "the red wolves of the Pampas."

They seized their weapons at once, and stationed themselves beside the Patagonian, who pointed toward the plain from whence the yelling resounded.

Robert drew back involuntarily.

"You are not afraid of wolves, my boy?" said Glenarvan.

"No, my Lord," said the lad in a firm tone, "and moreover, beside you I am afraid of nothing."

"So much the better. These AGUARAS are not very formidable either; and if it were not for their number I should not give them a thought."

"Never mind; we are all well armed; let them come."

"We'll certainly give them a warm reception," rejoined Glenarvan.

His Lordship only spoke thus to reassure the child, for a secret terror filled him at the sight of this legion of bloodthirsty animals let loose on them at midnight.

There might possibly be some hundreds, and what could three men do, even armed to the teeth, against such a multitude?

As soon as Thalcave said the word AGUARA, Glenarvan knew that he meant the red wolf, for this is the name given to it by the Pampas Indians. This voracious animal, called by naturalists the *Canis jubatus*, is in shape like a large dog, and has the head of a fox. Its fur is a reddish-cinnamon color, and there is a black mane all down the back. It is a strong, nimble animal, generally inhabiting marshy places, and pursuing aquatic animals by swimming, prowling about by night and sleeping during the day. Its attacks are particularly dreaded at the ESTANCIAS, or sheep stations, as it often commits considerable ravages, carrying off the finest of the flock. Singly, the AGUARA is not much to be feared; but they generally go in immense packs, and one had better have to deal with a jaguar or cougar than with them.

Both from the noise of the howling and the multitude of shadows leaping about, Glenarvan had a pretty good idea of the number of the wolves, and he knew they had scented a good meal of human flesh or horse flesh, and none of them would go back to their dens without a share. It was certainly a very alarming situation to be in.

The assailants were gradually drawing closer. The horses displayed signs of the liveliest terror, with the exception of Thaouka, who stamped his foot, and tried to break loose and get out. His master could only calm him by keeping up a low, continuous whistle.

Glenarvan and Robert had posted themselves so as to defend the opening of the RAMADA. They were just going to fire into the nearest ranks of the wolves when Thalcave lowered their weapons.

"What does Thalcave mean?" asked Robert.

"He forbids our firing."

"And why?"

"Perhaps he thinks it is not the right time."

But this was not the Indian's reason, and so Glenarvan saw when he lifted the powder-flask, showed him it was nearly empty.

"What's wrong?" asked Robert.

"We must husband our ammunition," was the reply. "To-day's shooting has cost us dear, and we are short of powder and shot. We can't fire more than twenty times."

The boy made no reply, and Glenarvan asked him if he was frightened.

"No, my Lord," he said.

"That's right," returned Glenarvan.

A fresh report resounded that instant. Thalcave had made short work of one assailant more audacious than the rest, and the infuriated pack had retreated to within a hundred steps of the inclosure.

On a sign from the Indian Glenarvan took his place, while Thalcave went back into the inclosure and gathered up all the dried grass and ALFAFARES, and, indeed, all the combustibles he could rake together, and made a pile of them at the entrance. Into this he flung one of the still-glowing embers, and soon the bright flames shot up into the dark night. Glenarvan could now get a good glimpse of his antagonists, and saw that it was impossible to exaggerate their numbers or their fury. The barrier of fire just raised by Thalcave had redoubled their anger, though it had cut off their approach. Several of them, however, urged on by the hindmost ranks, pushed forward into the very flames, and burned their paws for their pains.

From time to time another shot had to be fired, notwithstanding the fire, to keep off the howling pack, and in the course of an hour fifteen dead animals lay stretched on the prairie.

The situation of the besieged was, relatively speaking, less dangerous now. As long as the powder lasted and the barrier of fire burned on, there was no fear of being overmastered. But what was to be done afterward, when both means of defense failed at once?

Glenarvan's heart swelled as he looked at Robert. He forgot himself in thinking of this poor child, as he saw him showing a courage so far above his years. Robert was pale, but he kept his gun steady, and stood with firm foot ready to meet the attacks of the infuriated wolves.

However, after Glenarvan had calmly surveyed the actual state of affairs, he determined to bring things to a crisis.

"In an hour's time," he said, "we shall neither have powder nor fire.

It will never do to wait till then before we settle what to do."

Accordingly, he went up to Thalcave, and tried to talk to him by the help of the few Spanish words his memory could muster, though their conversation was often interrupted by one or the other having to fire a shot.

It was no easy task for the two men to understand each other, but, most fortunately, Glenarvan knew a great deal of the peculiarities of the red wolf; otherwise he could never have interpreted the Indian's words and gestures.

As it was, fully a quarter of an hour elapsed before he could get any answer from Thalcave to tell Robert in reply to his inquiry.

"What does he say?"

"He says that at any price we must hold out till daybreak. The AGUARA only prowls about at night, and goes back to his lair with the first streak of dawn. It is a cowardly beast, that loves the darkness and dreads the light—an owl on four feet."

"Very well, let us defend ourselves, then, till morning."

"Yes, my boy, and with knife-thrusts, when gun and shots fail."

Already Thalcave had set the example, for whenever a wolf came too near the burning pile, the long arm of the Patagonian dashed through the flames and came out again reddened with blood.

But very soon this means of defense would be at an end. About two o'clock, Thalcave flung his last armful of combustibles into the fire, and barely enough powder remained to load a gun five times.

Glenarvan threw a sorrowful glance round him. He thought of the lad standing there, and of his companions and those left behind, whom he loved so dearly.

Robert was silent. Perhaps the danger seemed less imminent to his imagination. But Glenarvan thought for him, and pictured to himself the horrible fate that seemed to await him inevitably. Quite overcome by his emotion, he took the child in his arms, and straining him convulsively to his heart, pressed his lips on his forehead, while tears he could not restrain streamed down his cheeks.

Robert looked up into his face with a smile, and said,

"I am not frightened."

"No, my child, no! and you are right. In two hours daybreak will come, and we shall be saved. Bravo, Thalcave! my brave Patagonian! Bravo!" he added as the Indian that moment leveled two enormous beasts who endeavored to leap across the barrier of flames.

But the fire was fast dying out, and the DENOUEMENT of the terrible drama was approaching. The flames got lower and lower. Once more the shadows of night fell on the prairie, and the glaring eyes of the wolves glowed like phosphorescent balls in the darkness. A few minutes longer, and the whole pack would be in the inclosure.

Thalcave loaded his carbine for the last time, killed one more enormous monster, and then folded his arms. His head sank on his chest, and he appeared buried in deep thought. Was he planning some daring, impossible, mad attempt to repulse the infuriated horde? Glenarvan did not venture to ask.

At this very moment the wolves began to change their tactics.

The deafening howls suddenly ceased: they seemed to be going away.

Gloomy silence spread over the prairie, and made Robert exclaim:

"They're gone!"

But Thalcave, guessing his meaning, shook his head. He knew they would never relinquish their sure prey till daybreak made them hasten back to their dens.

Still, their plan of attack had evidently been altered. They no longer attempted to force the entrance, but their new maneuvers only heightened the danger.

They had gone round the RAMADA, as by common consent, and were trying to get in on the opposite side.

The next minute they heard their claws attacking the moldering wood, and already formidable paws and hungry, savage jaws had found their way through the palings. The terrified horses broke loose from their halters and ran about the inclosure, mad with fear.

Glenarvan put his arms round the young lad, and resolved to defend him as long as his life held out. Possibly he might have made a useless attempt at flight when his eye fell on Thalcave.

The Indian had been stalking about the RAMADA like a stag, when he suddenly stopped short, and going up to his horse, who was trembling with impatience, began to saddle him with the most scrupulous care, without forgetting a single strap or buckle. He seemed no longer to disturb himself in the least about the wolves outside, though their yells had redoubled in intensity. A dark suspicion crossed Glenarvan's mind as he watched him.

"He is going to desert us," he exclaimed at last, as he saw him seize the reins, as if preparing to mount.

"He! never!" replied Robert. Instead of deserting them, the truth was that the Indian was going to try and save his friends by sacrificing himself.

Thaouka was ready, and stood champing his bit. He reared up, and his splendid eyes flashed fire; he understood his master.

But just as the Patagonian caught hold of the horse's mane, Glenarvan seized his arm with a convulsive grip, and said, pointing to the open prairie.

"You are going away?"

"Yes," replied the Indian, understanding his gesture. Then he said a few words in Spanish, which meant: "*Thaouka; good horse; quick; will draw all the wolves away after him.*"

"Oh, Thalcave," exclaimed Glenarvan.

"Quick, quick!" replied the Indian, while Glenarvan said, in a broken, agitated voice to Robert:

"Robert, my child, do you hear him? He wants to sacrifice himself for us. He wants to rush away over the Pampas, and turn off the wolves from us by attracting them to himself."

"Friend Thalcave," returned Robert, throwing himself at the feet of the Patagonian, "friend Thalcave, don't leave us!"

"No," said Glenarvan, "he shall not leave us."

And turning toward the Indian, he said, pointing to the frightened horses,

"Let us go together."

"No," replied Thalcave, catching his meaning.

"Bad beasts; frightened; Thaouka, good horse."

"Be it so then!" returned Glenarvan. "Thalcave will not leave you, Robert. He teaches me what I must do. It is for me to go, and for him to stay by you."

Then seizing Thaouka's bridle, he said, "I am going, Thalcave, not you."

"No," replied the Patagonian quietly.

"I am," exclaimed Glenarvan, snatching the bridle out of his hands.

"I, myself! Save this boy, Thalcave! I commit him to you."

Glenarvan was so excited that he mixed up English words with his Spanish. But what mattered the language at such a terrible moment. A gesture was enough. The two men understood each other.

However, Thalcave would not give in, and though every instant's delay but increased the danger, the discussion continued.

Neither Glenarvan nor Thalcave appeared inclined to yield. The Indian had dragged his companion towards the entrance of the RAMADA, and showed him the prairie, making him understand that now was the time when it was clear from the wolves; but that not a moment was to be lost, for should this maneuver not succeed, it would only render the situation of those left behind more desperate. and that he knew his horse well enough to be able to trust his wonderful lightness and swiftness to save them all. But Glenarvan was blind and obstinate, and determined to sacrifice himself at all hazards, when suddenly he felt himself violently pushed back. Thaouka pranced up, and reared himself bolt upright on his hind legs, and made a bound over the barrier of fire, while a clear, young voice called out:

"God save you, my lord."

But before either Thalcave or Glenarvan could get more than a glimpse of the boy, holding on fast by Thaouka's mane, he was out of sight.

"Robert! oh you unfortunate boy," cried Glenarvan.

But even Thalcave did not catch the words, for his voice was drowned in the frightful uproar made by the wolves, who had dashed off at a tremendous speed on the track of the horse.

Thalcave and Glenarvan rushed out of the RAMADA. Already the plain had recovered its tranquillity, and all that could be seen of the red wolves was a moving line far away in the distant darkness.

Glenarvan sank prostrate on the ground, and clasped his hands despairingly. He looked at Thalcave, who smiled with his accustomed calmness, and said:

"Thaouka, good horse. Brave boy. He will save himself!"

"And suppose he falls?" said Glenarvan.

"He'll not fall."

But notwithstanding Thalcave's assurances, poor Glenarvan spent the rest of the night in torturing anxiety. He seemed quite insensible now to the danger they had escaped through the departure of the wolves, and would have hastened immediately after Robert if the Indian had not kept him back by making him understand the impossibility of their horses overtaking Thaouka; and also that boy and horse had outdistanced the wolves long since, and that it would be useless going to look for them till daylight.

At four o'clock morning began to dawn. A pale glimmer appeared in the horizon, and pearly drops of dew lay thick on the plain and on the tall grass, already stirred by the breath of day.

The time for starting had arrived.

"Now!" cried Thalcave, "come."

Glenarvan made no reply, but took Robert's horse and sprung into the saddle. Next minute both men were galloping at full speed toward the west, in the line in which their companions ought to be advancing. They dashed along at a prodigious rate for a full hour, dreading every minute to come across the mangled corpse of Robert. Glenarvan had torn the flanks of his horse with his spurs in his mad haste, when at last gun-shots were heard in the distance at regular intervals, as if fired as a signal.

"There they are!" exclaimed Glenarvan; and both he and the Indian urged on their steeds to a still quicker pace, till in a few minutes more they came up to the little detachment conducted by Paganel. A cry broke from Glenarvan's lips, for Robert was there, alive and well, still mounted on the superb Thaouka, who neighed loudly with delight at the sight of his master.

"Oh, my child, my child!" cried Glenarvan, with indescribable tenderness in his tone.

Both he and Robert leaped to the ground, and flung themselves into each other's arms. Then the Indian hugged the brave boy in his arms.

"He is alive, he is alive," repeated Glenarvan again and again.

"Yes," replied Robert; "and thanks to Thaouka."

This great recognition of his favorite's services was wholly unexpected by the Indian, who was talking to him that minute, caressing and speaking to him, as if human blood flowed in the veins of the proud creature. Then turning to Paganel, he pointed to Robert, and said, "A brave!" and employing the Indian metaphor, he added, "his spurs did not tremble!"

But Glenarvan put his arms round the boy and said, "Why wouldn't you let me or Thalcave run the risk of this last chance of deliverance, my son?"

"My lord," replied the boy in tones of gratitude, "wasn't it my place to do it? Thalcave has saved my life already, and you— you are going to save my father."

CHAPTER XX STRANGE SIGNS

AFTER the first joy of the meeting was over, Paganel and his party, except perhaps the Major, were only conscious of one feeling— they were dying of thirst. Most fortunately for them, the Guamini ran not far off, and about seven in the morning the little troop reached the inclosure on its banks. The precincts were strewed with the dead wolves, and judging from their numbers, it was evident how violent the attack must have been, and how desperate the resistance.

As soon as the travelers had drunk their fill, they began to demolish the breakfast prepared in the RAMADA, and did ample justice to the extraordinary viands. The NANDOU fillets were pronounced first-rate, and the armadillo was delicious.

"To eat moderately," said Paganel, "would be positive ingratitude to Providence. We must eat immoderately."

And so they did, but were none the worse for it.

The water of the Guamini greatly aided digestion apparently.

Glenarvan, however, was not going to imitate Hannibal at Capua, and at ten o'clock next morning gave the signal for starting. The leathern bottles were filled with water, and the day's march commenced. The horses were so well rested that they were quite fresh again, and kept up a canter almost constantly. The country was not so parched up now, and consequently less sterile, but still a desert. No incident occurred of any importance during the 2d and 3d of November, and in the evening they reached the boundary of the Pampas, and camped for the night on the frontiers of the province of Buenos Ayres. Two-thirds of their journey was now accomplished. It was twenty-two days since they left the Bay of Talcahuano, and they had gone 450 miles.

Next morning they crossed the conventional line which separates the Argentine plains from the region of the Pampas. It was here that Thalcave hoped to meet the Caciques, in whose hands, he had no doubt, Harry Grant and his men were prisoners.

From the time of leaving the Guamini, there was marked change in the temperature, to the great relief of the travelers. It was much cooler, thanks to the violent and cold winds from Patagonia, which constantly agitate the atmospheric waves. Horses and men were glad enough of this, after what they had suffered from the heat and drought, and they felt animated with fresh ardor and confidence. But contrary to what Thalcave had said, the whole district appeared uninhabited, or rather abandoned.

Their route often led past or went right through small lagoons, sometimes of fresh water, sometimes of brackish. On the banks and bushes about these, king-wrens were hopping about and larks singing joyously in concert with the tangaras, the rivals in color of the brilliant humming birds. On the thorny bushes the nests of the ANNUBIS swung to and fro in the breeze like an Indian hammock; and on the shore magnificent flamingos stalked in regular order like soldiers marching, and spread out their flaming red wings. Their nests were seen in groups of thousands, forming a complete town, about a foot high, and resembling a truncated cone in shape. The flamingos did not disturb themselves in the least at the approach of the travelers, but this did not suit Paganel.

"I have been very desirous a long time," he said to the Major, "to see a flamingo flying."

"All right," replied McNabbs.

"Now while I have the opportunity, I should like to make the most of it," continued Paganel.

"Very well; do it, Paganel."

"Come with me, then, Major, and you too Robert. I want witnesses."

And all three went off towards the flamingos, leaving the others to go on in advance.

As soon as they were near enough, Paganel fired, only loading his gun, however, with powder, for he would not shed even the blood of a bird uselessly. The shot made the whole assemblage fly away *en masse*, while Paganel watched them attentively through his spectacles.

"Well, did you see them fly?" he asked the Major.

"Certainly I did," was the reply. "I could not help seeing them, unless I had been blind."

"Well and did you think they resembled feathered arrows when they were flying?"

"Not in the least."

"Not a bit," added Robert.

"I was sure of it," said the geographer, with a satisfied air; "and yet the very proudest of modest men, my illustrious countryman, Chateaubriand, made the inaccurate comparison. Oh, Robert, comparison is the most dangerous figure in rhetoric that I know. Mind you avoid it all your life, and only employ it in a last extremity."

"Are you satisfied with your experiment?" asked McNabbs.

"Delighted."

"And so am I. But we had better push on now, for your illustrious

Chateaubriand has put us more than a mile behind."

On rejoining their companions, they found Glenarvan busily engaged in conversation with the Indian, though apparently unable to make him understand. Thalcave's gaze was fixed intently on the horizon, and his face wore a puzzled expression.

The moment Paganel came in sight, Glenarvan called out:

"Come along, friend Paganel. Thalcave and I can't understand each other at all."

After a few minute's talk with the Patagonian, the interpreter turned to Glenarvan and said:

"Thalcave is quite astonished at the fact, and certainly it is very strange that there are no Indians, nor even traces of any to be seen in these plains, for they are generally thick with companies of them, either driving along cattle stolen from the ESTANCIAS, or going to the Andes to sell their zorillo cloths and plaited leather whips."

"And what does Thalcave think is the reason?"

"He does not know; he is amazed and that's all."

"But what description of Indians did he reckon on meeting in this part of the Pampas?"

"Just the very ones who had the foreign prisoners in their hands, the natives under the rule of the Caciques Calfoucoura, Catriel, or Yanchetruz."

"Who are these Caciques?"

"Chiefs that were all powerful thirty years ago, before they were driven beyond the sierras. Since then they have been reduced to subjection as much as Indians can be, and they scour the plains of the Pampas and the province of Buenos Ayres. I quite share Thalcave's surprise at not discovering any traces of them in regions which they usually infest as SALTEADORES, or bandits."

"And what must we do then?"

"I'll go and ask him," replied Paganel.

After a brief colloquy he returned and said:

"This is his advice, and very sensible it is, I think. He says we had better continue our route to the east as far as Fort Independence, and if we don't get news of Captain Grant there we shall hear, at any rate, what has become of the Indians of the Argentine plains."

"Is Fort Independence far away?" asked Glenarvan.

"No, it is in the Sierra Tandil, a distance of about sixty miles."

"And when shall we arrive?"

"The day after to-morrow, in the evening."

Glenarvan was considerably disconcerted by this circumstance. Not to find an Indian where in general there were only too many, was so unusual that there must be some grave cause for it; but worse still if Harry Grant were a prisoner in the hands of any of those tribes, had he been dragged away with them to the north or south? Glenarvan felt that, cost what it might, they must not lose his track, and therefore decided to follow the advice of Thalcave, and go to the village of Tandil. They would find some one there to speak to, at all events.

About four o'clock in the evening a hill, which seemed a mountain in so flat a country, was sighted in the distance. This was Sierra Tapalquem, at the foot of which the travelers camped that night.

The passage in the morning over this sierra, was accomplished without the slightest difficulty; after having crossed the Cordillera of the Andes, it was easy work to ascend the gentle heights of such a sierra as this. The horses scarcely slackened their speed. At noon they passed the deserted fort of Tapalquem, the first of the chain of forts which defend the southern frontiers from Indian marauders. But to the increasing surprise of Thalcave, they did not come across even the shadow of an Indian. About the middle of the day, however, three flying horsemen, well mounted and well armed came in sight, gazed at them for an instant, and then sped away with inconceivable rapidity. Glenarvan was furious.

"Gauchos," said the Patagonian, designating them by the name which had caused such a fiery discussion between the Major and Paganel.

"Ah! the Gauchos," replied McNabbs. "Well, Paganel, the north wind is not blowing to-day. What do you think of those fellows yonder?"

"I think they look like regular bandits."

"And how far is it from looking to being, my good geographer?"

"Only just a step, my dear Major."

Paganel's admission was received with a general laugh, which did not in the least disconcert him. He went on talking about the Indians however, and made this curious observation:

"I have read somewhere," he said, "that about the Arabs there is a peculiar expression of ferocity in the mouth, while the eyes have a kindly look. Now, in these American savages it is quite the reverse, for the eye has a particularly villainous aspect."

No physiognomist by profession could have better characterized the Indian race.

But desolate as the country appeared, Thalcave was on his guard against surprises, and gave orders to his party to form themselves in a close platoon. It was a useless precaution, however; for that same evening, they camped for the night in an immense TOLDERIA, which they not only found perfectly empty, but which the Patagonian declared, after he had examined it all round, must have been uninhabited for a long time.

Next day, the first ESTANCIAS of the Sierra Tandil came in sight. The ESTANCIAS are large cattle stations for breeding cattle; but Thalcave resolved not to stop at any of them, but to go straight on to Fort Independence. They passed several farms fortified by battlements and surrounded by a deep moat, the principal building being encircled by a terrace, from which the inhabitants could fire down on the marauders in the plain. Glenarvan might, perhaps, have got some information at these houses, but it was the surest plan to go straight on to the village of Tandil. Accordingly they went on without stopping, fording the RIO of Los Huasos and also the Chapaleofu, a few miles further on. Soon they were treading the grassy slopes of the first ridges of the Sierra Tandil, and an hour afterward the village appeared in the depths of a narrow gorge, and above it towered the lofty battlements of Fort Independence.

CHAPTER XXI A FALSE TRAIL

THE Sierra Tandil rises a thousand feet above the level of the sea. It is a primordial chain—that is to say, anterior to all organic and metamorphic creation. It is formed of a semi-circular ridge of gneiss hills, covered with fine short grass. The district of Tandil, to which it has given its name, includes all the south of the Province of Buenos Ayres, and terminates in a river which conveys north all the RIOS that take their rise on its slopes.

After making a short ascent up the sierra, they reached the postern gate, so carelessly guarded by an Argentine sentinel, that they passed through without difficulty, a circumstance which betokened extreme negligence or extreme security.

A few minutes afterward the Commandant appeared in person. He was a vigorous man about fifty years of age, of military aspect, with grayish hair, and an imperious eye, as far as one could see through the clouds of tobacco smoke which escaped from his short pipe. His walk reminded Paganel instantly of the old subalterns in his own country.

Thalcave was spokesman, and addressing the officer, presented Lord Glenarvan and his companions. While he was speaking, the Commandant kept staring fixedly at Paganel in rather an embarrassing manner. The geographer could not understand what he meant by it, and was just about to interrogate him, when the Commandant came forward, and seizing both his hands in the most free-and-easy fashion, said in a joyous voice, in the mother tongue of the geographer:

"A Frenchman!"

"Yes, a Frenchman," replied Paganel.

"Ah! delightful! Welcome, welcome. I am a Frenchman too," he added, shaking Paganel's hand with such vigor as to be almost alarming.

"Is he a friend of yours, Paganel?" asked the Major.

"Yes," said Paganel, somewhat proudly. "One has friends in every division of the globe."

After he had succeeded in disengaging his hand, though not without difficulty, from the living vise in which it was held, a lively conversation ensued. Glenarvan would fain have put in a word about the business on hand, but the Commandant related his entire history, and was not in a mood to stop till he had done. It was evident that the worthy man must have left his native country many years back, for his mother tongue had grown unfamiliar, and if he had not forgotten the words he certainly did not remember how to put them together. He spoke more like a negro belonging to a French colony.

The fact was that the Governor of Fort Independence was a French sergeant, an old comrade of Parachapee. He had never left the fort since it had been built in 1828; and, strange to say, he commanded it with the consent of the Argentine Government. He was a man about fifty years of age, a Basque by birth, and his name was Manuel Ipharaguerre, so that he was almost a Spaniard. A year after his arrival in the country he was naturalized, took service in the Argentine army, and married an Indian girl, who was then nursing twin babies six months old— two boys, be it understood, for the good wife of the Commandant would have never thought of presenting her husband with girls. Manuel could not conceive of any state but a military one, and he hoped in due time, with the help of God, to offer the republic a whole company of young soldiers.

"You saw them. Charming! good soldiers are Jose, Juan, and Miquele! Pepe, seven year old; Pepe can handle a gun."

Pepe, hearing himself complimented, brought his two little feet together, and presented arms with perfect grace.

"He'll get on!" added the sergeant. "He'll be colonel-major or brigadier-general some day."

Sergeant Manuel seemed so enchanted that it would have been useless to express a contrary opinion, either to the profession of arms or the probable future of his children. He was happy, and as Goethe says, "Nothing that makes us happy is an illusion."

All this talk took up a quarter of an hour, to the great astonishment of Thalcave. The Indian could not understand how so many words could come out of one throat. No one interrupted the Sergeant, but all things come to an end, and at last he was silent, but not till he had made his guests enter his dwelling, and be presented to Madame Ipharaguerre. Then, and not till then, did he ask his guests what had procured him the honor of their visit. Now or never was the moment to explain, and Paganel, seizing the chance at once, began an account of their journey across the Pampas, and ended by inquiring the reason of the Indians having deserted the country.

"Ah! there was no one!" replied the Sergeant, shrugging his shoulders—"really no one, and us, too, our arms crossed! Nothing to do!"

"But why?"

"War."

"War?"

"Yes, civil war between the Paraguayans and Buenos Ayriens," replied the Sergeant.

"Well?"

"Well, Indians all in the north, in the rear of General Flores.

Indian pillagers find pillage there."

"But where are the Caciques?"

"Caciques are with them."

"What! Catriel?"

"There is no Catriel."

"And Calfoucoura?"

"There is no Calfoucoura."

"And is there no Yanchetruz?"

"No; no Yanchetruz."

The reply was interpreted by Thalcave, who shook his head and gave an approving look. The Patagonian was either unaware of, or had forgotten that civil war was decimating the two parts of the republic—a war which ultimately required the intervention of Brazil. The Indians have everything to gain by these intestine strifes, and can not lose such fine opportunities of plunder. There was no doubt the Sergeant was right in assigning war then as the cause of the forsaken appearance of the plains.

But this circumstance upset all Glenarvan's projects, for if Harry Grant was a prisoner in the hands of the Caciques, he must have been dragged north with them. How and where should they ever find him if that were the case? Should they attempt a perilous and almost useless journey to the northern border of the Pampas? It was a serious question which would need to be well talked over.

However, there was one inquiry more to make to the Sergeant; and it was the Major who thought of it, for all the others looked at each other in silence.

"Had the Sergeant heard whether any Europeans were prisoners in the hands of the Caciques?"

Manuel looked thoughtful for a few minutes, like a man trying to ransack his memory. At last he said:

"Yes."

"Ah!" said Glenarvan, catching at the fresh hope.

They all eagerly crowded round the Sergeant, exclaiming,

"Tell us, tell us."

"It was some years ago," replied Manuel. "Yes; all I heard was that some Europeans were prisoners, but I never saw them."

"You are making a mistake," said Glenarvan. "It can't be some years ago; the date of the shipwreck is explicitly given. The BRITANNIA was wrecked in June, 1862. It is scarcely two years ago."

"Oh, more than that, my Lord."

"Impossible!" said Paganel.

"Oh, but it must be. It was when Pepe was born.

There were two prisoners."

"No, three!" said Glenarvan.

"Two!" replied the Sergeant, in a positive tone.

"Two?" echoed Glenarvan, much surprised. "Two Englishmen?"

"No, no. Who is talking of Englishmen? No; a Frenchman and an Italian."

"An Italian who was massacred by the Poyuches?" exclaimed Paganel.

"Yes; and I heard afterward that the Frenchman was saved."

"Saved!" exclaimed young Robert, his very life hanging on the lips of the Sergeant.

Yes; delivered out of the hands of the Indians."

Paganel struck his forehead with an air of desperation, and said at last,

"Ah! I understand. It is all clear now; everything is explained."

"But what is it?" asked Glenarvan, with as much impatience.

"My friends," replied Paganel, taking both Robert's hands in his own, "we must resign ourselves to a sad disaster. We have been on a wrong track. The prisoner mentioned is not the captain at all, but one of my own countrymen; and his companion, who was assassinated by the Poyuches, was Marco Vazello. The Frenchman was dragged along by the cruel Indians several times as far as the shores of the Colorado, but managed at length to make his escape, and return to Colorado. Instead of following the track of Harry Grant, we have fallen on that of young Guinnard."

This announcement was heard with profound silence. The mistake was palpable. The details given by the Sergeant, the nationality of the prisoner, the murder of his companions, his escape from the hands of the Indians, all evidenced the fact. Glenarvan looked at Thalcave with a crestfallen face, and the Indian, turning to the Sergeant, asked whether he had never heard of three English captives.

"Never," replied Manuel. "They would have known of them at Tandil, I am sure. No, it cannot be."

After this, there was nothing further to do at Fort Independence but to shake hands with the Commandant, and thank him and take leave.

Glenarvan was in despair at this complete overthrow of his hopes, and Robert walked silently beside him, with his eyes full of tears. Glenarvan could not find a word of comfort to say to him. Paganel gesticulated and talked away to himself. The Major never opened his mouth, nor Thalcave, whose *amour propre*, as an Indian, seemed quite wounded by having allowed himself to go on a wrong scent. No one, however, would have thought of reproaching him for an error so pardonable.

They went back to the FONDA, and had supper; but it was a gloomy party that surrounded the table. It was not that any one of them regretted the fatigue they had so heedlessly endured or the dangers they had run, but they felt their hope of success was gone, for there was no chance of coming across Captain Grant between the Sierra Tandil and the sea, as Sergeant Manuel must have heard if any prisoners had fallen into the hands of the Indians on the coast of the Atlantic. Any event of this nature would have attracted the notice of the Indian traders who traffic between Tandil and Carmen, at the mouth of the Rio Negro. The best thing to do now was to get to the DUNCAN as quick as possible at the appointed rendezvous.

Paganel asked Glenarvan, however, to let him have the document again, on the faith of which they had set out on so bootless a search. He read it over and over, as if trying to extract some new meaning out of it.

"Yet nothing can be clearer," said Glenarvan; "it gives the date of the shipwreck, and the manner, and the place of the captivity in the most categorical manner."

"That it does not—no, it does not!" exclaimed Paganel, striking the table with his fist. "Since Harry Grant is not in the Pampas, he is not in America; but where he is the document must say, and it shall say, my friends, or my name is not Jacques Paganel any longer."

CHAPTER XXII THE FLOOD

A DISTANCE of 150 miles separates Fort Independence from the shores of the Atlantic. Unless unexpected and certainly improbable delays should occur, in four days Glenarvan would rejoin the DUNCAN. But to return on board without Captain Grant, and after having so completely failed in his search, was what he could not bring himself to do. Consequently, when next day came, he gave no orders for departure; the Major took it upon himself to have the horses saddled, and make all preparations. Thanks to his activity, next morning at eight o'clock the little troop was descending the grassy slopes of the Sierra.

Glenarvan, with Robert at his side, galloped along without saying a word. His bold, determined nature made it impossible to take failure quietly. His heart throbbed as if it would burst, and his head was burning. Paganel, excited by the difficulty, was turning over and over the words of the document, and trying to discover some new meaning. Thalcave was perfectly silent, and left Thaouka to lead the way. The Major, always confident, remained firm at his post, like a man on whom discouragement takes no hold. Tom Austin and his two sailors shared the dejection of their master. A timid rabbit happened to run across their path, and the superstitious men looked at each other in dismay.

"A bad omen," said Wilson.

"Yes, in the Highlands," repeated Mulrady.

"What's bad in the Highlands is not better here," returned Wilson sententiously.

Toward noon they had crossed the Sierra, and descended into the undulating plains which extend to the sea. Limpid RIOS intersected these plains, and lost themselves among the tall grasses. The ground had once more become a dead level, the last mountains of the Pampas were passed, and a long carpet of verdure unrolled itself over the monotonous prairie beneath the horses' tread.

Hitherto the weather had been fine, but to-day the sky presented anything but a reassuring appearance. The heavy vapors, generated by the high temperature of the preceding days, hung in thick clouds, which ere long would empty themselves in torrents of rain. Moreover, the vicinity of the Atlantic, and the prevailing west wind, made the climate of this district particularly damp. This was evident by the fertility and abundance of the pasture and its dark color. However, the clouds remained unbroken for the present, and in the evening, after a brisk gallop of forty miles, the horses stopped on the brink of deep CANADAS, immense natural trenches filled with water. No shelter was near, and ponchos had to serve both for tents and coverlets as each man lay down and fell asleep beneath the threatening sky.

Next day the presence of water became still more sensibly felt; it seemed to exude from every pore of the ground. Soon large ponds, some just beginning to form, and some already deep, lay across the route to the east. As long as they had only to deal with lagoons, circumscribed pieces of water unencumbered with aquatic plants, the horses could get through well enough, but when they encountered moving sloughs called PENTANOS, it was harder work. Tall grass blocked them up, and they were involved in the peril before they were aware.

These bogs had already proved fatal to more than one living thing, for Robert, who had got a good bit ahead of the party, came rushing back at full gallop, calling out:

"Monsieur Paganel, Monsieur Paganel, a forest of horns."

"What!" exclaimed the geographer; "you have found a forest of horns?"

"Yes, yes, or at any rate a coppice."

"A coppice!" replied Paganel, shrugging his shoulders.

"My boy, you are dreaming."

"I am not dreaming, and you will see for yourself. Well, this is a strange country. They sow horns, and they sprout up like wheat. I wish I could get some of the seed."

"The boy is really speaking seriously," said the Major.

"Yes, Mr. Major, and you will soon see I am right."

The boy had not been mistaken, for presently they found themselves in front of an immense field of horns, regularly planted and stretching far out of sight. It was a complete copse, low and close packed, but a strange sort.

"Well," said Robert.

"This is peculiar certainly," said Paganel, and he turned round to question Thalcave on the subject.

"The horns come out of the ground," replied the Indian, "but the oxen are down below."

"What!" exclaimed Paganel; "do you mean to say that a whole herd was caught in that mud and buried alive?"

"Yes," said the Patagonian.

And so it was. An immense herd had been suffocated side by side in this enormous bog, and this was not the first occurrence of the kind which had taken place in the Argentine plains.

An hour afterward and the field of horns lay two miles behind.

Thalcave was somewhat anxiously observing a state of things which appeared to him unusual. He frequently stopped and raised himself on his stirrups and looked around. His great height gave him a commanding view of the whole horizon; but after a keen rapid survey, he quickly resumed his seat and went on. About a mile further he stopped again, and leaving the straight route, made a circuit of some miles north and south, and then returned and fell back in his place at the head of the troop, without saying a syllable as to what he hoped or feared. This strange behavior, several times repeated, made Glenarvan very uneasy, and quite puzzled Paganel. At last, at Glenarvan's request, he asked the Indian about it.

Thalcave replied that he was astonished to see the plains so saturated with water. Never, to his knowledge, since he had followed the calling of guide, had he found the ground in this soaking condition. Even in the rainy season, the Argentine plains had always been passable.

"But what is the cause of this increasing humidity?" said Paganel.

"I do not know, and what if I did?"

"Could it be owing to the RIOS of the Sierra being swollen to overflowing by the heavy rains?"

"Sometimes they are."

"And is it the case now?"

"Perhaps."

Paganel was obliged to be content with this unsatisfactory reply, and went back to Glenarvan to report the result of his conversation.

"And what does Thalcave advise us to do?" said Glenarvan.

Paganel went back to the guide and asked him.

"Go on fast," was the reply.

This was easier said than done. The horses soon tired of treading over ground that gave way at every step. It sank each moment more and more, till it seemed half under water.

They quickened their pace, but could not go fast enough to escape the water, which rolled in great sheets at their feet. Before two hours the cataracts of the sky opened and deluged the plain in true tropical torrents of rain. Never was there a finer occasion for displaying philosophic equanimity. There was no shelter, and nothing for it but to bear it stolidly. The ponchos were streaming like the overflowing gutter-spouts on the roof of a house, and the unfortunate horsemen had to submit to a double bath, for their horses dashed up the water to their waists at every step.

In this drenching, shivering state, and worn out with fatigue, they came toward evening to a miserable RANCHO, which could only have been called a shelter by people not very fastidious, and certainly only travelers in extremity would even have entered it; but Glenarvan and his companions had no choice, and were glad enough to burrow in this wretched hovel, though it would have been despised by even a poor Indian of the Pampas. A miserable fire of grass was kindled, which gave out more smoke than heat, and was very difficult to keep alight, as the torrents of rain which dashed against the ruined cabin outside found their way within and fell down in large drops from the roof. Twenty times over the fire would have been extinguished if Mulrady and Wilson had not kept off the water.

The supper was a dull meal, and neither appetizing nor reviving. Only the Major seemed to eat with any relish. The impassive McNabbs was superior to all circumstances. Paganel, Frenchman as he was, tried to joke, but the attempt was a failure.

"My jests are damp," he said, "they miss fire."

The only consolation in such circumstances was to sleep, and accordingly each one lay down and endeavored to find in slumber a temporary forgetfulness of his discomforts and his fatigues. The night was stormy, and the planks of the rancho cracked before the blast as if every instant they would give way. The poor horses outside, exposed to all the inclemency of the weather, were making piteous moans, and their masters were suffering quite as much inside the ruined RANCHO. However, sleep overpowered them at length. Robert was the first to close his eyes and lean his head against Glenarvan's shoulder, and soon all the rest were soundly sleeping too under the guardian eye of Heaven.

The night passed safely, and no one stirred till Thaouka woke them by tapping vigorously against the RANCHO with his hoof. He knew it was time to start, and at a push could give the signal as well as his master. They owed the faithful creature too much to disobey him, and set off immediately.

The rain had abated, but floods of water still covered the ground. Paganel, on consulting his map, came to the conclusion that the RIOS Grande and Vivarota, into which the water from the plains generally runs, must have been united in one large bed several miles in extent.

Extreme haste was imperative, for all their lives depended on it. Should the inundation increase, where could they find refuge? Not a single elevated point was visible on the whole circle of the horizon, and on such level plains water would sweep along with fearful rapidity.

The horses were spurred on to the utmost, and Thaouka led the way, bounding over the water as if it had been his natural element. Certainly he might justly have been called a sea-horse— better than many of the amphibious animals who bear that name.

All of a sudden, about ten in the morning, Thaouka betrayed symptoms of violent agitation. He kept turning round toward the south, neighing continually, and snorting with wide open nostrils. He reared violently, and Thalcave had some difficulty in keeping his seat. The foam from his mouth was tinged with blood from the action of the bit, pulled tightly by his master's strong hand, and yet the fiery animal would not be still. Had he been free, his master knew he would have fled away to the north as fast as his legs would have carried him.

"What is the matter with Thaouka?" asked Paganel. "Is he bitten by the leeches? They are very voracious in the Argentine streams."

"No," replied the Indian.

"Is he frightened at something, then?"

"Yes, he scents danger."

"What danger?"

"I don't know."

But, though no danger was apparent to the eye, the ear could catch the sound of a murmuring noise beyond the limits of the horizon, like the coming in of the tide. Soon a confused sound was heard of bellowing and neighing and bleating, and about a mile to the south immense flocks appeared, rushing and tumbling over each other in the greatest disorder, as they hurried pell-mell along with inconceivable rapidity. They raised such a whirlwind of water in their course that it was impossible to distinguish them clearly. A hundred whales of the largest size could hardly have dashed up the ocean waves more violently.

"*Anda, anda!*" (quick, quick), shouted Thalcave, in a voice like thunder.

"What is it, then?" asked Paganel.

"The rising," replied Thalcave.

"He means an inundation," exclaimed Paganel, flying with the others after Thalcave, who had spurred on his horse toward the north.

It was high time, for about five miles south an immense towering wave was seen advancing over the plain, and changing the whole country into an ocean. The tall grass disappeared before it as if cut down by a scythe, and clumps of mimosas were torn up and drifted about like floating islands.

The wave was speeding on with the rapidity of a racehorse, and the travelers fled before it like a cloud before a storm-wind. They looked in vain for some harbor of refuge, and the terrified horses galloped so wildly along that the riders could hardly keep their saddles.

"*Anda, anda!*" shouted Thalcave, and again they spurred on the poor animals till the blood ran from their lacerated sides. They stumbled every now and then over great cracks in the ground, or got entangled in the hidden grass below the water. They fell, and were pulled up only to fall again and again, and be pulled up again and again. The level of the waters was sensibly rising, and less than two miles off the gigantic wave reared its crested head.

For a quarter of an hour this supreme struggle with the most terrible of elements lasted. The fugitives could not tell how far they had gone, but, judging by the speed, the distance must have been considerable. The poor horses, however, were breast-high in water now, and could only advance with extreme difficulty. Glenarvan and Paganel, and, indeed, the whole party, gave themselves up for lost, as the horses were fast getting out of their depth, and six feet of water would be enough to drown them.

It would be impossible to tell the anguish of mind these eight men endured; they felt their own impotence in the presence of these cataclysms of nature so far beyond all human power. Their salvation did not lie in their own hands.

Five minutes afterward, and the horses were swimming; the current alone carried them along with tremendous force, and with a swiftness equal to their fastest gallop; they must have gone fully twenty miles an hour.

All hope of delivery seemed impossible, when the Major suddenly called out:

"A tree!"

"A tree?" exclaimed Glenarvan.

"Yes, there, there!" replied Thalcave, pointing with his finger to a species of gigantic walnut-tree, which raised its solitary head above the waters.

His companions needed no urging forward now; this tree, so opportunely discovered, they must reach at all hazards. The horses very likely might not be able to get to it, but, at all events, the men would, the current bearing them right down to it.

Just at that moment Tom Austin's horse gave a smothered neigh and disappeared. His master, freeing his feet from the stirrups, began to swim vigorously.

"Hang on to my saddle," called Glenarvan.

"Thanks, your honor, but I have good stout arms."

"Robert, how is your horse going?" asked his Lordship, turning to young Grant.

"Famously, my Lord, he swims like a fish."

"Lookout!" shouted the Major, in a stentorian voice.

The warning was scarcely spoken before the enormous billow, a monstrous wave forty feet high, broke over the fugitives with a fearful noise. Men and animals all disappeared in a whirl of foam; a liquid mass, weighing several millions of tons, engulfed them in its seething waters.

When it had rolled on, the men reappeared on the surface, and counted each other rapidly; but all the horses, except Thaouka, who still bore his master, had gone down forever.

"Courage, courage," repeated Glenarvan, supporting Paganel with one arm, and swimming with the other.

"I can manage, I can manage," said the worthy savant.

"I am even not sorry—"

But no one ever knew what he was not sorry about, for the poor man was obliged to swallow down the rest of his sentence with half a pint of muddy water. The Major advanced quietly, making regular strokes, worthy of a master swimmer. The sailors took to the water like porpoises, while Robert clung to Thaouka's mane, and was carried along with him. The noble animal swam superbly, instinctively making for the tree in a straight line.

The tree was only twenty fathoms off, and in a few minutes was safely reached by the whole party; but for this refuge they must all have perished in the flood.

The water had risen to the top of the trunk, just to where the parent branches fork out. It was consequently, quite easy to clamber up to it. Thalcave climbed up first, and got off his horse to hoist up Robert and help the others. His powerful arms had soon placed all the exhausted swimmers in a place of security.

But, meantime, Thaouka was being rapidly carried away by the current. He turned his intelligent face toward his master, and, shaking his long mane, neighed as if to summon him to his rescue.

"Are you going to forsake him, Thalcave?" asked Paganel.

"I!" replied the Indian, and forthwith he plunged down into the tumultuous waters, and came up again ten fathoms off. A few instants afterward his arms were round Thaouka's neck, and master and steed were drifting together toward the misty horizon of the north.

CHAPTER XXIII A SINGULAR ABODE

THE tree on which Glenarvan and his companions had just found refuge, resembled a walnut-tree, having the same glossy foliage and rounded form. In reality, however, it was the OMBU, which grows solitarily on the Argentine plains. The enormous and twisted trunk of this tree is planted firmly in the soil, not only by its great roots, but still more by its vigorous shoots, which fasten it down in the most tenacious manner. This was how it stood proof against the shock of the mighty billow.

This OMBU measured in height a hundred feet, and covered with its shadow a circumference of one hundred and twenty yards. All this scaffolding rested on three great boughs which sprang from the trunk. Two of these rose almost perpendicularly, and supported the immense parasol of foliage, the branches of which were so crossed and intertwined and entangled, as if by the hand of a basket-maker, that they formed an impenetrable shade. The third arm, on the contrary, stretched right out in a horizontal position above the roaring waters, into which the lower leaves dipped. There was no want of room in the interior of this gigantic tree, for there were great gaps in the foliage, perfect glades, with air in abundance, and freshness everywhere. To see the innumerable branches rising to the clouds, and the creepers running from bough to bough, and attaching them together while the sunlight glinted here and there among the leaves, one might have called it a complete forest instead of a solitary tree sheltering them all.

On the arrival of the fugitives a myriad of the feathered tribes fled away into the topmost branches, protesting by their outcries against this flagrant usurpation of their domicile. These birds, who themselves had taken refuge in the solitary OMBU, were in hundreds, comprising blackbirds, starlings, isacas, HILGUEROS, and especially the picaflor, humming-birds of most resplendent colors. When they flew away it seemed as though a gust of wind had blown all the flowers off the tree.

Such was the asylum offered to the little band of Glenarvan. Young Grant and the agile Wilson were scarcely perched on the tree before they had climbed to the upper branches and put their heads through the leafy dome to get a view of the vast horizon. The ocean made by the inundation surrounded them on all sides, and, far as the eye could reach, seemed to have no limits. Not a single tree was visible on the liquid plain; the OMBU stood alone amid the rolling waters, and trembled before them. In the distance, drifting from south to north, carried along by the impetuous torrent, they saw trees torn up by the roots, twisted branches, roofs torn off, destroyed RANCHOS, planks of sheds sto len by the deluge from ESTANCIAS, carcasses of drowned animals, blood-stained skins, and on a shaky tree a complete family of jaguars, howling and clutching hold of their frail raft. Still farther away, a black spot almost invisible, already caught Wilson's eye. It was Thalcave and his faithful Thaouka.

"Thalcave, Thalcave!" shouted Robert, stretching out his hands toward the courageous Patagonian.

"He will save himself, Mr. Robert," replied Wilson; "we must go down to his Lordship."

Next minute they had descended the three stages of boughs, and landed safely on the top of the trunk, where they found Glenarvan, Paganel, the Major, Austin, and Mulrady, sitting either astride or in some position they found more comfortable. Wilson gave an account of their investigations aloft, and all shared his opinion with respect to Thalcave. The only question was whether it was Thalcave who would save Thaouka, or Thaouka save Thalcave.

Their own situation meantime was much more alarming than his. No doubt the tree would be able to resist the current, but the waters might rise higher and higher, till the topmost branches were covered, for the depression of the soil made this part of the plain a deep reservoir. Glenarvan's first care, consequently, was to make notches by which to ascertain the progress of the inundation. For the present it was stationary, having apparently reached its height. This was reassuring.

"And now what are we going to do?" said Glenarvan.

"Make our nest, of course!" replied Paganel

"Make our nest!" exclaimed Robert.

"Certainly, my boy, and live the life of birds, since we can't that of fishes."

"All very well, but who will fill our bills for us?" said Glenarvan.

"I will," said the Major.

All eyes turned toward him immediately, and there he sat in a natural arm-chair, formed of two elastic boughs, holding out his ALFORJAS damp, but still intact.

"Oh, McNabbs, that's just like you," exclaimed Glenarvan, "you think of everything even under circumstances which would drive all out of your head."

"Since it was settled we were not going to be drowned,
I had no intention of starving of hunger."

"I should have thought of it, too," said Paganel, "but I am so DISTRAIT."

"And what is in the ALFORJAS?" asked Tom Austin.

"Food enough to last seven men for two days," replied McNabbs.

"And I hope the inundation will have gone down in twenty-four hours," said Glenarvan.

"Or that we shall have found some way of regaining *terra firma*," added Paganel.

"Our first business, then, now is to breakfast," said Glenarvan.

"I suppose you mean after we have made ourselves dry," observed the Major.

"And where's the fire?" asked Wilson.

"We must make it," returned Paganel.

"Where?"

"On the top of the trunk, of course."

"And what with?"

"With the dead wood we cut off the tree."

"But how will you kindle it?" asked Glenarvan. "Our tinder is just like wet sponge."

"We can dispense with it," replied Paganel. "We only want a little dry moss and a ray of sunshine, and the lens of my telescope, and you'll see what a fire I'll get to dry myself by. Who will go and cut wood in the forest?"

"I will," said Robert.

And off he scampered like a young cat into the depths of the foliage, followed by his friend Wilson. Paganel set to work to find dry moss, and had soon gathered sufficient.

This he laid on a bed of damp leaves, just where the large branches began to fork out, forming a natural hearth, where there was little fear of conflagration.

Robert and Wilson speedily reappeared, each with an armful of dry wood, which they threw on the moss. By the help of the lens it was easily kindled, for the sun was blazing overhead. In order to ensure a proper draught, Paganel stood over the hearth with his long legs straddled out in the Arab manner. Then stooping down and raising himself with a rapid motion, he made a violent current of air with his poncho, which made the wood take fire, and soon a bright flame roared in the improvised brasier. After drying themselves, each in his own fashion, and hanging their ponchos on the tree, where they were swung to and fro in the breeze, they breakfasted, carefully however rationing out the provisions, for the morrow had to be thought of; the immense basin might not empty so soon as Glenarvan expected, and, anyway, the supply was very limited. The OMBU produced no fruit, though fortunately, it would likely abound in fresh eggs, thanks to the numerous nests stowed away among the leaves, not to speak of their feathered proprietors. These resources were by no means to be despised.

The next business was to install themselves as comfortably as they could, in prospect of a long stay.

"As the kitchen and dining-room are on the ground floor," said Paganel, "we must sleep on the first floor. The house is large, and as the rent is not dear, we must not cramp ourselves for room. I can see up yonder natural cradles, in which once safely tucked up we shall sleep as if we were in the best beds in the world. We have nothing to fear. Besides, we will watch, and we are numerous enough to repulse a fleet of Indians and other wild animals."

"We only want fire-arms."

"I have my revolvers," said Glenarvan.

"And I have mine," replied Robert.

"But what's the good of them?" said Tom Austin, "unless Monsieur Paganel can find out some way of making powder."

"We don't need it," replied McNabbs, exhibiting a powder flask in a perfect state of preservation.

"Where did you get it from, Major," asked Paganel.

"From Thalcave. He thought it might be useful to us, and gave it to me before he plunged into the water to save Thaouka."

"Generous, brave Indian!" exclaimed Glenarvan.

"Yes," replied Tom Austin, "if all the Patagonians are cut after the same pattern, I must compliment Patagonia."

"I protest against leaving out the horse," said Paganel. "He is part and parcel of the Patagonian, and I'm much mistaken if we don't see them again, the one on the other's back."

"What distance are we from the Atlantic?" asked the Major.

"About forty miles at the outside," replied Paganel; "and now, friends, since this is Liberty Hall, I beg to take leave of you. I am going to choose an observatory for myself up there, and by the help of my telescope, let you know how things are going on in the world."

Forthwith the geographer set off, hoisting himself up very cleverly from bough to bough, till he disappeared beyond the thick foliage. His companions began to arrange the night quarters, and prepare their beds. But this was neither a long nor difficult task, and very soon they resumed their seats round the fire to have a talk.

As usual their theme was Captain Grant. In three days, should the water subside, they would be on board the DUNCAN once more. But Harry Grant and his two sailors, those poor shipwrecked fellows, would not be with them. Indeed, it even seemed after this ill success and this useless journey across America, that all chance of finding them was gone forever. Where could they commence a fresh quest? What grief Lady Helena and Mary Grant would feel on hearing there was no further hope.

"Poor sister!" said Robert. "It is all up with us."

For the first time Glenarvan could not find any comfort to give him.

What could he say to the lad?

Had they not searched exactly where the document stated?

"And yet," he said, "this thirty-seventh degree of latitude is not a mere figure, and that it applies to the shipwreck or captivity of Harry Grant, is no mere guess or supposition. We read it with our own eyes."

"All very true, your Honor," replied Tom Austin, "and yet our search has been unsuccessful."

"It is both a provoking and hopeless business," replied Glenarvan.

"Provoking enough, certainly," said the Major, "but not hopeless. It is precisely because we have an uncontestable figure, provided for us, that we should follow it up to the end."

"What do you mean?" asked Glenarvan. "What more can we do?"

"A very logical and simple thing, my dear Edward. When we go on board the DUNCAN, turn her beak head to the east, and go right along the thirty-seventh parallel till we come back to our starting point if necessary."

"Do you suppose that I have not thought of that, Mr. McNabbs?" replied Glenarvan. "Yes, a hundred times. But what chance is there of success? To leave the American continent, wouldn't it be to go away from the very spot indicated by Harry Grant, from this very Patagonia so distinctly named in the document."

"And would you recommence your search in the Pampas, when you have the certainty that the shipwreck of the BRITANNIA neither occurred on the coasts of the Pacific nor the Atlantic?"

Glenarvan was silent.

"And however small the chance of finding Harry Grant by following up the given parallel, ought we not to try?"

"I don't say no," replied Glenarvan.

"And are you not of my opinion, good friends," added the Major, addressing the sailors.

"Entirely," said Tom Austin, while Mulrady and Wilson gave an assenting nod.

"Listen to me, friends," said Glenarvan after a few minutes' reflection; "and remember, Robert, this is a grave discussion. I will do my utmost to find Captain Grant; I am pledged to it, and will devote my whole life to the task if needs be. All Scotland would unite with me to save so devoted a son as he has been to her. I too quite think with you that we must follow the thirty-seventh parallel round the globe if necessary, however slight our chance of finding him. But that is not the question we have to settle. There is one much more important than that is—should we from this time, and all together, give up our search on the American continent?"

No one made any reply. Each one seemed afraid to pronounce the word.

"Well?" resumed Glenarvan, addressing himself especially to the Major.

"My dear Edward," replied McNabbs, "it would be incurring too great a responsibility for me to reply *hic et nunc*. It is a question which requires reflection. I must know first, through which countries the thirty-seventh parallel of southern latitude passes?"

"That's Paganel's business; he will tell you that," said Glenarvan.

"Let's ask him, then," replied the Major.

But the learned geographer was nowhere to be seen. He was hidden among the thick leafage of the OMBU, and they must call out if they wanted him.

"Paganel, Paganel!" shouted Glenarvan.

"Here," replied a voice that seemed to come from the clouds.

"Where are you?"

"In my tower."

"What are you doing there?"

"Examining the wide horizon."

"Could you come down for a minute?"

"Do you want me?"

"Yes."

"What for?"

"To know what countries the thirty-seventh parallel passes through."

"That's easily said. I need not disturb myself to come down for that."

"Very well, tell us now."

"Listen, then. After leaving America the thirty-seventh parallel crosses the Atlantic Ocean."

"And then?"

"It encounters Isle Tristan d'Acunha."

"Yes."

"It goes on two degrees below the Cape of Good Hope."

"And afterwards?"

"Runs across the Indian Ocean, and just touches Isle St. Pierre, in the Amsterdam group."

"Go on."

"It cuts Australia by the province of Victoria."

"And then."

"After leaving Australia in—"

This last sentence was not completed. Was the geographer hesitating, or didn't he know what to say?

No; but a terrible cry resounded from the top of the tree.

Glenarvan and his friends turned pale and looked at each other.

What fresh catastrophe had happened now? Had the unfortunate

Paganel slipped his footing?

Already Wilson and Mulrady had rushed to his rescue when his long body appeared tumbling down from branch to branch.

But was he living or dead, for his hands made no attempt to seize anything to stop himself. A few minutes more, and he would have fallen into the roaring waters had not the Major's strong arm barred his passage.

"Much obliged, McNabbs," said Paganel.

"How's this? What is the matter with you? What came over you?

Another of your absent fits."

"Yes, yes," replied Paganel, in a voice almost inarticulate with emotion.

"Yes, but this was something extraordinary."

"What was it?"

"I said we had made a mistake. We are making it still, and have been all along."

"Explain yourself."

"Glenarvan, Major, Robert, my friends," exclaimed Paganel, "all you that hear me, we are looking for Captain Grant where he is not to be found."

"What do you say?" exclaimed Glenarvan.

"Not only where he is not now, but where he has never been."

CHAPTER XXIV PAGANEL'S DISCLOSURE

PROFOUND astonishment greeted these unexpected words of the learned geographer. What could he mean? Had he lost his sense? He spoke with such conviction, however, that all eyes turned toward Glenarvan, for Paganel's affirmation was a direct answer to his question, but Glenarvan shook his head, and said nothing, though evidently he was not inclined to favor his friend's views.

"Yes," began Paganel again, as soon as he had recovered himself a little; "yes, we have gone a wrong track, and read on the document what was never there."

"Explain yourself, Paganel," said the Major, "and more calmly if you can."

"The thing is very simple, Major. Like you, I was in error; like you, I had rushed at a false interpretation, until about an instant ago, on the top of the tree, when I was answering your questions, just as I pronounced the word 'Australia,' a sudden flash came across my mind, and the document became clear as day."

"What!" exclaimed Glenarvan, "you mean to say that Harry Grant—"

"I mean to say," replied Paganel, "that the word AUSTRAL that occurs in the document is not a complete word, as we have supposed up till now, but just the root of the word AUSTRALIE."

"Well, that would be strange," said the Major.

"Strange!" repeated Glenarvan, shrugging his shoulders; "it is simply impossible."

"Impossible?" returned Paganel. "That is a word we don't allow in France."

"What!" continued Glenarvan, in a tone of the most profound incredulity, "you dare to contend, with the document in your hand, that the shipwreck of the BRITANNIA happened on the shores of Australia."

"I am sure of it," replied Paganel.

"My conscience," exclaimed Glenarvan, "I must say I am surprised at such a declaration from the Secretary of a Geographical Society!"

"And why so?" said Paganel, touched in his weak point.

"Because, if you allow the word AUSTRALIE! you must also allow the word INDIENS, and Indians are never seen there."

Paganel was not the least surprised at this rejoinder.

Doubtless he expected it, for he began to smile, and said:

"My dear Glenarvan, don't triumph over me too fast.

I am going to floor you completely, and never was an

Englishman more thoroughly defeated than you will be.

It will be the revenge for Cressy and Agincourt."

"I wish nothing better. Take your revenge, Paganel."

"Listen, then. In the text of the document, there is neither mention of the Indians nor of Patagonia! The incomplete word INDI does not mean INDIENS, but of course, INDIGENES, aborigines! Now, do you admit that there are aborigines in Australia?"

"Bravo, Paganel!" said the Major.

"Well, do you agree to my interpretation, my dear Lord?" asked the geographer again.

"Yes," replied Glenarvan, "if you will prove to me that the fragment of a word GONIE, does not refer to the country of the Patagonians."

"Certainly it does not. It has nothing to do with Patagonia," said Paganel. "Read it any way you please except that."

"How?"

"*Cosmogonie, theogonie, agonie.*"

"AGONIE," said the Major.

"I don't care which," returned Paganel. "The word is quite unimportant; I will not even try to find out its meaning. The main point is that AUSTRAL means AUSTRALIE, and we must have gone blindly on a wrong track not to have discovered the explanation at the very beginning, it was so evident. If I had found the document myself, and my judgment had not been misled by your interpretation, I should never have read it differently."

A burst of hurrahs, and congratulations, and compliments followed Paganel's words. Austin and the sailors, and the Major and Robert, most all overjoyed at this fresh hope, applauded him heartily; while even Glenarvan, whose eyes were gradually getting open, was almost prepared to give in.

"I only want to know one thing more, my dear Paganel," he said, "and then I must bow to your perspicacity."

"What is it?"

"How will you group the words together according to your new interpretation? How will the document read?"

"Easily enough answered. Here is the document," replied Paganel, taking out the precious paper he had been studying so conscientiously for the last few days.

For a few minutes there was complete silence, while the worthy SAVANT took time to collect his thoughts before complying with his lordship's request. Then putting his finger on the words, and emphasizing some of them, he began as follows:

"'*Le 7 juin* 1862 *le trois-mats Britannia de Glasgow a sombre apres,*'— put, if you please, '*deux jours, trois jours,*' or '*une longue agonie,*' it doesn't signify, it is quite a matter of indifference,—'*sur les cotes de l'Australie. Se dirigeant a terre, deux matelots et le Capitaine Grant vont essayer d'aborder,*' or '*ont aborde le continent ou ils seront,*' or, '*sont prisonniers de cruels indigenes. Ils ont jete ce documents,*' etc. Is that clear?"

"Clear enough," replied Glenarvan, "if the word continent can be applied to Australia, which is only an island."

"Make yourself easy about that, my dear Glenarvan; the best geographers have agreed to call the island the Australian Continent."

"Then all I have now to say is, my friends," said Glenarvan, "away to Australia, and may Heaven help us!"

"To Australia!" echoed his companions, with one voice.

"I tell you what, Paganel," added Glenarvan, "your being on board the DUNCAN is a perfect providence."

"All right. Look on me as a messenger of providence, and let us drop the subject."

So the conversation ended—a conversation which great results were to follow; it completely changed the moral condition of the travelers; it gave the clew of the labyrinth in which they had thought themselves hopelessly entangled, and, amid their ruined projects, inspired them with fresh hope. They could now quit the American Continent without the least hesitation, and already their thoughts had flown to the Australias. In going on board the DUNCAN again they would not bring despair with them, and Lady Helena and Mary Grant would not have to mourn the irrevocable loss of Captain Grant. This thought so filled them with joy that they forgot all the dangers of their actual situation, and only regretted that they could not start immediately.

It was about four o'clock in the afternoon, and they determined to have supper at six. Paganel wished to get up a splendid spread in honor of the occasion, but as the materials were very scanty, he proposed to Robert to go and hunt in the neighboring forest. Robert clapped his hands at the idea, so they took Thalcave's powder flask, cleaned the revolvers and loaded them with small shot, and set off.

"Don't go too far," said the Major, gravely, to the two hunters.

After their departure, Glenarvan and McNabbs went down to examine the state of the water by looking at the notches they had made on the tree, and Wilson and Mulrady replenished the fire.

No sign of decrease appeared on the surface of the immense lake, yet the flood seemed to have reached its maximum height; but the violence with which it rushed from the south to north proved that the equilibrium of the Argentine rivers was not restored. Before getting lower the liquid mass must remain stationary, as in the case with the ocean before the ebb tide commences.

While Glenarvan and his cousin were making these observations, the report of firearms resounded frequently above their heads, and the jubilant outcries of the two sportsmen—for Paganel was every whit as much a child as Robert. They were having a fine time of it among the thick leaves, judging by the peals of laughter which rang out in the boy's clear treble voice and Paganel's deep bass. The chase was evidently successful, and wonders in culinary art might be expected. Wilson had a good idea to begin with, which he had skilfully carried out; for when Glenarvan came back to the brasier, he found that the brave fellow had actually managed to catch, with only a pin and a piece of string, several dozen small fish, as delicate as smelts, called MOJARRAS, which were all jumping about in a fold of his poncho, ready to be converted into an exquisite dish.

At the same moment the hunters reappeared. Paganel was carefully carrying some black swallows' eggs, and a string of sparrows, which he meant to serve up later under the name of field larks. Robert had been clever enough to bring down several brace of HILGUEROS, small green and yellow birds, which are excellent eating, and greatly in demand in the Montevideo market. Paganel, who knew fifty ways of dressing eggs, was obliged for this once to be content with simply hardening them on the hot embers. But notwithstanding this, the viands at the meal were both dainty and varied. The dried beef, hard eggs, grilled MOJARRAS, sparrows, and roast HILGUEROS, made one of those gala feasts the memory of which is imperishable.

The conversation was very animated. Many compliments were paid Paganel on his twofold talents as hunter and cook, which the SAVANT accepted with the modesty which characterizes true merit. Then he turned the conversation on the peculiarities of the OMBU, under whose canopy they had found shelter, and whose depths he declared were immense.

"Robert and I," he added, jestingly, "thought ourselves hunting in the open forest. I was afraid, for the minute, we should lose ourselves, for I could not find the road. The sun was sinking below the horizon; I sought vainly for footmarks; I began to feel the sharp pangs of hunger, and the gloomy depths of the forest resounded already with the roar of wild beasts. No, not that; there are no wild beasts here, I am sorry to say."

"What!" exclaimed Glenarvan, "you are sorry there are no wild beasts?"

"Certainly I am."

"And yet we should have every reason to dread their ferocity."

"Their ferocity is non-existent, scientifically speaking," replied the learned geographer.

"Now come, Paganel," said the Major, "you'll never make me admit the utility of wild beasts. What good are they?"

"Why, Major," exclaimed Paganel, "for purposes of classification into orders, and families, and species, and sub-species."

"A mighty advantage, certainly!" replied McNabbs, "I could dispense with all that. If I had been one of Noah's companions at the time of the deluge, I should most assuredly have hindered the imprudent patriarch from putting in pairs of lions, and tigers, and panthers, and bears, and such animals, for they are as malevolent as they are useless."

"You would have done that?" asked Paganel.

"Yes, I would."

"Well, you would have done wrong in a zoological point of view," returned Paganel.

"But not in a humanitarian one," rejoined the Major.

"It is shocking!" replied Paganel. "Why, for my part, on the contrary, I should have taken special care to preserve megatheriums and pterodactyles, and all the antediluvian species of which we are unfortunately deprived by his neglect."

"And I say," returned McNabbs, "that Noah did a very good thing when he abandoned them to their fate—that is, if they lived in his day."

"And I say he did a very bad thing," retorted Paganel, "and he has justly merited the malediction of SAVANTS to the end of time!"

The rest of the party could not help laughing at hearing the two friends disputing over old Noah. Contrary to all his principles, the Major, who all his life had never disputed with anyone, was always sparring with Paganel. The geographer seemed to have a peculiarly exciting effect on him.

Glenarvan, as usual, always the peacemaker, interfered in the debate, and said:

"Whether the loss of ferocious animals is to be regretted or not, in a scientific point of view, there is no help for it now; we must be content to do without them. Paganel can hardly expect to meet with wild beasts in this aerial forest."

"Why not?" asked the geographer.

"Wild beasts on a tree!" exclaimed Tom Austin.

"Yes, undoubtedly. The American tiger, the jaguar, takes refuge in the trees, when the chasė gets too hot for him. It is quite possible that one of these animals, surprised by the inundation, might have climbed up into this OMBU, and be hiding now among its thick foliage."

"You haven't met any of them, at any rate, I suppose?" said the Major.

"No," replied Paganel, "though we hunted all through the wood. It is vexing, for it would have been a splendid chase. A jaguar is a bloodthirsty, ferocious creature. He can twist the neck of a horse with a single stroke of his paw. When he has once tasted human flesh he scents it greedily. He likes to eat an Indian best, and next to him a negro, then a mulatto, and last of all a white man."

"I am delighted to hear we come number four," said McNabbs.

"That only proves you are insipid," retorted Paganel, with an air of disdain.

"I am delighted to be insipid," was the Major's reply.

"Well, it is humiliating enough," said the intractable Paganel. "The white man proclaimed himself chief of the human race; but Mr. Jaguar is of a different opinion it seems."

"Be that as it may, my brave Paganel, seeing there are
neither Indians, nor negroes, nor mulattoes among us,
I am quite rejoiced at the absence of your beloved jaguars.
Our situation is not so particularly agreeable."

"What! not agreeable!" exclaimed Paganel, jumping at the word as likely to give a new turn to the conversation. "You are complaining of your lot, Glenarvan."

"I should think so, indeed," replied Glenarvan. "Do you find these uncomfortable hard branches very luxurious?"

"I have never been more comfortable, even in my study. We live like the birds, we sing and fly about. I begin to believe men were intended to live on trees."

"But they want wings," suggested the Major.

"They'll make them some day."

"And till then," put in Glenarvan, "with your leave, I prefer the gravel of a park, or the floor of a house, or the deck of a ship, to this aerial dwelling."

"We must take things as they come, Glenarvan," returned Paganel. "If good, so much the better; if bad, never mind. Ah, I see you are wishing you had all the comforts of Malcolm Castle."

"No, but—"

"I am quite certain Robert is perfectly happy," interrupted Paganel, eager to insure one partisan at least.

"Yes, that I am!" exclaimed Robert, in a joyous tone.

"At his age it is quite natural," replied Glenarvan.

"And at mine, too," returned the geographer. "The fewer one's comforts, the fewer one's needs; and the fewer one's needs, the greater one's happiness."

"Now, now," said the Major, "here is Paganel running a tilt against riches and gilt ceilings."

"No, McNabbs," replied the SAVANT, "I'm not; but if you like, I'll tell you a little Arabian story that comes into my mind, very APROPOS this minute."

"Oh, do, do," said Robert.

"And what is your story to prove, Paganel?" inquired the Major.

"Much what all stories prove, my brave comrade."

"Not much then," rejoined McNabbs. "But go on, Scheherazade, and tell us the story."

"There was once," said Paganel, "a son of the great Haroun-al-Raschid, who was unhappy, and went to consult an old Dervish. The old sage told him that happiness was a difficult thing to find in this world. 'However,' he added, 'I know an infallible means of procuring your happiness.' 'What is it?' asked the young Prince. 'It is to put the shirt of a happy man on your shoulders.' Whereupon the Prince embraced the old man, and set out at once to search for his talisman. He visited all the capital cities in the world. He tried on the shirts of kings, and emperors, and princes and nobles; but all in vain: he could not find a man among them that was happy. Then he put on the shirts of artists, and warriors, and merchants; but these were no better. By this time he had traveled a long way, without finding what he sought. At last he began to despair of success, and began sorrowfully to retrace his steps back to his father's palace, when one day he heard an honest peasant singing so merrily as he drove the plow, that he thought, 'Surely this man is happy, if there is such a thing as happiness on earth.' Forthwith he accosted him, and said, 'Are you happy?' 'Yes,' was the reply. 'There is nothing you dcsirc'?' 'Nothing.' 'You would not change your lot for that of a king?' 'Never!' 'Well, then, sell me your shirt.' 'My shirt! I haven't one!'"

CHAPTER XXV BETWEEN FIRE AND WATER

BEFORE turning into "their nest," as Paganel had called it, he, and Robert, and Glenarvan climbed up into the observatory to have one more inspection of the liquid plain. It was about nine o'clock; the sun had just sunk behind the glowing mists of the western horizon.

The eastern horizon was gradually assuming a most stormy aspect. A thick dark bar of cloud was rising higher and higher, and by degrees extinguishing the stars. Before long half the sky was overspread. Evidently motive power lay in the cloud itself, for there was not a breath of wind. Absolute calm reigned in the atmosphere; not a leaf stirred on the tree, not a ripple disturbed the surface of the water. There seemed to be scarcely any air even, as though some vast pneumatic machine had rarefied it. The entire atmosphere was charged to the utmost with electricity, the presence of which sent a thrill through the whole nervous system of all animated beings.

"We are going to have a storm," said Paganel.

"You're not afraid of thunder, are you, Robert?" asked Glenarvan.

"No, my Lord!" exclaimed Robert. "Well, my boy, so much the better, for a storm is not far off."

"And a violent one, too," added Paganel, "if I may judge by the look of things."

"It is not the storm I care about," said Glenarvan, "so much as the torrents of rain that will accompany it. We shall be soaked to the skin. Whatever you may say, Paganel, a nest won't do for a man, and you will learn that soon, to your cost."

"With the help of philosophy, it will," replied Paganel.

"Philosophy! that won't keep you from getting drenched."

"No, but it will warm you."

"Well," said Glenarvan, "we had better go down to our friends, and advise them to wrap themselves up in their philosophy and their ponchos as tightly as possible, and above all, to lay in a stock of patience, for we shall need it before very long."

Glenarvan gave a last glance at the angry sky. The clouds now covered it entirely; only a dim streak of light shone faintly in the west. A dark shadow lay on the water, and it could hardly be distinguished from the thick vapors above it. There was no sensation of light or sound. All was darkness and silence around.

"Let us go down," said Glenarvan; "the thunder will soon burst over us."

On returning to the bottom of the tree, they found themselves, to their great surprise, in a sort of dim twilight, produced by myriads of luminous specks which appeared buzzing confusedly over the surface of the water.

"It is phosphorescence, I suppose," said Glenarvan.

"No, but phosphorescent insects, positive glow-worms, living diamonds, which the ladies of Buenos Ayres convert into magnificent ornaments."

"What!" exclaimed Robert, "those sparks flying about are insects!"

"Yes, my boy."

Robert caught one in his hand, and found Paganel was right. It was a kind of large drone, an inch long, and the Indians call it "tuco-tuco." This curious specimen of the COLEOPTERA sheds its radiance from two spots in the front of its breast-plate, and the light is sufficient to read by. Holding his watch close to the insect, Paganel saw distinctly that the time was 10 P. M.

On rejoining the Major and his three sailors, Glenarvan warned them of the approaching storm, and advised them to secure themselves in their beds of branches as firmly as possible, for there was no doubt that after the first clap of thunder the wind would become unchained, and the OMBU would be violently shaken. Though they could not defend themselves from the waters above, they might at least keep out of the rushing current beneath.

They wished one another "good-night," though hardly daring to hope for it, and then each one rolled himself in his poncho and lay down to sleep.

But the approach of the great phenomena of nature excites vague uneasiness in the heart of every sentient being, even in the most strong-minded. The whole party in the OMBU felt agitated and oppressed, and not one of them could close his eyes. The first peal of thunder found them wide awake. It occurred about 11 P. M., and sounded like a distant rolling. Glenarvan ventured to creep out of the sheltering foliage, and made his way to the extremity of the horizontal branch to take a look round.

The deep blackness of the night was already scarified with sharp bright lines, which were reflected back by the water with unerring exactness. The clouds had rent in many parts, but noiselessly, like some soft cotton material. After attentively observing both the zenith and horizon, Glenarvan went back to the center of the trunk.

"Well, Glenarvan, what's your report?" asked Paganel.

"I say it is beginning in good earnest, and if it goes on so we shall have a terrible storm."

"So much the better," replied the enthusiastic Paganel; "I should like a grand exhibition, since we can't run away."

"That's another of your theories," said the Major.

"And one of my best, McNabbs. I am of Glenarvan's opinion, that the storm will be superb. Just a minute ago, when I was trying to sleep, several facts occurred to my memory, that make me hope it will, for we are in the region of great electrical tempests. For instance, I have read somewhere, that in 1793, in this very province of Buenos Ayres, lightning struck thirty-seven times during one single storm. My colleague, M. Martin de Moussy, counted fifty-five minutes of uninterrupted rolling."

"Watch in hand?" asked the Major.

"Watch in hand. Only one thing makes me uneasy," added Paganel, "if it is any use to be uneasy, and that is, that the culminating point of this plain, is just this very OMBU where we are. A lightning conductor would be very serviceable to us at present. For it is this tree especially, among all that grow in the Pampas, that the thunder has a particular affection for. Besides, I need not tell you, friend, that learned men tell us never to take refuge under trees during a storm."

"Most seasonable advice, certainly, in our circumstances," said the Major.

"I must confess, Paganel," replied Glenarvan, "that you might have chosen a better time for this reassuring information."

"Bah!" replied Paganel, "all times are good for getting information.

Ha! now it's beginning."

Louder peals of thunder interrupted this inopportune conversation, the violence increasing with the noise till the whole atmosphere seemed to vibrate with rapid oscillations.

The incessant flashes of lightning took various forms. Some darted down perpendicularly from the sky five or six times in the same place in succession. Others would have excited the interest of a SAVANT to the highest degree, for though Arago, in his curious statistics, only cites two examples of forked lightning, it was visible here hundreds of times. Some of the flashes branched out in a thousand different directions, making coralliform zigzags, and threw out wonderful jets of arborescent light.

Soon the whole sky from east to north seemed supported by a phosphoric band of intense brilliancy. This kept increasing by degrees till it overspread the entire horizon, kindling the clouds which were faithfully mirrored in the waters as if they were masses of combustible material, beneath, and presented the appearance of an immense globe of fire, the center of which was the OMBU.

Glenarvan and his companions gazed silently at this terrifying spectacle. They could not make their voices heard, but the sheets of white light which enwrapped them every now and then, revealed the face of one and another, sometimes the calm features of the Major, sometimes the eager, curious glance of Paganel, or the energetic face of Glenarvan, and at others, the scared eyes of the terrified Robert, and the careless looks of the sailors, investing them with a weird, spectral aspect.

However, as yet, no rain had fallen, and the wind had not risen in the least. But this state of things was of short duration; before long the cataracts of the sky burst forth, and came down in vertical streams. As the large drops fell splashing into the lake, fiery sparks seemed to fly out from the illuminated surface.

Was the rain the FINALE of the storm? If so, Glenarvan and his companions would escape scot free, except for a few vigorous douche baths. No. At the very height of this struggle of the electric forces of the atmosphere, a large ball of fire appeared suddenly at the extremity of the horizontal parent branch, as thick as a man's wrist, and surrounded with black smoke. This ball, after turning round and round for a few seconds, burst like a bombshell, and with so much noise that the explosion was distinctly audible above the general FRACAS. A sulphurous smoke filled the air, and complete silence reigned till the voice of Tom Austin was heard shouting:

"The tree is on fire."

Tom was right. In a moment, as if some fireworks were being ignited, the flame ran along the west side of the OMBU; the dead wood and nests of dried grass, and the whole sap, which was of a spongy texture, supplied food for its devouring activity.

The wind had risen now and fanned the flame. It was time to flee, and Glenarvan and his party hurried away to the eastern side of their refuge, which was meantime untouched by the fire. They were all silent, troubled, and terrified, as they watched branch after branch shrivel, and crack, and writhe in the flame like living serpents, and then drop into the swollen torrent, still red and gleaming, as it was borne swiftly along on the rapid current. The flames sometimes rose to a prodigious height, and seemed almost lost in the atmosphere, and sometimes, beaten down by the hurricane, closely enveloped the OMBU like a robe of Nessus. Terror seized the entire group. They were almost suffocated with smoke, and scorched with the unbearable heat, for the conflagration had already reached the lower branches on their side of the OMBU. To extinguish it or check its progress was impossible; and they saw themselves irrevocably condemned to a torturing death, like the victims of Hindoo divinities.

CHAPTER XXV BETWEEN FIRE AND WATER

At last, their situation was absolutely intolerable. Of the two deaths staring them in the face, they had better choose the less cruel.

"To the water!" exclaimed Glenarvan.

Wilson, who was nearest the flames, had already plunged into the lake, but next minute he screamed out in the most violent terror:

"Help! Help!"

Austin rushed toward him, and with the assistance of the Major, dragged him up again on the tree.

"What's the matter?" they asked.

"Alligators! alligators!" replied Wilson.

The whole foot of the tree appeared to be surrounded by these formidable animals of the Saurian order. By the glare of the flames, they were immediately recognized by Paganel, as the ferocious species peculiar to America, called CAIMANS in the Spanish territories. About ten of them were there, lashing the water with their powerful tails, and attacking the OMBU with the long teeth of their lower jaw.

At this sight the unfortunate men gave themselves up to be lost. A frightful death was in store for them, since they must either be devoured by the fire or by the caimans. Even the Major said, in a calm voice:

"This is the beginning of the end, now."

There are circumstances in which men are powerless, when the unchained elements can only be combated by other elements. Glenarvan gazed with haggard looks at the fire and water leagued against him, hardly knowing what deliverance to implore from Heaven.

The violence of the storm had abated, but it had developed in the atmosphere a considerable quantity of vapors, to which electricity was about to communicate immense force. An enormous water-spout was gradually forming in the south— a cone of thick mists, but with the point at the bottom, and base at the top, linking together the turbulent water and the angry clouds. This meteor soon began to move forward, turning over and over on itself with dizzy rapidity, and sweeping up into its center a column of water from the lake, while its gyratory motions made all the surrounding currents of air rush toward it.

A few seconds more, and the gigantic water-spout threw itself on the OMBU, and caught it up in its whirl. The tree shook to its roots. Glenarvan could fancy the caimans' teeth were tearing it up from the soil; for as he and his companions held on, each clinging firmly to the other, they felt the towering OMBU give way, and the next minute it fell right over with a terrible hissing noise, as the flaming branches touched the foaming water.

It was the work of an instant. Already the water-spout had passed, to carry on its destructive work elsewhere. It seemed to empty the lake in its passage, by continually drawing up the water into itself.

The OMBU now began to drift rapidly along, impelled by wind and current. All the caimans had taken their departure, except one that was crawling over the upturned roots, and coming toward the poor refugees with wide open jaws. But Mulrady, seizing hold of a branch that was half-burned off, struck the monster such a tremendous blow, that it fell back into the torrent and disappeared, lashing the water with its formidable tail.

Glenarvan and his companions being thus delivered from the voracious SAURIANS, stationed themselves on the branches windward of the conflagration, while the OMBU sailed along like a blazing fire-ship through the dark night, the flames spreading themselves round like sails before the breath of the hurricane.

CHAPTER XXVI THE RETURN ON BOARD

FOR two hours the OMBU navigated the immense lake without reaching *terra firma*. The flames which were devouring it had gradually died out. The chief danger of their frightful passage was thus removed, and the Major went the length of saying, that he should not be surprised if they were saved after all.

The direction of the current remained unchanged, always running from southwest to northeast. Profound darkness had again set in, only illumined here and there by a parting flash of lightning. The storm was nearly over. The rain had given place to light mists, which a breath of wind dispersed, and the heavy masses of cloud had separated, and now streaked the sky in long bands.

The OMBU was borne onward so rapidly by the impetuous torrent, that anyone might have supposed some powerful locomotive engine was hidden in its trunk. It seemed likely enough they might continue drifting in this way for days. About three o'clock in the morning, however, the Major noticed that the roots were beginning to graze the ground occasionally, and by sounding the depth of the water with a long branch, Tom Austin found that they were getting on rising ground. Twenty minutes afterward, the OMBU stopped short with a violent jolt.

"Land! land!" shouted Paganel, in a ringing tone.

The extremity of the calcined bough had struck some hillock, and never were sailors more glad; the rock to them was the port.

Already Robert and Wilson had leaped on to the solid plateau with a loud, joyful hurrah! when a well-known whistle was heard. The gallop of a horse resounded over the plain, and the tall form of Thalcave emerged from the darkness.

"Thalcave! Thalcave!" they all cried with one voice.

"Amigos!" replied the Patagonian, who had been waiting for the travelers here in the same place where the current had landed himself.

As he spoke he lifted up Robert in his arms, and hugged him to his breast, never imagining that Paganel was hanging on to him. A general and hearty hand-shaking followed, and everyone rejoiced at seeing their faithful guide again. Then the Patagonian led the way into the HANGAR of a deserted ESTANCIA, where there was a good, blazing fire to warm them, and a substantial meal of fine, juicy slices of venison soon broiling, of which they did not leave a crumb. When their minds had calmed down a little, and they were able to reflect on the dangers they had come through from flood, and fire, and alligators, they could scarcely believe they had escaped.

Thalcave, in a few words, gave Paganel an account of himself since they parted, entirely ascribing his deliverance to his intrepid horse. Then Paganel tried to make him understand their new interpretation of the document, and the consequent hopes they were indulging. Whether the Indian actually understood his ingenious hypothesis was a question; but he saw that they were glad and confident, and that was enough for him.

As can easily be imagined, after their compulsory rest on the OMBU, the travelers were up betimes and ready to start. At eight o'clock they set off. No means of transport being procurable so far south, they were compelled to walk. However, it was not more than forty miles now that they had to go, and Thaouka would not refuse to give a lift occasionally to a tired pedestrian, or even to a couple at a pinch. In thirty-six hours they might reach the shores of the Atlantic.

The low-lying tract of marshy ground, still under water, soon lay behind them, as Thalcave led them upward to the higher plains. Here the Argentine territory resumed its monotonous aspect. A few clumps of trees, planted by European hands, might chance to be visible among the pasturage, but quite as rarely as in Tandil and Tapalquem Sierras. The native trees are only found on the edge of long prairies and about Cape Corrientes.

Next day, though still fifteen miles distant, the proximity of the ocean was sensibly felt. The VIRAZON, a peculiar wind, which blows regularly half of the day and night, bent down the heads of the tall grasses. Thinly planted woods rose to view, and small tree-like mimosas, bushes of acacia, and tufts of CURRA-MANTEL. Here and there, shining like pieces of broken glass, were salinous lagoons, which increased the difficulty of the journey as the travelers had to wind round them to get past. They pushed on as quickly as possible, hoping to reach Lake Salado, on the shores of the ocean, the same day; and at 8 P. M., when they found themselves in front of the sand hills two hundred feet high, which skirt the coast, they were all tolerably tired. But when the long murmur of the distant ocean fell on their ears, the exhausted men forgot their fatigue, and ran up the sandhills with surprising agility. But it was getting quite dark already, and their eager gaze could discover no traces of the DUNCAN on the gloomy expanse of water that met their sight.

"But she is there, for all that," exclaimed Glenarvan, "waiting for us, and running alongside."

"We shall see her to-morrow," replied McNabbs.

Tom Austin hailed the invisible yacht, but there was no response. The wind was very high and the sea rough. The clouds were scudding along from the west, and the spray of the waves dashed up even to the sand-hills. It was little wonder, then, if the man on the look-out could neither hear nor make himself heard, supposing the DUNCAN were there. There was no shelter on the coast for her, neither bay nor cove, nor port; not so much as a creek. The shore was composed of sand-banks which ran out into the sea, and were more dangerous to approach than rocky shoals. The sand-banks irritate the waves, and make the sea so particularly rough, that in heavy weather vessels that run aground there are invariably dashed to pieces.

Though, then, the DUNCAN would keep far away from such a coast, John Mangles is a prudent captain to get near. Tom Austin, however, was of the opinion that she would be able to keep five miles out.

The Major advised his impatient relative to restrain himself to circumstances. Since there was no means of dissipating the darkness, what was the use of straining his eyes by vainly endeavoring to pierce through it.

He set to work immediately to prepare the night's encampment beneath the shelter of the sand-hills; the last provisions supplied the last meal, and afterward, each, following the Major's example, scooped out a hole in the sand, which made a comfortable enough bed, and then covered himself with the soft material up to his chin, and fell into a heavy sleep.

But Glenarvan kept watch. There was still a stiff breeze of wind, and the ocean had not recovered its equilibrium after the recent storm. The waves, at all times tumultuous, now broke over the sand-banks with a noise like thunder. Glenarvan could not rest, knowing the DUNCAN was so near him. As to supposing she had not arrived at the appointed rendezvous, that was out of the question. Glenarvan had left the Bay of Talcahuano on the 14th of October, and arrived on the shores of the Atlantic on the 12th of November. He had taken thirty days to cross Chili, the Cordilleras, the Pampas, and the Argentine plains, giving the DUNCAN ample time to double Cape Horn, and arrive on the opposite side. For such a fast runner there were no impediments. Certainly the storm had been very violent, and its fury must have been terrible on such a vast battlefield as the Atlantic, but the yacht was a good ship, and the captain was a good sailor. He was bound to be there, and he would be there.

These reflections, however, did not calm Glenarvan. When the heart and the reason are struggling, it is generally the heart that wins the mastery. The laird of Malcolm Castle felt the presence of loved ones about him in the darkness as he wandered up and down the lonely strand. He gazed, and listened, and even fancied he caught occasional glimpses of a faint light.

"I am not mistaken," he said to himself; "I saw a ship's light, one of the lights on the DUNCAN! Oh! why can't I see in the dark?"

All at once the thought rushed across him that Paganel said he was a nyctalope, and could see at night. He must go and wake him.

The learned geographer was sleeping as sound as a mole.

A strong arm pulled him up out of the sand and made him call out:

"Who goes there?"

"It is I, Paganel."

"Who?"

"Glenarvan. Come, I need your eyes."

"My eyes," replied Paganel, rubbing them vigorously.

"Yes, I need your eyes to make out the DUNCAN in this darkness, so come."

"Confound the nyctalopia!" said Paganel, inwardly, though delighted to be of any service to his friend.

He got up and shook his stiffened limbs, and stretching and yawning as most people do when roused from sleep, followed Glenarvan to the beach.

Glenarvan begged him to examine the distant horizon across the sea, which he did most conscientiously for some minutes.

"Well, do you see nothing?" asked Glenarvan.

"Not a thing. Even a cat couldn't see two steps before her."

"Look for a red light or a green one—her larboard or starboard light."

"I see neither a red nor a green light, all is pitch dark," replied Paganel, his eyes involuntarily beginning to close.

For half an hour he followed his impatient friend, mechanically letting his head frequently drop on his chest, and raising it again with a start. At last he neither answered nor spoke, and he reeled about like a drunken man. Glenarvan looked at him, and found he was sound asleep!

Without attempting to wake him, he took his arm, led him back to his hole, and buried him again comfortably.

At dawn next morning, all the slumberers started to their feet and rushed to the shore, shouting "Hurrah, hurrah!" as Lord Glenarvan's loud cry, "The DUNCAN, the DUNCAN!" broke upon his ear.

CHAPTER XXVI THE RETURN ON BOARD

There she was, five miles out, her courses carefully reefed, and her steam half up. Her smoke was lost in the morning mist. The sea was so violent that a vessel of her tonnage could not have ventured safely nearer the sand-banks.

Glenarvan, by the aid of Paganel's telescope, closely observed the movements of the yacht. It was evident that John Mangles had not perceived his passengers, for he continued his course as before.

But at this very moment Thalcave fired his carbine in the direction of the yacht. They listened and looked, but no signal of recognition was returned. A second and a third time the Indian fired, awakening the echoes among the sand-hills.

At last a white smoke was seen issuing from the side of the yacht.

"They see us!" exclaimed Glenarvan. "That's the cannon of the DUNCAN."

A few seconds, and the heavy boom of the cannon came across the water and died away on the shore. The sails were instantly altered, and the steam got up, so as to get as near the coast as possible.

Presently, through the glass, they saw a boat lowered.

"Lady Helena will not be able to come," said Tom Austin.

"It is too rough."

"Nor John Mangles," added McNabbs; "he cannot leave the ship."

"My sister, my sister!" cried Robert, stretching out his arms toward the yacht, which was now rolling violently.

"Oh, how I wish I could get on board!" said Glenarvan.

"Patience, Edward! you will be there in a couple of hours," replied the Major.

Two hours! But it was impossible for a boat—a six-oared one— to come and go in a shorter space of time.

Glenarvan went back to Thalcave, who stood beside Thaouka, with his arms crossed, looking quietly at the troubled waves.

Glenarvan took his hand, and pointing to the yacht, said: "Come!"

The Indian gently shook his head.

"Come, friend," repeated Glenarvan.

"No," said Thalcave, gently. "Here is Thaouka, and there— the Pampas," he added, embracing with a passionate gesture the wide-stretching prairies.

Glenarvan understood his refusal. He knew that the Indian would never forsake the prairie, where the bones of his fathers were whitening, and he knew the religious attachment of these sons of the desert for their native land. He did not urge Thalcave longer, therefore, but simply pressed his hand. Nor could he find it in his heart to insist, when the Indian, smiling as usual, would not accept the price of his services, pushing back the money, and saying:

"For the sake of friendship."

Glenarvan could not reply; but he wished at least, to leave the brave fellow some souvenir of his European friends. What was there to give, however? Arms, horses, everything had been destroyed in the unfortunate inundation, and his friends were no richer than himself.

He was quite at a loss how to show his recognition of the disinterestedness of this noble guide, when a happy thought struck him. He had an exquisite portrait of Lady Helena in his pocket, a CHEF-D'OEUVRE of Lawrence. This he drew out, and offered to Thalcave, simply saying:

"My wife."

The Indian gazed at it with a softened eye, and said:

"Good and beautiful."

Then Robert, and Paganel, and the Major, and the rest, exchanged touching farewells with the faithful Patagonian. Thalcave embraced them each, and pressed them to his broad chest. Paganel made him accept a map of South America and the two oceans, which he had often seen the Indian looking at with interest. It was the most precious thing the geographer possessed. As for Robert, he had only caresses to bestow, and these he lavished on his friend, not forgetting to give a share to Thaouka.

The boat from the DUNCAN was now fast approaching, and in another minute had glided into a narrow channel between the sand-banks, and run ashore.

"My wife?" were Glenarvan's first words.

"My sister?" said Robert.

"Lady Helena and Miss Grant are waiting for you on board," replied the coxswain; "but lose no time your honor, we have not a minute, for the tide is beginning to ebb already."

The last kindly adieux were spoken, and Thalcave accompanied his friends to the boat, which had been pushed back into the water. Just as Robert was going to step in, the Indian took him in his arms, and gazed tenderly into his face. Then he said:

"Now go. You are a man."

"Good-by, good-by, friend!" said Glenarvan, once more.

"Shall we never see each other again?" Paganel called out.

"*Quien sabe?*" (Who knows?) replied Thalcave, lifting his arms toward heaven.

These were the Indian's last words, dying away on the breeze, as the boat receded gradually from the shore. For a long time, his dark, motionless SILHOUETTE stood out against the sky, through the white, dashing spray of the waves. Then by degrees his tall form began to diminish in size, till at last his friends of a day lost sight of him altogether.

An hour afterward Robert was the first to leap on board the DUNCAN. He flung his arms round Mary's neck, amid the loud, joyous hurrahs of the crew on the yacht.

Thus the journey across South America was accomplished, the given line of march being scrupulously adhered to throughout.

Neither mountains nor rivers had made the travelers change their course; and though they had not had to encounter any ill-will from men, their generous intrepidity had been often enough roughly put to the proof by the fury of the unchained elements.

AUSTRALIA

CHAPTER I A NEW DESTINATION

FOR the first few moments the joy of reunion completely filled the hearts. Lord Glenarvan had taken care that the ill-success of their expedition should not throw a gloom over the pleasure of meeting, his very first words being:

"Cheer up, friends, cheer up! Captain Grant is not with us, but we have a certainty of finding him!"

Only such an assurance as this would have restored hope to those on board the DUNCAN. Lady Helena and Mary Grant had been sorely tried by the suspense, as they stood on the poop waiting for the arrival of the boat, and trying to count the number of its passengers. Alternate hope and fear agitated the bosom of poor Mary. Sometimes she fancied she could see her father, Harry Grant, and sometimes she gave way to despair. Her heart throbbed violently; she could not speak, and indeed could scarcely stand. Lady Helena put her arm round her waist to support her, but the captain, John Mangles, who stood close beside them spoke no encouraging word, for his practiced eye saw plainly that the captain was not there.

"He is there! He is coming! Oh, father!" exclaimed the young girl. But as the boat came nearer, her illusion was dispelled; all hope forsook her, and she would have sunk in despair, but for the reassuring voice of Glenarvan.

After their mutual embraces were over, Lady Helena, and Mary Grant, and John Mangles, were informed of the principal incidents of the expedition, and especially of the new interpretation of the document, due to the sagacity of Jacques Paganel. His Lordship also spoke in the most eulogistic terms of Robert, of whom Mary might well be proud. His courage and devotion, and the dangers he had run, were all shown up in strong relief by his patron, till the modest boy did not know which way to look, and was obliged to hide his burning cheeks in his sister's arms.

"No need to blush, Robert," said John Mangles. "Your conduct has been worthy of your name." And he leaned over the boy and pressed his lips on his cheek, still wet with Mary's tears.

The Major and Paganel, it need hardly be said, came in for their due share of welcome, and Lady Helena only regretted she could not shake hands with the brave and generous Thalcave. McNabbs soon slipped away to his cabin, and began to shave himself as coolly and composedly as possible; while Paganel flew here and there, like a bee sipping the sweets of compliments and smiles. He wanted to embrace everyone on board the yacht, and beginning with Lady Helena and Mary Grant, wound up with M. Olbinett, the steward, who could only acknowledge so polite an attention by announcing that breakfast was ready.

"Breakfast!" exclaimed Paganel.

"Yes, Monsieur Paganel."

"A real breakfast, on a real table, with a cloth and napkins?"

"Certainly, Monsieur Paganel."

"And we shall neither have CHARQUI, nor hard eggs, nor fillets of ostrich?"

"Oh, Monsieur," said Olbinett in an aggrieved tone.

"I don't want to hurt your feelings, my friend," said the geographer smiling. "But for a month that has been our usual bill of fare, and when we dined we stretched ourselves full length on the ground, unless we sat astride on the trees. Consequently, the meal you have just announced seemed to me like a dream, or fiction, or chimera."

"Well, Monsieur Paganel, come along and let us prove its reality," said Lady Helena, who could not help laughing.

"Take my arm," replied the gallant geographer.

"Has his Lordship any orders to give me about the DUNCAN?" asked John Mangles.

"After breakfast, John," replied Glenarvan, "we'll discuss the program of our new expedition *en famille*."

M. Olbinett's breakfast seemed quite a FETE to the hungry guests. It was pronounced excellent, and even superior to the festivities of the Pampas. Paganel was helped twice to each dish, through "absence of mind," he said.

This unlucky word reminded Lady Helena of the amiable Frenchman's propensity, and made her ask if he had ever fallen into his old habits while they were away. The Major and Glenarvan exchanged smiling glances, and Paganel burst out laughing, and protested on his honor that he would never be caught tripping again once more during the whole voyage. After this prelude, he gave an amusing recital of his disastrous mistake in learning Spanish, and his profound study of Camoens. "After all," he added, "it's an ill wind that blows nobody good, and I don't regret the mistake."

"Why not, my worthy friend?" asked the Major.

"Because I not only know Spanish, but Portuguese. I can speak two languages instead of one."

"Upon my word, I never thought of that," said McNabbs. "My compliments,

Paganel—my sincere compliments."

But Paganel was too busily engaged with his knife and fork to lose a single mouthful, though he did his best to eat and talk at the same time. He was so much taken up with his plate, however, that one little fact quite escaped his observation, though Glenarvan noticed it at once. This was, that John Mangles had grown particularly attentive to Mary Grant. A significant glance from Lady Helena told him, moreover, how affairs stood, and inspired him with affectionate sympathy for the young lovers; but nothing of this was apparent in his manner to John, for his next question was what sort of a voyage he had made.

"We could not have had a better; but I must apprise your Lordship that I did not go through the Straits of Magellan again."

"What! you doubled Cape Horn, and I was not there!" exclaimed Paganel.

"Hang yourself!" said the Major.

"Selfish fellow! you advise me to do that because you want my rope," retorted the geographer.

"Well, you see, my dear Paganel, unless you have the gift of ubiquity you can't be in two places at once. While you were scouring the pampas you could not be doubling Cape Horn."

"That doesn't prevent my regretting it," replied Paganel.

Here the subject dropped, and John continued his account of his voyage. On arriving at Cape Pilares he had found the winds dead against him, and therefore made for the south, coasting along the Desolation Isle, and after going as far as the sixty-seventh degree southern latitude, had doubled Cape Horn, passed by Terra del Fuego and the Straits of Lemaire, keeping close to the Patagonian shore. At Cape Corrientes they encountered the terrible storm which had handled the travelers across the pampas so roughly, but the yacht had borne it bravely, and for the last three days had stood right out to sea, till the welcome signal-gun of the expedition was heard announcing the arrival of the anxiously-looked-for party. "It was only justice," the captain added, "that he should mention the intrepid bearing of Lady Helena and Mary Grant throughout the whole hurricane. They had not shown the least fear, unless for their friends, who might possibly be exposed to the fury of the tempest."

After John Mangles had finished his narrative, Glenarvan turned to Mary and said; "My dear Miss Mary, the captain has been doing homage to your noble qualities, and I am glad to think you are not unhappy on board his ship."

"How could I be?" replied Mary naively, looking at Lady Helena, and at the young captain too, likely enough.

"Oh, my sister is very fond of you, Mr. John, and so am I," exclaimed Robert.

"And so am I of you, my dear boy," returned the captain, a little abashed by Robert's innocent avowal, which had kindled a faint blush on Mary's cheek. Then he managed to turn the conversation to safer topics by saying: "And now that your Lordship has heard all about the doings of the DUNCAN, perhaps you will give us some details of your own journey, and tell us more about the exploits of our young hero."

Nothing could be more agreeable than such a recital to Lady Helena and Mary Grant; and accordingly Lord Glenarvan hastened to satisfy their curiosity—going over incident by incident, the entire march from one ocean to another, the pass of the Andes, the earthquake, the disappearance of Robert, his capture by the condor, Thalcave's providential shot, the episode of the red wolves, the devotion of the young lad, Sergeant Manuel, the inundations, the caimans, the waterspout, the night on the Atlantic shore— all these details, amusing or terrible, excited by turns laughter and horror in the listeners. Often and often Robert came in for caresses from his sister and Lady Helena. Never was a boy so much embraced, or by such enthusiastic friends.

"And now, friends," added Lord Glenarvan, when he had finished his narrative, "we must think of the present. The past is gone, but the future is ours. Let us come back to Captain Harry Grant."

As soon as breakfast was over they all went into Lord Glenarvan's private cabin and seated themselves round a table covered with charts and plans, to talk over the matter fully.

"My dear Helena," said Lord Glenarvan, "I told you, when we came on board a little while ago, that though we had not brought back Captain Grant, our hope of finding him was stronger than ever. The result of our journey across America is this: We have reached the conviction, or rather absolute certainty, that the shipwreck never occurred on the shores of the Atlantic nor Pacific. The natural inference is that, as far as regards Patagonia, our interpretation of the document was erroneous. Most fortunately, our friend Paganel, in a happy moment of inspiration, discovered the mistake. He has proved clearly that we have been on the wrong track, and so explained the document that all doubt whatever is removed from our minds. However, as the document is in French, I will ask Paganel to go over it for your benefit."

The learned geographer, thus called upon, executed his task in the most convincing manner, descanting on the syllables GONIE and INDI, and extracting AUSTRALIA out of AUSTRAL. He pointed out that Captain Grant, on leaving the coast of Peru to return to Europe, might have been carried away with his disabled ship by the southern currents of the Pacific right to the shores of Australia, and his hypotheses were so ingenious and his deductions so subtle that even the matter-of-fact John Mangles, a difficult judge, and most unlikely to be led away by any flights of imagination, was completely satisfied.

At the conclusion of Paganel's dissertation, Glenarvan announced that the DUNCAN would sail immediately for Australia.

But before the decisive orders were given, McNabbs asked for a few minutes' hearing.

"Say away, McNabbs," replied Glenarvan.

"I have no intention of weakening the arguments of my friend Paganel, and still less of refuting them. I consider them wise and weighty, and deserving our attention, and think them justly entitled to form the basis of our future researches. But still I should like them to be submitted to a final examination, in order to make their worth incontestable and uncontested."

"Go on, Major," said Paganel; "I am ready to answer all your questions."

"They are simple enough, as you will see. Five months ago, when we left the Clyde, we had studied these same documents, and their interpretation then appeared quite plain. No other coast but the western coast of Patagonia could possibly, we thought, have been the scene of the shipwreck. We had not even the shadow of a doubt on the subject."

"That's true," replied Glenarvan.

"A little later," continued the Major, "when a providential fit of absence of mind came over Paganel, and brought him on board the yacht, the documents were submitted to him and he approved our plan of search most unreservedly."

"I do not deny it," said Paganel.

"And yet we were mistaken," resumed the Major.

"Yes, we were mistaken," returned Paganel; "but it is only human to make a mistake, while to persist in it, a man must be a fool."

"Stop, Paganel, don't excite yourself; I don't mean to say that we should prolong our search in America."

"What is it, then, that you want?" asked Glenarvan.

"A confession, nothing more. A confession that Australia now as evidently appears to be the theater of the shipwreck of the BRITANNIA as America did before."

"We confess it willingly," replied Paganel.

"Very well, then, since that is the case, my advice is not to let your imagination rely on successive and contradictory evidence. Who knows whether after Australia some other country may not appear with equal certainty to be the place, and we may have to recommence our search?"

Glenarvan and Paganel looked at each other silently, struck by the justice of these remarks.

"I should like you, therefore," continued the Major, "before we actually start for Australia, to make one more examination of the documents. Here they are, and here are the charts. Let us take up each point in succession through which the 37th parallel passes, and see if we come across any other country which would agree with the precise indications of the document."

"Nothing can be more easily and quickly done," replied Paganel; "for countries are not very numerous in this latitude, happily."

"Well, look," said the Major, displaying an English planisphere on the plan of Mercator's Chart, and presenting the appearance of a terrestrial globe.

He placed it before Lady Helena, and then they all stood round, so as to be able to follow the argument of Paganel.

CHAPTER I A NEW DESTINATION

"As I have said already," resumed the learned geographer, "after having crossed South America, the 37th degree of latitude cuts the islands of Tristan d'Acunha. Now I maintain that none of the words of the document could relate to these islands."

The documents were examined with the most minute care, and the conclusion unanimously reached was that these islands were entirely out of the question.

"Let us go on then," resumed Paganel. "After leaving the Atlantic, we pass two degrees below the Cape of Good Hope, and into the Indian Ocean. Only one group of islands is found on this route, the Amsterdam Isles. Now, then, we must examine these as we did the Tristan d'Acunha group."

After a close survey, the Amsterdam Isles were rejected in their turn. Not a single word, or part of a word, French, English or German, could apply to this group in the Indian Ocean.

"Now we come to Australia," continued Paganel.

"The 37th parallel touches this continent at Cape Bernouilli, and leaves it at Twofold Bay. You will agree with me that, without straining the text, the English word STRA and the French one AUSTRAL may relate to Australia. The thing is too plain to need proof."

The conclusion of Paganel met with unanimous approval; every probability was in his favor.

"And where is the next point?" asked McNabbs.

"That is easily answered. After leaving Twofold Bay, we cross an arm of the sea which extends to New Zealand. Here I must call your attention to the fact that the French word CONTIN means a continent, irrefragably. Captain Grant could not, then, have found refuge in New Zealand, which is only an island. However that may be though, examine and compare, and go over and over each word, and see if, by any possibility, they can be made to fit this new country."

"In no way whatever," replied John Mangles, after a minute investigation of the documents and the planisphere.

"No," chimed in all the rest, and even the Major himself, "it cannot apply to New Zealand."

"Now," went on Paganel, "in all this immense space between this large island and the American coast, there is only one solitary barren little island crossed by the 37th parallel."

"And what is its name," asked the Major.

"Here it is, marked in the map. It is Maria Theresa—a name of which there is not a single trace in either of the three documents."

"Not the slightest," said Glenarvan.

"I leave you, then, my friends, to decide whether all these probabilities, not to say certainties, are not in favor of the Australian continent."

"Evidently," replied the captain and all the others.

"Well, then, John," said Glenarvan, "the next question is, have you provisions and coal enough?"

"Yes, your honor, I took in an ample store at Talcahuano, and, besides, we can easily replenish our stock of coal at Cape Town."

"Well, then, give orders."

"Let me make one more observation," interrupted McNabbs.

"Go on then."

"Whatever likelihood of success Australia may offer us, wouldn't it be advisable to stop a day or two at the Tristan d'Acunha Isles and the Amsterdam? They lie in our route, and would not take us the least out of the way. Then we should be able to ascertain if the BRITANNIA had left any traces of her shipwreck there?"

"Incredulous Major!" exclaimed Paganel, "he still sticks to his idea."

"I stick to this any way, that I don't want to have to retrace our steps, supposing that Australia should disappoint our sanguine hopes."

"It seems to me a good precaution," replied Glenarvan.

"And I'm not the one to dissuade you from it," returned Paganel; "quite the contrary."

"Steer straight for Tristan d'Acunha."

"Immediately, your Honor," replied the captain, going on deck, while Robert and Mary Grant overwhelmed Lord Glenarvan with their grateful thanks.

Shortly after, the DUNCAN had left the American coast, and was running eastward, her sharp keel rapidly cutting her way through the waves of the Atlantic Ocean.

CHAPTER II TRISTAN D'ACUNHA AND THE ISLE OF AMSTERDAM

IF the yacht had followed the line of the equator, the 196 degrees which separate Australia from America, or, more correctly, Cape Bernouilli from Cape Corrientes, would have been equal to 11,760 geographical miles; but along the 37th parallel these same degrees, owing to the form of the earth, only represent 9,480 miles. From the American coast to Tristan d'Acunha is reckoned 2,100 miles— a distance which John Mangles hoped to clear in ten days, if east winds did not retard the motion of the yacht. But he was not long uneasy on that score, for toward evening the breeze sensibly lulled and then changed altogether, giving the DUNCAN a fair field on a calm sea for displaying her incomparable qualities as a sailor.

The passengers had fallen back into their ordinary ship life, and it hardly seemed as if they really could have been absent a whole month. Instead of the Pacific, the Atlantic stretched itself out before them, and there was scarcely a shade of difference in the waves of the two oceans. The elements, after having handled them so roughly, seemed now disposed to favor them to the utmost. The sea was tranquil, and the wind kept in the right quarter, so that the yacht could spread all her canvas, and lend its aid, if needed to the indefatigable steam stored up in the boiler.

Under such conditions, the voyage was safely and rapidly accomplished. Their confidence increased as they found themselves nearer the Australian coast. They began to talk of Captain Grant as if the yacht were going to take him on board at a given port. His cabin was got ready, and berths for the men. This cabin was next to the famous *number six*, which Paganel had taken possession of instead of the one he had booked on the SCOTIA. It had been till now occupied by M. Olbinett, who vacated it for the expected guest. Mary took great delight in arranging it with her own hands, and adorning it for the reception of the loved inmate.

The learned geographer kept himself closely shut up. He was working away from morning till night at a work entitled "Sublime Impressions of a Geographer in the Argentine Pampas," and they could hear him repeating elegant periods aloud before committing them to the white pages of his day-book; and more than once, unfaithful to Clio, the muse of history, he invoked in his transports the divine Calliope, the muse of epic poetry.

Paganel made no secret of it either. The chaste daughters of Apollo willingly left the slopes of Helicon and Parnassus at his call. Lady Helena paid him sincere compliments on his mythological visitants, and so did the Major, though he could not forbear adding:

"But mind no fits of absence of mind, my dear Paganel; and if you take a fancy to learn Australian, don't go and study it in a Chinese grammar."

Things went on perfectly smoothly on board. Lady Helena and Lord Glenarvan found leisure to watch John Mangles' growing attachment to Mary Grant. There was nothing to be said against it, and, indeed, since John remained silent, it was best to take no notice of it.

"What will Captain Grant think?" Lord Glenarvan asked his wife one day.

"He'll think John is worthy of Mary, my dear Edward, and he'll think right."

Meanwhile, the yacht was making rapid progress. Five days after losing sight of Cape Corrientes, on the 16th of November, they fell in with fine westerly breezes, and the DUNCAN might almost have dispensed with her screw altogether, for she flew over the water like a bird, spreading all her sails to catch the breeze, as if she were running a race with the Royal Thames Club yachts.

Next day, the ocean appeared covered with immense seaweeds, looking like a great pond choked up with the DEBRIS of trees and plants torn off the neighboring continents. Commander Murray had specially pointed them out to the attention of navigators. The DUNCAN appeared to glide over a long prairie, which Paganel justly compared to the Pampas, and her speed slackened a little.

Twenty-four hours after, at break of day, the man on the look-out was heard calling out, "Land ahead!"

"In what direction?" asked Tom Austin, who was on watch.

"Leeward!" was the reply.

This exciting cry brought everyone speedily on deck. Soon a telescope made its appearance, followed by Jacques Paganel. The learned geographer pointed the instrument in the direction indicated, but could see nothing that resembled land.

"Look in the clouds," said John Mangles.

"Ah, now I do see a sort of peak, but very indistinctly."

"It is Tristan d'Acunha," replied John Mangles.

"Then, if my memory serves me right, we must be eighty miles from it, for the peak of Tristan, seven thousand feet high, is visible at that distance."

"That's it, precisely."

Some hours later, the sharp, lofty crags of the group of islands stood out clearly on the horizon. The conical peak of Tristan looked black against the bright sky, which seemed all ablaze with the splendor of the rising sun. Soon the principal island stood out from the rocky mass, at the summit of a triangle inclining toward the northeast.

Tristan d'Acunha is situated in 37 degrees 8' of southern latitude, and 10 degrees 44' of longitude west of the meridian at Greenwich. Inaccessible Island is eighteen miles to the southwest and Nightingale Island is ten miles to the southeast, and this completes the little solitary group of islets in the Atlantic Ocean. Toward noon, the two principal landmarks, by which the group is recognized were sighted, and at 3 P. M. the DUNCAN entered Falmouth Bay in Tristan d'Acunha.

Several whaling vessels were lying quietly at anchor there, for the coast abounds in seals and other marine animals.

John Mangle's first care was to find good anchorage, and then all the passengers, both ladies and gentlemen, got into the long boat and were rowed ashore. They stepped out on a beach covered with fine black sand, the impalpable DEBRIS of the calcined rocks of the island.

Tristan d'Acunha is the capital of the group, and consists of a little village, lying in the heart of the bay, and watered by a noisy, rapid stream. It contained about fifty houses, tolerably clean, and disposed with geometrical regularity. Behind this miniature town there lay 1,500 hectares of meadow land, bounded by an embankment of lava. Above this embankment, the conical peak rose 7,000 feet high.

Lord Glenarvan was received by a governor supplied from the English colony at the Cape. He inquired at once respecting Harry Grant and the BRITANNIA, and found the names entirely unknown. The Tristan d'Acunha Isles are out of the route of ships, and consequently little frequented. Since the wreck of the *Blendon Hall* in 1821, on the rocks of Inaccessible Island, two vessels have stranded on the chief island—the PRIMANGUET in 1845, and the three-mast American, PHILADELPHIA, in 1857. These three events comprise the whole catalogue of maritime disasters in the annals of the Acunhas.

Lord Glenarvan did not expect to glean any information, and only asked by the way of duty. He even sent the boats to make the circuit of the island, the entire extent of which was not more than seventeen miles at most.

In the interim the passengers walked about the village. The population does not exceed 150 inhabitants, and consists of English and Americans, married to negroes and Cape Hottentots, who might bear away the palm for ugliness. The children of these heterogeneous households are very disagreeable compounds of Saxon stiffness and African blackness.

It was nearly nightfall before the party returned to the yacht, chattering and admiring the natural riches displayed on all sides, for even close to the streets of the capital, fields of wheat and maize were waving, and crops of vegetables, imported forty years before; and in the environs of the village, herds of cattle and sheep were feeding.

The boats returned to the DUNCAN about the same time as Lord Glenarvan. They had made the circuit of the entire island in a few hours, but without coming across the least trace of the BRITANNIA. The only result of this voyage of circumnavigation was to strike out the name of Isle Tristan from the program of search.

CHAPTER III CAPE TOWN AND M. VIOT

As John Mangles intended to put in at the Cape of Good Hope for coals, he was obliged to deviate a little from the 37th parallel, and go two degrees north. In less than six days he cleared the thirteen hundred miles which separate the point of Africa from Tristan d'Acunha, and on the 24th of November, at 3 P. M. the Table Mountain was sighted. At eight o'clock they entered the bay, and cast anchor in the port of Cape Town. They sailed away next morning at daybreak.

Between the Cape and Amsterdam Island there is a distance of 2,900 miles, but with a good sea and favoring breeze, this was only a ten day's voyage. The elements were now no longer at war with the travelers, as on their journey across the Pampas— air and water seemed in league to help them forward.

"Ah! the sea! the sea!" exclaimed Paganel, "it is the field *par excellence* for the exercise of human energies, and the ship is the true vehicle of civilization. Think, my friends, if the globe had been only an immense continent, the thousandth part of it would still be unknown to us, even in this nineteenth century. See how it is in the interior of great countries. In the steppes of Siberia, in the plains of Central Asia, in the deserts of Africa, in the prairies of America, in the immense wilds of Australia, in the icy solitudes of the Poles, man scarcely dares to venture; the most daring shrinks back, the most courageous succumbs. They cannot penetrate them; the means of transport are insufficient, and the heat and disease, and savage disposition of the natives, are impassable obstacles. Twenty miles of desert separate men more than five hundred miles of ocean."

Paganel spoke with such warmth that even the Major had nothing to say against this panegyric of the ocean. Indeed, if the finding of Harry Grant had involved following a parallel across continents instead of oceans, the enterprise could not have been attempted; but the sea was there ready to carry the travelers from one country to another, and on the 6th of December, at the first streak of day, they saw a fresh mountain apparently emerging from the bosom of the waves.

This was Amsterdam Island, situated in 37 degrees 47 minutes latitude and 77 degrees 24 minutes longitude, the high cone of which in clear weather is visible fifty miles off. At eight o'clock, its form, indistinct though it still was, seemed almost a reproduction of Teneriffe.

"And consequently it must resemble Tristan d'Acunha," observed Glenarvan.

"A very wise conclusion," said Paganel, "according to the geometrographic axiom that two islands resembling a third must have a common likeness. I will only add that, like Tristan d'Acunha, Amsterdam Island is equally rich in seals and Robinsons."

"There are Robinsons everywhere, then?" said Lady Helena.

"Indeed, Madam," replied Paganel, "I know few islands without some tale of the kind appertaining to them, and the romance of your immortal countryman, Daniel Defoe, has been often enough realized before his day."

"Monsieur Paganel," said Mary, "may I ask you a question?"

"Two if you like, my dear young lady, and I promise to answer them."

"Well, then, I want to know if you would be very much frightened at the idea of being cast away alone on a desert island."

"I?" exclaimed Paganel.

"Come now, my good fellow," said the Major, "don't go and tell us that it is your most cherished desire."

"I don't pretend it is that, but still, after all, such an adventure would not be very unpleasant to me. I should begin a new life; I should hunt and fish; I should choose a grotto for my domicile in Winter and a tree in Summer. I should make storehouses for my harvests: in one word, I should colonize my island."

"All by yourself?"

"All by myself if I was obliged. Besides, are we ever obliged? Cannot one find friends among the animals, and choose some tame kid or eloquent parrot or amiable monkey? And if a lucky chance should send one a companion like the faithful Friday, what more is needed? Two friends on a rock, there is happiness. Suppose now, the Major and I—"

"Thank you," replied the Major, interrupting him; "I have no inclination in that line, and should make a very poor Robinson Crusoe."

"My dear Monsieur Paganel," said Lady Helena, "you are letting your imagination run away with you, as usual. But the dream is very different from the reality. You are thinking of an imaginary Robinson's life, thrown on a picked island and treated like a spoiled child by nature. You only see the sunny side."

"What, madam! You don't believe a man could be happy on a desert island?"

"I do not. Man is made for society and not for solitude, and solitude can only engender despair. It is a question of time. At the outset it is quite possible that material wants and the very necessities of existence may engross the poor shipwrecked fellow, just snatched from the waves; but afterward, when he feels himself alone, far from his fellow men, without any hope of seeing country and friends again, what must he think, what must he suffer? His little island is all his world. The whole human race is shut up in himself, and when death comes, which utter loneliness will make terrible, he will be like the last man on the last day of the world. Believe me, Monsieur Paganel, such a man is not to be envied."

Paganel gave in, though regretfully, to the arguments of Lady Helena, and still kept up a discussion on the advantages and disadvantages of Isolation, till the very moment the DUNCAN dropped anchor about a mile off Amsterdam Island.

This lonely group in the Indian Ocean consists of two distinct islands, thirty-three miles apart, and situated exactly on the meridian of the Indian peninsula. To the north is Amsterdam Island, and to the south St. Paul; but they have been often confounded by geographers and navigators.

At the time of the DUNCAN'S visit to the island, the population consisted of three people, a Frenchman and two mulattoes, all three employed by the merchant proprietor. Paganel was delighted to shake hands with a countryman in the person of good old Monsieur Viot. He was far advanced in years, but did the honors of the place with much politeness. It was a happy day for him when these kindly strangers touched at his island, for St. Peter's was only frequented by seal-fishers, and now and then a whaler, the crews of which are usually rough, coarse men.

M. Viot presented his subjects, the two mulattoes. They composed the whole living population of the island, except a few wild boars in the interior and myriads of penguins. The little house where the three solitary men lived was in the heart of a natural bay on the southeast, formed by the crumbling away of a portion of the mountain.

Twice over in the early part of the century, Amsterdam Island became the country of deserted sailors, providentially saved from misery and death; but since these events no vessel had been lost on its coast. Had any shipwreck occurred, some fragments must have been thrown on the sandy shore, and any poor sufferers from it would have found their way to M. Viot's fishing-huts. The old man had been long on the island, and had never been called upon to exercise such hospitality. Of the BRITANNIA and Captain Grant he knew nothing, but he was certain that the disaster had not happened on Amsterdam Island, nor on the islet called St. Paul, for whalers and fishing-vessels went there constantly, and must have heard of it.

Glenarvan was neither surprised nor vexed at the reply; indeed, his object in asking was rather to establish the fact that Captain Grant had not been there than that he had. This done, they were ready to proceed on their voyage next day.

They rambled about the island till evening, as its appearance was very inviting. Its FAUNA and FLORA, however, were poor in the extreme. The only specimens of quadrupeds, birds, fish and cetacea were a few wild boars, stormy petrels, albatrosses, perch and seals. Here and there thermal springs and chalybeate waters escaped from the black lava, and thin dark vapors rose above the volcanic soil. Some of these springs were very hot. John Mangles held his thermometer in one of them, and found the temperature was 176 degrees Fahrenheit. Fish caught in the sea a few yards off, cooked in five minutes in these all but boiling waters, a fact which made Paganel resolve not to attempt to bathe in them.

Toward evening, after a long promenade, Glenarvan and his party bade adieu to the good old M. Viot, and returned to the yacht, wishing him all the happiness possible on his desert island, and receiving in return the old man's blessing on their expedition.

CHAPTER IV A WAGER AND HOW DECIDED

ON the 7th of December, at three A. M., the DUNCAN lay puffing out her smoke in the little harbor ready to start, and a few minutes afterward the anchor was lifted, and the screw set in motion. By eight o'clock, when the passengers came on deck, the Amsterdam Island had almost disappeared from view behind the mists of the horizon. This was the last halting-place on the route, and nothing now was between them and the Australian coast but three thousand miles' distance. Should the west wind continue but a dozen days longer, and the sea remain favorable, the yacht would have reached the end of her voyage.

Mary Grant and her brother could not gaze without emotion at the waves through which the DUNCAN was speeding her course, when they thought that these very same waves must have dashed against the prow of the BRITANNIA but a few days before her shipwreck. Here, perhaps, Captain Grant, with a disabled ship and diminished crew, had struggled against the tremendous hurricanes of the Indian Ocean, and felt himself driven toward the coast with irresistible force. The Captain pointed out to Mary the different currents on the ship's chart, and explained to her their constant direction. Among others there was one running straight to the Australian continent, and its action is equally felt in the Atlantic and Pacific. It was doubtless against this that the BRITANNIA, dismasted and rudderless, had been unable to contend, and consequently been dashed against the coast, and broken in pieces.

A difficulty about this, however, presented itself. The last intelligence of Captain Grant was from Callao on the 30th of May, 1862, as appeared in the *Mercantile and Shipping Gazette*. "How then was it possible that on the 7th of June, only eight days after leaving the shores of Peru, that the BRITANNIA could have found herself in the Indian Ocean? But to this, Paganel, who was consulted on the subject, found a very plausible solution.

It was one evening, about six days after their leaving Amsterdam Island, when they were all chatting together on the poop, that the above-named difficulty was stated by Glenarvan. Paganel made no reply, but went and fetched the document. After perusing it, he still remained silent, simply shrugging his shoulders, as if ashamed of troubling himself about such a trifle.

"Come, my good friend," said Glenarvan, "at least give us an answer."

"No," replied Paganel, "I'll merely ask a question for

Captain John to answer."

"And what is it, Monsieur Paganel?" said John Mangles.

"Could a quick ship make the distance in a month over that part of the Pacific Ocean which lies between America and Australia?"

"Yes, by making two hundred miles in twenty-four hours."

"Would that be an extraordinary rate of speed?"

"Not at all; sailing clippers often go faster."

"Well, then, instead of '7 June' on this document, suppose that one figure has been destroyed by the sea-water, and read '17 June' or '27 June,' and all is explained."

"That's to say," replied Lady Helena, "that between the 31st of May and the 27th of June—"

"Captain Grant could have crossed the Pacific and found himself in the Indian Ocean."

Paganel's theory met with universal acceptance.

"That's one more point cleared up," said Glenarvan. "Thanks to our friend, all that remains to be done now is to get to Australia, and look out for traces of the wreck on the western coast."

"Or the eastern?" said John Mangles.

"Indeed, John, you may be right, for there is nothing in the document to indicate which shore was the scene of the catastrophe, and both points of the continent crossed by the 37th parallel, must, therefore, be explored."

"Then, my Lord, it is doubtful, after all," said Mary.

"Oh no, Miss Mary," John Mangles hastened to reply, seeing the young girl's apprehension. "His Lordship will please to consider that if Captain Grant had gained the shore on the east of Australia, he would almost immediately have found refuge and assistance. The whole of that coast is English, we might say, peopled with colonists. The crew of the BRITANNIA could not have gone ten miles without meeting a fellow-countryman."

"I am quite of your opinion, Captain John," said Paganel. "On the eastern coast Harry Grant would not only have found an English colony easily, but he would certainly have met with some means of transport back to Europe."

"And he would not have found the same resources on the side we are making for?" asked Lady Helena.

"No, madam," replied Paganel; "it is a desert coast, with no communication between it and Melbourne or Adelaide. If the BRITANNIA was wrecked on those rocky shores, she was as much cut off from all chance of help as if she had been lost on the inhospitable shores of Africa."

"But what has become of my father there, then, all these two years?" asked Mary Grant.

"My dear Mary," replied Paganel, "you have not the least doubt, have you, that Captain Grant reached the Australian continent after his shipwreck?"

"No, Monsieur Paganel."

"Well, granting that, what became of him? The suppositions we might make are not numerous. They are confined to three. Either Harry Grant and his companions have found their way to the English colonies, or they have fallen into the hands of the natives, or they are lost in the immense wilds of Australia."

"Go on, Paganel," said Lord Glenarvan, as the learned Frenchman made a pause.

"The first hypothesis I reject, then, to begin with, for Harry Grant could not have reached the English colonies, or long ago he would have been back with his children in the good town of Dundee."

"Poor father," murmured Mary, "away from us for two whole years."

"Hush, Mary," said Robert, "Monsieur Paganel will tell us."

"Alas! my boy, I cannot. All that I affirm is, that Captain Grant is in the hands of the natives."

"But these natives," said Lady Helena, hastily, "are they—"

"Reassure yourself, madam," said Paganel, divining her thoughts. "The aborigines of Australia are low enough in the scale of human intelligence, and most degraded and uncivilized, but they are mild and gentle in disposition, and not sanguinary like their New Zealand neighbors. Though they may be prisoners, their lives have never been threatened, you may be sure. All travelers are unanimous in declaring that the Australian natives abhor shedding blood, and many a time they have found in them faithful allies in repelling the attacks of evil-disposed convicts far more cruelly inclined."

"You hear what Monsieur Paganel tells us, Mary," said Lady Helena turning to the young girl. "If your father is in the hands of the natives, which seems probable from the document, we shall find him."

"And what if he is lost in that immense country?" asked Mary.

"Well, we'll find him still," exclaimed Paganel, in a confident tone.

"Won't we, friends?"

"Most certainly," replied Glenarvan; and anxious to give a less gloomy turn to the conversation, he added—

"But I won't admit the supposition of his being lost, not for an instant."

"Neither will I," said Paganel.

"Is Australia a big place?" inquired Robert.

"Australia, my boy, is about as large as four-fifths of Europe. It has somewhere about 775,000 HECTARES."

"So much as that?" said the Major.

"Yes, McNabbs, almost to a yard's breadth. Don't you think now it has a right to be called a continent?"

"I do, certainly."

"I may add," continued the SAVANT, "that there are but few accounts of travelers being lost in this immense country. Indeed, I believe Leichardt is the only one of whose fate we are ignorant, and some time before my departure I learned from the Geographical Society that Mcintyre had strong hopes of having discovered traces of him."

"The whole of Australia, then, is not yet explored?" asked Lady Helena.

"No, madam, but very little of it. This continent is not much better known than the interior of Africa, and yet it is from no lack of enterprising travelers. From 1606 to 1862, more than fifty have been engaged in exploring along the coast and in the interior."

"Oh, fifty!" exclaimed McNabbs incredulously.

"No, no," objected the Major; "that is going too far."

"And I might go farther, McNabbs," replied the geographer, impatient of contradiction.

"Yes, McNabbs, quite that number."

"Farther still, Paganel."

"If you doubt me, I can give you the names."

"Oh, oh," said the Major, coolly. "That's just like you SAVANTS. You stick at nothing."

"Major, will you bet your Purdy-Moore rifle against my telescope?"

"Why not, Paganel, if it would give you any pleasure."

"Done, Major!" exclaimed Paganel. "You may say good-by to your rifle, for it will never shoot another chamois or fox unless I lend it to you, which I shall always be happy to do, by the by."

"And whenever you require the use of your telescope, Paganel, I shall be equally obliging," replied the Major, gravely.

"Let us begin, then; and ladies and gentlemen, you shall be our jury.

Robert, you must keep count."

This was agreed upon, and Paganel forthwith commenced.

"Mnemosyne! Goddess of Memory, chaste mother of the Muses!" he exclaimed, "inspire thy faithful servant and fervent worshiper! Two hundred and fifty-eight years ago, my friends, Australia was unknown. Strong suspicions were entertained of the existence of a great southern continent. In the library of your British Museum, Glenarvan, there are two charts, the date of which is 1550, which mention a country south of Asia, called by the Portuguese Great Java. But these charts are not sufficiently authentic. In the seventeenth century, in 1606, Quiros, a Spanish navigator, discovered a country which he named Australia de Espiritu Santo. Some authors imagine that this was the New Hebrides group, and not Australia. I am not going to discuss the question, however. Count Quiros, Robert, and let us pass on to another."

"ONE," said Robert.

"In that same year, Louis Vas de Torres, the second in command of the fleet of Quiros, pushed further south. But it is to Theodore Hertoge, a Dutchman, that the honor of the great discovery belongs. He touched the western coast of Australia in 25 degrees latitude, and called it Eendracht, after his vessel. From this time navigators increased. In 1618, Zeachen discovered the northern parts of the coast, and called them Arnheim and Diemen. In 1618, Jan Edels went along the western coast, and christened it by his own name. In 1622, Leuwin went down as far as the cape which became his namesake." And so Paganel continued with name after name until his hearers cried for mercy.

"Stop, Paganel," said Glenarvan, laughing heartily, "don't quite crush poor McNabbs. Be generous; he owns he is vanquished."

"And what about the rifle?" asked the geographer, triumphantly.

"It is yours, Paganel," replied the Major, "and I am very sorry for it; but your memory might gain an armory by such feats."

"It is certainly impossible to be better acquainted with Australia; not the least name, not even the most trifling fact—"

"As to the most trifling fact, I don't know about that," said the Major, shaking his head.

"What do you mean, McNabbs?" exclaimed Paganel.

"Simply that perhaps all the incidents connected with the discovery of Australia may not be known to you."

"Just fancy," retorted Paganel, throwing back his head proudly.

"Come now. If I name one fact you don't know, will you give me back my rifle?" said McNabbs.

"On the spot, Major."

"Very well, it's a bargain, then."

"Yes, a bargain; that's settled."

"All right. Well now, Paganel, do you know how it is that Australia does not belong to France?"

"But it seems to me—"

"Or, at any rate, do you know what's the reason the English give?" asked the Major.

"No," replied Paganel, with an air of vexation.

"Just because Captain Baudin, who was by no means a timid man, was so afraid in 1802, of the croaking of the Australian frogs, that he raised his anchor with all possible speed, and quitted the coast, never to return."

"What!" exclaimed Paganel. "Do they actually give that version of it in England? But it is just a bad joke."

"Bad enough, certainly, but still it is history in the United Kingdom."

"It's an insult!" exclaimed the patriotic geographer; "and they relate that gravely?"

"I must own it is the case," replied Glenarvan, amidst a general outburst of laughter. "Do you mean to say you have never heard of it before?"

"Never! But I protest against it. Besides, the English call us 'frog-eaters.' Now, in general, people are not afraid of what they eat."

"It is said, though, for all that," replied McNabbs. So the Major kept his famous rifle after all.

CHAPTER V THE STORM ON THE INDIAN OCEAN

Two days after this conversation, John Mangles announced that the DUNCAN was in longitude 113 degrees 37 minutes, and the passengers found on consulting the chart that consequently Cape Bernouilli could not be more than five degrees off. They must be sailing then in that part of the Indian Ocean which washed the Australian continent, and in four days might hope to see Cape Bernouilli appear on the horizon.

Hitherto the yacht had been favored by a strong westerly breeze, but now there were evident signs that a calm was impending, and on the 13th of December the wind fell entirely; as the sailors say, there was not enough to fill a cap.

There was no saying how long this state of the atmosphere might last. But for the powerful propeller the yacht would have been obliged to lie motionless as a log. The young captain was very much annoyed, however, at the prospect of emptying his coal-bunkers, for he had covered his ship with canvas, intending to take advantage of the slightest breeze.

"After all, though," said Glenarvan, with whom he was talking over the subject, "it is better to have no wind than a contrary one."

"Your Lordship is right," replied John Mangles; "but the fact is these sudden calms bring change of weather, and this is why I dread them. We are close on the trade winds, and if we get them ever so little in our teeth, it will delay us greatly."

"Well, John, what if it does? It will only make our voyage a little longer."

"Yes, if it does not bring a storm with it."

"Do you mean to say you think we are going to have bad weather?" replied Glenarvan, examining the sky, which from horizon to zenith seemed absolutely cloudless.

"I do," returned the captain. "I may say so to your Lordship, but I should not like to alarm Lady Glenarvan or Miss Grant."

"You are acting wisely; but what makes you uneasy?"

"Sure indications of a storm. Don't trust, my Lord, to the appearance of the sky. Nothing is more deceitful. For the last two days the barometer has been falling in a most ominous manner, and is now at 27 degrees. This is a warning I dare not neglect, for there is nothing I dread more than storms in the Southern Seas; I have had a taste of them already. The vapors which become condensed in the immense glaciers at the South Pole produce a current of air of extreme violence. This causes a struggle between the polar and equatorial winds, which results in cyclones, tornadoes, and all those multiplied varieties of tempest against which a ship is no match."

"Well, John," said Glenarvan, "the DUNCAN is a good ship, and her captain is a brave sailor. Let the storm come, we'll meet it!"

CHAPTER V THE STORM ON THE INDIAN OCEAN

John Mangles remained on deck the whole night, for though as yet the sky was still unclouded, he had such faith in his weather-glass, that he took every precaution that prudence could suggest. About 11 P. M. the sky began to darken in the south, and the crew were called up, and all the sails hauled in, except the foresail, brigantine, top-sail, and jib-boom. At midnight the wind freshened, and before long the cracking of the masts, and the rattling of the cordage, and groaning of the timbers, awakened the passengers, who speedily made their appearance on deck— at least Paganel, Glenarvan, the Major and Robert.

"Is it the hurricane?" asked Glenarvan quietly.

"Not yet," replied the captain; "but it is close at hand."

And he went on giving his orders to the men, and doing his best to make ready for the storm, standing, like an officer commanding a breach, with his face to the wind, and his gaze fixed on the troubled sky. The glass had fallen to 26 degrees, and the hand pointed to tempest.

It was one o'clock in the morning when Lady Helena and Miss Grant ventured upstairs on deck. But they no sooner made their appearance than the captain hurried toward them, and begged them to go below again immediately. The waves were already beginning to dash over the side of the ship, and the sea might any moment sweep right over her from stem to stern. The noise of the warring elements was so great that his words were scarcely audible, but Lady Helena took advantage of a sudden lull to ask if there was any danger.

"None whatever," replied John Mangles; "but you cannot remain on deck, madam, no more can Miss Mary."

The ladies could not disobey an order that seemed almost an entreaty, and they returned to their cabin. At the same moment the wind redoubled its fury, making the masts bend beneath the weight of the sails, and completely lifting up the yacht.

"Haul up the foresail!" shouted the captain. "Lower the topsail and jib-boom!"

Glenarvan and his companions stood silently gazing at the struggle between their good ship and the waves, lost in wondering and half-terrified admiration at the spectacle.

Just then, a dull hissing was heard above the noise of the elements. The steam was escaping violently, not by the funnel, but from the safety-valves of the boiler; the alarm whistle sounded unnaturally loud, and the yacht made a frightful pitch, overturning Wilson, who was at the wheel, by an unexpected blow from the tiller. The DUNCAN no longer obeyed the helm.

"What is the matter?" cried the captain, rushing on the bridge.

"The ship is heeling over on her side," replied Wilson.

"The engine! the engine!" shouted the engineer.

Away rushed John to the engine-room. A cloud of steam filled the room. The pistons were motionless in their cylinders, and they were apparently powerless, and the engine-driver, fearing for his boilers, was letting off the steam.

"What's wrong?" asked the captain.

"The propeller is bent or entangled," was the reply.

"It's not acting at all."

"Can't you extricate it?"

"It is impossible."

An accident like this could not be remedied, and John's only resource was to fall back on his sails, and seek to make an auxiliary of his most powerful enemy, the wind. He went up again on deck, and after explaining in a few words to Lord Glenarvan how things stood, begged him to retire to his cabin, with the rest of the passengers. But Glenarvan wished to remain above.

"No, your Lordship," said the captain in a firm tone,
"I must be alone with my men. Go into the saloon.
The vessel will have a hard fight with the waves, and they
would sweep you over without mercy."

"But we might be a help."

"Go in, my Lord, go in. I must indeed insist on it.
There are times when I must be master on board, and retire you must."

Their situation must indeed be desperate for John Mangles to speak in such authoritative language. Glenarvan was wise enough to understand this, and felt he must set an example in obedience. He therefore quitted the deck immediately with his three companions, and rejoined the ladies, who were anxiously watching the DENOUEMENT of this war with the elements.

"He's an energetic fellow, this brave John of mine!" said Lord Glenarvan, as he entered the saloon.

"That he is," replied Paganel. "He reminds me of your great
Shakespeare's boatswain in the 'Tempest,' who says to the king
on board: 'Hence! What care these roarers for the name of king?
To cabin! Silence! Trouble us not.'"

However, John Mangles did not lose a second in extricating his ship from the peril in which she was placed by the condition of her screw propeller. He resolved to rely on the mainsail for keeping in the right route as far as possible, and to brace the yards obliquely, so as not to present a direct front to the storm. The yacht turned about like a swift horse that feels the spur, and presented a broadside to the billows. The only question was, how long would she hold out with so little sail, and what sail could resist such violence for any length of time. The great advantage of keeping up the mainsail was that it presented to the waves only the most solid portions of the yacht, and kept her in the right course. Still it involved some peril, for the vessel might get engulfed between the waves, and not be able to raise herself. But Mangles felt there was no alternative, and all he could do was to keep the crew ready to alter the sail at any moment, and stay in the shrouds himself watching the tempest.

The remainder of the night was spent in this manner, and it was hoped that morning would bring a calm. But this was a delusive hope. At 8 A. M. the wind had increased to a hurricane.

John said nothing, but he trembled for his ship, and those on board. The DUNCAN made a frightful plunge forward, and for an instant the men thought she would never rise again. Already they had seized their hatchets to cut away the shrouds from the mainmast, but the next minute the sails were torn away by the tempest, and had flown off like gigantic albatrosses.

The yacht had risen once more, but she found herself at the mercy of the waves entirely now, with nothing to steady or direct her, and was so fearfully pitched and tossed about that every moment the captain expected the masts would break short off. John had no resource but to put up a forestaysail, and run before the gale. But this was no easy task. Twenty times over he had all his work to begin again, and it was 3 P. M. before his attempt succeeded. A mere shred of canvas though it was, it was enough to drive the DUNCAN forward with inconceivable rapidity to the northeast, of course in the same direction as the hurricane. Swiftness was their only chance of safety. Sometimes she would get in advance of the waves which carried her along, and cutting through them with her sharp prow, bury herself in their depths. At others, she would keep pace with them, and make such enormous leaps that there was imminent danger of her being pitched over on her side, and then again, every now and then the storm-driven sea would out-distance the yacht, and the angry billows would sweep over the deck from stem to stern with tremendous violence.

In this alarming situation and amid dreadful alternations of hope and despair, the 12th of December passed away, and the ensuing night, John Mangles never left his post, not even to take food. Though his impassive face betrayed no symptoms of fear, he was tortured with anxiety, and his steady gaze was fixed on the north, as if trying to pierce through the thick mists that enshrouded it.

There was, indeed, great cause for fear. The DUNCAN was out of her course, and rushing toward the Australian coast with a speed which nothing could lessen. To John Mangles it seemed as if a thunderbolt were driving them along. Every instant he expected the yacht would dash against some rock, for he reckoned the coast could not be more than twelve miles off, and better far be in mid ocean exposed to all its fury than too near land.

John Mangles went to find Glenarvan, and had a private talk with him about their situation, telling him frankly the true state of affairs, stating the case with all the coolness of a sailor prepared for anything and everything and he wound up by saying he might, perhaps, be obliged to cast the yacht on shore.

"To save the lives of those on board, my Lord," he added.

"Do it then, John," replied Lord Glenarvan.

"And Lady Helena, Miss Grant?"

"I will tell them at the last moment when all hope of keeping out at sea is over. You will let me know?"

"I will, my Lord."

Glenarvan rejoined his companions, who felt they were in imminent danger, though no word was spoken on the subject. Both ladies displayed great courage, fully equal to any of the party. Paganel descanted in the most inopportune manner about the direction of atmospheric currents, making interesting comparisons, between tornadoes, cyclones, and rectilinear tempests. The Major calmly awaited the end with the fatalism of a Mussulman.

About eleven o'clock, the hurricane appeared to decrease slightly. The damp mist began to clear away, and a sudden gleam of light revealed a low-lying shore about six miles distant. They were driving right down on it. Enormous breakers fifty feet high were dashing over it, and the fact of their height showed John there must be solid ground before they could make such a rebound.

"Those are sand-banks," he said to Austin.

"I think they are," replied the mate.

"We are in God's hands," said John. "If we cannot find any opening for the yacht, and if she doesn't find the way in herself, we are lost."

"The tide is high at present, it is just possible we may ride over those sand-banks."

"But just see those breakers. What ship could stand them.

Let us invoke divine aid, Austin!"

Meanwhile the DUNCAN was speeding on at a frightful rate. Soon she was within two miles of the sand-banks, which were still veiled from time to time in thick mist. But John fancied he could see beyond the breakers a quiet basin, where the DUNCAN would be in comparative safety. But how could she reach it?

All the passengers were summoned on deck, for now that the hour of shipwreck was at hand, the captain did not wish anyone to be shut up in his cabin.

"John!" said Glenarvan in a low voice to the captain, "I will try to save my wife or perish with her. I put Miss Grant in your charge."

"Yes, my Lord," replied John Mangles, raising Glenarvan's hand to his moistened eyes.

The yacht was only a few cables' lengths from the sandbanks. The tide was high, and no doubt there was abundance of water to float the ship over the dangerous bar; but these terrific breakers alternately lifting her up and then leaving her almost dry, would infallibly make her graze the sand-banks.

Was there no means of calming this angry sea? A last expedient struck the captain. "The oil, my lads!" he exclaimed. "Bring the oil here!"

The crew caught at the idea immediately; this was a plan that had been successfully tried already. The fury of the waves had been allayed before this time by covering them with a sheet of oil. Its effect is immediate, but very temporary. The moment after a ship has passed over the smooth surface, the sea redoubles its violence, and woe to the bark that follows. The casks of seal-oil were forthwith hauled up, for danger seemed to have given the men double strength. A few hatchet blows soon knocked in the heads, and they were then hung over the larboard and starboard.

"Be ready!" shouted John, looking out for a favorable moment.

In twenty seconds the yacht reached the bar. Now was the time.

"Pour out!" cried the captain, "and God prosper it!"

The barrels were turned upside down, and instantly a sheet of oil covered the whole surface of the water. The billows fell as if by magic, the whole foaming sea seemed leveled, and the DUNCAN flew over its tranquil bosom into a quiet basin beyond the formidable bar; but almost the same minute the ocean burst forth again with all its fury, and the towering breakers dashed over the bar with increased violence.

CHAPTER VI A HOSPITABLE COLONIST

THE captain's first care was to anchor his vessel securely. He found excellent moorage in five fathoms' depth of water, with a solid bottom of hard granite, which afforded a firm hold. There was no danger now of either being driven away or stranded at low water. After so many hours of danger, the DUNCAN found herself in a sort of creek, sheltered by a high circular point from the winds outside in the open sea.

Lord Glenarvan grasped John Mangles' hand, and simply said:

"Thank you, John."

This was all, but John felt it ample recompense. Glenarvan kept to himself the secret of his anxiety, and neither Lady Helena, nor Mary, nor Robert suspected the grave perils they had just escaped.

One important fact had to be ascertained. On what part of the coast had the tempest thrown them? How far must they go to regain the parallel. At what distance S. W. was Cape Bernouilli? This was soon determined by taking the position of the ship, and it was found that she had scarcely deviated two degrees from the route. They were in longitude 36 degrees 12 minutes, and latitude 32 degrees 67 minutes, at Cape Catastrophe, three hundred miles from Cape Bernouilli. The nearest port was Adelaide, the Capital of Southern Australia.

Could the DUNCAN be repaired there? This was the question. The extent of the injuries must first be ascertained, and in order to do this he ordered some of the men to dive down below the stern. Their report was that one of the branches of the screw was bent, and had got jammed against the stern post, which of course prevented all possibility of rotation. This was a serious damage, so serious as to require more skilful workmen than could be found in Adelaide.

After mature reflection, Lord Glenarvan and John Mangles came to the determination to sail round the Australian coast, stopping at Cape Bernouilli, and continuing their route south as far as Melbourne, where the DUNCAN could speedily be put right. This effected, they would proceed to cruise along the eastern coast to complete their search for the BRITANNIA.

This decision was unanimously approved, and it was agreed that they should start with the first fair wind. They had not to wait long for the same night the hurricane had ceased entirely, and there was only a manageable breeze from the S. W. Preparations for sailing were instantly commenced, and at four o'clock in the morning the crew lifted the anchors, and got under way with fresh canvas outspread, and a wind blowing right for the Australian shores.

Two hours afterward Cape Catastrophe was out of sight. In the evening they doubled Cape Borda, and came alongside Kangaroo Island. This is the largest of the Australian islands, and a great hiding place for runaway convicts. Its appearance was enchanting. The stratified rocks on the shore were richly carpeted with verdure, and innumerable kangaroos were jumping over the woods and plains, just as at the time of its discovery in 1802. Next day, boats were sent ashore to examine the coast minutely, as they were now on the 36th parallel, and between that and the 38th Glenarvan wished to leave no part unexplored.

The boats had hard, rough work of it now, but the men never complained. Glenarvan and his inseparable companion, Paganel, and young Robert generally accompanied them. But all this painstaking exploration came to nothing. Not a trace of the shipwreck could be seen anywhere. The Australian shores revealed no more than the Patagonian. However, it was not time yet to lose hope altogether, for they had not reached the exact point indicated by the document.

On the 20th of December, they arrived off Cape Bernouilli, which terminates Lacepede Bay, and yet not a vestige of the BRITANNIA had been discovered. Still this was not surprising, as it was two years since the occurrence of the catastrophe, and the sea might, and indeed must, have scattered and destroyed whatever fragments of the brig had remained. Besides, the natives who scent a wreck as the vultures do a dead body, would have pounced upon it and carried off the smaller DEBRIS. There was no doubt whatever Harry Grant and his companions had been made prisoners the moment the waves threw them on the shore, and been dragged away into the interior of the continent.

But if so, what becomes of Paganel's ingenious hypothesis about the document? viz., that it had been thrown into a river and carried by a current into the sea. That was a plausible enough theory in Patagonia, but not in the part of Australia intersected by the 37th parallel. Besides the Patagonian rivers, the Rio Colorado and the Rio Negro, flow into the sea along deserted solitudes, uninhabited and uninhabitable; while, on the contrary, the principal rivers of Australia—the Murray, the Yarrow, the Torrens, the Darling—all connected with each other, throw themselves into the ocean by well-frequented routes, and their mouths are ports of great activity. What likelihood, consequently, would there be that a fragile bottle would ever find its way along such busy thoroughfares right out into the Indian Ocean?

Paganel himself saw the impossibility of it, and confessed to the Major, who raised a discussion on the subject, that his hypothesis would be altogether illogical in Australia. It was evident that the degrees given related to the place where the BRITANNIA was actually shipwrecked and not the place of captivity, and that the bottle therefore had been thrown into the sea on the western coast of the continent.

However, as Glenarvan justly remarked, this did not alter the fact of Captain Grant's captivity in the least degree, though there was no reason now for prosecuting the search for him along the 37th parallel, more than any other. It followed, consequently, that if no traces of the BRITANNIA were discovered at Cape Bernouilli, the only thing to be done was to return to Europe. Lord Glenarvan would have been unsuccessful, but he would have done his duty courageously and conscientiously.

But the young Grants did not feel disheartened. They had long since said to themselves that the question of their father's deliverance was about to be finally settled. Irrevocably, indeed, they might consider it, for as Paganel had judiciously demonstrated, if the wreck had occurred on the eastern side, the survivors would have found their way back to their own country long since.

"Hope on! Hope on, Mary!" said Lady Helena to the young girl, as they neared the shore; "God's hand will still lead us."

CHAPTER VI A HOSPITABLE COLONIST

"Yes, Miss Mary," said Captain John. "Man's extremity is God's opportunity. When one way is hedged up another is sure to open."

"God grant it," replied Mary.

Land was quite close now. The cape ran out two miles into the sea, and terminated in a gentle slope, and the boat glided easily into a sort of natural creek between coral banks in a state of formation, which in course of time would be a belt of coral reefs round the southern point of the Australian coast. Even now they were quite sufficiently formidable to destroy the keel of a ship, and the BRITANNIA might likely enough have been dashed to pieces on them.

The passengers landed without the least difficulty on an absolutely desert shore. Cliffs composed of beds of strata made a coast line sixty to eighty feet high, which it would have been difficult to scale without ladders or cramp-irons. John Mangles happened to discover a natural breach about half a mile south. Part of the cliff had been partially beaten down, no doubt, by the sea in some equinoctial gale. Through this opening the whole party passed and reached the top of the cliff by a pretty steep path. Robert climbed like a young cat, and was the first on the summit, to the despair of Paganel, who was quite ashamed to see his long legs, forty years old, out-distanced by a young urchin of twelve. However, he was far ahead of the Major, who gave himself no concern on the subject.

They were all soon assembled on the lofty crags, and from this elevation could command a view of the whole plain below. It appeared entirely uncultivated, and covered with shrubs and bushes. Glenarvan thought it resembled some glens in the lowlands of Scotland, and Paganel fancied it like some barren parts of Britanny. But along the coast the country appeared to be inhabited, and significant signs of industry revealed the presence of civilized men, not savages.

"A mill!" exclaimed Robert.

And, sure enough, in the distance the long sails of a mill appeared, apparently about three miles off.

"It certainly is a windmill," said Paganel, after examining the object in question through his telescope.

"Let us go to it, then," said Glenarvan.

Away they started, and, after walking about half an hour, the country began to assume a new aspect, suddenly changing its sterility for cultivation. Instead of bushes, quick-set hedges met the eye, inclosing recent clearings. Several bullocks and about half a dozen horses were feeding in meadows, surrounded by acacias supplied from the vast plantations of Kangaroo Island. Gradually fields covered with cereals came in sight, whole acres covered with bristling ears of corn, hay-ricks in the shape of large bee-hives, blooming orchards, a fine garden worthy of Horace, in which the useful and agreeable were blended; then came sheds; commons wisely distributed, and last of all, a plain comfortable dwelling-house, crowned by a joyous-sounding mill, and fanned and shaded by its long sails as they kept constantly moving round.

Just at that moment a pleasant-faced man, about fifty years of age, came out of the house, warned, by the loud barking of four dogs, of the arrival of strangers. He was followed by five handsome strapping lads, his sons, and their mother, a fine tall woman. There was no mistaking the little group. This was a perfect type of the Irish colonist—a man who, weary of the miseries of his country, had come, with his family, to seek fortune and happiness beyond the seas.

Before Glenarvan and his party had time to reach the house and present themselves in due form, they heard the cordial words: "Strangers! welcome to the house of Paddy O'Moore!"

"You are Irish," said Glenarvan, "if I am not mistaken," warmly grasping the outstretched hand of the colonist.

"I was," replied Paddy O'Moore, "but now I am Australian. Come in, gentlemen, whoever you may be, this house is yours."

It was impossible not to accept an invitation given with such grace. Lady Helena and Mary Grant were led in by Mrs. O'Moore, while the gentlemen were assisted by his sturdy sons to disencumber themselves of their fire-arms.

An immense hall, light and airy, occupied the ground floor of the house, which was built of strong planks laid horizontally. A few wooden benches fastened against the gaily-colored walls, about ten stools, two oak chests on tin mugs, a large long table where twenty guests could sit comfortably, composed the furniture, which looked in perfect keeping with the solid house and robust inmates.

The noonday meal was spread; the soup tureen was smoking between roast beef and a leg of mutton, surrounded by large plates of olives, grapes, and oranges. The necessary was there and there was no lack of the superfluous. The host and hostess were so pleasant, and the big table, with its abundant fare, looked so inviting, that it would have been ungracious not to have seated themselves. The farm servants, on equal footing with their master, were already in their places to take their share of the meal. Paddy O'Moore pointed to the seats reserved for the strangers, and said to Glenarvan:

"I was waiting for you."

"Waiting for us!" replied Glenarvan in a tone of surprise.

"I am always waiting for those who come," said the Irishman; and then, in a solemn voice, while the family and domestics reverently stood, he repeated the BENEDICITE.

Dinner followed immediately, during which an animated conversation was kept up on all sides. From Scotch to Irish is but a handsbreadth. The Tweed, several fathoms wide, digs a deeper trench between Scotland and England than the twenty leagues of Irish Channel, which separates Old Caledonia from the Emerald Isle. Paddy O'Moore related his history. It was that of all emigrants driven by misfortune from their own country. Many come to seek fortunes who only find trouble and sorrow, and then they throw the blame on chance, and forget the true cause is their own idleness and vice and want of commonsense. Whoever is sober and industrious, honest and economical, gets on.

Such a one had been and was Paddy O'Moore. He left Dundalk, where he was starving, and came with his family to Australia, landed at Adelaide, where, refusing employment as a miner, he got engaged on a farm, and two months afterward commenced clearing ground on his own account.

The whole territory of South Australia is divided into lots, each containing eighty acres, and these are granted to colonists by the government. Any industrious man, by proper cultivation, can not only get a living out of his lot, but lay by pounds 80 a year.

Paddy O'Moore knew this. He profited by his own former experience, and laid by every penny he could till he had saved enough to purchase new lots. His family prospered, and his farm also. The Irish peasant became a landed proprietor, and though his little estate had only been under cultivation for two years, he had five hundred acres cleared by his own hands, and five hundred head of cattle. He was his own master, after having been a serf in Europe, and as independent as one can be in the freest country in the world.

His guests congratulated him heartily as he ended his narration; and Paddy O'Moore no doubt expected confidence for confidence, but he waited in vain. However, he was one of those discreet people who can say, "I tell you who I am, but I don't ask who you are." Glenarvan's great object was to get information about the BRITANNIA, and like a man who goes right to the point, he began at once to interrogate O'Moore as to whether he had heard of the shipwreck.

The reply of the Irishman was not favorable; he had never heard the vessel mentioned. For two years, at least, no ship had been wrecked on that coast, neither above nor below the Cape. Now, the date of the catastrophe was within two years. He could, therefore, declare positively that the survivors of the wreck had not been thrown on that part of the western shore. Now, my Lord," he added, "may I ask what interest you have in making the inquiry?"

This pointed question elicited in reply the whole history of the expedition. Glenarvan related the discovery of the document, and the various attempts that had been made to follow up the precise indications given of the whereabouts of the unfortunate captives; and he concluded his account by expressing his doubt whether they should ever find the Captain after all.

His dispirited tone made a painful impression on the minds of his auditors. Robert and Mary could not keep back their tears, and Paganel had not a word of hope or comfort to give them. John Mangles was grieved to the heart, though he, too, was beginning to yield to the feeling of hopelessness which had crept over the rest, when suddenly the whole party were electrified by hearing a voice exclaim: "My Lord, praise and thank God! if Captain Grant is alive, he is on this Australian continent."

CHAPTER VII THE QUARTERMASTER OF THE "BRITANNIA"

THE surprise caused by these words cannot be described.

Glenarvan sprang to his feet, and pushing back his seat, exclaimed:

"Who spoke?"

"I did," said one of the servants, at the far end of the table.

"You, Ayrton!" replied his master, not less bewildered than Glenarvan.

"Yes, it was I," rejoined Ayrton in a firm tone, though somewhat agitated voice. "A Scotchman like yourself, my Lord, and one of the shipwrecked crew of the BRITANNIA."

The effect of such a declaration may be imagined. Mary Grant fell back, half-fainting, in Lady Helena's arms, overcome by joyful emotion, and Robert, and Mangles, and Paganel started up and toward the man that Paddy O'Moore had addressed as AYRTON. He was a coarse-looking fellow, about forty-five years of age, with very bright eyes, though half-hidden beneath thick, overhanging brows. In spite of extreme leanness there was an air of unusual strength about him. He seemed all bone and nerves, or, to use a Scotch expression, as if he had not wasted time in making fat. He was broad-shouldered and of middle height, and though his features were coarse, his face was so full of intelligence and energy and decision, that he gave one a favorable impression. The interest he excited was still further heightened by the marks of recent suffering imprinted on his countenance. It was evident that he had endured long and severe hardships, and that he had borne them bravely and come off victor.

"You are one of the shipwrecked sailors of the BRITANNIA?" was Glenarvan's first question.

"Yes, my Lord; Captain Grant's quartermaster."

"And saved with him after the shipwreck?"

"No, my Lord, no. I was separated from him at that terrible moment, for I was swept off the deck as the ship struck."

"Then you are not one of the two sailors mentioned in the document?"

"No; I was not aware of the existence of the document. The captain must have thrown it into the sea when I was no longer on board."

"But the captain? What about the captain?"

"I believed he had perished; gone down with all his crew.

I imagined myself the sole survivor."

"But you said just now, Captain Grant was living."

"No, I said, '*if the captain is living.*'"

"And you added, '*he is on the Australian continent.*'"

"And, indeed, he cannot be anywhere else."

"Then you don't know where he is?"

"No, my Lord. I say again, I supposed he was buried beneath the waves, or dashed to pieces against the rocks. It was from you I learned that he was still alive."

"What then do you know?"

"Simply this—if Captain Grant is alive, he is in Australia."

"Where did the shipwreck occur?" asked Major McNabbs.

This should have been the first question, but in the excitement caused by the unexpected incident, Glenarvan cared more to know where the captain was, than where the BRITANNIA had been lost. After the Major's inquiry, however, Glenarvan's examination proceeded more logically, and before long all the details of the event stood out clearly before the minds of the company.

To the question put by the Major, Ayrton replied:

"When I was swept off the forecastle, when I was hauling in the jib-boom, the BRITANNIA was running right on the Australian coast. She was not more than two cables' length from it and consequently she must have struck just there."

"In latitude 37 degrees?" asked John Mangles.

"Yes, in latitude 37 degrees."

"On the west coast?"

"No, on the east coast," was the prompt reply.

"And at what date?"

"It was on the night of the 27th of June, 1862."

"Exactly, just exactly," exclaimed Glenarvan.

"You see, then, my Lord," continued Ayrton, "I might justly say, *If Captain Grant* is alive, he is on the Australian continent, and it is useless looking for him anywhere else."

"And we will look for him there, and find him too, and save him," exclaimed Paganel. "Ah, precious document," he added, with perfect NAIVETE, "you must own you have fallen into the hands of uncommonly shrewd people."

But, doubtless, nobody heard his flattering words, for Glenarvan and Lady Helena, and Mary Grant, and Robert, were too much engrossed with Ayrton to listen to anyone else. They pressed round him and grasped his hands. It seemed as if this man's presence was the sure pledge of Harry Grant's deliverance. If this sailor had escaped the perils of the shipwreck, why should not the captain? Ayrton was quite sanguine as to his existence; but on what part of the continent he was to be found, that he could not say. The replies the man gave to the thousand questions that assailed him on all sides were remarkably intelligent and exact. All the while he spake, Mary held one of his hands in hers. This sailor was a companion of her father's, one of the crew of the BRITANNIA. He had lived with Harry Grant, crossed the seas with him and shared his dangers. Mary could not keep her eyes off his face, rough and homely though it was, and she wept for joy.

Up to this time no one had ever thought of doubting either the veracity or identity of the quartermaster; but the Major, and perhaps John Mangles, now began to ask themselves if this Ayrton's word was to be absolutely believed. There was something suspicious about this unexpected meeting. Certainly the man had mentioned facts and dates which corresponded, and the minuteness of his details was most striking. Still exactness of details was no positive proof. Indeed, it has been noticed that a falsehood has sometimes gained ground by being exceedingly particular in minutiae. McNabbs, therefore, prudently refrained from committing himself by expressing any opinion.

John Mangles, however, was soon convinced when he heard Ayrton speak to the young girl about her father. He knew Mary and Robert quite well. He had seen them in

Glasgow when the ship sailed. He remembered them at the farewell breakfast given on board the BRITANNIA to the captain's friends, at which Sheriff Mcintyre was present. Robert, then a boy of ten years old, had been given into his charge, and he ran away and tried to climb the rigging.

"Yes, that I did, it is quite right," said Robert.

He went on to mention several other trifling incidents, without attaching the importance to them that John Mangles did, and when he stopped Mary Grant said, in her soft voice: "Oh, go on, Mr. Ayrton, tell us more about our father."

The quartermaster did his best to satisfy the poor girl, and Glenarvan did not interrupt him, though a score of questions far more important crowded into his mind. Lady Helena made him look at Mary's beaming face, and the words he was about to utter remained unspoken.

Ayrton gave an account of the BRITANNIA'S voyage across the Pacific. Mary knew most of it before, as news of the ship had come regularly up to the month of May, 1862. In the course of the year Harry Grant had touched at all the principal ports. He had been to the Hebrides, to New Guinea, New Zealand, and New Caledonia, and had succeeded in finding an important point on the western coast of Papua, where the establishment of a Scotch colony seemed to him easy, and its prosperity certain. A good port on the Molucca and Philippine route must attract ships, especially when the opening of the Suez Canal would have supplanted the Cape route. Harry Grant was one of those who appreciated the great work of M. De Lesseps, and would not allow political rivalries to interfere with international interests.

After reconnoitering Papua, the BRITANNIA went to provision herself at Callao, and left that port on the 30th of May, 1862, to return to Europe by the Indian Ocean and the Cape. Three weeks afterward, his vessel was disabled by a fearful storm in which they were caught, and obliged to cut away the masts. A leak sprang in the hold, and could not be stopped. The crew were too exhausted to work the pumps, and for eight days the BRITANNIA was tossed about in the hurricane like a shuttlecock. She had six feet of water in her hold, and was gradually sinking. The boats had been all carried away by the tempest; death stared them in the face, when, on the night of the 22d of June, as Paganel had rightly supposed, they came in sight of the eastern coast of Australia.

The ship soon neared the shore, and presently dashed violently against it. Ayrton was swept off by a wave, and thrown among the breakers, where he lost consciousness. When he recovered, he found himself in the hands of natives, who dragged him away into the interior of the country. Since that time he had never heard the BRITANNIA's name mentioned, and reasonably enough came to the conclusion that she had gone down with all hands off the dangerous reefs of Twofold Bay.

This ended Ayrton's recital, and more than once sorrowful exclamations were evoked by the story. The Major could not, in common justice, doubt its authenticity. The sailor was then asked to narrate his own personal history, which was short and simple enough. He had been carried by a tribe of natives four hundred miles north of the 37th parallel. He spent a miserable existence there— not that he was ill-treated, but the natives themselves lived miserably. He passed two long years of painful slavery among them, but always cherished in his heart the hope of one day regaining his freedom, and watching for the slightest opportunity that might turn up, though he knew that his flight would be attended with innumerable dangers.

At length one night in October, 1864, he managed to escape the vigilance of the natives, and took refuge in the depths of immense forests. For a whole month he subsisted on roots, edible ferns and mimosa gums, wandering through vast solitudes, guiding himself by the sun during the day and by the stars at night. He went on, though often almost despairingly, through bogs and rivers, and across mountains, till he had traversed the whole of the uninhabited part of the continent, where only a few bold travelers have ventured; and at last, in an exhausted and all but dying condition, he reached the hospitable dwelling of Paddy O'Moore, where he said he had found a happy home in exchange for his labor.

"And if Ayrton speaks well of me," said the Irish settler, when the narrative ended, "I have nothing but good to say of him. He is an honest, intelligent fellow and a good worker; and as long as he pleases, Paddy O'Moore's house shall be his."

Ayrton thanked him by a gesture, and waited silently for any fresh question that might be put to him, though he thought to himself that he surely must have satisfied all legitimate curiosity. What could remain to be said that he had not said a hundred times already. Glenarvan was just about to open a discussion about their future plan of action, profiting by this rencontre with Ayrton, and by the information he had given them, when Major McNabbs, addressing the sailor said, "You were quartermaster, you say, on the BRITANNIA?"

"Yes," replied Ayrton, without the least hesitation.

But as if conscious that a certain feeling of mistrust, however slight, had prompted the inquiry, he added, "I have my shipping papers with me; I saved them from the wreck."

He left the room immediately to fetch his official document, and, though hardly absent a minute, Paddy O'Moore managed to say, "My Lord, you may trust Ayrton; I vouch for his being an honest man. He has been two months now in my service, and I have never had once to find fault with him. I knew all this story of his shipwreck and his captivity. He is a true man, worthy of your entire confidence."

Glenarvan was on the point of replying that he had never doubted his good faith, when the man came in and brought his engagement written out in due form. It was a paper signed by the shipowners and Captain Grant. Mary recognized her father's writing at once. It was to certify that "Tom Ayrton, able-bodied seaman, was engaged as quartermaster on board the three-mast vessel, the BRITANNIA, Glasgow."

There could not possibly be the least doubt now of Ayrton's identity, for it would have been difficult to account for his possession of the document if he were not the man named in it.

"Now then," said Glenarvan, "I wish to ask everyone's opinion as to what is best to be done. Your advice, Ayrton, will be particularly valuable, and I shall be much obliged if you would let us have it."

After a few minutes' thought, Ayrton replied—"I thank you, my Lord, for the confidence you show towards me, and I hope to prove worthy of it. I have some knowledge of the country, and the habits of the natives, and if I can be of any service to you—"

"Most certainly you can," interrupted Glenarvan.

"I think with you," resumed Ayrton, "that the captain and his two sailors have escaped alive from the wreck, but since they have not found their way to the English settlement, nor been seen any where, I have no doubt that their fate has been similar to my own, and that they are prisoners in the hands of some of the native tribes."

"That's exactly what I have always argued," said Paganel.

"The shipwrecked men were taken prisoners, as they feared.
But must we conclude without question that, like yourself,
they have been dragged away north of the 37th parallel?"

"I should suppose so, sir; for hostile tribes would hardly remain anywhere near the districts under the British rule."

"That will complicate our search," said Glenarvan, somewhat disconcerted. "How can we possibly find traces of the captives in the heart of so vast a continent?"

No one replied, though Lady Helena's questioning glances at her companions seemed to press for an answer. Paganel even was silent. His ingenuity for once was at fault. John Mangles paced the cabin with great strides, as if he fancied himself on the deck of his ship, evidently quite nonplussed.

"And you, Mr. Ayrton," said Lady Helena at last, "what would you do?"

"Madam," replied Ayrton, readily enough, "I should re-embark in the DUNCAN, and go right to the scene of the catastrophe. There I should be guided by circumstances, and by any chance indications we might discover."

"Very good," returned Glenarvan; "but we must wait till the DUNCAN is repaired."

"Ah, she has been injured then?" said Ayrton.

"Yes," replied Mangles.

"To any serious extent?"

"No; but such injuries as require more skilful workmanship than we have on board. One of the branches of the screw is twisted, and we cannot get it repaired nearer than Melbourne."

"Well, let the ship go to Melbourne then," said Paganel, "and we will go without her to Twofold Bay."

"And how?" asked Mangles.

"By crossing Australia as we crossed America, keeping along the 37th parallel."

"But the DUNCAN?" repeated Ayrton, as if particularly anxious on that score.

"The DUNCAN can rejoin us, or we can rejoin her, as the case may be. Should we discover Captain Grant in the course of our journey, we can all return together to Melbourne. If we have to go on to the coast, on the contrary, then the DUNCAN can come to us there. Who has any objection to make? Have you, Major?"

"No, not if there is a practicable route across Australia."

"So practicable, that I propose Lady Helena and Miss Grant should accompany us."

"Are you speaking seriously?" asked Glenarvan.

"Perfectly so, my Lord. It is a journey of 350 miles, not more. If we go twelve miles a day it will barely take us a month, just long enough to put the vessel in trim. If we had to cross the continent in a lower latitude, at its wildest part, and traverse immense deserts, where there is no water and where the heat is tropical, and go where the most adventurous travelers have never yet ventured, that would be a different matter. But the 37th parallel cuts only through the province of Victoria, quite an English country, with roads and railways, and well populated almost everywhere. It is a journey you might make, almost, in a chaise, though a wagon would be better. It is a mere trip from London to Edinburgh, nothing more."

"What about wild beasts, though?" asked Glenarvan, anxious to go into all the difficulties of the proposal.

"There are no wild beasts in Australia."

"And how about the savages?"

"There are no savages in this latitude, and if there were, they are not cruel, like the New Zealanders."

"And the convicts?"

"There are no convicts in the southern provinces, only in the eastern colonies. The province of Victoria not only refused to admit them, but passed a law to prevent any ticket-of-leave men from other provinces from entering her territories. This very year the Government threatened to withdraw its subsidy from the Peninsular Company if their vessels continued to take in coal in those western parts of Australia where convicts are admitted. What! Don't you know that, and you an Englishman?"

"In the first place, I beg leave to say I am not an Englishman," replied Glenarvan.

"What M. Paganel says is perfectly correct," said Paddy O'Moore. "Not only the province of Victoria, but also Southern Australia, Queensland, and even Tasmania, have agreed to expel convicts from their territories. Ever since I have been on this farm, I have never heard of one in this Province."

"And I can speak for myself. I have never come across one."

"You see then, friends," went on Jacques Paganel, "there are few if any savages, no ferocious animals, no convicts, and there are not many countries of Europe for which you can say as much. Well, will you go?"

"What do you think, Helena?" asked Glenarvan.

"What we all think, dear Edward," replied Lady Helena, turning toward her companions; "let us be off at once."

CHAPTER VIII PREPARATION FOR THE JOURNEY

GLENARVAN never lost much time between adopting an idea and carrying it out. As soon as he consented to Paganel's proposition, he gave immediate orders to make arrangements for the journey with as little delay as possible. The time of starting was fixed for the 22d of December, the next day but one.

What results might not come out of this journey. The presence of Harry Grant had become an indisputable fact, and the chances of finding him had increased. Not that anyone expected to discover the captain exactly on the 37th parallel, which they intended strictly to follow, but they might come upon his track, and at all events, they were going to the actual spot where the wreck had occurred. That was the principal point.

Besides, if Ayrton consented to join them and act as their guide through the forests of the province of Victoria and right to the eastern coast, they would have a fresh chance of success. Glenarvan was sensible of this, and asked his host whether he would have any great objection to his asking Ayrton to accompany them, for he felt particularly desirous of securing the assistance of Harry Grant's old companion.

Paddy O'Moore consented, though he would regret the loss of his excellent servant.

"Well, then, Ayrton, will you come with us in our search expedition?"

Ayrton did not reply immediately. He even showed signs of hesitation; but at last, after due reflection, said, "Yes, my Lord, I will go with you, and if I can not take you to Captain Grant, I can at least take you to the very place where his ship struck."

"Thanks, Ayrton."

"One question, my Lord."

"Well?"

"Where will you meet the DUNCAN again?"

"At Melbourne, unless we traverse the whole continent from coast to coast."

"But the captain?"

"The captain will await my instructions in the port of Melbourne."

"You may depend on me then, my Lord."

"I will, Ayrton."

The quartermaster was warmly thanked by the passengers of the DUNCAN, and the children loaded him with caresses. Everyone rejoiced in his decision except the Irishman, who lost in him an intelligent and faithful helper. But Paddy understood the importance Glenarvan attached to the presence of the man, and submitted. The whole party then returned to the ship, after arranging a rendezvous with Ayrton, and ordering him to procure the necessary means of conveyance across the country.

When John Mangles supported the proposition of Paganel, he took for granted that he should accompany the expedition. He began to speak to Glenarvan at once about it, and adduced all sorts of arguments to advance his cause—his devotion to Lady Helena and his Lordship, how useful could he be in organizing the party, and how useless on board the DUNCAN; everything, in fact, but the main reason, and that he had no need to bring forward.

"I'll only ask you one question, John," said Glenarvan. "Have you entire confidence in your chief officer?"

"Absolute," replied Mangles, "Tom Austin is a good sailor. He will take the ship to her destination, see that the repairs are skilfully executed, and bring her back on the appointed day. Tom is a slave to duty and discipline. Never would he take it upon himself to alter or retard the execution of an order. Your Lordship may rely on him as on myself."

"Very well then, John," replied Glenarvan. "You shall go with us, for it would be advisable," he added, smiling, "that you should be there when we find Mary Grant's father."

"Oh! your Lordship," murmured John, turning pale. He could say no more, but grasped Lord Glenarvan's hand.

Next day, John Mangles and the ship's carpenter, accompanied by sailors carrying provisions, went back to Paddy O'Moore's house to consult the Irishman about the best method of transport. All the family met him, ready to give their best help. Ayrton was there, and gave the benefit of his experience.

On one point both he and Paddy agreed, that the journey should be made in a bullock-wagon by the ladies, and that the gentlemen should ride on horseback. Paddy could furnish both bullocks and vehicle. The vehicle was a cart twenty feet long, covered over by a tilt, and resting on four large wheels without spokes or felloes, or iron tires— in a word, plain wooden discs. The front and hinder part were connected by means of a rude mechanical contrivance, which did not allow of the vehicle turning quickly. There was a pole in front thirty-five feet long, to which the bullocks were to be yoked in couples. These animals were able to draw both with head and neck, as their yoke was fastened on the nape of the neck, and to this a collar was attached by an iron peg. It required great skill to drive such a long, narrow, shaky concern, and to guide such a team by a goad; but Ayrton had served his apprenticeship to it on the Irishman's farm, and Paddy could answer for his competency. The role of conductor was therefore assigned to him.

There were no springs to the wagon, and, consequently, it was not likely to be very comfortable; but, such as it was, they had to take it. But if the rough construction could not be altered, John Mangles resolved that the interior should be made as easy as possible. His first care was to divide it into two compartments by a wooden partition. The back one was intended for the provisions and luggage, and M. Olbinett's portable kitchen. The front was set apart especially for the ladies, and, under the carpenter's hands, was to be speedily converted into a comfortable room, covered with a thick carpet, and fitted up with a toilet table and two couches. Thick leather curtains shut in this apartment, and protected the occupants from the chilliness of the nights. In case of necessity, the gentlemen might shelter themselves here, when the violent rains came on, but a tent was to be their usual resting-place when the caravan camped for the night. John Mangles exercised all his ingenuity in furnishing the small space with everything that the two ladies could possibly require, and he succeeded so well, that neither Lady Helena nor Mary had much reason to regret leaving their cosy cabins on board the DUNCAN.

For the rest of the party, the preparations were soon made, for they needed much less. Strong horses were provided for Lord Glenarvan, Paganel, Robert Grant, McNabbs, and John Mangles; also for the two sailors, Wilson and Mulrady, who were to accompany their captain. Ayrton's place was, of course, to be in front of the wagon, and M. Olbinett, who did not much care for equitation, was to make room for himself among the baggage.

Horses and bullocks were grazing in the Irishman's meadows, ready to fetch at a moment's notice.

After all arrangements were made, and the carpenter set to work, John Mangles escorted the Irishman and his family back to the vessel, for Paddy wished to return the visit of Lord Glenarvan. Ayrton thought proper to go too, and about four o'clock the party came over the side of the DUNCAN.

They were received with open arms. Glenarvan would not be outstripped in politeness, and invited his visitors to stop and dine. His hospitality was willingly accepted. Paddy was quite amazed at the splendor of the saloon, and was loud in admiration of the fitting up of the cabins, and the carpets and hangings, as well as of the polished maple-wood of the upper deck. Ayrton's approbation was much less hearty, for he considered it mere costly superfluity.

But when he examined the yacht with a sailor's eye, the quartermaster of the BRITANNIA was as enthusiastic about it as Paddy. He went down into the hold, inspected the screw department and the engine-room, examining the engine thoroughly, and inquired about its power and consumption. He explored the coal-bunkers, the store-room, the powder-store, and armory, in which last he seemed to be particularly attracted by a cannon mounted on the forecastle. Glenarvan saw he had to do with a man who understood such matters, as was evident from his questions. Ayrton concluded his investigations by a survey of the masts and rigging.

"You have a fine vessel, my Lord," he said after his curiosity was satisfied.

"A good one, and that is best," replied Glenarvan.

"And what is her tonnage?"

"Two hundred and ten tons."

"I don't think I am far out," continued Ayrton, "in judging her speed at fifteen knots. I should say she could do that easily."

"Say seventeen," put in John Mangles, "and you've hit the mark."

"Seventeen!" exclaimed the quartermaster. "Why, not a man-of-war— not the best among them, I mean—could chase her!"

"Not one," replied Mangles. "The DUNCAN is a regular racing yacht, and would never let herself be beaten."

"Even at sailing?" asked Ayrton.

"Even at sailing."

"Well, my Lord, and you too, captain," returned Ayrton, "allow a sailor who knows what a ship is worth, to compliment you on yours."

"Stay on board of her, then, Ayrton," said Glenarvan; "it rests with yourself to call it yours."

"I will think of it, my Lord," was all Ayrton's reply.

Just then M. Olbinett came to announce dinner, and his Lordship repaired with his guests to the saloon.

"That Ayrton is an intelligent man," said Paganel to the Major.

"Too intelligent!" muttered McNabbs, who, without any apparent reason, had taken a great dislike to the face and manners of the quartermaster.

During the dinner, Ayrton gave some interesting details about the Australian continent, which he knew perfectly. He asked how many sailors were going to accompany the expedition, and seemed astonished to hear that only two were going. He advised Glenarvan to take all his best men, and even urged him to do it, which advice, by the way, ought to have removed the Major's suspicion.

"But," said Glenarvan, "our journey is not dangerous, is it?"

"Not at all," replied Ayrton, quickly.
"Well then, we'll have all the men we can on board.
Hands will be wanted to work the ship, and to help in the repairs.
Besides, it is of the utmost importance that she should meet us
to the very day, at whatever place may be ultimately selected.
Consequently, we must not lessen her crew."
Ayrton said nothing more, as if convinced his Lordship was right.
When evening came, Scotch and Irish separated.
Ayrton and Paddy O'Moore and family returned home.
Horses and wagons were to be ready the next day, and eight
o'clock in the morning was fixed for starting.

Lady Helena and Mary Grant soon made their preparations. They had less to do than Jacques Paganel, for he spent half the night in arranging, and wiping, and rubbing up the lenses of his telescope. Of course, next morning he slept on till the Major's stentorian voice roused him.

The luggage was already conveyed to the farm, thanks to John Mangles, and a boat was waiting to take the passengers. They were soon seated, and the young captain gave his final orders to Tom Austin, his chief officer. He impressed upon him that he was to wait at Melbourne for Lord Glenarvan's commands, and to obey them scrupulously, whatever they might be.

The old sailor told John he might rely on him, and, in the name of the men, begged to offer his Lordship their best wishes for the success of this new expedition.

A storm of hurrahs burst forth from the yacht as the boat rowed off. In ten minutes the shore was reached, and a quarter of an hour afterward the Irishman's farm. All was ready. Lady Helena was enchanted with her installation. The huge chariot, with its primitive wheels and massive planks, pleased her particularly. The six bullocks, yoked in pairs, had a patriarchal air about them which took her fancy. Ayrton, goad in hand, stood waiting the orders of this new master.

"My word," said Paganel, "this is a famous vehicle; it beats all the mail-coaches in the world. I don't know a better fashion of traveling than in a mountebank's caravan— a movable house, which goes or stops wherever you please. What can one wish better? The Samaratians understood that, and never traveled in any other way."

"Monsieur Paganel," said Lady Helena, "I hope I shall have the pleasure of seeing you in my SALONS."

"Assuredly, madam, I should count it an honor. Have you fixed the day?"

"I shall be at home every day to my friends," replied Lady Helena; "and you are—"

"The most devoted among them all," interrupted Paganel, gaily.

These mutual compliments were interrupted by the arrival of the seven horses, saddled and ready. They were brought by Paddy's sons, and Lord Glenarvan paid the sum stipulated for his various purchases, adding his cordial thanks, which the worthy Irishman valued at least as much as his golden guineas.

The signal was given to start, and Lady Helena and Mary took their places in the reserved compartment. Ayrton seated himself in front, and Olbinett scrambled in among the luggage. The rest of the party, well armed with carbines and revolvers, mounted their horses. Ayrton gave a peculiar cry, and his team set off. The wagon shook and the planks creaked, and the axles grated in the naves of the wheels; and before long the hospitable farm of the Irishman was out of sight.

CHAPTER IX A COUNTRY OF PARADOXES

IT was the 23d of December, 1864, a dull, damp, dreary month in the northern hemisphere; but on the Australian continent it might be called June. The hottest season of the year had already commenced, and the sun's rays were almost tropical, when Lord Glenarvan started on his new expedition.

Most fortunately the 37th parallel did not cross the immense deserts, inaccessible regions, which have cost many martyrs to science already. Glenarvan could never have encountered them. He had only to do with the southern part of Australia—viz., with a narrow portion of the province of Adelaide, with the whole of Victoria, and with the top of the reversed triangle which forms New South Wales.

It is scarcely sixty-two miles from Cape Bernouilli to the frontiers of Victoria. It was not above a two days' march, and Ayrton reckoned on their sleeping next night at Apsley, the most westerly town of Victoria.

The commencement of a journey is always marked by ardor, both in the horses and the horsemen. This is well enough in the horsemen, but if the horses are to go far, their speed must be moderated and their strength husbanded. It was, therefore, fixed that the average journey every day should not be more than from twenty-five to thirty miles.

Besides, the pace of the horses must be regulated by the slower pace of the bullocks, truly mechanical engines which lose in time what they gain in power. The wagon, with its passengers and provisions, was the very center of the caravan, the moving fortress. The horsemen might act as scouts, but must never be far away from it.

As no special marching order had been agreed upon, everybody was at liberty to follow his inclinations within certain limits. The hunters could scour the plain, amiable folks could talk to the fair occupants of the wagon, and philosophers could philosophize. Paganel, who was all three combined, had to be and was everywhere at once.

The march across Adelaide presented nothing of any particular interest. A succession of low hills rich in dust, a long stretch of what they call in Australia "bush," several prairies covered with a small prickly bush, considered a great dainty by the ovine tribe, embraced many miles. Here and there they noticed a species of sheep peculiar to New Holland— sheep with pig's heads, feeding between the posts of the telegraph line recently made between Adelaide and the coast.

Up to this time there had been a singular resemblance in the country to the monotonous plains of the Argentine Pampas. There was the same grassy flat soil, the same sharply-defined horizon against the sky. McNabbs declared they had never changed countries; but Paganel told him to wait, and he would soon see a difference. And on the faith of this assurance marvelous things were expected by the whole party.

CHAPTER IX A COUNTRY OF PARADOXES

In this fashion, after a march of sixty miles in two days, the caravan reached the parish of Apsley, the first town in the Province of Victoria in the Wimerra district.

The wagon was put up at the Crown Inn. Supper was soon smoking on the table. It consisted solely of mutton served up in various ways.

They all ate heartily, but talked more than they ate, eagerly asking Paganel questions about the wonders of the country they were just beginning to traverse. The amiable geographer needed no pressing, and told them first that this part of it was called Australia Felix.

"Wrongly named!" he continued. "It had better have been called rich, for it is true of countries, as individuals, that riches do not make happiness. Thanks to her gold mines, Australia has been abandoned to wild devastating adventurers. You will come across them when we reach the gold fields."

"Is not the colony of Victoria of but a recent origin?" asked Lady Glenarvan.

"Yes, madam, it only numbers thirty years of existence.

It was on the 6th of June, 1835, on a Tuesday—"

"At a quarter past seven in the evening," put in the Major, who delighted in teasing the Frenchman about his precise dates.

"No, at ten minutes past seven," replied the geographer, gravely, "that Batman and Falckner first began a settlement at Port Phillip, the bay on which the large city of Melbourne now stands. For fifteen years the colony was part of New South Wales, and recognized Sydney as the capital; but in 1851, she was declared independent, and took the name of Victoria."

"And has greatly increased in prosperity since then,

I believe," said Glenarvan.

"Judge for yourself, my noble friend," replied Paganel. "Here are the numbers given by the last statistics; and let McNabbs say as he likes, I know nothing more eloquent than statistics."

"Go on," said the Major.

"Well, then, in 1836, the colony of Port Phillip had 224 inhabitants. To-day the province of Victoria numbers 550,000. Seven millions of vines produce annually 121,- 000 gallons of wine. There are 103,000 horses spreading over the plains, and 675,272 horned cattle graze in her wide-stretching pastures."

"Is there not also a certain number of pigs?" inquired McNabbs.

"Yes, Major, 79,625."

"And how many sheep?"

"7,115,943, McNabbs."

"Including the one we are eating at this moment."

"No, without counting that, since it is three parts devoured."

"Bravo, Monsieur Paganel," exclaimed Lady Helena, laughing heartily. "It must be owned you are posted up in geographical questions, and my cousin McNabbs need not try and find you tripping."

"It is my calling, Madam, to know this sort of thing, and to give you the benefit of my information when you please. You may therefore believe me when I tell you that wonderful things are in store for you in this strange country."

"It does not look like it at present," said McNabbs, on purpose to tease Paganel.

"Just wait, impatient Major," was his rejoinder. "You have hardly put your foot on the frontier, when you turn round and abuse it. Well, I say and say again, and will always maintain that this is the most curious country on the earth. Its formation, and nature, and products, and climate, and even its future disappearance have amazed, and are now amazing, and will amaze, all the SAVANTS in the world. Think, my friends, of a continent, the margin of which, instead of the center, rose out of the waves originally like a gigantic ring, which encloses, perhaps, in its center, a sea partly evaporated, the waves of which are drying up daily; where humidity does not exist either in the air or in the soil; where the trees lose their bark every year, instead of their leaves; where the leaves present their sides to the sun and not their face, and consequently give no shade; where the wood is often incombustible, where good-sized stones are dissolved by the rain; where the forests are low and the grasses gigantic; where the animals are strange; where quadrupeds have beaks, like the echidna, or ornithorhynchus, and naturalists have been obliged to create a special order for them, called monotremes; where the kangaroos leap on unequal legs, and sheep have pigs' heads; where foxes fly about from tree to tree; where the swans are black; where rats make nests; where the bower-bird opens her reception-rooms to receive visits from her feathered friends; where the birds astonish the imagination by the variety of their notes and their aptness; where one bird serves for a clock, and another makes a sound like a postilion cracking of a whip, and a third imitates a knife-grinder, and a fourth the motion of a pendulum; where one laughs when the sun rises, and another cries when the sun sets! Oh, strange, illogical country, land of paradoxes and anomalies, if ever there was one on earth—the learned botanist Grimard was right when he said, 'There is that Australia, a sort of parody, or rather a defiance of universal laws in the face of the rest of the world.'"

Paganel's tirade was poured forth in the most impetuous manner, and seemed as if it were never coming to an end. The eloquent secretary of the Geographical Society was no longer master of himself. He went on and on, gesticulating furiously, and brandishing his fork to the imminent danger of his neighbors. But at last his voice was drowned in a thunder of applause, and he managed to stop.

Certainly after such an enumeration of Australian peculiarities, he might have been left in peace but the Major said in the coolest tone possible: "And is that all, Paganel?"

"No, indeed not," rejoined the Frenchman, with renewed vehemence.

"What!" exclaimed Lady Helena; "there are more wonders still in Australia?"

"Yes, Madam, its climate. It is even stranger than its productions."

"Is it possible?" they all said.

"I am not speaking of the hygienic qualities of the climate," continued Paganel, "rich as it is in oxygen and poor in azote. There are no damp winds, because the trade winds blow regularly on the coasts, and most diseases are unknown, from typhus to measles, and chronic affections."

"Still, that is no small advantage," said Glenarvan.

"No doubt; but I am not referring to that, but to one quality it has which is incomparable."

"And what is that?"

"You will never believe me."

"Yes, we will," exclaimed his auditors, their curiosity aroused by this preamble.

"Well, it is—"

"It is what?"

"It is a moral regeneration."

"A moral regeneration?"

"Yes," replied the SAVANT, in a tone of conviction. "Here metals do not get rust on them by exposure to the air, nor men. Here the pure, dry atmosphere whitens everything rapidly, both linen and souls. The virtue of the climate must have been well known in England when they determined to send their criminals here to be reformed."

"What! do you mean to say the climate has really any such influence?" said Lady Helena.

"Yes, Madam, both on animals and men."

"You are not joking, Monsieur Paganel?"

"I am not, Madam. The horses and the cattle here are of incomparable docility. You see it?"

"It is impossible!"

"But it is a fact. And the convicts transported into this reviving, salubrious air, become regenerated in a few years. Philanthropists know this. In Australia all natures grow better."

"But what is to become of you then, Monsieur Paganel, in this privileged country—you who are so good already?" said Lady Helena. "What will you turn out?"

"Excellent, Madam, just excellent, and that's all."

CHAPTER X AN ACCIDENT

THE next day, the 24th of December, they started at daybreak. The heat was already considerable, but not unbearable, and the road was smooth and good, and allowed the cavalcade to make speedy progress. In the evening they camped on the banks of the White Lake, the waters of which are brackish and undrinkable.

Jacques Paganel was obliged to own that the name of this lake was a complete misnomer, for the waters were no more white than the Black Sea is black, or the Red Sea red, or the Yellow River yellow, or the Blue Mountains blue. However, he argued and disputed the point with all the *amour propre* of a geographer, but his reasoning made no impression.

M. Olbinett prepared the evening meal with his accustomed punctuality, and after this was dispatched, the travelers disposed themselves for the night in the wagon and in the tent, and were soon sleeping soundly, notwithstanding the melancholy howling of the "dingoes," the jackals of Australia.

A magnificent plain, thickly covered with chrysanthemums, stretched out beyond the lake, and Glenarvan and his friends would gladly have explored its beauties when they awoke next morning, but they had to start. As far as the eye could reach, nothing was visible but one stretch of prairie, enameled with flower, in all the freshness and abundance of spring. The blue flowers of the slender-leaved flax, combined with the bright hues of the scarlet acanthus, a flower peculiar to the country.

A few cassowaries were bounding over the plain, but it was impossible to get near them. The Major was fortunate enough, however, to hit one very rare animal with a ball in the leg. This was the jabiru, a species which is fast disappearing, the gigantic crane of the English colonies. This winged creature was five feet high, and his wide, conical, extremely pointed beak, measured eighteen inches in length. The violet and purple tints of his head contrasted vividly with the glossy green of his neck, and the dazzling whiteness of his throat, and the bright red of his long legs. Nature seems to have exhausted in its favor all the primitive colors on her palette.

Great admiration was bestowed on this bird, and the Major's spoil would have borne the honors of the day, had not Robert come across an animal a few miles further on, and bravely killed it. It was a shapeless creature, half porcupine, half ant-eater, a sort of unfinished animal belonging to the first stage of creation. A long glutinous extensible tongue hung out of his jaws in search of the ants, which formed its principal food.

"It is an echidna," said Paganel. "Have you ever seen such a creature?"

"It is horrible," replied Glenarvan.

"Horrible enough, but curious, and, what's more, peculiar to Australia. One might search for it in vain in any other part of the world."

CHAPTER X AN ACCIDENT

Naturally enough, the geographer wished to preserve this interesting specimen of monotremata, and wanted to stow it away in the luggage; but M. Olbinett resented the idea so indignantly, that the SAVANT was obliged to abandon his project.

About four o'clock in the afternoon, John Mangles descried an enormous column of smoke about three miles off, gradually overspreading the whole horizon. What could be the cause of this phenomenon? Paganel was inclined to think it was some description of meteor, and his lively imagination was already in search of an explanation, when Ayrton cut short all his conjectures summarily, by announcing that the cloud of dust was caused by a drove of cattle on the road.

The quartermaster proved right, for as the cloud came nearer, quite a chorus of bleatings and neighings, and bellowing's escaped from it, mingled with the loud tones of a human voice, in the shape of cries, and whistles, and vociferations.

Presently a man came out of the cloud. This was the leader-in-chief of the four-footed army. Glenarvan advanced toward him, and friendly relations were speedily established between them. The leader, or to give him his proper designation, the stock-keeper, was part owner of the drove. His name was Sam Machell, and he was on his way from the eastern provinces to Portland Bay.

The drove numbered 12,075 head in all, or 1,000 bullocks, 11,000 sheep, and 75 horses. All these had been bought in the Blue Mountains in a poor, lean condition, and were going to be fatted up on the rich pasture lands of Southern Australia, and sold again at a great profit. Sam Machell expected to get pounds 2 on each bullock, and 10s. on every sheep, which would bring him in pounds 3,750. This was doing good business; but what patience and energy were required to conduct such a restive, stubborn lot to their destination, and what fatigues must have to be endured. Truly the gain was hardly earned.

Sam Machell told his history in a few words, while the drove continued their march among the groves of mimosas. Lady Helena and Mary and the rest of the party seated themselves under the shade of a wide-spreading gum-tree, and listened to his recital.

It was seven months since Sam Machell had started. He had gone at the rate of ten miles a day, and his interminable journey would last three months longer. His assistants in the laborious task comprised twenty dogs and thirty men, five of whom were blacks, and very serviceable in tracking up any strayed beasts. Six wagons made the rear-guard. All the men were armed with stockwhips, the handles of which are eighteen inches long, and the lash nine feet, and they move about among the ranks, bringing refractory animals back into order, while the dogs, the light cavalry of the regiment, preserved discipline in the wings.

The travelers were struck with the admirable arrangement of the drove. The different stock were kept apart, for wild sheep and bullocks would not have got on together at all. The bullocks would never have grazed where the sheep had passed along, and consequently they had to go first, divided into two battalions. Five regiments of sheep followed, in charge of twenty men, and last of all came the horses.

Sam Machell drew the attention of his auditors to the fact that the real guides of the drove were neither the men nor the dogs, but the oxen themselves, beasts of superior intelligence, recognized as leaders by their congenitors. They advanced in front with perfect gravity, choosing the best route by instinct, and fully alive to their claim to respect. Indeed, they were obliged to be studied and humored in everything, for the whole drove obeyed them implicitly. If they took it into their heads to stop, it was a matter of necessity to yield to their good pleasure, for not a single animal would move a step till these leaders gave the signal to set off.

Sundry details, added by the stock-keeper, completed the history of this expedition, worthy of being written, if not commended by Xenophon himself. As long as the troop marched over the plains it was well enough, there was little difficulty or fatigue. The animals fed as they went along, and slaked their thirst at the numerous creeks that watered the plains, sleeping at night and making good progress in the day, always obedient and tractable to the dogs. But when they had to go through great forests and groves of eucalyptus and mimosas, the difficulties increased. Platoons, battalions and regiments got all mixed together or scattered, and it was a work of time to collect them again. Should a "leader" unfortunately go astray, he had to be found, cost what it might, on pain of a general disbandment, and the blacks were often long days in quest of him, before their search was successful. During the heavy rains the lazy beasts refused to stir, and when violent storms chanced to occur, the creatures became almost mad with terror, and were seized with a wild, disorderly panic.

However, by dint of energy and ambition, the stock-keeper triumphed over these difficulties, incessantly renewed though they were. He kept steadily on; mile after mile of plains and woods, and mountains, lay behind. But in addition to all his other qualities, there was one higher than all that he specially needed when they came to rivers. This was patience—patience that could stand any trial, and not only could hold out for hours and days, but for weeks. The stock-keeper would be himself forced to wait on the banks of a stream that might have been crossed at once. There was nothing to hinder but the obstinacy of the herd. The bullocks would taste the water and turn back. The sheep fled in all directions, afraid to brave the liquid element. The stock-keeper hoped when night came he might manage them better, but they still refused to go forward. The rams were dragged in by force, but the sheep would not follow. They tried what thirst would do, by keeping them without drink for several days, but when they were brought to the river again, they simply quenched their thirst, and declined a more intimate acquaintance with the water. The next expedient employed was to carry all the lambs over, hoping the mothers would be drawn after them, moved by their cries. But the lambs might bleat as pitifully as they liked, the mothers never stirred. Sometimes this state of affairs would last a whole month, and the stock-keeper would be driven to his wits' end by his bleating, bellowing, neighing army. Then all of a sudden, one fine day, without rhyme or reason, a detachment would take it into their heads to make a start across, and the only difficulty now was to keep the whole herd from rushing helter-skelter after them. The wildest confusion set in among the ranks, and numbers of the animals were drowned in the passage.

Such was the narrative of Sam Machell. During its recital, a considerable part of the troop had filed past in good order. It was time for him to return to his place at their head, that he might be able to choose the best pasturage. Taking leave of Lord Glenarvan, he sprang on a capital horse of the native breed, that one of his men held waiting for him, and after shaking hands cordially with everybody all round, took his departure. A few minutes later, nothing was visible of the stock-keeper and his troop but a cloud of dust.

The wagon resumed its course in the opposite direction, and did not stop again till they halted for the night at the foot of Mount Talbot.

Paganel made the judicious observation that it was the 25th of December, the Christmas Day so dear to English hearts. But the steward had not forgotten it, and an appetizing meal was soon ready under the tent, for which he deserved and received warm compliments from the guests. Indeed, M. Olbinett had quite excelled himself on this occasion. He produced from his stores such an array of European dishes as is seldom seen in the Australian desert. Reindeer hams, slices of salt beef, smoked salmon, oat cakes, and barley meal scones; tea *ad libitum*, and whisky in abundance, and several bottles of port, composed this astonishing meal. The little party might have thought themselves in the grand dining-hall of Malcolm Castle, in the heart of the Highlands of Scotland.

The next day, at 11 A. M., the wagon reached the banks of the Wimerra on the 143d meridian.

The river, half a mile in width, wound its limpid course between tall rows of gum-trees and acacias. Magnificent specimens of the MYRTACEA, among others, the *metrosideros speciosa*, fifteen feet high, with long drooping branches, adorned with red flowers. Thousands of birds, the lories, and greenfinches, and gold-winged pigeons, not to speak of the noisy paroquets, flew about in the green branches. Below, on the bosom of the water, were a couple of shy and unapproachable black swans. This *rara avis* of the Australian rivers soon disappeared among the windings of the Wimerra, which water the charming landscape in the most capricious manner.

The wagon stopped on a grassy bank, the long fringes of which dipped in the rapid current. There was neither raft nor bridge, but cross over they must. Ayrton looked about for a practicable ford. About a quarter of a mile up the water seemed shallower, and it was here they determined to try to pass over. The soundings in different parts showed a depth of three feet only, so that the wagon might safely enough venture.

"I suppose there is no other way of fording the river?" said Glenarvan to the quartermaster.

"No, my Lord; but the passage does not seem dangerous.

We shall manage it."

"Shall Lady Glenarvan and Miss Grant get out of the wagon?"

"Not at all. My bullocks are surefooted, and you may rely on me for keeping them straight."

"Very well, Ayrton; I can trust you."

The horsemen surrounded the ponderous vehicle, and all stepped boldly into the current. Generally, when wagons have to ford rivers, they have empty casks slung all round them, to keep them floating on the water; but they had no such swimming belt with them on this occasion, and they could only depend on the sagacity of the animals and the prudence of Ayrton, who directed the team. The Major and the two sailors were some feet in advance. Glenarvan and John Mangles went at the sides of the wagon, ready to lend any assistance the fair travelers might require, and Paganel and Robert brought up the rear.

All went well till they reached the middle of the Wimerra, but then the hollow deepened, and the water rose to the middle of the wheels. The bullocks were in danger of losing their footing, and dragging with them the oscillating vehicle. Ayrton devoted himself to his task courageously. He jumped into the water, and hanging on by the bullocks' horns, dragged them back into the right course.

Suddenly the wagon made a jolt that it was impossible to prevent; a crack was heard, and the vehicle began to lean over in a most precarious manner. The water now rose to the ladies' feet; the whole concern began to float, though John Mangles and Lord Glenarvan hung on to the side. It was an anxious moment.

Fortunately a vigorous effort drove the wagon toward the opposite shore, and the bank began to slope upward, so that the horses and bullocks were able to regain their footing, and soon the whole party found themselves on the other side, glad enough, though wet enough too.

The fore part of the wagon, however, was broken by the jolt, and Glenarvan's horse had lost a shoe.

This was an accident that needed to be promptly repaired. They looked at each other hardly knowing what to do, till Ayrton proposed he should go to Black Point Station, twenty miles further north, and bring back a blacksmith with him.

"Yes, go, my good fellow," said Glenarvan. "How long will it take you to get there and back?"

"About fifteen hours," replied Ayrton, "but not longer."

"Start at once, then, and we will camp here, on the banks of the Wimerra, till you return."

CHAPTER XI CRIME OR CALAMITY

IT was not without apprehension that the Major saw Ayrton quit the Wimerra camp to go and look for a blacksmith at the Black Point Station. But he did not breathe a word of his private misgivings, and contented himself with watching the neighborhood of the river; nothing disturbed the repose of those tranquil glades, and after a short night the sun reappeared on the horizon.

As to Glenarvan, his only fear was lest Ayrton should return alone.

If they fail to find a workman, the wagon could not resume the journey.

This might end in a delay of many days, and Glenarvan, impatient to

succeed, could brook no delay, in his eagerness to attain his object.

Ayrton luckily had lost neither his time nor his trouble. He appeared next morning at daybreak, accompanied by a man who gave himself out as the blacksmith from Black-Point Station. He was a powerful fellow, and tall, but his features were of a low, brutal type, which did not prepossess anyone in his favor. But that was nothing, provided he knew his business. He scarcely spoke, and certainly he did not waste his breath in useless words.

"Is he a good workman?" said John Mangles to the quartermaster.

"I know no more about him than you do, captain," said Ayrton.

"But we shall see."

The blacksmith set to work. Evidently that was his trade, as they could plainly see from the way he set about repairing the forepart of the wagon. He worked skilfully and with uncommon energy. The Major observed that the flesh of his wrists was deeply furrowed, showing a ring of extravasated blood. It was the mark of a recent injury, which the sleeve of an old woolen shirt could not conceal. McNabbs questioned the blacksmith about those sores which looked so painful. The man continued his work without answering. Two hours more and the damage the carriage had sustained was made good. As to Glenarvan's horse, it was soon disposed of. The blacksmith had had the forethought to bring the shoes with him. These shoes had a peculiarity which did not escape the Major; it was a trefoil clumsily cut on the back part. McNabbs pointed it out to Ayrton.

"It is the Black-Point brand," said the quartermaster. "That enables them to track any horses that may stray from the station, and prevents their being mixed with other herds."

The horse was soon shod. The blacksmith claimed his wage, and went off without uttering four words.

Half an hour later, the travelers were on the road. Beyond the grove of mimosas was a stretch of sparsely timbered country, which quite deserved its name of "open plain." Some fragments of quartz and ferruginous rock lay among the scrub and the tall grass, where numerous flocks were feeding. Some miles farther the wheels of the wagon plowed deep into the alluvial soil, where irregular creeks murmured in their beds, half hidden among giant reeds. By-and-by they skirted vast salt lakes, rapidly evaporating. The journey was accomplished without trouble, and, indeed, without fatigue.

Lady Helena invited the horsemen of the party to pay her a visit in turns, as her reception-room was but small, and in pleasant converse with this amiable woman they forgot the fatigue of their day's ride.

Lady Helena, seconded by Miss Mary, did the honors of their ambulatory house with perfect grace. John Mangles was not forgotten in these daily invitations, and his somewhat serious conversation was not unpleasing.

The party crossed, in a diagonal direction, the mail-coach road from Crowland to Horsham, which was a very dusty one, and little used by pedestrians.

The spurs of some low hills were skirted at the boundary of Talbot County, and in the evening the travelers reached a point about three miles from Maryborough. The fine rain was falling, which, in any other country, would have soaked the ground; but here the air absorbed the moisture so wonderfully that the camp did not suffer in the least.

Next day, the 29th of December, the march was delayed somewhat by a succession of little hills, resembling a miniature Switzerland. It was a constant repetition of up and down hill, and many a jolt besides, all of which were scarcely pleasant. The travelers walked part of the way, and thought it no hardship.

At eleven o'clock they arrived at Carisbrook, rather an important municipality. Ayrton was for passing outside the town without going through it, in order, he said, to save time. Glenarvan concurred with him, but Paganel, always eager for novelties, was for visiting Carisbrook. They gave him his way, and the wagon went on slowly.

Paganel, as was his custom, took Robert with him. His visit to the town was very short, but it sufficed to give him an exact idea of Australian towns. There was a bank, a court-house, a market, a church, and a hundred or so of brick houses, all exactly alike. The whole town was laid out in squares, crossed with parallel streets in the English fashion. Nothing could be more simple, nothing less attractive. As the town grows, they lengthen the streets as we lengthen the trousers of a growing child, and thus the original symmetry is undisturbed.

Carisbrook was full of activity, a remarkable feature in these towns of yesterday. It seems in Australia as if towns shot up like trees, owing to the heat of the sun. Men of business were hurrying along the streets; gold buyers were hastening to meet the incoming escort; the precious metal, guarded by the local police, was coming from the mines at Bendigo and Mount Alexander. All the little world was so absorbed in its own interests, that the strangers passed unobserved amid the laborious inhabitants.

After an hour devoted to visiting Carisbrook, the two visitors rejoined their companions, and crossed a highly cultivated district. Long stretches of prairie, known as the "Low Level Plains," next met their gaze, dotted with countless sheep, and shepherds' huts. And then came a sandy tract, without any transition, but with the abruptness of change so characteristic of Australian scenery. Mount Simpson and Mount Terrengower marked the southern point where the boundary of the Loddon district cuts the 144th meridian.

As yet they had not met with any of the aboriginal tribes living in the savage state. Glenarvan wondered if the Australians were wanting in Australia, as the Indians had been wanting in the Pampas of the Argentine district; but Paganel told him that, in that latitude, the natives frequented chiefly the Murray Plains, about one hundred miles to the eastward.

"We are now approaching the gold district," said he, "in a day or two we shall cross the rich region of Mount Alexander. It was here that the swarm of diggers alighted in 1852; the natives had to fly to the interior. We are in civilized districts without seeing any sign of it; but our road will, before the day is over, cross the railway which connects the Murray with the sea. Well, I must confess, a railway in Australia does seem to me an astonishing thing!"

"And pray, why, Paganel?" said Glenarvan.

"Why? because it jars on one's ideas. Oh! I know you English are so used to colonizing distant possessions. You, who have electric telegraphs and universal exhibitions in New Zealand, you think it is all quite natural. But it dumb-founders the mind of a Frenchman like myself, and confuses all one's notions of Australia!"

"Because you look at the past, and not at the present," said John Mangles.

A loud whistle interrupted the discussion. The party were within a mile of the railway. Quite a number of persons were hastening toward the railway bridge. The people from the neighboring stations left their houses, and the shepherds their flocks, and crowded the approaches to the railway. Every now and then there was a shout, "The railway! the railway!"

Something serious must have occurred to produce such an agitation.

Perhaps some terrible accident.

Glenarvan, followed by the rest, urged on his horse. In a few minutes he arrived at Camden Bridge and then he became aware of the cause of such an excitement.

A fearful accident had occurred; not a collision, but a train had gone off the line, and then there had been a fall. The affair recalled the worst disasters of American railways. The river crossed by the railway was full of broken carriages and the engine. Whether the weight of the train had been too much for the bridge, or whether the train had gone off the rails, the fact remained that five carriages out of six fell into the bed of the Loddon, dragged down by the locomotive. The sixth carriage, miraculously preserved by the breaking of the coupling chain, remained on the rails, six feet from the abyss. Below nothing was discernible but a melancholy heap of twisted and blackened axles, shattered wagons, bent rails, charred sleepers; the boiler, burst by the shock, had scattered its plates to enormous distances. From this shapeless mass of ruins flames and black smoke still rose. After the fearful fall came fire, more fearful still! Great tracks of blood, scattered limbs, charred trunks of bodies, showed here and there; none could guess how many victims lay dead and mangled under those ruins.

Glenarvan, Paganel, the Major, Mangles, mixing with the crowd, heard the current talk. Everyone tried to account for the accident, while doing his utmost to save what could be saved.

"The bridge must have broken," said one.

"Not a bit of it. The bridge is whole enough; they must have forgotten to close it to let the train pass. That is all."

It was, in fact, a swing bridge, which opened for the convenience of the boats. Had the guard, by an unpardonable oversight, omitted to close it for the passage of the train, so that the train, coming on at full speed, was precipitated into the Loddon? This hypothesis seemed very admissible; for although one-half of the bridge lay beneath the ruins of the train, the other half, drawn up to the opposite shore, hung, still unharmed, by its chains. No one could doubt that an oversight on the part of the guard had caused the catastrophe.

The accident had occurred in the night, to the express train which left Melbourne at 11:45 in the evening. About a quarter past three in the morning, twenty-five minutes after leaving Castlemaine, it arrived at Camden Bridge, where the terrible disaster befell. The passengers and guards of the last and only remaining carriage at once tried to obtain help. But the telegraph, whose posts were lying on the ground, could not be worked. It was three hours before the authorities from Castlemaine reached the scene of the accident, and it was six o'clock in the morning when the salvage party was organized, under the direction of Mr. Mitchell, the surveyor-general of the colony, and a detachment of police, commanded by an inspector. The squatters and their "hands" lent their aid, and directed their efforts first to extinguishing the fire which raged in the ruined heap with unconquerable violence. A few unrecognizable bodies lay on the slope of the embankment, but from that blazing mass no living thing could be saved. The fire had done its work too speedily. Of the passengers ten only survived—those in the last carriage. The railway authorities sent a locomotive to bring them back to Castlemaine.

Lord Glenarvan, having introduced himself to the surveyor-general, entered into conversation with him and the inspector of police. The latter was a tall, thin man, imperturbably cool, and, whatever he may have felt, allowed no trace of it to appear on his features. He contemplated this calamity as a mathematician does a problem; he was seeking to solve it, and to find the unknown; and when Glenarvan observed, "This is a great misfortune," he quietly replied, "Better than that, my Lord."

"Better than that?" cried Glenarvan. "I do not understand you."

"It is better than a misfortune, it is a crime!" he replied, in the same quiet tone.

Glenarvan looked inquiringly at Mr. Mitchell for a solution. "Yes, my Lord," replied the surveyor-general, "our inquiries have resulted in the conclusion that the catastrophe is the result of a crime. The last luggage-van has been robbed. The surviving passengers were attacked by a gang of five or six villains. The bridge was intentionally opened, and not left open by the negligence of the guard; and connecting with this fact the guard's disappearance, we may conclude that the wretched fellow was an accomplice of these ruffians."

The police-officer shook his head at this inference.

"You do not agree with me?" said Mr. Mitchell.

"No, not as to the complicity of the guard."

"Well, but granting that complicity, we may attribute the crime to the natives who haunt the Murray. Without him the blacks could never have opened a swing-bridge; they know nothing of its mechanism."

"Exactly so," said the police-inspector.

"Well," added Mr. Mitchell, "we have the evidence of a boatman whose boat passed Camden Bridge at 10:40 P. M., that the bridge was properly shut after he passed."

"True."

"Well, after that I cannot see any doubt as to the complicity of the guard."

The police-officer shook his head gently, but continuously.

"Then you don't attribute the crime to the natives?"

"Not at all."

"To whom then?"

Just at this moment a noise was heard from about half a mile up the river. A crowd had gathered, and quickly increased. They soon reached the station, and in their midst were two men carrying a corpse. It was the body of the guard, quite cold, stabbed to the heart. The murderers had no doubt hoped, by dragging their victim to a distance, that the police would be put on a wrong scent in their first inquiries. This discovery, at any rate, justified the doubts of the police-inspector. The poor blacks had had no hand in the matter.

"Those who dealt that blow," said he, "were already well used to this little instrument"; and so saying he produced a pair of "darbies," a kind of handcuff made of a double ring of iron secured by a lock. "I shall soon have the pleasure of presenting them with these bracelets as a New Year's gift."

"Then you suspect—"

"Some folks who came out free in Her Majesty's ships."

"What! convicts?" cried Paganel, who recognized the formula employed in the Australian colonies.

"I thought," said Glenarvan, "convicts had no right in the province of Victoria."

"Bah!" said the inspector, "if they have no right, they take it! They escape sometimes, and, if I am not greatly mistaken, this lot have come straight from Perth, and, take my word for it, they will soon be there again."

Mr. Mitchell nodded acquiescence in the words of the police-inspector. At this moment the wagon arrived at the level crossing of the railway. Glenarvan wished to spare the ladies the horrible spectacle at Camden Bridge. He took courteous leave of the surveyor-general, and made a sign to the rest to follow him. "There is no reason," said he, "for delaying our journey."

When they reached the wagon, Glenarvan merely mentioned to Lady Helena that there had been a railway accident, without a hint of the crime that had played so great a part in it; neither did he make mention of the presence of a band of convicts in the neighborhood, reserving that piece of information solely for Ayrton's ear. The little procession now crossed the railway some two hundred yards below the bridge, and then resumed their eastward course.

CHAPTER XII TOLINE OF THE LACHLAN

ABOUT two miles from the railway, the plain terminated in a range of low hills, and it was not long before the wagon entered a succession of narrow gorges and capricious windings, out of which it emerged into a most charming region, where grand trees, not closely planted, but in scattered groups, were growing with absolutely tropical luxuriance. As the party drove on they stumbled upon a little native boy lying fast asleep beneath the shade of a magnificent banksia. He was dressed in European garb, and seemed about eight years of age. There was no mistaking the characteristic features of his race; the crisped hair, the nearly black skin, the flattened nose, the thick lips, the unusual length of the arms, immediately classed him among the aborigines of the interior. But a degree of intelligence appeared in his face that showed some educational influences must have been at work on his savage, untamed nature.

Lady Helena, whose interest was greatly excited by this spectacle, got out of the wagon, followed by Mary, and presently the whole company surrounded the peaceful little sleeper. "Poor child!" said Mary Grant. "Is he lost, I wonder, in this desert?"

"I suppose," said Lady Helena, "he has come a long way to visit this part. No doubt some he loves are here."

"But he can't be left here," added Robert. "We must—"

His compassionate sentence remained unfinished, for, just at that moment the child turned over in his sleep, and, to the extreme surprise of everybody, there was a large label on his shoulders, on which the following was written:

TOLINE.
To be conducted to Echuca.
Care of Jeffries Smith, Railway Porter.
Prepaid.

"That's the English all over!" exclaimed Paganel. "They send off a child just as they would luggage, and book him like a parcel. I heard it was done, certainly; but I could not believe it before."

"Poor child!" said Lady Helena. "Could he have been in the train that got off the line at Camden Bridge? Perhaps his parents are killed, and he is left alone in the world!"

"I don't think so, madam," replied John Mangles. "That card rather goes to prove he was traveling alone."

"He is waking up!" said Mary.

And so he was. His eyes slowly opened and then closed again, pained by the glare of light. But Lady Helena took his hand, and he jumped up at once and looked about him in bewilderment at the sight of so many strangers. He seemed half frightened at first, but the presence of Lady Helena reassured him. "Do you understand English, my little man?" asked the young lady.

"I understand it and speak it," replied the child in fluent enough English, but with a marked accent. His pronunciation was like a Frenchman's.

"What is your name?" asked Lady Helena.

"Toline," replied the little native.

"Toline!" exclaimed Paganel. "Ah! I think that means 'bark of a tree' in Australian."

Toline nodded, and looked again at the travelers.

"Where do you come from?" inquired Lady Helena.

"From Melbourne, by the railway from Sandhurst."

"Were you in the accident at Camden Bridge?" said Glenarvan.

"Yes, sir," was Toline's reply; "but the God of the Bible protected me."

"Are you traveling alone?"

"Yes, alone; the Reverend Paxton put me in charge of Jeffries Smith; but unfortunately the poor man was killed."

"And you did not know any one else on the train?"

"No one, madam; but God watches over children and never forsakes them."

Toline said this in soft, quiet tones, which went to the heart. When he mentioned the name of God his voice was grave and his eyes beamed with all the fervor that animated his young soul.

This religious enthusiasm at so tender an age was easily explained. The child was one of the aborigines baptized by the English missionaries, and trained by them in all the rigid principles of the Methodist Church. His calm replies, proper behavior, and even his somber garb made him look like a little reverend already.

But where was he going all alone in these solitudes and why had he left Camden Bridge? Lady Helena asked him about this.

"I was returning to my tribe in the Lachlan," he replied.

"I wished to see my family again."

"Are they Australians?" inquired John Mangles.

"Yes, Australians of the Lachlan," replied Toline.

"Have you a father and mother?" said Robert Grant.

"Yes, my brother," replied Toline, holding out his hand to little Grant. Robert was so touched by the word brother that he kissed the black child, and they were friends forthwith.

The whole party were so interested in these replies of the little Australian savage that they all sat round him in a listening group. But the sun had meantime sunk behind the tall trees, and as a few miles would not greatly retard their progress, and the spot they were in would be suitable for a halt, Glenarvan gave orders to prepare their camp for the night at once. Ayrton unfastened the bullocks and turned them out to feed at will. The tent was pitched, and Olbinett got the supper ready. Toline consented, after some difficulty, to share it, though he was hungry enough. He took his seat beside Robert, who chose out all the titbits for his new friend. Toline accepted them with a shy grace that was very charming.

The conversation with him, however, was still kept up, for everyone felt an interest in the child, and wanted to talk to him and hear his history. It was simple enough. He was one of the poor native children confided to the care of charitable societies by the neighboring tribes. The Australian aborigines are gentle and inoffensive, never exhibiting the fierce hatred toward their conquerors which characterizes the New Zealanders, and possibly a few of the races of Northern Australia. They often go to the large towns, such as

Adelaide, Sydney and Melbourne, and walk about in very primitive costume. They go to barter their few articles of industry, hunting and fishing implements, weapons, etc., and some of the chiefs, from pecuniary motives, no doubt, willingly leave their children to profit by the advantages of a gratuitous education in English.

This was how Toline's parents had acted. They were true Australian savages living in the Lachlan, a vast region lying beyond the Murray. The child had been in Melbourne five years, and during that time had never once seen any of his own people. And yet the imperishable feeling of kindred was still so strong in his heart that he had dared to brave this journey over the wilds to visit his tribe once more, scattered though perchance it might be, and his family, even should he find it decimated.

"And after you have kissed your parents, are you coming back to Melbourne?" asked Lady Glenarvan.

"Yes, Madam," replied Toline, looking at the lady with a loving expression.

"And what are you going to be some day?" she continued.

"I am going to snatch my brothers from misery and ignorance. I am going to teach them, to bring them to know and love God. I am going to be a missionary."

Words like those, spoken with such animation from a child of only eight years, might have provoked a smile in light, scoffing auditors, but they were understood and appreciated by the grave Scotch, who admired the courage of this young disciple, already armed for the battle. Even Paganel was stirred to the depths of his heart, and felt his warmer sympathy awakened for the poor child.

To speak the truth, up to that moment he did not care much for a savage in European attire. He had not come to Australia to see Australians in coats and trousers. He preferred them simply tattooed, and this conventional dress jarred on his preconceived notions. But the child's genuine religious fervor won him over completely. Indeed, the wind-up of the conversation converted the worthy geographer into his best friend.

It was in reply to a question Lady Helena had asked, that Toline said he was studying at the Normal School in Melbourne, and that the principal was the Reverend Mr. Paxton.

"And what do they teach you?" she went on to say.

"They teach me the Bible, and mathematics, and geography."

Paganel pricked up his ears at this, and said, "Indeed, geography!"

"Yes, sir," said Toline; "and I had the first prize for geography before the Christmas holidays."

"You had the first prize for geography, my boy?"

"Yes, sir. Here it is," returned Toline, pulling a book out of his pocket.

It was a bible, 32mo size, and well bound. On the first page was written the words: "Normal School, Melbourne. First Prize for Geography. Toline of the Lachlan."

Paganel was beside himself. An Australian well versed in geography. This was marvelous, and he could not help kissing Toline on both cheeks, just as if he had been the Reverend Mr. Paxton himself, on the day of the distribution of prizes. Paganel need not have been so amazed at this circumstance, however, for it is frequent enough in Australian schools. The little savages are very quick in learning geography. They learn it eagerly, and on the other hand, are perfectly averse to the science of arithmetic.

Toline could not understand this outburst of affection on the part of the Frenchman, and looked so puzzled that Lady Helena thought she had better inform him that Paganel was a celebrated geographer and a distinguished professor on occasion.

"A professor of geography!" cried Toline. "Oh, sir, do question me!"

"Question you? Well, I'd like nothing better. Indeed, I was going to do it without your leave. I should very much like to see how they teach geography in the Normal School of Melbourne."

"And suppose Toline trips you up, Paganel!" said McNabbs.

"What a likely idea!" exclaimed the geographer. "Trip up the Secretary of the Geographical Society of France."

Their examination then commenced, after Paganel had settled his spectacles firmly on his nose, drawn himself up to his full height, and put on a solemn voice becoming to a professor.

"Pupil Toline, stand up."

As Toline was already standing, he could not get any higher, but he waited modestly for the geographer's questions.

"Pupil Toline, what are the five divisions of the globe?"

"Oceanica, Asia, Africa, America, and Europe."

"Perfectly so. Now we'll take Oceanica first; where are we at this moment? What are the principal divisions?"

"Australia, belonging to the English; New Zealand, belonging to the English; Tasmania, belonging to the English. The islands of Chatham, Auckland, Macquarie, Kermadec, Makin, Maraki, are also belonging to the English."

"Very good, and New Caledonia, the Sandwich Islands, the Mendana, the Pomotou?"

"They are islands under the Protectorate of Great Britain."

"What!" cried Paganel, "under the Protectorate of Great Britain. I rather think on the contrary, that France—"

"France," said the child, with an astonished look.

"Well, well," said Paganel; "is that what they teach you in the Melbourne Normal School?"

"Yes, sir. Isn't it right?"

"Oh, yes, yes, perfectly right. All Oceanica belongs to the English. That's an understood thing. Go on."

Paganel's face betrayed both surprise and annoyance, to the great delight of the Major.

"Let us go on to Asia," said the geographer.

"Asia," replied Toline, "is an immense country.

Capital—Calcutta. Chief Towns—Bombay, Madras, Calicut, Aden,

Malacca, Singapore, Pegu, Colombo. The Lacca-dive Islands,

the Maldives, the Chagos, etc., belonging to the English."

"Very good, pupil Toline. And now for Africa."

"Africa comprises two chief colonies—the Cape on the south, capital Capetown; and on the west the English settlements, chief city, Sierra Leone."

"Capital!" said Paganel, beginning to enter into this perfectly taught but Anglo-colored fanciful geography. "As to Algeria, Morocco, Egypt—they are all struck out of the Britannic cities."

"Let us pass on, pray, to America."

"It is divided," said Toline, promptly, "into North and South America. The former belongs to the English in Canada, New Brunswick, New Scotland, and the United States, under the government of President Johnson."

"President Johnson," cried Paganel, "the successor of the great and good Lincoln, assassinated by a mad fanatic of the slave party. Capital; nothing could be better. And as to South America, with its Guiana, its archipelago of South Shetland, its Georgia, Jamaica, Trinidad, etc., that belongs to the English, too! Well, I'll not be the one to dispute that point! But, Toline, I should like to know your opinion of Europe, or rather your professor's."

"Europe?" said Toline not at all understanding Paganel's excitement.

"Yes, Europe! Who does Europe belong to?"

"Why, to the English," replied Toline, as if the fact was quite settled.

"I much doubt it," returned Paganel. "But how's that, Toline, for I want to know that?"

"England, Ireland, Scotland, Malta, Jersey and Guernsey, the Ionian Islands, the Hebrides, the Shetlands, and the Orkneys."

"Yes, yes, my lad; but there are other states you forgot to mention."

"What are they?" replied the child, not the least disconcerted.

"Spain, Russia, Austria, Prussia, France," answered Paganel.

"They are provinces, not states," said Toline.

"Well, that beats all!" exclaimed Paganel, tearing off his spectacles.

"Yes," continued the child. "Spain—capital, Gibraltar."

"Admirable! perfect! sublime! And France, for I am French, and I should like to know to whom I belong."

"France," said Toline, quietly, "is an English province; chief city, Calais."

"Calais!" cried Paganel. "So you think Calais still belongs to the English?"

"Certainly."

"And that it is the capital of France?"

"Yes, sir; and it is there that the Governor, Lord Napoleon, lives."

This was too much for Paganel's risible faculties. He burst out laughing. Toline did not know what to make of him. He had done his best to answer every question put to him. But the singularity of the answers were not his blame; indeed, he never imagined anything singular about them. However, he took it all quietly, and waited for the professor to recover himself. These peals of laughter were quite incomprehensible to him.

"You see," said Major McNabbs, laughing, "I was right.

The pupil could enlighten you after all."

"Most assuredly, friend Major," replied the geographer. "So that's the way they teach geography in Melbourne! They do it well, these professors in the Normal School! Europe, Asia, Africa, America, Oceanica, the whole world belongs to the English. My conscience! with such an ingenious education it is no wonder the natives submit. Ah, well, Toline, my boy, does the moon belong to England, too?"

"She will, some day," replied the young savage, gravely.

This was the climax. Paganel could not stand any more. He was obliged to go away and take his laugh out, for he was actually exploding with mirth, and he went fully a quarter of a mile from the encampment before his equilibrium was restored.

Meanwhile, Glenarvan looked up a geography they had brought among their books. It was "Richardson's Compendium," a work in great repute in England, and more in agreement with modern science than the manual in use in the Normal School in Melbourne.

"Here, my child," he said to Toline, "take this book and keep it. You have a few wrong ideas about geography, which it would be well for you to rectify. I will give you this as a keepsake from me."

Toline took the book silently; but, after examining it attentively, he shook his head with an air of incredulity, and could not even make up his mind to put it in his pocket.

By this time night had closed in; it was 10 P. M. and time to think of rest, if they were to start betimes next day. Robert offered his friend Toline half his bed, and the little fellow accepted it. Lady Helena and Mary Grant withdrew to the wagon, and the others lay down in the tent, Paganel's merry peals still mingling with the low, sweet song of the wild magpie.

But in the morning at six o'clock, when the sunshine wakened the sleepers,

they looked in vain for the little Australian. Toline had disappeared.

Was he in haste to get to the Lachlan district? or was he hurt by

Paganel's laughter? No one could say.

But when Lady Helena opened her eyes she discovered a fresh branch of mimosa leaves lying across her, and Paganel found a book in his vest pocket, which turned out to be "Richardson's Geography."

CHAPTER XIII A WARNING

ON the 2d of January, at sunrise, the travelers forded the Colban and the Caupespe rivers. The half of their journey was now accomplished. In fifteen days more, should their journey continue to be prosperous, the little party would reach Twofold Bay.

They were all in good health. All that Paganel said of the hygienic qualities of the climate was realized. There was little or no humidity, and the heat was quite bearable. Neither horses nor bullocks could complain of it any more than human beings. The order of the march had been changed in one respect since the affair of Camden Bridge. That criminal catastrophe on the railway made Ayrton take sundry precautions, which had hitherto been unnecessary. The hunters never lost sight of the wagon, and whenever they camped, one was always placed on watch. Morning and evening the firearms were primed afresh. It was certain that a gang of ruffians was prowling about the country, and though there was no cause for actual fear, it was well to be ready for whatever might happen.

It need hardly be said these precautions were adopted without the knowledge of Lady Helena and Mary Grant, as Lord Glenarvan did not wish to alarm them.

They were by no means unnecessary, however, for any imprudence or carelessness might have cost the travelers dear. Others beside Glenarvan were on their guard. In lonely settlements and on stations, the inhabitants and the squatters prepared carefully against any attack or surprise. Houses are closed at nightfall; the dogs let loose inside the fences, barked at the slightest sound. Not a single shepherd on horseback gathered his numerous flocks together at close of day, without having a carbine slung from his saddle.

The outrage at Camden Bridge was the reason for all this, and many a colonist fastened himself in with bolts and bars now at dusk, who used to sleep with open doors and windows.

The Government itself displayed zeal and prudence, especially in the Post-office department. On this very day, just as Glenarvan and his party were on their way from Kilmore to Heathcote, the mail dashed by at full speed; but though the horses were at a gallop, Glenarvan caught sight of the glittering weapons of the mounted police that rode by its side, as they swept past in a cloud of dust. The travelers might have fancied themselves back in those lawless times when the discovery of the first gold-fields deluged the Australian continent with the scum of Europe.

A mile beyond the road to Kilmore, the wagon, for the first time since leaving Cape Bernouilli, struck into one of those forests of gigantic trees which extend over a superfices of several degrees. A cry of admiration escaped the travelers at the sight of the eucalyptus trees, two hundred feet high, with tough bark five inches thick. The trunks, measuring twenty feet round, and furrowed with foamy streaks of an odorous resin, rose one hundred and fifty feet above the soil. Not a branch, not a twig, not a stray shoot, not even a knot, spoilt the regularity of their outline. They could not have come out smoother from the hands of a turner. They stood like pillars all molded exactly alike, and could be counted by hundreds. At an enormous height they spread out in chaplets of branches, rounded and adorned at their extremity with alternate leaves. At the axle of these leaves solitary flowers drooped down, the calyx of which resembles an inverted urn.

Under this leafy dome, which never lost its greenness, the air circulated freely, and dried up the dampness of the ground. Horses, cattle, and wagon could easily pass between the trees, for they were standing in wide rows, and parceled out like a wood that was being felled. This was neither like the densely-packed woods choked up with brambles, nor the virgin forest barricaded with the trunks of fallen trees, and overgrown with inextricable tangles of creepers, where only iron and fire could open up a track. A grassy carpet at the foot of the trees, and a canopy of verdure above, long perspectives of bold colors, little shade, little freshness at all, a peculiar light, as if the rays came through a thin veil, dappled lights and shades sharply reflected on the ground, made up a whole, and constituted a peculiar spectacle rich in novel effects. The forests of the Oceanic continent do not in the least resemble the forests of the New World; and the Eucalyptus, the "Tara" of the aborigines, belonging to the family of MYRTACEA, the different varieties of which can hardly be enumerated, is the tree *par excellence* of the Australian flora.

The reason of the shade not being deep, nor the darkness profound, under these domes of verdure, was that these trees presented a curious anomaly in the disposition of the leaves. Instead of presenting their broad surface to the sunlight, only the side is turned. Only the profile of the leaves is seen in this singular foliage. Consequently the sun's rays slant down them to the earth, as if through the open slants of a Venetian blind.

Glenarvan expressed his surprise at this circumstance, and wondered what could be the cause of it. Paganel, who was never at a loss for an answer, immediately replied:

"What astonishes me is not the caprice of nature. She knows what she is about, but botanists don't always know what they are saying. Nature made no mistake in giving this peculiar foliage to the tree, but men have erred in calling them EUCALYPTUS."

"What does the word mean?" asked Mary Grant.

"It comes from a Greek word, meaning I *cover well*. They took care to commit the mistake in Greek, that it might not be so self-evident, for anyone can see that the ecualyptus covers badly."

"I agree with you there," said Glenarvan; "but now tell us, Paganel, how it is that the leaves grow in this fashion?"

"From a purely physical cause, friends," said Paganel, "and one that you will easily understand. In this country where the air is dry and rain seldom falls, and the ground is parched, the trees have no need of wind or sun. Moisture lacking, sap is lacking also. Hence these narrow leaves, which seek to defend themselves against the light, and prevent too great evaporation. This is why they present the profile and not the face to the sun's rays. There is nothing more intelligent than a leaf."

"And nothing more selfish," added the Major. "These only thought of themselves, and not at all of travelers."

Everyone inclined to the opinion of McNabbs except Paganel, who congratulated himself on walking under shadeless trees, though all the time he was wiping the perspiration from his forehead. However, this disposition of foliage was certainly to be regretted, for the journey through the forest was often long and painful, as the traveler had no protection whatever against the sun's fierce rays.

The whole of this day the wagon continued to roll along through interminable rows of eucalyptus, without meeting either quadruped or native. A few cockatoos lived in the tops of the trees, but at such a height they could scarcely be distinguished, and their noisy chatter was changed into an imperceptible murmur. Occasionally a swarm of par-roquets flew along a distant path, and lighted it up for an instant with gay colors; but otherwise, solemn silence reigned in this vast green temple, and the tramp of the horses, a few words exchanged with each other by the riders, the grinding noise of the wheels, and from time to time a cry from Ayrton to stir up his lazy team, were the only sounds which disturbed this immense solitude.

When night came they camped at the foot of some eucalyptus, which bore marks of a comparatively recent fire. They looked like tall factory chimneys, for the flame had completely hollowed them out their whole length. With the thick bark still covering them, they looked none the worse. However, this bad habit of squatters or natives will end in the destruction of these magnificent trees, and they will disappear like the cedars of Lebanon, those world monuments burnt by unlucky camp fires.

Olbinett, acting on Paganel's advice, lighted his fire to prepare supper in one of these tubular trunks. He found it drew capitally, and the smoke was lost in the dark foliage above. The requisite precautions were taken for the night, and Ayrton, Mulrady, Wilson and John Mangles undertook in turn to keep watch until sunrise.

On the 3d of January, all day long, they came to nothing but the same symmetrical avenues of trees; it seemed as if they never were going to end. However, toward evening the ranks of trees began to thin, and on a little plain a few miles off an assemblage of regular houses.

"Seymour!" cried Paganel; "that is the last town we come to in the province of Victoria."

"Is it an important one?" asked Lady Helena.

"It is a mere village, madam, but on the way to become a municipality."

"Shall we find a respectable hotel there?" asked Glenarvan.

"I hope so," replied Paganel.

"Very well; let us get on to the town, for our fair travelers, with all their courage, will not be sorry, I fancy, to have a good night's rest."

"My dear Edward, Mary and I will accept it gladly, but only on the condition that it will cause no delay, or take us the least out of the road."

"It will do neither," replied Lord Glenarvan. "Besides, our bullocks are fatigued, and we will start to-morrow at daybreak."

It was now nine o'clock; the moon was just beginning to rise, but her rays were only slanting yet, and lost in the mist. It was gradually getting dark when the little party entered the wide streets of Seymour, under Paganel's guidance, who seemed always to know what he had never seen; but his instinct led him right, and he walked straight to Campbell's North British Hotel.

The Major without even leaving the hotel, was soon aware that fear absorbed the inhabitants of the little town. Ten minutes' conversation with Dickson, the loquacious landlord, made him completely acquainted with the actual state of affairs; but he never breathed a word to any one.

When supper was over, though, and Lady Glenarvan, and Mary, and Robert had retired, the Major detained his companions a little, and said, "They have found out the perpetrators of the crime on the Sandhurst railroad."

"And are they arrested?" asked Ayrton, eagerly.

"No," replied McNabbs, without apparently noticing the EMPRESSMENT of the quartermaster—an EMPRESSMENT which, moreover, was reasonable enough under the circumstances.

"So much the worse," replied Ayrton.

"Well," said Glenarvan, "who are the authors of the crime?"

"Read," replied the Major, offering Glenarvan a copy of the *Australian and New Zealand Gazette*, "and you will see that the inspector of the police was not mistaken."

Glenarvan read aloud the following message:

SYDNEY, Jan. 2, 1866.

It will be remembered that on the night of the 29th or 30th of last December there was an accident at Camden Bridge, five miles beyond the station at Castlemaine, on the railway from Melbourne to Sandhurst. The night express, 11.45, dashing along at full speed, was precipitated into the Loddon River.

Camden Bridge had been left open. The numerous robberies committed after the accident, the body of the guard picked up about half a mile from Camden Bridge, proved that this catastrophe was the result of a crime.

Indeed, the coroner's inquest decided that the crime must be attributed to the band of convicts which escaped six months ago from the Penitentiary at Perth, Western Australia, just as they were about to be transferred to Norfolk Island.

The gang numbers twenty-nine men; they are under the command of a certain Ben Joyce, a criminal of the most dangerous class, who arrived in Australia a few months ago, by what ship is not known, and who has hitherto succeeded in evading the hands of justice.

The inhabitants of towns, colonists and squatters at stations, are hereby cautioned to be on their guard, and to communicate to the Surveyor-General any information that may aid his search. J. P. MITCHELL, S. G.

When Glenarvan had finished reading this article, McNabbs turned to the geographer and said, "You see, Paganel, there can be convicts in Australia."

"Escaped convicts, that is evident," replied Paganel, "but not regularly transported criminals. Those fellows have no business here."

"Well, they are here, at any rate," said Glenarvan; "but I don't suppose the fact need materially alter our arrangements. What do you think, John?"

John Mangles did not reply immediately; he hesitated between the sorrow it would cause the two children to give up the search, and the fear of compromising the expedition.

"If Lady Glenarvan, and Miss Grant were not with us," he said,

"I should not give myself much concern about these wretches."

Glenarvan understood him and added, "Of course I need not say that it is not a question of giving up our task; but would it perhaps be prudent, for the sake of our companions, to rejoin the DUNCAN at Melbourne, and proceed with our search for traces of Harry Grant on the eastern side. What do you think of it, McNabbs?"

"Before I give my opinion," replied the Major, "I should like to hear Ayrton's."

At this direct appeal, the quartermaster looked at Glenarvan, and said, "I think we are two hundred miles from Melbourne, and that the danger, if it exists, is as great on the route to the south as on the route to the east. Both are little frequented, and both will serve us. Besides, I do not think that thirty scoundrels can frighten eight well-armed, determined men. My advice, then, is to go forward."

"And good advice too, Ayrton," replied Paganel. "By going on we may come across the traces of Captain Grant. In returning south, on the contrary, we turn our backs to them. I think with you, then, and I don't care a snap for these escaped fellows. A brave man wouldn't care a bit for them!"

Upon this they agreed with the one voice to follow their original programme.

"Just one thing, my Lord," said Ayrton, when they were about to separate.

"Say on, Ayrton."

"Wouldn't it be advisable to send orders to the DUNCAN to be at the coast?"

"What good would that be," replied John Mangles. "When we reach Twofold Bay it will be time enough for that. If any unexpected event should oblige us to go to Melbourne, we might be sorry not to find the DUNCAN there. Besides, her injuries can not be repaired yet. For these reasons, then, I think it would be better to wait."

"All right," said Ayrton, and forbore to press the matter further.

CHAPTER XIV WEALTH IN THE WILDERNESS

ON January 6, at 7 A. M., after a tranquil night passed in longitude 146 degrees 15", the travelers continued their journey across the vast district. They directed their course steadily toward the rising sun, and made a straight line across the plain. Twice over they came upon the traces of squatters going toward the north, and their different footprints became confused, and Glenarvan's horse no longer left on the dust the Blackpoint mark, recognizable by its double shamrock.

The plain was furrowed in some places by fantastic winding creeks surrounded by box, and whose waters were rather temporary than permanent. They originated in the slopes of the Buffalo Ranges, a chain of mountains of moderate height, the undulating line of which was visible on the horizon. It was resolved to camp there the same night. Ayrton goaded on his team, and after a journey of thirty-five miles, the bullocks arrived, somewhat fatigued. The tent was pitched beneath the great trees, and as night had drawn on supper was served as quickly as possible, for all the party cared more for sleeping than eating, after such a day's march.

Paganel who had the first watch did not lie down, but shouldered his rifle and walked up and down before the camp, to keep himself from going to sleep. In spite of the absence of the moon, the night was almost luminous with the light of the southern constellations. The SAVANT amused himself with reading the great book of the firmament, a book which is always open, and full of interest to those who can read it. The profound silence of sleeping nature was only interrupted by the clanking of the hobbles on the horses' feet.

Paganel was engrossed in his astronomical meditations, and thinking more about the celestial than the terrestrial world, when a distant sound aroused him from his reverie. He listened attentively, and to his great amaze, fancied he heard the sounds of a piano. He could not be mistaken, for he distinctly heard chords struck.

"A piano in the wilds!" said Paganel to himself.

"I can never believe it is that."

It certainly was very surprising, but Paganel found it easier to believe it was some Australian bird imitating the sounds of a Pleyel or Erard, as others do the sounds of a clock or mill. But at this very moment, the notes of a clear ringing voice rose on the air. The PIANIST was accompanied by singing. Still Paganel was unwilling to be convinced. However, next minute he was forced to admit the fact, for there fell on his ear the sublime strains of Mozart's "Il mio tesoro tanto" from Don Juan.

"Well, now," said the geographer to himself, "let the Australian birds be as queer as they may, and even granting the paroquets are the most musical in the world, they can't sing Mozart!"

He listened to the sublime inspiration of the great master to the end. The effect of this soft melody on the still clear night was indescribable. Paganel remained as if spellbound for a time; the voice ceased and all was silence. When Wilson came to relieve the watch, he found the geographer plunged into a deep reverie. Paganel made no remark, however, to the sailor, but reserved his information for Glenarvan in the morning, and went into the tent to bed.

Next day, they were all aroused from sleep by the sudden loud barking of dogs, Glenarvan got up forthwith. Two magnificent pointers, admirable specimens of English hunting dogs, were bounding in front of the little wood, into which they had retreated at the approach of the travelers, redoubling their clamor.

"There is some station in this desert, then," said Glenarvan, "and hunters too, for these are regular setters."

Paganel was just about to recount his nocturnal experiences, when two young men appeared, mounted on horses of the most perfect breed, true "hunters."

The two gentlemen dressed in elegant hunting costume, stopped at the sight of the little group camping in gipsy fashion. They looked as if they wondered what could bring an armed party there, but when they saw the ladies get out of the wagon, they dismounted instantly, and went toward them hat in hand. Lord Glenarvan came to meet them, and, as a stranger, announced his name and rank.

The gentlemen bowed, and the elder of them said, "My Lord, will not these ladies and yourself and friends honor us by resting a little beneath our roof?"

"Mr.—," began Glenarvan.

"Michael and Sandy Patterson are our names, proprietors of

Hottam Station. Our house is scarcely a quarter of a mile distant."

"Gentlemen," replied Glenarvan, "I should not like to abuse such kindly-offered hospitality."

"My Lord," returned Michael Patterson, "by accepting it you will confer a favor on poor exiles, who will be only too happy to do the honors of the wilds."

Glenarvan bowed in token of acquiescence.

"Sir," said Paganel, addressing Michael Patterson, "if it is not an impudent question, may I ask whether it was you that sung an air from the divine Mozart last night?"

"It was, sir," replied the stranger, "and my cousin Sandy accompanied me."

"Well, sir," replied Paganel, holding out his hand to the young man, "receive the sincere compliments of a Frenchman, who is a passionate admirer of this music."

Michael grasped his hand cordially, and then pointing out the road to take, set off, accompanied by the ladies and Lord Glenarvan and his friends, for the station. The horses and the camp were left to the care of Ayrton and the sailors.

Hottam Station was truly a magnificent establishment, kept as scrupulously in order as an English park. Immense meadows, enclosed in gray fences, stretched away out of sight. In these, thousands of bullocks and millions of sheep were grazing, tended by numerous shepherds, and still more numerous dogs. The crack of the stock-whip mingled continually with the barking of the "collies" and the bellowing and bleating of the cattle and sheep.

Toward the east there was a boundary of myalls and gum-trees, beyond which rose Mount Hottam, its imposing peak towering 7,500 feet high. Long avenues of green trees were visible on all sides. Here and there was a thick clump of "grass trees," tall bushes ten feet high, like the dwarf palm, quite lost in their crown of long narrow leaves. The air was balmy and odorous with the perfume of scented laurels, whose white blossoms, now in full bloom, distilled on the breeze the finest aromatic perfume.

To these charming groups of native trees were added transplantations from European climates. The peach, pear, and apple trees were there, the fig, the orange, and even the oak, to the rapturous delight of the travelers, who greeted them with loud hurrahs! But astonished as the travelers were to find themselves walking beneath the shadow of the trees of their own native land, they were still more so at the sight of the birds that flew about in the branches— the "satin bird," with its silky plumage, and the "king-honeysuckers," with their plumage of gold and black velvet.

For the first time, too, they saw here the "Lyre" bird, the tail of which resembles in form the graceful instrument of Orpheus. It flew about among the tree ferns, and when its tail struck the branches, they were almost surprised not to hear the harmonious strains that inspired Amphion to rebuild the walls of Thebes. Paganel had a great desire to play on it.

However, Lord Glenarvan was not satisfied with admiring the fairy-like wonders of this oasis, improvised in the Australian desert. He was listening to the history of the young gentlemen. In England, in the midst of civilized countries, the new comer acquaints his host whence he comes and whither he is going; but here, by a refinement of delicacy, Michael and Sandy Patterson thought it a duty to make themselves known to the strangers who were about to receive their hospitality.

Michael and Sandy Patterson were the sons of London bankers.

When they were twenty years of age, the head of their family said,

"Here are some thousands, young men. Go to a distant colony;

and start some useful settlement there. Learn to know life by labor.

If you succeed, so much the better. If you fail, it won't matter much.

We shall not regret the money which makes you men."

The two young men obeyed. They chose the colony of Victoria in Australia, as the field for sowing the paternal bank-notes, and had no reason to repent the selection. At the end of three years the establishment was flourishing. In Victoria, New South Wales, and Southern Australia, there are more than three thousand stations, some belonging to squatters who rear cattle, and others to settlers who farm the ground. Till the arrival of the two Pattersons, the largest establishment of this sort was that of Mr. Jamieson, which covered an area of seventy-five miles, with a frontage of about eight miles along the Peron, one of the affluents of the Darling.

Now Hottam Station bore the palm for business and extent. The young men were both squatters and settlers. They managed their immense property with rare ability and uncommon energy.

The station was far removed from the chief towns in the midst of the unfrequented districts of the Murray. It occupied a long wide space of five leagues in extent, lying between the Buffalo Ranges and Mount Hottam. At the two angles north of this vast quadrilateral, Mount Aberdeen rose on the left, and the peaks of High Barven on the right. Winding, beautiful streams were not wanting, thanks to the creeks and affluents of the Oven's River, which throws itself at the north into the bed of the Murray. Consequently they were equally successful in cattle breeding and farming. Ten thousand acres of ground, admirably cultivated, produced harvests of native productions and exotics, and several millions of animals fattened in the fertile pastures. The products of Hottam Station fetched the very highest price in the markets of Castlemaine and Melbourne.

Michael and Sandy Patterson had just concluded these details of their busy life, when their dwelling came in sight, at the extremity of the avenue of the oaks.

It was a charming house, built of wood and brick, hidden in groves of emerophilis. Nothing at all, however, belonging to a station was visible—neither sheds, nor stables, nor cart-houses. All these out-buildings, a perfect village, comprising more than twenty huts and houses, were about a quarter of a mile off in the heart of a little valley. Electric communication was established between this village and the master's house, which, far removed from all noise, seemed buried in a forest of exotic trees.

At Sandy Patterson's bidding, a sumptuous breakfast was served in less than a quarter of an hour. The wines and viands were of the finest quality; but what pleased the guests most of all in the midst of these refinements of opulence, was the joy of the young squatters in offering them this splendid hospitality.

It was not long before they were told the history of the expedition, and had their liveliest interest awakened for its success. They spoke hopefully to the young Grants, and Michael said: "Harry Grant has evidently fallen into the hands of natives, since he has not turned up at any of the settlements on the coast. He knows his position exactly, as the document proves, and the reason he did not reach some English colony is that he must have been taken prisoner by the savages the moment he landed!"

"That is precisely what befell his quartermaster, Ayrton," said John Mangles.

"But you, gentlemen, then, have never heard the catastrophe of the BRITANNIA, mentioned?" inquired Lady Helena.

"Never, Madam," replied Michael.

"And what treatment, in your opinion, has Captain Grant met with among the natives?"

"The Australians are not cruel, Madam," replied the young squatter, "and Miss Grant may be easy on that score. There have been many instances of the gentleness of their nature, and some Europeans have lived a long time among them without having the least cause to complain of their brutality."

"King, among others, the sole survivor of the Burke expedition," put in Paganel.

"And not only that bold explorer," returned Sandy, "but also an English soldier named Buckley, who deserted at Port Philip in 1803, and who was welcomed by the natives, and lived thirty-three years among them."

"And more recently," added Michael," one of the last numbers of the AUSTRALASIA informs us that a certain Morrilli has just been restored to his countrymen after sixteen years of slavery. His story is exactly similar to the captain's, for it was at the very time of his shipwreck in the PRUVIENNE, in 1846, that he was made prisoner by the natives, and dragged away into the interior of the continent. I therefore think you have reason to hope still."

The young squatter's words caused great joy to his auditors.

They completely corroborated the opinions of Paganel and Ayrton.

The conversation turned on the convicts after the ladies had left the table. The squatters had heard of the catastrophe at Camden Bridge, but felt no uneasiness about the escaped gang. It was not a station, with more than a hundred men on it, that they would dare to attack. Besides, they would never go into the deserts of the Murray, where they could find no booty, nor near the colonies of New South Wales, where the roads were too well watched. Ayrton had said this too.

Glenarvan could not refuse the request of his amiable hosts, to spend the whole day at the station. It was twelve hours' delay, but also twelve hours' rest, and both horses and bullocks would be the better for the comfortable quarters they would find there. This was accordingly agreed upon, and the young squatters sketched out a programme of the day's amusements, which was adopted eagerly.

At noon, seven vigorous hunters were before the door. An elegant brake was intended for the ladies, in which the coachman could exhibit his skill in driving four-in-hand. The cavalcade set off preceded by huntsmen, and armed with first-rate rifles, followed by a pack of pointers barking joyously as they bounded through the bushes. For four hours the hunting party wandered through the paths and avenues of the park, which was as large as a small German state. The Reuiss-Schleitz, or Saxe-Coburg Gotha, would have gone inside it comfortably. Few people were to be met in it certainly, but sheep in abundance. As for game, there was a complete preserve awaiting the hunters. The noisy reports of guns were soon heard on all sides. Little Robert did wonders in company with Major McNabbs. The daring boy, in spite of his sister's injunctions, was always in front, and the first to fire. But John Mangles promised to watch over him, and Mary felt less uneasy.

During this BATTUE they killed certain animals peculiar to the country, the very names of which were unknown to Paganel; among others the "wombat" and the "bandicoot." The wombat is an herbivorous animal, which burrows in the ground like a badger. It is as large as a sheep, and the flesh is excellent.

The bandicoot is a species of marsupial animal which could outwit the European fox, and give him lessons in pillaging poultry yards. It was a repulsive-looking animal, a foot and a half long, but, as Paganel chanced to kill it, of course he thought it charming.

"An adorable creature," he called it.

But the most interesting event of the day, by far, was the kangaroo hunt. About four o'clock, the dogs roused a troop of these curious marsupials. The little ones retreated precipitately into the maternal pouch, and all the troop decamped in file. Nothing could be more astonishing than the enormous bounds of the kangaroo. The hind legs of the animal are twice as long as the front ones, and unbend like a spring. At the head of the flying troop was a male five feet high, a magnificent specimen of the *macropus giganteus*, an "old man," as the bushmen say.

For four or five miles the chase was vigorously pursued. The kangaroos showed no signs of weariness, and the dogs, who had reason enough to fear their strong paws and sharp nails, did not care to approach them. But at last, worn out with the race, the troop stopped, and the "old man" leaned against the trunk of a tree, ready to defend himself. One of the pointers, carried away by excitement, went up to him. Next minute the unfortunate beast leaped into the air, and fell down again completely ripped up.

The whole pack, indeed, would have had little chance with these powerful marsupia. They had to dispatch the fellow with rifles. Nothing but balls could bring down the gigantic animal.

Just at this moment, Robert was well nigh the victim of his own imprudence. To make sure of his aim, he had approached too near the kangaroo, and the animal leaped upon him immediately. Robert gave a loud cry and fell. Mary Grant saw it all from the brake, and in an agony of terror, speechless and almost unable even to see, stretched out her arms toward her little brother. No one dared to fire, for fear of wounding the child.

But John Mangles opened his hunting knife, and at the risk of being ripped up himself, sprang at the animal, and plunged it into his heart. The beast dropped forward, and Robert rose unhurt. Next minute he was in his sister's arms.

"Thank you, Mr. John, thank you!" she said, holding out her hand to the young captain.

"I had pledged myself for his safety," was all John said, taking her trembling fingers into his own.

This occurrence ended the sport. The band of marsupia
had disappeared after the death of their leader.
The hunting party returned home, bringing their game with them.
It was then six o'clock. A magnificent dinner was ready.
Among other things, there was one dish that was a great success.

It was kangaroo-tail soup, prepared in the native manner.

Next morning very early, they took leave of the young squatters, with hearty thanks and a positive promise from them of a visit to Malcolm Castle when they should return to Europe.

Then the wagon began to move away, round the foot of Mount Hottam, and soon the hospitable dwelling disappeared from the sight of the travelers like some brief vision which had come and gone.

For five miles further, the horses were still treading the station lands. It was not till nine o'clock that they had passed the last fence, and entered the almost unknown districts of the province of Victoria.

CHAPTER XV SUSPICIOUS OCCURRENCES

AN immense barrier lay across the route to the southeast. It was the Australian Alps, a vast fortification, the fantastic curtain of which extended 1,500 miles, and pierced the clouds at the height of 4,000 feet.

The cloudy sky only allowed the heat to reach the ground through a close veil of mist. The temperature was just bearable, but the road was toilsome from its uneven character. The extumescences on the plain became more and more marked. Several mounds planted with green young gum trees appeared here and there. Further on these protuberances rising sharply, formed the first steps of the great Alps. From this time their course was a continual ascent, as was soon evident in the strain it made on the bullocks to drag along the cumbrous wagon. Their yoke creaked, they breathed heavily, and the muscles of their houghs were stretched as if they would burst. The planks of the vehicle groaned at the unexpected jolts, which Ayrton with all his skill could not prevent. The ladies bore their share of discomfort bravely.

John Mangles and his two sailors acted as scouts, and went about a hundred steps in advance. They found out practical paths, or passes, indeed they might be called, for these projections of the ground were like so many rocks, between which the wagon had to steer carefully. It required absolute navigation to find a safe way over the billowy region.

It was a difficult and often perilous task. Many a time Wilson's hatchet was obliged to open a passage through thick tangles of shrubs. The damp argillaceous soil gave way under their feet. The route was indefinitely prolonged owing to the insurmountable obstacles, huge blocks of granite, deep ravines, suspected lagoons, which obliged them to make a thousand detours. When night came they found they had only gone over half a degree. They camped at the foot of the Alps, on the banks of the creek of Cobongra, on the edge of a little plain, covered with little shrubs four feet high, with bright red leaves which gladdened the eye.

"We shall have hard work to get over," said Glenarvan, looking at the chain of mountains, the outlines of which were fast fading away in the deepening darkness. "The very name Alps gives plenty of room for reflection."

"It is not quite so big as it sounds, my dear Glenarvan. Don't suppose you have a whole Switzerland to traverse. In Australia there are the Grampians, the Pyrenees, the Alps, the Blue Mountains, as in Europe and America, but in miniature. This simply implies either that the imagination of geographers is not infinite, or that their vocabulary of proper names is very poor."

"Then these Australian Alps," said Lord Glenarvan, "are—"

"Mere pocket mountains," put in Paganel; "we shall get over them without knowing it."

"Speak for yourself," said the Major. "It would certainly take a very absent man who could cross over a chain of mountains and not know it."

"Absent! But I am not an absent man now. I appeal to the ladies. Since ever I set foot on the Australian continent, have I been once at fault? Can you reproach me with a single blunder?"

"Not one. Monsieur Paganel," said Mary Grant. "You are now the most perfect of men."

"Too perfect," added Lady Helena, laughing; "your blunders suited you admirably."

"Didn't they, Madam? If I have no faults now, I shall soon get like everybody else. I hope then I shall make some outrageous mistake before long, which will give you a good laugh. You see, unless I make mistakes, it seems to me I fail in my vocation."

Next day, the 9th of January, notwithstanding the assurances of the confident geographer, it was not without great difficulty that the little troop made its way through the Alpine pass. They were obliged to go at a venture, and enter the depths of narrow gorges without any certainty of an outlet. Ayrton would doubtless have found himself very much embarrassed if a little inn, a miserable public house, had not suddenly presented itself.

"My goodness!" cried Paganel, "the landlord of this inn won't make his fortune in a place like this. What is the use of it here?"

"To give us the information we want about the route," replied Glenarvan. "Let us go in."

Glenarvan, followed by Ayrton, entered the inn forthwith. The landlord of the "Bush Inn," as it was called, was a coarse man with an ill-tempered face, who must have considered himself his principal customer for the gin, brandy and whisky he had to sell. He seldom saw any one but the squatters and rovers. He answered all the questions put to him in a surly tone. But his replies sufficed to make the route clear to Ayrton, and that was all that was wanted. Glenarvan rewarded him with a handful of silver for his trouble, and was about to leave the tavern, when a placard against the wall arrested his attention.

It was a police notice, and announcing the escape of the convicts from Perth, and offering a reward for the capture of Ben Joyce of pounds 100 sterling.

"He's a fellow that's worth hanging, and no mistake," said Glenarvan to the quartermaster.

"And worth capturing still more. But what a sum to offer!

He is not worth it!"

"I don't feel very sure of the innkeeper though, in spite of the notice," said Glenarvan.

"No more do I," replied Ayrton.

They went back to the wagon, toward the point where the route to Lucknow stopped. A narrow path wound away from this which led across the chain in a slanting direction. They had commenced the ascent.

It was hard work. More than once both the ladies and gentlemen had to get down and walk. They were obliged to help to push round the wheels of the heavy vehicle, and to support it frequently in dangerous declivities, to unharness the bullocks when the team could not go well round sharp turnings, prop up the wagon when it threatened to roll back, and more than once Ayrton had to reinforce his bullocks by harnessing the horses, although they were tired out already with dragging themselves along.

Whether it was this prolonged fatigue, or from some other cause altogether, was not known, but one of the horses sank suddenly, without the slightest symptom of illness. It was Mulrady's horse that fell, and on attempting to pull it up, the animal was found to be dead. Ayrton examined it immediately, but was quite at a loss to account for the disaster.

"The beast must have broken some blood vessels," said Glenarvan.

"Evidently," replied Ayrton.

"Take my horse, Mulrady," added Glenarvan. "I will join Lady Helena in the wagon."

Mulrady obeyed, and the little party continued their fatiguing ascent, leaving the carcass of the dead animal to the ravens.

The Australian Alps are of no great thickness, and the base is not more than eight miles wide. Consequently if the pass chosen by Ayrton came out on the eastern side, they might hope to get over the high barrier within forty-eight hours more. The difficulty of the route would then be surmounted, and they would only have to get to the sea.

During the 18th the travelers reached the top-most point of the pass, about 2,000 feet high. They found themselves on an open plateau, with nothing to intercept the view. Toward the north the quiet waters of Lake Omco, all alive with aquatic birds, and beyond this lay the vast plains of the Murray. To the south were the wide spreading plains of Gippsland, with its abundant gold-fields and tall forests. There nature was still mistress of the products and water, and great trees where the woodman's ax was as yet unknown, and the squatters, then five in number, could not struggle against her. It seemed as if this chain of the Alps separated two different countries, one of which had retained its primitive wildness. The sun went down, and a few solitary rays piercing the rosy clouds, lighted up the Murray district, leaving Gippsland in deep shadow, as if night had suddenly fallen on the whole region. The contrast was presented very vividly to the spectators placed between these two countries so divided, and some emotion filled the minds of the travelers, as they contemplated the almost unknown district they were about to traverse right to the frontiers of Victoria.

They camped on the plateau that night, and next day the descent commenced. It was tolerably rapid. A hailstorm of extreme violence assailed the travelers, and obliged them to seek a shelter among the rocks. It was not hail-stones, but regular lumps of ice, as large as one's hand, which fell from the stormy clouds. A waterspout could not have come down with more violence, and sundry big bruises warned Paganel and Robert to retreat. The wagon was riddled in several places, and few coverings would have held out against those sharp icicles, some of which had fastened themselves into the trunks of the trees. It was impossible to go on till this tremendous shower was over, unless the travelers wished to be stoned. It lasted about an hour, and then the march commenced anew over slanting rocks still slippery after the hail.

Toward evening the wagon, very much shaken and disjointed in several parts, but still standing firm on its wooden disks, came down the last slopes of the Alps, among great isolated pines. The passage ended in the plains of Gippsland. The chain of the Alps was safely passed, and the usual arrangements were made for the nightly encampment.

On the 21st, at daybreak, the journey was resumed with an ardor which never relaxed. Everyone was eager to reach the goal—that is to say the Pacific Ocean—at that part where the wreck of the BRITANNIA had occurred. Nothing could be done in the lonely wilds of Gippsland, and Ayrton urged Lord Glenarvan to send orders at once for the DUNCAN to repair to the coast, in order to have at hand all means of research. He thought it would certainly be advisable to take advantage of the Lucknow route to Melbourne. If they waited it would be difficult to find any way of direct communication with the capital.

This advice seemed good, and Paganel recommended that they should act upon it. He also thought that the presence of the yacht would be very useful, and he added, that if the Lucknow road was once passed, it would be impossible to communicate with Melbourne.

Glenarvan was undecided what to do, and perhaps he would have yielded to Ayrton's arguments, if the Major had not combated this decision vigorously. He maintained that the presence of Ayrton was necessary to the expedition, that he would know the country about the coast, and that if any chance should put them on the track of Harry Grant, the quartermaster would be better able to follow it up than any one else, and, finally, that he alone could point out the exact spot where the shipwreck occurred.

McNabbs voted therefore for the continuation of the voyage, without making the least change in their programme. John Mangles was of the same opinion. The young captain said even that orders would reach the DUNCAN more easily from Twofold Bay, than if a message was sent two hundred miles over a wild country.

His counsel prevailed. It was decided that they should wait till they came to Twofold Bay. The Major watched Ayrton narrowly, and noticed his disappointed look. But he said nothing, keeping his observations, as usual, to himself.

The plains which lay at the foot of the Australian Alps were level, but slightly inclined toward the east. Great clumps of mimosas and eucalyptus, and various odorous gum-trees, broke the uniform monotony here and there. The *gastrolobium grandiflorum* covered the ground, with its bushes covered with gay flowers. Several unimportant creeks, mere streams full of little rushes, and half covered up with orchids, often interrupted the route. They had to ford these. Flocks of bustards and emus fled at the approach of the travelers. Below the shrubs, kangaroos were leaping and springing like dancing jacks. But the hunters of the party were not thinking much of the sport, and the horses little needed any additional fatigue.

Moreover, a sultry heat oppressed the plain. The atmosphere was completely saturated with electricity, and its influence was felt by men and beasts. They just dragged themselves along, and cared for nothing else. The silence was only interrupted by the cries of Ayrton urging on his burdened team.

From noon to two o'clock they went through a curious forest of ferns, which would have excited the admiration of less weary travelers. These plants in full flower measured thirty feet in height. Horses and riders passed easily beneath their drooping leaves, and sometimes the spurs would clash against the woody stems. Beneath these immovable parasols there was a refreshing coolness which every one appreciated. Jacques Paganel, always demonstrative, gave such deep sighs of satisfaction that the paroquets and cockatoos flew out in alarm, making a deafening chorus of noisy chatter.

The geographer was going on with his sighs and jubilations with the utmost coolness, when his companions suddenly saw him reel forward, and he and his horse fell down in a lump. Was it giddiness, or worse still, suffocation, caused by the high temperature? They ran to him, exclaiming: "Paganel! Paganel! what is the matter?"

"Just this. I have no horse, now!" he replied, disengaging his feet from the stirrups.

"What! your horse?"

"Dead like Mulrady's, as if a thunderbolt had struck him."

Glenarvan, John Mangles, and Wilson examined the animal; and found

Paganel was right. His horse had been suddenly struck dead.

"That is strange," said John.

"Very strange, truly," muttered the Major.

Glenarvan was greatly disturbed by this fresh accident. He could not get a fresh horse in the desert, and if an epidemic was going to seize their steeds, they would be seriously embarrassed how to proceed.

Before the close of the day, it seemed as if the word epidemic was really going to be justified. A third horse, Wilson's, fell dead, and what was, perhaps equally disastrous, one of the bullocks also. The means of traction and transport were now reduced to three bullocks and four horses.

CHAPTER XV SUSPICIOUS OCCURRENCES

The situation became grave. The unmounted horsemen might walk, of course, as many squatters had done already; but if they abandoned the wagon, what would the ladies do? Could they go over the one hundred and twenty miles which lay between them and Twofold Bay? John Mangles and Lord Glenarvan examined the surviving horses with great uneasiness, but there was not the slightest symptom of illness or feebleness in them. The animals were in perfect health, and bravely bearing the fatigues of the voyage. This somewhat reassured Glenarvan, and made him hope the malady would strike no more victims. Ayrton agreed with him, but was unable to find the least solution of the mystery.

They went on again, the wagon serving, from time to time, as a house of rest for the pedestrians. In the evening, after a march of only ten miles, the signal to halt was given, and the tent pitched. The night passed without inconvenience beneath a vast mass of bushy ferns, under which enormous bats, properly called flying foxes, were flapping about.

The next day's journey was good; there were no new calamities. The health of the expedition remained satisfactory; horses and cattle did their task cheerily. Lady Helena's drawing-room was very lively, thanks to the number of visitors. M. Olbinett busied himself in passing round refreshments which were very acceptable in such hot weather. Half a barrel of Scotch ale was sent in bodily. Barclay and Co. was declared to be the greatest man in Great Britain, even above Wellington, who could never have manufactured such good beer. This was a Scotch estimate. Jacques Paganel drank largely, and discoursed still more *de omni re scibili.*

A day so well commenced seemed as if it could not but end well; they had gone fifteen good miles, and managed to get over a pretty hilly district where the soil was reddish. There was every reason to hope they might camp that same night on the banks of the Snowy River, an important river which throws itself into the Pacific, south of Victoria.

Already the wheels of the wagon were making deep ruts on the wide plains, covered with blackish alluvium, as it passed on between tufts of luxuriant grass and fresh fields of gastrolobium. As evening came on, a white mist on the horizon marked the course of the Snowy River. Several additional miles were got over, and a forest of tall trees came in sight at a bend of the road, behind a gentle eminence. Ayrton turned his team a little toward the great trunks, lost in shadow, and he had got to the skirts of the wood, about half-a-mile from the river, when the wagon suddenly sank up to the middle of the wheels.

"Stop!" he called out to the horsemen following him.

"What is wrong?" inquired Glenarvan.

"We have stuck in the mud," replied Ayrton.

He tried to stimulate the bullocks to a fresh effort by voice and goad, but the animals were buried half-way up their legs, and could not stir.

"Let us camp here," suggested John Mangles.

"It would certainly be the best place," said Ayrton. "We shall see by daylight tomorrow how to get ourselves out."

Glenarvan acted on their advice, and came to a halt. Night came on rapidly after a brief twilight, but the heat did not withdraw with the light. Stifling vapors filled the air, and occasionally bright flashes of lightning, the reflections of a distant storm, lighted up the sky with a fiery glare. Arrangements were made for the night immediately. They did the best they could with the sunk wagon, and the tent was pitched beneath the shelter of the great trees; and if the rain did not come, they had not much to complain about.

Ayrton succeeded, though with some difficulty, in extricating the three bullocks. These courageous beasts were engulfed up to their flanks. The quartermaster turned them out with the four horses, and allowed no one but himself to see after their pasturage. He always executed his task wisely, and this evening Glenarvan noticed he redoubled his care, for which he took occasion to thank him, the preservation of the team being of supreme importance.

Meantime, the travelers were dispatching a hasty supper. Fatigue and heat destroy appetite, and sleep was needed more than food. Lady Helena and Miss Grant speedily bade the company good-night, and retired. Their companions soon stretched themselves under the tent or outside under the trees, which is no great hardship in this salubrious climate.

Gradually they all fell into a heavy sleep. The darkness deepened owing to a thick current of clouds which overspread the sky. There was not a breath of wind. The silence of night was only interrupted by the cries of the "morepork" in the minor key, like the mournful cuckoos of Europe.

Towards eleven o'clock, after a wretched, heavy, unrefreshing sleep, the Major woke. His half-closed eyes were struck with a faint light running among the great trees. It looked like a white sheet, and glittered like a lake, and McNabbs thought at first it was the commencement of a fire.

He started up, and went toward the wood; but what was his surprise to perceive a purely natural phenomenon! Before him lay an immense bed of mushrooms, which emitted a phosphorescent light. The luminous spores of the cryptograms shone in the darkness with intensity.

The Major, who had no selfishness about him, was going to waken Paganel, that he might see this phenomenon with his own eyes, when something occurred which arrested him. This phosphorescent light illumined the distance half a mile, and McNabbs fancied he saw a shadow pass across the edge of it. Were his eyes deceiving him? Was it some hallucination?

McNabbs lay down on the ground, and, after a close scrutiny, he could distinctly see several men stooping down and lifting themselves up alternately, as if they were looking on the ground for recent marks.

The Major resolved to find out what these fellows were about, and without the least hesitation or so much as arousing his companions, crept along, lying flat on the ground, like a savage on the prairies, completely hidden among the long grass.

CHAPTER XVI A STARTLING DISCOVERY

IT was a frightful night. At two A. M. the rain began to fall in torrents from the stormy clouds, and continued till daybreak. The tent became an insufficient shelter. Glenarvan and his companions took refuge in the wagon; they did not sleep, but talked of one thing and another. The Major alone, whose brief absence had not been noticed, contented himself with being a silent listener. There was reason to fear that if the storm lasted longer the Snowy River would overflow its banks, which would be a very unlucky thing for the wagon, stuck fast as it was already in the soft ground. Mulrady, Ayrton and Mangles went several times to ascertain the height of the water, and came back dripping from head to foot.

At last day appeared; the rain ceased, but sunlight could not break through the thick clouds. Large patches of yellowish water— muddy, dirty ponds indeed they were— covered the ground. A hot steam rose from the soaking earth, and saturated the atmosphere with unhealthy humidity.

Glenarvan's first concern was the wagon; this was the main thing in his eyes. They examined the ponderous vehicle, and found it sunk in the mud in a deep hollow in the stiff clay. The forepart had disappeared completely, and the hind part up to the axle. It would be a hard job to get the heavy conveyance out, and would need the united strength of men, bullocks, and horses.

"At any rate, we must make haste," said John Mangles. "If the clay dries, it will make our task still more difficult."

"Let us be quick, then," replied Ayrton.

Glenarvan, his two sailors, John Mangles, and Ayrton went off at once into the wood, where the animals had passed the night. It was a gloomy-looking forest of tall gum-trees; nothing but dead trees, with wide spaces between, which had been barked for ages, or rather skinned like the cork-oak at harvest time. A miserable network of bare branches was seen above two hundred feet high in the air. Not a bird built its nest in these aerial skeletons; not a leaf trembled on the dry branches, which rattled together like bones. To what cataclysm is this phenomenon to be attributed, so frequent in Australia, entire forests struck dead by some epidemic; no one knows; neither the oldest natives, nor their ancestors who have lain long buried in the groves of the dead, have ever seen them green.

Glenarvan as he went along kept his eye fixed on the gray sky, on which the smallest branch of the gum-trees was sharply defined. Ayrton was astonished not to discover the horses and bullocks where he had left them the preceding night. They could not have wandered far with the hobbles on their legs.

They looked over the wood, but saw no signs of them, and Ayrton returned to the banks of the river, where magnificent mimosas were growing. He gave a cry well known to his team, but there was no reply. The quartermaster seemed uneasy, and his companions looked at him with disappointed faces. An hour had passed in vain endeavors, and Glenarvan was about to go back to the wagon, when a neigh struck on his ear, and immediately after a bellow.

"They are there!" cried John Mangles, slipping between the tall branches of gastrolobium, which grew high enough to hide a whole flock. Glenarvan, Mulrady, and Ayrton darted after him, and speedily shared his stupefaction at the spectacle which met their gaze.

Two bullocks and three horses lay stretched on the ground, struck down like the rest. Their bodies were already cold, and a flock of half-starved looking ravens croaking among the mimosas were watching the unexpected prey. Glenarvan and his party gazed at each other and Wilson could not keep back the oath that rose to his lips.

"What do you mean, Wilson?" said Glenarvan, with difficulty controlling himself. "Ayrton, bring away the bullock and the horse we have left; they will have to serve us now."

"If the wagon were not sunk in the mud," said John Mangles, "these two animals, by making short journeys, would be able to take us to the coast; so we must get the vehicle out, cost what it may."

"We will try, John," replied Glenarvan. "Let us go back now, or they will be uneasy at our long absence."

Ayrton removed the hobbles from the bullock and Mulrady from the horse, and they began to return to the encampment, following the winding margin of the river. In half an hour they rejoined Paganel, and McNabbs, and the ladies, and told them of this fresh disaster.

"Upon my honor, Ayrton," the Major could not help saying, "it is a pity that you hadn't had the shoeing of all our beasts when we forded the Wimerra."

"Why, sir?" asked Ayrton.

"Because out of all our horses only the one your blacksmith had in his hands has escaped the common fate."

"That's true," said John Mangles. "It's strange it happens so."

"A mere chance, and nothing more," replied the quartermaster, looking firmly at the Major.

Major McNabbs bit his lips as if to keep back something he was about to say. Glenarvan and the rest waited for him to speak out his thoughts, but the Major was silent, and went up to the wagon, which Ayrton was examining.

"What was he going to say. Mangles?" asked Glenarvan.

"I don't know," replied the young captain; "but the Major is not at all a man to speak without reason."

"No, John," said Lady Helena. "McNabbs must have suspicions about Ayrton."

"Suspicions!" exclaimed Paganel, shrugging his shoulders.

"And what can they be?" asked Glenarvan. "Does he suppose him capable of having killed our horses and bullocks? And for what purpose? Is not Ayrton's interest identical with our own?"

"You are right, dear Edward," said Lady Helena! "and what is more, the quartermaster has given us incontestable proofs of his devotion ever since the commencement of the journey."

"Certainly he has," replied Mangles; "but still, what could the Major mean? I wish he would speak his mind plainly out."

"Does he suppose him acting in concert with the convicts?" asked Paganel, imprudently.

"What convicts?" said Miss Grant.

"Monsieur Paganel is making a mistake," replied John Mangles, instantly.

"He knows very well there are no convicts in the province of Victoria."

"Ah, that is true," returned Paganel, trying to get out of his unlucky speech. "Whatever had I got in my head? Convicts! who ever heard of convicts being in Australia? Besides, they would scarcely have disembarked before they would turn into good, honest men. The climate, you know, Miss Mary, the regenerative climate—"

Here the poor SAVANT stuck fast, unable to get further, like the wagon in the mud. Lady Helena looked at him in surprise, which quite deprived him of his remaining *sang-froid;* but seeing his embarrassment, she took Mary away to the side of the tent, where M. Olbinett was laying out an elaborate breakfast.

"I deserve to be transported myself," said Paganel, woefully.

"I think so," said Glenarvan.

And after this grave reply, which completely overwhelmed the worthy geographer, Glenarvan and John Mangles went toward the wagon.

They found Ayrton and the two sailors doing their best to get it out of the deep ruts, and the bullock and horse, yoked together, were straining every muscle. Wilson and Mulrady were pushing the wheels, and the quartermaster urging on the team with voice and goad; but the heavy vehicle did not stir, the clay, already dry, held it as firmly as if sealed by some hydraulic cement.

John Mangles had the clay watered to loosen it, but it was of no use. After renewed vigorous efforts, men and animals stopped. Unless the vehicle was taken to pieces, it would be impossible to extricate it from the mud; but they had no tools for the purpose, and could not attempt such a task.

However, Ayrton, who was for conquering this obstacle at all costs, was about to commence afresh, when Glenarvan stopped him by saying: "Enough, Ayrton, enough. We must husband the strength of our remaining horse and bullock. If we are obliged to continue our journey on foot, the one animal can carry the ladies and the other the provisions. They may thus still be of great service to us."

"Very well, my Lord," replied the quartermaster, un-yoking the exhausted beasts.

"Now, friends," added Glenarvan, "let us return to the encampment and deliberately examine our situation, and determine on our course of action."

After a tolerably good breakfast to make up for their bad night, the discussion was opened, and every one of the party was asked to give his opinion. The first point was to ascertain their exact position, and this was referred to Paganel, who informed them, with his customary rigorous accuracy, that the expedition had been stopped on the 37th parallel, in longitude 147 degrees 53 minutes, on the banks of the Snowy River.

"What is the exact longitude of Twofold Bay?" asked Glenarvan.

"One hundred and fifty degrees," replied Paganel; "two degrees seven minutes distant from this, and that is equal to seventy-five miles."

"And Melbourne is?"

"Two hundred miles off at least."

"Very good. Our position being then settled, what is best to do?"

The response was unanimous to get to the coast without delay.

Lady Helena and Mary Grant undertook to go five miles a day.

The courageous ladies did not shrink, if necessary, from walking

the whole distance between the Snowy River and Twofold Bay.

"You are a brave traveling companion, dear Helena," said Lord Glenarvan. "But are we sure of finding at the bay all we want when we get there?"

"Without the least doubt," replied Paganel. "Eden is a municipality which already numbers many years in existence; its port must have frequent communication with Melbourne. I suppose even at Delegete, on the Victoria frontier, thirty-five miles from here, we might revictual our expedition, and find fresh means of transport."

"And the DUNCAN?" asked Ayrton. "Don't you think it advisable to send for her to come to the bay?"

"What do you think, John?" said Glenarvan.

"I don't think your lordship should be in any hurry about it," replied the young captain, after brief reflection. "There will be time enough to give orders to Tom Austin, and summon him to the coast."

"That's quite certain," added Paganel.

"You see," said John, "in four or five days we shall reach Eden."

"Four or five days!" repeated Ayrton, shaking his head; "say fifteen or twenty, Captain, if you don't want to repent your mistake when it is too late."

"Fifteen or twenty days to go seventy-five miles?" cried Glenarvan.

"At the least, my Lord. You are going to traverse the most difficult portion of Victoria, a desert, where everything is wanting, the squatters say; plains covered with scrub, where is no beaten track and no stations. You will have to walk hatchet or torch in hand, and, believe me, that's not quick work."

Ayrton had spoken in a firm tone, and Paganel, at whom all the others looked inquiringly, nodded his head in token of his agreement in opinion with the quartermaster.

But John Mangles said, "Well, admitting these difficulties, in fifteen days at most your Lordship can send orders to the DUNCAN."

"I have to add," said Ayrton, "that the principal difficulties are not the obstacles in the road, but the Snowy River has to be crossed, and most probably we must wait till the water goes down."

"Wait!" cried John. "Is there no ford?"

"I think not," replied Ayrton. "This morning I was looking for some practical crossing, but could not find any. It is unusual to meet with such a tumultuous river at this time of the year, and it is a fatality against which I am powerless."

"Is this Snowy River wide?" asked Lady Helena.

"Wide and deep, Madam," replied Ayrton; "a mile wide, with an impetuous current. A good swimmer could not go over without danger."

"Let us build a boat then," said Robert, who never stuck at anything. "We have only to cut down a tree and hollow it out, and get in and be off."

"He's going ahead, this boy of Captain Grant's!" said Paganel.

"And he's right," returned John Mangles. "We shall be forced to come to that, and I think it is useless to waste our time in idle discussion."

"What do you think of it, Ayrton?" asked Glenarvan seriously.

"I think, my Lord, that a month hence, unless some help arrives, we shall find ourselves still on the banks of the Snowy."

"Well, then, have you any better plan to propose?" said John Mangles, somewhat impatiently.

"Yes, that the DUNCAN should leave Melbourne, and go to the east coast."

"Oh, always the same story! And how could her presence at the bay facilitate our means of getting there?"

CHAPTER XVI A STARTLING DISCOVERY

Ayrton waited an instant before answering, and then said, rather evasively: "I have no wish to obtrude my opinions. What I do is for our common good, and I am ready to start the moment his honor gives the signal." And he crossed his arms and was silent.

"That is no reply, Ayrton," said Glenarvan. "Tell us your plan, and we will discuss it. What is it you propose?"

Ayrton replied in a calm tone of assurance: "I propose that we should not venture beyond the Snowy in our present condition. It is here we must wait till help comes, and this help can only come from the DUNCAN. Let us camp here, where we have provisions, and let one of us take your orders to Tom Austin to go on to Twofold Bay."

This unexpected proposition was greeted with astonishment, and by John Mangles with openly-expressed opposition.

"Meantime," continued Ayrton, "either the river will get lower, and allow us to ford it, or we shall have time to make a canoe. This is the plan I submit for your Lordship's approval."

"Well, Ayrton," replied Glenarvan, "your plan is worthy of serious consideration. The worst thing about it is the delay it would cause; but it would save us great fatigue, and perhaps danger. What do you think of it, friends?"

"Speak your mind, McNabbs," said Lady Helena. "Since the beginning of the discussion you have been only a listener, and very sparing of your words."

"Since you ask my advice," said the Major, "I will give it you frankly.

I think Ayrton has spoken wisely and well, and I side with him."

Such a reply was hardly looked for, as hitherto the Major had been strongly opposed to Ayrton's project. Ayrton himself was surprised, and gave a hasty glance at the Major. However, Paganel, Lady Helena, and the sailors were all of the same way of thinking; and since McNabbs had come over to his opinion, Glenarvan decided that the quartermaster's plan should be adopted in principle.

"And now, John," he added, "don't you think yourself it would be prudent to encamp here, on the banks of the river Snowy, till we can get some means of conveyance."

"Yes," replied John Mangles, "if our messenger can get across the Snowy when we cannot."

All eyes were turned on the quartermaster, who said, with the air of a man who knew what he was about: "The messenger will not cross the river."

"Indeed!" said John Mangles.

"He will simply go back to the Lucknow Road which leads straight to Melbourne."

"Go two hundred and fifty miles on foot!" cried the young Captain.

"On horseback," replied Ayrton. "There is one horse sound enough at present. It will only be an affair of four days. Allow the DUNCAN two days more to get to the bay and twenty hours to get back to the camp, and in a week the messenger can be back with the entire crew of the vessel."

The Major nodded approvingly as Ayrton spoke, to the profound astonishment of John Mangles; but as every one was in favor of the plan all there was to do was to carry it out as quickly as possible.

"Now, then, friends," said Glenarvan, "we must settle who is to be our messenger. It will be a fatiguing, perilous mission. I would not conceal the fact from you. Who is disposed, then, to sacrifice himself for his companions and carry our instructions to Melbourne?"

Wilson and Mulrady, and also Paganel, John Mangles and Robert instantly offered their services. John particularly insisted that he should be intrusted with the business; but Ayrton, who had been silent till that moment, now said: "With your Honor's permission I will go myself. I am accustomed to all the country round. Many a time I have been across worse parts. I can go through where another would stick. I ask then, for the good of all, that I may be sent to Melbourne. A word from you will accredit me with your chief officer, and in six days I guarantee the DUNCAN shall be in Twofold Bay."

"That's well spoken," replied Glenarvan. "You are a clever, daring fellow, and you will succeed."

It was quite evident the quartermaster was the fittest man for the mission. All the rest withdrew from the competition. John Mangles made this one last objection, that the presence of Ayrton was necessary to discover traces of the BRITANNIA or Harry Grant. But the Major justly observed that the expedition would remain on the banks of the Snowy till the return of Ayrton, that they had no idea of resuming their search without him, and that consequently his absence would not in the least prejudice the Captain's interests.

"Well, go, Ayrton," said Glenarvan. "Be as quick as you can, and come back by Eden to our camp."

A gleam of satisfaction shot across the quartermaster's face. He turned away his head, but not before John Mangles caught the look and instinctively felt his old distrust of Ayrton revive.

The quartermaster made immediate preparations for departure, assisted by the two sailors, one of whom saw to the horse and the other to the provisions. Glenarvan, meantime, wrote his letter for Tom Austin. He ordered his chief officer to repair without delay to Twofold Bay. He introduced the quartermaster to him as a man worthy of all confidence. On arriving at the coast, Tom was to dispatch a detachment of sailors from the yacht under his orders.

Glenarvan was just at this part of his letter, when McNabbs, who was following him with his eyes, asked him in a singular tone, how he wrote Ayrton's name.

"Why, as it is pronounced, of course," replied Glenarvan.

"It is a mistake," replied the Major quietly. "He pronounces it AYRTON, but he writes it *Ben Joyce!*"

CHAPTER XVII THE PLOT UNVEILED

THE revelation of Tom Ayrton's name was like a clap of thunder.

Ayrton had started up quickly and grasped his revolver.

A report was heard, and Glenarvan fell wounded by a ball.

Gunshots resounded at the same time outside.

John Mangles and the sailors, after their first surprise, would have seized Ben Joyce; but the bold convict had already disappeared and rejoined his gang scattered among the gum-trees.

The tent was no shelter against the balls. It was necessary to beat a retreat. Glenarvan was slightly wounded, but could stand up.

"To the wagon—to the wagon!" cried John Mangles, dragging Lady Helena and Mary Grant along, who were soon in safety behind the thick curtains.

John and the Major, and Paganel and the sailors seized their carbines in readiness to repulse the convicts. Glenarvan and Robert went in beside the ladies, while Olbinett rushed to the common defense.

These events occurred with the rapidity of lightning. John Mangles watched the skirts of the wood attentively. The reports had ceased suddenly on the arrival of Ben Joyce; profound silence had succeeded the noisy fusillade. A few wreaths of white smoke were still curling over the tops of the gum trees. The tall tufts of gastrolobium were motionless. All signs of attack had disappeared.

The Major and John Mangles examined the wood closely as far as the great trees; the place was abandoned. Numerous footmarks were there and several half-burned caps were lying smoking on the ground. The Major, like a prudent man, extinguished these carefully, for a spark would be enough to kindle a tremendous conflagration in this forest of dry trees.

"The convicts have disappeared!" said John Mangles.

"Yes," replied the Major; "and the disappearance of them

makes me uneasy. I prefer seeing them face to face.

Better to meet a tiger on the plain than a serpent in the grass.

Let us beat the bushes all round the wagon."

The Major and John hunted all round the country, but there was not a convict to be seen from the edge of the wood right down to the river. Ben Joyce and his gang seemed to have flown away like a flock of marauding birds. It was too sudden a disappearance to let the travelers feel perfectly safe; consequently they resolved to keep a sharp lookout. The wagon, a regular fortress buried in mud, was made the center of the camp, and two men mounted guard round it, who were relieved hour by hour.

The first care of Lady Helena and Mary was to dress Glenarvan's wound. Lady Helena rushed toward him in terror, as he fell down struck by Ben Joyce's ball. Controlling her agony, the courageous woman helped her husband into the wagon. Then his shoulder was bared, and the Major found, on examination, that the ball had only gone into the flesh, and there was no internal lesion. Neither bone nor muscle appeared to be injured. The wound bled profusely, but Glenarvan could use his fingers and forearm; and consequently there was no occasion for any uneasiness about the issue. As soon as his shoulder was dressed, he would not allow any more fuss to be made about himself, but at once entered on the business in hand.

All the party, except Mulrady and Wilson, who were on guard, were brought into the wagon, and the Major was asked to explain how this DENOUEMENT had come about.

Before commencing his recital, he told Lady Helena about the escape of the convicts at Perth, and their appearance in Victoria; as also their complicity in the railway catastrophe. He handed her the *Australian and New Zealand Gazette* they had bought in Seymour, and added that a reward had been offered by the police for the apprehension of Ben Joyce, a redoubtable bandit, who had become a noted character during the last eighteen months, for doing deeds of villainy and crime.

But how had McNabbs found out that Ayrton and Ben Joyce were one and the same individual? This was the mystery to be unraveled, and the Major soon explained it.

Ever since their first meeting, McNabbs had felt an instinctive distrust of the quartermaster. Two or three insignificant facts, a hasty glance exchanged between him and the blacksmith at the Wimerra River, his unwillingness to cross towns and villages, his persistence about getting the DUNCAN summoned to the coast, the strange death of the animals entrusted to his care, and, lastly, a want of frankness in all his behavior—all these details combined had awakened the Major's suspicions.

However, he could not have brought any direct accusation against him till the events of the preceding evening had occurred. He then told of his experience.

McNabbs, slipping between the tall shrubs, got within reach of the suspicious shadows he had noticed about half a mile away from the encampment. The phosphorescent furze emitted a faint light, by which he could discern three men examining marks on the ground, and one of the three was the blacksmith of Black Point.

"'It is them!' said one of the men. 'Yes,' replied another, 'there is the trefoil on the mark of the horseshoe. It has been like that since the Wimerra.' 'All the horses are dead.' 'The poison is not far off.' 'There is enough to kill a regiment of cavalry.' 'A useful plant this gastrolobium.'

"I heard them say this to each other, and then they were quite silent; but I did not know enough yet, so I followed them. Soon the conversation began again. 'He is a clever fellow, this Ben Joyce,' said the blacksmith. 'A capital quartermaster, with his invention of shipwreck.' 'If his project succeeds, it will be a stroke of fortune.' 'He is a very devil, is this Ayrton.' 'Call him Ben Joyce, for he has well earned his name.' And then the scoundrels left the forest.

"I had all the information I wanted now, and came back to the camp quite convinced, begging Paganel's pardon, that Australia does not reform criminals."

This was all the Major's story, and his companions sat silently thinking over it.

"Then Ayrton has dragged us here," said Glenarvan, pale with anger, "on purpose to rob and assassinate us."

"For nothing else," replied the Major; "and ever since we left the Wimerra, his gang has been on our track and spying on us, waiting for a favorable opportunity."

"Yes."

"Then the wretch was never one of the sailors on the BRITANNIA; he had stolen the name of Ayrton and the shipping papers."

They were all looking at McNabbs for an answer, for he must have put the question to himself already.

"There is no great certainty about the matter," he replied, in his usual calm voice; "but in my opinion the man's name is really Ayrton. Ben Joyce is his *nom de guerre*. It is an incontestible fact that he knew Harry Grant, and also that he was quartermaster on the BRITANNIA. These facts were proved by the minute details given us by Ayrton, and are corroborated by the conversation between the convicts, which I repeated to you. We need not lose ourselves in vain conjectures, but consider it as certain that Ben Joyce is Ayrton, and that Ayrton is Ben Joyce; that is to say, one of the crew of the BRITANNIA has turned leader of the convict gang."

The explanations of McNabbs were accepted without discussion.

"Now, then," said Glenarvan, "will you tell us how and why

Harry Grant's quartermaster comes to be in Australia?"

"How, I don't know," replied McNabbs; "and the police declare they are as ignorant on the subject as myself. Why, it is impossible to say; that is a mystery which the future may explain."

"The police are not even aware of Ayrton's identity with Ben Joyce," said John Mangles.

"You are right, John," replied the Major, "and this circumstance would throw light on their search."

"Then, I suppose," said Lady Helena, "the wicked wretch had got work on Paddy O'Moore's farm with a criminal intent?"

"There is not the least doubt of it. He was planning some evil design against the Irishman, when a better chance presented itself. Chance led us into his presence. He heard Paganel's story and all about the shipwreck, and the audacious fellow determined to act his part immediately. The expedition was decided on. At the Wimerra he found means of communicating with one of his gang, the blacksmith of Black Point, and left traces of our journey which might be easily recognized. The gang followed us. A poisonous plant enabled them gradually to kill our bullocks and horses. At the right moment he sunk us in the marshes of the Snowy, and gave us into the hands of his gang."

Such was the history of Ben Joyce. The Major had shown him up in his character—a bold and formidable criminal. His manifestly evil designs called for the utmost vigilance on the part of Glenarvan. Happily the unmasked bandit was less to be feared than the traitor.

But one serious consequence must come out of this revelation; no one had thought of it yet except Mary Grant. John Mangles was the first to notice her pale, despairing face; he understood what was passing in her mind at a glance.

"Miss Mary! Miss Mary!" he cried; "you are crying!"

"Crying, my child!" said Lady Helena.

"My father, madam, my father!" replied the poor girl.

She could say no more, but the truth flashed on every mind. They all knew the cause of her grief, and why tears fell from her eyes and her father's name came to her lips.

The discovery of Ayrton's treachery had destroyed all hope; the convict had invented a shipwreck to entrap Glenarvan. In the conversation overheard by McNabbs, the convicts had plainly said that the BRITANNIA had never been wrecked on the rocks in Twofold Bay. Harry Grant had never set foot on the Australian continent!

A second time they had been sent on the wrong track by an erroneous interpretation of the document. Gloomy silence fell on the whole party at the sight of the children's sorrow, and no one could find a cheering word to say. Robert was crying in his sister's arms. Paganel muttered in a tone of vexation: "That unlucky document! It may boast of having half-crazed a dozen peoples' wits!" The worthy geographer was in such a rage with himself, that he struck his forehead as if he would smash it in.

Glenarvan went out to Mulrady and Wilson, who were keeping watch. Profound silence reigned over the plain between the wood and the river. Ben Joyce and his band must be at considerable distance, for the atmosphere was in such a state of complete torpor that the slightest sound would have been heard. It was evident, from the flocks of birds on the lower branches of the trees, and the kangaroos feeding quietly on the young shoots, and a couple of emus whose confiding heads passed between the great clumps of bushes, that those peaceful solitudes were untroubled by the presence of human beings.

"You have neither seen nor heard anything for the last hour?" said Glenarvan to the two sailors.

"Nothing whatever, your honor," replied Wilson. "The convicts must be miles away from here."

"They were not in numbers enough to attack us, I suppose," added Mulrady. "Ben Joyce will have gone to recruit his party, with some bandits like himself, among the bushrangers who may be lurking about the foot of the Alps."

"That is probably the case, Mulrady," replied Glenarvan. "The rascals are cowards; they know we are armed, and well armed too. Perhaps they are waiting for nightfall to commence the attack. We must redouble our watchfulness. Oh, if we could only get out of this bog, and down the coast; but this swollen river bars our passage. I would pay its weight in gold for a raft which would carry us over to the other side."

"Why does not your honor give orders for a raft to be constructed?

We have plenty of wood."

"No, Wilson," replied Glenarvan; "this Snowy is not a river, it is an impassable torrent."

John Mangles, the Major, and Paganel just then came out of the wagon on purpose to examine the state of the river. They found it still so swollen by the heavy rain that the water was a foot above the level. It formed an impetuous current, like the American rapids. To venture over that foaming current and that rushing flood, broken into a thousand eddies and hollows and gulfs, was impossible.

John Mangles declared the passage impracticable. "But we must not stay here," he added, "without attempting anything. What we were going to do before Ayrton's treachery is still more necessary now."

"What do you mean, John?" asked Glenarvan.

"I mean that our need is urgent, and that since we cannot go to Twofold Bay, we must go to Melbourne. We have still one horse. Give it to me, my Lord, and I will go to Melbourne."

"But that will be a dangerous venture, John," said Glenarvan. "Not to speak of the perils of a journey of two hundred miles over an unknown country, the road and the by-ways will be guarded by the accomplices of Ben Joyce."

"I know it, my Lord, but I know also that things can't stay long as they are; Ayrton only asked a week's absence to fetch the crew of the DUNCAN, and I will be back to the Snowy River in six days. Well, my Lord, what are your commands?"

"Before Glenarvan decides," said Paganel, "I must make an observation.

That some one must go to Melbourne is evident, but that John Mangles should be the one to expose himself to the risk, cannot be.

He is the captain of the DUNCAN, and must be careful of his life.

I will go instead."

"That is all very well, Paganel," said the Major; "but why should you be the one to go?"

"Are we not here?" said Mulrady and Wilson.

"And do you think," replied McNabbs, "that a journey of two hundred miles on horseback frightens me."

"Friends," said Glenarvan, "one of us must go, so let it be decided by drawing lots. Write all our names, Paganel."

"Not yours, my Lord," said John Mangles.

"And why not?"

"What! separate you from Lady Helena, and before your wound is healed, too!"

"Glenarvan," said Paganel, "you cannot leave the expedition."

"No," added the Major. "Your place is here, Edward, you ought not to go."

"Danger is involved in it," said Glenarvan, "and I will take my share along with the rest. Write the names, Paganel, and put mine among them, and I hope the lot may fall on me."

His will was obeyed. The names were written, and the lots drawn.

Fate fixed on Mulrady. The brave sailor shouted hurrah! and said:

"My Lord, I am ready to start." Glenarvan pressed his hand, and then

went back to the wagon, leaving John Mangles and the Major on watch.

Lady Helena was informed of the determination to send a message to Melbourne, and that they had drawn lots who should go, and Mulrady had been chosen. Lady Helena said a few kind words to the brave sailor, which went straight to his heart. Fate could hardly have chosen a better man, for he was not only brave and intelligent, but robust and superior to all fatigue.

Mulrady's departure was fixed for eight o'clock, immediately after the short twilight. Wilson undertook to get the horse ready. He had a project in his head of changing the horse's left shoe, for one off the horses that had died in the night. This would prevent the convicts from tracking Mulrady, or following him, as they were not mounted.

While Wilson was arranging this, Glenarvan got his letter ready for Tom Austin, but his wounded arm troubled him, and he asked Paganel to write it for him. The SAVANT was so absorbed in one fixed idea that he seemed hardly to know what he was about. In all this succession of vexations, it must be said the document was always uppermost in Paganel's mind. He was always worrying himself about each word, trying to discover some new meaning, and losing the wrong interpretation of it, and going over and over himself in perplexities.

He did not hear Glenarvan when he first spoke, but on the request being made a second time, he said: "Ah, very well. I'm ready."

While he spoke he was mechanically getting paper from his note-book.

He tore a blank page off, and sat down pencil in hand to write.

Glenarvan began to dictate as follows: "Order to Tom Austin, Chief Officer, to get to sea without delay, and bring the DUNCAN to—"

Paganel was just finishing the last word, when his eye chanced to fall on the *Australian and New Zealand Gazette* lying on the ground. The paper was so folded that only the last two syllables of the title were visible. Paganel's pencil stopped, and he seemed to become oblivious of Glenarvan and the letter entirely, till his friends called out: "Come, Paganel!"

"Ah!" said the geographer, with a loud exclamation.

"What is the matter?" asked the Major.

"Nothing, nothing," replied Paganel. Then he muttered to himself, "*Aland! aland! aland!*"

He had got up and seized the newspaper. He shook it in his efforts to keep back the words that involuntarily rose to his lips.

Lady Helena, Mary, Robert, and Glenarvan gazed at him in astonishment,

at a loss to understand this unaccountable agitation.

Paganel looked as if a sudden fit of insanity had come over him.

But his excitement did not last. He became by degrees calmer.

The gleam of joy that shone in his eyes died away.

He sat down again, and said quietly:

"When you please, my Lord, I am ready." Glenarvan resumed his dictation at once, and the letter was soon completed. It read as follows: "Order to Tom Austin to go to sea without delay; and take the DUNCAN to Melbourne by the 37th degree of latitude to the eastern coast of Australia."

"Of Australia?" said Paganel. "Ah yes! of Australia."

Then he finished the letter, and gave it to Glenarvan to sign, who went through the necessary formality as well as he could, and closed and sealed the letter. Paganel, whose hand still trembled with emotion, directed it thus: "Tom Austin, Chief Officer on board the Yacht DUNCAN, Melbourne."

Then he got up and went out of the wagon, gesticulating and repeating the incomprehensible words:

"Aland aland! aland!"

CHAPTER XVIII FOUR DAYS OF ANGUISH

THE rest of the day passed on without any further incident. All the preparations for Mulrady's journey were completed, and the brave sailor rejoiced in being able to give his Lordship this proof of devotion.

Paganel had recovered his usual *sang-froid* and manners. His look, indeed, betrayed his preoccupation, but he seemed resolved to keep it secret. No doubt he had strong reasons for this course of action, for the Major heard him repeating, like a man struggling with himself: "No, no, they would not believe it; and, besides, what good would it be? It is too late!"

Having taken this resolution, he busied himself with giving Mulrady the necessary directions for getting to Melbourne, and showed him his way on the map. All the TRACKS, that is to say, paths through the prairie, came out on the road to Lucknow. This road, after running right down to the coast took a sudden bend in the direction of Melbourne. This was the route that must be followed steadily, for it would not do to attempt a short cut across an almost unknown country. Nothing, consequently, could be more simple. Mulrady could not lose his way.

As to dangers, there were none after he had gone a few miles beyond the encampment, out of the reach of Ben Joyce and his gang. Once past their hiding place, Mulrady was certain of soon being able to outdistance the convicts, and execute his important mission successfully.

At six o'clock they all dined together. The rain was falling in torrents. The tent was not protection enough, and the whole party had to take refuge in the wagon. This was a sure refuge. The clay kept it firmly imbedded in the soil, like a fortress resting on sure foundations. The arsenal was composed of seven carbines and seven revolvers, and could stand a pretty long siege, for they had plenty of ammunition and provisions. But before six days were over, the DUNCAN would anchor in Twofold Bay, and twenty-four hours after her crew would reach the other shore of the Snowy River; and should the passage still remain impracticable, the convicts at any rate would be forced to retire before the increased strength. But all depended on Mulrady's success in his perilous enterprise.

At eight o'clock it got very dark; now was the time to start. The horse prepared for Mulrady was brought out. His feet, by way of extra precaution, were wrapped round with cloths, so that they could not make the least noise on the ground. The animal seemed tired, and yet the safety of all depended on his strength and surefootedness. The Major advised Mulrady to let him go gently as soon as he got past the convicts. Better delay half-a-day than not arrive safely.

John Mangles gave his sailor a revolver, which he had loaded with the utmost care. This is a formidable weapon in the hand of a man who does not tremble, for six shots fired in a few seconds would easily clear a road infested with criminals. Mulrady seated himself in the saddle ready to start.

"Here is the letter you are to give to Tom Austin," said Glenarvan. "Don't let him lose an hour. He is to sail for Twofold Bay at once; and if he does not find us there, if we have not managed to cross the Snowy, let him come on to us without delay. Now go, my brave sailor, and God be with you."

He shook hands with him, and bade him good-by; and so did Lady Helena and Mary Grant. A more timorous man than the sailor would have shrunk back a little from setting out on such a dark, raining night on an errand so full of danger, across vast unknown wilds. But his farewells were calmly spoken, and he speedily disappeared down a path which skirted the wood.

At the same moment the gusts of wind redoubled their violence. The high branches of the eucalyptus clattered together noisily, and bough after bough fell on the wet ground. More than one great tree, with no living sap, but still standing hitherto, fell with a crash during this storm. The wind howled amid the cracking wood, and mingled its moans with the ominous roaring of the rain. The heavy clouds, driving along toward the east, hung on the ground like rays of vapor, and deep, cheerless gloom intensified the horrors of the night.

The travelers went back into the wagon immediately Mulrady had gone. Lady Helena, Mary Grant, Glenarvan and Paganel occupied the first compartment, which had been hermetically closed. The second was occupied by Olbinett, Wilson and Robert. The Major and John Mangles were on duty outside. This precaution was necessary, for an attack on the part of the convicts would be easy enough, and therefore probable enough.

The two faithful guardians kept close watch, bearing philosophically the rain and wind that beat on their faces. They tried to pierce through the darkness so favorable to ambushes, for nothing could be heard but the noise of the tempest, the sough of the wind, the rattling branches, falling trees, and roaring of the unchained waters.

At times the wind would cease for a few moments, as if to take breath. Nothing was audible but the moan of the Snowy River, as it flowed between the motionless reeds and the dark curtain of gum trees. The silence seemed deeper in these momentary lulls, and the Major and John Mangles listened attentively.

During one of these calms a sharp whistle reached them. John Mangles went hurriedly up to the Major. "You heard that?" he asked.

"Yes," said McNabbs. "Is it man or beast?"

"A man," replied John Mangles.

And then both listened. The mysterious whistle was repeated, and answered by a kind of report, but almost indistinguishable, for the storm was raging with renewed violence. McNabbs and John Mangles could not hear themselves speak. They went for comfort under the shelter of the wagon.

At this moment the leather curtains were raised and Glenarvan rejoined his two companions. He too had heard this ill-boding whistle, and the report which echoed under the tilt. "Which way was it?" asked he.

"There," said John, pointing to the dark track in the direction taken by Mulrady.

"How far?"

"The wind brought it; I should think, three or four miles, at least."

"Come," said Glenarvan, putting his gun on his shoulder.

"No," said the Major. "It is a decoy to get us away from the wagon."

"But if Mulrady has even now fallen beneath the blows of these rascals?" exclaimed Glenarvan, seizing McNabbs by the hand.

"We shall know by to-morrow," said the Major, coolly, determined to prevent Glenarvan from taking a step which was equally rash and futile.

"You cannot leave the camp, my Lord," said John. "I will go alone."

"You will do nothing of the kind!" cried McNabbs, energetically. "Do you want to have us killed one by one to diminish our force, and put us at the mercy of these wretches? If Mulrady has fallen a victim to them, it is a misfortune that must not be repeated. Mulrady was sent, chosen by chance. If the lot had fallen to me, I should have gone as he did; but I should neither have asked nor expected assistance."

In restraining Glenarvan and John Mangles, the Major was right in every aspect of the case. To attempt to follow the sailor, to run in the darkness of night among the convicts in their leafy ambush was madness, and more than that—it was useless. Glenarvan's party was not so numerous that it could afford to sacrifice another member of it.

Still Glenarvan seemed as if he could not yield; his hand was always on his carbine. He wandered about the wagon, and bent a listening ear to the faintest sound. The thought that one of his men was perhaps mortally wounded, abandoned to his fate, calling in vain on those for whose sake he had gone forth, was a torture to him. McNabbs was not sure that he should be able to restrain him, or if Glenarvan, carried away by his feelings, would not run into the arms of Ben Joyce.

"Edward," said he, "be calm. Listen to me as a friend.

Think of Lady Helena, of Mary Grant, of all who are left.

And, besides, where would you go? Where would you

find Mulrady? He must have been attacked two miles off.

In what direction? Which track would you follow?"

At that very moment, as if to answer the Major, a cry of distress was heard.

"Listen!" said Glenarvan.

This cry came from the same quarter as the report, but less than a quarter of a mile off.

Glenarvan, repulsing McNabbs, was already on the track, when at three hundred paces from the wagon they heard the exclamation: "Help! help!"

The voice was plaintive and despairing. John Mangles and the Major sprang toward the spot. A few seconds after they perceived among the scrub a human form dragging itself along the ground and uttering mournful groans. It was Mulrady, wounded, apparently dying; and when his companions raised him they felt their hands bathed in blood.

The rain came down with redoubled violence, and the wind raged among the branches of the dead trees. In the pelting storm, Glenarvan, the Major and John Mangles transported the body of Mulrady.

On their arrival everyone got up. Paganel, Robert, Wilson and Olbinett left the wagon, and Lady Helena gave up her compartment to poor Mulrady. The Major removed the poor fellow's flannel shirt, which was dripping with blood and rain. He soon found the wound; it was a stab in the right side.

McNabbs dressed it with great skill. He could not tell whether the weapon had touched any vital part. An intermittent jet of scarlet blood flowed from it; the patient's paleness and weakness showed that he was seriously injured. The Major washed the wound first with fresh water and then closed the orifice; after this he put on a thick pad of lint, and then folds of scraped linen held firmly in place with a bandage. He succeeded in stopping the hemorrhage. Mulrady was laid on his side, with his head and chest well raised, and Lady Helena succeeded in making him swallow a few drops of water.

After about a quarter of an hour, the wounded man, who till then had lain motionless, made a slight movement. His eyes unclosed, his lips muttered incoherent words, and the Major, bending toward him, heard him repeating: "My Lord—the letter—Ben Joyce."

The Major repeated these words, and looked at his companions. What did Mulrady mean? Ben Joyce had been the attacking party, of course; but why? Surely for the express purpose of intercepting him, and preventing his arrival at the DUNCAN. This letletter—

Glenarvan searched Mulrady's pockets. The letter addressed to Tom Austin was gone!

The night wore away amid anxiety and distress; every moment, they feared,

would be poor Mulrady's last. He suffered from acute fever.

The Sisters of Charity, Lady Helena and Mary Grant, never left him.

Never was patient so well tended, nor by such sympathetic hands.

Day came, and the rain had ceased. Great clouds filled the sky still; the ground was strewn with broken branches; the marly soil, soaked by the torrents of rain, had yielded still more; the approaches to the wagon became difficult, but it could not sink any deeper.

John Mangles, Paganel, and Glenarvan went, as soon as it was light enough, to reconnoiter in the neighborhood of the encampment. They revisited the track, which was still stained with blood. They saw no vestige of Ben Joyce, nor of his band. They penetrated as far as the scene of the attack. Here two corpses lay on the ground, struck down by Mulrady's bullets. One was the blacksmith of Blackpoint. His face, already changed by death, was a dreadful spectacle. Glenarvan searched no further. Prudence forbade him to wander from the camp. He returned to the wagon, deeply absorbed by the critical position of affairs.

"We must not think of sending another messenger to Melbourne," said he.

"But we must," said John Mangles; "and I must try to pass where my sailor could not succeed."

"No, John! it is out of the question. You have not even a horse for the journey, which is full two hundred miles!"

This was true, for Mulrady's horse, the only one that remained, had not returned. Had he fallen during the attack on his rider, or was he straying in the bush, or had the convicts carried him off?

"Come what will," replied Glenarvan, "we will not separate again. Let us wait a week, or a fortnight, till the Snowy falls to its normal level. We can then reach Twofold Bay by short stages, and from there we can send on to the DUNCAN, by a safer channel, the order to meet us."

"That seems the only plan," said Paganel.

"Therefore, my friends," rejoined Glenarvan, "no more parting. It is too great a risk for one man to venture alone into a robber-haunted waste. And now, may God save our poor sailor, and protect the rest of us!"

Glenarvan was right in both points; first in prohibiting all isolated attempts, and second, in deciding to wait till the passage of the Snowy River was practicable. He was scarcely thirty miles from Delegete, the first frontier village of New South Wales, where he would easily find the means of transport to Twofold Bay, and from there he could telegraph to Melbourne his orders about the DUNCAN.

These measures were wise, but how late! If Glenarvan had not sent Mulrady to Lucknow what misfortunes would have been averted, not to speak of the assassination of the sailor!

When he reached the camp he found his companions in better spirits. They seemed more hopeful than before. "He is better! he is better!" cried Robert, running out to meet Lord Glenarvan.

"Mulrady?—"

"Yes, Edward," answered Lady Helena. "A reaction has set in.

The Major is more confident. Our sailor will live."

"Where is McNabbs?" asked Glenarvan.

"With him. Mulrady wanted to speak to him, and they must not be disturbed."

He then learned that about an hour since, the wounded man had awakened from his lethargy, and the fever had abated. But the first thing he did on recovering his memory and speech was to ask for Lord Glenarvan, or, failing him, the Major. McNabbs seeing him so weak, would have forbidden any conversation; but Mulrady insisted with such energy that the Major had to give in. The interview had already lasted some minutes when Glenarvan returned. There was nothing for it but to await the return of McNabbs.

Presently the leather curtains of the wagon moved, and the Major appeared. He re-joined his friends at the foot of a gum-tree, where the tent was placed. His face, usually so stolid, showed that something disturbed him. When his eyes fell on Lady Helena and the young girl, his glance was full of sorrow.

Glenarvan questioned him, and extracted the following information: When he left the camp Mulrady followed one of the paths indicated by Paganel. He made as good speed as the darkness of the night would allow. He reckoned that he had gone about two miles when several men—five, he thought—sprang to his horse's head. The animal reared; Mulrady seized his revolver and fired. He thought he saw two of his assailants fall. By the flash he recognized Ben Joyce. But that was all. He had not time to fire all the barrels. He felt a violent blow on his side and was thrown to the ground.

Still he did not lose consciousness. The murderers thought he was dead.

He felt them search his pockets, and then heard one of them say:

"I have the letter."

"Give it to me," returned Ben Joyce, "and now the DUNCAN is ours."

At this point of the story, Glenarvan could not help uttering a cry.

McNabbs continued: "'Now you fellows,' added Ben Joyce, 'catch the horse. In two days I shall be on board the DUNCAN, and in six I shall reach Twofold Bay. This is to be the rendezvous. My Lord and his party will be still stuck in the marshes of the Snowy River. Cross the river at the bridge of Kemple Pier, proceed to the coast, and wait for me. I will easily manage to get you on board. Once at sea in a craft like the DUNCAN, we shall be masters of the Indian Ocean.' 'Hurrah for Ben Joyce!' cried the convicts. Mulrady's horse was brought, and Ben Joyce disappeared, galloping on the Lucknow Road, while the band took the road southeast of the Snowy River. Mulrady, though severely wounded, had the strength to drag himself to within three hundred paces from the camp, whence we found him almost dead. There," said McNabbs, "is the history of Mulrady; and now you can understand why the brave fellow was so determined to speak."

This revelation terrified Glenarvan and the rest of the party.

"Pirates! pirates!" cried Glenarvan. "My crew massacred! my DUNCAN in the hands of these bandits!"

"Yes, for Ben Joyce will surprise the ship," said the Major, "and then—"

"Well, we must get to the coast first," said Paganel.

"But how are we to cross the Snowy River?" said Wilson.

"As they will," replied Glenarvan. "They are to cross at
Kemple Pier Bridge, and so will we."

"But about Mulrady?" asked Lady Helena.

"We will carry him; we will have relays. Can I leave my crew to the mercy of Ben Joyce and his gang?"

To cross the Snowy River at Kemple Pier was practicable, but dangerous.

The convicts might entrench themselves at that point, and defend it.

They were at least thirty against seven! But there are moments when people do not deliberate, or when they have no choice but to go on.

"My Lord," said John Mangles, "before we throw away our chance, before venturing to this bridge, we ought to reconnoiter, and I will undertake it."

"I will go with you, John," said Paganel.

This proposal was agreed to, and John Mangles and Paganel prepared to start immediately. They were to follow the course of the Snowy River, follow its banks till they reached the place indicated by Ben Joyce, and especially they were to keep out of sight of the convicts, who were probably scouring the bush.

So the two brave comrades started, well provisioned and well armed, and were soon out of sight as they threaded their way among the tall reeds by the river. The rest anxiously awaited their return all day. Evening came, and still the scouts did not return. They began to be seriously alarmed. At last, toward eleven o'clock, Wilson announced their arrival. Paganel and John Mangles were worn out with the fatigues of a ten-mile walk.

"Well, what about the bridge? Did you find it?" asked Glenarvan, with impetuous eagerness.

"Yes, a bridge of supple-jacks," said John Mangles. "The convicts passed over, but—"

"But what?" said Glenarvan, who foreboded some new misfortune.

"They burned it after they passed!" said Paganel.

CHAPTER XIX HELPLESS AND HOPELESS

IT was not a time for despair, but action. The bridge at Kemple Pier was destroyed, but the Snowy River must be crossed, come what might, and they must reach Twofold Bay before Ben Joyce and his gang, so, instead of wasting time in empty words, the next day (the 16th of January) John Mangles and Glenarvan went down to examine the river, and arrange for the passage over.

The swollen and tumultuous waters had not gone down the least. They rushed on with indescribable fury. It would be risking life to battle with them. Glenarvan stood gazing with folded arms and downcast face.

"Would you like me to try and swim across?" said John Mangles.

"No, John, no!" said Lord Glenarvan, holding back the bold, daring young fellow, "let us wait."

And they both returned to the camp. The day passed in the most intense anxiety. Ten times Lord Glenarvan went to look at the river, trying to invent some bold way of getting over; but in vain. Had a torrent of lava rushed between the shores, it could not have been more impassable.

During these long wasted hours, Lady Helena, under the Major's advice, was nursing Mulrady with the utmost skill. The sailor felt a throb of returning life. McNabbs ventured to affirm that no vital part was injured. Loss of blood accounted for the patient's extreme exhaustion. The wound once closed and the hemorrhage stopped, time and rest would be all that was needed to complete his cure. Lady Helena had insisted on giving up the first compartment of the wagon to him, which greatly tried his modesty. The poor fellow's greatest trouble was the delay his condition might cause Glenarvan, and he made him promise that they should leave him in the camp under Wilson's care, should the passage of the river become practicable.

But, unfortunately, no passage was practicable, either that day or the next (January 17); Glenarvan was in despair. Lady Helena and the Major vainly tried to calm him, and preached patience.

Patience, indeed, when perhaps at this very moment Ben Joyce was boarding the yacht; when the DUNCAN, loosing from her moorings, was getting up steam to reach the fatal coast, and each hour was bringing her nearer.

John Mangles felt in his own breast all that Glenarvan was suffering. He determined to conquer the difficulty at any price, and constructed a canoe in the Australian manner, with large sheets of bark of the gum-trees. These sheets were kept together by bars of wood, and formed a very fragile boat. The captain and the sailor made a trial trip in it during the day. All that skill, and strength, and tact, and courage could do they did; but they were scarcely in the current before they were upside down, and nearly paid with their lives for the dangerous experiment. The boat disappeared, dragged down by the eddy. John Mangles and Wilson had not gone ten fathoms, and the river was a mile broad, and swollen by the heavy rains and melted snows.

Thus passed the 19th and 20th of January. The Major and Glenarvan went five miles up the river in search of a favorable passage, but everywhere they found the same roaring, rushing, impetuous torrent. The whole southern slope of the Australian Alps poured its liquid masses into this single bed.

All hope of saving the DUNCAN was now at an end. Five days had elapsed since the departure of Ben Joyce. The yacht must be at this moment at the coast, and in the hands of the convicts.

However, it was impossible that this state of things could last. The temporary influx would soon be exhausted, and the violence also. Indeed, on the morning of the 21st, Paganel announced that the water was already lower. "What does it matter now?" said Glenarvan. "It is too late!"

"That is no reason for our staying longer here," said the Major.

"Certainly not," replied John Mangles. "Perhaps tomorrow the river may be practicable."

"And will that save my unhappy men?" cried Glenarvan.

"Will your Lordship listen to me?" returned John Mangles. "I know Tom Austin. He would execute your orders, and set out as soon as departure was possible. But who knows whether the DUNCAN was ready and her injury repaired on the arrival of Ben Joyce. And suppose the yacht could not go to sea; suppose there was a delay of a day, or two days."

"You are right, John," replied Glenarvan. "We must get to Twofold Bay; we are only thirty-five miles from Delegete."

"Yes," added Paganel, "and that's a town where we shall find rapid means of conveyance. Who knows whether we shan't arrive in time to prevent a catastrophe."

"Let us start," cried Glenarvan.

John Mangles and Wilson instantly set to work to construct a canoe of larger dimensions. Experience had proved that the bark was powerless against the violence of the torrent, and John accordingly felled some of the gum-trees, and made a rude but solid raft with the trunks. It was a long task, and the day had gone before the work was ended. It was completed next morning.

By this time the waters had visibly diminished; the torrent had once more become a river, though a very rapid one, it is true. However, by pursuing a zigzag course, and overcoming it to a certain extent, John hoped to reach the opposite shore. At half-past twelve, they embarked provisions enough for a couple of days. The remainder was left with the wagon and the tent. Mulrady was doing well enough to be carried over; his convalescence was rapid.

At one o'clock, they all seated themselves on the raft, still moored to the shore. John Mangles had installed himself at the starboard, and entrusted to Wilson a sort of oar to steady the raft against the current, and lessen the leeway. He took his own stand at the back, to steer by means of a large scull; but, notwithstanding their efforts, Wilson and John Mangles soon found themselves in an inverse position, which made the action of the oars impossible.

There was no help for it; they could do nothing to arrest the gyratory movement of the raft; it turned round with dizzying rapidity, and drifted out of its course. John Mangles stood with pale face and set teeth, gazing at the whirling current.

However, the raft had reached the middle of the river, about half a mile from the starting point. Here the current was extremely strong, and this broke the whirling eddy, and gave the raft some stability. John and Wilson seized their oars again, and managed to push it in an oblique direction. This brought them nearer to the left shore. They were not more than fifty fathoms from it, when Wilson's oar snapped short off, and the raft, no longer supported, was dragged away. John tried to resist at the risk of breaking his own oar, too, and Wilson, with bleeding hands, seconded his efforts with all his might.

At last they succeeded, and the raft, after a passage of more than half an hour, struck against the steep bank of the opposite shore. The shock was so violent that the logs became disunited, the cords broke, and the water bubbled up between. The travelers had barely time to catch hold of the steep bank. They dragged out Mulrady and the two dripping ladies. Everyone was safe; but the provisions and firearms, except the carbine of the Major, went drifting down with the DEBRIS of the raft.

The river was crossed. The little company found themselves almost without provisions, thirty-five miles from Delegete, in the midst of the unknown deserts of the Victoria frontier. Neither settlers nor squatters were to be met with; it was entirely uninhabited, unless by ferocious bushrangers and bandits.

They resolved to set off without delay. Mulrady saw clearly that he would be a great drag on them, and he begged to be allowed to remain, and even to remain alone, till assistance could be sent from Delegete.

Glenarvan refused. It would be three days before he could reach Delegete, and five the shore—that is to say, the 26th of January. Now, as the DUNCAN had left Melbourne on the 16th, what difference would a few days' delay make?

"No, my friend," he said, "I will not leave anyone behind.

We will make a litter and carry you in turn."

The litter was made of boughs of eucalyptus covered with branches; and, whether he would or not, Mulrady was obliged to take his place on it. Glenarvan would be the first to carry his sailor. He took hold of one end and Wilson of the other, and all set off.

What a sad spectacle, and how lamentably was this expedition to end which had commenced so well. They were no longer in search of Harry Grant. This continent, where he was not, and never had been, threatened to prove fatal to those who sought him. And when these intrepid countrymen of his should reach the shore, they would find the DUNCAN waiting to take them home again. The first day passed silently and painfully. Every ten minutes the litter changed bearers. All the sailor's comrades took their share in this task without murmuring, though the fatigue was augmented by the great heat.

In the evening, after a journey of only five miles, they camped under the gum-trees. The small store of provisions saved from the raft composed the evening meal. But all they had to depend upon now was the Major's carbine.

It was a dark, rainy night, and morning seemed as if it would never dawn. They set off again, but the Major could not find a chance of firing a shot. This fatal region was only a desert, unfrequented even by animals. Fortunately, Robert discovered a bustard's nest with a dozen of large eggs in it, which Olbinett cooked on hot cinders. These, with a few roots of purslain which were growing at the bottom of a ravine, were all the breakfast of the 22d.

The route now became extremely difficult. The sandy plains were bristling with SPINIFEX, a prickly plant, which is called in Melbourne the porcupine. It tears the clothing to rags, and makes the legs bleed. The courageous ladies never complained, but footed it bravely, setting an example, and encouraging one and another by word or look.

They stopped in the evening at Mount Bulla Bulla, on the edge of the Jungalla Creek. The supper would have been very scant, if McNabbs had not killed a large rat, the *mus conditor*, which is highly spoken of as an article of diet. Olbinett roasted it, and it would have been pronounced even superior to its reputation had it equaled the sheep in size. They were obliged to be content with it, however, and it was devoured to the bones.

On the 23d the weary but still energetic travelers started off again. After having gone round the foot of the mountain, they crossed the long prairies where the grass seemed made of whalebone. It was a tangle of darts, a medley of sharp little sticks, and a path had to be cut through either with the hatchet or fire.

That morning there was not even a question of breakfast. Nothing could be more barren than this region strewn with pieces of quartz. Not only hunger, but thirst began to assail the travelers. A burning atmosphere heightened their discomfort. Glenarvan and his friends could only go half a mile an hour. Should this lack of food and water continue till evening, they would all sink on the road, never to rise again.

But when everything fails a man, and he finds himself without resources, at the very moment when he feels he must give up, then Providence steps in. Water presented itself in the CEPHALOTES, a species of cup-shaped flower, filled with refreshing liquid, which hung from the branches of coralliform-shaped bushes. They all quenched their thirst with these, and felt new life returning.

The only food they could find was the same as the natives were forced to subsist upon, when they could find neither game, nor serpents, nor insects. Paganel discovered in the dry bed of a creek, a plant whose excellent properties had been frequently described by one of his colleagues in the Geographical Society.

It was the NARDOU, a cryptogamous plant of the family Marsilacea, and the same which kept Burke and King alive in the deserts of the interior. Under its leaves, which resembled those of the trefoil, there were dried sporules as large as a lentil, and these sporules, when crushed between two stones, made a sort of flour. This was converted into coarse bread, which stilled the pangs of hunger at least. There was a great abundance of this plant growing in the district, and Olbinett gathered a large supply, so that they were sure of food for several days.

The next day, the 24th, Mulrady was able to walk part of the way. His wound was entirely cicatrized. The town of Delegete was not more than ten miles off, and that evening they camped in longitude 140 degrees, on the very frontier of New South Wales.

For some hours, a fine but penetrating rain had been falling. There would have been no shelter from this, if by chance John Mangles had not discovered a sawyer's hut, deserted and dilapidated to a degree. But with this miserable cabin they were obliged to be content. Wilson wanted to kindle a fire to prepare the NARDOU bread, and he went out to pick up the dead wood scattered all over the ground. But he found it would not light, the great quantity of albuminous matter which it contained prevented all combustion. This is the incombustible wood put down by Paganel in his list of Australian products.

They had to dispense with fire, and consequently with food too, and sleep in their wet clothes, while the laughing jackasses, concealed in the high branches, seemed to ridicule the poor unfortunates. However, Glenarvan was nearly at the end of his sufferings. It was time. The two young ladies were making heroic efforts, but their strength was hourly decreasing. They dragged themselves along, almost unable to walk.

Next morning they started at daybreak. At 11 A. M. Delegete came in sight in the county of Wellesley, and fifty miles from Twofold Bay.

Means of conveyance were quickly procured here. Hope returned to Glenarvan as they approached the coast. Perhaps there might have been some slight delay, and after all they might get there before the arrival of the DUNCAN. In twenty-four hours they would reach the bay.

At noon, after a comfortable meal, all the travelers installed in a mail-coach, drawn by five strong horses, left Delegete at a gallop. The postilions, stimulated by a promise of a princely DOUCEUR, drove rapidly along over a well-kept road. They did not lose a minute in changing horses, which took place every ten miles. It seemed as if they were infected with Glenarvan's zeal. All that day, and night, too, they traveled on at the rate of six miles an hour.

In the morning at sunrise, a dull murmur fell on their ears, and announced their approach to the Indian Ocean. They required to go round the bay to gain the coast at the 37th parallel, the exact point where Tom Austin was to wait their arrival.

When the sea appeared, all eyes anxiously gazed at the offing.

Was the DUNCAN, by a miracle of Providence, there running
close to the shore, as a month ago, when they crossed
Cape Corrientes, they had found her on the Argentine coast?

They saw nothing. Sky and earth mingled in the same horizon.

Not a sail enlivened the vast stretch of ocean.

One hope still remained. Perhaps Tom Austin had thought it his duty to cast anchor in Twofold Bay, for the sea was heavy, and a ship would not dare to venture near the shore. "To Eden!" cried Glenarvan. Immediately the mail-coach resumed the route round the bay, toward the little town of Eden, five miles distant. The postilions stopped not far from the lighthouse, which marks the entrance of the port. Several vessels were moored in the roadstead, but none of them bore the flag of Malcolm.

Glenarvan, John Mangles, and Paganel got out of the coach, and rushed to the custom-house, to inquire about the arrival of vessels within the last few days.

No ship had touched the bay for a week.

"Perhaps the yacht has not started," Glenarvan said, a sudden revulsion of feeling lifting him from despair. "Perhaps we have arrived first."

John Mangles shook his head. He knew Tom Austin. His first mate would not delay the execution of an order for ten days.

"I must know at all events how they stand," said Glenarvan.

"Better certainty than doubt."

A quarter of an hour afterward a telegram was sent to the syndicate of shipbrokers in Melbourne. The whole party then repaired to the Victoria Hotel.

At 2 P.M. the following telegraphic reply was received:

"LORD GLENARVAN, Eden.

"Twofold Bay.

"The DUNCAN left on the 16th current. Destination unknown.

J. ANDREWS, S. B."

The telegram dropped from Glenarvan's hands.

There was no doubt now. The good, honest Scotch yacht was now a pirate ship in the hands of Ben Joyce!

So ended this journey across Australia, which had commenced under circumstances so favorable. All trace of Captain Grant and his shipwrecked men seemed to be irrevocably lost. This ill success had cost the loss of a ship's crew. Lord Glenarvan had been vanquished in the strife; and the courageous searchers, whom the unfriendly elements of the Pampas had been unable to check, had been conquered on the Australian shore by the perversity of man.

NEW ZEALAND

CHAPTER I A ROUGH CAPTAIN

IF ever the searchers after Captain Grant were tempted to despair, surely it was at this moment when all their hopes were destroyed at a blow. Toward what quarter of the world should they direct their endeavors? How were they to explore new countries? The DUNCAN was no longer available, and even an immediate return to their own land was out of the question. Thus the enterprise of these generous Scots had failed! Failed! a despairing word that finds no echo in a brave soul; and yet under the repeated blows of adverse fate, Glenarvan himself was compelled to acknowledge his inability to prosecute his devoted efforts.

Mary Grant at this crisis nerved herself to the resolution never to utter the name of her father. She suppressed her own anguish, when she thought of the unfortunate crew who had perished. The daughter was merged in the friend, and she now took upon her to console Lady Glenarvan, who till now had been her faithful comforter. She was the first to speak of returning to Scotland. John Mangles was filled with admiration at seeing her so courageous and so resigned. He wanted to say a word further in the Captain's interest, but Mary stopped him with a glance, and afterward said to him: "No, Mr. John, we must think of those who ventured their lives. Lord Glenarvan must return to Europe!"

"You are right, Miss Mary," answered John Mangles; "he must. Beside, the English authorities must be informed of the fate of the DUNCAN. But do not despair. Rather than abandon our search I will resume it alone! I will either find Captain Grant or perish in the attempt!"

It was a serious undertaking to which John Mangles bound himself; Mary accepted, and gave her hand to the young captain, as if to ratify the treaty. On John Mangles' side it was a life's devotion; on Mary's undying gratitude.

During that day, their departure was finally arranged;

they resolved to reach Melbourne without delay.

Next day John went to inquire about the ships ready to sail.

He expected to find frequent communication between Eden and Victoria.

He was disappointed; ships were scarce. Three or four vessels, anchored in Twofold Bay, constituted the mercantile fleet of the place; none of them were bound for Melbourne, nor Sydney, nor Point de Galle, at any of which ports Glenarvan would have found ships loading for England. In fact, the Peninsular and Oriental Company has a regular line of packets between these points and England.

Under these circumstances, what was to be done? Waiting for a ship might be a tedious affair, for Twofold Bay is not much frequented. Numbers of ships pass by without touching. After due reflection and discussion, Glenarvan had nearly decided to follow the coast road to Sydney, when Paganel made an unexpected proposition.

The geographer had visited Twofold Bay on his own account, and was aware that there were no means of transport for Sydney or Melbourne. But of the three vessels anchored in the roadstead one was loading for Auckland, the capital of the northern island of New Zealand. Paganel's proposal was to take the ship in question, and get to Auckland, whence it would be easy to return to Europe by the boats of the Peninsular and Oriental Company.

This proposition was taken into serious consideration. Paganel on this occasion dispensed with the volley of arguments he generally indulged in. He confined himself to the bare proposition, adding that the voyage to New Zealand was only five or six days— the distance, in fact, being only about a thousand miles.

By a singular coincidence Auckland is situated on the self-same parallel— the thirty-seventh—which the explorers had perseveringly followed since they left the coast of Araucania. Paganel might fairly have used this as an argument in favor of his scheme; in fact, it was a natural opportunity of visiting the shores of New Zealand.

But Paganel did not lay stress on this argument. After two mistakes, he probably hesitated to attempt a third interpretation of the document. Besides, what could he make of it? It said positively that a "continent" had served as a refuge for Captain Grant, not an island. Now, New Zealand was nothing but an island. This seemed decisive. Whether, for this reason, or for some other, Paganel did not connect any idea of further search with this proposition of reaching Auckland. He merely observed that regular communication existed between that point and Great Britain, and that it was easy to take advantage of it.

John Mangles supported Paganel's proposal. He advised its adoption, as it was hopeless to await the problematical arrival of a vessel in Twofold Bay. But before coming to any decision, he thought it best to visit the ship mentioned by the geographer. Glenarvan, the Major, Paganel, Robert, and Mangles himself, took a boat, and a few strokes brought them alongside the ship anchored two cables' length from the quay.

It was a brig of 150 tons, named the MACQUARIE. It was engaged in the coasting trade between the various ports of Australia and New Zealand. The captain, or rather the "master," received his visitors gruffly enough. They perceived that they had to do with a man of no education, and whose manners were in no degree superior to those of the five sailors of his crew. With a coarse, red face, thick hands, and a broken nose, blind of an eye, and his lips stained with the pipe, Will Halley was a sadly brutal looking person. But they had no choice, and for so short a voyage it was not necessary to be very particular.

"What do you want?" asked Will Halley, when the strangers stepped on the poop of his ship.

"The captain," answered John Mangles.

"I am the captain," said Halley. "What else do you want?"

"The MACQUARIE is loading for Auckland, I believe?"

"Yes. What else?"

"What does she carry?"

"Everything salable and purchasable. What else?"

"When does she sail?"

"To-morrow at the mid-day tide. What else?"

"Does she take passengers?"

"That depends on who the passengers are, and whether they are satisfied with the ship's mess."

"They would bring their own provisions."

"What else?"

"What else?"

"Yes. How many are there?"

"Nine; two of them are ladies."

"I have no cabins."

"We will manage with such space as may be left at their disposal."

"What else?"

"Do you agree?" said John Mangles, who was not in the least put out by the captain's peculiarities.

"We'll see," said the master of the MACQUARIE.

Will Halley took two or three turns on the poop, making it resound with iron-heeled boots, and then he turned abruptly to John Mangles.

"What would you pay?" said he.

"What do you ask?" replied John.

"Fifty pounds."

Glenarvan looked consent.

"Very good! Fifty pounds," replied John Mangles.

"But passage only," added Halley.

"Yes, passage only."

"Food extra."

"Extra."

"Agreed. And now," said Will, putting out his hand, "what about the deposit money?"

"Here is half of the passage-money, twenty-five pounds," said Mangles, counting out the sum to the master.

"All aboard to-morrow," said he, "before noon. Whether or no,

I weigh anchor."

"We will be punctual."

This said, Glenarvan, the Major, Robert, Paganel, and John Mangles left the ship, Halley not so much as touching the oilskin that adorned his red locks.

"What a brute," exclaimed John.

"He will do," answered Paganel. "He is a regular sea-wolf."

"A downright bear!" added the Major.

"I fancy," said John Mangles, "that the said bear has dealt in human flesh in his time."

"What matter?" answered Glenarvan, "as long as he commands the MACQUARIE, and the MACQUARIE goes to New Zealand. From Twofold Bay to Auckland we shall not see much of him; after Auckland we shall see him no more."

Lady Helena and Mary Grant were delighted to hear that their departure was arranged for to-morrow. Glenarvan warned them that the MACQUARIE was inferior in comfort to the DUNCAN. But after what they had gone through, they were indifferent to trifling annoyances. Wilson was told off to arrange the accommodation on board the MACQUARIE. Under his busy brush and broom things soon changed their aspect.

Will Halley shrugged his shoulders, and let the sailor have his way. Glenarvan and his party gave him no concern. He neither knew, nor cared to know, their names. His new freight represented fifty pounds, and he rated it far below the two hundred tons of cured hides which were stowed away in his hold. Skins first, men after. He was a merchant. As to his sailor qualification, he was said to be skillful enough in navigating these seas, whose reefs make them very dangerous.

As the day drew to a close, Glenarvan had a desire to go again to the point on the coast cut by the 37th parallel. Two motives prompted him. He wanted to examine once more the presumed scene of the wreck. Ayrton had certainly been quartermaster on the BRITANNIA, and the BRITANNIA might have been lost on this part of the Australian coast; on the east coast if not on the west. It would not do to leave without thorough investigation, a locality which they were never to revisit.

And then, failing the BRITANNIA, the DUNCAN certainly had fallen into the hands of the convicts. Perhaps there had been a fight? There might yet be found on the coast traces of a struggle, a last resistance. If the crew had perished among the waves, the waves probably had thrown some bodies on the shore.

Glenarvan, accompanied by his faithful John, went to carry out the final search. The landlord of the Victoria Hotel lent them two horses, and they set out on the northern road that skirts Twofold Bay.

It was a melancholy journey. Glenarvan and Captain John trotted along without speaking, but they understood each other. The same thoughts, the same anguish harrowed both their hearts. They looked at the sea-worn rocks; they needed no words of question or answer. John's well-tried zeal and intelligence were a guarantee that every point was scrupulously examined, the least likely places, as well as the sloping beaches and sandy plains where even the slight tides of the Pacific might have thrown some fragments of wreck. But no indication was seen that could suggest further search in that quarter—all trace of the wreck escaped them still.

As to the DUNCAN, no trace either. All that part of Australia, bordering the ocean, was desert.

Still John Mangles discovered on the skirts of the shore evident traces of camping, remains of fires recently kindled under solitary Myall-trees. Had a tribe of wandering blacks passed that way lately? No, for Glenarvan saw a token which furnished incontestable proof that the convicts had frequented that part of the coast.

This token was a grey and yellow garment worn and patched, an ill-omened rag thrown down at the foot of a tree. It bore the convict's original number at the Perth Penitentiary. The felon was not there, but his filthy garments betrayed his passage. This livery of crime, after having clothed some miscreant, was now decaying on this desert shore.

"You see, John," said Glenarvan, "the convicts got as far as here! and our poor comrades of the DUNCAN—"

"Yes," said John, in a low voice, "they never landed, they perished!"

"Those wretches!" cried Glenarvan. "If ever they fall into my hands
I will avenge my crew—"

Grief had hardened Glenarvan's features. For some minutes he gazed at the expanse before him, as if taking a last look at some ship disappearing in the distance. Then his eyes became dim; he recovered himself in a moment, and without a word or look, set off at a gallop toward Eden.

The wanderers passed their last evening sadly enough. Their thoughts
recalled all the misfortunes they had encountered in this country.
They remembered how full of well-warranted hope they had been at
Cape Bernouilli, and how cruelly disappointed at Twofold Bay!

Paganel was full of feverish agitation. John Mangles, who had watched him since the affair at Snowy River, felt that the geographer was hesitating whether to speak or not to speak. A thousand times he had pressed him with questions, and failed in obtaining an answer.

But that evening, John, in lighting him to his room, asked him why he was so nervous.

"Friend John," said Paganel, evasively, "I am not more nervous to-night than I always am."

"Mr. Paganel," answered John, "you have a secret that chokes you."

"Well!" cried the geographer, gesticulating, "what can I do?

It is stronger than I!"

"What is stronger?"

"My joy on the one hand, my despair on the other."

"You rejoice and despair at the same time!"

"Yes; at the idea of visiting New Zealand."

"Why! have you any trace?" asked John, eagerly. "Have you recovered the lost tracks?"

"No, friend John. No one returns from New Zealand; but still— you know human nature. All we want to nourish hope is breath. My device is '*Spiro spero*,' and it is the best motto in the world!"

CHAPTER II NAVIGATORS AND THEIR DISCOVERIES

NEXT day, the 27th of January, the passengers of the MACQUARIE were installed on board the brig. Will Halley had not offered his cabin to his lady passengers. This omission was the less to be deplored, for the den was worthy of the bear.

At half past twelve the anchor was weighed, having been loosed from its holding-ground with some difficulty. A moderate breeze was blowing from the southwest. The sails were gradually unfurled; the five hands made slow work. Wilson offered to assist the crew; but Halley begged him to be quiet and not to interfere with what did not concern him. He was accustomed to manage his own affairs, and required neither assistance nor advice.

This was aimed at John Mangles, who had smiled at the clumsiness of some maneuver. John took the hint, but mentally resolved that he would nevertheless hold himself in readiness in case the incapacity of the crew should endanger the safety of the vessel.

However, in time, the sails were adjusted by the five sailors, aided by the stimulus of the captain's oaths. The MACQUARIE stood out to sea on the larboard tack, under all her lower sails, topsails, topgallants, cross-jack, and jib. By and by, the other sails were hoisted. But in spite of this additional canvas the brig made very little way. Her rounded bow, the width of her hold, and her heavy stern, made her a bad sailor, the perfect type of a wooden shoe.

They had to make the best of it. Happily, five days, or, at most, six, would take them to Auckland, no matter how bad a sailor the MACQUARIE was.

At seven o'clock in the evening the Australian coast and the lighthouse of the port of Eden had faded out of sight. The ship labored on the lumpy sea, and rolled heavily in the trough of the waves. The passengers below suffered a good deal from this motion. But it was impossible to stay on deck, as it rained violently. Thus they were condemned to close imprisonment.

Each one of them was lost in his own reflections. Words were few. Now and then Lady Helena and Miss Grant exchanged a few syllables. Glenarvan was restless; he went in and out, while the Major was impassive. John Mangles, followed by Robert, went on the poop from time to time, to look at the weather. Paganel sat in his corner, muttering vague and incoherent words.

What was the worthy geographer thinking of? Of New Zealand, the country to which destiny was leading him. He went mentally over all his history; he called to mind the scenes of the past in that ill-omened country.

But in all that history was there a fact, was there a solitary incident that could justify the discoverers of these islands in considering them as "a continent." Could a modern geographer or a sailor concede to them such a designation. Paganel was always revolving the meaning of the document. He was possessed with the idea; it became his ruling thought. After Patagonia, after Australia, his imagination, allured by a name, flew to New Zealand. But in that direction, one point, and only one, stood in his way.

"*Contin—contin,*" he repeated, "that must mean continent!"

And then he resumed his mental retrospect of the navigators who made known to us these two great islands of the Southern Sea.

It was on the 13th of December, 1642, that the Dutch navigator Tasman, after discovering Van Diemen's Land, sighted the unknown shores of New Zealand. He coasted along for several days, and on the 17th of December his ships penetrated into a large bay, which, terminating in a narrow strait, separated the two islands.

The northern island was called by the natives Ikana-Mani, a word which signifies the fish of Mani. The southern island was called Tavai-Pouna-Mou, "the whale that yields the green-stones."

Abel Tasman sent his boats on shore, and they returned accompanied by two canoes and a noisy company of natives. These savages were middle height, of brown or yellow complexion, angular bones, harsh voices, and black hair, which was dressed in the Japanese manner, and surmounted by a tall white feather.

This first interview between Europeans and aborigines seemed to promise amicable and lasting intercourse. But the next day, when one of Tasman's boats was looking for an anchorage nearer to the land, seven canoes, manned by a great number of natives, attacked them fiercely. The boat capsized and filled. The quartermaster in command was instantly struck with a badly-sharpened spear, and fell into the sea. Of his six companions four were killed; the other two and the quartermaster were able to swim to the ships, and were picked up and recovered.

After this sad occurrence Tasman set sail, confining his revenge to giving the natives a few musket-shots, which probably did not reach them. He left this bay—which still bears the name of Massacre Bay— followed the western coast, and on the 5th of January, anchored near the northern-most point. Here the violence of the surf, as well as the unfriendly attitude of the natives, prevented his obtaining water, and he finally quitted these shores, giving them the name Staten-land or the Land of the States, in honor of the States-General.

The Dutch navigator concluded that these islands were adjacent to the islands of the same name on the east of Terra del Fuego, at the southern point of the American continent. He thought he had found "the Great Southern Continent."

"But," said Paganel to himself, "what a seventeenth century sailor might call a 'continent' would never stand for one with a nineteenth century man. No such mistake can be supposed! No! there is something here that baffles me."

CHAPTER III THE MARTYR-ROLL OF NAVIGATORS

ON the 31st of January, four days after starting, the MACQUARIE had not done two-thirds of the distance between Australia and New Zealand. Will Halley took very little heed to the working of the ship; he let things take their chance. He seldom showed himself, for which no one was sorry. No one would have complained if he had passed all his time in his cabin, but for the fact that the brutal captain was every day under the influence of gin or brandy. His sailors willingly followed his example, and no ship ever sailed more entirely depending on Providence than the MACQUARIE did from Twofold Bay.

This unpardonable carelessness obliged John Mangles to keep a watchful eye ever open. Mulrady and Wilson more than once brought round the helm when some careless steering threatened to throw the ship on her beam-ends. Often Will Halley would interfere and abuse the two sailors with a volley of oaths. The latter, in their impatience, would have liked nothing better than to bind this drunken captain, and lower him into the hold, for the rest of the voyage. But John Mangles succeeded, after some persuasion, in calming their well-grounded indignation.

Still, the position of things filled him with anxiety; but, for fear of alarming Glenarvan, he spoke only to Paganel or the Major. McNabbs recommended the same course as Mulrady and Wilson.

"If you think it would be for the general good, John," said McNabbs, "you should not hesitate to take the command of the vessel. When we get to Auckland the drunken imbecile can resume his command, and then he is at liberty to wreck himself, if that is his fancy."

"All that is very true, Mr. McNabbs, and if it is absolutely necessary I will do it. As long as we are on open sea, a careful lookout is enough; my sailors and I are watching on the poop; but when we get near the coast, I confess I shall be uneasy if Halley does not come to his senses."

"Could not you direct the course?" asked Paganel.

"That would be difficult," replied John. "Would you believe it that there is not a chart on board?"

"Is that so?"

"It is indeed. The MACQUARIE only does a coasting trade between Eden and Auckland, and Halley is so at home in these waters that he takes no observations."

"I suppose he thinks the ship knows the way, and steers herself." "Ha! ha!" laughed John Mangles; "I do not believe in ships that steer themselves; and if Halley is drunk when we get among soundings, he will get us all into trouble."

"Let us hope," said Paganel, "that the neighborhood of land will bring him to his senses."

"Well, then," said McNabbs, "if needs were, you could not sail the MACQUARIE into Auckland?"

"Without a chart of the coast, certainly not. The coast is very dangerous. It is a series of shallow fiords as irregular and capricious as the fiords of Norway. There are many reefs, and it requires great experience to avoid them. The strongest ship would be lost if her keel struck one of those rocks that are submerged but a few feet below the water."

"In that case those on board would have to take refuge on the coast."

"If there was time."

"A terrible extremity," said Paganel, "for they are not hospitable shores, and the dangers of the land are not less appalling than the dangers of the sea."

"You refer to the Maories, Monsieur Paganel?" asked John Mangles.

"Yes, my friend. They have a bad name in these waters. It is not a matter of timid or brutish Australians, but of an intelligent and sanguinary race, cannibals greedy of human flesh, man-eaters to whom we should look in vain for pity."

"Well, then," exclaimed the Major, "if Captain Grant had been wrecked on the coast of New Zealand, you would dissuade us from looking for him."

"Oh, you might search on the coasts," replied the geographer, "because you might find traces of the BRITANNIA, but not in the interior, for it would be perfectly useless. Every European who ventures into these fatal districts falls into the hands of the Maories, and a prisoner in the hands of the Maories is a lost man. I have urged my friends to cross the Pampas, to toil over the plains of Australia, but I will never lure them into the mazes of the New Zealand forest. May heaven be our guide, and keep us from ever being thrown within the power of those fierce natives!"

CHAPTER IV THE WRECK OF THE "MACQUARIE"

STILL this wearisome voyage dragged on. On the 2d of February, six days from starting, the MACQUARIE had not yet made a nearer acquaintance with the shores of Auckland. The wind was fair, nevertheless, and blew steadily from the southwest; but the currents were against the ship's course, and she scarcely made any way. The heavy, lumpy sea strained her cordage, her timbers creaked, and she labored painfully in the trough of the sea. Her standing rigging was so out of order that it allowed play to the masts, which were violently shaken at every roll of the sea.

Fortunately, Will Halley was not a man in a hurry, and did not use a press of canvas, or his masts would inevitably have come down. John Mangles therefore hoped that the wretched hull would reach port without accident; but it grieved him that his companions should have to suffer so much discomfort from the defective arrangements of the brig.

But neither Lady Helena nor Mary Grant uttered a word of complaint, though the continuous rain obliged them to stay below, where the want of air and the violence of the motion were painfully felt. They often braved the weather, and went on the poop till driven down again by the force of a sudden squall. Then they returned to the narrow space, fitter for stowing cargo than accommodating passengers, especially ladies.

Their friends did their best to amuse them. Paganel tried to beguile the time with his stories, but it was a hopeless case. Their minds were so distracted at this change of route as to be quite unhinged. Much as they had been interested in his dissertation on the Pampas, or Australia, his lectures on New Zealand fell on cold and indifferent ears. Besides, they were going to this new and ill-reputed country without enthusiasm, without conviction, not even of their own free will, but solely at the bidding of destiny.

Of all the passengers on board the MACQUARIE, the most to be pitied was Lord Glenarvan. He was rarely to be seen below. He could not stay in one place. His nervous organization, highly excited, could not submit to confinement between four narrow bulkheads. All day long, even all night, regardless of the torrents of rain and the dashing waves, he stayed on the poop, sometimes leaning on the rail, sometimes walking to and fro in feverish agitation. His eyes wandered ceaselessly over the blank horizon. He scanned it eagerly during every short interval of clear weather. It seemed as if he sought to question the voiceless waters; he longed to tear away the veil of fog and vapor that obscured his view. He could not be resigned, and his features expressed the bitterness of his grief. He was a man of energy, till now happy and powerful, and deprived in a moment of power and happiness. John Mangles bore him company, and endured with him the inclemency of the weather. On this day Glenarvan looked more anxiously than ever at each point where a break in the mist enabled him to do so. John came up to him and said, "Your Lordship is looking out for land?"

Glenarvan shook his head in dissent.

"And yet," said the young captain, "you must be longing to quit this vessel. We ought to have seen the lights of Auckland thirty-six hours ago."

Glenarvan made no reply. He still looked, and for a moment his glass was pointed toward the horizon to windward.

"The land is not on that side, my Lord," said John Mangles.

"Look more to starboard."

"Why, John?" replied Glenarvan. "I am not looking for the land."

"What then, my Lord?"

"My yacht! the DUNCAN," said Glenarvan, hotly. "It must be here on these coasts, skimming these very waves, playing the vile part of a pirate! It is here, John; I am certain of it, on the track of vessels between Australia and New Zealand; and I have a presentiment that we shall fall in with her."

"God keep us from such a meeting!"

"Why, John?"

"Your Lordship forgets our position. What could we do in this ship if the DUNCAN gave chase. We could not even fly!"

"Fly, John?"

"Yes, my Lord; we should try in vain! We should be taken, delivered up to the mercy of those wretches, and Ben Joyce has shown us that he does not stop at a crime! Our lives would be worth little. We would fight to the death, of course, but after that! Think of Lady Glenarvan; think of Mary Grant!"

"Poor girls!" murmured Glenarvan. "John, my heart is broken; and sometimes despair nearly masters me. I feel as if fresh misfortunes awaited us, and that Heaven itself is against us. It terrifies me!"

"You, my Lord?"

"Not for myself, John, but for those I love—whom you love, also."

"Keep up your heart, my Lord," said the young captain. "We must not look out for troubles. The MACQUARIE sails badly, but she makes some way nevertheless. Will Halley is a brute, but I am keeping my eyes open, and if the coast looks dangerous, I will put the ship's head to sea again. So that, on that score, there is little or no danger. But as to getting alongside the DUNCAN! God forbid! And if your Lordship is bent on looking out for her, let it be in order to give her a wide berth."

John Mangles was right. An encounter with the DUNCAN would have been fatal to the MACQUARIE. There was every reason to fear such an engagement in these narrow seas, in which pirates could ply their trade without risk. However, for that day at least, the yacht did not appear, and the sixth night from their departure from Twofold Bay came, without the fears of John Mangles being realized.

But that night was to be a night of terrors. Darkness came on almost suddenly at seven o'clock in the evening; the sky was very threatening. The sailor instinct rose above the stupefaction of the drunkard and roused Will Halley. He left his cabin, rubbed his eyes, and shook his great red head. Then he drew a great deep breath of air, as other people swallow a draught of water to revive themselves. He examined the masts. The wind freshened, and veering a point more to the westward, blew right for the New Zealand coast.

Will Halley, with many an oath, called his men, tightened his topmast cordage, and made all snug for the night. John Mangles approved in silence. He had ceased to hold any conversation with the coarse seaman; but neither Glenarvan nor he left the poop. Two hours after a stiff breeze came on. Will Halley took in the lower reef of his topsails. The maneuver would have been a difficult job for five men if the MACQUARIE had not carried a double yard, on the American plan. In fact, they had only to lower the upper yard to bring the sail to its smallest size.

Two hours passed; the sea was rising. The MACQUARIE was struck so violently that it seemed as if her keel had touched the rocks. There was no real danger, but the heavy vessel did not rise easily to the waves. By and by the returning waves would break over the deck in great masses. The boat was washed out of the davits by the force of the water.

John Mangles never released his watch. Any other ship would have made no account of a sea like this; but with this heavy craft there was a danger of sinking by the bow, for the deck was filled at every lurch, and the sheet of water not being able to escape quickly by the scuppers, might submerge the ship. It would have been the wisest plan to prepare for emergency by knocking out the bulwarks with an ax to facilitate their escape, but Halley refused to take this precaution.

But a greater danger was at hand, and one that it was too late to prevent. About half-past eleven, John Mangles and Wilson, who stayed on deck throughout the gale, were suddenly struck by an unusual noise. Their nautical instincts awoke. John seized the sailor's hand. "The reef!" said he.

"Yes," said Wilson; "the waves breaking on the bank."

"Not more than two cables' length off?"

"At farthest? The land is there!"

John leaned over the side, gazed into the dark water, and called out,

"Wilson, the lead!"

The master, posted forward, seemed to have no idea of his position. Wilson seized the lead-line, sprang to the fore-chains, and threw the lead; the rope ran out between his fingers, at the third knot the lead stopped.

"Three fathoms," cried Wilson.

"Captain," said John, running to Will Halley, "we are on the breakers."

Whether or not he saw Halley shrug his shoulders is of very little importance. But he hurried to the helm, put it hard down, while Wilson, leaving the line, hauled at the main-topsail brace to bring the ship to the wind. The man who was steering received a smart blow, and could not comprehend the sudden attack.

"Let her go! Let her go!" said the young captain, working her to get away from the reefs.

For half a minute the starboard side of the vessel was turned toward them, and, in spite of the darkness, John could discern a line of foam which moaned and gleamed four fathoms away.

At this moment, Will Halley, comprehending the danger, lost his head. His sailors, hardly sobered, could not understand his orders. His incoherent words, his contradictory orders showed that this stupid sot had quite lost his self-control. He was taken by surprise at the proximity of the land, which was eight miles off, when he thought it was thirty or forty miles off. The currents had thrown him out of his habitual track, and this miserable slave of routine was left quite helpless.

Still the prompt maneuver of John Mangles succeeded in keeping the MACQUARIE off the breakers. But John did not know the position. For anything he could tell he was girdled in by reefs. The wind blew them strongly toward the east, and at every lurch they might strike.

In fact, the sound of the reef soon redoubled on the starboard side of the bow. They must luff again. John put the helm down again and brought her up. The breakers increased under the bow of the vessel, and it was necessary to put her about to regain the open sea. Whether she would be able to go about under shortened sail, and badly trimmed as she was, remained to be seen, but there was nothing else to be done.

"Helm hard down!" cried Mangles to Wilson.

The MACQUARIE began to near the new line of reefs:

in another moment the waves were seen dashing on submerged rocks.

It was a moment of inexpressible anxiety. The spray

was luminous, just as if lit up by sudden phosphorescence.

The roaring of the sea was like the voice of those ancient

Tritons whom poetic mythology endowed with life.

Wilson and Mulrady hung to the wheel with all their weight.

Some cordage gave way, which endangered the foremast.

It seemed doubtful whether she would go about without further damage.

Suddenly the wind fell and the vessel fell back, and turning her became hopeless. A high wave caught her below, carried her up on the reefs, where she struck with great violence. The foremast came down with all the fore-rigging. The brig rose twice, and then lay motionless, heeled over on her port side at an angle of 30 degrees.

The glass of the skylight had been smashed to powder. The passengers rushed out. But the waves were sweeping the deck from one side to the other, and they dared not stay there. John Mangles, knowing the ship to be safely lodged in the sand, begged them to return to their own quarters.

"Tell me the truth, John," said Glenarvan, calmly.

"The truth, my Lord, is that we are at a standstill. Whether the sea will devour us is another question; but we have time to consider."

"It is midnight?"

"Yes, my Lord, and we must wait for the day."

"Can we not lower the boat?"

"In such a sea, and in the dark, it is impossible.

And, besides, where could we land?"

"Well, then, John, let us wait for the daylight."

Will Halley, however, ran up and down the deck like a maniac. His crew had recovered their senses, and now broached a cask of brandy, and began to drink. John foresaw that if they became drunk, terrible scenes would ensue.

The captain could not be relied on to restrain them;

the wretched man tore his hair and wrung his hands.

His whole thought was his uninsured cargo. "I am ruined!

I am lost!" he would cry, as he ran from side to side.

John Mangles did not waste time on him. He armed his two companions, and they all held themselves in readiness to resist the sailors who were filling themselves with brandy, seasoned with fearful blasphemies.

"The first of these wretches that comes near the ladies,

I will shoot like a dog," said the Major, quietly.

The sailors doubtless saw that the passengers were determined to hold their own, for after some attempts at pillage, they disappeared to their own quarters. John Mangles thought no more of these drunken rascals, and waited impatiently for the dawn. The ship was now quite motionless. The sea became gradually calmer. The wind fell. The hull would be safe for some hours yet. At daybreak John examined the landing-place; the yawl, which was now their only boat, would carry the crew and the passengers. It would have to make three trips at least, as it could only hold four.

As he was leaning on the skylight, thinking over the situation of affairs, John Mangles could hear the roaring of the surf. He tried to pierce the darkness. He wondered how far it was to the land they longed for no less than dreaded. A reef sometimes extends for miles along the coast. Could their fragile boat hold out on a long trip?

While John was thus ruminating and longing for a little light from the murky sky, the ladies, relying on him, slept in their little berths. The stationary attitude of the brig insured them some hours of repose. Glenarvan, John, and their companions, no longer disturbed by the noise of the crew who were now wrapped in a drunken sleep, also refreshed themselves by a short nap, and a profound silence reigned on board the ship, herself slumbering peacefully on her bed of sand.

Toward four o'clock the first peep of dawn appeared in the east. The clouds were dimly defined by the pale light of the dawn. John returned to the deck. The horizon was veiled with a curtain of fog. Some faint outlines were shadowed in the mist, but at a considerable height. A slight swell still agitated the sea, but the more distant waves were undistinguishable in a motionless bank of clouds.

John waited. The light gradually increased, and the horizon acquired a rosy hue. The curtain slowly rose over the vast watery stage. Black reefs rose out of the waters. Then a line became defined on the belt of foam, and there gleamed a luminous beacon-light point behind a low hill which concealed the scarcely risen sun. There was the land, less than nine miles off.

"Land ho!" cried John Mangles.

His companions, aroused by his voice, rushed to the poop, and gazed in silence at the coast whose outline lay on the horizon. Whether they were received as friends or enemies, that coast must be their refuge.

"Where is Halley?" asked Glenarvan.

"I do not know, my Lord," replied John Mangles.

"Where are the sailors?"

"Invisible, like himself."

"Probably dead drunk, like himself," added McNabbs.

"Let them be called," said Glenarvan, "we cannot leave them on the ship."

Mulrady and Wilson went down to the forecastle, and two
minutes after they returned. The place was empty!

They then searched between decks, and then the hold.

But found no trace of Will Halley nor his sailors.

"What! no one?" exclaimed Glenarvan.

"Could they have fallen into the sea?" asked Paganel.

"Everything is possible," replied John Mangles, who was getting uneasy.

Then turning toward the stern: "To the boat!" said he.

Wilson and Mulrady followed to launch the yawl. The yawl was gone.

CHAPTER V CANNIBALS

WILL HALLEY and his crew, taking advantage of the darkness of night and the sleep of the passengers, had fled with the only boat. There could be no doubt about it. The captain, whose duty would have kept him on board to the last, had been the first to quit the ship.

"The cowards are off!" said John Mangles. "Well, my Lord, so much the better. They have spared us some trying scenes."

"No doubt," said Glenarvan; "besides we have a captain of our own, and courageous, if unskillful sailors, your companions, John. Say the word, and we are ready to obey."

The Major, Paganel, Robert, Wilson, Mulrady, Olbinett himself, applauded Glenarvan's speech, and ranged themselves on the deck, ready to execute their captain's orders.

"What is to be done?" asked Glenarvan.

It was evident that raising the MACQUARIE was out of the question, and no less evident that she must be abandoned. Waiting on board for succor that might never come, would have been imprudence and folly. Before the arrival of a chance vessel on the scene, the MACQUARIE would have broken up. The next storm, or even a high tide raised by the winds from seaward, would roll it on the sands, break it up into splinters, and scatter them on the shore. John was anxious to reach the land before this inevitable consummation.

He proposed to construct a raft strong enough to carry the passengers, and a sufficient quantity of provisions, to the coast of New Zealand.

There was no time for discussion, the work was to be set about at once, and they had made considerable progress when night came and interrupted them.

Toward eight o'clock in the evening, after supper, while Lady Helena and Mary Grant slept in their berths, Paganel and his friends conversed on serious matters as they walked up and down the deck. Robert had chosen to stay with them. The brave boy listened with all his ears, ready to be of use, and willing to enlist in any perilous adventure.

Paganel asked John Mangles whether the raft could not follow the coast as far as Auckland, instead of landing its freight on the coast.

John replied that the voyage was impossible with such an unmanageable craft.

"And what we cannot do on a raft could have been done in the ship's boat?"

"Yes, if necessary," answered John; "but we should have had to sail by day and anchor at night."

"Then those wretches who abandoned us—"

"Oh, as for them," said John, "they were drunk, and in the darkness
I have no doubt they paid for their cowardice with their lives."

"So much the worse for them and for us," replied Paganel; "for the boat would have been very useful to us."

"What would you have, Paganel? The raft will bring us to the shore," said Glenarvan.

"The very thing I would fain avoid," exclaimed the geographer.

"What! do you think another twenty miles after crossing the Pampas and Australia, can have any terrors for us, hardened as we are to fatigue?"

"My friend," replied Paganel, "I do not call in question our courage nor the bravery of our friends. Twenty miles would be nothing in any other country than New Zealand. You cannot suspect me of faint-heartedness. I was the first to persuade you to cross America and Australia. But here the case is different. I repeat, anything is better than to venture into this treacherous country."

"Anything is better, in my judgment," said John Mangles, "than braving certain destruction on a stranded vessel."

"What is there so formidable in New Zealand?" asked Glenarvan.

"The savages," said Paganel.

"The savages!" repeated Glenarvan. "Can we not avoid them by keeping to the shore? But in any case what have we to fear? Surely, two resolute and well-armed Europeans need not give a thought to an attack by a handful of miserable beings."

Paganel shook his head. "In this case there are no miserable beings to contend with. The New Zealanders are a powerful race, who are rebelling against English rule, who fight the invaders, and often beat them, and who always eat them!"

"Cannibals!" exclaimed Robert, "cannibals?" Then they heard him whisper,

"My sister! Lady Helena."

"Don't frighten yourself, my boy," said Glenarvan; "our friend Paganel exaggerates."

"Far from it," rejoined Paganel. "Robert has shown himself a man, and I treat him as such, in not concealing the truth from him."

Paganel was right. Cannibalism has become a fixed fact in New Zealand, as it is in the Fijis and in Torres Strait. Superstition is no doubt partly to blame, but cannibalism is certainly owing to the fact that there are moments when game is scarce and hunger great. The savages began by eating human flesh to appease the demands of an appetite rarely satiated; subsequently the priests regulated and satisfied the monstrous custom. What was a meal, was raised to the dignity of a ceremony, that is all.

Besides, in the eyes of the Maories, nothing is more natural than to eat one another. The missionaries often questioned them about cannibalism. They asked them why they devoured their brothers; to which the chiefs made answer that fish eat fish, dogs eat men, men eat dogs, and dogs eat one another. Even the Maori mythology has a legend of a god who ate another god; and with such a precedent, who could resist eating his neighbor?

Another strange notion is, that in eating a dead enemy they consume his spiritual being, and so inherit his soul, his strength and his bravery, which they hold are specially lodged in the brain. This accounts for the fact that the brain figures in their feasts as the choicest delicacy, and is offered to the most honored guest.

But while he acknowledged all this, Paganel maintained, not without a show of reason, that sensuality, and especially hunger, was the first cause of cannibalism among the New Zealanders, and not only among the Polynesian races, but also among the savages of Europe.

"For," said he, "cannibalism was long prevalent among the ancestors of the most civilized people, and especially (if the Major will not think me personal) among the Scotch."

"Really," said McNabbs.

CHAPTER V CANNIBALS

"Yes, Major," replied Paganel. "If you read certain passages of Saint Jerome, on the Atticoli of Scotland, you will see what he thought of your forefathers. And without going so far back as historic times, under the reign of Elizabeth, when Shakespeare was dreaming out his Shy-lock, a Scotch bandit, Sawney Bean, was executed for the crime of canni-cannibalism. Was it religion that prompted him to cannibalism? No! it was hunger."

"Hunger?" said John Mangles.

"Hunger!" repeated Paganel; "but, above all, the necessity of the carnivorous appetite of replacing the bodily waste, by the azote contained in animal tissues. The lungs are satisfied with a provision of vegetable and farinaceous food. But to be strong and active the body must be supplied with those plastic elements that renew the muscles. Until the Maories become members of the Vegetarian Association they will eat meat, and human flesh as meat."

"Why not animal flesh?" asked Glenarvan.

"Because they have no animals," replied Paganel; "and that ought to be taken into account, not to extenuate, but to explain, their cannibal habits. Quadrupeds, and even birds, are rare on these inhospitable shores, so that the Maories have always eaten human flesh. There are even 'man-eating seasons,' as there are in civilized countries hunting seasons. Then begin the great wars, and whole tribes are served up on the tables of the conquerors."

"Well, then," said Glenarvan, "according to your mode of reasoning, Paganel, cannibalism will not cease in New Zealand until her pastures teem with sheep and oxen."

"Evidently, my dear Lord; and even then it will take years to wean them from Maori flesh, which they prefer to all others; for the children will still have a relish for what their fathers so highly appreciated. According to them it tastes like pork, with even more flavor. As to white men's flesh, they do not like it so well, because the whites eat salt with their food, which gives a peculiar flavor, not to the taste of connoisseurs."

"They are dainty," said the Major. "But, black or white, do they eat it raw, or cook it?"

"Why, what is that to you, Mr. McNabbs?" cried Robert.

"What is that to me!" exclaimed the Major, earnestly. "If I am to make a meal for a cannibal, I should prefer being cooked."

"Why?"

"Because then I should be sure of not being eaten alive!"

"Very good. Major," said Paganel; "but suppose they cooked you alive?"

"The fact is," answered the Major, "I would not give half-a-crown for the choice!"

"Well, McNabbs, if it will comfort you—you may as well be told—

the New Zealanders do not eat flesh without cooking or smoking it.

They are very clever and experienced in cookery.

For my part, I very much dislike the idea of being eaten!

The idea of ending one's life in the maw of a savage! bah!"

"The conclusion of all," said John Mangles, "is that we must not fall into their hands. Let us hope that one day Christianity will abolish all these monstrous customs."

"Yes, we must hope so," replied Paganel; "but, believe me, a savage who has tasted human flesh, is not easily persuaded to forego it. I will relate two facts which prove it."

"By all means let us have the facts, Paganel," said Glenarvan.

"The first is narrated in the chronicles of the Jesuit Society in Brazil. A Portuguese missionary was one day visiting an old Brazilian woman who was very ill. She had only a few days to live. The Jesuit inculcated the truths of religion, which the dying woman accepted, without objection. Then having attended to her spiritual wants, he bethought himself of her bodily needs, and offered her some European delicacies. 'Alas,' said she, 'my digestion is too weak to bear any kind of food. There is only one thing I could fancy, and nobody here could get it for me.' 'What is it?' asked the Jesuit. 'Ah! my son,' said she, 'it is the hand of a little boy! I feel as if I should enjoy munching the little bones!'"

"Horrid! but I wonder is it so very nice?" said Robert.

"My second tale will answer you, my boy," said Paganel: "One day a missionary was reproving a cannibal for the horrible custom, so abhorrent to God's laws, of eating human flesh! 'And beside,' said he, 'it must be so nasty!' 'Oh, father,' said the savage, looking greedily at the missionary, 'say that God forbids it! That is a reason for what you tell us. But don't say it is nasty! If you had only tasted it!'"

CHAPTER VI A DREADED COUNTRY

PAGANEL'S facts were indisputable. The cruelty of the New Zealanders was beyond a doubt, therefore it was dangerous to land. But had the danger been a hundredfold greater, it had to be faced. John Mangles felt the necessity of leaving without delay a vessel doomed to certain and speedy destruction. There were two dangers, one certain and the other probable, but no one could hesitate between them.

As to their chance of being picked up by a passing vessel, they could not reasonably hope for it. The MACQUARIE was not in the track of ships bound to New Zealand. They keep further north for Auckland, further south for New Plymouth, and the ship had struck just between these two points, on the desert region of the shores of Ika-na-Mani, a dangerous, difficult coast, and infested by desperate characters.

"When shall we get away?" asked Glenarvan.

"To-morrow morning at ten o'clock," replied John Mangles. "The tide will then turn and carry us to land."

Next day, February 5, at eight o'clock, the raft was finished. John had given all his attention to the building of this structure. The foreyard, which did very well for mooring the anchors, was quite inadequate to the transport of passengers and provisions. What was needed was a strong, manageable raft, that would resist the force of the waves during a passage of nine miles. Nothing but the masts could supply suitable materials.

Wilson and Mulrady set to work; the rigging was cut clear, and the mainmast, chopped away at the base, fell over the starboard rail, which crashed under its weight. The MACQUARIE was thus razed like a pontoon.

When the lower mast, the topmasts, and the royals were sawn and split, the principal pieces of the raft were ready. They were then joined to the fragments of the foremast and the whole was fastened securely together. John took the precaution to place in the interstices half a dozen empty barrels, which would raise the structure above the level of the water. On this strong foundation, Wilson laid a kind of floor in open work, made of the gratings off the hatches. The spray could then dash on the raft without staying there, and the passengers would be kept dry. In addition to this, the hose-pipes firmly lashed together formed a kind of circular barrier which protected the deck from the waves.

That morning, John seeing that the wind was in their favor, rigged up the royal-yard in the middle of the raft as a mast. It was stayed with shrouds, and carried a makeshift sail. A large broad-bladed oar was fixed behind to act as a rudder in case the wind was sufficient to require it. The greatest pains had been expended on strengthening the raft to resist the force of the waves, but the question remained whether, in the event of a change of wind, they could steer, or indeed, whether they could hope ever to reach the land.

At nine o'clock they began to load. First came the provisions, in quantity sufficient to last till they should reach Auckland, for they could not count on the productions of this barren region.

Olbinett's stores furnished some preserved meat which remained of the purchase made for their voyage in the MACQUARIE. This was but a scanty resource. They had to fall back on the coarse viands of the ship; sea biscuits of inferior quality, and two casks of salt fish. The steward was quite crestfallen.

These provisions were put in hermetically sealed cases, staunch and safe from sea water, and then lowered on to the raft and strongly lashed to the foot of the mast. The arms and ammunition were piled in a dry corner. Fortunately the travelers were well armed with carbines and revolvers.

A holding anchor was also put on board in case John should be unable to make the land in one tide, and would have to seek moorings.

At ten o'clock the tide turned. The breeze blew gently from the northwest, and a slight swell rocked the frail craft.

"Are we ready?" asked John.

"All ready, captain," answered Wilson.

"All aboard!" cried John.

Lady Helena and Mary Grant descended by a rope ladder, and took their station at the foot of the mast on the cases of provisions, their companions near them. Wilson took the helm. John stood by the tackle, and Mulrady cut the line which held the raft to the ship's side.

The sail was spread, and the frail structure commenced its progress toward the land, aided by wind and tide. The coast was about nine miles off, a distance that a boat with good oars would have accomplished in three hours. But with a raft allowance must be made. If the wind held, they might reach the land in one tide. But if the breeze died away, the ebb would carry them away from the shore, and they would be compelled to anchor and wait for the next tide, a serious consideration, and one that filled John Mangles with anxiety.

Still he hoped to succeed. The wind freshened. The tide had turned at ten o'clock, and by three they must either make the land or anchor to save themselves from being carried out to sea. They made a good start. Little by little the black line of the reefs and the yellow banks of sand disappeared under the swelling tide. Extreme watchfulness and perfect skill were necessary to avoid these submerged rocks, and steer a bark that did not readily answer to the helm, and that constantly broke off.

At noon they were still five miles from shore. A tolerably clear sky allowed them to make out the principal features of the land. In the northeast rose a mountain about 2,300 feet high, whose sharply defined outline was exactly like the grinning face of a monkey turned toward the sky. It was Pirongia, which the map gave as exactly on the 38th parallel.

At half-past twelve, Paganel remarked that all the rocks had disappeared under the rising tide.

"All but one," answered Lady Helena.

"Which, Madam?" asked Paganel.

"There," replied she, pointing to a black speck a mile off.

"Yes, indeed," said Paganel. "Let us try to ascertain its position, so as not to get too near it, for the sea will soon conceal it."

"It is exactly in a line with the northern slope of the mountain," said John Mangles. "Wilson, mind you give it a wide berth."

"Yes, captain," answered the sailor, throwing his whole weight on the great oar that steered the raft.

In half an hour they had made half a mile. But, strange to say, the black point still rose above the waves.

John looked attentively, and in order to make it out, borrowed Paganel's telescope.

"That is no reef," said he, after a moment; "it is something floating, which rises and falls with the swell."

"Is it part of the mast of the MACQUARIE?" asked Lady Helena.

"No," said Glenarvan, "none of her timbers could have come so far."

"Stay!" said John Mangles; "I know it! It is the boat."

"The ship's boat?" exclaimed Glenarvan.

"Yes, my lord. The ship's boat, keel up."

"The unfortunate creatures," cried Lady Helena, "they have perished!"

"Yes, Madam," replied John Mangles, "they must have perished, for in the midst of these breakers in a heavy swell on that pitchy night, they ran to certain death."

For a few minutes the passengers were silent.

They gazed at the frail craft as they drew near it.

It must evidently have capsized about four miles from the shore,

and not one of the crew could have escaped.

"But this boat may be of use to us," said Glenarvan.

"That is true," answered John Mangles. "Keep her up, Wilson."

The direction was slightly changed, but the breeze fell gradually, and it was two hours before they reached the boat.

Mulrady, stationed forward, fended off the blow, and the yawl was drawn alongside.

"Empty?" asked John Mangles.

"Yes, captain," answered the sailor, "the boat is empty. and all its seams are open. It is of no use to us."

"No use at all?" said McNabbs.

"None at all," said John Mangles.

"It is good for nothing but to burn."

"I regret it," said Paganel, "for the yawl might have taken us to Auckland."

"We must bear our fate, Monsieur Paganel," replied John Mangles.

"But, for my part, in such a stormy sea I prefer our raft to that

crazy boat. A very slight shock would be enough to break her up.

Therefore, my lord, we have nothing to detain us further."

"As you think best, John."

"On then, Wilson," said John, "and bear straight for the land."

There was still an hour before the turn of the tide. In that time they might make two miles. But the wind soon fell almost entirely, and the raft became nearly motionless, and soon began to drift to seaward under the influence of the ebb-tide.

John did not hesitate a moment.

"Let go the anchor," said he.

Mulrady, who stood to execute this order, let go the anchor in five fathoms water. The raft backed about two fathoms on the line, which was then at full stretch. The sail was taken in, and everything made snug for a tedious period of inaction.

The returning tide would not occur till nine o'clock in the evening; and as John Mangles did not care to go on in the dark, the anchorage was for the night, or at least till five o'clock in the morning, land being in sight at a distance of less than three miles.

A considerable swell raised the waves, and seemed to set in continuously toward the coast, and perceiving this, Glenarvan asked John why he did not take advantage of this swell to get nearer to the land.

"Your Lordship is deceived by an optical illusion," said the young captain. "Although the swell seems to carry the waves landward, it does not really move at all. It is mere undulating molecular motion, nothing more. Throw a piece of wood overboard and you will see that it will remain quite stationary except as the tide affects it. There is nothing for it but patience."

"And dinner," said the Major.

Olbinett unpacked some dried meat and a dozen biscuits.

The steward blushed as he proffered the meager bill of fare.

But it was received with a good grace, even by the ladies,

who, however, had not much appetite, owing to the violent motion.

This motion, produced by the jerking of the raft on the cable, while she lay head on to the sea, was very severe and fatiguing. The blows of the short, tumbling seas were as severe as if she had been striking on a submerged rock. Sometimes it was hard to believe that she was not aground. The cable strained violently, and every half hour John had to take in a fathom to ease it. Without this precaution it would certainly have given way, and the raft must have drifted to destruction.

John's anxiety may easily be understood. His cable might break, or his anchor lose its hold, and in either case the danger was imminent.

Night drew on; the sun's disc, enlarged by refraction, was dipping blood-red below the horizon. The distant waves glittered in the west, and sparkled like sheets of liquid silver. Nothing was to be seen in that direction but sky and water, except one sharply-defined object, the hull of the MACQUARIE motionless on her rocky bed.

The short twilight postponed the darkness only by a few minutes, and soon the coast outline, which bounded the view on the east and north, was lost in darkness.

The shipwrecked party were in an agonizing situation on their narrow raft, and overtaken by the shades of night.

Some of the party fell into a troubled sleep, a prey to evil dreams; others could not close an eye. When the day dawned, the whole party were worn out with fatigue.

With the rising tide the wind blew again toward the land. It was six o'clock in the morning, and there was no time to lose. John arranged everything for resuming their voyage, and then he ordered the anchor to be weighed. But the anchor flukes had been so imbedded in the sand by the repeated jerks of the cable, that without a windlass it was impossible to detach it, even with the tackle which Wilson had improvised.

Half an hour was lost in vain efforts. John, impatient of delay, cut the rope, thus sacrificing his anchor, and also the possibility of anchoring again if this tide failed to carry them to land. But he decided that further delay was not to be thought of, and an ax-blow committed the raft to the mercy of the wind, assisted by a current of two knots an hour.

The sail was spread. They drifted slowly toward the land, which rose in gray, hazy masses, on a background of sky illumined by the rising sun. The reef was dexterously avoided and doubled, but with the fitful breeze the raft could not get near the shore. What toil and pain to reach a coast so full of danger when attained.

At nine o'clock, the land was less than a mile off. It was a steeply-shelving shore, fringed with breakers; a practicable landing-place had to be discovered.

Gradually the breeze grew fainter, and then ceased entirely. The sail flapped idly against the mast, and John had it furled. The tide alone carried the raft to the shore, but steering had become impossible, and its passage was impeded by immense bands of FUCUS.

At ten o'clock John found himself almost at a stand-still, not three cables' lengths from the shore. Having lost their anchor, they were at the mercy of the ebb-tide.

John clenched his hands; he was racked with anxiety, and cast frenzied glances toward this inaccessible shore.

In the midst of his perplexities, a shock was felt. The raft stood still. It had landed on a sand-bank, twenty-five fathoms from the coast.

Glenarvan, Robert, Wilson, and Mulrady, jumped into the water. The raft was firmly moored to the nearest rocks. The ladies were carried to land without wetting a fold of their dresses, and soon the whole party, with their arms and provisions, were finally landed on these much dreaded New Zealand shores.

CHAPTER VII THE MAORI WAR

GLENARVAN would have liked to start without an hour's delay, and follow the coast to Auckland. But since the morning heavy clouds had been gathering, and toward eleven o'clock, after the landing was effected, the vapors condensed into violent rain, so that instead of starting they had to look for shelter.

Wilson was fortunate enough to discover what just suited their wants: a grotto hollowed out by the sea in the basaltic rocks. Here the travelers took shelter with their arms and provisions. In the cave they found a ready-garnered store of dried sea-weed, which formed a convenient couch; for fire, they lighted some wood near the mouth of the cavern, and dried themselves as well as they could.

John hoped that the duration of this deluge of rain would be in an inverse ratio to its violence, but he was doomed to disappointment. Hours passed without any abatement of its fury. Toward noon the wind freshened, and increased the force of the storm. The most patient of men would have rebelled at such an untoward incident; but what could be done; without any vehicle, they could not brave such a tempest; and, after all, unless the natives appeared on the scene, a delay of twelve hours was not so much consequence, as the journey to Auckland was only a matter of a few days. During this involuntary halt, the conversation turned on the incidents of the New Zealand war. But to understand and appreciate the critical position into which these MACQUARIE passengers were thrown, something ought to be known of the history of the struggle which had deluged the island of Ika-na-Mani with blood.

Since the arrival of Abel Tasman in Cook's Strait, on the 16th of December, 1642, though the New Zealanders had often been visited by European vessels, they had maintained their liberty in their several islands. No European power had thought of taking possession of this archipelago, which commands the whole Pacific Ocean. The missionaries stationed at various points were the sole channels of Christian civilization. Some of them, especially the Anglicans, prepared the minds of the New Zealand chiefs for submitting to the English yoke. It was cleverly managed, and these chiefs were influenced to sign a letter addressed to Queen Victoria to ask her protection. But the most clearsighted of them saw the folly of this step; and one of them, after having affixed his tattoo-mark to the letter by way of signature, uttered these prophetic words: "We have lost our country! henceforth it is not ours; soon the stranger will come and take it, and we shall be his slaves."

And so it was; on January 29, 1840, the English corvette HERALD arrived to claim possession.

CHAPTER VII THE MAORI WAR

From the year 1840, till the day the DUNCAN left the Clyde, nothing had happened here that Paganel did not know and he was ready to impart his information to his companions.

"Madam," said he, in answer to Lady Helena's questions, "I must repeat what I had occasion to remark before, that the New Zealanders are a courageous people, who yielded for a moment, but afterward fought foot to foot against the English invaders. The Maori tribes are organized like the old clans of Scotland. They are so many great families owning a chief, who is very jealous of his prerogative. The men of this race are proud and brave, one tribe tall, with straight hair, like the Maltese, or the Jews of Bagdad; the other smaller, thickset like mulattoes, but robust, haughty, and warlike. They had a famous chief, named Hihi, a real Vercingetorix, so that you need not be astonished that the war with the English has become chronic in the Northern Island, for in it is the famous tribe of the Waikatos, who defend their lands under the leadership of William Thompson."

"But," said John Mangles, "are not the English in possession of the principal points in New Zealand?"

"Certainly, dear John," replied Paganel. "After Captain Hobson took formal possession, and became governor, nine colonies were founded at various times between 1840 and 1862, in the most favorable situations. These formed the nucleus of nine provinces, four in the North Island and five in the southern island, with a total population of 184,346 inhabitants on the 30th of June, 1864."

"But what about this interminable war?" asked John Mangles.

"Well," said Paganel, "six long months have gone by since we left Europe, and I cannot say what may have happened during that time, with the exception of a few facts which I gathered from the newspapers of Maryborough and Seymour during our Australian journey. At that time the fighting was very lively in the Northern Island."

"And when did the war commence?" asked Mary Grant.

"Recommence, you mean, my dear young lady," replied Paganel; "for there was an insurrection so far back as 1845. The present war began toward the close of 1863; but long before that date the Maories were occupied in making preparations to shake off the English yoke. The national party among the natives carried on an active propaganda for the election of a Maori ruler. The object was to make old Potatau king, and to fix as the capital of the new kingdom his village, which lay between the Waikato and Waipa Rivers. Potatau was an old man, remarkable rather for cunning than bravery; but he had a Prime Minister who was both intelligent and energetic, a descendant of the Ngatihahuas, who occupied the isthmus before the arrival of the strangers. This minister, William Thompson, became the soul of the War of Independence, and organized the Maori troops, with great skill. Under this guidance a Taranaki chief gathered the scattered tribes around the same flag; a Waikato chief formed a 'Land League,' intended to prevent the natives from selling their land to the English Government, and warlike feasts were held just as in civilized countries on the verge of revolution. The English newspapers began to notice these alarming symptoms, and the government became seriously disturbed at these 'Land League' proceedings. In short, the train was laid, and the mine was ready to explode. Nothing was wanted but the spark, or rather the shock of rival interests to produce the spark.

"This shock took place in 1860, in the Taranaki province on the southwest coast of Ika-na-Mani. A native had six hundred acres of land in the neighborhood of New Plymouth. He sold them to the English Government; but when the surveyor came to measure the purchased land, the chief Kingi protested, and by the month of March he had made the six hundred acres in question into a fortified camp, surrounded with high palisades. Some days after Colonel Gold carried this fortress at the head of his troops, and that day heard the first shot fired of the native war."

"Have the rebels been successful up to this time?"

"Yes, Madam, and the English themselves have often been compelled to admire the courage and bravery of the New Zealanders. Their mode of warfare is of the guerilla type; they form skirmishing parties, come down in small detachments, and pillage the colonists' homes. General Cameron had no easy time in the campaigns, during which every bush had to be searched. In 1863, after a long and sanguinary struggle, the Maories were entrenched in strong and fortified position on the Upper Waikato, at the end of a chain of steep hills, and covered by three miles of forts. The native prophets called on all the Maori population to defend the soil, and promised the extermination of the pakekas, or white men. General Cameron had three thousand volunteers at his disposal, and they gave no quarter to the Maories after the barbarous murder of Captain Sprent. Several bloody engagements took place; in some instances the fighting lasted twelve hours before the Maories yielded to the English cannonade. The heart of the army was the fierce Waikato tribe under William Thompson. This native general commanded at the outset 2,500 warriors, afterward increased to 8,000. The men of Shongi and Heki, two powerful chiefs, came to his assistance. The women took their part in the most trying labors of this patriotic war. But right has not always might. After severe struggles General Cameron succeeded in subduing the Waikato district, but empty and depopulated, for the Maories escaped in all directions. Some wonderful exploits were related. Four hundred Maories who were shut up in the fortress of Orakau, besieged by 1,000 English, under Brigadier-General Carey, without water or provisions, refused to surrender, but one day at noon cut their way through the then decimated 40th Regiment, and escaped to the marshes."

"But," asked John Mangles, "did the submission of the Waikato district put an end to this sanguinary war?"

"No, my friend," replied Paganel. "The English resolved to march on Taranaki province and besiege Mataitawa, William Thompson's fortress. But they did not carry it without great loss. Just as I was leaving Paris, I heard that the Governor and the General had accepted the submission of the Tauranga tribes, and left them in possession of three-fourths of their lands. It was also rumored that the principal chief of the rebellion, William Thompson, was inclined to surrender, but the Australian papers have not confirmed this, but rather the contrary, and I should not be surprised to find that at this moment the war is going on with renewed vigor."

"Then, according to you, Paganel," said Glenarvan, "this struggle is still going on in the provinces of Auckland and Taranaki?"

"I think so."

"This very province where the MACQUARIE'S wreck has deposited us."

"Exactly. We have landed a few miles above Kawhia harbor, where the Maori flag is probably still floating."

"Then our most prudent course would be to keep toward the north," remarked Glenarvan.

"By far the most prudent," said Paganel. "The New Zealanders are incensed against Europeans, and especially against the English. Therefore let us avoid falling into their hands."

"We might have the good fortune to fall in with a detachment of European troops," said Lady Helena.

"We may, Madam," replied the geographer; "but I do not expect it. Detached parties do not like to go far into the country, where the smallest tussock, the thinnest brushwood, may conceal an accomplished marksman. I don't fancy we shall pick up an escort of the 40th Regiment. But there are mission-stations on this west coast, and we shall be able to make them our halting-places till we get to Auckland."

CHAPTER VIII ON THE ROAD TO AUCKLAND

ON the 7th of February, at six o'clock in the morning, the signal for departure was given by Glenarvan. During the night the rain had ceased. The sky was veiled with light gray clouds, which moderated the heat of the sun, and allowed the travelers to venture on a journey by day.

Paganel had measured on the map a distance of eighty miles between Point Kawhia and Auckland; it was an eight days' journey if they made ten miles a day. But instead of following the windings of the coast, he thought it better to make for a point thirty miles off, at the confluence of the Waikato and the Waipa, at the village of Ngarnavahia. The "overland track" passes that point, and is rather a path than a road, practicable for the vehicles which go almost across the island, from Napier, in Hawke's Bay, to Auckland. From this village it would be easy to reach Drury, and there they could rest in an excellent hotel, highly recommended by Dr. Hochstetter.

The travelers, each carrying a share of the provisions, commenced to follow the shore of Aotea Bay. From prudential motives they did not allow themselves to straggle, and by instinct they kept a look-out over the undulating plains to the eastward, ready with their loaded carbines. Paganel, map in hand, took a professional pleasure in verifying the minutest details.

The country looked like an immense prairie which faded into distance, and promised an easy walk. But the travelers were undeceived when they came to the edge of this verdant plain. The grass gave way to a low scrub of small bushes bearing little white flowers, mixed with those innumerable tall ferns with which the lands of New Zealand abound. They had to cut a path across the plain, through these woody stems, and this was a matter of some difficulty, but at eight o'clock in the evening the first slopes of the Hakarihoata Ranges were turned, and the party camped immediately. After a fourteen miles' march, they might well think of resting.

Neither wagon or tent being available, they sought repose beneath some magnificent Norfolk Island pines. They had plenty of rugs which make good beds. Glenarvan took every possible precaution for the night. His companions and he, well armed, were to watch in turns, two and two, till daybreak. No fires were lighted. Barriers of fire are a potent preservation from wild beasts, but New Zealand has neither tiger, nor lion, nor bear, nor any wild animal, but the Maori adequately fills their place, and a fire would only have served to attract this two-footed jaguar.

The night passed pleasantly with the exception of the attack of the sand-flies, called by the natives, "ngamu," and the visit of the audacious family of rats, who exercised their teeth on the provisions.

CHAPTER VIII ON THE ROAD TO AUCKLAND

Next day, on the 8th of February, Paganel rose more sanguine, and almost reconciled to the country. The Maories, whom he particularly dreaded, had not yet appeared, and these ferocious cannibals had not molested him even in his dreams. "I begin to think that our little journey will end favorably. This evening we shall reach the confluence of the Waipa and Waikato, and after that there is not much chance of meeting natives on the way to Auckland."

"How far is it now," said Glenarvan, "to the confluence of the Waipa and Waikato?"

"Fifteen miles; just about what we did yesterday."

"But we shall be terribly delayed if this interminable scrub continues to obstruct our path."

"No," said Paganel, "we shall follow the banks of the Waipa, and then we shall have no obstacle, but on the contrary, a very easy road."

"Well, then," said Glenarvan, seeing the ladies ready, "let us make a start."

During the early part of the day, the thick brushwood seriously impeded their progress. Neither wagon nor horses could have passed where travelers passed, so that their Australian vehicle was but slightly regretted. Until practicable wagon roads are cut through these forests of scrub, New Zealand will only be accessible to foot passengers. The ferns, whose name is legion, concur with the Maories in keeping strangers off the lands.

The little party overcame many obstacles in crossing the plains in which the Hakarihoata Ranges rise. But before noon they reached the banks of the Waipa, and followed the northward course of the river.

The Major and Robert, without leaving their companions, shot some snipe and partridge under the low shrubs of the plain. Olbinett, to save time, plucked the birds as he went along.

Paganel was less absorbed by the culinary importance of the game than by the desire of obtaining some bird peculiar to New Zealand. His curiosity as a naturalist overcame his hunger as a traveler. He called to mind the peculiarities of the "tui" of the natives, sometimes called the mocking-bird from its incessant chuckle, and sometimes "the parson," in allusion to the white cravat it wears over its black, cassock-like plumage.

"The tui," said Paganel to the Major, "grows so fat during the Winter that it makes him ill, and prevents him from flying. Then he tears his breast with his beak, to relieve himself of his fat, and so becomes lighter. Does not that seem to you singular, McNabbs?"

"So singular that I don't believe a word of it," replied the Major.

Paganel, to his great regret, could not find a single specimen, or he might have shown the incredulous Major the bloody scars on the breast. But he was more fortunate with a strange animal which, hunted by men, cats and dogs, has fled toward the unoccupied country, and is fast disappearing from the fauna of New Zealand. Robert, searching like a ferret, came upon a nest made of interwoven roots, and in it a pair of birds destitute of wings and tail, with four toes, a long snipe-like beak, and a covering of white feathers over the whole body, singular creatures, which seemed to connect the oviparous tribes with the mam-mifers.

It was the New Zealand "kiwi," the *Apteryx australis* of naturalists, which lives with equal satisfaction on larvae, insects, worms or seeds. This bird is peculiar to the country. It has been introduced into very few of the zoological collections of Europe. Its graceless shape and comical motions have always attracted the notice of travelers, and during the great exploration of the Astrolabe and the Zelee, Dumont d'Urville was principally charged by the Academy of Sciences to bring back a specimen of these singular birds. But in spite of rewards offered to the natives, he could not obtain a single specimen.

Paganel, who was elated at such a piece of luck, tied the two birds together, and carried them along with the intention of presenting them to the Jardin des Plantes, in Paris. "Presented by M. Jacques Paganel." He mentally saw the flattering inscription on the handsomest cage in the gardens. Sanguine geographer!

The party pursued their way without fatigue along the banks of the Waipa. The country was quite deserted; not a trace of natives, nor any track that could betray the existence of man. The stream was fringed with tall bushes, or glided along sloping banks, so that nothing obstructed the view of the low range of hills which closed the eastern end of the valley. With their grotesque shapes, and their outlines lost in a deceptive haze, they brought to mind giant animals, worthy of antediluvian times. They might have been a herd of enormous whales, suddenly turned to stone. These disrupted masses proclaimed their essentially volcanic character. New Zealand is, in fact, a formation of recent plutonic origin. Its emergence from the sea is constantly increasing. Some points are known to have risen six feet in twenty years. Fire still runs across its center, shakes it, convulses it, and finds an outlet in many places by the mouths of geysers and the craters of volcanoes.

At four in the afternoon, nine miles had been easily accomplished. According to the map which Paganel constantly referred to, the confluence of the Waipa and Waikato ought to be reached about five miles further on, and there the night halt could be made. Two or three days would then suffice for the fifty miles which lay between them and the capital; and if Glenarvan happened to fall in with the mail coach that plies between Hawkes' Bay and Auckland twice a month, eight hours would be sufficient.

"Therefore," said Glenarvan, "we shall be obliged to camp during the night once more."

"Yes," said Paganel, "but I hope for the last time."

"I am very glad to think so, for it is very trying for Lady Helena and Mary Grant."

"And they never utter a murmur," added John Mangles. "But I think I heard you mention a village at the confluence of these rivers."

"Yes," said the geographer, "here it is, marked on Johnston's map. It is Ngarnavahia, two miles below the junction."

"Well, could we not stay there for the night? Lady Helena and Miss Grant would not grudge two miles more to find a hotel even of a humble character."

"A hotel!" cried Paganel, "a hotel in a Maori village! you would not find an inn, not a tavern! This village will be a mere cluster of huts, and so far from seeking rest there, my advice is that you give it a wide berth."

"Your old fears, Paganel!" retorted Glenarvan.

"My dear Lord, where Maories are concerned, distrust is safer than confidence. I do not know on what terms they are with the English, whether the insurrection is suppressed or successful, or whether indeed the war may not be going on with full vigor. Modesty apart, people like us would be a prize, and I must say, I would rather forego a taste of Maori hospitality. I think it certainly more prudent to avoid this village of Ngarnavahia, to skirt it at a distance, so as to avoid all encounters with the natives. When we reach Drury it will be another thing, and there our brave ladies will be able to recruit their strength at their leisure."

This advice prevailed. Lady Helena preferred to pass another night in the open air, and not to expose her companions to danger. Neither Mary Grant or she wished to halt, and they continued their march along the river.

Two hours later, the first shades of evening began to fall. The sun, before disappearing below the western horizon, darted some bright rays through an opening in the clouds. The distant eastern summits were empurpled with the parting glories of the day. It was like a flying salute addressed to the way-worn travelers.

Glenarvan and his friends hastened their steps, they knew how short the twilight is in this high latitude, and how quickly the night follows it. They were very anxious to reach the confluence of the two rivers before the darkness overtook them. But a thick fog rose from the ground, and made it very difficult to see the way.

Fortunately hearing stood them in the stead of sight; shortly a nearer sound of water indicated that the confluence was at hand. At eight o'clock the little troop arrived at the point where the Waipa loses itself in the Waikato, with a moaning sound of meeting waves.

"There is the Waikato!" cried Paganel, "and the road to Auckland is along its right bank."

"We shall see that to-morrow," said the Major, "Let us camp here. It seems to me that that dark shadow is that of a little clump of trees grown expressly to shelter us. Let us have supper and then get some sleep."

"Supper by all means," said Paganel, "but no fire; nothing but biscuit and dried meat. We have reached this spot incognito, let us try and get away in the same manner. By good luck, the fog is in our favor."

The clump of trees was reached and all concurred in the wish of the geographer. The cold supper was eaten without a sound, and presently a profound sleep overcame the travelers, who were tolerably fatigued with their fifteen miles' march.

CHAPTER IX INTRODUCTION TO THE CANNIBALS

THE next morning at daybreak a thick fog was clinging to the surface of the river. A portion of the vapors that saturated the air were condensed by the cold, and lay as a dense cloud on the water. But the rays of the sun soon broke through the watery mass and melted it away.

A tongue of land, sharply pointed and bristling with bushes, projected into the uniting streams. The swifter waters of the Waipa rushed against the current of the Waikato for a quarter of a mile before they mingled with it; but the calm and majestic river soon quieted the noisy stream and carried it off quietly in its course to the Pacific Ocean.

When the vapor disappeared, a boat was seen ascending the current of the Waikato. It was a canoe seventy feet long, five broad, and three deep; the prow raised like that of a Venetian gondola, and the whole hollowed out of a trunk of a kahikatea. A bed of dry fern was laid at the bottom. It was swiftly rowed by eight oars, and steered with a paddle by a man seated in the stern.

This man was a tall Maori, about forty-five years of age, broad-chested, muscular, with powerfully developed hands and feet. His prominent and deeply-furrowed brow, his fierce look, and sinister expression, gave him a formidable aspect.

Tattooing, or "moko," as the New Zealanders call it, is a mark of great distinction. None is worthy of these honorary lines, who has not distinguished himself in repeated fights. The slaves and the lower class can not obtain this decoration. Chiefs of high position may be known by the finish and precision and truth of the design, which sometimes covers their whole bodies with the figures of animals. Some are found to undergo the painful operation of "moko" five times. The more illustrious, the more illustrated, is the rule of New Zealand.

Dumont D'Urville has given some curious details as to this custom. He justly observes that "moko" is the counterpart of the armorial bearings of which many families in Europe are so vain. But he remarks that there is this difference: the armorial bearings of Europe are frequently a proof only of the merits of the first who bore them, and are no certificate of the merits of his descendants; while the individual coat-of-arms of the Maori is an irrefragible proof that it was earned by the display of extraordinary personal courage.

The practice of tattooing, independently of the consideration it procures, has also a useful aspect. It gives the cutaneous system an increased thickness, enabling it to resist the inclemency of the season and the incessant attacks of the mosquito.

As to the chief who was steering the canoe, there could be no mistake. The sharpened albatross bone used by the Maori tattooer, had five times scored his countenance. He was in his fifth edition, and betrayed it in his haughty bearing.

His figure, draped in a large mat woven of "phormium" trimmed with dogskins, was clothed with a pair of cotton drawers, blood-stained from recent combats. From the pendant lobe of his ears hung earrings of green jade, and round his neck a quivering necklace of "pounamous," a kind of jade stone sacred among the New Zealanders. At his side lay an English rifle, and a "patou-patou," a kind of two-headed ax of an emerald color, and eighteen inches long. Beside him sat nine armed warriors of inferior rank, ferocious-looking fellows, some of them suffering from recent wounds. They sat quite motionless, wrapped in their flax mantles. Three savage-looking dogs lay at their feet. The eight rowers in the prow seemed to be servants or slaves of the chief. They rowed vigorously, and propelled the boat against the not very rapid current of the Waikato, with extraordinary velocity.

In the center of this long canoe, with their feet tied together, sat ten European prisoners closely packed together.

It was Glenarvan and Lady Helena, Mary Grant, Robert, Paganel, the Major, John Mangles, the steward, and the two sailors.

The night before, the little band had unwittingly, owing to the mist, encamped in the midst of a numerous party of natives. Toward the middle of the night they were surprised in their sleep, were made prisoners, and carried on board the canoe. They had not been ill-treated, so far, but all attempts at resistance had been vain. Their arms and ammunition were in the hands of the savages, and they would soon have been targets for their own balls.

They were soon aware, from a few English words used by the natives, that they were a retreating party of the tribe who had been beaten and decimated by the English troops, and were on their way back to the Upper Waikato. The Maori chief, whose principal warriors had been picked off by the soldiers of the 42nd Regiment, was returning to make a final appeal to the tribes of the Waikato district, so that he might go to the aid of the indomitable William Thompson, who was still holding his own against the conquerors. The chief's name was "Kai-Koumou," a name of evil boding in the native language, meaning "He who eats the limbs of his enemy." He was bold and brave, but his cruelty was equally remarkable. No pity was to be expected at his hands. His name was well known to the English soldiers, and a price had been set on his head by the governor of New Zealand.

This terrible blow befell Glenarvan at the very moment when he was about to reach the long-desired haven of Auckland, and so regain his own country; but no one who looked at his cool, calm features, could have guessed the anguish he endured. Glenarvan always rose to his misfortunes. He felt that his part was to be the strength and the example of his wife and companions; that he was the head and chief; ready to die for the rest if circumstances required it. He was of a deeply religious turn of mind, and never lost his trust in Providence nor his belief in the sacred character of his enterprise. In the midst of this crowning peril he did not give way to any feeling of regret at having been induced to venture into this country of savages.

His companions were worthy of him; they entered into his lofty views; and judging by their haughty demeanor, it would scarcely have been supposed that they were hurrying to the final catastrophe. With one accord, and by Glenarvan's advice, they resolved to affect utter indifference before the natives. It was the only way to impress these ferocious natures. Savages in general, and particularly the Maories, have a notion of dignity from which they never derogate. They respect, above all things, coolness and courage. Glenarvan was aware that by this mode of procedure, he and his companions would spare themselves needless humiliation.

From the moment of embarking, the natives, who were very taciturn, like all savages, had scarcely exchanged a word, but from the few sentences they did utter, Glenarvan felt certain that the English language was familiar to them. He therefore made up his mind to question the chief on the fate that awaited them. Addressing himself to Kai-Koumou, he said in a perfectly unconcerned voice:

"Where are we going, chief?"

Kai-Koumou looked coolly at him and made no answer.

"What are you going to do with us?" pursued Glenarvan.

A sudden gleam flashed into the eyes of Kai-Koumou, and he said in a deep voice:

"Exchange you, if your own people care to have you; eat you if they don't."

Glenarvan asked no further questions; but hope revived in his heart. He concluded that some Maori chiefs had fallen into the hands of the English, and that the natives would try to get them exchanged. So they had a chance of salvation, and the case was not quite so desperate.

The canoe was speeding rapidly up the river. Paganel, whose excitable temperament always rebounded from one extreme to the other, had quite regained his spirits. He consoled himself that the natives were saving them the trouble of the journey to the English outposts, and that was so much gain. So he took it quite quietly and followed on the map the course of the Waikato across the plains and valleys of the province. Lady Helena and Mary Grant, concealing their alarm, conversed in a low voice with Glenarvan, and the keenest physiognomists would have failed to see any anxiety in their faces.

The Waikato is the national river in New Zealand. It is to the Maories what the Rhine is to the Germans, and the Danube to the Slavs. In its course of 200 miles it waters the finest lands of the North Island, from the province of Wellington to the province of Auckland. It gave its name to all those indomitable tribes of the river district, which rose *en masse* against the invaders.

The waters of this river are still almost strangers to any craft but the native canoe. The most audacious tourist will scarcely venture to invade these sacred shores; in fact, the Upper Waikato is sealed against profane Europeans.

Paganel was aware of the feelings of veneration with which the natives regard this great arterial stream. He knew that the English and German naturalists had never penetrated further than its junction with the Waipa. He wondered how far the good pleasure of Kai-Koumou would carry his captives? He could not have guessed, but for hearing the word "Taupo" repeatedly uttered between the chief and his warriors. He consulted his map and saw that "Taupo" was the name of a lake celebrated in geographical annals, and lying in the most mountainous part of the island, at the southern extremity of Auckland province. The Waikato passes through this lake and then flows on for 120 miles.

CHAPTER X A MOMENTOUS INTERVIEW

AN unfathomable gulf twenty-five miles long, and twenty miles broad was produced, but long before historic times, by the falling in of caverns among the trachytic lavas of the center of the island. And these waters falling from the surrounding heights have taken possession of this vast basin. The gulf has become a lake, but it is also an abyss, and no lead-line has yet sounded its depths.

Such is the wondrous lake of Taupo, lying 1,250 feet above the level of the sea, and in view of an amphitheater of mountains 2,400 feet high. On the west are rocky peaks of great size; on the north lofty summits clothed with low trees; on the east a broad beach with a road track, and covered with pumice stones, which shimmer through the leafy screen of the bushes; on the southern side rise volcanic cones behind a forest flat. Such is the majestic frame that incloses this vast sheet of water whose roaring tempests rival the cyclones of Ocean.

The whole region boils like an immense cauldron hung over subterranean fires. The ground vibrates from the agitation of the central furnace. Hot springs filter out everywhere. The crust of the earth cracks in great rifts like a cake, too quickly baked.

About a quarter of a mile off, on a craggy spur of the mountain stood a "pah," or Maori fortress. The prisoners, whose feet and hands were liberated, were landed one by one, and conducted into it by the warriors. The path which led up to the intrenchment, lay across fields of "phormium" and a grove of beautiful trees, the "kai-kateas" with persistent leaves and red berries; "dracaenas australis," the "ti-trees" of the natives, whose crown is a graceful counterpart of the cabbage-palm, and "huious," which are used to give a black dye to cloth. Large doves with metallic sheen on their plumage, and a world of starlings with reddish carmeles, flew away at the approach of the natives.

After a rather circuitous walk, Glenarvan and his party arrived at the "pah."

The fortress was defended by an outer inclosure of strong palisades, fifteen feet high; a second line of stakes; then a fence composed of osiers, with loop-holes, inclosed Verne the inner space, that is the plateau of the "pah," on which were erected the Maori buildings, and about forty huts arranged symmetrically.

When the captives approached they were horror-struck at the sight of the heads which adorned the posts of the inner circle. Lady Helena and Mary Grant turned away their eyes more with disgust than with terror. These heads were those of hostile chiefs who had fallen in battle, and whose bodies had served to feed the conquerors. The geographer recognized that it was so, from their eye sockets being hollow and deprived of eye-balls.

Glenarvan and his companions had taken in all this scene at a glance. They stood near an empty house, waiting the pleasure of the chief, and exposed to the abuse of a crowd of old crones. This troop of harpies surrounded them, shaking their fists, howling and vociferating. Some English words that escaped their coarse mouths left no doubt that they were clamoring for immediate vengeance.

In the midst of all these cries and threats, Lady Helena, tranquil to all outward seeming, affected an indifference she was far from feeling. This courageous woman made heroic efforts to restrain herself, lest she should disturb Glenarvan's coolness. Poor Mary Grant felt her heart sink within her, and John Mangles stood by ready to die in her behalf. His companions bore the deluge of invectives each according to his disposition; the Major with utter indifference, Paganel with exasperation that increased every moment.

Glenarvan, to spare Lady Helena the attacks of these witches, walked straight up to Kai-Koumou, and pointing to the hideous group:

"Send them away," said he.

The Maori chief stared fixedly at his prisoner without speaking; and then, with a nod, he silenced the noisy horde. Glenarvan bowed, as a sign of thanks, and went slowly back to his place.

At this moment a hundred Maories were assembled in the "pah," old men, full grown men, youths; the former were calm, but gloomy, awaiting the orders of Kai-Koumou; the others gave themselves up to the most violent sorrow, bewailing their parents and friends who had fallen in the late engagements.

Kai-Koumou was the only one of all the chiefs that obeyed the call of William Thompson, who had returned to the lake district, and he was the first to announce to his tribe the defeat of the national insurrection, beaten on the plains of the lower Waikato. Of the two hundred warriors who, under his orders, hastened to the defence of the soil, one hundred and fifty were missing on his return. Allowing for a number being made prisoners by the invaders, how many must be lying on the field of battle, never to return to the country of their ancestors!

This was the secret of the outburst of grief with which the tribe saluted the arrival of Kai-Koumou. Up to that moment nothing had been known of the last defeat, and the fatal news fell on them like a thunder clap.

Among the savages, sorrow is always manifested by physical signs; the parents and friends of deceased warriors, the women especially, lacerated their faces and shoulders with sharpened shells. The blood spurted out and blended with their tears. Deep wounds denoted great despair. The unhappy Maories, bleeding and excited, were hideous to look upon.

There was another serious element in their grief. Not only had they lost the relative or friend they mourned, but his bones would be missing in the family mausoleum. In the Maori religion the possession of these relics is regarded as indispensable to the destinies of the future life; not the perishable flesh, but the bones, which are collected with the greatest care, cleaned, scraped, polished, even varnished, and then deposited in the "oudoupa," that is the "house of glory." These tombs are adorned with wooden statues, representing with perfect exactness the tattoo of the deceased. But now their tombs would be left empty, the religious rites would be unsolemnized, and the bones that escaped the teeth of the wild dog would whiten without burial on the field of battle.

Then the sorrowful chorus redoubled. The menaces of the women were intensified by the imprecations of the men against the Europeans. Abusive epithets were lavished, the accompanying gestures became more violent. The howl was about to end in brutal action.

Kai-Koumou, fearing that he might be overpowered by the fanatics of his tribe, conducted his prisoners to a sacred place, on an abruptly raised plateau at the other end of the "pah." This hut rested against a mound elevated a hundred feet above it, which formed the steep outer buttress of the entrenchment. In this "Ware-Atoua," sacred house, the priests or arikis taught the Maories about a Triune God, father, son, and bird, or spirit. The large, well constructed hut, contained the sacred and choice food which Maoui-Ranga-Rangui eats by the mouths of his priests.

In this place, and safe for the moment from the frenzied natives, the captives lay down on the flax mats. Lady Helena was quite exhausted, her moral energies prostrate, and she fell helpless into her husband's arms.

Glenarvan pressed her to his bosom and said:

"Courage, my dear Helena; Heaven will not forsake us!"

Robert was scarcely in when he jumped on Wilson's shoulders, and squeezed his head through a crevice left between the roof and the walls, from which chaplets of amulets were hung. From that elevation he could see the whole extent of the "pah," and as far as Kai-Koumou's house.

"They are all crowding round the chief," said he softly.

"They are throwing their arms about. . . . They are howling. . . .

. Kai-Koumou is trying to speak."

Then he was silent for a few minutes.

"Kai-Koumou is speaking. . . . The savages are quieter.

. . . . They are listening. . . . ."

"Evidently," said the Major, "this chief has a personal interest in protecting us. He wants to exchange his prisoners for some chiefs of his tribe! But will his warriors consent?"

"Yes! . . . They are listening. . . . . They have dispersed, some are gone into their huts. . . . The others have left the intrenchment."

"Are you sure?" said the Major.

"Yes, Mr. McNabbs," replied Robert, "Kai-Koumou is left alone with the warriors of his canoe. . . . . Oh! one of them is coming up here. . . . ."

"Come down, Robert," said Glenarvan.

At this moment, Lady Helena who had risen, seized her husband's arm.

"Edward," she said in a resolute tone, "neither Mary Grant nor I must fall into the hands of these savages alive!"

And so saying, she handed Glenarvan a loaded revolver.

"Fire-arm!" exclaimed Glenarvan, with flashing eyes.

"Yes! the Maories do not search their prisoners. But, Edward, this is for us, not for them."

Glenarvan slipped the revolver under his coat; at the same moment the mat at the entrance was raised, and a native entered.

He motioned to the prisoners to follow him. Glenarvan and the rest walked across the "pah" and stopped before Kai-Koumou. He was surrounded by the principal warriors of his tribe, and among them the Maori whose canoe joined that of the Kai-Koumou at the confluence of Pohain-henna, on the Waikato. He was a man about forty years of age, powerfully built and of fierce and cruel aspect. His name was Kara-Tete, meaning "the irascible" in the native tongue. Kai-Koumou treated him with a certain tone of respect, and by the fineness of his tattoo, it was easy to perceive that Kara-Tete held a lofty position in the tribe, but a keen observer would have guessed the feeling of rivalry that existed between these two chiefs. The Major observed that the influence of Kara-Tete gave umbrage to Kai-Koumou. They both ruled the Waikato tribes, and were equal in authority. During this interview Kai-Koumou smiled, but his eyes betrayed a deep-seated enmity.

Kai-Koumou interrogated Glenarvan.

"You are English?" said he.

"Yes," replied Glenarvan, unhesitatingly, as his nationality would facilitate the exchange.

"And your companions?" said Kai-Koumou.

"My companions are English like myself. We are shipwrecked travelers, but it may be important to state that we have taken no part in the war."

"That matters little!" was the brutal answer of Kara-Tete.

"Every Englishman is an enemy. Your people invaded our island!

They robbed our fields! they burned our villages!"

"They were wrong!" said Glenarvan, quietly. "I say so, because I think it, not because I am in your power."

"Listen," said Kai-Koumou, "the Tohonga, the chief priest of Noui-Atoua has fallen into the hands of your brethren; he is a prisoner among the Pakekas. Our deity has commanded us to ransom him. For my own part, I would rather have torn out your heart, I would have stuck your head, and those of your companions, on the posts of that palisade. But Noui-Atoua has spoken."

As he uttered these words, Kai-Koumou, who till now had been quite unmoved, trembled with rage, and his features expressed intense ferocity.

Then after a few minutes' interval he proceeded more calmly.

"Do you think the English will exchange you for our Tohonga?"

Glenarvan hesitated, all the while watching the Maori chief.

"I do not know," said he, after a moment of silence.

"Speak," returned Kai-Koumou, "is your life worth that of our Tohonga?"

"No," replied Glenarvan. "I am neither a chief nor a priest among my own people."

Paganel, petrified at this reply, looked at Glenarvan in amazement.

Kai-Koumou appeared equally astonished.

"You doubt it then?" said he.

"I do not know," replied Glenarvan.

"Your people will not accept you as an exchange for Tohonga?"

"Me alone? no," repeated Glenarvan. "All of us perhaps they might."

"Our Maori custom," replied Kai-Koumou, "is head for head."

"Offer first these ladies in exchange for your priest," said Glenarvan, pointing to Lady Helena and Mary Grant.

Lady Helena was about to interrupt him. But the Major held her back.

"Those two ladies," continued Glenarvan, bowing respectfully toward Lady Helena and Mary Grant, "are personages of rank in their own country."

The warrior gazed coldly at his prisoner. An evil smile relaxed his lips for a moment; then he controlled himself, and in a voice of ill-concealed anger:

"Do you hope to deceive Kai-Koumou with lying words, accursed Pakeka? Can not the eyes of Kai-Koumou read hearts?"

And pointing to Lady Helena: "That is your wife?" he said.

"No! mine!" exclaimed Kara-Tete.

And then pushing his prisoners aside, he laid his hand on the shoulder of Lady Helena, who turned pale at his touch.

"Edward!" cried the unfortunate woman in terror.

Glenarvan, without a word, raised his arm, a shot! and Kara-Tete fell at his feet.

The sound brought a crowd of natives to the spot. A hundred arms were ready, and Glenarvan's revolver was snatched from him.

Kai-Koumou glanced at Glenarvan with a curious expression: then with one hand protecting Glenarvan, with the other he waved off the crowd who were rushing on the party.

At last his voice was heard above the tumult.

"Taboo! Taboo!" he shouted.

At that word the crowd stood still before Glenarvan and his companions, who for the time were preserved by a supernatural influence.

A few minutes after they were re-conducted to Ware-Atoua, which was their prison. But Robert Grant and Paganel were not with them.

CHAPTER XI THE CHIEF'S FUNERAL

KAI-KOUMOU, as frequently happens among the Maories, joined the title of ariki to that of tribal chief. He was invested with the dignity of priest, and, as such, he had the power to throw over persons or things the superstitious protection of the "taboo."

The "taboo," which is common to all the Polynesian races, has the primary effect of isolating the "tabooed" person and preventing the use of "tabooed" things. According to the Maori doctrine, anyone who laid sacrilegious hands on what had been declared "taboo," would be punished with death by the insulted deity, and even if the god delayed the vindication of his power, the priests took care to accelerate his vengeance.

By the chiefs, the "taboo" is made a political engine, except in some cases, for domestic reasons. For instance, a native is tabooed for several days when his hair is cut; when he is tattooed; when he is building a canoe, or a house; when he is seriously ill, and when he is dead. If excessive consumption threatens to exterminate the fish of a river, or ruin the early crop of sweet potatoes, these things are put under the protection of the taboo. If a chief wishes to clear his house of hangers-on, he taboos it; if an English trader displeases him he is tabooed. His interdict has the effect of the old royal "veto."

If an object is tabooed, no one can touch it with impunity. When a native is under the interdict, certain aliments are denied him for a prescribed period. If he is relieved, as regards the severe diet, his slaves feed him with the viands he is forbidden to touch with his hands; if he is poor and has no slaves, he has to take up the food with his mouth, like an animal.

In short, the most trifling acts of the Maories are directed and modified by this singular custom, the deity is brought into constant contact with their daily life. The taboo has the same weight as a law; or rather, the code of the Maories, indisputable and undisputed, is comprised in the frequent applications of the taboo.

As to the prisoners confined in the Ware-Atoua, it was an arbitrary taboo which had saved them from the fury of the tribe. Some of the natives, friends and partisans of Kai-Koumou, desisted at once on hearing their chief's voice, and protected the captives from the rest.

Glenarvan cherished no illusive hopes as to his own fate; nothing but his death could atone for the murder of a chief, and among these people death was only the concluding act of a martyrdom of torture. Glenarvan, therefore, was fully prepared to pay the penalty of the righteous indignation that nerved his arm, but he hoped that the wrath of Kai-Koumou would not extend beyond himself.

What a night he and his companions passed! Who could picture their agonies or measure their sufferings? Robert and Paganel had not been restored to them, but their fate was no doubtful matter. They were too surely the first victims of the frenzied natives.

Even McNabbs, who was always sanguine, had abandoned hope. John Mangles was nearly frantic at the sight of Mary Grant's despair at being separated from her brother. Glenarvan pondered over the terrible request of Lady Helena, who preferred dying by his hand to submitting to torture and slavery. How was he to summon the terrible courage!

"And Mary? who has a right to strike her dead?" thought John, whose heart was broken.

Escape was clearly impossible. Ten warriors, armed to the teeth, kept watch at the door of Ware-Atoua.

The morning of February 13th arrived. No communication had taken place between the natives and the "tabooed" prisoners. A limited supply of provisions was in the house, which the unhappy inmates scarcely touched. Misery deadened the pangs of hunger. The day passed without change, and without hope; the funeral ceremonies of the dead chief would doubtless be the signal for their execution.

Although Glenarvan did not conceal from himself the probability that Kai-Koumou had given up all idea of exchange, the Major still cherished a spark of hope.

"Who knows," said he, as he reminded Glenarvan of the effect produced on the chief by the death of Kara-Tete—"who knows but that Kai-Koumou, in his heart, is very much obliged to you?"

But even McNabbs' remarks failed to awaken hope in Glenarvan's mind. The next day passed without any appearance of preparation for their punishment; and this was the reason of the delay.

The Maories believe that for three days after death the soul inhabits the body, and therefore, for three times twenty-four hours, the corpse remains unburied. This custom was rigorously observed. Till February 15th the "pah" was deserted.

John Mangles, hoisted on Wilson's shoulders, frequently reconnoitered the outer defences. Not a single native was visible; only the watchful sentinels relieving guard at the door of the Ware-Atoua.

But on the third day the huts opened; all the savages, men, women, and children, in all several hundred Maories, assembled in the "pah," silent and calm.

Kai-Koumou came out of his house, and surrounded by the principal chiefs of his tribe, he took his stand on a mound some feet above the level, in the center of the enclosure. The crowd of natives formed in a half circle some distance off, in dead silence.

At a sign from Kai-Koumou, a warrior bent his steps toward Ware-Atoua.

"Remember," said Lady Helena to her husband. Glenarvan pressed her to his heart, and Mary Grant went closer to John Mangles, and said hurriedly:

"Lord and Lady Glenarvan cannot but think if a wife may claim death at her husband's hands, to escape a shameful life, a betrothed wife may claim death at the hands of her betrothed husband, to escape the same fate. John! at this last moment I ask you, have we not long been betrothed to each other in our secret hearts? May I rely on you, as Lady Helena relies on Lord Glenarvan?"

"Mary!" cried the young captain in his despair. "Ah! dear Mary—"

The mat was lifted, and the captives led to Kai-Koumou; the two women were resigned to their fate; the men dissembled their sufferings with superhuman effort.

They arrived in the presence of the Maori chief.

"You killed Kara-Tete," said he to Glenarvan.

"I did," answered Glenarvan.

"You die to-morrow at sunrise."

"Alone?" asked Glenarvan, with a beating heart.

"Oh! if our Tohonga's life was not more precious than yours!" exclaimed Kai-Koumou, with a ferocious expression of regret.

At this moment there was a commotion among the natives. Glenarvan looked quickly around; the crowd made way, and a warrior appeared heated by running, and sinking with fatigue.

Kai-Koumou, as soon as he saw him, said in English, evidently for the benefit of the captives:

"You come from the camp of the Pakekas?"

"Yes," answered the Maori.

"You have seen the prisoner, our Tohonga?"

"I have seen him."

"Alive?"

"Dead! English have shot him."

It was all over with Glenarvan and his companions.

"All!" cried Kai-Koumou; "you all die to-morrow at daybreak."

Punishment fell on all indiscriminately. Lady Helena and Mary Grant were grateful to Heaven for the boon.

The captives were not taken back to Ware-Atoua. They were destined to attend the obsequies of the chief and the bloody rites that accompanied them. A guard of natives conducted them to the foot of an immense kauri, and then stood on guard without taking their eyes off the prisoners.

The three prescribed days had elapsed since the death of Kara-Tete, and the soul of the dead warrior had finally departed; so the ceremonies commenced.

The body was laid on a small mound in the central enclosure. It was clothed in a rich dress, and wrapped in a magnificent flax mat. His head, adorned with feathers, was encircled with a crown of green leaves. His face, arms, and chest had been rubbed with oil, and did not show any sign of decay.

The parents and friends arrived at the foot of the mound, and at a certain moment, as if the leader of an orchestra were leading a funeral chant, there arose a great wail of tears, sighs, and sobs. They lamented the deceased with a plaintive rhythm and doleful cadence. The kinsmen beat their heads; the kinswomen tore their faces with their nails and lavished more blood than tears. But these demonstrations were not sufficient to propitiate the soul of the deceased, whose wrath might strike the survivors of his tribe; and his warriors, as they could not recall him to life, were anxious that he should have nothing to wish for in the other world. The wife of Kara-Tete was not to be parted from him; indeed, she would have refused to survive him. It was a custom, as well as a duty, and Maori history has no lack of such sacrifices.

This woman came on the scene; she was still young. Her disheveled hair flowed over her shoulders. Her sobs and cries filled the air. Incoherent words, regrets, sobs, broken phrases in which she extolled the virtues of the dead, alternated with her moans, and in a crowning paroxysm of sorrow, she threw herself at the foot of the mound and beat her head on the earth.

The Kai-Koumou drew near; suddenly the wretched victim rose; but a violent blow from a "MERE," a kind of club brandished by the chief, struck her to the ground; she fell senseless.

Horrible yells followed; a hundred arms threatened the terror-stricken captives. But no one moved, for the funeral ceremonies were not yet over.

The wife of Kara-Tete had joined her husband. The two bodies lay stretched side by side. But in the future life, even the presence of his faithful companion was not enough.

Who would attend on them in the realm of Noui-Atoua, if their slaves did not follow them into the other world.

Six unfortunate fellows were brought to the mound. They were attendants whom the pitiless usages of war had reduced to slavery. During the chief's lifetime they had borne the severest privations, and been subjected to all kinds of ill-usage; they had been scantily fed, and incessantly occupied like beasts of burden, and now, according to Maori ideas, they were to resume to all eternity this life of bondage.

These poor creatures appeared quite resigned to their destiny. They were not taken by surprise. Their unbound hands showed that they met their fate without resistance.

Their death was speedy and not aggravated by tedious suffering; torture was reserved for the authors of the murder, who, only twenty paces off, averted their eyes from the horrible scene which was to grow yet more horrible.

Six blows of the MERE, delivered by the hands of six powerful warriors, felled the victims in the midst of a sea of blood.

This was the signal for a fearful scene of cannibalism. The bodies of slaves are not protected by taboo like those of their masters. They belong to the tribe; they were a sort of small change thrown among the mourners, and the moment the sacrifice was over, the whole crowd, chiefs, warriors, old men, women, children, without distinction of age, or sex, fell upon the senseless remains with brutal appetite. Faster than a rapid pen could describe it, the bodies, still reeking, were dismembered, divided, cut up, not into morsels, but into crumbs. Of the two hundred Maories present everyone obtained a share. They fought, they struggled, they quarreled over the smallest fragment. The drops of hot blood splashed over these festive monsters, and the whole of this detestable crew groveled under a rain of blood. It was like the delirious fury of tigers fighting over their prey, or like a circus where the wild beasts devour the deer. This scene ended, a score of fires were lit at various points of the "pah"; the smell of charred flesh polluted the air; and but for the fearful tumult of the festival, but for the cries that emanated from these flesh-sated throats, the captives might have heard the bones crunching under the teeth of the cannibals.

Glenarvan and his companions, breathless with horror, tried to conceal this fearful scene from the eyes of the two poor ladies. They understood then what fate awaited them next day at dawn, and also with what cruel torture this death would be preceded. They were dumb with horror.

The funeral dances commenced. Strong liquors distilled from the "piper excelsum" animated the intoxication of the natives. They had nothing human left. It seemed possible that the "taboo" might be forgotten, and they might rush upon the prisoners, who were already terrified at their delirious gestures.

But Kai-Koumou had kept his own senses amidst the general delirium. He allowed an hour for this orgy of blood to attain its maximum and then cease, and the final scene of the obsequies was performed with the accustomed ceremonial.

The corpses of Kara-Tete and his wife were raised, the limbs were bent, and laid against the stomach according to the Maori usage; then came the funeral, not the final interment, but a burial until the moment when the earth had destroyed the flesh and nothing remained but the skeleton.

The place of "oudoupa," or the tomb, had been chosen outside the fortress, about two miles off at the top of a low hill called Maunganamu, situated on the right bank of the lake, and to this spot the body was to be taken. Two palanquins of a very primitive kind, hand-barrows, in fact, were brought to the foot of the mound, and the corpses doubled up so that they were sitting rather than lying, and their garments kept in place by a band of hanes, were placed on them. Four warriors took up the litters on their shoulders, and the whole tribe, repeating their funeral chant, followed in procession to the place of sepulture.

The captives, still strictly guarded, saw the funeral cortege leave the inner inclosure of the "pah"; then the chants and cries grew fainter. For about half an hour the funeral procession remained out of sight, in the hollow valley, and then came in sight again winding up the mountain side; the distance gave a fantastic effect to the undulating movement of this long serpentine column.

The tribe stopped at an elevation of about 800 feet, on the summit of Maunganamu, where the burial place of Kara-Tete had been prepared. An ordinary Maori would have had nothing but a hole and a heap of earth. But a powerful and formidable chief destined to speedy deification, was honored with a tomb worthy of his exploits.

The "oudoupa" had been fenced round, and posts, surmounted with faces painted in red ochre, stood near the grave where the bodies were to lie. The relatives had not forgotten that the "Waidoua," the spirit of the dead, lives on mortal food, as the body did in this life. Therefore, food was deposited in the inclosure as well as the arms and clothing of the deceased. Nothing was omitted for comfort. The husband and wife were laid side by side, then covered with earth and grass, after another series of laments.

Then the procession wound slowly down the mountain, and henceforth none dare ascend the slope of Maunganamu on pain of death, for it was "tabooed," like Tongariro, where lie the ashes of a chief killed by an earthquake in 1846.

CHAPTER XII STRANGELY LIBERATED

JUST as the sun was sinking beyond Lake Taupo, behind the peaks of
Tuhahua and Pukepapu, the captives were conducted back to their prison.
They were not to leave it again till the tops of the Wahiti Ranges
were lit with the first fires of day.

They had one night in which to prepare for death. Overcome as they were with horror and fatigue, they took their last meal together.

"We shall need all our strength," Glenarvan had said, "to look death in the face. We must show these savages how Europeans can die."

The meal ended. Lady Helena repeated the evening prayer aloud, her companions, bare-headed, repeated it after her. Who does not turn his thoughts toward God in the hour of death? This done, the prisoners embraced each other. Mary Grant and Helena, in a corner of the hut, lay down on a mat. Sleep, which keeps all sorrow in abeyance, soon weighed down their eyelids; they slept in each other's arms, overcome by exhaustion and prolonged watching.

Then Glenarvan, taking his friends aside, said: "My dear friends, our lives and the lives of these poor women are in God's hands. If it is decreed that we die to-morrow, let us die bravely, like Christian men, ready to appear without terror before the Supreme Judge. God, who reads our hearts, knows that we had a noble end in view. If death awaits us instead of success, it is by His will. Stern as the decree may seem, I will not repine. But death here, means not death only, it means torture, insult, perhaps, and here are two ladies—"

Glenarvan's voice, firm till now, faltered. He was silent a moment, and having overcome his emotion, he said, addressing the young captain:

"John, you have promised Mary what I promised Lady Helena.
What is your plan?"

"I believe," said John, "that in the sight of God I have a right to fulfill that promise."

"Yes, John; but we are unarmed."

"No!" replied John, showing him a dagger. "I snatched it from Kara-Tete when he fell at your feet. My Lord, whichever of us survives the other will fulfill the wish of Lady Helena and Mary Grant."

After these words were said, a profound silence ensued.

At last the Major said: "My friends, keep that to the last moment.
I am not an advocate of irremediable measures."

"I did not speak for ourselves," said Glenarvan. "Be it as it may,
we can face death! Had we been alone, I should ere now have cried,
'My friends, let us make an effort. Let us attack these wretches!'

But with these poor girls—"

At this moment John raised the mat, and counted twenty-five natives keeping guard on the Ware-Atoua. A great fire had been lighted, and its lurid glow threw into strong relief the irregular outlines of the "pah." Some of the savages were sitting round the brazier; the others standing motionless, their black outlines relieved against the clear background of flame. But they all kept watchful guard on the hut confided to their care.

It has been said that between a vigilant jailer and a prisoner who wishes to escape, the chances are in favor of the prisoner; the fact is, the interest of the one is keener than that of the other. The jailer may forget that he is on guard; the prisoner never forgets that he is guarded. The captive thinks oftener of escaping than the jailer of preventing his flight, and hence we hear of frequent and wonderful escapes.

But in the present instance hatred and revenge were the jailers— not an indifferent warder; the prisoners were not bound, but it was because bonds were useless when five-and-twenty men were watching the only egress from the Ware-Atoua.

This house, with its back to the rock which closed the fortress, was only accessible by a long, narrow promontory which joined it in front to the plateau on which the "pah" was erected. On its two other sides rose pointed rocks, which jutted out over an abyss a hundred feet deep. On that side descent was impossible, and had it been possible, the bottom was shut in by the enormous rock. The only outlet was the regular door of the Ware-Atoua, and the Maories guarded the promontory which united it to the "pah" like a drawbridge. All escape was thus hopeless, and Glenarvan having tried the walls for the twentieth time, was compelled to acknowledge that it was so.

The hours of this night, wretched as they were, slipped away. Thick darkness had settled on the mountain. Neither moon nor stars pierced the gloom. Some gusts of wind whistled by the sides of the "pah," and the posts of the house creaked: the fire outside revived with the puffs of wind, and the flames sent fitful gleams into the interior of Ware-Atoua. The group of prisoners was lit up for a moment; they were absorbed in their last thoughts, and a deathlike silence reigned in the hut.

It might have been about four o'clock in the morning when the Major's attention was called to a slight noise which seemed to come from the foundation of the posts in the wall of the hut which abutted on the rock. McNabbs was at first indifferent, but finding the noise continue, he listened; then his curiosity was aroused, and he put his ear to the ground; it sounded as if someone was scraping or hollowing out the ground outside.

As soon as he was sure of it, he crept over to Glenarvan and John Mangles, and startling them from their melancholy thoughts, led them to the end of the hut.

"Listen," said he, motioning them to stoop.

The scratching became more and more audible; they could hear the little stones grate on a hard body and roll away.

"Some animal in his burrow," said John Mangles.

Glenarvan struck his forehead.

"Who knows?" said he, "it might be a man."

"Animal or man," answered the Major, "I will soon find out!"

Wilson and Olbinett joined their companions, and all united to dig through the wall— John with his dagger, the others with stones taken from the ground, or with their nails, while Mulrady, stretched along the ground, watched the native guard through a crevice of the matting.

These savages sitting motionless around the fire, suspected nothing of what was going on twenty feet off.

CHAPTER XII STRANGELY LIBERATED

The soil was light and friable, and below lay a bed of silicious tufa; therefore, even without tools, the aperture deepened quickly. It soon became evident that a man, or men, clinging to the sides of the "pah," were cutting a passage into its exterior wall. What could be the object? Did they know of the existence of the prisoners, or was it some private enterprise that led to the undertaking?

The prisoners redoubled their efforts. Their fingers bled, but still they worked on; after half an hour they had gone three feet deep; they perceived by the increased sharpness of the sounds that only a thin layer of earth prevented immediate communication.

Some minutes more passed, and the Major withdrew his hand from the stroke of a sharp blade. He suppressed a cry.

John Mangles, inserting the blade of his poniard, avoided the knife which now protruded above the soil, but seized the hand that wielded it.

It was the hand of a woman or child, a European! On neither side had a word been uttered. It was evidently the cue of both sides to be silent.

"Is it Robert?" whispered Glenarvan.

But softly as the name was breathed, Mary Grant, already awakened by the sounds in the hut, slipped over toward Glenarvan, and seizing the hand, all stained with earth, she covered it with kisses.

"My darling Robert," said she, never doubting, "it is you! it is you!"

"Yes, little sister," said he, "it is I am here to save you all; but be very silent."

"Brave lad!" repeated Glenarvan.

"Watch the savages outside," said Robert.

Mulrady, whose attention was distracted for a moment by the appearance of the boy, resumed his post.

"It is all right," said he. "There are only four awake; the rest are asleep."

A minute after, the hole was enlarged, and Robert passed from the arms of his sister to those of Lady Helena. Round his body was rolled a long coil of flax rope.

"My child, my child," murmured Lady Helena, "the savages did not kill you!"

"No, madam," said he; "I do not know how it happened, but in the scuffle I got away; I jumped the barrier; for two days I hid in the bushes, to try and see you; while the tribe were busy with the chief's funeral, I came and reconnoitered this side of the path, and I saw that I could get to you. I stole this knife and rope out of the desert hut. The tufts of bush and the branches made me a ladder, and I found a kind of grotto already hollowed out in the rock under this hut; I had only to bore some feet in soft earth, and here I am."

Twenty noiseless kisses were his reward.

"Let us be off!" said he, in a decided tone.

"Is Paganel below?" asked Glenarvan.

"Monsieur Paganel?" replied the boy, amazed.

"Yes; is he waiting for us?"

"No, my Lord; but is he not here?" inquired Robert.

"No, Robert!" answered Mary Grant.

"Why! have you not seen him?" asked Glenarvan. "Did you lose each other in the confusion? Did you not get away together?"

"No, my Lord!" said Robert, taken aback by the disappearance of his friend Paganel.

"Well, lose no more time," said the Major. "Wherever Paganel is, he cannot be in worse plight than ourselves. Let us go."

Truly, the moments were precious. They had to fly. The escape was not very difficult, except the twenty feet of perpendicular fall outside the grotto.

After that the slope was practicable to the foot of the mountain. From this point the prisoners could soon gain the lower valleys; while the Maories, if they perceived the flight of the prisoners, would have to make a long round to catch them, being unaware of the gallery between the Ware-Atoua and the outer rock.

The escape was commenced, and every precaution was taken. The captives passed one by one through the narrow passage into the grotto. John Mangles, before leaving the hut, disposed of all the evidences of their work, and in his turn slipped through the opening and let down over it the mats of the house, so that the entrance to the gallery was quite concealed.

The next thing was to descend the vertical wall to the slope below, and this would have been impracticable, but that Robert had brought the flax rope, which was now unrolled and fixed to a projecting point of rock, the end hanging over.

John Mangles, before his friends trusted themselves to this flax rope, tried it; he did not think it very strong; and it was of importance not to risk themselves imprudently, as a fall would be fatal.

"This rope," said he, "will only bear the weight of two persons; therefore let us go in rotation. Lord and Lady Glenarvan first; when they arrive at the bottom, three pulls at the rope will be a signal to us to follow."

"I will go first," said Robert. "I discovered a deep hollow at the foot of the slope where those who come down can conceal themselves and wait for the rest."

"Go, my boy," said Glenarvan, pressing Robert's hand.

Robert disappeared through the opening out of the grotto. A minute after, the three pulls at the cord informed them the boy had alighted safely.

Glenarvan and Lady Helena immediately ventured out of the grotto. The darkness was still very great, though some grayish streaks were already visible on the eastern summits.

The biting cold of the morning revived the poor young lady.

She felt stronger and commenced her perilous descent.

Glenarvan first, then Lady Helena, let themselves down along the rope, till they came to the spot where the perpendicular wall met the top of the slope. Then Glenarvan going first and supporting his wife, began to descend backward.

He felt for the tufts and grass and shrubs able to afford a foothold; tried them and then placed Lady Helena's foot on them. Some birds, suddenly awakened, flew away, uttering feeble cries, and the fugitives trembled when a stone loosened from its bed rolled to the foot of the mountain.

They had reached half-way down the slope, when a voice was heard from the opening of the grotto.

"Stop!" whispered John Mangles.

Glenarvan, holding with one hand to a tuft of tetragonia, with the other holding his wife, waited with breathless anxiety.

Wilson had had an alarm. Having heard some unusual noise outside the Ware-Atoua, he went back into the hut and watched the Maories from behind the mat. At a sign from him, John stopped Glenarvan.

One of the warriors on guard, startled by an unusual sound, rose and drew nearer to the Ware-Atoua. He stood still about two paces from the hut and listened with his head bent forward. He remained in that attitude for a minute that seemed an hour, his ear intent, his eye peering into the darkness. Then shaking his head like one who sees he is mistaken, he went back to his companions, took an armful of dead wood, and threw it into the smouldering fire, which immediately revived. His face was lighted up by the flame, and was free from any look of doubt, and after having glanced to where the first light of dawn whitened the eastern sky, stretched himself near the fire to warm his stiffened limbs.

"All's well!" whispered Wilson.

John signaled to Glenarvan to resume his descent.

Glenarvan let himself gently down the slope; soon Lady Helena and he landed on the narrow track where Robert waited for them.

The rope was shaken three times, and in his turn John Mangles, preceding Mary Grant, followed in the dangerous route.

He arrived safely; he rejoined Lord and Lady Glenarvan in the hollow mentioned by Robert.

Five minutes after, all the fugitives had safely escaped from the Ware-Atoua, left their retreat, and keeping away from the inhabited shores of the lakes, they plunged by narrow paths into the recesses of the mountains.

They walked quickly, trying to avoid the points where they might be seen from the pah. They were quite silent, and glided among the bushes like shadows. Whither? Where chance led them, but at any rate they were free.

Toward five o'clock, the day began to dawn, bluish clouds marbled the upper stratum of clouds. The misty summits began to pierce the morning mists. The orb of day was soon to appear, and instead of giving the signal for their execution, would, on the contrary, announce their flight.

It was of vital importance that before the decisive moment arrived they should put themselves beyond the reach of the savages, so as to put them off their track. But their progress was slow, for the paths were steep. Lady Glenarvan climbed the slopes, supported, not to say carried, by Glenarvan, and Mary Grant leaned on the arm of John Mangles; Robert, radiant with joy, triumphant at his success, led the march, and the two sailors brought up the rear.

Another half an hour and the glorious sun would rise out of the mists of the horizon. For half an hour the fugitives walked on as chance led them. Paganel was not there to take the lead. He was now the object of their anxiety, and whose absence was a black shadow between them and their happiness. But they bore steadily eastward, as much as possible, and faced the gorgeous morning light. Soon they had reached a height of 500 feet above Lake Taupo, and the cold of the morning, increased by the altitude, was very keen. Dim outlines of hills and mountains rose behind one another; but Glenarvan only thought how best to get lost among them. Time enough by and by to see about escaping from the labyrinth.

At last the sun appeared and sent his first rays on their path.

Suddenly a terrific yell from a hundred throats rent the air.

It came from the pah, whose direction Glenarvan did not know.

Besides, a thick veil of fog, which, spread at his feet,

prevented any distinct view of the valleys below.

But the fugitives could not doubt that their escape had been discovered; and now the question was, would they be able to elude pursuit? Had they been seen? Would not their track betray them?

At this moment the fog in the valley lifted, and enveloped them for a moment in a damp mist, and at three hundred feet below they perceived the swarming mass of frantic natives.

While they looked they were seen. Renewed howls broke forth, mingled with the barking of dogs, and the whole tribe, after vainly trying to scale the rock of Ware-Atoua, rushed out of the pah, and hastened by the shortest paths in pursuit of the prisoners who were flying from their vengeance.

CHAPTER XIII THE SACRED MOUNTAIN

THE summit of the mountain was still a hundred feet above them. The fugitives were anxious to reach it that they might continue their flight on the eastern slope out of the view of their pursuers. They hoped then to find some practicable ridge that would allow of a passage to the neighboring peaks that were thrown together in an orographic maze, to which poor Paganel's genius would doubtless have found the clew.

They hastened up the slope, spurred on by the loud cries that drew nearer and nearer. The avenging crowd had already reached the foot of the mountain.

"Courage! my friends," cried Glenarvan, urging his companions by voice and look.

In less than five minutes they were at the top of the mountain, and then they turned to judge of their position, and decide on a route that would baffle their pursuers.

From their elevated position they could see over Lake Taupo, which stretched toward the west in its setting of picturesque mountains. On the north the peaks of Pirongia; on the south the burning crater of Tongariro. But eastward nothing but the rocky barrier of peaks and ridges that formed the Wahiti ranges, the great chain whose unbroken links stretch from the East Cape to Cook's Straits. They had no alternative but to descend the opposite slope and enter the narrow gorges, uncertain whether any outlet existed.

Glenarvan could not prolong the halt for a moment.

Wearied as they might be, they must fly or be discovered.

"Let us go down!" cried he, "before our passage is cut off."

But just as the ladies had risen with a despairing effort,

McNabbs stopped them and said:

"Glenarvan, it is useless. Look!"

And then they all perceived the inexplicable change that had taken place in the movements of the Maories.

Their pursuit had suddenly stopped. The ascent of the mountain had ceased by an imperious command. The natives had paused in their career, and surged like the sea waves against an opposing rock. All the crowd, thirsting for blood, stood at the foot of the mountain yelling and gesticulating, brandishing guns and hatchets, but not advancing a foot. Their dogs, rooted to the spot like themselves, barked with rage.

What stayed them? What occult power controlled these savages? The fugitives looked without understanding, fearing lest the charm that enchained Kai-Koumou's tribe should be broken.

Suddenly John Mangles uttered an exclamation which attracted the attention of his companions. He pointed to a little inclosure on the summit of the cone.

"The tomb of Kara-Tete!" said Robert.

"Are you sure, Robert?" said Glenarvan.

"Yes, my Lord, it is the tomb; I recognize it."

Robert was right. Fifty feet above, at the extreme peak of the mountain, freshly painted posts formed a small palisaded inclosure, and Glenarvan too was convinced that it was the chief's burial place. The chances of their flight had led them to the crest of Maunganamu.

Glenarvan, followed by the rest, climbed to the foot of the tomb.

A large opening, covered with mats, led into it.

Glenarvan was about to invade the sanctity of the "oudoupa," when he reeled backward.

"A savage!" said he.

"In the tomb?" inquired the Major.

"Yes, McNabbs."

"No matter; go in."

Glenarvan, the Major, Robert and John Mangles entered.

There sat a Maori, wrapped in a large flax mat; the darkness of the "oudoupa" preventing them from distinguishing his features.

He was very quiet, and was eating his breakfast quite coolly.

Glenarvan was about to speak to him when the native forestalled him by saying gayly and in good English:

"Sit down, my Lord; breakfast is ready."

It was Paganel. At the sound of his voice they all rushed into the "oudoupa," and he was cordially embraced all round. Paganel was found again. He was their salvation. They wanted to question him; to know how and why he was here on the summit of Maunganamu; but Glenarvan stopped this misplaced curiosity.

"The savages?" said he.

"The savages," said Paganel, shrugging his shoulders.

"I have a contempt for those people! Come and look at them."

They all followed Paganel out of the "oudoupa." The Maories were still in the same position round the base of the mountain, uttering fearful cries.

"Shout! yell! till your lungs are gone, stupid wretches!" said Paganel. "I dare you to come here!"

"But why?" said Glenarvan.

"Because the chief is buried here, and the tomb protects us, because the mountain is tabooed."

"Tabooed?"

"Yes, my friends! and that is why I took refuge here, as the malefactors used to flee to the sanctuaries in the middle ages."

"God be praised!" said Lady Helena, lifting her hands to heaven.

The fugitives were not yet out of danger, but they had a moment's respite, which was very welcome in their exhausted state.

Glenarvan was too much overcome to speak, and the Major nodded his head with an air of perfect content.

"And now, my friends," said Paganel, "if these brutes think to exercise their patience on us, they are mistaken. In two days we shall be out of their reach."

"By flight!" said Glenarvan. "But how?"

"That I do not know," answered Paganel, "but we shall manage it."

And now everybody wanted to know about their friend's adventures. They were puzzled by the reserve of a man generally so talkative; on this occasion they had to drag the words out of his mouth; usually he was a ready story-teller, now he gave only evasive answers to the questions of the rest.

"Paganel is another man!" thought McNabbs.

His face was really altered. He wrapped himself closely in his great flax mat and seemed to deprecate observation. Everyone noticed his embarrassment, when he was the subject of conversation, though nobody appeared to remark it; when other topics were under discussion, Paganel resumed his usual gayety.

Of his adventures all that could be extracted from him at this time was as follows:

After the murder of Kara-Tete, Paganel took advantage, like Robert, of the commotion among the natives, and got out of the inclosure. But less fortunate than young Grant, he walked straight into a Maori camp, where he met a tall, intelligent-looking chief, evidently of higher rank than all the warriors of his tribe. The chief spoke excellent English, and he saluted the new-comer by rubbing the end of his nose against the end of the geographer's nose.

Paganel wondered whether he was to consider himself a prisoner or not. But perceiving that he could not stir without the polite escort of the chief, he soon made up his mind on that point.

This chief, Hihi, or Sunbeam, was not a bad fellow. Paganel's spectacles and telescope seemed to give him a great idea of Paganel's importance, and he manifested great attachment to him, not only by kindness, but by a strong flax rope, especially at night.

This lasted for three days; to the inquiry whether he was well treated, he said "Yes and no!" without further answer; he was a prisoner, and except that he expected immediate execution, his state seemed to him no better than that in which he had left his unfortunate friends.

One night, however, he managed to break his rope and escape. He had seen from afar the burial of the chief, and knew that he was buried on the top of Maunganamu, and he was well acquainted with the fact that the mountain would be therefore tabooed. He resolved to take refuge there, being unwilling to leave the region where his companions were in durance. He succeeded in his dangerous attempt, and had arrived the previous night at the tomb of Kara-Tete, and there proposed to recruit his strength while he waited in the hope that his friends might, by Divine mercy, find the means of escape.

Such was Paganel's story. Did he designedly conceal some incident of his captivity? More than once his embarrassment led them to that conclusion. But however that might be, he was heartily congratulated on all sides. And then the present emergency came on for serious discussion. The natives dare not climb Maunganamu, but they, of course, calculated that hunger and thirst would restore them their prey. It was only a question of time, and patience is one of the virtues of all savages. Glenarvan was fully alive to the difficulty, but made up his mind to watch for an opportunity, or make one. First of all he made a thorough survey of Maunganamu, their present fortress; not for the purpose of defence, but of escape. The Major, John, Robert, Paganel, and himself, made an exact map of the mountain. They noted the direction, outlet and inclination of the paths. The ridge, a mile in length, which united Maunganamu to the Wahiti chain had a downward inclination. Its slope, narrow and jagged though it was, appeared the only practicable route, if they made good their escape at all. If they could do this without observation, under cover of night, they might possibly reach the deep valleys of the Range and put the Maories off the scent.

But there were dangers in this route; the last part of it was within pistol shot of natives posted on the lower slopes. Already when they ventured on the exposed part of the crest, they were saluted with a hail of shot which did not reach them. Some gun wads, carried by the wind, fell beside them; they were made of printed paper, which Paganel picked up out of curiosity, and with some trouble deciphered.

"That is a good idea! My friends, do you know what those creatures use for wads?"

"No, Paganel!" said Glenarvan.

"Pages of the Bible! If that is the use they make of the Holy Book, I pity the missionaries! It will be rather difficult to establish a Maori library."

"And what text of scripture did they aim at us?"

"A message from God Himself!" exclaimed John Mangles, who was in the act of reading the scorched fragment of paper. "It bids us hope in Him," added the young captain, firm in the faith of his Scotch convictions.

"Read it, John!" said Glenarvan.

And John read what the powder had left visible: "I will deliver him, for he hath trusted in me."

"My friends," said Glenarvan, "we must carry these words of hope to our dear, brave ladies. The sound will bring comfort to their hearts."

Glenarvan and his companions hastened up the steep path to the cone, and went toward the tomb. As they climbed they were astonished to perceive every few moments a kind of vibration in the soil. It was not a movement like earthquake, but that peculiar tremor that affects the metal of a boiler under high pressure. It was clear the mountain was the outer covering of a body of vapor, the product of subterranean fires.

This phenomenon of course excited no surprise in those that had just traveled among the hot springs of the Waikato. They knew that the central region of the Ika-na-Mani is essentially volcanic. It is a sieve, whose interstices furnish a passage for the earth's vapors in the shape of boiling geysers and solfataras.

Paganel, who had already noticed this, called the attention of his friends to the volcanic nature of the mountain. The peak of Maunganamu was only one of the many cones which bristle on this part of the island. It was a volcano of the future. A slight mechanical change would produce a crater of eruption in these slopes, which consisted merely of whitish silicious tufa.

"That may be," said Glenarvan, "but we are in no more danger here than standing by the boiler of the DUNCAN; this solid crust is like sheet iron."

"I agree with you," added the Major, "but however good a boiler may be, it bursts at last after too long service."

"McNabbs," said Paganel, "I have no fancy for staying on the cone.

When Providence points out a way, I will go at once."

"I wish," remarked John, "that Maunganamu could carry us himself, with all the motive power that he has inside. It is too bad that millions of horse-power should lie under our feet unavailable for our needs. Our DUNCAN would carry us to the end of the world with the thousandth part of it."

The recollections of the DUNCAN evoked by John Mangles turned Glenarvan's thoughts into their saddest channel; for desperate as his own case was he often forgot it, in vain regret at the fate of his crew.

His mind still dwelt on it when he reached the summit of Maunganamu and met his companions in misfortune.

Lady Helena, when she saw Glenarvan, came forward to meet him.

"Dear Edward," said she, "you have made up your mind?

Are we to hope or fear?"

"Hope, my dear Helena," replied Glenarvan. "The natives will never set foot on the mountain, and we shall have time to devise a plan of escape."

"More than that, madam, God himself has encouraged us to hope."

And so saying, John Mangles handed to Lady Helena the fragment of paper on which was legible the sacred words; and these young women, whose trusting hearts were always open to observe Providential interpositions, read in these words an indisputable sign of salvation.

"And now let us go to the 'oudoupa!'" cried Paganel, in his gayest mood. "It is our castle, our dining-room, our study! None can meddle with us there! Ladies! allow me to do the honors of this charming abode."

They followed Paganel, and when the savages saw them profaning anew the tabooed burial place, they renewed their fire and their fearful yells, the one as loud as the other. But fortunately the balls fell short of our friends, though the cries reached them.

Lady Helena, Mary Grant, and their companions were quite relieved to find that the Maories were more dominated by superstition than by anger, and they entered the monument.

It was a palisade made of red-painted posts. Symbolic figures, tattooed on the wood, set forth the rank and achievements of the deceased. Strings of amulets, made of shells or cut stones, hung from one part to another. In the interior, the ground was carpeted with green leaves, and in the middle, a slight mound betokened the place of the newly made grave. There lay the chief's weapons, his guns loaded and capped, his spear, his splendid ax of green jade, with a supply of powder and ball for the happy hunting grounds.

"Quite an arsenal!" said Paganel, "of which we shall make a better use.

What ideas they have! Fancy carrying arms in the other world!"

"Well!" said the Major, "but these are English firearms."

"No doubt," replied Glenarvan, "and it is a very unwise practice to give firearms to savages! They turn them against the invaders, naturally enough. But at any rate, they will be very valuable to us."

"Yes," said Paganel, "but what is more useful still is the food and water provided for Kara-Tete."

Things had been handsomely done for the deceased chief; the amount of provisions denoted their esteem for the departed. There was food enough to sustain ten persons for fifteen days, or the dead man forever.

The vegetable aliments consisted of edible ferns, sweet potatoes, the "convolvulus batatas," which was indigenous, and the potato which had been imported long before by the Europeans. Large jars contained pure water, and a dozen baskets artistically plaited contained tablets of an unknown green gum.

The fugitives were therefore provided for some days against hunger and thirst, and they needed no persuasion to begin their attack on the deceased chief's stores. Glenarvan brought out the necessary quantity and put them into Olbinett's hands. The steward, who never could forget his routine ideas, even in the most exceptional circumstances, thought the meal a slender one. He did not know how to prepare the roots, and, besides, had no fire.

But Paganel soon solved the difficulty by recommending him to bury his fern roots and sweet potatoes in the soil. The temperature of the surface stratum was very high, and a thermometer plunged into the soil would have marked from 160 to 170 degrees; in fact, Olbinett narrowly missed being scalded, for just as he had scooped a hole for the roots, a jet of vapor sprang up and with a whistling sound rose six feet above the ground.

The steward fell back in terror.

"Shut off steam!" cried the Major, running to close the hole with the loose drift, while Paganel pondering on the singular phenomenon muttered to himself:

"Let me see! ha! ha! Why not?"

"Are you hurt?" inquired McNabbs of Olbinett.

"No, Major," said the steward, "but I did not expect—"

"That Providence would send you fire," interrupted Paganel in a jovial tone. "First the larder of Kara-Tete and then fire out of the ground! Upon my word, this mountain is a paradise! I propose that we found a colony, and cultivate the soil and settle here for life! We shall be the Robinsons of Maunganamu. We should want for nothing."

"If it is solid ground," said John Mangles.

"Well! it is not a thing of yesterday," said Paganel. "It has stood against the internal fire for many a day, and will do so till we leave it, at any rate."

"Breakfast is ready," announced Olbinett with as much dignity as if he was in Malcolm Castle.

Without delay, the fugitives sat down near the palisade, and began one of the many meals with which Providence had supplied them in critical circumstances. Nobody was inclined to be fastidious, but opinions were divided as regarded the edible fern. Some thought the flavor sweet and agreeable, others pronounced it leathery, insipid, and resembling the taste of gum. The sweet potatoes, cooked in the burning soil, were excellent. The geographer remarked that Kara-Tete was not badly off after all.

And now that their hunger was appeased, it was time to decide on their plan of escape.

"So soon!" exclaimed Paganel in a piteous tone. "Would you quit the home of delight so soon?"

"But, Monsieur Paganel," interposed Lady Helena, "if this be Capua, you dare not intend to imitate Hannibal!"

"Madam, I dare not contradict you, and if discussion is the order of the day, let it proceed."

"First," said Glenarvan, "I think we ought to start before we are driven to it by hunger. We are revived now, and ought to take advantage of it. To-night we will try to reach the eastern valleys by crossing the cordon of natives under cover of the darkness."

"Excellent," answered Paganel, "if the Maories allow us to pass."

"And if not?" asked John Mangles.

"Then we will use our great resources," said Paganel.

"But have we great resources?" inquired the Major.

"More than we can use!" replied Paganel, without any further explanation.

And then they waited for the night.

The natives had not stirred. Their numbers seemed even greater, perhaps owing to the influx of the stragglers of the tribe. Fires lighted at intervals formed a girdle of flame round the base of the mountain, so that when darkness fell, Maunganamu appeared to rise out of a great brasier, and to hide its head in the thick darkness. Five hundred feet below they could hear the hum and the cries of the enemy's camp.

At nine o'clock the darkness being very intense, Glenarvan and John Mangles went out to reconnoiter before embarking the whole party on this critical journey. They made the descent noiselessly, and after about ten minutes, arrived on the narrow ridge that crossed the native lines, fifty feet above the camp.

All went well so far. The Maories, stretched beside the fires, did not appear to observe the two fugitives. But in an instant a double fusillade burst forth from both sides of the ridge.

"Back," exclaimed Glenarvan; "those wretches have the eyes of cats and the guns of riflemen!"

And they turned, and once more climbed the steep slope of the mountain, and then hastened to their friends who had been alarmed at the firing. Glenarvan's hat was pierced by two balls, and they concluded that it was out of the question to venture again on the ridge between two lines of marksmen.

"Wait till to-morrow," said Paganel, "and as we cannot elude their vigilance, let me try my hand on them."

The night was cold; but happily Kara-Tete had been furnished with his best night gear, and the party wrapped themselves each in a warm flax mantle, and protected by native superstition, slept quietly inside the inclosure, on the warm ground, still violating with the violence of the internal ebullition.

CHAPTER XIV A BOLD STRATAGEM

NEXT day, February 17th, the sun's first rays awoke the sleepers of the Maunganamu. The Maories had long since been astir, coming and going at the foot of the mountain, without leaving their line of observation. Furious clamor broke out when they saw the Europeans leave the sacred place they had profaned.

Each of the party glanced first at the neighboring mountains,
and at the deep valleys still drowned in mist, and over
Lake Taupo, which the morning breeze ruffled slightly.
And then all clustered round Paganel eager to hear his project.

Paganel soon satisfied their curiosity. "My friends," said he, "my plan has one great recommendation; if it does not accomplish all that I anticipate, we shall be no worse off than we are at present. But it must, it will succeed."

"And what is it?" asked McNabbs.

"It is this," replied Paganel, "the superstition of the natives has made this mountain a refuge for us, and we must take advantage of their superstition to escape. If I can persuade Kai-Koumou that we have expiated our profanation, that the wrath of the Deity has fallen on us: in a word, that we have died a terrible death, do you think he will leave the plateau of Maunganamu to return to his village?"

"Not a doubt of it," said Glenarvan.

"And what is the horrible death you refer to?" asked Lady Helena.

"The death of the sacrilegious, my friends," replied Paganel. "The avenging flames are under our feet. Let us open a way for them!"

"What! make a volcano!" cried John Mangles.

"Yes, an impromptu volcano, whose fury we can regulate. There are plenty of vapors ready to hand, and subterranean fires ready to issue forth. We can have an eruption ready to order."

"An excellent idea, Paganel; well conceived," said the Major.

"You understand," replied the geographer, "we are to pretend to fall victims to the flames of the Maori Pluto, and to disappear spiritually into the tomb of Kara-Tete. And stay there three, four, even five days if necessary—that is to say, till the savages are convinced that we have perished, and abandon their watch."

"But," said Miss Grant, "suppose they wish to be sure of our punishment, and climb up here to see?"

"No, my dear Mary," returned Paganel. "They will not do that. The mountain is tabooed, and if it devoured its sacrilegious intruders, it would only be more inviolably tabooed."

"It is really a very clever plan," said Glenarvan. "There is only one chance against it; that is, if the savages prolong their watch at the foot of Maunganamu, we may run short of provisions. But if we play our game well there is not much fear of that."

"And when shall we try this last chance?" asked Lady Helena.

"To-night," rejoined Paganel, "when the darkness is the deepest."

"Agreed," said McNabbs; "Paganel, you are a genius! and I, who seldom get up an enthusiasm, I answer for the success of your plan. Oh! those villains! They shall have a little miracle that will put off their conversion for another century. I hope the missionaries will forgive us."

The project of Paganel was therefore adopted, and certainly with the superstitious ideas of the Maories there seemed good ground for hope. But brilliant as the idea might be, the difficulty was in the *modus operandi*. The volcano might devour the bold schemers, who offered it a crater. Could they control and direct the eruption when they had succeeded in letting loose its vapor and flames, and lava streams? The entire cone might be engulfed. It was meddling with phenomena of which nature herself has the absolute monopoly.

Paganel had thought of all this; but he intended to act prudently and without pushing things to extremes. An appearance would be enough to dupe the Maories, and there was no need for the terrible realities of an eruption.

How long that day seemed. Each one of the party inwardly counted the hours. All was made ready for flight. The oudoupa provisions were divided and formed very portable packets. Some mats and firearms completed their light equipment, all of which they took from the tomb of the chief. It is needless to say that their preparations were made within the inclosure, and that they were unseen by the savages.

At six o'clock the steward served up a refreshing meal. Where or when they would eat in the valleys of the Ranges no one could foretell. So that they had to take in supplies for the future. The principal dish was composed of half a dozen rats, caught by Wilson and stewed. Lady Helena and Mary Grant obstinately refused to taste this game, which is highly esteemed by the natives; but the men enjoyed it like the real Maories. The meat was excellent and savory, and the six devourers were devoured down to the bones.

The evening twilight came on. The sun went down in a stormy-looking bank of clouds. A few flashes of lightning glanced across the horizon and distant thunder pealed through the darkened sky.

Paganel welcomed the storm, which was a valuable aid to his plans, and completed his program. The savages are superstitiously affected by the great phenomena of nature. The New Zealanders think that thunder is the angry voice of Noui-Atoua, and lightning the fierce gleam of his eyes. Thus their deity was coming personally to chastise the violators of the taboo.

At eight o'clock, the summit of the Maunganamu was lost in portentous darkness. The sky would supply a black background for the blaze which Paganel was about to throw on it. The Maories could no longer see their prisoners; and this was the moment for action. Speed was necessary. Glenarvan, Paganel, McNabbs, Robert, the steward, and the two sailors, all lent a hand.

The spot for the crater was chosen thirty paces from Kara-Tete's tomb. It was important to keep the oudoupa intact, for if it disappeared, the taboo of the mountain would be nullified. At the spot mentioned Paganel had noticed an enormous block of stone, round which the vapors played with a certain degree of intensity. This block covered a small natural crater hollowed in the cone, and by its own weight prevented the egress of the subterranean fire. If they could move it from its socket, the vapors and the lava would issue by the disencumbered opening.

The workers used as levers some posts taken from the interior of the oudoupa, and they plied their tools vigorously against the rocky mass. Under their united efforts the stone soon moved. They made a little trench so that it might roll down the inclined plane. As they gradually raised it, the vibrations under foot became more distinct. Dull roarings of flame and the whistling sound of a furnace ran along under the thin crust. The intrepid la-borers, veritable Cyclops handling Earth's fires, worked in silence; soon some fissures and jets of steam warned them that their place was growing dangerous. But a crowning effort moved the mass which rolled down and disappeared. Immediately the thin crust gave way. A column of fire rushed to the sky with loud detonations, while streams of boiling water and lava flowed toward the native camp and the lower valleys.

All the cone trembled as if it was about to plunge into a fathomless gulf.

Glenarvan and his companions had barely time to get out of the way; they fled to the enclosure of the oudoupa, not without having been sprinkled with water at 220 degrees. This water at first spread a smell like soup, which soon changed into a strong odor of sulphur.

Then the mud, the lava, the volcanic stones, all spouted forth in a torrent. Streams of fire furrowed the sides of Maunganamu. The neighboring mountains were lit up by the glare; the dark valleys were also filled with dazzling light.

All the savages had risen, howling under the pain inflicted by the burning lava, which was bubbling and foaming in the midst of their camp.

Those whom the liquid fire had not touched fled to the surrounding hills; then turned, and gazed in terror at this fearful phenomenon, this volcano in which the anger of their deity would swallow up the profane intruders on the sacred mountain. Now and then, when the roar of the eruption became less violent, their cry was heard:

"Taboo! taboo! taboo!"

An enormous quantity of vapors, heated stones and lava was escaping by this crater of Maunganamu. It was not a mere geyser like those that girdle round Mount Hecla, in Iceland, it was itself a Hecla. All this volcanic commotion was confined till then in the envelope of the cone, because the safety valve of Tangariro was enough for its expansion; but when this new issue was afforded, it rushed forth fiercely, and by the laws of equilibrium, the other eruptions in the island must on that night have lost their usual intensity.

An hour after this volcano burst upon the world, broad streams of lava were running down its sides. Legions of rats came out of their holes, and fled from the scene.

All night long, and fanned by the tempest in the upper sky, the crater never ceased to pour forth its torrents with a violence that alarmed Glenarvan. The eruption was breaking away the edges of the opening. The prisoners. hidden behind the inclosure of stakes, watched the fearful progress of the phenomenon.

Morning came. The fury of the volcano had not slackened. Thick yellowish fumes were mixed with the flames; the lava torrents wound their serpentine course in every direction.

Glenarvan watched with a beating heart, looking from all the interstices of the palisaded enclosure, and observed the movements in the native camp.

The Maories had fled to the neighboring ledges, out of the reach of the volcano. Some corpses which lay at the foot of the cone, were charred by the fire. Further off toward the "pah," the lava had reached a group of twenty huts, which were still smoking. The Maories, forming here and there groups, contemplated the canopied summit of Maunganamu with religious awe.

CHAPTER XIV A BOLD STRATAGEM

Kai-Koumou approached in the midst of his warriors, and Glenarvan recognized him. The chief advanced to the foot of the hill, on the side untouched by the lava, but he did not ascend the first ledge.

Standing there, with his arms stretched out like an exerciser, he made some grimaces, whose meaning was obvious to the prisoners. As Paganel had foreseen, Kai-Koumou launched on the avenging mountain a more rigorous taboo.

Soon after the natives left their positions and followed the winding paths that led toward the pah.

"They are going!" exclaimed Glenarvan. "They have left their posts! God be praised! Our stratagem has succeeded! My dear Lady Helena, my brave friends, we are all dead and buried! But this evening when night comes, we shall rise and leave our tomb, and fly these barbarous tribes!"

It would be difficult to conceive of the joy that pervaded the oudoupa. Hope had regained the mastery in all hearts. The intrepid travelers forgot the past, forgot the future, to enjoy the present delight! And yet the task before them was not an easy one—to gain some European outpost in the midst of this unknown country. But Kai-Koumou once off their track, they thought themselves safe from all the savages in New Zealand.

A whole day had to elapse before they could make a start, and they employed it in arranging a plan of flight. Paganel had treasured up his map of New Zealand, and on it could trace out the best roads.

After discussion, the fugitives resolved to make for the Bay of Plenty, towards the east. The region was unknown, but apparently desert. The travelers, who from their past experience, had learned to make light of physical difficulties, feared nothing but meeting Maories. At any cost they wanted to avoid them and gain the east coast, where the missionaries had several stations. That part of the country had hitherto escaped the horrors of war, and the natives were not in the habit of scouring the country.

As to the distance that separated Lake Taupo from the Bay of Plenty, they calculated it about a hundred miles. Ten days' march at ten miles a day, could be done, not without fatigue, but none of the party gave that a thought. If they could only reach the mission stations they could rest there while waiting for a favorable opportunity to get to Auckland, for that was the point they desired to reach.

This question settled, they resumed their watch of the native proceedings, and continued so doing till evening fell. Not a solitary native remained at the foot of the mountain, and when darkness set in over the Taupo valleys, not a fire indicated the presence of the Maories at the base. The road was free.

At nine o'clock, the night being unusually dark, Glenarvan gave the order to start. His companions and he, armed and equipped at the expense of Kara-Tete, began cautiously to descend the slopes of Maunganamu, John Mangles and Wilson leading the way, eyes and ears on the alert. They stopped at the slightest sound, they started at every passing cloud. They slid rather than walked down the spur, that their figures might be lost in the dark mass of the mountain. At two hundred feet below the summit, John Mangles and his sailors reached the dangerous ridge that had been so obstinately defended by the natives. If by ill luck the Maories, more cunning than the fugitives, had only pretended to retreat; if they were not really duped by the volcanic phenomenon, this was the spot where their presence would be betrayed. Glenarvan could not but shudder, in spite of his confidence, and in spite of the jokes of Paganel. The fate of the whole party would hang in the balance for the ten minutes required to pass along that ridge. He felt the beating of Lady Helena's heart, as she clung to his arm.

He had no thought of turning back. Neither had John. The young captain, followed closely by the whole party, and protected by the intense darkness, crept along the ridge, stopping when some loose stone rolled to the bottom. If the savages were still in the ambush below, these unusual sounds might provoke from both sides a dangerous fusillade.

But speed was impossible in their serpent-like progress down this sloping crest. When John Mangles had reached the lowest point, he was scarcely twenty-five feet from the plateau, where the natives were encamped the night before, and then the ridge rose again pretty steeply toward a wood for about a quarter of a mile.

All this lower part was crossed without molestation, and they commenced the ascent in silence. The clump of bush was invisible, though they knew it was there, and but for the possibility of an ambush, Glenarvan counted on being safe when the party arrived at that point. But he observed that after this point, they were no longer protected by the taboo. The ascending ridge belonged not to Maunganamu, but to the mountain system of the eastern side of Lake Taupo, so that they had not only pistol shots, but hand-to-hand fighting to fear. For ten minutes, the little band ascended by insensible degrees toward the higher table-land. John could not discern the dark wood, but he knew it ought to be within two hundred feet. Suddenly he stopped; almost retreated. He fancied he heard something in the darkness; his stoppage interrupted the march of those behind.

He remained motionless long enough to alarm his companions. They waited with unspeakable anxiety, wondering if they were doomed to retrace their steps, and return to the summit of Maunganamu.

But John, finding that the noise was not repeated, resumed the ascent of the narrow path of the ridge. Soon they perceived the shadowy outline of the wood showing faintly through the darkness. A few steps more and they were hid from sight in the thick foliage of the trees.

CHAPTER XV FROM PERIL TO SAFETY

THE night favored their escape, and prudence urged them to lose no time in getting away from the fatal neighborhood of Lake Taupo. Paganel took the post of leader, and his wonderful instinct shone out anew in this difficult mountain journey. His nyctalopia was a great advantage, his cat-like sight enabling him to distinguish the smallest object in the deepest gloom.

For three hours they walked on without halting along the far-reaching slope of the eastern side. Paganel kept a little to the southeast, in order to make use of a narrow passage between the Kaimanawa and the Wahiti Ranges, through which the road from Hawkes' Bay to Auckland passes. Once through that gorge, his plan was to keep off the road, and, under the shelter of the high ranges, march to the coast across the inhabited regions of the province.

At nine o'clock in the morning, they had made twelve miles in twelve hours. The courageous women could not be pressed further, and, besides, the locality was suitable for camping. The fugitives had reached the pass that separates the two chains. Paganel, map in hand, made a loop toward the northeast, and at ten o'clock the little party reached a sort of redan, formed by a projecting rock.

The provisions were brought out, and justice was done to their meal. Mary Grant and the Major, who had not thought highly of the edible fern till then, now ate of it heartily.

The halt lasted till two o'clock in the afternoon, then they resumed their journey; and in the evening they stopped eight miles from the mountains, and required no persuasion to sleep in the open air.

Next day was one of serious difficulties. Their route lay across this wondrous region of volcanic lakes, geysers, and solfataras, which extended to the east of the Wahiti Ranges. It is a country more pleasant for the eye to ramble over, than for the limbs. Every quarter of a mile they had to turn aside or go around for some obstacle, and thus incurred great fatigue; but what a strange sight met their eyes! What infinite variety nature lavishes on her great panoramas!

On this vast extent of twenty miles square, the subterranean forces had a field for the display of all their varied effects. Salt springs, of singular transparency, peopled by myriads of insects, sprang up from thickets of tea-tree scrub. They diffused a powerful odor of burnt powder, and scattered on the ground a white sediment like dazzling snow. The limpid waters were nearly at boiling point, while some neighboring springs spread out like sheets of glass. Gigantic tree-ferns grew beside them, in conditions analogous to those of the Silurian vegetation.

On every side jets of water rose like park fountains, out of a sea of vapor; some of them continuous, others intermittent, as if a capricious Pluto controlled their movements.

They rose like an amphitheater on natural terraces; their waters gradually flowed together under folds of white smoke, and corroding the edges of the semi-transparent steps of this gigantic staircase. They fed whole lakes with their boiling torrents.

Farther still, beyond the hot springs and tumultuous geysers, came the solfataras. The ground looked as if covered with large pustules. These were slumbering craters full of cracks and fissures from which rose various gases. The air was saturated with the acrid and unpleasant odor of sulphurous acid. The ground was encrusted with sulphur and crystalline concretions. All this incalculable wealth had been accumulating for centuries, and if the sulphur beds of Sicily should ever be exhausted, it is here, in this little known district of New Zealand, that supplies must be sought.

The fatigue in traveling in such a country as this will be best understood. Camping was very difficult, and the sportsmen of the party shot nothing worthy of Olbinett's skill; so that they had generally to content themselves with fern and sweet potato— a poor diet which was scarcely sufficient to recruit the exhausted strength of the little party, who were all anxious to escape from this barren region.

But four days at least must elapse before they could hope to leave it. On February 23, at a distance of fifty miles from Maunganamu, Glenarvan called a halt, and camped at the foot of a nameless mountain, marked on Paganel's map. The wooded plains stretched away from sight, and great forests appeared on the horizon.

That day McNabbs and Robert killed three kiwis, which filled the chief place on their table, not for long, however, for in a few moments they were all consumed from the beaks to the claws.

At dessert, between the potatoes and sweet potatoes, Paganel moved a resolution which was carried with enthusiasm. He proposed to give the name of Glenarvan to this unnamed mountain, which rose 3,000 feet high, and then was lost in the clouds, and he printed carefully on his map the name of the Scottish nobleman.

It would be idle to narrate all the monotonous and uninteresting details of the rest of the journey. Only two or three occurrences of any importance took place on the way from the lakes to the Pacific Ocean. The march was all day long across forests and plains. John took observations of the sun and stars. Neither heat nor rain increased the discomfort of the journey, but the travelers were so reduced by the trials they had undergone, that they made very slow progress; and they longed to arrive at the mission station.

They still chatted, but the conversation had ceased to be general. The little party broke up into groups, attracted to each other, not by narrow sympathies, but by a more personal communion of ideas.

Glenarvan generally walked alone; his mind seemed to recur to his unfortunate crew, as he drew nearer to the sea. He apparently lost sight of the dangers which lay before them on their way to Auckland, in the thought of his massacred men; the horrible picture haunted him.

Harry Grant was never spoken of; they were no longer in a position to make any effort on his behalf. If his name was uttered at all, it was between his daughter and John Mangles.

John had never reminded Mary of what she had said to him on that last night at Ware-Atoua. He was too wise to take advantage of a word spoken in a moment of despair. When he mentioned Captain Grant, John always spoke of further search. He assured Mary that Lord Glenarvan would re-embark in the enterprise. He persistently returned to the fact that the authenticity of the document was indisputable, and that therefore Harry Grant was somewhere to be found, and that they would find him, if they had to try all over the world. Mary drank in his words, and she and John, united by the same thought, cherished the same hope. Often Lady Helena joined in the conversation; but she did not participate in their illusions, though she refrained from chilling their enthusiasm.

McNabbs, Robert, Wilson, and Mulrady kept up their hunting parties, without going far from the rest, and each one furnished his QUOTA of game.

Paganel, arrayed in his flax mat, kept himself aloof, in a silent and pensive mood.

And yet, it is only justice to say, in spite of the general rule that, in the midst of trials, dangers, fatigues, and privations, the most amiable dispositions become ruffled and embittered, all our travelers were united, devoted, ready to die for one another.

On the 25th of February, their progress was stopped by a river which answered to the Wakari on Paganel's map, and was easily forded. For two days plains of low scrub succeeded each other without interruption. Half the distance from Lake Taupo to the coast had been traversed without accident, though not without fatigue.

Then the scene changed to immense and interminable forests, which reminded them of Australia, but here the kauri took the place of the eucalyptus. Although their enthusiasm had been incessantly called forth during their four months' journey, Glenarvan and his companions were compelled to admire and wonder at those gigantic pines, worthy rivals of the Cedars of Lebanon, and the "Mammoth trees" of California. The kauris measured a hundred feet high, before the ramification of the branches. They grew in isolated clumps, and the forest was not composed of trees, but of innumerable groups of trees, which spread their green canopies in the air two hundred feet from the ground.

Some of these pines, still young, about a hundred years old, resembled the red pine of Europe. They had a dark crown surmounted by a dark conical shoot. Their older brethren, five or six hundred years of age, formed great green pavilions supported on the inextricable network of their branches. These patriarchs of the New Zealand forest measured fifty yards in circumference, and the united arms of all the travelers could not embrace the giant trunk.

For three days the little party made their way under these vast arches, over a clayey soil which the foot of man had never trod. They knew this by the quantity of resinous gum that lay in heaps at the foot of the trees, and which would have lasted for native exportation many years.

The sportsmen found whole coveys of the kiwi, which are scarce in districts frequented by the Maories; the native dogs drive them away to the shelter of these inaccessible forests. They were an abundant source of nourishing food to our travelers.

Paganel also had the good fortune to espy, in a thicket, a pair of gigantic birds; his instinct as a naturalist was awakened. He called his companions, and in spite of their fatigue, the Major, Robert, and he set off on the track of these animals.

His curiosity was excusable, for he had recognized, or thought he had recognized, these birds as "moas" belonging to the species of "dinornis," which many naturalists class with the extinct birds. This, if Paganel was right, would confirm the opinion of Dr. Hochstetter and other travelers on the present existence of the wingless giants of New Zealand.

These moas which Paganel was chasing, the contemporaries of the Megatherium and the Pterodactyles, must have been eighteen feet high. They were huge ostriches, timid too, for they fled with extreme rapidity. But no shot could stay their course. After a few minutes of chase, these fleet-footed moas disappeared among the tall trees, and the sportsmen lost their powder and their pains.

That evening, March 1, Glenarvan and his companions, emerging at last from the immense kauri-forest, camped at the foot of Mount Ikirangi, whose summit rose five thousand five hundred feet into the air. At this point they had traveled a hundred miles from Maunganamu, and the shore was still thirty miles away. John Mangles had calculated on accomplishing the whole journey in ten days, but he did not foresee the physical difficulties of the country.

On the whole, owing to the circuits, the obstacles, and the imperfect observations, the journey had been extended by fully one-fifth, and now that they had reached Mount Ikirangi, they were quite worn out.

Two long days of walking were still to be accomplished, during which time all their activity and vigilance would be required, for their way was through a district often frequented by the natives. The little party conquered their weariness, and set out next morning at daybreak.

Between Mount Ikirangi which was left to the right, and Mount Hardy whose summit rose on the left to a height of 3,700 feet, the journey was very trying; for about ten miles the bush was a tangle of "supple-jack," a kind of flexible rope, appropriately called "stifling-creeper," that caught the feet at every step. For two days, they had to cut their way with an ax through this thousand-headed hydra. Hunting became impossible, and the sportsmen failed in their accustomed tribute. The provisions were almost exhausted, and there was no means of renewing them; their thirst was increasing by fatigue, and there was no water wherewith to quench it.

The sufferings of Glenarvan and his party became terrible, and for the first time their moral energy threatened to give way. They no longer walked, they dragged themselves along, soulless bodies, animated only by the instinct of self-preservation which survives every other feeling, and in this melancholy plight they reached Point Lottin on the shores of the Pacific.

Here they saw several deserted huts, the ruins of a village lately destroyed by the war, abandoned fields, and everywhere signs of pillage and incendiary fires.

They were toiling painfully along the shore, when they saw, at a distance of about a mile, a band of natives, who rushed toward them brandishing their weapons. Glenarvan, hemmed in by the sea, could not fly, and summoning all his remaining strength he was about to meet the attack, when John Mangles cried:

"A boat! a boat!"

And there, twenty paces off, a canoe with six oars lay on the beach. To launch it, jump in and fly from the dangerous shore, was only a minute's work. John Mangles, McNabbs, Wilson and Mulrady took the oars; Glenarvan the helm; the two women, Robert and Olbinett stretched themselves beside him. In ten minutes the canoe was a quarter of a mile from the shore. The sea was calm. The fugitives were silent. But John, who did not want to get too far from land, was about to give the order to go up the coast, when he suddenly stopped rowing.

He saw three canoes coming out from behind Point Lottin and evidently about to give chase.

"Out to sea! Out to sea!" he exclaimed. "Better to drown if we must!"

The canoe went fast under her four rowers. For half an hour she kept her distance; but the poor exhausted fellows grew weaker, and the three pursuing boats began to gain sensibly on them. At this moment, scarcely two miles lay between them. It was impossible to avoid the attack of the natives, who were already preparing to fire their long guns.

What was Glenarvan about?—standing up in the stern he was looking toward the horizon for some chimerical help. What did he hope for? What did he wish? Had he a presentiment?

In a moment his eyes gleamed, his hand pointed out into the distance.

"A ship! a ship!" he cried. "My friends, row! row hard!"

Not one of the rowers turned his head—not an oar-stroke must be lost.

Paganel alone rose, and turned his telescope to the point indicated.

"Yes," said he, "a ship! a steamer! they are under full steam! they are coming to us! Found now, brave comrades!"

The fugitives summoned new energy, and for another half hour, keeping their distance, they rowed with hasty strokes. The steamer came nearer and nearer. They made out her two masts, bare of sails, and the great volumes of black smoke. Glenarvan, handing the tiller to Robert, seized Paganel's glass, and watched the movements of the steamer.

John Mangles and his companions were lost in wonder when they saw Glenarvan's features contract and grow pale, and the glass drop from his hands. One word explained it.

"The DUNCAN!" exclaimed Glenarvan. "The DUNCAN, and the convicts!"

"The DUNCAN!" cried John, letting go his oar and rising.

"Yes, death on all sides!" murmured Glenarvan, crushed by despair.

It was indeed the yacht, they could not mistake her—the yacht and her bandit crew!

The major could scarcely restrain himself from cursing their destiny.

The canoe was meantime standing still. Where should they go? Whither fly? What choice was there between the convicts and the savages?

A shot was fired from the nearest of the native boats, and the ball struck Wilson's oar.

A few strokes then carried the canoe nearer to the DUNCAN.

The yacht was coming down at full speed, and was not more than half a mile off.

John Mangles, between two enemies, did not know what to advise, whither to fly! The two poor ladies on their knees, prayed in their agony.

The savages kept up a running fire, and shots were raining round the canoe, when suddenly a loud report was heard, and a ball from the yacht's cannon passed over their heads, and now the boat remained motionless between the DUNCAN and the native canoes.

John Mangles, frenzied with despair, seized his ax. He was about to scuttle the boat and sink it with his unfortunate companions, when a cry from Robert arrested his arm.

"Tom Austin! Tom Austin!" the lad shouted. "He is on board!

I see him! He knows us! He is waving his hat."

The ax hung useless in John's hand.

A second ball whistled over his head, and cut in two the nearest of the three native boats, while a loud hurrah burst forth on board the DUNCAN.

The savages took flight, fled and regained the shore.

"Come on, Tom, come on!" cried John Mangles in a joyous voice.

And a few minutes after, the ten fugitives, how, they knew not, were all safe on board the DUNCAN.

CHAPTER XVI WHY THE "DUNCAN" WENT TO NEW ZEALAND

IT would be vain to attempt to depict the feelings of Glenarvan and his friends when the songs of old Scotia fell on their ears. The moment they set foot on the deck of the DUNCAN, the piper blew his bagpipes, and commenced the national pibroch of the Malcolm clan, while loud hurrahs rent the air.

Glenarvan and his whole party, even the Major himself, were crying and embracing each other. They were delirious with joy. The geographer was absolutely mad. He frisked about, telescope in hand, pointing it at the last canoe approaching the shore.

But at the sight of Glenarvan and his companions, with their clothing in rags, and thin, haggard faces, bearing marks of horrible sufferings, the crew ceased their noisy demonstrations. These were specters who had returned—not the bright, adventurous travelers who had left the yacht three months before, so full of hope! Chance, and chance only, had brought them back to the deck of the yacht they never thought to see again. And in what a state of exhaustion and feebleness. But before thinking of fatigue, or attending to the imperious demands of hunger and thirst, Glenarvan questioned Tom Austin about his being on this coast.

Why had the DUNCAN come to the eastern coast of New Zealand? How was it not in the hands of Ben Joyce? By what providential fatality had God brought them in the track of the fugitives?

Why? how? and for what purpose? Tom was stormed with questions on all sides. The old sailor did not know which to listen to first, and at last resolved to hear nobody but Glenarvan, and to answer nobody but him.

"But the convicts?" inquired Glenarvan. "What did you do with them?"

"The convicts?" replied Tom, with the air of a man who does not in the least understand what he is being asked.

"Yes, the wretches who attacked the yacht."

"What yacht? Your Honor's?"

"Why, of course, Tom. The DUNCAN, and Ben Joyce, who came on board."

"I don't know this Ben Joyce, and have never seen him."

"Never seen him!" exclaimed Paganel, stupefied at the old sailor's replies. "Then pray tell me, Tom, how it is that the DUNCAN is cruising at this moment on the coast of New Zealand?"

But if Glenarvan and his friends were totally at a loss to understand the bewilderment of the old sailor, what was their amazement when he replied in a calm voice:

"The DUNCAN is cruising here by your Honor's orders."

"By my orders?" cried Glenarvan.

"Yes, my Lord. I only acted in obedience to the instructions sent in your letter of January fourteenth."

"My letter! my letter!" exclaimed Glenarvan.

The ten travelers pressed closer round Tom Austin, devouring him with their eyes. The letter dated from Snowy River had reached the DUNCAN, then.

"Let us come to explanations, pray, for it seems to me I am dreaming.

You received a letter, Tom?"

"Yes, a letter from your Honor."

"At Melbourne?"

"At Melbourne, just as our repairs were completed."

"And this letter?"

"It was not written by you, but bore your signature, my Lord."

"Just so; my letter was brought by a convict called Ben Joyce."

"No, by a sailor called Ayrton, a quartermaster on the BRITANNIA."

"Yes, Ayrton or Ben Joyce, one and the same individual.

Well, and what were the contents of this letter?"

"It contained orders to leave Melbourne without delay, and go and cruise on the eastern coast of—"

"Australia!" said Glenarvan with such vehemence that the old sailor was somewhat disconcerted.

"Of Australia?" repeated Tom, opening his eyes. "No, but New Zealand."

"Australia, Tom! Australia!" they all cried with one voice.

Austin's head began to feel in a whirl. Glenarvan spoke with such assurance that he thought after all he must have made a mistake in reading the letter. Could a faithful, exact old servant like himself have been guilty of such a thing! He turned red and looked quite disturbed.

"Never mind, Tom," said Lady Helena. "God so willed it."

"But, no, madam, pardon me," replied old Tom. "No, it is impossible, I was not mistaken. Ayrton read the letter as I did, and it was he, on the contrary, who wished to bring me to the Australian coast."

"Ayrton!" cried Glenarvan.

"Yes, Ayrton himself. He insisted it was a mistake: that you meant to order me to Twofold Bay."

"Have you the letter still, Tom?" asked the Major, extremely interested in this mystery.

"Yes, Mr. McNabbs," replied Austin. "I'll go and fetch it."

He ran at once to his cabin in the forecastle. During his momentary absence they gazed at each other in silence, all but the Major, who crossed his arms and said:

"Well, now, Paganel, you must own this would be going a little too far."

"What?" growled Paganel, looking like a gigantic note of interrogation, with his spectacles on his forehead and his stooping back.

Austin returned directly with the letter written by Paganel and signed by Glenarvan.

"Will your Honor read it?" he said, handing it to him.

Glenarvan took the letter and read as follows:

"Order to Tom Austin to put out to sea without delay, and to take the Duncan, by latitude 37 degrees to the eastern coast of New Zealand!"

"New Zealand!" cried Paganel, leaping up.

And he seized the letter from Glenarvan, rubbed his eyes, pushed down his spectacles on his nose, and read it for himself.

"New Zealand!" he repeated in an indescribable tone, letting the order slip between his fingers.

That same moment he felt a hand laid on his shoulder, and turning round found himself face to face with the Major, who said in a grave tone:

"Well, my good Paganel, after all, it is a lucky thing you did not send the DUNCAN to Cochin China!"

This pleasantry finished the poor geographer. The crew burst out into loud Homeric laughter. Paganel ran about like a madman, seized his head with both hands and tore his hair. He neither knew what he was doing nor what he wanted to do. He rushed down the poop stairs mechanically and paced the deck, nodding to himself and going straight before without aim or object till he reached the forecastle. There his feet got entangled in a coil of rope. He stumbled and fell, accidentally catching hold of a rope with both hands in his fall.

Suddenly a tremendous explosion was heard. The forecastle gun had gone off, riddling the quiet calm of the waves with a volley of small shot. The unfortunate Paganel had caught hold of the cord of the loaded gun. The geographer was thrown down the forecastle ladder and disappeared below.

A cry of terror succeeded the surprise produced by the explosion. Everybody thought something terrible must have happened. The sailors rushed between decks and lifted up Paganel, almost bent double. The geographer uttered no sound.

They carried his long body onto the poop. His companions were in despair. The Major, who was always the surgeon on great occasions, began to strip the unfortunate that he might dress his wounds; but he had scarcely put his hands on the dying man when he started up as if touched by an electrical machine.

"Never! never!" he exclaimed, and pulling his ragged coat tightly round him, he began buttoning it up in a strangely excited manner.

"But, Paganel," began the Major.

"No, I tell you!"

"I must examine—"

"You shall not examine."

"You may perhaps have broken—" continued McNabbs.

"Yes," continued Paganel, getting up on his long legs, "but what I have broken the carpenter can mend."

"What is it, then?"

"There."

Bursts of laughter from the crew greeted this speech.

Paganel's friends were quite reassured about him now.

They were satisfied that he had come off safe and sound from

his adventure with the forecastle gun.

"At any rate," thought the Major, "the geographer is wonderfully bashful."

But now Paganel was recovered a little, he had to reply to a question he could not escape.

"Now, Paganel," said Glenarvan, "tell us frankly all about it. I own that your blunder was providential. It is sure and certain that but for you the DUNCAN would have fallen into the hands of the convicts; but for you we should have been recaptured by the Maories. But for my sake tell me by what supernatural aberration of mind you were induced to write New Zealand instead of Australia?"

"Well, upon my oath," said Paganel, "it is—"

But the same instant his eyes fell on Mary and Robert Grant, and he stopped short and then went on:

"What would you have me say, my dear Glenarvan? I am mad, I am an idiot, an incorrigible fellow, and I shall live and die the most terrible absent man. I can't change my skin."

"Unless you get flayed alive."

"Get flayed alive!" cried the geographer, with a furious look.

"Is that a personal allusion?"

"An allusion to what?" asked McNabbs, quietly. This was all that passed. The mystery of the DUNCAN'S presence on the coast was explained, and all that the travelers thought about now was to get back to their comfortable cabins, and to have breakfast.

However, Glenarvan and John Mangles stayed behind with Tom Austin after the others had retired. They wished to put some further questions to him.

"Now, then, old Austin," said Glenarvan, "tell me, didn't it strike you as strange to be ordered to go and cruise on the coast of New Zealand?"

"Yes, your Honor," replied Tom. "I was very much surprised, but it is not my custom to discuss any orders I receive, and I obeyed. Could I do otherwise? If some catastrophe had occurred through not carrying out your injunctions to the letter, should not I have been to blame? Would you have acted differently, captain?"

"No, Tom," replied John Mangles.

"But what did you think?" asked Glenarvan.

"I thought, your Honor, that in the interest of Harry Grant, it was necessary to go where I was told to go. I thought that in consequence of fresh arrangements, you were to sail over to New Zealand, and that I was to wait for you on the east coast of the island. Moreover, on leaving Melbourne, I kept our destination a secret, and the crew only knew it when we were right out at sea, and the Australian continent was finally out of sight. But one circumstance occurred which greatly perplexed me."

"What was it, Tom?" asked Glenarvan.

"Just this, that when the quartermaster of the BRITANNIA heard our destination—"

"Ayrton!" cried Glenarvan. "Then he is on board?"

"Yes, your Honor."

"Ayrton here?" repeated Glenarvan, looking at John Mangles.

"God has so willed!" said the young captain.

In an instant, like lightning, Ayrton's conduct, his long-planned treachery, Glenarvan's wound, Mulrady's assassination, the sufferings of the expedition in the marshes of the Snowy River, the whole past life of the miscreant, flashed before the eyes of the two men. And now, by the strangest concourse of events, the convict was in their power.

"Where is he?" asked Glenarvan eagerly.

"In a cabin in the forecastle, and under guard."

"Why was he imprisoned?"

"Because when Ayrton heard the vessel was going to New Zealand, he was in a fury; because he tried to force me to alter the course of the ship; because he threatened me; and, last of all, because he incited my men to mutiny. I saw clearly he was a dangerous individual, and I must take precautions against him."

"And since then?"

"Since then he has remained in his cabin without attempting to go out."

"That's well, Tom."

Just at this moment Glenarvan and John Mangles were summoned to the saloon where breakfast, which they so sorely needed, was awaiting them. They seated themselves at the table and spoke no more of Ayrton.

But after the meal was over, and the guests were refreshed and invigorated, and they all went upon deck, Glenarvan acquainted them with the fact of the quartermaster's presence on board, and at the same time announced his intention of having him brought before them.

"May I beg to be excused from being present at his examination?" said Lady Helena. "I confess, dear Edward, it would be extremely painful for me to see the wretched man."

"He must be confronted with us, Helena," replied Lord Glenarvan; "I beg you will stay. Ben Joyce must see all his victims face to face."

Lady Helena yielded to his wish. Mary Grant sat beside her, near Glenarvan. All the others formed a group round them, the whole party that had been compromised so seriously by the treachery of the convict. The crew of the yacht, without understanding the gravity of the situation, kept profound silence.

"Bring Ayrton here," said Glenarvan.

CHAPTER XVII AYRTON'S OBSTINACY

AYRTON came. He crossed the deck with a confident tread, and mounted the steps to the poop. His eyes were gloomy, his teeth set, his fists clenched convulsively. His appearance betrayed neither effrontery nor timidity. When he found himself in the presence of Lord Glenarvan he folded his arms and awaited the questions calmly and silently.

"Ayrton," said Glenarvan, "here we are then, you and us, on this very DUNCAN that you wished to deliver into the hands of the convicts of Ben Joyce."

The lips of the quartermaster trembled slightly and a quick flush suffused his impassive features. Not the flush of remorse, but of shame at failure. On this yacht which he thought he was to command as master, he was a prisoner, and his fate was about to be decided in a few seconds.

However, he made no reply. Glenarvan waited patiently.

But Ayrton persisted in keeping absolute silence.

"Speak, Ayrton, what have you to say?" resumed Glenarvan.

Ayrton hesitated, the wrinkles in his forehead deepened, and at length he said in calm voice:

"I have nothing to say, my Lord. I have been fool enough to allow myself to be caught. Act as you please."

Then he turned his eyes away toward the coast which lay on the west, and affected profound indifference to what was passing around him. One would have thought him a stranger to the whole affair. But Glenarvan was determined to be patient. Powerful motives urged him to find out certain details concerning the mysterious life of Ayrton, especially those which related to Harry Grant and the BRITANNIA. He therefore resumed his interrogations, speaking with extreme gentleness and firmly restraining his violent irritation against him.

"I think, Ayrton," he went on, "that you will not refuse to reply to certain questions that I wish to put to you; and, first of all, ought I to call you Ayrton or Ben Joyce? Are you, or are you not, the quartermaster of the BRITANNIA?"

Ayrton remained impassive, gazing at the coast, deaf to every question.

Glenarvan's eyes kindled, as he said again:

"Will you tell me how you left the BRITANNIA, and why you are in Australia?"

The same silence, the same impassibility.

"Listen to me, Ayrton," continued Glenarvan; "it is to your interest to speak. Frankness is the only resource left to you, and it may stand you in good stead. For the last time, I ask you, will you reply to my questions?"

Ayrton turned his head toward Glenarvan, and looked into his eyes.

"My Lord," he said, "it is not for me to answer. Justice may witness against me, but I am not going to witness against myself."

"Proof will be easy," said Glenarvan.

"Easy, my Lord," repeated Ayrton, in a mocking tone. "Your honor makes rather a bold assertion there, it seems to me. For my own part, I venture to affirm that the best judge in the Temple would be puzzled what to make of me. Who will say why I came to Australia, when Captain Grant is not here to tell? Who will prove that I am the Ben Joyce placarded by the police, when the police have never had me in their hands, and my companions are at liberty? Who can damage me except yourself, by bringing forward a single crime against me, or even a blameable action? Who will affirm that I intended to take possession of this ship and deliver it into the hands of the convicts? No one, I tell you, no one. You have your suspicions, but you need certainties to condemn a man, and certainties you have none. Until there is a proof to the contrary, I am Ayrton, quartermaster of the BRITANNIA."

Ayrton had become animated while he was speaking, but soon relapsed into his former indifference.

He, no doubt, expected that his reply would close the examination, but Glenarvan commenced again, and said:

"Ayrton, I am not a Crown prosecutor charged with your indictment. That is no business of mine. It is important that our respective situations should be clearly defined. I am not asking you anything that could compromise you. That is for justice to do. But you know what I am searching for, and a single word may put me on the track I have lost. Will you speak?"

Ayrton shook his head like a man determined to be silent.

"Will you tell me where Captain Grant is?" asked Glenarvan.

"No, my Lord," replied Ayrton.

"Will you tell me where the BRITANNIA was wrecked?"

"No, neither the one nor the other."

"Ayrton," said Glenarvan, in almost beseeching tones, "if you know where Harry Grant is, will you, at least, tell his poor children, who are waiting for you to speak the word?"

Ayrton hesitated. His features contracted, and he muttered in a low voice, "I cannot, my Lord."

Then he added with vehemence, as if reproaching himself for a momentary weakness:

"No, I will not speak. Have me hanged, if you choose."

"Hanged!" exclaimed Glenarvan, overcome by a sudden feeling of anger.

But immediately mastering himself, he added in a grave voice:

"Ayrton, there is neither judge nor executioner here. At the first port we touch at, you will be given up into the hands of the English authorities."

"That is what I demand," was the quartermaster's reply.

Then he turned away and quietly walked back to his cabin, which served as his prison. Two sailors kept guard at the door, with orders to watch his slightest movement. The witnesses of this examination retired from the scene indignant and despairing.

As Glenarvan could make no way against Ayrton's obstinacy, what was to be done now? Plainly no course remained but to carry out the plan formed at Eden, of returning to Europe and giving up for the time this unsuccessful enterprise, for the traces of the BRITANNIA seemed irrevocably lost, and the document did not appear to allow any fresh interpretation. On the 37th parallel there was not even another country, and the DUNCAN had only to turn and go back.

CHAPTER XVII AYRTON'S OBSTINACY

After Glenarvan had consulted his friends, he talked over the question of returning, more particularly with the captain. John examined the coal bunkers, and found there was only enough to last fifteen days longer at the outside. It was necessary, therefore, to put in at the nearest port for a fresh supply.

John proposed that he should steer for the Bay of Talcahuano, where the DUNCAN had once before been revictualed before she commenced her voyage of circumnavigation. It was a direct route across, and lay exactly along the 37th parallel. From thence the yacht, being amply provisioned, might go south, double Cape Horn, and get back to Scotland by the Atlantic route.

This plan was adopted, and orders were given to the engineer to get up the steam. Half an hour afterward the beak-head of the yacht was turned toward Talcahuano, over a sea worthy of being called the Pacific, and at six P. M. the last mountains of New Zealand had disappeared in warm, hazy mist on the horizon.

The return voyage was fairly commenced. A sad voyage, for the courageous searching party to come back to the port without bringing home Harry Grant with them! The crew, so joyous at departure and so hopeful, were coming back to Europe defeated and discouraged. There was not one among the brave fellows whose heart did not swell at the thought of seeing his own country once more; and yet there was not one among them either who would not have been willing to brave the perils of the sea for a long time still if they could but find Captain Grant.

Consequently, the hurrahs which greeted the return of Lord Glenarvan to the yacht soon gave place to dejection. Instead of the close intercourse which had formerly existed among the passengers, and the lively conversations which had cheered the voyage, each one kept apart from the others in the solitude of his own cabin, and it was seldom that anyone appeared on the deck of the DUNCAN.

Paganel, who generally shared in an exaggerated form the feelings of those about him, whether painful or joyous— a man who could have invented hope if necessary—even Paganel was gloomy and taciturn. He was seldom visible; his natural loquacity and French vivacity gave place to silence and dejection. He seemed even more downhearted than his companions. If Glenarvan spoke at all of renewing the search, he shook his head like a man who has given up all hope, and whose convictions concerning the fate of the shipwrecked men appeared settled. It was quite evident he believed them irrevocably lost.

And yet there was a man on board who could have spoken the decisive word, and refused to break his silence. This was Ayrton. There was no doubt the fellow knew, if not the present whereabouts of the captain, at least the place of shipwreck. But it was evident that were Grant found, he would be a witness against him. Hence his persistent silence, which gave rise to great indignation on board, especially among the crew, who would have liked to deal summarily with him.

Glenarvan repeatedly renewed his attempts with the quartermaster, but promises and threats were alike useless. Ayrton's obstinacy was so great, and so inexplicable, that the Major began to believe he had nothing to reveal. His opinion was shared, moreover, by the geographer, as it corroborated his own notion about Harry Grant.

But if Ayrton knew nothing, why did he not confess his ignorance? It could not be turned against him. His silence increased the difficulty of forming any new plan. Was the presence of the quartermaster on the Australian continent a proof of Harry Grant's being there? It was settled that they must get this information out of Ayrton.

Lady Helena, seeing her husband's ill-success, asked his permission to try her powers against the obstinacy of the quartermaster. When a man had failed, a woman perhaps, with her gentler influence, might succeed. Is there not a constant repetition going on of the story of the fable where the storm, blow as it will, cannot tear the cloak from the shoulders of the traveler, while the first warm rays of sunshine make him throw it off immediately?

Glenarvan, knowing his young wife's good sense, allowed her to act as she pleased.

The same day (the 5th of March), Ayrton was conducted to Lady Helena's saloon. Mary Grant was to be present at the interview, for the influence of the young girl might be considerable, and Lady Helena would not lose any chance of success.

For a whole hour the two ladies were closeted with the quartermaster, but nothing transpired about their interview. What had been said, what arguments they used to win the secret from the convict, or what questions were asked, remained unknown; but when they left Ayrton, they did not seem to have succeeded, as the expression on their faces denoted discouragement.

In consequence of this, when the quartermaster was being taken back to his cabin, the sailors met him with violent menaces. He took no notice except by shrugging his shoulders, which so increased their rage, that John Mangles and Glenarvan had to interfere, and could only repress it with difficulty.

But Lady Helena would not own herself vanquished. She resolved to struggle to the last with this pitiless man, and went next day herself to his cabin to avoid exposing him again to the vindictiveness of the crew.

The good and gentle Scotchwoman stayed alone with the convict leader for two long hours. Glenarvan in a state of extreme nervous anxiety, remained outside the cabin, alternately resolved to exhaust completely this last chance of success, alternately resolved to rush in and snatch his wife from so painful a situation.

But this time when Lady Helena reappeared, her look was full of hope. Had she succeeded in extracting the secret, and awakening in that adamant heart a last faint touch of pity?

McNabbs, who first saw her, could not restrain a gesture of incredulity.

However the report soon spread among the sailors that the quartermaster had yielded to the persuasions of Lady Helena. The effect was electrical. The entire crew assembled on deck far quicker than Tom Austin's whistle could have brought them together.

Glenarvan had hastened up to his wife and eagerly asked:

"Has he spoken?"

"No," replied Lady Helena, "but he has yielded to my entreaties, and wishes to see you."

"Ah, dear Helena, you have succeeded!"

"I hope so, Edward."

"Have you made him any promise that I must ratify?"

"Only one; that you will do all in your power to mitigate his punishment."

"Very well, dear Helena. Let Ayrton come immediately."

Lady Helena retired to her cabin with Mary Grant, and the quartermaster was brought into the saloon where Lord Glenarvan was expecting him.

CHAPTER XVIII A DISCOURAGING CONFESSION

As soon as the quartermaster was brought into the presence of Lord Glenarvan, his keepers withdrew.

"You wanted to speak to me, Ayrton?" said Glenarvan.

"Yes, my Lord," replied the quartermaster.

"Did you wish for a private interview?"

"Yes, but I think if Major McNabbs and Mr. Paganel were present it would be better."

"For whom?"

"For myself."

Ayrton spoke quite calmly and firmly. Glenarvan looked at him for an instant, and then sent to summon McNabbs and Paganel, who came at once.

"We are all ready to listen to you," said Glenarvan, when his two friends had taken their place at the saloon table.

Ayrton collected himself, for an instant, and then said:

"My Lord, it is usual for witnesses to be present at every contract or transaction between two parties. That is why I desire the presence of Messrs. Paganel and McNabbs, for it is, properly speaking, a bargain which I propose to make."

Glenarvan, accustomed to Ayrton's ways, exhibited no surprise, though any bargaining between this man and himself seemed strange.

"What is the bargain?" he said.

"This," replied Ayrton. "You wish to obtain from me certain facts which may be useful to you. I wish to obtain from you certain advantages which would be valuable to me. It is giving for giving, my Lord. Do you agree to this or not?"

"What are the facts?" asked Paganel eagerly.

"No," said Glenarvan. "What are the advantages?"

Ayrton bowed in token that he understood Glenarvan's distinction.

"These," he said, "are the advantages I ask. It is still your intention,

I suppose, to deliver me up to the English authorities?"

"Yes, Ayrton, it is only justice."

"I don't say it is not," replied the quartermaster quietly.

"Then of course you would never consent to set me at liberty."

Glenarvan hesitated before replying to a question so plainly put.

On the answer he gave, perhaps the fate of Harry Grant might depend!

However, a feeling of duty toward human justice compelled him to say:

"No, Ayrton, I cannot set you at liberty."

"I do not ask it," said the quartermaster proudly.

"Then, what is it you want?"

"A middle place, my Lord, between the gibbet that awaits me and the liberty which you cannot grant me."

"And that is—"

"To allow me to be left on one of the uninhabited islands of the Pacific, with such things as are absolute necessaries. I will manage as best I can, and will repent if I have time."

Glenarvan, quite unprepared for such a proposal, looked at his two friends in silence. But after a brief reflection, he replied:

"Ayrton, if I agree to your request, you will tell me all I have an interest in knowing."

"Yes, my Lord, that is to say, all I know about Captain Grant and the BRITANNIA."

"The whole truth?"

"The whole."

"But what guarantee have I?"

"Oh, I see what you are uneasy about. You need a guarantee for me, for the truth of a criminal. That's natural. But what can you have under the circumstances. There is no help for it, you must either take my offer or leave it."

"I will trust to you, Ayrton," said Glenarvan, simply.

"And you do right, my Lord. Besides, if I deceive you, vengeance is in your own power."

"How?"

"You can come and take me again from where you left me, as I shall have no means of getting away from the island."

Ayrton had an answer for everything. He anticipated the difficulties and furnished unanswerable arguments against himself. It was evident he intended to affect perfect good faith in the business. It was impossible to show more complete confidence. And yet he was prepared to go still further in disinterestedness.

"My Lord and gentlemen," he added, "I wish to convince you of the fact that I am playing cards on the table. I have no wish to deceive you, and I am going to give you a fresh proof of my sincerity in this matter. I deal frankly with you, because I reckon on your honor."

"Speak, Ayrton," said Glenarvan.

"My Lord, I have not your promise yet to accede to my proposal, and yet I do not scruple to tell you that I know very little about Harry Grant."

"Very little," exclaimed Glenarvan.

"Yes, my Lord, the details I am in a position to give you relate to myself. They are entirely personal, and will not do much to help you to recover the lost traces of Captain Grant."

Keen disappointment was depicted on the faces of Glenarvan and the Major.

They thought the quartermaster in the possession of an important secret,

and he declared that his communications would be very nearly barren.

Paganel's countenance remained unmoved.

Somehow or other, this avowal of Ayrton, and surrender of himself, so to speak, unconditionally, singularly touched his auditors, especially when the quartermaster added:

"So I tell you beforehand, the bargain will be more to my profit than yours."

"It does not signify," replied Glenarvan. "I accept your proposal, Ayrton. I give you my word to land you on one of the islands of the Pacific Ocean."

"All right, my Lord," replied the quartermaster.

CHAPTER XVIII A DISCOURAGING CONFESSION

Was this strange man glad of this decision? One might have doubted it, for his impassive countenance betokened no emotion whatever. It seemed as if he were acting for someone else rather than himself.

"I am ready to answer," he said.

"We have no questions to put to you," said Glenarvan. "Tell us all you know, Ayrton, and begin by declaring who you are."

"Gentlemen," replied Ayrton, "I am really Tom Ayrton, the quartermaster of the BRITANNIA. I left Glasgow on Harry Grant's ship on the 12th of March, 1861. For fourteen months I cruised with him in the Pacific in search of an advantageous spot for founding a Scotch colony. Harry Grant was the man to carry out grand projects, but serious disputes often arose between us. His temper and mine could not agree. I cannot bend, and with Harry Grant, when once his resolution is taken, any resistance is impossible, my Lord. He has an iron will both for himself and others.

"But in spite of that, I dared to rebel, and I tried to get the crew to join me, and to take possession of the vessel. Whether I was to blame or not is of no consequence. Be that as it may, Harry Grant had no scruples, and on the 8th of April, 1862, he left me behind on the west coast of Australia."

"Of Australia!" said the Major, interrupting Ayrton in his narrative. "Then of course you had quitted the BRITANNIA before she touched at Callao, which was her last date?"

"Yes," replied the quartermaster, "for the BRITANNIA did not touch there while I was on board. And how I came to speak of Callao at Paddy O'Moore's farm was that I learned the circumstances from your recital."

"Go on, Ayrton," said Glenarvan.

"I found myself abandoned on a nearly desert coast, but only forty miles from the penal settlement at Perth, the capital of Western Australia. As I was wandering there along the shore, I met a band of convicts who had just escaped, and I joined myself to them. You will dispense, my Lord, with any account of my life for two years and a half. This much, however, I must tell you, that I became the leader of the gang, under the name of Ben Joyce. In September, 1864, I introduced myself at the Irish farm, where I engaged myself as a servant in my real name, Ayrton. I waited there till I should get some chance of seizing a ship. This was my one idea. Two months afterward the DUNCAN arrived. During your visit to the farm you related Captain Grant's history, and I learned then facts of which I was not previously aware— that the BRITANNIA had touched at Callao, and that her latest news was dated June, 1862, two months after my disembarkation, and also about the document and the loss of the ship somewhere along the 37th parallel; and, lastly, the strong reasons you had for supposing Harry Grant was on the Australian continent. Without the least hesitation I determined to appropriate the DUNCAN, a matchless vessel, able to outdistance the swiftest ships in the British Navy. But serious injuries had to be repaired. I therefore let it go to Melbourne, and joined myself to you in my true character as quartermaster, offering to guide you to the scene of the shipwreck, fictitiously placed by me on the east coast of Australia. It was in this way, followed or sometimes preceded by my gang of convicts, I directed your expedition toward the province of Victoria. My men committed a bootless crime at Camden Bridge; since the DUNCAN, if brought to the coast, could not escape me, and with the yacht once mine, I was master of the ocean. I led you in this way unsuspectingly as far as the Snowy River. The horses and bullocks dropped dead one by one, poisoned by the gastrolobium. I dragged the wagon into the marshes, where it got half buried. At my instance—but you know the rest, my Lord, and you may be sure that but for the blunder of Mr. Paganel, I should now command the DUNCAN. Such is my history, gentlemen. My disclosures, unfortunately, cannot put you on the track of Harry Grant, and you perceive that you have made but a poor bargain by coming to my terms."

The quartermaster said no more, but crossed his arms in his usual fashion and waited. Glenarvan and his friends kept silence. They felt that this strange criminal had spoken the whole truth. He had only missed his coveted prize, the DUNCAN, through a cause independent of his will. His accomplices had gone to Twofold Bay, as was proved by the convict blouse found by Glenarvan. Faithful to the orders of their chief, they had kept watch on the yacht, and at length, weary of waiting, had returned to the old haunt of robbers and incendiaries in the country parts of New South Wales.

The Major put the first question, his object being to verify the dates of the BRITANNIA.

"You are sure then," he said, "that it was on the 8th of April you were left on the west coast of Australia?"

"On that very day," replied Ayrton.

"And do you know what projects Harry Grant had in view at the time?"

"In an indefinite way I do."

"Say all you can, Ayrton," said Glenarvan, "the least indication may set us in the right course."

"I only know this much, my Lord," replied the quartermaster, "that Captain Grant intended to visit New Zealand. Now, as this part of the programme was not carried out while I was on board, it is not impossible that on leaving Callao the BRITANNIA went to reconnoiter New Zealand. This would agree with the date assigned by the document to the shipwreck—the 27th of June, 1862."

"Clearly," said Paganel.

"But," objected Glenarvan, "there is nothing in the fragmentary words in the document that could apply to New Zealand."

"That I cannot answer," said the quartermaster.

"Well, Ayrton," said Glenarvan, "you have kept your word, and I will keep mine. We have to decide now on what island of the Pacific Ocean you are to be left?"

"It matters little, my Lord," replied Ayrton.

"Return to your cabin," said Glenarvan, "and wait our decision."

The quartermaster withdrew, guarded by the two sailors.

"That villain might have been a man," said the Major.

"Yes," returned Glenarvan; "he is a strong, clear-headed fellow.
Why was it that he must needs turn his powers to such evil account?"

"But Harry Grant?"

"I must fear he is irrevocably lost. Poor children!
Who can tell them where their father is?"

"I can!" replied Paganel. "Yes; I can!" One could not help remarking that the geographer, so loquacious and impatient usually, had scarcely spoken during Ayrton's examination. He listened without opening his mouth. But this speech of his now was worth many others, and it made Glenarvan spring to his feet, crying out: "You, Paganel! you know where Captain Grant is?"

"Yes, as far as can be known."

"How do you know?"

"From that infernal document."

"Ah!" said the Major, in a tone of the most profound incredulity.

"Hear me first, and shrug your shoulders afterward," said Paganel. "I did not speak sooner, because you would not have believed me. Besides, it was useless; and I only speak to-day because Ayrton's opinion just supports my own."

"Then it is New Zealand?" asked Glenarvan.

"Listen and judge," replied Paganel. "It is not without reason, or, rather, I had a reason for making the blunder which has saved our lives. When I was in the very act of writing the letter to Glenarvan's dictation, the word ZEALAND was swimming in my brain. This is why. You remember we were in the wagon. McNabbs had just apprised Lady Helena about the convicts; he had given her the number of the *Australian and New Zealand Gazette* which contained the account of the catastrophe at Camden Bridge. Now, just as I was writing, the newspaper was lying on the ground, folded in such a manner that only two syllables of the title were visible; these two syllables were ALAND. What a sudden light flashed on my mind. ALAND was one of the words in the English document, one that hitherto we had translated *a terre*, and which must have been the termination of the proper noun, ZEALAND."

"Indeed!" said Glenarvan.

"Yes," continued Paganel, with profound conviction; "this meaning had escaped me, and do you know why? Because my wits were exercised naturally on the French document, as it was most complete, and in that this important word was wanting."

"Oh, oh!" said the Major; "your imagination goes too far, Paganel; and you forget your former deductions."

"Go on, Major; I am ready to answer you."

"Well, then, what do you make of your word AUSTRA?"

"What it was at first. It merely means southern countries."

"Well, and this syllable, INDI, which was first the root of the INDIANS, and second the root of the word *indigenes?*"

"Well, the third and last time," replied Paganel, "it will be the first syllable of the word INDIGENCE."

"And CONTIN?" cried McNabbs. "Does that still mean CONTINENT?"

"No; since New Zealand is only an island."

"What then?" asked Glenarvan.

"My dear lord," replied Paganel, "I am going to translate the document according to my third interpretation, and you shall judge. I only make two observations beforehand. First, forget as much as possible preceding interpretations, and divest your mind of all preconceived notions. Second, certain parts may appear to you strained, and it is possible that I translate them badly; but they are of no importance; among others, the word AGONIE, which chokes me; but I cannot find any other explanation. Besides, my interpretation was founded on the French document; and don't forget it was written by an Englishman, who could not be familiar with the idioms of the French language. Now then, having said this much, I will begin."

And slowly articulating each syllable, he repeated the following sentences:

"LE 27th JUIN, 1862, *le trois-mats Britannia*, de *Glasgow, a sombre* apres une longue AGONIE dans les mers AUSTRALES sur les cotes de la Nouvelle ZELANDE—in English *Zealand. Deux matelots* et le *Capitaine Grant* ont pu y ABORDER. La CONTINUEllement en PRoie a une CRUELle INDIgence, ils ont *jete ce document* par—*de lon*gitude ET 37 degrees 11' de LATItude. *Venex a leur* secours, ou ils sont PERDUS!" (On the 27th of June, 1865, the three-mast vessel BRITANNIA, of Glasgow, has foundered after a long AGOnie in the Southern Seas, on the coast of New Zealand. Two sailors and Captain Grant have succeeded in landing. Continually a prey to cruel indigence, they have thrown this document into the sea in— longitude and 37 degrees 11' latitude. Come to their help, or they are lost.)

Paganel stopped. His interpretation was admissible. But precisely because it appeared as likely as the preceding, it might be as false. Glenarvan and the Major did not then try and discuss it. However, since no traces of the BRITANNIA had yet been met with, either on the Patagonian or Australian coasts, at the points where these countries are crossed by the 37th parallel, the chances were in favor of New Zealand.

"Now, Paganel," said Glenarvan, "will you tell me why you have kept this interpretation secret for nearly two months?"

"Because I did not wish to buoy you up again with vain hopes. Besides, we were going to Auckland, to the very spot indicated by the latitude of the document."

"But since then, when we were dragged out of the route, why did you not speak?"

"Because, however just the interpretation, it could do nothing for the deliverance of the captain."

"Why not, Paganel?"

"Because, admitting that the captain was wrecked on the New Zealand coast, now that two years have passed and he has not reappeared, he must have perished by shipwreck or by the New Zealanders."

"Then you are of the opinion," said Glenarvan, "that—"

"That vestiges of the wreck might be found; but that the survivors of the BRITANNIA have, beyond doubt, perished."

"Keep all this silent, friends," said Glenarvan, "and let me choose a fitting moment to communicate these sad tidings to Captain Grant's children."

CHAPTER XIX A CRY IN THE NIGHT

THE crew soon heard that no light had been thrown on the situation of Captain Grant by the revelations of Ayrton, and it caused profound disappointment among them, for they had counted on the quartermaster, and the quartermaster knew nothing which could put the DUNCAN on the right track.

The yacht therefore continued her course. They had yet to select the island for Ayrton's banishment.

Paganel and John Mangles consulted the charts on board, and exactly on the 37th parallel found a little isle marked by the name of Maria Theresa, a sunken rock in the middle of the Pacific Ocean, 3,500 miles from the American coast, and 1,500 miles from New Zealand. The nearest land on the north was the Archipelago of Pomotou, under the protectorate of France; on the south there was nothing but the eternal ice-belt of the Polar Sea. No ship would come to reconnoiter this solitary isle. No echoes from the world would ever reach it. The storm birds only would rest awhile on it during their long flight, and in many charts the rock was not even marked.

If ever complete isolation was to be found on earth, it was on this little out-of-the-way island. Ayrton was informed of its situation, and expressed his willingness to live there apart from his fellows. The head of the vessel was in consequence turned toward it immediately.

Two days later, at two o'clock, the man on watch signaled land on the horizon. This was Maria Theresa, a low, elongated island, scarcely raised above the waves, and looking like an enormous whale. It was still thirty miles distant from the yacht, whose stem was rapidly cutting her way over the water at the rate of sixteen knots an hour.

Gradually the form of the island grew more distinct on the horizon. The orb of day sinking in the west, threw up its peculiar outlines in sharp relief. A few peaks of no great elevation stood out here and there, tipped with sunlight. At five o'clock John Mangles could discern a light smoke rising from it.

"Is it a volcano?" he asked of Paganel, who was gazing at this new land through his telescope.

"I don't know what to think," replied the geographer; "Maria Theresa is a spot little known; nevertheless, it would not be surprising if its origin were due to some submarine upheaval, and consequently it may be volcanic."

"But in that case," said Glenarvan, "is there not reason to fear that if an eruption produced it, an eruption may carry it away?"

"That is not possible," replied Paganel. "We know of its existence for several centuries, which is our security. When the Isle Julia emerged from the Mediterranean, it did not remain long above the waves, and disappeared a few months after its birth."

"Very good," said Glenarvan. "Do you think, John, we can get there to-night?"

"No, your honor, I must not risk the DUNCAN in the dark, for I am unacquainted with the coast. I will keep under steam, but go very slowly, and to-morrow, at daybreak, we can send off a boat."

At eight o'clock in the evening, Maria Theresa, though five miles to leeward, appeared only an elongated shadow, scarcely visible. The DUNCAN was always getting nearer.

At nine o'clock, a bright glare became visible, and flames shot up through the darkness. The light was steady and continued.

"That confirms the supposition of a volcano," said Paganel, observing it attentively.

"Yet," replied John Mangles, "at this distance we ought to hear the noise which always accompanies an eruption, and the east wind brings no sound whatever to our ear."

"That's true," said Paganel. "It is a volcano that blazes, but does not speak. The gleam seems intermittent too, sometimes, like that of a lighthouse."

"You are right," said John Mangles, "and yet we are not on a lighted coast."

"Ah!" he exclaimed, "another fire? On the shore this time!

Look! It moves! It has changed its place!"

John was not mistaken. A fresh fire had appeared, which seemed to die out now and then, and suddenly flare up again.

"Is the island inhabited then?" said Glenarvan.

"By savages, evidently," replied Paganel.

"But in that case, we cannot leave the quartermaster there."

"No," replied the Major, "he would be too bad a gift even to bestow on savages."

"We must find some other uninhabited island," said Glenarvan, who could not help smiling at the delicacy of McNabbs. "I promised Ayrton his life, and I mean to keep my promise."

"At all events, don't let us trust them," added Paganel.

"The New Zealanders have the barbarous custom of deceiving ships by

moving lights, like the wreckers on the Cornish coast in former times.

Now the natives of Maria Theresa may have heard of this proceeding."

"Keep her off a point," called out John to the man at the helm.

"To-morrow at sunrise we shall know what we're about."

At eleven o'clock, the passengers and John Mangles retired to their cabins. In the forepart of the yacht the man on watch was pacing the deck, while aft, there was no one but the man at the wheel.

At this moment Mary Grant and Robert came on the poop.

The two children of the captain, leaning over the rail, gazed sadly at the phosphorescent waves and the luminous wake of the DUNCAN. Mary was thinking of her brother's future, and Robert of his sister's. Their father was uppermost in the minds of both. Was this idolized parent still in existence? Must they give him up? But no, for what would life be without him? What would become of them without him? What would have become of them already, but for Lord Glenarvan and Lady Helena?

The young boy, old above his years through trouble, divined the thoughts that troubled his sister, and taking her hand in his own, said, "Mary, we must never despair. Remember the lessons our father gave us. Keep your courage up and no matter what befalls you, let us show this obstinate courage which can rise above everything. Up to this time, sister, you have been working for me, it is my turn now, and I will work for you."

"Dear Robert!" replied the young girl.

"I must tell you something," resumed Robert. "You mustn't be vexed, Mary!"

"Why should I be vexed, my child?"

"And you will let me do it?"

"What do you mean?" said Mary, getting uneasy.

"Sister, I am going to be a sailor!"

"You are going to leave me!" cried the young girl, pressing her brother's hand.

"Yes, sister; I want to be a sailor, like my father and Captain John. Mary, dear Mary, Captain John has not lost all hope, he says. You have confidence in his devotion to us, and so have I. He is going to make a grand sailor out of me some day, he has promised me he will; and then we are going to look for our father together. Tell me you are willing, sister mine. What our father would have done for us it is our duty, mine, at least, to do for him. My life has one purpose to which it should be entirely consecrated— that is to search, and never cease searching for my father, who would never have given us up. Ah, Mary, how good our father was!"

"And so noble, so generous!" added Mary. "Do you know, Robert, he was already a glory to our country, and that he would have been numbered among our great men if fate had not arrested his course."

"Yes, I know it," said Robert.

Mary put her arm around the boy, and hugged him fondly as he felt her tears fall on his forehead.

"Mary, Mary!" he cried, "it doesn't matter what our friends say, I still hope, and will always hope. A man like my father doesn't die till he has finished his work."

Mary Grant could not reply. Sobs choked her voice. A thousand feelings struggled in her breast at the news that fresh attempts were about to be made to recover Harry Grant, and that the devotion of the captain was so unbounded.

"And does Mr. John still hope?" she asked.

"Yes," replied Robert. "He is a brother that will never forsake us, never! I will be a sailor, you'll say yes, won't you, sister? And let me join him in looking for my father. I am sure you are willing."

"Yes, I am willing," said Mary. "But the separation!" she murmured.

"You will not be alone, Mary, I know that. My friend John told me so. Lady Helena will not let you leave her. You are a woman; you can and should accept her kindness. To refuse would be ungrateful, but a man, my father has said a hundred times, must make his own way."

"But what will become of our own dear home in Dundee, so full of memories?"

"We will keep it, little sister! All that is settled, and settled so well, by our friend John, and also by Lord Glenarvan. He is to keep you at Malcolm Castle as if you were his daughter. My Lord told my friend John so, and he told me. You will be at home there, and have someone to speak to about our father, while you are waiting till John and I bring him back to you some day. Ah! what a grand day that will be!" exclaimed Robert, his face glowing with enthusiasm.

"My boy, my brother," replied Mary, "how happy my father would be if he could hear you. How much you are like him, dear Robert, like our dear, dear father. When you grow up you'll be just himself."

"I hope I may," said Robert, blushing with filial and sacred pride.

"But how shall we requite Lord and Lady Glenarvan?" said Mary Grant.

"Oh, that will not be difficult," replied Robert, with boyish confidence. "We will love and revere them, and we will tell them so; and we will give them plenty of kisses, and some day, when we can get the chance, we will die for them."

"We'll live for them, on the contrary," replied the young girl, covering her brother's forehead with kisses. "They will like that better, and so shall I."

The two children then relapsed into silence, gazing out into the dark night, and giving way to long reveries, interrupted occasionally by a question or remark from one to the other. A long swell undulated the surface of the calm sea, and the screw turned up a luminous furrow in the darkness.

A strange and altogether supernatural incident now occurred. The brother and sister, by some of those magnetic communications which link souls mysteriously together, were the subjects at the same time and the same instant of the same hallucination.

Out of the midst of these waves, with their alternations of light and shadow, a deep plaintive voice sent up a cry, the tones of which thrilled through every fiber of their being.

"Come! come!" were the words which fell on their ears.

They both started up and leaned over the railing, and peered into the gloom with questioning eyes.

"Mary, you heard that? You heard that?" cried Robert.

But they saw nothing but the long shadow that stretched before them.

"Robert," said Mary, pale with emotion, "I thought—yes, I thought as you did, that—We must both be ill with fever, Robert."

A second time the cry reached them, and this time the illusion was so great, that they both exclaimed simultaneously, "My father! My father!"

It was too much for Mary. Overcome with emotion, she fell fainting into Robert's arms.

"Help!" shouted Robert. "My sister! my father! Help! Help!"

The man at the wheel darted forward to lift up the girl. The sailors on watch ran to assist, and John Mangles, Lady Helena, and Glenarvan were hastily roused from sleep.

"My sister is dying, and my father is there!" exclaimed Robert, pointing to the waves.

They were wholly at a loss to understand him.

"Yes!" he repeated, "my father is there! I heard my father's voice;
Mary heard it too!"

Just at this moment, Mary Grant recovering consciousness, but wandering and excited, called out, "My father! my father is there!"

And the poor girl started up, and leaning over the side of the yacht, wanted to throw herself into the sea.

"My Lord—Lady Helena!" she exclaimed, clasping her hands, "I tell you my father is there! I can declare that I heard his voice come out of the waves like a wail, as if it were a last adieu."

The young girl went off again into convulsions and spasms, which became so violent that she had to be carried to her cabin, where Lady Helena lavished every care on her. Robert kept on repeating, "My father! my father is there! I am sure of it, my Lord!"

The spectators of this painful scene saw that the captain's children were laboring under an hallucination. But how were they to be undeceived?

Glenarvan made an attempt, however. He took Robert's hand, and said,

"You say you heard your father's voice, my dear boy?"

"Yes, my Lord; there, in the middle of the waves.
He cried out, 'Come! come!'"

"And did you recognize his voice?"

"Yes, I recognized it immediately. Yes, yes; I can swear to it!
My sister heard it, and recognized it as well. How could we
both be deceived? My Lord, do let us go to my father's help.
A boat! a boat!"

Glenarvan saw it was impossible to undeceive the poor boy, but he tried once more by saying to the man at the wheel:

"Hawkins, you were at the wheel, were you not, when Miss Mary was so strangely attacked?"

"Yes, your Honor," replied Hawkins.

"And you heard nothing, and saw nothing?"

"Nothing."

"Now Robert, see?"

"If it had been Hawkins's father," returned the boy, with indomitable energy, "Hawkins would not say he had heard nothing. It was my father, my lord! my father."

Sobs choked his voice; he became pale and silent, and presently fell down insensible, like his sister.

Glenarvan had him carried to his bed, where he lay in a deep swoon.

"Poor orphans," said John Mangles. "It is a terrible trial they have to bear!"

"Yes," said Glenarvan; "excessive grief has produced the same hallucination in both of them, and at the same time."

"In both of them!" muttered Paganel; "that's strange, and pure science would say inadmissible."

He leaned over the side of the vessel, and listened attentively, making a sign to the rest to keep still.

But profound silence reigned around. Paganel shouted his loudest.

No response came.

"It is strange," repeated the geographer, going back to his cabin. "Close sympathy in thought and grief does not suffice to explain this phenomenon."

Next day, March 4, at 5 A. M., at dawn, the passengers, including Mary and Robert, who would not stay behind, were all assembled on the poop, each one eager to examine the land they had only caught a glimpse of the night before.

The yacht was coasting along the island at the distance of about a mile, and its smallest details could be seen by the eye.

Suddenly Robert gave a loud cry, and exclaimed he could see two men running about and gesticulating, and a third was waving a flag.

"The Union Jack," said John Mangles, who had caught up a spy-glass.

"True enough," said Paganel, turning sharply round toward Robert.

"My Lord," said Robert, trembling with emotion, "if you don't want me to swim to the shore, let a boat be lowered. Oh, my Lord, I implore you to let me be the first to land."

No one dared to speak. What! on this little isle, crossed by the 37th parallel, there were three men, shipwrecked Englishmen! Instantaneously everyone thought of the voice heard by Robert and Mary the preceding night. The children were right, perhaps, in the affirmation. The sound of a voice might have reached them, but this voice— was it their father's? No, alas, most assuredly no. And as they thought of the dreadful disappointment that awaited them, they trembled lest this new trial should crush them completely. But who could stop them from going on shore? Lord Glenarvan had not the heart to do it.

"Lower a boat," he called out.

Another minute and the boat was ready. The two children of Captain Grant, Glenarvan, John Mangles, and Paganel, rushed into it, and six sailors, who rowed so vigorously that they were presently almost close to the shore.

At ten fathoms' distance a piercing cry broke from Mary's lips.

"My father!" she exclaimed.

A man was standing on the beach, between two others. His tall, powerful form, and his physiognomy, with its mingled expression of boldness and gentleness, bore a resemblance both to Mary and Robert. This was indeed the man the children had so often described. Their hearts had not deceived them. This was their father, Captain Grant!

The captain had heard Mary's cry, for he held out his arms, and fell flat on the sand, as if struck by a thunderbolt.

CHAPTER XX CAPTAIN GRANT'S STORY

JOY does not kill, for both father and children recovered before they had reached the yacht. The scene which followed, who can describe? Language fails. The whole crew wept aloud at the sight of these three clasped together in a close, silent embrace.

The moment Harry Grant came on deck, he knelt down reverently. The pious Scotchman's first act on touching the yacht, which to him was the soil of his native land, was to return thanks to the God of his deliverance. Then, turning to Lady Helena and Lord Glenarvan, and his companions, he thanked them in broken words, for his heart was too full to speak. During the short passage from the isle to the yacht, his children had given him a brief sketch of the DUNCAN'S history.

What an immense debt he owed to this noble lady and her friends! From Lord Glenarvan, down to the lowest sailor on board, how all had struggled and suffered for him! Harry Grant expressed his gratitude with such simplicity and nobleness, his manly face suffused with pure and sweet emotion, that the whole crew felt amply recompensed for the trials they had undergone. Even the impassable Major himself felt a tear steal down his cheek in spite of all his self-command; while the good, simple Paganel cried like a child who does not care who sees his tears.

Harry Grant could not take his eyes off his daughter. He thought her beautiful, charming; and he not only said so to himself, but repeated it aloud, and appealed to Lady Helena for confirmation of his opinion, as if to convince himself that he was not blinded by his paternal affection. His boy, too, came in for admiration. "How he has grown! he is a man!" was his delighted exclamation. And he covered the two children so dear to him with the kisses he had been heaping up for them during his two years of absence.

Robert then presented all his friends successively, and found means always to vary the formula of introduction, though he had to say the same thing about each. The fact was, each and all had been perfect in the children's eyes.

John Mangles blushed like a child when his turn came, and his voice trembled as he spoke to Mary's father.

Lady Helena gave Captain Grant a narrative of the voyage, and made him proud of his son and daughter. She told him of the young hero's exploits, and how the lad had already paid back part of the paternal debt to Lord Glenarvan. John Mangles sang Mary's praises in such terms, that Harry Grant, acting on a hint from Lady Helena, put his daughter's hand into that of the brave young captain, and turning to Lord and Lady Glenarvan, said: "My Lord, and you, Madam, also give your blessing to our children."

When everything had been said and re-said over and over again, Glenarvan informed Harry Grant about Ayrton. Grant confirmed the quartermaster's confession as far as his disembarkation on the coast of Australia was concerned.

"He is an intelligent, intrepid man," he added, "whose passions have led him astray. May reflection and repentance bring him to a better mind!"

But before Ayrton was transferred, Harry Grant wished to do the honors of his rock to his friends. He invited them to visit his wooden house, and dine with him in Robinson Crusoe fashion.

Glenarvan and his friends accepted the invitation most willingly. Robert and Mary were eagerly longing to see the solitary house where their father had so often wept at the thought of them. A boat was manned, and the Captain and his two children, Lord and Lady Glenarvan, the Major, John Mangles, and Paganel, landed on the shores of the island.

A few hours sufficed to explore the whole domain of Harry Grant. It was in fact the summit of a submarine mountain, a plateau composed of basaltic rocks and volcanic DEBRIS. During the geological epochs of the earth, this mountain had gradually emerged from the depths of the Pacific, through the action of the subterranean fires, but for ages back the volcano had been a peaceful mountain, and the filled-up crater, an island rising out of the liquid plain. Then soil formed. The vegetable kingdom took possession of this new land. Several whalers landed domestic animals there in passing; goats and pigs, which multiplied and ran wild, and the three kingdoms of nature were now displayed on this island, sunk in mid ocean.

When the survivors of the shipwrecked BRITANNIA took refuge there, the hand of man began to organize the efforts of nature. In two years and a half, Harry Grant and his two sailors had metamorphosed the island. Several acres of well-cultivated land were stocked with vegetables of excellent quality.

The house was shaded by luxuriant gum-trees. The magnificent ocean stretched before the windows, sparkling in the sunlight. Harry Grant had the table placed beneath the grand trees, and all the guests seated themselves. A hind quarter of a goat, nardou bread, several bowls of milk, two or three roots of wild endive, and pure fresh water, composed the simple repast, worthy of the shepherds of Arcadia.

Paganel was enchanted. His old fancies about Robinson Crusoe revived in full force. "He is not at all to be pitied, that scoundrel, Ayrton!" he exclaimed, enthusiastically. "This little isle is just a paradise!"

"Yes," replied Harry Grant, "a paradise to these poor, shipwrecked fellows that Heaven had pity on, but I am sorry that Maria Theresa was not an extensive and fertile island, with a river instead of a stream, and a port instead of a tiny bay exposed to the open sea."

"And why, captain?" asked Glenarvan.

"Because I should have made it the foundation of the colony with which I mean to dower Scotland."

"Ah, Captain Grant, you have not given up the project, then, which made you so popular in our old country?"

"No, my Lord, and God has only saved me through your efforts that I might accomplish my task. My poor brothers in old Caledonia, all who are needy must have a refuge provided for them in another land against their misery, and my dear country must have a colony of her own, for herself alone, somewhere in these seas, where she may find that independence and comfort she so lacks in Europe."

"Ah, that is very true, Captain Grant," said Lady Helena. "This is a grand project of yours, and worthy of a noble heart. But this little isle—"

"No, madam, it is a rock only fit at most to support a few settlers; while what we need is a vast country, whose virgin soil abounds in untouched stores of wealth," replied the captain.

"Well, captain," exclaimed Glenarvan, "the future is ours, and this country we will seek for together."

And the two brave Scotchmen joined hands in a hearty grip and so sealed the compact.

A general wish was expressed to hear, while they were on the island, the account of the shipwreck of the BRITANNIA, and of the two years spent by the survivors in this very place. Harry Grant was delighted to gratify their curiosity, and commenced his narration forthwith.

"My story," he said, "is that of all the Robinson Crusoes cast upon an island, with only God and themselves to rely on, and feeling it a duty to struggle for life with the elements.

"It was during the night of the 26th or 27th of June, 1862, that the BRITANNIA, disabled by a six days' storm, struck against the rocks of Maria Theresa. The sea was mountains high, and lifeboats were useless. My unfortunate crew all perished, except Bob Learce and Joe Bell, who with myself managed to reach shore after twenty unsuccessful attempts.

"The land which received us was only an uninhabited island, two miles broad and five long, with about thirty trees in the interior, a few meadows, and a brook of fresh water, which fortunately never dried up. Alone with my sailors, in this corner of the globe, I did not despair. I put my trust in God, and accustomed myself to struggle resolutely for existence. Bob and Joe, my brave companions in misfortune, my friends, seconded me energetically.

"We began like the fictitious Robinson Crusoe of Defoe, our model, by collecting the planks of the ship, the tools, a little powder, and firearms, and a bag of precious seeds. The first few days were painful enough, but hunting and fishing soon afforded us a sure supply of food, for wild goats were in abundance in the interior of the island, and marine animals abounded on the coast. By degrees we fell into regular ways and habits of life.

"I had saved my instruments from the wreck, and knew exactly the position of the island. I found we were out of the route of vessels, and could not be rescued unless by some providential chance. I accepted our trying lot composedly, always thinking, however, of my dear ones, remembering them every day in my prayers, though never hoping to see them again.

"However, we toiled on resolutely, and before long several acres of land were sown with the seed off the BRITANNIA; potatoes, endive, sorrel, and other vegetables besides, gave wholesome variety to our daily fare. We caught some young kids, which soon grew quite tame. We had milk and butter. The nardou, which grew abundantly in dried up creeks, supplied us with tolerably substantial bread, and we had no longer any fears for our material life.

"We had built a log hut with the DEBRIS of the BRITANNIA, and this was covered over with sail cloth, carefully tarred over, and beneath this secure shelter the rainy season passed comfortably. Many a plan was discussed here, and many a dream indulged in, the brightest of which is this day realized.

"I had at first the idea of trying to brave the perils of the ocean in a canoe made out of the spars of the ship, but 1,500 miles lay between us and the nearest coast, that is to say the islands of the Archipelago of Pomotou. No boat could have stood so long a voyage. I therefore relinquished my scheme, and looked for no deliverance except from a divine hand.

"Ah, my poor children! how often we have stood on the top of the rocks and watched the few vessels passing in the distance far out at sea. During the whole period of our exile only two or three vessels appeared on the horizon, and those only to disappear again immediately. Two years and a half were spent in this manner. We gave up hoping, but yet did not despair. At last, early yesterday morning, when I was standing on the highest peak of the island, I noticed a light smoke rising in the west. It increased, and soon a ship appeared in sight. It seemed to be coming toward us. But would it not rather steer clear of an island where there was no harbor.

"Ah, what a day of agony that was! My heart was almost bursting.

My comrades kindled a fire on one of the peaks. Night came on,

but no signal came from the yacht. Deliverance was there, however.

Were we to see it vanish from our eyes?

"I hesitated no longer. The darkness was growing deeper. The ship might double the island during the night. I jumped into the sea, and attempted to make my way toward it. Hope trebled my strength, I cleft the waves with superhuman vigor, and had got so near the yacht that I was scarcely thirty fathoms off, when it tacked about.

"This provoked me to the despairing cry, which only my two children heard. It was no illusion.

"Then I came back to the shore, exhausted and overcome with emotion and fatigue. My two sailors received me half dead. It was a horrible night this last we spent on the island, and we believed ourselves abandoned forever, when day dawned, and there was the yacht sailing nearly alongside, under easy steam. Your boat was lowered—we were saved—and, oh, wonder of Divine goodness, my children, my beloved children, were there holding out their arms to me!"

Robert and Mary almost smothered their father with kisses and caresses as he ended his narrative.

It was now for the first time that the captain heard that he owed his deliverance to the somewhat hieroglyphical document which he had placed in a bottle and confined to the mercy of the ocean.

But what were Jacques Paganel's thoughts during Captain Grant's recital? The worthy geographer was turning over in his brain for the thousandth time the words of the document. He pondered his three successive interpretations, all of which had proved false. How had this island, called Maria Theresa, been indicated in the papers originally?

At last Paganel could contain himself no longer, and seizing

Harry Grant's hand, he exclaimed:

"Captain! will you tell me at last what really was in your indecipherable document?"

A general curiosity was excited by this question of the geographer, for the enigma which had been for nine months a mystery was about to be explained.

"Well, captain," repeated Paganel, "do you remember the precise words of the document?"

"Exactly," replied Harry Grant; "and not a day has passed without my recalling to memory words with which our last hopes were linked."

"And what are they, captain?" asked Glenarvan. "Speak, for our *amour propre* is wounded to the quick!"

"I am ready to satisfy you," replied Harry Grant; "but, you know, to multiply the chances of safety, I had inclosed three documents in the bottle, in three different languages. Which is it you wish to hear?"

"They are not identical, then?" cried Paganel.

"Yes, they are, almost to a word."

"Well, then, let us have the French document," replied Glenarvan. "That is the one that is most respected by the waves, and the one on which our interpretations have been mostly founded."

"My Lord, I will give it you word for word," replied Harry Grant.

"LE 27 JUIN, 1862, *le trois-mats Britannia, de Glasgow, s'est perdu a quinze cents lieues de la Patagonie, dans l'hemisphere austral. Partes a terre, deux matelots et le Capitaine Grant ont atteint l'ile Tabor—*"

"Oh!" exclaimed Paganel.

"LA," continued Harry Grant, "*continuellement en proie a une cruelle indigence, ils ont jete ce document par* 153 degrees *de longitude et* 37 degrees 11' *de latitude. Venes a leur secours, ou ils sont perdus.*"

At the name of Tabor, Paganel had started up hastily, and now being unable to restrain himself longer, he called out:

"How can it be Isle Tabor? Why, this is Maria Theresa!"

"Undoubtedly, Monsieur Paganel," replied Harry Grant. "It is
Maria Theresa on the English and German charts, but is named
Tabor on the French ones!"

At this moment a vigorous thump on Paganel's shoulder almost bent him double. Truth obliges us to say it was the Major that dealt the blow, though strangely contrary to his usual strict politeness.

"Geographer!" said McNabbs, in a tone of the most supreme contempt.

But Paganel had not even felt the Major's hand. What was that compared to the geographical blow which had stunned him?

He had been gradually getting nearer the truth, however, as he learned from Captain Grant. He had almost entirely deciphered the indecipherable document. The names Patagonia, Australia, New Zealand, had appeared to him in turn with absolute certainty. CONTIN, at first CONTINENT, had gradually reached its true meaning, *continuelle. Indi* had successively signified *indiens, indigenes*, and at last the right word was found—INDIGENCE. But one mutilated word, ABOR, had baffled the geographer's sagacity. Paganel had persisted in making it the root of the verb ABORDER, and it turned out to be a proper name, the French name of the Isle Tabor, the isle which had been a refuge for the shipwrecked sailors of the BRITANNIA. It was difficult to avoid falling into the error, however, for on the English planispheres on the DUNCAN, the little isle was marked Maria Theresa.

"No matter?" cried Paganel, tearing his hair; "I ought not to have forgotten its double appellation. It is an unpardonable mistake, one unworthy of a secretary of the Geographical Society. I am disgraced!"

"Come, come, Monsieur Paganel," said Lady Helena; "moderate your grief."

"No, madam, no; I am a mere ass!"

"And not even a learned one!" added the Major, by way of consolation.

When the meal was over, Harry Grant put everything in order in his house. He took nothing away, wishing the guilty to inherit the riches of the innocent. Then they returned to the vessel, and, as Glenarvan had determined to start the same day, he gave immediate orders for the disembarkation of the quartermaster. Ayrton was brought up on the poop, and found himself face to face with Harry Grant.

"It is I, Ayrton!" said Grant

"Yes, it is you, captain," replied Ayrton, without the least sign of surprise at Harry Grant's recovery. "Well, I am not sorry to see you again in good health."

"It seems, Ayrton, that I made a mistake in landing you on an inhabited coast."

"It seems so, captain."

"You are going to take my place on this uninhabited island.
May Heaven give you repentance!"

"Amen," said Ayrton, calmly.

Glenarvan then addressed the quartermaster.

"It is still your wish, then, Ayrton, to be left behind?"

"Yes, my Lord!"

"And Isle Tabor meets your wishes?"

"Perfectly."

"Now then, listen to my last words, Ayrton. You will be cut off here from all the world, and no communication with your fellows is possible. Miracles are rare, and you will not be able to quit this isle. You will be alone, with no eye upon you but that of God, who reads the deepest secrets of the heart; but you will be neither lost nor forsaken, as Captain Grant was. Unworthy as you are of anyone's remembrance, you will not be dropped out of recollection. I know where you are, Ayrton; I know where to find you— I shall never forget."

"God keep your Honor," was all Ayrton's reply.

These were the final words exchanged between Glenarvan and the quartermaster. The boat was ready and Ayrton got into it.

John Mangles had previously conveyed to the island several cases of preserved food, besides clothing, and tools and firearms, and a supply of powder and shot. The quartermaster could commence a new life of honest labor. Nothing was lacking, not even books; among others, the Bible, so dear to English hearts.

The parting hour had come. The crew and all the passengers were assembled on deck. More than one felt his heart swell with emotion. Mary Grant and Lady Helena could not restrain their feelings.

"Must it be done?" said the young wife to her husband.

"Must the poor man be left there?"

"He must, Helena," replied Lord Glenarvan. "It is in expiation of his crimes."

At that moment the boat, in charge of John Mangles, turned away. Ayrton, who remained standing, and still unmoved, took off his cap and bowed gravely.

Glenarvan uncovered, and all the crew followed his example, as if in presence of a man who was about to die, and the boat went off in profound silence.

On reaching land, Ayrton jumped on the sandy shore, and the boat returned to the yacht. It was then four o'clock in the afternoon, and from the poop the passengers could see the quartermaster gazing at the ship, standing with folded arms on a rock, motionless as a statue.

"Shall we set sail, my Lord?" asked John Mangles.

"Yes, John," replied Glenarvan, hastily, more moved than he cared to show.

"Go on!" shouted John to the engineer.

The steam hissed and puffed out, the screw began to stir the waves, and by eight o'clock the last peaks of Isle Tabor disappeared in the shadows of the night.

CHAPTER XXI PAGANEL'S LAST ENTANGLEMENT

ON the 19th of March, eleven days after leaving the island, the DUNCAN sighted the American coast, and next day dropped anchor in the bay of Talcahuano. They had come back again after a voyage of five months, during which, and keeping strictly along the 37th parallel, they had gone round the world. The passengers in this memorable expedition, unprecedented in the annals of the Travelers' Club, had visited Chili, the Pampas, the Argentine Republic, the Atlantic, the island of Tristan d'Acunha, the Indian Ocean, Amsterdam Island, Australia, New Zealand, Isle Tabor, and the Pacific. Their search had not been fruitless, for they were bringing back the survivors of the shipwrecked BRITANNIA.

Not one of the brave Scots who set out at the summons of their chief, but could answer to their names; all were returning to their old Scotia.

As soon as the DUNCAN had re-provisioned, she sailed along the coast of Patagonia, doubled Cape Horn, and made a swift run up the Atlantic Ocean. No voyage could be more devoid of incident. The yacht was simply carrying home a cargo of happiness. There was no secret now on board, not even John Mangles's attachment to Mary Grant.

Yes, there was one mystery still, which greatly excited McNabbs's curiosity. Why was it that Paganel remained always hermetically fastened up in his clothes, with a big comforter round his throat and up to his very ears? The Major was burning with desire to know the reason of this singular fashion. But in spite of interrogations, allusions, and suspicions on the part of McNabbs, Paganel would not unbutton.

Not even when the DUNCAN crossed the line, and the heat was so great that the seams of the deck were melting. "He is so DISTRAIT that he thinks he is at St. Petersburg," said the Major, when he saw the geographer wrapped in an immense great-coat, as if the mercury had been frozen in the thermometer.

At last on the 9th of May, fifty-three days from the time of leaving Talcahuano, John Mangles sighted the lights of Cape Clear. The yacht entered St. George's Channel, crossed the Irish Sea, and on the 10th of May reached the Firth of Clyde. At 11 o'clock she dropped anchor off Dunbarton, and at 2 P.M. the passengers arrived at Malcolm Castle amidst the enthusiastic cheering of the Highlanders.

As fate would have it then, Harry Grant and his two companions were saved. John Mangles wedded Mary Grant in the old cathedral of St. Mungo, and Mr. Paxton, the same clergyman who had prayed nine months before for the deliverance of the father, now blessed the marriage of his daughter and his deliverer. Robert was to become a sailor like Harry Grant and John Mangles, and take part with them in the captain's grand projects, under the auspices of Lord Glenarvan.

But fate also decreed that Paganel was not to die a bachelor?

Probably so.

The fact was, the learned geographer after his heroic exploits, could not escape celebrity. His blunders made quite a FURORE among the fashionables of Scotland, and he was overwhelmed with courtesies.

It was then that an amiable lady, about thirty years of age, in fact, a cousin of McNabbs, a little eccentric herself, but good and still charming, fell in love with the geographer's oddities, and offered him her hand. Forty thousand pounds went with it, but that was not mentioned.

Paganel was far from being insensible to the sentiments of Miss Arabella, but yet he did not dare to speak. It was the Major who was the medium of communication between these two souls, evidently made for each other. He even told Paganel that his marriage was the last freak he would be able to allow himself. Paganel was in a great state of embarrassment, but strangely enough could not make up his mind to speak the fatal word.

"Does not Miss Arabella please you then?" asked McNabbs.

"Oh, Major, she is charming," exclaimed Paganel, "a thousand times too charming, and if I must tell you all, she would please me better if she were less so. I wish she had a defect!"

"Be easy on that score," replied the Major, "she has, and more than one.

The most perfect woman in the world has always her quota.

So, Paganel, it is settled then, I suppose?"

"I dare not."

"Come, now, my learned friend, what makes you hesitate?"

"I am unworthy of Miss Arabella," was the invariable reply of the geographer. And to this he would stick.

At last, one day being fairly driven in a corner by the intractable Major, he ended by confiding to him, under the seal of secrecy, a certain peculiarity which would facilitate his apprehension should the police ever be on his track.

"Bah!" said the Major.

"It is really as I tell you," replied Paganel.

"What does it matter, my worthy friend?"

"Do you think so, Major?"

"On the contrary, it only makes you more uncommon. It adds to your personal merits. It is the very thing to make you the nonpareil husband that Arabella dreams about."

And the Major with imperturbable gravity left Paganel in a state of the utmost disquietude.

A short conversation ensued between McNabbs and Miss Arabella. A fortnight afterwards, the marriage was celebrated in grand style in the chapel of Malcolm Castle. Paganel looked magnificent, but closely buttoned up, and Miss Arabella was arrayed in splendor.

And this secret of the geographer would have been forever buried in oblivion, if the Major had not mentioned it to Glenarvan, and he could not hide it from Lady Helena, who gave a hint to Mrs. Mangles. To make a long story short, it got in the end to M. Olbinett's ears, and soon became noised abroad.

Jacques Paganel, during his three days' captivity among the Maories, had been tattooed from the feet to the shoulders, and he bore on his chest a heraldic kiwi with outspread wings, which was biting at his heart.

This was the only adventure of his grand voyage that Paganel could never get over, and he always bore a grudge to New Zealand on account of it. It was for this reason too, that, notwithstanding solicitation and regrets, he never would return to France. He dreaded lest he should expose the whole Geographical Society in his person to the jests of caricaturists and low newspapers, by their secretary coming back tattooed.

The return of the captain to Scotland was a national event, and Harry Grant was soon the most popular man in old Caledonia. His son Robert became a sailor like himself and Captain Mangles, and under the patronage of Lord Glenarvan they resumed the project of founding a Scotch colony in the Southern Seas.

TWENTY THOUSAND LEAGUES UNDER THE SEA

PART ONE

CHAPTER I A SHIFTING REEF

The year 1866 was signalised by a remarkable incident, a mysterious and puzzling phenomenon, which doubtless no one has yet forgotten. Not to mention rumours which agitated the maritime population and excited the public mind, even in the interior of continents, seafaring men were particularly excited. Merchants, common sailors, captains of vessels, skippers, both of Europe and America, naval officers of all countries, and the Governments of several States on the two continents, were deeply interested in the matter.

For some time past vessels had been met by "an enormous thing," a long object, spindle-shaped, occasionally phosphorescent, and infinitely larger and more rapid in its movements than a whale.

The facts relating to this apparition (entered in various log-books) agreed in most respects as to the shape of the object or creature in question, the untiring rapidity of its movements, its surprising power of locomotion, and the peculiar life with which it seemed endowed. If it was a whale, it surpassed in size all those hitherto classified in science. Taking into consideration the mean of observations made at divers times—rejecting the timid estimate of those who assigned to this object a length of two hundred feet, equally with the exaggerated opinions which set it down as a mile in width and three in length—we might fairly conclude that this mysterious being surpassed greatly all dimensions admitted by the learned ones of the day, if it existed at all. And that it DID exist was an undeniable fact; and, with that tendency which disposes the human mind in favour of the marvellous, we can understand the excitement produced in the entire world by this supernatural apparition. As to classing it in the list of fables, the idea was out of the question.

On the 20th of July, 1866, the steamer Governor Higginson, of the Calcutta and Burnach Steam Navigation Company, had met this moving mass five miles off the east coast of Australia. Captain Baker thought at first that he was in the presence of an unknown sandbank; he even prepared to determine its exact position when two columns of water, projected by the mysterious object, shot with a hissing noise a hundred and fifty feet up into the air. Now, unless the sandbank had been submitted to the intermittent eruption of a geyser, the Governor Higginson had to do neither more nor less than with an aquatic mammal, unknown till then, which threw up from its blow-holes columns of water mixed with air and vapour.

Similar facts were observed on the 23rd of July in the same year, in the Pacific Ocean, by the Columbus, of the West India and Pacific Steam Navigation Company. But this extraordinary creature could transport itself from one place to another with surprising velocity; as, in an interval of three days, the Governor Higginson and the Columbus had observed it at two different points of the chart, separated by a distance of more than seven hundred nautical leagues.

Fifteen days later, two thousand miles farther off, the Helvetia, of the Compagnie-Nationale, and the Shannon, of the Royal Mail Steamship Company, sailing to windward in that portion of the Atlantic lying between the United States and Europe, respectively signalled the monster to each other in 42° 15' N. lat. and 60° 35' W. long. In these simultaneous observations they thought themselves justified in estimating the minimum length of the mammal at more than three hundred and fifty feet, as the Shannon and Helvetia were of smaller dimensions than it, though they measured three hundred feet over all.

Now the largest whales, those which frequent those parts of the sea round the Aleutian, Kulammak, and Umgullich islands, have never exceeded the length of sixty yards, if they attain that.

In every place of great resort the monster was the fashion. They sang of it in the cafes, ridiculed it in the papers, and represented it on the stage. All kinds of stories were circulated regarding it. There appeared in the papers caricatures of every gigantic and imaginary creature, from the white whale, the terrible "Moby Dick" of sub-arctic regions, to the immense kraken, whose tentacles could entangle a ship of five hundred tons and hurry it into the abyss of the ocean. The legends of ancient times were even revived.

Then burst forth the unending argument between the believers and the unbelievers in the societies of the wise and the scientific journals. "The question of the monster" inflamed all minds. Editors of scientific journals, quarrelling with believers in the supernatural, spilled seas of ink during this memorable campaign, some even drawing blood; for from the sea-serpent they came to direct personalities.

During the first months of the year 1867 the question seemed buried, never to revive, when new facts were brought before the public. It was then no longer a scientific problem to be solved, but a real danger seriously to be avoided. The question took quite another shape. The monster became a small island, a rock, a reef, but a reef of indefinite and shifting proportions.

On the 5th of March, 1867, the Moravian, of the Montreal Ocean Company, finding herself during the night in 27° 30' lat. and 72° 15' long., struck on her starboard quarter a rock, marked in no chart for that part of the sea. Under the combined efforts of the wind and its four hundred horse power, it was going at the rate of thirteen knots. Had it not been for the superior strength of the hull of the Moravian, she would have been broken by the shock and gone down with the 237 passengers she was bringing home from Canada.

The accident happened about five o'clock in the morning, as the day was breaking. The officers of the quarter-deck hurried to the after-part of the vessel. They examined the sea with the most careful attention. They saw nothing but a strong eddy about three cables' length distant, as if the surface had been violently agitated. The bearings of the place were taken exactly, and the Moravian continued its route without apparent damage. Had it struck on a submerged rock, or on an enormous wreck? They could not tell; but, on examination of the ship's bottom when undergoing repairs, it was found that part of her keel was broken.

This fact, so grave in itself, might perhaps have been forgotten like many others if, three weeks after, it had not been re-enacted under similar circumstances. But, thanks to the nationality of the victim of the shock, thanks to the reputation of the company to which the vessel belonged, the circumstance became extensively circulated.

The 13th of April, 1867, the sea being beautiful, the breeze favourable, the Scotia, of the Cunard Company's line, found herself in 15° 12' long. and 45° 37' lat. She was going at the speed of thirteen knots and a half.

CHAPTER I A SHIFTING REEF

At seventeen minutes past four in the afternoon, whilst the passengers were assembled at lunch in the great saloon, a slight shock was felt on the hull of the Scotia, on her quarter, a little aft of the port-paddle.

The Scotia had not struck, but she had been struck, and seemingly by something rather sharp and penetrating than blunt. The shock had been so slight that no one had been alarmed, had it not been for the shouts of the carpenter's watch, who rushed on to the bridge, exclaiming, "We are sinking! we are sinking!" At first the passengers were much frightened, but Captain Anderson hastened to reassure them. The danger could not be imminent. The Scotia, divided into seven compartments by strong partitions, could brave with impunity any leak. Captain Anderson went down immediately into the hold. He found that the sea was pouring into the fifth compartment; and the rapidity of the influx proved that the force of the water was considerable. Fortunately this compartment did not hold the boilers, or the fires would have been immediately extinguished. Captain Anderson ordered the engines to be stopped at once, and one of the men went down to ascertain the extent of the injury. Some minutes afterwards they discovered the existence of a large hole, two yards in diameter, in the ship's bottom. Such a leak could not be stopped; and the Scotia, her paddles half submerged, was obliged to continue her course. She was then three hundred miles from Cape Clear, and, after three days' delay, which caused great uneasiness in Liverpool, she entered the basin of the company.

The engineers visited the Scotia, which was put in dry dock. They could scarcely believe it possible; at two yards and a half below water-mark was a regular rent, in the form of an isosceles triangle. The broken place in the iron plates was so perfectly defined that it could not have been more neatly done by a punch. It was clear, then, that the instrument producing the perforation was not of a common stamp and, after having been driven with prodigious strength, and piercing an iron plate 1 3/8 inches thick, had withdrawn itself by a backward motion.

Such was the last fact, which resulted in exciting once more the torrent of public opinion. From this moment all unlucky casualties which could not be otherwise accounted for were put down to the monster.

Upon this imaginary creature rested the responsibility of all these shipwrecks, which unfortunately were considerable; for of three thousand ships whose loss was annually recorded at Lloyd's, the number of sailing and steam-ships supposed to be totally lost, from the absence of all news, amounted to not less than two hundred!

Now, it was the "monster" who, justly or unjustly, was accused of their disappearance, and, thanks to it, communication between the different continents became more and more dangerous. The public demanded sharply that the seas should at any price be relieved from this formidable cetacean[1].

---

[1] Member of the whale family.

CHAPTER II PRO AND CON

At the period when these events took place, I had just returned from a scientific research in the disagreeable territory of Nebraska, in the United States. In virtue of my office as Assistant Professor in the Museum of Natural History in Paris, the French Government had attached me to that expedition. After six months in Nebraska, I arrived in New York towards the end of March, laden with a precious collection. My departure for France was fixed for the first days in May. Meanwhile I was occupying myself in classifying my mineralogical, botanical, and zoological riches, when the accident happened to the Scotia.

I was perfectly up in the subject which was the question of the day. How could I be otherwise? I had read and reread all the American and European papers without being any nearer a conclusion. This mystery puzzled me. Under the impossibility of forming an opinion, I jumped from one extreme to the other. That there really was something could not be doubted, and the incredulous were invited to put their finger on the wound of the Scotia.

On my arrival at New York the question was at its height. The theory of the floating island, and the unapproachable sandbank, supported by minds little competent to form a judgment, was abandoned. And, indeed, unless this shoal had a machine in its stomach, how could it change its position with such astonishing rapidity?

From the same cause, the idea of a floating hull of an enormous wreck was given up.

There remained, then, only two possible solutions of the question, which created two distinct parties: on one side, those who were for a monster of colossal strength; on the other, those who were for a submarine vessel of enormous motive power.

But this last theory, plausible as it was, could not stand against inquiries made in both worlds. That a private gentleman should have such a machine at his command was not likely. Where, when, and how was it built? and how could its construction have been kept secret? Certainly a Government might possess such a destructive machine. And in these disastrous times, when the ingenuity of man has multiplied the power of weapons of war, it was possible that, without the knowledge of others, a State might try to work such a formidable engine.

But the idea of a war machine fell before the declaration of Governments. As public interest was in question, and transatlantic communications suffered, their veracity could not be doubted. But how admit that the construction of this submarine boat had escaped the public eye? For a private gentleman to keep the secret under such circumstances would be very difficult, and for a State whose every act is persistently watched by powerful rivals, certainly impossible.

CHAPTER II PRO AND CON

Upon my arrival in New York several persons did me the honour of consulting me on the phenomenon in question. I had published in France a work in quarto, in two volumes, entitled Mysteries of the Great Submarine Grounds. This book, highly approved of in the learned world, gained for me a special reputation in this rather obscure branch of Natural History. My advice was asked. As long as I could deny the reality of the fact, I confined myself to a decided negative. But soon, finding myself driven into a corner, I was obliged to explain myself point by point. I discussed the question in all its forms, politically and scientifically; and I give here an extract from a carefully-studied article which I published in the number of the 30th of April. It ran as follows:

"After examining one by one the different theories, rejecting all other suggestions, it becomes necessary to admit the existence of a marine animal of enormous power.

"The great depths of the ocean are entirely unknown to us. Soundings cannot reach them. What passes in those remote depths—what beings live, or can live, twelve or fifteen miles beneath the surface of the waters—what is the organisation of these animals, we can scarcely conjecture. However, the solution of the problem submitted to me may modify the form of the dilemma. Either we do know all the varieties of beings which people our planet, or we do not. If we do NOT know them all—if Nature has still secrets in the deeps for us, nothing is more conformable to reason than to admit the existence of fishes, or cetaceans of other kinds, or even of new species, of an organisation formed to inhabit the strata inaccessible to soundings, and which an accident of some sort has brought at long intervals to the upper level of the ocean.

"If, on the contrary, we DO know all living kinds, we must necessarily seek for the animal in question amongst those marine beings already classed; and, in that case, I should be disposed to admit the existence of a gigantic narwhal.

"The common narwhal, or unicorn of the sea, often attains a length of sixty feet. Increase its size fivefold or tenfold, give it strength proportionate to its size, lengthen its destructive weapons, and you obtain the animal required. It will have the proportions determined by the officers of the Shannon, the instrument required by the perforation of the Scotia, and the power necessary to pierce the hull of the steamer.

"Indeed, the narwhal is armed with a sort of ivory sword, a halberd, according to the expression of certain naturalists. The principal tusk has the hardness of steel. Some of these tusks have been found buried in the bodies of whales, which the unicorn always attacks with success. Others have been drawn out, not without trouble, from the bottoms of ships, which they had pierced through and through, as a gimlet pierces a barrel. The Museum of the Faculty of Medicine of Paris possesses one of these defensive weapons, two yards and a quarter in length, and fifteen inches in diameter at the base.

"Very well! suppose this weapon to be six times stronger and the animal ten times more powerful; launch it at the rate of twenty miles an hour, and you obtain a shock capable of producing the catastrophe required. Until further information, therefore, I shall maintain it to be a sea-unicorn of colossal dimensions, armed not with a halberd, but with a real spur, as the armoured frigates, or the `rams' of war, whose massiveness and motive power it would possess at the same time. Thus may this puzzling phenomenon be explained, unless there be something over and above all that one has ever conjectured, seen, perceived, or experienced; which is just within the bounds of possibility."

These last words were cowardly on my part; but, up to a certain point, I wished to shelter my dignity as professor, and not give too much cause for laughter to the Americans, who laugh well when they do laugh. I reserved for myself a way of escape. In effect, however, I admitted the existence of the "monster." My article was warmly discussed, which procured it a high reputation. It rallied round it a certain number of partisans. The solution it proposed gave, at least, full liberty to the imagination. The human mind delights in grand conceptions of supernatural beings. And the sea is precisely their best vehicle, the only medium through which these giants (against which terrestrial animals, such as elephants or rhinoceroses, are as nothing) can be produced or developed.

The industrial and commercial papers treated the question chiefly from this point of view. The Shipping and Mercantile Gazette, the Lloyd's List, the Packet-Boat, and the Maritime and Colonial Review, all papers devoted to insurance companies which threatened to raise their rates of premium, were unanimous on this point. Public opinion had been pronounced. The United States were the first in the field; and in New York they made preparations for an expedition destined to pursue this narwhal. A frigate of great speed, the Abraham Lincoln, was put in commission as soon as possible. The arsenals were opened to Commander Farragut, who hastened the arming of his frigate; but, as it always happens, the moment it was decided to pursue the monster, the monster did not appear. For two months no one heard it spoken of. No ship met with it. It seemed as if this unicorn knew of the plots weaving around it. It had been so much talked of, even through the Atlantic cable, that jesters pretended that this slender fly had stopped a telegram on its passage and was making the most of it.

So when the frigate had been armed for a long campaign, and provided with formidable fishing apparatus, no one could tell what course to pursue. Impatience grew apace, when, on the 2nd of July, they learned that a steamer of the line of San Francisco, from California to Shanghai, had seen the animal three weeks before in the North Pacific Ocean. The excitement caused by this news was extreme. The ship was revictualled and well stocked with coal.

Three hours before the Abraham Lincoln left Brooklyn pier, I received a letter worded as follows:

To M. ARONNAX, Professor in the Museum of Paris, Fifth Avenue Hotel, New York.

SIR,—If you will consent to join the Abraham Lincoln in this expedition, the Government of the United States will with pleasure see France represented in the enterprise. Commander Farragut has a cabin at your disposal.

Very cordially yours, J.B. HOBSON, Secretary of Marine.

CHAPTER III I FORM MY RESOLUTION

Three seconds before the arrival of J. B. Hobson's letter I no more thought of pursuing the unicorn than of attempting the passage of the North Sea. Three seconds after reading the letter of the honourable Secretary of Marine, I felt that my true vocation, the sole end of my life, was to chase this disturbing monster and purge it from the world.

But I had just returned from a fatiguing journey, weary and longing for repose. I aspired to nothing more than again seeing my country, my friends, my little lodging by the Jardin des Plantes, my dear and precious collections—but nothing could keep me back! I forgot all—fatigue, friends and collections—and accepted without hesitation the offer of the American Government.

"Besides," thought I, "all roads lead back to Europe; and the unicorn may be amiable enough to hurry me towards the coast of France. This worthy animal may allow itself to be caught in the seas of Europe (for my particular benefit), and I will not bring back less than half a yard of his ivory halberd to the Museum of Natural History." But in the meanwhile I must seek this narwhal in the North Pacific Ocean, which, to return to France, was taking the road to the antipodes.

"Conseil," I called in an impatient voice.

Conseil was my servant, a true, devoted Flemish boy, who had accompanied me in all my travels. I liked him, and he returned the liking well. He was quiet by nature, regular from principle, zealous from habit, evincing little disturbance at the different surprises of life, very quick with his hands, and apt at any service required of him; and, despite his name, never giving advice—even when asked for it.

Conseil had followed me for the last ten years wherever science led. Never once did he complain of the length or fatigue of a journey, never make an objection to pack his portmanteau for whatever country it might be, or however far away, whether China or Congo. Besides all this, he had good health, which defied all sickness, and solid muscles, but no nerves; good morals are understood. This boy was thirty years old, and his age to that of his master as fifteen to twenty. May I be excused for saying that I was forty years old?

But Conseil had one fault: he was ceremonious to a degree, and would never speak to me but in the third person, which was sometimes provoking.

"Conseil," said I again, beginning with feverish hands to make preparations for my departure.

Certainly I was sure of this devoted boy. As a rule, I never asked him if it were convenient for him or not to follow me in my travels; but this time the expedition in question might be prolonged, and the enterprise might be hazardous in pursuit of an animal capable of sinking a frigate as easily as a nutshell. Here there was matter for reflection even to the most impassive man in the world. What would Conseil say?

"Conseil," I called a third time.

Conseil appeared.

"Did you call, sir?" said he, entering.

"Yes, my boy; make preparations for me and yourself too. We leave in two hours."

"As you please, sir," replied Conseil, quietly.

"Not an instant to lose; lock in my trunk all travelling utensils, coats, shirts, and stockings—without counting, as many as you can, and make haste."

"And your collections, sir?" observed Conseil.

"They will keep them at the hotel."

"We are not returning to Paris, then?" said Conseil.

"Oh! certainly," I answered, evasively, "by making a curve."

"Will the curve please you, sir?"

"Oh! it will be nothing; not quite so direct a road, that is all. We take our passage in the Abraham, Lincoln."

"As you think proper, sir," coolly replied Conseil.

"You see, my friend, it has to do with the monster—the famous narwhal. We are going to purge it from the seas. A glorious mission, but a dangerous one! We cannot tell where we may go; these animals can be very capricious. But we will go whether or no; we have got a captain who is pretty wide-awake."

Our luggage was transported to the deck of the frigate immediately. I hastened on board and asked for Commander Farragut. One of the sailors conducted me to the poop, where I found myself in the presence of a good-looking officer, who held out his hand to me.

"Monsieur Pierre Aronnax?" said he.

"Himself," replied I. "Commander Farragut?"

"You are welcome, Professor; your cabin is ready for you."

I bowed, and desired to be conducted to the cabin destined for me.

The Abraham Lincoln had been well chosen and equipped for her new destination. She was a frigate of great speed, fitted with high-pressure engines which admitted a pressure of seven atmospheres. Under this the Abraham Lincoln attained the mean speed of nearly eighteen knots and a third an hour—a considerable speed, but, nevertheless, insufficient to grapple with this gigantic cetacean.

The interior arrangements of the frigate corresponded to its nautical qualities. I was well satisfied with my cabin, which was in the after part, opening upon the gunroom.

"We shall be well off here," said I to Conseil.

"As well, by your honour's leave, as a hermit-crab in the shell of a whelk," said Conseil.

I left Conseil to stow our trunks conveniently away, and remounted the poop in order to survey the preparations for departure.

At that moment Commander Farragut was ordering the last moorings to be cast loose which held the Abraham Lincoln to the pier of Brooklyn. So in a quarter of an hour, perhaps less, the frigate would have sailed without me. I should have missed this extraordinary, supernatural, and incredible expedition, the recital of which may well meet with some suspicion.

But Commander Farragut would not lose a day nor an hour in scouring the seas in which the animal had been sighted. He sent for the engineer.

"Is the steam full on?" asked he.

"Yes, sir," replied the engineer.

"Go ahead," cried Commander Farragut.

CHAPTER IV NED LAND

Captain Farragut was a good seaman, worthy of the frigate he commanded. His vessel and he were one. He was the soul of it. On the question of the monster there was no doubt in his mind, and he would not allow the existence of the animal to be disputed on board. He believed in it, as certain good women believe in the leviathan—by faith, not by reason. The monster did exist, and he had sworn to rid the seas of it. Either Captain Farragut would kill the narwhal, or the narwhal would kill the captain. There was no third course.

The officers on board shared the opinion of their chief. They were ever chatting, discussing, and calculating the various chances of a meeting, watching narrowly the vast surface of the ocean. More than one took up his quarters voluntarily in the cross-trees, who would have cursed such a berth under any other circumstances. As long as the sun described its daily course, the rigging was crowded with sailors, whose feet were burnt to such an extent by the heat of the deck as to render it unbearable; still the Abraham Lincoln had not yet breasted the suspected waters of the Pacific. As to the ship's company, they desired nothing better than to meet the unicorn, to harpoon it, hoist it on board, and despatch it. They watched the sea with eager attention.

Besides, Captain Farragut had spoken of a certain sum of two thousand dollars, set apart for whoever should first sight the monster, were he cabin-boy, common seaman, or officer.

I leave you to judge how eyes were used on board the Abraham Lincoln.

For my own part I was not behind the others, and, left to no one my share of daily observations. The frigate might have been called the Argus, for a hundred reasons. Only one amongst us, Conseil, seemed to protest by his indifference against the question which so interested us all, and seemed to be out of keeping with the general enthusiasm on board.

I have said that Captain Farragut had carefully provided his ship with every apparatus for catching the gigantic cetacean. No whaler had ever been better armed. We possessed every known engine, from the harpoon thrown by the hand to the barbed arrows of the blunderbuss, and the explosive balls of the duck-gun. On the forecastle lay the perfection of a breech-loading gun, very thick at the breech, and very narrow in the bore, the model of which had been in the Exhibition of 1867. This precious weapon of American origin could throw with ease a conical projectile of nine pounds to a mean distance of ten miles.

Thus the Abraham Lincoln wanted for no means of destruction; and, what was better still she had on board Ned Land, the prince of harpooners.

Ned Land was a Canadian, with an uncommon quickness of hand, and who knew no equal in his dangerous occupation. Skill, coolness, audacity, and cunning he possessed in a superior degree, and it must be a cunning whale to escape the stroke of his harpoon.

Ned Land was about forty years of age; he was a tall man (more than six feet high), strongly built, grave and taciturn, occasionally violent, and very passionate when contradicted. His person attracted attention, but above all the boldness of his look, which gave a singular expression to his face.

Who calls himself Canadian calls himself French; and, little communicative as Ned Land was, I must admit that he took a certain liking for me. My nationality drew him to me, no doubt. It was an opportunity for him to talk, and for me to hear, that old language of Rabelais, which is still in use in some Canadian provinces. The harpooner's family was originally from Quebec, and was already a tribe of hardy fishermen when this town belonged to France.

Little by little, Ned Land acquired a taste for chatting, and I loved to hear the recital of his adventures in the polar seas. He related his fishing, and his combats, with natural poetry of expression; his recital took the form of an epic poem, and I seemed to be listening to a Canadian Homer singing the Iliad of the regions of the North.

I am portraying this hardy companion as I really knew him. We are old friends now, united in that unchangeable friendship which is born and cemented amidst extreme dangers. Ah, brave Ned! I ask no more than to live a hundred years longer, that I may have more time to dwell the longer on your memory.

Now, what was Ned Land's opinion upon the question of the marine monster? I must admit that he did not believe in the unicorn, and was the only one on board who did not share that universal conviction. He even avoided the subject, which I one day thought it my duty to press upon him. One magnificent evening, the 30th July (that is to say, three weeks after our departure), the frigate was abreast of Cape Blanc, thirty miles to leeward of the coast of Patagonia. We had crossed the tropic of Capricorn, and the Straits of Magellan opened less than seven hundred miles to the south. Before eight days were over the Abraham Lincoln would be ploughing the waters of the Pacific.

Seated on the poop, Ned Land and I were chatting of one thing and another as we looked at this mysterious sea, whose great depths had up to this time been inaccessible to the eye of man. I naturally led up the conversation to the giant unicorn, and examined the various chances of success or failure of the expedition. But, seeing that Ned Land let me speak without saying too much himself, I pressed him more closely.

"Well, Ned," said I, "is it possible that you are not convinced of the existence of this cetacean that we are following? Have you any particular reason for being so incredulous?"

The harpooner looked at me fixedly for some moments before answering, struck his broad forehead with his hand (a habit of his), as if to collect himself, and said at last, "Perhaps I have, Mr. Aronnax."

"But, Ned, you, a whaler by profession, familiarised with all the great marine mammalia—YOU ought to be the last to doubt under such circumstances!"

"That is just what deceives you, Professor," replied Ned. "As a whaler I have followed many a cetacean, harpooned a great number, and killed several; but, however strong or well-armed they may have been, neither their tails nor their weapons would have been able even to scratch the iron plates of a steamer."

"But, Ned, they tell of ships which the teeth of the narwhal have pierced through and through."

"Wooden ships—that is possible," replied the Canadian, "but I have never seen it done; and, until further proof, I deny that whales, cetaceans, or sea-unicorns could ever produce the effect you describe."

"Well, Ned, I repeat it with a conviction resting on the logic of facts. I believe in the existence of a mammal power fully organised, belonging to the branch of vertebrata, like the whales, the cachalots, or the dolphins, and furnished with a horn of defence of great penetrating power."

"Hum!" said the harpooner, shaking his head with the air of a man who would not be convinced.

"Notice one thing, my worthy Canadian," I resumed. "If such an animal is in existence, if it inhabits the depths of the ocean, if it frequents the strata lying miles below the surface of the water, it must necessarily possess an organisation the strength of which would defy all comparison."

"And why this powerful organisation?" demanded Ned.

"Because it requires incalculable strength to keep one's self in these strata and resist their pressure. Listen to me. Let us admit that the pressure of the atmosphere is represented by the weight of a column of water thirty-two feet high. In reality the column of water would be shorter, as we are speaking of sea water, the density of which is greater than that of fresh water. Very well, when you dive, Ned, as many times 32 feet of water as there are above you, so many times does your body bear a pressure equal to that of the atmosphere, that is to say, 15 lb. for each square inch of its surface. It follows, then, that at 320 feet this pressure equals that of 10 atmospheres, of 100 atmospheres at 3,200 feet, and of 1,000 atmospheres at 32,000 feet, that is, about 6 miles; which is equivalent to saying that if you could attain this depth in the ocean, each square three-eighths of an inch of the surface of your body would bear a pressure of 5,600 lb. Ah! my brave Ned, do you know how many square inches you carry on the surface of your body?"

"I have no idea, Mr. Aronnax."

"About 6,500; and as in reality the atmospheric pressure is about 15 lb. to the square inch, your 6,500 square inches bear at this moment a pressure of 97,500 lb."

"Without my perceiving it?"

"Without your perceiving it. And if you are not crushed by such a pressure, it is because the air penetrates the interior of your body with equal pressure. Hence perfect equilibrium between the interior and exterior pressure, which thus neutralise each other, and which allows you to bear it without inconvenience. But in the water it is another thing."

"Yes, I understand," replied Ned, becoming more attentive; "because the water surrounds me, but does not penetrate."

"Precisely, Ned: so that at 32 feet beneath the surface of the sea you would undergo a pressure of 97,500 lb.; at 320 feet, ten times that pressure; at 3,200 feet, a hundred times that pressure; lastly, at 32,000 feet, a thousand times that pressure would be 97,500,000 lb.—that is to say, that you would be flattened as if you had been drawn from the plates of a hydraulic machine!"

"The devil!" exclaimed Ned.

"Very well, my worthy harpooner, if some vertebrate, several hundred yards long, and large in proportion, can maintain itself in such depths—of those whose surface is represented by millions of square inches, that is by tens of millions of pounds, we must estimate the pressure they undergo. Consider, then, what must be the resistance of their bony structure, and the strength of their organisation to withstand such pressure!"

"Why!" exclaimed Ned Land, "they must be made of iron plates eight inches thick, like the armoured frigates."

"As you say, Ned. And think what destruction such a mass would cause, if hurled with the speed of an express train against the hull of a vessel."

"Yes—certainly—perhaps," replied the Canadian, shaken by these figures, but not yet willing to give in.

"Well, have I convinced you?"

"You have convinced me of one thing, sir, which is that, if such animals do exist at the bottom of the seas, they must necessarily be as strong as you say."

"But if they do not exist, mine obstinate harpooner, how explain the accident to the Scotia?"

CHAPTER V AT A VENTURE

The voyage of the Abraham Lincoln was for a long time marked by no special incident. But one circumstance happened which showed the wonderful dexterity of Ned Land, and proved what confidence we might place in him.

The 30th of June, the frigate spoke some American whalers, from whom we learned that they knew nothing about the narwhal. But one of them, the captain of the Monroe, knowing that Ned Land had shipped on board the Abraham Lincoln, begged for his help in chasing a whale they had in sight. Commander Farragut, desirous of seeing Ned Land at work, gave him permission to go on board the Monroe. And fate served our Canadian so well that, instead of one whale, he harpooned two with a double blow, striking one straight to the heart, and catching the other after some minutes' pursuit.

Decidedly, if the monster ever had to do with Ned Land's harpoon, I would not bet in its favour.

The frigate skirted the south-east coast of America with great rapidity. The 3rd of July we were at the opening of the Straits of Magellan, level with Cape Vierges. But Commander Farragut would not take a tortuous passage, but doubled Cape Horn.

The ship's crew agreed with him. And certainly it was possible that they might meet the narwhal in this narrow pass. Many of the sailors affirmed that the monster could not pass there, "that he was too big for that!"

The 6th of July, about three o'clock in the afternoon, the Abraham Lincoln, at fifteen miles to the south, doubled the solitary island, this lost rock at the extremity of the American continent, to which some Dutch sailors gave the name of their native town, Cape Horn. The course was taken towards the north-west, and the next day the screw of the frigate was at last beating the waters of the Pacific.

"Keep your eyes open!" called out the sailors.

And they were opened widely. Both eyes and glasses, a little dazzled, it is true, by the prospect of two thousand dollars, had not an instant's repose.

I myself, for whom money had no charms, was not the least attentive on board. Giving but few minutes to my meals, but a few hours to sleep, indifferent to either rain or sunshine, I did not leave the poop of the vessel. Now leaning on the netting of the forecastle, now on the taffrail, I devoured with eagerness the soft foam which whitened the sea as far as the eye could reach; and how often have I shared the emotion of the majority of the crew, when some capricious whale raised its black back above the waves! The poop of the vessel was crowded on a moment. The cabins poured forth a torrent of sailors and officers, each with heaving breast and troubled eye watching the course of the cetacean. I looked and looked till I was nearly blind, whilst Conseil kept repeating in a calm voice:

"If, sir, you would not squint so much, you would see better!"

But vain excitement! The Abraham Lincoln checked its speed and made for the animal signalled, a simple whale, or common cachalot, which soon disappeared amidst a storm of abuse.

But the weather was good. The voyage was being accomplished under the most favourable auspices. It was then the bad season in Australia, the July of that zone corresponding to our January in Europe, but the sea was beautiful and easily scanned round a vast circumference.

The 20th of July, the tropic of Capricorn was cut by 105d of longitude, and the 27th of the same month we crossed the Equator on the 110th meridian. This passed, the frigate took a more decided westerly direction, and scoured the central waters of the Pacific. Commander Farragut thought, and with reason, that it was better to remain in deep water, and keep clear of continents or islands, which the beast itself seemed to shun (perhaps because there was not enough water for him! suggested the greater part of the crew). The frigate passed at some distance from the Marquesas and the Sandwich Islands, crossed the tropic of Cancer, and made for the China Seas. We were on the theatre of the last diversions of the monster: and, to say truth, we no longer LIVED on board. The entire ship's crew were undergoing a nervous excitement, of which I can give no idea: they could not eat, they could not sleep—twenty times a day, a misconception or an optical illusion of some sailor seated on the taffrail, would cause dreadful perspirations, and these emotions, twenty times repeated, kept us in a state of excitement so violent that a reaction was unavoidable.

And truly, reaction soon showed itself. For three months, during which a day seemed an age, the Abraham Lincoln furrowed all the waters of the Northern Pacific, running at whales, making sharp deviations from her course, veering suddenly from one tack to another, stopping suddenly, putting on steam, and backing ever and anon at the risk of deranging her machinery, and not one point of the Japanese or American coast was left unexplored.

The warmest partisans of the enterprise now became its most ardent detractors. Reaction mounted from the crew to the captain himself, and certainly, had it not been for the resolute determination on the part of Captain Farragut, the frigate would have headed due southward. This useless search could not last much longer. The Abraham Lincoln had nothing to reproach herself with, she had done her best to succeed. Never had an American ship's crew shown more zeal or patience; its failure could not be placed to their charge—there remained nothing but to return.

This was represented to the commander. The sailors could not hide their discontent, and the service suffered. I will not say there was a mutiny on board, but after a reasonable period of obstinacy, Captain Farragut (as Columbus did) asked for three days' patience. If in three days the monster did not appear, the man at the helm should give three turns of the wheel, and the Abraham Lincoln would make for the European seas.

This promise was made on the 2nd of November. It had the effect of rallying the ship's crew. The ocean was watched with renewed attention. Each one wished for a last glance in which to sum up his remembrance. Glasses were used with feverish activity. It was a grand defiance given to the giant narwhal, and he could scarcely fail to answer the summons and "appear."

Two days passed, the steam was at half pressure; a thousand schemes were tried to attract the attention and stimulate the apathy of the animal in case it should be met in those parts. Large quantities of bacon were trailed in the wake of the ship, to the great satisfaction (I must say) of the sharks. Small craft radiated in all directions round the Abraham

Lincoln as she lay to, and did not leave a spot of the sea unexplored. But the night of the 4th of November arrived without the unveiling of this submarine mystery.

The next day, the 5th of November, at twelve, the delay would (morally speaking) expire; after that time, Commander Farragut, faithful to his promise, was to turn the course to the south-east and abandon for ever the northern regions of the Pacific.

The frigate was then in 31° 15' N. lat. and 136° 42' E. long. The coast of Japan still remained less than two hundred miles to leeward. Night was approaching. They had just struck eight bells; large clouds veiled the face of the moon, then in its first quarter. The sea undulated peaceably under the stern of the vessel.

At that moment I was leaning forward on the starboard netting. Conseil, standing near me, was looking straight before him. The crew, perched in the ratlines, examined the horizon which contracted and darkened by degrees. Officers with their night glasses scoured the growing darkness: sometimes the ocean sparkled under the rays of the moon, which darted between two clouds, then all trace of light was lost in the darkness.

In looking at Conseil, I could see he was undergoing a little of the general influence. At least I thought so. Perhaps for the first time his nerves vibrated to a sentiment of curiosity.

"Come, Conseil," said I, "this is the last chance of pocketing the two thousand dollars."

"May I be permitted to say, sir," replied Conseil, "that I never reckoned on getting the prize; and, had the government of the Union offered a hundred thousand dollars, it would have been none the poorer."

"You are right, Conseil. It is a foolish affair after all, and one upon which we entered too lightly. What time lost, what useless emotions! We should have been back in France six months ago."

"In your little room, sir," replied Conseil, "and in your museum, sir; and I should have already classed all your fossils, sir. And the Babiroussa would have been installed in its cage in the Jardin des Plantes, and have drawn all the curious people of the capital!"

"As you say, Conseil. I fancy we shall run a fair chance of being laughed at for our pains."

"That's tolerably certain," replied Conseil, quietly; "I think they will make fun of you, sir. And, must I say it——?"

"Go on, my good friend."

"Well, sir, you will only get your deserts."

"Indeed!"

"When one has the honour of being a savant as you are, sir, one should not expose one's self to——"

Conseil had not time to finish his compliment. In the midst of general silence a voice had just been heard. It was the voice of Ned Land shouting:

"Look out there! The very thing we are looking for—on our weather beam!"

CHAPTER VI AT FULL STEAM

At this cry the whole ship's crew hurried towards the harpooner—commander, officers, masters, sailors, cabin boys; even the engineers left their engines, and the stokers their furnaces.

The order to stop her had been given, and the frigate now simply went on by her own momentum. The darkness was then profound, and, however good the Canadian's eyes were, I asked myself how he had managed to see, and what he had been able to see. My heart beat as if it would break. But Ned Land was not mistaken, and we all perceived the object he pointed to. At two cables' length from the Abraham Lincoln, on the starboard quarter, the sea seemed to be illuminated all over. It was not a mere phosphoric phenomenon. The monster emerged some fathoms from the water, and then threw out that very intense but mysterious light mentioned in the report of several captains. This magnificent irradiation must have been produced by an agent of great SHINING power. The luminous part traced on the sea an immense oval, much elongated, the centre of which condensed a burning heat, whose overpowering brilliancy died out by successive gradations.

"It is only a massing of phosphoric particles," cried one of the officers.

"No, sir, certainly not," I replied. "That brightness is of an essentially electrical nature. Besides, see, see! it moves; it is moving forwards, backwards; it is darting towards us!"

A general cry arose from the frigate.

"Silence!" said the captain. "Up with the helm, reverse the engines."

The steam was shut off, and the Abraham Lincoln, beating to port, described a semicircle.

"Right the helm, go ahead," cried the captain.

These orders were executed, and the frigate moved rapidly from the burning light.

I was mistaken. She tried to sheer off, but the supernatural animal approached with a velocity double her own.

We gasped for breath. Stupefaction more than fear made us dumb and motionless. The animal gained on us, sporting with the waves. It made the round of the frigate, which was then making fourteen knots, and enveloped it with its electric rings like luminous dust.

Then it moved away two or three miles, leaving a phosphorescent track, like those volumes of steam that the express trains leave behind. All at once from the dark line of the horizon whither it retired to gain its momentum, the monster rushed suddenly towards the Abraham Lincoln with alarming rapidity, stopped suddenly about twenty feet from the hull, and died out—not diving under the water, for its brilliancy did not abate—but suddenly, and as if the source of this brilliant emanation was exhausted. Then it reappeared on the other side of the vessel, as if it had turned and slid under the hull. Any moment a collision might have occurred which would have been fatal to us. However, I was astonished at the manoeuvres of the frigate. She fled and did not attack.

On the captain's face, generally so impassive, was an expression of unaccountable astonishment.

"Mr. Aronnax," he said, "I do not know with what formidable being I have to deal, and I will not imprudently risk my frigate in the midst of this darkness. Besides, how attack this unknown thing, how defend one's self from it? Wait for daylight, and the scene will change."

"You have no further doubt, captain, of the nature of the animal?"

"No, sir; it is evidently a gigantic narwhal, and an electric one."

"Perhaps," added I, "one can only approach it with a torpedo."

"Undoubtedly," replied the captain, "if it possesses such dreadful power, it is the most terrible animal that ever was created. That is why, sir, I must be on my guard."

The crew were on their feet all night. No one thought of sleep. The Abraham Lincoln, not being able to struggle with such velocity, had moderated its pace, and sailed at half speed. For its part, the narwhal, imitating the frigate, let the waves rock it at will, and seemed decided not to leave the scene of the struggle. Towards midnight, however, it disappeared, or, to use a more appropriate term, it "died out" like a large glow-worm. Had it fled? One could only fear, not hope it. But at seven minutes to one o'clock in the morning a deafening whistling was heard, like that produced by a body of water rushing with great violence.

The captain, Ned Land, and I were then on the poop, eagerly peering through the profound darkness.

"Ned Land," asked the commander, "you have often heard the roaring of whales?"

"Often, sir; but never such whales the sight of which brought me in two thousand dollars. If I can only approach within four harpoons' length of it!"

"But to approach it," said the commander, "I ought to put a whaler at your disposal?"

"Certainly, sir."

"That will be trifling with the lives of my men."

"And mine too," simply said the harpooner.

Towards two o'clock in the morning, the burning light reappeared, not less intense, about five miles to windward of the Abraham Lincoln. Notwithstanding the distance, and the noise of the wind and sea, one heard distinctly the loud strokes of the animal's tail, and even its panting breath. It seemed that, at the moment that the enormous narwhal had come to take breath at the surface of the water, the air was engulfed in its lungs, like the steam in the vast cylinders of a machine of two thousand horse-power.

"Hum!" thought I, "a whale with the strength of a cavalry regiment would be a pretty whale!"

We were on the qui vive till daylight, and prepared for the combat. The fishing implements were laid along the hammock nettings. The second lieutenant loaded the blunder busses, which could throw harpoons to the distance of a mile, and long duck-guns, with explosive bullets, which inflicted mortal wounds even to the most terrible animals. Ned Land contented himself with sharpening his harpoon—a terrible weapon in his hands.

At six o'clock day began to break; and, with the first glimmer of light, the electric light of the narwhal disappeared. At seven o'clock the day was sufficiently advanced, but a very thick sea fog obscured our view, and the best spy glasses could not pierce it. That caused disappointment and anger.

I climbed the mizzen-mast. Some officers were already perched on the mast-heads. At eight o'clock the fog lay heavily on the waves, and its thick scrolls rose little by little. The horizon grew wider and clearer at the same time. Suddenly, just as on the day before, Ned Land's voice was heard:

"The thing itself on the port quarter!" cried the harpooner.

Every eye was turned towards the point indicated. There, a mile and a half from the frigate, a long blackish body emerged a yard above the waves. Its tail, violently agitated, produced a considerable eddy. Never did a tail beat the sea with such violence. An immense track, of dazzling whiteness, marked the passage of the animal, and described a long curve.

The frigate approached the cetacean. I examined it thoroughly.

The reports of the Shannon and of the Helvetia had rather exaggerated its size, and I estimated its length at only two hundred and fifty feet. As to its dimensions, I could only conjecture them to be admirably proportioned. While I watched this phenomenon, two jets of steam and water were ejected from its vents, and rose to the height of 120 feet; thus I ascertained its way of breathing. I concluded definitely that it belonged to the vertebrate branch, class mammalia.

The crew waited impatiently for their chief's orders. The latter, after having observed the animal attentively, called the engineer. The engineer ran to him.

"Sir," said the commander, "you have steam up?"

"Yes, sir," answered the engineer.

"Well, make up your fires and put on all steam."

Three hurrahs greeted this order. The time for the struggle had arrived. Some moments after, the two funnels of the frigate vomited torrents of black smoke, and the bridge quaked under the trembling of the boilers.

The Abraham Lincoln, propelled by her wonderful screw, went straight at the animal. The latter allowed it to come within half a cable's length; then, as if disdaining to dive, it took a little turn, and stopped a short distance off.

This pursuit lasted nearly three-quarters of an hour, without the frigate gaining two yards on the cetacean. It was quite evident that at that rate we should never come up with it.

"Well, Mr. Land," asked the captain, "do you advise me to put the boats out to sea?"

"No, sir," replied Ned Land; "because we shall not take that beast easily."

"What shall we do then?"

"Put on more steam if you can, sir. With your leave, I mean to post myself under the bowsprit, and, if we get within harpooning distance, I shall throw my harpoon."

"Go, Ned," said the captain. "Engineer, put on more pressure."

Ned Land went to his post. The fires were increased, the screw revolved forty-three times a minute, and the steam poured out of the valves. We heaved the log, and calculated that the Abraham Lincoln was going at the rate of 18 1/2 miles an hour.

But the accursed animal swam at the same speed.

For a whole hour the frigate kept up this pace, without gaining six feet. It was humiliating for one of the swiftest sailers in the American navy. A stubborn anger seized the crew; the sailors abused the monster, who, as before, disdained to answer them; the captain no longer contented himself with twisting his beard—he gnawed it.

The engineer was called again.

"You have turned full steam on?"

"Yes, sir," replied the engineer.

The speed of the Abraham Lincoln increased. Its masts trembled down to their stepping holes, and the clouds of smoke could hardly find way out of the narrow funnels.

They heaved the log a second time.

"Well?" asked the captain of the man at the wheel.

"Nineteen miles and three-tenths, sir."

"Clap on more steam."

The engineer obeyed. The manometer showed ten degrees. But the cetacean grew warm itself, no doubt; for without straining itself, it made 19 3/10 miles.

What a pursuit! No, I cannot describe the emotion that vibrated through me. Ned Land kept his post, harpoon in hand. Several times the animal let us gain upon it.—"We shall catch it! we shall catch it!" cried the Canadian. But just as he was going to strike, the cetacean stole away with a rapidity that could not be estimated at less than thirty miles an hour, and even during our maximum of speed, it bullied the frigate, going round and round it. A cry of fury broke from everyone!

At noon we were no further advanced than at eight o'clock in the morning.

The captain then decided to take more direct means.

"Ah!" said he, "that animal goes quicker than the Abraham Lincoln. Very well! we will see whether it will escape these conical bullets. Send your men to the forecastle, sir."

The forecastle gun was immediately loaded and slewed round. But the shot passed some feet above the cetacean, which was half a mile off.

"Another, more to the right," cried the commander, "and five dollars to whoever will hit that infernal beast."

An old gunner with a grey beard—that I can see now—with steady eye and grave face, went up to the gun and took a long aim. A loud report was heard, with which were mingled the cheers of the crew.

The bullet did its work; it hit the animal, and, sliding off the rounded surface, was lost in two miles depth of sea.

The chase began again, and the captain, leaning towards me, said:

"I will pursue that beast till my frigate bursts up."

"Yes," answered I; "and you will be quite right to do it."

I wished the beast would exhaust itself, and not be insensible to fatigue like a steam engine. But it was of no use. Hours passed, without its showing any signs of exhaustion.

However, it must be said in praise of the Abraham Lincoln that she struggled on indefatigably. I cannot reckon the distance she made under three hundred miles during this unlucky day, November the 6th. But night came on, and overshadowed the rough ocean.

Now I thought our expedition was at an end, and that we should never again see the extraordinary animal. I was mistaken. At ten minutes to eleven in the evening, the electric light reappeared three miles to windward of the frigate, as pure, as intense as during the preceding night.

The narwhal seemed motionless; perhaps, tired with its day's work, it slept, letting itself float with the undulation of the waves. Now was a chance of which the captain resolved to take advantage.

He gave his orders. The Abraham Lincoln kept up half steam, and advanced cautiously so as not to awake its adversary. It is no rare thing to meet in the middle of the ocean whales so sound asleep that they can be successfully attacked, and Ned Land had harpooned more than one during its sleep. The Canadian went to take his place again under the bowsprit.

The frigate approached noiselessly, stopped at two cables' lengths from the animal, and following its track. No one breathed; a deep silence reigned on the bridge. We were not a hundred feet from the burning focus, the light of which increased and dazzled our eyes.

At this moment, leaning on the forecastle bulwark, I saw below me Ned Land grappling the martingale in one hand, brandishing his terrible harpoon in the other, scarcely twenty feet from the motionless animal. Suddenly his arm straightened, and the harpoon was thrown; I heard the sonorous stroke of the weapon, which seemed to have struck a hard body. The electric light went out suddenly, and two enormous waterspouts broke over the bridge of the frigate, rushing like a torrent from stem to stern, overthrowing men, and breaking the lashings of the spars. A fearful shock followed, and, thrown over the rail without having time to stop myself, I fell into the sea.

CHAPTER VII AN UNKNOWN SPECIES OF WHALE

This unexpected fall so stunned me that I have no clear recollection of my sensations at the time. I was at first drawn down to a depth of about twenty feet. I am a good swimmer (though without pretending to rival Byron or Edgar Poe, who were masters of the art), and in that plunge I did not lose my presence of mind. Two vigorous strokes brought me to the surface of the water. My first care was to look for the frigate. Had the crew seen me disappear? Had the Abraham Lincoln veered round? Would the captain put out a boat? Might I hope to be saved?

The darkness was intense. I caught a glimpse of a black mass disappearing in the east, its beacon lights dying out in the distance. It was the frigate! I was lost.

"Help, help!" I shouted, swimming towards the Abraham Lincoln in desperation.

My clothes encumbered me; they seemed glued to my body, and paralysed my movements.

I was sinking! I was suffocating!

"Help!"

This was my last cry. My mouth filled with water; I struggled against being drawn down the abyss. Suddenly my clothes were seized by a strong hand, and I felt myself quickly drawn up to the surface of the sea; and I heard, yes, I heard these words pronounced in my ear:

"If master would be so good as to lean on my shoulder, master would swim with much greater ease."

I seized with one hand my faithful Conseil's arm.

"Is it you?" said I, "you?"

"Myself," answered Conseil; "and waiting master's orders."

"That shock threw you as well as me into the sea?"

"No; but, being in my master's service, I followed him."

The worthy fellow thought that was but natural.

"And the frigate?" I asked.

"The frigate?" replied Conseil, turning on his back; "I think that master had better not count too much on her."

"You think so?"

"I say that, at the time I threw myself into the sea, I heard the men at the wheel say, `The screw and the rudder are broken.'

"Broken?"

"Yes, broken by the monster's teeth. It is the only injury the Abraham Lincoln has sustained. But it is a bad look-out for us—she no longer answers her helm."

"Then we are lost!"

"Perhaps so," calmly answered Conseil. "However, we have still several hours before us, and one can do a good deal in some hours."

Conseil's imperturbable coolness set me up again. I swam more vigorously; but, cramped by my clothes, which stuck to me like a leaden weight, I felt great difficulty in bearing up. Conseil saw this.

"Will master let me make a slit?" said he; and, slipping an open knife under my clothes, he ripped them up from top to bottom very rapidly. Then he cleverly slipped them off me, while I swam for both of us.

Then I did the same for Conseil, and we continued to swim near to each other.

Nevertheless, our situation was no less terrible. Perhaps our disappearance had not been noticed; and, if it had been, the frigate could not tack, being without its helm. Conseil argued on this supposition, and laid his plans accordingly. This quiet boy was perfectly self-possessed. We then decided that, as our only chance of safety was being picked up by the Abraham Lincoln's boats, we ought to manage so as to wait for them as long as possible. I resolved then to husband our strength, so that both should not be exhausted at the same time; and this is how we managed: while one of us lay on our back, quite still, with arms crossed, and legs stretched out, the other would swim and push the other on in front. This towing business did not last more than ten minutes each; and relieving each other thus, we could swim on for some hours, perhaps till day-break. Poor chance! but hope is so firmly rooted in the heart of man! Moreover, there were two of us. Indeed I declare (though it may seem improbable) if I sought to destroy all hope—if I wished to despair, I could not.

The collision of the frigate with the cetacean had occurred about eleven o'clock in the evening before. I reckoned then we should have eight hours to swim before sunrise, an operation quite practicable if we relieved each other. The sea, very calm, was in our favour. Sometimes I tried to pierce the intense darkness that was only dispelled by the phosphorescence caused by our movements. I watched the luminous waves that broke over my hand, whose mirror-like surface was spotted with silvery rings. One might have said that we were in a bath of quicksilver.

Near one o'clock in the morning, I was seized with dreadful fatigue. My limbs stiffened under the strain of violent cramp. Conseil was obliged to keep me up, and our preservation devolved on him alone. I heard the poor boy pant; his breathing became short and hurried. I found that he could not keep up much longer.

"Leave me! leave me!" I said to him.

"Leave my master? Never!" replied he. "I would drown first."

Just then the moon appeared through the fringes of a thick cloud that the wind was driving to the east. The surface of the sea glittered with its rays. This kindly light reanimated us. My head got better again. I looked at all points of the horizon. I saw the frigate! She was five miles from us, and looked like a dark mass, hardly discernible. But no boats!

I would have cried out. But what good would it have been at such a distance! My swollen lips could utter no sounds. Conseil could articulate some words, and I heard him repeat at intervals, "Help! help!"

Our movements were suspended for an instant; we listened. It might be only a singing in the ear, but it seemed to me as if a cry answered the cry from Conseil.

"Did you hear?" I murmured.

"Yes! Yes!"

And Conseil gave one more despairing cry.

This time there was no mistake! A human voice responded to ours! Was it the voice of another unfortunate creature, abandoned in the middle of the ocean, some other victim of the shock sustained by the vessel? Or rather was it a boat from the frigate, that was hailing us in the darkness?

Conseil made a last effort, and, leaning on my shoulder, while I struck out in a desperate effort, he raised himself half out of the water, then fell back exhausted.

"What did you see?"

"I saw——" murmured he; "I saw—but do not talk—reserve all your strength!"

What had he seen? Then, I know not why, the thought of the monster came into my head for the first time! But that voice! The time is past for Jonahs to take refuge in whales' bellies! However, Conseil was towing me again. He raised his head sometimes, looked before us, and uttered a cry of recognition, which was responded to by a voice that came nearer and nearer. I scarcely heard it. My strength was exhausted; my fingers stiffened; my hand afforded me support no longer; my mouth, convulsively opening, filled with salt water. Cold crept over me. I raised my head for the last time, then I sank.

At this moment a hard body struck me. I clung to it: then I felt that I was being drawn up, that I was brought to the surface of the water, that my chest collapsed—I fainted.

It is certain that I soon came to, thanks to the vigorous rubbings that I received. I half opened my eyes.

"Conseil!" I murmured.

"Does master call me?" asked Conseil.

Just then, by the waning light of the moon which was sinking down to the horizon, I saw a face which was not Conseil's and which I immediately recognised.

"Ned!" I cried.

"The same, sir, who is seeking his prize!" replied the Canadian.

"Were you thrown into the sea by the shock to the frigate?"

"Yes, Professor; but more fortunate than you, I was able to find a footing almost directly upon a floating island."

"An island?"

"Or, more correctly speaking, on our gigantic narwhal."

"Explain yourself, Ned!"

"Only I soon found out why my harpoon had not entered its skin and was blunted."

"Why, Ned, why?"

"Because, Professor, that beast is made of sheet iron."

The Canadian's last words produced a sudden revolution in my brain. I wriggled myself quickly to the top of the being, or object, half out of the water, which served us for a refuge. I kicked it. It was evidently a hard, impenetrable body, and not the soft substance that forms the bodies of the great marine mammalia. But this hard body might be a bony covering, like that of the antediluvian animals; and I should be free to class this monster among amphibious reptiles, such as tortoises or alligators.

Well, no! the blackish back that supported me was smooth, polished, without scales. The blow produced a metallic sound; and, incredible though it may be, it seemed, I might say, as if it was made of riveted plates.

There was no doubt about it! This monster, this natural phenomenon that had puzzled the learned world, and over thrown and misled the imagination of seamen of both hemispheres, it must be owned was a still more astonishing phenomenon, inasmuch as it was a simply human construction.

We had no time to lose, however. We were lying upon the back of a sort of submarine boat, which appeared (as far as I could judge) like a huge fish of steel. Ned Land's mind was made up on this point. Conseil and I could only agree with him.

Just then a bubbling began at the back of this strange thing (which was evidently propelled by a screw), and it began to move. We had only just time to seize hold of the upper part, which rose about seven feet out of the water, and happily its speed was not great.

"As long as it sails horizontally," muttered Ned Land, "I do not mind; but, if it takes a fancy to dive, I would not give two straws for my life."

The Canadian might have said still less. It became really necessary to communicate with the beings, whatever they were, shut up inside the machine. I searched all over the outside for an aperture, a panel, or a manhole, to use a technical expression; but the lines of the iron rivets, solidly driven into the joints of the iron plates, were clear and uniform. Besides, the moon disappeared then, and left us in total darkness.

At last this long night passed. My indistinct remembrance prevents my describing all the impressions it made. I can only recall one circumstance. During some lulls of the wind and sea, I fancied I heard several times vague sounds, a sort of fugitive harmony produced by words of command. What was, then, the mystery of this submarine craft, of which the whole world vainly sought an explanation? What kind of beings existed in this strange boat? What mechanical agent caused its prodigious speed?

Daybreak appeared. The morning mists surrounded us, but they soon cleared off. I was about to examine the hull, which formed on deck a kind of horizontal platform, when I felt it gradually sinking.

"Oh! confound it!" cried Ned Land, kicking the resounding plate. "Open, you inhospitable rascals!"

Happily the sinking movement ceased. Suddenly a noise, like iron works violently pushed aside, came from the interior of the boat. One iron plate was moved, a man appeared, uttered an odd cry, and disappeared immediately.

Some moments after, eight strong men, with masked faces, appeared noiselessly, and drew us down into their formidable machine.

CHAPTER VIII MOBILIS IN MOBILI

This forcible abduction, so roughly carried out, was accomplished with the rapidity of lightning. I shivered all over. Whom had we to deal with? No doubt some new sort of pirates, who explored the sea in their own way. Hardly had the narrow panel closed upon me, when I was enveloped in darkness. My eyes, dazzled with the outer light, could distinguish nothing. I felt my naked feet cling to the rungs of an iron ladder. Ned Land and Conseil, firmly seized, followed me. At the bottom of the ladder, a door opened, and shut after us immediately with a bang.

We were alone. Where, I could not say, hardly imagine. All was black, and such a dense black that, after some minutes, my eyes had not been able to discern even the faintest glimmer.

Meanwhile, Ned Land, furious at these proceedings, gave free vent to his indignation.

"Confound it!" cried he, "here are people who come up to the Scotch for hospitality. They only just miss being cannibals. I should not be surprised at it, but I declare that they shall not eat me without my protesting."

"Calm yourself, friend Ned, calm yourself," replied Conseil, quietly. "Do not cry out before you are hurt. We are not quite done for yet."

"Not quite," sharply replied the Canadian, "but pretty near, at all events. Things look black. Happily, my bowie knife I have still, and I can always see well enough to use it. The first of these pirates who lays a hand on me——"

"Do not excite yourself, Ned," I said to the harpooner, "and do not compromise us by useless violence. Who knows that they will not listen to us? Let us rather try to find out where we are."

I groped about. In five steps I came to an iron wall, made of plates bolted together. Then turning back I struck against a wooden table, near which were ranged several stools. The boards of this prison were concealed under a thick mat, which deadened the noise of the feet. The bare walls revealed no trace of window or door. Conseil, going round the reverse way, met me, and we went back to the middle of the cabin, which measured about twenty feet by ten. As to its height, Ned Land, in spite of his own great height, could not measure it.

Half an hour had already passed without our situation being bettered, when the dense darkness suddenly gave way to extreme light. Our prison was suddenly lighted, that is to say, it became filled with a luminous matter, so strong that I could not bear it at first. In its whiteness and intensity I recognised that electric light which played round the submarine boat like a magnificent phenomenon of phosphorescence. After shutting my eyes involuntarily, I opened them, and saw that this luminous agent came from a half globe, unpolished, placed in the roof of the cabin.

"At last one can see," cried Ned Land, who, knife in hand, stood on the defensive.

"Yes," said I; "but we are still in the dark about ourselves."

"Let master have patience," said the imperturbable Conseil.

The sudden lighting of the cabin enabled me to examine it minutely. It only contained a table and five stools. The invisible door might be hermetically sealed. No noise was heard. All seemed dead in the interior of this boat. Did it move, did it float on the surface of the ocean, or did it dive into its depths? I could not guess.

A noise of bolts was now heard, the door opened, and two men appeared.

One was short, very muscular, broad-shouldered, with robust limbs, strong head, an abundance of black hair, thick moustache, a quick penetrating look, and the vivacity which characterises the population of Southern France.

The second stranger merits a more detailed description. I made out his prevailing qualities directly: self-confidence—because his head was well set on his shoulders, and his black eyes looked around with cold assurance; calmness—for his skin, rather pale, showed his coolness of blood; energy—evinced by the rapid contraction of his lofty brows; and courage—because his deep breathing denoted great power of lungs.

Whether this person was thirty-five or fifty years of age, I could not say. He was tall, had a large forehead, straight nose, a clearly cut mouth, beautiful teeth, with fine taper hands, indicative of a highly nervous temperament. This man was certainly the most admirable specimen I had ever met. One particular feature was his eyes, rather far from each other, and which could take in nearly a quarter of the horizon at once.

This faculty—(I verified it later)—gave him a range of vision far superior to Ned Land's. When this stranger fixed upon an object, his eyebrows met, his large eyelids closed around so as to contract the range of his vision, and he looked as if he magnified the objects lessened by distance, as if he pierced those sheets of water so opaque to our eyes, and as if he read the very depths of the seas.

The two strangers, with caps made from the fur of the sea otter, and shod with sea boots of seal's skin, were dressed in clothes of a particular texture, which allowed free movement of the limbs. The taller of the two, evidently the chief on board, examined us with great attention, without saying a word; then, turning to his companion, talked with him in an unknown tongue. It was a sonorous, harmonious, and flexible dialect, the vowels seeming to admit of very varied accentuation.

The other replied by a shake of the head, and added two or three perfectly incomprehensible words. Then he seemed to question me by a look.

I replied in good French that I did not know his language; but he seemed not to understand me, and my situation became more embarrassing.

"If master were to tell our story," said Conseil, "perhaps these gentlemen may understand some words."

I began to tell our adventures, articulating each syllable clearly, and without omitting one single detail. I announced our names and rank, introducing in person Professor Aronnax, his servant Conseil, and master Ned Land, the harpooner.

The man with the soft calm eyes listened to me quietly, even politely, and with extreme attention; but nothing in his countenance indicated that he had understood my story. When I finished, he said not a word.

There remained one resource, to speak English. Perhaps they would know this almost universal language. I knew it—as well as the German language—well enough to read it fluently, but not to speak it correctly. But, anyhow, we must make ourselves understood.

"Go on in your turn," I said to the harpooner; "speak your best Anglo-Saxon, and try to do better than I."

Ned did not beg off, and recommenced our story.

To his great disgust, the harpooner did not seem to have made himself more intelligible than I had. Our visitors did not stir. They evidently understood neither the language of England nor of France.

Very much embarrassed, after having vainly exhausted our speaking resources, I knew not what part to take, when Conseil said:

"If master will permit me, I will relate it in German."

But in spite of the elegant terms and good accent of the narrator, the German language had no success. At last, nonplussed, I tried to remember my first lessons, and to narrate our adventures in Latin, but with no better success. This last attempt being of no avail, the two strangers exchanged some words in their unknown language, and retired.

The door shut.

"It is an infamous shame," cried Ned Land, who broke out for the twentieth time. "We speak to those rogues in French, English, German, and Latin, and not one of them has the politeness to answer!"

"Calm yourself," I said to the impetuous Ned; "anger will do no good."

"But do you see, Professor," replied our irascible companion, "that we shall absolutely die of hunger in this iron cage?"

"Bah!" said Conseil, philosophically; "we can hold out some time yet."

"My friends," I said, "we must not despair. We have been worse off than this. Do me the favour to wait a little before forming an opinion upon the commander and crew of this boat."

"My opinion is formed," replied Ned Land, sharply. "They are rascals."

"Good! and from what country?"

"From the land of rogues!"

"My brave Ned, that country is not clearly indicated on the map of the world; but I admit that the nationality of the two strangers is hard to determine. Neither English, French, nor German, that is quite certain. However, I am inclined to think that the commander and his companion were born in low latitudes. There is southern blood in them. But I cannot decide by their appearance whether they are Spaniards, Turks, Arabians, or Indians. As to their language, it is quite incomprehensible."

"There is the disadvantage of not knowing all languages," said Conseil, "or the disadvantage of not having one universal language."

As he said these words, the door opened. A steward entered. He brought us clothes, coats and trousers, made of a stuff I did not know. I hastened to dress myself, and my companions followed my example. During that time, the steward—dumb, perhaps deaf—had arranged the table, and laid three plates.

"This is something like!" said Conseil.

"Bah!" said the angry harpooner, "what do you suppose they eat here? Tortoise liver, filleted shark, and beef steaks from seadogs."

"We shall see," said Conseil.

The dishes, of bell metal, were placed on the table, and we took our places. Undoubtedly we had to do with civilised people, and, had it not been for the electric light which flooded us, I could have fancied I was in the dining-room of the Adelphi Hotel at Liverpool, or at the Grand Hotel in Paris. I must say, however, that there was neither bread nor wine. The water was fresh and clear, but it was water and did not suit Ned Land's taste. Amongst the dishes which were brought to us, I recognised several fish delicately dressed; but of some, although excellent, I could give no opinion, neither could I tell to what kingdom they belonged, whether animal or vegetable. As to the dinner-service, it was elegant, and in perfect taste. Each utensil—spoon, fork, knife, plate—had a letter engraved on it, with a motto above it, of which this is an exact facsimile:

MOBILIS IN MOBILI N

The letter N was no doubt the initial of the name of the enigmatical person who commanded at the bottom of the seas.

Ned and Conseil did not reflect much. They devoured the food, and I did likewise. I was, besides, reassured as to our fate; and it seemed evident that our hosts would not let us die of want.

However, everything has an end, everything passes away, even the hunger of people who have not eaten for fifteen hours. Our appetites satisfied, we felt overcome with sleep.

"Faith! I shall sleep well," said Conseil.

"So shall I," replied Ned Land.

My two companions stretched themselves on the cabin carpet, and were soon sound asleep. For my own part, too many thoughts crowded my brain, too many insoluble questions pressed upon me, too many fancies kept my eyes half open. Where were we? What strange power carried us on? I felt—or rather fancied I felt—the machine sinking down to the lowest beds of the sea. Dreadful nightmares beset me; I saw in these mysterious asylums a world of unknown animals, amongst which this submarine boat seemed to be of the same kind, living, moving, and formidable as they. Then my brain grew calmer, my imagination wandered into vague unconsciousness, and I soon fell into a deep sleep.

CHAPTER IX NED LAND'S TEMPERS

How long we slept I do not know; but our sleep must have lasted long, for it rested us completely from our fatigues. I woke first. My companions had not moved, and were still stretched in their corner.

Hardly roused from my somewhat hard couch, I felt my brain freed, my mind clear. I then began an attentive examination of our cell. Nothing was changed inside. The prison was still a prison—the prisoners, prisoners. However, the steward, during our sleep, had cleared the table. I breathed with difficulty. The heavy air seemed to oppress my lungs. Although the cell was large, we had evidently consumed a great part of the oxygen that it contained. Indeed, each man consumes, in one hour, the oxygen contained in more than 176 pints of air, and this air, charged (as then) with a nearly equal quantity of carbonic acid, becomes unbreathable.

It became necessary to renew the atmosphere of our prison, and no doubt the whole in the submarine boat. That gave rise to a question in my mind. How would the commander of this floating dwelling-place proceed? Would he obtain air by chemical means, in getting by heat the oxygen contained in chlorate of potash, and in absorbing carbonic acid by caustic potash? Or—a more convenient, economical, and consequently more probable alternative—would he be satisfied to rise and take breath at the surface of the water, like a whale, and so renew for twenty-four hours the atmospheric provision?

In fact, I was already obliged to increase my respirations to eke out of this cell the little oxygen it contained, when suddenly I was refreshed by a current of pure air, and perfumed with saline emanations. It was an invigorating sea breeze, charged with iodine. I opened my mouth wide, and my lungs saturated themselves with fresh particles.

At the same time I felt the boat rolling. The iron-plated monster had evidently just risen to the surface of the ocean to breathe, after the fashion of whales. I found out from that the mode of ventilating the boat.

When I had inhaled this air freely, I sought the conduit pipe, which conveyed to us the beneficial whiff, and I was not long in finding it. Above the door was a ventilator, through which volumes of fresh air renewed the impoverished atmosphere of the cell.

I was making my observations, when Ned and Conseil awoke almost at the same time, under the influence of this reviving air. They rubbed their eyes, stretched themselves, and were on their feet in an instant.

"Did master sleep well?" asked Conseil, with his usual politeness.

"Very well, my brave boy. And you, Mr. Land?"

"Soundly, Professor. But, I don't know if I am right or not, there seems to be a sea breeze!"

A seaman could not be mistaken, and I told the Canadian all that had passed during his sleep.

"Good!" said he. "That accounts for those roarings we heard, when the supposed narwhal sighted the Abraham Lincoln."

"Quite so, Master Land; it was taking breath."

"Only, Mr. Aronnax, I have no idea what o'clock it is, unless it is dinner-time."

"Dinner-time! my good fellow? Say rather breakfast-time, for we certainly have begun another day."

"So," said Conseil, "we have slept twenty-four hours?"

"That is my opinion."

"I will not contradict you," replied Ned Land. "But, dinner or breakfast, the steward will be welcome, whichever he brings."

"Master Land, we must conform to the rules on board, and I suppose our appetites are in advance of the dinner hour."

"That is just like you, friend Conseil," said Ned, impatiently. "You are never out of temper, always calm; you would return thanks before grace, and die of hunger rather than complain!"

Time was getting on, and we were fearfully hungry; and this time the steward did not appear. It was rather too long to leave us, if they really had good intentions towards us. Ned Land, tormented by the cravings of hunger, got still more angry; and, notwithstanding his promise, I dreaded an explosion when he found himself with one of the crew.

For two hours more Ned Land's temper increased; he cried, he shouted, but in vain. The walls were deaf. There was no sound to be heard in the boat; all was still as death. It did not move, for I should have felt the trembling motion of the hull under the influence of the screw. Plunged in the depths of the waters, it belonged no longer to earth: this silence was dreadful.

I felt terrified, Conseil was calm, Ned Land roared.

Just then a noise was heard outside. Steps sounded on the metal flags. The locks were turned, the door opened, and the steward appeared.

Before I could rush forward to stop him, the Canadian had thrown him down, and held him by the throat. The steward was choking under the grip of his powerful hand.

Conseil was already trying to unclasp the harpooner's hand from his half-suffocated victim, and I was going to fly to the rescue, when suddenly I was nailed to the spot by hearing these words in French:

"Be quiet, Master Land; and you, Professor, will you be so good as to listen to me?"

CHAPTER X THE MAN OF THE SEAS

It was the commander of the vessel who thus spoke.

At these words, Ned Land rose suddenly. The steward, nearly strangled, tottered out on a sign from his master. But such was the power of the commander on board, that not a gesture betrayed the resentment which this man must have felt towards the Canadian. Conseil interested in spite of himself, I stupefied, awaited in silence the result of this scene.

The commander, leaning against the corner of a table with his arms folded, scanned us with profound attention. Did he hesitate to speak? Did he regret the words which he had just spoken in French? One might almost think so.

After some moments of silence, which not one of us dreamed of breaking, "Gentlemen," said he, in a calm and penetrating voice, "I speak French, English, German, and Latin equally well. I could, therefore, have answered you at our first interview, but I wished to know you first, then to reflect. The story told by each one, entirely agreeing in the main points, convinced me of your identity. I know now that chance has brought before me M. Pierre Aronnax, Professor of Natural History at the Museum of Paris, entrusted with a scientific mission abroad, Conseil, his servant, and Ned Land, of Canadian origin, harpooner on board the frigate Abraham Lincoln of the navy of the United States of America."

I bowed assent. It was not a question that the commander put to me. Therefore there was no answer to be made. This man expressed himself with perfect ease, without any accent. His sentences were well turned, his words clear, and his fluency of speech remarkable. Yet, I did not recognise in him a fellow-countryman.

He continued the conversation in these terms:

"You have doubtless thought, sir, that I have delayed long in paying you this second visit. The reason is that, your identity recognised, I wished to weigh maturely what part to act towards you. I have hesitated much. Most annoying circumstances have brought you into the presence of a man who has broken all the ties of humanity. You have come to trouble my existence."

"Unintentionally!" said I.

"Unintentionally?" replied the stranger, raising his voice a little. "Was it unintentionally that the Abraham Lincoln pursued me all over the seas? Was it unintentionally that you took passage in this frigate? Was it unintentionally that your cannon-balls rebounded off the plating of my vessel? Was it unintentionally that Mr. Ned Land struck me with his harpoon?"

I detected a restrained irritation in these words. But to these recriminations I had a very natural answer to make, and I made it.

"Sir," said I, "no doubt you are ignorant of the discussions which have taken place concerning you in America and Europe. You do not know that divers accidents, caused by collisions with your submarine machine, have excited public feeling in the two continents. I omit the theories without number by which it was sought to explain that of which you alone possess the secret. But you must understand that, in pursuing you over the high seas of the Pacific, the Abraham Lincoln believed itself to be chasing some powerful sea-monster, of which it was necessary to rid the ocean at any price."

A half-smile curled the lips of the commander: then, in a calmer tone:

"M. Aronnax," he replied, "dare you affirm that your frigate would not as soon have pursued and cannonaded a submarine boat as a monster?"

This question embarrassed me, for certainly Captain Farragut might not have hesitated. He might have thought it his duty to destroy a contrivance of this kind, as he would a gigantic narwhal.

"You understand then, sir," continued the stranger, "that I have the right to treat you as enemies?"

I answered nothing, purposely. For what good would it be to discuss such a proposition, when force could destroy the best arguments?

"I have hesitated some time," continued the commander; "nothing obliged me to show you hospitality. If I chose to separate myself from you, I should have no interest in seeing you again; I could place you upon the deck of this vessel which has served you as a refuge, I could sink beneath the waters, and forget that you had ever existed. Would not that be my right?"

"It might be the right of a savage," I answered, "but not that of a civilised man."

"Professor," replied the commander, quickly, "I am not what you call a civilised man! I have done with society entirely, for reasons which I alone have the right of appreciating. I do not, therefore, obey its laws, and I desire you never to allude to them before me again!"

This was said plainly. A flash of anger and disdain kindled in the eyes of the Unknown, and I had a glimpse of a terrible past in the life of this man. Not only had he put himself beyond the pale of human laws, but he had made himself independent of them, free in the strictest acceptation of the word, quite beyond their reach! Who then would dare to pursue him at the bottom of the sea, when, on its surface, he defied all attempts made against him?

What vessel could resist the shock of his submarine monitor? What cuirass, however thick, could withstand the blows of his spur? No man could demand from him an account of his actions; God, if he believed in one—his conscience, if he had one—were the sole judges to whom he was answerable.

These reflections crossed my mind rapidly, whilst the stranger personage was silent, absorbed, and as if wrapped up in himself. I regarded him with fear mingled with interest, as, doubtless, OEdiphus regarded the Sphinx.

After rather a long silence, the commander resumed the conversation.

"I have hesitated," said he, "but I have thought that my interest might be reconciled with that pity to which every human being has a right. You will remain on board my vessel, since fate has cast you there. You will be free; and, in exchange for this liberty, I shall only impose one single condition. Your word of honour to submit to it will suffice."

"Speak, sir," I answered. "I suppose this condition is one which a man of honour may accept?"

"Yes, sir; it is this: It is possible that certain events, unforeseen, may oblige me to consign you to your cabins for some hours or some days, as the case may be. As I desire never to use violence, I expect from you, more than all the others, a passive obedience. In thus acting, I take all the responsibility: I acquit you entirely, for I make it an impossibility for you to see what ought not to be seen. Do you accept this condition?"

Then things took place on board which, to say the least, were singular, and which ought not to be seen by people who were not placed beyond the pale of social laws. Amongst the surprises which the future was preparing for me, this might not be the least.

"We accept," I answered; "only I will ask your permission, sir, to address one question to you—one only."

"Speak, sir."

"You said that we should be free on board."

"Entirely."

"I ask you, then, what you mean by this liberty?"

"Just the liberty to go, to come, to see, to observe even all that passes here save under rare circumstances—the liberty, in short, which we enjoy ourselves, my companions and I."

It was evident that we did not understand one another.

"Pardon me, sir," I resumed, "but this liberty is only what every prisoner has of pacing his prison. It cannot suffice us."

"It must suffice you, however."

"What! we must renounce for ever seeing our country, our friends, our relations again?"

"Yes, sir. But to renounce that unendurable worldly yoke which men believe to be liberty is not perhaps so painful as you think."

"Well," exclaimed Ned Land, "never will I give my word of honour not to try to escape."

"I did not ask you for your word of honour, Master Land," answered the commander, coldly.

"Sir," I replied, beginning to get angry in spite of my self, "you abuse your situation towards us; it is cruelty."

"No, sir, it is clemency. You are my prisoners of war. I keep you, when I could, by a word, plunge you into the depths of the ocean. You attacked me. You came to surprise a secret which no man in the world must penetrate—the secret of my whole existence. And you think that I am going to send you back to that world which must know me no more? Never! In retaining you, it is not you whom I guard—it is myself."

These words indicated a resolution taken on the part of the commander, against which no arguments would prevail.

"So, sir," I rejoined, "you give us simply the choice between life and death?"

"Simply."

"My friends," said I, "to a question thus put, there is nothing to answer. But no word of honour binds us to the master of this vessel."

"None, sir," answered the Unknown.

Then, in a gentler tone, he continued:

"Now, permit me to finish what I have to say to you. I know you, M. Aronnax. You and your companions will not, perhaps, have so much to complain of in the chance which has bound you to my fate. You will find amongst the books which are my favourite study the work which you have published on `the depths of the sea.' I have often read it. You have carried out your work as far as terrestrial science permitted you. But you do not know all—you have not seen all. Let me tell you then, Professor, that you will not regret the time passed on board my vessel. You are going to visit the land of marvels."

These words of the commander had a great effect upon me. I cannot deny it. My weak point was touched; and I forgot, for a moment, that the contemplation of these sublime subjects was not worth the loss of liberty. Besides, I trusted to the future to decide this grave question. So I contented myself with saying:

"By what name ought I to address you?"

"Sir," replied the commander, "I am nothing to you but Captain Nemo; and you and your companions are nothing to me but the passengers of the Nautilus."

Captain Nemo called. A steward appeared. The captain gave him his orders in that strange language which I did not understand. Then, turning towards the Canadian and Conseil:

"A repast awaits you in your cabin," said he. "Be so good as to follow this man.

"And now, M. Aronnax, our breakfast is ready. Permit me to lead the way."

"I am at your service, Captain."

I followed Captain Nemo; and as soon as I had passed through the door, I found myself in a kind of passage lighted by electricity, similar to the waist of a ship. After we had proceeded a dozen yards, a second door opened before me.

I then entered a dining-room, decorated and furnished in severe taste. High oaken sideboards, inlaid with ebony, stood at the two extremities of the room, and upon their shelves glittered china, porcelain, and glass of inestimable value. The plate on the table sparkled in the rays which the luminous ceiling shed around, while the light was tempered and softened by exquisite paintings.

In the centre of the room was a table richly laid out. Captain Nemo indicated the place I was to occupy.

The breakfast consisted of a certain number of dishes, the contents of which were furnished by the sea alone; and I was ignorant of the nature and mode of preparation of some of them. I acknowledged that they were good, but they had a peculiar flavour, which I easily became accustomed to. These different aliments appeared to me to be rich in phosphorus, and I thought they must have a marine origin.

Captain Nemo looked at me. I asked him no questions, but he guessed my thoughts, and answered of his own accord the questions which I was burning to address to him.

"The greater part of these dishes are unknown to you," he said to me. "However, you may partake of them without fear. They are wholesome and nourishing. For a long time I have renounced the food of the earth, and I am never ill now. My crew, who are healthy, are fed on the same food."

"So," said I, "all these eatables are the produce of the sea?"

"Yes, Professor, the sea supplies all my wants. Sometimes I cast my nets in tow, and I draw them in ready to break. Sometimes I hunt in the midst of this element, which appears to be inaccessible to man, and quarry the game which dwells in my submarine forests. My flocks, like those of Neptune's old shepherds, graze fearlessly in the immense prairies of the ocean. I have a vast property there, which I cultivate myself, and which is always sown by the hand of the Creator of all things."

"I can understand perfectly, sir, that your nets furnish excellent fish for your table; I can understand also that you hunt aquatic game in your submarine forests; but I cannot understand at all how a particle of meat, no matter how small, can figure in your bill of fare."

"This, which you believe to be meat, Professor, is nothing else than fillet of turtle. Here are also some dolphins' livers, which you take to be ragout of pork. My cook is a clever fellow, who excels in dressing these various products of the ocean. Taste all these dishes. Here is a preserve of sea-cucumber, which a Malay would declare to be unrivalled in the world; here is a cream, of which the milk has been furnished by the cetacea, and the sugar by the great fucus of the North Sea; and, lastly, permit me to offer you some preserve of anemones, which is equal to that of the most delicious fruits."

I tasted, more from curiosity than as a connoisseur, whilst Captain Nemo enchanted me with his extraordinary stories.

"You like the sea, Captain?"

"Yes; I love it! The sea is everything. It covers seven tenths of the terrestrial globe. Its breath is pure and healthy. It is an immense desert, where man is never lonely, for he feels life stirring on all sides. The sea is only the embodiment of a supernatural and wonderful existence. It is nothing but love and emotion; it is the `Living Infinite,' as one of your poets has said. In fact, Professor, Nature manifests herself in it by her three kingdoms—mineral, vegetable, and animal. The sea is the vast reservoir of Nature. The globe began with sea, so to speak; and who knows if it will not end with it? In it is supreme tranquillity. The sea does not belong to despots. Upon its surface men can still exercise unjust laws, fight, tear one another to pieces, and be carried away with terrestrial horrors. But at thirty feet below its level, their reign ceases, their influence is quenched, and their power disappears. Ah! sir, live—live in the bosom of the waters! There only is independence! There I recognise no masters! There I am free!"

Captain Nemo suddenly became silent in the midst of this enthusiasm, by which he was quite carried away. For a few moments he paced up and down, much agitated. Then he became more calm, regained his accustomed coldness of expression, and turning towards me:

"Now, Professor," said he, "if you wish to go over the Nautilus, I am at your service."

Captain Nemo rose. I followed him. A double door, contrived at the back of the dining-room, opened, and I entered a room equal in dimensions to that which I had just quitted.

It was a library. High pieces of furniture, of black violet ebony inlaid with brass, supported upon their wide shelves a great number of books uniformly bound. They followed the shape of the room, terminating at the lower part in huge divans, covered with brown leather, which were curved, to afford the greatest comfort. Light movable desks, made to slide in and out at will, allowed one to rest one's book while reading. In the centre stood an immense table, covered with pamphlets, amongst which were some newspapers, already of old date. The electric light flooded everything; it was shed from four unpolished globes half sunk in the volutes of the ceiling. I looked with real admiration at this room, so ingeniously fitted up, and I could scarcely believe my eyes.

"Captain Nemo," said I to my host, who had just thrown himself on one of the divans, "this is a library which would do honour to more than one of the continental palaces, and I am absolutely astounded when I consider that it can follow you to the bottom of the seas."

"Where could one find greater solitude or silence, Professor?" replied Captain Nemo. "Did your study in the Museum afford you such perfect quiet?"

"No, sir; and I must confess that it is a very poor one after yours. You must have six or seven thousand volumes here."

"Twelve thousand, M. Aronnax. These are the only ties which bind me to the earth. But I had done with the world on the day when my Nautilus plunged for the first time beneath the waters. That day I bought my last volumes, my last pamphlets, my last papers, and from that time I wish to think that men no longer think or write. These books, Professor, are at your service besides, and you can make use of them freely."

I thanked Captain Nemo, and went up to the shelves of the library. Works on science, morals, and literature abounded in every language; but I did not see one single work on political economy; that subject appeared to be strictly proscribed. Strange to say, all these books were irregularly arranged, in whatever language they were written; and this medley proved that the Captain of the Nautilus must have read indiscriminately the books which he took up by chance.

"Sir," said I to the Captain, "I thank you for having placed this library at my disposal. It contains treasures of science, and I shall profit by them."

"This room is not only a library," said Captain Nemo, "it is also a smoking-room."

"A smoking-room!" I cried. "Then one may smoke on board?"

"Certainly."

"Then, sir, I am forced to believe that you have kept up a communication with Havannah."

"Not any," answered the Captain. "Accept this cigar, M. Aronnax; and, though it does not come from Havannah, you will be pleased with it, if you are a connoisseur."

I took the cigar which was offered me; its shape recalled the London ones, but it seemed to be made of leaves of gold. I lighted it at a little brazier, which was supported upon an elegant bronze stem, and drew the first whiffs with the delight of a lover of smoking who has not smoked for two days.

"It is excellent, but it is not tobacco."

"No!" answered the Captain, "this tobacco comes neither from Havannah nor from the East. It is a kind of sea-weed, rich in nicotine, with which the sea provides me, but somewhat sparingly."

At that moment Captain Nemo opened a door which stood opposite to that by which I had entered the library, and I passed into an immense drawing-room splendidly lighted.

It was a vast, four-sided room, thirty feet long, eighteen wide, and fifteen high. A luminous ceiling, decorated with light arabesques, shed a soft clear light over all the marvels accumulated in this museum. For it was in fact a museum, in which an intelligent and prodigal hand had gathered all the treasures of nature and art, with the artistic confusion which distinguishes a painter's studio.

Thirty first-rate pictures, uniformly framed, separated by bright drapery, ornamented the walls, which were hung with tapestry of severe design. I saw works of great value, the greater part of which I had admired in the special collections of Europe, and in the exhibitions of paintings. The several schools of the old masters were represented by a Madonna of Raphael, a Virgin of Leonardo da Vinci, a nymph of Corregio, a woman of Titan, an Adoration of Veronese, an Assumption of Murillo, a portrait of Holbein, a monk of Velasquez, a martyr of Ribera, a fair of Rubens, two Flemish landscapes of Teniers, three little "genre" pictures of Gerard Dow, Metsu, and Paul Potter, two specimens of Gericault and Prudhon, and some sea-pieces of Backhuysen and Vernet. Amongst the works of modern painters were pictures with the signatures of Delacroix, Ingres, Decamps, Troyon, Meissonier, Daubigny, etc.; and some admirable statues in marble and bronze, after the finest antique models, stood upon pedestals in the corners of this magnificent museum. Amazement, as the Captain of the Nautilus had predicted, had already begun to take possession of me.

"Professor," said this strange man, "you must excuse the unceremonious way in which I receive you, and the disorder of this room."

"Sir," I answered, "without seeking to know who you are, I recognise in you an artist."

"An amateur, nothing more, sir. Formerly I loved to collect these beautiful works created by the hand of man. I sought them greedily, and ferreted them out indefatigably, and I have been able to bring together some objects of great value. These are my last souvenirs of that world which is dead to me. In my eyes, your modern artists are already old; they have two or three thousand years of existence; I confound them in my own mind. Masters have no age."

"And these musicians?" said I, pointing out some works of Weber, Rossini, Mozart, Beethoven, Haydn, Meyerbeer, Herold, Wagner, Auber, Gounod, and a number of others, scattered over a large model piano-organ which occupied one of the panels of the drawing-room.

"These musicians," replied Captain Nemo, "are the contemporaries of Orpheus; for in the memory of the dead all chronological differences are effaced; and I am dead, Professor; as much dead as those of your friends who are sleeping six feet under the earth!"

Captain Nemo was silent, and seemed lost in a profound reverie. I contemplated him with deep interest, analysing in silence the strange expression of his countenance. Leaning on his elbow against an angle of a costly mosaic table, he no longer saw me,—he had forgotten my presence.

I did not disturb this reverie, and continued my observation of the curiosities which enriched this drawing-room.

Under elegant glass cases, fixed by copper rivets, were classed and labelled the most precious productions of the sea which had ever been presented to the eye of a naturalist. My delight as a professor may be conceived.

The division containing the zoophytes presented the most curious specimens of the two groups of polypi and echinodermes. In the first group, the tubipores, were gorgones arranged like a fan, soft sponges of Syria, ises of the Moluccas, pennatules, an admirable virgularia of the Norwegian seas, variegated unbellulairae, alcyonariae, a whole series of madrepores, which my master Milne Edwards has so cleverly classified, amongst which I remarked some wonderful flabellinae oculinae of the Island of Bourbon, the "Neptune's car" of the Antilles, superb varieties of corals—in short, every species of those curious polypi of which entire islands are formed, which will one day become continents. Of the echinodermes, remarkable for their coating of spines, asteri, sea-stars, pantacrinae, comatules, asterophons, echini, holothuri, etc., represented individually a complete collection of this group.

A somewhat nervous conchyliologist would certainly have fainted before other more numerous cases, in which were classified the specimens of molluscs. It was a collection of inestimable value, which time fails me to describe minutely. Amongst these specimens I will quote from memory only the elegant royal hammer-fish of the Indian Ocean, whose regular white spots stood out brightly on a red and brown ground, an imperial spondyle, bright-coloured, bristling with spines, a rare specimen in the European museums—(I estimated its value at not less than L1000); a common hammer-fish of the seas of New Holland, which is only procured with difficulty; exotic buccardia of Senegal; fragile white bivalve shells, which a breath might shatter like a soap-bubble; several varieties of the aspirgillum of Java, a kind of calcareous tube, edged with leafy folds, and much debated by amateurs; a whole series of trochi, some a greenish-yellow, found in the American seas, others a reddish-brown, natives of Australian waters; others from the Gulf of Mexico, remarkable for their imbricated shell; stellari found in the Southern Seas; and last, the rarest of all, the magnificent spur of New Zealand; and every description of delicate and fragile shells to which science has given appropriate names.

Apart, in separate compartments, were spread out chaplets of pearls of the greatest beauty, which reflected the electric light in little sparks of fire; pink pearls, torn from the pinna-marina of the Red Sea; green pearls of the haliotyde iris; yellow, blue and black pearls, the curious productions of the divers molluscs of every ocean, and certain mussels of the water-courses of the North; lastly, several specimens of inestimable value which had been gathered from the rarest pintadines. Some of these pearls were larger than a pigeon's egg, and were worth as much, and more than that which the traveller Tavernier sold to the Shah of Persia for three millions, and surpassed the one in the possession of the Imaum of Muscat, which I had believed to be unrivalled in the world.

Therefore, to estimate the value of this collection was simply impossible. Captain Nemo must have expended millions in the acquirement of these various specimens, and I was thinking what source he could have drawn from, to have been able thus to gratify his fancy for collecting, when I was interrupted by these words:

"You are examining my shells, Professor? Unquestionably they must be interesting to a naturalist; but for me they have a far greater charm, for I have collected them all with my own hand, and there is not a sea on the face of the globe which has escaped my researches."

"I can understand, Captain, the delight of wandering about in the midst of such riches. You are one of those who have collected their treasures themselves. No museum in Europe possesses such a collection of the produce of the ocean. But if I exhaust all my admiration upon it, I shall have none left for the vessel which carries it. I do not wish to pry into your secrets: but I must confess that this Nautilus, with the motive power which is confined in it, the contrivances which enable it to be worked, the powerful agent which propels it, all excite my curiosity to the highest pitch. I see suspended on the walls of this room instruments of whose use I am ignorant."

"You will find these same instruments in my own room, Professor, where I shall have much pleasure in explaining their use to you. But first come and inspect the cabin which is set apart for your own use. You must see how you will be accommodated on board the Nautilus."

I followed Captain Nemo who, by one of the doors opening from each panel of the drawing-room, regained the waist. He conducted me towards the bow, and there I found, not a cabin, but an elegant room, with a bed, dressing-table, and several other pieces of excellent furniture.

I could only thank my host.

"Your room adjoins mine," said he, opening a door, "and mine opens into the drawing-room that we have just quitted."

I entered the Captain's room: it had a severe, almost a monkish aspect. A small iron bedstead, a table, some articles for the toilet; the whole lighted by a skylight. No comforts, the strictest necessaries only.

Captain Nemo pointed to a seat.

"Be so good as to sit down," he said. I seated myself, and he began thus:

CHAPTER XI ALL BY ELECTRICITY

"Sir," said Captain Nemo, showing me the instruments hanging on the walls of his room, "here are the contrivances required for the navigation of the Nautilus. Here, as in the drawing-room, I have them always under my eyes, and they indicate my position and exact direction in the middle of the ocean. Some are known to you, such as the thermometer, which gives the internal temperature of the Nautilus; the barometer, which indicates the weight of the air and foretells the changes of the weather; the hygrometer, which marks the dryness of the atmosphere; the storm-glass, the contents of which, by decomposing, announce the approach of tempests; the compass, which guides my course; the sextant, which shows the latitude by the altitude of the sun; chronometers, by which I calculate the longitude; and glasses for day and night, which I use to examine the points of the horizon, when the Nautilus rises to the surface of the waves."

"These are the usual nautical instruments," I replied, "and I know the use of them. But these others, no doubt, answer to the particular requirements of the Nautilus. This dial with movable needle is a manometer, is it not?"

"It is actually a manometer. But by communication with the water, whose external pressure it indicates, it gives our depth at the same time."

"And these other instruments, the use of which I cannot guess?"

"Here, Professor, I ought to give you some explanations. Will you be kind enough to listen to me?"

He was silent for a few moments, then he said:

"There is a powerful agent, obedient, rapid, easy, which conforms to every use, and reigns supreme on board my vessel. Everything is done by means of it. It lights, warms it, and is the soul of my mechanical apparatus. This agent is electricity."

"Electricity?" I cried in surprise.

"Yes, sir."

"Nevertheless, Captain, you possess an extreme rapidity of movement, which does not agree well with the power of electricity. Until now, its dynamic force has remained under restraint, and has only been able to produce a small amount of power."

"Professor," said Captain Nemo, "my electricity is not everybody's. You know what sea-water is composed of. In a thousand grammes are found 96 1/2 per cent. of water, and about 2 2/3 per cent. of chloride of sodium; then, in a smaller quantity, chlorides of magnesium and of potassium, bromide of magnesium, sulphate of magnesia, sulphate and carbonate of lime. You see, then, that chloride of sodium forms a large part of it. So it is this sodium that I extract from the sea-water, and of which I compose my ingredients. I owe all to the ocean; it produces electricity, and electricity gives heat, light, motion, and, in a word, life to the Nautilus."

"But not the air you breathe?"

"Oh! I could manufacture the air necessary for my consumption, but it is useless, because I go up to the surface of the water when I please. However, if electricity does not furnish me with air to breathe, it works at least the powerful pumps that are stored in spacious reservoirs, and which enable me to prolong at need, and as long as I will, my stay in the depths of the sea. It gives a uniform and unintermittent light, which the sun does not. Now look at this clock; it is electrical, and goes with a regularity that defies the best chronometers. I have divided it into twenty-four hours, like the Italian clocks, because for me there is neither night nor day, sun nor moon, but only that factitious light that I take with me to the bottom of the sea. Look! just now, it is ten o'clock in the morning."

"Exactly."

"Another application of electricity. This dial hanging in front of us indicates the speed of the Nautilus. An electric thread puts it in communication with the screw, and the needle indicates the real speed. Look! now we are spinning along with a uniform speed of fifteen miles an hour."

"It is marvelous! And I see, Captain, you were right to make use of this agent that takes the place of wind, water, and steam."

"We have not finished, M. Aronnax," said Captain Nemo, rising. "If you will allow me, we will examine the stern of the Nautilus."

Really, I knew already the anterior part of this submarine boat, of which this is the exact division, starting from the ship's head: the dining-room, five yards long, separated from the library by a water-tight partition; the library, five yards long; the large drawing-room, ten yards long, separated from the Captain's room by a second water-tight partition; the said room, five yards in length; mine, two and a half yards; and, lastly a reservoir of air, seven and a half yards, that extended to the bows. Total length thirty five yards, or one hundred and five feet. The partitions had doors that were shut hermetically by means of india-rubber instruments, and they ensured the safety of the Nautilus in case of a leak.

I followed Captain Nemo through the waist, and arrived at the centre of the boat. There was a sort of well that opened between two partitions. An iron ladder, fastened with an iron hook to the partition, led to the upper end. I asked the Captain what the ladder was used for.

"It leads to the small boat," he said.

"What! have you a boat?" I exclaimed, in surprise.

"Of course; an excellent vessel, light and insubmersible, that serves either as a fishing or as a pleasure boat."

"But then, when you wish to embark, you are obliged to come to the surface of the water?"

"Not at all. This boat is attached to the upper part of the hull of the Nautilus, and occupies a cavity made for it. It is decked, quite water-tight, and held together by solid bolts. This ladder leads to a man-hole made in the hull of the Nautilus, that corresponds with a similar hole made in the side of the boat. By this double opening I get into the small vessel. They shut the one belonging to the Nautilus; I shut the other by means of screw pressure. I undo the bolts, and the little boat goes up to the surface of the sea with prodigious rapidity. I then open the panel of the bridge, carefully shut till then; I mast it, hoist my sail, take my oars, and I'm off."

"But how do you get back on board?"

"I do not come back, M. Aronnax; the Nautilus comes to me."

"By your orders?"

"By my orders. An electric thread connects us. I telegraph to it, and that is enough."

"Really," I said, astonished at these marvels, "nothing can be more simple."

After having passed by the cage of the staircase that led to the platform, I saw a cabin six feet long, in which Conseil and Ned Land, enchanted with their repast, were devouring it with avidity. Then a door opened into a kitchen nine feet long, situated between the large store-rooms. There electricity, better than gas itself, did all the cooking. The streams under the furnaces gave out to the sponges of platina a heat which was regularly kept up and distributed. They also heated a distilling apparatus, which, by evaporation, furnished excellent drinkable water. Near this kitchen was a bathroom comfortably furnished, with hot and cold water taps.

Next to the kitchen was the berth-room of the vessel, sixteen feet long. But the door was shut, and I could not see the management of it, which might have given me an idea of the number of men employed on board the Nautilus.

At the bottom was a fourth partition that separated this office from the engine-room. A door opened, and I found myself in the compartment where Captain Nemo—certainly an engineer of a very high order—had arranged his locomotive machinery. This engine-room, clearly lighted, did not measure less than sixty-five feet in length. It was divided into two parts; the first contained the materials for producing electricity, and the second the machinery that connected it with the screw. I examined it with great interest, in order to understand the machinery of the Nautilus.

"You see," said the Captain, "I use Bunsen's contrivances, not Ruhmkorff's. Those would not have been powerful enough. Bunsen's are fewer in number, but strong and large, which experience proves to be the best. The electricity produced passes forward, where it works, by electro-magnets of great size, on a system of levers and cog-wheels that transmit the movement to the axle of the screw. This one, the diameter of which is nineteen feet, and the thread twenty-three feet, performs about 120 revolutions in a second."

"And you get then?"

"A speed of fifty miles an hour."

"I have seen the Nautilus manoeuvre before the Abraham Lincoln, and I have my own ideas as to its speed. But this is not enough. We must see where we go. We must be able to direct it to the right, to the left, above, below. How do you get to the great depths, where you find an increasing resistance, which is rated by hundreds of atmospheres? How do you return to the surface of the ocean? And how do you maintain yourselves in the requisite medium? Am I asking too much?"

"Not at all, Professor," replied the Captain, with some hesitation; "since you may never leave this submarine boat. Come into the saloon, it is our usual study, and there you will learn all you want to know about the Nautilus."

CHAPTER XII SOME FIGURES

A moment after we were seated on a divan in the saloon smoking. The Captain showed me a sketch that gave the plan, section, and elevation of the Nautilus. Then he began his description in these words:

"Here, M. Aronnax, are the several dimensions of the boat you are in. It is an elongated cylinder with conical ends. It is very like a cigar in shape, a shape already adopted in London in several constructions of the same sort. The length of this cylinder, from stem to stern, is exactly 232 feet, and its maximum breadth is twenty-six feet. It is not built quite like your long-voyage steamers, but its lines are sufficiently long, and its curves prolonged enough, to allow the water to slide off easily, and oppose no obstacle to its passage. These two dimensions enable you to obtain by a simple calculation the surface and cubic contents of the Nautilus. Its area measures 6,032 feet; and its contents about 1,500 cubic yards; that is to say, when completely immersed it displaces 50,000 feet of water, or weighs 1,500 tons.

"When I made the plans for this submarine vessel, I meant that nine-tenths should be submerged: consequently it ought only to displace nine-tenths of its bulk, that is to say, only to weigh that number of tons. I ought not, therefore, to have exceeded that weight, constructing it on the aforesaid dimensions.

"The Nautilus is composed of two hulls, one inside, the other outside, joined by T-shaped irons, which render it very strong. Indeed, owing to this cellular arrangement it resists like a block, as if it were solid. Its sides cannot yield; it coheres spontaneously, and not by the closeness of its rivets; and its perfect union of the materials enables it to defy the roughest seas.

"These two hulls are composed of steel plates, whose density is from .7 to .8 that of water. The first is not less than two inches and a half thick and weighs 394 tons. The second envelope, the keel, twenty inches high and ten thick, weighs only sixty-two tons. The engine, the ballast, the several accessories and apparatus appendages, the partitions and bulkheads, weigh 961.62 tons. Do you follow all this?"

"I do."

"Then, when the Nautilus is afloat under these circumstances, one-tenth is out of the water. Now, if I have made reservoirs of a size equal to this tenth, or capable of holding 150 tons, and if I fill them with water, the boat, weighing then 1,507 tons, will be completely immersed. That would happen, Professor. These reservoirs are in the lower part of the Nautilus. I turn on taps and they fill, and the vessel sinks that had just been level with the surface."

"Well, Captain, but now we come to the real difficulty. I can understand your rising to the surface; but, diving below the surface, does not your submarine contrivance encounter a pressure, and consequently undergo an upward thrust of one atmosphere for every thirty feet of water, just about fifteen pounds per square inch?"

"Just so, sir."

"Then, unless you quite fill the Nautilus, I do not see how you can draw it down to those depths."

"Professor, you must not confound statics with dynamics or you will be exposed to grave errors. There is very little labour spent in attaining the lower regions of the ocean, for all bodies have a tendency to sink. When I wanted to find out the necessary increase of weight required to sink the Nautilus, I had only to calculate the reduction of volume that sea-water acquires according to the depth."

"That is evident."

"Now, if water is not absolutely incompressible, it is at least capable of very slight compression. Indeed, after the most recent calculations this reduction is only .000436 of an atmosphere for each thirty feet of depth. If we want to sink 3,000 feet, I should keep account of the reduction of bulk under a pressure equal to that of a column of water of a thousand feet. The calculation is easily verified. Now, I have supplementary reservoirs capable of holding a hundred tons. Therefore I can sink to a considerable depth. When I wish to rise to the level of the sea, I only let off the water, and empty all the reservoirs if I want the Nautilus to emerge from the tenth part of her total capacity."

I had nothing to object to these reasonings.

"I admit your calculations, Captain," I replied; "I should be wrong to dispute them since daily experience confirms them; but I foresee a real difficulty in the way."

"What, sir?"

"When you are about 1,000 feet deep, the walls of the Nautilus bear a pressure of 100 atmospheres. If, then, just now you were to empty the supplementary reservoirs, to lighten the vessel, and to go up to the surface, the pumps must overcome the pressure of 100 atmospheres, which is 1,500 lbs. per square inch. From that a power——"

"That electricity alone can give," said the Captain, hastily. "I repeat, sir, that the dynamic power of my engines is almost infinite. The pumps of the Nautilus have an enormous power, as you must have observed when their jets of water burst like a torrent upon the Abraham Lincoln. Besides, I use subsidiary reservoirs only to attain a mean depth of 750 to 1,000 fathoms, and that with a view of managing my machines. Also, when I have a mind to visit the depths of the ocean five or six miles below the surface, I make use of slower but not less infallible means."

"What are they, Captain?"

"That involves my telling you how the Nautilus is worked."

"I am impatient to learn."

"To steer this boat to starboard or port, to turn, in a word, following a horizontal plan, I use an ordinary rudder fixed on the back of the stern-post, and with one wheel and some tackle to steer by. But I can also make the Nautilus rise and sink, and sink and rise, by a vertical movement by means of two inclined planes fastened to its sides, opposite the centre of flotation, planes that move in every direction, and that are worked by powerful levers from the interior. If the planes are kept parallel with the boat, it moves horizontally. If slanted, the Nautilus, according to this inclination, and under the influence of the screw, either sinks diagonally or rises diagonally as it suits me. And even if I wish to rise more quickly to the surface, I ship the screw, and the pressure of the water causes the Nautilus to rise vertically like a balloon filled with hydrogen."

"Bravo, Captain! But how can the steersman follow the route in the middle of the waters?"

"The steersman is placed in a glazed box, that is raised about the hull of the Nautilus, and furnished with lenses."

"Are these lenses capable of resisting such pressure?"

"Perfectly. Glass, which breaks at a blow, is, nevertheless, capable of offering considerable resistance. During some experiments of fishing by electric light in 1864 in the Northern Seas, we saw plates less than a third of an inch thick resist a pressure of sixteen atmospheres. Now, the glass that I use is not less than thirty times thicker."

"Granted. But, after all, in order to see, the light must exceed the darkness, and in the midst of the darkness in the water, how can you see?"

"Behind the steersman's cage is placed a powerful electric reflector, the rays from which light up the sea for half a mile in front."

"Ah! bravo, bravo, Captain! Now I can account for this phosphorescence in the supposed narwhal that puzzled us so. I now ask you if the boarding of the Nautilus and of the Scotia, that has made such a noise, has been the result of a chance rencontre?"

"Quite accidental, sir. I was sailing only one fathom below the surface of the water when the shock came. It had no bad result."

"None, sir. But now, about your rencontre with the Abraham Lincoln?"

"Professor, I am sorry for one of the best vessels in the American navy; but they attacked me, and I was bound to defend myself. I contented myself, however, with putting the frigate hors de combat; she will not have any difficulty in getting repaired at the next port."

"Ah, Commander! your Nautilus is certainly a marvellous boat."

"Yes, Professor; and I love it as if it were part of myself. If danger threatens one of your vessels on the ocean, the first impression is the feeling of an abyss above and below. On the Nautilus men's hearts never fail them. No defects to be afraid of, for the double shell is as firm as iron; no rigging to attend to; no sails for the wind to carry away; no boilers to burst; no fire to fear, for the vessel is made of iron, not of wood; no coal to run short, for electricity is the only mechanical agent; no collision to fear, for it alone swims in deep water; no tempest to brave, for when it dives below the water it reaches absolute tranquillity. There, sir! that is the perfection of vessels! And if it is true that the engineer has more confidence in the vessel than the builder, and the builder than the captain himself, you understand the trust I repose in my Nautilus; for I am at once captain, builder, and engineer."

"But how could you construct this wonderful Nautilus in secret?"

"Each separate portion, M. Aronnax, was brought from different parts of the globe."

"But these parts had to be put together and arranged?"

"Professor, I had set up my workshops upon a desert island in the ocean. There my workmen, that is to say, the brave men that I instructed and educated, and myself have put together our Nautilus. Then, when the work was finished, fire destroyed all trace of our proceedings on this island, that I could have jumped over if I had liked."

"Then the cost of this vessel is great?"

"M. Aronnax, an iron vessel costs L145 per ton. Now the Nautilus weighed 1,500. It came therefore to L67,500, and L80,000 more for fitting it up, and about L200,000, with the works of art and the collections it contains."

"One last question, Captain Nemo."

"Ask it, Professor."

"You are rich?"

"Immensely rich, sir; and I could, without missing it, pay the national debt of France."

CHAPTER XII SOME FIGURES

I stared at the singular person who spoke thus. Was he playing upon my credulity? The future would decide that.

CHAPTER XIII THE BLACK RIVER

The portion of the terrestrial globe which is covered by water is estimated at upwards of eighty millions of acres. This fluid mass comprises two billions two hundred and fifty millions of cubic miles, forming a spherical body of a diameter of sixty leagues, the weight of which would be three quintillions of tons. To comprehend the meaning of these figures, it is necessary to observe that a quintillion is to a billion as a billion is to unity; in other words, there are as many billions in a quintillion as there are units in a billion. This mass of fluid is equal to about the quantity of water which would be discharged by all the rivers of the earth in forty thousand years.

During the geological epochs the ocean originally prevailed everywhere. Then by degrees, in the silurian period, the tops of the mountains began to appear, the islands emerged, then disappeared in partial deluges, reappeared, became settled, formed continents, till at length the earth became geographically arranged, as we see in the present day. The solid had wrested from the liquid thirty-seven million six hundred and fifty-seven square miles, equal to twelve billions nine hundred and sixty millions of acres.

The shape of continents allows us to divide the waters into five great portions: the Arctic or Frozen Ocean, the Antarctic, or Frozen Ocean, the Indian, the Atlantic, and the Pacific Oceans.

The Pacific Ocean extends from north to south between the two Polar Circles, and from east to west between Asia and America, over an extent of 145 degrees of longitude. It is the quietest of seas; its currents are broad and slow, it has medium tides, and abundant rain. Such was the ocean that my fate destined me first to travel over under these strange conditions.

"Sir," said Captain Nemo, "we will, if you please, take our bearings and fix the starting-point of this voyage. It is a quarter to twelve; I will go up again to the surface."

The Captain pressed an electric clock three times. The pumps began to drive the water from the tanks; the needle of the manometer marked by a different pressure the ascent of the Nautilus, then it stopped.

"We have arrived," said the Captain.

I went to the central staircase which opened on to the platform, clambered up the iron steps, and found myself on the upper part of the Nautilus.

The platform was only three feet out of water. The front and back of the Nautilus was of that spindle-shape which caused it justly to be compared to a cigar. I noticed that its iron plates, slightly overlaying each other, resembled the shell which clothes the bodies of our large terrestrial reptiles. It explained to me how natural it was, in spite of all glasses, that this boat should have been taken for a marine animal.

CHAPTER XIII THE BLACK RIVER

Toward the middle of the platform the longboat, half buried in the hull of the vessel, formed a slight excrescence. Fore and aft rose two cages of medium height with inclined sides, and partly closed by thick lenticular glasses; one destined for the steersman who directed the Nautilus, the other containing a brilliant lantern to give light on the road.

The sea was beautiful, the sky pure. Scarcely could the long vehicle feel the broad undulations of the ocean. A light breeze from the east rippled the surface of the waters. The horizon, free from fog, made observation easy. Nothing was in sight. Not a quicksand, not an island. A vast desert.

Captain Nemo, by the help of his sextant, took the altitude of the sun, which ought also to give the latitude. He waited for some moments till its disc touched the horizon. Whilst taking observations not a muscle moved, the instrument could not have been more motionless in a hand of marble.

"Twelve o'clock, sir," said he. "When you like——"

I cast a last look upon the sea, slightly yellowed by the Japanese coast, and descended to the saloon.

"And now, sir, I leave you to your studies," added the Captain; "our course is E.N.E., our depth is twenty-six fathoms. Here are maps on a large scale by which you may follow it. The saloon is at your disposal, and, with your permission, I will retire." Captain Nemo bowed, and I remained alone, lost in thoughts all bearing on the commander of the Nautilus.

For a whole hour was I deep in these reflections, seeking to pierce this mystery so interesting to me. Then my eyes fell upon the vast planisphere spread upon the table, and I placed my finger on the very spot where the given latitude and longitude crossed.

The sea has its large rivers like the continents. They are special currents known by their temperature and their colour. The most remarkable of these is known by the name of the Gulf Stream. Science has decided on the globe the direction of five principal currents: one in the North Atlantic, a second in the South, a third in the North Pacific, a fourth in the South, and a fifth in the Southern Indian Ocean. It is even probable that a sixth current existed at one time or another in the Northern Indian Ocean, when the Caspian and Aral Seas formed but one vast sheet of water.

At this point indicated on the planisphere one of these currents was rolling, the Kuro-Scivo of the Japanese, the Black River, which, leaving the Gulf of Bengal, where it is warmed by the perpendicular rays of a tropical sun, crosses the Straits of Malacca along the coast of Asia, turns into the North Pacific to the Aleutian Islands, carrying with it trunks of camphor-trees and other indigenous productions, and edging the waves of the ocean with the pure indigo of its warm water. It was this current that the Nautilus was to follow. I followed it with my eye; saw it lose itself in the vastness of the Pacific, and felt myself drawn with it, when Ned Land and Conseil appeared at the door of the saloon.

My two brave companions remained petrified at the sight of the wonders spread before them.

"Where are we, where are we?" exclaimed the Canadian. "In the museum at Quebec?"

"My friends," I answered, making a sign for them to enter, "you are not in Canada, but on board the Nautilus, fifty yards below the level of the sea."

"But, M. Aronnax," said Ned Land, "can you tell me how many men there are on board? Ten, twenty, fifty, a hundred?"

"I cannot answer you, Mr. Land; it is better to abandon for a time all idea of seizing the Nautilus or escaping from it. This ship is a masterpiece of modern industry, and I should be sorry not to have seen it. Many people would accept the situation forced upon us, if only to move amongst such wonders. So be quiet and let us try and see what passes around us."

"See!" exclaimed the harpooner, "but we can see nothing in this iron prison! We are walking—we are sailing—blindly."

Ned Land had scarcely pronounced these words when all was suddenly darkness. The luminous ceiling was gone, and so rapidly that my eyes received a painful impression.

We remained mute, not stirring, and not knowing what surprise awaited us, whether agreeable or disagreeable. A sliding noise was heard: one would have said that panels were working at the sides of the Nautilus.

"It is the end of the end!" said Ned Land.

Suddenly light broke at each side of the saloon, through two oblong openings. The liquid mass appeared vividly lit up by the electric gleam. Two crystal plates separated us from the sea. At first I trembled at the thought that this frail partition might break, but strong bands of copper bound them, giving an almost infinite power of resistance.

The sea was distinctly visible for a mile all round the Nautilus. What a spectacle! What pen can describe it? Who could paint the effects of the light through those transparent sheets of water, and the softness of the successive gradations from the lower to the superior strata of the ocean?

We know the transparency of the sea and that its clearness is far beyond that of rock-water. The mineral and organic substances which it holds in suspension heightens its transparency. In certain parts of the ocean at the Antilles, under seventy-five fathoms of water, can be seen with surprising clearness a bed of sand. The penetrating power of the solar rays does not seem to cease for a depth of one hundred and fifty fathoms. But in this middle fluid travelled over by the Nautilus, the electric brightness was produced even in the bosom of the waves. It was no longer luminous water, but liquid light.

On each side a window opened into this unexplored abyss. The obscurity of the saloon showed to advantage the brightness outside, and we looked out as if this pure crystal had been the glass of an immense aquarium.

"You wished to see, friend Ned; well, you see now."

"Curious! curious!" muttered the Canadian, who, forgetting his ill-temper, seemed to submit to some irresistible attraction; "and one would come further than this to admire such a sight!"

"Ah!" thought I to myself, "I understand the life of this man; he has made a world apart for himself, in which he treasures all his greatest wonders."

For two whole hours an aquatic army escorted the Nautilus. During their games, their bounds, while rivalling each other in beauty, brightness, and velocity, I distinguished the green labre; the banded mullet, marked by a double line of black; the round-tailed goby, of a white colour, with violet spots on the back; the Japanese scombrus, a beautiful mackerel of these seas, with a blue body and silvery head; the brilliant azurors, whose name alone defies description; some banded spares, with variegated fins of blue and yellow; the woodcocks of the seas, some specimens of which attain a yard in length; Japanese salamanders, spider lampreys, serpents six feet long, with eyes small and lively, and a huge mouth bristling with teeth; with many other species.

Our imagination was kept at its height, interjections followed quickly on each other. Ned named the fish, and Conseil classed them. I was in ecstasies with the vivacity of their movements and the beauty of their forms. Never had it been given to me to surprise these animals, alive and at liberty, in their natural element. I will not mention all the varieties which passed before my dazzled eyes, all the collection of the seas of China and Japan.

These fish, more numerous than the birds of the air, came, attracted, no doubt, by the brilliant focus of the electric light.

Suddenly there was daylight in the saloon, the iron panels closed again, and the enchanting vision disappeared. But for a long time I dreamt on, till my eyes fell on the instruments hanging on the partition. The compass still showed the course to be E.N.E., the manometer indicated a pressure of five atmospheres, equivalent to a depth of twenty five fathoms, and the electric log gave a speed of fifteen miles an hour. I expected Captain Nemo, but he did not appear. The clock marked the hour of five.

Ned Land and Conseil returned to their cabin, and I retired to my chamber. My dinner was ready. It was composed of turtle soup made of the most delicate hawks bills, of a surmullet served with puff paste (the liver of which, prepared by itself, was most delicious), and fillets of the emperor-holocanthus, the savour of which seemed to me superior even to salmon.

I passed the evening reading, writing, and thinking. Then sleep overpowered me, and I stretched myself on my couch of zostera, and slept profoundly, whilst the Nautilus was gliding rapidly through the current of the Black River.

CHAPTER XIV A NOTE OF INVITATION

The next day was the 9th of November. I awoke after a long sleep of twelve hours. Conseil came, according to custom, to know "how I passed the night," and to offer his services. He had left his friend the Canadian sleeping like a man who had never done anything else all his life. I let the worthy fellow chatter as he pleased, without caring to answer him. I was preoccupied by the absence of the Captain during our sitting of the day before, and hoping to see him to-day.

As soon as I was dressed I went into the saloon. It was deserted. I plunged into the study of the shell treasures hidden behind the glasses.

The whole day passed without my being honoured by a visit from Captain Nemo. The panels of the saloon did not open. Perhaps they did not wish us to tire of these beautiful things.

The course of the Nautilus was E.N.E., her speed twelve knots, the depth below the surface between twenty-five and thirty fathoms.

The next day, 10th of November, the same desertion, the same solitude. I did not see one of the ship's crew: Ned and Conseil spent the greater part of the day with me. They were astonished at the puzzling absence of the Captain. Was this singular man ill?—had he altered his intentions with regard to us?

After all, as Conseil said, we enjoyed perfect liberty, we were delicately and abundantly fed. Our host kept to his terms of the treaty. We could not complain, and, indeed, the singularity of our fate reserved such wonderful compensation for us that we had no right to accuse it as yet.

That day I commenced the journal of these adventures which has enabled me to relate them with more scrupulous exactitude and minute detail.

11th November, early in the morning. The fresh air spreading over the interior of the Nautilus told me that we had come to the surface of the ocean to renew our supply of oxygen. I directed my steps to the central staircase, and mounted the platform.

It was six o'clock, the weather was cloudy, the sea grey, but calm. Scarcely a billow. Captain Nemo, whom I hoped to meet, would he be there? I saw no one but the steersman imprisoned in his glass cage. Seated upon the projection formed by the hull of the pinnace, I inhaled the salt breeze with delight.

By degrees the fog disappeared under the action of the sun's rays, the radiant orb rose from behind the eastern horizon. The sea flamed under its glance like a train of gunpowder. The clouds scattered in the heights were coloured with lively tints of beautiful shades, and numerous "mare's tails," which betokened wind for that day. But what was wind to this Nautilus, which tempests could not frighten!

CHAPTER XIV A NOTE OF INVITATION

I was admiring this joyous rising of the sun, so gay, and so life-giving, when I heard steps approaching the platform. I was prepared to salute Captain Nemo, but it was his second (whom I had already seen on the Captain's first visit) who appeared. He advanced on the platform, not seeming to see me. With his powerful glass to his eye, he scanned every point of the horizon with great attention. This examination over, he approached the panel and pronounced a sentence in exactly these terms. I have remembered it, for every morning it was repeated under exactly the same conditions. It was thus worded:

"Nautron respoc lorni virch."

What it meant I could not say.

These words pronounced, the second descended. I thought that the Nautilus was about to return to its submarine navigation. I regained the panel and returned to my chamber.

Five days sped thus, without any change in our situation. Every morning I mounted the platform. The same phrase was pronounced by the same individual. But Captain Nemo did not appear.

I had made up my mind that I should never see him again, when, on the 16th November, on returning to my room with Ned and Conseil, I found upon my table a note addressed to me. I opened it impatiently. It was written in a bold, clear hand, the characters rather pointed, recalling the German type. The note was worded as follows:

TO PROFESSOR ARONNAX, On board the Nautilus. 16th of November, 1867.

Captain Nemo invites Professor Aronnax to a hunting-party, which will take place tomorrow morning in the forests of the Island of Crespo. He hopes that nothing will prevent the Professor from being present, and he will with pleasure see him joined by his companions.

CAPTAIN NEMO, Commander of the Nautilus.

"A hunt!" exclaimed Ned.

"And in the forests of the Island of Crespo!" added Conseil.

"Oh! then the gentleman is going on terra firma?" replied Ned Land.

"That seems to me to be clearly indicated," said I, reading the letter once more.

"Well, we must accept," said the Canadian. "But once more on dry ground, we shall know what to do. Indeed, I shall not be sorry to eat a piece of fresh venison."

Without seeking to reconcile what was contradictory between Captain Nemo's manifest aversion to islands and continents, and his invitation to hunt in a forest, I contented myself with replying:

"Let us first see where the Island of Crespo is."

I consulted the planisphere, and in 32° 40' N. lat. and 157° 50' W. long., I found a small island, recognised in 1801 by Captain Crespo, and marked in the ancient Spanish maps as Rocca de la Plata, the meaning of which is The Silver Rock. We were then about eighteen hundred miles from our starting-point, and the course of the Nautilus, a little changed, was bringing it back towards the southeast.

I showed this little rock, lost in the midst of the North Pacific, to my companions.

"If Captain Nemo does sometimes go on dry ground," said I, "he at least chooses desert islands."

Ned Land shrugged his shoulders without speaking, and Conseil and he left me.

After supper, which was served by the steward, mute and impassive, I went to bed, not without some anxiety.

The next morning, the 17th of November, on awakening, I felt that the Nautilus was perfectly still. I dressed quickly and entered the saloon.

Captain Nemo was there, waiting for me. He rose, bowed, and asked me if it was convenient for me to accompany him. As he made no allusion to his absence during the last eight days, I did not mention it, and simply answered that my companions and myself were ready to follow him.

We entered the dining-room, where breakfast was served.

"M. Aronnax," said the Captain, "pray, share my breakfast without ceremony; we will chat as we eat. For, though I promised you a walk in the forest, I did not undertake to find hotels there. So breakfast as a man who will most likely not have his dinner till very late."

I did honour to the repast. It was composed of several kinds of fish, and slices of sea-cucumber, and different sorts of seaweed. Our drink consisted of pure water, to which the Captain added some drops of a fermented liquor, extracted by the Kamschatcha method from a seaweed known under the name of Rhodomenia palmata. Captain Nemo ate at first without saying a word. Then he began:

"Sir, when I proposed to you to hunt in my submarine forest of Crespo, you evidently thought me mad. Sir, you should never judge lightly of any man."

"But Captain, believe me——"

"Be kind enough to listen, and you will then see whether you have any cause to accuse me of folly and contradiction."

"I listen."

"You know as well as I do, Professor, that man can live under water, providing he carries with him a sufficient supply of breathable air. In submarine works, the workman, clad in an impervious dress, with his head in a metal helmet, receives air from above by means of forcing pumps and regulators."

"That is a diving apparatus," said I.

"Just so, but under these conditions the man is not at liberty; he is attached to the pump which sends him air through an india-rubber tube, and if we were obliged to be thus held to the Nautilus, we could not go far."

"And the means of getting free?" I asked.

"It is to use the Rouquayrol apparatus, invented by two of your own countrymen, which I have brought to perfection for my own use, and which will allow you to risk yourself under these new physiological conditions without any organ whatever suffering. It consists of a reservoir of thick iron plates, in which I store the air under a pressure of fifty atmospheres. This reservoir is fixed on the back by means of braces, like a soldier's knapsack. Its upper part forms a box in which the air is kept by means of a bellows, and therefore cannot escape unless at its normal tension. In the Rouquayrol apparatus such as we use, two india rubber pipes leave this box and join a sort of tent which holds the nose and mouth; one is to introduce fresh air, the other to let out the foul, and the tongue closes one or the other according to the wants of the respirator. But I, in encountering great pressures at the bottom of the sea, was obliged to shut my head, like that of a diver in a ball of copper; and it is to this ball of copper that the two pipes, the inspirator and the expirator, open."

"Perfectly, Captain Nemo; but the air that you carry with you must soon be used; when it only contains fifteen per cent. of oxygen it is no longer fit to breathe."

"Right! But I told you, M. Aronnax, that the pumps of the Nautilus allow me to store the air under considerable pressure, and on those conditions the reservoir of the apparatus can furnish breathable air for nine or ten hours."

"I have no further objections to make," I answered. "I will only ask you one thing, Captain—how can you light your road at the bottom of the sea?"

"With the Ruhmkorff apparatus, M. Aronnax; one is carried on the back, the other is fastened to the waist. It is composed of a Bunsen pile, which I do not work with bichromate of potash, but with sodium. A wire is introduced which collects the electricity produced, and directs it towards a particularly made lantern. In this lantern is a spiral glass which contains a small quantity of carbonic gas. When the apparatus is at work this gas becomes luminous, giving out a white and continuous light. Thus provided, I can breathe and I can see."

"Captain Nemo, to all my objections you make such crushing answers that I dare no longer doubt. But, if I am forced to admit the Rouquayrol and Ruhmkorff apparatus, I must be allowed some reservations with regard to the gun I am to carry."

"But it is not a gun for powder," answered the Captain.

"Then it is an air-gun."

"Doubtless! How would you have me manufacture gun powder on board, without either saltpetre, sulphur, or charcoal?"

"Besides," I added, "to fire under water in a medium eight hundred and fifty-five times denser than the air, we must conquer very considerable resistance."

"That would be no difficulty. There exist guns, according to Fulton, perfected in England by Philip Coles and Burley, in France by Furcy, and in Italy by Landi, which are furnished with a peculiar system of closing, which can fire under these conditions. But I repeat, having no powder, I use air under great pressure, which the pumps of the Nautilus furnish abundantly."

"But this air must be rapidly used?"

"Well, have I not my Rouquayrol reservoir, which can furnish it at need? A tap is all that is required. Besides M. Aronnax, you must see yourself that, during our submarine hunt, we can spend but little air and but few balls."

"But it seems to me that in this twilight, and in the midst of this fluid, which is very dense compared with the atmosphere, shots could not go far, nor easily prove mortal."

"Sir, on the contrary, with this gun every blow is mortal; and, however lightly the animal is touched, it falls as if struck by a thunderbolt."

"Why?"

"Because the balls sent by this gun are not ordinary balls, but little cases of glass. These glass cases are covered with a case of steel, and weighted with a pellet of lead; they are real Leyden bottles, into which the electricity is forced to a very high tension. With the slightest shock they are discharged, and the animal, however strong it may be, falls dead. I must tell you that these cases are size number four, and that the charge for an ordinary gun would be ten."

"I will argue no longer," I replied, rising from the table. "I have nothing left me but to take my gun. At all events, I will go where you go."

Captain Nemo then led me aft; and in passing before Ned's and Conseil's cabin, I called my two companions, who followed promptly. We then came to a cell near the machinery-room, in which we put on our walking-dress.

CHAPTER XV A WALK ON THE BOTTOM OF THE SEA

This cell was, to speak correctly, the arsenal and wardrobe of the Nautilus. A dozen diving apparatuses hung from the partition waiting our use.

Ned Land, on seeing them, showed evident repugnance to dress himself in one.

"But, my worthy Ned, the forests of the Island of Crespo are nothing but submarine forests."

"Good!" said the disappointed harpooner, who saw his dreams of fresh meat fade away. "And you, M. Aronnax, are you going to dress yourself in those clothes?"

"There is no alternative, Master Ned."

"As you please, sir," replied the harpooner, shrugging his shoulders; "but, as for me, unless I am forced, I will never get into one."

"No one will force you, Master Ned," said Captain Nemo.

"Is Conseil going to risk it?" asked Ned.

"I follow my master wherever he goes," replied Conseil.

At the Captain's call two of the ship's crew came to help us dress in these heavy and impervious clothes, made of india-rubber without seam, and constructed expressly to resist considerable pressure. One would have thought it a suit of armour, both supple and resisting. This suit formed trousers and waistcoat. The trousers were finished off with thick boots, weighted with heavy leaden soles. The texture of the waistcoat was held together by bands of copper, which crossed the chest, protecting it from the great pressure of the water, and leaving the lungs free to act; the sleeves ended in gloves, which in no way restrained the movement of the hands. There was a vast difference noticeable between these consummate apparatuses and the old cork breastplates, jackets, and other contrivances in vogue during the eighteenth century.

Captain Nemo and one of his companions (a sort of Hercules, who must have possessed great strength), Conseil and myself were soon enveloped in the dresses. There remained nothing more to be done but to enclose our heads in the metal box. But, before proceeding to this operation, I asked the Captain's permission to examine the guns.

One of the Nautilus men gave me a simple gun, the butt end of which, made of steel, hollow in the centre, was rather large. It served as a reservoir for compressed air, which a valve, worked by a spring, allowed to escape into a metal tube. A box of projectiles in a groove in the thickness of the butt end contained about twenty of these electric balls, which, by means of a spring, were forced into the barrel of the gun. As soon as one shot was fired, another was ready.

"Captain Nemo," said I, "this arm is perfect, and easily handled: I only ask to be allowed to try it. But how shall we gain the bottom of the sea?"

"At this moment, Professor, the Nautilus is stranded in five fathoms, and we have nothing to do but to start."

"But how shall we get off?"

"You shall see."

Captain Nemo thrust his head into the helmet, Conseil and I did the same, not without hearing an ironical "Good sport!" from the Canadian. The upper part of our dress terminated in a copper collar upon which was screwed the metal helmet. Three holes, protected by thick glass, allowed us to see in all directions, by simply turning our head in the interior of the head-dress. As soon as it was in position, the Rouquayrol apparatus on our backs began to act; and, for my part, I could breathe with ease.

With the Ruhmkorff lamp hanging from my belt, and the gun in my hand, I was ready to set out. But to speak the truth, imprisoned in these heavy garments, and glued to the deck by my leaden soles, it was impossible for me to take a step.

But this state of things was provided for. I felt myself being pushed into a little room contiguous to the wardrobe room. My companions followed, towed along in the same way. I heard a water-tight door, furnished with stopper plates, close upon us, and we were wrapped in profound darkness.

After some minutes, a loud hissing was heard. I felt the cold mount from my feet to my chest. Evidently from some part of the vessel they had, by means of a tap, given entrance to the water, which was invading us, and with which the room was soon filled. A second door cut in the side of the Nautilus then opened. We saw a faint light. In another instant our feet trod the bottom of the sea.

And now, how can I retrace the impression left upon me by that walk under the waters? Words are impotent to relate such wonders! Captain Nemo walked in front, his companion followed some steps behind. Conseil and I remained near each other, as if an exchange of words had been possible through our metallic cases. I no longer felt the weight of my clothing, or of my shoes, of my reservoir of air, or my thick helmet, in the midst of which my head rattled like an almond in its shell.

The light, which lit the soil thirty feet below the surface of the ocean, astonished me by its power. The solar rays shone through the watery mass easily, and dissipated all colour, and I clearly distinguished objects at a distance of a hundred and fifty yards. Beyond that the tints darkened into fine gradations of ultramarine, and faded into vague obscurity. Truly this water which surrounded me was but another air denser than the terrestrial atmosphere, but almost as transparent. Above me was the calm surface of the sea. We were walking on fine, even sand, not wrinkled, as on a flat shore, which retains the impression of the billows. This dazzling carpet, really a reflector, repelled the rays of the sun with wonderful intensity, which accounted for the vibration which penetrated every atom of liquid. Shall I be believed when I say that, at the depth of thirty feet, I could see as if I was in broad daylight?

For a quarter of an hour I trod on this sand, sown with the impalpable dust of shells. The hull of the Nautilus, resembling a long shoal, disappeared by degrees; but its lantern, when darkness should overtake us in the waters, would help to guide us on board by its distinct rays.

Soon forms of objects outlined in the distance were discernible. I recognised magnificent rocks, hung with a tapestry of zoophytes of the most beautiful kind, and I was at first struck by the peculiar effect of this medium.

It was then ten in the morning; the rays of the sun struck the surface of the waves at rather an oblique angle, and at the touch of their light, decomposed by refraction as through a prism, flowers, rocks, plants, shells, and polypi were shaded at the edges by the seven solar colours. It was marvellous, a feast for the eyes, this complication of coloured tints, a perfect kaleidoscope of green, yellow, orange, violet, indigo, and blue; in one word, the whole palette of an enthusiastic colourist! Why could I not communicate to Conseil the lively sensations which were mounting to my brain, and rival him in expressions of admiration? For aught I knew, Captain Nemo and his companion might be able to exchange thoughts by means of signs previously agreed upon. So, for want of better, I talked to myself; I declaimed in the copper box which covered my head, thereby expending more air in vain words than was perhaps wise.

Various kinds of isis, clusters of pure tuft-coral, prickly fungi, and anemones formed a brilliant garden of flowers, decked with their collarettes of blue tentacles, sea-stars studding the sandy bottom. It was a real grief to me to crush under my feet the brilliant specimens of molluscs which strewed the ground by thousands, of hammerheads, donaciae (veritable bounding shells), of staircases, and red helmet-shells, angel-wings, and many others produced by this inexhaustible ocean. But we were bound to walk, so we went on, whilst above our heads waved medusae whose umbrellas of opal or rose-pink, escalloped with a band of blue, sheltered us from the rays of the sun and fiery pelagiae, which, in the darkness, would have strewn our path with phosphorescent light.

All these wonders I saw in the space of a quarter of a mile, scarcely stopping, and following Captain Nemo, who beckoned me on by signs. Soon the nature of the soil changed; to the sandy plain succeeded an extent of slimy mud which the Americans call "ooze," composed of equal parts of silicious and calcareous shells. We then travelled over a plain of seaweed of wild and luxuriant vegetation. This sward was of close texture, and soft to the feet, and rivalled the softest carpet woven by the hand of man. But whilst verdure was spread at our feet, it did not abandon our heads. A light network of marine plants, of that inexhaustible family of seaweeds of which more than two thousand kinds are known, grew on the surface of the water.

I noticed that the green plants kept nearer the top of the sea, whilst the red were at a greater depth, leaving to the black or brown the care of forming gardens and parterres in the remote beds of the ocean.

We had quitted the Nautilus about an hour and a half. It was near noon; I knew by the perpendicularity of the sun's rays, which were no longer refracted. The magical colours disappeared by degrees, and the shades of emerald and sapphire were effaced. We walked with a regular step, which rang upon the ground with astonishing intensity; the slightest noise was transmitted with a quickness to which the ear is unaccustomed on the earth; indeed, water is a better conductor of sound than air, in the ratio of four to one. At this period the earth sloped downwards; the light took a uniform tint. We were at a depth of a hundred and five yards and twenty inches, undergoing a pressure of six atmospheres.

At this depth I could still see the rays of the sun, though feebly; to their intense brilliancy had succeeded a reddish twilight, the lowest state between day and night; but we could still see well enough; it was not necessary to resort to the Ruhmkorff apparatus as yet. At this moment Captain Nemo stopped; he waited till I joined him, and then pointed to an obscure mass, looming in the shadow, at a short distance.

"It is the forest of the Island of Crespo," thought I; and I was not mistaken.

CHAPTER XVI A SUBMARINE FOREST

We had at last arrived on the borders of this forest, doubtless one of the finest of Captain Nemo's immense domains. He looked upon it as his own, and considered he had the same right over it that the first men had in the first days of the world. And, indeed, who would have disputed with him the possession of this submarine property? What other hardier pioneer would come, hatchet in hand, to cut down the dark copses?

This forest was composed of large tree-plants; and the moment we penetrated under its vast arcades, I was struck by the singular position of their branches—a position I had not yet observed.

Not an herb which carpeted the ground, not a branch which clothed the trees, was either broken or bent, nor did they extend horizontally; all stretched up to the surface of the ocean. Not a filament, not a ribbon, however thin they might be, but kept as straight as a rod of iron. The fuci and llianas grew in rigid perpendicular lines, due to the density of the element which had produced them. Motionless yet, when bent to one side by the hand, they directly resumed their former position. Truly it was the region of perpendicularity!

I soon accustomed myself to this fantastic position, as well as to the comparative darkness which surrounded us. The soil of the forest seemed covered with sharp blocks, difficult to avoid. The submarine flora struck me as being very perfect, and richer even than it would have been in the arctic or tropical zones, where these productions are not so plentiful. But for some minutes I involuntarily confounded the genera, taking animals for plants; and who would not have been mistaken? The fauna and the flora are too closely allied in this submarine world.

These plants are self-propagated, and the principle of their existence is in the water, which upholds and nourishes them. The greater number, instead of leaves, shoot forth blades of capricious shapes, comprised within a scale of colours pink, carmine, green, olive, fawn, and brown.

"Curious anomaly, fantastic element!" said an ingenious naturalist, "in which the animal kingdom blossoms, and the vegetable does not!"

In about an hour Captain Nemo gave the signal to halt; I, for my part, was not sorry, and we stretched ourselves under an arbour of alariae, the long thin blades of which stood up like arrows.

This short rest seemed delicious to me; there was nothing wanting but the charm of conversation; but, impossible to speak, impossible to answer, I only put my great copper head to Conseil's. I saw the worthy fellow's eyes glistening with delight, and, to show his satisfaction, he shook himself in his breastplate of air, in the most comical way in the world.

After four hours of this walking, I was surprised not to find myself dreadfully hungry. How to account for this state of the stomach I could not tell. But instead I felt an insurmountable desire to sleep, which happens to all divers. And my eyes soon closed behind the thick glasses, and I fell into a heavy slumber, which the movement alone had prevented before. Captain Nemo and his robust companion, stretched in the clear crystal, set us the example.

How long I remained buried in this drowsiness I cannot judge, but, when I woke, the sun seemed sinking towards the horizon. Captain Nemo had already risen, and I was beginning to stretch my limbs, when an unexpected apparition brought me briskly to my feet.

A few steps off, a monstrous sea-spider, about thirty-eight inches high, was watching me with squinting eyes, ready to spring upon me. Though my diver's dress was thick enough to defend me from the bite of this animal, I could not help shuddering with horror. Conseil and the sailor of the Nautilus awoke at this moment. Captain Nemo pointed out the hideous crustacean, which a blow from the butt end of the gun knocked over, and I saw the horrible claws of the monster writhe in terrible convulsions. This incident reminded me that other animals more to be feared might haunt these obscure depths, against whose attacks my diving-dress would not protect me. I had never thought of it before, but I now resolved to be upon my guard. Indeed, I thought that this halt would mark the termination of our walk; but I was mistaken, for, instead of returning to the Nautilus, Captain Nemo continued his bold excursion. The ground was still on the incline, its declivity seemed to be getting greater, and to be leading us to greater depths. It must have been about three o'clock when we reached a narrow valley, between high perpendicular walls, situated about seventy-five fathoms deep. Thanks to the perfection of our apparatus, we were forty-five fathoms below the limit which nature seems to have imposed on man as to his submarine excursions.

I say seventy-five fathoms, though I had no instrument by which to judge the distance. But I knew that even in the clearest waters the solar rays could not penetrate further. And accordingly the darkness deepened. At ten paces not an object was visible. I was groping my way, when I suddenly saw a brilliant white light. Captain Nemo had just put his electric apparatus into use; his companion did the same, and Conseil and I followed their example. By turning a screw I established a communication between the wire and the spiral glass, and the sea, lit by our four lanterns, was illuminated for a circle of thirty-six yards.

As we walked I thought the light of our Ruhmkorff apparatus could not fail to draw some inhabitant from its dark couch. But if they did approach us, they at least kept at a respectful distance from the hunters. Several times I saw Captain Nemo stop, put his gun to his shoulder, and after some moments drop it and walk on. At last, after about four hours, this marvellous excursion came to an end. A wall of superb rocks, in an imposing mass, rose before us, a heap of gigantic blocks, an enormous, steep granite shore, forming dark grottos, but which presented no practicable slope; it was the prop of the Island of Crespo. It was the earth! Captain Nemo stopped suddenly. A gesture of his brought us all to a halt; and, however desirous I might be to scale the wall, I was obliged to stop. Here ended Captain Nemo's domains. And he would not go beyond them. Further on was a portion of the globe he might not trample upon.

The return began. Captain Nemo had returned to the head of his little band, directing their course without hesitation. I thought we were not following the same road to return to the Nautilus. The new road was very steep, and consequently very painful. We approached the surface of the sea rapidly. But this return to the upper strata was not so sudden as to cause relief from the pressure too rapidly, which might have produced serious disorder in our organisation, and brought on internal lesions, so fatal to divers. Very soon light reappeared and grew, and, the sun being low on the horizon, the refraction edged the different objects with a spectral ring. At ten yards and a half deep, we walked amidst a shoal of little fishes of all kinds, more numerous than the birds of the air, and also more agile; but no aquatic game worthy of a shot had as yet met our gaze, when at that moment I saw the Captain shoulder his gun quickly, and follow a moving object into the shrubs. He fired; I heard a slight hissing, and a creature fell stunned at some distance from us. It was a magnificent sea-otter, an enhydrus, the only exclusively marine quadruped. This otter was five feet long, and must have been very valuable. Its skin, chestnut-brown above and silvery underneath, would have made one of those beautiful furs so sought after in the Russian and Chinese markets: the fineness and the lustre of its coat would certainly fetch L80. I admired this curious mammal, with its rounded head ornamented with short ears, its round eyes, and white whiskers like those of a cat, with webbed feet and nails, and tufted tail. This precious animal, hunted and tracked by fishermen, has now become very rare, and taken refuge chiefly in the northern parts of the Pacific, or probably its race would soon become extinct.

Captain Nemo's companion took the beast, threw it over his shoulder, and we continued our journey. For one hour a plain of sand lay stretched before us. Sometimes it rose to within two yards and some inches of the surface of the water. I then saw our image clearly reflected, drawn inversely, and above us appeared an identical group reflecting our movements and our actions; in a word, like us in every point, except that they walked with their heads downward and their feet in the air.

Another effect I noticed, which was the passage of thick clouds which formed and vanished rapidly; but on reflection I understood that these seeming clouds were due to the varying thickness of the reeds at the bottom, and I could even see the fleecy foam which their broken tops multiplied on the water, and the shadows of large birds passing above our heads, whose rapid flight I could discern on the surface of the sea.

On this occasion I was witness to one of the finest gun shots which ever made the nerves of a hunter thrill. A large bird of great breadth of wing, clearly visible, approached, hovering over us. Captain Nemo's companion shouldered his gun and fired, when it was only a few yards above the waves. The creature fell stunned, and the force of its fall brought it within the reach of dexterous hunter's grasp. It was an albatross of the finest kind.

Our march had not been interrupted by this incident. For two hours we followed these sandy plains, then fields of algae very disagreeable to cross. Candidly, I could do no more when I saw a glimmer of light, which, for a half mile, broke the darkness of the waters. It was the lantern of the Nautilus. Before twenty minutes were over we should be on board, and I should be able to breathe with ease, for it seemed that my reservoir supplied air very deficient in oxygen. But I did not reckon on an accidental meeting which delayed our arrival for some time.

I had remained some steps behind, when I presently saw Captain Nemo coming hurriedly towards me. With his strong hand he bent me to the ground, his companion doing the same to Conseil. At first I knew not what to think of this sudden attack, but I was soon reassured by seeing the Captain lie down beside me, and remain immovable.

I was stretched on the ground, just under the shelter of a bush of algae, when, raising my head, I saw some enormous mass, casting phosphorescent gleams, pass blusteringly by.

My blood froze in my veins as I recognised two formidable sharks which threatened us. It was a couple of tintoreas, terrible creatures, with enormous tails and a dull glassy stare, the phosphorescent matter ejected from holes pierced around the muzzle. Monstrous brutes! which would crush a whole man in their iron jaws. I did not know whether Conseil stopped to classify them; for my part, I noticed their silver bellies, and their huge mouths bristling with teeth, from a very unscientific point of view, and more as a possible victim than as a naturalist.

Happily the voracious creatures do not see well. They passed without seeing us, brushing us with their brownish fins, and we escaped by a miracle from a danger certainly greater than meeting a tiger full-face in the forest. Half an hour after, guided by the electric light we reached the Nautilus. The outside door had been left open, and Captain Nemo closed it as soon as we had entered the first cell. He then pressed a knob. I heard the pumps working in the midst of the vessel, I felt the water sinking from around me, and in a few moments the cell was entirely empty. The inside door then opened, and we entered the vestry.

There our diving-dress was taken off, not without some trouble, and, fairly worn out from want of food and sleep, I returned to my room, in great wonder at this surprising excursion at the bottom of the sea.

CHAPTER XVII FOUR THOUSAND LEAGUES UNDER THE PACIFIC

The next morning, the 18th of November, I had quite recovered from my fatigues of the day before, and I went up on to the platform, just as the second lieutenant was uttering his daily phrase.

I was admiring the magnificent aspect of the ocean when Captain Nemo appeared. He did not seem to be aware of my presence, and began a series of astronomical observations. Then, when he had finished, he went and leant on the cage of the watch-light, and gazed abstractedly on the ocean. In the meantime, a number of the sailors of the Nautilus, all strong and healthy men, had come up onto the platform. They came to draw up the nets that had been laid all night. These sailors were evidently of different nations, although the European type was visible in all of them. I recognised some unmistakable Irishmen, Frenchmen, some Sclaves, and a Greek, or a Candiote. They were civil, and only used that odd language among themselves, the origin of which I could not guess, neither could I question them.

The nets were hauled in. They were a large kind of "chaluts," like those on the Normandy coasts, great pockets that the waves and a chain fixed in the smaller meshes kept open. These pockets, drawn by iron poles, swept through the water, and gathered in everything in their way. That day they brought up curious specimens from those productive coasts.

I reckoned that the haul had brought in more than nine hundredweight of fish. It was a fine haul, but not to be wondered at. Indeed, the nets are let down for several hours, and enclose in their meshes an infinite variety. We had no lack of excellent food, and the rapidity of the Nautilus and the attraction of the electric light could always renew our supply. These several productions of the sea were immediately lowered through the panel to the steward's room, some to be eaten fresh, and others pickled.

The fishing ended, the provision of air renewed, I thought that the Nautilus was about to continue its submarine excursion, and was preparing to return to my room, when, without further preamble, the Captain turned to me, saying:

"Professor, is not this ocean gifted with real life? It has its tempers and its gentle moods. Yesterday it slept as we did, and now it has woke after a quiet night. Look!" he continued, "it wakes under the caresses of the sun. It is going to renew its diurnal existence. It is an interesting study to watch the play of its organisation. It has a pulse, arteries, spasms; and I agree with the learned Maury, who discovered in it a circulation as real as the circulation of blood in animals.

"Yes, the ocean has indeed circulation, and to promote it, the Creator has caused things to multiply in it—caloric, salt, and animalculae."

When Captain Nemo spoke thus, he seemed altogether changed, and aroused an extraordinary emotion in me.

"Also," he added, "true existence is there; and I can imagine the foundations of nautical towns, clusters of submarine houses, which, like the Nautilus, would ascend every morning to breathe at the surface of the water, free towns, independent cities. Yet who knows whether some despot——"

Captain Nemo finished his sentence with a violent gesture. Then, addressing me as if to chase away some sorrowful thought:

"M. Aronnax," he asked, "do you know the depth of the ocean?"

"I only know, Captain, what the principal soundings have taught us."

"Could you tell me them, so that I can suit them to my purpose?"

"These are some," I replied, "that I remember. If I am not mistaken, a depth of 8,000 yards has been found in the North Atlantic, and 2,500 yards in the Mediterranean. The most remarkable soundings have been made in the South Atlantic, near the thirty-fifth parallel, and they gave 12,000 yards, 14,000 yards, and 15,000 yards. To sum up all, it is reckoned that if the bottom of the sea were levelled, its mean depth would be about one and three-quarter leagues."

"Well, Professor," replied the Captain, "we shall show you better than that I hope. As to the mean depth of this part of the Pacific, I tell you it is only 4,000 yards."

Having said this, Captain Nemo went towards the panel, and disappeared down the ladder. I followed him, and went into the large drawing-room. The screw was immediately put in motion, and the log gave twenty miles an hour.

During the days and weeks that passed, Captain Nemo was very sparing of his visits. I seldom saw him. The lieutenant pricked the ship's course regularly on the chart, so I could always tell exactly the route of the Nautilus.

Nearly every day, for some time, the panels of the drawing-room were opened, and we were never tired of penetrating the mysteries of the submarine world.

The general direction of the Nautilus was south-east, and it kept between 100 and 150 yards of depth. One day, however, I do not know why, being drawn diagonally by means of the inclined planes, it touched the bed of the sea. The thermometer indicated a temperature of 4.25 (cent.): a temperature that at this depth seemed common to all latitudes.

At three o'clock in the morning of the 26th of November the Nautilus crossed the tropic of Cancer at 172° long. On 27th instant it sighted the Sandwich Islands, where Cook died, February 14, 1779. We had then gone 4,860 leagues from our starting-point. In the morning, when I went on the platform, I saw two miles to windward, Hawaii, the largest of the seven islands that form the group. I saw clearly the cultivated ranges, and the several mountain-chains that run parallel with the side, and the volcanoes that overtop Mouna-Rea, which rise 5,000 yards above the level of the sea. Besides other things the nets brought up, were several flabellariae and graceful polypi, that are peculiar to that part of the ocean. The direction of the Nautilus was still to the south-east. It crossed the equator December 1, in 142° long.; and on the 4th of the same month, after crossing rapidly and without anything in particular occurring, we sighted the Marquesas group. I saw, three miles off, Martin's peak in Nouka-Hiva, the largest of the group that belongs to France. I only saw the woody mountains against the horizon, because Captain Nemo did not wish to bring the ship to the wind. There the nets brought up beautiful specimens of fish: some with azure fins and tails like gold, the flesh of which is unrivalled; some nearly destitute of scales, but of exquisite flavour; others, with bony jaws, and yellow-tinged gills, as good as bonitos; all fish that would be of use to us. After leaving these charming islands protected by the French flag, from the 4th to the 11th of December the Nautilus sailed over about 2,000 miles.

During the daytime of the 11th of December I was busy reading in the large drawing-room. Ned Land and Conseil watched the luminous water through the half-open panels. The Nautilus was immovable. While its reservoirs were filled, it kept at a depth of 1,000 yards, a region rarely visited in the ocean, and in which large fish were seldom seen.

I was then reading a charming book by Jean Mace, The Slaves of the Stomach, and I was learning some valuable lessons from it, when Conseil interrupted me.

"Will master come here a moment?" he said, in a curious voice.

"What is the matter, Conseil?"

"I want master to look."

I rose, went, and leaned on my elbows before the panes and watched.

In a full electric light, an enormous black mass, quite immovable, was suspended in the midst of the waters. I watched it attentively, seeking to find out the nature of this gigantic cetacean. But a sudden thought crossed my mind. "A vessel!" I said, half aloud.

"Yes," replied the Canadian, "a disabled ship that has sunk perpendicularly."

Ned Land was right; we were close to a vessel of which the tattered shrouds still hung from their chains. The keel seemed to be in good order, and it had been wrecked at most some few hours. Three stumps of masts, broken off about two feet above the bridge, showed that the vessel had had to sacrifice its masts. But, lying on its side, it had filled, and it was heeling over to port. This skeleton of what it had once been was a sad spectacle as it lay lost under the waves, but sadder still was the sight of the bridge, where some corpses, bound with ropes, were still lying. I counted five—four men, one of whom was standing at the helm, and a woman standing by the poop, holding an infant in her arms. She was quite young. I could distinguish her features, which the water had not decomposed, by the brilliant light from the Nautilus. In one despairing effort, she had raised her infant above her head—poor little thing!—whose arms encircled its mother's neck. The attitude of the four sailors was frightful, distorted as they were by their convulsive movements, whilst making a last effort to free themselves from the cords that bound them to the vessel. The steersman alone, calm, with a grave, clear face, his grey hair glued to his forehead, and his hand clutching the wheel of the helm, seemed even then to be guiding the three broken masts through the depths of the ocean.

What a scene! We were dumb; our hearts beat fast before this shipwreck, taken as it were from life and photographed in its last moments. And I saw already, coming towards it with hungry eyes, enormous sharks, attracted by the human flesh.

However, the Nautilus, turning, went round the submerged vessel, and in one instant I read on the stern—"The Florida, Sunderland."

CHAPTER XVIII VANIKORO

This terrible spectacle was the forerunner of the series of maritime catastrophes that the Nautilus was destined to meet with in its route. As long as it went through more frequented waters, we often saw the hulls of shipwrecked vessels that were rotting in the depths, and deeper down cannons, bullets, anchors, chains, and a thousand other iron materials eaten up by rust. However, on the 11th of December we sighted the Pomotou Islands, the old "dangerous group" of Bougainville, that extend over a space of 500 leagues at E.S.E. to W.N.W., from the Island Ducie to that of Lazareff. This group covers an area of 370 square leagues, and it is formed of sixty groups of islands, among which the Gambier group is remarkable, over which France exercises sway. These are coral islands, slowly raised, but continuous, created by the daily work of polypi. Then this new island will be joined later on to the neighboring groups, and a fifth continent will stretch from New Zealand and New Caledonia, and from thence to the Marquesas.

One day, when I was suggesting this theory to Captain Nemo, he replied coldly:

"The earth does not want new continents, but new men."

Chance had conducted the Nautilus towards the Island of Clermont-Tonnere, one of the most curious of the group, that was discovered in 1822 by Captain Bell of the Minerva. I could study now the madreporal system, to which are due the islands in this ocean.

Madrepores (which must not be mistaken for corals) have a tissue lined with a calcareous crust, and the modifications of its structure have induced M. Milne Edwards, my worthy master, to class them into five sections. The animalcule that the marine polypus secretes live by millions at the bottom of their cells. Their calcareous deposits become rocks, reefs, and large and small islands. Here they form a ring, surrounding a little inland lake, that communicates with the sea by means of gaps. There they make barriers of reefs like those on the coasts of New Caledonia and the various Pomoton islands. In other places, like those at Reunion and at Maurice, they raise fringed reefs, high, straight walls, near which the depth of the ocean is considerable.

Some cable-lengths off the shores of the Island of Clermont I admired the gigantic work accomplished by these microscopical workers. These walls are specially the work of those madrepores known as milleporas, porites, madrepores, and astraeas. These polypi are found particularly in the rough beds of the sea, near the surface; and consequently it is from the upper part that they begin their operations, in which they bury themselves by degrees with the debris of the secretions that support them. Such is, at least, Darwin's theory, who thus explains the formation of the *atolls*, a superior theory (to my mind) to that given of the foundation of the madreporical works, summits of mountains or volcanoes, that are submerged some feet below the level of the sea.

I could observe closely these curious walls, for perpendicularly they were more than 300 yards deep, and our electric sheets lighted up this calcareous matter brilliantly. Replying to a question Conseil asked me as to the time these colossal barriers took to be raised, I astonished him much by telling him that learned men reckoned it about the eighth of an inch in a hundred years.

Towards evening Clermont-Tonnerre was lost in the distance, and the route of the Nautilus was sensibly changed. After having crossed the tropic of Capricorn in 135° longitude, it sailed W.N.W., making again for the tropical zone. Although the summer sun was very strong, we did not suffer from heat, for at fifteen or twenty fathoms below the surface, the temperature did not rise above from ten to twelve degrees.

On 15th of December, we left to the east the bewitching group of the Societies and the graceful Tahiti, queen of the Pacific. I saw in the morning, some miles to the windward, the elevated summits of the island. These waters furnished our table with excellent fish, mackerel, bonitos, and some varieties of a sea-serpent.

On the 25th of December the Nautilus sailed into the midst of the New Hebrides, discovered by Quiros in 1606, and that Bougainville explored in 1768, and to which Cook gave its present name in 1773. This group is composed principally of nine large islands, that form a band of 120 leagues N.N.S. to S.S.W., between 15° and 2° S. lat., and 164 deg. and 168° long. We passed tolerably near to the Island of Aurou, that at noon looked like a mass of green woods, surmounted by a peak of great height.

That day being Christmas Day, Ned Land seemed to regret sorely the non-celebration of "Christmas," the family fete of which Protestants are so fond. I had not seen Captain Nemo for a week, when, on the morning of the 27th, he came into the large drawing-room, always seeming as if he had seen you five minutes before. I was busily tracing the route of the Nautilus on the planisphere. The Captain came up to me, put his finger on one spot on the chart, and said this single word.

"Vanikoro."

The effect was magical! It was the name of the islands on which La Perouse had been lost! I rose suddenly.

"The Nautilus has brought us to Vanikoro?" I asked.

"Yes, Professor," said the Captain.

"And I can visit the celebrated islands where the Boussole and the Astrolabe struck?"

"If you like, Professor."

"When shall we be there?"

"We are there now."

Followed by Captain Nemo, I went up on to the platform, and greedily scanned the horizon.

To the N.E. two volcanic islands emerged of unequal size, surrounded by a coral reef that measured forty miles in circumference. We were close to Vanikoro, really the one to which Dumont d'Urville gave the name of Isle de la Recherche, and exactly facing the little harbour of Vanou, situated in 16° 4' S. lat., and 164° 32' E. long. The earth seemed covered with verdure from the shore to the summits in the interior, that were crowned by Mount Kapogo, 476 feet high. The Nautilus, having passed the outer belt of rocks by a narrow strait, found itself among breakers where the sea was from thirty to forty fathoms deep. Under the verdant shade of some mangroves I perceived some savages, who appeared greatly surprised at our approach. In the long black body, moving between wind and water, did they not see some formidable cetacean that they regarded with suspicion?

Just then Captain Nemo asked me what I knew about the wreck of La Perouse.

"Only what everyone knows, Captain," I replied.

"And could you tell me what everyone knows about it?" he inquired, ironically.

"Easily."

I related to him all that the last works of Dumont d'Urville had made known—works from which the following is a brief account.

La Perouse, and his second, Captain de Langle, were sent by Louis XVI, in 1785, on a voyage of circumnavigation. They embarked in the corvettes Boussole and the Astrolabe, neither of which were again heard of. In 1791, the French Government, justly uneasy as to the fate of these two sloops, manned two large merchantmen, the Recherche and the Esperance, which left Brest the 28th of September under the command of Bruni d'Entrecasteaux.

Two months after, they learned from Bowen, commander of the Albemarle, that the debris of shipwrecked vessels had been seen on the coasts of New Georgia. But D'Entrecasteaux, ignoring this communication—rather uncertain, besides—directed his course towards the Admiralty Islands, mentioned in a report of Captain Hunter's as being the place where La Perouse was wrecked.

They sought in vain. The Esperance and the Recherche passed before Vanikoro without stopping there, and, in fact, this voyage was most disastrous, as it cost D'Entrecasteaux his life, and those of two of his lieutenants, besides several of his crew.

Captain Dillon, a shrewd old Pacific sailor, was the first to find unmistakable traces of the wrecks. On the 15th of May, 1824, his vessel, the St. Patrick, passed close to Tikopia, one of the New Hebrides. There a Lascar came alongside in a canoe, sold him the handle of a sword in silver that bore the print of characters engraved on the hilt. The Lascar pretended that six years before, during a stay at Vanikoro, he had seen two Europeans that belonged to some vessels that had run aground on the reefs some years ago.

Dillon guessed that he meant La Perouse, whose disappearance had troubled the whole world. He tried to get on to Vanikoro, where, according to the Lascar, he would find numerous debris of the wreck, but winds and tides prevented him.

Dillon returned to Calcutta. There he interested the Asiatic Society and the Indian Company in his discovery. A vessel, to which was given the name of the Recherche, was put at his disposal, and he set out, 23rd January, 1827, accompanied by a French agent.

The Recherche, after touching at several points in the Pacific, cast anchor before Vanikoro, 7th July, 1827, in that same harbour of Vanou where the Nautilus was at this time.

There it collected numerous relics of the wreck—iron utensils, anchors, pulley-strops, swivel-guns, an 18 lb. shot, fragments of astronomical instruments, a piece of crown work, and a bronze clock, bearing this inscription—"Bazin m'a fait," the mark of the foundry of the arsenal at Brest about 1785. There could be no further doubt.

Dillon, having made all inquiries, stayed in the unlucky place till October. Then he quitted Vanikoro, and directed his course towards New Zealand; put into Calcutta, 7th April, 1828, and returned to France, where he was warmly welcomed by Charles X.

But at the same time, without knowing Dillon's movements, Dumont d'Urville had already set out to find the scene of the wreck. And they had learned from a whaler that some medals and a cross of St. Louis had been found in the hands of some savages of Louisiade and New Caledonia. Dumont d'Urville, commander of the Astrolabe, had then sailed, and two months after Dillon had left Vanikoro he put into Hobart Town. There he learned the results of Dillon's inquiries, and found that a certain James Hobbs, second lieutenant of the Union of Calcutta, after landing on an island situated 8° 18' S. lat., and 156° 30' E. long., had seen some iron bars and red stuffs used by the natives of these parts. Dumont d'Urville, much perplexed, and not knowing how to credit the reports of low-class journals, decided to follow Dillon's track.

On the 10th of February, 1828, the Astrolabe appeared off Tikopia, and took as guide and interpreter a deserter found on the island; made his way to Vanikoro, sighted it on the 12th inst., lay among the reefs until the 14th, and not until the 20th did he cast anchor within the barrier in the harbour of Vanou.

On the 23rd, several officers went round the island and brought back some unimportant trifles. The natives, adopting a system of denials and evasions, refused to take them to the unlucky place. This ambiguous conduct led them to believe that the natives had ill-treated the castaways, and indeed they seemed to fear that Dumont d'Urville had come to avenge La Perouse and his unfortunate crew.

However, on the 26th, appeased by some presents, and understanding that they had no reprisals to fear, they led M. Jacquireot to the scene of the wreck.

There, in three or four fathoms of water, between the reefs of Pacou and Vanou, lay anchors, cannons, pigs of lead and iron, embedded in the limy concretions. The large boat and the whaler belonging to the Astrolabe were sent to this place, and, not without some difficulty, their crews hauled up an anchor weighing 1,800 lbs., a brass gun, some pigs of iron, and two copper swivel-guns.

Dumont d'Urville, questioning the natives, learned too that La Perouse, after losing both his vessels on the reefs of this island, had constructed a smaller boat, only to be lost a second time. Where, no one knew.

But the French Government, fearing that Dumont d'Urville was not acquainted with Dillon's movements, had sent the sloop Bayonnaise, commanded by Legoarant de Tromelin, to Vanikoro, which had been stationed on the west coast of America. The Bayonnaise cast her anchor before Vanikoro some months after the departure of the Astrolabe, but found no new document; but stated that the savages had respected the monument to La Perouse. That is the substance of what I told Captain Nemo.

"So," he said, "no one knows now where the third vessel perished that was constructed by the castaways on the island of Vanikoro?"

"No one knows."

Captain Nemo said nothing, but signed to me to follow him into the large saloon. The Nautilus sank several yards below the waves, and the panels were opened.

I hastened to the aperture, and under the crustations of coral, covered with fungi, syphonules, alcyons, madrepores, through myriads of charming fish—girelles, glyphisidri, pompherides, diacopes, and holocentres—I recognised certain debris that the drags had not been able to tear up—iron stirrups, anchors, cannons, bullets, capstan fittings, the stem of a ship, all objects clearly proving the wreck of some vessel, and now carpeted with living flowers. While I was looking on this desolate scene, Captain Nemo said, in a sad voice:

"Commander La Perouse set out 7th December, 1785, with his vessels La Boussole and the Astrolabe. He first cast anchor at Botany Bay, visited the Friendly Isles, New Caledonia, then directed his course towards Santa Cruz, and put into Namouka, one of the Hapai group. Then his vessels struck on the unknown reefs of Vanikoro. The Boussole, which went first, ran aground on the southerly coast. The Astrolabe went to its help, and ran aground too. The first vessel was destroyed almost immediately. The second, stranded under the wind, resisted some days. The natives made the castaways welcome. They installed themselves in the island, and constructed a smaller boat with the debris of the two large ones. Some sailors stayed willingly at Vanikoro; the others, weak and ill, set out with La Perouse. They directed their course towards the Solomon Islands, and there perished, with everything, on the westerly coast of the chief island of the group, between Capes Deception and Satisfaction."

"How do you know that?"

"By this, that I found on the spot where was the last wreck."

Captain Nemo showed me a tin-plate box, stamped with the French arms, and corroded by the salt water. He opened it, and I saw a bundle of papers, yellow but still readable.

They were the instructions of the naval minister to Commander La Perouse, annotated in the margin in Louis XVI's handwriting.

"Ah! it is a fine death for a sailor!" said Captain Nemo, at last. "A coral tomb makes a quiet grave; and I trust that I and my comrades will find no other."

CHAPTER XIX TORRES STRAITS

During the night of the 27th or 28th of December, the Nautilus left the shores of Vanikoro with great speed. Her course was south-westerly, and in three days she had gone over the 750 leagues that separated it from La Perouse's group and the south-east point of Papua.

Early on the 1st of January, 1863, Conseil joined me on the platform.

"Master, will you permit me to wish you a happy New Year?"

"What! Conseil; exactly as if I was at Paris in my study at the Jardin des Plantes? Well, I accept your good wishes, and thank you for them. Only, I will ask you what you mean by a `Happy New Year' under our circumstances? Do you mean the year that will bring us to the end of our imprisonment, or the year that sees us continue this strange voyage?"

"Really, I do not know how to answer, master. We are sure to see curious things, and for the last two months we have not had time for dullness. The last marvel is always the most astonishing; and, if we continue this progression, I do not know how it will end. It is my opinion that we shall never again see the like. I think then, with no offence to master, that a happy year would be one in which we could see everything."

On 2nd January we had made 11,340 miles, or 5,250 French leagues, since our starting-point in the Japan Seas. Before the ship's head stretched the dangerous shores of the coral sea, on the north-east coast of Australia. Our boat lay along some miles from the redoubtable bank on which Cook's vessel was lost, 10th June, 1770. The boat in which Cook was struck on a rock, and, if it did not sink, it was owing to a piece of coral that was broken by the shock, and fixed itself in the broken keel.

I had wished to visit the reef, 360 leagues long, against which the sea, always rough, broke with great violence, with a noise like thunder. But just then the inclined planes drew the Nautilus down to a great depth, and I could see nothing of the high coral walls. I had to content myself with the different specimens of fish brought up by the nets. I remarked, among others, some germons, a species of mackerel as large as a tunny, with bluish sides, and striped with transverse bands, that disappear with the animal's life.

These fish followed us in shoals, and furnished us with very delicate food. We took also a large number of gilt-heads, about one and a half inches long, tasting like dorys; and flying pyrapeds like submarine swallows, which, in dark nights, light alternately the air and water with their phosphorescent light. Among the molluscs and zoophytes, I found in the meshes of the net several species of alcyonarians, echini, hammers, spurs, dials, cerites, and hyalleae. The flora was represented by beautiful floating seaweeds, laminariae, and macrocystes, impregnated with the mucilage that transudes through their pores;

and among which I gathered an admirable Nemastoma Geliniarois, that was classed among the natural curiosities of the museum.

Two days after crossing the coral sea, 4th January, we sighted the Papuan coasts. On this occasion, Captain Nemo informed me that his intention was to get into the Indian Ocean by the Strait of Torres. His communication ended there.

The Torres Straits are nearly thirty-four leagues wide; but they are obstructed by an innumerable quantity of islands, islets, breakers, and rocks, that make its navigation almost impracticable; so that Captain Nemo took all needful precautions to cross them. The Nautilus, floating betwixt wind and water, went at a moderate pace. Her screw, like a cetacean's tail, beat the waves slowly.

Profiting by this, I and my two companions went up on to the deserted platform. Before us was the steersman's cage, and I expected that Captain Nemo was there directing the course of the Nautilus. I had before me the excellent charts of the Straits of Torres, and I consulted them attentively. Round the Nautilus the sea dashed furiously. The course of the waves, that went from south-east to north-west at the rate of two and a half miles, broke on the coral that showed itself here and there.

"This is a bad sea!" remarked Ned Land.

"Detestable indeed, and one that does not suit a boat like the Nautilus."

"The Captain must be very sure of his route, for I see there pieces of coral that would do for its keel if it only touched them slightly."

Indeed the situation was dangerous, but the Nautilus seemed to slide like magic off these rocks. It did not follow the routes of the Astrolabe and the Zelee exactly, for they proved fatal to Dumont d'Urville. It bore more northwards, coasted the Islands of Murray, and came back to the south-west towards Cumberland Passage. I thought it was going to pass it by, when, going back to north-west, it went through a large quantity of islands and islets little known, towards the Island Sound and Canal Mauvais.

I wondered if Captain Nemo, foolishly imprudent, would steer his vessel into that pass where Dumont d'Urville's two corvettes touched; when, swerving again, and cutting straight through to the west, he steered for the Island of Gilboa.

It was then three in the afternoon. The tide began to recede, being quite full. The Nautilus approached the island, that I still saw, with its remarkable border of screw-pines. He stood off it at about two miles distant. Suddenly a shock overthrew me. The Nautilus just touched a rock, and stayed immovable, laying lightly to port side.

When I rose, I perceived Captain Nemo and his lieutenant on the platform. They were examining the situation of the vessel, and exchanging words in their incomprehensible dialect.

She was situated thus: Two miles, on the starboard side, appeared Gilboa, stretching from north to west like an immense arm. Towards the south and east some coral showed itself, left by the ebb. We had run aground, and in one of those seas where the tides are middling—a sorry matter for the floating of the Nautilus. However, the vessel had not suffered, for her keel was solidly joined. But, if she could neither glide off nor move, she ran the risk of being for ever fastened to these rocks, and then Captain Nemo's submarine vessel would be done for.

I was reflecting thus, when the Captain, cool and calm, always master of himself, approached me.

"An accident?" I asked.

"No; an incident."

"But an incident that will oblige you perhaps to become an inhabitant of this land from which you flee?"

Captain Nemo looked at me curiously, and made a negative gesture, as much as to say that nothing would force him to set foot on terra firma again. Then he said:

"Besides, M. Aronnax, the Nautilus is not lost; it will carry you yet into the midst of the marvels of the ocean. Our voyage is only begun, and I do not wish to be deprived so soon of the honour of your company."

"However, Captain Nemo," I replied, without noticing the ironical turn of his phrase, "the Nautilus ran aground in open sea. Now the tides are not strong in the Pacific; and, if you cannot lighten the Nautilus, I do not see how it will be reinflated."

"The tides are not strong in the Pacific: you are right there, Professor; but in Torres Straits one finds still a difference of a yard and a half between the level of high and low seas. To-day is 4th January, and in five days the moon will be full. Now, I shall be very much astonished if that satellite does not raise these masses of water sufficiently, and render me a service that I should be indebted to her for."

Having said this, Captain Nemo, followed by his lieutenant, redescended to the interior of the Nautilus. As to the vessel, it moved not, and was immovable, as if the coralline polypi had already walled it up with their in destructible cement.

"Well, sir?" said Ned Land, who came up to me after the departure of the Captain.

"Well, friend Ned, we will wait patiently for the tide on the 9th instant; for it appears that the moon will have the goodness to put it off again."

"Really?"

"Really."

"And this Captain is not going to cast anchor at all since the tide will suffice?" said Conseil, simply.

The Canadian looked at Conseil, then shrugged his shoulders.

"Sir, you may believe me when I tell you that this piece of iron will navigate neither on nor under the sea again; it is only fit to be sold for its weight. I think, therefore, that the time has come to part company with Captain Nemo."

"Friend Ned, I do not despair of this stout Nautilus, as you do; and in four days we shall know what to hold to on the Pacific tides. Besides, flight might be possible if we were in sight of the English or Provencal coast; but on the Papuan shores, it is another thing; and it will be time enough to come to that extremity if the Nautilus does not recover itself again, which I look upon as a grave event."

"But do they know, at least, how to act circumspectly? There is an island; on that island there are trees; under those trees, terrestrial animals, bearers of cutlets and roast beef, to which I would willingly give a trial."

"In this, friend Ned is right," said Conseil, "and I agree with him. Could not master obtain permission from his friend Captain Nemo to put us on land, if only so as not to lose the habit of treading on the solid parts of our planet?"

"I can ask him, but he will refuse."

"Will master risk it?" asked Conseil, "and we shall know how to rely upon the Captain's amiability."

To my great surprise, Captain Nemo gave me the permission I asked for, and he gave it very agreeably, without even exacting from me a promise to return to the vessel; but flight across New Guinea might be very perilous, and I should not have counselled Ned Land to attempt it. Better to be a prisoner on board the Nautilus than to fall into the hands of the natives.

At eight o'clock, armed with guns and hatchets, we got off the Nautilus. The sea was pretty calm; a slight breeze blew on land. Conseil and I rowing, we sped along quickly, and Ned steered in the straight passage that the breakers left between them. The boat was well handled, and moved rapidly.

Ned Land could not restrain his joy. He was like a prisoner that had escaped from prison, and knew not that it was necessary to re-enter it.

"Meat! We are going to eat some meat; and what meat!" he replied. "Real game! no, bread, indeed."

"I do not say that fish is not good; we must not abuse it; but a piece of fresh venison, grilled on live coals, will agreeably vary our ordinary course."

"Glutton!" said Conseil, "he makes my mouth water."

"It remains to be seen," I said, "if these forests are full of game, and if the game is not such as will hunt the hunter himself."

"Well said, M. Aronnax," replied the Canadian, whose teeth seemed sharpened like the edge of a hatchet; "but I will eat tiger—loin of tiger—if there is no other quadruped on this island."

"Friend Ned is uneasy about it," said Conseil.

"Whatever it may be," continued Ned Land, "every animal with four paws without feathers, or with two paws without feathers, will be saluted by my first shot."

"Very well! Master Land's imprudences are beginning."

"Never fear, M. Aronnax," replied the Canadian; "I do not want twenty-five minutes to offer you a dish, of my sort."

At half-past eight the Nautilus boat ran softly aground on a heavy sand, after having happily passed the coral reef that surrounds the Island of Gilboa.

CHAPTER XX A FEW DAYS ON LAND

I was much impressed on touching land. Ned Land tried the soil with his feet, as if to take possession of it. However, it was only two months before that we had become, according to Captain Nemo, "passengers on board the Nautilus," but, in reality, prisoners of its commander.

In a few minutes we were within musket-shot of the coast. The whole horizon was hidden behind a beautiful curtain of forests. Enormous trees, the trunks of which attained a height of 200 feet, were tied to each other by garlands of bindweed, real natural hammocks, which a light breeze rocked. They were mimosas, figs, hibisci, and palm trees, mingled together in profusion; and under the shelter of their verdant vault grew orchids, leguminous plants, and ferns.

But, without noticing all these beautiful specimens of Papuan flora, the Canadian abandoned the agreeable for the useful. He discovered a coco-tree, beat down some of the fruit, broke them, and we drunk the milk and ate the nut with a satisfaction that protested against the ordinary food on the Nautilus.

"Excellent!" said Ned Land.

"Exquisite!" replied Conseil.

"And I do not think," said the Canadian, "that he would object to our introducing a cargo of coco-nuts on board."

"I do not think he would, but he would not taste them."

"So much the worse for him," said Conseil.

"And so much the better for us," replied Ned Land. "There will be more for us."

"One word only, Master Land," I said to the harpooner, who was beginning to ravage another coco-nut tree. "Coco-nuts are good things, but before filling the canoe with them it would be wise to reconnoitre and see if the island does not produce some substance not less useful. Fresh vegetables would be welcome on board the Nautilus."

"Master is right," replied Conseil; "and I propose to reserve three places in our vessel, one for fruits, the other for vegetables, and the third for the venison, of which I have not yet seen the smallest specimen."

"Conseil, we must not despair," said the Canadian.

"Let us continue," I returned, "and lie in wait. Although the island seems uninhabited, it might still contain some individuals that would be less hard than we on the nature of game."

"Ho! ho!" said Ned Land, moving his jaws significantly.

"Well, Ned!" said Conseil.

"My word!" returned the Canadian, "I begin to understand the charms of anthropophagy."

"Ned! Ned! what are you saying? You, a man-eater? I should not feel safe with you, especially as I share your cabin. I might perhaps wake one day to find myself half devoured."

"Friend Conseil, I like you much, but not enough to eat you unnecessarily."

"I would not trust you," replied Conseil. "But enough. We must absolutely bring down some game to satisfy this cannibal, or else one of these fine mornings, master will find only pieces of his servant to serve him."

While we were talking thus, we were penetrating the sombre arches of the forest, and for two hours we surveyed it in all directions.

Chance rewarded our search for eatable vegetables, and one of the most useful products of the tropical zones furnished us with precious food that we missed on board. I would speak of the bread-fruit tree, very abundant in the island of Gilboa; and I remarked chiefly the variety destitute of seeds, which bears in Malaya the name of "rima."

Ned Land knew these fruits well. He had already eaten many during his numerous voyages, and he knew how to prepare the eatable substance. Moreover, the sight of them excited him, and he could contain himself no longer.

"Master," he said, "I shall die if I do not taste a little of this bread-fruit pie."

"Taste it, friend Ned—taste it as you want. We are here to make experiments—make them."

"It won't take long," said the Canadian.

And, provided with a lentil, he lighted a fire of dead wood that crackled joyously. During this time, Conseil and I chose the best fruits of the bread-fruit. Some had not then attained a sufficient degree of maturity; and their thick skin covered a white but rather fibrous pulp. Others, the greater number yellow and gelatinous, waited only to be picked.

These fruits enclosed no kernel. Conseil brought a dozen to Ned Land, who placed them on a coal fire, after having cut them in thick slices, and while doing this repeating:

"You will see, master, how good this bread is. More so when one has been deprived of it so long. It is not even bread," added he, "but a delicate pastry. You have eaten none, master?"

"No, Ned."

"Very well, prepare yourself for a juicy thing. If you do not come for more, I am no longer the king of harpooners."

After some minutes, the part of the fruits that was exposed to the fire was completely roasted. The interior looked like a white pasty, a sort of soft crumb, the flavour of which was like that of an artichoke.

It must be confessed this bread was excellent, and I ate of it with great relish.

"What time is it now?" asked the Canadian.

"Two o'clock at least," replied Conseil.

"How time flies on firm ground!" sighed Ned Land.

"Let us be off," replied Conseil.

We returned through the forest, and completed our collection by a raid upon the cabbage-palms, that we gathered from the tops of the trees, little beans that I recognised as the "abrou" of the Malays, and yams of a superior quality.

We were loaded when we reached the boat. But Ned Land did not find his provisions sufficient. Fate, however, favoured us. Just as we were pushing off, he perceived several trees, from twenty-five to thirty feet high, a species of palm-tree.

At last, at five o'clock in the evening, loaded with our riches, we quitted the shore, and half an hour after we hailed the Nautilus. No one appeared on our arrival. The enormous iron-plated cylinder seemed deserted. The provisions embarked, I descended to my chamber, and after supper slept soundly.

The next day, 6th January, nothing new on board. Not a sound inside, not a sign of life. The boat rested along the edge, in the same place in which we had left it. We resolved to return to the island. Ned Land hoped to be more fortunate than on the day before with regard to the hunt, and wished to visit another part of the forest.

At dawn we set off. The boat, carried on by the waves that flowed to shore, reached the island in a few minutes.

We landed, and, thinking that it was better to give in to the Canadian, we followed Ned Land, whose long limbs threatened to distance us. He wound up the coast towards the west: then, fording some torrents, he gained the high plain that was bordered with admirable forests. Some kingfishers were rambling along the water-courses, but they would not let themselves be approached. Their circumspection proved to me that these birds knew what to expect from bipeds of our species, and I concluded that, if the island was not inhabited, at least human beings occasionally frequented it.

After crossing a rather large prairie, we arrived at the skirts of a little wood that was enlivened by the songs and flight of a large number of birds.

"There are only birds," said Conseil.

"But they are eatable," replied the harpooner.

"I do not agree with you, friend Ned, for I see only parrots there."

"Friend Conseil," said Ned, gravely, "the parrot is like pheasant to those who have nothing else."

"And," I added, "this bird, suitably prepared, is worth knife and fork."

Indeed, under the thick foliage of this wood, a world of parrots were flying from branch to branch, only needing a careful education to speak the human language. For the moment, they were chattering with parrots of all colours, and grave cockatoos, who seemed to meditate upon some philosophical problem, whilst brilliant red lories passed like a piece of bunting carried away by the breeze, papuans, with the finest azure colours, and in all a variety of winged things most charming to behold, but few eatable.

However, a bird peculiar to these lands, and which has never passed the limits of the Arrow and Papuan islands, was wanting in this collection. But fortune reserved it for me before long.

After passing through a moderately thick copse, we found a plain obstructed with bushes. I saw then those magnificent birds, the disposition of whose long feathers obliges them to fly against the wind. Their undulating flight, graceful aerial curves, and the shading of their colours, attracted and charmed one's looks. I had no trouble in recognising them.

"Birds of paradise!" I exclaimed.

The Malays, who carry on a great trade in these birds with the Chinese, have several means that we could not employ for taking them. Sometimes they put snares on the top of high trees that the birds of paradise prefer to frequent. Sometimes they catch them with a viscous birdlime that paralyses their movements. They even go so far as to poison the fountains that the birds generally drink from. But we were obliged to fire at them during flight, which gave us few chances to bring them down; and, indeed, we vainly exhausted one half our ammunition.

About eleven o'clock in the morning, the first range of mountains that form the centre of the island was traversed, and we had killed nothing. Hunger drove us on. The hunters had relied on the products of the chase, and they were wrong. Happily Conseil, to his great surprise, made a double shot and secured breakfast. He brought down a white pigeon and a wood-pigeon, which, cleverly plucked and suspended from a skewer, was roasted before a red fire of dead wood. While these interesting birds were cooking, Ned prepared the fruit of the bread-tree. Then the wood-pigeons were devoured to the bones, and declared excellent. The nutmeg, with which they are in the habit of stuffing their crops, flavours their flesh and renders it delicious eating.

"Now, Ned, what do you miss now?"

"Some four-footed game, M. Aronnax. All these pigeons are only side-dishes and trifles; and until I have killed an animal with cutlets I shall not be content."

"Nor I, Ned, if I do not catch a bird of paradise."

"Let us continue hunting," replied Conseil. "Let us go towards the sea. We have arrived at the first declivities of the mountains, and I think we had better regain the region of forests."

That was sensible advice, and was followed out. After walking for one hour we had attained a forest of sago-trees. Some inoffensive serpents glided away from us. The birds of paradise fled at our approach, and truly I despaired of getting near one when Conseil, who was walking in front, suddenly bent down, uttered a triumphal cry, and came back to me bringing a magnificent specimen.

"Ah! bravo, Conseil!"

"Master is very good."

"No, my boy; you have made an excellent stroke. Take one of these living birds, and carry it in your hand."

"If master will examine it, he will see that I have not deserved great merit."

"Why, Conseil?"

"Because this bird is as drunk as a quail."

"Drunk!"

"Yes, sir; drunk with the nutmegs that it devoured under the nutmeg-tree, under which I found it. See, friend Ned, see the monstrous effects of intemperance!"

"By Jove!" exclaimed the Canadian, "because I have drunk gin for two months, you must needs reproach me!"

However, I examined the curious bird. Conseil was right. The bird, drunk with the juice, was quite powerless. It could not fly; it could hardly walk.

This bird belonged to the most beautiful of the eight species that are found in Papua and in the neighbouring islands. It was the "large emerald bird, the most rare kind." It measured three feet in length. Its head was comparatively small, its eyes placed near the opening of the beak, and also small. But the shades of colour were beautiful, having a yellow beak, brown feet and claws, nut-coloured wings with purple tips, pale yellow at the back of the neck and head, and emerald colour at the throat, chestnut on the breast and belly. Two horned, downy nets rose from below the tail, that prolonged the long light feathers of admirable fineness, and they completed the whole of this marvellous bird, that the natives have poetically named the "bird of the sun."

But if my wishes were satisfied by the possession of the bird of paradise, the Canadian's were not yet. Happily, about two o'clock, Ned Land brought down a magnificent hog; from the brood of those the natives call "bari-outang." The animal came in time for us to procure real quadruped meat, and he was well received. Ned Land was very proud of his shot. The hog, hit by the electric ball, fell stone dead. The Canadian skinned and cleaned it properly, after having taken half a dozen cutlets, destined to furnish us with a grilled repast in the evening. Then the hunt was resumed, which was still more marked by Ned and Conseil's exploits.

Indeed, the two friends, beating the bushes, roused a herd of kangaroos that fled and bounded along on their elastic paws. But these animals did not take to flight so rapidly but what the electric capsule could stop their course.

"Ah, Professor!" cried Ned Land, who was carried away by the delights of the chase, "what excellent game, and stewed, too! What a supply for the Nautilus! Two! three! five down! And to think that we shall eat that flesh, and that the idiots on board shall not have a crumb!"

I think that, in the excess of his joy, the Canadian, if he had not talked so much, would have killed them all. But he contented himself with a single dozen of these interesting marsupians. These animals were small. They were a species of those "kangaroo rabbits" that live habitually in the hollows of trees, and whose speed is extreme; but they are moderately fat, and furnish, at least, estimable food. We were very satisfied with the results of the hunt. Happy Ned proposed to return to this enchanting island the next day, for he wished to depopulate it of all the eatable quadrupeds. But he had reckoned without his host.

At six o'clock in the evening we had regained the shore; our boat was moored to the usual place. The Nautilus, like a long rock, emerged from the waves two miles from the beach. Ned Land, without waiting, occupied himself about the important dinner business. He understood all about cooking well. The "bari-outang," grilled on the coals, soon scented the air with a delicious odour.

Indeed, the dinner was excellent. Two wood-pigeons completed this extraordinary menu. The sago pasty, the artocarpus bread, some mangoes, half a dozen pineapples, and the liquor fermented from some coco-nuts, overjoyed us. I even think that my worthy companions' ideas had not all the plainness desirable.

"Suppose we do not return to the Nautilus this evening?" said Conseil.

"Suppose we never return?" added Ned Land.

Just then a stone fell at our feet and cut short the harpooner's proposition.

CHAPTER XXI CAPTAIN NEMO'S THUNDERBOLT

We looked at the edge of the forest without rising, my hand stopping in the action of putting it to my mouth, Ned Land's completing its office.

"Stones do not fall from the sky," remarked Conseil, "or they would merit the name aerolites."

A second stone, carefully aimed, that made a savoury pigeon's leg fall from Conseil's hand, gave still more weight to his observation. We all three arose, shouldered our guns, and were ready to reply to any attack.

"Are they apes?" cried Ned Land.

"Very nearly—they are savages."

"To the boat!" I said, hurrying to the sea.

It was indeed necessary to beat a retreat, for about twenty natives armed with bows and slings appeared on the skirts of a copse that masked the horizon to the right, hardly a hundred steps from us.

Our boat was moored about sixty feet from us. The savages approached us, not running, but making hostile demonstrations. Stones and arrows fell thickly.

Ned Land had not wished to leave his provisions; and, in spite of his imminent danger, his pig on one side and kangaroos on the other, he went tolerably fast. In two minutes we were on the shore. To load the boat with provisions and arms, to push it out to sea, and ship the oars, was the work of an instant. We had not gone two cable-lengths, when a hundred savages, howling and gesticulating, entered the water up to their waists. I watched to see if their apparition would attract some men from the Nautilus on to the platform. But no. The enormous machine, lying off, was absolutely deserted.

Twenty minutes later we were on board. The panels were open. After making the boat fast, we entered into the interior of the Nautilus.

I descended to the drawing-room, from whence I heard some chords. Captain Nemo was there, bending over his organ, and plunged in a musical ecstasy.

"Captain!"

He did not hear me.

"Captain!" I said, touching his hand.

He shuddered, and, turning round, said, "Ah! it is you, Professor? Well, have you had a good hunt, have you botanised successfully?"

"Yes Captain; but we have unfortunately brought a troop of bipeds, whose vicinity troubles me."

"What bipeds?"

"Savages."

"Savages!" he echoed, ironically. "So you are astonished, Professor, at having set foot on a strange land and finding savages? Savages! where are there not any? Besides, are they worse than others, these whom you call savages?"

"But Captain——"

"How many have you counted?"

"A hundred at least."

"M. Aronnax," replied Captain Nemo, placing his fingers on the organ stops, "when all the natives of Papua are assembled on this shore, the Nautilus will have nothing to fear from their attacks."

The Captain's fingers were then running over the keys of the instrument, and I remarked that he touched only the black keys, which gave his melodies an essentially Scotch character. Soon he had forgotten my presence, and had plunged into a reverie that I did not disturb. I went up again on to the platform: night had already fallen; for, in this low latitude, the sun sets rapidly and without twilight. I could only see the island indistinctly; but the numerous fires, lighted on the beach, showed that the natives did not think of leaving it. I was alone for several hours, sometimes thinking of the natives—but without any dread of them, for the imperturbable confidence of the Captain was catching—sometimes forgetting them to admire the splendours of the night in the tropics. My remembrances went to France in the train of those zodiacal stars that would shine in some hours' time. The moon shone in the midst of the constellations of the zenith.

The night slipped away without any mischance, the islanders frightened no doubt at the sight of a monster aground in the bay. The panels were open, and would have offered an easy access to the interior of the Nautilus.

At six o'clock in the morning of the 8th January I went up on to the platform. The dawn was breaking. The island soon showed itself through the dissipating fogs, first the shore, then the summits.

The natives were there, more numerous than on the day before—five or six hundred perhaps—some of them, profiting by the low water, had come on to the coral, at less than two cable-lengths from the Nautilus. I distinguished them easily; they were true Papuans, with athletic figures, men of good race, large high foreheads, large, but not broad and flat, and white teeth. Their woolly hair, with a reddish tinge, showed off on their black shining bodies like those of the Nubians. From the lobes of their ears, cut and distended, hung chaplets of bones. Most of these savages were naked. Amongst them, I remarked some women, dressed from the hips to knees in quite a crinoline of herbs, that sustained a vegetable waistband. Some chiefs had ornamented their necks with a crescent and collars of glass beads, red and white; nearly all were armed with bows, arrows, and shields and carried on their shoulders a sort of net containing those round stones which they cast from their slings with great skill. One of these chiefs, rather near to the Nautilus, examined it attentively. He was, perhaps, a "mado" of high rank, for he was draped in a mat of banana-leaves, notched round the edges, and set off with brilliant colours.

I could easily have knocked down this native, who was within a short length; but I thought that it was better to wait for real hostile demonstrations. Between Europeans and savages, it is proper for the Europeans to parry sharply, not to attack.

During low water the natives roamed about near the Nautilus, but were not troublesome; I heard them frequently repeat the word "Assai," and by their gestures I understood that they invited me to go on land, an invitation that I declined.

So that, on that day, the boat did not push off, to the great displeasure of Master Land, who could not complete his provisions.

This adroit Canadian employed his time in preparing the viands and meat that he had brought off the island. As for the savages, they returned to the shore about eleven o'clock in the morning, as soon as the coral tops began to disappear under the rising tide; but I saw their numbers had increased considerably on the shore. Probably they came from the neighbouring islands, or very likely from Papua. However, I had not seen a single native canoe. Having nothing better to do, I thought of dragging these beautiful limpid waters, under which I saw a profusion of shells, zoophytes, and marine plants. Moreover, it was the last day that the Nautilus would pass in these parts, if it float in open sea the next day, according to Captain Nemo's promise.

I therefore called Conseil, who brought me a little light drag, very like those for the oyster fishery. Now to work! For two hours we fished unceasingly, but without bringing up any rarities. The drag was filled with midas-ears, harps, melames, and particularly the most beautiful hammers I have ever seen. We also brought up some sea-slugs, pearl-oysters, and a dozen little turtles that were reserved for the pantry on board.

But just when I expected it least, I put my hand on a wonder, I might say a natural deformity, very rarely met with. Conseil was just dragging, and his net came up filled with divers ordinary shells, when, all at once, he saw me plunge my arm quickly into the net, to draw out a shell, and heard me utter a cry.

"What is the matter, sir?" he asked in surprise. "Has master been bitten?"

"No, my boy; but I would willingly have given a finger for my discovery."

"What discovery?"

"This shell," I said, holding up the object of my triumph.

"It is simply an olive porphyry, genus olive, order of the pectinibranchidae, class of gasteropods, sub-class mollusca."

"Yes, Conseil; but, instead of being rolled from right to left, this olive turns from left to right."

"Is it possible?"

"Yes, my boy; it is a left shell."

Shells are all right-handed, with rare exceptions; and, when by chance their spiral is left, amateurs are ready to pay their weight in gold.

Conseil and I were absorbed in the contemplation of our treasure, and I was promising myself to enrich the museum with it, when a stone unfortunately thrown by a native struck against, and broke, the precious object in Conseil's hand. I uttered a cry of despair! Conseil took up his gun, and aimed at a savage who was poising his sling at ten yards from him. I would have stopped him, but his blow took effect and broke the bracelet of amulets which encircled the arm of the savage.

"Conseil!" cried I. "Conseil!"

"Well, sir! do you not see that the cannibal has commenced the attack?"

"A shell is not worth the life of a man," said I.

"Ah! the scoundrel!" cried Conseil; "I would rather he had broken my shoulder!"

Conseil was in earnest, but I was not of his opinion. However, the situation had changed some minutes before, and we had not perceived. A score of canoes surrounded the Nautilus. These canoes, scooped out of the trunk of a tree, long, narrow, well adapted for speed, were balanced by means of a long bamboo pole, which floated on the water. They were managed by skilful, half-naked paddlers, and I watched their advance with some uneasiness. It was evident that these Papuans had already had dealings with the Europeans and knew their ships. But this long iron cylinder anchored in the bay, without masts or chimneys, what could they think of it? Nothing good, for at first they kept at a respectful distance. However, seeing it motionless, by degrees they took courage, and sought to familiarise themselves with it. Now this familiarity was precisely what it was necessary to avoid. Our arms, which were noiseless, could only produce a moderate effect on the savages, who have little respect for aught but blustering things. The thunderbolt without the reverberations of thunder would frighten man but little, though the danger lies in the lightning, not in the noise.

At this moment the canoes approached the Nautilus, and a shower of arrows alighted on her.

I went down to the saloon, but found no one there. I ventured to knock at the door that opened into the Captain's room. "Come in," was the answer.

I entered, and found Captain Nemo deep in algebraical calculations of *x* and other quantities.

"I am disturbing you," said I, for courtesy's sake.

"That is true, M. Aronnax," replied the Captain; "but I think you have serious reasons for wishing to see me?"

"Very grave ones; the natives are surrounding us in their canoes, and in a few minutes we shall certainly be attacked by many hundreds of savages."

"Ah!" said Captain Nemo quietly, "they are come with their canoes?"

"Yes, sir."

"Well, sir, we must close the hatches."

"Exactly, and I came to say to you——"

"Nothing can be more simple," said Captain Nemo. And, pressing an electric button, he transmitted an order to the ship's crew.

"It is all done, sir," said he, after some moments. "The pinnace is ready, and the hatches are closed. You do not fear, I imagine, that these gentlemen could stave in walls on which the balls of your frigate have had no effect?"

"No, Captain; but a danger still exists."

"What is that, sir?"

"It is that to-morrow, at about this hour, we must open the hatches to renew the air of the Nautilus. Now, if, at this moment, the Papuans should occupy the platform, I do not see how you could prevent them from entering."

"Then, sir, you suppose that they will board us?"

"I am certain of it."

"Well, sir, let them come. I see no reason for hindering them. After all, these Papuans are poor creatures, and I am unwilling that my visit to the island should cost the life of a single one of these wretches."

Upon that I was going away; But Captain Nemo detained me, and asked me to sit down by him. He questioned me with interest about our excursions on shore, and our hunting; and seemed not to understand the craving for meat that possessed the Canadian. Then the conversation turned on various subjects, and, without being more communicative, Captain Nemo showed himself more amiable.

Amongst other things, we happened to speak of the situation of the Nautilus, run aground in exactly the same spot in this strait where Dumont d'Urville was nearly lost. Apropos of this:

"This D'Urville was one of your great sailors," said the Captain to me, "one of your most intelligent navigators. He is the Captain Cook of you Frenchmen. Unfortunate man of science, after having braved the icebergs of the South Pole, the coral reefs of Oceania, the cannibals of the Pacific, to perish miserably in a railway train! If this energetic man could have reflected during the last moments of his life, what must have been uppermost in his last thoughts, do you suppose?"

So speaking, Captain Nemo seemed moved, and his emotion gave me a better opinion of him. Then, chart in hand, we reviewed the travels of the French navigator, his voyages of circumnavigation, his double detention at the South Pole, which led to the discovery of Adelaide and Louis Philippe, and fixing the hydrographical bearings of the principal islands of Oceania.

"That which your D'Urville has done on the surface of the seas," said Captain Nemo, "that have I done under them, and more easily, more completely than he. The Astrolabe and the Zelee, incessantly tossed about by the hurricane, could not be worth the Nautilus, quiet repository of labour that she is, truly motionless in the midst of the waters.

"To-morrow," added the Captain, rising, "to-morrow, at twenty minutes to three p.m., the Nautilus shall float, and leave the Strait of Torres uninjured."

Having curtly pronounced these words, Captain Nemo bowed slightly. This was to dismiss me, and I went back to my room.

There I found Conseil, who wished to know the result of my interview with the Captain.

"My boy," said I, "when I feigned to believe that his Nautilus was threatened by the natives of Papua, the Captain answered me very sarcastically. I have but one thing to say to you: Have confidence in him, and go to sleep in peace."

"Have you no need of my services, sir?"

"No, my friend. What is Ned Land doing?"

"If you will excuse me, sir," answered Conseil, "friend Ned is busy making a kangaroo-pie which will be a marvel."

I remained alone and went to bed, but slept indifferently. I heard the noise of the savages, who stamped on the platform, uttering deafening cries. The night passed thus, without disturbing the ordinary repose of the crew. The presence of these cannibals affected them no more than the soldiers of a masked battery care for the ants that crawl over its front.

At six in the morning I rose. The hatches had not been opened. The inner air was not renewed, but the reservoirs, filled ready for any emergency, were now resorted to, and discharged several cubic feet of oxygen into the exhausted atmosphere of the Nautilus.

I worked in my room till noon, without having seen Captain Nemo, even for an instant. On board no preparations for departure were visible.

I waited still some time, then went into the large saloon. The clock marked half-past two. In ten minutes it would be high-tide: and, if Captain Nemo had not made a rash promise, the Nautilus would be immediately detached. If not, many months would pass ere she could leave her bed of coral.

However, some warning vibrations began to be felt in the vessel. I heard the keel grating against the rough calcareous bottom of the coral reef.

At five-and-twenty minutes to three, Captain Nemo appeared in the saloon.

"We are going to start," said he.

"Ah!" replied I.

"I have given the order to open the hatches."

"And the Papuans?"

"The Papuans?" answered Captain Nemo, slightly shrugging his shoulders.

"Will they not come inside the Nautilus?"

"How?"

"Only by leaping over the hatches you have opened."

"M. Aronnax," quietly answered Captain Nemo, "they will not enter the hatches of the Nautilus in that way, even if they were open."

I looked at the Captain.

"You do not understand?" said he.

"Hardly."

"Well, come and you will see."

I directed my steps towards the central staircase. There Ned Land and Conseil were slyly watching some of the ship's crew, who were opening the hatches, while cries of rage and fearful vociferations resounded outside.

The port lids were pulled down outside. Twenty horrible faces appeared. But the first native who placed his hand on the stair-rail, struck from behind by some invisible force, I know not what, fled, uttering the most fearful cries and making the wildest contortions.

Ten of his companions followed him. They met with the same fate.

Conseil was in ecstasy. Ned Land, carried away by his violent instincts, rushed on to the staircase. But the moment he seized the rail with both hands, he, in his turn, was overthrown.

"I am struck by a thunderbolt," cried he, with an oath.

This explained all. It was no rail; but a metallic cable charged with electricity from the deck communicating with the platform. Whoever touched it felt a powerful shock—and this shock would have been mortal if Captain Nemo had discharged into the conductor the whole force of the current. It might truly be said that between his assailants and himself he had stretched a network of electricity which none could pass with impunity.

Meanwhile, the exasperated Papuans had beaten a retreat paralysed with terror. As for us, half laughing, we consoled and rubbed the unfortunate Ned Land, who swore like one possessed.

But at this moment the Nautilus, raised by the last waves of the tide, quitted her coral bed exactly at the fortieth minute fixed by the Captain. Her screw swept the waters slowly and majestically. Her speed increased gradually, and, sailing on the surface of the ocean, she quitted safe and sound the dangerous passes of the Straits of Torres.

CHAPTER XXII "AEGRI SOMNIA"

The following day 10th January, the Nautilus continued her course between two seas, but with such remarkable speed that I could not estimate it at less than thirty-five miles an hour. The rapidity of her screw was such that I could neither follow nor count its revolutions. When I reflected that this marvellous electric agent, after having afforded motion, heat, and light to the Nautilus, still protected her from outward attack, and transformed her into an ark of safety which no profane hand might touch without being thunderstricken, my admiration was unbounded, and from the structure it extended to the engineer who had called it into existence.

Our course was directed to the west, and on the 11th of January we doubled Cape Wessel, situation in 135° long. and 10° S. lat., which forms the east point of the Gulf of Carpentaria. The reefs were still numerous, but more equalised, and marked on the chart with extreme precision. The Nautilus easily avoided the breakers of Money to port and the Victoria reefs to starboard, placed at 130° long. and on the 10th parallel, which we strictly followed.

On the 13th of January, Captain Nemo arrived in the Sea of Timor, and recognised the island of that name in 122° long.

From this point the direction of the Nautilus inclined towards the south-west. Her head was set for the Indian Ocean. Where would the fancy of Captain Nemo carry us next? Would he return to the coast of Asia or would he approach again the shores of Europe? Improbable conjectures both, to a man who fled from inhabited continents. Then would he descend to the south? Was he going to double the Cape of Good Hope, then Cape Horn, and finally go as far as the Antarctic pole? Would he come back at last to the Pacific, where his Nautilus could sail free and independently? Time would show.

After having skirted the sands of Cartier, of Hibernia, Seringapatam, and Scott, last efforts of the solid against the liquid element, on the 14th of January we lost sight of land altogether. The speed of the Nautilus was considerably abated, and with irregular course she sometimes swam in the bosom of the waters, sometimes floated on their surface.

During this period of the voyage, Captain Nemo made some interesting experiments on the varied temperature of the sea, in different beds. Under ordinary conditions these observations are made by means of rather complicated instruments, and with somewhat doubtful results, by means of thermometrical sounding-leads, the glasses often breaking under the pressure of the water, or an apparatus grounded on the variations of the resistance of metals to the electric currents. Results so obtained could not be correctly calculated. On the contrary, Captain Nemo went himself to test the temperature in the depths of the sea, and his thermometer, placed in communication with the different sheets of water, gave him the required degree immediately and accurately.

CHAPTER XXII "AEGRI SOMNIA"

It was thus that, either by overloading her reservoirs or by descending obliquely by means of her inclined planes, the Nautilus successively attained the depth of three, four, five, seven, nine, and ten thousand yards, and the definite result of this experience was that the sea preserved an average temperature of four degrees and a half at a depth of five thousand fathoms under all latitudes.

On the 16th of January, the Nautilus seemed becalmed only a few yards beneath the surface of the waves. Her electric apparatus remained inactive and her motionless screw left her to drift at the mercy of the currents. I supposed that the crew was occupied with interior repairs, rendered necessary by the violence of the mechanical movements of the machine.

My companions and I then witnessed a curious spectacle. The hatches of the saloon were open, and, as the beacon light of the Nautilus was not in action, a dim obscurity reigned in the midst of the waters. I observed the state of the sea, under these conditions, and the largest fish appeared to me no more than scarcely defined shadows, when the Nautilus found herself suddenly transported into full light. I thought at first that the beacon had been lighted, and was casting its electric radiance into the liquid mass. I was mistaken, and after a rapid survey perceived my error.

The Nautilus floated in the midst of a phosphorescent bed which, in this obscurity, became quite dazzling. It was produced by myriads of luminous animalculae, whose brilliancy was increased as they glided over the metallic hull of the vessel. I was surprised by lightning in the midst of these luminous sheets, as though they had been rivulets of lead melted in an ardent furnace or metallic masses brought to a white heat, so that, by force of contrast, certain portions of light appeared to cast a shade in the midst of the general ignition, from which all shade seemed banished. No; this was not the calm irradiation of our ordinary lightning. There was unusual life and vigour: this was truly living light!

In reality, it was an infinite agglomeration of coloured infusoria, of veritable globules of jelly, provided with a threadlike tentacle, and of which as many as twenty-five thousand have been counted in less than two cubic half-inches of water.

During several hours the Nautilus floated in these brilliant waves, and our admiration increased as we watched the marine monsters disporting themselves like salamanders. I saw there in the midst of this fire that burns not the swift and elegant porpoise (the indefatigable clown of the ocean), and some swordfish ten feet long, those prophetic heralds of the hurricane whose formidable sword would now and then strike the glass of the saloon. Then appeared the smaller fish, the balista, the leaping mackerel, wolf-thorn-tails, and a hundred others which striped the luminous atmosphere as they swam. This dazzling spectacle was enchanting! Perhaps some atmospheric condition increased the intensity of this phenomenon. Perhaps some storm agitated the surface of the waves. But at this depth of some yards, the Nautilus was unmoved by its fury and reposed peacefully in still water.

So we progressed, incessantly charmed by some new marvel. The days passed rapidly away, and I took no account of them. Ned, according to habit, tried to vary the diet on board. Like snails, we were fixed to our shells, and I declare it is easy to lead a snail's life.

Thus this life seemed easy and natural, and we thought no longer of the life we led on land; but something happened to recall us to the strangeness of our situation.

On the 18th of January, the Nautilus was in 105° long. and 15° S. lat. The weather was threatening, the sea rough and rolling. There was a strong east wind. The barometer, which had been going down for some days, foreboded a coming storm. I went up on to the platform just as the second lieutenant was taking the measure of the horary angles, and waited, according to habit till the daily phrase was said. But on this day it was exchanged for another phrase not less incomprehensible. Almost directly, I saw Captain Nemo appear with a glass, looking towards the horizon.

For some minutes he was immovable, without taking his eye off the point of observation. Then he lowered his glass and exchanged a few words with his lieutenant. The latter seemed to be a victim to some emotion that he tried in vain to repress. Captain Nemo, having more command over himself, was cool. He seemed, too, to be making some objections to which the lieutenant replied by formal assurances. At least I concluded so by the difference of their tones and gestures. For myself, I had looked carefully in the direction indicated without seeing anything. The sky and water were lost in the clear line of the horizon.

However, Captain Nemo walked from one end of the platform to the other, without looking at me, perhaps without seeing me. His step was firm, but less regular than usual. He stopped sometimes, crossed his arms, and observed the sea. What could he be looking for on that immense expanse?

The Nautilus was then some hundreds of miles from the nearest coast.

The lieutenant had taken up the glass and examined the horizon steadfastly, going and coming, stamping his foot and showing more nervous agitation than his superior officer. Besides, this mystery must necessarily be solved, and before long; for, upon an order from Captain Nemo, the engine, increasing its propelling power, made the screw turn more rapidly.

Just then the lieutenant drew the Captain's attention again. The latter stopped walking and directed his glass towards the place indicated. He looked long. I felt very much puzzled, and descended to the drawing-room, and took out an excellent telescope that I generally used. Then, leaning on the cage of the watch-light that jutted out from the front of the platform, set myself to look over all the line of the sky and sea.

But my eye was no sooner applied to the glass than it was quickly snatched out of my hands.

I turned round. Captain Nemo was before me, but I did not know him. His face was transfigured. His eyes flashed sullenly; his teeth were set; his stiff body, clenched fists, and head shrunk between his shoulders, betrayed the violent agitation that pervaded his whole frame. He did not move. My glass, fallen from his hands, had rolled at his feet.

Had I unwittingly provoked this fit of anger? Did this incomprehensible person imagine that I had discovered some forbidden secret? No; I was not the object of this hatred, for he was not looking at me; his eye was steadily fixed upon the impenetrable point of the horizon. At last Captain Nemo recovered himself. His agitation subsided. He addressed some words in a foreign language to his lieutenant, then turned to me. "M. Aronnax," he said, in rather an imperious tone, "I require you to keep one of the conditions that bind you to me."

"What is it, Captain?"

"You must be confined, with your companions, until I think fit to release you."

"You are the master," I replied, looking steadily at him. "But may I ask you one question?"

"None, sir."

There was no resisting this imperious command, it would have been useless. I went down to the cabin occupied by Ned Land and Conseil, and told them the Captain's determination. You may judge how this communication was received by the Canadian.

But there was not time for altercation. Four of the crew waited at the door, and conducted us to that cell where we had passed our first night on board the Nautilus.

Ned Land would have remonstrated, but the door was shut upon him.

"Will master tell me what this means?" asked Conseil.

I told my companions what had passed. They were as much astonished as I, and equally at a loss how to account for it.

Meanwhile, I was absorbed in my own reflections, and could think of nothing but the strange fear depicted in the Captain's countenance. I was utterly at a loss to account for it, when my cogitations were disturbed by these words from Ned Land:

"Hallo! breakfast is ready."

And indeed the table was laid. Evidently Captain Nemo had given this order at the same time that he had hastened the speed of the Nautilus.

"Will master permit me to make a recommendation?" asked Conseil.

"Yes, my boy."

"Well, it is that master breakfasts. It is prudent, for we do not know what may happen."

"You are right, Conseil."

"Unfortunately," said Ned Land, "they have only given us the ship's fare."

"Friend Ned," asked Conseil, "what would you have said if the breakfast had been entirely forgotten?"

This argument cut short the harpooner's recriminations.

We sat down to table. The meal was eaten in silence.

Just then the luminous globe that lighted the cell went out, and left us in total darkness. Ned Land was soon asleep, and what astonished me was that Conseil went off into a heavy slumber. I was thinking what could have caused his irresistible drowsiness, when I felt my brain becoming stupefied. In spite of my efforts to keep my eyes open, they would close. A painful suspicion seized me. Evidently soporific substances had been mixed with the food we had just taken. Imprisonment was not enough to conceal Captain Nemo's projects from us, sleep was more necessary. I then heard the panels shut. The undulations of the sea, which caused a slight rolling motion, ceased. Had the Nautilus quitted the surface of the ocean? Had it gone back to the motionless bed of water? I tried to resist sleep. It was impossible. My breathing grew weak. I felt a mortal cold freeze my stiffened and half-paralysed limbs. My eye lids, like leaden caps, fell over my eyes. I could not raise them; a morbid sleep, full of hallucinations, bereft me of my being. Then the visions disappeared, and left me in complete insensibility.

CHAPTER XXIII THE CORAL KINGDOM

The next day I woke with my head singularly clear. To my great surprise, I was in my own room. My companions, no doubt, had been reinstated in their cabin, without having perceived it any more than I. Of what had passed during the night they were as ignorant as I was, and to penetrate this mystery I only reckoned upon the chances of the future.

I then thought of quitting my room. Was I free again or a prisoner? Quite free. I opened the door, went to the half-deck, went up the central stairs. The panels, shut the evening before, were open. I went on to the platform.

Ned Land and Conseil waited there for me. I questioned them; they knew nothing. Lost in a heavy sleep in which they had been totally unconscious, they had been astonished at finding themselves in their cabin.

As for the Nautilus, it seemed quiet and mysterious as ever. It floated on the surface of the waves at a moderate pace. Nothing seemed changed on board.

The second lieutenant then came on to the platform, and gave the usual order below.

As for Captain Nemo, he did not appear.

Of the people on board, I only saw the impassive steward, who served me with his usual dumb regularity.

About two o'clock, I was in the drawing-room, busied in arranging my notes, when the Captain opened the door and appeared. I bowed. He made a slight inclination in return, without speaking. I resumed my work, hoping that he would perhaps give me some explanation of the events of the preceding night. He made none. I looked at him. He seemed fatigued; his heavy eyes had not been refreshed by sleep; his face looked very sorrowful. He walked to and fro, sat down and got up again, took a chance book, put it down, consulted his instruments without taking his habitual notes, and seemed restless and uneasy. At last, he came up to me, and said:

"Are you a doctor, M. Aronnax?"

I so little expected such a question that I stared some time at him without answering.

"Are you a doctor?" he repeated. "Several of your colleagues have studied medicine."

"Well," said I, "I am a doctor and resident surgeon to the hospital. I practised several years before entering the museum."

"Very well, sir."

My answer had evidently satisfied the Captain. But, not knowing what he would say next, I waited for other questions, reserving my answers according to circumstances.

"M. Aronnax, will you consent to prescribe for one of my men?" he asked.

"Is he ill?"

"Yes."

"I am ready to follow you."

"Come, then."

I own my heart beat, I do not know why. I saw certain connection between the illness of one of the crew and the events of the day before; and this mystery interested me at least as much as the sick man.

Captain Nemo conducted me to the poop of the Nautilus, and took me into a cabin situated near the sailors' quarters.

There, on a bed, lay a man about forty years of age, with a resolute expression of countenance, a true type of an Anglo-Saxon.

I leant over him. He was not only ill, he was wounded. His head, swathed in bandages covered with blood, lay on a pillow. I undid the bandages, and the wounded man looked at me with his large eyes and gave no sign of pain as I did it. It was a horrible wound. The skull, shattered by some deadly weapon, left the brain exposed, which was much injured. Clots of blood had formed in the bruised and broken mass, in colour like the dregs of wine.

There was both contusion and suffusion of the brain. His breathing was slow, and some spasmodic movements of the muscles agitated his face. I felt his pulse. It was intermittent. The extremities of the body were growing cold already, and I saw death must inevitably ensue. After dressing the unfortunate man's wounds, I readjusted the bandages on his head, and turned to Captain Nemo.

"What caused this wound?" I asked.

"What does it signify?" he replied, evasively. "A shock has broken one of the levers of the engine, which struck myself. But your opinion as to his state?"

I hesitated before giving it.

"You may speak," said the Captain. "This man does not understand French."

I gave a last look at the wounded man.

"He will be dead in two hours."

"Can nothing save him?"

"Nothing."

Captain Nemo's hand contracted, and some tears glistened in his eyes, which I thought incapable of shedding any.

For some moments I still watched the dying man, whose life ebbed slowly. His pallor increased under the electric light that was shed over his death-bed. I looked at his intelligent forehead, furrowed with premature wrinkles, produced probably by misfortune and sorrow. I tried to learn the secret of his life from the last words that escaped his lips.

"You can go now, M. Aronnax," said the Captain.

I left him in the dying man's cabin, and returned to my room much affected by this scene. During the whole day, I was haunted by uncomfortable suspicions, and at night I slept badly, and between my broken dreams I fancied I heard distant sighs like the notes of a funeral psalm. Were they the prayers of the dead, murmured in that language that I could not understand?

The next morning I went on to the bridge. Captain Nemo was there before me. As soon as he perceived me he came to me.

"Professor, will it be convenient to you to make a submarine excursion to-day?"

"With my companions?" I asked.

"If they like."

"We obey your orders, Captain."

"Will you be so good then as to put on your cork jackets?"

It was not a question of dead or dying. I rejoined Ned Land and Conseil, and told them of Captain Nemo's proposition. Conseil hastened to accept it, and this time the Canadian seemed quite willing to follow our example.

It was eight o'clock in the morning. At half-past eight we were equipped for this new excursion, and provided with two contrivances for light and breathing. The double door was open; and, accompanied by Captain Nemo, who was followed by a dozen of the crew, we set foot, at a depth of about thirty feet, on the solid bottom on which the Nautilus rested.

A slight declivity ended in an uneven bottom, at fifteen fathoms depth. This bottom differed entirely from the one I had visited on my first excursion under the waters of the Pacific Ocean. Here, there was no fine sand, no submarine prairies, no sea-forest. I immediately recognised that marvellous region in which, on that day, the Captain did the honours to us. It was the coral kingdom.

The light produced a thousand charming varieties, playing in the midst of the branches that were so vividly coloured. I seemed to see the membraneous and cylindrical tubes tremble beneath the undulation of the waters. I was tempted to gather their fresh petals, ornamented with delicate tentacles, some just blown, the others budding, while a small fish, swimming swiftly, touched them slightly, like flights of birds. But if my hand approached these living flowers, these animated, sensitive plants, the whole colony took alarm. The white petals re-entered their red cases, the flowers faded as I looked, and the bush changed into a block of stony knobs.

Chance had thrown me just by the most precious specimens of the zoophyte. This coral was more valuable than that found in the Mediterranean, on the coasts of France, Italy and Barbary. Its tints justified the poetical names of "Flower of Blood," and "Froth of Blood," that trade has given to its most beautiful productions. Coral is sold for L20 per ounce; and in this place the watery beds would make the fortunes of a company of coral-divers. This precious matter, often confused with other polypi, formed then the inextricable plots called "macciota," and on which I noticed several beautiful specimens of pink coral.

But soon the bushes contract, and the arborisations increase. Real petrified thickets, long joints of fantastic architecture, were disclosed before us. Captain Nemo placed himself under a dark gallery, where by a slight declivity we reached a depth of a hundred yards. The light from our lamps produced sometimes magical effects, following the rough outlines of the natural arches and pendants disposed like lustres, that were tipped with points of fire.

At last, after walking two hours, we had attained a depth of about three hundred yards, that is to say, the extreme limit on which coral begins to form. But there was no isolated bush, nor modest brushwood, at the bottom of lofty trees. It was an immense forest of large mineral vegetations, enormous petrified trees, united by garlands of elegant sea-bindweed, all adorned with clouds and reflections. We passed freely under their high branches, lost in the shade of the waves.

Captain Nemo had stopped. I and my companions halted, and, turning round, I saw his men were forming a semi-circle round their chief. Watching attentively, I observed that four of them carried on their shoulders an object of an oblong shape.

We occupied, in this place, the centre of a vast glade surrounded by the lofty foliage of the submarine forest. Our lamps threw over this place a sort of clear twilight that singularly elongated the shadows on the ground. At the end of the glade the darkness increased, and was only relieved by little sparks reflected by the points of coral.

Ned Land and Conseil were near me. We watched, and I thought I was going to witness a strange scene. On observing the ground, I saw that it was raised in certain places by slight excrescences encrusted with limy deposits, and disposed with a regularity that betrayed the hand of man.

In the midst of the glade, on a pedestal of rocks roughly piled up, stood a cross of coral that extended its long arms that one might have thought were made of petrified blood. Upon a sign from Captain Nemo one of the men advanced; and at some feet from the cross he began to dig a hole with a pickaxe that he took from his belt. I understood all! This glade was a cemetery, this hole a tomb, this oblong object the body of the man who had died in the night! The Captain and his men had come to bury their companion in this general resting-place, at the bottom of this inaccessible ocean!

The grave was being dug slowly; the fish fled on all sides while their retreat was being thus disturbed; I heard the strokes of the pickaxe, which sparkled when it hit upon some flint lost at the bottom of the waters. The hole was soon large and deep enough to receive the body. Then the bearers approached; the body, enveloped in a tissue of white linen, was lowered into the damp grave. Captain Nemo, with his arms crossed on his breast, and all the friends of him who had loved them, knelt in prayer.

The grave was then filled in with the rubbish taken from the ground, which formed a slight mound. When this was done, Captain Nemo and his men rose; then, approaching the grave, they knelt again, and all extended their hands in sign of a last adieu. Then the funeral procession returned to the Nautilus, passing under the arches of the forest, in the midst of thickets, along the coral bushes, and still on the ascent. At last the light of the ship appeared, and its luminous track guided us to the Nautilus. At one o'clock we had returned.

As soon as I had changed my clothes I went up on to the platform, and, a prey to conflicting emotions, I sat down near the binnacle. Captain Nemo joined me. I rose and said to him:

"So, as I said he would, this man died in the night?"

"Yes, M. Aronnax."

"And he rests now, near his companions, in the coral cemetery?"

"Yes, forgotten by all else, but not by us. We dug the grave, and the polypi undertake to seal our dead for eternity." And, burying his face quickly in his hands, he tried in vain to suppress a sob. Then he added: "Our peaceful cemetery is there, some hundred feet below the surface of the waves."

"Your dead sleep quietly, at least, Captain, out of the reach of sharks."

"Yes, sir, of sharks and men," gravely replied the Captain.

PART TWO

CHAPTER I THE INDIAN OCEAN

We now come to the second part of our journey under the sea. The first ended with the moving scene in the coral cemetery which left such a deep impression on my mind. Thus, in the midst of this great sea, Captain Nemo's life was passing, even to his grave, which he had prepared in one of its deepest abysses. There, not one of the ocean's monsters could trouble the last sleep of the crew of the Nautilus, of those friends riveted to each other in death as in life. "Nor any man, either," had added the Captain. Still the same fierce, implacable defiance towards human society!

I could no longer content myself with the theory which satisfied Conseil.

That worthy fellow persisted in seeing in the Commander of the Nautilus one of those unknown servants who return mankind contempt for indifference. For him, he was a misunderstood genius who, tired of earth's deceptions, had taken refuge in this inaccessible medium, where he might follow his instincts freely. To my mind, this explains but one side of Captain Nemo's character. Indeed, the mystery of that last night during which we had been chained in prison, the sleep, and the precaution so violently taken by the Captain of snatching from my eyes the glass I had raised to sweep the horizon, the mortal wound of the man, due to an unaccountable shock of the Nautilus, all put me on a new track. No; Captain Nemo was not satisfied with shunning man. His formidable apparatus not only suited his instinct of freedom, but perhaps also the design of some terrible retaliation.

At this moment nothing is clear to me; I catch but a glimpse of light amidst all the darkness, and I must confine myself to writing as events shall dictate.

That day, the 24th of January, 1868, at noon, the second officer came to take the altitude of the sun. I mounted the platform, lit a cigar, and watched the operation. It seemed to me that the man did not understand French; for several times I made remarks in a loud voice, which must have drawn from him some involuntary sign of attention, if he had understood them; but he remained undisturbed and dumb.

As he was taking observations with the sextant, one of the sailors of the Nautilus (the strong man who had accompanied us on our first submarine excursion to the Island of Crespo) came to clean the glasses of the lantern. I examined the fittings of the apparatus, the strength of which was increased a hundredfold by lenticular rings, placed similar to those in a lighthouse, and which projected their brilliance in a horizontal plane. The electric lamp was combined in such a way as to give its most powerful light. Indeed, it was produced in vacuo, which insured both its steadiness and its intensity. This vacuum economised the graphite points between which the luminous arc was developed—an important point of economy for Captain Nemo, who could not easily have replaced them; and under these conditions their waste was imperceptible. When the Nautilus was ready to continue its submarine journey, I went down to the saloon. The panel was closed, and the course marked direct west.

We were furrowing the waters of the Indian Ocean, a vast liquid plain, with a surface of 1,200,000,000 of acres, and whose waters are so clear and transparent that any one leaning over them would turn giddy. The Nautilus usually floated between fifty and a hundred fathoms deep. We went on so for some days. To anyone but myself, who had a great love for the sea, the hours would have seemed long and monotonous; but the daily walks on the platform, when I steeped myself in the reviving air of the ocean, the sight of the rich waters through the windows of the saloon, the books in the library, the compiling of my memoirs, took up all my time, and left me not a moment of ennui or weariness.

For some days we saw a great number of aquatic birds, sea-mews or gulls. Some were cleverly killed and, prepared in a certain way, made very acceptable water-game. Amongst large-winged birds, carried a long distance from all lands and resting upon the waves from the fatigue of their flight, I saw some magnificent albatrosses, uttering discordant cries like the braying of an ass, and birds belonging to the family of the longwings.

As to the fish, they always provoked our admiration when we surprised the secrets of their aquatic life through the open panels. I saw many kinds which I never before had a chance of observing.

I shall notice chiefly ostracions peculiar to the Red Sea, the Indian Ocean, and that part which washes the coast of tropical America. These fishes, like the tortoise, the armadillo, the sea-hedgehog, and the Crustacea, are protected by a breastplate which is neither chalky nor stony, but real bone. In some it takes the form of a solid triangle, in others of a solid quadrangle. Amongst the triangular I saw some an inch and a half in length, with wholesome flesh and a delicious flavour; they are brown at the tail, and yellow at the fins, and I recommend their introduction into fresh water, to which a certain number of sea-fish easily accustom themselves. I would also mention quadrangular ostracions, having on the back four large tubercles; some dotted over with white spots on the lower part of the body, and which may be tamed like birds; trigons provided with spikes formed by the lengthening of their bony shell, and which, from their strange gruntings, are called "seapigs"; also dromedaries with large humps in the shape of a cone, whose flesh is very tough and leathery.

I now borrow from the daily notes of Master Conseil. "Certain fish of the genus petrodon peculiar to those seas, with red backs and white chests, which are distinguished by three rows of longitudinal filaments; and some electrical, seven inches long, decked in the liveliest colours. Then, as specimens of other kinds, some ovoides, resembling an egg of a dark brown colour, marked with white bands, and without tails; diodons, real sea-porcupines, furnished with spikes, and capable of swelling in such a way as to look like cushions bristling with darts; hippocampi, common to every ocean; some pegasi with lengthened snouts, which their pectoral fins, being much elongated and formed in the shape of wings, allow, if not to fly, at least to shoot into the air; pigeon spatulae, with tails covered with many rings of shell; macrognathi with long jaws, an excellent fish, nine inches long, and bright with most agreeable colours; pale-coloured calliomores, with rugged heads; and plenty of chaetpdons, with long and tubular muzzles, which kill insects by shooting them, as from an air-gun, with a single drop of water. These we may call the flycatchers of the seas.

"In the eighty-ninth genus of fishes, classed by Lacepede, belonging to the second lower class of bony, characterised by opercules and bronchial membranes, I remarked the scorpaena, the head of which is furnished with spikes, and which has but one dorsal fin;

these creatures are covered, or not, with little shells, according to the sub-class to which they belong. The second sub-class gives us specimens of didactyles fourteen or fifteen inches in length, with yellow rays, and heads of a most fantastic appearance. As to the first sub-class, it gives several specimens of that singular looking fish appropriately called a 'seafrog,' with large head, sometimes pierced with holes, sometimes swollen with protuberances, bristling with spikes, and covered with tubercles; it has irregular and hideous horns; its body and tail are covered with callosities; its sting makes a dangerous wound; it is both repugnant and horrible to look at."

From the 21st to the 23rd of January the Nautilus went at the rate of two hundred and fifty leagues in twenty-four hours, being five hundred and forty miles, or twenty-two miles an hour. If we recognised so many different varieties of fish, it was because, attracted by the electric light, they tried to follow us; the greater part, however, were soon distanced by our speed, though some kept their place in the waters of the Nautilus for a time. The morning of the 24th, in 12° 5' S. lat., and 94° 33' long., we observed Keeling Island, a coral formation, planted with magnificent cocos, and which had been visited by Mr. Darwin and Captain Fitzroy. The Nautilus skirted the shores of this desert island for a little distance. Its nets brought up numerous specimens of polypi and curious shells of mollusca. Some precious productions of the species of delphinulae enriched the treasures of Captain Nemo, to which I added an astraea punctifera, a kind of parasite polypus often found fixed to a shell.

Soon Keeling Island disappeared from the horizon, and our course was directed to the north-west in the direction of the Indian Peninsula.

From Keeling Island our course was slower and more variable, often taking us into great depths. Several times they made use of the inclined planes, which certain internal levers placed obliquely to the waterline. In that way we went about two miles, but without ever obtaining the greatest depths of the Indian Sea, which soundings of seven thousand fathoms have never reached. As to the temperature of the lower strata, the thermometer invariably indicated 4° above zero. I only observed that in the upper regions the water was always colder in the high levels than at the surface of the sea.

On the 25th of January the ocean was entirely deserted; the Nautilus passed the day on the surface, beating the waves with its powerful screw and making them rebound to a great height. Who under such circumstances would not have taken it for a gigantic cetacean? Three parts of this day I spent on the platform. I watched the sea. Nothing on the horizon, till about four o'clock a steamer running west on our counter. Her masts were visible for an instant, but she could not see the Nautilus, being too low in the water. I fancied this steamboat belonged to the P.O. Company, which runs from Ceylon to Sydney, touching at King George's Point and Melbourne.

At five o'clock in the evening, before that fleeting twilight which binds night to day in tropical zones, Conseil and I were astonished by a curious spectacle.

It was a shoal of argonauts travelling along on the surface of the ocean. We could count several hundreds. They belonged to the tubercle kind which are peculiar to the Indian seas.

These graceful molluscs moved backwards by means of their locomotive tube, through which they propelled the water already drawn in. Of their eight tentacles, six were elongated, and stretched out floating on the water, whilst the other two, rolled up flat, were spread to the wing like a light sail. I saw their spiral-shaped and fluted shells, which Cuvier justly compares to an elegant skiff. A boat indeed! It bears the creature which secretes it without its adhering to it.

For nearly an hour the Nautilus floated in the midst of this shoal of molluscs. Then I know not what sudden fright they took. But as if at a signal every sail was furled, the arms folded, the body drawn in, the shells turned over, changing their centre of gravity, and the whole fleet disappeared under the waves. Never did the ships of a squadron manoeuvre with more unity.

At that moment night fell suddenly, and the reeds, scarcely raised by the breeze, lay peaceably under the sides of the Nautilus.

The next day, 26th of January, we cut the equator at the eighty-second meridian and entered the northern hemisphere. During the day a formidable troop of sharks accompanied us, terrible creatures, which multiply in these seas and make them very dangerous. They were "cestracio philippi" sharks, with brown backs and whitish bellies, armed with eleven rows of teeth—eyed sharks—their throat being marked with a large black spot surrounded with white like an eye. There were also some Isabella sharks, with rounded snouts marked with dark spots. These powerful creatures often hurled themselves at the windows of the saloon with such violence as to make us feel very insecure. At such times Ned Land was no longer master of himself. He wanted to go to the surface and harpoon the monsters, particularly certain smooth-hound sharks, whose mouth is studded with teeth like a mosaic; and large tiger-sharks nearly six yards long, the last named of which seemed to excite him more particularly. But the Nautilus, accelerating her speed, easily left the most rapid of them behind.

The 27th of January, at the entrance of the vast Bay of Bengal, we met repeatedly a forbidding spectacle, dead bodies floating on the surface of the water. They were the dead of the Indian villages, carried by the Ganges to the level of the sea, and which the vultures, the only undertakers of the country, had not been able to devour. But the sharks did not fail to help them at their funeral work.

About seven o'clock in the evening, the Nautilus, half-immersed, was sailing in a sea of milk. At first sight the ocean seemed lactified. Was it the effect of the lunar rays? No; for the moon, scarcely two days old, was still lying hidden under the horizon in the rays of the sun. The whole sky, though lit by the sidereal rays, seemed black by contrast with the whiteness of the waters.

Conseil could not believe his eyes, and questioned me as to the cause of this strange phenomenon. Happily I was able to answer him.

"It is called a milk sea," I explained. "A large extent of white wavelets often to be seen on the coasts of Amboyna, and in these parts of the sea."

"But, sir," said Conseil, "can you tell me what causes such an effect? for I suppose the water is not really turned into milk."

"No, my boy; and the whiteness which surprises you is caused only by the presence of myriads of infusoria, a sort of luminous little worm, gelatinous and without colour, of the thickness of a hair, and whose length is not more than seven-thousandths of an inch. These insects adhere to one another sometimes for several leagues."

"Several leagues!" exclaimed Conseil.

"Yes, my boy; and you need not try to compute the number of these infusoria. You will not be able, for, if I am not mistaken, ships have floated on these milk seas for more than forty miles."

Towards midnight the sea suddenly resumed its usual colour; but behind us, even to the limits of the horizon, the sky reflected the whitened waves, and for a long time seemed impregnated with the vague glimmerings of an aurora borealis.

CHAPTER II A NOVEL PROPOSAL OF CAPTAIN NEMO'S

On the 28th of February, when at noon the Nautilus came to the surface of the sea, in 9° 4' N. lat., there was land in sight about eight miles to westward. The first thing I noticed was a range of mountains about two thousand feet high, the shapes of which were most capricious. On taking the bearings, I knew that we were nearing the island of Ceylon, the pearl which hangs from the lobe of the Indian Peninsula.

Captain Nemo and his second appeared at this moment. The Captain glanced at the map. Then turning to me, said:

"The Island of Ceylon, noted for its pearl-fisheries. Would you like to visit one of them, M. Aronnax?"

"Certainly, Captain."

"Well, the thing is easy. Though, if we see the fisheries, we shall not see the fishermen. The annual exportation has not yet begun. Never mind, I will give orders to make for the Gulf of Manaar, where we shall arrive in the night."

The Captain said something to his second, who immediately went out. Soon the Nautilus returned to her native element, and the manometer showed that she was about thirty feet deep.

"Well, sir," said Captain Nemo, "you and your companions shall visit the Bank of Manaar, and if by chance some fisherman should be there, we shall see him at work."

"Agreed, Captain!"

"By the bye, M. Aronnax you are not afraid of sharks?"

"Sharks!" exclaimed I.

This question seemed a very hard one.

"Well?" continued Captain Nemo.

"I admit, Captain, that I am not yet very familiar with that kind of fish."

"We are accustomed to them," replied Captain Nemo, "and in time you will be too. However, we shall be armed, and on the road we may be able to hunt some of the tribe. It is interesting. So, till to-morrow, sir, and early."

This said in a careless tone, Captain Nemo left the saloon. Now, if you were invited to hunt the bear in the mountains of Switzerland, what would you say?

"Very well! to-morrow we will go and hunt the bear." If you were asked to hunt the lion in the plains of Atlas, or the tiger in the Indian jungles, what would you say?

"Ha! ha! it seems we are going to hunt the tiger or the lion!" But when you are invited to hunt the shark in its natural element, you would perhaps reflect before accepting the invitation. As for myself, I passed my hand over my forehead, on which stood large drops of cold perspiration. "Let us reflect," said I, "and take our time. Hunting otters in submarine forests, as we did in the Island of Crespo, will pass; but going up and down at the bottom of the sea, where one is almost certain to meet sharks, is quite another thing! I know well that in certain countries, particularly in the Andaman Islands, the negroes never hesitate to attack them with a dagger in one hand and a running noose in the other; but I also know that few who affront those creatures ever return alive. However, I am not a negro, and if I were I think a little hesitation in this case would not be ill-timed."

At this moment Conseil and the Canadian entered, quite composed, and even joyous. They knew not what awaited them.

"Faith, sir," said Ned Land, "your Captain Nemo—the devil take him!—has just made us a very pleasant offer."

"Ah!" said I, "you know?"

"If agreeable to you, sir," interrupted Conseil, "the commander of the Nautilus has invited us to visit the magnificent Ceylon fisheries to-morrow, in your company; he did it kindly, and behaved like a real gentleman."

"He said nothing more?"

"Nothing more, sir, except that he had already spoken to you of this little walk."

"Sir," said Conseil, "would you give us some details of the pearl fishery?"

"As to the fishing itself," I asked, "or the incidents, which?"

"On the fishing," replied the Canadian; "before entering upon the ground, it is as well to know something about it."

"Very well; sit down, my friends, and I will teach you."

Ned and Conseil seated themselves on an ottoman, and the first thing the Canadian asked was:

"Sir, what is a pearl?"

"My worthy Ned," I answered, "to the poet, a pearl is a tear of the sea; to the Orientals, it is a drop of dew solidified; to the ladies, it is a jewel of an oblong shape, of a brilliancy of mother-of-pearl substance, which they wear on their fingers, their necks, or their ears; for the chemist it is a mixture of phosphate and carbonate of lime, with a little gelatine; and lastly, for naturalists, it is simply a morbid secretion of the organ that produces the mother-of-pearl amongst certain bivalves."

"Branch of molluscs," said Conseil.

"Precisely so, my learned Conseil; and, amongst these testacea the earshell, the tridacnae, the turbots, in a word, all those which secrete mother-of-pearl, that is, the blue, bluish, violet, or white substance which lines the interior of their shells, are capable of producing pearls."

"Mussels too?" asked the Canadian.

"Yes, mussels of certain waters in Scotland, Wales, Ireland, Saxony, Bohemia, and France."

"Good! For the future I shall pay attention," replied the Canadian.

"But," I continued, "the particular mollusc which secretes the pearl is the pearl-oyster, the meleagrina margaritiferct, that precious pintadine. The pearl is nothing but a nacreous formation, deposited in a globular form, either adhering to the oyster shell, or buried in the folds of the creature. On the shell it is fast; in the flesh it is loose; but always has for a kernel a small hard substance, may be a barren egg, may be a grain of sand, around which the pearly matter deposits itself year after year successively, and by thin concentric layers."

"Are many pearls found in the same oyster?" asked Conseil.

"Yes, my boy. Some are a perfect casket. One oyster has been mentioned, though I allow myself to doubt it, as having contained no less than a hundred and fifty sharks."

"A hundred and fifty sharks!" exclaimed Ned Land.

"Did I say sharks?" said I hurriedly. "I meant to say a hundred and fifty pearls. Sharks would not be sense."

"Certainly not," said Conseil; "but will you tell us now by what means they extract these pearls?"

"They proceed in various ways. When they adhere to the shell, the fishermen often pull them off with pincers; but the most common way is to lay the oysters on mats of the seaweed which covers the banks. Thus they die in the open air; and at the end of ten days they are in a forward state of decomposition. They are then plunged into large reservoirs of sea-water; then they are opened and washed."

"The price of these pearls varies according to their size?" asked Conseil.

"Not only according to their size," I answered, "but also according to their shape, their water (that is, their colour), and their lustre: that is, that bright and diapered sparkle which makes them so charming to the eye. The most beautiful are called virgin pearls, or paragons. They are formed alone in the tissue of the mollusc, are white, often opaque, and sometimes have the transparency of an opal; they are generally round or oval. The round are made into bracelets, the oval into pendants, and, being more precious, are sold singly. Those adhering to the shell of the oyster are more irregular in shape, and are sold by weight. Lastly, in a lower order are classed those small pearls known under the name of seed-pearls; they are sold by measure, and are especially used in embroidery for church ornaments."

"But," said Conseil, "is this pearl-fishery dangerous?"

"No," I answered, quickly; "particularly if certain precautions are taken."

"What does one risk in such a calling?" said Ned Land, "the swallowing of some mouthfuls of sea-water?"

"As you say, Ned. By the bye," said I, trying to take Captain Nemo's careless tone, "are you afraid of sharks, brave Ned?"

"I!" replied the Canadian; "a harpooner by profession? It is my trade to make light of them."

"But," said I, "it is not a question of fishing for them with an iron-swivel, hoisting them into the vessel, cutting off their tails with a blow of a chopper, ripping them up, and throwing their heart into the sea!"

"Then, it is a question of——"

"Precisely."

"In the water?"

"In the water."

"Faith, with a good harpoon! You know, sir, these sharks are ill-fashioned beasts. They turn on their bellies to seize you, and in that time——"

Ned Land had a way of saying "seize" which made my blood run cold.

"Well, and you, Conseil, what do you think of sharks?"

"Me!" said Conseil. "I will be frank, sir."

"So much the better," thought I.

"If you, sir, mean to face the sharks, I do not see why your faithful servant should not face them with you."

CHAPTER III A PEARL OF TEN MILLIONS

The next morning at four o'clock I was awakened by the steward whom Captain Nemo had placed at my service. I rose hurriedly, dressed, and went into the saloon.

Captain Nemo was awaiting me.

"M. Aronnax," said he, "are you ready to start?"

"I am ready."

"Then please to follow me."

"And my companions, Captain?"

"They have been told and are waiting."

"Are we not to put on our diver's dresses?" asked I.

"Not yet. I have not allowed the Nautilus to come too near this coast, and we are some distance from the Manaar Bank; but the boat is ready, and will take us to the exact point of disembarking, which will save us a long way. It carries our diving apparatus, which we will put on when we begin our submarine journey."

Captain Nemo conducted me to the central staircase, which led on the platform. Ned and Conseil were already there, delighted at the idea of the "pleasure party" which was preparing. Five sailors from the Nautilus, with their oars, waited in the boat, which had been made fast against the side.

The night was still dark. Layers of clouds covered the sky, allowing but few stars to be seen. I looked on the side where the land lay, and saw nothing but a dark line enclosing three parts of the horizon, from south-west to north west. The Nautilus, having returned during the night up the western coast of Ceylon, was now west of the bay, or rather gulf, formed by the mainland and the Island of Manaar. There, under the dark waters, stretched the pintadine bank, an inexhaustible field of pearls, the length of which is more than twenty miles.

Captain Nemo, Ned Land, Conseil, and I took our places in the stern of the boat. The master went to the tiller; his four companions leaned on their oars, the painter was cast off, and we sheered off.

The boat went towards the south; the oarsmen did not hurry. I noticed that their strokes, strong in the water, only followed each other every ten seconds, according to the method generally adopted in the navy. Whilst the craft was running by its own velocity, the liquid drops struck the dark depths of the waves crisply like spats of melted lead. A little billow, spreading wide, gave a slight roll to the boat, and some samphire reeds flapped before it.

We were silent. What was Captain Nemo thinking of? Perhaps of the land he was approaching, and which he found too near to him, contrary to the Canadian's opinion, who thought it too far off. As to Conseil, he was merely there from curiosity.

CHAPTER III A PEARL OF TEN MILLIONS

About half-past five the first tints on the horizon showed the upper line of coast more distinctly. Flat enough in the east, it rose a little to the south. Five miles still lay between us, and it was indistinct owing to the mist on the water. At six o'clock it became suddenly daylight, with that rapidity peculiar to tropical regions, which know neither dawn nor twilight. The solar rays pierced the curtain of clouds, piled up on the eastern horizon, and the radiant orb rose rapidly. I saw land distinctly, with a few trees scattered here and there. The boat neared Manaar Island, which was rounded to the south. Captain Nemo rose from his seat and watched the sea.

At a sign from him the anchor was dropped, but the chain scarcely ran, for it was little more than a yard deep, and this spot was one of the highest points of the bank of pintadines.

"Here we are, M. Aronnax," said Captain Nemo. "You see that enclosed bay? Here, in a month will be assembled the numerous fishing boats of the exporters, and these are the waters their divers will ransack so boldly. Happily, this bay is well situated for that kind of fishing. It is sheltered from the strongest winds; the sea is never very rough here, which makes it favourable for the diver's work. We will now put on our dresses, and begin our walk."

I did not answer, and, while watching the suspected waves, began with the help of the sailors to put on my heavy sea-dress. Captain Nemo and my companions were also dressing. None of the Nautilus men were to accompany us on this new excursion.

Soon we were enveloped to the throat in india-rubber clothing; the air apparatus fixed to our backs by braces. As to the Ruhmkorff apparatus, there was no necessity for it. Before putting my head into the copper cap, I had asked the question of the Captain.

"They would be useless," he replied. "We are going to no great depth, and the solar rays will be enough to light our walk. Besides, it would not be prudent to carry the electric light in these waters; its brilliancy might attract some of the dangerous inhabitants of the coast most inopportunely."

As Captain Nemo pronounced these words, I turned to Conseil and Ned Land. But my two friends had already encased their heads in the metal cap, and they could neither hear nor answer.

One last question remained to ask of Captain Nemo.

"And our arms?" asked I; "our guns?"

"Guns! What for? Do not mountaineers attack the bear with a dagger in their hand, and is not steel surer than lead? Here is a strong blade; put it in your belt, and we start."

I looked at my companions; they were armed like us, and, more than that, Ned Land was brandishing an enormous harpoon, which he had placed in the boat before leaving the Nautilus.

Then, following the Captain's example, I allowed myself to be dressed in the heavy copper helmet, and our reservoirs of air were at once in activity. An instant after we were landed, one after the other, in about two yards of water upon an even sand. Captain Nemo made a sign with his hand, and we followed him by a gentle declivity till we disappeared under the waves.

Over our feet, like coveys of snipe in a bog, rose shoals of fish, of the genus monoptera, which have no other fins but their tail. I recognized the Javanese, a real serpent two and a half feet long, of a livid colour underneath, and which might easily be mistaken for a conger eel if it were not for the golden stripes on its side. In the genus stromateus, whose bodies are very flat and oval, I saw some of the most brilliant colours, carrying their dorsal fin like a scythe; an excellent eating fish, which, dried and pickled, is known by the name of Karawade; then some tranquebars, belonging to the genus apsiphoroides, whose body is covered with a shell cuirass of eight longitudinal plates.

The heightening sun lit the mass of waters more and more. The soil changed by degrees. To the fine sand succeeded a perfect causeway of boulders, covered with a carpet of molluscs and zoophytes. Amongst the specimens of these branches I noticed some placenae, with thin unequal shells, a kind of ostracion peculiar to the Red Sea and the Indian Ocean; some orange lucinae with rounded shells; rockfish three feet and a half long, which raised themselves under the waves like hands ready to seize one. There were also some panopyres, slightly luminous; and lastly, some oculines, like magnificent fans, forming one of the richest vegetations of these seas.

In the midst of these living plants, and under the arbours of the hydrophytes, were layers of clumsy articulates, particularly some raninae, whose carapace formed a slightly rounded triangle; and some horrible looking parthenopes.

At about seven o'clock we found ourselves at last surveying the oyster-banks on which the pearl-oysters are reproduced by millions.

Captain Nemo pointed with his hand to the enormous heap of oysters; and I could well understand that this mine was inexhaustible, for Nature's creative power is far beyond man's instinct of destruction. Ned Land, faithful to his instinct, hastened to fill a net which he carried by his side with some of the finest specimens. But we could not stop. We must follow the Captain, who seemed to guide him self by paths known only to himself. The ground was sensibly rising, and sometimes, on holding up my arm, it was above the surface of the sea. Then the level of the bank would sink capriciously. Often we rounded high rocks scarped into pyramids. In their dark fractures huge crustacea, perched upon their high claws like some war-machine, watched us with fixed eyes, and under our feet crawled various kinds of annelides.

At this moment there opened before us a large grotto dug in a picturesque heap of rocks and carpeted with all the thick warp of the submarine flora. At first it seemed very dark to me. The solar rays seemed to be extinguished by successive gradations, until its vague transparency became nothing more than drowned light. Captain Nemo entered; we followed. My eyes soon accustomed themselves to this relative state of darkness. I could distinguish the arches springing capriciously from natural pillars, standing broad upon their granite base, like the heavy columns of Tuscan architecture. Why had our incomprehensible guide led us to the bottom of this submarine crypt? I was soon to know. After descending a rather sharp declivity, our feet trod the bottom of a kind of circular pit. There Captain Nemo stopped, and with his hand indicated an object I had not yet perceived. It was an oyster of extraordinary dimensions, a gigantic tridacne, a goblet which could have contained a whole lake of holy-water, a basin the breadth of which was more than two yards and a half, and consequently larger than that ornamenting the saloon of the Nautilus. I approached this extraordinary mollusc. It adhered by its filaments to a table of granite, and there, isolated, it developed itself in the calm waters of the grotto. I estimated the weight of this tridacne at 600 lb. Such an oyster would contain 30 lb. of meat; and one must have the stomach of a Gargantua to demolish some dozens of them.

Captain Nemo was evidently acquainted with the existence of this bivalve, and seemed to have a particular motive in verifying the actual state of this tridacne. The shells were a little open; the Captain came near and put his dagger between to prevent them from closing; then with his hand he raised the membrane with its fringed edges, which formed a cloak for the creature. There, between the folded plaits, I saw a loose pearl, whose size equalled that of a coco-nut. Its globular shape, perfect clearness, and admirable lustre made it altogether a jewel of inestimable value. Carried away by my curiosity, I stretched out my hand to seize it, weigh it, and touch it; but the Captain stopped me, made a sign of refusal, and quickly withdrew his dagger, and the two shells closed suddenly. I then understood Captain Nemo's intention. In leaving this pearl hidden in the mantle of the tridacne he was allowing it to grow slowly. Each year the secretions of the mollusc would add new concentric circles. I estimated its value at L500,000 at least.

After ten minutes Captain Nemo stopped suddenly. I thought he had halted previously to returning. No; by a gesture he bade us crouch beside him in a deep fracture of the rock, his hand pointed to one part of the liquid mass, which I watched attentively.

About five yards from me a shadow appeared, and sank to the ground. The disquieting idea of sharks shot through my mind, but I was mistaken; and once again it was not a monster of the ocean that we had anything to do with.

It was a man, a living man, an Indian, a fisherman, a poor devil who, I suppose, had come to glean before the harvest. I could see the bottom of his canoe anchored some feet above his head. He dived and went up successively. A stone held between his feet, cut in the shape of a sugar loaf, whilst a rope fastened him to his boat, helped him to descend more rapidly. This was all his apparatus. Reaching the bottom, about five yards deep, he went on his knees and filled his bag with oysters picked up at random. Then he went up, emptied it, pulled up his stone, and began the operation once more, which lasted thirty seconds.

The diver did not see us. The shadow of the rock hid us from sight. And how should this poor Indian ever dream that men, beings like himself, should be there under the water watching his movements and losing no detail of the fishing? Several times he went up in this way, and dived again. He did not carry away more than ten at each plunge, for he was obliged to pull them from the bank to which they adhered by means of their strong byssus. And how many of those oysters for which he risked his life had no pearl in them! I watched him closely; his manoeuvres were regular; and for the space of half an hour no danger appeared to threaten him.

I was beginning to accustom myself to the sight of this interesting fishing, when suddenly, as the Indian was on the ground, I saw him make a gesture of terror, rise, and make a spring to return to the surface of the sea.

I understood his dread. A gigantic shadow appeared just above the unfortunate diver. It was a shark of enormous size advancing diagonally, his eyes on fire, and his jaws open. I was mute with horror and unable to move.

The voracious creature shot towards the Indian, who threw himself on one side to avoid the shark's fins; but not its tail, for it struck his chest and stretched him on the ground.

This scene lasted but a few seconds: the shark returned, and, turning on his back, prepared himself for cutting the Indian in two, when I saw Captain Nemo rise suddenly, and then, dagger in hand, walk straight to the monster, ready to fight face to face with him. The very moment the shark was going to snap the unhappy fisherman in two, he perceived his new adversary, and, turning over, made straight towards him.

I can still see Captain Nemo's position. Holding himself well together, he waited for the shark with admirable coolness; and, when it rushed at him, threw himself on one side with wonderful quickness, avoiding the shock, and burying his dagger deep into its side. But it was not all over. A terrible combat ensued.

The shark had seemed to roar, if I might say so. The blood rushed in torrents from its wound. The sea was dyed red, and through the opaque liquid I could distinguish nothing more. Nothing more until the moment when, like lightning, I saw the undaunted Captain hanging on to one of the creature's fins, struggling, as it were, hand to hand with the monster, and dealing successive blows at his enemy, yet still unable to give a decisive one.

The shark's struggles agitated the water with such fury that the rocking threatened to upset me.

I wanted to go to the Captain's assistance, but, nailed to the spot with horror, I could not stir.

I saw the haggard eye; I saw the different phases of the fight. The Captain fell to the earth, upset by the enormous mass which leant upon him. The shark's jaws opened wide, like a pair of factory shears, and it would have been all over with the Captain; but, quick as thought, harpoon in hand, Ned Land rushed towards the shark and struck it with its sharp point.

The waves were impregnated with a mass of blood. They rocked under the shark's movements, which beat them with indescribable fury. Ned Land had not missed his aim. It was the monster's death-rattle. Struck to the heart, it struggled in dreadful convulsions, the shock of which overthrew Conseil.

But Ned Land had disentangled the Captain, who, getting up without any wound, went straight to the Indian, quickly cut the cord which held him to his stone, took him in his arms, and, with a sharp blow of his heel, mounted to the surface.

We all three followed in a few seconds, saved by a miracle, and reached the fisherman's boat.

Captain Nemo's first care was to recall the unfortunate man to life again. I did not think he could succeed. I hoped so, for the poor creature's immersion was not long; but the blow from the shark's tail might have been his death-blow.

Happily, with the Captain's and Conseil's sharp friction, I saw consciousness return by degrees. He opened his eyes. What was his surprise, his terror even, at seeing four great copper heads leaning over him! And, above all, what must he have thought when Captain Nemo, drawing from the pocket of his dress a bag of pearls, placed it in his hand! This munificent charity from the man of the waters to the poor Cingalese was accepted with a trembling hand. His wondering eyes showed that he knew not to what super-human beings he owed both fortune and life.

At a sign from the Captain we regained the bank, and, following the road already traversed, came in about half an hour to the anchor which held the canoe of the Nautilus to the earth.

Once on board, we each, with the help of the sailors, got rid of the heavy copper helmet.

Captain Nemo's first word was to the Canadian.

"Thank you, Master Land," said he.

"It was in revenge, Captain," replied Ned Land. "I owed you that."

A ghastly smile passed across the Captain's lips, and that was all.

"To the Nautilus," said he.

The boat flew over the waves. Some minutes after we met the shark's dead body floating. By the black marking of the extremity of its fins, I recognised the terrible melanopteron of the Indian Seas, of the species of shark so properly called. It was more than twenty-five feet long; its enormous mouth occupied one-third of its body. It was an adult, as was known by its six rows of teeth placed in an isosceles triangle in the upper jaw.

Whilst I was contemplating this inert mass, a dozen of these voracious beasts appeared round the boat; and, without noticing us, threw themselves upon the dead body and fought with one another for the pieces.

CHAPTER III A PEARL OF TEN MILLIONS

At half-past eight we were again on board the Nautilus. There I reflected on the incidents which had taken place in our excursion to the Manaar Bank.

Two conclusions I must inevitably draw from it—one bearing upon the unparalleled courage of Captain Nemo, the other upon his devotion to a human being, a representative of that race from which he fled beneath the sea. Whatever he might say, this strange man had not yet succeeded in entirely crushing his heart.

When I made this observation to him, he answered in a slightly moved tone:

"That Indian, sir, is an inhabitant of an oppressed country; and I am still, and shall be, to my last breath, one of them!"

CHAPTER IV THE RED SEA

In the course of the day of the 29th of January, the island of Ceylon disappeared under the horizon, and the Nautilus, at a speed of twenty miles an hour, slid into the labyrinth of canals which separate the Maldives from the Laccadives. It coasted even the Island of Kiltan, a land originally coraline, discovered by Vasco da Gama in 1499, and one of the nineteen principal islands of the Laccadive Archipelago, situated between 10° and 14° 30' N. lat., and 69° 50' 72" E. long.

We had made 16,220 miles, or 7,500 (French) leagues from our starting-point in the Japanese Seas.

The next day (30th January), when the Nautilus went to the surface of the ocean there was no land in sight. Its course was N.N.E., in the direction of the Sea of Oman, between Arabia and the Indian Peninsula, which serves as an outlet to the Persian Gulf. It was evidently a block without any possible egress. Where was Captain Nemo taking us to? I could not say. This, however, did not satisfy the Canadian, who that day came to me asking where we were going.

"We are going where our Captain's fancy takes us, Master Ned."

"His fancy cannot take us far, then," said the Canadian. "The Persian Gulf has no outlet: and, if we do go in, it will not be long before we are out again."

"Very well, then, we will come out again, Master Land; and if, after the Persian Gulf, the Nautilus would like to visit the Red Sea, the Straits of Bab-el-mandeb are there to give us entrance."

"I need not tell you, sir," said Ned Land, "that the Red Sea is as much closed as the Gulf, as the Isthmus of Suez is not yet cut; and, if it was, a boat as mysterious as ours would not risk itself in a canal cut with sluices. And again, the Red Sea is not the road to take us back to Europe."

"But I never said we were going back to Europe."

"What do you suppose, then?"

"I suppose that, after visiting the curious coasts of Arabia and Egypt, the Nautilus will go down the Indian Ocean again, perhaps cross the Channel of Mozambique, perhaps off the Mascarenhas, so as to gain the Cape of Good Hope."

"And once at the Cape of Good Hope?" asked the Canadian, with peculiar emphasis.

"Well, we shall penetrate into that Atlantic which we do not yet know. Ah! friend Ned, you are getting tired of this journey under the sea; you are surfeited with the incessantly varying spectacle of submarine wonders. For my part, I shall be sorry to see the end of a voyage which it is given to so few men to make."

CHAPTER IV THE RED SEA

For four days, till the 3rd of February, the Nautilus scoured the Sea of Oman, at various speeds and at various depths. It seemed to go at random, as if hesitating as to which road it should follow, but we never passed the Tropic of Cancer.

In quitting this sea we sighted Muscat for an instant, one of the most important towns of the country of Oman. I admired its strange aspect, surrounded by black rocks upon which its white houses and forts stood in relief. I saw the rounded domes of its mosques, the elegant points of its minarets, its fresh and verdant terraces. But it was only a vision! The Nautilus soon sank under the waves of that part of the sea.

We passed along the Arabian coast of Mahrah and Hadramaut, for a distance of six miles, its undulating line of mountains being occasionally relieved by some ancient ruin. The 5th of February we at last entered the Gulf of Aden, a perfect funnel introduced into the neck of Bab-el-mandeb, through which the Indian waters entered the Red Sea.

The 6th of February, the Nautilus floated in sight of Aden, perched upon a promontory which a narrow isthmus joins to the mainland, a kind of inaccessible Gibraltar, the fortifications of which were rebuilt by the English after taking possession in 1839. I caught a glimpse of the octagon minarets of this town, which was at one time the richest commercial magazine on the coast.

I certainly thought that Captain Nemo, arrived at this point, would back out again; but I was mistaken, for he did no such thing, much to my surprise.

The next day, the 7th of February, we entered the Straits of Bab-el-mandeb, the name of which, in the Arab tongue, means The Gate of Tears.

To twenty miles in breadth, it is only thirty-two in length. And for the Nautilus, starting at full speed, the crossing was scarcely the work of an hour. But I saw nothing, not even the Island of Perim, with which the British Government has fortified the position of Aden. There were too many English or French steamers of the line of Suez to Bombay, Calcutta to Melbourne, and from Bourbon to the Mauritius, furrowing this narrow passage, for the Nautilus to venture to show itself. So it remained prudently below. At last about noon, we were in the waters of the Red Sea.

I would not even seek to understand the caprice which had decided Captain Nemo upon entering the gulf. But I quite approved of the Nautilus entering it. Its speed was lessened: sometimes it kept on the surface, sometimes it dived to avoid a vessel, and thus I was able to observe the upper and lower parts of this curious sea.

The 8th of February, from the first dawn of day, Mocha came in sight, now a ruined town, whose walls would fall at a gunshot, yet which shelters here and there some verdant date-trees; once an important city, containing six public markets, and twenty-six mosques, and whose walls, defended by fourteen forts, formed a girdle of two miles in circumference.

The Nautilus then approached the African shore, where the depth of the sea was greater. There, between two waters clear as crystal, through the open panels we were allowed to contemplate the beautiful bushes of brilliant coral and large blocks of rock clothed with a splendid fur of green variety of sites and landscapes along these sandbanks and algae and fuci. What an indescribable spectacle, and what variety of sites and landscapes along these sandbanks and volcanic islands which bound the Libyan coast! But where these shrubs appeared in all their beauty was on the eastern coast, which the Nautilus soon gained. It was on the coast of Tehama, for there not only did this display of zoophytes flourish beneath the level of the sea, but they also formed picturesque interlacings which unfolded themselves about sixty feet above the surface, more capricious but less highly coloured than those whose freshness was kept up by the vital power of the waters.

What charming hours I passed thus at the window of the saloon! What new specimens of submarine flora and fauna did I admire under the brightness of our electric lantern!

The 9th of February the Nautilus floated in the broadest part of the Red Sea, which is comprised between Souakin, on the west coast, and Komfidah, on the east coast, with a diameter of ninety miles.

That day at noon, after the bearings were taken, Captain Nemo mounted the platform, where I happened to be, and I was determined not to let him go down again without at least pressing him regarding his ulterior projects. As soon as he saw me he approached and graciously offered me a cigar.

"Well, sir, does this Red Sea please you? Have you sufficiently observed the wonders it covers, its fishes, its zoophytes, its parterres of sponges, and its forests of coral? Did you catch a glimpse of the towns on its borders?"

"Yes, Captain Nemo," I replied; "and the Nautilus is wonderfully fitted for such a study. Ah! it is an intelligent boat!"

"Yes, sir, intelligent and invulnerable. It fears neither the terrible tempests of the Red Sea, nor its currents, nor its sandbanks."

"Certainly," said I, "this sea is quoted as one of the worst, and in the time of the ancients, if I am not mistaken, its reputation was detestable."

"Detestable, M. Aronnax. The Greek and Latin historians do not speak favourably of it, and Strabo says it is very dangerous during the Etesian winds and in the rainy season. The Arabian Edrisi portrays it under the name of the Gulf of Colzoum, and relates that vessels perished there in great numbers on the sandbanks and that no one would risk sailing in the night. It is, he pretends, a sea subject to fearful hurricanes, strewn with inhospitable islands, and `which offers nothing good either on its surface or in its depths.'"

"One may see," I replied, "that these historians never sailed on board the Nautilus."

"Just so," replied the Captain, smiling; "and in that respect moderns are not more advanced than the ancients. It required many ages to find out the mechanical power of steam. Who knows if, in another hundred years, we may not see a second Nautilus? Progress is slow, M. Aronnax."

"It is true," I answered; "your boat is at least a century before its time, perhaps an era. What a misfortune that the secret of such an invention should die with its inventor!"

Captain Nemo did not reply. After some minutes' silence he continued:

"You were speaking of the opinions of ancient historians upon the dangerous navigation of the Red Sea."

"It is true," said I; "but were not their fears exaggerated?"

"Yes and no, M. Aronnax," replied Captain Nemo, who seemed to know the Red Sea by heart. "That which is no longer dangerous for a modern vessel, well rigged, strongly built, and master of its own course, thanks to obedient steam, offered all sorts of perils to the ships of the ancients. Picture to yourself those first navigators venturing in ships made of planks sewn with the cords of the palmtree, saturated with the grease of the seadog, and covered with powdered resin! They had not even instruments wherewith to take their bearings, and they went by guess amongst currents of which they scarcely knew anything. Under such conditions shipwrecks were, and must have been, numerous. But in our time, steamers running between Suez and the South Seas have nothing more to fear from the fury of this gulf, in spite of contrary trade-winds. The captain and passengers do not prepare for their departure by offering propitiatory sacrifices; and, on their return, they no longer go ornamented with wreaths and gilt fillets to thank the gods in the neighbouring temple."

"I agree with you," said I; "and steam seems to have killed all gratitude in the hearts of sailors. But, Captain, since you seem to have especially studied this sea, can you tell me the origin of its name?"

"There exist several explanations on the subject, M. Aronnax. Would you like to know the opinion of a chronicler of the fourteenth century?"

"Willingly."

"This fanciful writer pretends that its name was given to it after the passage of the Israelites, when Pharaoh perished in the waves which closed at the voice of Moses."

"A poet's explanation, Captain Nemo," I replied; "but I cannot content myself with that. I ask you for your personal opinion."

"Here it is, M. Aronnax. According to my idea, we must see in this appellation of the Red Sea a translation of the Hebrew word `Edom'; and if the ancients gave it that name, it was on account of the particular colour of its waters."

"But up to this time I have seen nothing but transparent waves and without any particular colour."

"Very likely; but as we advance to the bottom of the gulf, you will see this singular appearance. I remember seeing the Bay of Tor entirely red, like a sea of blood."

"And you attribute this colour to the presence of a microscopic seaweed?"

"Yes."

"So, Captain Nemo, it is not the first time you have overrun the Red Sea on board the Nautilus?"

"No, sir."

"As you spoke a while ago of the passage of the Israelites and of the catastrophe to the Egyptians, I will ask whether you have met with the traces under the water of this great historical fact?"

"No, sir; and for a good reason."

"What is it?"

"It is that the spot where Moses and his people passed is now so blocked up with sand that the camels can barely bathe their legs there. You can well understand that there would not be water enough for my Nautilus."

"And the spot?" I asked.

"The spot is situated a little above the Isthmus of Suez, in the arm which formerly made a deep estuary, when the Red Sea extended to the Salt Lakes. Now, whether this passage were miraculous or not, the Israelites, nevertheless, crossed there to reach the Promised Land, and Pharaoh's army perished precisely on that spot; and I think that excavations made in the middle of the sand would bring to light a large number of arms and instruments of Egyptian origin."

"That is evident," I replied; "and for the sake of archaeologists let us hope that these excavations will be made sooner or later, when new towns are established on the isthmus, after the construction of the Suez Canal; a canal, however, very useless to a vessel like the Nautilus."

"Very likely; but useful to the whole world," said Captain Nemo. "The ancients well understood the utility of a communication between the Red Sea and the Mediterranean for their commercial affairs: but they did not think of digging a canal direct, and took the Nile as an intermediate. Very probably the canal which united the Nile to the Red Sea was begun by Sesostris, if we may believe tradition. One thing is certain, that in the year 615 before Jesus Christ, Necos undertook the works of an alimentary canal to the waters of the Nile across the plain of Egypt, looking towards Arabia. It took four days to go up this canal, and it was so wide that two triremes could go abreast. It was carried on by Darius, the son of Hystaspes, and probably finished by Ptolemy II. Strabo saw it navigated: but its decline from the point of departure, near Bubastes, to the Red Sea was so slight that it was only navigable for a few months in the year. This canal answered all commercial purposes to the age of Antonius, when it was abandoned and blocked up with sand. Restored by order of the Caliph Omar, it was definitely destroyed in 761 or 762 by Caliph Al-Mansor, who wished to prevent the arrival of provisions to Mohammed-ben-Abdallah, who had revolted against him. During the expedition into Egypt, your General Bonaparte discovered traces of the works in the Desert of Suez; and, surprised by the tide, he nearly perished before regaining Hadjaroth, at the very place where Moses had encamped three thousand years before him."

"Well, Captain, what the ancients dared not undertake, this junction between the two seas, which will shorten the road from Cadiz to India, M. Lesseps has succeeded in doing; and before long he will have changed Africa into an immense island."

"Yes, M. Aronnax; you have the right to be proud of your countryman. Such a man brings more honour to a nation than great captains. He began, like so many others, with disgust and rebuffs; but he has triumphed, for he has the genius of will. And it is sad to think that a work like that, which ought to have been an international work and which would have sufficed to make a reign illustrious, should have succeeded by the energy of one man. All honour to M. Lesseps!"

"Yes! honour to the great citizen," I replied, surprised by the manner in which Captain Nemo had just spoken.

"Unfortunately," he continued, "I cannot take you through the Suez Canal; but you will be able to see the long jetty of Port Said after to-morrow, when we shall be in the Mediterranean."

"The Mediterranean!" I exclaimed.

"Yes, sir; does that astonish you?"

"What astonishes me is to think that we shall be there the day after to-morrow."

"Indeed?"

"Yes, Captain, although by this time I ought to have accustomed myself to be surprised at nothing since I have been on board your boat."

"But the cause of this surprise?"

"Well! it is the fearful speed you will have to put on the Nautilus, if the day after to-morrow she is to be in the Mediterranean, having made the round of Africa, and doubled the Cape of Good Hope!"

"Who told you that she would make the round of Africa and double the Cape of Good Hope, sir?"

"Well, unless the Nautilus sails on dry land, and passes above the isthmus——"

"Or beneath it, M. Aronnax."

"Beneath it?"

"Certainly," replied Captain Nemo quietly. "A long time ago Nature made under this tongue of land what man has this day made on its surface."

"What! such a passage exists?"

"Yes; a subterranean passage, which I have named the Arabian Tunnel. It takes us beneath Suez and opens into the Gulf of Pelusium."

"But this isthmus is composed of nothing but quick sands?"

"To a certain depth. But at fifty-five yards only there is a solid layer of rock."

"Did you discover this passage by chance?" I asked more and more surprised.

"Chance and reasoning, sir; and by reasoning even more than by chance. Not only does this passage exist, but I have profited by it several times. Without that I should not have ventured this day into the impassable Red Sea. I noticed that in the Red Sea and in the Mediterranean there existed a certain number of fishes of a kind perfectly identical. Certain of the fact, I asked myself was it possible that there was no communication between the two seas? If there was, the subterranean current must necessarily run from the Red Sea to the Mediterranean, from the sole cause of difference of level. I caught a large number of fishes in the neighbourhood of Suez. I passed a copper ring through their tails, and threw them back into the sea. Some months later, on the coast of Syria, I caught some of my fish ornamented with the ring. Thus the communication between the two was proved. I then sought for it with my Nautilus; I discovered it, ventured into it, and before long, sir, you too will have passed through my Arabian tunnel!"

CHAPTER V THE ARABIAN TUNNEL

That same evening, in 21° 30' N. lat., the Nautilus floated on the surface of the sea, approaching the Arabian coast. I saw Djeddah, the most important counting-house of Egypt, Syria, Turkey, and India. I distinguished clearly enough its buildings, the vessels anchored at the quays, and those whose draught of water obliged them to anchor in the roads. The sun, rather low on the horizon, struck full on the houses of the town, bringing out their whiteness. Outside, some wooden cabins, and some made of reeds, showed the quarter inhabited by the Bedouins. Soon Djeddah was shut out from view by the shadows of night, and the Nautilus found herself under water slightly phosphorescent.

The next day, the 10th of February, we sighted several ships running to windward. The Nautilus returned to its submarine navigation; but at noon, when her bearings were taken, the sea being deserted, she rose again to her waterline.

Accompanied by Ned and Conseil, I seated myself on the platform. The coast on the eastern side looked like a mass faintly printed upon a damp fog.

We were leaning on the sides of the pinnace, talking of one thing and another, when Ned Land, stretching out his hand towards a spot on the sea, said:

"Do you see anything there, sir?"

"No, Ned," I replied; "but I have not your eyes, you know."

"Look well," said Ned, "there, on the starboard beam, about the height of the lantern! Do you not see a mass which seems to move?"

"Certainly," said I, after close attention; "I see something like a long black body on the top of the water."

And certainly before long the black object was not more than a mile from us. It looked like a great sandbank deposited in the open sea. It was a gigantic dugong!

Ned Land looked eagerly. His eyes shone with covetousness at the sight of the animal. His hand seemed ready to harpoon it. One would have thought he was awaiting the moment to throw himself into the sea and attack it in its element.

At this instant Captain Nemo appeared on the platform. He saw the dugong, understood the Canadian's attitude, and, addressing him, said:

"If you held a harpoon just now, Master Land, would it not burn your hand?"

"Just so, sir."

"And you would not be sorry to go back, for one day, to your trade of a fisherman and to add this cetacean to the list of those you have already killed?"

"I should not, sir."

"Well, you can try."

"Thank you, sir," said Ned Land, his eyes flaming.

"Only," continued the Captain, "I advise you for your own sake not to miss the creature."

"Is the dugong dangerous to attack?" I asked, in spite of the Canadian's shrug of the shoulders.

"Yes," replied the Captain; "sometimes the animal turns upon its assailants and overturns their boat. But for Master Land this danger is not to be feared. His eye is prompt, his arm sure."

At this moment seven men of the crew, mute and immovable as ever, mounted the platform. One carried a harpoon and a line similar to those employed in catching whales. The pinnace was lifted from the bridge, pulled from its socket, and let down into the sea. Six oarsmen took their seats, and the coxswain went to the tiller. Ned, Conseil, and I went to the back of the boat.

"You are not coming, Captain?" I asked.

"No, sir; but I wish you good sport."

The boat put off, and, lifted by the six rowers, drew rapidly towards the dugong, which floated about two miles from the Nautilus.

Arrived some cables-length from the cetacean, the speed slackened, and the oars dipped noiselessly into the quiet waters. Ned Land, harpoon in hand, stood in the fore part of the boat. The harpoon used for striking the whale is generally attached to a very long cord which runs out rapidly as the wounded creature draws it after him. But here the cord was not more than ten fathoms long, and the extremity was attached to a small barrel which, by floating, was to show the course the dugong took under the water.

I stood and carefully watched the Canadian's adversary. This dugong, which also bears the name of the halicore, closely resembles the manatee; its oblong body terminated in a lengthened tail, and its lateral fins in perfect fingers. Its difference from the manatee consisted in its upper jaw, which was armed with two long and pointed teeth which formed on each side diverging tusks.

This dugong which Ned Land was preparing to attack was of colossal dimensions; it was more than seven yards long. It did not move, and seemed to be sleeping on the waves, which circumstance made it easier to capture.

The boat approached within six yards of the animal. The oars rested on the rowlocks. I half rose. Ned Land, his body thrown a little back, brandished the harpoon in his experienced hand.

Suddenly a hissing noise was heard, and the dugong disappeared. The harpoon, although thrown with great force; had apparently only struck the water.

"Curse it!" exclaimed the Canadian furiously; "I have missed it!"

"No," said I; "the creature is wounded—look at the blood; but your weapon has not stuck in his body."

"My harpoon! my harpoon!" cried Ned Land.

The sailors rowed on, and the coxswain made for the floating barrel. The harpoon regained, we followed in pursuit of the animal.

The latter came now and then to the surface to breathe. Its wound had not weakened it, for it shot onwards with great rapidity.

The boat, rowed by strong arms, flew on its track. Several times it approached within some few yards, and the Canadian was ready to strike, but the dugong made off with a sudden plunge, and it was impossible to reach it.

Imagine the passion which excited impatient Ned Land! He hurled at the unfortunate creature the most energetic expletives in the English tongue. For my part, I was only vexed to see the dugong escape all our attacks.

We pursued it without relaxation for an hour, and I began to think it would prove difficult to capture, when the animal, possessed with the perverse idea of vengeance of which he had cause to repent, turned upon the pinnace and assailed us in its turn.

This manoeuvre did not escape the Canadian.

"Look out!" he cried.

The coxswain said some words in his outlandish tongue, doubtless warning the men to keep on their guard.

The dugong came within twenty feet of the boat, stopped, sniffed the air briskly with its large nostrils (not pierced at the extremity, but in the upper part of its muzzle). Then, taking a spring, he threw himself upon us.

The pinnace could not avoid the shock, and half upset, shipped at least two tons of water, which had to be emptied; but, thanks to the coxswain, we caught it sideways, not full front, so we were not quite overturned. While Ned Land, clinging to the bows, belaboured the gigantic animal with blows from his harpoon, the creature's teeth were buried in the gunwale, and it lifted the whole thing out of the water, as a lion does a roebuck. We were upset over one another, and I know not how the adventure would have ended, if the Canadian, still enraged with the beast, had not struck it to the heart.

I heard its teeth grind on the iron plate, and the dugong disappeared, carrying the harpoon with him. But the barrel soon returned to the surface, and shortly after the body of the animal, turned on its back. The boat came up with it, took it in tow, and made straight for the Nautilus.

It required tackle of enormous strength to hoist the dugong on to the platform. It weighed 10,000 lb.

The next day, 11th February, the larder of the Nautilus was enriched by some more delicate game. A flight of sea-swallows rested on the Nautilus. It was a species of the Sterna nilotica, peculiar to Egypt; its beak is black, head grey and pointed, the eye surrounded by white spots, the back, wings, and tail of a greyish colour, the belly and throat white, and claws red. They also took some dozen of Nile ducks, a wild bird of high flavour, its throat and upper part of the head white with black spots.

About five o'clock in the evening we sighted to the north the Cape of Ras-Mohammed. This cape forms the extremity of Arabia Petraea, comprised between the Gulf of Suez and the Gulf of Acabah.

The Nautilus penetrated into the Straits of Jubal, which leads to the Gulf of Suez. I distinctly saw a high mountain, towering between the two gulfs of Ras-Mohammed. It was Mount Horeb, that Sinai at the top of which Moses saw God face to face.

At six o'clock the Nautilus, sometimes floating, sometimes immersed, passed some distance from Tor, situated at the end of the bay, the waters of which seemed tinted with red, an observation already made by Captain Nemo. Then night fell in the midst of a heavy silence, sometimes broken by the cries of the pelican and other night-birds, and the noise of the waves breaking upon the shore, chafing against the rocks, or the panting of some far-off steamer beating the waters of the Gulf with its noisy paddles.

From eight to nine o'clock the Nautilus remained some fathoms under the water. According to my calculation we must have been very near Suez. Through the panel of the saloon I saw the bottom of the rocks brilliantly lit up by our electric lamp. We seemed to be leaving the Straits behind us more and more.

At a quarter-past nine, the vessel having returned to the surface, I mounted the platform. Most impatient to pass through Captain Nemo's tunnel, I could not stay in one place, so came to breathe the fresh night air.

Soon in the shadow I saw a pale light, half discoloured by the fog, shining about a mile from us.

"A floating lighthouse!" said someone near me.

I turned, and saw the Captain.

"It is the floating light of Suez," he continued. "It will not be long before we gain the entrance of the tunnel."

"The entrance cannot be easy?"

"No, sir; for that reason I am accustomed to go into the steersman's cage and myself direct our course. And now, if you will go down, M. Aronnax, the Nautilus is going under the waves, and will not return to the surface until we have passed through the Arabian Tunnel."

Captain Nemo led me towards the central staircase; half way down he opened a door, traversed the upper deck, and landed in the pilot's cage, which it may be remembered rose at the extremity of the platform. It was a cabin measuring six feet square, very much like that occupied by the pilot on the steamboats of the Mississippi or Hudson. In the midst worked a wheel, placed vertically, and caught to the tiller-rope, which ran to the back of the Nautilus. Four light-ports with lenticular glasses, let in a groove in the partition of the cabin, allowed the man at the wheel to see in all directions.

This cabin was dark; but soon my eyes accustomed themselves to the obscurity, and I perceived the pilot, a strong man, with his hands resting on the spokes of the wheel. Outside, the sea appeared vividly lit up by the lantern, which shed its rays from the back of the cabin to the other extremity of the platform.

"Now," said Captain Nemo, "let us try to make our passage."

Electric wires connected the pilot's cage with the machinery room, and from there the Captain could communicate simultaneously to his Nautilus the direction and the speed. He pressed a metal knob, and at once the speed of the screw diminished.

I looked in silence at the high straight wall we were running by at this moment, the immovable base of a massive sandy coast. We followed it thus for an hour only some few yards off.

Captain Nemo did not take his eye from the knob, suspended by its two concentric circles in the cabin. At a simple gesture, the pilot modified the course of the Nautilus every instant.

I had placed myself at the port-scuttle, and saw some magnificent substructures of coral, zoophytes, seaweed, and fucus, agitating their enormous claws, which stretched out from the fissures of the rock.

At a quarter-past ten, the Captain himself took the helm. A large gallery, black and deep, opened before us. The Nautilus went boldly into it. A strange roaring was heard round its sides. It was the waters of the Red Sea, which the incline of the tunnel precipitated violently towards the Mediterranean. The Nautilus went with the torrent, rapid as an arrow, in spite of the efforts of the machinery, which, in order to offer more effective resistance, beat the waves with reversed screw.

On the walls of the narrow passage I could see nothing but brilliant rays, straight lines, furrows of fire, traced by the great speed, under the brilliant electric light. My heart beat fast.

At thirty-five minutes past ten, Captain Nemo quitted the helm, and, turning to me, said:

"The Mediterranean!"

In less than twenty minutes, the Nautilus, carried along by the torrent, had passed through the Isthmus of Suez.

CHAPTER VI THE GRECIAN ARCHIPELAGO

The next day, the 12th of February, at the dawn of day, the Nautilus rose to the surface. I hastened on to the platform. Three miles to the south the dim outline of Pelusium was to be seen. A torrent had carried us from one sea to another. About seven o'clock Ned and Conseil joined me.

"Well, Sir Naturalist," said the Canadian, in a slightly jovial tone, "and the Mediterranean?"

"We are floating on its surface, friend Ned."

"What!" said Conseil, "this very night."

"Yes, this very night; in a few minutes we have passed this impassable isthmus."

"I do not believe it," replied the Canadian.

"Then you are wrong, Master Land," I continued; "this low coast which rounds off to the south is the Egyptian coast. And you who have such good eyes, Ned, you can see the jetty of Port Said stretching into the sea."

The Canadian looked attentively.

"Certainly you are right, sir, and your Captain is a first-rate man. We are in the Mediterranean. Good! Now, if you please, let us talk of our own little affair, but so that no one hears us."

I saw what the Canadian wanted, and, in any case, I thought it better to let him talk, as he wished it; so we all three went and sat down near the lantern, where we were less exposed to the spray of the blades.

"Now, Ned, we listen; what have you to tell us?"

"What I have to tell you is very simple. We are in Europe; and before Captain Nemo's caprices drag us once more to the bottom of the Polar Seas, or lead us into Oceania, I ask to leave the Nautilus."

I wished in no way to shackle the liberty of my companions, but I certainly felt no desire to leave Captain Nemo.

Thanks to him, and thanks to his apparatus, I was each day nearer the completion of my submarine studies; and I was rewriting my book of submarine depths in its very element. Should I ever again have such an opportunity of observing the wonders of the ocean? No, certainly not! And I could not bring myself to the idea of abandoning the Nautilus before the cycle of investigation was accomplished.

"Friend Ned, answer me frankly, are you tired of being on board? Are you sorry that destiny has thrown us into Captain Nemo's hands?"

The Canadian remained some moments without answering. Then, crossing his arms, he said:

"Frankly, I do not regret this journey under the seas. I shall be glad to have made it; but, now that it is made, let us have done with it. That is my idea."

"It will come to an end, Ned."

"Where and when?"

"Where I do not know—when I cannot say; or, rather, I suppose it will end when these seas have nothing more to teach us."

"Then what do you hope for?" demanded the Canadian.

"That circumstances may occur as well six months hence as now by which we may and ought to profit."

"Oh!" said Ned Land, "and where shall we be in six months, if you please, Sir Naturalist?"

"Perhaps in China; you know the Nautilus is a rapid traveller. It goes through water as swallows through the air, or as an express on the land. It does not fear frequented seas; who can say that it may not beat the coasts of France, England, or America, on which flight may be attempted as advantageously as here."

"M. Aronnax," replied the Canadian, "your arguments are rotten at the foundation. You speak in the future, `We shall be there! we shall be here!' I speak in the present, `We are here, and we must profit by it.'"

Ned Land's logic pressed me hard, and I felt myself beaten on that ground. I knew not what argument would now tell in my favour.

"Sir," continued Ned, "let us suppose an impossibility: if Captain Nemo should this day offer you your liberty; would you accept it?"

"I do not know," I answered.

"And if," he added, "the offer made you this day was never to be renewed, would you accept it?"

"Friend Ned, this is my answer. Your reasoning is against me. We must not rely on Captain Nemo's good-will. Common prudence forbids him to set us at liberty. On the other side, prudence bids us profit by the first opportunity to leave the Nautilus."

"Well, M. Aronnax, that is wisely said."

"Only one observation—just one. The occasion must be serious, and our first attempt must succeed; if it fails, we shall never find another, and Captain Nemo will never forgive us."

"All that is true," replied the Canadian. "But your observation applies equally to all attempts at flight, whether in two years' time, or in two days'. But the question is still this: If a favourable opportunity presents itself, it must be seized."

"Agreed! And now, Ned, will you tell me what you mean by a favourable opportunity?"

"It will be that which, on a dark night, will bring the Nautilus a short distance from some European coast."

"And you will try and save yourself by swimming?"

"Yes, if we were near enough to the bank, and if the vessel was floating at the time. Not if the bank was far away, and the boat was under the water."

"And in that case?"

"In that case, I should seek to make myself master of the pinnace. I know how it is worked. We must get inside, and the bolts once drawn, we shall come to the surface of the water, without even the pilot, who is in the bows, perceiving our flight."

"Well, Ned, watch for the opportunity; but do not forget that a hitch will ruin us."

"I will not forget, sir."

"And now, Ned, would you like to know what I think of your project?"

"Certainly, M. Aronnax."

"Well, I think—I do not say I hope—I think that this favourable opportunity will never present itself."

"Why not?"

"Because Captain Nemo cannot hide from himself that we have not given up all hope of regaining our liberty, and he will be on his guard, above all, in the seas and in the sight of European coasts."

"We shall see," replied Ned Land, shaking his head determinedly.

"And now, Ned Land," I added, "let us stop here. Not another word on the subject. The day that you are ready, come and let us know, and we will follow you. I rely entirely upon you."

Thus ended a conversation which, at no very distant time, led to such grave results. I must say here that facts seemed to confirm my foresight, to the Canadian's great despair. Did Captain Nemo distrust us in these frequented seas? or did he only wish to hide himself from the numerous vessels, of all nations, which ploughed the Mediterranean? I could not tell; but we were oftener between waters and far from the coast. Or, if the Nautilus did emerge, nothing was to be seen but the pilot's cage; and sometimes it went to great depths, for, between the Grecian Archipelago and Asia Minor we could not touch the bottom by more than a thousand fathoms.

Thus I only knew we were near the Island of Carpathos, one of the Sporades, by Captain Nemo reciting these lines from Virgil:

"Est Carpathio Neptuni gurgite vates,
Caeruleus Proteus,"

as he pointed to a spot on the planisphere.

It was indeed the ancient abode of Proteus, the old shepherd of Neptune's flocks, now the Island of Scarpanto, situated between Rhodes and Crete. I saw nothing but the granite base through the glass panels of the saloon.

The next day, the 14th of February, I resolved to employ some hours in studying the fishes of the Archipelago; but for some reason or other the panels remained hermetically sealed. Upon taking the course of the Nautilus, I found that we were going towards Candia, the ancient Isle of Crete. At the time I embarked on the Abraham Lincoln, the whole of this island had risen in insurrection against the despotism of the Turks. But how the insurgents had fared since that time I was absolutely ignorant, and it was not Captain Nemo, deprived of all land communications, who could tell me.

I made no allusion to this event when that night I found myself alone with him in the saloon. Besides, he seemed to be taciturn and preoccupied. Then, contrary to his custom, he ordered both panels to be opened, and, going from one to the other, observed the mass of waters attentively. To what end I could not guess; so, on my side, I employed my time in studying the fish passing before my eyes.

In the midst of the waters a man appeared, a diver, carrying at his belt a leathern purse. It was not a body abandoned to the waves; it was a living man, swimming with a strong hand, disappearing occasionally to take breath at the surface.

I turned towards Captain Nemo, and in an agitated voice exclaimed:

"A man shipwrecked! He must be saved at any price!"

The Captain did not answer me, but came and leaned against the panel.

The man had approached, and, with his face flattened against the glass, was looking at us.

To my great amazement, Captain Nemo signed to him. The diver answered with his hand, mounted immediately to the surface of the water, and did not appear again.

"Do not be uncomfortable," said Captain Nemo. "It is Nicholas of Cape Matapan, surnamed Pesca. He is well known in all the Cyclades. A bold diver! water is his element, and he lives more in it than on land, going continually from one island to another, even as far as Crete."

"You know him, Captain?"

"Why not, M. Aronnax?"

Saying which, Captain Nemo went towards a piece of furniture standing near the left panel of the saloon. Near this piece of furniture, I saw a chest bound with iron, on the cover of which was a copper plate, bearing the cypher of the Nautilus with its device.

At that moment, the Captain, without noticing my presence, opened the piece of furniture, a sort of strong box, which held a great many ingots.

They were ingots of gold. From whence came this precious metal, which represented an enormous sum? Where did the Captain gather this gold from? and what was he going to do with it?

I did not say one word. I looked. Captain Nemo took the ingots one by one, and arranged them methodically in the chest, which he filled entirely. I estimated the contents at more than 4,000 lb. weight of gold, that is to say, nearly L200,000.

The chest was securely fastened, and the Captain wrote an address on the lid, in characters which must have belonged to Modern Greece.

This done, Captain Nemo pressed a knob, the wire of which communicated with the quarters of the crew. Four men appeared, and, not without some trouble, pushed the chest out of the saloon. Then I heard them hoisting it up the iron staircase by means of pulleys.

At that moment, Captain Nemo turned to me.

"And you were saying, sir?" said he.

"I was saying nothing, Captain."

"Then, sir, if you will allow me, I will wish you good night."

Whereupon he turned and left the saloon.

I returned to my room much troubled, as one may believe. I vainly tried to sleep—I sought the connecting link between the apparition of the diver and the chest filled with gold. Soon, I felt by certain movements of pitching and tossing that the Nautilus was leaving the depths and returning to the surface.

Then I heard steps upon the platform; and I knew they were unfastening the pinnace and launching it upon the waves. For one instant it struck the side of the Nautilus, then all noise ceased.

Two hours after, the same noise, the same going and coming was renewed; the boat was hoisted on board, replaced in its socket, and the Nautilus again plunged under the waves.

So these millions had been transported to their address. To what point of the continent? Who was Captain Nemo's correspondent?

The next day I related to Conseil and the Canadian the events of the night, which had excited my curiosity to the highest degree. My companions were not less surprised than myself.

"But where does he take his millions to?" asked Ned Land.

To that there was no possible answer. I returned to the saloon after having breakfast and set to work. Till five o'clock in the evening I employed myself in arranging my notes. At that moment—(ought I to attribute it to some peculiar idiosyncrasy)—I felt so great a heat that I was obliged to take off my coat. It was strange, for we were under low latitudes; and even then the Nautilus, submerged as it was, ought to experience no change of temperature. I looked at the manometer; it showed a depth of sixty feet, to which atmospheric heat could never attain.

I continued my work, but the temperature rose to such a pitch as to be intolerable.

"Could there be fire on board?" I asked myself.

I was leaving the saloon, when Captain Nemo entered; he approached the thermometer, consulted it, and, turning to me, said:

"Forty-two degrees."

"I have noticed it, Captain," I replied; "and if it gets much hotter we cannot bear it."

"Oh, sir, it will not get better if we do not wish it."

"You can reduce it as you please, then?"

"No; but I can go farther from the stove which produces it."

"It is outward, then!"

"Certainly; we are floating in a current of boiling water."

"Is it possible!" I exclaimed.

"Look."

The panels opened, and I saw the sea entirely white all round. A sulphurous smoke was curling amid the waves, which boiled like water in a copper. I placed my hand on one of the panes of glass, but the heat was so great that I quickly took it off again.

"Where are we?" I asked.

"Near the Island of Santorin, sir," replied the Captain. "I wished to give you a sight of the curious spectacle of a submarine eruption."

"I thought," said I, "that the formation of these new islands was ended."

"Nothing is ever ended in the volcanic parts of the sea," replied Captain Nemo; "and the globe is always being worked by subterranean fires. Already, in the nineteenth year of our era, according to Cassiodorus and Pliny, a new island, Theia (the divine), appeared in the very place where these islets have recently been formed. Then they sank under the waves, to rise again in the year 69, when they again subsided. Since that time to our days the Plutonian work has been suspended. But on the 3rd of February, 1866, a new island, which they named George Island, emerged from the midst of the sulphurous vapour near Nea Kamenni, and settled again the 6th of the same month. Seven days after, the 13th of February, the Island of Aphroessa appeared, leaving between Nea Kamenni and itself a canal ten yards broad. I was in these seas when the phenomenon occurred, and I was able therefore to observe all the different phases. The Island of Aphroessa, of round form, measured 300 feet in diameter, and 30 feet in height. It was composed of black and vitreous lava, mixed with fragments of felspar. And lastly, on the 10th of March, a smaller island, called Reka, showed itself near Nea Kamenni, and since then these three have joined together, forming but one and the same island."

"And the canal in which we are at this moment?" I asked.

"Here it is," replied Captain Nemo, showing me a map of the Archipelago. "You see, I have marked the new islands."

I returned to the glass. The Nautilus was no longer moving, the heat was becoming unbearable. The sea, which till now had been white, was red, owing to the presence of salts of iron. In spite of the ship's being hermetically sealed, an insupportable smell of sulphur filled the saloon, and the brilliancy of the electricity was entirely extinguished by bright scarlet flames. I was in a bath, I was choking, I was broiled.

"We can remain no longer in this boiling water," said I to the Captain.

"It would not be prudent," replied the impassive Captain Nemo.

An order was given; the Nautilus tacked about and left the furnace it could not brave with impunity. A quarter of an hour after we were breathing fresh air on the surface. The thought then struck me that, if Ned Land had chosen this part of the sea for our flight, we should never have come alive out of this sea of fire.

The next day, the 16th of February, we left the basin which, between Rhodes and Alexandria, is reckoned about 1,500 fathoms in depth, and the Nautilus, passing some distance from Cerigo, quitted the Grecian Archipelago after having doubled Cape Matapan.

CHAPTER VII THE MEDITERRANEAN IN FORTY-EIGHT HOURS

The Mediterranean, the blue sea par excellence, "the great sea" of the Hebrews, "the sea" of the Greeks, the "mare nostrum" of the Romans, bordered by orange-trees, aloes, cacti, and sea-pines; embalmed with the perfume of the myrtle, surrounded by rude mountains, saturated with pure and transparent air, but incessantly worked by underground fires; a perfect battlefield in which Neptune and Pluto still dispute the empire of the world!

It is upon these banks, and on these waters, says Michelet, that man is renewed in one of the most powerful climates of the globe. But, beautiful as it was, I could only take a rapid glance at the basin whose superficial area is two million of square yards. Even Captain Nemo's knowledge was lost to me, for this puzzling person did not appear once during our passage at full speed. I estimated the course which the Nautilus took under the waves of the sea at about six hundred leagues, and it was accomplished in forty-eight hours. Starting on the morning of the 16th of February from the shores of Greece, we had crossed the Straits of Gibraltar by sunrise on the 18th.

It was plain to me that this Mediterranean, enclosed in the midst of those countries which he wished to avoid, was distasteful to Captain Nemo. Those waves and those breezes brought back too many remembrances, if not too many regrets. Here he had no longer that independence and that liberty of gait which he had when in the open seas, and his Nautilus felt itself cramped between the close shores of Africa and Europe.

Our speed was now twenty-five miles an hour. It may be well understood that Ned Land, to his great disgust, was obliged to renounce his intended flight. He could not launch the pinnace, going at the rate of twelve or thirteen yards every second. To quit the Nautilus under such conditions would be as bad as jumping from a train going at full speed—an imprudent thing, to say the least of it. Besides, our vessel only mounted to the surface of the waves at night to renew its stock of air; it was steered entirely by the compass and the log.

I saw no more of the interior of this Mediterranean than a traveller by express train perceives of the landscape which flies before his eyes; that is to say, the distant horizon, and not the nearer objects which pass like a flash of lightning.

We were then passing between Sicily and the coast of Tunis. In the narrow space between Cape Bon and the Straits of Messina the bottom of the sea rose almost suddenly. There was a perfect bank, on which there was not more than nine fathoms of water, whilst on either side the depth was ninety fathoms.

The Nautilus had to manoeuvre very carefully so as not to strike against this submarine barrier.

I showed Conseil, on the map of the Mediterranean, the spot occupied by this reef.

"But if you please, sir," observed Conseil, "it is like a real isthmus joining Europe to Africa."

"Yes, my boy, it forms a perfect bar to the Straits of Lybia, and the soundings of Smith have proved that in former times the continents between Cape Boco and Cape Furina were joined."

"I can well believe it," said Conseil.

"I will add," I continued, "that a similar barrier exists between Gibraltar and Ceuta, which in geological times formed the entire Mediterranean."

"What if some volcanic burst should one day raise these two barriers above the waves?"

"It is not probable, Conseil."

"Well, but allow me to finish, please, sir; if this phenomenon should take place, it will be troublesome for M. Lesseps, who has taken so much pains to pierce the isthmus."

"I agree with you; but I repeat, Conseil, this phenomenon will never happen. The violence of subterranean force is ever diminishing. Volcanoes, so plentiful in the first days of the world, are being extinguished by degrees; the internal heat is weakened, the temperature of the lower strata of the globe is lowered by a perceptible quantity every century to the detriment of our globe, for its heat is its life."

"But the sun?"

"The sun is not sufficient, Conseil. Can it give heat to a dead body?"

"Not that I know of."

"Well, my friend, this earth will one day be that cold corpse; it will become uninhabitable and uninhabited like the moon, which has long since lost all its vital heat."

"In how many centuries?"

"In some hundreds of thousands of years, my boy."

"Then," said Conseil, "we shall have time to finish our journey—that is, if Ned Land does not interfere with it."

And Conseil, reassured, returned to the study of the bank, which the Nautilus was skirting at a moderate speed.

During the night of the 16th and 17th February we had entered the second Mediterranean basin, the greatest depth of which was 1,450 fathoms. The Nautilus, by the action of its crew, slid down the inclined planes and buried itself in the lowest depths of the sea.

On the 18th of February, about three o'clock in the morning, we were at the entrance of the Straits of Gibraltar. There once existed two currents: an upper one, long since recognised, which conveys the waters of the ocean into the basin of the Mediterranean; and a lower counter-current, which reasoning has now shown to exist. Indeed, the volume of water in the Mediterranean, incessantly added to by the waves of the Atlantic and by rivers falling into it, would each year raise the level of this sea, for its evaporation is not sufficient to restore the equilibrium. As it is not so, we must necessarily admit the existence of an under-current, which empties into the basin of the Atlantic through the Straits of Gibraltar the surplus waters of the Mediterranean. A fact indeed; and it was this counter-current by which the Nautilus profited. It advanced rapidly by the narrow pass. For one instant I caught a glimpse of the beautiful ruins of the temple of Hercules, buried in the ground, according to Pliny, and with the low island which supports it; and a few minutes later we were floating on the Atlantic.

CHAPTER VIII VIGO BAY

The Atlantic! a vast sheet of water whose superficial area covers twenty-five millions of square miles, the length of which is nine thousand miles, with a mean breadth of two thousand seven hundred—an ocean whose parallel winding shores embrace an immense circumference, watered by the largest rivers of the world, the St. Lawrence, the Mississippi, the Amazon, the Plata, the Orinoco, the Niger, the Senegal, the Elbe, the Loire, and the Rhine, which carry water from the most civilised, as well as from the most savage, countries! Magnificent field of water, incessantly ploughed by vessels of every nation, sheltered by the flags of every nation, and which terminates in those two terrible points so dreaded by mariners, Cape Horn and the Cape of Tempests.

The Nautilus was piercing the water with its sharp spur, after having accomplished nearly ten thousand leagues in three months and a half, a distance greater than the great circle of the earth. Where were we going now, and what was reserved for the future? The Nautilus, leaving the Straits of Gibraltar, had gone far out. It returned to the surface of the waves, and our daily walks on the platform were restored to us.

I mounted at once, accompanied by Ned Land and Conseil. At a distance of about twelve miles, Cape St. Vincent was dimly to be seen, forming the south-western point of the Spanish peninsula. A strong southerly gale was blowing. The sea was swollen and billowy; it made the Nautilus rock violently. It was almost impossible to keep one's foot on the platform, which the heavy rolls of the sea beat over every instant. So we descended after inhaling some mouthfuls of fresh air.

I returned to my room, Conseil to his cabin; but the Canadian, with a preoccupied air, followed me. Our rapid passage across the Mediterranean had not allowed him to put his project into execution, and he could not help showing his disappointment. When the door of my room was shut, he sat down and looked at me silently.

"Friend Ned," said I, "I understand you; but you cannot reproach yourself. To have attempted to leave the Nautilus under the circumstances would have been folly."

Ned Land did not answer; his compressed lips and frowning brow showed with him the violent possession this fixed idea had taken of his mind.

"Let us see," I continued; "we need not despair yet. We are going up the coast of Portugal again; France and England are not far off, where we can easily find refuge. Now if the Nautilus, on leaving the Straits of Gibraltar, had gone to the south, if it had carried us towards regions where there were no continents, I should share your uneasiness. But we know now that Captain Nemo does not fly from civilised seas, and in some days I think you can act with security."

Ned Land still looked at me fixedly; at length his fixed lips parted, and he said, "It is for to-night."

I drew myself up suddenly. I was, I admit, little prepared for this communication. I wanted to answer the Canadian, but words would not come.

"We agreed to wait for an opportunity," continued Ned Land, "and the opportunity has arrived. This night we shall be but a few miles from the Spanish coast. It is cloudy. The wind blows freely. I have your word, M. Aronnax, and I rely upon you."

As I was silent, the Canadian approached me.

"To-night, at nine o'clock," said he. "I have warned Conseil. At that moment Captain Nemo will be shut up in his room, probably in bed. Neither the engineers nor the ship's crew can see us. Conseil and I will gain the central staircase, and you, M. Aronnax, will remain in the library, two steps from us, waiting my signal. The oars, the mast, and the sail are in the canoe. I have even succeeded in getting some provisions. I have procured an English wrench, to unfasten the bolts which attach it to the shell of the Nautilus. So all is ready, till to-night."

"The sea is bad."

"That I allow," replied the Canadian; "but we must risk that. Liberty is worth paying for; besides, the boat is strong, and a few miles with a fair wind to carry us is no great thing. Who knows but by to-morrow we may be a hundred leagues away? Let circumstances only favour us, and by ten or eleven o'clock we shall have landed on some spot of terra firma, alive or dead. But adieu now till to-night."

With these words the Canadian withdrew, leaving me almost dumb. I had imagined that, the chance gone, I should have time to reflect and discuss the matter. My obstinate companion had given me no time; and, after all, what could I have said to him? Ned Land was perfectly right. There was almost the opportunity to profit by. Could I retract my word, and take upon myself the responsibility of compromising the future of my companions? To-morrow Captain Nemo might take us far from all land.

At that moment a rather loud hissing noise told me that the reservoirs were filling, and that the Nautilus was sinking under the waves of the Atlantic.

A sad day I passed, between the desire of regaining my liberty of action and of abandoning the wonderful Nautilus, and leaving my submarine studies incomplete.

What dreadful hours I passed thus! Sometimes seeing myself and companions safely landed, sometimes wishing, in spite of my reason, that some unforeseen circumstance, would prcvcnt thc rcalisation of Ncd Land's projcct.

Twice I went to the saloon. I wished to consult the compass. I wished to see if the direction the Nautilus was taking was bringing us nearer or taking us farther from the coast. But no; the Nautilus kept in Portuguese waters.

I must therefore take my part and prepare for flight. My luggage was not heavy; my notes, nothing more.

As to Captain Nemo, I asked myself what he would think of our escape; what trouble, what wrong it might cause him and what he might do in case of its discovery or failure. Certainly I had no cause to complain of him; on the contrary, never was hospitality freer than his. In leaving him I could not be taxed with ingratitude. No oath bound us to him. It was on the strength of circumstances he relied, and not upon our word, to fix us for ever.

I had not seen the Captain since our visit to the Island of Santorin. Would chance bring me to his presence before our departure? I wished it, and I feared it at the same time. I listened if I could hear him walking the room contiguous to mine. No sound reached my ear. I felt an unbearable uneasiness. This day of waiting seemed eternal. Hours struck too slowly to keep pace with my impatience.

My dinner was served in my room as usual. I ate but little; I was too preoccupied. I left the table at seven o'clock. A hundred and twenty minutes (I counted them) still separated me from the moment in which I was to join Ned Land. My agitation redoubled. My pulse beat violently. I could not remain quiet. I went and came, hoping to calm my troubled spirit by constant movement. The idea of failure in our bold enterprise was the least painful of my anxieties; but the thought of seeing our project discovered before leaving the Nautilus, of being brought before Captain Nemo, irritated, or (what was worse) saddened, at my desertion, made my heart beat.

I wanted to see the saloon for the last time. I descended the stairs and arrived in the museum, where I had passed so many useful and agreeable hours. I looked at all its riches, all its treasures, like a man on the eve of an eternal exile, who was leaving never to return.

These wonders of Nature, these masterpieces of art, amongst which for so many days my life had been concentrated, I was going to abandon them for ever! I should like to have taken a last look through the windows of the saloon into the waters of the Atlantic: but the panels were hermetically closed, and a cloak of steel separated me from that ocean which I had not yet explored.

In passing through the saloon, I came near the door let into the angle which opened into the Captain's room. To my great surprise, this door was ajar. I drew back involuntarily. If Captain Nemo should be in his room, he could see me. But, hearing no sound, I drew nearer. The room was deserted. I pushed open the door and took some steps forward. Still the same monklike severity of aspect.

Suddenly the clock struck eight. The first beat of the hammer on the bell awoke me from my dreams. I trembled as if an invisible eye had plunged into my most secret thoughts, and I hurried from the room.

There my eye fell upon the compass. Our course was still north. The log indicated moderate speed, the manometer a depth of about sixty feet.

I returned to my room, clothed myself warmly—sea boots, an otterskin cap, a great coat of byssus, lined with sealskin; I was ready, I was waiting. The vibration of the screw alone broke the deep silence which reigned on board. I listened attentively. Would no loud voice suddenly inform me that Ned Land had been surprised in his projected flight. A mortal dread hung over me, and I vainly tried to regain my accustomed coolness.

At a few minutes to nine, I put my ear to the Captain's door. No noise. I left my room and returned to the saloon, which was half in obscurity, but deserted.

I opened the door communicating with the library. The same insufficient light, the same solitude. I placed myself near the door leading to the central staircase, and there waited for Ned Land's signal.

At that moment the trembling of the screw sensibly diminished, then it stopped entirely. The silence was now only disturbed by the beatings of my own heart. Suddenly a slight shock was felt; and I knew that the Nautilus had stopped at the bottom of the ocean. My uneasiness increased. The Canadian's signal did not come. I felt inclined to join Ned Land and beg of him to put off his attempt. I felt that we were not sailing under our usual conditions.

At this moment the door of the large saloon opened, and Captain Nemo appeared. He saw me, and without further preamble began in an amiable tone of voice:

"Ah, sir! I have been looking for you. Do you know the history of Spain?"

Now, one might know the history of one's own country by heart; but in the condition I was at the time, with troubled mind and head quite lost, I could not have said a word of it.

"Well," continued Captain Nemo, "you heard my question! Do you know the history of Spain?"

"Very slightly," I answered.

"Well, here are learned men having to learn," said the Captain. "Come, sit down, and I will tell you a curious episode in this history. Sir, listen well," said he; "this history will interest you on one side, for it will answer a question which doubtless you have not been able to solve."

"I listen, Captain," said I, not knowing what my interlocutor was driving at, and asking myself if this incident was bearing on our projected flight.

"Sir, if you have no objection, we will go back to 1702. You cannot be ignorant that your king, Louis XIV, thinking that the gesture of a potentate was sufficient to bring the Pyrenees under his yoke, had imposed the Duke of Anjou, his grandson, on the Spaniards. This prince reigned more or less badly under the name of Philip V, and had a strong party against him abroad. Indeed, the preceding year, the royal houses of Holland, Austria, and England had concluded a treaty of alliance at the Hague, with the intention of plucking the crown of Spain from the head of Philip V, and placing it on that of an archduke to whom they prematurely gave the title of Charles III.

"Spain must resist this coalition; but she was almost entirely unprovided with either soldiers or sailors. However, money would not fail them, provided that their galleons, laden with gold and silver from America, once entered their ports. And about the end of 1702 they expected a rich convoy which France was escorting with a fleet of twenty-three vessels, commanded by Admiral Chateau-Renaud, for the ships of the coalition were already beating the Atlantic. This convoy was to go to Cadiz, but the Admiral, hearing that an English fleet was cruising in those waters, resolved to make for a French port.

"The Spanish commanders of the convoy objected to this decision. They wanted to be taken to a Spanish port, and, if not to Cadiz, into Vigo Bay, situated on the northwest coast of Spain, and which was not blocked.

"Admiral Chateau-Renaud had the rashness to obey this injunction, and the galleons entered Vigo Bay.

"Unfortunately, it formed an open road which could not be defended in any way. They must therefore hasten to unload the galleons before the arrival of the combined fleet; and time would not have failed them had not a miserable question of rivalry suddenly arisen.

"You are following the chain of events?" asked Captain Nemo.

"Perfectly," said I, not knowing the end proposed by this historical lesson.

"I will continue. This is what passed. The merchants of Cadiz had a privilege by which they had the right of receiving all merchandise coming from the West Indies. Now, to disembark these ingots at the port of Vigo was depriving them of their rights. They complained at Madrid, and obtained the consent of the weak-minded Philip that the convoy, without discharging its cargo, should remain sequestered in the roads of Vigo until the enemy had disappeared.

"But whilst coming to this decision, on the 22nd of October, 1702, the English vessels arrived in Vigo Bay, when Admiral Chateau-Renaud, in spite of inferior forces, fought bravely. But, seeing that the treasure must fall into the enemy's hands, he burnt and scuttled every galleon, which went to the bottom with their immense riches."

Captain Nemo stopped. I admit I could not see yet why this history should interest me.

"Well?" I asked.

"Well, M. Aronnax," replied Captain Nemo, "we are in that Vigo Bay; and it rests with yourself whether you will penetrate its mysteries."

The Captain rose, telling me to follow him. I had had time to recover. I obeyed. The saloon was dark, but through the transparent glass the waves were sparkling. I looked.

For half a mile around the Nautilus, the waters seemed bathed in electric light. The sandy bottom was clean and bright. Some of the ship's crew in their diving-dresses were clearing away half-rotten barrels and empty cases from the midst of the blackened wrecks. From these cases and from these barrels escaped ingots of gold and silver, cascades of piastres and jewels. The sand was heaped up with them. Laden with their precious booty, the men returned to the Nautilus, disposed of their burden, and went back to this inexhaustible fishery of gold and silver.

I understood now. This was the scene of the battle of the 22nd of October, 1702. Here on this very spot the galleons laden for the Spanish Government had sunk. Here Captain Nemo came, according to his wants, to pack up those millions with which he burdened the Nautilus. It was for him and him alone America had given up her precious metals. He was heir direct, without anyone to share, in those treasures torn from the Incas and from the conquered of Ferdinand Cortez.

"Did you know, sir," he asked, smiling, "that the sea contained such riches?"

"I knew," I answered, "that they value money held in suspension in these waters at two millions."

"Doubtless; but to extract this money the expense would be greater than the profit. Here, on the contrary, I have but to pick up what man has lost—and not only in Vigo Bay, but in a thousand other ports where shipwrecks have happened, and which are marked on my submarine map. Can you understand now the source of the millions I am worth?"

"I understand, Captain. But allow me to tell you that in exploring Vigo Bay you have only been beforehand with a rival society."

"And which?"

"A society which has received from the Spanish Government the privilege of seeking those buried galleons. The shareholders are led on by the allurement of an enormous bounty, for they value these rich shipwrecks at five hundred millions."

"Five hundred millions they were," answered Captain Nemo, "but they are so no longer."

"Just so," said I; "and a warning to those shareholders would be an act of charity. But who knows if it would be well received? What gamblers usually regret above all is less the loss of their money than of their foolish hopes. After all, I pity them less than the thousands of unfortunates to whom so much riches well-distributed would have been profitable, whilst for them they will be for ever barren."

I had no sooner expressed this regret than I felt that it must have wounded Captain Nemo.

"Barren!" he exclaimed, with animation. "Do you think then, sir, that these riches are lost because I gather them? Is it for myself alone, according to your idea, that I take the trouble to collect these treasures? Who told you that I did not make a good use of it? Do you think I am ignorant that there are suffering beings and oppressed races on this earth, miserable creatures to console, victims to avenge? Do you not understand?"

Captain Nemo stopped at these last words, regretting perhaps that he had spoken so much. But I had guessed that, whatever the motive which had forced him to seek independence under the sea, it had left him still a man, that his heart still beat for the sufferings of humanity, and that his immense charity was for oppressed races as well as individuals. And I then understood for whom those millions were destined which were forwarded by Captain Nemo when the Nautilus was cruising in the waters of Crete.

CHAPTER IX A VANISHED CONTINENT

The next morning, the 19th of February, I saw the Canadian enter my room. I expected this visit. He looked very disappointed.

"Well, sir?" said he.

"Well, Ned, fortune was against us yesterday."

"Yes; that Captain must needs stop exactly at the hour we intended leaving his vessel."

"Yes, Ned, he had business at his bankers."

"His bankers!"

"Or rather his banking-house; by that I mean the ocean, where his riches are safer than in the chests of the State."

I then related to the Canadian the incidents of the preceding night, hoping to bring him back to the idea of not abandoning the Captain; but my recital had no other result than an energetically expressed regret from Ned that he had not been able to take a walk on the battlefield of Vigo on his own account.

"However," said he, "all is not ended. It is only a blow of the harpoon lost. Another time we must succeed; and to-night, if necessary——"

"In what direction is the Nautilus going?" I asked.

"I do not know," replied Ned.

"Well, at noon we shall see the point."

The Canadian returned to Conseil. As soon as I was dressed, I went into the saloon. The compass was not reassuring. The course of the Nautilus was S.S.W. We were turning our backs on Europe.

I waited with some impatience till the ship's place was pricked on the chart. At about half-past eleven the reservoirs were emptied, and our vessel rose to the surface of the ocean. I rushed towards the platform. Ned Land had preceded me. No more land in sight. Nothing but an immense sea. Some sails on the horizon, doubtless those going to San Roque in search of favourable winds for doubling the Cape of Good Hope. The weather was cloudy. A gale of wind was preparing. Ned raved, and tried to pierce the cloudy horizon. He still hoped that behind all that fog stretched the land he so longed for.

At noon the sun showed itself for an instant. The second profited by this brightness to take its height. Then, the sea becoming more billowy, we descended, and the panel closed.

An hour after, upon consulting the chart, I saw the position of the Nautilus was marked at 16° 17' long., and 33° 22' lat., at 150 leagues from the nearest coast. There was no means of flight, and I leave you to imagine the rage of the Canadian when I informed him of our situation.

For myself, I was not particularly sorry. I felt lightened of the load which had oppressed me, and was able to return with some degree of calmness to my accustomed work.

That night, about eleven o'clock, I received a most unexpected visit from Captain Nemo. He asked me very graciously if I felt fatigued from my watch of the preceding night. I answered in the negative.

"Then, M. Aronnax, I propose a curious excursion."

"Propose, Captain?"

"You have hitherto only visited the submarine depths by daylight, under the brightness of the sun. Would it suit you to see them in the darkness of the night?"

"Most willingly."

"I warn you, the way will be tiring. We shall have far to walk, and must climb a mountain. The roads are not well kept."

"What you say, Captain, only heightens my curiosity; I am ready to follow you."

"Come then, sir, we will put on our diving-dresses."

Arrived at the robing-room, I saw that neither of my companions nor any of the ship's crew were to follow us on this excursion. Captain Nemo had not even proposed my taking with me either Ned or Conseil.

In a few moments we had put on our diving-dresses; they placed on our backs the reservoirs, abundantly filled with air, but no electric lamps were prepared. I called the Captain's attention to the fact.

"They will be useless," he replied.

I thought I had not heard aright, but I could not repeat my observation, for the Captain's head had already disappeared in its metal case. I finished harnessing myself. I felt them put an iron-pointed stick into my hand, and some minutes later, after going through the usual form, we set foot on the bottom of the Atlantic at a depth of 150 fathoms. Midnight was near. The waters were profoundly dark, but Captain Nemo pointed out in the distance a reddish spot, a sort of large light shining brilliantly about two miles from the Nautilus. What this fire might be, what could feed it, why and how it lit up the liquid mass, I could not say. In any case, it did light our way, vaguely, it is true, but I soon accustomed myself to the peculiar darkness, and I understood, under such circumstances, the uselessness of the Ruhmkorff apparatus.

As we advanced, I heard a kind of pattering above my head. The noise redoubling, sometimes producing a continual shower, I soon understood the cause. It was rain falling violently, and crisping the surface of the waves. Instinctively the thought flashed across my mind that I should be wet through! By the water! in the midst of the water! I could not help laughing at the odd idea. But, indeed, in the thick diving-dress, the liquid element is no longer felt, and one only seems to be in an atmosphere somewhat denser than the terrestrial atmosphere. Nothing more.

After half an hour's walk the soil became stony. Medusae, microscopic crustacea, and pennatules lit it slightly with their phosphorescent gleam. I caught a glimpse of pieces of stone covered with millions of zoophytes and masses of sea weed. My feet often slipped upon this sticky carpet of sea weed, and without my iron-tipped stick I should have fallen more than once. In turning round, I could still see the whitish lantern of the Nautilus beginning to pale in the distance.

But the rosy light which guided us increased and lit up the horizon. The presence of this fire under water puzzled me in the highest degree. Was I going towards a natural phenomenon as yet unknown to the savants of the earth? Or even (for this thought crossed my brain) had the hand of man aught to do with this conflagration? Had he fanned this flame? Was I to meet in these depths companions and friends of Captain Nemo whom he was going to visit, and who, like him, led this strange existence? Should I find down there a whole colony of exiles who, weary of the miseries of this earth, had sought and found independence in the deep ocean? All these foolish and unreasonable ideas pursued me. And in this condition of mind, over-excited by the succession of wonders continually passing before my eyes, I should not have been surprised to meet at the bottom of the sea one of those submarine towns of which Captain Nemo dreamed.

Our road grew lighter and lighter. The white glimmer came in rays from the summit of a mountain about 800 feet high. But what I saw was simply a reflection, developed by the clearness of the waters. The source of this inexplicable light was a fire on the opposite side of the mountain.

In the midst of this stony maze furrowing the bottom of the Atlantic, Captain Nemo advanced without hesitation. He knew this dreary road. Doubtless he had often travelled over it, and could not lose himself. I followed him with unshaken confidence. He seemed to me like a genie of the sea; and, as he walked before me, I could not help admiring his stature, which was outlined in black on the luminous horizon.

It was one in the morning when we arrived at the first slopes of the mountain; but to gain access to them we must venture through the difficult paths of a vast copse.

Yes; a copse of dead trees, without leaves, without sap, trees petrified by the action of the water and here and there overtopped by gigantic pines. It was like a coal-pit still standing, holding by the roots to the broken soil, and whose branches, like fine black paper cuttings, showed distinctly on the watery ceiling. Picture to yourself a forest in the Hartz hanging on to the sides of the mountain, but a forest swallowed up. The paths were encumbered with seaweed and fucus, between which grovelled a whole world of crustacea. I went along, climbing the rocks, striding over extended trunks, breaking the sea bind-weed which hung from one tree to the other; and frightening the fishes, which flew from branch to branch. Pressing onward, I felt no fatigue. I followed my guide, who was never tired. What a spectacle! How can I express it? how paint the aspect of those woods and rocks in this medium—their under parts dark and wild, the upper coloured with red tints, by that light which the reflecting powers of the waters doubled? We climbed rocks which fell directly after with gigantic bounds and the low growling of an avalanche. To right and left ran long, dark galleries, where sight was lost. Here opened vast glades which the hand of man seemed to have worked; and I sometimes asked myself if some inhabitant of these submarine regions would not suddenly appear to me.

But Captain Nemo was still mounting. I could not stay behind. I followed boldly. My stick gave me good help. A false step would have been dangerous on the narrow passes sloping down to the sides of the gulfs; but I walked with firm step, without feeling any giddiness. Now I jumped a crevice, the depth of which would have made me hesitate had it been among the glaciers on the land; now I ventured on the unsteady trunk of a tree thrown across from one abyss to the other, without looking under my feet, having only eyes to admire the wild sites of this region.

There, monumental rocks, leaning on their regularly-cut bases, seemed to defy all laws of equilibrium. From between their stony knees trees sprang, like a jet under heavy pressure, and upheld others which upheld them. Natural towers, large scarps, cut perpendicularly, like a "curtain," inclined at an angle which the laws of gravitation could never have tolerated in terrestrial regions.

Two hours after quitting the Nautilus we had crossed the line of trees, and a hundred feet above our heads rose the top of the mountain, which cast a shadow on the brilliant irradiation of the opposite slope. Some petrified shrubs ran fantastically here and there. Fishes got up under our feet like birds in the long grass. The massive rocks were rent with impenetrable fractures, deep grottos, and unfathomable holes, at the bottom of which formidable creatures might be heard moving. My blood curdled when I saw enormous antennae blocking my road, or some frightful claw closing with a noise in the shadow of some cavity. Millions of luminous spots shone brightly in the midst of the darkness. They were the eyes of giant crustacea crouched in their holes; giant lobsters setting themselves up like halberdiers, and moving their claws with the clicking sound of pincers; titanic crabs, pointed like a gun on its carriage; and frightful-looking poulps, interweaving their tentacles like a living nest of serpents.

We had now arrived on the first platform, where other surprises awaited me. Before us lay some picturesque ruins, which betrayed the hand of man and not that of the Creator. There were vast heaps of stone, amongst which might be traced the vague and shadowy forms of castles and temples, clothed with a world of blossoming zoophytes, and over which, instead of ivy, sea-weed and fucus threw a thick vegetable mantle. But what was this portion of the globe which had been swallowed by cataclysms? Who had placed those rocks and stones like cromlechs of prehistoric times? Where was I? Whither had Captain Nemo's fancy hurried me?

I would fain have asked him; not being able to, I stopped him—I seized his arm. But, shaking his head, and pointing to the highest point of the mountain, he seemed to say:

"Come, come along; come higher!"

I followed, and in a few minutes I had climbed to the top, which for a circle of ten yards commanded the whole mass of rock.

I looked down the side we had just climbed. The mountain did not rise more than seven or eight hundred feet above the level of the plain; but on the opposite side it commanded from twice that height the depths of this part of the Atlantic. My eyes ranged far over a large space lit by a violent fulguration. In fact, the mountain was a volcano.

At fifty feet above the peak, in the midst of a rain of stones and scoriae, a large crater was vomiting forth torrents of lava which fell in a cascade of fire into the bosom of the liquid mass. Thus situated, this volcano lit the lower plain like an immense torch, even to the extreme limits of the horizon. I said that the submarine crater threw up lava, but no flames. Flames require the oxygen of the air to feed upon and cannot be developed under water; but streams of lava, having in themselves the principles of their incandescence, can attain a white heat, fight vigorously against the liquid element, and turn it to vapour by contact.

Rapid currents bearing all these gases in diffusion and torrents of lava slid to the bottom of the mountain like an eruption of Vesuvius on another Terra del Greco.

There indeed under my eyes, ruined, destroyed, lay a town—its roofs open to the sky, its temples fallen, its arches dislocated, its columns lying on the ground, from which one would still recognise the massive character of Tuscan architecture. Further on, some remains of a gigantic aqueduct; here the high base of an Acropolis, with the floating outline of a Parthenon; there traces of a quay, as if an ancient port had formerly abutted on the borders of the ocean, and disappeared with its merchant vessels and its war-galleys. Farther on again, long lines of sunken walls and broad, deserted streets—a perfect Pompeii escaped beneath the waters. Such was the sight that Captain Nemo brought before my eyes!

Where was I? Where was I? I must know at any cost. I tried to speak, but Captain Nemo stopped me by a gesture, and, picking up a piece of chalk-stone, advanced to a rock of black basalt, and traced the one word:

ATLANTIS

What a light shot through my mind! Atlantis! the Atlantis of Plato, that continent denied by Origen and Humbolt, who placed its disappearance amongst the legendary tales. I had it there now before my eyes, bearing upon it the unexceptionable testimony of its catastrophe. The region thus engulfed was beyond Europe, Asia, and Lybia, beyond the columns of Hercules, where those powerful people, the Atlantides, lived, against whom the first wars of ancient Greeks were waged.

Thus, led by the strangest destiny, I was treading under foot the mountains of this continent, touching with my hand those ruins a thousand generations old and contemporary with the geological epochs. I was walking on the very spot where the contemporaries of the first man had walked.

Whilst I was trying to fix in my mind every detail of this grand landscape, Captain Nemo remained motionless, as if petrified in mute ecstasy, leaning on a mossy stone. Was he dreaming of those generations long since disappeared? Was he asking them the secret of human destiny? Was it here this strange man came to steep himself in historical recollections, and live again this ancient life—he who wanted no modern one? What would I not have given to know his thoughts, to share them, to understand them! We remained for an hour at this place, contemplating the vast plains under the brightness of the lava, which was some times wonderfully intense. Rapid tremblings ran along the mountain caused by internal bubblings, deep noise, distinctly transmitted through the liquid medium were echoed with majestic grandeur. At this moment the moon appeared through the mass of waters and threw her pale rays on the buried continent. It was but a gleam, but what an indescribable effect! The Captain rose, cast one last look on the immense plain, and then bade me follow him.

We descended the mountain rapidly, and, the mineral forest once passed, I saw the lantern of the Nautilus shining like a star. The Captain walked straight to it, and we got on board as the first rays of light whitened the surface of the ocean.

CHAPTER X THE SUBMARINE COAL-MINES

The next day, the 20th of February, I awoke very late: the fatigues of the previous night had prolonged my sleep until eleven o'clock. I dressed quickly, and hastened to find the course the Nautilus was taking. The instruments showed it to be still toward the south, with a speed of twenty miles an hour and a depth of fifty fathoms.

The species of fishes here did not differ much from those already noticed. There were rays of giant size, five yards long, and endowed with great muscular strength, which enabled them to shoot above the waves; sharks of many kinds; amongst others, one fifteen feet long, with triangular sharp teeth, and whose transparency rendered it almost invisible in the water.

Amongst bony fish Conseil noticed some about three yards long, armed at the upper jaw with a piercing sword; other bright-coloured creatures, known in the time of Aristotle by the name of the sea-dragon, which are dangerous to capture on account of the spikes on their back.

About four o'clock, the soil, generally composed of a thick mud mixed with petrified wood, changed by degrees, and it became more stony, and seemed strewn with conglomerate and pieces of basalt, with a sprinkling of lava. I thought that a mountainous region was succeeding the long plains; and accordingly, after a few evolutions of the Nautilus, I saw the southerly horizon blocked by a high wall which seemed to close all exit. Its summit evidently passed the level of the ocean. It must be a continent, or at least an island—one of the Canaries, or of the Cape Verde Islands. The bearings not being yet taken, perhaps designedly, I was ignorant of our exact position. In any case, such a wall seemed to me to mark the limits of that Atlantis, of which we had in reality passed over only the smallest part.

Much longer should I have remained at the window admiring the beauties of sea and sky, but the panels closed. At this moment the Nautilus arrived at the side of this high, perpendicular wall. What it would do, I could not guess. I returned to my room; it no longer moved. I laid myself down with the full intention of waking after a few hours' sleep; but it was eight o'clock the next day when I entered the saloon. I looked at the manometer. It told me that the Nautilus was floating on the surface of the ocean. Besides, I heard steps on the platform. I went to the panel. It was open; but, instead of broad daylight, as I expected, I was surrounded by profound darkness. Where were we? Was I mistaken? Was it still night? No; not a star was shining and night has not that utter darkness.

I knew not what to think, when a voice near me said:

"Is that you, Professor?"

"Ah! Captain," I answered, "where are we?"

"Underground, sir."

"Underground!" I exclaimed. "And the Nautilus floating still?"

"It always floats."

"But I do not understand."

"Wait a few minutes, our lantern will be lit, and, if you like light places, you will be satisfied."

I stood on the platform and waited. The darkness was so complete that I could not even see Captain Nemo; but, looking to the zenith, exactly above my head, I seemed to catch an undecided gleam, a kind of twilight filling a circular hole. At this instant the lantern was lit, and its vividness dispelled the faint light. I closed my dazzled eyes for an instant, and then looked again. The Nautilus was stationary, floating near a mountain which formed a sort of quay. The lake, then, supporting it was a lake imprisoned by a circle of walls, measuring two miles in diameter and six in circumference. Its level (the manometer showed) could only be the same as the outside level, for there must necessarily be a communication between the lake and the sea. The high partitions, leaning forward on their base, grew into a vaulted roof bearing the shape of an immense funnel turned upside down, the height being about five or six hundred yards. At the summit was a circular orifice, by which I had caught the slight gleam of light, evidently daylight.

"Where are we?" I asked.

"In the very heart of an extinct volcano, the interior of which has been invaded by the sea, after some great convulsion of the earth. Whilst you were sleeping, Professor, the Nautilus penetrated to this lagoon by a natural canal, which opens about ten yards beneath the surface of the ocean. This is its harbour of refuge, a sure, commodious, and mysterious one, sheltered from all gales. Show me, if you can, on the coasts of any of your continents or islands, a road which can give such perfect refuge from all storms."

"Certainly," I replied, "you are in safety here, Captain Nemo. Who could reach you in the heart of a volcano? But did I not see an opening at its summit?"

"Yes; its crater, formerly filled with lava, vapour, and flames, and which now gives entrance to the life-giving air we breathe."

"But what is this volcanic mountain?"

"It belongs to one of the numerous islands with which this sea is strewn—to vessels a simple sandbank—to us an immense cavern. Chance led me to discover it, and chance served me well."

"But of what use is this refuge, Captain? The Nautilus wants no port."

"No, sir; but it wants electricity to make it move, and the wherewithal to make the electricity—sodium to feed the elements, coal from which to get the sodium, and a coal-mine to supply the coal. And exactly on this spot the sea covers entire forests embedded during the geological periods, now mineralised and transformed into coal; for me they are an inexhaustible mine."

"Your men follow the trade of miners here, then, Captain?"

"Exactly so. These mines extend under the waves like the mines of Newcastle. Here, in their diving-dresses, pick axe and shovel in hand, my men extract the coal, which I do not even ask from the mines of the earth. When I burn this combustible for the manufacture of sodium, the smoke, escaping from the crater of the mountain, gives it the appearance of a still-active volcano."

"And we shall see your companions at work?"

"No; not this time at least; for I am in a hurry to continue our submarine tour of the earth. So I shall content myself with drawing from the reserve of sodium I already possess. The time for loading is one day only, and we continue our voyage. So, if you wish to go over the cavern and make the round of the lagoon, you must take advantage of to-day, M. Aronnax."

I thanked the Captain and went to look for my companions, who had not yet left their cabin. I invited them to follow me without saying where we were. They mounted the platform. Conseil, who was astonished at nothing, seemed to look upon it as quite natural that he should wake under a mountain, after having fallen asleep under the waves. But Ned Land thought of nothing but finding whether the cavern had any exit. After breakfast, about ten o'clock, we went down on to the mountain.

"Here we are, once more on land," said Conseil.

"I do not call this land," said the Canadian. "And besides, we are not on it, but beneath it."

Between the walls of the mountains and the waters of the lake lay a sandy shore which, at its greatest breadth, measured five hundred feet. On this soil one might easily make the tour of the lake. But the base of the high partitions was stony ground, with volcanic locks and enormous pumice-stones lying in picturesque heaps. All these detached masses, covered with enamel, polished by the action of the subterraneous fires, shone resplendent by the light of our electric lantern. The mica dust from the shore, rising under our feet, flew like a cloud of sparks. The bottom now rose sensibly, and we soon arrived at long circuitous slopes, or inclined planes, which took us higher by degrees; but we were obliged to walk carefully among these conglomerates, bound by no cement, the feet slipping on the glassy crystal, felspar, and quartz.

The volcanic nature of this enormous excavation was confirmed on all sides, and I pointed it out to my companions.

"Picture to yourselves," said I, "what this crater must have been when filled with boiling lava, and when the level of the incandescent liquid rose to the orifice of the mountain, as though melted on the top of a hot plate."

"I can picture it perfectly," said Conseil. "But, sir, will you tell me why the Great Architect has suspended operations, and how it is that the furnace is replaced by the quiet waters of the lake?"

"Most probably, Conseil, because some convulsion beneath the ocean produced that very opening which has served as a passage for the Nautilus. Then the waters of the Atlantic rushed into the interior of the mountain. There must have been a terrible struggle between the two elements, a struggle which ended in the victory of Neptune. But many ages have run out since then, and the submerged volcano is now a peaceable grotto."

"Very well," replied Ned Land; "I accept the explanation, sir; but, in our own interests, I regret that the opening of which you speak was not made above the level of the sea."

"But, friend Ned," said Conseil, "if the passage had not been under the sea, the Nautilus could not have gone through it."

We continued ascending. The steps became more and more perpendicular and narrow. Deep excavations, which we were obliged to cross, cut them here and there; sloping masses had to be turned. We slid upon our knees and crawled along. But Conseil's dexterity and the Canadian's strength surmounted all obstacles. At a height of about 31 feet the nature of the ground changed without becoming more practicable. To the conglomerate and trachyte succeeded black basalt, the first dispread in layers full of bubbles, the latter forming regular prisms, placed like a colonnade supporting the spring of the immense vault, an admirable specimen of natural architecture. Between the blocks of basalt wound long streams of lava, long since grown cold, encrusted with bituminous rays; and in some places there were spread large carpets of sulphur. A more powerful light shone through the upper crater, shedding a vague glimmer over these volcanic depressions for ever buried in the bosom of this extinguished mountain. But our upward march was soon stopped at a height of about two hundred and fifty feet by impassable obstacles. There was a complete vaulted arch overhanging us, and our ascent was changed to a circular walk. At the last change vegetable life began to struggle with the mineral. Some shrubs, and even some trees, grew from the fractures of the walls. I recognised some euphorbias, with the caustic sugar coming from them; heliotropes, quite incapable of justifying their name, sadly drooped their clusters of flowers, both their colour and perfume half gone. Here and there some chrysanthemums grew timidly at the foot of an aloe with long, sickly-looking leaves. But between the streams of lava, I saw some little violets still slightly perfumed, and I admit that I smelt them with delight. Perfume is the soul of the flower, and sea-flowers have no soul.

We had arrived at the foot of some sturdy dragon-trees, which had pushed aside the rocks with their strong roots, when Ned Land exclaimed:

"Ah! sir, a hive! a hive!"

"A hive!" I replied, with a gesture of incredulity.

"Yes, a hive," repeated the Canadian, "and bees humming round it."

I approached, and was bound to believe my own eyes. There at a hole bored in one of the dragon-trees were some thousands of these ingenious insects, so common in all the Canaries, and whose produce is so much esteemed. Naturally enough, the Canadian wished to gather the honey, and I could not well oppose his wish. A quantity of dry leaves, mixed with sulphur, he lit with a spark from his flint, and he began to smoke out the bees. The humming ceased by degrees, and the hive eventually yielded several pounds of the sweetest honey, with which Ned Land filled his haversack.

"When I have mixed this honey with the paste of the bread-fruit," said he, "I shall be able to offer you a succulent cake."

"'Pon my word," said Conseil, "it will be gingerbread."

"Never mind the gingerbread," said I; "let us continue our interesting walk."

At every turn of the path we were following, the lake appeared in all its length and breadth. The lantern lit up the whole of its peaceable surface, which knew neither ripple nor wave. The Nautilus remained perfectly immovable. On the platform, and on the mountain, the ship's crew were working like black shadows clearly carved against the luminous atmosphere. We were now going round the highest crest of the first layers of rock which upheld the roof. I then saw that bees were not the only representatives of the animal kingdom in the interior of this volcano. Birds of prey hovered here and there in the shadows, or fled from their nests on the top of the rocks. There were sparrow hawks, with white breasts, and kestrels, and down the slopes scampered, with their long legs, several fine fat bustards. I leave anyone to imagine the covetousness of the Canadian at the sight of this savoury game, and whether he did not regret having no gun. But he did his best to replace the lead by stones, and, after several fruitless attempts, he succeeded in wounding a magnificent bird. To say that he risked his life twenty times before reaching it is but the truth; but he managed so well that the creature joined the honey-cakes in his bag. We were now obliged to descend toward the shore, the crest becoming impracticable. Above us the crater seemed to gape like the mouth of a well. From this place the sky could be clearly seen, and clouds, dissipated by the west wind, leaving behind them, even on the summit of the mountain, their misty remnants—certain proof that they were only moderately high, for the volcano did not rise more than eight hundred feet above the level of the ocean. Half an hour after the Canadian's last exploit we had regained the inner shore. Here the flora was represented by large carpets of marine crystal, a little umbelliferous plant very good to pickle, which also bears the name of pierce-stone and sea-fennel. Conseil gathered some bundles of it. As to the fauna, it might be counted by thousands of crustacea of all sorts, lobsters, crabs, spider-crabs, chameleon shrimps, and a large number of shells, rockfish, and limpets. Three-quarters of an hour later we had finished our circuitous walk and were on board. The crew had just finished loading the sodium, and the Nautilus could have left that instant. But Captain Nemo gave no order. Did he wish to wait until night, and leave the submarine passage secretly? Perhaps so. Whatever it might be, the next day, the Nautilus, having left its port, steered clear of all land at a few yards beneath the waves of the Atlantic.

CHAPTER XI THE SARGASSO SEA

That day the Nautilus crossed a singular part of the Atlantic Ocean. No one can be ignorant of the existence of a current of warm water known by the name of the Gulf Stream. After leaving the Gulf of Florida, we went in the direction of Spitzbergen. But before entering the Gulf of Mexico, about 45° of N. lat., this current divides into two arms, the principal one going towards the coast of Ireland and Norway, whilst the second bends to the south about the height of the Azores; then, touching the African shore, and describing a lengthened oval, returns to the Antilles. This second arm—it is rather a collar than an arm—surrounds with its circles of warm water that portion of the cold, quiet, immovable ocean called the Sargasso Sea, a perfect lake in the open Atlantic: it takes no less than three years for the great current to pass round it. Such was the region the Nautilus was now visiting, a perfect meadow, a close carpet of seaweed, fucus, and tropical berries, so thick and so compact that the stem of a vessel could hardly tear its way through it. And Captain Nemo, not wishing to entangle his screw in this herbaceous mass, kept some yards beneath the surface of the waves. The name Sargasso comes from the Spanish word "sargazzo" which signifies kelp. This kelp, or berry-plant, is the principal formation of this immense bank. And this is the reason why these plants unite in the peaceful basin of the Atlantic. The only explanation which can be given, he says, seems to me to result from the experience known to all the world. Place in a vase some fragments of cork or other floating body, and give to the water in the vase a circular movement, the scattered fragments will unite in a group in the centre of the liquid surface, that is to say, in the part least agitated. In the phenomenon we are considering, the Atlantic is the vase, the Gulf Stream the circular current, and the Sargasso Sea the central point at which the floating bodies unite.

I share Maury's opinion, and I was able to study the phenomenon in the very midst, where vessels rarely penetrate. Above us floated products of all kinds, heaped up among these brownish plants; trunks of trees torn from the Andes or the Rocky Mountains, and floated by the Amazon or the Mississippi; numerous wrecks, remains of keels, or ships' bottoms, side-planks stove in, and so weighted with shells and barnacles that they could not again rise to the surface. And time will one day justify Maury's other opinion, that these substances thus accumulated for ages will become petrified by the action of the water and will then form inexhaustible coal-mines—a precious reserve prepared by far-seeing Nature for the moment when men shall have exhausted the mines of continents.

In the midst of this inextricable mass of plants and sea weed, I noticed some charming pink halcyons and actiniae, with their long tentacles trailing after them, and medusae, green, red, and blue.

All the day of the 22nd of February we passed in the Sargasso Sea, where such fish as are partial to marine plants find abundant nourishment. The next, the ocean had returned to its accustomed aspect. From this time for nineteen days, from the 23rd of February to the 12th of March, the Nautilus kept in the middle of the Atlantic, carrying us at a constant speed of a hundred leagues in twenty-four hours. Captain Nemo evidently intended accomplishing his submarine programme, and I imagined that he intended, after doubling Cape Horn, to return to the Australian seas of the Pacific. Ned Land had cause for fear. In these large seas, void of islands, we could not attempt to leave the boat. Nor had we any means of opposing Captain Nemo's will. Our only course was to submit; but what we could neither gain by force nor cunning, I liked to think might be obtained by persuasion. This voyage ended, would he not consent to restore our liberty, under an oath never to reveal his existence?—an oath of honour which we should have religiously kept. But we must consider that delicate question with the Captain. But was I free to claim this liberty? Had he not himself said from the beginning, in the firmest manner, that the secret of his life exacted from him our lasting imprisonment on board the Nautilus? And would not my four months' silence appear to him a tacit acceptance of our situation? And would not a return to the subject result in raising suspicions which might be hurtful to our projects, if at some future time a favourable opportunity offered to return to them?

During the nineteen days mentioned above, no incident of any kind happened to signalise our voyage. I saw little of the Captain; he was at work. In the library I often found his books left open, especially those on natural history. My work on submarine depths, conned over by him, was covered with marginal notes, often contradicting my theories and systems; but the Captain contented himself with thus purging my work; it was very rare for him to discuss it with me. Sometimes I heard the melancholy tones of his organ; but only at night, in the midst of the deepest obscurity, when the Nautilus slept upon the deserted ocean. During this part of our voyage we sailed whole days on the surface of the waves. The sea seemed abandoned. A few sailing-vessels, on the road to India, were making for the Cape of Good Hope. One day we were followed by the boats of a whaler, who, no doubt, took us for some enormous whale of great price; but Captain Nemo did not wish the worthy fellows to lose their time and trouble, so ended the chase by plunging under the water. Our navigation continued until the 13th of March; that day the Nautilus was employed in taking soundings, which greatly interested me. We had then made about 13,000 leagues since our departure from the high seas of the Pacific. The bearings gave us 45° 37' S. lat., and 37° 53' W. long. It was the same water in which Captain Denham of the Herald sounded 7,000 fathoms without finding the bottom. There, too, Lieutenant Parker, of the American frigate Congress, could not touch the bottom with 15,140 fathoms. Captain Nemo intended seeking the bottom of the ocean by a diagonal sufficiently lengthened by means of lateral planes placed at an angle of 45° with the water-line of the Nautilus. Then the screw set to work at its maximum speed, its four blades beating the waves with in describable force. Under this powerful pressure, the hull of the Nautilus quivered like a sonorous chord and sank regularly under the water.

At 7,000 fathoms I saw some blackish tops rising from the midst of the waters; but these summits might belong to high mountains like the Himalayas or Mont Blanc, even higher; and the depth of the abyss remained incalculable. The Nautilus descended still lower, in spite of the great pressure. I felt the steel plates tremble at the fastenings of the bolts; its bars bent, its partitions groaned; the windows of the saloon seemed to curve under the pressure of the waters. And this firm structure would doubtless have yielded, if, as its Captain had said, it had not been capable of resistance like a solid block. We had attained a depth of 16,000 yards (four leagues), and the sides of the Nautilus then bore a pressure of 1,600 atmospheres, that is to say, 3,200 lb. to each square two-fifths of an inch of its surface.

"What a situation to be in!" I exclaimed. "To overrun these deep regions where man has never trod! Look, Captain, look at these magnificent rocks, these uninhabited grottoes, these lowest receptacles of the globe, where life is no longer possible! What unknown sights are here! Why should we be unable to preserve a remembrance of them?"

"Would you like to carry away more than the remembrance?" said Captain Nemo.

"What do you mean by those words?"

"I mean to say that nothing is easier than to make a photographic view of this submarine region."

I had not time to express my surprise at this new proposition, when, at Captain Nemo's call, an objective was brought into the saloon. Through the widely-opened panel, the liquid mass was bright with electricity, which was distributed with such uniformity that not a shadow, not a gradation, was to be seen in our manufactured light. The Nautilus remained motionless, the force of its screw subdued by the inclination of its planes: the instrument was propped on the bottom of the oceanic site, and in a few seconds we had obtained a perfect negative.

But, the operation being over, Captain Nemo said, "Let us go up; we must not abuse our position, nor expose the Nautilus too long to such great pressure."

"Go up again!" I exclaimed.

"Hold well on."

I had not time to understand why the Captain cautioned me thus, when I was thrown forward on to the carpet. At a signal from the Captain, its screw was shipped, and its blades raised vertically; the Nautilus shot into the air like a balloon, rising with stunning rapidity, and cutting the mass of waters with a sonorous agitation. Nothing was visible; and in four minutes it had shot through the four leagues which separated it from the ocean, and, after emerging like a flying-fish, fell, making the waves rebound to an enormous height.

CHAPTER XII CACHALOTS AND WHALES

During the nights of the 13th and 14th of March, the Nautilus returned to its southerly course. I fancied that, when on a level with Cape Horn, he would turn the helm westward, in order to beat the Pacific seas, and so complete the tour of the world. He did nothing of the kind, but continued on his way to the southern regions. Where was he going to? To the pole? It was madness! I began to think that the Captain's temerity justified Ned Land's fears. For some time past the Canadian had not spoken to me of his projects of flight; he was less communicative, almost silent. I could see that this lengthened imprisonment was weighing upon him, and I felt that rage was burning within him. When he met the Captain, his eyes lit up with suppressed anger; and I feared that his natural violence would lead him into some extreme. That day, the 14th of March, Conseil and he came to me in my room. I inquired the cause of their visit.

"A simple question to ask you, sir," replied the Canadian.

"Speak, Ned."

"How many men are there on board the Nautilus, do you think?"

"I cannot tell, my friend."

"I should say that its working does not require a large crew."

"Certainly, under existing conditions, ten men, at the most, ought to be enough."

"Well, why should there be any more?"

"Why?" I replied, looking fixedly at Ned Land, whose meaning was easy to guess. "Because," I added, "if my surmises are correct, and if I have well understood the Captain's existence, the Nautilus is not only a vessel: it is also a place of refuge for those who, like its commander, have broken every tie upon earth."

"Perhaps so," said Conseil; "but, in any case, the Nautilus can only contain a certain number of men. Could not you, sir, estimate their maximum?"

"How, Conseil?"

"By calculation; given the size of the vessel, which you know, sir, and consequently the quantity of air it contains, knowing also how much each man expends at a breath, and comparing these results with the fact that the Nautilus is obliged to go to the surface every twenty-four hours."

Conseil had not finished the sentence before I saw what he was driving at.

"I understand," said I; "but that calculation, though simple enough, can give but a very uncertain result."

"Never mind," said Ned Land urgently.

"Here it is, then," said I. "In one hour each man consumes the oxygen contained in twenty gallons of air; and in twenty-four, that contained in 480 gallons. We must, therefore find how many times 480 gallons of air the Nautilus contains."

"Just so," said Conseil.

"Or," I continued, "the size of the Nautilus being 1,500 tons; and one ton holding 200 gallons, it contains 300,000 gallons of air, which, divided by 480, gives a quotient of 625. Which means to say, strictly speaking, that the air contained in the Nautilus would suffice for 625 men for twenty-four hours."

"Six hundred and twenty-five!" repeated Ned.

"But remember that all of us, passengers, sailors, and officers included, would not form a tenth part of that number."

"Still too many for three men," murmured Conseil.

The Canadian shook his head, passed his hand across his forehead, and left the room without answering.

"Will you allow me to make one observation, sir?" said Conseil. "Poor Ned is longing for everything that he can not have. His past life is always present to him; everything that we are forbidden he regrets. His head is full of old recollections. And we must understand him. What has he to do here? Nothing; he is not learned like you, sir; and has not the same taste for the beauties of the sea that we have. He would risk everything to be able to go once more into a tavern in his own country."

Certainly the monotony on board must seem intolerable to the Canadian, accustomed as he was to a life of liberty and activity. Events were rare which could rouse him to any show of spirit; but that day an event did happen which recalled the bright days of the harpooner. About eleven in the morning, being on the surface of the ocean, the Nautilus fell in with a troop of whales—an encounter which did not astonish me, knowing that these creatures, hunted to death, had taken refuge in high latitudes.

We were seated on the platform, with a quiet sea. The month of October in those latitudes gave us some lovely autumnal days. It was the Canadian—he could not be mistaken—who signalled a whale on the eastern horizon. Looking attentively, one might see its black back rise and fall with the waves five miles from the Nautilus.

"Ah!" exclaimed Ned Land, "if I was on board a whaler, now such a meeting would give me pleasure. It is one of large size. See with what strength its blow-holes throw up columns of air an steam! Confound it, why am I bound to these steel plates?"

"What, Ned," said I, "you have not forgotten your old ideas of fishing?"

"Can a whale-fisher ever forget his old trade, sir? Can he ever tire of the emotions caused by such a chase?"

"You have never fished in these seas, Ned?"

"Never, sir; in the northern only, and as much in Behring as in Davis Straits."

"Then the southern whale is still unknown to you. It is the Greenland whale you have hunted up to this time, and that would not risk passing through the warm waters of the equator. Whales are localised, according to their kinds, in certain seas which they never leave. And if one of these creatures went from Behring to Davis Straits, it must be simply because there is a passage from one sea to the other, either on the American or the Asiatic side."

"In that case, as I have never fished in these seas, I do not know the kind of whale frequenting them!"

"I have told you, Ned."

"A greater reason for making their acquaintance," said Conseil.

"Look! look!" exclaimed the Canadian, "they approach: they aggravate me; they know that I cannot get at them!"

Ned stamped his feet. His hand trembled, as he grasped an imaginary harpoon.

"Are these cetaceans as large as those of the northern seas?" asked he.

"Very nearly, Ned."

"Because I have seen large whales, sir, whales measuring a hundred feet. I have even been told that those of Hullamoch and Umgallick, of the Aleutian Islands, are sometimes a hundred and fifty feet long."

"That seems to me exaggeration. These creatures are only balaeaopterons, provided with dorsal fins; and, like the cachalots, are generally much smaller than the Greenland whale."

"Ah!" exclaimed the Canadian, whose eyes had never left the ocean, "they are coming nearer; they are in the same water as the Nautilus."

Then, returning to the conversation, he said:

"You spoke of the cachalot as a small creature. I have heard of gigantic ones. They are intelligent cetacea. It is said of some that they cover themselves with seaweed and fucus, and then are taken for islands. People encamp upon them, and settle there; lights a fire——"

"And build houses," said Conseil.

"Yes, joker," said Ned Land. "And one fine day the creature plunges, carrying with it all the inhabitants to the bottom of the sea."

"Something like the travels of Sinbad the Sailor," I replied, laughing.

"Ah!" suddenly exclaimed Ned Land, "it is not one whale; there are ten—there are twenty—it is a whole troop! And I not able to do anything! hands and feet tied!"

"But, friend Ned," said Conseil, "why do you not ask Captain Nemo's permission to chase them?"

Conseil had not finished his sentence when Ned Land had lowered himself through the panel to seek the Captain. A few minutes afterwards the two appeared together on the platform.

Captain Nemo watched the troop of cetacea playing on the waters about a mile from the Nautilus.

"They are southern whales," said he; "there goes the fortune of a whole fleet of whalers."

"Well, sir," asked the Canadian, "can I not chase them, if only to remind me of my old trade of harpooner?"

"And to what purpose?" replied Captain Nemo; "only to destroy! We have nothing to do with the whale-oil on board."

"But, sir," continued the Canadian, "in the Red Sea you allowed us to follow the dugong."

"Then it was to procure fresh meat for my crew. Here it would be killing for killing's sake. I know that is a privilege reserved for man, but I do not approve of such murderous pastime. In destroying the southern whale (like the Greenland whale, an inoffensive creature), your traders do a culpable action, Master Land. They have already depopulated the whole of Baffin's Bay, and are annihilating a class of useful animals. Leave the unfortunate cetacea alone. They have plenty of natural enemies—cachalots, swordfish, and sawfish—without you troubling them."

The Captain was right. The barbarous and inconsiderate greed of these fishermen will one day cause the disappearance of the last whale in the ocean. Ned Land whistled "Yankee-doodle" between his teeth, thrust his hands into his pockets, and turned his back upon us. But Captain Nemo watched the troop of cetacea, and, addressing me, said:

"I was right in saying that whales had natural enemies enough, without counting man. These will have plenty to do before long. Do you see, M. Aronnax, about eight miles to leeward, those blackish moving points?"

"Yes, Captain," I replied.

"Those are cachalots—terrible animals, which I have met in troops of two or three hundred. As to those, they are cruel, mischievous creatures; they would be right in exterminating them."

The Canadian turned quickly at the last words.

"Well, Captain," said he, "it is still time, in the interest of the whales."

"It is useless to expose one's self, Professor. The Nautilus will disperse them. It is armed with a steel spur as good as Master Land's harpoon, I imagine."

The Canadian did not put himself out enough to shrug his shoulders. Attack cetacea with blows of a spur! Who had ever heard of such a thing?

"Wait, M. Aronnax," said Captain Nemo. "We will show you something you have never yet seen. We have no pity for these ferocious creatures. They are nothing but mouth and teeth."

Mouth and teeth! No one could better describe the macrocephalous cachalot, which is sometimes more than seventy-five feet long. Its enormous head occupies one-third of its entire body. Better armed than the whale, whose upper jaw is furnished only with whalebone, it is supplied with twenty-five large tusks, about eight inches long, cylindrical and conical at the top, each weighing two pounds. It is in the upper part of this enormous head, in great cavities divided by cartilages, that is to be found from six to eight hundred pounds of that precious oil called spermaceti. The cachalot is a disagreeable creature, more tadpole than fish, according to Fredol's description. It is badly formed, the whole of its left side being (if we may say it), a "failure," and being only able to see with its right eye. But the formidable troop was nearing us. They had seen the whales and were preparing to attack them. One could judge beforehand that the cachalots would be victorious, not only because they were better built for attack than their inoffensive adversaries, but also because they could remain longer under water without coming to the surface. There was only just time to go to the help of the whales. The Nautilus went under water. Conseil, Ned Land, and I took our places before the window in the saloon, and Captain Nemo joined the pilot in his cage to work his apparatus as an engine of destruction. Soon I felt the beatings of the screw quicken, and our speed increased. The battle between the cachalots and the whales had already begun when the Nautilus arrived. They did not at first show any fear at the sight of this new monster joining in the conflict. But they soon had to guard against its blows. What a battle! The Nautilus was nothing but a formidable harpoon, brandished by the hand of its Captain. It hurled itself against the fleshy mass, passing through from one part to the other, leaving behind it two quivering halves of the animal. It could not feel the formidable blows from their tails upon its sides, nor the shock which it produced itself, much more. One cachalot killed, it ran at the next, tacked on the spot that it might not miss its prey, going forwards and backwards, answering to its helm, plunging when the cetacean dived into the deep waters, coming up with it when it returned to the surface, striking it front or sideways, cutting or tearing in all directions and at any pace, piercing it with its terrible spur. What carnage! What a noise on the surface of the waves! What sharp hissing, and what snorting peculiar to these enraged animals! In the midst of these waters, generally so peaceful, their tails made perfect billows. For one hour this wholesale massacre continued, from which the cachalots could not escape. Several times ten or twelve united tried to crush the Nautilus by their weight. From the window we could see their enormous mouths, studded with tusks, and their formidable eyes. Ned Land could not contain himself; he threatened and swore at them. We could feel them clinging to our vessel like dogs worrying a wild boar in a copse. But the Nautilus, working its screw, carried them here and there, or to the upper levels of the ocean, without caring for their enormous weight, nor the powerful strain on the vessel. At length the mass of cachalots broke up, the waves became quiet, and I felt that we were rising to the surface. The panel opened, and we hurried on to the platform. The sea was covered with mutilated bodies. A formidable explosion could not have divided and torn this fleshy mass with more violence. We were floating amid gigantic bodies, bluish on the back and white underneath, covered with enormous protuberances. Some terrified cachalots were flying towards the horizon. The waves were dyed red for several miles, and the Nautilus floated in a sea of blood: Captain Nemo joined us.

"Well, Master Land?" said he.

"Well, sir," replied the Canadian, whose enthusiasm had somewhat calmed; "it is a terrible spectacle, certainly. But I am not a butcher. I am a hunter, and I call this a butchery."

"It is a massacre of mischievous creatures," replied the Captain; "and the Nautilus is not a butcher's knife."

"I like my harpoon better," said the Canadian.

"Every one to his own," answered the Captain, looking fixedly at Ned Land.

I feared he would commit some act of violence, which would end in sad consequences. But his anger was turned by the sight of a whale which the Nautilus had just come up with. The creature had not quite escaped from the cachalot's teeth. I recognised the southern whale by its flat head, which is entirely black. Anatomically, it is distinguished from the white whale and the North Cape whale by the seven cervical vertebrae, and it has two more ribs than its congeners. The unfortunate cetacean was lying on its side, riddled with holes from the bites, and quite dead. From its mutilated fin still hung a young whale which it could not save from the massacre. Its open mouth let the water flow in and out, murmuring like the waves breaking on the shore. Captain Nemo steered close to the corpse of the creature. Two of his men mounted its side, and I saw, not without surprise, that they were drawing from its breasts all the milk which they contained, that is to say, about two or three tons. The Captain offered me a cup of the milk, which was still warm. I could not help showing my repugnance to the drink; but he assured me that it was excellent, and not to be distinguished from cow's milk. I tasted it, and was of his opinion. It was a useful reserve to us, for in the shape of salt butter or cheese it would form an agreeable variety from our ordinary food. From that day I noticed with uneasiness that Ned Land's ill-will towards Captain Nemo increased, and I resolved to watch the Canadian's gestures closely.

CHAPTER XIII THE ICEBERG

The Nautilus was steadily pursuing its southerly course, following the fiftieth meridian with considerable speed. Did he wish to reach the pole? I did not think so, for every attempt to reach that point had hitherto failed. Again, the season was far advanced, for in the Antarctic regions the 13th of March corresponds with the 13th of September of northern regions, which begin at the equinoctial season. On the 14th of March I saw floating ice in latitude 55°, merely pale bits of debris from twenty to twenty-five feet long, forming banks over which the sea curled. The Nautilus remained on the surface of the ocean. Ned Land, who had fished in the Arctic Seas, was familiar with its icebergs; but Conseil and I admired them for the first time. In the atmosphere towards the southern horizon stretched a white dazzling band. English whalers have given it the name of "ice blink." However thick the clouds may be, it is always visible, and announces the presence of an ice pack or bank. Accordingly, larger blocks soon appeared, whose brilliancy changed with the caprices of the fog. Some of these masses showed green veins, as if long undulating lines had been traced with sulphate of copper; others resembled enormous amethysts with the light shining through them. Some reflected the light of day upon a thousand crystal facets. Others shaded with vivid calcareous reflections resembled a perfect town of marble. The more we neared the south the more these floating islands increased both in number and importance.

At 60° lat. every pass had disappeared. But, seeking carefully, Captain Nemo soon found a narrow opening, through which he boldly slipped, knowing, however, that it would close behind him. Thus, guided by this clever hand, the Nautilus passed through all the ice with a precision which quite charmed Conseil; icebergs or mountains, ice-fields or smooth plains, seeming to have no limits, drift-ice or floating ice-packs, plains broken up, called palchs when they are circular, and streams when they are made up of long strips. The temperature was very low; the thermometer exposed to the air marked 2 deg. or 3° below zero, but we were warmly clad with fur, at the expense of the sea-bear and seal. The interior of the Nautilus, warmed regularly by its electric apparatus, defied the most intense cold. Besides, it would only have been necessary to go some yards beneath the waves to find a more bearable temperature. Two months earlier we should have had perpetual daylight in these latitudes; but already we had had three or four hours of night, and by and by there would be six months of darkness in these circumpolar regions. On the 15th of March we were in the latitude of New Shetland and South Orkney. The Captain told me that formerly numerous tribes of seals inhabited them; but that English and American whalers, in their rage for destruction, massacred both old and young; thus, where there was once life and animation, they had left silence and death.

About eight o'clock on the morning of the 16th of March the Nautilus, following the fifty-fifth meridian, cut the Antarctic polar circle. Ice surrounded us on all sides, and closed the horizon. But Captain Nemo went from one opening to another, still going higher. I cannot express my astonishment at the beauties of these new regions. The ice took most surprising forms. Here the grouping formed an oriental town, with innumerable mosques and minarets; there a fallen city thrown to the earth, as it were, by some convulsion of nature. The whole aspect was constantly changed by the oblique rays of the sun, or lost in the greyish fog amidst hurricanes of snow. Detonations and falls were heard on all sides, great overthrows of icebergs, which altered the whole landscape like a diorama. Often seeing no exit, I thought we were definitely prisoners; but, instinct guiding him at the slightest indication, Captain Nemo would discover a new pass. He was never mistaken when he saw the thin threads of bluish water trickling along the ice-fields; and I had no doubt that he had already ventured into the midst of these Antarctic seas before. On the 16th of March, however, the ice-fields absolutely blocked our road. It was not the iceberg itself, as yet, but vast fields cemented by the cold. But this obstacle could not stop Captain Nemo: he hurled himself against it with frightful violence. The Nautilus entered the brittle mass like a wedge, and split it with frightful crackings. It was the battering ram of the ancients hurled by infinite strength. The ice, thrown high in the air, fell like hail around us. By its own power of impulsion our apparatus made a canal for itself; some times carried away by its own impetus, it lodged on the ice-field, crushing it with its weight, and sometimes buried beneath it, dividing it by a simple pitching movement, producing large rents in it. Violent gales assailed us at this time, accompanied by thick fogs, through which, from one end of the platform to the other, we could see nothing. The wind blew sharply from all parts of the compass, and the snow lay in such hard heaps that we had to break it with blows of a pickaxe. The temperature was always at 5 deg. below zero; every outward part of the Nautilus was covered with ice. A rigged vessel would have been entangled in the blocked up gorges. A vessel without sails, with electricity for its motive power, and wanting no coal, could alone brave such high latitudes. At length, on the 18th of March, after many useless assaults, the Nautilus was positively blocked. It was no longer either streams, packs, or ice-fields, but an interminable and immovable barrier, formed by mountains soldered together.

"An iceberg!" said the Canadian to me.

I knew that to Ned Land, as well as to all other navigators who had preceded us, this was an inevitable obstacle. The sun appearing for an instant at noon, Captain Nemo took an observation as near as possible, which gave our situation at 51° 30' long. and 67° 39' of S. lat. We had advanced one degree more in this Antarctic region. Of the liquid surface of the sea there was no longer a glimpse. Under the spur of the Nautilus lay stretched a vast plain, entangled with confused blocks. Here and there sharp points and slender needles rising to a height of 200 feet; further on a steep shore, hewn as it were with an axe and clothed with greyish tints; huge mirrors, reflecting a few rays of sunshine, half drowned in the fog. And over this desolate face of nature a stern silence reigned, scarcely broken by the flapping of the wings of petrels and puffins. Everything was frozen—even the noise. The Nautilus was then obliged to stop in its adventurous course amid these fields of ice. In spite of our efforts, in spite of the powerful means employed to break up the ice, the Nautilus remained immovable. Generally, when we can proceed no further, we have return still open to us; but here return was as impossible as advance, for every pass had closed behind us; and for the few moments when we were stationary, we were likely to be entirely blocked, which did indeed happen about two o'clock in the afternoon, the fresh ice forming around its sides with astonishing rapidity. I was obliged to admit that Captain

Nemo was more than imprudent. I was on the platform at that moment. The Captain had been observing our situation for some time past, when he said to me:

"Well, sir, what do you think of this?"

"I think that we are caught, Captain."

"So, M. Aronnax, you really think that the Nautilus cannot disengage itself?"

"With difficulty, Captain; for the season is already too far advanced for you to reckon on the breaking of the ice."

"Ah! sir," said Captain Nemo, in an ironical tone, "you will always be the same. You see nothing but difficulties and obstacles. I affirm that not only can the Nautilus disengage itself, but also that it can go further still."

"Further to the South?" I asked, looking at the Captain.

"Yes, sir; it shall go to the pole."

"To the pole!" I exclaimed, unable to repress a gesture of incredulity.

"Yes," replied the Captain, coldly, "to the Antarctic pole—to that unknown point from whence springs every meridian of the globe. You know whether I can do as I please with the Nautilus!"

Yes, I knew that. I knew that this man was bold, even to rashness. But to conquer those obstacles which bristled round the South Pole, rendering it more inaccessible than the North, which had not yet been reached by the boldest navigators—was it not a mad enterprise, one which only a maniac would have conceived? It then came into my head to ask Captain Nemo if he had ever discovered that pole which had never yet been trodden by a human creature?

"No, sir," he replied; "but we will discover it together. Where others have failed, I will not fail. I have never yet led my Nautilus so far into southern seas; but, I repeat, it shall go further yet."

"I can well believe you, Captain," said I, in a slightly ironical tone. "I believe you! Let us go ahead! There are no obstacles for us! Let us smash this iceberg! Let us blow it up; and, if it resists, let us give the Nautilus wings to fly over it!"

"Over it, sir!" said Captain Nemo, quietly; "no, not over it, but under it!"

"Under it!" I exclaimed, a sudden idea of the Captain's projects flashing upon my mind. I understood; the wonderful qualities of the Nautilus were going to serve us in this superhuman enterprise.

"I see we are beginning to understand one another, sir," said the Captain, half smiling. "You begin to see the possibility—I should say the success—of this attempt. That which is impossible for an ordinary vessel is easy to the Nautilus. If a continent lies before the pole, it must stop before the continent; but if, on the contrary, the pole is washed by open sea, it will go even to the pole."

"Certainly," said I, carried away by the Captain's reasoning; "if the surface of the sea is solidified by the ice, the lower depths are free by the Providential law which has placed the maximum of density of the waters of the ocean one degree higher than freezing-point; and, if I am not mistaken, the portion of this iceberg which is above the water is as one to four to that which is below."

"Very nearly, sir; for one foot of iceberg above the sea there are three below it. If these ice mountains are not more than 300 feet above the surface, they are not more than 900 beneath. And what are 900 feet to the Nautilus?"

"Nothing, sir."

"It could even seek at greater depths that uniform temperature of sea-water, and there brave with impunity the thirty or forty degrees of surface cold."

"Just so, sir—just so," I replied, getting animated.

"The only difficulty," continued Captain Nemo, "is that of remaining several days without renewing our provision of air."

"Is that all? The Nautilus has vast reservoirs; we can fill them, and they will supply us with all the oxygen we want."

"Well thought of, M. Aronnax," replied the Captain, smiling. "But, not wishing you to accuse me of rashness, I will first give you all my objections."

"Have you any more to make?"

"Only one. It is possible, if the sea exists at the South Pole, that it may be covered; and, consequently, we shall be unable to come to the surface."

"Good, sir! but do you forget that the Nautilus is armed with a powerful spur, and could we not send it diagonally against these fields of ice, which would open at the shocks."

"Ah! sir, you are full of ideas to-day."

"Besides, Captain," I added, enthusiastically, "why should we not find the sea open at the South Pole as well as at the North? The frozen poles of the earth do not coincide, either in the southern or in the northern regions; and, until it is proved to the contrary, we may suppose either a continent or an ocean free from ice at these two points of the globe."

"I think so too, M. Aronnax," replied Captain Nemo. "I only wish you to observe that, after having made so many objections to my project, you are now crushing me with arguments in its favour!"

The preparations for this audacious attempt now began. The powerful pumps of the Nautilus were working air into the reservoirs and storing it at high pressure. About four o'clock, Captain Nemo announced the closing of the panels on the platform. I threw one last look at the massive iceberg which we were going to cross. The weather was clear, the atmosphere pure enough, the cold very great, being 12° below zero; but, the wind having gone down, this temperature was not so unbearable. About ten men mounted the sides of the Nautilus, armed with pickaxes to break the ice around the vessel, which was soon free. The operation was quickly performed, for the fresh ice was still very thin. We all went below. The usual reservoirs were filled with the newly-liberated water, and the Nautilus soon descended. I had taken my place with Conseil in the saloon; through the open window we could see the lower beds of the Southern Ocean. The thermometer went up, the needle of the compass deviated on the dial. At about 900 feet, as Captain Nemo had foreseen, we were floating beneath the undulating bottom of the iceberg. But the Nautilus went lower still—it went to the depth of four hundred fathoms. The temperature of the water at the surface showed twelve degrees, it was now only ten; we had gained two. I need not say the temperature of the Nautilus was raised by its heating apparatus to a much higher degree; every manoeuvre was accomplished with wonderful precision.

"We shall pass it, if you please, sir," said Conseil.

"I believe we shall," I said, in a tone of firm conviction.

In this open sea, the Nautilus had taken its course direct to the pole, without leaving the fifty-second meridian. From 67° 30' to 90 deg., twenty-two degrees and a half of latitude remained to travel; that is, about five hundred leagues. The Nautilus kept up a mean speed of twenty-six miles an hour—the speed of an express train. If that was kept up, in forty hours we should reach the pole.

For a part of the night the novelty of the situation kept us at the window. The sea was lit with the electric lantern; but it was deserted; fishes did not sojourn in these imprisoned waters; they only found there a passage to take them from the Antarctic Ocean to the open polar sea. Our pace was rapid; we could feel it by the quivering of the long steel body. About two in the morning I took some hours' repose, and Conseil did the same. In crossing the waist I did not meet Captain Nemo: I supposed him to be in the pilot's cage. The next morning, the 19th of March, I took my post once more in the saloon. The electric log told me that the speed of the Nautilus had been slackened. It was then going towards the surface; but prudently emptying its reservoirs very slowly. My heart beat fast. Were we going to emerge and regain the open polar atmosphere? No! A shock told me that the Nautilus had struck the bottom of the iceberg, still very thick, judging from the deadened sound. We had in deed "struck," to use a sea expression, but in an inverse sense, and at a thousand feet deep. This would give three thousand feet of ice above us; one thousand being above the water-mark. The iceberg was then higher than at its borders—not a very reassuring fact. Several times that day the Nautilus tried again, and every time it struck the wall which lay like a ceiling above it. Sometimes it met with but 900 yards, only 200 of which rose above the surface. It was twice the height it was when the Nautilus had gone under the waves. I carefully noted the different depths, and thus obtained a submarine profile of the chain as it was developed under the water. That night no change had taken place in our situation. Still ice between four and five hundred yards in depth! It was evidently diminishing, but, still, what a thickness between us and the surface of the ocean! It was then eight. According to the daily custom on board the Nautilus, its air should have been renewed four hours ago; but I did not suffer much, although Captain Nemo had not yet made any demand upon his reserve of oxygen. My sleep was painful that night; hope and fear besieged me by turns: I rose several times. The groping of the Nautilus continued. About three in the morning, I noticed that the lower surface of the iceberg was only about fifty feet deep. One hundred and fifty feet now separated us from the surface of the waters. The iceberg was by degrees becoming an ice-field, the mountain a plain. My eyes never left the manometer. We were still rising diagonally to the surface, which sparkled under the electric rays. The iceberg was stretching both above and beneath into lengthening slopes; mile after mile it was getting thinner. At length, at six in the morning of that memorable day, the 19th of March, the door of the saloon opened, and Captain Nemo appeared.

"The sea is open!!" was all he said.

CHAPTER XIV THE SOUTH POLE

I rushed on to the platform. Yes! the open sea, with but a few scattered pieces of ice and moving icebergs—a long stretch of sea; a world of birds in the air, and myriads of fishes under those waters, which varied from intense blue to olive green, according to the bottom. The thermometer marked 3° C. above zero. It was comparatively spring, shut up as we were behind this iceberg, whose lengthened mass was dimly seen on our northern horizon.

"Are we at the pole?" I asked the Captain, with a beating heart.

"I do not know," he replied. "At noon I will take our bearings."

"But will the sun show himself through this fog?" said I, looking at the leaden sky.

"However little it shows, it will be enough," replied the Captain.

About ten miles south a solitary island rose to a height of one hundred and four yards. We made for it, but carefully, for the sea might be strewn with banks. One hour afterwards we had reached it, two hours later we had made the round of it. It measured four or five miles in circumference. A narrow canal separated it from a considerable stretch of land, perhaps a continent, for we could not see its limits. The existence of this land seemed to give some colour to Maury's theory. The ingenious American has remarked that, between the South Pole and the sixtieth parallel, the sea is covered with floating ice of enormous size, which is never met with in the North Atlantic. From this fact he has drawn the conclusion that the Antarctic Circle encloses considerable continents, as icebergs cannot form in open sea, but only on the coasts. According to these calculations, the mass of ice surrounding the southern pole forms a vast cap, the circumference of which must be, at least, 2,500 miles. But the Nautilus, for fear of running aground, had stopped about three cable-lengths from a strand over which reared a superb heap of rocks. The boat was launched; the Captain, two of his men, bearing instruments, Conseil, and myself were in it. It was ten in the morning. I had not seen Ned Land. Doubtless the Canadian did not wish to admit the presence of the South Pole. A few strokes of the oar brought us to the sand, where we ran ashore. Conseil was going to jump on to the land, when I held him back.

"Sir," said I to Captain Nemo, "to you belongs the honour of first setting foot on this land."

"Yes, sir," said the Captain, "and if I do not hesitate to tread this South Pole, it is because, up to this time, no human being has left a trace there."

Saying this, he jumped lightly on to the sand. His heart beat with emotion. He climbed a rock, sloping to a little promontory, and there, with his arms crossed, mute and motionless, and with an eager look, he seemed to take possession of these southern regions. After five minutes passed in this ecstasy, he turned to us.

"When you like, sir."

I landed, followed by Conseil, leaving the two men in the boat. For a long way the soil was composed of a reddish sandy stone, something like crushed brick, scoriae, streams of lava, and pumice-stones. One could not mistake its volcanic origin. In some parts, slight curls of smoke emitted a sulphurous smell, proving that the internal fires had lost nothing of their expansive powers, though, having climbed a high acclivity, I could see no volcano for a radius of several miles. We know that in those Antarctic countries, James Ross found two craters, the Erebus and Terror, in full activity, on the 167th meridian, latitude 77° 32'. The vegetation of this desolate continent seemed to me much restricted. Some lichens lay upon the black rocks; some microscopic plants, rudimentary diatomas, a kind of cells placed between two quartz shells; long purple and scarlet weed, supported on little swimming bladders, which the breaking of the waves brought to the shore. These constituted the meagre flora of this region. The shore was strewn with molluscs, little mussels, and limpets. I also saw myriads of northern clios, one-and-a-quarter inches long, of which a whale would swallow a whole world at a mouthful; and some perfect sea-butterflies, animating the waters on the skirts of the shore.

There appeared on the high bottoms some coral shrubs, of the kind which, according to James Ross, live in the Antarctic seas to the depth of more than 1,000 yards. Then there were little kingfishers and starfish studding the soil. But where life abounded most was in the air. There thousands of birds fluttered and flew of all kinds, deafening us with their cries; others crowded the rock, looking at us as we passed by without fear, and pressing familiarly close by our feet. There were penguins, so agile in the water, heavy and awkward as they are on the ground; they were uttering harsh cries, a large assembly, sober in gesture, but extravagant in clamour. Albatrosses passed in the air, the expanse of their wings being at least four yards and a half, and justly called the vultures of the ocean; some gigantic petrels, and some damiers, a kind of small duck, the underpart of whose body is black and white; then there were a whole series of petrels, some whitish, with brown-bordered wings, others blue, peculiar to the Antarctic seas, and so oily, as I told Conseil, that the inhabitants of the Ferroe Islands had nothing to do before lighting them but to put a wick in.

"A little more," said Conseil, "and they would be perfect lamps! After that, we cannot expect Nature to have previously furnished them with wicks!"

About half a mile farther on the soil was riddled with ruffs' nests, a sort of laying-ground, out of which many birds were issuing. Captain Nemo had some hundreds hunted. They uttered a cry like the braying of an ass, were about the size of a goose, slate-colour on the body, white beneath, with a yellow line round their throats; they allowed themselves to be killed with a stone, never trying to escape. But the fog did not lift, and at eleven the sun had not yet shown itself. Its absence made me uneasy. Without it no observations were possible. How, then, could we decide whether we had reached the pole? When I rejoined Captain Nemo, I found him leaning on a piece of rock, silently watching the sky. He seemed impatient and vexed. But what was to be done? This rash and powerful man could not command the sun as he did the sea. Noon arrived without the orb of day showing itself for an instant. We could not even tell its position behind the curtain of fog; and soon the fog turned to snow.

"Till to-morrow," said the Captain, quietly, and we returned to the Nautilus amid these atmospheric disturbances.

The tempest of snow continued till the next day. It was impossible to remain on the platform. From the saloon, where I was taking notes of incidents happening during this excursion to the polar continent, I could hear the cries of petrels and albatrosses sporting in the midst of this violent storm. The Nautilus did not remain motionless, but skirted the coast, advancing ten miles more to the south in the half-light left by the sun as it skirted the edge of the horizon. The next day, the 20th of March, the snow had ceased. The cold was a little greater, the thermometer showing 2° below zero. The fog was rising, and I hoped that that day our observations might be taken. Captain Nemo not having yet appeared, the boat took Conseil and myself to land. The soil was still of the same volcanic nature; everywhere were traces of lava, scoriae, and basalt; but the crater which had vomited them I could not see. Here, as lower down, this continent was alive with myriads of birds. But their rule was now divided with large troops of sea-mammals, looking at us with their soft eyes. There were several kinds of seals, some stretched on the earth, some on flakes of ice, many going in and out of the sea. They did not flee at our approach, never having had anything to do with man; and I reckoned that there were provisions there for hundreds of vessels.

"Sir," said Conseil, "will you tell me the names of these creatures?"

"They are seals and morses."

It was now eight in the morning. Four hours remained to us before the sun could be observed with advantage. I directed our steps towards a vast bay cut in the steep granite shore. There, I can aver that earth and ice were lost to sight by the numbers of sea-mammals covering them, and I involuntarily sought for old Proteus, the mythological shepherd who watched these immense flocks of Neptune. There were more seals than anything else, forming distinct groups, male and female, the father watching over his family, the mother suckling her little ones, some already strong enough to go a few steps. When they wished to change their place, they took little jumps, made by the contraction of their bodies, and helped awkwardly enough by their imperfect fin, which, as with the lamantin, their cousins, forms a perfect forearm. I should say that, in the water, which is their element—the spine of these creatures is flexible; with smooth and close skin and webbed feet—they swim admirably. In resting on the earth they take the most graceful attitudes. Thus the ancients, observing their soft and expressive looks, which cannot be surpassed by the most beautiful look a woman can give, their clear voluptuous eyes, their charming positions, and the poetry of their manners, metamorphosed them, the male into a triton and the female into a mermaid. I made Conseil notice the considerable development of the lobes of the brain in these interesting cetaceans. No mammal, except man, has such a quantity of brain matter; they are also capable of receiving a certain amount of education, are easily domesticated, and I think, with other naturalists, that if properly taught they would be of great service as fishing-dogs. The greater part of them slept on the rocks or on the sand. Amongst these seals, properly so called, which have no external ears (in which they differ from the otter, whose ears are prominent), I noticed several varieties of seals about three yards long, with a white coat, bulldog heads, armed with teeth in both jaws, four incisors at the top and four at the bottom, and two large canine teeth in the shape of a fleur-de-lis. Amongst them glided sea-elephants, a kind of seal, with short, flexible trunks. The giants of this species measured twenty feet round and ten yards and a half in length; but they did not move as we approached.

"These creatures are not dangerous?" asked Conseil.

"No; not unless you attack them. When they have to defend their young their rage is terrible, and it is not uncommon for them to break the fishing-boats to pieces."

"They are quite right," said Conseil.

"I do not say they are not."

Two miles farther on we were stopped by the promontory which shelters the bay from the southerly winds. Beyond it we heard loud bellowings such as a troop of ruminants would produce.

"Good!" said Conseil; "a concert of bulls!"

"No; a concert of morses."

"They are fighting!"

"They are either fighting or playing."

We now began to climb the blackish rocks, amid unforeseen stumbles, and over stones which the ice made slippery. More than once I rolled over at the expense of my loins. Conseil, more prudent or more steady, did not stumble, and helped me up, saying:

"If, sir, you would have the kindness to take wider steps, you would preserve your equilibrium better."

Arrived at the upper ridge of the promontory, I saw a vast white plain covered with morses. They were playing amongst themselves, and what we heard were bellowings of pleasure, not of anger.

As I passed these curious animals I could examine them leisurely, for they did not move. Their skins were thick and rugged, of a yellowish tint, approaching to red; their hair was short and scant. Some of them were four yards and a quarter long. Quieter and less timid than their cousins of the north, they did not, like them, place sentinels round the outskirts of their encampment. After examining this city of morses, I began to think of returning. It was eleven o'clock, and, if Captain Nemo found the conditions favourable for observations, I wished to be present at the operation. We followed a narrow pathway running along the summit of the steep shore. At half-past eleven we had reached the place where we landed. The boat had run aground, bringing the Captain. I saw him standing on a block of basalt, his instruments near him, his eyes fixed on the northern horizon, near which the sun was then describing a lengthened curve. I took my place beside him, and waited without speaking. Noon arrived, and, as before, the sun did not appear. It was a fatality. Observations were still wanting. If not accomplished to-morrow, we must give up all idea of taking any. We were indeed exactly at the 20th of March. To-morrow, the 21st, would be the equinox; the sun would disappear behind the horizon for six months, and with its disappearance the long polar night would begin. Since the September equinox it had emerged from the northern horizon, rising by lengthened spirals up to the 21st of December. At this period, the summer solstice of the northern regions, it had begun to descend; and to-morrow was to shed its last rays upon them. I communicated my fears and observations to Captain Nemo.

"You are right, M. Aronnax," said he; "if to-morrow I cannot take the altitude of the sun, I shall not be able to do it for six months. But precisely because chance has led me into these seas on the 21st of March, my bearings will be easy to take, if at twelve we can see the sun."

"Why, Captain?"

"Because then the orb of day described such lengthened curves that it is difficult to measure exactly its height above the horizon, and grave errors may be made with instruments."

"What will you do then?"

"I shall only use my chronometer," replied Captain Nemo. "If to-morrow, the 21st of March, the disc of the sun, allowing for refraction, is exactly cut by the northern horizon, it will show that I am at the South Pole."

"Just so," said I. "But this statement is not mathematically correct, because the equinox does not necessarily begin at noon."

"Very likely, sir; but the error will not be a hundred yards and we do not want more. Till to-morrow, then!"

Captain Nemo returned on board. Conseil and I remained to survey the shore, observing and studying until five o'clock. Then I went to bed, not, however, without invoking, like the Indian, the favour of the radiant orb. The next day, the 21st of March, at five in the morning, I mounted the platform. I found Captain Nemo there.

"The weather is lightening a little," said he. "I have some hope. After breakfast we will go on shore and choose a post for observation."

That point settled, I sought Ned Land. I wanted to take him with me. But the obstinate Canadian refused, and I saw that his taciturnity and his bad humour grew day by day. After all, I was not sorry for his obstinacy under the circumstances. Indeed, there were too many seals on shore, and we ought not to lay such temptation in this unreflecting fisherman's way. Breakfast over, we went on shore. The Nautilus had gone some miles further up in the night. It was a whole league from the coast, above which reared a sharp peak about five hundred yards high. The boat took with me Captain Nemo, two men of the crew, and the instruments, which consisted of a chronometer, a telescope, and a barometer. While crossing, I saw numerous whales belonging to the three kinds peculiar to the southern seas; the whale, or the English "right whale," which has no dorsal fin; the "humpback," with reeved chest and large, whitish fins, which, in spite of its name, do not form wings; and the fin-back, of a yellowish brown, the liveliest of all the cetacea. This powerful creature is heard a long way off when he throws to a great height columns of air and vapour, which look like whirlwinds of smoke. These different mammals were disporting themselves in troops in the quiet waters; and I could see that this basin of the Antarctic Pole serves as a place of refuge to the cetacea too closely tracked by the hunters. I also noticed large medusae floating between the reeds.

At nine we landed; the sky was brightening, the clouds were flying to the south, and the fog seemed to be leaving the cold surface of the waters. Captain Nemo went towards the peak, which he doubtless meant to be his observatory. It was a painful ascent over the sharp lava and the pumice-stones, in an atmosphere often impregnated with a sulphurous smell from the smoking cracks. For a man unaccustomed to walk on land, the Captain climbed the steep slopes with an agility I never saw equalled and which a hunter would have envied. We were two hours getting to the summit of this peak, which was half porphyry and half basalt. From thence we looked upon a vast sea which, towards the north, distinctly traced its boundary line upon the sky. At our feet lay fields of dazzling whiteness. Over our heads a pale azure, free from fog. To the north the disc of the sun seemed like a ball of fire, already horned by the cutting of the horizon. From the bosom of the water rose sheaves of liquid jets by hundreds. In the distance lay the Nautilus like a cetacean asleep on the water. Behind us, to the south and east, an immense country and a chaotic heap of rocks and ice, the limits of which were not visible. On arriving at the summit Captain Nemo carefully took the mean height of the barometer, for he would have to consider that in taking his observations. At a quarter to twelve the sun, then seen only by refraction, looked like a golden disc shedding its last rays upon this deserted continent and seas which never man had yet ploughed. Captain Nemo, furnished with a lenticular glass which, by means of a mirror, corrected the refraction, watched the orb sinking below the horizon by degrees, following a lengthened diagonal. I held the chronometer. My heart beat fast. If the disappearance of the half-disc of the sun coincided with twelve o'clock on the chronometer, we were at the pole itself.

"Twelve!" I exclaimed.

"The South Pole!" replied Captain Nemo, in a grave voice, handing me the glass, which showed the orb cut in exactly equal parts by the horizon.

I looked at the last rays crowning the peak, and the shadows mounting by degrees up its slopes. At that moment Captain Nemo, resting with his hand on my shoulder, said:

"I, Captain Nemo, on this 21st day of March, 1868, have reached the South Pole on the ninetieth degree; and I take possession of this part of the globe, equal to one-sixth of the known continents."

"In whose name, Captain?"

"In my own, sir!"

Saying which, Captain Nemo unfurled a black banner, bearing an "N" in gold quartered on its bunting. Then, turning towards the orb of day, whose last rays lapped the horizon of the sea, he exclaimed:

"Adieu, sun! Disappear, thou radiant orb! rest beneath this open sea, and let a night of six months spread its shadows over my new domains!"

CHAPTER XV ACCIDENT OR INCIDENT?

The next day, the 22nd of March, at six in the morning, preparations for departure were begun. The last gleams of twilight were melting into night. The cold was great, the constellations shone with wonderful intensity. In the zenith glittered that wondrous Southern Cross—the polar bear of Antarctic regions. The thermometer showed 120 below zero, and when the wind freshened it was most biting. Flakes of ice increased on the open water. The sea seemed everywhere alike. Numerous blackish patches spread on the surface, showing the formation of fresh ice. Evidently the southern basin, frozen during the six winter months, was absolutely inaccessible. What became of the whales in that time? Doubtless they went beneath the icebergs, seeking more practicable seas. As to the seals and morses, accustomed to live in a hard climate, they remained on these icy shores. These creatures have the instinct to break holes in the ice-field and to keep them open. To these holes they come for breath; when the birds, driven away by the cold, have emigrated to the north, these sea mammals remain sole masters of the polar continent. But the reservoirs were filling with water, and the Nautilus was slowly descending. At 1,000 feet deep it stopped; its screw beat the waves, and it advanced straight towards the north at a speed of fifteen miles an hour. Towards night it was already floating under the immense body of the iceberg. At three in the morning I was awakened by a violent shock. I sat up in my bed and listened in the darkness, when I was thrown into the middle of the room. The Nautilus, after having struck, had rebounded violently. I groped along the partition, and by the staircase to the saloon, which was lit by the luminous ceiling. The furniture was upset. Fortunately the windows were firmly set, and had held fast. The pictures on the starboard side, from being no longer vertical, were clinging to the paper, whilst those of the port side were hanging at least a foot from the wall. The Nautilus was lying on its starboard side perfectly motionless. I heard footsteps, and a confusion of voices; but Captain Nemo did not appear. As I was leaving the saloon, Ned Land and Conseil entered.

"What is the matter?" said I, at once.

"I came to ask you, sir," replied Conseil.

"Confound it!" exclaimed the Canadian, "I know well enough! The Nautilus has struck; and, judging by the way she lies, I do not think she will right herself as she did the first time in Torres Straits."

"But," I asked, "has she at least come to the surface of the sea?"

"We do not know," said Conseil.

"It is easy to decide," I answered. I consulted the manometer. To my great surprise, it showed a depth of more than 180 fathoms. "What does that mean?" I exclaimed.

"We must ask Captain Nemo," said Conseil.

"But where shall we find him?" said Ned Land.

"Follow me," said I, to my companions.

We left the saloon. There was no one in the library. At the centre staircase, by the berths of the ship's crew, there was no one. I thought that Captain Nemo must be in the pilot's cage. It was best to wait. We all returned to the saloon. For twenty minutes we remained thus, trying to hear the slightest noise which might be made on board the Nautilus, when Captain Nemo entered. He seemed not to see us; his face, generally so impassive, showed signs of uneasiness. He watched the compass silently, then the manometer; and, going to the planisphere, placed his finger on a spot representing the southern seas. I would not interrupt him; but, some minutes later, when he turned towards me, I said, using one of his own expressions in the Torres Straits:

"An incident, Captain?"

"No, sir; an accident this time."

"Serious?"

"Perhaps."

"Is the danger immediate?"

"No."

"The Nautilus has stranded?"

"Yes."

"And this has happened—how?"

"From a caprice of nature, not from the ignorance of man. Not a mistake has been made in the working. But we cannot prevent equilibrium from producing its effects. We may brave human laws, but we cannot resist natural ones."

Captain Nemo had chosen a strange moment for uttering this philosophical reflection. On the whole, his answer helped me little.

"May I ask, sir, the cause of this accident?"

"An enormous block of ice, a whole mountain, has turned over," he replied. "When icebergs are undermined at their base by warmer water or reiterated shocks their centre of gravity rises, and the whole thing turns over. This is what has happened; one of these blocks, as it fell, struck the Nautilus, then, gliding under its hull, raised it with irresistible force, bringing it into beds which are not so thick, where it is lying on its side."

"But can we not get the Nautilus off by emptying its reservoirs, that it might regain its equilibrium?"

"That, sir, is being done at this moment. You can hear the pump working. Look at the needle of the manometer; it shows that the Nautilus is rising, but the block of ice is floating with it; and, until some obstacle stops its ascending motion, our position cannot be altered."

Indeed, the Nautilus still held the same position to starboard; doubtless it would right itself when the block stopped. But at this moment who knows if we may not be frightfully crushed between the two glassy surfaces? I reflected on all the consequences of our position. Captain Nemo never took his eyes off the manometer. Since the fall of the iceberg, the Nautilus had risen about a hundred and fifty feet, but it still made the same angle with the perpendicular. Suddenly a slight movement was felt in the hold. Evidently it was righting a little. Things hanging in the saloon were sensibly returning to their normal position. The partitions were nearing the upright. No one spoke. With beating hearts we watched and felt the straightening. The boards became horizontal under our feet. Ten minutes passed.

"At last we have righted!" I exclaimed.

"Yes," said Captain Nemo, going to the door of the saloon.

"But are we floating?" I asked.

"Certainly," he replied; "since the reservoirs are not empty; and, when empty, the Nautilus must rise to the surface of the sea."

We were in open sea; but at a distance of about ten yards, on either side of the Nautilus, rose a dazzling wall of ice. Above and beneath the same wall. Above, because the lower surface of the iceberg stretched over us like an immense ceiling. Beneath, because the overturned block, having slid by degrees, had found a resting-place on the lateral walls, which kept it in that position. The Nautilus was really imprisoned in a perfect tunnel of ice more than twenty yards in breadth, filled with quiet water. It was easy to get out of it by going either forward or backward, and then make a free passage under the iceberg, some hundreds of yards deeper. The luminous ceiling had been extinguished, but the saloon was still resplendent with intense light. It was the powerful reflection from the glass partition sent violently back to the sheets of the lantern. I cannot describe the effect of the voltaic rays upon the great blocks so capriciously cut; upon every angle, every ridge, every facet was thrown a different light, according to the nature of the veins running through the ice; a dazzling mine of gems, particularly of sapphires, their blue rays crossing with the green of the emerald. Here and there were opal shades of wonderful softness, running through bright spots like diamonds of fire, the brilliancy of which the eye could not bear. The power of the lantern seemed increased a hundredfold, like a lamp through the lenticular plates of a first-class lighthouse.

"How beautiful! how beautiful!" cried Conseil.

"Yes," I said, "it is a wonderful sight. Is it not, Ned?"

"Yes, confound it! Yes," answered Ned Land, "it is superb! I am mad at being obliged to admit it. No one has ever seen anything like it; but the sight may cost us dear. And, if I must say all, I think we are seeing here things which God never intended man to see."

Ned was right, it was too beautiful. Suddenly a cry from Conseil made me turn.

"What is it?" I asked.

"Shut your eyes, sir! Do not look, sir!" Saying which, Conseil clapped his hands over his eyes.

"But what is the matter, my boy?"

"I am dazzled, blinded."

My eyes turned involuntarily towards the glass, but I could not stand the fire which seemed to devour them. I understood what had happened. The Nautilus had put on full speed. All the quiet lustre of the ice-walls was at once changed into flashes of lightning. The fire from these myriads of diamonds was blinding. It required some time to calm our troubled looks. At last the hands were taken down.

"Faith, I should never have believed it," said Conseil.

It was then five in the morning; and at that moment a shock was felt at the bows of the Nautilus. I knew that its spur had struck a block of ice. It must have been a false manoeuvre, for this submarine tunnel, obstructed by blocks, was not very easy navigation. I thought that Captain Nemo, by changing his course, would either turn these obstacles or else follow the windings of the tunnel. In any case, the road before us could not be entirely blocked. But, contrary to my expectations, the Nautilus took a decided retrograde motion.

"We are going backwards?" said Conseil.

"Yes," I replied. "This end of the tunnel can have no egress."

"And then?"

"Then," said I, "the working is easy. We must go back again, and go out at the southern opening. That is all."

In speaking thus, I wished to appear more confident than I really was. But the retrograde motion of the Nautilus was increasing; and, reversing the screw, it carried us at great speed.

"It will be a hindrance," said Ned.

"What does it matter, some hours more or less, provided we get out at last?"

"Yes," repeated Ned Land, "provided we do get out at last!"

For a short time I walked from the saloon to the library. My companions were silent. I soon threw myself on an ottoman, and took a book, which my eyes overran mechanically. A quarter of an hour after, Conseil, approaching me, said, "Is what you are reading very interesting, sir?"

"Very interesting!" I replied.

"I should think so, sir. It is your own book you are reading."

"My book?"

And indeed I was holding in my hand the work on the Great Submarine Depths. I did not even dream of it. I closed the book and returned to my walk. Ned and Conseil rose to go.

"Stay here, my friends," said I, detaining them. "Let us remain together until we are out of this block."

"As you please, sir," Conseil replied.

Some hours passed. I often looked at the instruments hanging from the partition. The manometer showed that the Nautilus kept at a constant depth of more than three hundred yards; the compass still pointed to south; the log indicated a speed of twenty miles an hour, which, in such a cramped space, was very great. But Captain Nemo knew that he could not hasten too much, and that minutes were worth ages to us. At twenty-five minutes past eight a second shock took place, this time from behind. I turned pale. My companions were close by my side. I seized Conseil's hand. Our looks expressed our feelings better than words. At this moment the Captain entered the saloon. I went up to him.

"Our course is barred southward?" I asked.

"Yes, sir. The iceberg has shifted and closed every outlet."

"We are blocked up then?"

"Yes."

CHAPTER XVI WANT OF AIR

Thus around the Nautilus, above and below, was an impenetrable wall of ice. We were prisoners to the iceberg. I watched the Captain. His countenance had resumed its habitual imperturbability.

"Gentlemen," he said calmly, "there are two ways of dying in the circumstances in which we are placed." (This puzzling person had the air of a mathematical professor lecturing to his pupils.) "The first is to be crushed; the second is to die of suffocation. I do not speak of the possibility of dying of hunger, for the supply of provisions in the Nautilus will certainly last longer than we shall. Let us, then, calculate our chances."

"As to suffocation, Captain," I replied, "that is not to be feared, because our reservoirs are full."

"Just so; but they will only yield two days' supply of air. Now, for thirty-six hours we have been hidden under the water, and already the heavy atmosphere of the Nautilus requires renewal. In forty-eight hours our reserve will be exhausted."

"Well, Captain, can we be delivered before forty-eight hours?"

"We will attempt it, at least, by piercing the wall that surrounds us."

"On which side?"

"Sound will tell us. I am going to run the Nautilus aground on the lower bank, and my men will attack the iceberg on the side that is least thick."

Captain Nemo went out. Soon I discovered by a hissing noise that the water was entering the reservoirs. The Nautilus sank slowly, and rested on the ice at a depth of 350 yards, the depth at which the lower bank was immersed.

"My friends," I said, "our situation is serious, but I rely on your courage and energy."

"Sir," replied the Canadian, "I am ready to do anything for the general safety."

"Good! Ned," and I held out my hand to the Canadian.

"I will add," he continued, "that, being as handy with the pickaxe as with the harpoon, if I can be useful to the Captain, he can command my services."

"He will not refuse your help. Come, Ned!"

I led him to the room where the crew of the Nautilus were putting on their cork-jackets. I told the Captain of Ned's proposal, which he accepted. The Canadian put on his sea-costume, and was ready as soon as his companions. When Ned was dressed, I re-entered the drawing-room, where the panes of glass were open, and, posted near Conseil, I examined the ambient beds that supported the Nautilus. Some instants after, we saw a dozen of the crew set foot on the bank of ice, and among them Ned Land, easily known by his stature. Captain Nemo was with them. Before proceeding to dig the walls, he took the soundings, to be sure of working in the right direction. Long sounding lines were sunk in the side walls, but after fifteen yards they were again stopped by the thick wall. It was useless to attack it on the ceiling-like surface, since the iceberg itself measured more than 400 yards in height. Captain Nemo then sounded the lower surface. There ten yards of wall separated us from the water, so great was the thickness of the ice-field. It was necessary, therefore, to cut from it a piece equal in extent to the waterline of the Nautilus. There were about 6,000 cubic yards to detach, so as to dig a hole by which we could descend to the ice-field. The work had begun immediately and carried on with indefatigable energy. Instead of digging round the Nautilus which would have involved greater difficulty, Captain Nemo had an immense trench made at eight yards from the port-quarter. Then the men set to work simultaneously with their screws on several points of its circumference. Presently the pickaxe attacked this compact matter vigorously, and large blocks were detached from the mass. By a curious effect of specific gravity, these blocks, lighter than water, fled, so to speak, to the vault of the tunnel, that increased in thickness at the top in proportion as it diminished at the base. But that mattered little, so long as the lower part grew thinner. After two hours' hard work, Ned Land came in exhausted. He and his comrades were replaced by new workers, whom Conseil and I joined. The second lieutenant of the Nautilus superintended us. The water seemed singularly cold, but I soon got warm handling the pickaxe. My movements were free enough, although they were made under a pressure of thirty atmospheres. When I re-entered, after working two hours, to take some food and rest, I found a perceptible difference between the pure fluid with which the Rouquayrol engine supplied me and the atmosphere of the Nautilus, already charged with carbonic acid. The air had not been renewed for forty-eight hours, and its vivifying qualities were considerably enfeebled. However, after a lapse of twelve hours, we had only raised a block of ice one yard thick, on the marked surface, which was about 600 cubic yards! Reckoning that it took twelve hours to accomplish this much it would take five nights and four days to bring this enterprise to a satisfactory conclusion. Five nights and four days! And we have only air enough for two days in the reservoirs! "Without taking into account," said Ned, "that, even if we get out of this infernal prison, we shall also be imprisoned under the iceberg, shut out from all possible communication with the atmosphere." True enough! Who could then foresee the minimum of time necessary for our deliverance? We might be suffocated before the Nautilus could regain the surface of the waves? Was it destined to perish in this ice-tomb, with all those it enclosed? The situation was terrible. But everyone had looked the danger in the face, and each was determined to do his duty to the last.

As I expected, during the night a new block a yard square was carried away, and still further sank the immense hollow. But in the morning when, dressed in my cork-jacket, I traversed the slushy mass at a temperature of six or seven degrees below zero, I remarked that the side walls were gradually closing in. The beds of water farthest from the trench, that were not warmed by the men's work, showed a tendency to solidification. In presence of this new and imminent danger, what would become of our chances of safety, and how hinder the solidification of this liquid medium, that would burst the partitions of the Nautilus like glass?

I did not tell my companions of this new danger. What was the good of damping the energy they displayed in the painful work of escape? But when I went on board again, I told Captain Nemo of this grave complication.

"I know it," he said, in that calm tone which could counteract the most terrible apprehensions. "It is one danger more; but I see no way of escaping it; the only chance of safety is to go quicker than solidification. We must be beforehand with it, that is all."

On this day for several hours I used my pickaxe vigorously. The work kept me up. Besides, to work was to quit the Nautilus, and breathe directly the pure air drawn from the reservoirs, and supplied by our apparatus, and to quit the impoverished and vitiated atmosphere. Towards evening the trench was dug one yard deeper. When I returned on board, I was nearly suffocated by the carbonic acid with which the air was filled—ah! if we had only the chemical means to drive away this deleterious gas. We had plenty of oxygen; all this water contained a considerable quantity, and by dissolving it with our powerful piles, it would restore the vivifying fluid. I had thought well over it; but of what good was that, since the carbonic acid produced by our respiration had invaded every part of the vessel? To absorb it, it was necessary to fill some jars with caustic potash, and to shake them incessantly. Now this substance was wanting on board, and nothing could replace it. On that evening, Captain Nemo ought to open the taps of his reservoirs, and let some pure air into the interior of the Nautilus; without this precaution we could not get rid of the sense of suffocation. The next day, March 26th, I resumed my miner's work in beginning the fifth yard. The side walls and the lower surface of the iceberg thickened visibly. It was evident that they would meet before the Nautilus was able to disengage itself. Despair seized me for an instant; my pickaxe nearly fell from my hands. What was the good of digging if I must be suffocated, crushed by the water that was turning into stone?—a punishment that the ferocity of the savages even would not have invented! Just then Captain Nemo passed near me. I touched his hand and showed him the walls of our prison. The wall to port had advanced to at least four yards from the hull of the Nautilus. The Captain understood me, and signed me to follow him. We went on board. I took off my cork-jacket and accompanied him into the drawing-room.

"M. Aronnax, we must attempt some desperate means, or we shall be sealed up in this solidified water as in cement."

"Yes; but what is to be done?"

"Ah! if my Nautilus were strong enough to bear this pressure without being crushed!"

"Well?" I asked, not catching the Captain's idea.

"Do you not understand," he replied, "that this congelation of water will help us? Do you not see that by its solidification, it would burst through this field of ice that imprisons us, as, when it freezes, it bursts the hardest stones? Do you not perceive that it would be an agent of safety instead of destruction?"

"Yes, Captain, perhaps. But, whatever resistance to crushing the Nautilus possesses, it could not support this terrible pressure, and would be flattened like an iron plate."

"I know it, sir. Therefore we must not reckon on the aid of nature, but on our own exertions. We must stop this solidification. Not only will the side walls be pressed together; but there is not ten feet of water before or behind the Nautilus. The congelation gains on us on all sides."

"How long will the air in the reservoirs last for us to breathe on board?"

The Captain looked in my face. "After to-morrow they will be empty!"

A cold sweat came over me. However, ought I to have been astonished at the answer? On March 22, the Nautilus was in the open polar seas. We were at 26°. For five days we had lived on the reserve on board. And what was left of the respirable air must be kept for the workers. Even now, as I write, my recollection is still so vivid that an involuntary terror seizes me and my lungs seem to be without air. Meanwhile, Captain Nemo reflected silently, and evidently an idea had struck him; but he seemed to reject it. At last, these words escaped his lips:

"Boiling water!" he muttered.

"Boiling water?" I cried.

"Yes, sir. We are enclosed in a space that is relatively confined. Would not jets of boiling water, constantly injected by the pumps, raise the temperature in this part and stay the congelation?"

"Let us try it," I said resolutely.

"Let us try it, Professor."

The thermometer then stood at 7° outside. Captain Nemo took me to the galleys, where the vast distillatory machines stood that furnished the drinkable water by evaporation. They filled these with water, and all the electric heat from the piles was thrown through the worms bathed in the liquid. In a few minutes this water reached 100°. It was directed towards the pumps, while fresh water replaced it in proportion. The heat developed by the troughs was such that cold water, drawn up from the sea after only having gone through the machines, came boiling into the body of the pump. The injection was begun, and three hours after the thermometer marked 6° below zero outside. One degree was gained. Two hours later the thermometer only marked 4°.

"We shall succeed," I said to the Captain, after having anxiously watched the result of the operation.

"I think," he answered, "that we shall not be crushed. We have no more suffocation to fear."

During the night the temperature of the water rose to 1° below zero. The injections could not carry it to a higher point. But, as the congelation of the sea-water produces at least 2°, I was at least reassured against the dangers of solidification.

The next day, March 27th, six yards of ice had been cleared, twelve feet only remaining to be cleared away. There was yet forty-eight hours' work. The air could not be renewed in the interior of the Nautilus. And this day would make it worse. An intolerable weight oppressed me. Towards three o'clock in the evening this feeling rose to a violent degree. Yawns dislocated my jaws. My lungs panted as they inhaled this burning fluid, which became rarefied more and more. A moral torpor took hold of me. I was powerless, almost unconscious. My brave Conseil, though exhibiting the same symptoms and suffering in the same manner, never left me. He took my hand and encouraged me, and I heard him murmur, "Oh! if I could only not breathe, so as to leave more air for my master!"

Tears came into my eyes on hearing him speak thus. If our situation to all was intolerable in the interior, with what haste and gladness would we put on our cork-jackets to work in our turn! Pickaxes sounded on the frozen ice-beds. Our arms ached, the skin was torn off our hands. But what were these fatigues, what did the wounds matter? Vital air came to the lungs! We breathed! we breathed!

All this time no one prolonged his voluntary task beyond the prescribed time. His task accomplished, each one handed in turn to his panting companions the apparatus that supplied him with life. Captain Nemo set the example, and submitted first to this severe discipline. When the time came, he gave up his apparatus to another and returned to the vitiated air on board, calm, unflinching, unmurmuring.

On that day the ordinary work was accomplished with unusual vigour. Only two yards remained to be raised from the surface. Two yards only separated us from the open sea. But the reservoirs were nearly emptied of air. The little that remained ought to be kept for the workers; not a particle for the Nautilus. When I went back on board, I was half suffocated. What a night! I know not how to describe it. The next day my breathing was oppressed. Dizziness accompanied the pain in my head and made me like a drunken man. My companions showed the same symptoms. Some of the crew had rattling in the throat.

On that day, the sixth of our imprisonment, Captain Nemo, finding the pickaxes work too slowly, resolved to crush the ice-bed that still separated us from the liquid sheet. This man's coolness and energy never forsook him. He subdued his physical pains by moral force.

By his orders the vessel was lightened, that is to say, raised from the ice-bed by a change of specific gravity. When it floated they towed it so as to bring it above the immense trench made on the level of the water-line. Then, filling his reservoirs of water, he descended and shut himself up in the hole.

Just then all the crew came on board, and the double door of communication was shut. The Nautilus then rested on the bed of ice, which was not one yard thick, and which the sounding leads had perforated in a thousand places. The taps of the reservoirs were then opened, and a hundred cubic yards of water was let in, increasing the weight of the Nautilus to 1,800 tons. We waited, we listened, forgetting our sufferings in hope. Our safety depended on this last chance. Notwithstanding the buzzing in my head, I soon heard the humming sound under the hull of the Nautilus. The ice cracked with a singular noise, like tearing paper, and the Nautilus sank.

"We are off!" murmured Conseil in my ear.

I could not answer him. I seized his hand, and pressed it convulsively. All at once, carried away by its frightful overcharge, the Nautilus sank like a bullet under the waters, that is to say, it fell as if it was in a vacuum. Then all the electric force was put on the pumps, that soon began to let the water out of the reservoirs. After some minutes, our fall was stopped. Soon, too, the manometer indicated an ascending movement. The screw, going at full speed, made the iron hull tremble to its very bolts and drew us towards the north. But if this floating under the iceberg is to last another day before we reach the open sea, I shall be dead first.

Half stretched upon a divan in the library, I was suffocating. My face was purple, my lips blue, my faculties suspended. I neither saw nor heard. All notion of time had gone from my mind. My muscles could not contract. I do not know how many hours passed thus, but I was conscious of the agony that was coming over me. I felt as if I was going to die. Suddenly I came to. Some breaths of air penetrated my lungs. Had we risen to the surface of the waves? Were we free of the iceberg? No! Ned and Conseil, my two brave friends, were sacrificing themselves to save me. Some particles of air still remained at the bottom of one apparatus. Instead of using it, they had kept it for me, and, while they were being suffocated, they gave me life, drop by drop. I wanted to push back the thing; they held my hands, and for some moments I breathed freely. I looked at the clock; it was eleven in the morning. It ought to be the 28th of March. The Nautilus went at a frightful pace, forty miles an hour. It literally tore through the water. Where was Captain Nemo? Had he succumbed? Were his companions dead with him? At the moment the manometer indicated that we were not more than twenty feet from the surface. A mere plate of ice separated us from the atmosphere. Could we not break it? Perhaps. In any case the Nautilus was going to attempt it. I felt that it was in an oblique position, lowering the stern, and raising the bows. The introduction of water had been the means of disturbing its equilibrium. Then, impelled by its powerful screw, it attacked the ice-field from beneath like a formidable battering-ram. It broke it by backing and then rushing forward against the field, which gradually gave way; and at last, dashing suddenly against it, shot forwards on the ice-field, that crushed beneath its weight. The panel was opened—one might say torn off—and the pure air came in in abundance to all parts of the Nautilus.

CHAPTER XVII FROM CAPE HORN TO THE AMAZON

How I got on to the platform, I have no idea; perhaps the Canadian had carried me there. But I breathed, I inhaled the vivifying sea-air. My two companions were getting drunk with the fresh particles. The other unhappy men had been so long without food, that they could not with impunity indulge in the simplest aliments that were given them. We, on the contrary, had no end to restrain ourselves; we could draw this air freely into our lungs, and it was the breeze, the breeze alone, that filled us with this keen enjoyment.

"Ah!" said Conseil, "how delightful this oxygen is! Master need not fear to breathe it. There is enough for everybody."

Ned Land did not speak, but he opened his jaws wide enough to frighten a shark. Our strength soon returned, and, when I looked round me, I saw we were alone on the platform. The foreign seamen in the Nautilus were contented with the air that circulated in the interior; none of them had come to drink in the open air.

The first words I spoke were words of gratitude and thankfulness to my two companions. Ned and Conseil had prolonged my life during the last hours of this long agony. All my gratitude could not repay such devotion.

"My friends," said I, "we are bound one to the other for ever, and I am under infinite obligations to you."

"Which I shall take advantage of," exclaimed the Canadian.

"What do you mean?" said Conseil.

"I mean that I shall take you with me when I leave this infernal Nautilus."

"Well," said Conseil, "after all this, are we going right?"

"Yes," I replied, "for we are going the way of the sun, and here the sun is in the north."

"No doubt," said Ned Land; "but it remains to be seen whether he will bring the ship into the Pacific or the Atlantic Ocean, that is, into frequented or deserted seas."

I could not answer that question, and I feared that Captain Nemo would rather take us to the vast ocean that touches the coasts of Asia and America at the same time. He would thus complete the tour round the submarine world, and return to those waters in which the Nautilus could sail freely. We ought, before long, to settle this important point. The Nautilus went at a rapid pace. The polar circle was soon passed, and the course shaped for Cape Horn. We were off the American point, March 31st, at seven o'clock in the evening. Then all our past sufferings were forgotten. The remembrance of that imprisonment in the ice was effaced from our minds. We only thought of the future. Captain Nemo did not appear again either in the drawing-room or on the platform. The point shown each day on the planisphere, and, marked by the lieutenant, showed me the exact direction of the Nautilus. Now, on that evening, it was evident, to, my great satisfaction, that we were going back to the North by the Atlantic. The next day, April 1st, when the Nautilus ascended to the surface some minutes before noon, we sighted land to the west. It was Terra del Fuego, which the first navigators named thus from seeing the quantity of smoke that rose from the natives' huts. The coast seemed low to me, but in the distance rose high mountains. I even thought I had a glimpse of Mount Sarmiento, that rises 2,070 yards above the level of the sea, with a very pointed summit, which, according as it is misty or clear, is a sign of fine or of wet weather. At this moment the peak was clearly defined against the sky. The Nautilus, diving again under the water, approached the coast, which was only some few miles off. From the glass windows in the drawing-room, I saw long seaweeds and gigantic fuci and varech, of which the open polar sea contains so many specimens, with their sharp polished filaments; they measured about 300 yards in length—real cables, thicker than one's thumb; and, having great tenacity, they are often used as ropes for vessels. Another weed known as velp, with leaves four feet long, buried in the coral concretions, hung at the bottom. It served as nest and food for myriads of crustacea and molluscs, crabs, and cuttlefish. There seals and otters had splendid repasts, eating the flesh of fish with sea-vegetables, according to the English fashion. Over this fertile and luxuriant ground the Nautilus passed with great rapidity. Towards evening it approached the Falkland group, the rough summits of which I recognised the following day. The depth of the sea was moderate. On the shores our nets brought in beautiful specimens of sea weed, and particularly a certain fucus, the roots of which were filled with the best mussels in the world. Geese and ducks fell by dozens on the platform, and soon took their places in the pantry on board.

When the last heights of the Falklands had disappeared from the horizon, the Nautilus sank to between twenty and twenty-five yards, and followed the American coast. Captain Nemo did not show himself. Until the 3rd of April we did not quit the shores of Patagonia, sometimes under the ocean, sometimes at the surface. The Nautilus passed beyond the large estuary formed by the Uraguay. Its direction was northwards, and followed the long windings of the coast of South America. We had then made 1,600 miles since our embarkation in the seas of Japan. About eleven o'clock in the morning the Tropic of Capricorn was crossed on the thirty-seventh meridian, and we passed Cape Frio standing out to sea. Captain Nemo, to Ned Land's great displeasure, did not like the neighbourhood of the inhabited coasts of Brazil, for we went at a giddy speed. Not a fish, not a bird of the swiftest kind could follow us, and the natural curiosities of these seas escaped all observation.

This speed was kept up for several days, and in the evening of the 9th of April we sighted the most westerly point of South America that forms Cape San Roque. But then the Nautilus swerved again, and sought the lowest depth of a submarine valley which is between this Cape and Sierra Leone on the African coast. This valley bifurcates to the parallel of the Antilles, and terminates at the mouth by the enormous depression of 9,000 yards. In this place, the geological basin of the ocean forms, as far as the Lesser Antilles, a cliff to three and a half miles perpendicular in height, and, at the parallel of the Cape Verde Islands, another wall not less considerable, that encloses thus all the sunk continent of the Atlantic. The bottom of this immense valley is dotted with some mountains, that give to these submarine places a picturesque aspect. I speak, moreover, from the manuscript charts that were in the library of the Nautilus—charts evidently due to Captain Nemo's hand, and made after his personal observations. For two days the desert and deep waters were visited by means of the inclined planes. The Nautilus was furnished with long diagonal broadsides which carried it to all elevations. But on the 11th of April it rose suddenly, and land appeared at the mouth of the Amazon River, a vast estuary, the embouchure of which is so considerable that it freshens the sea-water for the distance of several leagues.

The equator was crossed. Twenty miles to the west were the Guianas, a French territory, on which we could have found an easy refuge; but a stiff breeze was blowing, and the furious waves would not have allowed a single boat to face them. Ned Land understood that, no doubt, for he spoke not a word about it. For my part, I made no allusion to his schemes of flight, for I would not urge him to make an attempt that must inevitably fail. I made the time pass pleasantly by interesting studies. During the days of April 11th and 12th, the Nautilus did not leave the surface of the sea, and the net brought in a marvellous haul of Zoophytes, fish and reptiles. Some zoophytes had been fished up by the chain of the nets; they were for the most part beautiful phyctallines, belonging to the actinidian family, and among other species the phyctalis protexta, peculiar to that part of the ocean, with a little cylindrical trunk, ornamented With vertical lines, speckled with red dots, crowning a marvellous blossoming of tentacles. As to the molluscs, they consisted of some I had already observed—turritellas, olive porphyras, with regular lines intercrossed, with red spots standing out plainly against the flesh; odd pteroceras, like petrified scorpions; translucid hyaleas, argonauts, cuttle-fish (excellent eating), and certain species of calmars that naturalists of antiquity have classed amongst the flying-fish, and that serve principally for bait for cod-fishing. I had now an opportunity of studying several species of fish on these shores. Amongst the cartilaginous ones, petromyzons-pricka, a sort of eel, fifteen inches long, with a greenish head, violet fins, grey-blue back, brown belly, silvered and sown with bright spots, the pupil of the eye encircled with gold—a curious animal, that the current of the Amazon had drawn to the sea, for they inhabit fresh waters—tuberculated streaks, with pointed snouts, and a long loose tail, armed with a long jagged sting; little sharks, a yard long, grey and whitish skin, and several rows of teeth, bent back, that are generally known by the name of pantouffles; vespertilios, a kind of red isosceles triangle, half a yard long, to which pectorals are attached by fleshy prolongations that make them look like bats, but that their horny appendage, situated near the nostrils, has given them the name of sea-unicorns; lastly, some species of balistae, the curassavian, whose spots were of a brilliant gold colour, and the capriscus of clear violet, and with varying shades like a pigeon's throat.

I end here this catalogue, which is somewhat dry perhaps, but very exact, with a scrics of bony fish that I observed in passing belonging to the apteronotes, and whose snout is white as snow, the body of a beautiful black, marked with a very long loose fleshy strip; odontognathes, armed with spikes; sardines nine inches long, glittering with a bright silver light; a species of mackerel provided with two anal fins; centronotes of a blackish tint, that are fished for with torches, long fish, two yards in length, with fat flesh, white and firm, which, when they arc fresh, taste like eel, and when dry, like smoked salmon; labres, half red, covered with scales only at the bottom of the dorsal and anal fins; chrysoptera, on which gold and silver blend their brightness with that of the ruby and topaz; golden-tailed spares, the flesh of which is extremely delicate, and whose phosphorescent properties betray them in the midst of the waters; orange-coloured spares with long tongues; maigres, with gold caudal fins, dark thorn-tails, anableps of Surinam, etc.

Notwithstanding this "et cetera," I must not omit to mention fish that Conseil will long remember, and with good reason. One of our nets had hauled up a sort of very flat ray fish, which, with the tail cut off, formed a perfect disc, and weighed twenty ounces. It was white underneath, red above, with large round spots of dark blue encircled with black, very glossy skin, terminating in a bilobed fin. Laid out on the platform, it struggled, tried to turn itself by convulsive movements, and made so many efforts, that one last turn had nearly sent it into the sea. But Conseil, not wishing to let the fish go, rushed to it, and, before I could prevent him, had seized it with both hands. In a moment he was overthrown, his legs in the air, and half his body paralysed, crying—

"Oh! master, master! help me!"

It was the first time the poor boy had spoken to me so familiarly. The Canadian and I took him up, and rubbed his contracted arms till he became sensible. The unfortunate Conseil had attacked a cramp-fish of the most dangerous kind, the cumana. This odd animal, in a medium conductor like water, strikes fish at several yards' distance, so great is the power of its electric organ, the two principal surfaces of which do not measure less than twenty-seven square feet. The next day, April 12th, the Nautilus approached the Dutch coast, near the mouth of the Maroni. There several groups of sea-cows herded together; they were manatees, that, like the dugong and the stellera, belong to the skenian order. These beautiful animals, peaceable and inoffensive, from eighteen to twenty-one feet in length, weigh at least sixteen hundredweight. I told Ned Land and Conseil that provident nature had assigned an important role to these mammalia. Indeed, they, like the seals, are designed to graze on the submarine prairies, and thus destroy the accumulation of weed that obstructs the tropical rivers.

"And do you know," I added, "what has been the result since men have almost entirely annihilated this useful race? That the putrefied weeds have poisoned the air, and the poisoned air causes the yellow fever, that desolates these beautiful countries. Enormous vegetations are multiplied under the torrid seas, and the evil is irresistibly developed from the mouth of the Rio de la Plata to Florida. If we are to believe Toussenel, this plague is nothing to what it would be if the seas were cleaned of whales and seals. Then, infested with poulps, medusae, and cuttle-fish, they would become immense centres of infection, since their waves would not possess 'these vast stomachs that God had charged to infest the surface of the seas.'"

CHAPTER XVIII THE POULPS

For several days the Nautilus kept off from the American coast. Evidently it did not wish to risk the tides of the Gulf of Mexico or of the sea of the Antilles. April 16th, we sighted Martinique and Guadaloupe from a distance of about thirty miles. I saw their tall peaks for an instant. The Canadian, who counted on carrying out his projects in the Gulf, by either landing or hailing one of the numerous boats that coast from one island to another, was quite disheartened. Flight would have been quite practicable, if Ned Land had been able to take possession of the boat without the Captain's knowledge. But in the open sea it could not be thought of. The Canadian, Conseil, and I had a long conversation on this subject. For six months we had been prisoners on board the Nautilus. We had travelled 17,000 leagues; and, as Ned Land said, there was no reason why it should come to an end. We could hope nothing from the Captain of the Nautilus, but only from ourselves. Besides, for some time past he had become graver, more retired, less sociable. He seemed to shun me. I met him rarely. Formerly he was pleased to explain the submarine marvels to me; now he left me to my studies, and came no more to the saloon. What change had come over him? For what cause? For my part, I did not wish to bury with me my curious and novel studies. I had now the power to write the true book of the sea; and this book, sooner or later, I wished to see daylight. The land nearest us was the archipelago of the Bahamas. There rose high submarine cliffs covered with large weeds. It was about eleven o'clock when Ned Land drew my attention to a formidable pricking, like the sting of an ant, which was produced by means of large seaweeds.

"Well," I said, "these are proper caverns for poulps, and I should not be astonished to see some of these monsters."

"What!" said Conseil; "cuttlefish, real cuttlefish of the cephalopod class?"

"No," I said, "poulps of huge dimensions."

"I will never believe that such animals exist," said Ned.

"Well," said Conseil, with the most serious air in the world, "I remember perfectly to have seen a large vessel drawn under the waves by an octopus's arm."

"You saw that?" said the Canadian.

"Yes, Ned."

"With your own eyes?"

"With my own eyes."

"Where, pray, might that be?"

"At St. Malo," answered Conseil.

"In the port?" said Ned, ironically.

"No; in a church," replied Conseil.

"In a church!" cried the Canadian.

"Yes; friend Ned. In a picture representing the poulp in question."

"Good!" said Ned Land, bursting out laughing.

"He is quite right," I said. "I have heard of this picture; but the subject represented is taken from a legend, and you know what to think of legends in the matter of natural history. Besides, when it is a question of monsters, the imagination is apt to run wild. Not only is it supposed that these poulps can draw down vessels, but a certain Olaus Magnus speaks of an octopus a mile long that is more like an island than an animal. It is also said that the Bishop of Nidros was building an altar on an immense rock. Mass finished, the rock began to walk, and returned to the sea. The rock was a poulp. Another Bishop, Pontoppidan, speaks also of a poulp on which a regiment of cavalry could manoeuvre. Lastly, the ancient naturalists speak of monsters whose mouths were like gulfs, and which were too large to pass through the Straits of Gibraltar."

"But how much is true of these stories?" asked Conseil.

"Nothing, my friends; at least of that which passes the limit of truth to get to fable or legend. Nevertheless, there must be some ground for the imagination of the story-tellers. One cannot deny that poulps and cuttlefish exist of a large species, inferior, however, to the cetaceans. Aristotle has stated the dimensions of a cuttlefish as five cubits, or nine feet two inches. Our fishermen frequently see some that are more than four feet long. Some skeletons of poulps are preserved in the museums of Trieste and Montpelier, that measure two yards in length. Besides, according to the calculations of some naturalists, one of these animals only six feet long would have tentacles twenty-seven feet long. That would suffice to make a formidable monster."

"Do they fish for them in these days?" asked Ned.

"If they do not fish for them, sailors see them at least. One of my friends, Captain Paul Bos of Havre, has often affirmed that he met one of these monsters of colossal dimensions in the Indian seas. But the most astonishing fact, and which does not permit of the denial of the existence of these gigantic animals, happened some years ago, in 1861."

"What is the fact?" asked Ned Land.

"This is it. In 1861, to the north-east of Teneriffe, very nearly in the same latitude we are in now, the crew of the despatch-boat Alector perceived a monstrous cuttlefish swimming in the waters. Captain Bouguer went near to the animal, and attacked it with harpoon and guns, without much success, for balls and harpoons glided over the soft flesh. After several fruitless attempts the crew tried to pass a slip-knot round the body of the mollusc. The noose slipped as far as the tail fins and there stopped. They tried then to haul it on board, but its weight was so considerable that the tightness of the cord separated the tail from the body, and, deprived of this ornament, he disappeared under the water."

"Indeed! is that a fact?"

"An indisputable fact, my good Ned. They proposed to name this poulp `Bouguer's cuttlefish.'"

"What length was it?" asked the Canadian.

"Did it not measure about six yards?" said Conseil, who, posted at the window, was examining again the irregular windings of the cliff.

"Precisely," I replied.

"Its head," rejoined Conseil, "was it not crowned with eight tentacles, that beat the water like a nest of serpents?"

"Precisely."

"Had not its eyes, placed at the back of its head, considerable development?"

"Yes, Conseil."

"And was not its mouth like a parrot's beak?"

"Exactly, Conseil."

"Very well! no offence to master," he replied, quietly; "if this is not Bouguer's cuttlefish, it is, at least, one of its brothers."

I looked at Conseil. Ned Land hurried to the window.

"What a horrible beast!" he cried.

I looked in my turn, and could not repress a gesture of disgust. Before my eyes was a horrible monster worthy to figure in the legends of the marvellous. It was an immense cuttlefish, being eight yards long. It swam crossways in the direction of the Nautilus with great speed, watching us with its enormous staring green eyes. Its eight arms, or rather feet, fixed to its head, that have given the name of cephalopod to these animals, were twice as long as its body, and were twisted like the furies' hair. One could see the 250 air holes on the inner side of the tentacles. The monster's mouth, a horned beak like a parrot's, opened and shut vertically. Its tongue, a horned substance, furnished with several rows of pointed teeth, came out quivering from this veritable pair of shears. What a freak of nature, a bird's beak on a mollusc! Its spindle-like body formed a fleshy mass that might weigh 4,000 to 5,000 lb.; the, varying colour changing with great rapidity, according to the irritation of the animal, passed successively from livid grey to reddish brown. What irritated this mollusc? No doubt the presence of the Nautilus, more formidable than itself, and on which its suckers or its jaws had no hold. Yet, what monsters these poulps are! what vitality the Creator has given them! what vigour in their movements! and they possess three hearts! Chance had brought us in presence of this cuttlefish, and I did not wish to lose the opportunity of carefully studying this specimen of cephalopods. I overcame the horror that inspired me, and, taking a pencil, began to draw it.

"Perhaps this is the same which the Alector saw," said Conseil.

"No," replied the Canadian; "for this is whole, and the other had lost its tail."

"That is no reason," I replied. "The arms and tails of these animals are re-formed by renewal; and in seven years the tail of Bouguer's cuttlefish has no doubt had time to grow."

By this time other poulps appeared at the port light. I counted seven. They formed a procession after the Nautilus, and I heard their beaks gnashing against the iron hull. I continued my work. These monsters kept in the water with such precision that they seemed immovable. Suddenly the Nautilus stopped. A shock made it tremble in every plate.

"Have we struck anything?" I asked.

"In any case," replied the Canadian, "we shall be free, for we are floating."

The Nautilus was floating, no doubt, but it did not move. A minute passed. Captain Nemo, followed by his lieutenant, entered the drawing-room. I had not seen him for some time. He seemed dull. Without noticing or speaking to us, he went to the panel, looked at the poulps, and said something to his lieutenant. The latter went out. Soon the panels were shut. The ceiling was lighted. I went towards the Captain.

"A curious collection of poulps?" I said.

"Yes, indeed, Mr. Naturalist," he replied; "and we are going to fight them, man to beast."

I looked at him. I thought I had not heard aright.

"Man to beast?" I repeated.

"Yes, sir. The screw is stopped. I think that the horny jaws of one of the cuttlefish is entangled in the blades. That is what prevents our moving."

"What are you going to do?"

"Rise to the surface, and slaughter this vermin."

"A difficult enterprise."

"Yes, indeed. The electric bullets are powerless against the soft flesh, where they do not find resistance enough to go off. But we shall attack them with the hatchet."

"And the harpoon, sir," said the Canadian, "if you do not refuse my help."

"I will accept it, Master Land."

"We will follow you," I said, and, following Captain Nemo, we went towards the central staircase.

There, about ten men with boarding-hatchets were ready for the attack. Conseil and I took two hatchets; Ned Land seized a harpoon. The Nautilus had then risen to the surface. One of the sailors, posted on the top ladderstep, unscrewed the bolts of the panels. But hardly were the screws loosed, when the panel rose with great violence, evidently drawn by the suckers of a poulp's arm. Immediately one of these arms slid like a serpent down the opening and twenty others were above. With one blow of the axe, Captain Nemo cut this formidable tentacle, that slid wriggling down the ladder. Just as we were pressing one on the other to reach the platform, two other arms, lashing the air, came down on the seaman placed before Captain Nemo, and lifted him up with irresistible power. Captain Nemo uttered a cry, and rushed out. We hurried after him.

What a scene! The unhappy man, seized by the tentacle and fixed to the suckers, was balanced in the air at the caprice of this enormous trunk. He rattled in his throat, he was stifled, he cried, "Help! help!" These words, spoken in French, startled me! I had a fellow-countryman on board, perhaps several! That heart-rending cry! I shall hear it all my life. The unfortunate man was lost. Who could rescue him from that powerful pressure? However, Captain Nemo had rushed to the poulp, and with one blow of the axe had cut through one arm. His lieutenant struggled furiously against other monsters that crept on the flanks of the Nautilus. The crew fought with their axes. The Canadian, Conseil, and I buried our weapons in the fleshy masses; a strong smell of musk penetrated the atmosphere. It was horrible!

For one instant, I thought the unhappy man, entangled with the poulp, would be torn from its powerful suction. Seven of the eight arms had been cut off. One only wriggled in the air, brandishing the victim like a feather. But just as Captain Nemo and his lieutenant threw themselves on it, the animal ejected a stream of black liquid. We were blinded with it. When the cloud dispersed, the cuttlefish had disappeared, and my unfortunate countryman with it. Ten or twelve poulps now invaded the platform and sides of the Nautilus. We rolled pell-mell into the midst of this nest of serpents, that wriggled on the platform in the waves of blood and ink. It seemed as though these slimy tentacles sprang up like the hydra's heads. Ned Land's harpoon, at each stroke, was plunged into the staring eyes of the cuttle fish. But my bold companion was suddenly overturned by the tentacles of a monster he had not been able to avoid.

Ah! how my heart beat with emotion and horror! The formidable beak of a cuttlefish was open over Ned Land. The unhappy man would be cut in two. I rushed to his succour. But Captain Nemo was before me; his axe disappeared between the two enormous jaws, and, miraculously saved, the Canadian, rising, plunged his harpoon deep into the triple heart of the poulp.

"I owed myself this revenge!" said the Captain to the Canadian.

Ned bowed without replying. The combat had lasted a quarter of an hour. The monsters, vanquished and mutilated, left us at last, and disappeared under the waves. Captain Nemo, covered with blood, nearly exhausted, gazed upon the sea that had swallowed up one of his companions, and great tears gathered in his eyes.

CHAPTER XIX THE GULF STREAM

This terrible scene of the 20th of April none of us can ever forget. I have written it under the influence of violent emotion. Since then I have revised the recital; I have read it to Conseil and to the Canadian. They found it exact as to facts, but insufficient as to effect. To paint such pictures, one must have the pen of the most illustrious of our poets, the author of The Toilers of the Deep.

I have said that Captain Nemo wept while watching the waves; his grief was great. It was the second companion he had lost since our arrival on board, and what a death! That friend, crushed, stifled, bruised by the dreadful arms of a poulp, pounded by his iron jaws, would not rest with his comrades in the peaceful coral cemetery! In the midst of the struggle, it was the despairing cry uttered by the unfortunate man that had torn my heart. The poor Frenchman, forgetting his conventional language, had taken to his own mother tongue, to utter a last appeal! Amongst the crew of the Nautilus, associated with the body and soul of the Captain, recoiling like him from all contact with men, I had a fellow-countryman. Did he alone represent France in this mysterious association, evidently composed of individuals of divers nationalities? It was one of these insoluble problems that rose up unceasingly before my mind!

Captain Nemo entered his room, and I saw him no more for some time. But that he was sad and irresolute I could see by the vessel, of which he was the soul, and which received all his impressions. The Nautilus did not keep on in its settled course; it floated about like a corpse at the will of the waves. It went at random. He could not tear himself away from the scene of the last struggle, from this sea that had devoured one of his men. Ten days passed thus. It was not till the 1st of May that the Nautilus resumed its northerly course, after having sighted the Bahamas at the mouth of the Bahama Canal. We were then following the current from the largest river to the sea, that has its banks, its fish, and its proper temperatures. I mean the Gulf Stream. It is really a river, that flows freely to the middle of the Atlantic, and whose waters do not mix with the ocean waters. It is a salt river, salter than the surrounding sea. Its mean depth is 1,500 fathoms, its mean breadth ten miles. In certain places the current flows with the speed of two miles and a half an hour. The body of its waters is more considerable than that of all the rivers in the globe. It was on this ocean river that the Nautilus then sailed.

I must add that, during the night, the phosphorescent waters of the Gulf Stream rivalled the electric power of our watch-light, especially in the stormy weather that threatened us so frequently. May 8th, we were still crossing Cape Hatteras, at the height of the North Caroline. The width of the Gulf Stream there is seventy-five miles, and its depth 210 yards. The Nautilus still went at random; all supervision seemed abandoned. I thought that, under these circumstances, escape would be possible. Indeed, the inhabited shores offered anywhere an easy refuge. The sea was incessantly ploughed by the steamers that ply between New York or Boston and the Gulf of Mexico, and overrun day and night by the little schooners coasting about the several parts of the American coast. We could hope to be picked up. It was a favourable opportunity, notwithstanding the thirty miles that separated the Nautilus from the coasts of the Union. One unfortunate circumstance thwarted the Canadian's plans. The weather was very bad. We were nearing those shores where tempests are so frequent, that country of waterspouts and cyclones actually engendered by the current of the Gulf Stream. To tempt the sea in a frail boat was certain destruction. Ned Land owned this himself. He fretted, seized with nostalgia that flight only could cure.

"Master," he said that day to me, "this must come to an end. I must make a clean breast of it. This Nemo is leaving land and going up to the north. But I declare to you that I have had enough of the South Pole, and I will not follow him to the North."

"What is to be done, Ned, since flight is impracticable just now?"

"We must speak to the Captain," said he; "you said nothing when we were in your native seas. I will speak, now we are in mine. When I think that before long the Nautilus will be by Nova Scotia, and that there near New foundland is a large bay, and into that bay the St. Lawrence empties itself, and that the St. Lawrence is my river, the river by Quebec, my native town—when I think of this, I feel furious, it makes my hair stand on end. Sir, I would rather throw myself into the sea! I will not stay here! I am stifled!"

The Canadian was evidently losing all patience. His vigorous nature could not stand this prolonged imprisonment. His face altered daily; his temper became more surly. I knew what he must suffer, for I was seized with home-sickness myself. Nearly seven months had passed without our having had any news from land; Captain Nemo's isolation, his altered spirits, especially since the fight with the poulps, his taciturnity, all made me view things in a different light.

"Well, sir?" said Ned, seeing I did not reply.

"Well, Ned, do you wish me to ask Captain Nemo his intentions concerning us?"

"Yes, sir."

"Although he has already made them known?"

"Yes; I wish it settled finally. Speak for me, in my name only, if you like."

"But I so seldom meet him. He avoids me."

"That is all the more reason for you to go to see him."

I went to my room. From thence I meant to go to Captain Nemo's. It would not do to let this opportunity of meeting him slip. I knocked at the door. No answer. I knocked again, then turned the handle. The door opened, I went in. The Captain was there. Bending over his work-table, he had not heard me. Resolved not to go without having spoken, I approached him. He raised his head quickly, frowned, and said roughly, "You here! What do you want?"

"To speak to you, Captain."

"But I am busy, sir; I am working. I leave you at liberty to shut yourself up; cannot I be allowed the same?"

This reception was not encouraging; but I was determined to hear and answer everything.

"Sir," I said coldly, "I have to speak to you on a matter that admits of no delay."

"What is that, sir?" he replied, ironically. "Have you discovered something that has escaped me, or has the sea delivered up any new secrets?"

We were at cross-purposes. But, before I could reply, he showed me an open manuscript on his table, and said, in a more serious tone, "Here, M. Aronnax, is a manuscript written in several languages. It contains the sum of my studies of the sea; and, if it please

God, it shall not perish with me. This manuscript, signed with my name, complete with the history of my life, will be shut up in a little floating case. The last survivor of all of us on board the Nautilus will throw this case into the sea, and it will go whither it is borne by the waves."

This man's name! his history written by himself! His mystery would then be revealed some day.

"Captain," I said, "I can but approve of the idea that makes you act thus. The result of your studies must not be lost. But the means you employ seem to me to be primitive. Who knows where the winds will carry this case, and in whose hands it will fall? Could you not use some other means? Could not you, or one of yours——"

"Never, sir!" he said, hastily interrupting me.

"But I and my companions are ready to keep this manuscript in store; and, if you will put us at liberty——"

"At liberty?" said the Captain, rising.

"Yes, sir; that is the subject on which I wish to question you. For seven months we have been here on board, and I ask you to-day, in the name of my companions and in my own, if your intention is to keep us here always?"

"M. Aronnax, I will answer you to-day as I did seven months ago: Whoever enters the Nautilus, must never quit it."

"You impose actual slavery upon us!"

"Give it what name you please."

"But everywhere the slave has the right to regain his liberty."

"Who denies you this right? Have I ever tried to chain you with an oath?"

He looked at me with his arms crossed.

"Sir," I said, "to return a second time to this subject will be neither to your nor to my taste; but, as we have entered upon it, let us go through with it. I repeat, it is not only myself whom it concerns. Study is to me a relief, a diversion, a passion that could make me forget everything. Like you, I am willing to live obscure, in the frail hope of bequeathing one day, to future time, the result of my labours. But it is otherwise with Ned Land. Every man, worthy of the name, deserves some consideration. Have you thought that love of liberty, hatred of slavery, can give rise to schemes of revenge in a nature like the Canadian's; that he could think, attempt, and try——"

I was silenced; Captain Nemo rose.

"Whatever Ned Land thinks of, attempts, or tries, what does it matter to me? I did not seek him! It is not for my pleasure that I keep him on board! As for you, M. Aronnax, you are one of those who can understand everything, even silence. I have nothing more to say to you. Let this first time you have come to treat of this subject be the last, for a second time I will not listen to you."

I retired. Our situation was critical. I related my conversation to my two companions.

"We know now," said Ned, "that we can expect nothing from this man. The Nautilus is nearing Long Island. We will escape, whatever the weather may be."

But the sky became more and more threatening. Symptoms of a hurricane became manifest. The atmosphere was becoming white and misty. On the horizon fine streaks of cirrhous clouds were succeeded by masses of cumuli. Other low clouds passed swiftly by. The swollen sea rose in huge billows. The birds disappeared with the exception of the petrels, those friends of the storm. The barometer fell sensibly, and indicated an extreme extension of the vapours. The mixture of the storm glass was decomposed under the influence of the electricity that pervaded the atmosphere. The tempest burst on the 18th of May, just as the Nautilus was floating off Long Island, some miles from the port of New

York. I can describe this strife of the elements! for, instead of fleeing to the depths of the sea, Captain Nemo, by an unaccountable caprice, would brave it at the surface. The wind blew from the south-west at first. Captain Nemo, during the squalls, had taken his place on the platform. He had made himself fast, to prevent being washed overboard by the monstrous waves. I had hoisted myself up, and made myself fast also, dividing my admiration between the tempest and this extraordinary man who was coping with it. The raging sea was swept by huge cloud-drifts, which were actually saturated with the waves. The Nautilus, sometimes lying on its side, sometimes standing up like a mast, rolled and pitched terribly. About five o'clock a torrent of rain fell, that lulled neither sea nor wind. The hurricane blew nearly forty leagues an hour. It is under these conditions that it overturns houses, breaks iron gates, displaces twenty-four pounders. However, the Nautilus, in the midst of the tempest, confirmed the words of a clever engineer, "There is no well-constructed hull that cannot defy the sea." This was not a resisting rock; it was a steel spindle, obedient and movable, without rigging or masts, that braved its fury with impunity. However, I watched these raging waves attentively. They measured fifteen feet in height, and 150 to 175 yards long, and their speed of propagation was thirty feet per second. Their bulk and power increased with the depth of the water. Such waves as these, at the Hebrides, have displaced a mass weighing 8,400 lb. They are they which, in the tempest of December 23rd, 1864, after destroying the town of Yeddo, in Japan, broke the same day on the shores of America. The intensity of the tempest increased with the night. The barometer, as in 1860 at Reunion during a cyclone, fell seven-tenths at the close of day. I saw a large vessel pass the horizon struggling painfully. She was trying to lie to under half steam, to keep up above the waves. It was probably one of the steamers of the line from New York to Liverpool, or Havre. It soon disappeared in the gloom. At ten o'clock in the evening the sky was on fire. The atmosphere was streaked with vivid lightning. I could not bear the brightness of it; while the captain, looking at it, seemed to envy the spirit of the tempest. A terrible noise filled the air, a complex noise, made up of the howls of the crushed waves, the roaring of the wind, and the claps of thunder. The wind veered suddenly to all points of the horizon; and the cyclone, rising in the east, returned after passing by the north, west, and south, in the inverse course pursued by the circular storm of the southern hemisphere. Ah, that Gulf Stream! It deserves its name of the King of Tempests. It is that which causes those formidable cyclones, by the difference of temperature between its air and its currents. A shower of fire had succeeded the rain. The drops of water were changed to sharp spikes. One would have thought that Captain Nemo was courting a death worthy of himself, a death by lightning. As the Nautilus, pitching dreadfully, raised its steel spur in the air, it seemed to act as a conductor, and I saw long sparks burst from it. Crushed and without strength I crawled to the panel, opened it, and descended to the saloon. The storm was then at its height. It was impossible to stand upright in the interior of the Nautilus. Captain Nemo came down about twelve. I heard the reservoirs filling by degrees, and the Nautilus sank slowly beneath the waves. Through the open windows in the saloon I saw large fish terrified, passing like phantoms in the water. Some were struck before my eyes. The Nautilus was still descending. I thought that at about eight fathoms deep we should find a calm. But no! the upper beds were too violently agitated for that. We had to seek repose at more than twenty-five fathoms in the bowels of the deep. But there, what quiet, what silence, what peace! Who could have told that such a hurricane had been let loose on the surface of that ocean?

CHAPTER XX FROM LATITUDE 47° 24' TO LONGITUDE 17° 28'

In consequence of the storm, we had been thrown eastward once more. All hope of escape on the shores of New York or St. Lawrence had faded away; and poor Ned, in despair, had isolated himself like Captain Nemo. Conseil and I, however, never left each other. I said that the Nautilus had gone aside to the east. I should have said (to be more exact) the north-east. For some days, it wandered first on the surface, and then beneath it, amid those fogs so dreaded by sailors. What accidents are due to these thick fogs! What shocks upon these reefs when the wind drowns the breaking of the waves! What collisions between vessels, in spite of their warning lights, whistles, and alarm bells! And the bottoms of these seas look like a field of battle, where still lie all the conquered of the ocean; some old and already encrusted, others fresh and reflecting from their iron bands and copper plates the brilliancy of our lantern.

On the 15th of May we were at the extreme south of the Bank of Newfoundland. This bank consists of alluvia, or large heaps of organic matter, brought either from the Equator by the Gulf Stream, or from the North Pole by the counter-current of cold water which skirts the American coast. There also are heaped up those erratic blocks which are carried along by the broken ice; and close by, a vast charnel-house of molluscs, which perish here by millions. The depth of the sea is not great at Newfoundland—not more than some hundreds of fathoms; but towards the south is a depression of 1,500 fathoms. There the Gulf Stream widens. It loses some of its speed and some of its temperature, but it becomes a sea.

It was on the 17th of May, about 500 miles from Heart's Content, at a depth of more than 1,400 fathoms, that I saw the electric cable lying on the bottom. Conseil, to whom I had not mentioned it, thought at first that it was a gigantic sea-serpent. But I undeceived the worthy fellow, and by way of consolation related several particulars in the laying of this cable. The first one was laid in the years 1857 and 1858; but, after transmitting about 400 telegrams, would not act any longer. In 1863 the engineers constructed another one, measuring 2,000 miles in length, and weighing 4,500 tons, which was embarked on the Great Eastern. This attempt also failed.

On the 25th of May the Nautilus, being at a depth of more than 1,918 fathoms, was on the precise spot where the rupture occurred which ruined the enterprise. It was within 638 miles of the coast of Ireland; and at half-past two in the afternoon they discovered that communication with Europe had ceased. The electricians on board resolved to cut the cable before fishing it up, and at eleven o'clock at night they had recovered the damaged part. They made another point and spliced it, and it was once more submerged. But some days after it broke again, and in the depths of the ocean could not be recaptured. The

Americans, however, were not discouraged. Cyrus Field, the bold promoter of the enterprise, as he had sunk all his own fortune, set a new subscription on foot, which was at once answered, and another cable was constructed on better principles. The bundles of conducting wires were each enveloped in gutta-percha, and protected by a wadding of hemp, contained in a metallic covering. The Great Eastern sailed on the 13th of July, 1866. The operation worked well. But one incident occurred. Several times in unrolling the cable they observed that nails had recently been forced into it, evidently with the motive of destroying it. Captain Anderson, the officers, and engineers consulted together, and had it posted up that, if the offender was surprised on board, he would be thrown without further trial into the sea. From that time the criminal attempt was never repeated.

On the 23rd of July the Great Eastern was not more than 500 miles from Newfoundland, when they telegraphed from Ireland the news of the armistice concluded between Prussia and Austria after Sadowa. On the 27th, in the midst of heavy fogs, they reached the port of Heart's Content. The enterprise was successfully terminated; and for its first despatch, young America addressed old Europe in these words of wisdom, so rarely understood: "Glory to God in the highest, and on earth peace, goodwill towards men."

I did not expect to find the electric cable in its primitive state, such as it was on leaving the manufactory. The long serpent, covered with the remains of shells, bristling with foraminiferae, was encrusted with a strong coating which served as a protection against all boring molluscs. It lay quietly sheltered from the motions of the sea, and under a favourable pressure for the transmission of the electric spark which passes from Europe to America in .32 of a second. Doubtless this cable will last for a great length of time, for they find that the gutta-percha covering is improved by the sea-water. Besides, on this level, so well chosen, the cable is never so deeply submerged as to cause it to break. The Nautilus followed it to the lowest depth, which was more than 2,212 fathoms, and there it lay without any anchorage; and then we reached the spot where the accident had taken place in 1863. The bottom of the ocean then formed a valley about 100 miles broad, in which Mont Blanc might have been placed without its summit appearing above the waves. This valley is closed at the east by a perpendicular wall more than 2,000 yards high. We arrived there on the 28th of May, and the Nautilus was then not more than 120 miles from Ireland.

Was Captain Nemo going to land on the British Isles? No. To my great surprise he made for the south, once more coming back towards European seas. In rounding the Emerald Isle, for one instant I caught sight of Cape Clear, and the light which guides the thousands of vessels leaving Glasgow or Liverpool. An important question then arose in my mind. Did the Nautilus dare entangle itself in the Manche? Ned Land, who had reappeared since we had been nearing land, did not cease to question me. How could I answer? Captain Nemo remained invisible. After having shown the Canadian a glimpse of American shores, was he going to show me the coast of France?

But the Nautilus was still going southward. On the 30th of May, it passed in sight of Land's End, between the extreme point of England and the Scilly Isles, which were left to starboard. If we wished to enter the Manche, he must go straight to the east. He did not do so.

During the whole of the 31st of May, the Nautilus described a series of circles on the water, which greatly interested me. It seemed to be seeking a spot it had some trouble in finding. At noon, Captain Nemo himself came to work the ship's log. He spoke no word to me, but seemed gloomier than ever. What could sadden him thus? Was it his proximity to European shores? Had he some recollections of his abandoned country? If not, what did he feel? Remorse or regret? For a long while this thought haunted my mind, and I had a kind of presentiment that before long chance would betray the captain's secrets.

The next day, the 1st of June, the Nautilus continued the same process. It was evidently seeking some particular spot in the ocean. Captain Nemo took the sun's altitude as he had done the day before. The sea was beautiful, the sky clear. About eight miles to the east, a large steam vessel could be discerned on the horizon. No flag fluttered from its mast, and I could not discover its nationality. Some minutes before the sun passed the meridian, Captain Nemo took his sextant, and watched with great attention. The perfect rest of the water greatly helped the operation. The Nautilus was motionless; it neither rolled nor pitched.

I was on the platform when the altitude was taken, and the Captain pronounced these words: "It is here."

He turned and went below. Had he seen the vessel which was changing its course and seemed to be nearing us? I could not tell. I returned to the saloon. The panels closed, I heard the hissing of the water in the reservoirs. The Nautilus began to sink, following a vertical line, for its screw communicated no motion to it. Some minutes later it stopped at a depth of more than 420 fathoms, resting on the ground. The luminous ceiling was darkened, then the panels were opened, and through the glass I saw the sea brilliantly illuminated by the rays of our lantern for at least half a mile round us.

I looked to the port side, and saw nothing but an immensity of quiet waters. But to starboard, on the bottom appeared a large protuberance, which at once attracted my attention. One would have thought it a ruin buried under a coating of white shells, much resembling a covering of snow. Upon examining the mass attentively, I could recognise the ever-thickening form of a vessel bare of its masts, which must have sunk. It certainly belonged to past times. This wreck, to be thus encrusted with the lime of the water, must already be able to count many years passed at the bottom of the ocean.

What was this vessel? Why did the Nautilus visit its tomb? Could it have been aught but a shipwreck which had drawn it under the water? I knew not what to think, when near me in a slow voice I heard Captain Nemo say:

"At one time this ship was called the Marseillais. It carried seventy-four guns, and was launched in 1762. In 1778, the 13th of August, commanded by La Poype-Ver trieux, it fought boldly against the Preston. In 1779, on the 4th of July, it was at the taking of Grenada, with the squadron of Admiral Estaing. In 1781, on the 5th of September, it took part in the battle of Comte de Grasse, in Chesapeake Bay. In 1794, the French Republic changed its name. On the 16th of April, in the same year, it joined the squadron of Villaret Joyeuse, at Brest, being entrusted with the escort of a cargo of corn coming from America, under the command of Admiral Van Stebel. On the 11th and 12th Prairal of the second year, this squadron fell in with an English vessel. Sir, to-day is the 13th Prairal, the first of June, 1868. It is now seventy-four years ago, day for day on this very spot, in latitude 47° 24', longitude 17° 28', that this vessel, after fighting heroically, losing its three masts, with the water in its hold, and the third of its crew disabled, preferred sinking with its 356 sailors to surrendering; and, nailing its colours to the poop, disappeared under the waves to the cry of `Long live the Republic!'"

"The Avenger!" I exclaimed.

"Yes, sir, the Avenger! A good name!" muttered Captain Nemo, crossing his arms.

CHAPTER XXI A HECATOMB

The way of describing this unlooked-for scene, the history of the patriot ship, told at first so coldly, and the emotion with which this strange man pronounced the last words, the name of the Avenger, the significance of which could not escape me, all impressed itself deeply on my mind. My eyes did not leave the Captain, who, with his hand stretched out to sea, was watching with a glowing eye the glorious wreck. Perhaps I was never to know who he was, from whence he came, or where he was going to, but I saw the man move, and apart from the savant. It was no common misanthropy which had shut Captain Nemo and his companions within the Nautilus, but a hatred, either monstrous or sublime, which time could never weaken. Did this hatred still seek for vengeance? The future would soon teach me that. But the Nautilus was rising slowly to the surface of the sea, and the form of the Avenger disappeared by degrees from my sight. Soon a slight rolling told me that we were in the open air. At that moment a dull boom was heard. I looked at the Captain. He did not move.

"Captain?" said I.

He did not answer. I left him and mounted the platform. Conseil and the Canadian were already there.

"Where did that sound come from?" I asked.

"It was a gunshot," replied Ned Land.

I looked in the direction of the vessel I had already seen. It was nearing the Nautilus, and we could see that it was putting on steam. It was within six miles of us.

"What is that ship, Ned?"

"By its rigging, and the height of its lower masts," said the Canadian, "I bet she is a ship-of-war. May it reach us; and, if necessary, sink this cursed Nautilus."

"Friend Ned," replied Conseil, "what harm can it do to the Nautilus? Can it attack it beneath the waves? Can its cannonade us at the bottom of the sea?"

"Tell me, Ned," said I, "can you recognise what country she belongs to?"

The Canadian knitted his eyebrows, dropped his eyelids, and screwed up the corners of his eyes, and for a few moments fixed a piercing look upon the vessel.

"No, sir," he replied; "I cannot tell what nation she belongs to, for she shows no colours. But I can declare she is a man-of-war, for a long pennant flutters from her main mast."

For a quarter of an hour we watched the ship which was steaming towards us. I could not, however, believe that she could see the Nautilus from that distance; and still less that she could know what this submarine engine was. Soon the Canadian informed me that she was a large, armoured, two-decker ram. A thick black smoke was pouring from her two funnels. Her closely-furled sails were stopped to her yards. She hoisted no flag at her mizzen-peak. The distance prevented us from distinguishing the colours of her pennant, which floated like a thin ribbon. She advanced rapidly. If Captain Nemo allowed her to approach, there was a chance of salvation for us.

"Sir," said Ned Land, "if that vessel passes within a mile of us I shall throw myself into the sea, and I should advise you to do the same."

I did not reply to the Canadian's suggestion, but continued watching the ship. Whether English, French, American, or Russian, she would be sure to take us in if we could only reach her. Presently a white smoke burst from the fore part of the vessel; some seconds after, the water, agitated by the fall of a heavy body, splashed the stern of the Nautilus, and shortly afterwards a loud explosion struck my ear.

"What! they are firing at us!" I exclaimed.

"So please you, sir," said Ned, "they have recognised the unicorn, and they are firing at us."

"But," I exclaimed, "surely they can see that there are men in the case?"

"It is, perhaps, because of that," replied Ned Land, looking at me.

A whole flood of light burst upon my mind. Doubtless they knew now how to believe the stories of the pretended monster. No doubt, on board the Abraham Lincoln, when the Canadian struck it with the harpoon, Commander Farragut had recognised in the supposed narwhal a submarine vessel, more dangerous than a supernatural cetacean. Yes, it must have been so; and on every sea they were now seeking this engine of destruction. Terrible indeed! if, as we supposed, Captain Nemo employed the Nautilus in works of vengeance. On the night when we were imprisoned in that cell, in the midst of the Indian Ocean, had he not attacked some vessel? The man buried in the coral cemetery, had he not been a victim to the shock caused by the Nautilus? Yes, I repeat it, it must be so. One part of the mysterious existence of Captain Nemo had been unveiled; and, if his identity had not been recognised, at least, the nations united against him were no longer hunting a chimerical creature, but a man who had vowed a deadly hatred against them. All the formidable past rose before me. Instead of meeting friends on board the approaching ship, we could only expect pitiless enemies. But the shot rattled about us. Some of them struck the sea and ricochetted, losing themselves in the distance. But none touched the Nautilus. The vessel was not more than three miles from us. In spite of the serious cannonade, Captain Nemo did not appear on the platform; but, if one of the conical projectiles had struck the shell of the Nautilus, it would have been fatal. The Canadian then said, "Sir, we must do all we can to get out of this dilemma. Let us signal them. They will then, perhaps, understand that we are honest folks."

Ned Land took his handkerchief to wave in the air; but he had scarcely displayed it, when he was struck down by an iron hand, and fell, in spite of his great strength, upon the deck.

"Fool!" exclaimed the Captain, "do you wish to be pierced by the spur of the Nautilus before it is hurled at this vessel?"

Captain Nemo was terrible to hear; he was still more terrible to see. His face was deadly pale, with a spasm at his heart. For an instant it must have ceased to beat. His pupils were fearfully contracted. He did not speak, he roared, as, with his body thrown forward, he wrung the Canadian's shoulders. Then, leaving him, and turning to the ship of war, whose shot was still raining around him, he exclaimed, with a powerful voice, "Ah, ship of an accursed nation, you know who I am! I do not want your colours to know you by! Look! and I will show you mine!"

And on the fore part of the platform Captain Nemo unfurled a black flag, similar to the one he had placed at the South Pole. At that moment a shot struck the shell of the Nautilus obliquely, without piercing it; and, rebounding near the Captain, was lost in the sea. He shrugged his shoulders; and, addressing me, said shortly, "Go down, you and your companions, go down!"

"Sir," I cried, "are you going to attack this vessel?"

"Sir, I am going to sink it."

"You will not do that?"

"I shall do it," he replied coldly. "And I advise you not to judge me, sir. Fate has shown you what you ought not to have seen. The attack has begun; go down."

"What is this vessel?"

"You do not know? Very well! so much the better! Its nationality to you, at least, will be a secret. Go down!"

We could but obey. About fifteen of the sailors surrounded the Captain, looking with implacable hatred at the vessel nearing them. One could feel that the same desire of vengeance animated every soul. I went down at the moment another projectile struck the Nautilus, and I heard the Captain exclaim:

"Strike, mad vessel! Shower your useless shot! And then, you will not escape the spur of the Nautilus. But it is not here that you shall perish! I would not have your ruins mingle with those of the Avenger!"

I reached my room. The Captain and his second had remained on the platform. The screw was set in motion, and the Nautilus, moving with speed, was soon beyond the reach of the ship's guns. But the pursuit continued, and Captain Nemo contented himself with keeping his distance.

About four in the afternoon, being no longer able to contain my impatience, I went to the central staircase. The panel was open, and I ventured on to the platform. The Captain was still walking up and down with an agitated step. He was looking at the ship, which was five or six miles to leeward.

He was going round it like a wild beast, and, drawing it eastward, he allowed them to pursue. But he did not attack. Perhaps he still hesitated? I wished to mediate once more. But I had scarcely spoken, when Captain Nemo imposed silence, saying:

"I am the law, and I am the judge! I am the oppressed, and there is the oppressor! Through him I have lost all that I loved, cherished, and venerated—country, wife, children, father, and mother. I saw all perish! All that I hate is there! Say no more!"

I cast a last look at the man-of-war, which was putting on steam, and rejoined Ned and Conseil.

"We will fly!" I exclaimed.

"Good!" said Ned. "What is this vessel?"

"I do not know; but, whatever it is, it will be sunk before night. In any case, it is better to perish with it, than be made accomplices in a retaliation the justice of which we cannot judge."

"That is my opinion too," said Ned Land, coolly. "Let us wait for night."

Night arrived. Deep silence reigned on board. The compass showed that the Nautilus had not altered its course. It was on the surface, rolling slightly. My companions and I resolved to fly when the vessel should be near enough either to hear us or to see us; for the moon, which would be full in two or three days, shone brightly. Once on board the ship, if we could not prevent the blow which threatened it, we could, at least we would, do all that circumstances would allow. Several times I thought the Nautilus was preparing for attack; but Captain Nemo contented himself with allowing his adversary to approach, and then fled once more before it.

CHAPTER XXI A HECATOMB

Part of the night passed without any incident. We watched the opportunity for action. We spoke little, for we were too much moved. Ned Land would have thrown himself into the sea, but I forced him to wait. According to my idea, the Nautilus would attack the ship at her waterline, and then it would not only be possible, but easy to fly.

At three in the morning, full of uneasiness, I mounted the platform. Captain Nemo had not left it. He was standing at the fore part near his flag, which a slight breeze displayed above his head. He did not take his eyes from the vessel. The intensity of his look seemed to attract, and fascinate, and draw it onward more surely than if he had been towing it. The moon was then passing the meridian. Jupiter was rising in the east. Amid this peaceful scene of nature, sky and ocean rivalled each other in tranquillity, the sea offering to the orbs of night the finest mirror they could ever have in which to reflect their image. As I thought of the deep calm of these elements, compared with all those passions brooding imperceptibly within the Nautilus, I shuddered.

The vessel was within two miles of us. It was ever nearing that phosphorescent light which showed the presence of the Nautilus. I could see its green and red lights, and its white lantern hanging from the large foremast. An indistinct vibration quivered through its rigging, showing that the furnaces were heated to the uttermost. Sheaves of sparks and red ashes flew from the funnels, shining in the atmosphere like stars.

I remained thus until six in the morning, without Captain Nemo noticing me. The ship stood about a mile and a half from us, and with the first dawn of day the firing began afresh. The moment could not be far off when, the Nautilus attacking its adversary, my companions and myself should for ever leave this man. I was preparing to go down to remind them, when the second mounted the platform, accompanied by several sailors. Captain Nemo either did not or would not see them. Some steps were taken which might be called the signal for action. They were very simple. The iron balustrade around the platform was lowered, and the lantern and pilot cages were pushed within the shell until they were flush with the deck. The long surface of the steel cigar no longer offered a single point to check its manoeuvres. I returned to the saloon. The Nautilus still floated; some streaks of light were filtering through the liquid beds. With the undulations of the waves the windows were brightened by the red streaks of the rising sun, and this dreadful day of the 2nd of June had dawned.

At five o'clock, the log showed that the speed of the Nautilus was slackening, and I knew that it was allowing them to draw nearer. Besides, the reports were heard more distinctly, and the projectiles, labouring through the ambient water, were extinguished with a strange hissing noise.

"My friends," said I, "the moment is come. One grasp of the hand, and may God protect us!"

Ned Land was resolute, Conseil calm, myself so nervous that I knew not how to contain myself. We all passed into the library; but the moment I pushed the door opening on to the central staircase, I heard the upper panel close sharply. The Canadian rushed on to the stairs, but I stopped him. A well-known hissing noise told me that the water was running into the reservoirs, and in a few minutes the Nautilus was some yards beneath the surface of the waves. I understood the manoeuvre. It was too late to act. The Nautilus did not wish to strike at the impenetrable cuirass, but below the water-line, where the metallic covering no longer protected it.

We were again imprisoned, unwilling witnesses of the dreadful drama that was preparing. We had scarcely time to reflect; taking refuge in my room, we looked at each other without speaking. A deep stupor had taken hold of my mind: thought seemed to stand still. I was in that painful state of expectation preceding a dreadful report. I waited, I listened, every sense was merged in that of hearing! The speed of the Nautilus was accelerated. It was preparing to rush. The whole ship trembled. Suddenly I screamed. I felt the shock, but comparatively light. I felt the penetrating power of the steel spur. I heard rattlings and scrapings. But the Nautilus, carried along by its propelling power, passed through the mass of the vessel like a needle through sailcloth!

I could stand it no longer. Mad, out of my mind, I rushed from my room into the saloon. Captain Nemo was there, mute, gloomy, implacable; he was looking through the port panel. A large mass cast a shadow on the water; and, that it might lose nothing of her agony, the Nautilus was going down into the abyss with her. Ten yards from me I saw the open shell, through which the water was rushing with the noise of thunder, then the double line of guns and the netting. The bridge was covered with black, agitated shadows.

The water was rising. The poor creatures were crowding the ratlines, clinging to the masts, struggling under the water. It was a human ant-heap overtaken by the sea. Paralysed, stiffened with anguish, my hair standing on end, with eyes wide open, panting, without breath, and without voice, I too was watching! An irresistible attraction glued me to the glass! Suddenly an explosion took place. The compressed air blew up her decks, as if the magazines had caught fire. Then the unfortunate vessel sank more rapidly. Her topmast, laden with victims, now appeared; then her spars, bending under the weight of men; and, last of all, the top of her mainmast. Then the dark mass disappeared, and with it the dead crew, drawn down by the strong eddy.

I turned to Captain Nemo. That terrible avenger, a perfect archangel of hatred, was still looking. When all was over, he turned to his room, opened the door, and entered. I followed him with my eyes. On the end wall beneath his heroes, I saw the portrait of a woman, still young, and two little children. Captain Nemo looked at them for some moments, stretched his arms towards them, and, kneeling down, burst into deep sobs.

CHAPTER XXII THE LAST WORDS OF CAPTAIN NEMO

The panels had closed on this dreadful vision, but light had not returned to the saloon: all was silence and darkness within the Nautilus. At wonderful speed, a hundred feet beneath the water, it was leaving this desolate spot. Whither was it going? To the north or south? Where was the man flying to after such dreadful retaliation? I had returned to my room, where Ned and Conseil had remained silent enough. I felt an insurmountable horror for Captain Nemo. Whatever he had suffered at the hands of these men, he had no right to punish thus. He had made me, if not an accomplice, at least a witness of his vengeance. At eleven the electric light reappeared. I passed into the saloon. It was deserted. I consulted the different instruments. The Nautilus was flying northward at the rate of twenty-five miles an hour, now on the surface, and now thirty feet below it. On taking the bearings by the chart, I saw that we were passing the mouth of the Manche, and that our course was hurrying us towards the northern seas at a frightful speed. That night we had crossed two hundred leagues of the Atlantic. The shadows fell, and the sea was covered with darkness until the rising of the moon. I went to my room, but could not sleep. I was troubled with dreadful nightmare. The horrible scene of destruction was continually before my eyes. From that day, who could tell into what part of the North Atlantic basin the Nautilus would take us? Still with unaccountable speed. Still in the midst of these northern fogs. Would it touch at Spitzbergen, or on the shores of Nova Zembla? Should we explore those unknown seas, the White Sea, the Sea of Kara, the Gulf of Obi, the Archipelago of Liarrov, and the unknown coast of Asia? I could not say. I could no longer judge of the time that was passing. The clocks had been stopped on board. It seemed, as in polar countries, that night and day no longer followed their regular course. I felt myself being drawn into that strange region where the foundered imagination of Edgar Poe roamed at will. Like the fabulous Gordon Pym, at every moment I expected to see "that veiled human figure, of larger proportions than those of any inhabitant of the earth, thrown across the cataract which defends the approach to the pole." I estimated (though, perhaps, I may be mistaken)—I estimated this adventurous course of the Nautilus to have lasted fifteen or twenty days. And I know not how much longer it might have lasted, had it not been for the catastrophe which ended this voyage. Of Captain Nemo I saw nothing whatever now, nor of his second. Not a man of the crew was visible for an instant. The Nautilus was almost incessantly under water. When we came to the surface to renew the air, the panels opened and shut mechanically. There were no more marks on the planisphere. I knew not where we were. And the Canadian, too, his strength and patience at an end, appeared no more. Conseil could not draw a word from him; and, fearing that, in a dreadful fit of madness, he might kill himself, watched him with constant devotion. One morning (what date it was I could not say) I had fallen into a heavy sleep towards the early hours, a sleep both painful and unhealthy, when I suddenly awoke. Ned Land was leaning over me, saying, in a low voice, "We are going to fly." I sat up.

"When shall we go?" I asked.

"To-night. All inspection on board the Nautilus seems to have ceased. All appear to be stupefied. You will be ready, sir?"

"Yes; where are we?"

"In sight of land. I took the reckoning this morning in the fog—twenty miles to the east."

"What country is it?"

"I do not know; but, whatever it is, we will take refuge there."

"Yes, Ned, yes. We will fly to-night, even if the sea should swallow us up."

"The sea is bad, the wind violent, but twenty miles in that light boat of the Nautilus does not frighten me. Unknown to the crew, I have been able to procure food and some bottles of water."

"I will follow you."

"But," continued the Canadian, "if I am surprised, I will defend myself; I will force them to kill me."

"We will die together, friend Ned."

I had made up my mind to all. The Canadian left me. I reached the platform, on which I could with difficulty support myself against the shock of the waves. The sky was threatening; but, as land was in those thick brown shadows, we must fly. I returned to the saloon, fearing and yet hoping to see Captain Nemo, wishing and yet not wishing to see him. What could I have said to him? Could I hide the involuntary horror with which he inspired me? No. It was better that I should not meet him face to face; better to forget him. And yet—— How long seemed that day, the last that I should pass in the Nautilus. I remained alone. Ned Land and Conseil avoided speaking, for fear of betraying themselves. At six I dined, but I was not hungry; I forced myself to eat in spite of my disgust, that I might not weaken myself. At half-past six Ned Land came to my room, saying, "We shall not see each other again before our departure. At ten the moon will not be risen. We will profit by the darkness. Come to the boat; Conseil and I will wait for you."

The Canadian went out without giving me time to answer. Wishing to verify the course of the Nautilus, I went to the saloon. We were running N.N.E. at frightful speed, and more than fifty yards deep. I cast a last look on these wonders of nature, on the riches of art heaped up in this museum, upon the unrivalled collection destined to perish at the bottom of the sea, with him who had formed it. I wished to fix an indelible impression of it in my mind. I remained an hour thus, bathed in the light of that luminous ceiling, and passing in review those treasures shining under their glasses. Then I returned to my room.

I dressed myself in strong sea clothing. I collected my notes, placing them carefully about me. My heart beat loudly. I could not check its pulsations. Certainly my trouble and agitation would have betrayed me to Captain Nemo's eyes. What was he doing at this moment? I listened at the door of his room. I heard steps. Captain Nemo was there. He had not gone to rest. At every moment I expected to see him appear, and ask me why I wished to fly. I was constantly on the alert. My imagination magnified everything. The impression became at last so poignant that I asked myself if it would not be better to go to the Captain's room, see him face to face, and brave him with look and gesture.

It was the inspiration of a madman; fortunately I resisted the desire, and stretched myself on my bed to quiet my bodily agitation. My nerves were somewhat calmer, but in my excited brain I saw over again all my existence on board the Nautilus; every incident, either happy or unfortunate, which had happened since my disappearance from the Abraham Lincoln—the submarine hunt, the Torres Straits, the savages of Papua, the running ashore, the coral cemetery, the passage of Suez, the Island of Santorin, the Cretan diver, Vigo Bay, Atlantis, the iceberg, the South Pole, the imprisonment in the ice, the fight among the poulps, the storm in the Gulf Stream, the Avenger, and the horrible scene of the vessel sunk with all her crew. All these events passed before my eyes like scenes in a drama. Then Captain Nemo seemed to grow enormously, his features to assume superhuman proportions. He was no longer my equal, but a man of the waters, the genie of the sea.

It was then half-past nine. I held my head between my hands to keep it from bursting. I closed my eyes; I would not think any longer. There was another half-hour to wait, another half-hour of a nightmare, which might drive me mad.

At that moment I heard the distant strains of the organ, a sad harmony to an undefinable chant, the wail of a soul longing to break these earthly bonds. I listened with every sense, scarcely breathing; plunged, like Captain Nemo, in that musical ecstasy, which was drawing him in spirit to the end of life.

Then a sudden thought terrified me. Captain Nemo had left his room. He was in the saloon, which I must cross to fly. There I should meet him for the last time. He would see me, perhaps speak to me. A gesture of his might destroy me, a single word chain me on board.

But ten was about to strike. The moment had come for me to leave my room, and join my companions.

I must not hesitate, even if Captain Nemo himself should rise before me. I opened my door carefully; and even then, as it turned on its hinges, it seemed to me to make a dreadful noise. Perhaps it only existed in my own imagination.

I crept along the dark stairs of the Nautilus, stopping at each step to check the beating of my heart. I reached the door of the saloon, and opened it gently. It was plunged in profound darkness. The strains of the organ sounded faintly. Captain Nemo was there. He did not see me. In the full light I do not think he would have noticed me, so entirely was he absorbed in the ecstasy.

I crept along the carpet, avoiding the slightest sound which might betray my presence. I was at least five minutes reaching the door, at the opposite side, opening into the library.

I was going to open it, when a sigh from Captain Nemo nailed me to the spot. I knew that he was rising. I could even see him, for the light from the library came through to the saloon. He came towards me silently, with his arms crossed, gliding like a spectre rather than walking. His breast was swelling with sobs; and I heard him murmur these words (the last which ever struck my ear):

"Almighty God! enough! enough!"

Was it a confession of remorse which thus escaped from this man's conscience?

In desperation, I rushed through the library, mounted the central staircase, and, following the upper flight, reached the boat. I crept through the opening, which had already admitted my two companions.

"Let us go! let us go!" I exclaimed.

"Directly!" replied the Canadian.

The orifice in the plates of the Nautilus was first closed, and fastened down by means of a false key, with which Ned Land had provided himself; the opening in the boat was also closed. The Canadian began to loosen the bolts which still held us to the submarine boat.

Suddenly a noise was heard. Voices were answering each other loudly. What was the matter? Had they discovered our flight? I felt Ned Land slipping a dagger into my hand.

"Yes," I murmured, "we know how to die!"

The Canadian had stopped in his work. But one word many times repeated, a dreadful word, revealed the cause of the agitation spreading on board the Nautilus. It was not we the crew were looking after!

"The maelstrom! the maelstrom!" Could a more dreadful word in a more dreadful situation have sounded in our ears! We were then upon the dangerous coast of Norway. Was the Nautilus being drawn into this gulf at the moment our boat was going to leave its sides? We knew that at the tide the pent-up waters between the islands of Ferroe and Loffoden rush with irresistible violence, forming a whirlpool from which no vessel ever escapes. From every point of the horizon enormous waves were meeting, forming a gulf justly called the "Navel of the Ocean," whose power of attraction extends to a distance of twelve miles. There, not only vessels, but whales are sacrificed, as well as white bears from the northern regions.

It is thither that the Nautilus, voluntarily or involuntarily, had been run by the Captain.

It was describing a spiral, the circumference of which was lessening by degrees, and the boat, which was still fastened to its side, was carried along with giddy speed. I felt that sickly giddiness which arises from long-continued whirling round.

We were in dread. Our horror was at its height, circulation had stopped, all nervous influence was annihilated, and we were covered with cold sweat, like a sweat of agony! And what noise around our frail bark! What roarings repeated by the echo miles away! What an uproar was that of the waters broken on the sharp rocks at the bottom, where the hardest bodies are crushed, and trees worn away, "with all the fur rubbed off," according to the Norwegian phrase!

What a situation to be in! We rocked frightfully. The Nautilus defended itself like a human being. Its steel muscles cracked. Sometimes it seemed to stand upright, and we with it!

"We must hold on," said Ned, "and look after the bolts. We may still be saved if we stick to the Nautilus."

He had not finished the words, when we heard a crashing noise, the bolts gave way, and the boat, torn from its groove, was hurled like a stone from a sling into the midst of the whirlpool.

My head struck on a piece of iron, and with the violent shock I lost all consciousness.

CHAPTER XXIII CONCLUSION

Thus ends the voyage under the seas. What passed during that night—how the boat escaped from the eddies of the maelstrom—how Ned Land, Conseil, and myself ever came out of the gulf, I cannot tell.

But when I returned to consciousness, I was lying in a fisherman's hut, on the Loffoden Isles. My two companions, safe and sound, were near me holding my hands. We embraced each other heartily.

At that moment we could not think of returning to France. The means of communication between the north of Norway and the south are rare. And I am therefore obliged to wait for the steamboat running monthly from Cape North.

And, among the worthy people who have so kindly received us, I revise my record of these adventures once more. Not a fact has been omitted, not a detail exaggerated. It is a faithful narrative of this incredible expedition in an element inaccessible to man, but to which Progress will one day open a road.

Shall I be believed? I do not know. And it matters little, after all. What I now affirm is, that I have a right to speak of these seas, under which, in less than ten months, I have crossed 20,000 leagues in that submarine tour of the world, which has revealed so many wonders.

But what has become of the Nautilus? Did it resist the pressure of the maelstrom? Does Captain Nemo still live? And does he still follow under the ocean those frightful retaliations? Or, did he stop after the last hecatomb?

Will the waves one day carry to him this manuscript containing the history of his life? Shall I ever know the name of this man? Will the missing vessel tell us by its nationality that of Captain Nemo?

I hope so. And I also hope that his powerful vessel has conquered the sea at its most terrible gulf, and that the Nautilus has survived where so many other vessels have been lost! If it be so—if Captain Nemo still inhabits the ocean, his adopted country, may hatred be appeased in that savage heart! May the contemplation of so many wonders extinguish for ever the spirit of vengeance! May the judge disappear, and the philosopher continue the peaceful exploration of the sea! If his destiny be strange, it is also sublime. Have I not understood it myself? Have I not lived ten months of this unnatural life? And to the question asked by Ecclesiastes three thousand years ago, "That which is far off and exceeding deep, who can find it out?" two men alone of all now living have the right to give an answer——

CAPTAIN NEMO AND MYSELF.

The Complete Richard Hannay - 39 Steps, Greenmantle, Mr Steadfast, Three Hostages, Island of Sheep.
John Buchan
Benediction Classics, 2012
908 pages
ISBN: 978-1-78139-203-4

Available from www.amazon.com, www.amazon.co.uk

The Complete Richard Hannay includes the five John Buchan novels that feature the hero: 39 Steps, Greenmantle, Mr Steadfast, Three Hostages, Island of Sheep. Richard Hannay was one of the first modern spy thriller heroes and has shaped the genre. Hannay is strong and silent, combining the Scottish dourness with the English "stiff upper lip". He is tough and shrewd, courageous and resourceful. However, unlike later spy thrillers he has a greater breadth of emotion. He is philosophical and refuses to demonise his enemies, he falls in love, he is dependent upon his friends and he is religious. These books are exciting, with Richard Hannay being chased over moor and glen, they are page turning thrillers.

The Complete Sherlock Holmes - unabridged and illustrated - A Study In Scarlet, The Sign Of The Four, The Hound Of The Baskervilles, The Valley Of Fear, The Adventures Of Sherlock Holmes, The Memoirs Of Sherlock Holmes, The Return Of Sherlock Holmes, His Last Bow, and The Case-Book Of Sherlock Holmes
Arthur Conan Doyle
Benediction Classics, 2012
1108 pages
ISBN: 978-1-78139-210-2

Available from www.amazon.com, www.amazon.co.uk

The Complete Sherlock Holmes - Illustrated. This edition brings together the four Sherlock Holmes Novels: A Study In Scarlet, The Sign Of The Four, The Hound Of The Baskervilles and The Valley Of Fear. In addition, it includes the five Sherlock Holmes Collections, bringing together the 56 short stories: The Adventures Of Sherlock Holmes, The Memoirs Of Sherlock Holmes, The Return Of Sherlock Holmes, His Last Bow and The Case-Book Of Sherlock Holmes. This book is a must have for any Sherlock Holmes lover.

The Chronicles of Captain Blood
Rafael Sabatini
Benediction Classics, 2011
188 pages
ISBN: 978-1-84902-469-3

Available from www.amazon.com, www.amazon.co.uk

First published in 1931, this new edition is now available. It is a collection of short stories set within the timeframe of Sabatini's best-selling novel 'Captain Blood'. A second collection of short stories 'The Fortunes of Captain Blood (1936) is also available.

The Fortunes of Captain Blood
Rafael Sabatini
Oxford City Press, 2012
162 pages
ISBN: 978-1-78139-128-0

Available from www.amazon.com, www.amazon.co.uk

Rafael Sabatini is a master storyteller. The Daily Telegraph described him thus: 'One wonders if there is another storyteller so adroit at filling his pages with intrigue and counter-intrigue, with danger threaded with romance, with a background of lavish colour, of silks and velvets, of swords and jewels'. 'The Fortunes of Captain Blood' (1936) is a collection of short stories. Captain Blood is handsome, brilliant and skilled with his blade, always one step ahead of his enemies. Perils upon perils challenge him but with his faithful crew, ever willing to follow him into danger, he manages to be both chivalrous and victorious. 'The Chronicles of Captain Blood' (1931), another collection of his short stories is also available.

Also from Benediction Books ...

Wandering Between Two Worlds: Essays on Faith and Art
Anita Mathias
Benediction Books, 2007
152 pages
ISBN: 0955373700

Available from www.amazon.com, www.amazon.co.uk

In these wide-ranging lyrical essays, Anita Mathias writes, in lush, lovely prose, of her naughty Catholic childhood in Jamshedpur, India; her large, eccentric family in Mangalore, a sea-coast town converted by the Portuguese in the sixteenth century; her rebellion and atheism as a teenager in her Himalayan boarding school, run by German missionary nuns, St. Mary's Convent, Nainital; and her abrupt religious conversion after which she entered Mother Teresa's convent in Calcutta as a novice. Later rich, elegant essays explore the dualities of her life as a writer, mother, and Christian in the United States-- Domesticity and Art, Writing and Prayer, and the experience of being "an alien and stranger" as an immigrant in America, sensing the need for roots.

About the Author

Anita Mathias is the author of *Wandering Between Two Worlds: Essays on Faith and Art*. She has a B.A. and M.A. in English from Somerville College, Oxford University, and an M.A. in Creative Writing from the Ohio State University, USA. Anita won a National Endowment of the Arts fellowship in Creative Non-fiction in 1997. She lives in Oxford, England with her husband, Roy, and her daughters, Zoe and Irene.

Anita's website:
    http://www.anitamathias.com, and
Anita's blog Dreaming Beneath the Spires:
    http://dreamingbeneaththespires.blogspot.com

The Church That Had Too Much
Anita Mathias
Benediction Books, 2010
52 pages
ISBN: 9781849026567

Available from www.amazon.com, www.amazon.co.uk

The Church That Had Too Much was very well-intentioned. She wanted to love God, she wanted to love people, but she was both hampered by her muchness and the abundance of her possessions, and beset by ambition, power struggles and snobbery. Read about the surprising way The Church That Had Too Much began to resolve her problems in this deceptively simple and enchanting fable.

About the Author

Anita Mathias is the author of *Wandering Between Two Worlds: Essays on Faith and Art*. She has a B.A. and M.A. in English from Somerville College, Oxford University, and an M.A. in Creative Writing from the Ohio State University, USA. Anita won a National Endowment of the Arts fellowship in Creative Non-fiction in 1997. She lives in Oxford, England with her husband, Roy, and her daughters, Zoe and Irene.

Anita's website:
    http://www.anitamathias.com, and
Anita's blog Dreaming Beneath the Spires:
    http://dreamingbeneaththespires.blogspot.com

www.ingramcontent.com/pod-product-compliance
Lightning Source LLC
Chambersburg PA
CBHW081129300726
48982CB00005B/903

* 9 7 8 1 7 8 1 3 9 2 4 8 5 *